The

Cliff Richard

Recording Catalogue

1958-2010

Victor Rust

First Edition: September 2010

To obtain additional copies of this book, or to monitor future editions of the book, please visit the author's page at the Lulu website, http://www.lulu.com/victorrust, or order it from any bookshop.

Published by: Victor Rust

ISBN: 978-0-9567384-0-0

For the memory of my Uncle John
whose wit and love of music were an inspiration

And especially for My own Pretty One

Author's Note and Acknowledgments

During the research process for this marvellously large book, every reasonable attempt has been made to validate the facts by using verifiable sources where available and reliable sources wherever possible. However, there may be instances where the author has inadvertently perpetuated the odd myth or incorrect fact and this is entirely unintentional.

On a project of this enormity, it is possible that there are some such statements, which may be incorrect, in spite of the efforts extended to ensure that this has not happened. If any such issues are identified then the author unreservedly regrets the oversight and would be pleased to rectify the position in future editions.

Where such errata are unearthed in the encyclopædia, the author invites anyone who finds them to send the details and the associated citation for the change to the email address attached to the author's web page highlighted in the copyright statement of this book. Once checked and accepted, the author will make the changes. For the trouble the finder of the error has gone to, any such changes will be associated with their name in print if that is appropriate and what they would want.

Ultimately, it is absolutely the author's desire that the entries in the encyclopædia should be factually correct and 100% precise in the detail. After all, it's what is expected from the principal subject of this volume - Cliff Richard - in his recording and performance ventures.

The contents of this book are based on all commercial disc releases up to **30th June 2010** and cover all the songs released in aural format (LPs, singles, CDs, downloads, etc.) and those tracks recorded and available for issue in aural format but not released. It does not cover those songs only released on video, DVD, film-only versions or television (that's a whole other enterprise altogether!).

I am indebted to the variety of sources used to check and verify certain facts. In particular, the following sources are acknowledged:

allmusic.com - a superb site for checking credits, songwriters and song and album output
allmovies.com - the sister site for all things relating to film
answers.com - a great comparison site consolidating the information from a number of other sites
cliffchartsite.co uk - a great site with loads of information about the UK charts and international single releases
cliffrichard.org - background of Cliff's biography and discography
cliffrichardsongs.com - a marvellous site itemising nearly all songs that Cliff has performed on record, film and video
en.wikipedia.org - a useful starting point for a number of biographies and other information
youtube.com - a very useful source of rare video performances

Cliff Richard: The Biography by Steve Turner
The Complete Chronicles by Mike Read, Peter Lewry and Nigel Goodall
The Complete Recording Sessions 1958-1990 by Peter Lewry and Nigel Goodall
Guinness Book of British Hit Singles and Albums
The Moody Blues Encyclopaedia by Victor Rust
My Life, My Way by Cliff Richard
On the Continent complementary booklet
Rock 'n' Roll - I Gave You the Best Years of My Life: A Life in the Shadows by Bruce Welch
The Ultimate Beatles Encyclopædia by Bill Harry
The album and track listings, DVDs and videos of films and live performances
The liner notes from albums, where available

...but, ultimately, obtaining and listening to all the tracks held within this volume.

I would also like to thank two people, in particular:
My wife, **Jane**, who has supported me in this authoring endeavour and indulged my whims to get this book finished
My friend, **Beth Johnson**, for her help in some of the research and for the discussions on music and for suggestions on appropriate translations

I couldn't have done this without either of you and I can only proffer my inadequate thanks.

Victor Rust
Pembury, Kent

THE CLIFF RICHARD RECORDING CATALOGUE

INTRODUCTION

Well!

This has been an extraordinary journey: almost an epiphany, if you like. The subject of this book, Sir Cliff Richard, has been at the top of his profession for over fifty years and still shows no sign of slowing down. Although he has gone in and out of fashion over the years, no-one can deny the achievements and accolades he has accrued: the only artist to reach number one in five successive decades, the biggest selling British artist, the artist who has spent most weeks at number one, the artist to have released the most singles... and so it goes on (see the final section of this book for more).

But when I started out on pulling this book together, I was not prepared for the wealth and enormity of Cliff's output over the years. Of course, I knew that he had recorded so many singles and albums but hadn't understood just how that would pan out in terms of the number of songs. Neither was I prepared for the breadth of the material he has recorded. It was and remains a labour of love to go through his back catalogue and listen to hours of glorious tracks.

But I'm getting ahead of myself in my excitement!

* * *

I was born in the spring of Cliff's fifth year in the music business so wasn't really aware of him until the end of the sixties when I began to listen to more music than just albums of children's songs. I was then given a boxed set of Cliff and The Shadows singles and fell in love with his earlier material, listening spellbound to musicianship spilling out of the speakers and the sheer beauty of Cliff's voice blending with Hank's and Bruce's; I was captivated by the guitar intro to *Move It* and the simple emotion of *It's All Over*. As a trained musician myself, I could fully appreciate the perfect pitch of Cliff's voice and I was a firm fan.

Even when it was seriously uncool to like Cliff in the seventies, I was happy to list him as one of my formative musical influences, alongside the Moody Blues and Genesis. I was irritated by the perceived association applied to Cliff's music and the lurid preoccupation in the media with his private life. And, more than anything else, I could guarantee that, regardless of the personal tastes, anyone going to one of his concerts, they couldn't fail to be completely entertained.

By the middle of the seventies, I had begun to collect his new material (even being one of the people to get a copy of *(There's a) Honky Tonk Angel* and continued to do so to the present day. In parallel, I was also collecting the complete works of the Moody Blues – the band has a stronger sway over me even than Cliff – and, ten yearsago, I began to research and write an encyclopedia on the band, which was published in 2008. I thoroughly enjoyed the process of creating that book and I decided that I would work on an encyclopedia of Cliff's recorded material.

I followed exactly the same procedure as for the Moody Blues book, by locating songs that I had not had in my collection from iTunes and other sites, eBay, Amazon, and anywhere else that I could pick up on the rarities. The hardest, but paradoxically most enjoyable, part of the research was listening to all of these tracks in chronological order and aurally undersanding the passage of the change in Cliff's musical output.

If I had to specify any particular songs, it would be hard but probably a toss-up between *Move It*, *From a Distance*, *The Old Accordion*, *Peace in Our Time*, *Butterfly Kisses*... okay, I really can't do it. The list is so long because of the quality of the songs and the brilliance of the performance. Suffice it to say that all my favourites are held within this book. And I have been known to sing *Bachelor Boy* at karaoke parties (but don't tell anyone).

Of course, I should say that what you are holding in your hands is not an official publication endorsed by Sir Cliff, but I have been in contact with the Organisation in order to make them aware of this hefty tome. Because of his busy commitments when he returns to Britain for his seventieth birthday *Bold as Brass* concerts, it has not been possible to get any time with the great man, but I was afforded the opportunity of asking a handful of questions, the answers to which will appear in a later edition.

* * *

Well, that's about it; I hope you enjoy the information in the book and that you find a number of relevatory facts within the covers as I did when researching. One final vote of thanks should go to Sir Cliff Richard himself, without whom the project would have been utterly pointless!

Keep the faith!

Vic Rust
Pembury, Kent
September 2010

THE CLIFF RICHARD RECORDING CATALOGUE

HOW TO USE THIS ENCYCLOPÆDIA

Each entry is treated in straightforward alphabetical order – i.e. without the spaces or punctuation. As ever there are conventional differences: anything starting with definite or indefinite article ('The' or 'A') or their equivalent in other languages, is entered in the encyclopædia with that word appearing at the end (for example: *Voice in the Wilderness, A* or *Minute You're Gone, The*). Where there are multiple entries of the same title or name but are different entities, these entries are differentiated by a numerical suffix and presented, as far as is practically known, in chronological order (for example: *Do You Remember?* (the song from the *Wonderful Life* film soundtrack) and *Do You Remember?* (one of the candidates for the 1968 Eurovision Song Contest)).

The structure of the entries is shown below:

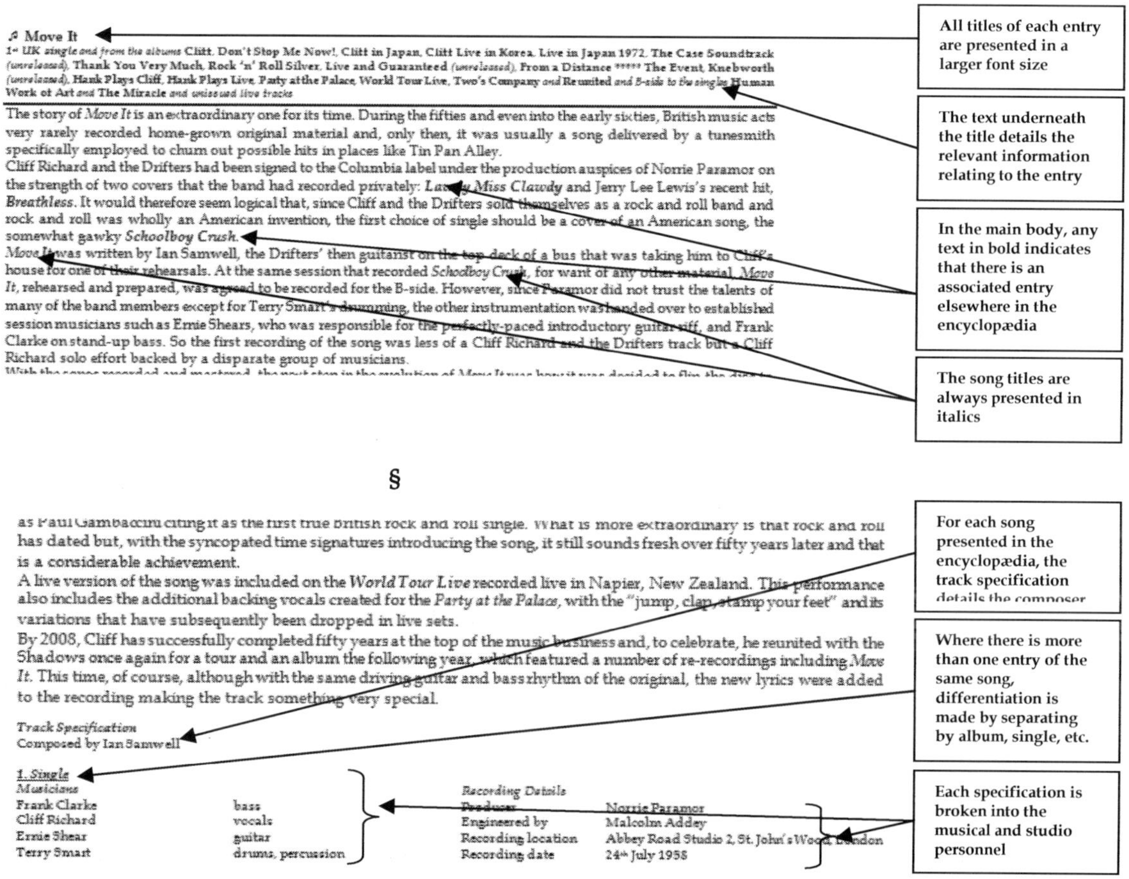

THE

CLIFF RICHARD

RECORDING CATALOGUE

1958-2010

—

The Songs

THE CLIFF RICHARD RECORDING CATALOGUE

NUMERICS

♫ 21st Century Christmas
138th UK double A-side single

Cliff Richard knowingly bowed to his critics expectations in 2006 and recorded another Christmas song; this time, rather than adopting the chintzy Christmas clichés, he took the themes of a new century to express what needs to happen to obtain peace and goodwill in the frenetic new world of the millennium. But it was much more than a cheesy Christmas record, because underlying the melody is a perfect piece of pure pop.
Released as a double A-side with a version of ***Move It***, which was the new recording made for the ***Two's Company*** album, *21st Century Christmas* was issued on the EMI label as a seven-inch vinyl record (catalogue number CLIFFX217) and CD with the songs reversed as the lead (00946 3799312 5) on 11th December 2006 and reached number two in the UK singles charts. In reality, taking the download chart in isolation, he was number one (although this is a deceit to maintain his record of a number one every decade since the start of his music career). The version that appears on the ***50th Anniversary*** album is edited so that the final ten seconds are excised from the original single release.
Evoking modern images of mobile phones, DVDs and satellite tracking, the song demonstrates that the twenty-first century Christmas really doesn't need to dispense with the story of the Nativity, even though it is positively a challenge in comparison with much of what is materially itemized in the lyrics. The strength of the song is not only the message but the backing vocal arrangement, most obviously effective in the middle eight section, and the foot-tapping instrumentation accompaniment, assisted by the beautifully-executed key change.

Track Specification
Composed by Paul Brady and Ralph Murphy

Musicians

Richard Cardwell	keyboards
Gavin Harrison	drums, percussion
Jakko M. Jakszyk	backing vocals
Phil Palmer	guitar
Cliff Richard	vocals, backing vocals

Recording Details

Producer	Chris Porter
Engineered by	Chris Porter
Recording location	Stanley House Studios, west London
Recording date	2006

♫ 23rd Psalm (Crimond)
From the album **Good News**

Of the one hundred and fifty psalms in the Bible, the twenty-third is probably amongst the most familiar, given that it is often sung at funerals. In addition it was used as the theme tune lyrics for the situation comedy *The Vicar of Dibley*, composed for the series by Howard Goodall. The psalm was written, according to religious lore, by King David, and it describes his God as a shepherd leading his bewildered sheep through danger providing protection, through famine with abundance and so on. Metrical versions have been written from as early as the sixteenth century and set to music but by far the most familiar is Jessie Seymour Irvine's *Crimond*, which was originally a hymn tune, although other versions such as the melody for ***Amazing Grace*** are used as well. The metrical settings have also been used in classical arrangements by composers such as Ralph Vaughan Williams, Leonard Bernstein, Franz Schubert and John Rutter, but it has also appeared in popular and gospel song recordings by artists such as Bobby McFerrin, Pink Floyd, Duke Ellington and Katherine Jenkins (the latter covering Goodall's television theme tune).
Often called *The Lord Is My Shepherd* after the first line of the song, for Cliff Richard's ***Good News*** album, he chose to record the traditional setting to the *Crimond* hymn tune, calling it the *23rd Psalm*. It was the first song to be completed at the session – four others were attempted but only two were accepted – with the sixth take and edit being used for issue.
Backed with a simple harp arrangement and gentle backing vocals, Cliff is at his most reverent in this song during the introduction. The orchestral strings join in to replace the backing vocals as Cliff gives the sustained notes a vibrato that injects an energetic passion. The second verse is sung as a hymn with the backing vocalists taking over the handling of the harmonized tune.

Track Specification
Composed by Jessie Seymour Irvine, arranged by Norrie Paramor

Musicians

Norrie Paramor Orchestra	orchestra
Mike Leander	arranger, conductor
Cliff Richard	vocals
Unknown	backing vocals

Recording Details

Producer	Norrie Paramor
Engineered by	Peter Vince and Mike Stone
Recording location	Abbey Road Studio 2, St. John's Wood, London
Recording date	4th May 1967

♫ 31st of February Street (Closing)

From the album **The 31st of February Street**

As with the prior book-end song ***31st of February Street (Opening)***, the closing track on the titular album loses the definite article. Written by Cliff Richard, it completes his first concept album (about leaving home and the variety of emotions associated with being away and wanting to return). The song was recorded at the final session for the album, with this track being the last of three – it is likely that the album title was chosen and Cliff then created the songs rather than the other way around.

Now at half a minute compared with the song's opening length of a minute, the closing version is simply a reprise of the opening with Cliff accompanied by guitar and bass.

Track Specification

Composed by Cliff Richard

Musicians

Kevin Peek	acoustic guitar
Cliff Richard	vocals
Alan Tarney	bass

Recording Details

Producer	David MacKay
Engineered by	Tony Clark and Mike Jarrett
Recording location	Abbey Road Studio 2, St. John's Wood, London
Recording date	25th February 1974

♫ 31st of February Street (Opening)

From the album **The 31st of February Street**

The titular song from the album (along with ***31st of February Street (Closing)***) was recorded at the final session for the album at the end of February 1974 and was written by Cliff Richard. Intended to be the opening track to the concept album (Cliff's first attempt at such), the song loses the definite article from the album's title, and was probably written as a response to the album's title rather than the other way around.

Naturally, the date is a fabrication since the month of February never has more than twenty-nine days and this gives some indication to the yearning that is created throughout the concept of longing and sense of displacement when being away from home. The gentle song is accompanied by a variety of percussion and tom-toms, as well as a prominent rhythm guitar, a steel guitar and electronic keyboards. Short at around a minute, Cliff's voice is muted in its production and the minor keys predominantly used on the track make it a reflective rather than sad song. Cliff's own backing vocals are fed through a vocoder.

Track Specification

Composed by Cliff Richard

Musicians

Cliff Hall	keyboards
Gordon Huntley	steel guitar
Dave MacRae	keyboards
Kevin Peek	acoustic guitar
Cliff Richard	vocals, backing vocals
Trevor Spencer	drums, percussion
Alan Tarney	bass

Recording Details

Producer	David MacKay
Engineered by	Tony Clark and Mike Jarrett
Recording location	Abbey Road Studio 2, St. John's Wood, London
Recording date	25th February 1974

THE CLIFF RICHARD RECORDING CATALOGUE

A - A - A - A - A - A - A - A - A - A - A - A - A - A - A - A - A

♫ Abraham, Martin and John

From the album **Tracks 'n' Groves**

First recorded by Dion in late 1968, *Abraham, Martin and John* is perhaps most familiar in the version that was recorded by Marvin Gaye, and which reached a high of number nine in the UK charts in May 1970. Written by Dick Holler as a tribute to those public figures that he considered to be agents of change in American society, with Abraham being Abraham Lincoln, Martin being Martin Luther King, Jr. and the John is John F. Kennedy. It also mentions Kennedy's brother, Robert, in the lyrics and what ties each of these iconic people together is that they were all assassinated while trying to effect the change about which they were so passionate. In addition to the aforementioned record, it has also been covered by a number of artists including Smokey Robinson and the Miracles, Harry Belafonte, Emmylou Harris, Paul Weller, Ray Charles, Eartha Kitt, Andy Williams, Kenny Rogers and there even exists a version by *Star Trek* actor and film director Leonard Nimoy.

Cliff recorded his version for the ***Tracks 'n' Grooves*** album at a dual session in September 1969 and it was the preliminary song to be completed in that first session. The song appears on the primary side of the original album and is one of the first of Cliff's songs to be released in stereo only, although it is possible that a mono edit might have been created. Cliff's version begins with a typical bass-heavy orchestral introduction that was prevalent at the end of the sixties and into the seventies and particularly with Cliff's work of the period. Imbuing the lead vocals with significant emotion that perfectly matches the tenor of the lyrical acknowledgment to these great American men, Cliff carries off the lead vocal with aplomb.

Track Specification

Composed by Dick Holler

Musicians

Nick Ingman Orchestra	orchestra
Nick Ingman	arranger, conductor
Cliff Richard	vocals
Unknown	backing vocals

Recording Details

Producer	Norrie Paramor
Engineered by	Peter Vince
Recording location	Abbey Road Studio 2, St. John's Wood, London
Recording date	22nd September 1969

♫ After This Love

B-side of **Can't Keep This Feeling In**

Recorded during the sessions for Cliff Richard's late nineties album, ***Real as I Wanna Be***, *After This Love* was not immediately issued on its track listing. It was held back until it was chosen as an extra track for the second of the dual disc CD release of the first single from the project, ***Can't Keep This Feeling In***.

Heavy on the synthesized percussion and the bass, as had been the case for much of the parent album project, *After This Love* drives along with a strong dance-like beat. The backing vocals come in at the chorus and help build up the drama in this story of a man realizing that he needs to think about what happens after a relationship begins to creak and fall apart.

Track Specification

Composed by Sheppard Soloman, John Clifford and Larry Tag

Musicians

Vinnie Colaiuta	drums, percussion
Paul Jackson Jr.	guitar
Cliff Richard	vocals, backing vocals
Michelle Wolf	backing vocals
Peter Wolf	arranger, bass, keyboards, synclavier, percussion

Recording Details

Producer	Peter Wolf
Engineered by	Christian Leitgeb, Chris Heil, Paul Erickson and/or Keith Bessey
Recording location	Little America Recording Studios, Weiler, Austria, Ocean Recording Studios, Burbank, California, USA, Arco Recording Studios, Munich, Germany, R. G. Jones Recording Studios, Wimbledon, London, England and/or The Pierce Room, London, England
Recording date	1997 or 1998

♫ Again

From the album **Cliff Richard**

One of the many songs recorded in the prolific American Columbia sessions in Nashville and New York by Cliff Richard in the summer of 1964, *Again* was one of the tracks that would eventually appear on the track listing of the self-titled ***Cliff Richard*** album. The ninth and final take and edit were used for the mono and stereo recordings but with different mixes for the requirements of the separate audio channels.

The syrupy orchestral arrangement and vocal accompaniment would drown many singers but, with Cliff's performance, his strong vocals ensure that he is never overwhelmed and, indeed, he imbues the lyrics with the intended emotion that are missing from the lush but disappointing string arrangement.

Track Specification
Composed by Lionel Newman and Dorcas Cochran

Musicians

Stan Applebaum	conductor
Cliff Richard	vocals
Unknown	backing vocals
Unknown	orchestra
Unknown	guitar
Unknown	piano
Unknown	drums

Recording Details

Producer	Bob Morgan
Engineered by	Frank Laico
Recording location	Columbia Studios, New York
Recording date	19th August 1964

♬ Ah! Quelle Histoire
French single

Although Cliff Richard came second (by one point after some dubious voting from Germany) at the 1968 Eurovision Song Contest, it was his song, ***Congratulations***, that was the most memorable tune from the contest with the Spanish winner *La La La* being almost lost to history. It was therefore no surprise that Cliff would be asked to record foreign language versions, which he did in the four main European languages of German, French, Spanish and Italian.

The first of these to be recorded was ***Man Gratuliert Mir*** just three days after the contest on 6th April 1968. Erroneously, some publications have stated that the backing track used for all four new versions was that for the English version that was recorded on 3rd February. However, in fact, the German version was an original recording, while the other three languages used that backing track for their versions with Cliff's new vocals overdubbed on to it. There is no information available on who the backing singers are although it is possible that it is the Ladybirds who sang on the English original.

Ah! Quelle Histoire (literally translated as *Ah! What a Story*, and with lyrics that are completely different from the message of love in the original, preferring to focus on obtaining riches and becoming a millionaire instead) was recorded at the same session as the Spanish ***Qué Buena Suerte***. It was released as a single in France, backed with the English B-side ***Girl, You'll Be a Woman Soon***, on the Columbia label (catalogue number CF 155) in May 1968. Released in mono only as was the Columbia policy, the rare track was eventually reissued in stereo as part of the 1997 ***On the Continent*** album.

With an arrangement that brings the original guitar line more up front in the mix, there is very little difference otherwise in the recording other than the inclusion of Cliff and the backing singers singing along with the accelerando section.

Track Specification
Composed by Bill Martin and Phil Coulter; French lyrics by André Salvet

Musicians

Norrie Paramor Orchestra	orchestra
Norrie Paramor	arranger, conductor
Cliff Richard	vocals
Unknown	backing vocals
Unknown	hand claps

Recording Details

Producer	Norrie Paramor (backing track and vocals)
Engineered by	Peter Vince (backing track and vocals)
Recording location	Abbey Road Studio 2 (backing track) and Abbey Road Studio 1 (vocals), St. John's Wood, London
Recording date	9th April 1968 (backing track) and 23rd April 1968 (vocals)

♬ Ain't Nothing but a House Party
From the albums **Live at the Talk of the Town** *and* **Cliff Live in Korea**

Originally a March 1968 hit for the Showstoppers, a product of the strident success of Northern Soul, the American band reached number eleven in the UK charts. *Ain't Nothing but a House Party* charted eighteen years later when Phil Fearon reached number sixty with his final single in November 1986. Also covered by the Contours, the Tremeloes and the Paper Dolls, the song's appeal and popularity ensured its position on the Cliff Richard's set lists during 1968 and 1969.

Cliff began to feature the song in concert towards the end of the sixties and it showed up on the track listing of two of his live albums, ***Live at the Talk of the Town*** and the much rarer *Cliff Live in Korea*. The latter album was issued in mono format and only for the Korean market.

Track Specification
Composed by Joseph Thomas and Del Sharah

1. Live at the Talk of the Town

Musicians

Breakaways:	backing vocals
Vicki Hasemen	
Margo Quantrell	
Jean Ryder	
Norrie Paramor	arranger, conductor
Cliff Richard	vocals
Talk of the Town Orchestra	orchestra

Recording Details

Producer	Norrie Paramor
Engineered by	Peter Vince
Recording location	Talk of the Town Theatre, London
Recording date	30th May 1968

2. *Cliff Live in Korea*

Musicians

Brian Bennett	drums, percussion
Alan Hawkshaw	keyboards
Hank Marvin	backing vocals, guitar
Cliff Richard	vocals
John Rostill	backing vocals, bass
Bruce Welch	backing vocals, rhythm guitar

Recording Details

Producer	Unknown
Engineered by	Unknown
Recording location	Citizen Hall, Seoul, South Korea
Recording date	16th October 1969

♫ All at Once

From the film soundtrack album of **Summer Holiday**

During the set-up for ***A Swingin' Affair***, Don (played by Cliff Richard) had stated that he wanted a romance with runaway American heiress Barbara Winters (Lauri Peters). But he also wants to keep things casual and light because he doesn't like to feel owned – this is something that upsets Barbara because she is clearly in love with him. Later, after some wine and food, the company dance and sing in ***Really Waltzing***, after which Don takes Barbara aside and professes his love for her and confirms that his original attitude to romance with her is now completely reversed. He begins singing *All at Once* to her to prove the effect that she has had on him and to underline his feelings for her. She seems reluctant to believe he has changed and, after repeating the fact that he loves her several times, she reveals that she had loved him from the first time they had met on the bus (when she was dressed as a boy to hide). As the camera pans away from them up into the trees, the pair leans into each other and kiss gently for the first time.

The song was recorded as the final track in the two sessions planned for the day, with a splice of the sixth and seventh take creating the released track. The same spliced takes and edits were used for the mono and stereo recordings but with different mixes for the requirements of the audio channels. The film version of the song is very similar to the studio version but with character dialogue in the middle over the orchestral break, but it has never been released in any other commercially available format. The soundtrack album version was also made available on the track listing of the ***More Hits from Summer Holiday*** EP.

Saccharine strings and woodwind introduce the song and continue throughout underlining the theme of the burgeoning love expressed in the lyrics. Cliff sings naturally well as usual but, although he has a proven track record of being able to sing these slow love songs, it is the faster tracks in the film that show off his skills better in comparison.

Track Specification

Composed by Peter Myers and Ronald Cass

Musicians

Associated British Studio Orchestra	orchestra
Stanley Black	conductor
Cliff Richard	vocals

Recording Details

Producer	Norrie Paramor
Engineered by	Malcolm Addey and Richard Langham
Recording location	Abbey Road Studio 2, St. John's Wood, London
Recording date	26th August 1962

♫ All by Myself

Unissued live track

Probably the best-known of Eric Carmen's solo material, *All by Myself* is an achingly beautiful love song that regrets the break-up of a relationship. It wasn't without its controversy, however, because Carmen had used the melody from Rachmaninoff's second piano concerto, in the firm belief that it was in the public domain and that no copyright existed on it. Unfortunately, this was not the case and Carmen had to come to an agreement with the late composer's estate, meaning that Rachmaninoff should also have a compositional credit (as here). When it was released as a single in 1976, it reached the number two slot in the US Billboard Hot 100 charts and number twelve in the UK charts. Twenty years later, Céline Dion took her version to number six, incorporating vocal histrionics to add to the melodrama. It has also been covered by Frank Sinatra, Tom Jones, Sheryl Crow, Richard Clayderman, Michael Ball and John Barrowman among several others.

Cliff Richard picked up on the song for the set list of his ***Live and Guaranteed 1988!*** tour, the Danish leg of which was filmed and recorded for video release. Fewer than half of the songs were included on the track listing and, in 1995, it was re-released with an accompanying CD. Once again, neither formats had *All by Myself* included.

Track Specification

Composed by Eric Carmen and Sergei Rachmaninoff

Musicians

John Clark	guitar
Rosemarie Ford	backing vocals
Mark Griffiths	bass
Peter Howarth	backing vocals
Steve Lauri	guitar
Paul Moessl	keyboards
Mick Mullins	backing vocals
Alan Park	keyboards
Cliff Richard	vocals
Henry Spinetti	drums, percussion

Recording Details

Producer	Unknown
Engineered by	Unknown
Recording location	Fyens Forum, Odense, Denmark
Recording date	22nd May 1988

♫ All for One

From the film soundtrack album of **The Young Ones**

Based on the oft-repeated phrase of camaraderie bond from Alexander Dumas's *The Three Musketeers* ('All for one and one for all'), the song is performed in the Simpkin's Youth Club after Nicky Black (Cliff Richard) has revealed to his girlfriend Toni Crowthier (Carole Black) that he is Hamilton Black's son, as he fears a backlash after Black Senior is responsible for the impending closure. All of the young adults at the club are despondent, until Toni suggests that they put on a show to get the £1,500 required to extend the lease that is now owned by Hamilton Black. There is excitement as the characters express their ideas for the show, which leads into a routine after Nicky professes that they can do anything together. The first line of the song mentions Dumas and the chorus of amity. During the performance, there is a solo by Cliff as Nicky playing the drums and cymbals (although what is seen is occasionally out of step with the soundtrack but cleverly covered nonetheless). The song is revisited later in the film (although not appearing on the soundtrack album) when singing star Dorinder Morell announces that she is leaving the show having signed to Hamilton Black's other theatre on the same night, leaving Nicky (as The Mystery Singer) to become the new star of the club's effort.

One of six songs to be completed at the 9th August session, the same take was used for the mono and stereo edit, although different mixes were required for the audio channels. The version of the song used in the film was recorded separately from the album sessions and, to date, it has not been released on any other format than the film itself. This version features the vocals of the actors taking part rather than the Mike Sammes Singers.

The mild orchestral backing to the song and the change in tempo all are familiar film musical techniques that had been in use for a number of years but, inevitably, the film required something to link it back to what was known and comfortable rather than alienating parts of the audience with full rock and roll songs – or so the producers presumably thought, because the song, while pleasant enough, seems to sit in juxtaposition with the more contemporary songs.

Track Specification

Composed by Peter Myers and Ronald Cass

Musicians

Associated British Studio Orchestra	orchestra
Stanley Black	conductor
Mike Sammes Singers	vocals, backing vocals
Cliff Richard	vocals

Recording Details

Producer	Norrie Paramor
Engineered by	Malcolm Addey and Alan Kane
Recording location	Abbey Road Studio 2, St. John's Wood, London
Recording date	9th August 1961

♫ All Glory, Laud and Honour

From the album **Good News**

A much-loved hymn from traditional church services, *All Glory, Laud and Honour* has been covered by a number of artists including the Hosanna Chorus, Michael Silverman, the King's College Cambridge Choir, Mike Curb and the Peter Knight Singers.

Cliff Richard recorded his version at the end of a long session for the ***Good News*** album that saw five songs attempted and only three completed, with *All Glory, Laud and Honour* successfully closing the session with just two takes.

Initiated with a full choral version in male voices singing the first couple of lines, Cliff sings the hymnal lyrics with impassioned gusto, successfully closing the first side of the vinyl version of the album. The backing vocalists are uncredited but it is possible that they are representatives from the Mike Sammes Singers although this is yet to be confirmed.

Track Specification

Composed by John M. Neale

Musicians

Norrie Paramor Orchestra	orchestra
Mike Leander	arranger, conductor
Cliff Richard	vocals
Unknown	backing vocals

Recording Details

Producer	Norrie Paramor
Engineered by	Peter Vince and Mike Stone
Recording location	Abbey Road Studio 2, St. John's Wood, London
Recording date	4th May 1967

♫ All I Ask of You

99th UK single

The eighties seemed to be the pinnacle of Cliff Richard's collaborations with other artists, including Phil Everly, Elton John, Sheila Walsh, Janet Jackson, Olivia Newton-John and the Young Ones, and the latest came in 1986 when Andrew Lloyd Webber invited him to record *All I Ask of You* with his then wife Sarah Brightman and the star of the upcoming musical theatre extravaganza that was to become *The Phantom of the Opera*. The song is performed at the point in the narrative where Christine (Brightman) has become increasingly frightened of the activities of the Phantom (eventually to be played by Michael Crawford) and shares her anxieties with Raoul (played by Cliff for the purposes of the record). In the course of the song, Raoul asks Christine to marry him and she accepts the proposal but, unbeknownst to them, the jealous Phantom is in hiding, listening to what they are saying.

Backed with one of the most dramatic orchestral openings to a musical, *Phantom Overture Act II*, *All I Ask of You* was released as a single on the Polydor label (catalogue number POSP 802) on 26th September 1986 and reached number three in the UK charts. At the same, a twelve-inch single was released with the same B-side track and the addition of ***Only You*** (taken from *Starlight Express*), which was another Cliff and Sarah Brightman duet (catalogue number POSPX 802). A promotional CD disc, which had *All I Ask of You* and three other tracks (Brightman on *Wishing You Were Here*, Michael Crawford and Brightman on *Phantom of the Opera* and Crawford on *The Music of the Night*), was released to preview the show's music (catalogue number 731488-2). As well as appearing on CD commercially for the first time on Cliff's 1988 album, ***Private Collection***, it was subsequently released on ***Two's Company*** in 2006. The promotional video featured a torrid red sunset with Cliff and Brightman in white. The sky turns to blue when her vocals come in as Cliff gazes at her adoringly, as the backing melts to a seascape returning to the sky. Cliff acts well but the back-drops look very tacky.

As is expected from Lloyd Webber, there is a complex and lush accompaniment, here provided by the Royal Philharmonic Orchestra and conducted by The Really Useful Company's resident music director, David Caddick. Brightman's vocal over-emphasises the lyrics and consonants which distracts slightly from the performance but the overall product is strong both lyrically and musically and is best when Cliff is singing and when the pair are singing in harmony or unison, particularly in the dramatic moments such as the dénouement of the song.

Track Specification

Composed by Andrew Lloyd Webber and Charles Hart

Musicians		*Recording Details*	
Sarah Brightman	vocals	Producer	Andrew Lloyd Webber
David Caddick	conductor	Engineered by	Martin Levan
Cliff Richard	vocals	Recording location	Abbey Road Studios, St. John's Wood, London
Royal Philharmonic Orchestra	orchestra	Recording date	6th August 1986

♬ All I Do Is Dream of You

From the EP **Dream**

Originally written for the 1934 musical *Sadie McKee, All I Do Is Dream of You* has since become a standard for many artists plundering the catalogue of songs from the first half of the twentieth century. The following year, Chico Marx performed a piano instrumental version of it in the Marx Brothers' film *A Night at the Opera*. It was then revived twice for 1952's *Singin' in the Rain* (Debbie Reynolds and Gene Kelly) and 1953's *The Affairs of Dobie Gills* (Debbie Reynolds (again) and Bobby Van). The first version was recorded in 1934 by Dick Robertson with Angelo Ferdinando's Orchestra and has since been issued by a number of different artists including Alma Cogan, Michael Bublé, Twiggy, Ella Fitzgerald, Dean Martin, Perry Como, Johnny Ray, Patti Page and Judy Garland among many others.

One of three songs recorded for the ***Dream*** EP (the first EP to be of new material not featured on any other Cliff Richard release) at the early May 1961 session, the final and thirteenth take was used for the mono and stereo edits, although different mixes were required for the respective audio channels. Until the 1989 See For Miles compilation album release of EP tracks, *All I Do Is Dream of You* was a substantial rarity and it was much sought after by fans. The song has since been released on a French album and on the collection of ***Cliff Sings the Standards*** in 2003.

Like the preceding ***Dream*** song track, *All I Do Is Dream of You* is introduced with a complex melody played on a classical guitar before the entry of Cliff's vocals that leads into a swinging rhythm supported by brushed drums and gentle lead guitar. Not as strong as *Dream, All I Do Is Dream of You* is nevertheless a good track that is an exemplar of Cliff's output at the time. The Shadows' accompaniment is subdued with the emphasis primarily on the vocal line in the mix, although the introduction, completion and middle eight all allow them same free rein to improvise.

Track Specification

Composed by Arthur Freed and Nacio Herb Brown

Musicians		*Recording Details*	
Jet Harris	bass	Producer	Norrie Paramor
Hank Marvin	guitar	Engineered by	Malcolm Addey
Tony Meehan	drums, percussion	Recording location	Abbey Road Studio 2, St. John's Wood, London
Cliff Richard	vocals	Recording date	4th May 1961
Bruce Welch	rhythm guitar		

♬ All I Have to Do Is Dream

122nd UK single

All I Have to Do Is Dream was written by the husband and wife songwriting partnership of Felice and Boudleaux Bryant and was published in 1958. There have been three versions that have made a showing in the British singles charts with the Everly Brothers being by far the most familiar and successful, when it reached the number one spot as a double A-side with ***Claudette*** and stayed for seven weeks in the late summer of 1958. It was later picked up by Bobbie Gentry and Glen Campbell in 1969, reaching number three at the beginning of 1970. The third was, of course, the 1994 release of the duet by Phil Everly and Cliff Richard. The actor Richard Chamberlain attempted the song in 1963, reaching number fourteen in the US Billboard charts and Andy Gibb and Victoria Principal had another duet in 1981, although that only reached number fifty-one in the US.

The 1994 single release by Cliff and Everly was mixed from a 1981 recording at the Hammersmith Odeon as part of a BBC documentary about Cliff. This programme ensured a strong single in ***Daddy's Home*** at the time of recording but it would

take another thirteen years for three further tracks to be licensed from the BBC: *All I Have to Do Is Dream*, ***When Will I Be Loved*** and ***Tribute to the Legends Medley***, all accompanied by Phil Everly. The tracks were remixed in September of 1994 and, for *All I Have to Do Is Dream*, the applause was technologically removed to give the sound of being recorded in a studio. During the early nineties, as inducement to buy the then new format CD versions, Cliff's singles often were issued in two parts usually over two weeks, while still offering the alternative vinyl version but with more limited content. The vinyl single was backed with a remixed version of ***Miss You Nights*** as a double A-side on the EMI label (catalogue number EM 359) on 28th November 1994; the first CD single had the same tracks as the vinyl singles with the addition of the aforementioned *When Will I Be Loved* and the *Tribute to the Legends Medley* and was issued on the EMI label (catalogue number CDEMS 359) also on 28th November; the second part of the CD single release reiterated the double A-side tracks but included ***True Love Ways*** and ***Party Megamix*** as bonus tracks (catalogue number CDEM 359) on 5th December 1994. Combining the sales of all formats of the double A-side single ensured that it reached number fourteen in the UK charts.
As had already been proven to the public with ***She Means Nothing to Me***, Cliff's voice matches well with Phil Everly's and this makes *All I Have to Do Is Dream* another piece of evidence to prove the effectiveness of their duetting capabilities. Cliff takes the melody predominantly, while Everly, when not singing in unison, provides the higher harmonies as he did on the original with his brother. There is an effective key change leading into the final verse and the song ends on a sudden rallentando with both men singing *a capella*.

Track Specification
Composed by Felice Bryant and Boudleaux Bryant

Musicians

Stuart Calver	backing vocals
John Clark	guitar
Phil Everly	vocal
Mark Griffiths	bass
Graham Jarvis	drums, percussion
Martin Jenner	guitar
Alan Park	keyboards
John Perry	backing vocals
Cliff Richard	vocals
Tony Rivers	backing vocals
Graham Todd	keyboards

Recording Details

Producer	Cliff Richard
Engineered by	Unknown
Recording location	Hammersmith Odeon, London
Remixed at	R. G. Jones Studio, London
Recording date	1st May 1981 (live track), 7th September 1994 (remix) and 5th October 1994 (applause removal)

♫ All in the April Evening

Unissued track

The signature song of the Glasgow Orpheus Choir, which records many modern religious works, and covered by several other choirs, *All in the April Evening* was the first song to be recorded by Cliff Richard in the 28th April session for the ***Good News*** album, although, after three takes, further attempts were abandoned and the song remains unissued. Pat Clark was present at these sessions but, without access to the recording, it is unclear whether she performs on this song or not.

Track Specification
Composed by Hugh S. Roberton

Musicians

Pat Clark	vocals
Norrie Paramor Orchestra	orchestra
Mike Leander	arranger, conductor
Cliff Richard	vocals

Recording Details

Producer	Norrie Paramor
Engineered by	Peter Vince and Mike Stone
Recording location	Abbey Road Studio 2, St. John's Wood, London
Recording date	28th April 1967

♫ All Kinds of People

From the film soundtrack album of **Wonderful Life**

In the narrative of ***Wonderful Life***, the group has tried to make another film alongside the main film, but is thwarted by the director (Walter Slezak) who bars them from using company equipment or facilities. Johnny (Cliff Richard), desperate to finish his film, remembers fashion photographer Miguel and agrees that it takes different people to make a film. The song uses several visual ideas for getting things done (digging a hole needs a spade and so on) and it turns into a major dance routine featuring both Cliff and Una Stubbs prominently. Briefly, it is reprised as part of ***Youth and Experience***.
Recorded at a session that completed four tracks for the *Wonderful Life* soundtrack, *All Kinds of People* was the last to be finished. The same (unknown) take and edit was used for the mono and stereo recordings but with different mixes to cater for the separate audio channel requirements, and it appeared on the track listing of the ***Hits from Wonderful Life*** EP. The film version was probably recorded in the first three months of 1964, although the details of the musicians, studio personnel and location are unknown. The film version differs in that the section featuring the dancing is extended, while the lyrics and arrangement remain close to the soundtrack version. To date, the film version has not been released.
Sounding similar to the ***Summer Holiday*** song ***Let Us Take You for a Ride***, this song is one of the better Myers and Cass compositions from the film. With time signature and key changes, the interest is maintained, particularly with the involvement of the members of the Mike Sammes Singers. However, it is yet another track that doesn't work well when listening to the soundtrack since it has obviously been created solely for the dance routine that it supports.

Track Specification
Composed by Peter Myers and Ronald Cass

Musicians

Associated British Studio Orchestra	orchestra
Stanley Black	conductor
Mike Sammes Singers	backing vocals
Cliff Richard	vocals

Recording Details

Producer	Norrie Paramor
Engineered by	Malcolm Addey
Recording location	Abbey Road Studio 2, St. John's Wood, London
Recording date	22nd April 1964

♫ All My Love

***40th UK single** and from the albums* **...And They Said It Wouldn't Last! (My 50 Years in Music)** *and* **Live at the Talk of the Town**

Often subtitled in brackets with its original Italian title of *Solo Tu* (literally *Only You*), *All My Love* has been covered by only a few artists in its English language incarnation, including Vikki Carr and Cliff Richard's friend and fellow singer Cilla Black. But it was Cliff's version that was the most successful, even though some critics may have considered the choice of song a retrograde step for him after the innovative ***The Day I Met Marie***. Backed with the Christmas song ***Sweet Little Jesus Boy***, *All My Love* was released as a single on the Columbia label (catalogue number DB 8293) on 10th November 1967, rising to a high of number six in the UK singles charts. It was originally issued in mono only, which was the practice and policy of Columbia at that time, reserving stereo for the album releases only alongside the mono versions. It was subsequently issued in stereo format on the 1969 compilation ***The Best of Cliff***.

Supported by strings, a harp and a lugubrious xylophone, this sort of song has Cliff in his element and he complements the accompaniment by giving a strong and emotional performance that occasionally borders on the operatic. For the second verse, the instrumentation becomes fuller as he is accompanied, too, by the Mike Sammes Singers. This continues until the final chorus, with its rallentando as he finishes on the song's title.

In 2008, as part of the rarity collection ***...And They Said It Wouldn't Last! (My 50 Years in Music)***, the first take from the session was issued on the *Lost and Found* selection. There are very slight differences in the backing accompaniment but otherwise, this issue is very close to the original single released recording.

Track Specification
Composed by Monti Arduini; English lyrics by Peter Callender

1. Single

Musicians

Bernard Ebbinghouse Orchestra	orchestra
Bernard Ebbinghouse	arranger, conductor
Mike Sammes Singers	backing vocals
Cliff Richard	vocals

Recording Details

Producer	Norrie Paramor
Engineered by	Peter Vince
Recording location	Abbey Road Studio 2, St. John's Wood, London
Recording date	5th October 1967

2. ...And They Said It Wouldn't Last! (My 50 Years in Music)

Musicians

Bernard Ebbinghouse Orchestra	orchestra
Bernard Ebbinghouse	arranger, conductor
Mike Sammes Singers	backing vocals
Cliff Richard	vocals

Recording Details

Producer	Norrie Paramor
Engineered by	Peter Vince
Recording location	Abbey Road Studio 2, St. John's Wood, London
Recording date	5th October 1967

3. Live at the Talk of the Town

Musicians

Breakaways: Vicki Hasemen, Margo Quantrell, Jean Ryder	backing vocals
Norrie Paramor	arranger, conductor
Cliff Richard	vocals
Talk of the Town Orchestra	orchestra

Recording Details

Producer	Norrie Paramor
Engineered by	Peter Vince
Recording location	Talk of the Town Theatre, London
Recording date	30th May 1968

♫ All out of Love

From the album **Love... The Album**

The familiar pop ballad, *All out of Love*, was first recorded by Air Supply and was released in 1980. It reached number two in the US charts and number eleven in Britain with what was the band's first single in the early autumn. Irish boy band Westlife recorded the song as a duet with ex-*Neighbours* actress Delta Goodrem and it has also been covered by John Barrowman, One Voice, Jenny Drey, Keira Green, Donny Osmond and Soft Cell among others.

Cliff Richard recorded his version as the final song of five new tracks to be added to the compilation of ballads album ***Love... The Album*** in 2007. The musicians in the band performing on the track remain unknown until further research reveals the details for this entry to be updated.

A flowing piano introduces the song, which is taken at a slightly faster pace than the original. Cliff's anguished vocals are supported by a full string orchestra and rock band, while female voices provide the backing vocals during each chorus. In the mid-section, there is an almost *a capella* vocal arrangement that includes Cliff providing his own harmonies.

Track Specification
Composed by Graham Russell and Clive Davis

Musicians		*Recording Details*	
Cliff Richard	vocals, backing vocals	Producer	Michael Omartian
Unknown	backing vocals	Engineered by	Terry Christian
Unknown	guitar	Recording location	Sound Kitchen, Franklin, Tennessee, USA, Sound House, Franklin, Tennessee, USA and/or Blue Wave Studios, Bayley's Plantation, St. Phillip, Barbados
Unknown	bass		
Unknown	piano		
Unknown	drums, percussion		
Unknown	arranger, conductor	Recording date	2007
Unknown	orchestra		

♫ All Shook Up

From the albums **Thank You Very Much**, **Wanted** *and* **World Tour Live**

Elvis Presley's first UK number one came with his eleventh release in July 1957, but it only reached number three in the US. Co-written by Presley, the song gave its title to the theatrical musical featuring a number of his songs, the plot of which was roughly based on William Shakespeare's *Twelfth Night* with the songs interpolated into the narrative. In 1992, Billy Joel took his version of *All Shook Up* into the UK charts where it settled at number twenty-seven. A number of other artists have covered the song including Suzi Quatro, the Beatles, the Jeff Beck Group and Paul McCartney.

Often citing Presley as a formative influence, it is no surprise that Cliff Richard should choose one of his songs to celebrate twenty years in showbusiness. Performing the song with Hank Marvin and Bruce Welch as an acoustic set for the ***Thank You Very Much*** concerts and album, the guitar introduction is played principally by Hank but Cliff and Bruce are also strumming as they sing in close harmony; a blend that is exquisite. Sitting on stools, they bring in humour as they raise up from the seats and down during the final chorus. The mid-section has a perfect *a capella* rendition that is perfect.

It was an obvious choice when it came to picking the track listing for Cliff's first album of the new millennium, ***Wanted***, which featured covers of songs that were recognizable and popular, as well as a few original songs to add to the mixture. Since Presley was a confirmed influence, two songs (the other was ***Love Me Tender***) were recorded. However, this version is far more upbeat than the original or the live version (and also gets in a couple of uncredited lines from ***Devil Woman***), with a hefty bass drum beat driving the song while the keyboards play a repetitive motif. Cliff performs the song with a quiet confidentiality that is in juxtaposition to the lyrical meaning; however, this adds an extraordinary dimension to the song that is augmented further by the backing vocal arrangement, which includes some vocoder treatment.

For the tour to support the release of the album, the New Zealand leg was filmed for DVD release later in the year. The following year, a selection of the songs was chosen for the track listing of a CD album and this included *All Shook Up*. The live version includes a saxophone accompaniment, while Cliff is joined on stage by the dancers dressed in black, but the song is a faithful reproduction of his studio track in all other respects.

Track Specification
Composed by Otis Blackwell and Elvis Presley

1. Thank You Very Much

Musicians		*Recording Details*	
Hank Marvin	backing vocals, guitar	Producer	Bruce Welch
Cliff Richard	vocals, guitar	Engineered by	Tony Clark, remixed by Peter Vince
Bruce Welch	backing vocals, rhythm guitar	Recording location	London Palladium, London
		Remix location	Abbey Road Studios, St. John's Wood, London
		Recording date	4th March 1978

2. Wanted

Musicians		*Recording Details*	
John Brant	additional programming	Producer	Alan Tarney
Anthony Clark	backing vocals	Engineered by	John Brant and Gerry Kitchingham
Cliff Richard	vocals, backing vocals	Recording location	Wilmer Studios, London
Alan Tarney	arranger, backing vocals, keyboards, programming	Recording date	January-April 2001

3. World Tour Live

Musicians		*Recording Details*	
Anthony Clark	backing vocals, guitar	Producer	Keith Bessey
John Clark	guitar	Engineered by	Keith Bessey
Dave Cooke	keyboards	Recording location	The Mission Winery, Napier, New Zealand
Mike Haughton	saxophone	Recording date	22nd February 2003
Peter Howarth	backing vocals		
Pete May	drums, percussion		
Mick Mullins	backing vocals		
Keith Murrell	backing vocals		
Alan Park	keyboards		
Cliff Richard	vocals		
Steve Stroud	bass		

♬ All That Matters

From the album **Diana Princess of Wales Tribute** *and* **Something Special**

On the 31st August 1997, Britain went into an extraordinary and unprecedented period of mourning after learning of the death of Diana, Princess of Wales. She suffered terrible injuries after the car in which she was travelling crashed into a pillar in the tunnel by the Pont de l'Alma in Paris because the chauffeur, believed to be under the influence of alcohol, was trying to get away from the chasing paparazzi. At her funeral a week later, Elton John performed a modified version of *Candle in the Wind*, which was subsequently recorded and issued as a single with all proceeds going to her charity. This inspired a full concert, at which Cliff Richard made an appearance to sing *All That Matters*, which was written by his old friend Paul Field. The subsequent tribute album featuring the track was also sold in aid of her charities.
As is expected from an Alan Tarney production, the performance is littered with shimmering keyboards and synthesisers. The track is a gentle song of reflection, a tinge of regret but also happy memories. Cliff provides his own backing vocals alongside Tarney's, which are successfully layered and brought together under the insistent beat created on the synthesized drums. In the middle eight, there is a sophisticated guitar solo, which gives way to a percussion accompaniment and then a short vocal passage by Cliff before relinquishing control back to a repeat of the chorus.
Cliff revisited the song for a charity performance at the Brighton Centre in aid of NASS (the National Asylum Support Service), which was later released on a special album, *Something Special*, and featured Cliff and a simple accompaniment on guitar.

Track Specification
Composed by Paul Field

1. Diana, Princess of Wales Tribute

Musicians		*Recording Details*	
Cliff Richard	vocals, backing vocals	Producer	Alan Tarney
Alan Tarney	backing vocals, guitar, bass, synthesisers, drum programming	Engineered by	Unknown
		Recording location	Unknown
		Recording date	1997

2. Something Special

Musicians		*Recording Details*	
Cliff Richard	vocals, guitar	Producer	Paul Raynor-Brown
		Engineered by	Julius Warren
		Recording location	Brighton Centre, Brighton
		Recording date	7th June 1998

♬ All the Time

From the album **I'm Grateful** *(Garth Hewitt)*

Also featuring future Wings guitarist Laurence Juber, *All the Time* was one of the three songs on which Cliff Richard helped to record backing vocals for Garth Hewitt's solo album, *I'm Grateful*. Recorded in between the spread out sessions for Cliff's next album, ***Rock 'n' Roll Juvenile***, the suite of songs for Hewitt's album was finished in the summer of 1978, with *All the Time* being issued on CD for the first time as part of the collection *30 Songs in 30 Years 1973-2003*.
The lovely guitar introduction leads into Hewitt's lead vocal, which is held back as if not wanting to reveal his inner thoughts. For the second verse, the choir-like backing vocals appear and slowly the power of the song builds up. Cliff contributes backing vocals but these are almost like a duet, as he sings the lyrics gently under Hewitt's main performance.

Track Specification
Composed by Garth Hewitt

Musicians		*Recording Details*	
Rod Edwards	piano, electric piano	Producer	Jon Miller, Rod Edwards and Roger Hand
Mike Giles	drums, percussion	Engineered by	Roger T. Wake
Garth Hewitt	vocals	Recording location	Redan Recorders, London
Jessy Dixon Singers	backing vocals	Recording date	August 1978
Laurence Juber	guitar		
John G. Perry	bass		
Cliff Richard	backing vocals		
Bob Weston	guitar solo		

♬ All the Time You Need

From the album **Live & Guaranteed 1988!** *and B-side of* **Silhouettes** *(twelve-inch and CD single only)*

Before Cliff Richard recorded a new Chris Eaton song, *All the Time You Need*, it was tried out in concert during the *Live & Guaranteed 1988!* tour. The Danish leg of the performances was filmed and recorded for video release, which was subsequently reissued on VHS with an accompanying CD. Over half of the set list remains unissued in aural format but *All the Time You Need* was incorporated as the opening track, although it was the fourth to be performed in the concert and also had not been added to the original VHS release.

Cliff took the song into the studios a couple of months after the tour and, along with another eventual B-side ***Marmaduke***, recorded it for future release. When ***Silhouettes*** was issued as a single in August 1990, *All the Time You Need* was chosen as a bonus B-side track on the twelve-inch and CD versions of the single. It was later included on the original album release of ***From a Distance* ***** *The Event*** in 1990, although it was removed, presumably for space considerations and the fact it was a studio recording, from the track listing of the 2005 remaster of the album.

The song begins as a straightforward love ballad but, as Cliff enters the chorus, the drama is built up allowing him to express the lyrics which talk of a relationship that is faltering and the mixture of emotions between wanting to hug someone and accepting that they should be given space. Ultimately, he looks to God to guide him in the mid-section making it a quasi-religious song in addition to being a love ballad.

Track Specification
Composed by Chris Eaton

1. Unissued track (Live & Guaranteed 1988!)

Musicians		*Recording Details*	
John Clark	guitar	Producer	Unknown
Rosemarie Ford	backing vocals	Engineered by	Unknown
Mark Griffiths	bass	Recording location	Fyens Forum, Odense, Denmark
Peter Howarth	backing vocals	Recording date	22nd May 1988
Steve Lauri	guitar		
Paul Moessl	keyboards		
Mick Mullins	backing vocals		
Alan Park	keyboards		
Cliff Richard	vocals		
Henry Spinetti	drums, percussion		

2. B-side (Silhouettes - twelve-inch and CD only)

Musicians		*Recording Details*	
John Clark	guitar	Producer	Cliff Richard
Mark Griffiths	bass	Engineered by	Gerry Kitchingham and Ben Robbins
Peter Howarth	backing vocals	Recording location	R. G. Jones Studios, Wimbledon, London
Steve Lauri	guitar	Recording date	August 1988
Paul Moessl	synthesisers		
Mick Mullins	backing vocals		
Keith Murrell	backing vocals		
Alan Park	piano		
Cliff Richard	vocals		
Henry Spinetti	drums, percussion		

♫ All You Need Is Love

From the album **Party at the Park**

As with all of the Beatles songs credited to John Lennon and Paul McCartney, it was almost always one or the other's song with perhaps some contribution from the other during the development; however, some were totally down to the one writer with no input from the other (for McCartney, such an example is *Yesterday* or *Eleanor Rigby*) and *All You Need Is Love* was totally created by Lennon. The song was the result of a commission by the BBC for the Beatles to perform at the first global satellite broadcast. Starting with a brass band playing *La Marseillaise* (the French national anthem), it leads into relatively simplistic lyrics that can be understood easily even if English is not necessarily the first language. This was part of the brief and subsequently it was watched by over 400 million people in twenty-six different countries. The song was released as a single and became an instant success on the back of the broadcast and the fact that it was the Beatles singing about love during the early part of the Summer of Love, reaching number one in many countries around the world.

The song was employed to help close the pop concert in the grounds of Buckingham Palace in June 2002, taking place in honour of Queen Elizabeth II's fiftieth anniversary of her accession to the throne. Driven by Rod Stewart, Joe Cocker and Paul McCartney, several other guests including Cliff Richard appeared on the stage to help out with the supporting vocals. The introduction is changed from *La Marseillaise* to become the first few bars of the British National Anthem (more appropriate to the occasion). The sing-along quality of the song is exploited in this performance, featuring the different lead vocalists, the band, the orchestra and solo efforts from the likes of Eric Clapton.

Track Specification
Composed by John Lennon and Paul McCartney

Musicians		*Recording Details*	
Rusty Anderson	guitar	Producer	Giles Martin
Sam Brown	backing vocals	Engineered by	Andy Rose
Margo Buchanan	backing vocals	Recording location	Buckingham Palace, London
Eric Clapton	guitar solo	Mixed by	Paul Hicks (Abbey Road) and John Hudson and Greg Jackman (Mayfair)
Joe Cocker	vocals		
Phil Collins	drums, percussion	Mixed at	Abbey Road Studios, St. John's Wood, London and Mayfair Studios, London
Ray Cooper	percussion		
Claudia Fontaine	backing vocals	Recording date	3rd June 2002

Abe Laboriel Jr.	drums, percussion
Ladysmith Black Mambazo	backing vocals
Paul McCartney	vocals, piano
Pino Palladino	bass
Phil Palmer	guitar
Brian Ray	guitar
Cliff Richard	backing vocals
Eric Robison	saxophone
Royal Academy of Music Symphony Orchestra	orchestra
Rod Stewart	vocals
Wix Wickens	keyboards

♬ Almost Like Being in Love

From the album **Listen to Cliff!**

Written for the musical *Brigadoon* in 1947 by one of the most enduring writing partnerships of Lerner and Loewe, it was famously performed by Gene Kelly in the 1954 film of the musical play. It has since been covered by a variety of artists including Frank Sinatra, Shirley Bassey, Michael Johnson (who had a US hit with his version), Ella Fitzgerald, Dean Martin and Judy Garland. Nat King Cole's recording was used in the credits of the 1993 comedy film *Groundhog Day*, in which the main character relives the same day over and over until he learns to express his emotions and love for the girl sincerely.
The final track from the first side of ***Listen to Cliff!*** album was recorded in both stereo and mono. The same take (the third and final from the session) was used for each version but mixed differently for the requisite aural channels. *Almost Like Being in Love* was also included on the track listing of the ***Listen to Cliff! No.*** **2** EP.
A swinging beat in the orchestral brass gives way to the keyboards as Cliff almost carelessly takes up the vocal. What is extraordinary in this upbeat song is that Cliff was a young man when this was recorded but he is able to perform all styles of music and, with the genre of big band swing, he holds the tune and the energy of the song as if he were a much older performer.

Track Specification
Composed by Frederick Loewe and Alan Jay Lerner
Musicians

Bernard Ebbinghouse Orchestra	orchestra
Cliff Richard	vocals

Recording Details

Producer	Norrie Paramor
Engineered by	Malcolm Addey and David Lloyd
Recording location	Abbey Road Studio 2, St. John's Wood, London
Recording date	11th January 1961

♬ Alpha Omega

From the album **Don't Hide Your Heart** *(Sheila Walsh)*

Written by long-term Cliff Richard collaborator Chris Eaton, *Alpha Omega* is the theological idea that God is the beginning and the end, as in the first and last characters of the Greek alphabet. The song was featured on Sheila Walsh's third album, ***Don't Hide Your Heart***, on which Cliff principally provided backing vocals in a year when he did very little recording, joined by Eaton himself as well as two members of Network 3, for whom Cliff had produced two singles earlier in the decade.
With a foot-tapping beat initiating the song, the synthesiser backing and the lead vocal have all the hallmarks of a mid-eighties pop song by the likes of female artists such as Sheena Easton. Cliff's vocals are still discernible in the group singing the backing harmonies.

Track Specification
Composed by Chris Eaton
Musicians

Chris Eaton	backing vocals
Rick Fenn	guitar
London Community Gospel Choir	choir
Annie McCaig	backing vocals
Craig Pruess	keyboards, electronics
Cliff Richard	backing vocals
Mo Turner	backing vocals
Sheila Walsh	vocals
Mark Williamson	backing vocals

Recording Details

Producer	Craig Pruess and Keith Bessey
Engineered by	Keith Bessey
Recording location	Gallery Studios, Chertsey, Surrey
Recording date	November 1984-February 1985

♬ Alright, It's Alright

From the album **I'm Nearly Famous**

The closing track of Cliff Richard's ***I'm Nearly Famous*** album was completed at the first session in December 1975, with three takes sealing the recording, while additional vocal overdubs were recorded at a follow-up session nine days later. The American issue of the vinyl album (on Elton John's Rocket Records) incorrectly lists this song as ***It's Alright Now***.

The synthesiser- and guitar-driven song is riven with syncopation that, at the time, was an extraordinary gear-change for Cliff to be singing. The chorus is quieter than the brashness of the verse, but it is the instrumentation that comes to the fore on this song. Taking an unusual approach to the album, Cliff provides much of his own backing vocals during the verses, and is only joined by his choir – the first time he had employed a singing group on non-ballad tracks – in the choruses.

Track Specification
Composed by Michael Allison and Peter Sills

Musicians	
Terry Britten	guitar
Clem Cattini	drums, percussion
Tony Harding	backing vocals
John Perry	backing vocals
Cliff Richard	vocals, backing vocals
Tony Rivers	backing vocals
Alan Tarney	bass
Graham Todd	keyboards

Recording Details	
Producer	Bruce Welch
Engineered by	Tony Clark and John Barrett
Recording location	Abbey Road Studio 3, St. John's Wood, London
Recording date	1st and 10th December 1975

♫ Always (1)

From the album **Sincerely Cliff Richard**

Always was written by Terry Britten, who would be so instrumental in engineering Cliff Richard's renaissance in the mid-seventies with his beautiful tunes and it started with this gently yearning ballad.

Always was recorded at the beginning of July 1968 but only released towards the end of the following year on *Sincerely Cliff Richard*. The first of two songs to be completed at the session, *Always* was accepted as one of Cliff's favourite songs from the period.

With flutes and interesting rhythm created by the percussion and strings, Cliff brings the song in gently as the instrumentation slowly builds up behind it. With an uncredited female backing vocal group producing strong harmonies and the arrangement creating interesting augmented intervals, the performance is deceptively strong while being held back at the same time.

Track Specification
Composed by Terry Britten

Musicians	
Mike Leander	conductor
Mike Leander Orchestra	orchestra
Cliff Richard	vocals
Unknown	backing vocals

Recording Details	
Producer	Norrie Paramor
Engineered by	Peter Vince
Recording location	Abbey Road Studio 2, St. John's Wood, London
Recording date	6th July 1968

♫ Always (2)

From the album **From a Distance ***** The Event**

Not to be confused with the song of the same nam recorded for the ***Sincerely Cliff Richard*** album in 1968, *Always* was written by Irving Berlin in 1925 and proffered as a wedding gift for Ellin McKay when they married the following year. Originally intended for a Marx Brothers musical and film *The Cocoanuts*, it was cut from the project by Berlin himself. Since its publication in the twenties, the song has been covered by hundreds of artists including Frank Sinatra, Phil Collins, Patsy Cline (who had a hit with the most familiar version in 1964), the Ink Spots, Guy Lombardo and Leonard Cohen.

Recorded at the *From a Distance ***** The Event*, where it segues from the Dallas Boys singing their version of *Zing Went the Strings of My Heart* and moving on to a spirited rendition of *When* by the Kalin Twins, both of which didn't feature Cliff.

Saxophones drive the harmonies and the bass line keeps the rhythm moving ever onwards underneath Cliff's exemplary vocals. The arrangement is pure rock and roll ballad in spite of it being written some sixty-four years before.

Track Specification
Composed by Irving Berlin

Musicians	
Oh Boy! Band	rock 'n' roll band
Cliff Richard	vocals

Recording Details	
Producer	Cliff Richard
Engineered by	Keith Bessey and Mick McKenna
Recording location	Rolling Stones Mobile Studio, Wembley Stadium, Wembley, North-west London
Recording date	16th-17th June 1989

♫ Always Guaranteed

From the albums **Always Guaranteed** *and* **Live & Guaranteed 1988!**

The title song from Cliff Richard's ***Always Guaranteed*** album closes the original album and, like all the other tracks, was composed and driven by the producer Alan Tarney. At the time, Cliff was heavily involved in his lead role as the Rock Star in the London-based ***Time – the Musical*** making his availability for recording limited. As it happened, Tarney would develop the songs and lay down the backing track in time for Cliff to come in and quickly apply his vocals.

A strong melody matched with the sputtering synthesiser accompaniment, Cliff sings the song with a kind of confidentiality as if he is singing to the listener alone and this is reflected by the engineering of the track. The upbeat nature of the rhythm makes it a suitable song to complete the album and leaves the listener wanting more.
The title track was performed at the ***Live & Guaranteed 1988!*** Performances, with the Danish concert filmed and recorded for release as a video. In 1995, it was reissued but included a CD of the songs, too, which featured *Always Guaranteed*.

Track Specification
Composed by Alan Tarney

1. *Always Guaranteed*

Musicians	
Cliff Richard	vocals, backing vocals
Alan Tarney	backing vocals, guitars, bass, keyboards, drum and percussion programming

Recording Details	
Producer	Alan Tarney
Engineered by	Gerry Kitchingham and Keith Bessey
Recording location	R. G. Jones Studios, Wimbledon, London
Recording date	13th October-November 1986

2. *Live & Guaranteed 1988!*

Musicians	
John Clark	guitar
Rosemarie Ford	backing vocals
Mark Griffiths	bass
Peter Howarth	backing vocals
Steve Lauri	guitar
Paul Moessl	keyboards
Mick Mullins	backing vocals
Alan Park	keyboards
Cliff Richard	vocals
Henry Spinetti	drums, percussion

Recording Details	
Producer	Unknown
Engineered by	Unknown
Recording location	Fyens Forum, Odense, Denmark
Recording date	22nd May 1988

♫ Always on the Run

From the album **Did He Jump... Or Was He Pushed?** *(Garth Hewitt)*

Written by the protagonist of the album ***Did He Jump... Or Was He Pushed?***, Garth Hewitt, *Always on the Run* also featured Cliff Richard on guitar, backing vocals and production duties.
After two tracks of rock and roll on the album, *Always on the Run* takes the pace down and exhibits a slight country feel. Cliff supplies occasional backing vocals to Hewitt's lead vocal, which is strong and well executed.

Track Specification
Composed by Garth Hewitt

Musicians	
Garth Hewitt	vocals
Graham Jarvis	drums, percussion
Adrian Lee	synthesiser
Mike Moran	keyboards
Jo Partridge	guitar
Cliff Richard	backing vocals
Dave Wintour	bass

Recording Details	
Producer	Cliff Richard
Engineered by	Tony Clark and Haydn Bendall
Recording location	Odyssey Studios, London
Recording date	1979

♫ Amandier Sauvage, L'

B-side of **La Ballade de Baltimore**

Cliff Richard recorded a number of songs in French, often covers of English versions he had already recorded, although the output was limited since there was a preference to release foreign songs in the German language. Nevertheless, in June 1971, he was back in the studio recording a French version of ***The Lady Came from Baltimore***, which was retitled ***La Ballade de Baltimore***, for single release. To partner it as a B-side, recorded at the same session, Cliff completed *L'Amandier Sauvage* – literally translated as *The Wild Almond* – which is an original French song.
Initially released in mono format as part of the single issue, the stereo mix of the song was added to the track listing of the French language compilation ***When in France... Chante en Français*** in 1975. It was finally issued in digital format (also in stereo) as part of the 1997 collation of Cliff's foreign language songs, ***On the Continent***.
Cliff sings competently in a variety of languages but particularly well in French and German. Supported by an uncredited backing chorus, the song is pleasant enough, although it sounds a little distracting as it leads into the chorus from the verse and back again because the pace strangely picks up and slows.

Track Specification
Composed by Pierre-André Dousset and Guy Bonnet

Musicians	
Nick Ingman	arranger, conductor
Nick Ingman Orchestra	orchestra
Cliff Richard	vocals
Unknown	backing vocals

Recording Details	
Producer	Norrie Paramor
Engineered by	Peter Vince
Recording location	Abbey Road Studio 2, St. John's Wood, London
Recording date	2nd June 1971

♫ Amazing Grace

From the albums **Help It Along** *and* **Japan Tour 74**

Written in 1773 and published in 1779 as a hymn by an English clergyman, John Newton, *Amazing Grace* is imbued with the meaning of forgiveness and the enticing possibility of redemption for those who sin. The hymn was composed from personal experience, since Newton grew up without much religious awareness but was press-ganged into joining the navy; one night, a violent storm forced him to call out to God for mercy and sparked his conversion. Ordained in 1964, he began writing hymns, occasionally with William Cowper and *Amazing Grace* was written in order to illustrate a sermon he was giving about the redemption of sinners.

Amazing Grace was first recorded in 1922 with an *a capella* version by the Sacred Harp Choir. Since then, it has become a recording favourite and has been covered by Joan Baez, Aretha Franklin, Rod Stewart, Sam Cooke, Elvis Presley, The Byrds, Willie Nelson and the Lemonheads among several others. Its popularity was given a further boost when Arlo Guthrie performed it at the Woodstock festival, but it is Judy Collins' version that is by far the most famous. In the UK, she reached number one in 1970 and re-entered a phenomenal seven times. This was followed by a bagpipe version, which also reached number one, by the Pipes and Drums and Military Band of the Royal Scots Dragoon Guards in 1972.

At that time, not only was it a familiar song but it had topped the charts twice in recent years and so it was unsurprising that Cliff Richard would include it on the set list of his studio-based concerts at the Morgan Studios in London in front of a small audience. Here it was recorded as part of seventeen songs in a seven-session marathon over three days for inclusion on the charity album ***Help It Along***, which was sold in aid of the Tear Fund.

Starting with a guitar introduction, this gives way to a unison *a capella* rendition of the familiar melody featuring Cliff and the backing vocalists before the guitar returns for the second verse. By the third verse, the rest of the instruments have come in building up on the exquisite musical drama that unfolds, before returning to the *a capella* in the final verse - this time featuring the male voices in addition to the women.

It was subsequently incorporated into the ***Gospel Medley*** section of his tour of Japan: ***Jesus***, *Amazing Grace* and ***Jesus Is My Kind of People***. The instrumentation from *Jesus* stops abruptly and leads into a string segue before Cliff sings the first verse unaccompanied and is then joined by the other singers in an *a capella* rendition of the second verse before the jazzy piano kicks in to introduce *Jesus Is My Kind of People*.

Track Specification

Composed by John Newton

1. Help It Along

Musicians		*Recording Details*	
Terry Britten	backing vocals, guitar	Producer	David MacKay
Cliff Hall	keyboards	Engineered by	Roger Quested
Jean Hawker	backing vocals	Recording location	Morgan Studios, London
Anna Peacock	backing vocals	Recording date	24th, 25th and 26th September 1973
Kevin Peek	guitar		
Cliff Richard	vocals		
Trevor Spencer	backing vocals, drums, percussion		
Alan Tarney	backing vocals, bass		

2. Japan Tour '74

Musicians		*Recording Details*	
Brian Lewis	backing vocals	Producer	Toshiba EMI (no individual detailed)
Cliff Richard	vocals	Engineered by	Toshiba EMI (no individual detailed)
Alan Tarney	backing vocals	Recording location	Shinjuku Koseinenkin, Tokyo, Japan
Bruce Welch	backing vocals	Recording date	7th-8th October 1974

♫ Amor, Amor, Amor

From the album **When in Spain** *and unissued track*

Literally translated into the English language as *Love, Love, Love*, the Spanish ballad *Amor, Amor, Amor* was recorded in Barcelona for Cliff Richard's ***When in Spain*** album. Later in January 1965, Cliff recorded several vocal lines translated into English for several of these Spanish tracks from the album. On the session listing for those tracks is the title *Amor, Amor, Amor* (note that it has not been translated to English) and, given the purpose of those sessions, it is likely that this is an English version, although it remains unreleased to date.

The Spanish album version was one of four tracks completed at the session, being the last of the four to be recorded. The fourth and final take and edit were used for the mono and stereo recordings but with different mixes for the needs of the audio channel.

The song is very gentle with a mandolin-like accompaniment on the lead guitar backed with arpeggiated rhythm and strings backing Cliff's vocal line. To the layman's ear, Cliff expresses the Spanish pronunciation very well- the result of the phonetic notation of the lyrics and a lot of hard work in the studio. Because the album was in Spanish, it was less played than others (although it reached the top ten in the UK) and this is a shame since this is a most beautiful track from Cliff and the Shadows.

Track Specification
Composed by Ricardo Lopez Mendez and Gabriel Ruiz

1. When in Spain

Musicians

Brian Bennett	drums, percussion
Brian 'Licorice' Locking	bass
Hank Marvin	guitar
Norrie Paramor Strings	orchestra
Norrie Paramor	arranger, conductor
Cliff Richard	vocals
Bruce Welch	rhythm guitar

Recording Details

Producer	Norrie Paramor
Engineered by	Malcolm Addey
Recording location	EMI Studios, Barcelona and Abbey Road Studio 2, St. John's Wood, London (strings)
Recording date	28th April 1963 (main recording) and 14th May 1963 (strings)

2. Unissued track (possible English vocal recording)

Musicians

Brian Bennett	drums, percussion
Brian 'Licorice' Locking	bass
Hank Marvin	guitar
Norrie Paramor Strings	orchestra
Norrie Paramor	arranger, conductor
Cliff Richard	vocals
Bruce Welch	rhythm guitar

Recording Details

Producer	Norrie Paramor
Engineered by	Malcolm Addey
Recording location	EMI Studios, Barcelona and Abbey Road Studio 2, St. John's Wood, London (strings, English vocal)
Recording date	28th April 1963 (main recording), 4th May 1963 (strings) and 31st January 1965 (English vocal)

♬ And I Love Her
From the album **Wanted**

Many of the writing credits for the Beatles were given to John Lennon and Paul McCartney, although there was often little or no input from the other besides suggestions during recording (an example is *Yesterday*, which was solely McCartney and didn't even feature Lennon on the recording). Although *And I Love Her* was principally written by McCartney, Lennon claimed in a *Playboy* interview that he had contributed the middle eight, thereby warranting his compositional credit, while McCartney maintains that Lennon had no such influence. Whatever the story behind its creation, the song shows the maturing Beatles sound. Although not a UK single, it was backed with *Tell Me Why* in the US to promote *A Hard Day's Night* and reached number twelve there. It has since been covered by several people including Bob Marley and the Wailers, Bobby Womack, Barry Manilow, Richard Marx, Carla Bruni and Smokey Robinson and the Miracles.

Cliff Richard picked the song for ***Wanted***, his first album since parting company with EMI, and, working with Alan Tarney again for the first time in twelve years, produced a version that is quintessentially Cliff while nodding towards the provenance of the Beatles colossus.

While the Beatles version was quiet, subdued and performed with gentle guitars and rhythm, Cliff's version is more upbeat with a strong percussive element in its accompaniment. Cliff imbues the lyrics with the requisite emotion and the backing vocal arrangement lifts the cover version further, with ad libbed comments throughout by Alan Tarney.

Track Specification
Composed by John Lennon and Paul McCartney

Musicians

John Brant	additional programming
Anthony Clark	backing vocals
Cliff Richard	vocals, backing vocals
Alan Tarney	arranger, backing vocals, spoken vocals, keyboards, programming

Recording Details

Producer	Alan Tarney
Engineered by	John Brant and Gerry Kitchingham
Recording location	Wilmer Studios, London
Recording date	January-April 2001

♬ And Me (I'm on the Outside Now)
From the album **Two a Penny**

One of two songs written by Cliff Richard and Mike Leander that were recorded at the second session of the day, *And Me (I'm on the Outside Now)* was recorded directly after the first song to be completed, ***Lonely Girl***. The two sessions were set up with the orchestra and Shadows at the beginning and then finishing with just the Shadows backing songs.

A Greek-style guitar with accidentals giving the song a rocking motion and the brass concoction work through the song, which Cliff sings with emotion as he tells of a break-up with a girl and observing her happiness from a distance. Gradually and subtly, the pace picks up as the verses follow on, although it's unclear whether this is intentional or not (certainly it matches the style and the *faux* Greco music).

Track Specification
Composed by Cliff Richard and Mike Leander

Musicians

Breakaways:	backing vocals
Vicki Hasemen	
Margo Quantrell	
Jean Ryder	
Mike Leander	arranger, conductor
Mike Leander Orchestra	orchestra

Recording Details

Producer	Norrie Paramor
Engineered by	Peter Vince
Recording location	Abbey Road Studio 2, St. John's Wood, London
Recording date	8th March 1968

♫ Angel

From the album **Cliff Richard** *and unissued live tracks*

One of the twenty-one tracks provided to Cliff Richard by Sid Tepper and Roy Bennett for recording over the first few years of the sixties, *Angel* was recorded during the American Columbia sessions in Nashville and New York in the summer of 1964. The song gave its title to the ***Angel*** EP, the track listing of which was only released in mono; the international single release was also only issued in mono, backed with ***Razzle Dazzle*** on the Columbia label (catalogue number DC 762) in May 1965, and it reached the top ten in places such as Australia and Hong Kong. Although this single version was not an official UK release, it found its way into record outlets, although it didn't chart as a single. The stereo version of the song was released on the stereo issue of the ***Cliff Richard*** album. The same (unknown) take and edit were used for the mono and stereo recordings but with different mixes for the separate audio channels.

The bass line is the most interesting part of the accompaniment since it is so complex in comparison with much of the instrumentation. There are key changes, an organ instrumental break and female backing vocals (although no Jordanaires this time) and a racing rhythm that keeps the toes tapping.

Part of the set for his tours after the release of the album, particularly with *Angel* being a popular single in the Far East, it was recorded at the performance that made up the ***Cliff in Japan*** album but, to date, has not been issued.

Resurrected for the world tour in 2003, Cliff's New Zealand concert was filmed for DVD release later that year. While all of the tracks performed were issued on the DVD, the complementary CD album, *World Tour Live*, only featured a subset of the songs and missing from it was this version of *Angel*.

Track Specification

Composed by Sid Tepper and Roy C. Bennett

1. Cliff Richard

Musicians

Cliff Richard	vocals
Unknown	female backing vocals
Unknown	hand claps
Unknown	guitar
Unknown	bass
Unknown	piano
Unknown	organ
Unknown	drums, percussion

Recording Details

Producer	Bob Morgan and Billy Sherrill
Engineered by	Mort Thomason
Recording location	Columbia Studios, Nashville
Recording date	24th August 1964

2. Unissued track (Cliff in Japan)

Musicians

Norrie Paramor Orchestra	orchestra
Norrie Paramor	arranger, conductor
Cliff Richard	vocals
Unknown	backing vocals

Recording Details

Producer	Norrie Paramor
Engineered by	Unknown
Recording location	Shibuya Public Hall, Tokyo, Japan
Recording date	18th October 1967

3. Unissued track (World Tour Live)

Musicians

Anthony Clark	backing vocals, guitar
John Clark	guitar
Dave Cooke	keyboards
Mike Haughton	saxophone
Peter Howarth	backing vocals
Pete May	drums, percussion
Mick Mullins	backing vocals
Keith Murrell	backing vocals
Alan Park	keyboards
Cliff Richard	vocals
Steve Stroud	bass

Recording Details

Producer	Keith Bessey
Engineered by	Keith Bessey
Recording location	The Mission Winery, Napier, New Zealand
Recording date	22nd February 2003

♫ Annabella Umbrella

B-side of **Silvery Rain**

Back in the London-based Chappell Studios rather than the familiar Abbey Road complex, Cliff Richard recorded two B-side songs at this session. The first was ***Pigeon***, while the second was *Annabella Umbrella*, although this was not the first introduction to that song. For Cliff's second German language album, *Ich Träume Deine Träume*, he had recorded a large amount of original material, including a song called ***Umbarella*** (so derived from the three syllables stretched across four notes, thereby forcing an additional syllable and taking the phonetic word as the title). It was recorded at a marathon session in November of 1970 and, secondarily with the original English lyrics, recorded in February the next year.

Annabella Umbrella was included as part of a maxi-single, backing Cliff's fifty-third UK single, ***Silvery Rain***, alongside its B-side partner, ***Time Flies***. It was originally released in mono, with Columbia reverting back to its policy of not releasing stereo singles, and it would take another thirty-seven years before the stereo version was added to the track listing of the rare B-sides section of the celebratory collation ***...And They Said It Wouldn't Last! (My 50 Years in Music)***.

The production of the English interpretation of the song is a significant improvement on the German version, principally because Cliff's vocal line is mixed further forward. The chorus is more upbeat than the verse and each time is introduced by drums and a tripping bass guitar. The uncredited backing vocals are a little too strident and mature for the original intent of the lyrics that talk about a childhood sweetheart and simple early memories of love.

Track Specification
Composed by Valerie Avon and Harold Spiro

Musicians		*Recording Details*	
Nick Ingman	arranger, conductor	Producer	Norrie Paramor
Nick Ingman Orchestra	orchestra	Engineered by	Unknown
Cliff Richard	vocals	Recording location	Chappell Studios, London
Unknown	backing vocals	Recording date	12th February 1971

♫ Another Christmas Day
B-side of **Remember Me**

Other than carols and their modernized variants over the years (for example, ***Little Town***), *Another Christmas Day* was the first original Cliff Richard recording to touch on the season of Christmas – something for which Cliff would forever be associated and occasionally castigated. After his run as the Rock Star in ***Time – the Musical***, during which period Cliff recorded the entire ***Always Guaranteed*** album in his time off during the day, he returned to the studio in the early spring of 1987 to record a number of additional tracks that were used as B-sides. The self-penned *Another Christmas Day* was slightly different, however, because, while it was the official B-side of the third single from that album, ***Remember Me***, in all its formats, the track was also released on a bonus one-sided seven-inch vinyl single (EMI label; catalogue number XMAS 87A) as part of the *Always Guaranteed* special boxed set release and it included an etched signature and message on the blank side. Cliff recorded the song in the studio at his Cliff Richard Organisation offices based in Esher. The song was included as a bonus track on the 2004 remaster of *Always Guaranteed*.
The twinkling of the synthesisers is the first clue that the song has a Christmas theme. However, it eschews the desire to add other Christmas effects such as bells of any variety. As it was composed by Cliff, it is obviously well-suited for his voice and it is difficult to imagine another singer improving upon it.

Track Specification
Composed by Cliff Richard

Musicians		*Recording Details*	
John Clark	guitar, bass	Producer	Cliff Richard
Alan Park	keyboards, drum and percussion programming	Engineered by	Keith Bessey
		Recording location	C. R. O. Studios, Esher, Surrey
Cliff Richard	vocals, backing vocals	Recording date	April 1987

♫ Anti-Brotherhood of Man, The
From the film soundtrack album of **Take Me High**

Possibly due to timing restrictions on the original release, the soundtrack album for ***Take Me High*** presented the songs in a different sequence from what is heard during the film's narrative. This is most obvious with *The Anti-Brotherhood of Man*, which appears as the ninth song after ***Take Me High*** and before ***Winning*** on the soundtrack, while it is actually the fourth song appearing *after Winning* and before ***Why?*** in the film. However, this random sequence of the songs doesn't detract from the listenability of the album as a suite of songs.
Sarah (Debbie Watling) has a struggling French café-cum-restaurant that is losing money because of her boyfriend's lack of business acumen (and cooking skills, it is revealed). She attempts to get money from the Furness Orlando merchant bank and is strung along by Hugo Flaxman (Anthony Andrews). Flaxman then leaves Tim Matthews (Cliff Richard) to impart the news that there is no more money to be had and hides as Tim tells her the bad news but his hiding place is revealed. Sarah loses her temper and there is a wordless argument that ensues with this song performed over the top.
The Anti-Brotherhood of Man was completed in just one take at a set of sessions in May 1973 for the film. There is some suggestion that a selection of the songs were recorded in May with vocal overdubs in September; however, there is no information to confirm that this track was one of them. Until further information is found, it is assumed that the song was successfully completed at the May sessions.
This short atmospheric song, which slowly builds up in drama, starts with Cliff singing pianissimo backed with him also talking the vocals underneath the main melody line, as more instrumentation and then an uncredited backing choir are led in and brought to sharp conclusion by the sound effect of a door slamming.

Track Specification
Composed by Tony Cole

Musicians		*Recording Details*	
David MacKay Orchestra	orchestra	Producer	David MacKay
David MacKay	arranger, conductor	Engineered by	Tony Clark and Mike Jarrett
Cliff Richard	vocals, spoken vocals	Recording location	Abbey Road Studio 3, St. John's Wood, London
Unknown	backing vocals	Recording date	27th-28th May 1973

♫ Anyone Who Had a Heart

From the album **Two's Company**

The song *Anyone Who Had a Heart* was offered to Dionne Warwick before Hal David and Burt Bacharach had finished its composition and she loved it. It is quirky in its changes of time signature throughout from common time to five/four time to seven/eight. Recorded by Warwick in New York in November 1963, the same sessions also produced ***Walk on By***. Released later that month, *Anyone Who Had a Heart* reached number one in the US in December. In February 1964, it was released as her first single in the UK, reaching number forty-two, but it was Cilla Black who had the bigger hit when her cover reached number one and stayed for three weeks during the same period. Two weeks after these two versions were released, UK singer Mary May released another version. Given the popularity of Black's record, it is unsurprising that this only reached number forty-nine. Petula Clark, signed to the same label as Warwick, released foreign language versions on the continent, while a host of other artists covered the song including, Dusty Springfield, Atomic Kitten, Shirley Bassey, the Four Seasons, Luther Vandross, Vicky Leandros, Olivia Newton-John and Linda Ronstadt among several others.

In the middle of the first decade of the new millennium, Cliff Richard decided to record an album of duets, extrapolating the track listing from those he had already recorded. One of the new songs he recorded was *Anyone Who Had a Heart* with the original artist, Dionne Warwick. Music press suggested that the track was to be released on a duets album recorded by Warwick but this project failed to materialize, while the duet she definitely recorded appeared on Cliff's ***Two's Company***.

The dramatic string introduction leads into Warwick's introduction, joined by Cliff who takes over the verse and they share the duties on the chorus. Quite faithful to the original, Dionne Warwick's voice has deepened over the years but they successfully blend their vocals.

Track Specification

Composed by Burt Bacharach and Hal David

Musicians

Chris Cameron	arranger, conductor
Mickey Féat	bass
Peter Gordeno	keyboards
Katie Kissoon	backing vocals
Tessa Niles	backing vocals
Phil Palmer	guitar
Cliff Richard	vocals, backing vocals
Unknown	orchestra
Dionne Warwick	vocals
Gavin Wright	leader, violin

Recording Details

Producer	Chris Porter
Engineered by	Chris Porter
Recording location	Metropolis Studios, London and Abbey Road Studios, St. John's Wood, London
Recording date	Summer 2005

♫ Anything I Can Do

From the album **I'm No Hero**

Having had a long association with both Cliff Richard and the Shadows in the late sixties and seventies, Alan Tarney increased his dominance in Cliff's output in the eighties, starting with a number of tracks for the ***I'm No Hero*** album in 1980. The recording sessions were transplanted from the more familiar Abbey Road to the Riverside Studios.

The synthesiser and bass-heavy song is typical of the material Cliff was recording during the period and specifically for the *I'm No Hero* album. The beat is strong as was the style dictated by songs of the era, while the melody is enhanced by the vocal harmonies created by the multiple layering Cliff's and Tarney's vocals.

Track Specification

Composed by Alan Tarney

Musicians

Michael Boddicker	synthesiser
Nick Glennie-Smith	synthesiser
Cliff Richard	vocals, backing vocals
Trevor Spencer	drums, percussion
Alan Tarney	arranger, backing vocals, bass

Recording Details

Producer	Alan Tarney
Engineered by	Ashley Howe
Recording location	Riverside Studios, London
Recording date	12th May-27th June 1980

♫ Apache

Single by **The Shadows**

Ostensibly set up as Cliff Richard's backing band, The Shadows had attempted a parallel recording career since their inception. In their former guise of The Drifters (the release and success of ***Living Doll*** in America in the latter part of 1959 forced the name change to The Shadows to avoid confusion with the pre-existing US vocal group of the same name), they had released two singles – *Feelin' Fine* and *Jet Black* – while, as The Shadows, they had released *Saturday Dance*. What was odd, with the benefit of hindsight, was that these were all vocal tracks and the record-buying public seemed to have a problem with Cliff's band also recording vocal singles. This all changed in the middle of 1960, when they picked up a tune called *Apache*, much vaunted at the time by Bert Weedon in his shows, and the start of a long and happy relationship with the composer Jerry Lordan, who would go on to write a number of other instrumental tracks for the band.

The other problem with the first three singles, while reasonably strong in their own right, they were somewhat derivative and appeared to be copying others' sounds rather than generating their own definitive style. In parallel, Hank Marvin and

Bruce Welch (principally) and Jet Harris and Tony Meehan were sculpting what would be quintessentially The Shadows sound as part of their backing with Cliff (and none more so obvious than on the ***Me and My Shadows*** album). With *Apache*, this was fully formed and, despite having many imitators – the tune was desperately copied by acts such as The Surfaris, The Challengers, Aki Aleong, The Rockets, The Ventures and Bert Weedon himself – but none of them exhibited the magical ingredient that made The Shadows' version of *Apache* superlative and a template for the copycats.
The tune was recorded in between the sessions for *Me and My Shadows*, along with the B-side *Quatermasster's Stores* – this being a cultural play on words, because the most watched programme of the time was the thriller series following Professor Bernard Quatermass's exploits; contemporaneously, National Service was still in force and one of the campfire songs the cadets would have learned would have been *Quartermaster's Stores*. The sense of humour that would make many future Shadows titles brought the elements together. Cliff Richard was on hand to play the distinctive thumping native drums at the start and end of the *Apache* track.
Initially, Norrie Paramor wanted to release *Quatermasster's Stores* as the A-side on the premise that those leaving National Service would be more likely to buy a rocked up version of a familiar tune. However, it was agreed that *Apache* was the stronger tune and Paramor's decision was overturned. The single was released on the Columbia label (catalogue number 45-DB 4484) in July 1960, and reached number one, usurping Cliff's ***Please Don't Tease*** in the process, and stayed there for five weeks, cementing the Shadows' reputation as an instrumental band and giving them a lengthy parallel career.
Apache has, of course, appeared on several compilations and is held up as the apogee of guitar instrumentals and the defining tune of the Shadows' recorded output. In addition to being a single, it was also included on the *Shadows to the Fore* EP, which was released on the Columbia label (catalogue number SEGM 8094) a couple of years later in 1962. A clear favourite with fans in concert, the thrumming drum introduction leaves no doubt what is about to be played.
The recording has been released in slightly differing formats, the mono and stereo single versions, of course, but also two to be found on *The Shadows at EMI* and *20 Golden Greats*, both of which enhance the instrumentation rather than change or add anything to them. As such, since these are the same recordings, they will not qualify for a separate track specification.

Track Specification
Composed by Jerry Lordan

Musicians		*Recording Details*	
Jet Harris	bass	Producer	Norrie Paramor
Hank Marvin	lead guitar	Engineered by	Malcolm Addey
Tony Meehan	drums, percussion	Recording location	Abbey Road Studio 2, St. John's Wood, London
Cliff Richard	Chinese drum	Recording date	17th June 1960
Bruce Welch	rhythm guitar		

♫ Apron Strings
From the album **Cliff** *and the B-side of* **Living Doll**

Cliff Richard and the Drifters first recorded *Apron Strings* during the 'live' session in front of invited fans at Abbey Road. Throughout the song, there are screams from the girls, presumably in response to some gyration or other from their idol. This 'live' version of the song was also included on Cliff's first EP, *Cliff No. 1*.
The performance of the song is the closest that Cliff got to emulate *his* idol, Elvis Presley, with a sort of choked vocal, particularly in the chorus with the repetition of the word 'tied'. The song is about a man professing his love to a woman and his willingness to settle down with her and be, as the title suggests, tied to her apron strings. It's an interesting social documentary because, in that era, the man went out to work while the woman stayed in the house, wearing the ubiquitous apron. That has changed over the fifty years since and the idea of being tied to anyone's apron strings regarded as a potentially sexist slight. In addition, it is interesting to note that the phrase 'being tied to apron strings' also referred to grown children refusing to fly the domestic nest: in other words, being mollycoddled by the matriarch.
The song has been covered by an esoteric sequence of artists including Curtis Hoback, Johnny and the Roccos and, of course, Marty Wilde. Since Wilde covered the song, it was reasonable that Cliff and the Drifters should include it in their 'live' set as it would still be fresh in the record-buying public's mind.
The B-side of ***Living Doll*** was a new recording (without audience) of *Apron Strings*, which allowed the vocal and instrumentation to come more to the fore, with the driving drums, the twanging guitar solo, the running bass line and Cliff's jerking vocal style he had adopted for the song. However, it possible that the version used for publication may have been an error since the paperwork from the sessions indicate that this is a rehearsal take only. The mono and stereo versions are the same recording but with different mixes for the additional aural channel.

Track Specification
Composed by George Weiss and Aaron Schroeder

1. Cliff

Musicians		*Recording Details*	
Jet Harris	bass	Producer	Norrie Paramor
Hank Marvin	guitar	Engineered by	Peter Bown and Stuart Eltham
Tony Meehan	drums, percussion	Recording location	Abbey Road Studio 2, St. John's Wood, London
Cliff Richard	vocals	Recording date	9th February 1959
Bruce Welch	rhythm guitar		

2. B-side (Living Doll)

Musicians		*Recording Details*	
Jet Harris	bass	Producer	Norrie Paramor
Hank Marvin	guitar	Engineered by	Peter Bown and Stuart Eltham
Tony Meehan	drums, percussion	Recording location	Abbey Road Studio 2, St. John's Wood, London
Cliff Richard	vocals	Recording date	25th May 1959
Bruce Welch	rhythm guitar		

♫ Are You Only Fooling Me?

From the album **Tracks 'n' Grooves**

Written by the Raymond Froggatt, who was responsible for one of Cliff's biggest recent hits, ***Big Ship***, *Are You Only Fooling Me?* was recorded at the second of two sessions planned for the 22nd September 1969. The second song to be recorded, it was the only song to be released, with the other two (***Postmark Heaven*** and ***When You Are There***) being held back by EMI for almost forty years. Songs like *Are You Fooling Me?* fit Cliff's voice perfectly and the uncredited backing vocals, for once, meld to wonderful effect with his lead and this is because they are Cliff working with himself.

Track Specification

Composed by Raymond Froggatt

Musicians		*Recording Details*	
Mike Vickers Orchestra	orchestra	Producer	Norrie Paramor
Cliff Richard	vocals, backing vocals	Engineered by	Peter Vince
Mike Vickers	arranger, conductor	Recording location	Abbey Road Studio 2, St. John's Wood, London
		Recording date	22nd September 1969

♫ Are You Sincere?

B-side of **Wonderful Summer** *(Richard Loring)*

In 1977, Cliff Richard had few appointments in the recording studio for his own material but he helped others out. He worked as producer for five tracks by Richard Loring, one of which, ***Wonderful Summer***, was released as a single in South Africa only in 1978. For the B-side, *Are You Sincere?* was was a country song from the early sixties and had already been covered by Elvis Presley, Floyd Cramer, Marty Robbins, the Platters, Gene McDaniels and several others.

Track Specification

Composed by Wayne Walker

Musicians		*Recording Details*	
Richard Loring	vocals	Producer	Cliff Richard
Unknown	other instrumentation	Engineered by	Unknown
		Recording location	Abbey Road Studios, St. John's Wood, London
		Recording date	August 1977

♫ Arrivederci Roma

From the album **When in Rome**

Written in 1955, *Arrivederci Roma* (or *Goodbye Rome*) was included in the score for Mario Lanza's 1957 film *Seven Hills of Rome*, with the Italian film release taking the title of the song. English lyrics were added by Jack Fishman with the title changed to *Arrivederci Darling*. In this latter incarnation, it was a hit for Anne Shelton, who reached number seventeen in late 1955 as her first charting single. It was swiftly followed within a week a two by Edna Savage who had her only chart entry with this song when it reached number nineteen but stayed in the charts for just one week. It has also been covered by Jo Stafford, the Three Suns and Francisco Cavez. In the original Italian version, it has been covered by a much larger community of artists including Claudio Villa, Edmundo Ros, Percy Faith, Vic Damone, Mantovani, Dean Martin, Connie Francis, Nat King Cole, Guy Lombardo, Chet Atkins and Perry Como amongst many others.

Cliff Richard's version was recorded for his album ***When in Rome***, which featured covers of several Italian originals. *Arrivederci Roma* was one of the very few songs in a foreign language that he recorded that didn't have an English counterpart. The final (unknown) vocal take was overdubbed on the fourth and final orchestral take that was recorded seven months earlier. The track was only released in mono format, which included the EP ***Hits from When in Rome***.

Cliff had difficulty with learning to enunciate the Italian lyrics, which were written phonetically for him, but it is not obvious from the evidence in this song and his performance here is one of the best on the album.

Track Specification

Composed by Pierre Garinei, Sandor Giovannini and Renato Rascel

Musicians		*Recording Details*	
Norrie Paramor Orchestra	orchestra	Producer	John Lee and M. DiPonti (backing track) and Norrie Paramor (vocals)
Norrie Paramor	arranger, conductor	Engineered by	Malcolm Addey
Cliff Richard	vocals	Recording location	EMI Studios, Milan (backing track) and Estudios Valentim, De Carvalho, Lisbon (vocals)
		Recording date	2nd-3rd October 1964 (backing track) and 13th May 1965 (vocals)

♫ Ashes to Ashes

B-side of **Help It Along/Tomorrow Rising**

Written by Tony Cole, who would go on to write much of the material for Cliff Richard's final film, ***Take Me High***, *Ashes to Ashes* was one of the six contenders for the UK song in the 1973 Eurovision Song Contest. Cliff performed each of the songs over a period of weeks on the BBC1 Saturday night variety show, *Cilla*, which was hosted by his friend Cilla Black. *Ashes to Ashes* was the second song to be performed before being reprised at the end of the run and presented for the public postal vote. Unfortunately, it came last, polling 7.1% just behind ***The Days of Love*** (7.6%), but it was obvious that the winner was ***Power to All Our Friends*** (51.8%).

Recorded as the first song in a two-day session that saw all six contending songs wrapped up, the first session also yielded *The Day of Love* and the second-placed ***Come Back Billie Jo***. Usually, the winner and runner-up were released as a single with the four remaining songs forming a complementary EP; however, on this occasion, the third- and fourth-placed songs (***Help It Along*** and ***Tomorrow Rising***) were combined to form a literal double A-side, released as a maxi-single with *The Days of Love* and *Ashes to Ashes* forming a joint B-side. A major rarity for many years, it was eventually reissued on the remastered version of ***The 31st of February Street*** in 2004.

Unsurprisingly, *Ashes to Ashes* has an echo of the score for *Take Me High* as it crashes into life with a dramatic orchestral accompaniment. The verses are lighter in touch than the chorus, which is fast-paced and optimistic but, unfortunately, while the music progression is surprisingly intricate, there are insufficient expected hooks for the song to be a serious contender for the Eurovision Song Contest.

Track Specification

Composed by Tony Cole

Musicians

Terry Britten	backing vocals, guitar
David MacKay Orchestra	orchestra
David MacKay	backing vocals, arranger, conductor
Kevin Peek	guitar
Cliff Richard	vocals
Trevor Spencer	backing vocals, drums, percussion
Alan Tarney	backing vocals, bass

Recording Details

Producer	David MacKay
Engineered by	Peter Vince
Recording location	Abbey Road Studio 2, St. John's Wood, London
Recording date	27th December 1972

♫ As I Walk into the Morning of Your Life

From the album **Tracks 'n' Grooves**

As I Walk into the Morning of Your Life was the first of five songs to be successfully recorded at the session that was a departure from the previous ten years with the operation transferred to London's Chappell Studios rather than the familiar Abbey Road Studios. The second song on the ***Tracks 'n' Grooves*** album, it would remain in the vaults of EMI for over two years until the album was eventually pulled together and released. This timing delay meant that only the stereo version was issued, although a mono version would have been created at the time of recording since it wasn't clear when the song would be released.

With a Latin rhythm, *As I Walk into the Morning of Your Life* is a typical song that Cliff recorded and released during this period. The song features a gradual move down the scale through most of the verses and then enters into an almost baroque orchestral interlude in the middle eight. There is a female backing group but these are uncredited, although it is quite possible that it is the Breakaways who were regularly recording with Cliff at the time.

Track Specification

Composed by Joey Brooks

Musicians

Mike Leander	arranger, conductor
Mike Leander Orchestra	orchestra
Cliff Richard	vocals
Unknown	backing vocals

Recording Details

Producer	Norrie Paramor
Engineered by	Peter Vince
Recording location	Chappell Studios, London
Recording date	2nd July 1968

♫ As Time Goes By

From the album **Cliff Sings**

Cliff's second album – and actually the first true studio album since the first, *Cliff*, was presented live in front of an audience in the studio – was divided between accompaniment from the Drifters (so named at the time of recording but they would have changed their name to The Shadows by the time of the *Cliff Sings* album release) and the Norrie Paramor Orchestra. *As Time Goes By* has, for many years, been a much loved standard for balladeers and crooners and it was also chosen for the theme tune for the BBC situation comedy of the same name starring Geoffrey Palmer and Dame Judi Dench. The song was originally recorded by Rudy Vallee for RCA Victor in the early thirties and was later included in the musical *Everybody's Welcome*. Murray Burnett had heard Vallee's recording and, when travelling in Europe heard another singer's version. Against the warmongering backdrop of late thirties Europe, he wrote the stage play *Everybody Goes to*

Rick's, which also featured the song. Of course, it is a matter of historical record this was picked up by Warner Brothers as a film option and it was transmogrified into *Casablanca*, from which the song's use is its most powerful and famous.
Because of the popularity of the film and its leading actors in Ingrid Bergman and Humphrey Bogart, *As Time Goes By* has been covered over the years by a wide variety of acts such as Barbra Streisand, Jason Donovan, Frank Sinatra, Tony Bennett, Carly Simon, Harry Nilsson, Kenny G, Kenny Rogers and Jimmy Durante.
The swooping strings and supporting brass give suitable support to Cliff Richard's liquid vocals in his interpretation of the song. It is very difficult to do something different with a song that has been covered by so many people yet Cliff manages to bring something a little different to it. Using the same take for both mono and stereo releases (for the album and the mono *Cliff Sings No. 3* EP and the stereo version of the EP), Norrie Paramor and his engineers remixed it for use in the second audio channel.

Track Specification
Composed by Herman Hupfeld
Musicians

Norrie Paramor Orchestra	orchestra
Norrie Paramor	arranger, conductor
Cliff Richard	vocals

Recording Details

Producer	Norrie Paramor
Engineered by	Malcolm Addey and Alan Kane (mono) and Stuart Eltham and Norman Smith (stereo)
Recording location	Abbey Road Studio 2, St. John's Wood, London
Recording date	10th September 1959

♫ At the Hop

From the album **From a Distance ***** The Event**

Although Cliff Richard had recorded an alternative version, retitled to ***TV Hop***, for his appearances on the *Oh Boy!* television show, he included the original Danny and the Juniors hit when he performed a ***Medley*** of rock and roll era songs to close the *Oh Boy! Set* at ***The Event*** in 1989. *At the Hop* was a number three for them in early 1958 in the UK and was reissued in July 1976 during a period of rock and roll revival; this time, it reached number thirty-nine. It was given a new lease of life in 1969, when Sha Na Na performed their version at the seminal Woodstock Festival and has since appeared in many a nostalgic American film to conjure up the feeling of the era. It has since been covered by Shakin' Stevens, Bobbie Vee, Frankie Valens and the Bloomfields and it has also been sampled by Jive Bunny and the Mastermixers.
Cliff's version is performed with the assistance of the Kalin Twins as principal shared vocals alongside the Vernons Girls, while Cliff joins in at the end just as it changes gear and shifts key to segue into ***Rock 'n' Roll Is Here to Stay***.

Track Specification
Composed by Arthur Singer, John Medora and David White
Musicians

Dallas Boys:	
Nicky Clarke	backing vocals
Leon Fisk	backing vocals
Stan Jones	backing vocals
Joe Smith	backing vocals
Bob Wragg	backing vocals
Kalin Twins:	
Harold Kalin	vocals, backing vocals
Herbie Kalin	vocals, backing vocals
Oh Boy! Band	rock 'n' roll band
Cliff Richard	vocals
Vernons Girls:	
Lyn Cornell	vocals, backing vocals
Maureen Kennedy	vocals, backing vocals
Frances Lee	vocals, backing vocals
Jean Owen	vocals, backing vocals

Recording Details

Producer	Cliff Richard
Engineered by	Keith Bessey and Mick McKenna
Recording location	Rolling Stones Mobile Studio, Wembley Stadium, Wembley, North-west London
Recording date	16th-17th June 1989

THE CLIFF RICHARD RECORDING CATALOGUE

B – B – B – B – B – B – B – B – B – B – B – B – B – B – B – B– B– B– B

♫ Baby I Could Be So Good at Loving You

From the album **Sincerely Cliff Richard**

Following its release on the Lou Rawls album *You're Good for Me, Baby I Could Be So Good at Loving You* was recorded by Cliff Richard at the beginning of July 1968 as the last song at the session. The song was included fifteen months later on the selection of songs recorded across a two-year period for the ***Sincerely Cliff Richard*** album, where it opened the second side of the original vinyl long-player. It would later be resurrected for the set list for Cliff's 1984 tour.

Employing a Mellotron, which was generally the purview of the progressive rock groups of the period, this song moves along steadily with a strong vocal arrangement backed by an uncredited male vocal group. It's not the best song on the album but there is still much to recommend it.

Track Specification

Composed by Buzz Clifford

Musicians

Mike Leander	conductor
Mike Leander Orchestra	orchestra
Cliff Richard	vocals
Unknown	backing vocals

Recording Details

Producer	Norrie Paramor
Engineered by	Peter Vince
Recording location	Abbey Road Studio 3, St. John's Wood, London
Recording date	1st July 1968

♫ Baby I Don't Care

From the album **Cliff**

The most famous and memorable version of *Baby I Don't Care* is, of course, by Elvis Presley (one of Cliff Richard's great rock and roll idols and formative influences), although several other artists have covered it including Buddy Holly, Bryan Ferry and Queen. A typical song from the Lieber and Stoller hit-making factory, it was first a singles chart hit in the UK for Holly, who reached number twelve three years after his death and then finally for Presley in 1983, when it only reached number sixty-one. However, Presley's version had been released in the US in 1958 and enjoyed much success there; it was a popular tune in the UK too but RCA never saw fit to release it at the time. Nevertheless, because both Holly and Presley had enjoyed their success with it, it was chosen as part of the repertoire for the 'live' set list at Abbey Road Studios for the album ***Cliff***, which was recorded in front of a selected audience picked from the band's fan base.

Starting with a driving bass line, Cliff gives a great vocal performance that is marred by the incessant screaming of the present fans. Tony Meehan's percussion is at the forefront of this track alongside Hank Marvin's subdued lead guitar.

The song was included on the first Cliff Richard and the Drifters EP, *Cliff No. 1*, itself released in the June of 1959.

Track Specification

Composed by Jerry Lieber and Mike Stoller

Musicians

Jet Harris	bass
Hank Marvin	guitar
Tony Meehan	drums, percussion
Cliff Richard	vocals
Bruce Welch	rhythm guitar

Recording Details

Producer	Norrie Paramor
Engineered by	Peter Bown and Stuart Eltham
Recording location	Abbey Road Studio 2, St. John's Wood, London
Recording date	9th February 1959

♫ Baby It's You

From the album **Don't Stop Me Now!**

Originally a hit for the Shirelles in 1961 when they reached the number eight position in the US Billboard chart, it was left to Britain's Dave Berry to achieve a hit with it in the UK, when his version reached number twenty-four in May 1964. But, for most people, the definitive version is the one recorded by the Beatles for their debut album *Please Please Me*, after having regularly performed it at their live gigs; the band also released a live version on the *Live at the BBC* collection in 1994, which was subsequently issued as an EP single in April 1994, and reaching the number seven spot. Popular as a song to cover, it has been recorded by artists as varied as its co-writer Burt Bacharach, Dave Berry, Pia Zadora, the Carpenters, Nick Lowe, Foxy Brown, Steve Salas, Jenny Wolfe and Shakin' Stevens.

For the album ***Don't Stop Me Now!***, released in 1967, Cliff Richard recorded his version of the song at his first studio session of the year. *Baby It's You* was the first song to be completed out of four for the album with the fourth and final take and edit being used for both the mono and stereo recordings. There is scant information available on the musicians employed on the session and they are therefore marked as unknown in the track specification.

With brass accompaniment relinquishing control to the strings and guitar, Cliff's version of the clipped original is a *tour de force* on an album made of such covers. The arrangement of the orchestra (possibly Mike Leander, Norrie Paramor or Bernard Ebbinghouse, all of whom were regularly working with Cliff at the time) is entirely sympathetic to the song, while Cliff's vocal is strong making this track one of the best on the album.

Track Specification
Composed by Hal David, Burt Bacharach and Barney Williams

Musicians

Cliff Richard	vocals
Unknown	arranger, conductor
Unknown	orchestra

Recording Details

Producer	Norrie Paramor
Engineered by	Peter Vince and Richard Lush
Recording location	Abbey Road Studio 2, St. John's Wood, London
Recording date	15th January 1967

♫ Baby You're Dynamite

***91st UK single** (seven- and twelve-inch versions) and from the album* **Silver**

Recorded at Cliff Richard's final session in 1984, *Baby You're Dynamite* brought together several names from Cliff's career history: first, it was written by Guy Fletcher and Doug Flett, who were responsible for a number of Cliff tracks in the late sixties and early seventies; second, it saw Cliff working with Bruce Welch as producer; third, Brian Bennett was brought in to play drums on the track; fourth, Cliff and the Shadows recording engineer was involved at the mixing desk; and last, while most of the recording sessions for ***Silver*** had taken place in other studios around London, *Baby You're Dynamite* was completed at the Abbey Road Studio complex. An additional point is that Cliff is reported as suggesting that the song could have – contemporaneously – won the Eurovision Song Contest, with which Cliff has a long association.

Backed with ***Ocean Deep***, the song was issued as a single on the EMI label (catalogue number EMI 5457) on 19th March 1984, reaching number twenty-seven in the British charts. As the single was slipping back down, the tracks were flipped and reissued with *Ocean Deep* pushed as the A-side on the same label and catalogue number on 7th May 1984. First time around, *Baby You're Dynamite* was also issued as a twelve-inch single, also on the EMI label (catalogue number 12EMI 5457). This release had the same tracks as the seven-inch but also included an extended mixed version of *Baby You're Dynamite*. The track that appears ***Silver*** is the same as the single version but includes extra music in between the third and final chorus and at the fade out. For the German, Dutch and Australian issues of *Baby You're Dynamite*, a completely different song, ***Back in Vaudeville***, was chosen for the B-side. The associated promotional video features Cliff playing a number of parts as he observes himself being the target for plates thrown by his girlfriend at a villa before trying to fob off her anger with a proffered rose and a goofy grin. He even gets to break a tennis racquet over his knee in emulation of John McEnroe. Eventually running down deserted tracks with a crowd, the message is enough for her anger to subside.

Exploiting the electronic drums to great effect in the introduction, the simple melody is sung with great gusto by Cliff. The backing vocals are provided by Cliff and one of the writers, Guy Fletcher, and the arrangement ensures a perfect blend with the accompaniment. As it is Bruce Welch producing, it is perhaps inevitable that there would be at least some use of Cliff's falsetto, which appears at the end of the chorus.

Track Specification
Composed by Guy Fletcher and Doug Flett

1. Single (seven-inch)

Musicians

Brian Bennett	drums, percussion
Guy Fletcher	backing vocals, keyboards
Nigel Jenkins	guitar
Alan Jones	bass
Cliff Richard	vocals, backing vocals
Bruce Welch	arranger

Recording Details

Producer	Bruce Welch
Engineered by	Peter Vince
Recording location	Abbey Road Studio, St. John's Wood, London
Recording date	August 1983

2. Single (twelve-inch)

Musicians

Brian Bennett	drums, percussion
Guy Fletcher	backing vocals, keyboards
Nigel Jenkins	guitar
Alan Jones	bass
Cliff Richard	vocals, backing vocals
Bruce Welch	arranger

Recording Details

Producer	Bruce Welch
Engineered by	Peter Vince
Recording location	Abbey Road Studio, St. John's Wood, London
Recording date	August 1983

3. Silver

Musicians

Brian Bennett	drums, percussion
Guy Fletcher	backing vocals, keyboards
Nigel Jenkins	guitar
Alan Jones	bass
Cliff Richard	vocals
Bruce Welch	arranger

Recording Details

Producer	Bruce Welch
Engineered by	Peter Vince
Recording location	Abbey Road Studio, St. John's Wood, London
Recording date	August 1983

♫ Bachelor Boy

B-side of and double A-side with **The Next Time** *and from the film soundtrack album of* **Summer Holiday –Special Edition** *and from the albums* **Hits from the Original Soundtrack of Summer Holiday**, **Cliff Richard at the Movies 1959-1974**, **Cliff Live in Korea**, **Cliff "Live" in Japan '72**, **Japan Tour '74** *and* **Reunited** *and unissued live tracks and B-side of* **Be with Me Always**

For one of the most enduring and popular of Cliff Richard's songs, it is ironic that, as far as the ***Summer Holiday*** film was concerned at any rate, it was very much an afterthought once the producers realized the film was coming in too short. It was written by Cliff and Bruce Welch who were in Norrie Paramor's office when the call came in. As many commentators like to point out (usually with a sneer), it is also quite prophetic given Cliff's eventual marital status, and is often used as a prefix for many stories in the press regarding his relationships; but that salaciousness detracts from the song itself.

Because of the lateness of establishing that the final edited version of the film was several minutes short of what was desired for a full cinema release, Norrie Paramor at Elstree contacted Cliff and Bruce Welch who happened to be at his London office. A couple of hours later, Bruce and Cliff had produced *Bachelor Boy*, with Cliff adding to the principal lyrics laid down to Bruce's music. Because the film had already wrapped, rather than increase the expense further by going on location, a sound stage was used at Elstree Studio to complete the sequence so that it could be easily spliced into the film at the requisite point. As far as the narrative is concerned, it doesn't move the story on, although it does help to underline Cliff's character's reluctance to get into a romance without knowing what he is getting into (heeding his father's warning that he will be a bachelor until he dies). Even though this is the case, it doesn't detract from the action in the film prior to and immediately after *Bachelor Boy* is performed.

In the narrative of the film, Melvyn Hayes's character makes innuendo about Barbara (Lauri Peters), who has just joined the bus, but Don (Cliff Richard) confirms that he is not interested as he enters into the familiar song. Hayes, Cliff and the four Shadows are all on hand to assist with the dancing and the singing. Hank Marvin pretends to be the young Don on his knees during the lyrics referring to what his father said and Brian Bennett uses a bicycle pump to pretend he is adding air into Hank as he gradually stands up. The dance routine is not polished but this adds to the charm as the men skip about the set. The only slight visual jarring is that the Shadows are not travelling with them but have suddenly appeared (although there are bicycles in the background linking it cleverly to the prior sequence during the performance of ***Summer Holiday***) and the other two actors (Teddy Green and Jeremy Bulloch) are not around to join in (although conceivably they are inside with the girls): presumably, the actors were on different engagements by the time this scene was shot.

In his autobiography, *Rock 'n' Roll: I Gave You the Best Years of My Life*, Bruce Welch comments that their overall skills as songwriters were very much in development at the time, which is why they thought there was nothing wrong with the lyrics at the time. However, he recognizes now that the scanning of the lyrics forces the wrong emphasis on 'have *A* wife and *A* child', leaving the nouns languishing unemphasized.

The song has been covered by Darren Day (released as an uncharting single from his stage show soundtrack based on the film), Norrie Paramor, The Bachelors, The Shadows and the Toy Dolls (an album track with altered lyrics). The soundtrack version of the song was recorded along with ***Big News*** and is a splice of takes ten and eleven, with the same edit used for the mono and stereo recordings but with different mixes for the audio channels. The soundtrack song also appeared on the ***Hits from Summer Holiday*** EP. A number of different Cliff and the Shadows versions have subsequently been released: first, on the bonus tracks of the soundtrack CD of ***Summer Holiday – Special Edition*** is the ninth take, which features lyric changes and the count-in after messing up the first few bars but with no backing vocals; second, from the American album to accompany the film, *Hits from the Original Soundtrack of Summer Holiday*, which is a different mix of the original recording but with minor differences in lyrics and in Cliff's vocal performance; and, third, the film version itself, which was recorded later at Elstree Studios and released on the album ***Cliff Richard at the Movies 1959-1974***, and is very similar to the single with the exception that it is only in mono and the backing vocals are mixed more prominently.

Originally released as the backing to another song from the film, ***The Next Time***, however, the record-buying public began to ask for the B-side as well. Issued on the Columbia label (catalogue number 45-DB 4950) on 6th December 1962, *The Next Time* hit the number one spot in the UK singles charts on 3rd January 1963. *Bachelor Boy* was subsequently listed as a double A-side from the following week with both tracks remaining at number one for a further two weeks.

With the vocals in the right channel and instrumentation in the left, there is an uncredited piano (possibly Hank Marvin or Norrie Paramor) that drives the rhythm supported by the guitars, bass and drums. *Bachelor Boy* is a prime example of the exquisite harmonies provided by Cliff and the Shadows and this is particularly emphasized during the choruses.

On the original release of ***Cliff in Japan***, the live album from his Tokyo concert on 18th October 1967, *Bachelor Boy* was left off the track listing in Britain even though it had been a strong number one in the UK. It was, however, included on the Japanese version of the album in 1968 but subsequently restored to the track listing in 2007 with the remastering of the album allowing additional tracks on the release. It has only ever been released in stereo although, since the original album was issued in both mono and stereo, it is reasonable to presume that a mono version also exists.

There exists an ultra-rare live version of *Bachelor Boy*, which appeared on the *Cliff Live in Korea*, an album that was released in 1970 in mono only for the Korean market. For the ***Cliff "Live" in Japan '72*** release, it is introduced with guitars rather than piano and includes a completely new guitar line to accompany it. *Bachelor Boy* was part of the ***Hit Medley: Living Doll***, *Bachelor Boy* and ***The Young Ones***.

Having sung ***Don't Talk to Him*** in the Japan tour in 1974, *Bachelor Boy* followed on naturally and featured Bruce Welch on prominent backing vocals. In addition, Bruce stepped forward and sang the lead on the second verse.

Again performed at the twentieth anniversary concert, ***Thank You Very Much***, the song has never been released on either the original or remastered versions of the album or on the associated video.
In spite of the restoration of all other previously unreleased tracks to the remaster of ***From a Distance ***** The Event***, *Bachelor Boy* was one of six performances to remain unissued (with no information given for the decision).
Cliff's love of tennis meant that he regularly spectates at the annual Wimbledon tournament. In 1996, the weather was particularly inclement and Cliff was invited to entertain the crowds with an impromptu concert of a number of rock and roll tracks and hits. *Bachelor Boy* was one of the few that were subsequently issued as a B-side of ***Be with Me Always***.
For the 2009 tour, Cliff got back together with the Shadows to promote the ***Reunited*** album – a twenty-two track album of re-recordings of their early popular material – and performed *Bachelor Boy*. Having introduced the song as being written by a great composer, Cliff points to himself after Bruce had started preening, once again showing the closeness that was still maintained after fifty years of working together. Once again, the performance is close to the original but it is always worth listening to it for the exquisite blending of the vocals created by Cliff, Hank and Bruce.

Track Specification
Composed by Cliff Richard and Bruce Welch

1. Single

Musicians	
Brian Bennett	drums, percussion
Brian 'Licorice' Locking	bass
Hank Marvin	backing vocals, guitar, piano
Cliff Richard	vocals
Unknown	piano
Bruce Welch	backing vocals, rhythm guitar

Recording Details	
Producer	Norrie Paramor
Engineered by	Malcolm Addey
Recording location	Abbey Road Studio 2, St. John's Wood, London
Recording date	16th November 1962

2. Summer Holiday – Special Edition

Musicians	
Brian Bennett	drums, percussion
Brian 'Licorice' Locking	bass
Hank Marvin	guitar, piano
Cliff Richard	vocals
Unknown	piano
Bruce Welch	rhythm guitar

Recording Details	
Producer	Norrie Paramor
Engineered by	Malcolm Addey
Recording location	Abbey Road Studio 2, St. John's Wood, London
Recording date	16th November 1962

3. Hits from the Original Soundtrack of Summer Holiday

Musicians	
Brian Bennett	drums, percussion
Brian 'Licorice' Locking	bass
Hank Marvin	backing vocals, guitar, piano
Cliff Richard	vocals
Unknown	piano
Bruce Welch	backing vocals, rhythm guitar

Recording Details	
Producer	Norrie Paramor
Engineered by	Malcolm Addey
Recording location	Abbey Road Studio 2, St. John's Wood, London
Recording date	16th November 1962

4. Cliff Richard at the Movies 1959-1974

Musicians	
Brian Bennett	drums, percussion
Brian 'Licorice' Locking	bass
Hank Marvin	backing vocals, guitar, piano
Cliff Richard	vocals
Unknown	piano
Bruce Welch	backing vocals, rhythm guitar

Recording Details	
Producer	Norrie Paramor
Engineered by	Malcolm Addey
Recording location	Elstree Studios, Hertfordshire
Recording date	1962

5. Cliff in Japan

Musicians	
Norrie Paramor Orchestra	orchestra
Norrie Paramor	arranger, conductor
Cliff Richard	vocals

Recording Details	
Producer	Norrie Paramor
Engineered by	Unknown
Recording location	Shibuya Public Hall, Tokyo, Japan
Recording date	18th October 1967

6. Cliff Live in Korea

Musicians	
Brian Bennett	drums, percussion
Alan Hawkshaw	keyboards
Hank Marvin	backing vocals, guitar
Cliff Richard	vocals
John Rostill	backing vocals, bass
Bruce Welch	backing vocals, rhythm guitar

Recording Details	
Producer	Unknown
Engineered by	Unknown
Recording location	Citizen Hall, Seoul, South Korea
Recording date	16th October 1969

7. Cliff "Live" in Japan '72

Musicians	
Brian Bennett	drums, percussion
Pat Carroll	backing vocals

Recording Details	
Producer	Norrie Paramor
Engineered by	Unknown

John Farrar	bass	Recording location	Kosei Nenkin Hall, Tokyo, Japan
Alan Hawkshaw	piano	Recording date	22nd-23rd September 1972
Hank Marvin	guitar		
Olivia Newton-John	backing vocals		
Cliff Richard	vocals		
Bruce Welch	rhythm guitar		

8. Japan Tour '74

Musicians		*Recording Details*	
Cliff Hall	piano	Producer	Toshiba EMI (no individual detailed)
Brian Lewis	guitar	Engineered by	Toshiba EMI (no individual detailed)
Kevin Peak	acoustic guitar	Recording location	Shinjuku Koseinenkin, Tokyo, Japan
Cliff Richard	vocals, backing vocals	Recording date	7th-8th October 1974
Trevor Spencer	drums, percussion		
Alan Tarney	bass		
Bruce Welch	vocals, backing vocals, rhythm Guitar		

9. Thank You Very Much

Musicians		*Recording Details*	
Brian Bennett	drums, percussion	Producer	Bruce Welch
Alan Jones	bass	Engineered by	Tony Clark
Cliff Hall	keyboards	Recording location	London Palladium, London
Hank Marvin	guitar	Recording date	4th March 1978
Cliff Richard	vocals		
Bruce Welch	rhythm guitar		

10. Unissued track (From a Distance ** The Event)***

Musicians		*Recording Details*	
Ray Beavis	saxophone	Producer	Cliff Richard
Brian Bennett	drums, percussion	Engineered by	Keith Bessey and Mick McKenna
Mark Griffiths	bass	Recording location	Rolling Stones Mobile Studio, Wembley Stadium, Wembley, North-west London
Cliff Hall	keyboards	Recording date	16th-17th June 1989
Hank Marvin	backing vocals, guitar		
Cliff Richard	vocals		
Bruce Welch	backing vocals, rhythm guitar		

11. Unissued (Knebworth - The Album)

Musicians		*Recording Details*	
Ray Beavis	saxophone	Producer	Chris Kimsey and Steve Smith
Brian Bennett	drums, percussion	Engineered by	Unknown
John Earle	saxophone	Recording location	Knebworth House, Hertfordshire, England
Chris Gower	trombone	Recording date	30th June 1990
Mark Griffiths	bass		
Cliff Hall	keyboards		
Dick Hanson	trumpet		
Peter Howarth	backing vocals		
Hank Marvin	backing vocals, guitar		
Paul Moessl	keyboards		
Mick Mullins	backing vocals		
Keith Murrell	backing vocals		
Cliff Richard	vocals		
Bruce Welch	backing vocals, guitar		

12. B-side (Be with Me Always)

Musicians		*Recording Details*	
Cliff Richard	vocals	Producer	Unknown
		Engineered by	Unknown
		Recording location	Wimbledon Lawn Tennis Association
		Recording date	3rd July 1996

13. Reunited

Musicians		*Recording Details*	
Brian Bennett	drums, percussion	Producer	Warren Bennett (co-ordination)
Warren Bennett	piano	Engineered by	James Collins (Honeyhill Studios), Ethan Carlson (Middle Ear Studios), Les Williams (Nivram Studios) and Keith Bessey (mixing and mastering)
Mark Griffiths	bass	Recording location	Middle Ear Studios, Miami, Florida, USA (Cliff's vocals), Nivram Studios, Perth, Western Australia (Hank's guitars and vocals) and Honeyhill Studios, Hertfordshire, England (all other vocals and instruments)
Hank Marvin	backing vocals, guitar	Recording date	Early 2009
Cliff Richard	vocals, backing vocals		
Bruce Welch	backing vocals, rhythm guitar		

♫ Back in Vaudeville

B-side of **Baby You're Dynamite** *(German, Dutch and Australian releases only)*

In the spring of 1984, while most territories enjoyed the single ***Baby You're Dynamite*** backed with ***Ocean Deep***, Cliff Richard's ninety-first single was issued in Germany (EMI label, catalogue number 1C-0061078337), Holland (EMI label, catalogue number 1A-006107837) and Australia (EMI label, catalogue number EMI-1154) with an entirely different song, *Back in Vaudeville*, which had been recorded in March 1983 a few months before Cliff started the ***Silver*** sessions. *Back in Vaudeville* was a major rarity, particularly in Britain, until it was included on the rare B-sides section as a bonus track as part of the celebratory ***...And They Said It Wouldn't Last! (My 50 Years in Music)*** album in 2008. The song, notably, was the only one that Cliff recorded in the then newly-refurbished Penthouse studio at the Abbey Road Studio complex.

The upbeat nature of the song perfectly matches the material that Cliff was recording during this period. The musicians are unknown, although they are likely to comprise those band members who were regularly performing with Cliff at the time. As would be expected from a Bruce Welch production, one of the best parts of the ensemble piece is the backing vocals which are in close harmony and feature Cliff prominently among their number.

Track Specification

Composed by Dave Hacker, Keith Wilford and Dave Heap

Musicians

Cliff Richard	vocals, backing vocals
Unknown	backing vocals
Unknown	guitar
Unknown	bass
Unknown	synthesisers
Unknown	saxophone
Unknown	drums, percussion

Recording Details

Producer	Bruce Welch
Engineered by	Unknown
Recording location	Abbey Road Penthouse Studio, St. John's Wood, London
Recording date	7th–12th March 1983

♫ Ballade de Baltimore, La

French single

There is some suggestion that this French song is a translation of ***The Lady Came from Baltimore***, a Tim Hardin song that Cliff Richard never recorded in the studio but regularly performed on stage, but the ***On the Continent*** boxed set collation of Cliff's foreign language songs, clearly indicates that the composers are different. However, listening to both pieces of music, and although the French version is more melodramatic in its accompaniment and pace, there are too many similarities for them not to be the same tune.

Recorded at the same session as its eventual B-side, ***L'Amandier Sauvage***, as the only two songs slated for that day, *La Ballade de Baltimore* (literally *The Ballad of Baltimore*, of course) was issued as a single on the Columba label (catalogue number 2C 006-04841) in June 1971 in mono format only. It was later added to the French language collection of Cliff's songs, *When in France... Chante en Français*, which was released in October 1975 in stereo.

As is always expected, Cliff carries off the performance with self-assurance and confidence as he not only sings the lead vocal but provides his own backing vocals in the chorus sections, which always works well. The spirited orchestral accompaniment with a prominent string, trumpet and harp section drive the song onwards.

Track Specification

Composed by Tim Hardin; French lyrics provided by Jean-Max Rivière and Maryland

Musicians

Nick Ingman	arranger, conductor
Nick Ingman Orchestra	orchestra
Cliff Richard	vocals, backing vocals

Recording Details

Producer	Norrie Paramor
Engineered by	Peter Vince
Recording location	Abbey Road Studio 2, St. John's Wood, London
Recording date	2nd June 1971

♫ Bang Bang (My Baby Shot Me Down)

From the album **Tracks 'n' Grooves**

Recorded by American singer Cher and written by her then husband, the late Sonny Bono, *Bang Bang (My Baby Shot Me Down)* was released as a single in 1966, reaching number two in her native US and number three in the UK in April of that year. It was covered later that year by Nancy Sinatra and again by Cher twenty-two years later, although that single didn't fare so well. It has also been covered by the Beau Brummels, Stevie Wonder, Vanilla Fudge and Paul Weller among others and a version by French first lady Carla Bruni was recorded to accompany a television advertisement for Lancia Musa.

Cliff Richard recorded his version in October 1968, although the track would have to wait until two years later to be included on the ***Tracks 'n' Grooves*** album. Between this dates, Columbia's policy changed regarding albums: ***Established 1958*** was the last studio album to be issued in both mono and stereo. Therefore, *Bang Bang (My Baby Shot Me Down)* has only ever been released in stereo, although a mono version was probably edited at the time of recording.

Performed with even more orchestral melodrama than Cher's version, it sounds quite different with Cliff singing the lead: in some ways the lack of Americanisation in his lyrics makes it sound rather odd. The mid-section picks up the pace with an almost Greek-like dance rhythm applied before it settles back to the original. Quirky it is certainly but not the best track on the album for all that.

Track Specification
Composed by Sonny Bono
Musicians

Brian Bennett	arranger
Norrie Paramor Orchestra	orchestra
Norrie Paramor	conductor
Cliff Richard	vocals

Recording Details

Producer	Norrie Paramor
Engineered by	Peter Vince
Recording location	Abbey Road Studio 2, St. John's Wood, London
Recording date	10th October 1968

♫ Beat out Dat Rhythm on a Drum

From the album **Listen to Cliff!**

Undoubtedly one of the most familiar pieces of dramatic classical music, the operetta *Carmen* was written by Georges Bizet with a libretto by Henri Meilhac and Ludovic Halévy. Completed in the first part of the 1840s, *Carmen* was given its first public performance in 1845. Following the story of love and treachery through the central character of the peasant girl Carmen, it has been changed and updated to make it more contemporary several times in its history. Most considerable in this change was Oscar Hammerstein II's version, which he called *Carmen Jones* and this was first performed almost a hundred years later in 1943. Basically taking Bizet's original score and using his own lyrics, the characters were changed from Spaniards to African-Americans, the time period from early nineteenth century Spain to a World War II-era Southern state military base, and the central character working in a parachute factory rather than a cigar sweatshop. A film version was made in 1954 directed by Otto Preminger and with Dorothy Dandridge and Harry Belafonte in the lead roles, even though their voices were dubbed by other singers.

One of the principal songs from the updated musical version was *Beat out Dat Rhythm on a Drum*, which is essentially the *Gypsy Song* from the original operetta. Recorded by Pearl Bailey, Marc Almond, Mandy Patinkin, the London Symphony Orchestra, Madeline Bell, June Hawkins and even the Caribbean Steel Orchestra, it has never been a single success in the UK charts, although Cliff Richard's version from ***Listen to Cliff!*** was released in Holland, where it reached a top placing of number five in September 1961.

The mono and stereo versions of the song used the same take and edit but were mixed differently for the needs of the aural channels. *Beat out Dat Rhythm on a Drum* also appeared on track listing of the associated release of ***Listen to Cliff! No. 2*** EP and features as the opening track of the second side of the parent album.

Drums and brass introduce Cliff's version of this classic from the musical. From a performance standpoint, the vocal line is technically difficult, with light and shade, changes of key and unusual musical intervals. Although Cliff doesn't have the raucousness (or southern US accent) to fully complement the song, he displays the usual competence that makes even the most complex song sound easy to perform in his vocal cords.

Track Specification
Composed by Oscar Hammerstein II and Georges Bizet
Musicians

Bernard Ebbinghouse Orchestra	orchestra
Cliff Richard	vocals

Recording Details

Producer	Norrie Paramor
Engineered by	Malcolm Addey and David Lloyd
Recording location	Abbey Road Studio 2, St. John's Wood, London
Recording date	11th January 1961

♫ Be-Bop-a-Lula

From the album **Rock 'n' Roll Silver** *and unissued live track*

One of the classic songs from the heart of the rock 'n' roll era in the mid-fifties, *Be-Bop-a-Lula* was first recorded by the author Gene Vincent and His Blue Caps. Although credited to Vincent and his manager Bill 'Sheriff Tex' Davis, there is evidence that it was started a year earlier while Vincent was recuperating from an accident. At the hospital he met Donald Graves, who allegedly wrote the lyrics to Vincent's melody. Davis then reportedly bought out Graves and credited himself as the writer. Vincent's version was the first of his singles to chart in the UK, when it reached number sixteen in July 1956. Well-known covers are those by the Beatles, John Lennon, Stray Cats, Queen, David Cassidy, the Everly Brothers, Jerry Lee Lewis and Carl Perkins, among several others.

When planning the twenty-fifth anniversary album, ***Rock 'n' Roll Silver***, Cliff Richard brought in a hand-picked band, which he dubbed Thunder, and together they chose the track listing, jointly arranging and producing the resultant tracks, one of which was *Be-Bop-a-Lula*, which was the penultimate song on the list. The following year, with little fresh material to complete the album ***The Rock Connection***, this track was also included on that album.

Taken at a slower pace than the first recording by Vincent or any of his followers with an almost jazz club feel created by brushes on the drums, Cliff performs the song almost entirely in falsetto in the chorus, while the verses are sung in a normal vocal tone. As with most of the tracks on *Rock 'n' Roll Silver*, the arrangements of familiar tunes are highly effective while still managing to be faithful to the original.

The first live recording of the song was made on the New Zealand leg of the 2003 world tour to support the then new album, ***Wanted***, which also featured a number of covers, revisited tracks and old hits. The show was filmed for DVD release and, in 2004, the release of the complementary *World Tour Live* CD album only had a selection of the tracks, missing off *Be-Bop-a-Lula*.

Track Specification
Composed by Gene Vincent and Bill 'Sheriff Tex' Davis

1. Rock 'n' Roll Silver

Musicians

Stuart Calver	backing vocals
Dave Cooke	keyboards
John Clark	electric guitar
Mark Griffiths	bass
Graham Jarvis	drums, percussion
Mart Jenner	guitar
John Perry	backing vocals
Alan Park	keyboards
Cliff Richard	vocals
Tony Rivers	backing vocals
Thunder	arranger

Recording Details

Producer	Thunder
Engineered by	Keith Bessey
Recording location	Strawberry Studios South, Surrey
Recording date	9th-18th May 1983

2. Unissued track (World Tour Live)

Musicians

Anthony Clark	backing vocals, guitar
John Clark	guitar
Dave Cooke	keyboards
Cornelia Didenco	violin
Gina Ferguson	violin
Mike Haughton	saxophone
Cathy Irons	violin
Pete May	drums, percussion
Alan Park	keyboards
Hee-Jung Park	violin
Cliff Richard	vocals
Eva Schwanen-Lilley	violin
Steve Stroud	bass

Recording Details

Producer	Keith Bessey
Engineered by	Keith Bessey
Recording location	The Mission Winery, Napier, New Zealand
Recording date	22nd February 2003

♫ Be in My Heart

From the album **Now You See Me, Now You Don't**

Written by one of Cliff Richard's backing singers, John Perry, *Be in My Heart* is one of only two songs on the ***Now You See Me... Now You Don't*** album to feature additional backing singers (Cliff provided his own backing on the other tracks). But, instead of using Perry, Cliff opted to go back to using the Mike Sammes Singers, giving the track a slightly old-fashioned but curiously comfortable air on an album very much at the forefront of musical and technical techniques.
The use of the harmonium, played by co-producer Craig Pruess, creates a feel that is part folk and part religious reverence. Cliff's vibrato is exceptional on this emotive song and is helped by his own backing vocals that are then replaced by the Mike Sammes Singers.

Track Specification
Composed by John Perry

Musicians

Mike Sammes Singers	backing vocals
Carole Allum	
Valerie Bain	
Michael Clarke	
Enid Heard	
Tom Saffery	
Mike Sammes	
Danny Street	
Angela Young	
Craig Pruess	harmonium, synthesisers
Cliff Richard	vocals, backing vocals

Recording Details

Producer	Cliff Richard and Craig Pruess
Engineered by	Keith Bessey and Steve Cook
Recording location	Strawberry Studios South, Surrey
Recording date	29th March and 2nd-5th April 1982

♫ Bellman's Speech, The

From the album **The Hunting of the Snark** *(Mike Batt)*

Lewis Carroll's nonsense poem *The Hunting of the Snark (An Agony in Eight Fits)* was written in 1874 and many scholars and commentators have since tried to apply some sense: a fool's errand. The narrative, however, is clear, with a group of disparate characters embarking on a quest for the Snark, a mythical character than can also be a Boojum. Of course, many have suggested that the Snark equals good, while the Boojum is evil and is therefore an allegory about religion and seeking enlightenment. Perhaps it is, but it is just as likely to be a joyful poem that excels in its use of words and imagery. Some points to note are that each of the travellers has an occupation that starts with the letter 'B', so there is the Barrister, the Billiard-Player, the Bonnet-maker, the Butcher, the Baker, the Beaver (a curious addition but it is a nonsense poem!) and the Bellman. A Bellman was essentially the person that looked after the ship, while not being grand enough to be called a captain, and was so called because he had a bell with which to attract attention.

In the early eighties, Mike Batt, who had previously been associated with the musical version of children's characters The Wombles and Cliff Richard's ***Please Don't Fall in Love*** single, wrote his musical version of *The Hunting of the Snark*. Being as complete as he could get it, Batt contacted a number of stars to take part, including Art Garfunkel (the Butcher), Julian Lennon (the Baker), Roger Daltrey (the Barrister), Deniece Williams (the Beaver), Captain Sensible (the Billiard-Player) and Cliff (the Bellman). The following year, a charity extravaganza was staged at the Royal Albert Hall on 1st April and broadcast on the BBC but with Justin Hayward replacing Art Garfunkel and comedian Billy Connolly replacing Cliff. The song is, as expected from Batt's pen, a highly catchy and moving tune with brilliant harmonies. In addition, the technical requirements of singing the song are extraordinary with falsetto octave jumps, which are exceptionally difficult to pitch: on this point, Cliff is perfect, while Connolly was struggling given that he is not really a trained singer. For those who have not heard the song, it comes as a surprise when they listen to Cliff showing off his innate capabilities.
The introduction includes a reading of a couple of verses read by Sir John Gielgud and John Hurt, before handing off to the orchestra with its ebullient string section creating a dancelike quality to the music that leads into Cliff's wonderful rendition in the lead vocal. This has a slight echo behind it, while Mike Batt provides the backing vocals and this is used effectively on the repetition of the musical's title. For its beauty, it would have been interesting to know how the song would have fared as a single. The song quickly segues into the main journey, ***The Escapade***.

Track Specification
Composed by Mike Batt

Musicians

Mike Batt	arranger, backing vocals, conductor
Sir John Gielgud	narration
John Hurt	narration
London Symphony Orchestra	orchestra
Cliff Richard	vocals

Recording Details

Producer	Mike Batt
Engineered by	Nick Patrick, Robert Butterworth and Dick Lewsey (orchestra)
Recording location	C. T. S., Wembley, Odyssey Studios, London, Mayfair Studios, London, Wessex Studios, London, Maison Rouge Studios, London and/or Comfort's Place, London (main track) and Abbey Road Studio 1, St. John's Wood, London (orchestra)
Recording date	1986

♫ Best of Me, The

106th UK single *and from the albums* **Stronger** *and* **From a Distance** ******* The Event Remaster**

The song chosen as the first single to be released from the ***Stronger*** album project was the subject of a huge publicity exercise. *The Best of Me* was one of the candidates touted for release as Cliff Richard's one hundredth single – and caused much argument when Aswad claimed that ***Share a Dream*** would take that accolade. Except that it wasn't. *The Best of Me* was actually the one hundred and sixth single to be released by Cliff in the capacity of being a lead vocalist and, in fact, the minor hit with Elton John, ***Slow Rivers***, was the hundredth single. In the otherwise excellent *The Complete Chronicle* by Mike Read, Peter Lewry and Nigel Goodall, the successive singles are highlighted by their release sequence but peters out in the nineties until the fanfare entry for this song, after which it picks up the numerical sequence again.
There are two elements of truth that can be gleaned to support the inexorable publicity that *The Best of Me* was the hundredth single: first, counting the number of placed songs in the charts (and assuming true double A-sides count as one chart entry) reveals that *The Best of Me* is indeed the hundredth single – however, this arrogantly assumes that the single would also chart and ignores the fact that ***Never Mind*** and ***Dynamite*** were B-sides that happened to chart independently so were not official single releases; second, ignoring the duets with Olivia Newton-John, Phil Everly, Sheila Walsh, Janet Jackson, Sarah Brightman and Elton John indicates that *The Best of Me* becomes the one hundredth single – but this overlooks the fact that two of Cliff's singles, ***Throw Down a Line*** and ***The Joy of Living*** were credited to Cliff and Hank Marvin, while the second version of ***Living Doll*** was a collaboration with the Young Ones comedy troupe. Neither stands up to close scrutiny and, as a result, the only true measure of the number of singles is the linear progression of single releases with Cliff in official lead vocalist role.
After all the songs were recorded during February and March 1989, Cliff and Mike Read compèred a session at the London Palladium on 3rd April, where two thousand fans were invited to listen to six tracks from the forthcoming *Stronger* album. *The Best of Me* came second in the subsequent poll behind the album's opening track and fourth single, ***Stronger than That***. Originally, *The Best of Me* had been a duet between Olivia Newton-John and co-writer David Foster and had been covered by Phil Perry, Barry Manilow, Kenny Rogers and Kiri Te Kanawa, before Cliff picked it up to record for his new album. Backed with ***Move It*** to book-end his thirty-year career anniversary (although it was released in his thirty-first year), *The Best of Me* was released on the EMI label (catalogue number EM 92) on 30th May 1989 and reached number two in the UK charts, where it was held off the top position by Jason Donovan's version of *Sealed with a Kiss*. Different versions of the single were released: a seven-inch issue with a gold cover (catalogue number EMS 92); the twelve-inch (12EM 92) and CD (CDEMS 92) versions, which included the original ***High Class Baby*** track and non-album track ***Lindsay Jane*** as bonus tracks; and a twelve-inch release with a gold cover (12EMS 92). The version that appeared on ***...And They Said It Wouldn't Last! (My 50 Years in Music)***, is edited down by fading the last ten seconds down earlier. The promotional video is in black and white and features lots of cross-fades to different profiles of Cliff.

The song is introduced by the sad minor key melody played out on a shimmering synthesiser. Cliff sings the song with meaning as he looks back over a love affair and how it has gone wrong in the mean time. The accompaniment is kept quite sparse, while the occasional bursts of harmonized vocals, which include Cliff's own voice, are arranged superbly to blend in a highly effective manner.
The Best of Me was included as the penultimate song of the night at ***The Event***, the concerts to celebrate Cliff's thirtieth year in showbusiness. Originally, the song was left off the track listing of the resultant accompanying album, ***From a Distance ***** The Event***, but was restored fifteen years later in 2005 when it was reinstated on the two-CD album remaster. Prior to the performance, Cliff emotionally dedicates the performance of the song to his fans in the crowd. Truly the set list was exactly what is stated in the title and the live version of the single is a faithful reproduction of the song with its synthesiser accompaniment behind Cliff's impassioned and reflective vocal performance.

Track Specification
Composed by Jeremy Lubbock, David Foster and Richard Marx

1. Single

Musicians		*Recording Details*	
Keith Bessey	drum and percussion programming	Producer	Cliff Richard
John Clark	guitar	Engineered by	Gerry Kitchingham and Ben Robbins
Mark Griffiths	bass	Recording location	R. G. Jones Studios, Wimbledon, London
Paul Moessl	arranger	Recording date	27th February 1989, 9th March 1989, 13th-17th March 1989 and 22nd-23rd March 1989
Mick Mullins	backing vocals		
Keith Murrell	backing vocals		
Cliff Richard	vocals, backing vocals		

*2. From a Distance ***** The Event Remaster*

Musicians		*Recording Details*	
John Clark	guitar	Producer	Cliff Richard
Sonia Jones-Morgan	backing vocals	Engineered by	Keith Bessey and Mick McKenna
Steve Lauri	guitar	Recording location	Rolling Stones Mobile Studio, Wembley Stadium, Wembley, North-west London
Peter May	drums, percussion	Recording date	16th-17th June 1989
Paul Moessl	keyboards		
Tessa Niles	backing vocals		
Alan Park	keyboards		
Provox:			
Peter Howarth	backing vocals		
Mick Mullins	backing vocals		
Keith Murrell	backing vocals		
Cliff Richard	vocals		
Steve Stroud	bass		

♫ Better Day

From the album **Stronger**

The last song on the ***Stronger*** album to be produced and written by Alan Tarney, *Better Day* was the penultimate track on the eventual album. Cliff Richard and Tarney had developed an approach during the ***Always Guaranteed*** album sessions whereby Tarney would lay down the backing track, often composing on the spot, before Cliff arrived to add his vocals and one such song was *Better Day*.
The sequenced cymbals introduce this driving rock song that employs a fuzzed guitar underneath Cliff's foreboding vocals. The unusual backing vocals and percussion in the background create some surprises.

Track Specification
Composed by Alan Tarney

Musicians		*Recording Details*	
Cliff Richard	vocals, backing vocals	Producer	Alan Tarney
Alan Tarney	arranger, backing vocals, synthesisers, drum and percussion sequencers	Engineered by	Gerry Kitchingham and Ben Robbins
		Recording location	R. G. Jones Studios, Wimbledon, London
		Recording date	27th February 1989, 9th March 1989, 13th-17th March 1989 and 22nd-23rd March 1989

♫ Better than I Know Myself

From the album **Wired for Sound**

The first song on the ***Wired for Sound*** album that was not written by Alan Tarney, *Better than I Know Myself* is one of those songs that Cliff Richard does so well: a gospel song disguised as a pop or rock song. This is why it was later issued on the many Christian song-related compendiums issued by Cliff. *Better than I Know Myself* was written by husband and wife team David Cooke and Judy Mackenzie – Cooke was instrumental in Christian music recording throughout the seventies and, indeed, regularly co-wrote with Garth Hewitt, for whom Cliff worked as producer on several tracks.
There are muted guitar and bass in the introduction and less emphasis on the synthesisers than is otherwise present on other tracks on the album. The particular highlight of *Better than I Know Myself* is the arrangement of the backing vocals,

created by layering Cliff's and Tarney's backing to create a group feel, and the blend with Cliff's lead vocal. The simplicity of the track makes it stand out from the rest of the album.

Track Specification
Composed by David Cooke and Judy Mackenzie

Musicians	
Graham Jarvis	drums, percussion
Cliff Richard	vocals, backing vocals
Alan Tarney	arranger, backing vocals, guitar, bass, keyboards

Recording Details	
Producer	Alan Tarney
Engineered by	Michael Boddicker and Ian Little
Recording location	Gallery Studios, Chertsey, Surrey
Recording date	27th May-9th July 1981

♫ Be with Me Always

***126th UK single** and from the album* **Heathcliff Live**

Heathcliff (Cliff Richard) is grieving the death of his beloved Cathy in childbirth and knows that he is to be tormented forever by the loss, having beseeched her not to leave him in this hell and to remain with him forever, which is the principal tenet of this final song from the original studio album ***Songs from Heathcliff***. Not believing that he is fault for the tragic circumstances, he calls on any forces to bring her back but it is not to be. The song is subsequently reprised by Helen Hobson (as Cathy) echoing in the ears of the distraught Heathcliff.

Backed with three of the four songs that Cliff recorded at an impromptu concert in the rain during the Wimbledon fortnight in 1996, at which someone passed him a microphone with which to entertain the crowd, ***Summer Holiday, The Young Ones*** and ***Bachelor Boy***, the studio version of *Be with Me Always* was issued as a single on the EMI label (catalogue number CDEM 453) on 13th January 1997 and reached number fifty-two in the UK singles charts. A cassette version of the single was released (catalogue number TCEM 453) with a fourth song from the Wimbledon centre court sing-along, ***Congratulations***. A promotional CD was also issued with just the album track (catalogue number CDEMDJ 453).

The minor key of the song completely underlines the sadness that Heathcliff is feeling, even though there is a lack of admission on his part as to how he and Cathy got to this point. Accompanied by sweeping synthesiser sequences and backing vocals that Cliff provides himself with help from John Farrar, the song descends into further sadness as the reality dawns. The live version's introduction has a spooky keyboard introduction as Cathy dies before him ushering in the song. This version is sung with even more emotion and passion than the original as Cliff imbues the lyrics with the meaning of the events that have transpired.

The following year after the ***Heathcliff*** tour was completed, featured guitarist Gordon Giltrap recorded a solo album called *Troubadour*, which featured his own version of ***I Do Not Love You Isabella*** and the medley ***A Misunderstood Man/Be with Me Always***, the latter of which featured Cliff on backing vocals.

Track Specification
Composed by Tim Rice and John Farrar

1. Single

Musicians	
Sean Callery	orchestrator, synclavier, keyboards
John Farrar	backing vocals, guitar, synclavier
Cliff Richard	vocals, backing vocals
Bob Sabellico	drum programming
Michael Thompson	guitar

Recording Details	
Producer	John Farrar
Engineered by	Chris Fogel, Eric Rudd and Joe Schiff (Moonee Ponds Studio), Darren Goodwin and Guy Massey (Abbey Road Studios) and James Collins and Caroline Daniel (CTS Studios)
Recording location	Moonee Ponds Studio, Los Angeles, Abbey Road Studios, St. John's Wood, London and CTS Studios, Wembley, London
Mixed by	Allen Sides and Chris Fogel
Mixed at	Moonee Ponds Studio, Los Angeles
Recording date	February-April 1994 and May-August 1995

2. Heathcliff Live

Musicians	
Sean Callery	orchestrator, orchestra
David Combes	backing vocals
John Clark	guitar
Keith Hayman	keyboards
Helen Hobson	spoken vocals
Peter May	drums, percussion
Bob Noble	keyboards
Alan Park	keyboards
John Perry	backing vocals
Cliff Richard	spoken vocals, vocals
Steve Stroud	bass
Kevin Townend	orchestration
Unknown	orchestra
Mick Wilson	backing vocals

Recording Details	
Producer	John Farrar
Engineered by	Keith Bessey, John Pearson and Tom Tranter
Recording location	National Indoor Arena, Birmingham, England
Recording date	17th-18th October 1996

♬ Big Black Mamba

From the album **Did He Jump... Or Was He Pushed?** *(Garth Hewitt)*

Cliff Richard had increasingly become involved in production of his own work and other artists' recordings, particularly friends from the Christian fraternity such as Garth Hewitt. The songs on Hewitt's second album, ***Did He Jump... Or Was He Pushed?*** were all written by Hewitt but also featured a number of musicians who had worked with Cliff. For *Big Black Mamba* – a large Asian poisonous snake – this included Bryn Haworth, for whom Cliff sang on a couple of songs.
With a drum beat straight from the glam rock period and a rocking guitar and piano from a decade or so before, this quirky little song is performed with gusto and an extraordinary energy that would have made a successful single were it not for the changing tastes of the period. Cliff's layered backing vocals are brought in in the middle eight and makes this feel like an upbeat forties period number.

Track Specification
Composed by Garth Hewitt

Musicians	
Bryn Haworth	slide guitar
Garth Hewitt	vocals
Graham Jarvis	drums, percussion
Mike Moran	keyboards
Jo Partridge	guitar
Cliff Richard	backing vocals
Dave Wintour	bass

Recording Details	
Producer	Cliff Richard
Engineered by	Tony Clark and Haydn Bendall
Recording location	Odyssey Studios, London
Recording date	1979

♬ Big News

From the film soundtrack albums of **Summer Holiday** *and* **Summer Holiday – Special Edition**

As with ***Bachelor Boy***, *Big News* was a last minute addition to the film. Norrie Paramor identified that the final edit of the film was too short by several minutes, contacted Cliff Richard and Bruce Welch and they composed *Bachelor Boy*, while *Big News* was written within hours on set by Cliff, their roadie Mike Conlon and the film's screenwriter Ronald Cass.
Big News is the final song of the film and takes place at a press conference arranged by the pushy mother of Barbara Winters (Lauri Peters), whom she has kept locked in a bedroom (although rescued by the boys and girls from the bus). Mrs. Winters states that she would give 'those hoodlums' a piece of her mind if she saw any one of them, just as Don Preston (Cliff) enters to provide a statement about Barbara's alleged kidnapping. The journalists are all ears as he professes his love for Barbara. When asked if she would give her consent to marriage, Mrs. Winters, thinking the girl is still safely locked in her room, says that if her daughter confessed her love, she would drop all charges. Barbara appears and says she loves Don, after which Mrs. Winters can't be seen to backtrack on the promise. Then, as she realizes that Don's Red Bus Holiday company has two hundred buses lined up, she realizes her future son-in-law will be rich.
Big News was recorded for the soundtrack at the same late session as *Bachelor Boy*. Splicing the twelfth and thirteenth takes together, the same edit was used for both mono and stereo but with different mixes for the audio channels. The film version of the song was recorded at a similar time as the soundtrack version at Elstree Studios and has the interaction with the journalists to the sensational and revelatory lyrics sung by Cliff, while the brass of the orchestra is very prominent and the Shadows backing swamped. This version was released on the *Summer Holiday – Special Edition* album.
There is a slight echo behind Cliff's lead vocals in this rock and roll song that is driven along by Brian Bennett's drums and Bruce Welch's rhythm guitar, and Hank Marvin performs a short instrumental break. Unfortunately, the vocals are mixed into the right channel and instrumentation into the left rather than separated more equally – a practice that was common during stereo's infancy – and this makes it an odd listening experience particularly through headphones.

Track Specification
Composed by Cliff Richard, Mike Conlon and Ronald Cass

1. Summer Holiday

Musicians	
Brian Bennett	drums, percussion
Brian 'Licorice' Locking	bass
Hank Marvin	backing vocals, guitar
Cliff Richard	vocals
Bruce Welch	backing vocals, rhythm guitar

Recording Details	
Producer	Norrie Paramor
Engineered by	Malcolm Addey
Recording location	Abbey Road Studio 2, St. John's Wood, London
Recording date	16th November 1962

2. Summer Holiday – Special Edition

Musicians	
Associated British Studio Orchestra	orchestra
Brian Bennett	drums, percussion
Stanley Black	conductor
Brian 'Licorice' Locking	bass
Hank Marvin	backing vocals, guitar
Cliff Richard	vocals
Bruce Welch	backing vocals, rhythm guitar

Recording Details	
Producer	Norrie Paramor
Engineered by	Unknown
Recording location	Elstree Studios, Hertfordshire
Recording date	1962

♫ Big Ship

***46th UK single** and from the album* **Cliff Live in Korea**

By 1969, many commentators considered Cliff Richard to be producing dull, predictable and low quality material; where he had been at the vanguard of the music revolution at the start of the decade, by the end, it was becoming almost commercial singles by numbers. However, there were some critics that appreciated the different direction he was going in. No more did he have the Shadows supporting him, so the material tended to be orchestral in nature, thus moving away from the rock and roll image Cliff had carefully developed and nurtured at the start of his career. Because of this, a large group of fans felt that the apparently stodgy material wasn't worth buying and 1969 was therefore seen as the turning point in his fortunes before the mid-seventies renaissance.

The recording and release of *Big Ship* had many critics divided, particularly following on the heels of ***Good Times (Better Times)***. Nevertheless, *Big Ship* was Cliff's biggest chart success since ***Congratulations*** the previous year and his first top ten single in that same period, reaching as it did number eight. Backed with ***She's Leaving You***, which was recorded at a session a week later, *Big Ship* was released as a single on the Columbia label (catalogue number DB 8581) on 23rd May 1969 in mono format only. The stereo version was issued over three years later when it was included on the compilation album ***The Best of Cliff Vol. 2*** in November 1972.

The bass line is a sound that was created on many songs in the early seventies and this makes *Big Ship* of its moment. Introduced with brass, Cliff sings lyrics that are somewhat simplistic with the *Big Ship* of the title being an allegory for love. There is a backing vocal group that is uncredited but they help make the result better than it would have otherwise been with some other vocalists – the timbre and blend work well here. There are key changes, unusual lyrics and strong brass and woodwind arrangement that set this song apart from much of what Cliff had previously recorded.

Having recently issued the song as a single, it became part of the set list for the Far East tour in 1969 by Cliff and the Shadows, back together again after being offered lots of money to do so. Issued in mono only on the ultra-rare *Cliff Live in Korea* album in 1970, it has never been reissued in any other format.

Track Specification

Composed by Raymond Froggatt

1. Single

Musicians		*Recording Details*	
Mike Vickers Orchestra	orchestra	Producer	Norrie Paramor
Cliff Richard	vocals	Engineered by	Peter Vince
Mike Vickers	arranger, conductor	Recording location	Abbey Road Studio 2, St. John's Wood, London
Unknown	backing vocals	Recording date	22nd April 1969

2. Cliff Live in Korea

Musicians		*Recording Details*	
Brian Bennett	drums, percussion	Producer	Unknown
Alan Hawkshaw	keyboards	Engineered by	Unknown
Hank Marvin	backing vocals, guitar	Recording location	Citizen Hall, Seoul, South Korea
Cliff Richard	vocals	Recording date	16th October 1969
John Rostill	backing vocals, bass		
Bruce Welch	backing vocals, rhythm guitar		

♫ Bilder von Dir

B-side of **Ein Girl Wie Du**

For Cliff Richard's tenth German language single, a German version of ***Words*** was released and retitled ***Ein Girl Wie Du*** (not to be confused with ***A Girl Like You***, the 1961 English language hit written by Jerry Lordan). Backing it as a B-side, was a German translation of Cliff's then recent hit ***Visions***, which was retitled *Bilder von Dir* with German lyrics added by Kurt Hertha, who had provided translations for other German songs earlier in Cliff's career. Recorded at the same session as the A-side, *Bilder von Dir* translates literally as *Pictures of You*, which is close to the original intent of the song. As was the custom at the time, particularly with Columbia, stereo was reserved only for albums and so *Bilder von Dir* was released in mono only before the stereo version was included thirty years later on the foreign language compilation ***On the Continent*** in 1997.

Presented at a slower pace than the English equivalent, the instrumentation is also edited further up front in the mix. Cliff performs the song with the same emotion and passion as he does the English original. Where *Visions* had a female backing group providing the harmonies, in the German version, they are replaced by a lovely arrangement for orchestral strings.

Track Specification

Composed by Paul Ferris; German lyrics by Kurt Hertha

Musicians		*Recording Details*	
Mike Leander Orchestra	orchestra	Producer	Norrie Paramor
Mike Leander	arranger, conductor	Engineered by	Peter Vince
Cliff Richard	vocals	Recording location	Abbey Road Studio 2, St. John's Wood, London
		Recording date	25th April 1967

♫ Bin Verliebt

German single

Cliff Richard started an extraordinary continental career by recording new versions or completely new songs in French, German, Spanish and Italian that would continue into the very early seventies. The first such recording was made in the last few weeks of 1960 with a German version of Cliff Richard and the Shadows' eighth single, Ian Samwell's ***Fall in Love with You***, which had been a number two hit in Germany. While Cliff and the Shadows recorded the instrumental line and the lead vocals in mono only, further overdubs (no information available on the dates or studio personnel) were recorded in Germany using The Hansen Boys to provide the German backing vocals, with additional instruments provided by Berlipp's Band, a decision that detracts from the sound that Cliff and the Shadows had developed as a close-knit band.
Bin Verliebt – literally translated as '*Am Loved*' – was released in Germany in January 1961 on the German Columbia label (catalogue number C 21703) and backed with ***Die Stimme der Liebe***, which was a translated version of ***A Voice in the Wilderness***. The single reached number forty in the German charts, the relatively low placing possibly due to it being a translation of an earlier hit in Germany, and, until the release of the boxed set of CDs ***On the Continent***, remained a considerable rarity.
The structure of this song is very different from the original English version, with a clanking piano taking over the rhythm and lead melody that is normally played by Bruce Welch and Hank Marvin. The backing vocals, too, are not as much of an ensemble as Cliff and Shadows were able to produce. Although Cliff has had good schooling in German pronunciation, his performance sounds a little more coy than usual, perhaps due to unfamiliarity. The staccato instrumentation also helps to give the overall performance a stuttering quality but, in spite of these slight issues, it is nevertheless a good recording and an interesting historic record of Cliff's growing career.

Track Specification
Composed by Ian Samwell, German translation by Fleming
Musicians

Friedel Berlipp	conductor
Berlipp's Band	additional instruments
The Hansen Boys	backing vocals
Jet Harris	bass
Hank Marvin	guitar
Tony Meehan	drums, percussion
Cliff Richard	vocals
Bruce Welch	rhythm guitar

Recording Details

Producer	Norrie Paramor
Engineered by	Malcolm Addey
Recording location	Abbey Road Studio 2, St. John's Wood, London plus overdubs in unknown location in Germany
Recording date	5th December 1960

♫ Bird Dog

From the album **From a Distance ***** The Event**

Originally a number two hit in September 1958 for the Everly Brothers, *Bird Dog* appeared as part of the opening ***Oh Boy! Medley*** at Cliff Richard's thirtieth anniversary ***The Event*** celebrations that took place at Wembley Stadium in June 1989. Since the Everly Brothers' success with the song, it has also been covered by a variety of artists including Joan Jett and the Blackhearts, Carl Perkins, the Bluegrass Cardinals, the Hep Stars and Alvin Stardust among others.
Faithful to the original, the Kalin Twins sing the principal lyrics, while Cliff sings the responses. For the second part, the roles are reversed. The Kalin Twins sound unfortunately aged, while Cliff sounds fresh and energetic.

Track Specification
Composed by Boudleaux Bryant and Felice Bryant
Musicians

Dallas Boys:	
Nicky Clarke	backing vocals
Leon Fisk	backing vocals
Stan Jones	backing vocals
Joe Smith	backing vocals
Bob Wragg	backing vocals
Kalin Twins:	
Harold Kalin	backing vocals
Herbie Kalin	backing vocals
Oh Boy! Band	rock 'n' roll band
Cliff Richard	vocals

Recording Details

Producer	Cliff Richard
Engineered by	Keith Bessey and Mick McKenna
Recording location	Rolling Stones Mobile Studio, Wembley Stadium, Wembley, North-west London
Recording date	16th-17th June 1989

♫ Birth of John the Baptist and the Birth of Jesus, The

From the album **About that Man**

On most of the ***About That Man*** album, Cliff Richard reads principally from the Bible rather than performing songs. For the first track, he reads from the book of Luke, chapter one, verses 5 to 38, 57 to 66 and 80 (the birth of John the Baptist) and Luke, chapter two, verses 1 to 20 (the birth of Jesus). Cliff reads the tracts with passion and imbues the passages with meaning and character. The recording was probably completed in one or two takes since there are no obvious splices, except between the readings of the two births.

Track Specification
From the King James Bible

Musicians		*Recording Details*	
Cliff Richard	vocals	Producer	Norrie Paramor
		Engineered by	Richard Lush
		Recording location	Abbey Road Studio 2, St. John's Wood, London
		Recording date	20th February 1970

♫ Blame It on the Bossa Nova

From the album **Kinda Latin**

The Mann-Weil song was made famous by Latin singer Eydie Gormé, who recorded both English and Spanish versions. A love song about a couple falling for each other through their love of the dance, Gormé took the song to number seven in the US charts but only managed number thirty-two in the UK in February 1963. It has since been covered by artists such as Edmundo Ros, Bobby Vee, Scooter Lee, Annette Funkicello, Ted Heath and Dave Rooney.

Recorded at the second of three intensive October 1965 sessions for the album ***Kinda Latin***, *Blame It on the Bossa Nova* was recorded by Cliff Richard in just three takes. The last song from the session, that final take and edit were used for both the mono and stereo recordings but with different mixes for the separation in audio channels.

Introduced with an uncredited vocal group (that is likely to be the Mike Sammes Singers, who were heavily used in Cliff's recordings of the period), Cliff is obviously his performance of the song, which is, as the title suggests, a bossa nova rhythm. This style was a favourite and appears on a number of his recordings, most notably the single ***On the Beach***. The Mexican sounding trumpet and percussion accompaniment make this a superb opener to the album.

Track Specification
Composed by Barry Mann and Cynthia Weil

Musicians		*Recording Details*	
Reg Guest	arranger, conductor	Producer	Norrie Paramor
Reg Guest Orchestra	orchestra	Engineered by	Peter Bown
Cliff Richard	vocals	Recording location	Abbey Road Studio 2, St. John's Wood, London
Unknown	backing vocals	Recording date	7th October 1965

♫ Blowin' in the Wind

From the album **Kinda Latin**

Perhaps one of the most famous songs to be written by American folk legend Bob Dylan, *Blowin' in the Wind* was first released on his album *The Freewheelin' Bob Dylan* in 1963. Now a folk classic, it started its long life as a protest song and has been inducted into the Grammy Hall of Fame. It became the subject of a plagiarism claim with an article in *Newsweek* suggesting that it was the work of a student, although this was found to be deception on the part of a man named Wyatt, who later put the lie down to panicking about his own songwriting abilities. Other than Dylan's, the most famous version is by Peter, Paul and Mary, who hit the number two spot in the US and number thirteen in the UK charts with what was their first of four charting singles. Stevie Wonder (with the prefix 'Little') was the only other artist to chart with it in the UK when he achieved number thirty-six in August 1966, although he reached the top ten stateside. Other covers have been recorded by artists such as Marlene Dietrich, Judy Collins, Neil Young, Joan Baez, Bruce Springsteen, Elvis Presley, Marianne Faithfull (released as a single that didn't chart), The Seekers, Chet Atkins, Dolly Parton and Bobby Darin.

In October 1965, Cliff Richard took part in three intensive recording sessions that produced the track listing for his upcoming album ***Kinda Latin***. At the third of those, he recorded the seminal *Blowin' in the Wind* with an orchestral backing. The ninth and final take and edit were used for the mono and stereo recordings but with different mixes for the audio channel separation.

With an arrangement that gives the song a tango beat (this making it fit the album's title), it is an unusual version by Cliff. It would be all too easy to do a straightforward cover of Dylan's protest song but instead Cliff gives it the light and shade to bring out the importance of the lyrics. His impeccable pitch and timing improve immeasurably on the original.

Track Specification
Composed by Bob Dylan

Musicians		*Recording Details*	
Les Reed Orchestra	orchestra	Producer	Norrie Paramor
Les Reed	arranger, conductor	Engineered by	Peter Bown
Cliff Richard	vocals	Recording location	Abbey Road Studio 3, St. John's Wood, London
		Recording date	22nd October 1965

♫ Blueberry Hill

From the album **32 Minutes and 17 Seconds with Cliff Richard**

Written in 1940, *Blueberry Hill* was first recorded in that year by the Sammy Kaye Orchestra, with the lead vocals taken by Tommy Ryan and was subsequently recorded by a number of other acts that same year, including Glenn Miller and Gene Autry (who sang it in his film *The Singing Hill*). The biggest hit that year was the Glenn Miller Band, but it was when Fats Domino recorded his version in 1956 that the song became firmly associated with him. It reached number two in the US

Billboard singles charts and gave him his only British top ten single when it reached number six in December 1956; it was later reissued in 1976 when it hit number forty-one. The only other successful entry came in August 1960, when the John Barry Orchestra took an instrumental version to number thirty-four, although it has been recorded by a number of other artists including Little Richard, Ricky Nelson, Elvis Presley, Louis Armstrong, The Beach Boys, Led Zeppelin, Duane Eddy, Bill Haley and His Comets, Elton John and the Rolling Stones to name but a few.
For the ***32 Minutes and 17 Seconds with Cliff Richard*** album version, the same take and edit was used for the mono and stereo recordings but employed different mixes to match the requirements of the audio channels. The song was also featured on the track listing of the ***Time for Cliff and the Shadows*** EP.
As would be expected on a Fats Domino cover, the principal instrument is an uncredited piano (either producer Norrie Paramor or Hank Marvin). While certainly not as gruff a performance as Domino's, Cliff Richard manages to bring something different to the version, with syncopated guitar chords and a differently arranged melody line coming through in the final verse, which ends with Cliff speaking the song's title.

Track Specification
Composed by Vincent Roze, Al Lewis and Larry Stock

Musicians

Brian Bennett	drums, percussion
Brian 'Licorice' Locking	bass
Hank Marvin	guitar
Cliff Richard	vocals
Unknown	piano
Bruce Welch	rhythm guitar

Recording Details

Producer	Norrie Paramor
Engineered by	Malcolm Addey
Recording location	Abbey Road Studio 2, St. John's Wood, London
Recording date	17th May 1962

♫ Blue Moon

From the albums **Listen to Cliff!** *and* **From a Distance ***** The Event**

A perennial favourite, *Blue Moon* has been recorded by a wide variety of artists and is a staple at sixties karaoke parties – Vic Damone, Louis Armstrong, Chet Baker, Ella Fitzgerald, Julie London, Conway Twitty, El Riot and the Rebels, Mud, Tony Bennett, Chet Baker and Frank Sinatra are but some of the diverse acts who have committed the song to vinyl but, in the UK, only the Marcels (number one in 1961), Showaddywaddy (number thirty in 1980), actor John Alford (number nine in 1996) and Elvis Presley (number nine in 1956) have had any commercial single success with the song.
The version of *Blue Moon* that was chosen for the ***Listen to Cliff!*** album was the third and final take from the session, which was used for both mono and stereo releases but with different mixes for the needs of the aural channels. In early 1962, the mono edit of the song was chosen as the B-side for the international export single, ***What'd I Say?***, also from the same album, which was in demand from the domestic market, although it sold insufficient numbers to dent the charts. The mono and stereo versions were included on the ***Listen to Cliff! No. 1*** EP. On the 2001 2-on-1 release of ***Me and My Shadows*** and *Listen to Cliff!*, *Blue Moon* is severely edited losing almost one and a half minutes from the original, presumably in order to allow both albums to fit on one CD.
With Tony Meehan's gently-paced drums played with brushes to accompany the tinkling woodwind and muted brass of the orchestra, Cliff reveals a slower-paced version of this perennial standard. The haunting oboe and flutes in particular lend a counterpoint to the reflective mood projected in the lyrics of the song. As with much of Cliff's work, the performance is highly assured and, rather than opting for a straight copy of the then most recently familiar version by the Marcels, the vocal arrangement and laidback delivery ensures that his version is just different enough.
Blue Moon was a natural choice for ***The Event***, which showcased Cliff's career and where he started, with the song forming part of a ***Medley*** to close the *Oh Boy! Set* with which the concert had opened. This version features the Dallas Boys and Vernons Girls singing the backing vocals, while Cliff and the Kalin Twins take turns to sing the leads. The version is the more upbeat version rather than the slower one that was created by the Platters and other artists.

Track Specification
Composed by Richard Rodgers and Lorenz Hart

1. Listen to Cliff!
Musicians

Tony Meehan	drums, percussion
Norrie Paramor Orchestra	orchestra
Norrie Paramor	arranger, conductor
Cliff Richard	vocals

Recording Details

Producer	Norrie Paramor
Engineered by	Malcolm Addey and Norman Smith
Recording location	Abbey Road Studio 2, St. John's Wood, London
Recording date	17th November 1960

2. From a Distance ** The Event***
Musicians

Dallas Boys:	
Nicky Clarke	backing vocals
Leon Fisk	backing vocals
Stan Jones	backing vocals
Joe Smith	backing vocals
Bob Wragg	backing vocals

Recording Details

Producer	Cliff Richard
Engineered by	Keith Bessey and Mick McKenna
Recording location	Rolling Stones Mobile Studio, Wembley Stadium, Wembley, North-west London
Recording date	16th-17th June 1989

Kalin Twins:	
Harold Kalin	backing vocals
Herbie Kalin	backing vocals
Oh Boy! Band	rock 'n' roll band
Cliff Richard	vocals
Vernons Girls:	
Lyn Cornell	backing vocals
Maureen Kennedy	backing vocals
Frances Lee	backing vocals
Jean Owen	backing vocals

♫ Blue Suede Shoes

From the album **Cliff Sings** *and CD B-side of* **All I Have to Do Is Dream/Miss You Nights**

For the first true Cliff Richard studio album, ***Cliff Sings***, the repertoire was divided up between eight songs with backing by The Drifters (who would have become The Shadows by the time the album was released) and a similar number of ballads and standards accompanied by the Norrie Paramor Orchestra, but all songs were covers rather than original material. The intention was to give an insight into the breadth of material and versatility that Cliff could sing.

The first song on the album was what was becoming a standard in the rock and roll repertoire: *Blue Suede Shoes*. Written by Carl Perkins, according to Jerry Naylor and Steve Halliday in their book *Rockabilly Legends*, it was inspired by Johnny Cash in the mid-fifties, when he remembered a man in the Airforce while serving his military service in Germany, who called his regulation boots his 'blue suede shoes' (the specific reason is unclear). Accordingly, Cash suggested to Perkins that he write a song about these shoes, although Perkins was unsure. It was only on observing a couple wearing blue suede shoes while dancing during one of his sets that he resumed his attempts to write the song.

Carl Perkins was the first to release the song in January 1956 in the US. It reached number ten in the UK, where it became his only UK hit. As was the vogue of the times, several other acts queued up to record the song and none more famous than touring partner Elvis Presley, who released his version five months after Perkins's and managed to get one placing better than the original at number nine. It has been covered by several musicians, many citing it as a formative influence: Eddie Cochran, Buddy Holly, Jimi Hendrix, Paul McCartney, Mary J. Blige and Bruce Springsteen among them.

The melodic result of Cliff's recording is helped by the racing rhythm guitar (Bruce Welch) and the subtly running bass lines (Jet Harris) and, of course, Hank Marvin's guitar solos. It is impossible to keep still while listening to this version of the song, which is presented at a faster pace than the original. Although the album version was released in mono only, there was a stereo version created from the same take of the song that was only released on the stereo version of the ***Cliff Sings No. 1*** EP. Since then, though, both mono and stereo versions have been made available on a variety of compilations as well as the re-issued version of the *Cliff Sings* album remastered into stereo.

Fast-forwarding twenty-two years and Cliff was performing *Blue Suede Shoes* as part of the ***Tribute to the Legends***; this and ***Great Balls of Fire*** featured Cliff on his own before Phil Everly joined him for the remainder of the medley, which was recorded by the BBC as part of the four-part documentary they were making about Cliff. Although ***Daddy's Home*** and a couple of other tracks were licensed for release at the time, it would take another thirteen years before the Everly section was dusted off and licensed for release with ***All I Have to Do Is Dream*** being issued as a double A-side along with a remixed version of ***Miss You Nights***. While the vinyl single had only the two tracks, the dual CD release had several other tracks, with the first section including ***When Will I Be Loved?*** and this medley incorporated as bonus tracks.

The performance by Cliff shows that rock and roll is what he enjoys best. While not as raucous as the original recordings from the fifties, Cliff has the rock and roll timing that is required to engender the spirit of the genre.

Track Specification

Composed by Carl Perkins

1. Cliff

Musicians

Jet Harris	bass
Hank Marvin	guitar
Tony Meehan	drums, percussion
Cliff Richard	vocals
Bruce Welch	rhythm guitar

Recording Details

Producer	Norrie Paramor
Engineered by	Malcolm Addey and Alan Kane (mono) and Stuart Eltham and Norman Smith (stereo)
Recording location	Abbey Road Studio 2, St. John's Wood, London
Recording date	7th September 1959

2. CD B-side (All I Have to Do Is Dream)

Musicians

Stuart Calver	backing vocals
John Clark	guitar
Mark Griffiths	bass
Graham Jarvis	drums, percussion
Martin Jenner	guitar
Alan Park	keyboards
John Perry	backing vocals
Cliff Richard	vocals
Tony Rivers	backing vocals
Graham Todd	keyboards

Recording Details

Producer	Cliff Richard
Engineered by	Unknown
Recording location	Hammersmith Odeon, London
Remixed at	R. G. Jones Studio, London
Recording date	1st May 1981 (live track) and 7th September 1994 (remix)

♫ Blue Turns to Grey

33rd UK single

Written in 1965 at the height of their creative powers, *Blue Turns to Grey* was the result of one of the many collaborations between chief Rolling Stones writers Mick Jagger and Keith Richards. It appeared on the track listing of the band's late 1965 album *December's Children and Everybody's* but earlier in the year in February, it was covered by the Mighty Avengers and Dick and Dee Dee, although neither charted in the UK. It has also been covered by Diana Darby, the Epics, Don and the Goodtimes and the Flamin' Groovies.

The following year that it was announced that Cliff Richard and the Shadows were going to cover the song for a future single release. Recorded at the first session of 1966, the band recorded the single and its B-side together. Backed with ***Somebody Loses***, *Blue Turns to Grey* was released on the Columbia label (catalogue number DB 7866) on 18th March 1966, reaching number fifteen in the UK singles charts. The final (unknown) take and edit were used for mono and stereo recordings but with different mixes for the separation of audio channels. The single and B-side were only released in mono format, although the stereo version *Blue Turns to Grey* was released on the compilation album ***The Best of Cliff*** three years later and has frequently appeared on hit compilations since.

The choice of a Rolling Stones song seems at odds with what Cliff was generally recording during this period but he makes the song work very well for him. With a guitar by Hank Marvin that has a vibrato throughout as well as the powerhouse rhythm created by the other Shadows, Cliff's vocal as an edge that is surprising in comparison to the previous singles he had released. It is also another song that exhibits the perfection of the vocal harmonies created by the Shadows against Cliff's lead.

Track Specification

Composed by Mick Jagger and Keith Richards

Musicians

Brian Bennett	drums, percussion
Hank Marvin	backing vocals, guitar
Cliff Richard	vocals
John Rostill	backing vocals, bass
Bruce Welch	backing vocals, rhythm guitar

Recording Details

Producer	Norrie Paramor
Engineered by	Unknown
Recording location	Abbey Road Studio 2, St. John's Wood, London
Recording date	17th January 1966

♫ Bony Maronie

From the album **Japan Tour '74**

A major hit for the writer of the song, Larry Williams, when it was released in early 1958, *Bony Maronie* reached number eleven in the UK charts. With a variety of spellings based on the –y and –ie suffixes, the song has been covered by a number of artists including Boxcar Willie, John Lennon, Ritchie Valens, Alvin Stardust, Johnny Winter and the Who.

Cliff Richard regularly performed songs in concert that were popular or resonated in some other way but that he had never (and would never) record in the studio. For the 1974 tour of Japan, this included *Bony Maronie*, which helped to represent some of the favourite songs that had inspired him over the years as part of a ***Rock Medley***: ***His Latest Flame, Chantilly Lace***, *Bony Maronie*, ***Do You Wanna Dance?***, ***Crocodile Rock*** and ***Do You Wanna Dance?*** again to complete the medley. After the frenetic pace of the first two songs, the rhythm is halved for *Bony Maronie* and at a slower pace than the original, although the performance works well as a contrast.

Track Specification

Composed by Larry Williams

Musicians

Cliff Hall	piano
Brian Lewis	backing vocals, guitar
Kevin Peak	acoustic guitar
Cliff Richard	vocals
Trevor Spencer	drums, percussion
Alan Tarney	backing vocals, bass
Bruce Welch	backing vocals, rhythm guitar

Recording Details

Producer	Toshiba EMI (no individual detailed)
Engineered by	Toshiba EMI (no individual detailed)
Recording location	Shinjuku Koseinenkin, Tokyo, Japan
Recording date	7th-8th October 1974

♫ Book of Love

From the album **From a Distance ***** The Event**

Incorrectly missing the definite article on the track listings of ***From a Distance ***** The Event***, Cliff Richard opened his thirtieth anniversary concerts at Wembley Stadium with a sequence of songs from the era when he started out in music. To complete the set, he performed another medley of songs, starting with *The Book of Love*.

Written by three members of the Monotones to record, their single reached number five in the American Billboard Hot 100 charts in 1958, although, to British audiences, it was the Mudlarks' cover later that year that is more familiar when it went to number eight in the parochial charts. In the intervening time, a few artists have covered it including the Carpenters, the Four Seasons, the Alley Cats, Mud, Sha Na Na, the Raindrops and the Underbeats.

With assistance from the Dallas Boys and the Vernons Girls and then the Kalin Twins, Cliff comes in not singing the melody but rather the upper harmony. His overall contribution is shortened to two lines from the lyrics.

Track Specification
Composed by Warren Davis, George Malone and Charles Patrick
Musicians

Dallas Boys:	
Nicky Clarke	backing vocals
Leon Fisk	backing vocals
Stan Jones	backing vocals
Joe Smith	backing vocals
Bob Wragg	backing vocals
Kalin Twins:	
Harold Kalin	backing vocals
Herbie Kalin	backing vocals
Oh Boy! Band	rock 'n' roll band
Cliff Richard	vocals
Vernons Girls:	
Lyn Cornell	backing vocals
Maureen Kennedy	backing vocals
Frances Lee	backing vocals
Jean Owen	backing vocals

Recording Details

Producer	Cliff Richard
Engineered by	Keith Bessey and Mick McKenna
Recording location	Rolling Stones Mobile Studio, Wembley Stadium, Wembley, North-west London
Recording date	16th-17th June 1989

♬ Boom Boom (That's How My Heart Beats)

From the EP **Take Four**

Written by prolific composer and music manager Gordon Mills, who had also written ***I'm the Lonely One***, *Boom Boom (That's How My Heart Beats)* was recorded on its own and released on the ***Take Four*** EP in mono only. The final take and edit were used for both mono and stereo recordings but with different mixes for the separate channels. The song was a major rarity, until the stereo version was issued on ***The EP Collection: Ballads and Love Songs*** in 1989, itself a significant rarity over the years until the stereo version was reissued on the 2001 French compilation *I Could Easily Fall*.
It is possible that the song was attempted to be recorded prior to this session: on 4th April, a song called ***Whatcha Gonna Do About It?*** was listed on the session notes. Since this was ten days prior to the successful completion of *Boom Boom (That's How My Heart Beats)* and because that different title is a prominent lyric in the song, the evidence seems to suggest that it might have been an earlier attempt of this song under a different title rather than a separate song.
This upbeat song is driven along by strummed electric guitar chords and the powerhouse rhythm by Bruce Welch. On the record, there is a perfect example of the Shadows vocals blending with Cliff's that became quintessentially their sound.

Track Specification
Composed by Gordon Mills
Musicians

Brian Bennett	drums, percussion
Hank Marvin	backing vocals, guitar
Cliff Richard	vocals
John Rostill	backing vocals, bass
Bruce Welch	backing vocals, rhythm guitar

Recording Details

Producer	Norrie Paramor
Engineered by	Unknown
Recording location	Abbey Road Studio 2, St. John's Wood, London
Recording date	14th April 1965

♬ Born to Rock 'n' Roll

98th UK single *(seven- and twelve-inch) and from the albums* **Dave Clark's Time – The Album**, **My Kinda Life** *and* **World Tour Live** *and unissued live track*

In the sixties, Dave Clark and his five-piece band created some of the most memorable music of the era with hits such as *Glad All Over*, *Bits and Pieces* and *Catch Us if You Can*, although, by the seventies, the band's popularity was on the wane. By the eighties, Clark had begun work on a stage musical that ostensibly was about the salvation of the human race by a group of intergalactic beings (a loose allegory to a Supreme Being). The result was ***Time***, performed first in London at the Dominion Theatre with Cliff Richard in the lead. To support his latest excursion into the theatre, Cliff recorded a number of songs from the show, starting with ***She's So Beautiful***, ***It's in Every One of Us*** and the first song from the show, *Born to Rock 'n' Roll*. It comes as part of a stadium-like rock gig, with Cliff's back to the theatre audience as if they are looking out on the stadium's audience. The singer's popularity means that he is chosen to represent humanity for all their failings at a court of justice, which, of course, he does and saves the world. To represent the stage audience, the album version of the song has sound effects of applause at the start and end that are unconvincing but these are left off the single version.
Born to Rock 'n' Roll is autobiographical for Cliff in many ways and, backed with *Law of the Universe* (a non-Cliff track performed by Chris Thompson, Miriam Stockley and Michael Mullens), it was issued on the EMI label (catalogue number EMI 5545) on 6th May 1986 but, unlike the other two singles, it failed to chart in the UK. Simultaneously, a twelve-inch version of the single was released (catalogue number 12EMI 5545) with the original songs plus an extended version of the A-side. The original single was released in CD format for the first time on the 2002 compilation, ***The Singles Collection***.
Percussion representing a beating heart starts before the guitars, bass and drums take over amidst the cheers of the audience to whom the Rock Star is performing. The song is strong and defies the listener to stop their foot from tapping.
During the *Live & Guaranteed 1988!* tour to support the associated album ***Always Guaranteed***, *Born to Rock 'n' Roll* opened the set, appropriate because of the lyrics and the fact that it opened the musical. The Denmark leg of the tour was filmed and released as a video tape and then later on an accompanying CD. However, *Born to Rock 'n' Roll* remains unreleased.

In 1992, Cliff revisited a number of his tracks for a different kind of album release, ***My Kinda Life***, which featured the original tracks but with additional instrumentation and occasional vocals. The first track was *Born to Rock 'n' Roll*, which featured extra electronic drums, synthesisers and guitar arranged by Cliff's new music director Paul Moessl.

In 2003, for his world tour to support the release of the ***Wanted*** album, Cliff chose *Born to Rock 'n' Roll* for the set list. Filmed and recorded at the New Zealand concert for a later DVD, the following year the complementary *World Tour Live* CD was issued with a subset of the DVD tracks and included the performance of this song. Joined by the four dancers, Cliff returns to the stage in dark sunglasses and leather trousers as he performs a spirited version of the song.

Track Specification

Composed by Dave Clark, Jeff Daniels and David Soames

1. Single (seven-inch)

Musicians

Peter Collins	arranger
John Edwards	bass
Jerry Hay	bass
Graham Jarvis	drums, percussion
Stuart Mather	backing vocals
Cliff Richard	vocals
Billy Squire	backing vocals, guitar
Dave Stewart	arranger, keyboards
Paul Wickens	keyboards

Recording Details

Producer	Peter Collins
Engineered by	Chris Porter
Recording location	Marcus Studios, London
Recording date	25th August 1985

2. Single (twelve-inch)

Musicians

John Edwards	bass
Jerry Hay	bass
Graham Jarvis	drums, percussion
Stuart Mather	backing vocals
Cliff Richard	vocals
Billy Squire	backing vocals, guitar
Dave Stewart	keyboards
Paul Wickens	keyboards

Recording Details

Producer	Peter Collins
Engineered by	Chris Porter
Recording location	Marcus Studios, London
Recording date	25th August 1985

3. Dave Clark's Time – The Album

Musicians

John Edwards	bass
Jerry Hay	bass
Graham Jarvis	drums, percussion
Stuart Mather	backing vocals
Cliff Richard	vocals
Billy Squire	backing vocals, guitar
Dave Stewart	keyboards
Unknown	audience effects
Paul Wickens	keyboards

Recording Details

Producer	Peter Collins
Engineered by	Chris Porter
Recording location	Marcus Studios, London
Recording date	25th August 1985

4. Unissued track (Live & Guaranteed 1988!)

Musicians

John Clark	guitar
Rosemarie Ford	backing vocals
Mark Griffiths	bass
Peter Howarth	backing vocals
Steve Lauri	guitar
Paul Moessl	keyboards
Mick Mullins	backing vocals
Alan Park	keyboards
Cliff Richard	vocals
Henry Spinetti	drums, percussion

Recording Details

Producer	Unknown
Engineered by	Unknown
Recording location	Fyens Forum, Odense, Denmark
Recording date	22nd May 1988

5. My Kinda Life

Musicians

John Clark	guitar
Peter Collins	arranger (original track)
John Edwards	bass
Jerry Hay	bass
Graham Jarvis	drums, percussion
Stuart Mather	backing vocals
Paul Moessl	arranger (new instrumentation), drum programming, keyboards
Cliff Richard	vocals
Billy Squire	backing vocals, guitar
Dave Stewart	arranger, keyboards
Paul Wickens	keyboards

Recording Details

Producer	Peter Collins (original track) and Cliff Richard and Paul Moessl (new instrumentation)
Engineered by	Chris Porter (original track) and Gerry Kitchingham and Ben Robbins (new instrumentation)
Recording location	Marcus Studios, London (original track) and R. G. Jones Studios, Wimbledon, London (new instrumentation)
Recording date	25th August 1985 (original track) and 20th-23rd April 1992 (new instrumentation)

6. World Tour Live

Musicians

Anthony Clark	backing vocals, guitar
John Clark	guitar
Dave Cooke	keyboards
Mike Haughton	saxophone
Peter Howarth	backing vocals
Pete May	drums, percussion
Mick Mullins	backing vocals
Keith Murrell	backing vocals
Alan Park	keyboards
Cliff Richard	vocals
Steve Stroud	bass

Recording Details

Producer	Keith Bessey
Engineered by	Keith Bessey
Recording location	The Mission Winery, Napier, New Zealand
Recording date	22nd February 2003

♫ Boum

From the EP **When in France**

Written by the prolific composer Charles Trenet (who also wrote ***La Mer***) in 1938, *Boum* (often appearing with an exclamation mark but not on the ***When in France*** EP) won a coveted Grand Prix du Disque in his native France. Pronounced similarly to the English onomatopoeic word 'boom' and meaning pretty much the same in translation, Trenet's intention was for it to be light-hearted reflection of the mood of the French people when it was released.
Cliff Richard and the Shadows recorded it in the first of three sessions over five days while they were performing in the summer season in Blackpool. Released in mono format, *Boum* is one of the few foreign language songs not be re-recorded by Cliff into English. One of three songs to be recorded in the session for the EP, *Boum* was completed in ten takes. Until twelve years later, when it appeared on Belgian LP *When in France... Chante en Français*, the song remained a relative rarity – but it would take another twenty-two years to appear on CD in the foreign language compilation ***On the Continent***.
Performed with gusto by the Shadows, the driving force behind the song lies with the staccato bass line by Brian Locking and Bruce Welch's perfect chord structure. The middle eight break features a Hank Marvin solo but it is the lead vocal line by Cliff that, while not imitating the original quirkiness, tops off a brilliant version of this continental track.

Track Specification

Composed by Charles Trenet

Musicians

Brian 'Licorice' Locking	bass
Hank Marvin	backing vocals, guitar
Brian Bennett	drums, percussion
Cliff Richard	vocals
Bruce Welch	backing vocals, rhythm guitar

Recording Details

Producer	Norrie Paramor
Engineered by	Malcolm Addey and Jimmy Johnson
Recording location	Jubilee Hall, Blackpool
Recording date	5th August 1963

♫ Brand New Song, A

58th UK single

A brand new song in a few respects: it marked a departure in musical style for Cliff Richard, it was the last Cliff single to be released on the Columbia label, it was the first song to be recorded with new producer David MacKay, after Norrie Paramor's retirement, and it was the first song to register Cliff's first real commercial disaster. Although that last point should resonate, the song was recorded by the New Seekers and was a popular part of their repertoire. The song was found for Cliff by MacKay and all concerned thought the recording would be a massive hit. However, it was not to be. *A Brand New Song* was recorded at a session that saw two tracks completed for the upcoming ***The 31st of February Street***.
The track was issued as a single, backed with ***The Old Accordion***, on the Columbia label (catalogue number DB 8957) on 24th November 1972 and went on to claim the ignominious accolade of being the first of a very small number of singles that would not chart for Cliff; once again, it was seen as a final nail in the coffin for Cliff's career by some critics who thought he was now too middle-of-the-road to make much of an impression on the current music scene. Because of its poor reception and lack of sales, the single was extraordinarily rare until it was added to the track listing of the compilation album *1970s* and later on the 2002 boxed set *The Singles Collection*.
A spirited performance is introduced with tinkling guitar strings hit with implements in a similar way to that of the psalter. The song is not bad but it is probably, in retrospect, not single material in spite of the fun that the new band is having with it. The production, sharper than on Cliff's prior singles, is maybe due to the new broom of David MacKay.

Track Specification

Composed by Jeff Barry and Paul Williams

Musicians

Terry Britten	backing vocals, guitar
Barrie Guard	percussion
David MacKay	arranger
Kevin Peek	guitar
Cliff Richard	vocals, backing vocals
Trevor Spencer	drums, percussion
Alan Tarney	backing vocals, bass

Recording Details

Producer	David MacKay
Engineered by	Peter Vince
Recording location	Abbey Road Studio 3, St. John's Wood, London
Recording date	11th October 1972

♫ Brave New World

B-side of **Remember Me** *(twelve-inch and CD single formats)*

In the spring of 1987, fresh from the rigours of performing in ***Time – the Musical*** at night and recording ***Always Guaranteed*** by day at the end of 1986, Cliff Richard went back into the studios to record a number of songs that would provide a suite of B-sides. *Brave New World* was one such track and it was chosen as a bonus B-side track for the twelve-inch and CD single releases of ***Remember Me***, the third single from the album project. It remained somewhat a rarity until it was added as one of eight bonus tracks on the 2004 remaster of *Always Guaranteed.*

Cliff's vocals are engineered with a slight echo running behind them, while he also provides the backing vocals. The synthesiser introduction sounds like an Australian didgeridoo, while the performance stays principally on one or two chords throughout. The beauty of the song though is derived from the construction of the vocal arrangement.

Track Specification
Composed by Alan Tarney

Musicians	
John Clark	guitar
Alan Park	keyboards
Cliff Richard	vocals, backing vocals
Unknown	bass
Unknown	drums, percussion

Recording Details	
Producer	Cliff Richard, Keith Bessey and Alan Park
Engineered by	Keith Bessey
Recording location	C. R. O. Studios, Esher, Surrey
Recording date	April 1987

♫ Breathless

Private demo (subsequently released on ***The Rock and Roll Years 1958-1963***) and unreleased live track

A significant hit for American rock and roller Jerry Lee Lewis in the April of 1958, when his version reached number eight in the UK charts, the song has also been covered by a variety of artists, particularly at the time of Lewis's successful single in order to pick up on some of the cachet associated with it, including Albert Lee, Mike Berry, Wanda Jackson, the writer of the song Otis Blackwell, Tom Jones and, of course, Little Richard who also turned out a memorable version.

In the July (or thereabouts) of 1958, a young Harry Webb and a group of friends visited the HMV shop in Oxford Street in London. With the increase in popularity of singles, entrepreneurial record shops converted store rooms and other available space into small recording studios, giving members of the public the opportunity to cut a disc for themselves. This was a boon for ambitious new singers and groups, since they were able to record demonstration material, which they could then tout around the various record companies. Armed with ten pounds provided by his parents – a significant sum of money in a Britain still struggling in the post-war austerity years of rationing and tightening belts that would be the equivalent of around one hundred pounds or more in today's prices – the young Webb and his mates entered the studio on the first floor of the shop and recorded their versions of *Breathless* and ***Lawdy Miss Clawdy***, which had been a recent hit for Elvis Presley and Little Richard.

The song presented on this private recording shows that Cliff Richard had an immense musical and vocal talent even at the young age of seventeen, incorporating falsetto and a strong understanding for performing rock and roll. The guitars are slightly out of synch with each other and it sounds as if the solo middle eight was a bit of struggle to perform; however, it is the lead vocals that are the key interest here with the promise of what was to come in a long and fruitful recording career for Cliff.

There is no information regarding the studio personnel available and these will be annotated as unknown until fresh research material comes to light. However, the group of friends is known and the instruments that they played.

As it was a private pressing, it remained in the hands of Cliff and was only heard by friends, family and record company executives, including Norrie Paramor at Columbia who signed Cliff Richard and the Drifters on the strength of the raw musicianship shown in these demos. It was eventually given public release on the rarities and summary anthology and profile of Cliff's first five years in rock and roll, *The Rock and Roll Years 1958-1963*. On a special edition release of this album, a special 78 r.p.m. record was issued with *Breathless* as the B-side of *Lawdy Miss Clawdy*.

Another version of the song was recorded during the residency secured by Cliff Richard and the Drifters (actually only Cliff, Ian Samwell and Terry Smart) at the Butlin's Holiday Camp in Clacton, where they would perform their own versions of popular American rock and roll and country music. Recorded on to a two-track tape machine by Stan Edwards, while some tracks were good enough (from a technical quality standpoint) for release on *The Rock and Roll Years 1958-1963* retrospective, others were too poor to be considered for release. One such casualty was this live recording of *Breathless*.

Track Specification
Composed by Otis Blackwell

1. Private demo *(The Rock and Roll Years 1958-1963)*

Musicians	
Norman Mitham	guitar
Ken Pavey	guitar
Cliff Richard	vocals, guitar
Ian Samwell	guitar
Terry Smart	drums, percussion

Recording Details	
Producer	Unknown
Engineered by	Unknown
Recording location	HMV Record Shop, First Floor studio, Oxford Street, London
Recording date	Early summer, 1958 (possibly July)

2. *Unreleased live track (Butlin's)*

Musicians

Cliff Richard	vocals, guitar
Ian Samwell	guitar
Terry Smart	drums, percussion

Recording Details

Producer	Unknown
Engineered by	Stan Edwards
Recording location	Rock 'n' Roll Ballroom, Butlin's Holiday Camp, Clacton-on-Sea, Essex
Recording date	August 1958

♫ Broken Doll

From the album **Wired for Sound**

The opening track to the second vinyl side of Cliff Richard's ***Wired or Sound***, *Broken Doll* was one of the small handful of songs not written by Alan Tarney, although his dominance of Cliff's recordings is still evident as he plays nearly all the instruments, produces the track and arranges the song too. Originally recorded by Wreckless Eric, who was one of the drivers behind the punk rock movement in the late seventies, *Broken Doll* therefore seems to be an odd choice for Cliff to record – but it also demonstrates his versatility behind the microphone and is a strong song for inclusion on the record.

In spite of the perceived sadness created by the song's title, the rhythm and major key in which it is presented belies the meaning of the lyrics, which talk of observing a friend's failing relationship with a girl who is crushed by the man's dalliances. This is a surprisingly different song in some respects for Cliff to sing and confirms his ability to turn his hand to a number of styles, even though it is overlaid by Tarney's electronica.

Track Specification

Composed by Eric Goulden and Walter Hacon

Musicians

Graham Jarvis	drums, percussion
Cliff Richard	vocals, backing vocals
Alan Tarney	arranger, backing vocals, guitar, bass, keyboards

Recording Details

Producer	Alan Tarney
Engineered by	Michael Boddicker and Ian Little
Recording location	Gallery Studios, Chertsey, Surrey
Recording date	27th May-9th July 1981

♫ Brother to Brother

From the album **Cliff Richard - The Album**

The final track on Cliff Richard's ***Cliff Richard - The Album*** is a beautifully presented song of faith and friendship that begins with an *a capella* section with close harmonies. It exemplifies what Cliff is absolutely best at in singing either solo in a close harmony group. The song is performed over an electric piano before the choral section is brought back in. The instrumentation is built up with strings, bass and guitar but these quieten down leaving Cliff singing on his own. The guitar creates an effective solo underneath the lead vocal before relinquishing the control to the strings arranged by Richard Hewson and finally, there is an ensemble piece that has everyone joining in as the track slowly fades.

Track Specification

Composed by Paul Moessl and Steve Glen

Musicians

John Bradbury	violin
John Clark	guitar
Richard Hewson	arranger, conductor
Peter Howarth	backing vocals
Peter May	drums, percussion
Paul Moessl	arranger, drum programming, keyboards
Keith Murrell	backing vocals
Cliff Richard	vocals, backing vocals
Steve Stroud	bass
Unknown	orchestra (other strings)
David Woodcock	violin

Recording Details

Producer	Paul Moessl and Cliff Richard
Engineered by	Gerry Kitchingham and Ben Robbins
Recording location	R. G. Jones Studios, Wimbledon, London
Recording date	25th-31st May 1992, 8th June 1992 (backing track) and 6th July 1992 (vocals)

♫ Brumburger Duet

From the film soundtrack album of **Take Me High**

In the days when ***Take Me High*** was filmed, there was nowhere near the dominance of the fast food market that burger giant McDonald's holds today and, as a result of this, the prospect of setting up a market-dominating business in the existing burger restaurants would have seemed like a good one. So the main storyline of *Take Me High* that sees Tim Matthews (Cliff Richard) and Sarah (Debbie Watling) setting up the Brumburger business with a view to turning it into a tremendous success is not such a preposterous one with that hindsight. The prefix 'Brum-', of course, is derived from the location of the filming in Birmingham, where the residents are known as Brummagems.

In the film, having sowed the seed of the idea of a Brumburger in Sarah's mind, Tim invites her over to his houseboat so that they can work on the recipe and the requisite slogans required for marketing the new food. With a quirky, clown-like melody, they work through a few ideas in duet as they taste the results of her cooking, interspersed with dialogue that doesn't occur on the soundtrack. At the end of the song, the pair kisses for the first time.

Recorded in a set of sessions for the film over a four-day period, the *Brumburger Duet*, featuring both Cliff and Debbie Watling on vocals, took five takes to complete. On the soundtrack album, the track appears out of sequence when compared with the narrative of the film, appearing before ***Take Me High***, where it appears before ***Driving*** in the film.
Employing the sounds of the fairground – such as the pipe organ, the duck whistles and other instruments – the song is great fun and Cliff appears to be having a good time recording it. There is a rallentando at the end before the original time signature is resumed adding to the seething drama underneath the apparently simplistic little song.

Track Specification
Composed by Tony Cole

Musicians		*Recording Details*	
David MacKay Orchestra	orchestra	Producer	David MacKay
David MacKay	arranger, conductor	Engineered by	Tony Clark and Mike Jarrett
Cliff Richard	vocals	Recording location	Abbey Road Studio 3, St. John's Wood, London
Debbie Watling	vocals	Recording date	27th-28th May 1973

♫ Brumburger Finale

From the film soundtrack album of **Take Me High**

This joyous and upbeat song features at the end of the film (as the title might suggest). The premise of a burger restaurant being so new and a huge business proposition may seem strange today but, back in 1973, fast food outlets were few and far between and what there were available were generally awful, so seems a strong idea with the benefit of this hindsight. With a police escort from the bank headquarters in Birmingham to the Brumburger restaurant, Tim Matthews (Cliff Richard) leads everyone else through the doors to a crowded floor filled with people (even though it is supposed to be a seated restaurant and not a buffet). He hugs Sarah (Debbie Watling) as the camera pans out and the end titles begin rolling to the dying strains of the song.
Recorded in at the final set of sessions for the film, *Brumburger Finale* was the last song to be recorded for the soundtrack. With quacking guitar – prevalent on songs of the era – the track is a perfect ending to a feel-good film that is part advert for the new Brumburger and part recollection of how far the central character has come in his emotional development since the start. The foot-tapping principal melody is picked up in the guitar before the pace is slowed to about half of the original as Cliff invites everyone to his restaurant whatever their status might be.

Track Specification
Composed by Tony Cole

Musicians		*Recording Details*	
David MacKay Orchestra	orchestra	Producer	David MacKay
David MacKay	arranger, conductor	Engineered by	Tony Clark and Mike Jarrett
Cliff Richard	vocals, backing vocals	Recording location	Abbey Road Studio 3, St. John's Wood, London
Unknown	backing vocals	Recording date	3rd September 1973

♫ Bulange Downpour

B-side of **I Still Believe in You**

Written by Cliff Richard and recorded during the 1992 sessions for ***Cliff Richard - The Album***, *Bulange Downpour* was inspired by a sudden rainstorm when he visited the little village of Bulange in Uganda for his charity. The water flowed through the village, turning the mud into what he thought looked like blood. Built of the same clay, Cliff also recalls witnessing the houses being washed away by the storm. The track was chosen as the principal B-side of the first single released from the parent album, ***I Still Believe in You***, and was subsequently issued on the track listing of the compilation of Cliff's compositions, ***My Songs***.
Twinkling bells (sounding like bicycles) and the sound effects of the thunderstorm bring in this beautifully observed song that is principally accompanied by pizzicato strings and sustained chords. Cliff supplies his own backing vocals, which are kept simple. The percussion is exotically created on tom-toms, while there is a lovely male chorus (no details available as to who they are but likely to be local villagers) repeating a vocal motif until the song fades. This is a lovely song that is unfortunate in that it was tucked away on the B-side of a single, when it deserved much greater exposure to prove how good Cliff is at writing songs that are inspirational to him.

Track Specification
Composed by Cliff Richard

Musicians		*Recording Details*	
John Bradbury	violin	Producer	Paul Moessl and Cliff Richard
Richard Hewson	arranger, conductor	Engineered by	Gerry Kitchingham and Ben Robbins
Paul Moessl	arranger, drum programming, keyboards	Recording location	R. G. Jones Studios, Wimbledon, London
Cliff Richard	vocals, backing vocals	Recording date	25th-31st May 1992, 8th June 1992 (backing track) and 19th July1992 (vocals)
Unknown	orchestra (other strings)		
Unknown	male chorus		
David Woodcock	violin		

♫ Burn On!

From the album **The Kendrick Collection** *(Graham Kendrick)*

Having been a supporter of Graham Kendrick's songs, recording and performing them himself as well as choosing some for his various protégées such as Sheila Walsh, it was not a significant issue for Cliff Richard to agree to perform on record a number of songs by the man. Working with the All Souls Orchestra based at the church of the same name, in Langham, *Burn On* was the first of three songs involving Cliff.

The gentle woodwind and a horn usher in this mellow song that has Cliff employing his vibrato to add to the emotion of the lyrics. There is a syncopated rhythm underpinning the accompaniment but it is Cliff's precise lead that engenders the beauty of the song, and this assisted by Cliff supplying his own backing vocals as the song slowly builds up in its drama.

Track Specification

Composed by Graham Kendrick

Musicians		*Recording Details*	
All Souls Orchestra	orchestra	Producer	Burt Rhodes
Cliff Richard	vocals, backing vocals	Engineered by	Graham McHutchon
Noël Tredinnick	arranger, conductor	Recording location	All Souls Church, Langham, London
		Recording date	2nd February 1989

♫ Butterfly Kisses

From the album **Real as I Wanna Be**

Butterfly Kisses is an extraordinarily beautiful song that is a bittersweet tearjerker as it follows the reminiscences of a father regarding his daughter and the transition as she grows up and leaves home to get married and have kids of her own. The exceptional emotion that is imbued in the lyrics and the accompanying melody defies anyone not to be moved as the butterfly kisses are placed first on his daughter by him and then on him by her at her wedding in order to make them feel loved and secure. The song was a bewilderingly minor hit for its writer Bob Carlisle when he reached number fifty-six in the late August of 1997, although it did better in the US, while it has also been covered by Jeff Carson, the Raybon Brothers, Obscure, Carousel, Carol Lang and Westlife among others. Unsurprisingly, given the heart-wrenching content, it is a favourite song to be played at weddings.

Although Cliff Richard is unmarried and, naturally, has no children, he sings the song perfectly and confirms that he had tears in his eyes while recording the song because the love within a family is universal and not specific to individual relationships. The extraordinary beauty of the song is imitated by the synthesized strings and piano, which are kept reverentially quiet behind the cracked emotion in Cliff's lead vocals.

Track Specification

Composed by Bob Carlisle and Randy Thomas

Musicians		*Recording Details*	
Charlie Bonat	acoustic guitar	Producer	Peter Wolf
Munich Symphony Orchestra	orchestra	Engineered by	Christian Leitgeb, Chris Heil, Paul Erickson and/or Keith Bessey
Cliff Richard	vocals, backing vocals		
Michelle Wolf	backing vocals		
Peter Wolf	arranger, conductor, keyboards	Recording location	Little America Recording Studios, Weiler, Austria, Ocean Recording Studios, Burbank, California, USA, Arco Recording Studios, Munich, Germany, R. G. Jones Recording Studios, Wimbledon, London, England and/or The Pierce Room, London, England
		Recording date	March-April 1996 and November 1997

♫ Canción de Orfeo

From the album **When in Spain**

With an English version entitled ***Carnival*** (which Cliff Richard recorded for his ***Holiday Carnival*** EP), *Canción de Orfeo* (or *Orfeo's Song*) is sometimes referred to as *Manhã de Carnaval* (or *Morning of the Carnival*). The song was originally written by its Brazilian writers for the 1959 Portuguese language film *Orfeu Negro* (or *Black Orpheus*). Performed in a bossanova rhythm, it has become a jazz standard, particularly in the US. Luis Bonfá has recorded a version of the song, as has a variety of other artists including Perry Como, Stan Getz, Frank Sinatra, Joan Baez, Carly Simon, Dinah Shore, Julio Iglesias, Clare Nunes and Chet Atkins among many others.

Cliff Richard's Spanish language version is a completely new recording, rather than taking the English version from the *Holiday Carnival* EP and applying re-recorded vocals. Instead, *Canción de Orfeo* was recorded at the Barcelona-based EMI Studios as one of four tracks from the session for the ***When in Spain*** album. The fifth and final take and edit were used for the mono and stereo recordings but with different mixes for the needs of the audio channels.

For once on the album, the stereo recording techniques are used to great effect on this track, with the guitar solo accompaniment from Hank Marvin spread out between the predominant right channel and into the left. Cliff's vocals are suitably anguished and show his abilities to express himself in any language he chose to record in. The strings, overdubbed at a later date, add an extra dimension to the song that is a missing nugget from Cliff's oeuvre.

Track Specification

Composed by Luiz Bonfá, Hugo Peretti, Luigi Creatore, George Weiss and Jesus Maria de Arozamena

Musicians		*Recording Details*	
Brian Bennett	drums, percussion	Producer	Norrie Paramor
Brian 'Licorice' Locking	bass	Engineered by	Malcolm Addey
Hank Marvin	guitar	Recording location	EMI Studios, Barcelona (main) and Abbey Road Studio 2 (strings)
Norrie Paramor Strings	orchestra		
Norrie Paramor	arranger, conductor	Recording date	29th April 1963 (main recording) and 14th May 1963 (strings)
Cliff Richard	vocals		
Bruce Welch	rhythm guitar		

♫ Can It Be True? (1)

Unissued track

In early 1969, Tyne Tees Television commissioned a series of six playlets for their religious broadcast slot called *Life with Johnny*, featuring Cliff Richard in the title role as each episode updated a well-known parable told by Jesus in the Bible. Records are unclear on most of the episodes although *Johnny Come Home* and *Johnny Faces Facts* are complete, *Johnny and the Good Samaritan* is partially available, while the remainder are unavailable in either records or film form.

The songs performed had some relevance to the parable being performed and, in all, there were generally five songs per episode. *Can It Be True?*, recorded at the Abbey Road studios with a putative album tie-in project that didn't materialize, appeared in one of the *Johnny on the Rocks*, *Johnny and the Blind Rage* or *Johnny in Love* episodes. The end credits of the available episodes stated that all songs were original and written in collaboration between Cliff, the Settlers and the programme's writer David Winter, and it is not the same as the song of the same name from ***About That Man***. The instrumentation and performance details are unknown and so are expressed as those known to be present.

Track Specification

Composed by Cliff Richard, David Winter, Cindy Kent, Mike Jones, John Fyffe and Geoffrey Srodzinski

Musicians		*Recording Details*	
John Fyffe	backing vocals, guitar	Producer	Norrie Paramor
Cindy Kent	backing vocals	Engineered by	Peter Vince
Mike Jones	backing vocals, guitar	Recording location	Abbey Road Studio 3, St. John's Wood, London
Cliff Richard	vocals	Recording date	24th March 1969
Geoffrey Srodzinski	backing vocals, bass		

♫ Can It Be True? (2)

From the album **About That Man**

One of four songs to be recorded for the ***About That Man*** religious album, it is not the same song that was used for the Tyne Tees programme *Life with Johnny*, featuring Cliff Richard, of the same name, because of the stated different writers:

however, the first version is unavailable for musical comparison. All of the tracks for the album were recorded at the one session, since most are readings of Bible tracts and the musical accompaniment for the songs was kept deliberately simple. The song was included on the 1988 *Carols* LP and later on the *Carol and Christmas Songs* album seven years later. Accompanying himself on the guitar, the gentle song is well-suited to Cliff's voice, which employs a perfect vibrato that underlines the meaning of the lyrics.

Track Specification
Composed by Brother William

Musicians		*Recording Details*	
Cliff Richard	vocals, guitar	Producer	Norrie Paramor
		Engineered by	Richard Lush
		Recording location	Abbey Road Studio 2, St. John's Wood, London
		Recording date	20th February 1970

♫ Can't Keep This Feeling In

***127th UK single** and B-sides to* **Can't Keep This Feeling In**

By the end of the nineties, Cliff Richard was suffering again at the hands of the critics. The BBC radio had been reorganized and music that allegedly catered for the youth market was on the playlist. Given that Cliff had completed forty years in the business when *Can't Keep This Feeling In* was released as a single, he was monumentally uncool in the eyes of the station controllers. However unfair this attitude was – and hurtful to Cliff, as he expressed later in interview – he managed to achieve a publicity coup. Having set up the Blackknight label subsidiary with friend Clive Black (the first part of the title, with Knight being a reference to Cliff's recent investiture as a Knight of the Realm), the song was issued under that name rather than Cliff's. Black music stations and the more mainstream trendy radio stations picked it up and gave it a lot of airplay. Because most of the song is performed in falsetto, which Cliff had mastered after guidance from Bruce Welch twenty years earlier, many people were fooled because it simply didn't sound like a singer in his mid-fifties; they imagined that it was a much younger newcomer singing a perfect soul song. However, as soon as it was revealed exactly who it was, the stations promptly stopped playing it, purely on the premise that it was Cliff singing it; an argument that doesn't stand up to any kind of scrutiny other than the bloody-mindedness and ignorant narrow-minded outlook of those controlling the playlist. After all, were they really concerned that Cliff could threaten their stability?
The single was released in a number of formats and packages: primarily backed with non-album track ***Larger Design*** and the 5AM Little America mix of the main track, it was issued on the EMI label (catalogue number CDEM 526) on 12th October 1998 on both of the dual CD single releases. The second CD single featured the main track along with another non-album track, ***After This Love***, and another remix of the title track, this time called the Step Child mix. Four promotional copies were created: first, a radio copy of the main track (catalogue number CDEMDJ 526); second, the Phil Chills Remix version; third, a twelve-inch vinyl DJ promotional copy (BKNIGHT001), which was the one that fooled the radio stations and was subsequently pulled from the schedules – this featured the Step Child and Phil Chills R & B Mixes; and finally the CD version of the vinyl (also BKNIGHT001). The song reached number ten in the UK charts and became Cliff's first top ten hit since ***Peace in Our Time*** at the beginning of the decade.
Although it is very different from what Cliff has performed before, there is no mistaking the timbre and vibrato, even when singing in falsetto. The gentle song is kept together by an insistent percussion sequence but it is Cliff's spirited performance, which includes supplying his own backing vocals, that is the key to the track's success.
The Step Child Mix uses a lot of studio trickery with voices appearing as if on the telephone, while Cliff's vocal line is supported by a much heavier bass mix. It might have gone down well in clubs but it doesn't make for pleasant frequent listening. By contrast, the 5AM Little America Mix is much stronger, with a more fluid accompaniment that takes much of the original album recording and keeps it in place. Cliff's vocals are kept stark in the introduction before the supporting instrumentation joins in. The promotional video was recorded in Portugal, judging from the locations and the people in the background. Cliff is seen leaning against sun-blistered walls and sitting in the shade of doorways and at bar tables in poses that were very much of this period of his career.

Track Specification
Composed by Dennis Lambert, Steve Skinner and Arnie Roman

1. Single

Musicians		*Recording Details*	
Vinnie Colaiuta	drums, percussion	Producer	Peter Wolf
Paul Jackson Jr.	guitar, sitar	Engineered by	Christian Leitgeb, Chris Heil, Paul Erickson and/or Keith Bessey
Cliff Richard	vocals, backing vocals	Recording location	Little America Recording Studios, Weiler, Austria, Ocean Recording Studios, Burbank, California, USA, Arco Recording Studios, Munich, Germany, R. G. Jones Recording Studios, Wimbledon, London, England and/or The Pierce Room, London, England
Unknown	spoken vocals	Recording date	March-April 1996 and November 1997
Peter Wolf	arranger, bass, keyboards, synclavier, percussion		

2. B-side (*Can't Keep This Feeling In 5AM Little America Mix*)

Musicians

Vinnie Colaiuta	drums, percussion
Paul Jackson Jr.	guitar, sitar
Cliff Richard	vocals, backing vocals
Michelle Wolf	backing vocals
Peter Wolf	arranger, bass, keyboards, synclavier, percussion

Recording Details

Producer	Peter Wolf
Engineered by	Christian Leitgeb, Chris Heil, Paul Erickson and/or Keith Bessey
Recording location	Little America Recording Studios, Weiler, Austria, Ocean Recording Studios, Burbank, California, USA, Arco Recording Studios, Munich, Germany, R. G. Jones Recording Studios, Wimbledon, London, England and/or The Pierce Room, London, England
Recording date	March-April 1996 and November 1997

3. B-side (*Can't Keep This Feeling In Step Child Mix*)

Musicians

Vinnie Colaiuta	drums, percussion
Paul Jackson Jr.	guitar, sitar
Cliff Richard	vocals, backing vocals
Michelle Wolf	backing vocals
Peter Wolf	arranger, bass, keyboards, synclavier, percussion

Recording Details

Producer	Peter Wolf
Engineered by	Christian Leitgeb, Chris Heil, Paul Erickson and/or Keith Bessey
Recording location	Little America Recording Studios, Weiler, Austria, Ocean Recording Studios, Burbank, California, USA, Arco Recording Studios, Munich, Germany, R. G. Jones Recording Studios, Wimbledon, London, England and/or The Pierce Room, London, England
Recording date	March-April 1996 and November 1997

4. B-side (*Can't Keep This Feeling In Phil Chills R & B Mix*)

Musicians

Vinnie Colaiuta	drums, percussion
Paul Jackson Jr.	guitar, sitar
Cliff Richard	vocals, backing vocals
Michelle Wolf	backing vocals
Peter Wolf	arranger, bass, keyboards, synclavier, percussion

Recording Details

Producer	Peter Wolf
Engineered by	Christian Leitgeb, Chris Heil, Paul Erickson and/or Keith Bessey
Recording location	Little America Recording Studios, Weiler, Austria, Ocean Recording Studios, Burbank, California, USA, Arco Recording Studios, Munich, Germany, R. G. Jones Recording Studios, Wimbledon, London, England and/or The Pierce Room, London, England
Remixed by	Phil Chills
Recording date	March-April 1996 and November 1997

♫ Can't Let You Go

From the album **Cliff "Live" in Japan '72**

Made famous by Barry Ryan, who had a UK hit with the song as his last single in January 1972, when it reached number thirty-two, *Can't Let You Go* was picked up by Cliff Richard and performed during his Far East tour later that year, reforming the Shadows and employing friends Olivia Newton-John and Pat Carroll on backing vocals.

A foot-tapping song, never recorded in the studio, that gets a strong reception from the crowd at the start, Cliff employs his vocals well on the exposition of a typical rock and roll song. Featuring a riproaring piano and guitar accompaniment by Alan Hawkshaw and Hank Marvin, the girls' backing vocals are also featured prominently in the performance.

Track Specification

Composed by Russ Ballard

Musicians

Brian Bennett	drums, percussion
Pat Carroll	backing vocals
John Farrar	bass
Alan Hawkshaw	piano
Hank Marvin	guitar
Olivia Newton-John	backing vocals
Cliff Richard	vocals
Bruce Welch	rhythm guitar

Recording Details

Producer	Norrie Paramor
Engineered by	Unknown
Recording location	Kosei Nenkin Hall, Tokyo, Japan
Recording date	22nd-23rd September 1972

♫ Can't Take the Hurt Any More

73rd UK single

Recorded at Cliff Richard's final recording session of 1977, *Can't Take the Hurt Anymore* was not intended for the ***Green Light*** album, although it was added to its track listing when the songs were brought together. It was the first song to be completed at the session that also saw its eventual B-side added and a long-time unreleased song ***Mobile Alabama School Leaving Hullabaloo***. Issued with its B-side, ***Needing a Friend***, on the EMI label (catalogue number EMI 2885) on 3rd November 1978, and in spite of the quality of the song, the single failed to chart. The second of three singles from the album and the third single in a row not to chart, it was included on the track listing of the ***Love Songs*** album.

The flowing rhythm guitar is matched with a twinkling piano that flows around the stereo channels. The simplicity of the instrumentation - guitar, piano, bass, drums and percussion: the classic rock band set up - keeps the frustration and sadness of the lyrics firmly in the mind while the additional beauty of the complex backing vocal arrangements makes the song a perfect single for Cliff.

Track Specification
Composed by Laurie Andrew

Musicians	
Terry Britten	guitar
Stuart Calver	backing vocals
Alan Hawkshaw	keyboards
John Perry	backing vocals
Cliff Richard	vocals, backing vocals
Tony Rivers	backing vocals
Trevor Spencer	drums, percussion
Alan Tarney	backing vocals, bass

Recording Details	
Producer	Bruce Welch
Engineered by	Tony Clark and Haydn Bendall
Recording location	Abbey Road Studio 3, St. John's Wood, London
Recording date	11th July 1977

♬ Captain Ginjah

From the film soundtrack album of **The Young Ones**

Taken from the ***Vaudeville Routine*** section of the film, this snippet of action features Nicky Black (played by Cliff Richard) and two others in pith helmets and preposterous clothes, performing against a jungle backdrop. Cliff sings this song solo with no backing vocals.

The entire sequence was recorded in one session along with the segments of ***What D'You Know, We've Got a Show***. Several takes were recorded of each of the sections of the *Vaudeville Routine*, with the same takes chosen for the stereo and mono edits, but with different mixes for the audio channel requirements. The film version of the sequence was recorded later on the year (probably in the same month) but has not been formally released in any other commercial format.

Track Specification
Composed by Leigh and Baston (no first names available)

Musicians	
Associated British Studio Orchestra	orchestra
Stanley Black	conductor
Cliff Richard	vocals

Recording Details	
Producer	Norrie Paramor
Engineered by	Malcolm Addey and Alan Kane
Recording location	Abbey Road Studio 2, St. John's Wood, London
Recording date	9th August 1961

♬ Carina

From the album **When in Rome**

The title of this song, *Carina*, could either be a girl's name or the Italian translation of the English word *Cute* - either way, the song refers to a particular love interest. The foreign language song was picked for inclusion on Cliff Richard's foreign language album ***When in Rome***. Recorded in a marathon two-day session that saw Cliff provide overdubbed vocals on previously recorded backing tracks (whether new orchestral arrangements or previous English or Italian backing tracks), *Carina* was one of the few foreign language recordings that he made that didn't have an English equivalent. The fifth and final orchestral take was added to the unknown vocal take and edited for release in mono format only.

Cliff appears to be enjoying singing this song which bounces along at a fair pace. Although he had difficulty with the pronunciation, that is not obvious from the evidence of this track, which is one of the highlights to be found on the album.

Track Specification
Composed by Alberto Testa and R. Poes

Musicians	
Norrie Paramor Orchestra	orchestra
Norrie Paramor	arranger, conductor
Cliff Richard	vocals

Recording Details	
Producer	John Lee and M. DiPonti (backing track) and Norrie Paramor (vocals)
Engineered by	Malcolm Addey
Recording location	EMI Studios, Milan (backing track) and Estudios Valentim, De Carvalho, Lisbon (vocals)
Recording date	2nd-3rd October 1964 (backing track) and 14th May 1965 (vocals)

♬ Carnival

From the EP **Holiday Carnival**

The early December 1962 studio session produced three original tracks destined for three different EPs (***Holiday Carnival, Love Songs*** and ***Why Don't They Understand?***). The first to be completed was *Carnival* and is the splice of the third and sixth takes, from which the same edit was used for the mono and stereo recordings with different mixes for the audio channels. In April 1963, the song was revisited when a Spanish version was recorded for ***When in Spain*** under the title ***Canción de Orfeo***, although that was a completely new recording rather than using base tracks that had already been

recorded for the English version. Released only on the *Holiday Carnival* EP, *Carnival* remained a real rarity until the release of the album ***The EP Collection: Ballads and Love Songs***, itself becoming a rarity until the release of *Carnival* on the track listing of ***...And They Said It Wouldn't Last! (My 50 Years in Music)***.
The introduction features a Spanish style guitar and military snare drum and is then backed by orchestral strings and lightly humming backing vocals. The session notes indicate that the Shadows were not involved although the guitar does sound suspiciously like Hank Marvin's particular way of playing and the drum may also be Brian Bennett's performance. Cliff sings the song with conviction, including the humming bridge – a technique that can be surprisingly difficult to achieve in the lead singing position – and it is a beautiful song that justly gets a late airing.

Track Specification
Composed by Luiz Bonfà, Hugo Peretti, Luigi Creatore and George Weiss

Musicians	
Mike Sammes Singers	backing vocals
Norrie Paramor Orchestra	orchestra
Norrie Paramor	arranger, conductor
Cliff Richard	vocals
Unknown	guitar
Unknown	drums

Recording Details	
Producer	Norrie Paramor
Engineered by	Malcolm Addey and Peter Vince
Recording location	Abbey Road Studio 2, St. John's Wood, London
Recording date	6th December 1962

♫ Carnival's Just for Me, The

Unissued track

In early 1969, Tyne Tees Television commissioned a series of six playlets for their religious broadcast slot called *Life with Johnny*, featuring Cliff Richard in the title role as each episode updated a well-known parable told by Jesus in the Bible. Records are unclear on most of the episodes although *Johnny Come Home* and *Johnny Faces Facts* are complete, *Johnny and the Good Samaritan* is partially available, while the remainder are unavailable in either records or film form.
The songs performed had some relevance to the parable being performed and, in all, there were usually five songs per episode. *The Carnival's Just for Me*, recorded at the Abbey Road studios for a putative album tie-in project that didn't materialize, appeared in one of *Johnny on the Rocks*, *Johnny and the Blind Rage* or *Johnny in Love*. The end credits of the episode stated that all songs were original and written in collaboration between Cliff, the Settlers and the programme's writer David Winter. The instrumentation and performance details are unknown and are given as those present.

Track Specification
Composed by Cliff Richard, David Winter, Cindy Kent, Mike Jones, John Fyffe and Geoffrey Srodzinski

Musicians	
John Fyffe	backing vocals, guitar
Cindy Kent	backing vocals
Mike Jones	backing vocals, guitar
Cliff Richard	vocals
Geoffrey Srodzinski	backing vocals, bass

Recording Details	
Producer	Norrie Paramor
Engineered by	Peter Vince
Recording location	Abbey Road Studio 3, St. John's Wood, London
Recording date	24th March 1969

♫ Carrie

***77th UK single** and from the albums* **Dressed for the Occasion**, **My Kinda Life** *and* **Hank Plays Cliff**

The result of the continuing collaboration between Terry Britten and B. A. Robertson, *Carrie* is by far and away the most successful of all of their songs. Recorded as part of the ***Rock 'n' Roll Juvenile*** album sessions, it was completed in two parts with the first in Paris providing the backing track and the second, back in Britain, for the vocal overdubs. As with many of Britten's collaborations, his partner provided the story and he composed the musical hooks and riffs.
It was the third single to be released from the album by Cliff Richard, backed with non-album track ***Moving In***, on the EMI label (catalogue number EMI 5006) on 18th January 1980 and it reached number four in the UK charts. It was also a major seller in the US, where it reached the highest point of thirty-four in the Billboard charts. The single edit is taken from the album track but is presented at a slightly faster speed, encouraging the single to be completed quicker than the album version and the fade out appears some fifteen or so seconds earlier, removing part of the end synthesiser solo.
As B. A. Robertson has said in interview, the key to the ingenuity of the song is the musical accompaniment to the mystery of the lyrics. It's not made clear who the central character of Carrie is, or what her domestic status is, or what her relationship to the singer (Cliff) is.
The lazy feel to what is a strict rhythm is brought about courtesy of a running bass line accompanied by a synthesiser and thumping bass drum in the right stereo channel. Cliff sings his own backing vocals aided by Britten, which are occasionally fed through a vocoder, and, although the song is not rock and roll, it fits perfectly in the album track listing.
Inevitably, given its recent release, the song was included on the set list for Cliff's ***Dressed for the Occasion*** performance with the London Philharmonic Orchestra. Whereas the original recording sounded quite claustrophobic and almost paranoid, the inclusion of the orchestra opens the sound up, making it more expansive in its performance.
For ***My Kinda Life***, the 1992 French album, Cliff and music director Paul Moessl revisited a number of tracks from the mid-seventies to early eighties and, taking the original track, embellished it with new instrumentation and, occasionally, vocals. *Carrie* was one such song that had a major overhaul with a new vocal and additional guitars recorded. The fade-

out is later than the original with more lyrics performed by Cliff. This version was included as the B-side of the seven-inch and CD single releases of ***Healing Love*** in December 1993.

In 1995, Hank Marvin recorded a new, mostly instrumental, album based on Cliff's hits, called *Hank Plays Cliff*, featuring Cliff on vocals on four tracks, including *Carrie*. An acoustic guitar sequence introduces the largely instrumental version, which features Cliff at the beginning singing "Carrie, where are you?". Hank's signature electric guitar mellifluously flows into the verse and onwards through the track. Cliff sings the song title occasionally throughout and adds his own harmonizing vocals to the utterance. In the mid-point, Cliff adds more lyrics but these merely counterpoint the clever guitar work by Hank.

The song was performed on Cliff's 2003 World Tour but, unusually, it was left to the backing vocalists to perform, as the last in a medley with ***Devil Woman*** and ***Green Light***, while Cliff went off stage to change.

Track Specification
Composed by Terry Britten and B. A. Robertson

1. Single

Musicians		*Recording Details*	
Terry Britten	backing vocals, guitar	Producer	Cliff Richard and Terry Britten
Mel Collins	saxophone	Engineered by	Tony Clark and Haydn Bendall
Herbie Flowers	bass	Recording location	Pathé Marconi, Paris, France (backing track) and Abbey Road Studio, St. John's Wood, London (vocals)
Tristan Fry	percussion		
Graham Jarvis	drums, percussion		
Bill Livesy	keyboards	Recording date	7th-12th January 1979 (backing track) and 2nd February 1979 (vocals)
Cliff Richard	vocals, backing vocals		

2. Dressed for the Occasion

Musicians		*Recording Details*	
Stuart Calver	backing vocals	Producer	Cliff Richard and Richard Hewson
David Cooke	synthesiser	Engineered by	John Kurlander
Steve Gray	piano	Mixed by	Keith Bessey
Mark Griffiths	bass	Recording location	Royal Albert Hall, London
Tony Harding	backing vocals	Mixed at	Strawberry Studios South, Surrey
Richard Hewson	arranger, conductor	Recording date	23rd November 1982
Graham Jarvis	drums, percussion		
London Philharmonic Orchestra	orchestra		
John Perry	backing vocals		
Cliff Richard	vocals		
Tony Rivers	backing vocals		

3. My Kinda Life

Musicians		*Recording Details*	
Terry Britten	backing vocals, guitar	Producer	Cliff Richard and Terry Britten (original track) and Cliff Richard and Paul Moessl (new instrumentation and vocal)
John Clark	guitar		
Mel Collins	saxophone		
Herbie Flowers	bass	Engineered by	Tony Clark and Haydn Bendall (original track) and Gerry Kitchingham and Ben Robbins (new instrumentation and vocal)
Tristan Fry	percussion		
Graham Jarvis	drums, percussion		
Bill Livesy	keyboards	Recording location	Pathé Marconi, Paris, France (backing track) and R. G. Jones Studios, Wimbledon, London (new instrumentation and vocal)
Cliff Richard	vocals		
		Recording date	7th-12th January 1979 (backing track) and 1st-2nd February 1992 (new vocals) and 20th-23rd April 1992 (new instrumentation)

4. Hank Plays Cliff

Musicians		*Recording Details*	
Warren Bennett	arranger, keyboards	Producer	Hank Marvin
Ben Marvin	guitar	Engineered by	Les Williams (Planet Sound Studios) and Dick Plant (Honeyhill Studios)
Hank Marvin	acoustic guitar, electric guitar		
Cliff Richard	vocals, backing vocals	Recording location	Planet Sound Studios, Subiaco, Perth, Australia (instruments) and Honeyhill Studios, Hertfordshire (vocals)
Gary Ridge	percussion		
Trevor Spencer	drums, percussion		
Gary Taylor	bass	Recording date	1995

♫ Casa senza Finestre
From the album **When in Rome**

Originally recorded in English title as ***House without Windows*** (a direct translation) for his ***Cliff Richard*** album, *Casa senza Finestre* was recorded at a marathon two-day session at studios in Lisbon, where Cliff overdubbed most of the vocals for his Italian language album ***When in Rome***. Using the backing track from the 1964 English recording, Cliff's new vocals were applied in May 1965, with the English album having just been released contemporaneously. The final (unknown) take and edit of the vocals were overdubbed on the original track and the result was only ever released in mono format.

The mix of this track is less lugubrious and menacing than the English equivalent but other than that there is little to distinguish the two versions, largely because the same backing track has been used for both. In the echo behind the accompaniment, there are vague ghosts of the backing vocals from the original but they are largely edited out.

Track Specification
Composed by Lee Pockriss and Alberto Testa

Musicians		*Recording Details*	
Norrie Paramor Orchestra	orchestra	Producer	Norrie Paramor (backing track and vocals)
Norrie Paramor	arranger, conductor	Engineered by	Malcolm Addey (backing track and vocals)
Cliff Richard	vocals	Recording location	Abbey Road Studio 2, St. John's Wood, London (backing track) and Estudios Valentim De Carvalho, Lisbon, Portugal (vocals)
		Recording date	24th July 1964 (backing track) and 14th May 1965 (vocals)

♫ Catch Me

From the albums **21 Today** *and* **The Rock and Roll Years 1958-1963**

The first of two Sid Tepper and Roy Bennett collaborations on the ***21 Today*** album, *Catch Me* was the first track to be recorded (although it is likely that it was possibly intended for release on ***Listen to Cliff!*** but left off for reasons of space). There were ten takes recorded, of which the final one was used for the stereo and mono edits with different mixes for the respective audio channels. There are uncredited female backing vocals, although these are likely to the Mike Sammes Singers, much employed as session singers at the time.
The anthology of rarities and Cliff's early work ***The Rock and Roll Years 1958-1963*** featured the same take as appeared on the *21 Today* album but missing the female backing vocals and incorporating additional overdubs by Cliff and extra repeats of the line 'I'm falling for you'. In addition, the take number announcement (ten) is also left on the recording. Because of the differences and additional recording, it is included here as a separate track listing entry.
The song is a typical song of the period, exhorting a girl to catch him as he has fallen for her – a little corny but fitting for the times. The female backing vocals are a little irritating in their tweeness but there is a subtle energy to the song that cannot be undermined by what is essentially a minor quibble.

Track Specification
Composed by Sid Tepper and Roy C. Bennett

1. 21 Today

Musicians		*Recording Details*	
Jet Harris	bass	Producer	Norrie Paramor
Hank Marvin	guitar	Engineered by	Malcolm Addey and David Lloyd
Tony Meehan	drums, percussion	Recording location	Abbey Road Studio 2, St. John's Wood, London
Cliff Richard	vocals	Recording date	9th September 1960
Unknown	female backing vocals		
Bruce Welch	rhythm guitar		

2. The Rock 'n' Roll Years 1958-1963

Musicians		*Recording Details*	
Jet Harris	bass	Producer	Norrie Paramor
Hank Marvin	guitar	Engineered by	Malcolm Addey and David Lloyd
Tony Meehan	drums, percussion	Recording location	Abbey Road Studio 2, St. John's Wood, London
Cliff Richard	vocals	Recording date	9th September 1960
Bruce Welch	rhythm guitar		

♫ 'Cause I Believe in Loving

From the album **...And They Said It Wouldn't Last! (My 50 Years in Music)**

Also covered by Roger Williams for an easy listening album, *'Cause I Believe in Loving* was recorded by Cliff Richard at the second session of 1971, which took place at the Chappell Studios rather than Abbey Road for unknown reasons (although possibly due to Abbey Road's period of refurbishment). Two songs were recorded that day, the other being ***I, Who Have Nothing***, but neither was released until they were both added to the track listing of the 'lost and found' section of the celebratory ***...And They Said It Wouldn't Last! (My 50 Years in Music)*** in 2008.
A beautiful rendition of the song, Cliff is clearly at home with performing ballads of this type. The syrupy orchestral string accompaniment is typical of a Marvin Hamlisch composition but doesn't detract from the overall performance.

Track Specification
Composed by Marvin Hamlisch and Howard Liebling

Musicians		*Recording Details*	
Cliff Richard	vocals	Producer	Norrie Paramor
Unknown	arranger, conductor	Engineered by	Unknown
Unknown	orchestra	Recording location	Chappell Studios, London
		Recording date	5th March 1971

♫ Celebrate
Unissued track

At the end of the *Life with Johnny* episode entitled *Johnny Come Home* – a modern-day setting of the prodigal son parable – with Cliff Richard playing the title role, Johnny has admitted his mistakes after going to London to seek fame and fortune and ultimately failing, returning home worried about what his father (played by William Hartnell) will say to him. Instead, his father welcomes him home with open arms and puts on a party, at which point *Celebrate* is performed.

With a gospel-like, upbeat performance led by the guitars and tambourine, Cliff's vocals are matched with the Settlers' harmonies, as he relates the biblical parable in the lyrics. The song, as with all of the tracks in the series, was recorded at Abbey Road, with an album tie-in planned but dropped as a project. It was written, according to the programme's end titles, as an original song by Cliff in collaboration with the Settlers and the programme's screenwriter David Winter.

Track Specification
Composed by Cliff Richard, David Winter, Cindy Kent, Mike Jones, John Fyffe and Geoffrey Srodzinski

Musicians		*Recording Details*	
John Fyffe	backing vocals, guitar	Producer	Norrie Paramor
Cindy Kent	backing vocals, tambourine	Engineered by	Peter Vince
Mike Jones	backing vocals, guitar	Recording location	Abbey Road Studio 3, St. John's Wood, London
Cliff Richard	vocals	Recording date	11th January 1969
Geoffrey Srodzinski	backing vocals, bass		

♫ Celestial Houses
B-side of **Take Me High** *and from the album* **Help It Along**

Increasingly, Terry Britten was becoming a favourite writer for Cliff Richard during the early seventies and he wrote one of the songs that were included in the studio concert in aid of the Tear Fund charity and the subsequent album ***Help It Along***, *Celestial Houses*. It was later chosen and edited for inclusion as the B-side, with the orchestra and some guitar and backing chorus removed, of the eponymous and only single released from the ***Take Me High*** film project. It was one of the thirteen songs of seventeen performed and recorded to be issued from the charity album project, while the B-side version was eventually included on the remastered ***The 31st of February Street*** as a bonus track in 2004.

Guitar-driven in the first instance, the instrumentation builds up to the second verse as Cliff sings of the celestial houses (churches) and how we need to give love to God. The song is not a particularly strong one, it has to be said, but the intent is focused in the bouncing choruses.

Track Specification
Composed by Terry Britten

1. B-side (Take Me High)

Musicians		*Recording Details*	
Terry Britten	guitar	Producer	David MacKay
Barrie Guard	arranger, conductor, percussion	Engineered by	Roger Quested
Cliff Hall	keyboards	Recording location	Morgan Studios, London
Jean Hawker	backing vocals	Recording date	24th, 25th and 26th September 1973
Anna Peacock	backing vocals		
Kevin Peek	guitar		
Cliff Richard	vocals		
Trevor Spencer	drums, percussion		
Alan Tarney	bass		

2. Help It Along

Musicians		*Recording Details*	
Terry Britten	guitar	Producer	David MacKay
Barrie Guard	arranger, conductor, percussion	Engineered by	Roger Quested
Cliff Hall	keyboards	Recording location	Morgan Studios, London
Jean Hawker	backing vocals	Recording date	24th, 25th and 26th September 1973
Anna Peacock	backing vocals		
Kevin Peek	guitar		
Cliff Richard	vocals		
Trevor Spencer	drums, percussion		
Alan Tarney	bass		
Unknown	orchestra		

♫ C'est Si Bon
From the EP **When in France**

Originally released in French by the Belgian-German chanteuse Angèle Durand (who sang a German version that was a hit Germany), *C'est Si Bon* (literally *It's So Good*) was written in 1947, with English lyrics by Jerry Seelen added later. The most popular covers are by Louis Armstrong, Danny Kaye and Johnny Desmond, although it has been parodied by Allan Sherman (as the hospital-based *I See Bones*).

The version by Cliff Richard and the Shadows is one of the very few foreign language originals by him not to be re-recorded with English lyrics. Recorded at a suite of three sessions across five days while the band was in Blackpool enjoying a summer season at the Jubilee Hall, *C'est Si Bon* was the last of three songs completed (and four attempted) at the first session, with the twelfth take being used for issue of the ***When in France*** EP, although it as only ever been released in mono format. Appearing, as all the other EP tracks did, on the Belgian LP *When in France... Chante en Français* in 1975, it would take another twenty-two years for it to be made more widely available and in CD format on the foreign language Cliff Richard compilation boxed set ***On the Continent***.
As with the other tracks on the EP, *C'est Si Bon* is a prime example of Cliff and the Shadows and their ensemble creations. Cliff's vocals take him to the upper part of his vocal range, while the middle eight sees Hank Marvin providing a guitar solo, and the whole is supported by Bruce Welch's chord structure, Brian Locking's bass line and Brian Bennett's complex drum rhythms. The wonderful harmonies created by Hank, Bruce and Cliff are reserved for the final two repetitions of the song title.

Track Specification
Composed by Henri Betti and André Hornez

Musicians

Brian Bennett	drums, percussion
Brian 'Licorice' Locking	bass
Hank Marvin	backing vocals, guitar
Cliff Richard	vocals
Bruce Welch	backing vocals, rhythm guitar

Recording Details

Producer	Norrie Paramor
Engineered by	Malcolm Addey and Jimmy Johnson
Recording location	Jubilee Hall, Blackpool
Recording date	5th August 1963

♫ Chantilly Lace

From the albums **Japan Tour '74** *and* **From a Distance ***** The Event**

Written J. P. Richardson and recorded by him under his stage name of The Big Bopper, *Chantilly Lace* is obstensively an itemized list of the characteristics that a man finds appealing about his girlfriend. It was a number twelve hit in the UK in the late December of 1958 and into the new year. In 1972, it was covered by rocker Jerry Lee Lewis, who took it to number thirty-three.
For the Japanese tour in 1974, Cliff Richard performed the song as part of a ***Rock Medley***: ***His Latest Flame***, *Chantilly Lace*, ***Bony Maronie***, ***Do You Wanna Dance?***, ***Crocodile Rock*** and ***Do You Wanna Dance?*** again to complete the medley, although he has, to date, never recorded it in the studio. The Japanese performance segues neatly from *His Latest Flame* and, although taken at a faster pace than the original, he band are clearly having fun with it, including the excellent guitar solo performed by Brian Lewis.
Later included at *The Event* as part of the ***Medley*** in the *Oh Boy! Set*, it successfully segues from a rocking version of ***Do You Wanna Dance?***. Cliff takes the lead vocal, although he is supported by the Vernons Girls, the Dallas Boys and the Kalin Twins as backing vocalists.

Track Specification
Composed by J. P. Richardson

1. Japan Tour '74

Musicians

Cliff Hall	piano
Brian Lewis	guitar
Kevin Peak	acoustic guitar
Cliff Richard	vocals
Trevor Spencer	drums, percussion
Alan Tarney	bass
Bruce Welch	rhythm guitar

Recording Details

Producer	Toshiba EMI (no individual detailed)
Engineered by	Toshiba EMI (no individual detailed)
Recording location	Shinjuku Koseinenkin, Tokyo, Japan
Recording date	7th-8th October 1974

2. From a Distance ** The Event***

Musicians

Dallas Boys:	
Nicky Clarke	backing vocals
Leon Fisk	backing vocals
Stan Jones	backing vocals
Joe Smith	backing vocals
Bob Wragg	backing vocals
Kalin Twins:	
Harold Kalin	backing vocals
Herbie Kalin	backing vocals
Oh Boy! Band	rock 'n' roll band
Cliff Richard	vocals
Vernons Girls:	
Lyn Cornell	backing vocals
Maureen Kennedy	backing vocals
Frances Lee	backing vocals
Jean Owen	backing vocals

Recording Details

Producer	Cliff Richard
Engineered by	Keith Bessey and Mick McKenna
Recording location	Rolling Stones Mobile Studio, Wembley Stadium, Wembley, North-west London
Recording date	16th-17th June 1989

♫ Chaser

Unissued track

Uncertain and with no ready information on its pedigree, *Chaser* was included in the set list of Cliff Richard's charity album project, ***Help It Along,*** which was performed in front of a small group of people at the Morgan Studios in seven sessions over three days but was not included in the final track listing of the album and remains unissued.

Track Specification
Composed by Unknown

Musicians	
Terry Britten	guitar
Barrie Guard	arranger, conductor, percussion
Cliff Hall	keyboards
Jean Hawker	backing vocals
Anna Peacock	backing vocals
Kevin Peek	guitar
Cliff Richard	vocals
Trevor Spencer	drums, percussion
Alan Tarney	bass
Unknown	orchestra

Recording Details	
Producer	David MacKay
Engineered by	Roger Quested
Recording location	Morgan Studios, London
Recording date	24th, 25th and 26th September 1973

♫ Che Cosa del Farai Mia Amore?

From the album **When in Rome**

Roughly translating to *What Are You Doing About It, My Love?, Che Cosa del Farai Mia Amore?* was one of the Italian originals chosen for inclusion on the Italian language album ***When in Rome*** by Cliff Richard. Purporting to have had most difficulty with that language out of all the continental languages he recorded in, this song is one of the very small handful that has only ever been recorded in the parochial language with no English translated version. Cliff's vocals, recorded at a long two-day session at studios in Lisbon in May 1965, were overdubbed on an orchestral track that had already been finished in preparation for the album seven months earlier. The fifth and final orchestral take and edit were applied to the unknown vocal take and edit but only ever mixed and released in mono format.

Although Cliff believes he had most difficulty with the enunciation of the Italian language, which was written phonetically for him, he found it the better European language to sing in since it is naturally musical in its pronunciation and Cliff shows few flaws in the result.

Track Specification
Composed by Vito Pallavincini and Di Ponti

Musicians	
Norrie Paramor Orchestra	orchestra
Norrie Paramor	arranger, conductor
Cliff Richard	vocals

Recording Details	
Producer	John Lee and M. DiPonti (backing track) and Norrie Paramor (vocals)
Engineered by	Malcolm Addey
Recording location	EMI Studios, Milan (backing track) and Estudios Valentim, De Carvalho, Lisbon (vocals)
Recording date	2nd-3rd October 1964 (backing track) and 14th May 1965 (vocals)

♫ Children of the King

From the album **Triumph in the Air** *(Sheila Walsh)*

The third song by Chris Eaton was the closer of the second album, ***Triumph in the Air,*** by Cliff Richard protégée Sheila Walsh and features Cliff on backing vocals. In addition to Eaton himself, Mo Turner and Annie McCaig, who were both in Network 3 (for whom Cliff produced two singles), and session singer Mark Williamson joined him in the chorus.

The synthesized brass and crashing percussion initiates this reverent song, which has Walsh performing in an almost operatic way as the accompaniment gives way to synthesized strings. Slowly the performance builds up in pace and energy, supported by the backing vocals singing in almost gospel-like intensity, into the choruses. Cliff's contribution is the most obvious of the group singing behind her but this adds to the beauty of the ensemble piece rather than detracting from it.

Track Specification
Composed by Chris Eaton

Musicians	
Chris Eaton	backing vocals
Graham Jarvis	drums, percussion
Annie McCaig	backing vocals
Craig Pruess	arranger, keyboards, electronics
Cliff Richard	backing vocals
Mo Turner	backing vocals
Sheila Walsh	vocals
Mark Williamson	backing vocals

Recording Details	
Producer	Craig Pruess, assisted by Keith Bessey
Engineered by	Keith Bessey
Recording location	Cloud 9 Studios, London, Strawberry Studios, London and/or Jacobs Studios, Farnham, Surrey
Recording date	September 1983-January 1984

♫ Chi Lo Sà

B-side of **Non Dimenticare Chi Ti Ama** *and from the album* **On the Continent**

In the last few months of 1968 and the first of 1969, Cliff Richard spent time in the studio recording foreign language versions of his songs from albums and recent singles. What was unusual, at the end of February of 1969, is that he recorded an Italian single B-side version of his 1964 UK hit ***On the Beach***, called *Chi Lo Sà* (or, as it translates back to English, *Search Me!*, which is a departure from the original English intent of the lyrics).

Chosen as the B-side of *Non Dimenticare Chi Ti Ama* (the Italian language version of ***Don't Forget to Catch Me***) and issued in April 1969 in Italy, *Chi Lo Sà* was originally released in mono format only. However, the stereo version was released first on the *When in Rome* compilation in 1977 and then on the foreign language compilation ***On the Continent*** boxed set in 1997. Also on that album, a track subtitled 'original version' is included on the track listing but there is no information available as which take this is, although there are a several differences between the versions. The first version on the album uses the original Shadows backing track from 1963 with new vocals by Cliff and a different (uncredited) backing vocal group, while the second is an orchestral accompaniment with a very prominent male vocal group, also uncredited. In addition, on the orchestral version, Cliff sings slightly differently to the one with the Shadows' original backing track. It is presumed that Cliff's vocals and the backing vocals were recorded for both versions at the same session.

As with all songs that use an original backing track, there are very few differences to comment on. However, Cliff carries out the vocal duties with apparent natural ease and, while the backing vocals are pleasant enough, the track misses the beauty of Hank Marvin's and Bruce Welch's blend of vocal harmonies with Cliff's.

Track Specification

Composed by Hank Marvin, Bruce Welch and Cliff Richard; Italian lyrics by Cino Tortorella

1. On the Continent

Musicians

Brian Bennett	drums, percussion
Brian 'Licorice' Locking	bass
Hank Marvin	backing vocals, guitar
Cliff Richard	vocals
Unknown	backing vocals
Bruce Welch	backing vocals, rhythm guitar

Recording Details

Producer	Norrie Paramor (backing track and vocals)
Engineered by	Malcolm Addey (backing track) and Peter Vince (vocals)
Recording location	Abbey Road Studio 3 (backing track) and Abbey Road Studio 2 (vocals), St. John's Wood, London
Recording date	5th November 1963 (backing track) and 24th February 1969 (vocals)

2. B-side Non Dimenticare Chi Ti Ama)

Musicians

Norrie Paramor Orchestra	orchestra
Norrie Paramor	arranger, conductor
Cliff Richard	vocals
Unknown	backing vocals

Recording Details

Producer	Norrie Paramor
Engineered by	Peter Vince
Recording location	Abbey Road Studio 2, St. John's Wood, London
Recording date	24th February 1969

♫ Chim Chim Cheree

From the album **...And They Said It Wouldn't Last! (My 50 Years in Music)**

One of the most phenomenally successful and favourite Disney films is *Mary Poppins*, which was based on the story written by Pamela L. Travers. Starring Julie Andrews in the eponymous role and Dick van Dyke as her friend Bert, she comes into the lives of two children whose parents are typically Victorian in an Edwardian era and their childhood is suffering as a result. They go on adventures with Bert to different lands and have tea on the ceiling and so on. *Chim Chim Cheree*, one of the most popular tunes from film, it was sung by Dick van Dyke during the dance routine sequence among the chimney pots of London. Other than van Dyke's film version, it has also been covered by John Coltrane, Louis Armstrong, Ray Conniff, Charlie Byrd, Karen Dotrice (who played the young Jane in the film), Allan Sherman (a parody), Burl Ives, Mantovani, Duke Ellington, Freddie and the Dreamers, Peggy March and Bobby Vinton.

At the final recording session of 1965, Cliff Richard recorded four Disney songs: two from *Mary Poppins* (***A Spoonful of Sugar*** and *Chim Chim Cheree*) and two from *Song of the South* (***Zip-a-Dee-Doo-Dah*** and ***Sooner or Later***). *Mary Poppins* had been released in 1964 and the songs were still fresh in people's minds. However, the four songs remained unreleased for over forty years until the issue of the rarity compilation ***...And They Said It Wouldn't Last! (My 50 Years in Music)***. The fifth and final take and edit were used for both mono and stereo recordings, although it has only been released in stereo.

Although Disney songs seem to be a strange choice for Cliff to sing, he carries it off well, although the mock cockney is largely ignored since Cliff sings the lyrics too precisely. This is helped by the jazzed up arrangement that is reminiscent of a late night club. Cliff is enjoying the opportunity to sing the songs, it's clear, and given the brilliance of the result, it is surprising that the four tracks, including this one, languished in the EMI vaults for so long.

Track Specification

Composed by Richard M. Sherman and Robert B. Sherman

Musicians

Cliff Richard	vocals
Unknown	orchestra
Unknown	arranger, conductor

Recording Details

Producer	Norrie Paramor
Engineered by	Malcolm Addey
Recording location	Abbey Road Studio 2, St. John's Wood, London
Recording date	18th November 1965

♫ Choosing When It's Too Late

From the albums **Songs from Heathcliff** *and* **Heathcliff Live**

After the farcical and cruel wedding ceremony between Heathcliff (Cliff Richard) and Isabella (Sara Haggerty in the stage show), Isabella's brother Edgar (Darryl Knock in the show) finds Heathcliff to tell him his thoughts on his brother-in-law and how despicable he finds him and how he's held back from saying anything for the sake of Cathy (Olivia Newton-John on ***Songs from Heathcliff*** and Helen Hobson in the stage show). The essence of the song is that he has chosen to speak out to Heathcliff when it is too late to do anything about it. Heathcliff responds by name-calling in front of Cathy and a fight ensues as Cathy beseeches Heathcliff to disappear and protects him from Edgar's gun. Cathy's madness comes on as she runs on to the moors in the middle of a storm. The song segues into *The Madness of Cathy*, which uses the same melody and harmonies but is only sung by Helen Hobson and is her rail against the injustice of love as she feels the pain of her failing pregnancy.

The bass sustained chords and the staccato higher pitched chords as well as the almost breathless performance by Cliff create an air of menace from the start. Naturally, Cliff performs all of the lead male vocals on the studio recording, which are shared out between the characters in the show. When Olivia joins him, the blend of their vocal harmonies lifts the musical aspects of the song, although the menacing accompaniment continues. The live version is similar with the exception of the division of lead vocal responsibilities and the inclusion of some spoken dialogue. There is an extraordinary beauty in the ensemble vocal arrangement and the harmonies it generates.

Track Specification

Composed by John Farrar and Tim Rice

__*1. Songs from Heathcliff*__

Musicians		*Recording Details*	
Sean Callery	orchestrator, synclavier, keyboards	Producer	John Farrar
John Farrar	guitar, synclavier	Engineered by	Chris Fogel, Eric Rudd and Joe Schiff (Moonee Ponds Studio), Darren Goodwin and Guy Massey (Abbey Road Studios) and James Collins and Caroline Daniel (CTS Studios)
Olivia Newton-John	vocals	Recording location	Moonee Ponds Studio, Los Angeles, Abbey Road Studios, St. John's Wood, London and CTS Studios, Wembley, London
Cliff Richard	vocals	Mixed by	Elliot Scheiner
Bob Sabellico	drum programming	Mixed at	Moonee Ponds Studio, Los Angeles
Michael Thompson	guitar	Recording date	February-April 1994 and May-August 1995

__*2. Heathcliff Live*__

Musicians		*Recording Details*	
Sean Callery	orchestrator, orchestra	Producer	John Farrar
John Clark	guitar	Engineered by	Keith Bessey, John Pearson and Tom Tranter
Keith Hayman	keyboards	Recording location	Earl's Court Hall 2, London and/or The Academy, National Indoor Arena, Birmingham, England
Sara Haggerty	spoken vocals, vocals	Recording date	October 1996
Helen Hobson	spoken vocals, vocals		
Darryl Knock	spoken vocals, vocals		
Peter May	drums, percussion		
Bob Noble	keyboards		
Alan Park	keyboards		
Cliff Richard	spoken vocals, vocals		
Steve Stroud	bass		
Kevin Townend	orchestration		
Unknown	orchestra		

♫ Choppin' 'n' Changin'

Unissued track and from the album **Me and My Shadows**

Choppin' 'n' Changin' was first attempted in the 6th September 1959 session but remained unissued. The song was untouched again until 24th June 1960 when it was attempted again. This time it was successful and the seventh take was used for the eventual album release, where it formed the first track of the second side of ***Me and My Shadows***. Stereo and mono versions were recorded simultaneously but different mixes were used for the stereo channels plus additional later work was carried out. Eventually a completely different take was used for the stereo version, which was slower in pace, had a few minor changes to the lyrics and the guitar lead was different. The song also appears on the associated ***Me and My Shadows No. 2*** EP.

One of six Ian Samwell compositions on the album, it is a moody rock and roll song that talks of a girl unable to make up her mind (hence the title). The traditional guitar solo is performed in the middle eight, while the expected bass guitar run appears here too. A competent song of its ilk, it is a good opening song to the second side of the album, though there are better songs available on it.

Track Specification
Composed by Ian Samwell

1. Unissued track (Me and My Shadows)

Musicians		*Recording Details*	
Jet Harris	bass	Producer	Norrie Paramor
Hank Marvin	guitar	Engineered by	Peter Bown and Norman Smith
Tony Meehan	drums, percussion	Recording location	Abbey Road Studio 2, St. John's Wood, London
Cliff Richard	vocals	Recording date	6th September 1959
Bruce Welch	rhythm guitar		

2. Me and My Shadows

Musicians		*Recording Details*	
Jet Harris	bass	Producer	Norrie Paramor
Hank Marvin	guitar	Engineered by	Malcolm Addey and Alan Kane
Tony Meehan	drums, percussion	Recording location	Abbey Road Studio 2, St. John's Wood, London
Cliff Richard	vocals	Recording date	24th June 1960
Bruce Welch	rhythm guitar		

♫ Christmas Alphabet

From the album **Together with Cliff Richard**

Most associated with Dickie Valentine who first had a hit with *Christmas Alphabet* in 1955 reaching number one in the UK, it is also a favourite with children since it spells out the word 'Christmas' by using imagery of the season – candy-trimmed trees, happiness, reindeer and so on – and, although this isn't strictly an alphabet but an acrostic, it certainly captures the imagination. Since Valentine's version, there have been a few covers and these include those by artists such as the Allisons, Bing Crosby, the McGuire Sisters and Paul Brooks.

Cliff Richard's version was recorded in the early summer of 1991, the juxtaposition of long days and fine weather being at odds with the material being recorded, and included on his 1991 album ***Together with Cliff Richard***.

The inevitable sleighbells make their first appearance on the sixth track of this Christmas album, leading into a jazzy rhythm version of the song. The syncopation lifts the song from the original while the brass accompaniment lends it more sophistication. Cliff provides his own backing vocals helped by the female singers, which are employed to introduce a few of the letters. Cliff also gives an explosive kiss at the requisite place in the lyrics.

Track Specification
Composed by Buddy Kaye and Jules Loman

Musicians		*Recording Details*	
Dave Bishop	saxophone	Producer	Cliff Richard and Paul Moessl
John Clark	guitar	Engineered by	Gerry Kitchingham, Andrew Greasley and Ben Robbins
Paul Dunne	guitar		
Dave Cunliffe	violin	Recording location	R. G. Jones Studios, Wimbledon, London
Andrew Greasley	violin	Recording date	24th June 1991 to July 1991
Mark Griffiths	bass		
Mae McKenna	backing vocals		
Peter May	drums, percussion		
Paul Moessl	drum programming, keyboards		
Sonia Morgan	backing vocals		
Tessa Niles	backing vocals		
Cliff Richard	arranger, vocals, backing vocals		
Frank Ricotti	drums, percussion		
Miriam Stockley	backing vocals		
Steve Stroud	bass		
Derek Watkins	trumpet		

♫ Christmas Is Quiet

From the album **Cliff at Christmas**

Written by Peter Wolf, who had been the producer of Cliff Richard's ***Real as I Wanna Be*** album in the nineties, *Christmas Is Quiet* is actually a reworking of the song *Night of Nights* that Cliff had been singing on his gospel tours. Given that the liner notes of ***Cliff at Christmas*** indicate that the song was recorded in Austria and produced by Wolf with the same musician personnel, it is quite possible that the song was at least started during the *Real as I Wanna Be* sessions, since Wolf was no longer recording in Austria by the time the collation process for the Christmas album had started in 2003.

Track Specification
Composed by Peter Wolf

Musicians		*Recording Details*	
Cliff Richard	vocals	Producer	Peter Wolf
Jeff Richman	guitar	Engineered by	Christian Leitgeb
Michelle Wolf	backing vocals	Recording location	Little America Studios, Austria
Peter Wolf	keyboards, synthesized strings	Recording date	1998 and possibly 203 (additional mixing)

♫ Christmas Medley

Unissued live track

In 2003, Cliff Richard embarked on a world tour to promote his then new album, ***Wanted***. The result was filmed during the show in New Zealand and issued on DVD later that year and included the entire concert. A CD album to complement the film, *World Tour Live*, was released in 2004 but only included fourteen of the tracks performed. In spite of the timing and unseasonality at that time of year, Cliff performed a medley of his well-known Christmas hits. Of the tracks not included on the CD, one of those included was the *Christmas Medley*, which covered:

a) ***Mistletoe and Wine***
b) ***We Should Be Together***
c) ***Saviour's Day***
d) ***Little Town***

The entries for those songs carry the information on the recording details and musicians.

♫ Christmas Never Comes

From the album **Together with Cliff Richard**

Cliff Richard produced two singles for Network 3 in 1981, ***Last Train Home*** and ***Dangerous Game***, which featured Paul Field as the lead singer. Since that collaboration, Field had written a number of songs for Cliff to record on various albums as well as forging a solo career of his own. The very latest song was for Cliff's seasonal album, ***Together with Cliff Richard***, and *Christmas Never Comes* was the result. Recorded in the summer of 1991, it was one of the ten original tracks and new covers that Cliff completed for the album.

A beautiful piano and string introduction brings the song in, as Cliff gently and liltingly sings of the things he considers to be important at Christmas and looking for love that never happens. Cliff sings his own backing vocals for the most part and this helps the languid beauty of the song.

Track Specification

Composed by Paul Field

Musicians

Dave Cunliffe	violin
Andrew Greasley	violin
Mark Griffiths	bass
Mae McKenna	backing vocals
Peter May	drums, percussion
Paul Moessl	drum programming, piano
Sonia Morgan	backing vocals
Tessa Niles	backing vocals
Cliff Richard	arranger, vocals, backing vocals
Frank Ricotti	drums, percussion
Miriam Stockley	backing vocals
Steve Stroud	bass

Recording Details

Producer	Cliff Richard and Paul Moessl
Engineered by	Gerry Kitchingham, Andrew Greasley and Ben Robbins
Recording location	R. G. Jones Studios, Wimbledon, London
Recording date	24th June 1991 to July 1991

♫ Christmas Song, The

Song title on **Cliff at Christmas**

On ***Together with Cliff Richard***, *The Christmas Song* was incorrectly subtitled ***(Merry Christmas to You)***. This was corrected for ***Cliff at Christmas***. Although ostensibly the same song, sleighbells are added to various sections of the song.

♫ Christmas Song, The (Merry Christmas to You)

From the albums **Together with Cliff Richard** *and* **Cliff at Christmas**

Often called *Merry Christmas to You*, after the pay-off line from its chorus, or occasionally *Chestnuts Roasting on an Open Fire*, after the opening line, the song is correctly called simply ***The Christmas Song***. When EMI was collating the information for the liner notes of Cliff Richard's 1991 album ***Together with Cliff Richard***, they subtitled the song *Merry Christmas to You*, possibly to let the listener know what song it was by referring to a more familiar line from it. This issue was rectified on the release of ***Cliff at Christmas*** fifteen or so years later.

Most familiar in the perennial version that is played by Nat King Cole, his cover was only released in 1991 and reached number fifty-one, although it was recorded in 1946, two years after it has been written. Alexander O'Neal was there first with his version in 1988 (with the 'chestnuts' subtitle) and reached number thirty. Other artists to have covered the song include N'Sync, Andrea Bocelli, Kenny Loggins, Johnny Mathis, Amy Grant, Andy Williams, Lou Rawls, Bing Crosby, Michael Bublé, Charlotte Church, Bob Dylan, Christina Aguilera, Sheryl Crow, Smokey Robinson and the Miracles, Doris Day, the Carpenters, Hayley Westenra, James Taylor and James Brown among many others. In modern culture, it has also been parodied by the Simpsons in an episode entitled *Simpsons Roasting on an Open Fire*.

Cliff recorded his version in the beginning of the summer in 1991 – mirroring the time of year when Mel Tormé and Robert Wells wrote it with the sun streaming down in hot waves – and it appeared on the *Together with Cliff Richard* album which was released later that year.

Introduced with an echoing saxophone, the synthesized keyboards take over the control, with the guitar rhythm and percussion injects the song with a jazz-like rhythm that raises the sophistication and arrangement. The beautiful backing vocals create an exquisite mid-section as the saxophones take over.

The version on ***Cliff at Christmas*** is the same take and arrangement as the original but there are sleigh-bells added to various parts of the chorus and it is more percussive overall.

Track Specification
Composed by Mel Tormé and Robert Wells

1. Together with Cliff Richard

Musicians

Dave Bishop	alto saxophone
John Clark	guitar
Mick Clarke	backing vocals
Paul Dunne	guitar
Dave Cunliffe	violin
Andrew Greasley	violin
Mark Griffiths	bass
Peter Howarth	backing vocals
Peter May	drums, percussion
Paul Moessl	drum programming, keyboards
Mick Mullins	backing vocals
Keith Murrell	backing vocals
Cliff Richard	arranger, vocals, backing vocals
Frank Ricotti	drums, percussion
Tony Rivers	backing vocals
Steve Stroud	bass
Anthony Thompson	backing vocals

Recording Details

Producer	Cliff Richard and Paul Moessl
Engineered by	Gerry Kitchingham, Andrew Greasley and Ben Robbins
Recording location	R. G. Jones Studios, Wimbledon, London
Recording date	24th June 1991 to July 1991

2. Cliff at Christmas

Musicians

Dave Bishop	alto saxophone
John Clark	guitar
Mick Clarke	backing vocals
Paul Dunne	guitar
Dave Cunliffe	violin
Andrew Greasley	violin
Mark Griffiths	bass
Peter Howarth	backing vocals
Peter May	drums, percussion
Paul Moessl	drum programming, keyboards
Mick Mullins	backing vocals
Keith Murrell	backing vocals
Cliff Richard	arranger, vocals, backing vocals
Frank Ricotti	drums, percussion
Steve Stroud	bass
Anthony Thompson	backing vocals
Unknown	sleighbells

Recording Details

Producer	Cliff Richard and Paul Moessl (original track) and Unknown (sleigh-bells)
Engineered by	Gerry Kitchingham, Andrew Greasley and Ben Robbins (original track) and Unknown (sleigh-bells)
Recording location	R. G. Jones Studios, Wimbledon, London (original track) and Unknown (sleigh-bells)
Recording date	24th June 1991 to July 1991 (original track) and Unknown (sleigh-bells)

♬ Cities May Fall

From the album **Rock 'n' Roll Juvenile**

Of the twelve tracks released on the ***Rock 'n' Roll Juvenile*** album, Cliff Richard's co-producer Terry Britten wrote or co-wrote ten of them. *Cities May Fall* was the third track on the first side of the original album and was recorded in the EMI Studios in Paris where the backing track was completed, followed by a vocal overdub session a fortnight later.

With a similar vibe to ***Carrie***, Cliff's lead vocal is fed through a small vocoder that effectively shuts his voice down a little. The expansive saxophone as well as the relentless rhythm created in the guitar and percussion makes *Cities May Fall* a memorable song and one of the best on the album.

Track Specification
Composed by Terry Britten and B. A. Robertson

Musicians

Terry Britten	guitar
Stuart Calver	backing vocals
Martin Dobson	saxophone
Herbie Flowers	bass
Graham Jarvis	drums, percussion
Bill Livesy	keyboards
John Perry	backing vocals
Cliff Richard	vocals
Tony Rivers	backing vocals

Recording Details

Producer	Cliff Richard and Terry Britten
Engineered by	Tony Clark and Haydn Bendall
Recording location	Pathé Marconi, Paris, France (backing track) and Abbey Road Studio, St. John's Wood, London (vocals)
Recording date	7th-12th July 1979 (backing track) and 27th January 1979 (vocals)

♫ Claudette

From the album **World Tour Live**

Since the early eighties when he performed ***She Means Nothing to Me*** with Phil Everly, Cliff Richard has had a close association with the Everly Brothers. Even before that, Cliff was an admirer of their work and regularly included a cover or two of their songs in concert and occasionally on record. *Claudette* was a Roy Orbison composition that was recorded by the Brothers and released as a double A-side single partnered with ***All I Have to Do Is Dream*** in June 1958, making it their first number one in the UK charts. Since then, it has been covered by composer Orbison, Status Quo, John Denver, Showaddywaddy and the Everly Brothers version was also sampled by Jive Bunny and the Mastermixers.
Cliff chose the song to be on the set list for his 2003 world tour. The New Zealand show was filmed ostensibly for DVD release later in the year and, in 2004, it was decided to issue a complementary CD album also called ***World Tour Live***. While many tracks from the DVD were not included, *Claudette* was added to the track listing. Joined by guitarist Anthony Clark, they sing the version as the Everly Brothers arranged it. It is a lovely rendition and Clark's voice combines well with Cliff's. The instrumentalists then surround Mike Haughton as he plays a saxophone solo in the middle eight.

Track Specification
Composed by Roy Orbison and Howard Greenfield
Musicians

Anthony Clark	vocals, guitar
John Clark	guitar
Dave Cooke	keyboards
Mike Haughton	saxophone
Peter Howarth	backing vocals
Pete May	drums, percussion
Mick Mullins	backing vocals
Keith Murrell	backing vocals
Alan Park	keyboards
Cliff Richard	vocals, guitar
Steve Stroud	bass

Recording Details

Producer	Keith Bessey
Engineered by	Keith Bessey
Recording location	The Mission Winery, Napier, New Zealand
Recording date	22nd February 2003

♫ Clear Blue Skies

From the album **Stronger**

For the follow-up to Cliff Richard's career best-seller, ***Always Guaranteed***, he returned to the studio once again with Alan Tarney, although this time not all of the songs were written or produced by him. However, the majority of the tracks had some involvement, including *Clear Blue Skies*, although it was written by guitarist Dave Cooke and Chris Turner.
An upbeat and optimistic number, *Clear Blue Skies* looks forward to the future in a new relationship. With an effective use of Cliff's own vocals to harmonize with his lead, the song is driven on by a relentless bass line that sticks predominantly to the one note.

Track Specification
Composed by Dave Cooke and Chris Turner
Musicians

Cliff Richard	vocals, backing vocals
Alan Tarney	arranger, synthesisers, drum and percussion sequencers

Recording Details

Producer	Alan Tarney
Engineered by	Gerry Kitchingham and Ben Robbins
Recording location	R. G. Jones Studios, Wimbledon, London
Mixed by	John Hudson and Noel Rafferty
Mixing location	Mayfair Studios, London
Recording date	27th February 1989, 9th March 1989, 13th-17th March 1989 and 22nd-23rd March 1989

♫ Cliff's Personal Message to You

Flexi-disc single issued with **Serenade** *magazine*

On occasion, Cliff Richard would record a number of messages for his fans as part of a personal thanks to them for their support, particularly in other countries where he might not have been touring for a while or at all. There were also sporadic commercial recordings required by EMI to help boost sales of his records. *Cliff's Personal Message to You* was recorded in March of 1960 and issued on flexi-disc as a free incentive with the now defunct *Serenade* magazine and was subsequently reissued as part of the track listing for the anthology ***The Rock 'n' Roll Years 1958-1963***.
In the speech, Cliff thanks the fans, talks about how he prepares himself for performances and how much fun he has making music and tells amusing anecdotes.

Track Specification
Composed by Cliff Richard
Musicians

Cliff Richard	spoken vocals

Recording Details

Producer	Norrie Paramor
Engineered by	Malcolm Addey and Norman Smith
Recording location	Abbey Road Studio 2, St. John's Wood, London
Recording date	17th March 1960

♫ Climbing Up Mount Everest

From the album **Real as I Wanna Be**

Used as a metaphor for the struggle to keep a relationship together, *Climbing Up Mount Everest* appears on Cliff Richard's first studio album for three years, ***Real as I Wanna Be***. The track continues in the same vein as much of the other material, which is a departure from what many would expect from Cliff, with its soul flavours and synthesiser-driven arrangement. The synthesiser introduction flutters around the stereo channels, while the fuzzed guitar and insistent bass line drives the song onwards, as Cliff performs in a breathy anxiety, that brightens at the chorus. Cliff provides his own backing vocals in a throaty hoarseness and this adds to the interest of the track.

Track Specification

Composed by Tommy Lee James and Robin Lerner

Musicians

Michael Landau	guitar
Anastasios Panos	drums, percussion
Cliff Richard	vocals, backing vocals
Jeff Richman	guitar
Michelle Wolf	backing vocals
Peter Wolf	arranger, bass, keyboards, percussion

Recording Details

Producer	Peter Wolf
Engineered by	Christian Leitgeb, Chris Heil, Paul Erickson and/or Keith Bessey
Recording location	Little America Recording Studios, Weiler, Austria, Ocean Recording Studios, Burbank, California, USA, Arco Recording Studios, Munich, Germany, R. G. Jones Recording Studios, Wimbledon, London, England and/or The Pierce Room, London, England
Recording date	1997 or 1998

♫ Closer to You

Unissued track

One of a number of tracks to be recorded during the sessions for Cliff Richard's ***Now You See Me... Now You Don't*** album in early 1962 that didn't make it on to the track listing, *Closer to You* has not, to date, been issued in any format.

Track Specification

Composed by Unknown

Musicians

Mel Collins	saxophone
Mark Griffiths	bass
Graham Jarvis	drums, percussion
Mart Jenner	electric guitar
Craig Pruess	piano, synthesisers, sequencers, electronic percussion
Cliff Richard	vocals, backing vocals
Bill Roberts	electric guitar

Recording Details

Producer	Cliff Richard and Craig Pruess
Engineered by	John Walker and Steve Cook
Recording location	Strawberry Studios South, Surrey
Recording date	4th-15th January 1982

♫ Close to Kathy

From the film soundtrack album of **Two a Penny**

Recorded over a year and half before the next session for the film soundtrack of ***Two a Penny***, Cliff Richard recorded *Close to Kathy* at the penultimate session of 1965. Not originally anticipated for the soundtrack album, it was simply recorded as a pleasant song. However, once the film was in the works, it was decided that it would be an excellent addition to the track listing, since there were only four songs featured from the film. The final (unknown) take and edit were used for both the mono and stereo recordings but with different mixes for the needs of the separate audio channels. Sometimes the song is erroneously titled *Close to Cathy*; the track listing clearly states it to be *Close to Kathy*.

The stereo edit mixes Cliff's vocal into the right channel with the remainder in the left. The staccato accompaniment on guitar and woodwind underlines the emotion that Cliff imbues in the lyrics. His vibrato and ability to express the words are exemplified on this track. During the recording a reverberating echo has been added that is half a beat behind the lead.

Track Specification

Composed by Bob Goodman and Earl Shuman

Musicians

Bernard Ebbinghouse Orchestra	orchestra
Bernard Ebbinghouse	arranger, conductor
Cliff Richard	vocals

Recording Details

Producer	Norrie Paramor
Engineered by	Malcolm Addey
Recording location	Abbey Road Studio 2, St. John's Wood, London
Recording date	17th November 1965

♫ Cloudy

From the film soundtrack album of **Two a Penny**

The best known version of *Cloudy* is by the Cyrkle, who had already had a hit with ***Red Rubber Ball*** after being offered the song by writer Paul Simon when they supported the Simon and Garfunkel tour and it was logical that they would then record other material by Simon. Correspondingly, it has also been covered by the Seekers (as they did with *Red Rubber Ball*) and, of course, Simon and Garfunkel recorded a version for their *Parsley, Sage, Rosemary and Thyme* album.

Cliff Richard had long been an admirer of Paul Simon's compositions and had already recorded *Red Rubber Ball* himself for the ***Two a Penny*** album and ***Homeward Bound*** for ***Don't Stop Me Now!***, so including *Cloudy* for the track listing of *Two a Penny* seemed a logical step forward.
Cliff turns his hand to the change in style of song and creates a lovely version that is supported by tinkling percussion, a thudding orchestral accompaniment and an uncredited female vocal group, which could quite possibly be the Breakaways since they were involved professionally with Cliff at the time.

Track Specification
Composed by Paul Simon
Musicians

Mike Leander	arranger, conductor
Mike Leander Orchestra	orchestra
Cliff Richard	vocals
Unknown	backing vocals

Recording Details

Producer	Norrie Paramor
Engineered by	Peter Vince
Recording location	Abbey Road Studio 2, St. John's Wood, London
Recording date	11th October 1967

♬ C'mon Everybody

From the albums **Rock Dreams** *(The Brian Bennett Band),* **From a Distance ***** The Event** *and* **Reunited**

Originally released as a B-side of *Don't Ever Let Me Go* by its co-writer, Eddie Cochrane, such was his growing popularity in the UK that the song was released in its own right in March 1959 and reached number six. It was reissued in February 1988, following a successful television advertising campaign for Levi's 501 jeans, although this time the single only reached number fourteen. Most memorably, during the punk rock era of the latter half of the seventies, the Sex Pistols recorded their version, which was released as a single, reaching number three in July 1979. Not to be confused with the song of the same name by Elvis Presley from *Viva Las Vegas*, *C'mon Everybody* has been covered by a number of other artists including Humble Pie, UFO, Led Zeppelin and Cliff Richard and the Shadows (more of which later in this entry).
In 1977, Cliff didn't carry out much in the way of recording sessions or his own material but he was increasingly involved in helping others. Brian Bennett, the Shadows' drummer, had created his own band and recorded a number of tracks for his first solo album, *Rock Dreams*. Two tracks featured Cliff on backing vocals as well as members of his own then backing band, including Tony Rivers on lead vocals. One song was released as a single, ***The Girls Back Home***, while the other, *C'mon Everybody*, was used as a track on the album.
Rivers was also Cliff's backing vocalist at the time, and Brian Bennett's version of the song is competently driven along but there does seem to be something lacking; there appears to be a lack of energy that's difficult to pinpoint. However, that denigrates the performance unintentionally because the arrangement is interesting and refreshing, although Cliff's vocals cannot be immediately identified in the mix.
The song was a natural choice for inclusion in the ***Oh Boy! Medley***, which was the opening suite of numbers at ***The Event*** in 1989, which Cliff used as a nod towards those artists from the fifties and early sixties who had inspired him as a singer. Taking the lead, Cliff sings the song with his natural flair for this type of song and receives some of the biggest applause during the performance of the medley.
Along with the single from the project, ***Singing the Blues***, and a re-recording of ***Sea Cruise***, *C'mon Everybody* was one of three songs that were recorded for the 2009 ***Reunited*** album to celebrate fifty years in the music business with the Shadows that were not specifically their own material. The performance is strong with Cliff enjoying the exercising of his vocals including the wild whoops, while the driving guitars and bass give the song pace. The middle eight features a rocking guitar solo by Hank that leads into the strong rhythm guitar by Bruce for the remainder of the song.

Track Specification
Composed by Jerry Capehart and Eddie Cochran

1. Rock Dreams
Musicians

Brian Bennett	drums, percussion
Stuart Calver	backing vocals
Alan Hawkshaw	keyboards
Les Hurtle	bass
Alan Parkes	guitar
John Perry	backing vocals
Cliff Richard	backing vocals
Tony Rivers	vocals
Unknown	hand claps

Recording Details

Producer	Brian Bennett
Engineered by	Dick Plant
Recording location	Honey Hill Studios, Hertfordshire
Recording date	April 1977

2. From a Distance ** The Event***
Musicians
Dallas Boys:

Nicky Clarke	backing vocals
Leon Fisk	backing vocals
Stan Jones	backing vocals
Joe Smith	backing vocals
Bob Wragg	backing vocals

Recording Details

Producer	Cliff Richard
Engineered by	Keith Bessey and Mick McKenna
Recording location	Rolling Stones Mobile Studio, Wembley Stadium, Wembley, North-west London
Recording date	16th-17th June 1989

Kalin Twins:	
Harold Kalin	backing vocals
Herbie Kalin	backing vocals
Oh Boy! Band	rock 'n' roll band
Cliff Richard	vocals
Unknown	hand claps
Vernons Girls:	
Lyn Cornell	backing vocals
Maureen Kennedy	backing vocals
Frances Lee	backing vocals
Jean Owen	backing vocals

3. Reunited

Musicians

Brian Bennett	drums, percussion
Mark Griffiths	bass
Hank Marvin	backing vocals, guitar
Cliff Richard	vocals, backing vocals
Bruce Welch	backing vocals, rhythm guitar

Recording Details

Producer	Warren Bennett (co-ordination)
Engineered by	James Collins (Honeyhill Studios), Ethan Carlson (Middle Ear Studios), Les Williams (Nivram Studios) and Keith Bessey (mixing and mastering)
Recording location	Middle Ear Studios, Miami, Florida, USA (Cliff's vocals), Nivram Studios, Perth, Western Australia (Hank's guitars and vocals) and Honeyhill Studios, Hertfordshire, England (all other vocals and instruments)
Recording date	Early 2009

♫ Come Back Billie Jo

B-side of **Power to All Our Friends**

Five years after narrowly missing out on being the winner with ***Congratulations*** at the 1968 Eurovision Song Contest, Cliff Richard was asked to sing at the Contest to represent the United Kingdom once again in 1973. As was the custom, the shortlist of six songs vying for the coveted Song for Europe was chosen by industry representatives and each one was performed over six weeks on a Saturday night television variety show and, that year, it fell to a programme hosted by his friend Cilla Black, simply titled *Cilla*. The first song of the six candidate entries to be performed, *Come Back Billie Jo* went on to become the second favourite behind ***Power to All Our Friends***, which went on to be sung on 7th April 1973 in Luxembourg. Polling 14.1% of the total votes (to the winner's huge portion of 51.8%), *Come Back Billie Jo* came ahead of the third-placed ***Help It Along*** (one of Cliff's favourites) by 3.4 percentage points.

Come Back Billie Jo was recorded with the other five songs in a two-day session at the end of December 1972 and was the last of three tracks to be completed (along with ***Ashes to Ashes*** and ***The Days of Love***) on the first day. As it was the second choice of the British public's postal vote, it was the traditional choice for the B-side of the winning entry and the single was released four weeks before the contest. Of all the subsequent re-recordings of *Power to All Our Friends* into the three main European languages, all had the same B-side, but not translated from English. The track was a significant rarity for many years until it was included on the rare B-side CD section of the celebratory ***...And They Said It Wouldn't Last! (My 50 Years in Music)*** in 2008.

The emphasis in the accompanying orchestra is on the bass clarinet and banjo, as Cliff sings to a girl who is off doing her own thing and that he wants her to return to him. A fine song, certainly, but it doesn't quite have the magic of *Power to All Our Friends*, although it is a worthy runner up.

Track Specification

Composed by Mitch Murray and Tony MacAuley

Musicians

Terry Britten	backing vocals, guitar
David MacKay Orchestra	orchestra
David MacKay	backing vocals, arranger, conductor
Kevin Peek	banjo
Cliff Richard	vocals
Trevor Spencer	backing vocals, drums, percussion
Alan Tarney	backing vocals, bass

Recording Details

Producer	David MacKay
Engineered by	Peter Vince
Recording location	Abbey Road Studio 2, St. John's Wood, London
Recording date	27th December 1972

♫ Come Back to Me

From the album **Real as I Wanna Be**

Written by the married writing partnership of producer Peter Wolf and backing singer Michelle Wolf, Cliff Richard provides many of his backing vocals, counterpointing the main melody with more creativity than many of the songs on the parent album ***Real as I Wanna Be***.

A straightforward pop song, the echoing vocals are used to great effect in the introduction. Cliff's vocals are mixed to the forefront of the edit, giving it a confidential air. Once again, the backing vocals, provided by Cliff, blend in with the lead vocal and add extra beauty to the emotion held within the lyrics.

Track Specification
Composed by Peter Wolf and Michelle Wolf

Musicians		*Recording Details*	
Paul Jackson Jr.	guitar	Producer	Peter Wolf
Michael Landau	guitar	Engineered by	Christian Leitgeb, Chris Heil, Paul Erickson and/or Keith Bessey
Christian Leitgeb	guitar	Recording location	Little America Recording Studios, Weiler, Austria, Ocean Recording Studios, Burbank, California, USA, Arco Recording Studios, Munich, Germany, R. G. Jones Recording Studios, Wimbledon, London, England and/or The Pierce Room, London, England
Cliff Richard	vocals, backing vocals	Recording date	1997 or 1998
Michelle Wolf	backing vocals		
Peter Wolf	arranger, bass, keyboards, percussion		

♫ Come Closer to Me
From the album **Kinda Latin**

Recorded by artists including Julie London, Nat King Cole, Pérez Prado, Ben E. King and Hugo Winterhalter and his Orchestra, *Come Closer to Me* began life as a Spanish song that was subsequently translated into English by John Stewart. The English version was recorded by Cliff Richard for his album ***Kinda Latin*** at the final session of three that took place in October 1965. The last song to be completed for the album at that session, the sixth and final take and edit of *Come Closer to Me* were used for the mono and stereo recordings but with different mixes for the separation of the channels.
Although the rhythm is definitely a Latin one, as per the concept of the album, the instrumentation is unusual, certainly in comparison with other tracks on the album. Cliff excels when singing this style of song, with a touch of vibrato on the sustained notes while providing light and shade in his phrasing of the lyrics.

Track Specification
Composed by Osvaldo Farrés; English lyrics by John Stewart

Musicians		*Recording Details*	
Les Reed Orchestra	orchestra	Producer	Norrie Paramor
Les Reed	arranger, conductor	Engineered by	Peter Bown
Cliff Richard	vocals	Recording location	Abbey Road Studio 3, St. John's Wood, London
		Recording date	22nd October 1965

♫ Come Go with Me
B-side of **Dangerous Game** *(Network 3) and from the album* **World Tour Live**

Written by Clarence Quick, who, as a member of the Del-Vikings, recorded *Come Go with Me* and hit number four in the American charts, the song has also been memorably covered by the Beach Boys who had a number eighteen US hit in 1982, while the original also featured on the soundtracks of fifties nostalgia movies *Stand By Me* and *American Graffiti*. Other acts to cover the song include Dion and the Belmonts, the Everly Brothers, Bobby Vee, the Fleetwoods, Sha Na Na, the Quarrymen and a sample was used by Jive Bunny and the Mastermixers.
With Cliff Richard producing the two Network 3 tracks singles and their B-sides in 1980 for release the following year, it was only a short while before the Christian vocal group split up for good. *Come Go with Me* was released as the B-side of the second and final of those singles: ***Dangerous Game***. There is a paucity of information from the sessions – technical personnel, other musicians, date and location – but these will be remedied should further information come to light.
The track begins with the vocalists singing non-lyrical vocals in *a capella*, as Paul Field joins in with the lead vocal matched by the strength of Cliff's backing vocal. Although it has strong evocations of a bygone era in the arrangement, it is an excellent contemporary production by Cliff. By the mid-point, a saxophone is added to the mix but the *a capella* vocals return and continue to be a great study in pitching vocal performances such as these. The vocals die down and the track completes on a jammed saxophone performance.
The track was chosen to initiate the ***Doo-Wop Medley*** for the 2003 world tour. The performance was filmed at the New Zealand show for DVD release later in that year, while the complementary CD album, *World Tour Live*, featured only a selection of those songs, which included the entire *Doo-Wop Medley*. Cliff is joined on stage by the troupe of dancers as he sings the style of song that he excels at. The backing vocals are pure doo-wop and the execution of the ensemble is perfect, including the subtle key change.

Track Specification
Composed by Clarence Quick

1. B-side (Dangerous Game)

Musicians		*Recording Details*	
Paul Field	vocals	Producer	Cliff Richard
Mo McCafferty	vocals	Engineered by	Unknown
Annie McCaig	vocals	Recording location	Unknown
Cliff Richard	backing vocals	Recording date	1980
Unknown	saxophone		
Unknown	percussion		

2. *World Tour Live*

Musicians		*Recording Details*	
Anthony Clark	backing vocals, guitar	Producer	Keith Bessey
John Clark	guitar	Engineered by	Keith Bessey
Dave Cooke	keyboards	Recording location	The Mission Winery, Napier, New Zealand
Mike Haughton	saxophone	Recording date	22nd February 2003
Peter Howarth	backing vocals		
Pete May	drums, percussion		
Mick Mullins	backing vocals		
Keith Murrell	backing vocals		
Alan Park	keyboards		
Cliff Richard	vocals		
Steve Stroud	bass		

♫ Come out Fighting

B-side of **I Can Hear Love** *(Garth Hewitt) and single by* **Garth Hewitt**

At the end of the seventies, Cliff Richard became heavily involved in production of recordings by other artists (in addition to some of his own tracks) and he had a particularly long association with fellow Christian singer Garth Hewitt. In 1980, Cliff was at work again on Hewitt's 1980 single ***I Can Hear Love***, for which *Come out Fighting* was chosen as the B-side. Curiously, the single was flipped over and reissued on the same label (Pye) and given a fresh catalogue number (PAR 108) and rereleased in the same year. There is very little information on the musicians, location and technical staff on the recording, although it is likely that the two tracks were recorded at a studio in London.

The initial rhythm is quirky with crashing percussion and guitar chords and leads to a standard rock rhythm. Hewitt's vocals are assertive enough for the meaning of the song where he is fighting for his beliefs and it is improved further when Cliff's gentle backing vocals come in to support the choruses. An excellent guitar solo is deployed in the middle eight and the contrast between the verses and the ensemble performance would have made a better choice for the A-side.

Track Specification

Composed by Garth Hewitt

Musicians		*Recording Details*	
Garth Hewitt	vocals	Producer	Cliff Richard
Cliff Richard	backing vocals	Engineered by	Unknown
Unknown	guitar	Recording location	Unknown
Unknown	bass	Recording date	1980
Unknown	keyboards		
Unknown	drums, percussion		

♫ Come Prima

From the album **When in Rome**

Made popular in Italy by Tony Dallara, *Come Prima* (literally translated as *As Before* or *As the First Time*, which is often used in musical annotation and direction to instruct the musician to repeat the style from the start of the piece of music) has been translated into French (*Tu Me Donnes*) and two versions in English: *More than Ever* and *For the First Time*. *More than Ever* was a hit for the Mike Sammes Singers (the long-time backing vocalists on many of Cliff Richard's recordings) backing Michael Vaughan, who reached number five in late 1958, and Robert Earl, who hit number twenty-eight contemporaneously. It has also been covered by the Platters, Dean Martin, Eve Boswell, and Polly Bergen.

The Italian version with its original title was recorded by Cliff Richard at the first two sessions in May at Lisbon studios, dubbing the vocals on pre-recorded backing tracks. Cliff often recorded foreign language songs in English and vice versa during the sixties, but *Come Prima* is one that he only recorded in Italian. He is quoted as saying that he found Italian the most difficult language to enunciate and he had to work with a teacher who taught him the Italian phonetically, although this doesn't notice in the eventual track. The final vocal take and edit were combined with the fourth and final orchestral take for the mono-only release. *Come Prima* also appeared on the track listing for the EP ***Hits from When in Rome***, also only released in mono format. There is confusion over the studio personnel involved in the recording: while Malcolm Addey might have been involved in the vocal tracks, it is unlikely that he was engineering the orchestral backing track.

Cliff imbues the performance with a vibrato in his voice that would later be one of his trademarks. The song is performed in six-eight time that gives it a lilt that perfectly matches Cliff's lines.

Track Specification

Composed by Mario Panzeri, Vincenzo DiPaolo and Sandro Taccani

Musicians		*Recording Details*	
Norrie Paramor Orchestra	orchestra	Producer	John Lee and M. DiPonti (backing track) and Norrie Paramor (vocals)
Norrie Paramor	arranger, conductor	Engineered by	Malcolm Addey
Cliff Richard	vocals	Recording location	EMI Studios, Milan (backing track) and Estudios Valentim De Carvalho, Lisbon (vocals)
		Recording date	2nd-3rd October 1964 (backing track) and 13th May 1965 (vocals)

♬ Come Sunday

From the pantomime cast recording album of **Cinderella**

This gentle song, taken from the soundtrack of the ***Cinderella*** pantomime that was performed at the London Palladium over Christmas 1966 and into the new year, is another of the many songs from the prolific Shadows (they wrote the previous year's pantomime, ***Aladdin and His Wonderful Lamp***, as well as all the music for the film ***Finders Keepers*** during the same period). From the first session for the *Cinderella* soundtrack, *Come Sunday* was the only song to be completed. The sixth and final take and edit were used for the mono and stereo recordings – while the mono version was released later as part of the ***Cinderella*** EP, the stereo version was issued on the dual LP releases.

As would be expected from the Shadows, they have composed a very pretty and emotive song with cleverly constructed arrangements, while Cliff performs with his customary grace with acknowledgments to the song's lyrics in his phrasing. Elevating the song further are the beautiful close harmony vocals, particularly in the last few bars of the song.

Track Specification

Composed by Hank Marvin, Bruce Welch, Brian Bennett and John Rostill

Musicians

Brian Bennett	drums, percussion
Hank Marvin	backing vocals, guitar
Cliff Richard	vocals
John Rostill	backing vocals, bass
Bruce Welch	backing vocals, rhythm guitar

Recording Details

Producer	Norrie Paramor
Engineered by	Peter Vince and Richard Lush
Recording location	Abbey Road Studio 2, St. John's Wood, London
Recording date	14th October 1966

♬ Come to Us

From the album **Cliff at Christmas**

Recorded at the same sessions that produced ***Santa's List***, *Come to Us* was chosen as an addition to the track listing of Cliff Richard's second album of seasonal and festive material, ***Cliff at Christmas***. Written by non-English composers, the jazz trio of Jacqui Dankworth (daughter of Johnny and Cleo Laine), Sara Colman and Liane Carroll added the English lyrics.

A tinkling piano and guitar introduce the song, which has Cliff singing the lyrics in a gentle way. The strength of the song comes from the fact that the tune and lyrics are not overly-familiar and, by this method, the track sounds fresh and unusual on the album. Cliff provides his own backing vocals and this adds further aspects of interest.

Track Specification

Composed by Zbigniew Preisner, Liane Carroll, Sara Colman, Jacqui Dankworth and Dan Mucha

Musicians

Chris Cameron	conductor
Peter Gordeno	keyboards
Rick Mitra	drums, percussion
Phil Palmer	guitar
Cliff Richard	vocals, backing vocals
Unknown	orchestra
Gavin Wright	violin, leader

Recording Details

Producer	Chris Porter
Engineered by	Chris Porter
Recording location	Sony Studios, London (orchestra) and Porterhouse Studios, London (other instruments and vocals)
Recording date	2003

♬ Compassion Road

Unissued track

Having found the help he sought from a stranger in one of the episodes dramatically retelling the famous parables in the Tyne Tees Television series *Life with Johnny*, Johnny (played by Cliff Richard) suddenly recognizes what he has been missing all these years: compassion to strangers. The lyrics of the song are more connected to the biblical parable than the new setting although there is a zigzagging road lad out on the studio floor, with the opening lyrics stating that Compassion Road lies between Jerusalem and Jericho.

Performed in a spiritual style with close harmonies provided by the Settlers, the verses are gentle and thought-provoking while the chorus is upbeat and glorious in praise of God. The song was recorded with the other songs appearing in the programmes at Abbey Road, although any expected album tie-in failed to materialize as a project (its limited appeal is not necessarily the reason since EMI indulged Cliff with a number of gospel and religious albums over the years). According to the final credits, the songs were all original and written by the screenwriter David Winter along with Cliff and the four members of the Settlers. Some sources claim that the song was called ***Confession Road***, although this is at odds with the lyrics, the performance and the story of the Good Samaritan.

Track Specification

Composed by Cliff Richard, David Winter, Cindy Kent, Mike Jones, John Fyffe and Geoffrey Srodzinski

Musicians

John Fyffe	backing vocals, guitar
Cindy Kent	backing vocals
Mike Jones	backing vocals, guitar
Cliff Richard	vocals, finger-clicks
Geoffrey Srodzinski	backing vocals, bass
Unknown	drums, percussion

Recording Details

Producer	Norrie Paramor
Engineered by	Peter Vince
Recording location	Abbey Road Studio 3, St. John's Wood, London
Recording date	2nd-3rd December 1968

♫ Concerto
From the album **Ich Träume Deine Träume**

Concerto was recorded by Cliff Richard for his second German language album, *Ich Träume Deine Träume*, released in 1971. *Concerto* was the second song recorded in the third of a marathon four sessions over two days in November 1970, which was made easier by having the orchestral backing tracks recorded prior to the event. The song was eventually remastered and reissued on the anthology of Cliff's foreign language recordings, ***On the Continent***, in 1997.

The arrangement is unusual as it seems to be competing with Cliff's vocal line in parts, while the chorus sounds as if it has been inspired by *Muss I Denn* (or *Wooden Heart*, in the Elvis Presley's version). Overall, it feels as if it has been quickly cobbled together without consideration to the end product but, for all that, it is an interesting addition to Cliff's oeuvre.

Track Specification

Composed by Gordini and Kurt Hertha

Musicians

Bernard Ebbinghouse	arranger, conductor
Norrie Paramor Orchestra	orchestra
Cliff Richard	vocals
Unknown	backing vocals

Recording Details

Producer	Norrie Paramor (backing track and vocals)
Engineered by	Phil McDonald (backing track and vocals)
Recording location	Cologne, Germany (backing track) and Abbey Road Studio 2, St. John's Wood, London (vocals)
Recording date	November 1970 (backing track) and 25th November 1970 (vocals)

♫ Concerto d'Autumno
From the album **When in Rome**

One of the fourteen tracks recorded over two days in a Lisbon studio, the Italian song *Concerto d'Autumno* (or *Autumn Concerto*) is one of the very few foreign language songs recorded by Cliff Richard that was not subsequently dubbed into English. Destined for ***When in Rome***, the song's vocals were recorded in May 1965 and overdubbed on an orchestral track recorded seven months previously (at a point when Cliff was too busy to record his vocals). The final and unknown vocal take and edit were applied to the fourth and final orchestral take and edit but have only ever been released in mono format only. There is some confusion over the studio personnel involved in the recording: while Malcolm Addey might have been involved in the vocal tracks, it is unlikely that he was engineering the orchestral backing track.

Played as a muted tango, Cliff sings the song with the vocals produced from the back of his throat, giving it an emotion that would otherwise have been lost. Cliff had the greatest trouble with enunciating the Italian language but found it ultimately the most satisfactory and this comes through in this song.

Track Specification

Composed by Danpa and Camillo Bargoni

Musicians

Norrie Paramor Orchestra	orchestra
Norrie Paramor	arranger, conductor
Cliff Richard	vocals

Recording Details

Producer	John Lee and M. DiPonti (backing track) and Norrie Paramor (vocals)
Engineered by	Malcolm Addey
Recording location	EMI Studios, Milan (backing track) and Estudios Valentim De Carvalho, Lisbon (vocals)
Recording date	2nd-3rd October 1964 (backing track) and 13th May 1965 (vocals)

♫ Concrete and Clay
From the album **Kinda Latin**

Best known for the rendering by British group Unit 4 + 2, it was a number one hit for them in March 1965, whence it was removed by Cliff Richard's ***The Minute You're Gone*** the following week. Based on a bossa nova beat, it was covered by Eddie Rambeau who had the hit in the US. In 1976, this was followed by Randy Edelman, who reached number eleven in the UK singles chart with his first release in the March of that year. It has since been covered by a number of artists including Pete Byrne, Kevin Rowland, Eddie Rambeau, Gary Lewis and the Playboys, Joe Longthorne and Jesse Boyce.

The first song to be completed at the final session for Cliff Richard's ***Kinda Latin*** album in October 1965, the seventh and final take and edit of *Concrete and Clay* were used for both the mono and stereo recordings but with different mixes for the requirements of the separate audio channels.

With a full brass arrangement to accompany the percussive Latin rhythm, Cliff's version of what was a very familiar song at the time is very different. Although he over-emphasizes the 'r' consonant, this doesn't detract from an excellent closing track to the album.

Track Specification

Composed by Brian Parker and Thomas Moeller

Musicians

Les Reed Orchestra	orchestra
Les Reed	arranger, conductor
Cliff Richard	vocals

Recording Details

Producer	Norrie Paramor
Engineered by	Peter Bown
Recording location	Abbey Road Studio 3, St. John's Wood, London
Recording date	22nd October 1965

♫ Confession Road

Misnomer for **Compassion Road**

Some sources suggest that the song ***Compassion Road*** from the *Life with Johnny* religious broadcasts is *Confession Road*, but this does not match up with the lyrics or the story-line of the Good Samaritan. Refer to the entry for *Compassion Road.*

♫ Confidential

Unissued track

Recorded by a number of acts in the late fifties and early sixties, the most familiar covers are those by the Fleetwoods, Sonny Knight, Charles Brown and Bobby Russell. In 1977, while Cliff was taking a sabbatical from recording his own material, he took the producer's chair for a number of tracks by actor and singer Richard Loring, which resulted in a single, ***Wonderful Summer***, and its B-side as well as three tracks never released. One of these was *Confidential*, and, as with all of these recordings, there is scant information available on the recording and musical personnel involved.

Track Specification

Composed by Dorinda Morgan

Musicians

Richard Loring	vocals
Unknown	other instrumentation

Recording Details

Producer	Cliff Richard
Engineered by	Unknown
Recording location	Abbey Road Studios, St. John's Wood, London
Recording date	August 1977

♫ Congratulations

***41st UK single** and from the albums* **Live at the Talk of the Town**, **Cliff Live in Korea**, **Cliff "Live" in Japan '72**, **Cliff Live in Japan** *and* **Japan Tour '74** *and B-side of* **Be with Me Always**

With the possible exception of ***Summer Holiday*** and ***Living Doll***, *Congratulations* is the one song that is indelibly linked to Cliff Richard. Written by Phil Coulter and Bill Martin, who had written the winning UK entry for the 1967 Eurovision Song Contest, *Puppet on a String*, *Congratulations* was one of the six candidates for the 1968 contest. The song started its existence as an affirmative love song called *I Think I Love You* by Coulter, although he wasn't happy with the lyrics. When he handed the song over to his writing partner, Martin changed it to *Congratulations*, becoming the familiar song.
Cliff performed one of the six candidate songs each week on the *Cilla Black Show*, with a public mail vote at the end. *Congratulations* received a staggering 69% of the vote, with its closest rival, ***High 'n' Dry***, only receiving 12%.The strength of the song made journalists question what would come second to it, believing it unlikely that any other song could beat it. Indeed, for most of voting at the contest held at the Royal Albert Hall on 6th April 1968, *Congratulations* was in the lead. But then something changed: Germany, voting towards the end, gave Spain (UK's nearest rival) six points and the UK two. This put Spain one point in the lead and gavethem the contest. In 2008, in a documentary by Montse Fernandez Vila, it was suggested that General Franco had engineered vote-rigging in order to force a Spanish win. Whatever the case, *Congratulations* was the commercial winner, with Cliff selling over two million records, while Spain's *La La La*, performed by Massiel, has been long-forgotten.
Now used for celebratory occasions such as weddings, sporting achievements and returning troops, *Congratulations* was released as a single, backed with *High 'n' Dry*, on the Columbia label (catalogue number DB 8376) on 20th March 1968 and reached number one in the UK singles charts – the first number one for Cliff since ***The Minute You're Gone*** almost exactly three years before (and his last for another eleven), staying at the top for two weeks before being displaced by Louis Armstrong's ***What a Wonderful World***; it even just made it into the US Billboard charts hitting number ninety-nine. As was the Columbia policy at the time, the single, featuring future Led Zeppelin bassist John Paul Jones, was released in mono only; the stereo version was first released (ironically) in Germany on the album *Congratulations und 13 Weitere Hits* later in the year and then made more widely available on the compilation ***The Best of Cliff*** in 1969. In terms of musical direction, *Congratulations* was a double-edged sword in that, while hugely popular, it set the template for Cliff's musical style over the next few years, something that waned in commercial popularity as the new decade dawned. After huge demand, Cliff recorded versions in the four main European languages immediately after the contest: ***Man Gratuliert Mir*** (Germany), ***Que Buena Suerte (Felicidades)*** (Spain), ***A Quelle Histoire*** (France) and ***Il Mondo et Tondo*** (Italy).
The stuttering orchestral chords followed by the thumping bass drum are one of the most recognizable introductions of any popular songs. Matched with the swooping string echoes, the subtle female backing vocals, followed by the slow accelerando at the end (which he later repeated on his ***Living in Harmony*** single, almost using the same introductory notes) and it is no surprise why the British public and the Eurovision panels had little trouble voting for the song. It is upbeat and optimistic as per the song's title and Cliff sings it with appropriate gusto. The backing vocals are by ex-Vernons Girls breakaway group the Ladybirds, who also sang on Sandie Shaw's Eurovision hit from the previous year, and by coincidence another Vernons splinter group, the Breakaways, would accompany him on his concert at the Talk of the Town, where the song was performed as the first of two encores.
It was Olivia Newton-John and Pat Carroll that provided the backing vocals for the version that was performed on ***Cliff "Live" in Japan '72***, which also featured a spirited accompaniment by the assembled band. The break starts with Cliff saying "Altogether now" and slowly brings up each syllable with laughter from the audience.

For the Japanese tour in 1974, Cliff performed a ***Hit Medley*** that featured a number of his sixties hits: *Congratulations*, ***In the Country, Dancing Shoes, The Day I Met Marie, On the Beach*** and ***Sing a Song of Freedom***. Cliff interrupts the orchestral thumping introduction and suggests that they shouldn't sing it and then relents but only if the audience sings it with him. The inevitable introduction features Cliff singing each syllable and then stopping to lead the audience on.
The song was released again as the principal B-side of the 1993 single from ***Cliff Richard - The Album***, ***Never Let Go***, and also included the original *The Young Ones* track on the CD single release.
A new version was released as the B-side of ***Be with Me Always***, which was taken from the live performance at the Centre Court during the Wimbledon tennis tournament after a continuous downpour prevented further games being played. *Congratulations* was one of for tracks to be subsequently released for the B-side but this only appeared on the cassette version of the single (unusual in itself since CDs had pretty much become the principal format).

Track Specification
Composed by Bill Martin and Phil Coulter

1. Single

Musicians

John Paul Jones	bass
Ladybirds	backing vocals
Marian Davies	
Gloria George	
Maggie Stredder	
Norrie Paramor Orchestra	orchestra
Norrie Paramor	arranger, conductor
Cliff Richard	vocals

Recording Details

Producer	Norrie Paramor
Engineered by	Peter Vince
Recording location	Abbey Road Studio 2, St. John's Wood, London
Recording date	3rd February 1968

2. Live at the Talk of the Town

Musicians

Breakaways:	backing vocals
Vicki Hasemen	
Margo Quantrell	
Jean Ryder	
Norrie Paramor	arranger, conductor
Cliff Richard	vocals
Talk of the Town Orchestra	orchestra

Recording Details

Producer	Norrie Paramor
Engineered by	Peter Vince
Recording location	Talk of the Town Theatre, London
Recording date	30th May 1968

3. Cliff Live in Korea

Musicians

Brian Bennett	drums, percussion
Alan Hawkshaw	keyboards
Hank Marvin	backing vocals, guitar
Cliff Richard	vocals
John Rostill	backing vocals, bass
Bruce Welch	backing vocals, rhythm guitar

Recording Details

Producer	Unknown
Engineered by	Unknown
Recording location	Citizen Hall, Seoul, South Korea
Recording date	16th October 1969

4. Cliff "Live" in Japan '72

Musicians

Brian Bennett	drums, percussion
Pat Carroll	backing vocals
John Farrar	bass
Alan Hawkshaw	piano
Hank Marvin	guitar
Olivia Newton-John	backing vocals
Cliff Richard	vocals
Bruce Welch	rhythm guitar

Recording Details

Producer	Norrie Paramor
Engineered by	Unknown
Recording location	Kosei Nenkin Hall, Tokyo, Japan
Recording date	22nd-23rd September 1972

5. Japan Tour '74

Musicians

Barrie Guard	arranger, conductor
Cliff Hall	piano
Brian Lewis	guitar
Kevin Peak	acoustic guitar
Cliff Richard	vocals
Shambles Symphonet	orchestra
Trevor Spencer	drums, percussion
Alan Tarney	bass
Bruce Welch	rhythm guitar

Recording Details

Producer	Toshiba EMI (no individual detailed)
Engineered by	Toshiba EMI (no individual detailed)
Recording location	Shinjuku Koseinenkin, Tokyo, Japan
Recording date	7th-8th October 1974

6. B-side (Be with Me Always)

Musicians

Cliff Richard	vocals

Recording Details

Producer	Unknown
Engineered by	Unknown
Recording location	Wimbledon Lawn Tennis Association
Recording date	3rd July 1996

♫ Constantly

25th UK single and from the album **Japan Tour '74**

Found and chosen for Cliff Richard to record by his producer Norrie Paramor, *Constantly* is an English version of an Italian hit called *L'Edera* (itself occasionally used as a subtitle for Cliff's hit and translated literally as *The Ivy*). In its original Italian form, it has been recorded by Nilla Pizzi, Elena Camerini, Manuela Zanier, Tonina Torrielli and Julia De Palma, amongst others.

Recorded at the penultimate recording session of 1963 with Norrie Paramor's orchestrations, *Constantly* was one of three songs to be recorded. The (unknown) take and edit were used for the mono and stereo recordings with different mixes for the audio channels. One of the other songs to be recorded at that session, ***I Only Know I Love You,*** was only released as the B-side in Italy (for no readily available reason) on the Columbia label (catalogue number SCMQ-1751) in May 1964 in mono only. *Constantly* was issued as a single in other territories, backed with ***True, True Lovin'*** (in all other countries than Italy) on the Columbia label (catalogue number DB 7272) on 24th April 1964, reaching the number four position in the UK singles charts. In addition to the single, the song also featured on the track listing of the ***A Forever Kind of Love*** EP and is a regular choice in the huge variety of compilations of Cliff's work.

The beautiful string and horn arrangement by Norrie Paramor elevates this pretty little love song, which Cliff sings with restrained passion. Although critics would have expected him to churn out fast-paced rock songs, it is tracks like *Constantly* that prove Cliff's worth as an all-round singer.

Performed during the Japanese our in 1974, the predominant accompaniment is the strings of the orchestra, while there are virtuoso performances on the acoustic guitar, the piano and the bass as well as Cliff's lead vocals.

Track Specification

Composed by Saverio Seracini and Vincenzo d'Acquisito; English translation and lyrics by Michael Julien

1. Single

Musicians		*Recording Details*	
Brian Bennett	drums, percussion	Producer	Norrie Paramor
Norrie Paramor Orchestra	orchestra	Engineered by	Malcolm Addey
Norrie Paramor	arranger, conductor	Recording location	Abbey Road Studio 2, St. John's Wood, London
Cliff Richard	vocals	Recording date	17th November 1963

2. Japan Tour '74

Musicians		*Recording Details*	
Barrie Guard	arranger, conductor	Producer	Toshiba EMI (no individual detailed)
Cliff Hall	piano	Engineered by	Toshiba EMI (no individual detailed)
Brian Lewis	guitar	Recording location	Shinjuku Koseinenkin, Tokyo, Japan
Kevin Peak	acoustic guitar	Recording date	7th-8th October 1974
Cliff Richard	vocals		
Shambles Symphonet	orchestra		
Trevor Spencer	drums, percussion		
Alan Tarney	bass		
Bruce Welch	rhythm guitar		

♫ 'Cos I Love That Rock 'n' Roll

From the album **Wired for Sound**

The final song on the first side of Cliff Richard's ***Wired for Sound*** album was written by Alan Tarney, demonstrating his increasing domination in Cliff's recordings, particularly as he not only produced it but also played all of the instruments with the exception of drums.

After the exuberance of ***Oh No, Don't Let Go*** on the album, *'Cos I Love That Rock 'n' Roll* sounds a bit flat in comparison but, slowly, the energy builds up towards the chorus, which features the multi-layered backing vocals created by Tarney and Cliff. There are also some interesting key progressions and Cliff carries off the song with simple assuredness although this track is probably not the best song with which to complete the first side of the vinyl album.

Track Specification

Composed by Alan Tarney

Musicians		*Recording Details*	
Graham Jarvis	drums, percussion	Producer	Alan Tarney
Cliff Richard	vocals, backing vocals	Engineered by	Michael Boddicker and Ian Little
Alan Tarney	arranger, backing vocals, guitar, bass, keyboards	Recording location	Gallery Studios, Chertsey, Surrey
		Recording date	27th May-9th July 1981

♫ Couldn't Care Less

From the album **Sail Away** *(Dave Pope)*

The opening song of the second side to Dave Pope's album, ***Sail Away,*** was produced by Cliff Richard. As the sleeve and the other reference material available do not provide the details of the specific musicians, they will be annotated as unknown until further information is found.

The quirky introduction featuring a guitar motif over stuttering drums breaks into a standard pop song with Pope's singing voice gathering more strength than can be heard on much of the first side of the album. The guitar is performed with rapidly plucked strings similar in style to the mandolin. It is essentially a love song that juxtaposes the suggestion that someone couldn't care less because they couldn't care more. The backing vocals are subtly placed behind the lead vocal in the last verse. *Couldn't Care Less* is one of the strongest songs on the album.

Track Specification
Composed by John Daniels

Musicians

Dave Pope	vocals
Cliff Richard	backing vocals
Unknown	backing vocals
Unknown	guitar
Unknown	bass
Unknown	keyboards
Unknown	drums, percussion

Recording Details

Producer	Cliff Richard
Engineered by	Tony Clark
Recording location	Morgan Studios, London
Recording date	April 1978

♫ Count Me Out

B-side of **We Don't Talk Anymore**

Until the release of the ***Green Light*** album, the working title for *Count Me Out* was *New Song*, presumably until composers Alan Tarney and Bruce Welch could come up with a better title that reflected the song's lyrics. It was chosen as the B-side for the phenomenally big international best-seller, ***We Don't Talk Anymore***. The single was subsequently re-released in its original format, with the same B-side, three years later. Recorded as the only complete song at the session and finished in two takes, additional overdubs were recorded three months later.

A tremulous synthesiser line introduces the song over arpeggiated guitar chords leading to Cliff's tender vocal line as the other instruments join in. A sad love song, it features backing vocals supplied by Cliff on the second verse onwards.

Track Specification
Composed by Bruce Welch and Alan Tarney

Musicians

Brian Bennett	drums, percussion
Terry Britten	guitar
Alan Jones	bass
Duncan MacKay	keyboards
Alan Parker	guitar
Tim Renwick	guitar
Cliff Richard	vocals, backing vocals
Trevor Spencer	drums, percussion
Alan Tarney	backing vocals, guitar, bass, keyboards
Graham Todd	keyboards

Recording Details

Producer	Bruce Welch
Engineered by	Tony Clark and Haydn Bendall
Recording location	Abbey Road Studio 3, St. John's Wood, London
Recording date	15th January 1978 and 25th April 1978

♫ Count Us Out

Unissued track

The first of the five songs that appear in the *Life with Johnny* episode entitled *Johnny Come Home* featuring Cliff Richard as Johnny, *Count Us Out* is a short piece sung at the pub when Johnny moans to his friends and talks about making his fortune in London (made by Tyne Tees Television, the action takes place somewhere in the north-east of England). As he continues, he starts to sing this song that makes a mockery of the town and pub (and the song) by asking who would want to sing about 'this dump'. He reveals at the end that, while he has plans, he has no job lined up to go to in London.

The song is a straightforward tune with close harmony underpinning the sheer ennui that Johnny is trying to portray, with a guitar-led accompaniment that would do well on any of Cliff's albums. The song was recorded at Abbey Road but has never been released: an unusual step for EMI in those days, which may have been due to nervousness of limited appeal, although this is unlikely given the fact that they released other religious material by Cliff. The closing credits of the programme indicated that the songs were original (they are) and that they were written together by Cliff, David Winter, the programme's writer, and the four members of the Settlers – this is borne out in the credits for ***Where Is That Man?***, which was re-recorded and released on the album ***About That Man***.

Track Specification
Composed by Cliff Richard, David Winter, Cindy Kent, Mike Jones, John Fyffe and Geoffrey Srodzinski

Musicians

John Fyffe	backing vocals, guitar
Cindy Kent	backing vocals
Mike Jones	backing vocals, guitar
Cliff Richard	vocals
Geoffrey Srodzinski	backing vocals, bass
Unknown	organ

Recording Details

Producer	Norrie Paramor
Engineered by	Peter Vince
Recording location	Abbey Road Studio 3, St. John's Wood, London
Recording date	11th January 1969

♫ Crocodile Rock

From the album **Japan Tour '74**

Elton John's star was very much in the ascendency when he recorded the self-penned hit *Crocodile Rock* in 1972 as part of his *Don't Shoot Me, I'm Only the Piano-Player* album. When the song was released as a single in late 1972, it gave him his first number one in the US but it only reached number five in the UK. The song is a look back with nostalgia at rock and roll (that is, when it was relatively young) and the lyrics talk of a relationship with Suzie, a name that crops up in many early rock and roll standards. It has been covered by the Beach Boys, children's cartoon character Bob the Builder, the Baha Men, the Hit Crew, the Chipmunks, Ray Hamilton, David Osborne, the Moods Unlimited Orchestra and Joey Welz among several others.

Cliff Richard regularly performed songs in concert that were popular or resonated in some other way but that he had never (and would never) record in the studio. For the 1974 tour of Japan, he included *Crocodile Rock* as part of a ***Rock Medley***, bringing the selection right up to date: ***His Latest Flame, Chantilly Lace, Bony Maronie, Do You Wanna Dance?***, *Crocodile Rock* and *Do You Wanna Dance?* again to complete the medley. With the expected falsetto vocal introduction from the backing vocalists, Cliff takes the song at a faster pace than John's original but carries off the song off with his standard assuredness. In many respects, it is unfortunate for fans that he never attempted a studio version of the song because it is a superlative version.

Track Specification

Composed by Bernie Taupin and Elton John

Musicians

Cliff Hall	piano
Brian Lewis	backing vocals, guitar
Kevin Peak	acoustic guitar
Cliff Richard	vocals
Trevor Spencer	drums, percussion
Alan Tarney	backing vocals, bass
Bruce Welch	backing vocals, rhythm guitar

Recording Details

Producer	Toshiba EMI (no individual detailed)
Engineered by	Toshiba EMI (no individual detailed)
Recording location	Shinjuku Koseinenkin, Tokyo, Japan
Recording date	7th-8th October 1974

♫ Daddy's Home

82nd ***UK single*** *and from the albums* **Dressed for the Occasion Remaster** *and* **From a Distance ***** The Event Remaster** *and unissued live track*

Originally written and recorded by James Sheppard under the name Shep and the Limelites in 1961, *Daddy's Home* was in essence a sequel to the song that he had recorded five years earlier in another band called the Heartbeats, *A Thousand Miles Away*. Without too much originality, the melody was pretty similar to the earlier tune, although the lyrics were more meaningful and captured the audience's imagination. Both songs were a hit in Shep's homeland of the USA but didn't fare well in Britain. As with many popular tunes of the era, *Daddy's Home* was also covered by other artists including Gene Chandler, P. J. Proby, Barbra Streisand, Paul Anka, Montell Jordan, the Carpenters and the Jackson 5.

Cliff Richard regularly performed songs that he had not recorded in the studio, often because he had the records on the jukebox at his home (see also ***Silhouettes***) and really liked the song. In 1981, the BBC was constructing a four-part documentary about Cliff and, in order to support the narrative, they recorded a number of items from shows at the Hammersmith Odeon in London and the Manchester Apollo. Of the dozen or so tracks that were recorded, three of them were licensed for subsequent release: *Daddy's Home*, its eventual B-side ***Shakin' All Over*** and ***Stood Up*** (although this last remained unissued). Over a decade later, the three songs, one a medley, performed with Phil Everly were also released as part of the single ***All I Have to Do Is Dream***. Backed with the aforementioned *Shakin' All Over*, *Daddy's Home* was released as a single on the EMI label (licensed from the BBC, catalogue number EMI 5251) on 6th November 1981. It gave Cliff his ninth number two chart placing in the UK, while it sailed up the US charts, reaching the highest point of number twenty-three. The track was subsequently issued on the CD single release of ***Healing Love*** in 1993. The associated publicity video was filmed at Ewart's Studio based in Wimbledon, south London and featured Cliff in a mock bar-cum-café with pool tables that are initially empty and then filled with people who play the game, dance and lip-synch to back Cliff. He has a few days stubble on his face; possibly the first time that he has ever been filmed looking so – deliberately, of course - dishevelled and he is met by the mother of his child and the daughter, who carries a doll. The girl doesn't look too convinced about Cliff but she hands him the doll she has been carrying, which he brings out at the end of the song as the bar completely empties. This proffering of the gift is timed with the live performance where he utters "Thank you". While it matches the receipt of the doll, it was in fact to one of the front row fans who had given him a rose.

The song's gentleness is initiated by electric keyboards, while the close harmony backing vocals are what make the song a perfect choice for him to perform. Cliff is never better than when he has an effective chorale of harmonized vocals to support him and there are sections when it is *a capella*, while his anguished vocals match the lyrics' emotion in the lyrics.

The song was included in the Royal Albert Hall concert recorded for the ***Dressed for the Occasion*** album and, although it was mixed ready for release, it was left off, possibly due to space considerations but also to make way for songs not recorded in the studio, such as ***Treasure of Love*** and ***Softly as I Leave You***. However, it was included on the remastered album. The close harmonies, keyboards and string arrangement reflect an almost perfect replica of the original recording.

The song was on the set list of the 1988 *Live & Guaranteed 1988!* tour and, while the whole performance was filmed and recorded for a video release and the subsequent accompanying CD, *Daddy's Home* remains unissued. Similarly, when it was performed at Wembley Stadium for the thirtieth anniversary concerts, it was not issued on the 1990 album release of ***From a Distance ***** The Event*** although it was restored on a two-CD remaster of the album in 2005. Since the song as released was a live track originally, it is hardly surprising that this version should be so close to it, replete with the languid saxophone accompaniment.

Track Specification
Composed by James Sheppard and William Miller

1. Single
Musicians

Stuart Calver	backing vocals
Howie Casey	saxophone
John Clark	guitar
Mark Griffiths	bass
Graham Jarvis	drums, percussion
Martin Jenner	guitar
Alan Park	keyboards
John Perry	backing vocals
Cliff Richard	vocals
Tony Rivers	backing vocals
Graham Todd	keyboards

Recording Details

Producer	Cliff Richard
Engineered by	Unknown
Recording location	Hammersmith Odeon, London
Recording date	1st May 1981

2. *Dressed for the Occasion Remaster*

Musicians	
Stuart Calver	backing vocals
David Cooke	synthesiser
Steve Gray	piano
Mark Griffiths	bass
Tony Harding	backing vocals
Richard Hewson	arranger, conductor
Graham Jarvis	drums, percussion
London Philharmonic Orchestra	orchestra
John Perry	backing vocals
Cliff Richard	vocals
Tony Rivers	backing vocals

Recording Details	
Producer	Cliff Richard and Richard Hewson
Engineered by	John Kurlander
Mixed by	Keith Bessey
Recording location	Royal Albert Hall, London
Mixed at	Strawberry Studios South, Surrey
Recording date	23rd November 1982

3. *Unissued track (Live & Guaranteed 1988!)*

Musicians	
John Clark	guitar
Rosemarie Ford	backing vocals
Mark Griffiths	bass
Peter Howarth	backing vocals
Steve Lauri	guitar
Paul Moessl	keyboards
Mick Mullins	backing vocals
Alan Park	keyboards
Cliff Richard	vocals
Henry Spinetti	drums, percussion

Recording Details	
Producer	Unknown
Engineered by	Unknown
Recording location	Fyens Forum, Odense, Denmark
Recording date	22nd May 1988

4. *From a Distance *** The Event***

Musicians	
Ray Beavis	saxophone
John Clark	guitar
Sonia Jones-Morgan	backing vocals
Steve Lauri	guitar
Peter May	drums, percussion
Paul Moessl	keyboards
Tessa Niles	backing vocals
Alan Park	keyboards
Provox:	
Peter Howarth	backing vocals
Mick Mullins	backing vocals
Keith Murrell	backing vocals
Cliff Richard	vocals
Steve Stroud	bass

Recording Details	
Producer	Cliff Richard
Engineered by	Keith Bessey and Mick McKenna
Recording location	Rolling Stones Mobile Studio, Wembley Stadium, Wembley, North-west London
Recording date	16th-17th June 1989

♫ Dancing Shoes

B-sides to **Summer Holiday** *and* **Singing the Blues** *(download only) and from the albums* **The Rock 'n' Roll Years 1958-1963** *and* **Japan Tour '74**

One of the songs that were written for the film ***Summer Holiday*** by Hank Marvin and Bruce Welch, the rocking track was composed in just a day and entitled *Dancing Shoes,* which features as the four bus mechanic friends go off into the Yugoslavian fields to try and find some food, while the girls they have picked up remain back at the bus. Don (Cliff Richard) stops a peasant woman by a large hayrick and tries to impress on her that they need sustenance and to find out how they can get it. With much stereotypical Englander abroad, the four men talk slowly and loudly, adding the embarrassing 'o' and 'ee' on the end of words in vain to try to get themselves understood. One of the group (played by Teddy Green) tries to mime eating the straw but then falls over causing the woman to laugh. But then, for no reason, she begins to cry and Don is exhorted to sing her a song to cheer up, the result of which is *Dancing Shoes.* She tries to get away from the boys' antics before succumbing and joining in with the twist on the hay. After the song, a misunderstanding over a dictionary translation makes her think that Don has proposed and the boys are taken to the village for the wedding.

Although the sequence was purported to be the former Yugoslavia, the scene was actually shot in a hay-field in Greece. The song was chosen as the B-side of the second single and theme tune for the film, ***Summer Holiday***, and was the first song to be recorded in the session that produced both the A- and B-sides. The fourth and final take and edit was used or the mono and stereo recordings with different mixes for the audio channels and it featured on the track listing of the ***Hits from Summer Holiday*** EP. The recording session was noteworthy particularly for this song as it was the first studio recording for a Cliff Richard song to feature Brian Locking on bass guitar, replacing Jet Harris at very short shrift (his last recording session had been just four days before). The film version was recorded at the Elstree Studios later that same year but has not been released in any other format. That version, though, is very similar to that released as the B-side and on the soundtrack album.

A classic Shadows-driven track, the backing vocals harmonies against the lead vocal disappear into the right channel, while the unaccompanied lead vocal is centred. The song uses characters from nursery rhymes and children's stories (something that Hank Marvin and Bruce Welch would use in later songs), usually who have some calamity to deal with, and, following the advice of dancing to soothe their woes, their outlook will automatically improve. With hand-claps providing additional rhythm to the drums and driving guitar and bass, Cliff's vocals are never better in this genre than when singing this style of song.

The live track that was released on the album ***The Rock 'n' Roll Years 1958-1963*** was taken from Cliff and the Shadows' debut performance in France, recorded at the Paris Olympia Theatre and broadcast live on Europe 1 and, at the time, *Dancing Shoes* was a considerable favourite being in the proximity of the release of the *Summer Holiday* film. This version is a pretty faithful live revisioning of the film track, although there are some vocal differences as Cliff exhorts all to 'come on'. For the Japanese tour in 1974, Cliff created a ***Hit Medley*** that featured a number of his sixties hits: ***Congratulations, In the Country***, *Dancing Shoes*, ***The Day I Met Marie, On the Beach*** and ***Sing a Song of Freedom***. Here the guitar and bass are the principal instruments as Cliff clearly relishes the opportunity to dust the song off once again.

In 2009, while compiling the fiftieth anniversary album ***Reunited***, Cliff and the Shadows chose to re-record *Dancing Shoes*. Although not issued on the album, it was released on the download-only version of the only single to be released from the enterprise, ***Singing the Blues***. The rhythm guitar is much more in evidence in this version than the original, while the beauty of the blend of the backing vocals is once again in evidence.

Track Specification
Composed by Hank Marvin and Bruce Welch

1. B-side (Summer Holiday)

Musicians		*Recording Details*	
Brian Bennett	drums, percussion	Producer	Norrie Paramor
Brian 'Licorice' Locking	bass	Engineered by	Malcolm Addey
Hank Marvin	backing vocals, guitar	Recording location	Abbey Road Studio 2, St. John's Wood, London
Cliff Richard	vocals	Recording date	5th May 1962
Unknown	hand-claps		
Bruce Welch	backing vocals, rhythm guitar		

2. The Rock 'n' Roll Years 1958-1963

Musicians		*Recording Details*	
Brian Bennett	drums, percussion	Producer	Unknown
Brian 'Licorice' Locking	bass	Engineered by	Unknown
Hank Marvin	guitar	Recording location	Olympia Theatre, Paris
Cliff Richard	vocals	Recording date	14th May 1963
Unknown	hand-claps		
Bruce Welch	rhythm guitar		

3. Japan Tour '74

Musicians		*Recording Details*	
Cliff Hall	piano	Producer	Toshiba EMI (no individual detailed)
Brian Lewis	backing vocals, guitar	Engineered by	Toshiba EMI (no individual detailed)
Kevin Peak	acoustic guitar	Recording location	Shinjuku Koseinenkin, Tokyo, Japan
Cliff Richard	vocals	Recording date	7th-8th October 1974
Trevor Spencer	drums, percussion		
Alan Tarney	backing vocals, bass		
Bruce Welch	backing vocals, rhythm guitar		

4. B-side (Singing the Blues - download)

Musicians		*Recording Details*	
Brian Bennett	drums, percussion	Producer	Warren Bennett (co-ordination)
Mark Griffiths	bass	Engineered by	James Collins (Honeyhill Studios), Ethan Carlson (Middle Ear Studios), Les Williams (Nivram Studios) and Keith Bessey (mixing and mastering)
Hank Marvin	backing vocals, guitar	Recording location	Middle Ear Studios, Miami, Florida, USA (Cliff's vocals), Nivram Studios, Perth, Western Australia (Hank's guitars and vocals) and Honeyhill Studios, Hertfordshire, England (all other vocals and instruments)
Cliff Richard	vocals, backing vocals	Recording date	Early 2009
Bruce Welch	backing vocals, rhythm guitar		

♫ Dangerous Game

Single by **Network 3**

The second and final single to be recorded by Network 3 was, like its predecessor, produced by Cliff Richard. Having changed their name from Nutshell prior to these recordings in 1980, Network 3 were a Christian folk group who had been recording since 1976, although the group split up shortly after the single's release leaving Paul Field to forge a solo career and Mo McCafferty and Annie McCaig to become sought-after session vocalists. Backed with ***Come Go with Me***, *Dangerous Game* was issued on the EMI label (catalogue number EMI 5205) later in 1981, although, like ***Last Train Home***, it also failed to make an impression on the charts, in spite of its pedigree. There is very little information available regarding

the recording sessions – technical and performing personnel, location, dates and so on – so these have been left as unknown until additional information becomes available.
As was the musical vogue for the period, Network 3 opt for a performance that is supported more by synthesisers and piano than the guitars of the first single, and *Dangerous Game* sounds more like a performance from a stage show, although it has the sound of the period too with the strong vocal arrangement. This features Cliff in a minor capacity supplying backing vocals and there is a synthesiser solo in the middle eight and a saxophone solo over the repeating chorus to the end.

Track Specification
Composed by Paul Field and Dave Cooke

Musicians

Paul Field	vocals
Mo McCafferty	vocals
Annie McCaig	vocals
Cliff Richard	backing vocals
Unknown	guitar
Unknown	bass
Unknown	piano
Unknown	keyboards
Unknown	saxophone
Unknown	drums, percussion

Recording Details

Producer	Cliff Richard
Engineered by	Unknown
Recording location	Unknown
Recording date	1980

♫ Danny

From the album **Cliff**

The song *Danny* had been recorded by both Elvis Presley and Marty Wilde in the late fifties and so it had good provenance for inclusion on the 'live' set list for the *Cliff* album, the first long-player issued by Cliff Richard and the Drifters. It was performed over two consecutive nights in front of an invited audience drawn from the band's and Cliff's fan base, which explains a lot of the screaming on the tracks. However, that noted and as with the earlier ***Donna***, on the issued recording there is no screaming during the performance. Both tracks feature backing vocals by the Mike Sammes singers and it is suggested that they were recorded separately with the initial and ending screams edited in.
Another ballad, it is a gentle song that talks of the singer's concerns about a relationship. Unlike *Donna*, which Cliff later said was a terrible recording, this is a brilliant rendition of *Danny* with assured vocals by Cliff and perfect accompaniment from the Drifters. The Mike Sammes Singers seem too much for the minimalist approach to the song and it's a shame that it would take a few more recordings to establish the perfect blend particularly of Cliff's, Hanks and Bruce's voices.

Track Specification
Composed by Ben Weisman and Fred Wise

Musicians

Jet Harris	bass
Hank Marvin	guitar
Tony Meehan	drums, percussion
Mike Sammes Singers	backing vocals
Cliff Richard	vocals
Bruce Welch	rhythm guitar

Recording Details

Producer	Norrie Paramor
Engineered by	Peter Bown and Stuart Eltham
Recording location	Abbey Road Studio 2, St. John's Wood, London
Recording date	10th February 1959

♫ Danny Boy

From the album **Two's Company**

More often than not set to the tune of *Londonderry Air*, the lyrics were written by Frederick Weatherly in 1910 with the intended purpose of using a different tune. Published in 1913, it was only afterwards that the words were adjusted for application to the *Londonderry Air*. As would be expected given the tune setting, it is a song that is most associated with Ireland and, in particular, the Northern Irish. It was originally intended as a love ballad from a woman to a man, although Weatherly suggested the alternative 'Eily dear' for male singers to perform; however, more often than not, it is men singing the original and it is since taken on a subtext of a parent waving off a son going to war or even the Irish mass emigration particularly to America in the nineteenth century. It has been covered by artists from a wide variety of genres including the Calico Consort, Hayley Westenra, the Ten Tenors, G4, Bryn Terfel, Johnny Cash, Nigel Kennedy, Eva Cassidy, Harry Connick Jr., Carly Simon, Mary O'Hara, Charlotte Church, Elvis Presley, Joan Baez, Cher, the Bachelors, Conway Twitty, Sinéad O'Connor, Paul Robeson and Daniel O'Donnell among several others.
In 2002, the Belgian singer-songwriter Helmut Lotti invited Cliff Richard to duet with him on his version for the upcoming *Pop Classics in Symphony* album to be released the following year. It was later included as the penultimate track on the collection of duets by Cliff, ***Two's Company***.
The swelling strings of the orchestra and piano introduce the song with Cliff taking the first honours at singing, with a slight echo added to his vocal line. Helmut Lotti joins Cliff in harmony in the chorus, creating a lovely intensity that is matched by Cliff's pitch-perfect high notes. Lotti takes control for the second part of the song with Cliff in a supporting role, singing in the highest part of his range, creating a brilliant and unique performance from a song that is so familiar.

Track Specification
Composed by Frederick Weatherly set to a traditional tune

Musicians

Golden Symphonic Orchestra	orchestra
Helmut Lotti	vocals
Cliff Richard	vocals
Unknown	backing vocals
Unknown	piano
André Walschaerts	conductor

Recording Details

Producer	Peter Koelewijn
Engineered by	Hans von Vondelen
Recording location	Fendal Sound Studio, Netherlands
Recording date	2002

♫ Das Ist Die Frage Aller Fragen

German single

The German version of the popular tune ***Spanish Harlem*** literally translates to *That Is the Question of All Questions* and was recorded by Cliff Richard in November 1964 for single release in Germany, as well as being covered by parochial artists such as Howard Carpendale and Lose Skiffle Gemeinschaft. Although research indicates that the original instrumentation track from the English version in 1961 was used with Cliff's new vocals overdubs, listening to the performance appears to show that instruments were added or that the edit was remixed to bring those instruments forward. The same combined take and edit were used for the mono and stereo recordings but with different mixes for the separate audio channels.

The single was initially released in mono format only, backed with the German language version of ***On the Beach*** from the recently released ***Wonderful Life*** film, ***Nur Mit Dir***, on the German Columbia label (catalogue number C-22811) in November 1964 shortly after Cliff added his new vocals. Simultaneously, the English version of *Spanish Harlem* was also issued and both versions hit the number one spot in Germany. The song was a considerable rarity in the UK, since it was never issued in that country, and the stereo version was eventually issued on the 1997 German compilation of all Cliff's foreign language recordings ***On the Continent***, along with its B-side.

Since the song uses the same backing track as the English version, there is very little to distinguish the later version other than the different language in which it is sung. Cliff manages the foreign language pronunciation very well coupled with ensuring another pitch-perfect rendition.

Track Specification
Composed by Jerry Leiber and Phil Spector; German lyrics by Carl Ulrich Blecher

Musicians

Mike Sammes Singers	backing vocals
Norrie Paramor Orchestra	orchestra
Norrie Paramor	arranger, conductor
Cliff Richard	vocals

Recording Details

Producer	Norrie Paramor (backing track and vocals)
Engineered by	Malcolm Addey and Norman Smith (backing track) and Malcolm Addey (vocals)
Recording location	Abbey Road Studio 2, St. John's Wood, London (backing track and vocals)
Recording date	4th December 1961 (backing track) and 10th October 1964 (vocals)

♫ Dawn Down in Durban

Single by **Garth Hewitt**

Cliff Richard continued his association with Christian singer Garth Hewitt when he sang backing vocals on his 1981 South Africa released single *Dawn Down in Durban*. Also accompanying Hewitt were Paul Field, Mo McCafferty and Annie McCaig, who were recording their singles under the name Network 3, with Cliff producing. The other technical and musician information is not readily available and has been noted as unknown in the track specification. *Dawn Down in Durban* was conceived and written in the Umhlanga Rocks above the South African city of Durban. Backed with Hewitt's version of ***Under the Influence*** (recorded without Cliff's involvement), it was released as a single on the EMI label (catalogue number EMIJ 4371) in 1981 but in South Africa only and is a considerable rarity on vinyl. The track can now be found on the CD collection of Hewitt's African-inspired songs, *Wings of Love over Africa*, which was released in 2007.

Track Specification
Composed by Garth Hewitt

Musicians

Paul Field	backing vocals
Garth Hewitt	vocals
Mo McCafferty	backing vocals
Annie McCaig	backing vocals
Cliff Richard	backing vocals
Unknown	all instrumentation

Recording Details

Producer	Tom Blades
Engineered by	Unknown
Recording location	Unknown
Recording date	1981

♫ Day by Day

From the album **Help It Along**

One of the most recognisable and frequently covered songs from the *Godspell* musical, *Day by Day* is also featured in a number of films such as *Meet the Parents* (where Ben Stiller's character recites the lyrics instead of saying grace) and it is used for a song in a talent show in *Wet Hot American Summer*. The musical is essentially a modern take on the Christian

story and, for this reason, the song is often used as an inspiration by gospel singers. Covered by many acts including Jacqueline Dankworth, Percy Faith, Judy Collins, Shirley Bassey, Hot Butter and the New Seekers, it was Holly Sherwood who had a minor chart hit with it when her version reached number twenty-nine in February 1972.
The idea of the ***Help It Along*** album was to record a number of religiously motivated songs in aid of the Tear Fund, of which charity Cliff Richard remains a patron. Performed in front of a small audience in the Morgan Studios across seven sessions in three consecutive days, *Day by Day* was one of thirteen tracks released out of seventeen recorded.
With a slightly swinging feel to the tempo at the start, it relinquishes itself to the rocking rhythm of the principal performance, accompanied by a clucking, wowing guitar that was the choice of the day. Cliff comes in to rapturous applause and he sings the song well, with the female backing vocalists harmonizing well behind him on the opening bars although they become a little too strident in the later stages of the song.

Track Specification
Composed by Stephen Schwartz

Musicians		*Recording Details*	
Terry Britten	guitar	Producer	David MacKay
Barrie Guard	arranger, conductor, percussion	Engineered by	Roger Quested
Cliff Hall	keyboards	Recording location	Morgan Studios, London
Jean Hawker	backing vocals	Recording date	24th, 25th and 26th September 1973
Anna Peacock	backing vocals		
Kevin Peek	guitar		
Cliff Richard	vocals		
Trevor Spencer	drums, percussion		
Alan Tarney	bass		
Unknown	orchestra		

♫ Day I Met Marie, The

***39th UK single** and from the albums* **...And They Said It Wouldn't Last! (My 50 Years in Music)**, **Live at the Talk of the Town**, **Live in Japan**, **Cliff Live in Korea**, **Cliff "Live" in Japan '72**, **Japan Tour '74** *and* **Thank You Very Much** *and unissued live track*

Recorded separately by Hank Marvin (for his *Hank Plays Cliff* album) and the Shadows on the live albums of their final tours, *The Day I Met Marie* was Cliff Richard's thirty-ninth UK single. For a long time, Cliff Richard confirmed that *The Day I Met Marie* was his favourite song and still remains among his most much-loved songs from the hundreds he has recorded.
It was issued as a single, backed with ***Our Story Book*** from an earlier session, on the Columbia label (catalogue number DB 8245) on 11th August 1967, and it reached number ten in the UK singles charts. The single version was only released in mono format only, which was the protocol adopted by Columbia at the time, referring the stereo releases to albums only alongside the mono partner. The stereo version was first released two years later on the ***Best of Cliff*** compilation album in 1969. On the celebratory rarity and favourites compilation album ***...And They Said It Wouldn't Last! (My 50 Years in Music)*** in 2008, another take was released (the first of an unknown number from the session) but this only in mono.
What marks this song as a brilliant composition is the light and shade exhibited throughout by Cliff as he sings the slower passage set to a plucked guitar, setting the scene of his day with a girl, and the juxtaposition of the upbeat choruses accompanied by what is almost a German brass band style of rousing, as he remembers how the day turned out. There is a group of backing vocalists – quite possibly the Breakaways, who were regularly recording and touring with Cliff at this time – who are uncredited and sing during the upbeat choruses.
At the end of September 1967, Cliff went back into the Abbey Road studios to record original material and vocal overdubs in Italian and German. On this occasion, he recorded a German translation of *The Day I Met Marie* (***Ein Sonntag mit Marie***), which became the B-side of the German single ***Es Ist Nicht Gut, Allein zu Sein*** and an Italian translation (***Imagina un Giorno***), which was released as a single in Italy. Both vocal lines were overdubbed on the same orchestral backing track that had been recorded in a session on the previous day.
The song was on the set list for his Far East tour at the end of 1967 and, although it was recorded as part of the ***Cliff in Japan*** concert album, the track remains unissued. It also formed part of a medley of Hank Marvin compositions on the ***Live at the Talk of the Town*** album along with ***London's Not Too Far*** and ***The Dreams I Dream***. The version on *Cliff Live in Korea* was recorded for the Korean market only and has only ever been issued in mono format. For the Japanese tour in 1974, Cliff developed a ***Hit Medley*** that featured a number of his sixties hits: ***Congratulations, In the Country, Dancing Shoes***, *The Day I Met Marie*, ***On the Beach*** and ***Sing a Song of Freedom***. The transition into the song feels awkward but the song is picked up cleverly in the middle of the first chorus and onwards to the end of the song.
On the ***Cliff "Live" in Japan '72*** album, it is Hank who plays the introductory guitar and the initial verse sounds very similar to the studio original, while the upbeat central section is brought to life with the girls' backing vocals and the fun the band is having in its performance of the ebullient choruses.
In 1978, the song was resurrected again for ***Thank You Very Much*** at the London Palladium, and is introduced by Cliff with much joshing towards Bruce Welch and Hank Marvin about age of suits, dandruff and brilliant songs that have yet to be given to him. The same approach to the live version is taken as the original with the gentle verses and the upbeat choruses, although the latter have less emphasis because of the lack of orchestra.

Track Specification
Composed by Hank Marvin

1. Single

Musicians

Mike Leander Orchestra	orchestra
Mike Leander	arranger, conductor
Cliff Richard	vocals
Unknown	backing vocals

Recording Details

Producer	Norrie Paramor
Engineered by	Peter Vince
Recording location	Abbey Road Studio 2, St. John's Wood, London
Recording date	1st June 1967

2. ...And They Said It Wouldn't Last! (My 50 Years in Music)

Musicians

Mike Leander Orchestra	orchestra
Mike Leander	arranger, conductor
Cliff Richard	vocals

Recording Details

Producer	Norrie Paramor
Engineered by	Peter Vince
Recording location	Abbey Road Studio 2, St. John's Wood, London
Recording date	1st June 1967

3. Unissued track (Cliff in Japan)

Musicians

Norrie Paramor Orchestra	orchestra
Norrie Paramor	arranger, conductor
Cliff Richard	vocals
Unknown	backing vocals

Recording Details

Producer	Norrie Paramor
Engineered by	Unknown
Recording location	Shibuya Public Hall, Tokyo, Japan
Recording date	18th October 1967

4. Live at the Talk of the Town

Musicians

Breakaways:	backing vocals
Vicki Hasemen	
Margo Quantrell	
Jean Ryder	
Norrie Paramor	arranger, conductor
Cliff Richard	vocals
Talk of the Town Orchestra	orchestra

Recording Details

Producer	Norrie Paramor
Engineered by	Peter Vince
Recording location	Talk of the Town Theatre, London
Recording date	30th May 1968

5. Cliff Live in Korea

Musicians

Brian Bennett	drums, percussion
Alan Hawkshaw	keyboards
Hank Marvin	backing vocals, guitar
Cliff Richard	vocals
John Rostill	backing vocals, bass
Bruce Welch	backing vocals, rhythm guitar

Recording Details

Producer	Unknown
Engineered by	Unknown
Recording location	Citizen Hall, Seoul, South Korea
Recording date	16th October 1969

6. Cliff "Live" in Japan '72

Musicians

Brian Bennett	drums, percussion
Pat Carroll	backing vocals
John Farrar	bass
Alan Hawkshaw	piano
Hank Marvin	guitar
Olivia Newton-John	backing vocals
Cliff Richard	vocals
Bruce Welch	rhythm guitar

Recording Details

Producer	Norrie Paramor
Engineered by	Unknown
Recording location	Kosei Nenkin Hall, Tokyo, Japan
Recording date	22nd-23rd September 1972

7. Japan Tour '74

Musicians

Barrie Guard	arranger, conductor, piano
Cliff Hall	piano
Brian Lewis	backing vocals, guitar
Kevin Peak	acoustic guitar
Cliff Richard	vocals
Shambles Symphonet	orchestra
Trevor Spencer	drums, percussion
Alan Tarney	backing vocals, bass
Bruce Welch	backing vocals, rhythm guitar

Recording Details

Producer	Toshiba EMI (no individual detailed)
Engineered by	Toshiba EMI (no individual detailed)
Recording location	Shinjuku Koseinenkin, Tokyo, Japan
Recording date	7th-8th October 1974

8. Thank You Very Much

Musicians

Brian Bennett	drums, percussion
Alan Jones	bass
Cliff Hall	keyboards
Hank Marvin	backing vocals, guitar
Cliff Richard	vocals
Bruce Welch	backing vocals, rhythm guitar

Recording Details

Producer	Bruce Welch
Engineered by	Tony Clark, remixed by Peter Vince
Recording location	London Palladium, London
Remix location	Abbey Road Studios, St. John's Wood, London
Recording date	4th March 1978

♫ Days Go By

From the album **Days Go By** *(Aleksander John)*

The eponymous song from the 1974 solo album by Aleksander John (the pseudonym of Aleksander Mežek) features Cliff Richard on backing vocals and represents the first example of Cliff assisting other artists outside of the Shadows that started in the seventies. The album is very rare and, by association, so is the track.

Employing the same basic instrumental group as Cliff used on his recordings of the time, the song is an upbeat guitar-driven track that suggests that the successive generations believe they know what is going on, although, more often than not, they don't. Cliff's voice in the backing vocal section is discernible but he keeps it tight to avoid overwhelming the other performers. The song keeps an uplifted, summery feel to its exposition and it becomes one of the best tracks on the album.

Track Specification

Composed by Unknown

Musicians

Terry Britten	acoustic guitar, electric guitar
Cliff Hall	keyboards
Aleksander John	vocals, backing vocals
Sally Kemp	backing vocals
Dave MacRae	keyboards
Kevin Peek	acoustic guitar
Cliff Richard	backing vocals
Trevor Spencer	drums, percussion
Alan Tarney	backing vocals, bass

Recording Details

Producer	Barrie Guard
Engineered by	Greg Jackman and Roger Quested
Recording location	Morgan Studios, London
Recording date	Summer 1974

♫ Days of Love, The

B-side of **Help It Along/Tomorrow Rising**

Over several weeks on Saturday nights, Cliff Richard performed each of the six shortlisted Song for Europe contenders for the 1973 Eurovision Song Contest. Performing them on *Cilla* hosted by Cilla Black on BBC1, *The Days of Love* was the fourth song to be performed before being reprised on the seventh week and opening it up to the public with a postal vote. Polling just 7.6% of the votes cast (against 51.8% of the eventual winner ***Power to All Our Friends***), it narrowly avoided being last of the group by coming just ahead of ***Ashes to Ashes*** (7.1%) and behind ***Tomorrow Rising*** (9%).

The song was recorded along with the other five contenders across a two-day session at the end of December 1972, with *The Days of Love* being the second of three to be completed (alongside *Ashes to Ashes* and ***Come Back Billie Jo***). As was customary, the winner and the second-placed song were released as a single, while the remaining four were usually released as an EP to accompany the single release. Unusually, the third- and fourth-placed songs, ***Help It Along*** and *Tomorrow Rising* were released as a literal joint A-side with *The Days of Love* and *Ashes to Ashes* forming a double B-side – and, while the cover had the correct title on it, the label suggested that it was incorrectly called just *Days of Love*. A significant rarity because of the low chart placing (twenty-nine), it did not appear in any other format until it was included on the remastered version of ***The 31st of February Street*** in 2004.

After *Help It Along*, *The Days of Love* has many more elements of Eurovision about it. Cliff is in his element and comfort zone with the song. Although it is a pleasant enough song, particularly in the middle eight with the dramatic orchestration and harmony vocals, it doesn't however have the immediate impact of the eventual winner.

Track Specification

Composed by Alan Hawkshaw and Dougie Wright

Musicians

Terry Britten	backing vocals, guitar
David MacKay Orchestra	orchestra
David MacKay	backing vocals, arranger, conductor
Kevin Peek	guitar
Cliff Richard	vocals
Trevor Spencer	backing vocals, drums, percussion
Alan Tarney	backing vocals, bass

Recording Details

Producer	David MacKay
Engineered by	Peter Vince
Recording location	Abbey Road Studio 2, St. John's Wood, London
Recording date	27th December 1972

♫ Day That I Stopped Loving You, The

From the album **Something's Goin' On**

Recorded during the sessions that also completed ***Santa's List***, *The Day That I Stopped Loving You* was one of the many songs submitted to Cliff Richard after he commissioned American writers to compose material for his new ***Something's Goin' On*** album, which was also recorded primarily in Nashville with American personnel to give it a genuine American feel. On Cliff's website in February 2005, it was suggested that *The Day That I Stopped Loving You* was going to be the next single to be released from the project, something that was backed up by a radio interview by Cliff in Chicago; however, this failed to materialize and the song was never issued other than on the parent album. It was made available as a download (as were the other album tracks) and, for this purpose, a radio edit was created with minor cuts to the introduction, the instrumental pause in the final chorus and the repeated final lines.

The sustained bass note and tinkling percussion initiate the track as the other instrumentation is brought in. The gentleness of touch in Cliff's lead vocal is sustained throughout the verse and opened up in the chorus, where Cliff has to sing complex musical intervals in this song that analyzes whether he would ever stop loving a partner or not.

Track Specification
Composed by Jennifer Kimball, Darrell Brown and Bobby Huff

Musicians

Andy Chrisman	backing vocals
Carl Gorodetsky	conductor
Mark Harris	backing vocals
John Hammond	drums, percussion
George Marinelli	guitar
Nashville String Machine	strings
Craig Nelson	bass
Amanda Omartian	backing vocals
Michael Omartian	keyboards
Cliff Richard	vocals
Biff Watson	drums, percussion

Recording Details

Producer	Michael Omartian
Engineered by	Terry Christian
Recording location	Sound House, Brentwood, Tennessee, USA, The Blue Room, Nashville, Tennessee, USA and Tennessee Sound Kitchen, Franklin, Tennessee, USA
Recording date	2003

♫ Deeper Meaning

From the album **Triumph in the Air** *(Sheila Walsh)*

For Sheila Walsh's second album, ***Triumph in the Air***, Cliff Richard relinquished the control of production to Craig Pruess (assisted by engineer Keith Bessey) and performed backing vocals on only a few of the tracks, including *Deeper Meaning*. The gentleness of the track is introduced on twinkling synthesisers. Walsh sings the song with a slight cracking anguish in her vocal as she tells of how God has shown her what her life means. More overtly religious than her previous album, it is a pleasant song that crosses effectively over into pop and is lifted by Cliff's backing vocals when they are employed.

Track Specification
Composed by Teri de Sario Purse and Bill Purse

Musicians

Graham Jarvis	drums, percussion
Craig Pruess	arranger, keyboards, electronics
Cliff Richard	backing vocals
Sheila Walsh	vocals, backing vocals

Recording Details

Producer	Craig Pruess, assisted by Keith Bessey
Engineered by	Keith Bessey
Recording location	Cloud 9 Studios, London, Strawberry Studios, London and/or Jacobs Studios, Farnham, Surrey
Recording date	September 1983-January 1984

♫ Deep Purple

From the album **...And They Said It Wouldn't Last! (My 50 Years in Music)**

American pianist Peter DeRose regularly performed on the NBC radio network with May Singhi and wrote and published the melody for *Deep Purple* to be played specifically as a piano work on the show. The sales of the sheet music soared after Paul Whiteman arranged a version for his orchestra in the late thirties and, as a result, lyricist Mitchell Parish added the now familiar words. Since then, it has become a classic and a much-covered song, with Larry Clinton's Orchestra being by far the most popular of the time. It has since been covered by a many different artists over the years, including Pat Boone, Ray Anthony, Bing Crosby, Val Doonican, Count Basie, Screaming Jay Hawkins, Ambrose and His Orchestra, Art Pepper, Benny Carter, Jack Hylton, Chet Baker, Artie Shaw, Dave Brubeck, Vic Damone, Woody Herman, Oscar Peterson, Duke Ellington, Spike Jones and Peter Skellern among many others. In the UK, the song has been taken into the charts three times: first in November 1957, when Billy Ward and His Dominoes reached number thirty for just one week; second by Nino Tempo and April Stevens, who hit number seventeen in the latter part of 1963; while the most famous contemporary version is probably by Donny and Marie Osmond, who reached number twenty-five with their last single in 1976. It was also chosen for the name of the heavy metal group after guitarist Ritchie Blackmore's grandmother reportedly kept requesting that his group play her favourite song (although there are no records of whether they did!).

Already issued as an instrumental by the Shadows on their album *Dance with the Shadows*, *Deep Purple* was included on the list of songs for Cliff Richard to record during the dual session at the Portuguese studios in May 1965. Of the six songs completed at that session, *Deep Purple* was the only one to remain unissued, although it was released as a forgotten gem on the celebratory rarity anthology ***...And They Said It Wouldn't Last! (My 50 Years in Music)***, but only in mono format. It is unclear why the song was not released at the time – Cliff was recording songs for two albums simultaneously (***Kinda Latin*** and ***Love Is Forever***) and it would have fit well with the track listing of the latter album. An acetate of the song was sold at auction in London in the mid-eighties, alerting collectors to the song's existence, although it would be over twenty years later that it would be formally released commercially by EMI.

With an emphasis on the bass guitar in the mix, Cliff's version sounds beautifully mellifluous as per the song's title. With a similar performance to that on their own version, the Shadows rhythm is driven on by the guitars and the drums and ticking cymbals, while there is a piano performing alongside them, which is likely to be Norrie Paramor.

Track Specification
Composed by Peter DeRose and Mitchell Parish

Musicians		*Recording Details*	
Brian Bennett	drums, percussion	Producer	Norrie Paramor
Hank Marvin	guitar	Engineered by	Unknown
Cliff Richard	vocals	Recording location	Estudios Valentim de Carvalho, Lisbon, Portugal
John Rostill	bass	Recording date	10th May 1965
Unknown	piano		
Bruce Welch	rhythm guitar		

♫ Deine Augen Träumen Mary

From the album **Hier Ist Cliff**

Cliff Richard's 1968 album ***Established 1958*** was plundered for many of the tracks found on ***Hier Ist Cliff***, his first fully German LP release. One such was ***What's Behind the Eyes of Mary?***, which was translated into German under the title *Deine Augen Träumen Mary* (or in English: *Your Eyes Dream of Mary*, which changes the meaning slightly). During the sixties, it was a cost-saving strategy to record new vocals and overdub them on a previously recorded backing track. Where Cliff's foreign language songs were concerned, this usually meant recording translated vocals and adding them to the original English backing track. However, for *Hier Ist Cliff*, all tracks were recorded anew. Released only in stereo, the track's rarity was diminished when it was included on the foreign language compilation ***On the Continent*** in 1997.

Once again, Norrie Paramor's arrangement has successfully replicated the Shadows sound from the original album. Cliff's vocal performance is as impassioned as the English version and he is clearly comfortable with singing in the German language. The instrumental break in the mid-section is a beautiful play-off between the members of the woodwind section, particularly the bassoon and oboe.

Track Specification
Composed by Hank Marvin and Brian Bennett; German lyrics by Joachim Relin

Musicians		*Recording Details*	
Norrie Paramor Orchestra	orchestra	Producer	Norrie Paramor
Norrie Paramor	arranger, director	Engineered by	Peter Vince
Cliff Richard	vocals	Recording location	Abbey Road Studio 2, St. John's Wood, London
		Recording date	27th November 1968

♫ Devil Woman

66th UK single *and from the albums* **40 Golden Greats**, **Thank You Very Much**, **Dressed for the Occasion**, **Live & Guaranteed 1988!** *and* **My Kinda Life**

Terry Britten had written a number of songs for Cliff Richard to record and was a fully-fledged member of his backing band but he struck gold with *Devil Woman*. Written in partnership with Christine Holmes, a sometime singer with Family Dogg (also performing under the name Kristine Sparkle) and occasional television presenter, Britten has stated in interview that he didn't know how it transpired but it appears that he didn't enjoy the experience particularly. It was Holmes who provided the story and title, although Britten didn't like it at first because there was already a Marty Robbins song of the same name. But he decided to run with the title anyway, while he provided the catchy riffs and hooks and the melody. Holmes was the first to record it, under her now shortened stage name of Kristine, although it didn't get anywhere in the charts.

Terry Britten had given Cliff a demo tape of the song but it remained in the stack at the office until Bruce Welch, looking for material, happened to play it and raved about it to Cliff, who subsequently agreed to record it. It was completed at the beginning of September 1975 in the first of two sessions that provided three A-sides (including ***Miss You Nights***, which was another important single to Cliff's chart rehabilitation and renaissance). Initially, the song was scheduled to be released as a single at the beginning of 1976; however, the Electric Light Orchestra had just released their single entitled *Evil Woman*. Fearing confusion amongst record-buyers, the single issue of *Devil Woman* was delayed until ELO's song was dropping back down the charts. Recorded in just three takes with an additional session for vocal overdubs, *Devil Woman* was backed with ***Love On***, which was recorded over six months later, and was issued on the EMI label (catalogue number EMI 2448) on 23rd April 1976. It reached number nine in the UK charts, giving Cliff his first top ten single since the Eurovision Song Contest entry ***Power to All Our Friends*** three years earlier.

The release created more controversy on top of the furore that erupted the year before with ***(There's a) Honky Tonk Angel***, which is a song about a prostitute trawling seedy bars for custom; something that Cliff admits he was naive about before pulling the single and refusing to sing it at events. Ignorant critics pounced on the *Devil Woman* title, without looking at the lyrics for the meaning, and took great joy in ripping into Cliff because the title had the word 'devil' and the word 'woman' in it, which for the perceived wholesome do-gooder such as Cliff was wrong because it talked about Satan and sex in just the title. There were many patronising critiques written at the time but it was Cliff who won through the battle with the requisite chart placing, and extraordinarily, his highest chart placing ever in the US Billboard charts when it settled at number six. Unfortunately for Cliff, there was an expectation that he would produce similar music from thereon in and therefore his next single ***I Can't Ask for Anything More Than You*** failed to get anywhere.

Cliff had taken the original *Devil Woman* song, a story of a man who perceives his bad luck is brought about by a woman who reads palms, and changed some of the lyrics in order to make it more upbeat and anti-occult – a point that many

critics missed as has been observed. Cliff often tells the story of a letter he received from an Australian fan, who was mixed up with the occult: a worried friend had suggested that she listen to Cliff's new single as she was a fan and, having taken the positive lyrics to heart, had turned her back on occultism and was now a member of the local church. It is this reaction, as well the groundbreaking sound that was created on the record, that made it such an important song for him and he regularly introduces the song in concerts prefaced with this story.
A number of other artists have recorded their version of the song, including Hayseed Dixie, James Last, Hank Marvin (on his *Hank Plays Cliff* and *Hank Plays Live* albums), Cradle of Filth, Shy, the Slingsby Hornets, Riot and Wolf Weiss. Cliff's version was reissued in the same single format in 1982 but didn't re-enter the charts. Later in the eighties, the original edit was revisited and remixed with more emphasis on the bass drums and cutting the song short in the fifth verse. This was released on the 1989 CD reissue of ***40 Golden Greats*** and has been issued in this format on subsequent compilations. There is no information available as to who remixed the song – or indeed why.
As with ***Miss You Nights***, it is difficult to appreciate the impact of first hearing the song and how extraordinary it was that Cliff was releasing such material. Starting with a shimmering synthesiser that oscillates between the stereo channels, this already generates a mystical quality. Cliff's vocal line is performed with slight hesitation and fear, underlining the lyrical and pursues the song to its end as he talk-sings some warnings to the woman he is trying to avoid.
It was included in the ***Thank You Very Much*** concerts at the London Palladium and showed how effective the song could be in performance with the judicious use of lighting. Closing the original release of ***Dressed for the Occasion***, the arrangement is focused more on the rock band element than on the orchestra, although the London Philharmonic makes itself felt. The performance feels more open than the foreboding original but it loses nothing for all that.
The Danish leg of the *Live & Guaranteed 1988!* tour was filmed for video release, although fewer than half the songs were issued. In 1995, the video was re-released with a CD album to accompany it, which incorporated *Devil Woman*.
Cliff revisited what he confirms is the song he wants to be most remembered for when putting together a new kind of album in 1992, ***My Kinda Life***. All of the tracks were to be the original recordings but tarted up to give them a fresher, more contemporary feel. For *Devil Woman*, there are additional guitars and the fade-out occurs fifteen or so seconds after the original, although this may be a product of the album generation process rather than a particular intent. This version was subsequently released as a bonus track on the second of the dual single release of ***Human Work of Art*** in June 1993.
The track listing on the DVD for the *World Tour Live* suggests that *Devil Woman* was the first of a medley of hits but this is incorrect since it begins with ***Green Light***, then *Devil Woman* and finishing with ***Carrie***, but, even so, it is unusually performed by the backing vocalists while Cliff left the stage to change into a different wardrobe.

Track Specification
Composed by Terry Britten and Christine Holmes; additional lyrics by Cliff Richard

1. Single

Musicians		*Recording Details*	
Terry Britten	guitar	Producer	Bruce Welch
Clem Cattini	drums, percussion	Engineered by	Tony Clark and John Barrett
Tony Harding	backing vocals	Recording location	Abbey Road Studio 2, St. John's Wood, London
John Perry	backing vocals	Recording date	8th and 9th September 1975
Cliff Richard	vocals		
Tony Rivers	backing vocals		
Alan Tarney	bass		
Graham Todd	keyboards		

2. 40 Golden Greats (CD version)

Musicians		*Recording Details*	
Terry Britten	guitar	Producer	Bruce Welch
Clem Cattini	drums, percussion	Engineered by	Tony Clark and John Barrett
Tony Harding	backing vocals	Recording location	Abbey Road Studio 2, St. John's Wood, London
John Perry	backing vocals	Recording date	8th and 9th September 1975
Cliff Richard	vocals		
Tony Rivers	backing vocals		
Alan Tarney	bass		
Graham Todd	keyboards		

3. Thank You Very Much

Musicians		*Recording Details*	
Terry Britten	guitar	Producer	Bruce Welch
Stuart Calver	backing vocals	Engineered by	Tony Clark, remixed by Peter Vince
Clem Cattini	drums, percussion	Recording location	London Palladium, London
Dave Christopher	guitar	Remix location	Abbey Road Studios, St. John's Wood, London
Mo Foster	bass	Recording date	4th March 1978
Graham Jarvis	drums, percussion		
Graham Murray	guitar		
John Perry	backing vocals		
Cliff Richard	vocals		
Tony Rivers	backing vocals		
Graham Todd	keyboards		

4. *Dressed for the Occasion*

Musicians		*Recording Details*	
Stuart Calver	backing vocals	Producer	Cliff Richard and Richard Hewson
David Cooke	synthesiser	Engineered by	John Kurlander
Steve Gray	piano	Mixed by	Keith Bessey
Mark Griffiths	bass	Recording location	Royal Albert Hall, London
Tony Harding	backing vocals	Mixed at	Strawberry Studios South, Surrey
Richard Hewson	arranger, conductor	Recording date	23rd November 1982
Graham Jarvis	drums, percussion		
London Philharmonic Orchestra	orchestra		
John Perry	backing vocals		
Cliff Richard	vocals		
Tony Rivers	backing vocals		

5. *Live & Guaranteed 1988!*

Musicians		*Recording Details*	
John Clark	guitar	Producer	Unknown
Rosemarie Ford	backing vocals	Engineered by	Unknown
Mark Griffiths	bass	Recording location	Fyens Forum, Odense, Denmark
Peter Howarth	backing vocals	Recording date	22nd May 1988
Steve Lauri	guitar		
Paul Moessl	keyboards		
Mick Mullins	backing vocals		
Alan Park	keyboards		
Cliff Richard	vocals		
Henry Spinetti	drums, percussion		

6. *My Kinda Life*

Musicians		*Recording Details*	
Terry Britten	guitar	Producer	Bruce Welch (original track) and Cliff Richard and Paul Moessl (new instrumentation)
Clem Cattini	drums, percussion	Engineered by	Tony Clark and John Barrett (original track) and Gerry Kitchingham and Ben Robbins (new instrumentation)
John Clark	guitar	Recording location	Abbey Road Studio 2, St. John's Wood, London (original track) and R. G. Jones Studios, Wimbledon, London (new instrumentation)
Tony Harding	backing vocals	Recording date	8th-9th September 1975 (original track) and 20th-23rd April 1992 (new instrumentation)
Richard Hewson	arranger, conductor		
John Perry	backing vocals		
Cliff Richard	vocals		
Tony Rivers	backing vocals		
Alan Tarney	bass		
Graham Todd	keyboards		
Unknown	orchestra		

♬ Devoted to You

From the album **The Coronation St Album** *(Various)*

Best known by the version that was recorded by the Everly Brothers, and which was released as the B-side of their version of ***Bird Dog***, *Devoted to You* managed to achieve a US chart entry on its merits when it reached number ten in the US, while it reached to top position in neighbouring Canada. *Devoted to You* has since been recorded by James Taylor and Carly Simon (the then married couple covered it for Simon's solo album *Boys in the Trees* in 1978), Skeeter Davies, the Seekers, Ali Campbell, the Beach Boys, Linda Ronstadt, Brian Hyland and Sandy Posey among others.

In the early days of *Coronation Street*, which originally premiered in late 1960 as an intended six-part kitchen-sink drama but then went on to become one of the longest-running continuing television serials in the world, the character of Ena Sharples was discussing the cherubic pop singer Cliff Richard and she suggested that he was a bit chubby. This had two immediate effects: one for Cliff to make sure he continued to watch his weight throughout his life and the next to confirm Cliff's love of the programme, often suggesting that he would be happy to do a cameo role as one of the actors in the background in the Rover's Return. So it made sense for him to contribute to the 1995 album that featured contributions from the programme's stars of the period. The choice of song was *Devoted to You* and, produced by Alan Tarney, Cliff performed the song with Denise Black, who played recurring character Denise Mitchell. On the issue of *The Coronation St. Album*, the song was the first found on the track listing.

Starting with signature keyboards and drum sequencing by producer Alan Tarney, who also provides backing vocals, Cliff and Denise Black's vocals come in singing in harmony. Cliff sings the main melody, while Black performs the simpler harmony line but the ensemble performance is extremely effective. The problem with these sorts of collections is that they can be excruciating but this track is expertly crafted and performed.

Track Specification

Composed by Felice Bryant and Boudleaux Bryant

Musicians		*Recording Details*	
Denise Black	vocals	Producer	Alan Tarney
Cliff Richard	vocals	Engineered by	Gerry Kitchingham
Alan Tarney	arranger, backing vocals, synthesisers, drum programming	Recording location	R. G. Jones Studios, Wimbledon, London
		Recording date	August-September 1995

♫ Diamonds on a Chain

B-side of **What Car?** *(DVD single)*

Recorded during the sessions for Cliff Richard's 2004 album, ***Something's Goin' On***, *Diamonds on a Chain* was held back from the album's release and instead added as a B-side of the DVD issue of the ***What Car?*** audio single release (with the promotional video for that song and others on it). It was subsequently added as an extra track on ***For Life***, which is essentially a reissue of the parent album with four tracks recorded at the sessions but released in a variety of other formats.

A curious diminished interval is played on the synthesiser at the beginning of the track before being joined by a simple guitar and Cliff's lead vocal. Gradually, the song builds up as Cliff emotes unspoken love for the object of his affection. The accompaniment and the backing vocals create an understated beauty running under Cliff's vocal. Unfortunately, the melody is not immediately memorable and takes a number of listens before the truth of the performance can be understood.

Track Specification

Composed by Don Poythress and Brian White

Musicians

George Cocchini	electric guitar
Scott Dente	acoustic guitar
Mark Hill	bass
Ken Lewis	percussion
Michael Mellett	backing vocals
Dan Needham	drums, percussion
Cliff Richard	vocals, backing vocals
Jeff Roach	keyboards

Recording Details

Producer	Monroe Jones
Engineered by	Jim Dineen
Recording location	The Bennett House, Nashville, Tennessee, USA and The Hideout, Franklin, Tennessee, USA
Recording date	2003-2004

♫ Dicitencello Vuie

From the album **When in Rome**

A song that was originally written in the Neapolitan dialect, *Dicitencello Vuie* (literally translated as *Say to You* but often taking the subtitle or English translation of *Just Say I Love Her*) has been recorded by a number of artists including Angelo Petisi, Mario Lanza, Jimmy Alleva, Nino Rossano, Jerry Hadley, Matt Morgan and Ion Piso, while its English equivalent has seen covers by artists such as Dean Martin, Vic Damone, Remo Capra, Tony Bennett, Eddie Fisher, Engelbert Humperdinck and Johnny Desmond among others.

Often it was the case that Cliff Richard recorded an English song – or the English equivalent of a foreign tune – and then applied overdubbed foreign vocals for release in the particular country. For *Dicitencello Vuie*, which was recorded for the ***When in Rome*** album, it was one of the few foreign language songs by Cliff that doesn't have a version he recorded in English. *Dicitencello Vuie* was recorded along with the bulk of the album's vocals across two days in May 1965 and overdubbed on a pre-recorded orchestral track completed seven months earlier. The unknown take and edit were used for the release in mono format only and was subsequently included on the ***Hits from When in Rome*** EP.

The simple love song sounds as if it has come straight from a continental film soundtrack to back some love disaster in the narrative. Cliff sings the first verse and chorus in Italian but the second is performed in English before reverting back to the Italian. The transition is seamless and the song suits Cliff's voice well.

Track Specification

Composed by Martin Kalmanoff, Sam Ward, Enzo Fusco, Jack Val, Jimmy Dale and Rodolfo Falvo

Musicians

Norrie Paramor Orchestra	orchestra
Norrie Paramor	arranger, conductor
Cliff Richard	vocals

Recording Details

Producer	John Lee and M. DiPonti (backing track) and Norrie Paramor (vocals)
Engineered by	Malcolm Addey
Recording location	EMI Studios, Milan (backing track) and Estudios Valentim De Carvalho, Lisbon (vocals)
Recording date	2nd-3rd October 1964 (backing track) and 14th May 1965 (vocals)

♫ Did He Jump?

From the album **Did He Jump... Or Was He Pushed?** *(Garth Hewitt)*

The title track from Garth Hewitt's ***Did He Jump... Or Was He Pushed?*** album was produced by Cliff Richard and, backed with ***Roll On*** (also from the album), was released as a single on the EMI label (catalogue number EMI 5017) at some point in 1979. Although it had the Cliff association and his star was once more in the ascendency at the time, the single didn't trouble the British charts.

After the raw energy and quirkiness of ***Big Black Mamba*** on the album, Hewitt returns to the safe ground of standard rock ballad driven by a throbbing bass, drums and percussion and an excellent guitar virtuoso performance by Jo Partridge. In the second chorus, Cliff's multiple backing vocals are brought in and the exquisite harmonies created add a level to the song that was somewhat sedentary to that point. But then he pushes it further by performing falsetto vocals and then a bass *sotto voce* accompaniment to the lead.

Track Specification
Composed by Garth Hewitt

Musicians	
Garth Hewitt	vocals, guitar
Graham Jarvis	drums, percussion
Mike Moran	guitar, keyboards
Jo Partridge	guitar
Cliff Richard	backing vocals, guitar
Dave Wintour	bass

Recording Details	
Producer	Cliff Richard
Engineered by	Tony Clark and Haydn Bendall
Recording location	Odyssey Studios, London
Recording date	1979

♬ Didn't He?

Unissued track

As a committed Christian, Cliff Richard regularly performed at or took part in close-knit gospel sessions or fronted large rallies such as the Way of Life, which took place at the Empire Pool (now the Arena) at Wembley. In April, 1975, he performed three songs: ***Love Never Gives Up, Why Me?*** and ***Didn't He?*** In addition, he spoke of his conversion to Christianity and what his faith meant to him. All three songs were recorded but only the first was issued when it appeared on the album *10th Way of Life Rally* later in 1975 to raise funds for charity. The album is a major rarity and many of the details regarding the recording are unknown or unavailable.

Track Specification
Composed by Unknown

Musicians	
Cliff Richard	vocals
Unknown	all instrumentation

Recording Details	
Producer	Unknown
Engineered by	Unknown
Recording location	Empire Pool, Wembley, Middlesex
Recording date	19th April 1975

♬ Different Is Beautiful

From the album **Progression** *(Vincenzo La Scola)*

Another song written by Peter and Michele Wolf, who had been instrumental in pulling together the tracks and recording of Cliff Richard's ***Real as I Wanna Be*** album, *Different Is Beautiful* is a duet between Cliff and Vincenzo La Scola who had worked together on the song ***Vita Mia***. It is quite possible that this track was recorded at the same sessions that produced that track for Cliff's album, although there is no available information to confirm that.

Track Specification
Composed by Peter Wolf and Michelle Wolf

Musicians	
Coolio	backing vocals
James Ingram	backing vocals
Vincenzo La Scola	vocals
Steve Lukather	guitar
Jennifer Paige	backing vocals
Cliff Richard	vocals
Unknown	keyboards
Unknown	conductor
Unknown	orchestra
Michelle Wolf	backing vocals

Recording Details	
Producer	Peter Wolf
Engineered by	Unknown
Recording location	Little America Recording Studios, Weiler, Austria
Recording date	1997 or 1998

♬ Dim Dim the Lights

From the album **Live at the ABC Kingston 1962**

Recorded by Bill Haley and His Comets as one of the first examples of rock and roll and covered by Eddie Rabbitt, *Dim Dim the Lights* is one of the few tracks that Cliff Richard (with the Shadows in this event) performed on stage but did not record in the studio. Performed live at the ABC Theatre in Kingston, the track was released first on the compilation album ***The Rock 'n' Roll Years 1958-1963***, before the entire concert was issued on the 2003 CD ***Live at the ABC Kingston 1962***, although this was in stereo only.

A typical rock and roll performance, the song has the familiar bass line, the chunking guitar, and the various pauses. At times the instrumentation threatens to overwhelm Cliff's lead vocals but he is clearly in his element with a fast-paced song such as this and it is obviously much appreciated by the adoring fans in the audience listening to the performance.

Track Specification
Composed by Beverley Ross and Julius Dixon

Musicians	
Brian Bennett	drums, percussion
Jet Harris	bass
Hank Marvin	guitar
Cliff Richard	vocals
Bruce Welch	rhythm guitar

Recording Details	
Producer	Norrie Paramor
Engineered by	Malcolm Addey and Ken Townsend
Recording location	ABC Theatre, Kingston, Surrey
Recording date	7th March 1962

♫ 'D' in Love

B-side of **I Love You** *and unissued live track*

One of a number of songs that Sid Tepper and Roy Bennett wrote for Cliff Richard during the early years, *'D' in Love* was chosen as the B-side of Cliff's first Christmas number one single, ***I Love You***. The identical take and edit were used for both mono and stereo issues but mixed differently for the benefit of the stereo channels. A further version was included on the anthology ***The Rock 'n' Roll Years 1958-1963***, which is effectively the same mix as used for the stereo but with the initial studio banter and count-in included; otherwise there is no difference between the two tracks. *'D' in Love* remained only available on copies of the single until it was included on the eighties album ***Rock on with Cliff Richard***.

The song is an excoriation of a girlfriend by the singer as to how she is shaping up in the love game – the 'D' of the title is a reference to school grades where 'C' is satisfactory and anything below that is less so. The introduction of the song elucidates further as he indicates how well she is doing academically but how bad she is when school is over and it's time for loving. Cliff's vocal is very strong, ably supported by the Shadows' instrumentation but there are few musical hooks to be instantly memorable. But that denigrates the qualities of the track, which is a functional rock and roll song.

Over forty years later, Cliff dusted the song down for his 2003 world tour to support the release of ***Wanted***. The set list included tracks from the album as well as songs never before performed and others that he had not performed for some years. The New Zealand concert was filmed for DVD release later in the year but a complementary CD album, *World Tour Live*, released the following year, only included a small subset of those performed and *'D' in Love* was one of those left off the track listing. This has Cliff on the rhythm guitar in a performance that is sadly missed from the track listing.

Track Specification

Composed by Sid Tepper and Roy C. Bennett

1. B-side (I Love You)

Musicians		*Recording Details*	
Jet Harris	bass	Producer	Norrie Paramor
Hank Marvin	guitar	Engineered by	Malcolm Addey and Norman Smith
Tony Meehan	drums, percussion	Recording location	Abbey Road Studio 2, St. John's Wood, London
Cliff Richard	vocals	Recording date	9th September 1960
Bruce Welch	rhythm guitar		

2. Unissued track (World Tour Live)

Musicians		*Recording Details*	
Anthony Clark	guitar	Producer	Keith Bessey
Dave Cooke	keyboards	Engineered by	Keith Bessey
Pete May	drums, percussion	Recording location	The Mission Winery, Napier, New Zealand
Alan Park	keyboards	Recording date	22nd February 2003
Cliff Richard	vocals, guitar		
Steve Stroud	bass		

♫ Discovering

B-side of **Where Do We Go from Here?** *and from the album* **Dressed for the Occasion Remaster**

The final track on the ***Now You See Me... Now You Don't*** album by Cliff Richard was the last of three written by Chris Eaton. As with many of his compositions and fitting in with the general tenor of the album, it is a gospel song dressed up with a modern pop sound. The second single from the project, ***Where Do We Go from Here?***, was also written by Eaton and *Discovering* was paired with it as the B-side. The song was subsequently reissued on the album *Yesterday Today Forever* album but with an earlier fade cutting off sixteen seconds of the synthesiser sounds that are on the album's trail-out.

Wind chimes usher in synthesisers and lead into Cliff's vocal in this six-eight swiftly moving song. Cliff's voice is engineered further back in the mix with a little echo and gradually, it comes forward as the song develops. Cliff sings his own backing vocals but these are not as prominently used as other album tracks, since they only appear on the trail out.

Discovering was on the set list of Cliff's Royal Albert Hall concert which was recorded for the ***Dressed for the Occasion*** album but not included in the final track listing, possibly for space consideration reasons. In 2004, because the song had been mixed ready for release at the time, it was successfully restored in the remastered version of the album along with four other tracks. The principal instrumentation is provided by the London Philharmonic Orchestra, although the drums, synthesiser and piano are in evidence from the rock band element.

Track Specification

Composed by Chris Eaton

1. B-side (Where Do We Go from Here?)

Musicians		*Recording Details*	
Mark Griffiths	fretless bass	Producer	Cliff Richard and Craig Pruess
Mart Jenner	acoustic guitar	Engineered by	John Walker and Steve Cook
Craig Pruess	piano, synthesisers, sequencer, electronic percussion, wind chimes	Recording location	Strawberry Studios South, Surrey
		Recording date	4th-15th January 1982
Cliff Richard	vocals, backing vocals		

2. *Dressed for the Occasion Remaster*

Musicians	
Stuart Calver	backing vocals
David Cooke	synthesiser
Steve Gray	piano
Tony Harding	backing vocals
Richard Hewson	arranger, conductor
Graham Jarvis	drums, percussion
London Philharmonic Orchestra	orchestra
John Perry	backing vocals
Cliff Richard	vocals
Tony Rivers	backing vocals

Recording Details	
Producer	Cliff Richard and Richard Hewson
Engineered by	John Kurlander
Mixed by	Keith Bessey
Recording location	Royal Albert Hall, London
Mixed at	Strawberry Studios South, Surrey
Recording date	23rd November 1982

♬ Dizzy Miss Lizzy

From the album **Don't Stop Me Now!** *and unissued live track*

One of the most familiar rock and roll songs from the fifties era that was never a hit in the UK, *Dizzy Miss Lizzy* has had a high profile after being covered by a number of different artists such as the Beatles, Gerry and the Pacemakers, Ronnie Hawkins, Jess Conrad, the Flying Lizards, Canned Heat, the Plastic Ono Band, the Saints and the writer Larry Williams.
One of the first recordings that were made by Cliff Richard with Mike Leander's arrangements, Cliff cites this as one of his most favourite. Recorded at one of the first sessions for the ***Don't Stop Me Now!*** album, *Dizzy Miss Lizzy* was the last song to be completed that day, requiring only one take, which was used for both the mono and stereo recordings.
A thumping bass and cow-bell percussion mixed with a brass section introduce the song, made less raucous by the treatment, but Cliff is clearly enjoying the opportunity to sing rock and roll. The Breakaways provide tongue-twisting backing vocals, which are better than the wavering quality of the Mike Sammes Singers on prior recordings.
Dizzy Miss Lizzy featured frequently on the subsequent tours and it was performed at the Tokyo show that was released as ***Cliff in Japan*** but this particular version, also with orchestral accompaniment, remains unissued to date.

Track Specification
Composed by Larry Williams

1. *Don't Stop Me Now!*

Musicians	
Breakaways:	backing vocals
Vicki Hasemen	
Margo Quantrell	
Jean Ryder	
Mike Leander Orchestra	orchestra
Mike Leander	arranger, conductor
Cliff Richard	vocals
Unknown	piano

Recording Details	
Producer	Norrie Paramor
Engineered by	Peter Vincent and Richard Lush
Recording location	Abbey Road Studio 2, St. John's Wood, London
Recording date	19th October 1966

2. *Unissued track (Cliff in Japan)*

Musicians	
Norrie Paramor Orchestra	orchestra
Norrie Paramor	arranger, conductor
Cliff Richard	vocals
Unknown	backing vocals

Recording Details	
Producer	Norrie Paramor
Engineered by	Unknown
Recording location	Shibuya Public Hall, Tokyo, Japan
Recording date	18th October 1967

♬ Doing Fine

From the album **Rock 'n' Roll Juvenile**

One of ten songs written or co-written by Terry Britten for ***Rock 'n' Roll Juvenile***, *Doing Fine* was recorded initially in a number of sessions at the EMI studios in Paris with vocals added at a separate session nine months later.
With a more choppy rhythm than the first track, *Doing Fine* relies more on synthesisers than the standard rock band set-up; however, this creates a fresh sound for a new era in Cliff Richard's career. The song features an abridged version of ***Travellin' Light*** in the second verse and this effectively matches with the tenor of that song with *Doing Fine*.

Track Specification
Composed by Terry Britten

Musicians	
Terry Britten	guitar, synthesiser
Stuart Calver	backing vocals
Lance Dixon	synthesiser
Herbie Flowers	bass
Graham Jarvis	drums, percussion
Bill Livesy	keyboards
John Perry	backing vocals
Cliff Richard	vocals
Tony Rivers	backing vocals
Graham Todd	keyboards

Recording Details	
Producer	Cliff Richard and Terry Britten
Engineered by	Tony Clark and Haydn Bendall
Recording location	Pathé Marconi, Paris, France (backing track) and Abbey Road Studio, St. John's Wood, London (vocals)
Recording date	18th-20th July 1978 (backing track) and 18th April 1979 (vocals)

♬ Donna

From the albums **Cliff** *and* **Rock 'n' Roll Silver**

Popularized by the single success by Ritchie Valens, which reached number twenty-nine in the UK charts, *Donna* was subsequently covered and released by Cliff Richard's rival Marty Wilde in March 1959, who took it to the number three spot. It has since been covered by Johnny Crawford, Donny Osmond and Daniel O'Donnell and was chosen for inclusion in the set list of Cliff and the Drifters' 'live' recording set at Abbey Road in February of 1959. Later, it was also featured on the band's second EP, entitled *Cliff No. 2*.

Cliff stated in an interview for the *From the Heart* album liner notes that he considered his first recording of the song was terrible. It's not that bad but he does sound less self-assured than on other tracks on the *Cliff* album. Given the amount of screaming that went on during the other songs, it is curiously absent from this song. The screaming of the fans is mixed in to the start and end of the track instead to create a streamlined segue between all the tracks. Along with ***Danny*** towards the end of the album, they are the only tracks to include the Mike Sammes Singers on backing vocals and it is suggested that the recordings of these two songs were done at a different time to manage the expense of bringing in the vocal group.

The second version, made twenty-four years later, for the ***Rock 'n' Roll Silver*** album was arranged and produced by Thunder, the group of musicians brought in by Cliff for the sessions and through which they treated the work as a kind of co-operative. The subdued version of *Donna* is introduced by a guitar solo that feeds into a vocal group, which includes Cliff's contribution in addition t the lead. Faithful to the original, this is brought up to date for the album.

Track Specification

Composed by Ritchie Valens

1. Cliff

Musicians

Jet Harris	bass
Hank Marvin	guitar
Tony Meehan	drums, percussion
Mike Sammes Singers	backing vocals
Cliff Richard	vocals
Bruce Welch	rhythm guitar

Recording Details

Producer	Norrie Paramor
Engineered by	Peter Bown and Stuart Eltham
Recording location	Abbey Road Studio 2, St. John's Wood, London
Recording date	9th February 1959

2. Rock 'n' Roll Silver

Musicians

Stuart Calver	backing vocals
Dave Cooke	keyboards
John Clark	electric guitar
Mark Griffiths	bass
Graham Jarvis	drums, percussion
Mart Jenner	guitar
John Perry	backing vocals
Alan Park	keyboards
Cliff Richard	vocals, backing vocals
Tony Rivers	backing vocals
Thunder	arranger

Recording Details

Producer	Thunder
Engineered by	Keith Bessey
Recording location	Strawberry Studios South, Surrey
Recording date	9th-18th May 1983

♬ Don't

From the album **Don't Stop Me Now!**

Another classic from the pen of rock and roll balladeers Jerry Leiber and Mike Stoller, *Don't* – as with much of what they had written – is most associated with Elvis Presley. His single was released in early 1958 and rose to the top of the US charts, giving him his eleventh American number one, while, in the UK, it reached number two in March of the same year. Among those who have covered the song are Graham Bonnet, Chuck Jackson, P. J. Proby, the Hep Stars, Emile Ford, Presley's vocal group the Jordanaires (who appeared on Cliff Richard's Nashville sessions), Albert Lee and Don McLean.

Cliff's version appeared on his 1967 album ***Don't Stop Me Now!***, and was recorded at the first main session for the album in October 1966. The fifth and final take and edit were used for both the mono and stereo recordings.

Initially unaccompanied, Cliff's version is somewhat slower than the familiar Elvis Presley version but this doesn't detract from the beauty of it. Cliff is in his element when singing songs such as this and the stentorian bass and the sympathetic accompaniment in the orchestra make it something unusual and quite different from the familiar rendering.

Track Specification

Composed by Jerry Leiber and Mike Stoller

Musicians

Breakaways:	backing vocals
Vicki Hasemen	
Margo Quantrell	
Jean Ryder	
Mike Leander Orchestra	orchestra
Mike Leander	arranger, conductor
Cliff Richard	vocals

Recording Details

Producer	Norrie Paramor
Engineered by	Peter Vincent and Richard Lush
Recording location	Abbey Road Studio 2, St. John's Wood, London
Recording date	19th October 1966

♬ Don't Ask Me to Be Friends

From the album **Tracks 'n' Grooves**

More well-known as an Everly Brothers album track, Cliff Richard covered *Don't Ask Me to Be Friends* at a late 1967 session but the track was not released until it was included on the 1970 ***Tracks 'n' Grooves*** album. As a consequence of its late release, it has only ever been issued in stereo format (Columbia had converted all album releases to stereo only by 1970), although, given the timing of the recording, it would almost certainly have been edited in mono too. Subsequently translated and retitled to *Laß Uns Schnell Vergessen*, it was recorded by Cliff for his second German language album.
A very pretty song that Cliff sings with a slight vibrato, it is a sad love song that reflects on a break-up and the impossibility of thinking of just being friends after the relationship they had.

Track Specification
Composed by Gerry Goffin and Jack Keller

Musicians

Bernard Ebbinghouse Orchestra	orchestra
Bernard Ebbinghouse	arranger, conductor
Mike Sammes Singers	backing vocals
Cliff Richard	vocals

Recording Details

Producer	Norrie Paramor
Engineered by	Peter Vince
Recording location	Abbey Road Studio 2, St. John's Wood, London
Recording date	5th October 1967

♬ Don't Be Cruel

From the album **World Tour Live**

One of the first songs that Elvis Presley recorded at the sessions for RCA after leaving Sun Records in 1956, *Don't Be Cruel* was actually written solely by Otis Blackwell. Blackwell, though, was happy to have a dual composition credit with Presley because of his status as the hottest singer around at the time. The credit to Presley is perhaps not as much of a conceit as it first appeared because he created the arrangement in the studio on the piano. He also produced the track although it was Steve Sholes at RCA who was given that credit. Recording twenty-eight takes to perfect the song, it was released backed with *Hound Dog* in America and became a number one with *Hound Dog* reaching number two. Curiously, it wasn't issued in the UK in its own right as a single until after Presley's death in August 1977, when it reached number twenty-four in June 1978. In fact, the first act to have a hit in the UK with the song was Bill Black's Combo, a short-lived US instrumental group, who achieved a number thirty-two hit in November 1960 with their last single. In May 1975, Billy Swan took his last UK single to number forty-two and it has also been covered by a variety of artists including John Lennon, Jerry Lee Lewis, Neil Diamond, Cheap Trick, Merle Haggard and Jackie Wilson, the latter of which impressed Presley so much that he incorporated some of Wilson's inflections into his own performances on stage.
Cliff included the song in the ***Elvis Medley*** as part of the set list for his 2003 world tour. The New Zealand show was filmed ostensibly for DVD release later in the year and, in 2004, it was decided to issue a complementary CD album also called *World Tour Live*. While many tracks from the DVD were not included, *Don't Be Cruel* was added to the track listing. The song picks up the pace after *Too Much* and the backing vocals are very much like the Jordanaires. In this version, Cliff sings the song in a similar choked style to the Presley original but still adds elements of his own.

Track Specification
Composed by Otis Blackwell and Elvis Presley

Musicians

Anthony Clark	backing vocals, guitar
John Clark	guitar
Dave Cooke	keyboards
Mike Haughton	saxophone
Peter Howarth	backing vocals
Pete May	drums, percussion
Mick Mullins	backing vocals
Keith Murrell	backing vocals
Alan Park	keyboards
Cliff Richard	vocals, guitar
Steve Stroud	bass

Recording Details

Producer	Keith Bessey
Engineered by	Keith Bessey
Recording location	The Mission Winery, Napier, New Zealand
Recording date	22nd February 2003

♬ Don't Be Mad at Me

B-side of **A Voice in the Wilderness** *and unissued tracks*

Written by the enduring partnership of Tepper and Bennett, who had composed Cliff Richard's second UK number one, ***Travellin' Light***, *Don't Be Mad at Me* was slated for the B-side of Cliff's seventh single, ***A Voice in the Wilderness***. Prior to the accepted take from the 18th November 1959 sessions, there had been two unsuccessful attempts to get the song into the can (on 6th November and 17th November). At the final session, the mono and stereo versions of the song were recorded at the same time on different machines and mixed down separately for the purposes of the dual listening channels.
Using bongos to introduce the song (and thereby giving it a link back to the A-side, which was featured in the film ***Expresso Bongo***), it is a joyful piece of syncopation between the guitars, the bongos and lyrics. What marks this song aside from what had gone on before in any of Cliff's recordings is that he is backed for the first time by the chorale made up from the singers in the Shadows: Hank Marvin, Bruce Welch and Jet Harris. Once again, the song is about having an

argument with a girl (much like the A-side) and how they are going to get through it and it typifies much of what was being recorded in the early sixties with Cliff and the Shadows being in the vanguard. The moody touches of Cliff's main vocal line also bring an extra emotional dimension to the song.

Track Specification
Composed by Sid Tepper and Roy C. Bennett

1. Unissued track

Musicians		*Recording Details*	
Jet Harris	backing vocals, bass	Producer	Norrie Paramor
Hank Marvin	backing vocals, guitar	Engineered by	Malcolm Addey and Alan Kane (mono) and Stuart Eltham and Peter Bown (stereo)
Tony Meehan	drums, percussion		
Cliff Richard	vocals	Recording location	Abbey Road Studio 2, St. John's Wood, London
Bruce Welch	backing vocals, rhythm guitar	Recording date	6th November 1959

2. Unissued track

Musicians		*Recording Details*	
Jet Harris	backing vocals, bass	Producer	Norrie Paramor
Hank Marvin	backing vocals, guitar	Engineered by	Malcolm Addey and Alan Kane (mono) and Stuart Eltham and Peter Bown (stereo)
Tony Meehan	drums, percussion		
Cliff Richard	vocals	Recording location	Abbey Road Studio 2, St. John's Wood, London
Bruce Welch	backing vocals, rhythm guitar	Recording date	17th November 1959

3. B-side (A Voice in the Wilderness)

Musicians		*Recording Details*	
Jet Harris	backing vocals, bass	Producer	Norrie Paramor
Hank Marvin	backing vocals, guitar	Engineered by	Malcolm Addey and Alan Kane (mono) and Stuart Eltham and Peter Bown (stereo)
Tony Meehan	drums, percussion		
Cliff Richard	vocals	Recording location	Abbey Road Studio 2, St. John's Wood, London
Bruce Welch	backing vocals, rhythm guitar	Recording date	19th November 1959

♫ Don't Blame Me

Unissued track

One of the five songs that appear in the ***Life with Johnny*** episode entitled *Johnny Faces Facts* featuring Cliff Richard in the title role, *Don't Blame Me* cements the message of the parable of the speck and plank in people's eyes. Johnny has been waiting at the pub for his girlfriend Cindy (played by Cindy Kent from the Settlers) and she is late. Pouring scorn on her with his friends, he decides to go, bumping into her outside, where she apologizes for being late but she had to look after getting a meal for her father. However, Johnny takes the opportunity to use this as a way of telling her through the song that she shouldn't blame him any more whenever he is late after being at the football, staying with friends, picking up his suit and so on, to the point that she can't blame him for anything. They arrive back home just in time to catch the thought at bedtime delivered by their local vicar.

The song is an upbeat four-four rhythm, with a guitar-led accompaniment that would do well on any of Cliff's albums, regardless of their religious nature – indeed, it fits in a non-religious environment too. The song was recorded at Abbey Road but has never been released: an unusual step for EMI in those days, which may have been due to nervousness of limited appeal, although this is unlikely given the fact that they released other religious material by Cliff. The closing credits of the programme indicated that the songs were original (they are) and that they were written together by Cliff, David Winter, the programme's writer, and the four members of the Settlers – this is borne out in the credits for ***Where Is That Man?***, which was re-recorded and released on the album ***About That Man***.

Track Specification
Composed by Cliff Richard, David Winter, Cindy Kent, Mike Jones, John Fyffe and Geoffrey Srodzinski

Musicians		*Recording Details*	
John Fyffe	backing vocals, guitar	Producer	Norrie Paramor
Cindy Kent	backing vocals, tambourine	Engineered by	Peter Vince
Mike Jones	backing vocals, guitar	Recording location	Abbey Road Studio 3, St. John's Wood, London
Cliff Richard	vocals	Recording date	8th January 1969
Geoffrey Srodzinski	backing vocals, bass		

♫ Don't Bug Me Baby

Unreleased track (subsequently released on **The Rock and Roll Years 1958 -1963***) and from the album* **Cliff**

A version of a song made famous by Milton Allen and subsequently covered by the Blue J's, Ruthie and the Wranglers, Bobby Horton and others, *Don't Bug Me Baby* was long mooted to be a contender as a follow-up single to Cliff Richard's ***Move It***, which had received accolades and significant commercial success throughout the summer of 1958. But it was also felt that Ian Samwell, the writer of that first single, had the necessary creativity to muster subsequent songs as single material. At the same recording sessions that produced *Don't Bug Me Baby*, ***High Class Baby*** was also recorded and it was chosen as the successor, along with ***My Feet Hit the Ground***, also completed at the same time.

Don't Bug Me Baby remained unissued and languished in EMI's vaults for almost forty years until the release of the rarity collection and summary of Cliff's first five years in the charts as a rock and roll star, *The Rock and Roll Years 1958 - 1963*. With a more American feel than the Samwell tunes, it did indeed seem to be a suitably strong contender for the second single release, with its rock and roll bass riffs and snare drum interludes. The song is well suited to Cliff's style and it is surprising that such a gem should remain away from public ears for so long, although that is now remedied.
The track is a love song but with a twist - the girl that Cliff is in love with is also irritating him (hence the tenor of the title) and he spends the song trying to tell her that she should back off from him, give him space, so that he doesn't feel compelled to get rid of her purely because she is exasperating him.
Norrie Paramor initially preferred to employ established session musicians for the recordings he produced and it is likely that this track incorporates the sound of Ernie Shears on guitar and Frank Clarke on stand-up bass, although this is unsubstantiated since there are no records or fixed memories of those involved. For the moment and until relevant research material is unearthed, these will be stated as unknown in the trak specification of this entry.
A second recording was made of the song for the album ***Cliff*** (his first LP issue), which was a selection of songs recorded at Abbey Road studios at two sessions over two days but in front of an invited audience, although the wild screaming of the girls somewhat detracts from the performance. Two versions were made - one in mono; the other in stereo - with only small minor variants according to the amount of audience noise heard in the separate channels on the stereo version. After the issue of the LP, this 'live' version was also included on the track listing of the *Cliff No. 2* EP (released in both a mono and a stereo version), while the LP has been rereleased in different formats in subsequent years and includes the stereo version of the track only on CD.

Track Specification
Composed by Leon Luallen and Johnny Bragg

1. The Rock and Roll Years 1958-1963

Musicians		*Recording Details*	
Cliff Richard	vocals	Producer	Norrie Paramor
Unknown	guitar	Engineered by	Malcolm Addey
Unknown	bass	Recording location	Abbey Road Studio 2, St. John's Wood, London
Unknown	drums, percussion	Recording date	3rd October 1958
Unknown	hand-claps		

2. Cliff

Musicians		*Recording Details*	
Jet Harris	bass	Producer	Norrie Paramor
Hank Marvin	backing vocals, guitar	Engineered by	Peter Brown and Stuart Eltham
Tony Meehan	drums, percussion	Recording location	Abbey Road Studio 2, St. John's Wood, London
Cliff Richard	vocals	Recording date	10th November 1959
Bruce Welch	backing vocals, guitar		

♫ Don't Forget to Catch Me

Unissued tracks and ***44th UK single***

As with all of the tracks on ***Established 1958***, *Don't Forget to Catch Me* was written by the prolific compositional talents of Shadows. The opening track on the album, it was also chosen for release as Cliff Richard's forty-fourth UK single. The song divided critics with some considering him to be serving up boring material that was too similar to the early days, while others thought it brilliant. However, to the record-buyers, too, it was neither one nor the other as it settled for a highest chart placing of twenty-one, ending temporarily a run of three singles in the region of the twenties. It was also the last time that Cliff and the Shadows would be in the singles charts as an act until 2009 when they issued a new version of ***Singing the Blues***. *Don't Forget to Catch Me* was backed with ***What's More (I Don't Need Her)*** and issued on the Columbia label (catalogue number DB 8503) on 15th November 1968 but in mono only, although both the mono and stereo versions had already been released a couple of months earlier on the parent album. In addition, a radio promotional disc was produced (also on Columbia with a catalogue number of PRS 316), this time coupled with the Shadows' *The Magical Mrs. Clamps*, which also from the same album.
As with many Shadows compositions, there is a beautiful melody that transposes through related keys, while the harmonies are exquisite, particularly when performing their trademark close harmony vocals. Having said all that, it seems a strange choice for a single when there was much stronger material to choose from the album's recording sessions.
Cliff had recorded a number of German language singles and B-sides in the sixties but it took until 1968 to record a full album of new material - translated versions of songs that appear primarily on *Established 1958* and ***Two a Penny***. The German version of *Don't Forget to Catch Me*, which became ***Zärtliche Sekunden***, was the only song to be released as a single from the project backed with the non-album track ***Wonderful World*** (aGerman language song in spite of the English title). In the following February, Cliff recorded a number of French translation songs, one of which included *Don't Forget to Catch Me*; however, the translated title is unavailable and, to date, the song has not been issued. Later that month, Cliff completed a recording of an Italian version of the song, which was released in single form as ***Non Dimenticare Chi Ti Ama***, backed with ***Chi Lo Sà***, which was a translation of ***On the Beach***.

Track Specification

1. Unissued track (single)

Composed by Hank Marvin, Bruce Welch and Brian Bennett

Musicians		*Recording Details*	
Brian Bennett	drums, percussion	Producer	Norrie Paramor
Mike Leander	arranger, conductor	Engineered by	Peter Vince
Hank Marvin	backing vocals, guitar	Recording location	Abbey Road Studio 2, St. John's Wood, London
Mike Leander Orchestra	orchestra	Recording date	29th May 1968
Cliff Richard	vocals, backing vocals		
John Rostill	backing vocals, bass		
Bruce Welch	backing vocals, rhythm guitar		

2. Single

Composed by Hank Marvin, Bruce Welch and Brian Bennett

Musicians		*Recording Details*	
Brian Bennett	drums, percussion	Producer	Norrie Paramor
Mike Leander	arranger, conductor	Engineered by	Peter Vince
Hank Marvin	guitar	Recording location	Abbey Road Studio 2, St. John's Wood, London
Mike Leander Orchestra	orchestra	Recording date	31st May 1968
Cliff Richard	vocals		
John Rostill	bass		
Bruce Welch	rhythm guitar		

3. Unissued track (French version)

Composed by Hank Marvin, Bruce Welch and Brian Bennett; French lyrics by Unknown

Musicians		*Recording Details*	
Norrie Paramor Orchestra	orchestra	Producer	Norrie Paramor
Norrie Paramor	arranger, conductor	Engineered by	Peter Vince
Cliff Richard	vocals	Recording location	Abbey Road Studio 3, St. John's Wood, London
		Recording date	21st February 1969

♫ Don't Let Tonight Ever End

From the album **Tracks 'n' Grooves**

One of five songs recorded at the then unusual location of London's Chappell Studios rather than the more familiar Abbey Road Studios, *Don't Let Tonight Ever End* was the fourth song to be completed at the session, although it would be another two years before it was released as part of the album ***Tracks 'n' Grooves***. In between these dates, Columbia's policy on album releases changed: indeed ***Established 1958*** was the last studio album by Cliff Richard to be released in both mono and stereo format. Thereafter, all new albums were released solely in stereo, which meant that *Don't Let Tonight Ever End* has only been released in stereo format, although, given the timing of the session, it is quite likely that a mono edit was also created from the recording.

Twinkling instrumentation and shimmering strings that evoke memories of *Lara's Theme* from *Doctor Zhivago*, introduce the song, with Cliff coming in gently on the lead vocal, albeit with a slight echo applied to his voice. A typically continental style of song that could have been part of a film soundtrack, it features occasional uncredited female backing vocals that might possibly be the Breakaways, with whom Cliff regularly worked during this period, although that remains unconfirmed.

Track Specification

Composed by Simoni, Libano and C. Shane

Musicians		*Recording Details*	
Mike Leander	arranger, conductor	Producer	Norrie Paramor
Mike Leander Orchestra	orchestra	Engineered by	Peter Vince
Cliff Richard	vocals	Recording location	Chappell Studios, London
Unknown	backing vocals	Recording date	2nd July 1968

♫ Don't Listen to Him

Unissued track

Recorded for the Tyne Tees Television religious broadcasting series *Life with Johnny*, which featured Cliff Richard in the lead role, *Don't Listen to Him* is highlighted in the episode entitled *Johnny Faces Facts*, although it doesn't appear on any of the recording sheets connected to the sessions. In the playlet, having heard a businessman on television appearing to talk down to his audience and telling them what to do, Johnny suggests to his friends that this man is talking rubbish, while they advocate telling the businessman what to do instead. The scene cuts to an internal set at a studio with demanding placards and Johnny, the friends and other dancers in bowler hats with UK flags in the ribbon stating that no-one should listen to the businessman and that, instead they should just chuck a brick – this at a time when union unrest was at its height with demands and counterdemands but with no sight of the other's viewpoints and therefore no possibility of compromise because the other side is always deemed to be in the wrong. The scene ends with the group picking up imaginary bricks and throwing them towards the camera with a smashing glass sound effect.

Presented in a cockney knees-up dance style, the pace is kept up nicely by the lyrics and the meaning behind them as well as the visual dance routine itself. The song was recorded at Abbey Road, possibly with a view to releasing the songs as a tie-in album but, if so, this project was abandoned and *Don't Listen to Him* remains unissued. The credits of the program indicate that the songs were all original and written by Cliff, the programme's writer David Winter and the four members of the Settlers – something which is confirmed by the re-recording of ***Where Is That Man?*** on ***About That Man*** – and so these are all assigned credits to this track.

Track Specification
Composed by Cliff Richard, David Winter, Cindy Kent, Mike Jones, John Fyffe and Geoffrey Srodzinski

Musicians

John Fyffe	backing vocals, guitar
Cindy Kent	backing vocals
Mike Jones	backing vocals, guitar
Cliff Richard	vocals
Geoffrey Srodzinski	backing vocals
Unknown	drums, percussion

Recording Details

Producer	Norrie Paramor
Engineered by	Peter Vince
Recording location	Abbey Road Studio 3, St. John's Wood, London
Recording date	8th–9th January 1969

♬ Don't Make Promises
From the album **Don't Stop Me Now!**

Self-composed by Tim Hardin for his debut album, *Tim Hardin 1*, in 1966, *Don't Make Promises* has been rated highly by critics in both America and Britain. One of two major hits drawn from that first album (although this song was not a hit in the UK), it has been covered by a number of other artists including Bobby Darin, the Beau Brummels, Joan Baez, Marianne Faithfull, Scott MacKenzie, Peter Keane, Gary Puckett, Rick Nelson, Three Dog Night, Helen Reddy and Paul Weller amongst others.

One of four songs completed at the session for the ***Don't Stop Me Now!*** album, Cliff Richard's version of *Don't Make Promises* was finalized in just three takes, with that third and final take and edit used for both the mono and stereo recordings.

With a jaunty rhythm created in a guitar and pizzicato harp, the thudding bass and brass backing make this arrangement of the song for Cliff's album interesting. The orchestra is uncredited and is most likely to be Mike Leander's outfit, since he was working prominently with Cliff at the time, although the orchestra could also be that of Norrie Paramor or Bernard Ebbinghouse who were regulars in the studio in this period, too.

Track Specification
Composed by Tim Hardin

Musicians

Cliff Richard	vocals
Unknown	arranger, conductor
Unknown	orchestra

Recording Details

Producer	Norrie Paramor
Engineered by	Peter Vince and Richard Lush
Recording location	Abbey Road Studio 2, St. John's Wood, London
Recording date	15th January 1967

♬ Don't Meet the Band
From the album **Japan Tour '74**

This track featured as the opener for the fourth side of the original vinyl version of ***Japan Tour '74***, which was released in Japan only in 1975. The liner notes suggest that it was written by Cliff Richard and Bruce Welch, and the track was not included on the transference of the CD in 2009. Whether it is a musical track or just a witty introduction to each member of the band is not clear and, as a result, this entry is incomplete until the original track can be accessed for closer scrutiny.

♬ Don't Move Away
B-side of **Sunny Honey Girl**

Aside from ***Throw Down a Line*** that saw Cliff Richard in partnership with then erstwhile Shadows guitarist Hank Marvin, *Don't Move Away* was the first (of many) collaborations and duets and the first of three that Cliff recorded with Olivia Newton-John (the other two being ***Suddenly*** and ***Had to Be***). Olivia is reported as saying that she was petrified about going into the studio with such a big star as Cliff and having to sing along with an orchestra, neither of which she had ever done before. *Don't Move Away* was recorded at the same session as the two other songs that formed the maxi-single: the A-side was ***Sunny Honey Girl*** and the other song on the B-side was a Cliff solo ***I Was Only Fooling Myself***. *Don't Move Away* was the first track to be completed with the third and last take being used for the final edit. Quite a rarity in that it had not been released in any other medium than the single, it was added to the aforementioned duet *Had to Be* single in 1995 and a succession of 1970s-related Cliff compilations before being remastered and added as a bonus track on the reissued ***Tracks 'n' Grooves*** album in 2004.

A bittersweet love song sung in duet with the familiar breathy style of Olivia Newton-John, the song is somewhat short on musical hooks although the template of the combination of Cliff's and Olivia's voices was set here for future collaborations. At the time, there was much speculation about a possible romantic liaison and this track helped (however unintentionally) pique the public's expectation.

Track Specification
Composed by Valerie Avon and Harold Spiro

Musicians	
Brian Bennett	arranger, conductor
Brian Bennett Orchestra	orchestra
Olivia Newton-John	vocals
Cliff Richard	vocals

Recording Details	
Producer	Norrie Paramor
Engineered by	Peter Vince and Richard Lush
Recording location	Abbey Road Studio 2, St. John's Wood, London
Recording date	16th November 1970

♫ Don't Talk to Him

23rd ***UK single*** *and from the albums* **Japan Tour '74** *and* **Reunited**

Although Cliff Richard had tried his hand at writing songs, he has admitted in interview that he found it a frightening experience, possibly because of the prolific output of Hank Marvin and Bruce Welch, and he preferred to write, whenever he did, with someone else providing the music. Often forging a collaboration with Bruce, so it was with *Don't Talk to Him,* a tune that Welch had and played to Cliff. He took it away and wrote the lyrics that same evening accompanying himself on guitar at a rented cottage where he was staying for the Blackpool summer season. It has since been covered by The Shadows on their own, by Norrie Paramor and his orchestra and esoteric acts such as Bachman Cummings and Sally Yeh.
The only song to be recorded at the session, the eleventh take and edit were used for the mono and stereo mixed differently for each. Backed with ***Say You're Mine***, it was released as a single on the Columbia label (catalogue number DB 7150) on 1st November 1963, reaching number two, where it was held off the top position by the Beatles' *She Loves You*. A regular track on Cliff compilations, it was also released on the track listing of ***Cliff Sings Don't Talk to Him*** EP.
The guitar introduction and thumping drums lead into Cliff's almost urgent announcement to his lover not to listen to whoever is saying things about him. Bruce is the unsung hero of a lot of the recordings featuring the Shadows since it is principally his work on the guitar that keeps the pace moving. Other points of note are the beautiful guitar line from Hank Marvin and the beautiful harmonies created by the exquisite musical intervals by Hank, Bruce and Cliff together.
Don't Talk to Him was translated into German as ***Sag 'No' zu Ihm*** and recorded by Cliff for the German market as a B-side of ***Zuviel Allein*** but only in mono. For this recording, the Shadows original English instrumental backing was used with Cliff adding his new vocals at a later session in March 1964 with overdubs of backing vocals by a German vocal group. It was subsequently translated into Italian for Cliff's album ***When in Rome***, entitled ***Non l'Ascoltare***.
Bruce joined Cliff on his 1974 Japanese tour, so it was an obvious choice and Bruce's voice is the one that can be heard harmonising with Cliff's. The guitar solo is not as slick as Hank's original but it is good enough for the performance.
A completely new recording by Cliff and the Shadows was included on the 2009 album ***Reunited***, before being one of the most popular performances at the concerts scheduled to promote the album. The recording is cleaner than the original and the arrangement is very similar but sounds fresher and more contemporary.

Track Specification
Composed by Bruce Welch and Cliff Richard

1. Single

Musicians	
Brian Bennett	drums, percussion
Brian 'Licorice' Locking	bass
Hank Marvin	backing vocals, guitar
Cliff Richard	vocals, backing vocals
Bruce Welch	backing vocals, rhythm guitar

Recording Details	
Producer	Norrie Paramor
Engineered by	Malcolm Addey
Recording location	Abbey Road Studio 3, St. John's Wood, London
Recording date	13th October 1963

2. Japan Tour '74

Musicians	
Cliff Hall	piano
Brian Lewis	backing vocals, guitar
Kevin Peak	acoustic guitar
Cliff Richard	vocals
Trevor Spencer	drums, percussion
Alan Tarney	backing vocals, bass
Bruce Welch	backing vocals, rhythm guitar

Recording Details	
Producer	Toshiba EMI (no individual detailed)
Engineered by	Toshiba EMI (no individual detailed)
Recording location	Shinjuku Koseinenkin, Tokyo, Japan
Recording date	7th–8th October 1974

3. Reunited

Musicians	
Brian Bennett	drums, percussion
Mark Griffiths	bass
Hank Marvin	backing vocals, guitar
Cliff Richard	vocals, backing vocals
Bruce Welch	backing vocals, rhythm guitar

Recording Details	
Producer	Warren Bennett (co-ordination)
Engineered by	James Collins (Honeyhill Studios), Ethan Carlson (Middle Ear Studios), Les Williams (Nivram Studios) and Keith Bessey (mixing and mastering)
Recording location	Middle Ear Studios, Miami, Florida, USA (Cliff's vocals), Nivram Studios, Perth, Western Australia (Hank's guitars and vocals) and Honeyhill Studios, Hertfordshire, England (all other vocals and instruments)
Recording date	Early 2009

♫ Don't Turn the Light Out

From the album **Every Face Tells a Story**

Guy Fletcher and Doug Flett had written many songs for Cliff Richard to record over his then recent career and *Don't Turn the Light Out* was one of the last. First attempted at the first session for the ***Every Face Tells a Story***, *Don't Turn the Light Out* was abandoned after three takes, presumably because it was the last song and time had run out before a good take could be recorded. It was next tried as the first song on the next day's session, where it was finished after three takes with additional vocal overdubs recorded a week later. Although not issued as a single in the UK, it was released in the US, backed with ***Nothing Left for Me to Say***, on the Rocket Records label (catalogue number 40724) in 1977, reaching number fifty-seven in the Billboard charts.

After the gentleness of the preceding track, *Up in the World*, Cliff follows with an upbeat song that talks about getting back together with someone after a possible misunderstanding. Highly driven by synthesisers, the song also has the by now standard backing vocal mix that marks much of Cliff's material from this period.

Track Specification

Composed by Guy Fletcher and Doug Flett

1. Unissued track (Every Face Tells a Story)

Musicians

Brian Bennett	drums, percussion
Terry Britten	guitar
John Perry	backing vocals
Cliff Richard	vocals
Frank Ricotti	percussion
Tony Rivers	backing vocals
Alan Tarney	bass
Graham Todd	keyboards

Recording Details

Producer	Bruce Welch
Engineered by	Tony Clark and John Barrett
Recording location	Abbey Road Studio 2, St. John's Wood, London
Recording date	6th September 1976

2. Every Face Tells a Story

Musicians

Brian Bennett	drums, percussion
Terry Britten	guitar
John Perry	backing vocals
Cliff Richard	vocals
Frank Ricotti	percussion
Tony Rivers	backing vocals
Alan Tarney	bass
Graham Todd	keyboards

Recording Details

Producer	Bruce Welch
Engineered by	Tony Clark, Mike Jarrett and Alan Rouse
Recording location	Abbey Road Studio 2, St. John's Wood, London
Recording date	7th and 14th September 1976

♫ Doo-Wop Medley

From the album **World Tour Live**

In 2003, Cliff Richard embarked on a world tour to promote ***Wanted***. The result was filmed during the New Zealand show and issued on DVD later that year and included the entire concert. A CD album to complement the film, *World Tour Live*, was released the following year but included fourteen of the tracks. Of those, one was the *Doo-Wop Medley*, which covered:

a) ***Come Go with Me***
b) ***Dream Lover***
c) ***Since I Don't Have You***

The entries for those songs carry the information on the recording details and musicians.

♫ Do They Know It's Christmas?

Single by **Band Aid II**

The story of *Do They Know It's Christmas?* is as dramatic and as close to heart-warming and equally heart-wrenching embrace of humanity as the tragic events that triggered it. In late 1984, the BBC dispatched reporter Michael Buerk to Ethiopia to cover one of the worst famines that the country had ever endured. Nothing could have prepared the public for the disturbing images of the dying, starving Ethiopian people living in destitution in makeshift hospital camps – what was worse was the painfully emotional pictures of listless children with distended, food-starved bellies with eyes haunted by the desire for death, so hungry and ill were they by that time.

In England, Boomtown Rats lead singer Bob Geldof was watching the report with uneasy and growing anger – the angry feelings were created by disparity between the want of one group of people in the world and the wanton waste of another and the unease formed because of his relative affluence and comfort and want for nothing. It is this mixed feeling that particularly moved him to try and do something to increase awareness and raise money. Falling back on what he knew – the music business – he came up with the idea of planning a recording and subsequent release of a charity record.

Calling on Midge Ure to help him, they wrote the seminal *Do They Know It's Christmas?* very quickly. Next, he began 'phoning performers who were contemporaneously at the pinnacle of their careers (including U2, Phil Collins, Duran Duran, Bananarama, Big Country, Culture Club, Paul McCartney, Wham!, Spandau Ballet and many others) to convene at a recording studio in London. The song was sliced up with one or two lines of the lyrics being apportioned to each act – originally, the opening section was intended for David Bowie, who was unable to take part, and were taken so memorably by Paul Young.

Geldof spent time contacting various music businesses and record companies, playing one off against the other to convince them to give their services for free (or at least cost) and succeeded in his quest. He even fought against the huge sales tax (VAT at 18%) applied by the government, which initially refused the refund. However, the popular backlash was unexpected and eventually they relented. The song was released on 3rd December 1984 and went straight to number one. Originally, Geldof had thought that £70,000 would be a good target to achieve but, with the record selling almost 3,000,000, it far exceeded even his wildest expectations and paved the way for *Live Aid*.

The song was re-released the following Christmas in 1985, making the number one spot again, and appears on many Christmas compilations. In 1989, a new group of artists was brought together, this time produced by Stock, Aitken and Waterman, and included chart acts such as Kylie, Jason Donovan, Big Fun, Bananarama (again), Bros and Cliff Richard. Backed with an instrumental version of the song (the backing track), it was released as a single on the PWL Records label (catalogue number POL 102/FEED 2) on 11th December 1989. It was also released as a CD single but in Holland only (catalogue number PWCS 006). Also reaching number one, like its predecessor, it has largely been ignored as inferior by CD compilers and is only trotted out as an attempt at wit on music channel video compilations of the season's 'worst turkeys'. In truth, it is simply different and has a distinct quality to it and, given that it kept the profile high at the time of the African plight, it served its purpose. In 2004, to mark the continuing problems in Africa and the twentieth anniversary of the original charity record, a third version was recorded, this time with the likes of Chris Martin, Joss Stone, the Sugababes, McCartney (again), Rachel Stevens, Justin Hawkins, Robbie Williams and Dizzee Rascal.

By far the most recognizable voices on the song are Chris Rea, Kylie Minogue and Cliff as they sing the individual slivers of lyrics. The problem with the record is that it has a lot to prove against the original. By far the best voice is Cliff's and he is used more than the other participants, making it almost a Cliff recording with a few friends joining him. The forgotten song from the canon of the Band Aid phenomenon, there is still much to commend it, with the youthful sound created by the corral of talent in the Stock, Aitken and Waterman camp as well as the individual performances.

Track Specification

Composed by Bob Geldof and Midge Ure

Musicians

Matt Aitken	keyboards
Bananarama:	
Sarah Dallin	backing vocals
Siobhan Fahey	backing vocals
Keren Woodward	backing vocals
Big Fun:	
Phil Creswick	backing vocals
Mark Gillespie	backing vocals
Jason John	backing vocals
Bros:	
Luke Goss	backing vocals, drums, percussion
Matt Goss	vocals, backing vocals
Craig Logan	backing vocals
Cathy Dennis	vocals, backing vocals
D Mob	backing vocals
Jason Donovan	vocals, backing vocals
Kevin Godley	backing vocals
Glen Goldsmith	backing vocals
A. Linn	drums, percussion
Kylie Minogue	vocals, backing vocals
Pasadenas:	
Andrew Banfield	backing vocals
Aaron Brown	backing vocals
David Milliner	backing vocals
Mike Milliner	backing vocals
Hamish Seelochan	backing vocals
Chris Rea	vocals, backing vocals, guitar
Cliff Richard	vocals, backing vocals
Jimmy Somerville	vocals, backing vocals
Sonia	vocals, backing vocals
Lisa Stansfield	vocals, backing vocals
Mike Stock	keyboards
Technotronic:	
Thomas DeQuincey	backing vocals
Wet Wet Wet:	
Graeme Clark	backing vocals
Tommy Cunningham	backing vocals
Neil Mitchell	backing vocals
Marti Pellow	vocals, backing vocals

Recording Details

Producer	Mike Stock, Matt Aitken and Pete Waterman
Engineered by	Karen Hewitt and Yoyo
Recording location	PWL Studios, London
Recording date	3rd-4th December 1984

♬ Do What You Gotta Do

Unissued track

Not much is known about *Do What You Gotta Do* other than it being one of a number of tracks recorded during the ***Green Light*** album sessions by Cliff Richard but not issued. Unlike many of the others, the composer is unknown and neither is the musician set up involved, this forcing those known to be involved to be added in their entirety to be added to the track specification. The song was stopped after the first take and overdubs added the following month, indicating that it was prepared for release, although it still remains unissued.

Track Specification

Composed by Unknown

Musicians

Brian Bennett	drums, percussion
Terry Britten	guitar
Stuart Calver	backing vocals
Richard Hewson	arranger, conductor
Alan Jones	bass
Duncan MacKay	keyboards
Alan Parker	guitar
John Perry	backing vocals
Tim Renwick	guitar
Cliff Richard	vocals
Tony Rivers	backing vocals
Trevor Spencer	drums, percussion
Alan Tarney	backing vocals, guitar, bass, keyboards
Graham Todd	keyboards
Unknown	orchestra

Recording Details

Producer	Bruce Welch
Engineered by	Tony Clark and Haydn Bendall
Recording location	Abbey Road Studio 3, St. John's Wood, London
Recording date	12th January 1978 and 19th February 1978

♬ Down the Line

From the album **Cliff**

The song has been recorded by a wide variety of artists and is a staple to croon at sixties karaoke parties – Vic Damone, Louis Armstrong, Ella Fitzgerald, Julie London, Conway Twitty, Frankie Lymon and the Teenagers, Mud, Tony Bennett, Billie Holliday, Chet Baker and Frank Sinatra are but some of the diverse acts who have committed the song to vinyl but, in the UK, only the Marcels (number one in 1961), Showaddywaddy (number thirty in 1980), actor John Alford (number nine in 1996) and Elvis Presley (number nine in 1956) have had any commercial single success with the song. With Presley's success with singing a Roy Orbison song, it was a natural choice for inclusion in the 'live' set recorded at Abbey Road in front of an invited guest list comprising Cliff Richard fans.

The screaming occasionally overwhelms the recording but Cliff's assured performance is driven onwards by the chugging guitar line by Hank Marvin and Bruce Welch. The rhythm is maintained by the drums but also by Cliff using hand-claps, which seems to have a curious effect on the listening girls. The perfectly executed rock song is one of the highlights on the *Cliff* album.

This 'live' version of the song was included on Cliff's first EP, *Cliff No. 1.*

Track Specification

Composed by Roy Orbison

Musicians

Jet Harris	bass
Hank Marvin	guitar
Tony Meehan	drums, percussion
Cliff Richard	vocals, hand-claps
Bruce Welch	rhythm guitar

Recording Details

Producer	Norrie Paramor
Engineered by	Peter Bown and Stuart Eltham
Recording location	Abbey Road Studio 2, St. John's Wood, London
Recording date	9th February 1959

♬ Do You Remember? (1)

From the film soundtrack album of **Wonderful Life** *and from the album* **The Rock 'n' Roll Years 1958-1963**

Two years before the soundtrack to the film ***Wonderful Life*** was recorded, Cliff Richard tried a version of *Do You Remember?* at the end of 1961 with Norrie Paramor's orchestra. For over thirty-five years, this remained unreleased with the film's version being the familiar one. In 1997, when the rarity anthology ***The Rock 'n' Roll Years 1958-1963*** was created, it included a take from this December 1961 session, which differs in its slower pace, the muting of the backing vocals and the removal of the guitar introduction (since it is an orchestrally backed version). This track was subsequently included on the 2005 remastered reissue of the film's soundtrack CD.

For the film, the song comes at the point of a Kasbah love scene between Johnny (Cliff Richard) and Jenny (Susan Hampshire), for a film being created by the group of friends without Jenny's knowledge. Johnny convinces Jenny to go to the café in their film-set clothes so that they can be in character ostensibly while they learn their lines together. Tables are cleared, screens put up and the Shadows perform in fezzes behind them as Jerry (Melvyn Hayes) and Edward (Richard O'Sullivan) convert the place temporarily into a Moroccan restaurant. Johnny suggests singing the lines to help the mood

while the whole sequence is filmed on a camera hidden in a cake. Sung as a duet between Johnny and Jenny, they complete the song as Jerry and Edward close a bead curtain on them.
Recorded in Cliff's own session in November 1963, the bassist was Brian Locking, even though it is his successor John Rostill who appears in the film. The sixteenth and final take and edit were used for the mono and stereo recordings but with different mixes for the separate requirements of the audio channels and it also features on the track listing of the ***Wonderful Life No. 1*** EP. The principal difference between the released soundtrack and the film version of the song is that the soundtrack is a solo performance, while Susan Hampshire performs with Cliff as a duet in the film. The film version was probably recorded in the first three months of 1964 and has never been released in any other commercial format.
Elevated above the standard British musical fare that was written by Peter Myers and Ronal Cass for the soundtrack, the beautiful *Do You Remember?* is a romantic toe-tapper that features swooping strings but a lovely guitar solo played in thirds by Hank Marvin and, throughout, a rhythm played by Bruce Welch. Cliff sings the lyrics with meaning and, in the rallentando towards the end, imbues the sustained notes with the vibrato that would be one of his later trademarks.

Track Specification
Composed by Bruce Welch and Hank Marvin

1. The Rock 'n' Roll Years 1958-1963

Musicians		*Recording Details*	
Mike Sammes Singers	backing vocals	Producer	Norrie Paramor
Norrie Paramor Orchestra	orchestra	Engineered by	Malcolm Addey
Norrie Paramor	arranger, conductor	Recording location	Abbey Road Studio 2, St. John's Wood, London
Cliff Richard	vocals	Recording date	4th December 1961

2. Wonderful Life

Musicians		*Recording Details*	
Brian Bennett	drums, percussion	Producer	Norrie Paramor
Brian 'Licorice' Locking	bass	Engineered by	Malcolm Addey and Jimmy Johnson
Hank Marvin	guitar	Recording location	Abbey Road Studio 2, St. John's Wood, London
Mike Sammes Singers	backing vocals	Recording date	1st November 1963
Norrie Paramor Orchestra	orchestra		
Norrie Paramor	arranger, conductor		
Cliff Richard	vocals		
Bruce Welch	rhythm guitar		

♫ Do You Remember? (2)

From the EP **Congratulations**

Not the song of the same name that appeared in the film ***Wonderful Life***, *Do You Remember?* was one of the candidates for the 1968 UK entry for the Eurovision Song Contest. Cliff Richard sang one song each week on the *Cilla Black Show* in the first few months of 1968 and then the choice was opened up to a public postal vote. With one of the contenders being ***Congratulations***, which polled 69% of the votes, it is unsurprising that the remaining five songs should take such a relatively low percentage of the overall vote. *Do You Remember?* was the least favourite, polling just 1.7% of the votes with its nearest challenger being ***Little Rag Doll*** which received 4.2%. The orchestra used at the session is either fronted by Bernard Ebbinghouse or Norrie Paramor – records are unclear on which but both are confirmed to have played at the session – and the track also features Shadows Hank Marvin and Bruce Welch on backing vocals and Led Zeppelin bassist-in-waiting John Paul Jones. Appearing on the ***Congratulations*** EP, *Do You Remember?* has only ever been released in mono format with the exception of the stereo version that was on the track listing of the German 1968 compilation *Congratulations und 13 Weitere Hits*. In 2007, the mono version was made more widely available when it was included as a bonus track on ***Live at the Talk of the Town***.
With its guitar introduction and the driving beat created by the intricate bass line, a frenetic tambourine and rushing orchestral instrumentation, it is a surprise that this song polled so few votes in comparison to the other contenders in the competition. With the addition of Hank's and Bruce's backing vocals every time the song's title is sung, along with a catchy instrumental break, it deserved far more recognition that it received. Since the session notes indicate that both the Bernard Ebbinghouse and the Norrie Paramor Orchestras were involved in the session, there is no further information to indicate which played on which track and so both are listed.

Track Specification
Composed by Tommy Scott

Musicians		*Recording Details*	
Bernard Ebbinghouse Orchestra	orchestra	Producer	Norrie Paramor
Bernard Ebbinghouse	conductor	Engineered by	Peter Vince
John Paul Jones	bass	Recording location	Abbey Road Studio 2, St. John's Wood, London
Hank Marvin	backing vocals	Recording date	2nd February 1968
Norrie Paramor Orchestra	orchestra		
Norrie Paramor	arranger, conductor		
Cliff Richard	vocals		
Bruce Welch	backing vocals		

♫ Do You Wanna Dance?

B-side of **I'm Looking out the Window**, *seventeenth double A-side single and from the albums* **Cliff's Hit Album** *(stereo version)*, **The Rock 'n' Roll Years 1958-1963**, **Live at the ABC Kingston 1962** , **Cliff "Live" in Japan '72**, **Japan Tour '74**, **Thank You Very Much**, **Dressed for the Occasion**, **From a Distance ***** The Event**, **Knebworth – the Album**, **Summer Holiday** *(Darren Day) and* **Reunited** *and single by* **Marietta**

Often referred to as *Do You Wanna Dance*, the *Guinness Book of British Singles* states that the song is officially titled *Do You Want to Dance?* However, many of Cliff Richard's albums refer to it using the former spelling and it would be churlish to push the point of pedantry as a result.

Recorded in the final session of 1961, there is one incorrect part of the song – down to the writer, rather than the performer – and it is that, in order to maintain the flow and rhythm correctly, the singer is forced to stress the second syllable of 'under' ('UnDER the moonlight') rather than the correct inflection on the first (for reference, see also ***Bachelor Boy***). In Cliff's many versions of *Do You Wanna Dance?*, he tends to sing this line by leaving the 'under' until a beat later and shortening the remaining notes of the sentence, thereby creating a stronger rhythm and rectifying the linguistic error.

Written and originally recorded by Bobby Freeman at the height of the rock and roll popularity, it was a minor hit for him and was later covered by Eddie Cochran, The Mamas and the Papas, T. Rex, the Ramones, Ray Stevens and John Lennon. It was Bette Midler's first US single release in 1973, reaching number seventeen in the Billboard charts, while the Beach Boys covered it in 1965 when it reached number twelve.

In the UK, the only artist to secure a hit with the song was Cliff Richard and the Shadows, of course, although it was never intended to be released as a single in its own right. Because it was a cover version rather than an original tune, it was chosen as the B-side of the juxtaposed ***I'm Looking out the Window***, which was much slower in pace and tenor. But the fans began asking for the B-side as well when purchasing the record. While the A-side hit the number two slot in the UK singles charts, *Do You Wanna Dance?*, now a double A-side of sorts, pitched in at a creditable number ten. The record was issued on the Columbia label (catalogue number 45-DB 4828) on 4th May 1962 and Cliff's version of the song was identified as Bobby Freeman's favourite version when asked around the time of the record's release.

Recorded in just three takes, the mono and stereo edits differ slightly at the end of the song, missing many of Cliff's shouts that appear on the stereo version, which was eventually released on the 1971 ***Cliff's Hits*** album. A mock stereo version was also created, which was based on the original mono edit. All three takes from the studio session have been released on the rarity compilation album ***The Rock 'n' Roll Years 1958-1963***: the first is a rehearsal take, featuring Hank Marvin trying a different guitar line but without backing vocals or the hand-claps that featured on the final release; the second is similar to the released single version (take three) but breaks down towards the end and doesn't have the harmonized choruses; the third is the final take that was released as the single but without the overdubs (the harmonized vocals and hand claps) and starting with shushing from those in the studio before the drums kick in. The single version was also included on the track listing for the ***Cliff's Hits*** EP.

With the drum introduction and the rollicking guitar underpinning the vocal line, *Do You Wanna Dance?* is an ideal illustration of the close harmony perfection that Cliff, Hank and Bruce managed to achieve on their recordings and was so successful in creating the sound that was associated with band. The hand-claps provide most of the percussive elements of the song while Cliff's tuneful howls before the instrumental bridges add something special to the mix and to the energy of the overall performance.

The song has become a regular standard on the set list for Cliff's concerts, the first of which after the single's release was the ABC Kingston concert, which was recorded on 7th March 1962 but remained unreleased until the CD album ***Live at the ABC Kingston 1962***, which was also only issued in stereo. The performance is an almost exact replica of the single including the close harmonies and hand claps.

For the Japanese tour in 1974, Cliff not only performed the song separately but also as part of a ***Rock Medley***: ***His Latest Flame***, ***Chantilly Lace***, ***Bony Maronie***, *Do You Wanna Dance?*, ***Crocodile Rock*** and *Do You Wanna Dance?* again to complete the medley. In the separate performance, the guitar is more heavily in evidence, as is the bass drum, than in previous live recordings but this was simply a feature of the overall performance. The guitar is more subdued in the medley version but it is only the opening two lines of the song before the falsetto la-laing of the introduction to *Crocodile Rock*. After this, the medley recapitulates with *Do You Wanna Dance?* to complete the medley but this time repeats the opening two lines three times before finishing with a rallentando and a high note to rapturous applause.

The approach taken to the reunion concert in 1978 that was issued on the ***Thank You Very Much*** album is a fast-paced and rocking version that is curiously driven along by the complex bass line and the rocking piano. Hank Marvin's guitar is featured brilliantly during the solo jam in the middle eight.

Around four years later, following a small earlier collaboration with Marietta Parfitt on her January single ***You're Only Lonely***, Cliff was invited back to assist on the backing vocals once more for her follow-up single, which was a cover of Cliff's seventeenth single – as with many of the compilation releases by Cliff, Marietta's cover uses the contraction 'wanna' rather than 'want to'. Backed with a song written by Marietta, *Only in Your Eyes I See*, *Do You Wanna Dance?* was released as a single on the Polydor label (catalogue number POSP 483) in late 1982, but, in spite of its pedigree, the song failed to make an impression on the charts. There is scant information on the technical and musical personnel and location and these are highlighted as unknown in the track specification. This version is heavy on the saxophones and has a much more bouncing rhythm of the twelve bar blues associated with Status Quo, unsurprisingly. Marietta's vocal is pleasant enough, if a little nasal, but it is the instrumentation and the 'oohing' backing vocals that make the track stand out.

Part of the ***Medley*** towards the end of the *Oh Boy! Set* at his 1989 Wembley Stadium concerts, Cliff sang this rocking version with the Dallas Boys, the Vernons Girls and the Kalin Twins but, in other respects, it is the familiar arrangement replete with guitar solo. The song segues neatly into ***Chantilly Lace***.

Cliff was back together with the Shadows for a short set at a festival that took place in June 1990 in the grounds of Knebworth House in Hertfordshire. Although the full thirteen-song performance was broadcast in full on BBC radio, only two tracks appeared on the charity album, *Knebworth – The Album*, sold in aid of the Nordoff-Robbins Music Therapy Centre: ***On the Beach*** and *Do You Wanna Dance?*; however, two other tracks appeared alongside these on the DVD: ***Good Golly Miss Molly*** and ***We Don't Talk Anymore***.

A musical based around the hits of Cliff Richard toured the UK in 1997 and into 1998 with Darren Day in the lead role. The associated album that was recorded (and produced by Brian Bennett) featured Cliff on backing vocals on four of the tracks, including *Do You Wanna Dance?*, which also featured in the final track, ***The Summer Holiday Megamix***. There is some energy lacking in Day's performance, although he possesses the same pitch-perfection of his model. Cliff provides the layered backing vocals that were originally the preserve of Hank and Bruce and this instantly elevates the song, whenever they are performed.

A hugely popular song in Cliff Richard and the Shadows' oeuvre, *Do You Wanna Dance?* was one of the songs that was inevitably chosen for the track listing of ***Reunited***, which saw the band together and re-recording material from their early days. The song is built up in a different way from the original and includes some additional guitar work but this only improves it. The best part is the performance of the close harmony vocals crated by Cliff, Bruce and Hank proving they have lost none of their technique.

Track Specification
Composed by Bobby Freeman

1. B-side (I'm Looking out the Window)/double A-side

Musicians		*Recording Details*	
Jet Harris	backing vocals, bass	Producer	Norrie Paramor
Hank Marvin	backing vocals, guitar	Engineered by	Malcolm Addey
Tony Meehan	drums, percussion	Recording location	Abbey Road Studio 2, St. John's Wood, London
Cliff Richard	vocals, hand claps	Recording date	19th December 1961
Bruce Welch	backing vocals, rhythm guitar		

2. Cliff's Hit Album (alternative stereo version)

Musicians		*Recording Details*	
Jet Harris	backing vocals, bass	Producer	Norrie Paramor .
Hank Marvin	backing vocals, guitar	Engineered by	Malcolm Addey
Tony Meehan	drums, percussion	Recording location	Abbey Road Studio 2, St. John's Wood, London
Cliff Richard	vocals, hand claps	Recording date	19th December 1961
Bruce Welch	backing vocals, rhythm guitar		

3. The Rock 'n' Roll Years 1958-1963 (take one – rehearsal take)

Musicians		*Recording Details*	
Jet Harris	bass	Producer	Norrie Paramor
Hank Marvin	guitar	Engineered by	Malcolm Addey
Tony Meehan	drums, percussion	Recording location	Abbey Road Studio 2, St. John's Wood, London
Cliff Richard	vocals	Recording date	19th December 1961
Bruce Welch	rhythm guitar		

4. The Rock 'n' Roll Years 1958-1963 (take two)

Musicians		*Recording Details*	
Jet Harris	bass	Producer	Norrie Paramor
Hank Marvin	guitar	Engineered by	Malcolm Addey
Tony Meehan	drums, percussion	Recording location	Abbey Road Studio 2, St. John's Wood, London
Cliff Richard	vocals	Recording date	19th December 1961
Bruce Welch	rhythm guitar		

5. The Rock 'n' Roll Years 1958-1963 (take three – basic single take)

Musicians		*Recording Details*	
Jet Harris	bass	Producer	Norrie Paramor
Hank Marvin	guitar	Engineered by	Malcolm Addey
Tony Meehan	drums, percussion	Recording location	Abbey Road Studio 2, St. John's Wood, London
Cliff Richard	vocals	Recording date	19th December 1961
Bruce Welch	rhythm guitar		

6. Live at the ABC Kingston 1962

Musicians		*Recording Details*	
Brian Bennett	drums, percussion	Producer	Norrie Paramor
Jet Harris	backing vocals, bass	Engineered by	Malcolm Addey and Ken Townsend
Hank Marvin	backing vocals, guitar	Recording location	ABC Theatre, Kingston, Surrey
Cliff Richard	vocals, hand claps	Recording date	7th March 1962
Bruce Welch	backing vocals, rhythm guitar		

7. Cliff "Live" in Japan '72

Musicians	
Brian Bennett	drums, percussion
Pat Carroll	backing vocals
John Farrar	bass
Alan Hawkshaw	piano
Hank Marvin	guitar
Olivia Newton-John	backing vocals
Cliff Richard	vocals
Bruce Welch	rhythm guitar

Recording Details	
Producer	Norrie Paramor
Engineered by	Unknown
Recording location	Kosei Nenkin Hall, Tokyo, Japan
Recording date	22nd-23rd September 1972

8. Japan Tour '74

Musicians	
Cliff Hall	piano
Brian Lewis	backing vocals, guitar
Kevin Peak	acoustic guitar
Cliff Richard	vocals
Trevor Spencer	drums, percussion
Alan Tarney	backing vocals, bass
Bruce Welch	backing vocals, rhythm guitar

Recording Details	
Producer	Toshiba EMI (no individual detailed)
Engineered by	Toshiba EMI (no individual detailed)
Recording location	Shinjuku Koseinenkin, Tokyo, Japan
Recording date	7th-8th October 1974

9. Japan Tour '74 (Rock Medley)

Musicians	
Cliff Hall	piano
Brian Lewis	backing vocals, guitar
Kevin Peak	acoustic guitar
Cliff Richard	vocals
Trevor Spencer	drums, percussion
Alan Tarney	backing vocals, bass
Bruce Welch	backing vocals, rhythm guitar

Recording Details	
Producer	Toshiba EMI (no individual detailed)
Engineered by	Toshiba EMI (no individual detailed)
Recording location	Shinjuku Koseinenkin, Tokyo, Japan
Recording date	7th-8th October 1974

10. Thank You Very Much

Musicians	
Brian Bennett	drums, percussion
Alan Jones	bass
Cliff Hall	keyboards
Hank Marvin	backing vocals, guitar
Cliff Richard	vocals
Bruce Welch	backing vocals, rhythm guitar

Recording Details	
Producer	Bruce Welch
Engineered by	Tony Clark, remixed by Peter Vince
Recording location	London Palladium, London
Remix location	Abbey Road Studios, St. John's Wood, London
Recording date	4th March 1978

11. Single (Marietta)

Musicians	
Marietta Parfitt	vocals
Rick Parfitt	guitar
Cliff Richard	backing vocals
Unknown	bass
Unknown	saxophones
Unknown	keyboards
Unknown	drums, percussion

Recording Details	
Producer	Craig Pruess, John Eden and Rick Parfitt
Engineered by	Unknown
Recording location	Unknown
Recording date	1982

12. From a Distance *** The Event**

Musicians	
Dallas Boys:	
Nicky Clarke	backing vocals
Leon Fisk	backing vocals
Stan Jones	backing vocals
Joe Smith	backing vocals
Bob Wragg	backing vocals
Kalin Twins:	
Harold Kalin	backing vocals
Herbie Kalin	backing vocals
Oh Boy! Band	rock 'n' roll band
Cliff Richard	vocals
Vernons Girls:	
Lyn Cornell	backing vocals
Maureen Kennedy	backing vocals
Frances Lee	backing vocals
Jean Owen	backing vocals

Recording Details	
Producer	Cliff Richard
Engineered by	Keith Bessey and Mick McKenna
Recording location	Rolling Stones Mobile Studio, Wembley Stadium, Wembley, North-west London
Recording date	16th-17th June 1989

13. Knebworth – The Album

Musicians	
Ray Beavis	saxophone
Brian Bennett	drums, percussion
John Earle	saxophone
Chris Gower	trombone

Recording Details	
Producer	Chris Kimsey and Steve Smith
Engineered by	Unknown
Recording location	Knebworth House, Hertfordshire, England
Recording date	30th June 1990

Mark Griffiths	bass
Cliff Hall	keyboards
Dick Hanson	trumpet
Peter Howarth	backing vocals
Hank Marvin	backing vocals, guitar
Paul Moessl	keyboards
Mick Mullins	backing vocals
Keith Murrell	backing vocals
Cliff Richard	vocals
Bruce Welch	backing vocals, guitar

14. Summer Holiday (Darren Day)

Musicians

Darren Day	vocals
Mark Griffiths	lead guitar
Cliff Richard	backing vocals
Warren Bennett	arranger, guitar, bass, drums, percussion

Recording Details

Producer	Brian Bennett
Engineered by	Dick Plant
Recording location	Honeyhill Studios, Hertfordshire, England
Recording date	1996

15. Reunited

Musicians

Brian Bennett	drums, percussion
Warren Bennett	piano
Mark Griffiths	bass
Hank Marvin	backing vocals, guitar
Cliff Richard	vocals, backing vocals
Bruce Welch	backing vocals, rhythm guitar

Recording Details

Producer	Warren Bennett (co-ordination)
Engineered by	James Collins (Honeyhill Studios), Ethan Carlson (Middle Ear Studios), Les Williams (Nivram Studios) and Keith Bessey (mixing and mastering)
Recording location	Middle Ear Studios, Miami, Florida, USA (Cliff's vocals), Nivram Studios, Perth, Western Australia (Hank's guitars and vocals) and Honeyhill Studios, Hertfordshire, England (all other vocals and instruments)
Recording date	Early 2009

♫ Do You Want to Dance?

Published title for **Do You Wanna Dance?**

The *Guinness Book of British Hit Singles* defines the song as ***Do You Want to Dance?*** in its official listing of Cliff Richard's singles. Often, the Americanized version with the words *Want* and *to* combined into *Wanna* is listed as the song's title on a variety of albums. Although the singles authority lists it as *Do You Want to Dance?*, the preference is to follow the track listings of the albums and the popular culture assocxiated with Cliff's recording of the song, and use the more familiar ***Do You Wanna Dance?***.

♫ Do You Wonder?

From the album **Wanted**

Alan Tarney had worked with Cliff since the late sixties in the capacity of supporting musician, songwriter, arranger and later on as producer of his most influential songs and albums: ***We Don't Talk Anymore*** and ***Always Guaranteed*** respectively. After ***Stronger*** in 1989, Tarney and Cliff had only worked together sporadically but they came together to work on Cliff's first album since EMI decided to drop him from their artist list, ***Wanted***, with Tarney arranging and providing most of the instrumentation for the choice of songs on the track listing. Most of the songs were covers of well-known and influential songs but there was a small handful of original compositions by Tarney and Chris Eaton that were incorporated into the album, one of which was *Do You Wonder?*

Swooping electronic strings introduce the song, which picks up the pace and matches the rhythm with a blipping percussive arrangement. Not the best song on the album, but it is suitably functional and any issues with it are lifted by the inevitable strong backing vocal arrangement.

Track Specification

Composed by Alan Tarney

Musicians

John Brant	additional programming
Anthony Clark	backing vocals
Cliff Richard	vocals, backing vocals
Alan Tarney	arranger, backing vocals, keyboards, programming

Recording Details

Producer	Alan Tarney
Engineered by	John Brant and Gerry Kitchingham
Recording location	Wilmer Studios, London
Recording date	January-April 2001

♫ Dream

From the EP **Dream**

Forming one of four tracks on the first Cliff Richard EP (***Dream***) not to include any album tracks or singles, *Dream* was written in 1944 by Johnny Mercer and had since become a standard in the fifties and sixties for acts from Frank Sinatra through Roy Orbison to Michael Bublé. The song was included in the 1955 musical film *Daddy Long Legs*, featuring Freed Astaire and Leslie Caron and has since been recorded by a variety of artists including Ella Fitzgerald, Doris Day, Vaughn Monroe, Julie London, The Bachelors, Woody Herman, The Pied Pipers, Little Anthony and the Imperials among many others.

Dream was the first track to be recorded in the session that produced the Cliff EP with six takes being concluded before an acceptable recording was complete. The sixth and final take was used for the record with the stereo and mono releases using the same edit but with different mixes for the requirements of the audio channels. Prior to a French CD album in 2008 and then the celebratory ***...And They Said It Wouldn't Last! (My 50 Years in Music)***, *Dream* remained a complete rarity and much sought after by Cliff Richard fans and collectors.

The classical guitar introduction, matched with the arpeggiated bass and the tinkling percussive finger-bells and tambourine, create the perfect atmosphere of a sleepy dream. There are no drums and Cliff's vocals are as competent as ever and are well suited to this style of ballad love song. The middle eight has a brief instrumental interlude but it is a simple continuation of the musical accompaniment that continues throughout the song. It would have been a strong choice for a single were it not leading the charge as the eponymous title of the EP.

Track Specification
Composed by Johnny Mercer

Musicians		*Recording Details*	
Jet Harris	bass	Producer	Norrie Paramor
Hank Marvin	guitar	Engineered by	Malcolm Addey
Tony Meehan	finger-bells, tambourine	Recording location	Abbey Road Studio 2, St. John's Wood, London
Cliff Richard	vocals	Recording date	4th May 1961
Bruce Welch	rhythm guitar		

♫ Dreamin'

***78th UK single** and from B-side of* **From a Distance** *(twelve-inch and CD versions) and from the album* **World Tour Live**

With the melody written by Alan Tarney and featuring lyrics provided by seventies pop star Leo Sayer, *Dreamin'* was the first single to be released from the ***I'm No Hero*** project, when it became Cliff Richard's seventy-eighth UK single release. Backed with ***Dynamite***, which was a completely new recording of the Ian Samwell song that had been first recorded in 1959, *Dreamin'* was released as a single on the EMI label (catalogue number EMI 5095) on 8th August 1980 and reached number eight in the UK singles charts. It also cemented his short-lived (and resurgent) success in America at the time, when it hit number seven in the Billboard charts and, along with the duet with Olivia Newton-John, ***Suddenly*** from the film *Xanadu*, and ***A Little in Love*** (also from *I'm No Hero*), Cliff had achieved the feat of having three songs in the Billboard Hot 100 chart for the first time since the start of his career. It was also the first time that he had greater chart success in the US with a single than he had in his native land. The associated promotional video was essentially a studio-based 'live' version of the song interspersed with Cliff sitting or standing in a large box with metal bars and mirrors. The band behind him is the one that appears on the track and the set appears to be that of a night club with a number of neon lights littered around them.

One of the most familiar songs from the period has a certain ***We Don't Talk Anymore*** vibe about it in its structure and rhythmic devices. Cliff's lead vocal line is echoed around two beats behind, while he and Tarney provide the supporting vocals, with Cliff's voice being the most prominently built in the layers.

Naturally, in a set of important songs from the latter period of Cliff's career, *Dreamin'* would be among them and it was performed at Wembley Stadium in June 1989 as part of ***The Event***. However, probably for reasons of space, it was not issued on the track listing of ***From a Distance ***** The Event*** in 1990 and would have to await the 2005 remaster of the album for it to be restored to its programmed position. Following on from ***Wired for Sound***, *Dreamin'* is of the same mould and perfectly evokes memories of that period of Cliff's recordings. The performance feels a little subdued behind Cliff's vocal line but it is still a great addition to the songs that run through Cliff's history.

Fourteen years later, Cliff incorporated *Dreamin'* into the set list for his world tour in 2003 to support his then new album ***Wanted***. The New Zealand show as filmed for the planned DVD release later in the year and, in 2004, a selection of the songs was issued on the complementary *World Tour Live* CD album and the track listing included *Dreamin'*. This version sounds somewhat sanitized until Cliff begins his vocals and the memories flood back. In the video, he is joined by the black-clad dancers as the stage is brightly lit.

Track Specification
Composed by Alan Tarney and Leo Sayer

1. Single

Musicians		*Recording Details*	
Michael Boddicker	synthesiser	Producer	Alan Tarney
Nick Glennie-Smith	synthesiser	Engineered by	Ashley Howe
Cliff Richard	vocals, backing vocals	Recording location	Riverside Studios, London
Trevor Spencer	drums, percussion	Recording date	12th May-27th June 1980
Alan Tarney	arranger, backing vocals, bass		

2. B-side (From a Distance)

Musicians

John Clark	guitar
Sonia Jones-Morgan	backing vocals
Steve Lauri	guitar
Peter May	drums, percussion
Paul Moessl	keyboards
Tessa Niles	backing vocals
Alan Park	keyboards
Provox:	
Peter Howarth	backing vocals
Mick Mullins	backing vocals
Keith Murrell	backing vocals
Cliff Richard	vocals
Steve Stroud	bass

Recording Details

Producer	Cliff Richard
Engineered by	Keith Bessey and Mick McKenna
Recording location	Rolling Stones Mobile Studio, Wembley Stadium, Wembley, North-west London
Recording date	16th-17th June 1989

3. World Tour Live

Musicians

Anthony Clark	backing vocals, guitar
John Clark	guitar
Dave Cooke	keyboards
Peter Howarth	backing vocals
Pete May	drums, percussion
Mick Mullins	backing vocals
Keith Murrell	backing vocals
Alan Park	keyboards
Cliff Richard	vocals
Steve Stroud	bass

Recording Details

Producer	Keith Bessey
Engineered by	Keith Bessey
Recording location	The Mission Winery, Napier, New Zealand
Recording date	22nd February 2003

♫ Dream Lover

From the album **World Tour Live**

Written and recorded by Bobby Darin, it became his first number one when released as a single in the UK in the middle of 1959. In his native USA, he reached number two in the Billboard charts with the recording that features Neil Sedaka accompanying him on the piano. In the UK, *Dream Lover* was reissued as a double A-side with *Mack the Knife* in 1979, but only reached number sixty-four. It has been covered a number of artists and a small sample includes Jason Donovan, Ricky Nelson, Daniel O'Donnell, Glen Campbell with Tanya Tucker and Dion and the Belmonts.
Never recorded by Cliff Richard, he included it in the ***Doo-Wop Medley*** section of his 2003 world tour. The New Zealand show was filmed for DVD release and, in 2004, it was decided to issue a complementary CD album also called *World Tour Live*. While many tracks from the DVD were not included, the *Doo-Wop Medley* was issued.The performance sits well in this musical genre, which Cliff sings well. The backing vocalists help recreate the era in this perfect slice of live doo-wop.

Track Specification

Composed by Bobby Darin

Musicians

Anthony Clark	backing vocals, guitar
John Clark	guitar
Dave Cooke	keyboards
Mike Haughton	saxophone
Peter Howarth	backing vocals
Pete May	drums, percussion
Mick Mullins	backing vocals
Keith Murrell	backing vocals
Alan Park	keyboards
Cliff Richard	vocals
Steve Stroud	bass

Recording Details

Producer	Keith Bessey
Engineered by	Keith Bessey
Recording location	The Mission Winery, Napier, New Zealand
Recording date	22nd February 2003

♫ Dreams I Dream, The

From the albums **Established 1958** *and* **Live at the Talk of the Town**

Originally a Shadows' single which reached number forty-two in November 1966, Cliff Richard recorded *The Dreams I Dream* in March 1968, although it wouldn't be released until the issue of ***Established 1958*** and is the only track on that album by Cliff that doesn't have the Shadows accompaniment. Cliff took to performing a medley of songs composed by Hank Marvin in his shows, with the Talk of the Town line-up being: ***London's Not Too Far*** (also recorded in the studio but not released until 1970 on ***Sincerely Cliff***), *The Dreams I Dream* and his single ***The Day I Met Marie***.
Cliff's performance matches the Shadows' original and it would have been great to be joined by them on this track. Nevertheless the brass accompaniment and strong backing vocals by the Breakaways make for an interesting track.
The story of the song didn't stop there as it was chosen as one of the songs to be translated into German for the album ***Hier Ist Cliff***, taking the title ***Geh' Deinen Weg Nicht So Allein***.

Track Specification
Composed by Hank Marvin

1. Established 1958

Musicians		*Recording Details*	
Breakaways:	backing vocals	Producer	Norrie Paramor
Vicki Hasemen		Engineered by	Peter Vince
Margo Quantrell		Recording location	Abbey Road Studio 2, St. John's Wood, London
Jean Ryder		Recording date	8th March 1968
Mike Leander	arranger, conductor		
Mike Leander Orchestra	orchestra		
Cliff Richard	vocals		

2. Live at the Talk of the Town

Musicians		*Recording Details*	
Breakaways:	backing vocals	Producer	Norrie Paramor
Vicki Hasemen		Engineered by	Peter Vince
Margo Quantrell		Recording location	Talk of the Town Theatre, London
Jean Ryder		Recording date	30th May 1968
Norrie Paramor	arranger, conductor		
Cliff Richard	vocals		
Talk of the Town Orchestra	orchestra		

♫ Dream Tomorrow

From the albums **Songs from Heathcliff** *and* **Heathcliff Live**

Another duet between Cliff Richard and Olivia Newton-John from the ***Songs from Heathcliff*** album, *Dream Tomorrow* features at the beginning of the second act when Heathcliff (Cliff) and Cathy (Olivia on the studio album, Helen Hobson in the stage musical) meet again after Heathcliff's lengthy absence abroad accruing wealth by beating down the native peoples of the countries he visited. The pompous Edgar Linton, to whom Cathy is betrothed, is somewhat jealous to see the return of his newly rich rival, while Cathy is ebullient with joy to see her old friend again. The song is sung principally by Cathy while Heathcliff responds as they sing together but realize that getting back together is merely a dream, in spite of his offers of gold and money and other meaningless trinkets and jewellery. He leaves Isabella Linton with a silk scarf, which gives her the wrong message about his intentions, as he reveals that he is living at Wuthering Heights with Cathy's brother Hindley, while Linton orders Cathy to come home with him immediately.

With exotic percussion to indicate the travelled nature of Heathcliff's character, Olivia begins the duet and, in her performance, it sounds very much like her early eighties material. The flute-like synthesiser motif in the accompaniment creates a passing interesting as Cliff begins his section. At the mid-point of the song, Olivia and Cliff sing together in perfect harmony. Helen Hobson executes the song well on the live track, supported by the backing vocalists of her friends. Cliff sings the song as well as he ever did on the studio recording and the harmony vocals between Hobson and Cliff work exceptionally well on the stage version and are improved over the original.

A promotional edit of the *Songs from Heathcliff* recording of the first two and half minutes was included on a Tower Records cassette handed out at an appearance in store, which was called *Cliff Richard at Tower.*

Track Specification
Composed by John Farrar and Tim Rice

1. Songs from Heathcliff

Musicians		*Recording Details*	
Sean Callery	orchestrator, synclavier, keyboards	Producer	John Farrar
Liz Constantino	backing vocals	Engineered by	Chris Fogel, Eric Rudd and Joe Schiff (Moonee Ponds Studio), Darren Goodwin and Guy Massey (Abbey Road Studios) and James Collins and Caroline Daniel (CTS Studios)
Linda Dalziel	backing vocals		
John Farrar	guitar, synclavier		
Steve Kipner	backing vocals		
Clif Magness	backing vocals	Recording location	Moonee Ponds Studio, Los Angeles, Abbey Road Studios, St. John's Wood, London and CTS Studios, Wembley, London
Olivia Newton-John	vocals		
Kristina Nichols	backing vocals		
Cliff Richard	vocals	Mixed by	Elliot Scheiner
Bob Sabellico	drum programming	Mixed at	Moonee Ponds Studio, Los Angeles
Michael Thompson	guitar	Recording date	February-April 1994 and May-August 1995

2. Heathcliff Live

Musicians		*Recording Details*	
Sean Callery	orchestrator, orchestra	Producer	John Farrar
John Clark	guitar	Engineered by	Keith Bessey, John Pearson and Tom Tranter
Friends of Cathy:		Recording location	Earl's Court Hall 2, London and/or The Academy, National Indoor Arena, Birmingham, England
Sonia Jones	backing vocals		
Niki Kitt	backing vocals		
Suzanne Parry	backing vocals	Recording date	October 1996
Keith Hayman	keyboards		

Helen Hobson	spoken vocals, vocals
Darryl Knock	spoken vocals
Peter May	drums, percussion
Bob Noble	keyboards
Alan Park	keyboards
Cliff Richard	spoken vocals, vocals
Steve Stroud	bass
Kevin Townend	orchestration
Unknown	orchestra

♫ Drifting

88th UK single

Cliff Richard's eighty-eighth UK single took many by surprise, in part because it was another duet but mainly because his protégée, Sheila Walsh, was pretty unknown in most musical circles. However, it shows his generosity of spirit to lend his name to the project in spite of the likelihood that many record-buyers might be turned off an unknown singing a faith-related song. The song was recorded during the sessions for Walsh's first album under Cliff's direction, also called ***Drifting***. Backed with ***It's Lonely When the Lights Go On***, which was also found on the album, *Drifting* was issued as a single on the DJM Records label (catalogue number SHEIL 1) on 27th May 1983. Although it had good airplay, the song settled at number sixty-four, which, of Cliff's charting singles, was the worst placing of his career to date. A picture disc version of the single (essentially the misty-pictured portrait shot of Cliff and Sheila Walsh that appears on the picture sleeve) was simultaneously released (same label but with a catalogue number of SHEIL 100); the rarity value of this single issue is enormous. Cliff continued to work with Walsh and issue singles but no other releases managed to chart.

Cliff begins the duet by singing the first couple of lines before handing over to Sheila Walsh. The gentle sustained chords on the synthesiser slowly build up to the chorus, which allows the drifting idea to be a reality as Cliff and Walsh sing their harmonies. During this section, Walsh has a vocal projection that is reminiscent of Olivia Newton-John, while Cliff also provides backing vocals. The pace picks up in the middle eight with an electric guitar solo but this returns to the pace of the original verse with Walsh adding her own backing vocals. It is a beautiful love song and is a surprise that it was well-received commercially.

Track Specification

Composed by Bruce Woolley and Simon Darlow

Musicians

John Clark	electric guitar
Rick Fenn	acoustic guitar
Craig Pruess	arranger, synthesiser, piano
Cliff Richard	vocals, backing vocals
Sheila Walsh	vocals, backing vocals

Recording Details

Producer	Cliff Richard and Craig Pruess
Engineered by	Keith Bessey
Recording location	Riverside Studios, London, Strawberry Studios, London, Ramp Studios, London and/or Sonoptics Studios, London
Recording date	September 1982-January 1983

♫ Driving

From the film soundtrack album of **Take Me High**

For some unknown reason, most of the songs on the soundtrack album for the ***Take Me High*** film are presented in a different sequence to those in the narrative on the film. Thus *Driving* appears as the fifth song on the album but in reality is the ninth in the film and should appear between ***Brumburger Duet*** and the eponymous film song ***Take Me High***; however, while the songs were written to support the story, the narrative is not necessarily lost on the album by being out of sequence.

Driving appears at the point in the film where Tim Matthews (played by Cliff Richard) and now girlfriend Sarah (Debbie Watling) are trying to find Sir Hugh Cunningham in order to talk to him about the City Cross scheme in which he can invest. Cunningham is out fox-hunting and Tim drives his Mini Cooper across fields and up dirt-tracks, eventually getting stuck in the mud. To help balance the weight and get traction, Sarah gets out and straddles the bonnet helping Tim to get driving. She paints pictures in the frosting of her breath in the windscreen and this is used as a device to show the pair falling in love. The song itself, though, is by far the weakest in the film, because it feels uncertain and out of tune and, by attrition, lower quality than the other tracks. An instrumental version of the song, which also appears on the soundtrack, is used a little later on as the hunted fox jumps into the car and curls up on the back seat. The vocals are then repeated very briefly at the end of this sequence, although this does not appear on the album as a separate entity.

The lovely guitar line is accompanied by Cliff's falsetto 'ooh'ings but he appears uncomfortable on the top notes for some reason, although he does also provide his own backing vocals on this very short piece.

Track Specification

Composed by Tony Cole

Musicians

David MacKay Orchestra	orchestra
David MacKay	arranger, conductor
Cliff Richard	vocals, backing vocals

Recording Details

Producer	David MacKay
Engineered by	Tony Clark and Mike Jarrett
Recording location	Abbey Road Studio 3, St. John's Wood, London
Recording date	26th May 1973

♬ Du Bist Mein Erster Gedanke

German single

Originally a Spanish popular song by the name of *Quiereme Mucho*, the song is much more famously known simply as *Yours*, after English lyrics were applied and it was recorded by Jimmy Dorsey in 1941. In that incarnation, it was also covered by Mantovani, the Three Degrees, Benny Goodman, Bing Crosby, Chet Atkins, Engelbert Humperdinck, Jim Reeves, Vera Lynn and Billy Vaughn among others. The original Spanish version literally translates to *I Love You So Much*, while the German version, *Du Bist Mein Erster Gedanke*, means *You Are My First Thought*, all having the same message.
Cliff Richard recorded his version in the German language specifically for a single release in Germany in May 1966 in the middle of a sequence of sessions set aside to record the soundtrack for his next film project, ***Finders Keepers***. The final (unknown) take and edit were used for both the mono and stereo recordings but with different mixes for the separate audio channels. When it was released as a single, it was issued in mono format and it was only when the 1997 foreign language compilation ***On the Continent*** was released that the stereo version was issued. Backed with a German translation of ***The Time in Between, Was Ist Dabei?***, the song was issued as a single in Germany on the international Columbia label (catalogue number C-23211) in July 1966, and it reached number fifteen in the German singles charts.
The song has a specifically Teutonic feel to its performance and the song suits Cliff's voice so well. There is unfortunately little information available on the recording sessions so the orchestra and backing vocals remain unknown.

Track Specification

Composed by Gonzalo Roig and Augustin Torres Rodriguez; German lyrics by Ralph Maria Siegel

Musicians		*Recording Details*	
Cliff Richard	vocals	Producer	Norrie Paramor
Unknown	backing vocals	Engineered by	Peter Vince
Unknown	arranger, conductor	Recording location	Abbey Road Studio 3, St. John's Wood, London
Unknown	orchestra	Recording date	13th May 1966

♬ Du, Du Gefällst Mir So

German single

Written and recorded by Barry McGuire in its original English title form of *Green, Green*, this parochial version has also been recorded by Bobby Darin, Glenn Campbell, the New Christy Minstrels, Trini Lopez, the Village Stompers and Johnny Rivers among others. In its German form, with new lyrics by Georg Buscher, it was retitled to *Du, Du Gefällst Mir So* (literally translated as *You, You Give Me So Much Pleasure*) and recorded by Cliff Richard at a convened session at the London-based Chappell Studios, the relocation possibly due to refurbishment of the Abbey Road Studio complex. At this session, four songs were attempted, three German and one unissued for the ***His Land*** album and film project.
Du, Du Gefällst Mir So was backed with ***Lieben Kann Man Einmal Nur*** (or *You Can Only Be in Love Once*), a German original, and released as a single on the international Columbia label (catalogue number 1C 006-04364) in March 1970. Although a strong song, there was insufficient following from fans for it to break into the German singles charts. Released solely in stereo (as per the Columbia singles policy entering the seventies) and was a significant rarity until it was included on the 1997 foreign language compilation ***On the Continent***.
Cliff provides his own backing vocals alongside those of an uncredited group and this is made highly effective on this bass-heavy song that moves along at a fast walking pace but is arranged in an undeniably Teutonic way. The middle eight features a lighter touch and a change of key worthy of any self-respecting Eurovision Song Contest entry.

Track Specification

Composed by Barry McGuire and Randy Sparks; German lyrics by Georg Buscher

Musicians		*Recording Details*	
Mike Vickers Orchestra	orchestra	Producer	Norrie Paramor
Cliff Richard	vocals, backing vocals	Engineered by	Unknown
Unknown	backing vocals	Recording location	Chappell Studios, London
Mike Vickers	arranger, conductor	Recording date	21st January 1970

♬ Du Fragst Mich Immer Wieder

From the album **Ich Träume Deine Träume**

Following the success of his first German language album, *Hier Ist Cliff*, Cliff Richard returned to the studios in late November 1970 to record some tracks for the follow-up, *Ich Träume Deine Träume*, released the following year. Other than previous singles recorded earlier that year, *Du Fragst Mich Immer Wieder* was one of five songs completed at the first of two dual sessions spread over the 24th and 25th of November. The process was simplified by recording the orchestral track earlier so that the focus of the later session was solely on Cliff's vocals. *Du Fragst Mich Immer Wieder* –translated as *You Ask Me Time and Time Again* – is an original German composition and Cliff has never recorded an English equivalent. The track was incorporated on the track listing of Cliff's foreign language tracks, ***On the Continent***, released in 1997.
The pumping orchestral accompaniment creates a driving force as it emphasises the offbeat in this German original song. Although there is an uncredited backing vocal group, Cliff forms his own principal harmony vocals that elevates the song further since the arrangement of his own duet brings out perfect musical intervals.

Track Specification
Composed by Müller and Werner

Musicians	
Norrie Paramor Orchestra	orchestra
Norrie Paramor	arranger, conductor
Cliff Richard	vocals, backing vocals
Unknown	backing vocals

Recording Details	
Producer	Norrie Paramor (backing track and vocals)
Engineered by	Phil McDonald (backing track and vocals)
Recording location	Cologne, Germany (backing track) and Abbey Road Studio 2, St. John's Wood, London (vocals)
Recording date	November 1970 (backing track) and 24th November 1970 (vocals)

♫ Dying Embers

From the album **Sail Away** *(Dave Pope)*

Recorded in the spring of 1978 for Dave Pope's solo album, ***Sail Away***, *Dying Embers* was produced by Cliff Richard. As with all the other album tracks, there is no information regarding the musicians involved on the album sleeve or in other reference material; as a consequence, these are highlighted as unknown in the track specification until further research unearths the detail.

A luscious piano introduction leads into Pope's gentle and emotional lead vocal, which he imbues with some subtle vibrato that adds further to the meaning of the lyrics, which talk of a relationship burning out. Cliff supplies backing vocals with other uncredited singers and this lifts the song and its meaning further whenever they are employed.

Track Specification
Composed by John Daniels

Musicians	
Dave Pope	vocals
Cliff Richard	backing vocals
Unknown	backing vocals
Unknown	guitar
Unknown	bass
Unknown	piano
Unknown	synthesiser
Unknown	drums, percussion

Recording Details	
Producer	Cliff Richard
Engineered by	Tony Clark
Recording location	Morgan Studios, London
Recording date	April 1978

♫ Dynamite

B-sides of **Travellin' Light** *and* **Dreamin'** *and taken from the albums* **Time to Rock!** *(Dutch),* **Cliff in Japan** *and* **...And They Said It Wouldn't Last (My Fifty Years in Music)** *and unissued live track*

The choice for a B-side of ***Travellin' Light***, which was Cliff's sixth single and second number one, returned to Ian Samwell, the erstwhile Drifters guitarist who had written a number of earlier hits including ***Move It*** and B-sides. The driving guitar and the sussurating cymbals and percussion ensure an energy throughout, while Cliff's vocals continue to improve with shouts and crystal clear enunciation and pitch.

Another two versions were released, one of which was issued in Holland (possibly by mistake) on the *Time to Rock* ten-inch long-player and another (take four from the session) on the *...And They Said It Wouldn't Last (My Fifty Years in Music)* anthology. The Dutch version was added to the 1987 issue of *Rock On with Cliff Richard* album and is quite different from the original B-side version in the changed lyrics. The version released as take four on the anthology is much closer to this Dutch version where the guitar and the lyric changes are very similar. In all three cases, the mono and stereo versions are the same recording but with different mixes for the additional channel.

Dynamite, an increasing favourite with Cliff's fans, was eventually listed in the UK charts as a separate song from the single's A-side, *Travellin' Light*, and reached number sixteen, while the main song reached number one. The single and its B-side were released on the Columbia label (catalogue number DB 4351 (78 r.p.m. format) and 45-DB 4351 (seven-inch single)) on 2nd October 1959 with both songs entering the chart simultaneously.

Unusually, for the live album ***Cliff in Japan***, the accompaniment for the entire concert at the Shibuya Public Hall in Tokyo is by Norrie Paramor conducting his orchestra rather than the expected rock and roll instrumentation for this type of song.

Over twenty years later, Cliff revisited *Dynamite* for the ***I'm No Hero*** album sessions in the early summer of 1980. Although the song was not included on the album (in spite of having enough space as it was his shortest album to date with just ten songs on it), it was released as the B-side of Cliff's seventy-eighth UK single release, ***Dreamin'***. It would have remained a rarity in any other format were it not for a paucity of material recorded for ***The Rock Connection*** album in 1984, when the decision was taken to include *Dynamite* in the track listing since it fitted with the tenor of the other material that was completed. It was incorporated finally as a bonus track on the 2001 remaster of *I'm No Hero*. This version of the song is far less rock and roll than the original with a bilious synthesiser bubbling behind Cliff's lead vocals, which are presented in a very sedate way rather than the raucous screaming of the familiar original. The change in recording techniques also facilitates Cliff singing his own backing vocals alongside those of producer Alan Tarney.

In spite of the restoration of all other previously unreleased tracks to the 2005 remaster of ***From a Distance ***** The Event***, *Dynamite* was one of six Cliff and the Shadows performances to remain unissued (with no information given as to why the decision was taken).

Track Specification
Composed by Ian Samwell

1. B-side (Travellin' Light)

Musicians

Jet Harris	bass
Hank Marvin	guitar
Tony Meehan	drums, percussion
Cliff Richard	vocals
Bruce Welch	rhythm guitar

Recording Details

Producer	Norrie Paramor
Engineered by	Peter Bown and Stuart Eltham
Recording location	Abbey Road Studio 2, St. John's Wood, London
Recording date	6th September 1959

2. Time to Rock!

Musicians

Jet Harris	bass
Hank Marvin	guitar
Tony Meehan	drums, percussion
Cliff Richard	vocals
Bruce Welch	rhythm guitar

Recording Details

Producer	Norrie Paramor
Engineered by	Peter Bown and Stuart Eltham
Recording location	Abbey Road Studio 2, St. John's Wood, London
Recording date	6th September 1959

3. ...And They Said It Wouldn't Last (My Fifty Years in Music)

Musicians

Jet Harris	bass
Hank Marvin	guitar
Tony Meehan	drums, percussion
Cliff Richard	vocals
Bruce Welch	rhythm guitar

Recording Details

Producer	Norrie Paramor
Engineered by	Peter Bown and Stuart Eltham
Recording location	Abbey Road Studio 2, St. John's Wood, London
Recording date	6th September 1959

4. Cliff in Japan

Musicians

Norrie Paramor Orchestra	orchestra
Norrie Paramor	arranger, conductor
Cliff Richard	vocals

Recording Details

Producer	Norrie Paramor
Engineered by	Unknown
Recording location	Shibuya Public Hall, Tokyo, Japan
Recording date	18th October 1967

5. B-side (Dreamin')

Musicians

Michael Boddicker	synthesiser
Nick Glennie-Smith	synthesiser
Cliff Richard	vocals, backing vocals
Trevor Spencer	drums, percussion
Alan Tarney	arranger, backing vocals, guitar, bass

Recording Details

Producer	Alan Tarney
Engineered by	Ashley Howe
Recording location	Riverside Studios, London
Recording date	12th May-27th June 1980

6. Unissued track (From a Distance ** The Event)***

Musicians

Ray Beavis	saxophone
Brian Bennett	drums, percussion
Mark Griffiths	bass
Cliff Hall	keyboards
Hank Marvin	guitar
Cliff Richard	vocals
Bruce Welch	rhythm guitar

Recording Details

Producer	Cliff Richard
Engineered by	Keith Bessey and Mick McKenna
Recording location	Rolling Stones Mobile Studio, Wembley Stadium, Wembley, North-west London
Recording date	16th-17th June 1989

♫ Each to His Own
From the album **Heathcliff Live**

At the grand house of Edgar Linton and his sister Isabella, there was a hugely ostentatious display of wealth each Christmas and Cathy Earnshaw (Helen Hobson) and Heathcliff (Cliff Richard) would walk across their beloved moors to watch as the guests indulged in dancing, singing carols and playing party games. During the waltz, Edgar asks Cathy to dance, with Heathcliff growing jealous as he observes her having fun. Heathcliff pulls her away from Linton and she storms off – with him angrily professing his love. Cathy later taunts him about the Lintons and how great – and clean – they are in comparison. The song begins with Cathy deriding Heathcliff's intellectual powers but underlying the words is her love for Heathcliff although she is cutting him off romantically. Cliff sings very little in the song, only providing harmonies to Hobson's main vocal line when it comes to the later utterances of the song title and then counterpointing with a repeat of the chorus to the song's end. Cathy runs away to meet up with Edgar leaving Heathcliff to observe.
The first new song featuring Cliff not on ***Songs from Heathcliff***, *Each to His Own* came in the show after *The Grange Waltz*. There is a lengthy spoken introduction as Heathcliff and Cathy talk before suddenly entering into this song. Hobson performs the song first chiding and then in mollification as she reveals her intentions. The accompaniment is simple synthesiser keyboards revealing the heaviness of the lovers' hearts. Cliff joins halfway through with harmony vocals.

Track Specification
Composed by John Farrar and Tim Rice
Musicians

Sean Callery	orchestrator, conductor
John Clark	guitar
Keith Hayman	keyboards
Helen Hobson	spoken vocals, vocals
Peter May	drums, percussion
Bob Noble	keyboards
Alan Park	keyboards
Cliff Richard	spoken vocals, vocals
Steve Stroud	bass
Kevin Townend	orchestration
Unknown	orchestra

Recording Details

Producer	John Farrar
Engineered by	Keith Bessey, John Pearson and Tom Tranter
Recording location	Earl's Court Hall 2, London and/or The Academy, National Indoor Arena, Birmingham, England
Recording date	October 1996

♫ Early in the Morning (1)
From the album **Oh Boy!**

Originally a major hit for its writer Bobby Darrin around the world but particularly in the US, it became more popular in the UK when Buddy Holly covered it for a single released on the same day as Cliff Richard's ***Move It***. Although Holly's version only reached number nineteen in the UK charts, it was enough for aspiring bands and singers to want to cover it. Cliff became a regular favourite on Jack Good's *Oh Boy!* show, performing covers and some original material. Following the show's success, an album was recorded. *Early in the Morning* was chosen for Cliff to record.
The backing track and Cliff's vocals were recorded on separate days and, instead of using the Drifters, the musicians were from the Oh Boy! Band. There is no record of who the individual performers are and will be highlighted as unknown in this entry. The energy of the performance is improved on some songs by the band, with a better set of backing vocals, which sound far enhanced from the lacklustre performances elsewhere. Although the album was re-released in the late seventies, it wasn't until the issue of *The Rock and Roll Years 1958-1963* that it saw release in digital format.

Track Specification
Composed by Bobby Darrin and Woody Harris
Musicians

Dallas Boys:	
Nicky Clarke	backing vocals
Leon Fisk	backing vocals
Stan Jones	backing vocals
Joe Smith	backing vocals
Bob Wragg	backing vocals
Oh Boy! Band	guitars, stand-up bass, piano, drums, percussion, tambourine
Cliff Richard	vocals

Recording Details

Producer	Harry Robinson (backing track) and Norrie Paramor (vocals)
Engineered by	Norman Newell (backing track) and Malcolm Addey (vocals)
Recording location	Abbey Road Studio 2, St. John's Wood, London
Recording date	19th October 1958 (backing track) and 21st October 1958 (vocals)

♫ Early in the Morning (2)

From the albums **Tracks 'n' Grooves**, **Cliff Live in Korea**, **Cliff "Live" in Japan '72** *and* **Japan Tour '74**

Not to be confused with the Bobby Darrin hit of the same name, in the UK, *Early in the Morning* is most familiarly associated with Vanity Fare. The vocal group recorded the song to serve as their second single and it became their only top ten chart hit when it reached number eight in August 1969. In the Far East, though, it was Cliff Richard's version that was the most popular, even though the Vanity Fare single was also available and Cliff himself was reported to be slightly embarrassed since he considered the group's recording to be the superior version.

Co-written by Mike Leander, who had been involved in arranging and conducting a number of tracks in the previous few years for Cliff's singles and albums, the track was released on the Odeon label (catalogue number OR-2373) in September 1969 in Japan, backed with ***Ooh La La*** from the ***Established 1958*** album and it reached the number one spot in the Japanese charts. Cliff's recording is quite different from the Vanity Fair version, although the bouncy, quirky nature is maintained from the original. Detracting from Cliff's lead vocals is an uncredited female backing group who are too raucous against the purity of Cliff's voice.

Throughout his tour in the Far East in the latter part of 1969, Cliff included *Early in the Morning* on the set list and it is probably this that drove the demand from the Japanese fans for a regional release of the song and then became a self-fulfilling prophecy as he had to to perform it as it was so successful commercially in Japan. It was included on the album *Cliff Live in Korea* and twice more on live recordings of his 1972 and 1974 Far East tours. In November 1970, Cliff was back in the studios recording material in German for his second album to be released in that country; while most of it was original material, there were some translated items from his English oeuvre, one of which was *Early in the Morning*, which was given German lyrics and retitled ***Neben Dir Wird's Keine Geben*** (or loosely *No-one Compares with You*).

Because of the single's success in the region, *Early in the Morning* was on the set list recorded for ***Cliff "Live" in Japan '72*** and it is executed with perfection by Cliff backed up by the band who are clearly enjoying the foot-tapping performance. It was revisited once more for his 1974 tour of Japan and appeared on the four-disc ***Japan Tour '74***. Once again, it is an upbeat and foot-tapping performance but sounds different from the earlier tour because the backing vocals are all male rather than all female.

Track Specification
Composed by Mike Leander and Eddie Seago

1. Tracks 'n' Grooves

Musicians		*Recording Details*	
Mike Vickers Orchestra	orchestra	Producer	Norrie Paramor
Cliff Richard	vocals	Engineered by	Peter Vince
Unknown	female backing vocals	Recording location	Abbey Road Studio 2, St. John's Wood, London
Mike Vickers	arranger, conductor	Recording date	2nd May 1969

2. Cliff Live in Korea

Musicians		*Recording Details*	
Brian Bennett	drums, percussion	Producer	Unknown
Alan Hawkshaw	keyboards	Engineered by	Unknown
Hank Marvin	guitar	Recording location	Citizen Hall, Seoul, South Korea
Cliff Richard	vocals	Recording date	16th October 1969
John Rostill	bass		
Bruce Welch	rhythm guitar		

3. Cliff "Live" in Japan '72

Musicians		*Recording Details*	
Brian Bennett	drums, percussion	Producer	Norrie Paramor
Pat Carroll	backing vocals	Engineered by	Unknown
John Farrar	bass	Recording location	Kosei Nenkin Hall, Tokyo, Japan
Alan Hawkshaw	piano	Recording date	22nd-23rd September 1972
Hank Marvin	guitar		
Olivia Newton-John	backing vocals		
Cliff Richard	vocals		
Bruce Welch	rhythm guitar		

4. Japan Tour '74

Musicians		*Recording Details*	
Barrie Guard	arranger, conductor	Producer	Toshiba EMI (no individual detailed)
Cliff Hall	piano	Engineered by	Toshiba EMI (no individual detailed)
Brian Lewis	backing vocals, guitar	Recording location	Shinjuku Koseinenkin, Tokyo, Japan
Kevin Peak	acoustic guitar	Recording date	7th-8th October 1974
Cliff Richard	vocals		
Shambles Symphonet	orchestra		
Trevor Spencer	drums, percussion		
Alan Tarney	backing vocals, bass		
Bruce Welch	backing vocals, rhythm guitar		

♫ Ease Along

From the album **Green Light**

Prolific Cliff Richard songwriters Alan Tarney and Trevor Spencer wrote *Ease Along* for Cliff's next project, ***Green Light***, where it was positioned as the album's original closer. Recorded at the first session for the album and the last of two songs completed, it was finished in three takes, while additional overdubs were recorded almost a month later.
Called *Easy Along* in the misprinted track listing for the album, *Ease Along* is introduced by synthesisers and staccato rhythms on the guitar and bass. Cliff's vocals are set back in the mix with reverb added.

Track Specification

Composed by Alan Tarney and Trevor Spencer

Musicians

Brian Bennett	drums, percussion
Terry Britten	guitar
Stuart Calver	backing vocals
Richard Hewson	arranger, conductor
Alan Jones	bass
Duncan MacKay	keyboards
Alan Parker	guitar
John Perry	backing vocals
Tim Renwick	guitar
Cliff Richard	vocals
Tony Rivers	backing vocals
Trevor Spencer	drums, percussion
Alan Tarney	backing vocals, guitar, bass, keyboards
Graham Todd	keyboards
Unknown	orchestra

Recording Details

Producer	Bruce Welch
Engineered by	Tony Clark and Haydn Bendall
Recording location	Abbey Road Studio 3, St. John's Wood, London
Recording date	9th January 1978 and 7th February 1978

♫ Elvis Medley

From the album **World Tour Live**

In 2003, Cliff Richard embarked on a world tour to promote his then new album, ***Wanted***. The result was filmed during the show in New Zealand and issued on DVD later that year and included the entire concert. A CD album to complement the film, *World Tour Live*, was released the following year but the disc only included fourteen of the tracks performed. Of the chosen tracks, one of those included was the *Elvis Medley*, which covered:

a) ***Too Much***
b) ***Don't Be Cruel***

The entries for those songs carry the information on the recording details and musicians.

♫ Embraceable You

From the album **Cliff Sings**

For the ***Cliff Sings*** albu, half of the songs were backed by the Norrie Paramor Orchestra and half by the Drifters in order to demonstrate Cliff Richard's vocal versatility. *Embraceable You* was written by brothers George and Ira Gershwin for a defunct musical entitled *East Is West* in 1928 and was then used in 1930 as part of the Broadway musical *Girl Crazy*, which featured Freed Astaire and Ginger Rogers. It has been covered by a variety of acts over the years including Billie Holiday, Ella Fitzgerald, Rod Stewart, Frank Sinatra, Chet Baker, Nat King Cole, Charlie Parker and Judy Garland.
With swelling strings and plodding double bass, this slow standard fits Cliff's voice well and he manages to sound sultry, while exuding sex appeal. The song is technically difficult but he has an innate ability to pitch the notes perfectly. The song was released on the *Cliff Richard Sings No. 3* EP in both mono and stereo, although the same take and edit was used to for both issues but with a different mix for each format. Both have since been reissued in CD format of the original album.

Track Specification

Composed by George Gershwin and Ira Gershwin

Musicians

Norrie Paramor Orchestra	orchestra
Norrie Paramor	arranger, conductor
Cliff Richard	vocals

Recording Details

Producer	Norrie Paramor
Engineered by	Malcolm Addey and Alan Kane (mono) and Stuart Eltham and Norman Smith (stereo)
Recording location	Abbey Road Studio 2, St. John's Wood, London
Recording date	10th September 1959

♫ Empty Chairs

B-side of **Living in Harmony**

Written by Don McLean, whose popularity was sealed at the time of Cliff Richard's recording with the enormously successful *American Pie* and its follow-up *Vincent*, *Empty Chairs* was a good choice for the B-side of Cliff's fifty-seventh single, ***Living in Harmony***. As well as its author, the song has been recorded by Harry Belafonte and Terence James Coffman, among a few others. Featuring married couple John Farrar (who was then working with Hank Marvin and

Bruce Welch on the Marvin, Welch & Farrar projects) and Pat Farrar (formerly Carroll, who had sung with Olivia Newton-John), the song was recorded in studio three of the Abbey Road complex rather than the more familiar studio two.
Like its A-side, it took a long time for the song to be released in another format, with *Empty Chairs* having to wait a further ten years before it was included on the rare B-sides section of the celebratory ***...And They Said It Wouldn't Last! (My 50 Years in Music)*** compilation in 2008.
A sad guitar introduction brings in Cliff's vocal line, which is sung with much emotion to underline the loneliness he feels with the parting of a girlfriend, who has left nothing but empty chairs for him to stare at. The song is one of reminiscence and its sadness comes out through the portrayed minor key as well as the sympathetic orchestral arrangement.

Track Specification
Composed by Don McLean

Musicians		*Recording Details*	
Nick Ingman	arranger, conductor	Producer	Norrie Paramor
Nick Ingman Orchestra	orchestra	Engineered by	Unknown
Cliff Richard	vocals	Recording location	Abbey Road Studio 3, St. John's Wood, London
		Recording date	28th April 1972

♬ End of the Show

From the album **Thank You Very Much**

A perfect song to complete a concert, *End of the Show* with it lyrics thanking everybody was written and performed by Dennis Wilson of the Beach Boys as the final track on his 1977 solo album *Pacific Ocean Blue*. Because Cliff Richard and the Shadows had been in showbusiness for twenty years in 1978, thanks in large part to their huge fan-base, not only was it suitable to close the show – apposite because of the lyrical meaning and the title – but it also gave the concerts their title: ***Thank You Very Much***. The song was one of the few over the years that Cliff has never revisited in the studio.
Introduced on a gentle piano chord structure, Cliff's vocals are quiet, subdued and almost tremulous with the use of his vibrato while the song builds up within the instrumentation. Bruce Welch and Hank Marvin provide their reliable backing vocal harmonies as the song increaees the drama into a foot-stomping song that would not be out of place in the Eurovision Song Contest. The song is sad and occasionally regretful because the show is over but over-riding this is the optimism and joy of coming together in spite of it being the end of the show.

Track Specification
Composed by Dennis Wilson and Gregg Jakobson

Musicians		*Recording Details*	
Brian Bennett	drums, percussion	Producer	Bruce Welch
Alan Jones	bass	Engineered by	Tony Clark, remixed by Peter Vince
Cliff Hall	keyboards	Recording location	London Palladium, London
Hank Marvin	backing vocals, guitar	Remix location	Abbey Road Studios, St. John's Wood, London
Cliff Richard	vocals	Recording date	4th March 1978
Bruce Welch	backing vocals, rhythm guitar		

♬ Escapade, The

From the album **The Hunting of the Snark** *(Mike Batt)*

The Escapade is the start of the fantasy journey to seek the Snark by the characters in Lewis Carroll's nonsense poem. Featuring as a dramatic showstopper at the start of the musical version of *The Hunting of the Snark*, composed and adapted from the poem by Mike Batt, it features each of the main characters introducing themselves: the Bellman (Cliff Richard in the CD version, replaced by Billy Connolly in the subsequent stage performance), the Baker (Julian Lennon), the Billiard-player (Captain Sensible), the Beaver (Deniece Williams), the Butcher (performed by Art Garfunkel on CD but replaced by Justin Hayward in the live performance), the Barrister (Roger Daltrey), the Banker (Midge Ure) and the Narrator (John Hurt, joined by Sir John Gielgud on the CD), who links the musical pieces by reciting stanzas of Carroll's original poem.
The dramatic presentation of the tune is a fusion of rock and classical styles of music and the wit of the nonsense poem is expertly carried through into the songs, the music and acting asides from the performers. Technically and musically complex, *The Escapade* is a true showstopper that was embellished for the West End run of the stage show in the early nineties, playing on the interaction between the Bellman and the conductor (eventually ripping the bell out of his hands and chucking it off-stage after "angrily tinkling" it just once too often).
Batt's genius at composing such songs and the arrangements that are achingly beautiful reaches its pinnacle in the performance of this song, which is a foot-tapping stomper and creates the atmosphere of excitement that surrounds this disparate bunch of misfits as they embark on the journey to find their Snark. The middle break, featuring Mike Batt, Cliff Richard and Vaughan Thomas in close harmony, is imbued with the danger of the journey as it comes as a surprisingly stark juxtaposition to the excitement of the rest of the piece.
The track is made up of a number of slow sections as the characters introduce themselves but the extraordinary excitement that is brought about on the thumping rhythm and exquisite melody of the representation of the journey is one of the best moments of the entire performance. Cliff's recital is short and only limited to the close harmony vocals warning the assembled crew before embarking on the journey, following on from his *tour de force* in ***The Bellman's Speech***.

Track Specification
Composed by Lewis Carroll (poem) and Mike Batt (additional lyrics and music)

Musicians	
Mike Batt	arranger, backing vocals, conductor, keyboards
Ray Cooper	percussion
Mitch Dalton	guitar
Art Garfunkel	vocals
Sir John Gielgud	spoken vocals
Stéphane Grapelli	violin solo
John Hurt	spoken vocals
Julian Lennon	vocals
London Symphony Orchestra	orchestra
Frank McDonald	bass
Tom Nicholl	drums, percussion
Alan Park	guitar
Cliff Richard	vocals, backing vocals
Ray Russell	guitar
Chris Spedding	guitar
Vaughan Thomas	backing vocals
Deniece Williams	vocals

Recording Details	
Producer	Mike Batt
Engineered by	Nick Patrick, Robert Butterworth (main track), Joe Laux (Deniece Williams' vocal) and Dick Lewsey (orchestra)
Recording location	C. T. S., Wembley, Odyssey Studios, London, Mayfair Studios, London, Wessex Studios, London, Maison Rouge Studios, London and/or Comfort's Place, London (main track), Kendon Recorders, Los Angeles (Deniece Williams' vocal) and Abbey Road Studio 1, St. John's Wood, London (orchestra)
Recording date	1986

♫ Es Gehören Zwei zum Glücklichsein

German single

In June 1974, Cliff Richard recorded his final German language single, a translation of ***(You Keep Me) Hangin' On***, which was a top twenty UK hit for Cliff and the only English single he released that year. Recorded at the Morgan Studios, *Es Gehören Zwei zum Glücklichsein* – translated back to *Happiness Takes Two* – it is a completely new recording rather than using the backing track of the original English version and overdubbing the new vocals. Backed with ***Liebeslied*** (a German translation of the B-side of the *(You Keep Me) Hangin' On* single, **Love Is Here**), the track was issued as a single on the EMI label (catalogue number 1C 006-05609) in August 1974 but didn't register in the German singles charts. A rarity for a number of years, the track was reissued on the foreign language compilation album ***On the Continent*** in 1997.
The recording session notes indicate that it is solely an orchestra with Cliff, although the instrumentation used is very much that associated with a country band, except where the strings come in to link the chorus to the verses and pretty much are used exclusively throughout. There is also an uncredited female vocal group, who sing along with the last two lines of the chorus. The English version is better because it feels tighter and more claustrophobic while this is far brighter and expansive, going against the meaning of the lyrics.

Track Specification
Composed by Buddy Mize and Ira Allen; German lyrics by Bert Olden

Musicians	
Nick Ingman	conductor, arranger
Nick Ingman Orchestra	orchestra
Cliff Richard	vocals
Unknown	female backing vocals

Recording Details	
Producer	David MacKay
Engineered by	Roger Quested
Recording location	Morgan Studios, London
Recording date	24th June 1974

♫ Es Ist Nicht Gut, Allein zu Sein

German single

During the sixties, Cliff Richard recorded a number of foreign language tracks, with Spanish, French and Italian reserved for EP and album tracks in the main. For Germany, though, he recorded a number of specific German singles, with most of them charting highly. In particular, he re-recorded a number of his English language hits with new German lyrics. Towards the latter half of the decade, though, he began to record original German songs (or songs with a foreign pedigree translated into German) for which he hadn't recorded an English equivalent. One such example was *Es Ist Nicht Gut, Allein zu Sein* – literally *It's Not Good to Be Alone* – which was recorded at a couple of sessions designed to complete a number of foreign language tracks with many of them being in German.
Es Ist Nicht Gut, Allein zu Sein was the first song to be completed in the session in an unknown number of takes. It was issued, backed with ***Ein Sonntag mit Marie*** (a German translation of his recent hit ***The Day I Met Marie***), on the international Columbia label (catalogue number C-23611) in October 1967, reaching number twenty-one in the German charts. Originally only released in mono, as was the practice by Columbia at the time for singles and EPs, it was eventually issued in stereo as part of the track listing of the foreign language song compilation ***On the Continent***.
A piccolo trumpet introduces the song and the predominant instrumentation following it comes from the brass section with a supporting and plodding bass. It is a typically Teutonic arrangement throughout, until the middle eight is reached and then a harpsichord and reeded instruments take over, sounding quite medieval in their performance, which is repeated towards the end of the track. Cliff sings the song with his customary assurance and he is supported by a group of female backing singers, who are uncredited in any of the session notes.

Track Specification
Composed by Carl Niessen and Peter Stroem

Musicians	
Bernard Ebbinghouse Orchestra	orchestra
Bernard Ebbinghouse	arranger, conductor
Cliff Richard	vocals
Unknown	backing vocals

Recording Details	
Producer	Norrie Paramor
Engineered by	Peter Vince
Recording location	Abbey Road Studio 2, St. John's Wood, London
Recording date	28th September 1967

♫ Es Könnte Schön Morgen Sein
B-side of **Es War Keine So Wunderbar Wie Du**

With German lyrics provided by Kurt Hertha, who had previously translated ***I'm the Lonely One*** into ***Zuviel Allein*** for Cliff Richard's fourth German language single, *Es Könnte Schön Morgen Sein* (literally translated as *It Could Already Be Morning* – a deviation from the original) is a German language version of Cliff's hit ***The Minute You're Gone***. This had been recorded in Nashville in the August of the previous year and, using the base track from that session, Cliff's new vocals (and some new instrumentation, possibly a different mix to bring those instruments forward) were overdubbed in the session in London that provided the A-side song, ***Es War Keine So Wunderbar Wie Du*** (a translation of another English hit, ***I Could Easily Fall (in Love with You)*** from the pantomime show ***Aladdin and His Wonderful Lamp***).
The combined final take and edit were used for the mono and stereo recordings but with different mixes for the needs of the audio channels. However, in its single form, it was only issued in mono, becoming a considerable rarity, particularly as it was not available in the UK and also failed to chart in Germany. In 1997, the German compilation album, ***On the Continent***, was released and featured a remastered stereo version of the song.
The mix for this track is clearer than the original with some of the instrumentation brought further forward. In addition, there are uncredited German backing vocalists, who manage to replicate the sound of the English original.

Track Specification
Composed by Jimmy Gately; German lyrics by Kurt Hertha

Musicians	
Jordanaires	male backing vocals
Cliff Richard	vocals
Unknown	female backing vocals
Unknown	guitar
Unknown	slide guitar
Unknown	bass
Unknown	piano
Unknown	violin
Unknown	drums, percussion

Recording Details	
Producer	Bob Morgan and Billy Sherrill (backing track), Norrie Paramor (vocals) and Unknown (backing vocals)
Engineered by	Mort Thomason (backing track), Malcolm Addey (vocals) and Unknown (backing vocals)
Recording location	Columbia Studios, Nashville (backing track), Abbey Road Studio 3, St. John's Wood, London (vocals) and Germany (backing vocals)
Recording date	25th August 1964 (backing track), 15th April 1965 (vocals) and April 1965 (backing vocals)

♫ Eso Beso
From the album **Kinda Latin**

Translated directly as *That Kiss*, it is primarily Paul Anka and Nancy Ames who are separately most associated with performing the song *Eso Beso*. It has also been covered by Emma Bunton, Jenna Esposito and Georgie Fame and the Blue Flames among others, although no version has been a hit in the UK.
One of four songs destined for Cliff Richard's upcoming ***Kinda Latin*** album to be recorded at the second of three October 1965 sessions, *Eso Beso* was the second track to be completed on that night. The third and final take and edit were used for the mono and stereo recordings but with different mixes for the needs of the separation in audio channels.
It is another song with a samba rhythm that Cliff performs with exuberance and he is clearly enjoying himself on the recording. There is an uncredited vocal group, singing wordlessly behind him, which is likely to be the Mike Sammes Singers, who readily appeared on many of Cliff's recordings of the period.

Track Specification
Composed by Joe Sherman and Noel Sherman

Musicians	
Reg Guest	arranger, conductor
Reg Guest Orchestra	orchestra
Cliff Richard	vocals
Unknown	backing vocals

Recording Details	
Producer	Norrie Paramor
Engineered by	Peter Bown
Recording location	Abbey Road Studio 2, St. John's Wood, London
Recording date	7th October 1965

♫ Es War Keine So Wunderbar Wie Du
German single

By 1965, Cliff Richard was becoming highly proficient in recording in other tongues than English. For his sixth German language single, Carl Ulrich Blecher, who had already translated ***Don't Talk to Him*** into ***Sag 'No' zu Ihm*** for Cliff's fourth German single B-side, provided the new lyrics to the hit from the ***Aladdin and His Wonderful Lamp*** pantomime show earlier that year, ***I Could Easily Fall (in Love with You)***. The title translates to *It Wasn't so Wonderful as You* and has even been covered by German rock band Wirtschaftswunder.

The combined final take and edit were used for both the mono and stereo recordings but with different mixes for the needs of the separate audio channels. Curiously, Cliff couldn't repeat the success of two of his previous singles – ***Das Ist die Frage der Aller Fragen*** and ***Rote Lippen Soll Man Küssen*** – which went to number one in Germany as did their English counterparts – ***Spanish Harlem*** and ***Lucky Lips***. While the English version of *I Could Easily Fall (in Love with You)* reached number five, *Es War Keine So Wunderbar Wie Du* remained unplaced. Originally released only in mono backed with ***Es Könnte Schön Morgen Sein*** (the German translation of Cliff's hit ***The Minute You're Gone***), it was issued on the German Columbia label (catalogue number C-22962) in May 1965. A considerable rarity for UK fans, it was eventually released in restored stereo format on the 1997 German compilation set of all of Cliff's foreign language recordings, ***On the Continent***.
Apart from the language change, it is difficult to identify anything noteworthy in the differences between the English and German versions other than the mix of the bass guitar further forward and, while the original backing vocals of Hank Marvin, John Rostill and Bruce Welch are in place, whenever there are no words to sung, Cliff provides his own backing harmonies when there are and this is highly effective.

Track Specification
Composed by Hank Marvin, Bruce Welch, Brian Bennett and John Rostill; German lyrics by Carl Ulrich Blecher

Musicians		*Recording Details*	
Brian Bennett	drums, percussion	Producer	Norrie Paramor (backing track and vocals)
Hank Marvin	backing vocals, guitar	Engineered by	Malcolm Addey and Ken Scott (backing track) and Malcolm Addey (vocals)
Cliff Richard	vocals, backing vocals		
John Rostill	backing vocals, bass	Recording location	Abbey Road Studio 2 (backing track) and Abbey Road Studio 3 (vocals), St. John's Wood, London
Unknown	hand claps		
Bruce Welch	backing vocals, rhythm guitar	Recording date	15th October 1964 (backing track) and 15th April 1965 (vocals)

♫ Even If It Breaks My Heart
From the album **Real as I Wanna Be**

Cliff Richard had, for a long time, expertly used falsetto to get more out of a song and, on *Even If It Breaks My Heart*, he uses it effectively on the opening lines of the first verse. As with much of the material on the ***Real as I Wanna Be*** album, Cliff raises some eyebrows as he continues the track listing with a synth and percussion-driven song that is a clear departure from what is normally expected from him.
The synclavier strings playing in broad strokes as well as pizzicato hide what is coming in the rest of the song, which picks up its pace and becomes a synthesiser-driven song with a heavy bass and rhythm section. Cliff is stretched vocally as he sings at all levels of his natural register, but it is the bopping chorus that makes the song great with its gentle backing vocal harmonies. The saxophone solo in the middle eight elevates the track even further.

Track Specification
Composed by Shelly Peiken, Adam Gorgoni and Phil Roy

Musicians		*Recording Details*	
Vinnie Colaiuta	drums, percussion	Producer	Peter Wolf
Everette Harp	alto saxophone	Engineered by	Christian Leitgeb, Chris Heil, Paul Erickson and/or Keith Bessey
Paul Jackson Jr.	guitar		
Cliff Richard	vocals, backing vocals		
Michelle Wolf	backing vocals	Recording location	Little America Recording Studios, Weiler, Austria, Ocean Recording Studios, Burbank, California, USA, Arco Recording Studios, Munich, Germany, R. G. Jones Recording Studios, Wimbledon, London, England and/or The Pierce Room, London, England
Peter Wolf	arranger, bass, keyboards, synclavier, percussion		
		Recording date	1997 or 1998

♫ Evening Comes
From the pantomime cast recording album of **Aladdin and His Wonderful Lamp**

The penultimate track from the 1964 London Palladium version of the pantomime ***Aladdin and His Wonderful Lamp*** was one of eighteen written by the Shadows and features Cliff Richard on vocals. One of four tracks to be recorded at a double session, the third and final take and edit were used for the mono and stereo recordings but with different mixes for the separate requirements of the audio channels. The mono version was also released on the EP ***Cliff's Hits from Aladdin and His Wonderful Lamp*** with no stereo format generated.
With a typical guitar accompaniment, Cliff sings what is actually a quite complex melody. As with any Shadows compositions, the melody is pretty and the musical intervals and chord structure highly and musically interesting and flowing. There are several unexpected key changes throughout before resolving back to the base key signature. There is an uncredited piano that is quite possibly Norrie Paramor although this has not been confirmed and remains noted as unknown.

Track Specification
Composed by Hank Marvin, Bruce Welch, Brian Bennett and John Rostill

Musicians

Brian Bennett	drums, percussion
Hank Marvin	guitar
Mike Sammes Singers	backing vocals
Norrie Paramor Orchestra	orchestra
Norrie Paramor	arranger, conductor
Cliff Richard	vocals
John Rostill	bass
Unknown	piano
Bruce Welch	rhythm guitar

Recording Details

Producer	Norrie Paramor
Engineered by	Malcolm Addey and Ken Scott
Recording location	Abbey Road Studio 2, St. John's Wood, London
Recording date	15th October 1964

♬ Evergreen Tree

From the albums **Me and My Shadows** *and* **Cliff in Japan**

For the first time since the first two singles, an extra musician was brought in to record with Cliff Richard and the Shadows (excluding Norrie Paramor's orchestra on some earlier album tracks) in the shape of Jerry Furst. Furst was a renowned harmonica-player and his instrument adds a blues or country and western feel to this fourth track from the ***Me and My Shadows*** album. Recorded in stereo and mono, the same take was used (the fifth from the session) but different mixes for the stereo channels employed. The song also featured on the ***Me and My Shadows No. 1*** EP.

A slower paced song, it starts with a rhythm guitar setting the pace before Furst's harmonica is brought in. Tony Meehan plays percussion here, rather than drums, tapping on wooden blocks and using a tambourine. It is an expression of enduring and promised eternal love (the evergreen nature of the song title). Cliff carries out his gentle vocals with aplomb and the subtle accompaniment brings together an underrated song from Cliff's early years.

Backed with album track ***Choppin' 'n' Changin'***, *Evergreen Tree* was issued as a single in the Far East territories only on the Odeon label (catalogue number OR-1168) in December 1964 and was successful in a number of countries: in Malaysia, it reached number five, India number four, Singapore number three but it was in Thailand that it reached number one. As a consequence, *Evergreen Tree* was a perennial favourite in any concert set list when touring the Asian continent and the Japanese concert in 1967, which was recorded for ***Cliff in Japan***, included the song to rapturous reception.

Track Specification
Composed by Aaron Schroeder and Wally Gold

1. Me and My Shadows

Musicians

Jerry Furst	harmonica
Jet Harris	bass
Hank Marvin	guitar
Tony Meehan	blocks, tambourine
Cliff Richard	vocals
Bruce Welch	rhythm guitar

Recording Details

Producer	Norrie Paramor
Engineered by	Malcolm Addey and Norman Smith (mono) and Peter Bown and Alan Kane (stereo)
Recording location	Abbey Road Studio 2, St. John's Wood, London
Recording date	16th March 1960

2. Cliff in Japan

Musicians

Norrie Paramor Orchestra	orchestra
Norrie Paramor	arranger, conductor
Cliff Richard	vocals

Recording Details

Producer	Norrie Paramor
Engineered by	Unknown
Recording location	Shibuya Public Hall, Tokyo, Japan
Recording date	18th October 1967

♬ Everybody Knows

From the album **Stronger**

Written and produced by Alan Tarney in the studio, following the same process that Cliff Richard and he had initiated during the recording of the ***Always Guaranteed*** album and continued into the ***Stronger*** sessions, *Everybody Knows* was generated in the studio with an initial backing track laid down for Cliff to add his vocals later.

The insistent beat is created in the synthesized drums and doesn't let up throughout. The synthesiser keyboards are used to great effect to underpin the lyrics, while Cliff's own backing vocals blend well with his lead.

Track Specification
Composed by Alan Tarney

Musicians

Cliff Richard	vocals, backing vocals
Alan Tarney	arranger, synthesisers, drum and percussion sequencers

Recording Details

Producer	Alan Tarney
Engineered by	Gerry Kitchingham and Ben Robbins
Recording location	R. G. Jones Studios, Wimbledon, London
Mixed by	John Hudson and Noel Rafferty
Mixing location	Mayfair Studios, London
Recording date	27th February 1989, 9th March 1989, 13th-17th March 1989 and 22nd-23rd March 1989

♬ Everybody's Got a Crisis in Their Lives

Charity single

This single was recorded by a group of musicians, including Cliff Richard, to raise money for the Leukæmia Research Fund, Great Ormond Street Children's Hospital and the Queen Elizabeth Hospital for Children, Hackney. A group of quite disparate musicians met at the Black Barn Studios in Ripley, Surrey to record this song written by Jim Cozens and sung by co-conspirator Simon Cummings, a Guildford-based DJ who was revealed to be suffering from the disease.

It was difficult to find a distributor but it was eventually released on the EMI label, backed with *Make Your Dreams Come True* (which has no contribution from Cliff), with a catalogue number set up for the purpose of supporting the Leukæmia Research Fund (LRF001) on 14th January 1990. In spite of minor coverage in separate interviews with Cliff and the Moody Blues guitarist and principal singer Justin Hayward at the time, there was insufficient impetus for it to be anything more than a parochial success and is now a massively rare single for collectors of Cliff memorabilia.

Cliff's contribution to this performance is clear from the *a capella* vocal introduction, where his voice can be heard above everyone else and then throughout the supporting performance. The video accompanying the song features the assembled cast on a stage singing to patients and nursing staff in a hospital canteen. The song is very memorable and has an inner strength and it is surprising it was not a commercial success as a result.

Track Specification

Composed by Jim Cozens

Musicians

Ann Bryson	backing vocals
Jim Cozens	acoustic guitar
David Croft	electric guitar
Jill Croft	backing vocals
Simon Cummings	vocals
Stephanie de Sykes	backing vocals
Adam Fenton	backing vocals
Justin Hayward	backing vocals, acoustic guitar
Ian Herron	backing vocals
Tank James	backing vocals
Julie Morgan	backing vocals
Marietta Parfitt	backing vocals
Cliff Richard	backing vocals
Mike Smith	backing vocals, keyboards
Diane Solomon	backing vocals
Alvin Stardust	backing vocals
Rick Wakeman	keyboards
Carl Wayne	backing vocals
John Wetton	backing vocals, bass
Joanne Zorian	backing vocals

Recording Details

Produced by	Jim Cozens and David Croft
Engineered by	Robin Black, assisted by Matthew Ollivier
Recording location	Black Barn Studios, Ripley
Mixed by	Ian Herron at Studio 125, Burgess Hill
Final editing by	Teo Miller
Recording date	5th February 1989

♬ Every Face Tells a Story (It Never Tells a Lie)

Unissued tracks and from the album **Every Face Tells a Story**

Having written the title track to the previous album, ***I'm Nearly Famous***, Michael Allison and Peter Sills came up with the title song, but without the parentheses, of the next album, ***Every Face Tells a Story***. The song was attempted originally during the early sessions for the previous album but dropped after three takes. Picked up again in the September sessions, the ninth take on the first of its sessions was taken and the seventh take of overdubs at the second used for the final edit.

To promote the parent album, the title track was issued as a promotional sampler single, backed with ***Spider Man*** and ***You Got Me Wondering***, on the EMI label (catalogue number PSR 410) in 1977.

Guitars are the emphasized instrument split over the stereo channels and the foot-tapping rhythm ushers in Cliff's vocals. He provides his own backing vocals on the second verse and chorus in almost perfect thirds throughout but he is joined by the chorale of other vocalists from the mid-section onwards.

The song was performed at the twentieth anniversary concert, recorded for video and the album release ***Thank You Very Much*** but has not been issued on either the original or remastered version of the album.

Track Specification

Composed by Michael Allison and Peter Sills

1. Unissued track (I'm Nearly Famous)

Musicians

Terry Britten	guitar
Clem Cattini	drums, percussion
Tony Harding	backing vocals
John Perry	backing vocals
Cliff Richard	vocals, backing vocals
Tony Rivers	backing vocals
Alan Tarney	bass
Graham Todd	keyboards

Recording Details

Producer	Bruce Welch
Engineered by	Tony Clark and John Barrett
Recording location	Abbey Road Studio 3, St. John's Wood, London
Recording date	2nd December 1975

2. *Every Face Tells a Story*

Musicians		*Recording Details*	
Brian Bennett	drums, percussion	Producer	Bruce Welch
Terry Britten	guitar	Engineered by	Tony Clark and Alan Rouse
John Perry	backing vocals	Recording location	Abbey Road Studio 2, St. John's Wood, London
Cliff Richard	vocals, backing vocals	Recording date	10th and 18th September 1976
Frank Ricotti	percussion		
Tony Rivers	backing vocals		
Alan Tarney	bass		
Graham Todd	keyboards		

3. *Unissued track (Thank You Very Much)*

Musicians		*Recording Details*	
Terry Britten	guitar	Producer	Bruce Welch
Stuart Calver	backing vocals	Engineered by	Tony Clark
Clem Cattini	drums, percussion	Recording location	London Palladium, London
Dave Christopher	guitar	Recording date	4th March 1978
Mo Foster	bass		
Graham Jarvis	drums, percussion		
Graham Murray	guitar		
John Perry	backing vocals		
Cliff Richard	vocals		
Tony Rivers	backing vocals		
Graham Todd	keyboards		

♬ Everyman

From the album **I'm No Hero**

Cliff Richard's thirty-fourth studio album, ***I'm No Hero***, was the shortest to date in terms of the number of tracks and *Everyman* came in as the tenth and final song on the listing. It is an exemplar of the album's producer Alan Tarney's increased dominance on Cliff's recordings, particularly through the eighties, acting as writer, arranger, performer, backing singer as well as producer. In the UK and many other territories, ***A Little in Love*** was released as a single backed with a non-album track, ***Keep on Looking***, while, in the US, where Cliff was enjoying great success with his singles at the time, the decision was taken to use *Everyman* for the single's B-side.

A straightforward synthesiser-led rock song, *Everyman* is a medium-paced track that has Cliff's vocals engineered further back in the mix with a small amount of echo. As was the practice in Cliff's recordings from the seventies onwards, the backing vocals frequently incorporated Cliff overdubbing his own harmonies, and when Tarney was producing, a wall of sound was built up in layers from multiple recordings by Cliff and Tarney.

Track Specification

Composed by Alan Tarney

Musicians		*Recording Details*	
Michael Boddicker	synthesiser	Producer	Alan Tarney
Nick Glennie-Smith	synthesiser	Engineered by	Ashley Howe
Cliff Richard	vocals, backing vocals	Recording location	Riverside Studios, London
Trevor Spencer	drums, percussion	Recording date	12th May-27th June 1980
Alan Tarney	arranger, backing vocals, guitar, bass		

♬ Everyone Needs Someone to Love

From the album **Love Is Forever**

Written by the prolific composer team of Burt Bacharach and Hal David specifically for Cliff Richard to record during his recording sojourn in New York and Nashville in the summer of 1964, *Everyone Needs Someone to Love* was destined for his 1965 album ***Love Is Forever*** and the similarly titled EP (although that format was only ever released in mono). The fifteenth and final take and edit from the session were used for the mono and stereo recordings but with different mixes for the needs of the separate audio channels.

Cliff's voice is mixed to the forefront of the recording with a lightly swinging orchestral and shuffling drum accompaniment. The melody is simplistic in its structure, although the key modulations elevate it successfully. The musical intervals in some of the sections are also impressively handled in the vocal line.

Track Specification

Composed by Burt Bacharach and Hal David

Musicians		*Recording Details*	
Cliff Richard	vocals	Producer	Bob Morgan
Gary Sherman	conductor	Engineered by	Frank Laico
Unknown	backing vocals	Recording location	Columbia Studios, New York
Unknown	orchestra	Recording date	21st August 1964

♫ Extract from St. Matthew's Gospel Ch. 2 (1)

From the album **The Christmas Story**

In 2007, Cliff Richard was invited to take part in a recording of the traditional Christmas story directed by Premier Christian Radio. Reading through most of the second chapter of the Gospel according to St. Matthew across the album, this was broken up into six segments across the track listing interspersed with performances of traditional carols sung by the choristers of Exeter Cathedral. The first segment covered verses one to two from the Gospel and is the story of the three wise men from the East, who are directed to Christ's birthplace by a star. Cliff reads the section with expected reverence, wonder and passion and the introductory organ from *We Three Kings* can be heard underneath the last few words.

Track Specification
Written by St. Matthew
Musicians
Cliff Richard — spoken vocals

Recording Details

Producer	Gordon Lorenz
Engineered by	Richard Scott
Recording location	Exeter Cathedral, Exeter, England
Recording date	2007

♫ Extract from St. Matthew's Gospel Ch. 2 (2)

From the album **The Christmas Story**

For the 2007 album ***The Christmas Story***, Cliff Richard read extracts from two psalms and most of the second chapter of St. Matthew's Gospel, which was divided into six segments. The second of those covered verses three to six, where Herod is troubled by the news of Christ's birth and demands to know exactly where he is to be born. Cliff reads the passage with reverential passion, while the introductory organ passage from *O Little Town of Bethlehem* may be heard underneath the last few words.

Track Specification
Written by St. Matthew
Musicians
Cliff Richard — spoken vocals

Recording Details

Producer	Gordon Lorenz
Engineered by	Richard Scott
Recording location	Exeter Cathedral, Exeter, England
Recording date	2007

♫ Extract from St. Matthew's Gospel Ch. 2 (3)

From the album **The Christmas Story**

The third segment of the second chapter of St. Matthew's Gospel covers verses seven through to the first half of verse eleven. Read by Cliff Richard with a joyous passion, it covers the story of the three wise men's arrival in Bethlehem and their worship of the infant Jesus. The introductory organ notes of *The Rocking Carol* can be heard coming in on the end of the passage.

Track Specification
Written by St. Matthew
Musicians
Cliff Richard — spoken vocals

Recording Details

Producer	Gordon Lorenz
Engineered by	Richard Scott
Recording location	Exeter Cathedral, Exeter, England
Recording date	2007

♫ Extract from St. Matthew's Gospel Ch. 2 (4)

From the album **The Christmas Story**

Recorded at the cathedral in Exeter, the fourth of six segments of the second chapter of the Gospel according to St. Matthew covers the second half of verse eleven and verse twelve, telling the familiar story of the gifts of gold, frankincense and myrrh by the three wise men before they return to their own lands, thereby avoiding Herod's instructions to return with the information on the precise location of Christ's birth. Cliff Richard reads all of the passages with reverential fervour and successfully gets the elements of the story over succinctly in the short time that he has available.

Track Specification
Written by St. Matthew
Musicians
Cliff Richard — spoken vocals

Recording Details

Producer	Gordon Lorenz
Engineered by	Richard Scott
Recording location	Exeter Cathedral, Exeter, England
Recording date	2007

♫ Extract from St. Matthew's Gospel Ch. 2 (5)
From the album **The Christmas Story**

Cliff Richard recorded two psalms and most of the second chapter from the Gospel according to St. Matthew at Exeter Cathedral for the album ***The Christmas Story***. The latter was segmented into six sections with the penultimate being verses thirteen and fourteen, which tells of God's message to Joseph warning him to flee to Egypt with Mary and Jesus to avoid Herod's intent to slay the newborn child. Cliff reads the passage with reverence and a frisson of excitement, imbuing the words as he does with the spirit of the thriller narrative in the story. The initial bars of the next track, ***Silent Night***, may be heard underneath the final few words of the section.

Track Specification
Written by St. Matthew
Musicians

Cliff Richard	spoken vocals

Recording Details

Producer	Gordon Lorenz
Engineered by	Richard Scott
Recording location	Exeter Cathedral, Exeter, England
Recording date	2007

♫ Extract from St. Matthew's Gospel Ch. 2 (6)
From the album **The Christmas Story**

The final section of the second chapter of the Gospel according to St. Matthew covers verse fifteen (Herod slays all the infant children and then dies himself) and verses nineteen to twenty-one (Joseph receiving word from God that he may return to Israel safely with Mary and Jesus). Recorded at Exeter Cathedral, Cliff Richard reads the excerpts with joyous reverence, passion and with a real sense of telling the Christmas story. Underneath the final words, the choristers of Exeter Cathedral can be heard singing the opening phrase of *Ding Dong Merrily on High*.

Track Specification
Written by St. Matthew
Musicians

Cliff Richard	spoken vocals

Recording Details

Producer	Gordon Lorenz
Engineered by	Richard Scott
Recording location	Exeter Cathedral, Exeter, England
Recording date	2007

THE CLIFF RICHARD RECORDING CATALOGUE

F – F – F – F – F – F – F – F – F – F – F – F – F – F – F – F – F – F – F – F

♫ Faithful One

From the album **Something's Goin' On**

The final track on Cliff Richard's 2004 studio album, ***Something's Goin' On***, was co-written by long-term friend and provider of songs such as ***Saviour's Day*** and ***Little Town***, Chris Eaton, and *Faithful One* is the third composed by him on the album. As with many of Eaton's songs, there is an obvious religious or spiritual overtone to his compositions with *Faithful One* being more obvious than many, particularly with the whispered, almost reverential 'keep the faith' to close the album. It was therefore a greatly significant choice for inclusion on the faith and inspiration section of the 2008 celebratory ***...And They Said It Wouldn't Last! (My 50 Years in Music)***.

An almost ecclesiastical introduction is performed on strings that evoke memories of classical music symphonies, which then makes way for Cliff to sing his song with nearly no accompaniment from the simplistic instrumentation and plenty of echo. The second verse witnesses the accompaniment beginning to build up and there are flashes of the drama previously experienced in *Saviour's Day*. Cliff sings his own harmonizing vocals and this adds a further depth of beauty to the performance.

Track Specification

Composed by Brian White and Chris Eaton

Musicians

Ziggie Diaz	programming
Carl Gorodetsky	conductor
Tom Henby	guitar
Nashville String Machine	strings
Michael Omartian	arranger, keyboards
Richard Pena	programming
Cliff Richard	vocals, backing vocals
Tommy Sims	guitar, bass, drum programming

Recording Details

Producer	Tommy Sims
Engineered by	Terry Christian
Recording location	Sound House, Brentwood, Tennessee, USA (vocals and instruments) and Starstruck Studios, Nashville, Tennessee, USA (strings)
Recording date	2003-2004

♫ Falling in Love with Love

From the album **32 Minutes and 17 Seconds with Cliff Richard**

One of the more familiar songs from the Rodgers and Hart 1938 musical *The Boys from Syracuse*, *Falling in Love with Love* was performed by Allan Jones in the 1940 film version. It was later used in the Oscar Hammerstein II and Richard Rodgers version of ***Cinderella***, itself made into a film in 1997, where the lead vocal was taken by Bernadette Peters. It has been covered by Tony Bennett, Harry Secombe, Paul Anka, Sammy Davis, Jr., Julie Andrews, Mario Lanza, Diana Ross and the Supremes, Dinah Shore, Stanley Black, Cannonball Adderley, Carmen MacRae, Frank Sinatra, Sarah Vaughan and Andy Williams, who exemplify a huge number of artists who took the song into the studio.

One of four songs recorded and three completed in the session by Cliff Richard, *Falling in Love with Love* was the last song to be attempted. The sixth and final take and edit was used for the mono and stereo recordings released on the ***32 Minutes and 17 Seconds with Cliff Richard*** album but with different mixes for the requirements of the audio channels. The song also appeared on the track listing of the ***Cliff Sings Don't Talk to Him*** EP.

Cliff's version of the song has a film soundtrack feel to the performance, purely because of the orchestral arrangement and the upbeat rhythm; there is almost an expectation that Cliff will break into a dance routine at any minute. It's not a great song, in comparison to the wealth of other material that he recorded but, as with most of his career, he carries the song off with sincere aplomb.

Track Specification

Composed by Richard Rodgers and Lorenz Hart

Musicians

Norrie Paramor Orchestra	orchestra
Norrie Paramor	arranger, conductor
Cliff Richard	vocals

Recording Details

Producer	Norrie Paramor
Engineered by	Malcolm Addey and Norman Smith
Recording location	Abbey Road Studio 2, St. John's Wood, London
Recording date	5th December 1961

♫ Fallin' in Luv

From the album **Rock 'n' Roll Juvenile**

With the assistance of solo performer and songwriter B. A. Robertson, co-producer Terry Britten wrote a number of tracks for Cliff Richard to record for his ***Rock 'n' Roll Juvenile*** album, including *Fallin' in Luv*. The track was, as with most of the

album, recorded in two parts, with the backing track completed in the Parisian EMI studios and the vocal overdubs added almost a year later. The title is deliberately misspelled reflecting an adolescent way of expressing the emotion.
Providing his own backing vocals that elevate the introduction, Cliff sings one of the first songs that doesn't truly conform to the rock and roll rhythm, as per the title concept of the album. The song is simple in its structure but the running bass line in addition to the synthesiser accompaniment makes it quirkily interesting. The vocal arrangements work well underneath the guitar solo in the middle eight as a change of pace temporarily leads into a key change before returning to the final verse and chorus sequence.

Track Specification
Composed by Terry Britten and B. A. Robertson

Musicians		*Recording Details*	
Terry Britten	guitar	Producer	Cliff Richard and Terry Britten
Herbie Flowers	bass	Engineered by	Tony Clark and Haydn Bendall
Graham Jarvis	drums, percussion	Recording location	Pathé Marconi, Paris, France (backing track) and Abbey Road Studio, St. John's Wood, London (vocals)
Cliff Richard	vocals, backing vocals		
Graham Todd	keyboards		
		Recording date	18th-20th July 1978 (backing track) and 30th July 1979 (vocals)

♫ Fall in Love with You

***8th UK single** and from the album **...And They Said It Wouldn't Last! (My 50 Years in Music)** and unissued live track*

With the release of Cliff Richard's eighth single, the choice was again made to use a song by erstwhile bandmate Ian Samwell, who had written many of Cliff's early hits and B-sides including his debut, ***Move It***. This time, rather than run with another rock and roller that had been Samwell's trademark to this point, Cliff and the Shadows chose to extrapolate from the previous hits of ***Living Doll***, ***Travellin' Light*** and ***A Voice in the Wilderness*** by keeping it gentle. The recording also consolidates what is the quintessential sound of the Shadows backing Cliff with the choral accompaniment in close harmony understated but extremely effective.
The single was released, backed with a version of ***Willie and the Hand Jive***, on 10th March 1960 on the Columbia label (catalogue number 45-DB 4431). Although many people were asking for *Willie and the Hand Jive* by name in the record shops, the B-side was never officially elevated to the status of a double A-side. The first of Cliff's singles not to be released on the by then antiquated shellac of the 78 r.p.m. format, *Fall in Love with You* reached number two in the chart and was held off the top by Lonnie Donegan's novelty skiffle hit *My Old Man's a Dustman*. The stereo version of this release was mocked from the original mono edit rather than being recorded individually and mixed and edited separately for the two aural channels.
For the celebratory album ***...And They Said It Wouldn't Last (My 50 Years in Music)*** in 2008, a number of different takes of several of the early songs were incorporated in the track listing including another version of *Fall in Love with You*. Musically, it is very similar to the single version with the only major differences being the lack of reverberation echo on Cliff's lead vocals and there are no backing vocals.
The introductory guitar solo, running bass line and rhythm guitar are now so much connected to the Cliff and the Shadows sound that it is difficult to appreciate how fresh and new it would have sounded on release back in the early sixties. The song is a love ballad – indeed a first romance – with the date coming to an end and Cliff wanting to romance the girl and finding difficulty in understanding why he should not fall in love with her. The song moves along with the instrumentation coming to the fore and, of course, the beautiful cadences in the combined voices of the singing members of the Shadows combining so eloquently with Cliff's almost laidback delivery. *Fall in Love with You* is perhaps the first indication of the band beginning to get in their collective stride.
A month later in December 1960, Cliff and the Shadows recorded a German version, entitled ***Bin Verliebt*** (literally, '*Am Loved*'), which was released as a single, reaching number forty in Germany.

Track Specification
Composed by Ian Samwell

1. Single

Musicians		*Recording Details*	
Jet Harris	backing vocals, bass	Producer	Norrie Paramor
Hank Marvin	backing vocals, guitar	Engineered by	Malcolm Addey and Alan Kane (mono) and Stuart Eltham and Peter Bown (stereo)
Tony Meehan	drums, percussion		
Cliff Richard	vocals	Recording location	Abbey Road Studio 2, St. John's Wood, London
Bruce Welch	backing vocals, rhythm guitar	Recording date	19th November 1959

2. ...And They Said It Wouldn't Last! (My 50 Years in Music)

Musicians		*Recording Details*	
Jet Harris	bass	Producer	Norrie Paramor
Hank Marvin	guitar	Engineered by	Malcolm Addey and Alan Kane (mono) and Stuart Eltham and Peter Bown (stereo)
Tony Meehan	drums, percussion		
Cliff Richard	vocals	Recording location	Abbey Road Studio 2, St. John's Wood, London
Bruce Welch	rhythm guitar	Recording date	19th November 1959

3. Unissued (Knebworth - The Album)

Musicians

Ray Beavis	saxophone
Brian Bennett	drums, percussion
John Earle	saxophone
Chris Gower	trombone
Mark Griffiths	bass
Cliff Hall	keyboards
Dick Hanson	trumpet
Peter Howarth	backing vocals
Hank Marvin	backing vocals, guitar
Paul Moessl	keyboards
Mick Mullins	backing vocals
Keith Murrell	backing vocals
Cliff Richard	vocals
Bruce Welch	backing vocals, guitar

Recording Details

Producer	Chris Kimsey and Steve Smith
Engineered by	Unknown
Recording location	Knebworth House, Hertfordshire, England
Recording date	30th June 1990

♫ Fellow Next to Me, The

Unissued track

In early 1969, Cliff Richard took part in a six-episode series for the religious broadcasting at Tyne Tees Television. Called *Life with Johnny*, each episode revisited a parable from the Bible as told by Jesus and updated so that it was set in modern times, with Cliff playing the role of Johnny. For *Johnny Faces the Facts*, it was the turn of the mote and the beam or the splinter and the plank (depending on the age of the book used). In the introduction of the episode, Cliff sings *The Fellow Next to Me* straight to the camera, with three dancers (possibly the three male members of the Settlers) acting out the lyrics, which refer to someone, anyone other than Johnny himself, thereby laying down the basis of the playlet the audience is about to see.

The track is performed in a shuffling rock style with guitars and an uncredited organ (possibly Norrie Paramor, who used to play keyboards on Cliff's earlier recordings when one was required). The song was recorded at Abbey Road, possibly with a view to releasing them as an album later on but, if so, the idea was abandoned. The show's credits state that the original songs are down to Cliff, the writer of the episodes David Winter and the four members of the Settlers, a fact borne out by ***Where Is That Man?*** which appears on the album ***About That Man***.

Track Specification

Composed by Cliff Richard, David Winter, Cindy Kent, Mike Jones, John Fyffe and Geoffrey Srodzinski

Musicians

John Fyffe	backing vocals, guitar
Mike Jones	backing vocals, guitar
Cliff Richard	vocals
Geoffrey Srodzinski	backing vocals
Unknown	organ

Recording Details

Producer	Norrie Paramor
Engineered by	Peter Vince
Recording location	Abbey Road Studio 3, St. John's Wood, London
Recording date	8th January 1969

♫ Field of Love

From the album **Something's Goin' On**

The beautiful and gentle *Field of Love* was co-written by producer Tommy Sims for Cliff Richard's album ***Something's Goin' On***. An American musician, Sims was one of the writers commissioned to write music for the album, which was recorded principally in Nashville and also featuring American musicians in order to give the project an American feel.

One of the most beautiful songs on the album, *Field of Love* starts with sustained synthesiser chords, before a rattling drum and percussion are brought in under Cliff's lead vocals. The transposition between keys and the chord progressions are what make the song such a brilliant performance. Cliff sings the song with emotion and the echoing backing vocals elevate it further until the middle eight, when Cliff's voice takes off through complex musical intervals.

Track Specification

Composed by Tommy Sims, Jennifer Kimball and Will Robinson

Musicians

Susan Ashton	backing vocals
Ziggie Diaz	programming
Carl Gorodetsky	conductor
Barry Green	trombone
Tony Harrell	keyboards
Mike Haynes	trumpet, flugelhorn
Jennifer Kummer	French horn
Ken Lewis	percussion
Nashville String Machine	strings
Cliff Richard	vocals
Richie Pena	programming
Tommy Sims	guitar, bass, keyboards
Curtis Zackery	drum programming

Recording Details

Producer	Tommy Sims
Engineered by	Bryan Lenox and Tommy Sims (vocals and instruments) and Ronnie Brookshire (strings)
Recording location	Uncle Tom's Cabin, Franklin, Tennessee, USA (vocals and instruments) and The Tracking Room, Nashville, Tennessee, USA (strings)
Recording date	2003-2004

♫ Fields of Gold

From the album **Two's Company**

Gordon Sumner, or Sting as he is better known, wrote this beautiful love song for his single in 1993 and successfully reached number sixteen in the UK charts in the June of that year. It is often picked as an exemplar of a ballad on many of the reality television talent shows and has since been covered by a variety of artists including Eva Cassidy, Mary Black, Lisa Lynne and Amy Nutall among a number of others.

Cliff Richard recorded a number of duets to flesh out the track listing of his ***Two's Company*** album and chose *Fields of Gold* to record with Barry Gibb, with whom he had recorded for his previous studio album, ***Something's Goin' On***. Guitar harmonics, saxophone and keyboards bring in the song, which has Cliff taking first lead vocal responsibility before singing in harmony with Gibb and then reversing roles. The pair had already proved how well they worked together on Cliff's *Something's Goin' On* project and later on the ***Grief Never Grows Old*** charity record and this is the next step. Sting's original project was stark and overwrought, whereas this version is a lot warmer, assisted by the blending vocals and the mellifluous saxophone.

Track Specification

Composed by Sting

Musicians		*Recording Details*	
Richard Cardwell	keyboards	Producer	Chris Porter
Pandit Dinesh	percussion	Engineered by	Chris Porter
Mickey Féat	bass	Recording location	Metropolis Studio, London and Stanley House Studios, west London
Barry Gibb	vocals	Recording date	2006
Andy Hamilton	saxophone		
Phil Palmer	guitar		
Cliff Richard	vocals		

♫ Fiesta

From the film soundtrack album of **Finders Keepers**

Often melded together with an instrumental by the Shadows, *Spanish Music*, *Fiesta* is performed during the finale of the film ***Finders Keepers***. Cliff Richard and the Shadows (all playing themselves in the film) have found the bomb that had been inadvertently dropped near the town that they were supposed to be performing in (San Carlos) and the residents celebrate in Spanish style with much dancing in the streets, fireworks and a carnival. *Fiesta* dissolves into a slightly more upbeat instrumental version by the Shadows as the band and Cliff leave on the back of the truck with the bomb as the words 'The End' are displayed.

Recorded as part of the session that laid down the Shadows' own tracks for the film soundtrack, this was the only track that required Cliff's vocals. The final (unknown) take and edit were used for the mono and stereo recordings but with different mixes for the requirements of the audio channels. Although the song is performed in the film, it is the same as the soundtrack but, because it backs the scripted action, there is no lip-synching or miming to instruments required.

Fiesta is an example of Cliff and the Shadows at their best. Buried away on the soundtrack, it is unfortunate that it never gets an airing. The excitement generated from the melody and the supporting instrumentation is enhanced exponentially by the beautiful vocal harmonies created by Cliff, Hank Marvin, Bruce Welch and John Rostill. At the end, they transition through several keys and this, more than any other song, shows their collective musicianship and performance talents.

Track Specification

Composed by Hank Marvin, Bruce Welch, Brian Bennett and John Rostill

Musicians		*Recording Details*	
Brian Bennett	drums, percussion	Producer	Norrie Paramor
Hank Marvin	backing vocals, guitar	Engineered by	Unknown
Cliff Richard	vocals	Recording location	Abbey Road Studio 2, St. John's Wood, London
John Rostill	backing vocals, bass	Recording date	30th April 1966
Bruce Welch	backing vocals, rhythm guitar		

♫ Fifty Tears for Every Kiss

From the album **21 Today**

Some track listings that feature *Fifty Tears for Every Kiss* suggest that it is entitled *Fifty* Years *for Every Kiss* but, since this makes little sense (other than the presumed jail-term that the singer thinks he'll get for stealing each kiss) and given that Cliff clearly enunciates the 't' at the beginning of *Tears*, the correct title is *Fifty Tears for Every Kiss*. This also matches the tenor of the lachrymose emotion of the song.

The fourth and final take from the first orchestral session for the ***21 Today*** album was used for both the mono and stereo edits, although the differing audio requirements employed different mixes and the song was included on the track listing of the ***Cliff Richard No. 2*** EP.

This gentle little love song employs a plinking piano and strident string chords and subtle backing vocals to accompany Cliff's anguished lead vocal. Technically complex to sing with passages of *a capella* performance required, there are very few problems with it and it becomes one of the best tracks on the album.

Track Specification
Composed by Bella

Musicians		*Recording Details*	
Mike Sammes Singers	backing vocals	Producer	Norrie Paramor
Norrie Paramor Orchestra	orchestra	Engineered by	Malcolm Addey
Norrie Paramor	arranger, conductor	Recording location	Abbey Road Studio 2, St. John's Wood, London
Cliff Richard	vocals	Recording date	30th January 1961

♫ Fighter

From the albums **Drifting** *(Sheila Walsh),* **The Kendrick Collection** *(Graham Kendrick) and* **From a Distance ***** The Event**

The second Graham Kendrick composition on the first album by Cliff Richard's protégée Sheila Walsh, ***Drifting***, *Fighter* was positioned as the closing track of the album. It was then picked up by Cliff and recorded for his own release. Walsh's version first appeared on CD on the US-only album release of *Compact Favorites* in 1988.
Wheeling synthesiser swirls lead into timpani and a shuffling percussive motif. The militaristic march effect is at odds with the vocal line injected with fear by Walsh, sung in reverence to the meaning of the religious fight. Cliff's backing vocals are joined by Walsh's and the dread that runs through the performance is allayed by the building drama in the synthesisers as she becomes more assured in her belief than she can fight.
In 1989, Cliff was invited to sing three songs written by Kendrick at a session at the All Souls Church in Langham, one of which was *Fighter*. A militaristic drum and brass section lead into the song, while Cliff sings reverentially with respect to the lyrics of the King. As with ***Burn On!*** on the same album, Cliff also provides his own multi-layered backing vocals. The march rhythm continues into the mid-section where his blended vocals are most effective. The final verse and chorus are presented in a syncopated rhythm against the military beat, which remains underpinned by the snare drum.
Combined with ***Thief in the Night*** as a sort of medley, Cliff incorporated *Fighter* into his set for the second part of his celebratory thirtieth anniversary concerts at Wembley Stadium in June 1989. The track starts with the standard dramatic chords, and Cliff's vocal is given some echo. The instrumentation creates a picture to match the lyrics and, in many respects, the rock band is more effective than the orchestral backing. The song segues into *Thief in the Night*.

Track Specification
Composed by Graham Kendrick

1. Drifting

Musicians		*Recording Details*	
Clem Clemson	electric guitar	Producer	Cliff Richard and Craig Pruess
Graham Jarvis	drums, percussion	Engineered by	Keith Bessey
Craig Pruess	arranger, backing vocals, synthesiser, brass, timpani	Recording location	Riverside Studios, London, Strawberry Studios, London, Ramp Studios, London and/or Sonoptics Studios, London
Cliff Richard	backing vocals		
Sheila Walsh	vocals	Recording date	September 1982-January 1983

2. The Kendrick Collection

Musicians		*Recording Details*	
All Souls Orchestra	orchestra	Producer	Burt Rhodes
Cliff Richard	vocals, backing vocals	Engineered by	Graham McHutchon
Noël Tredinnick	arranger, conductor	Recording location	All Souls Church, Langham, London
		Recording date	2nd February 1989

3. From a Distance ** The Event***

Musicians		*Recording Details*	
John Clark	guitar	Producer	Cliff Richard
Sonia Jones-Morgan	backing vocals	Engineered by	Keith Bessey and Mick McKenna
Steve Lauri	guitar	Recording location	Rolling Stones Mobile Studio, Wembley Stadium, Wembley, North-west London
Peter May	drums, percussion	Recording date	16th-17th June 1989
Paul Moessl	keyboards		
Tessa Niles	backing vocals		
Alan Park	keyboards		
Provox:			
Peter Howarth	backing vocals		
Mick Mullins	backing vocals		
Keith Murrell	backing vocals		
Cliff Richard	vocals		
Steve Stroud	bass		

♫ Final Extract Psalm 106

From the album **The Christmas Story**

In 2007, Cliff Richard took part in a recording ***The Christmas Story***, where he supplied the readings punctuated by the relevant carols sung by the choristers of Exeter Cathedral. Two extracts from Psalm 106 were recorded, running straight into each other: the first was verses one to five (tagged as ***Palm 106 Extract***) and verses forty-seven to forty-eight, which is a simple prayer and praise of God. Cliff reads these verses with reverence finishing with a passionately ebullient 'Amen!'

Track Specification
Written by Traditional

Musicians		*Recording Details*	
Cliff Richard	spoken vocals	Producer	Gordon Lorenz
		Engineered by	Richard Scott
		Recording location	Exeter Cathedral, Exeter, England
		Recording date	2007

♫ Find a Little Faith

From the album **A Celebration in Song** *(Olivia Newton-John)*

Cliff Richard's association with Olivia Newton-John stretches back to the late sixties when she was a regular performer on his television shows and backed him on concerts. Over the years, the pair has recorded a number of duets and, in 2007, they teamed up for *Find a Little Faith*, which was one of the tracks on Olivia's new duets album, *A Celebration in Song*. *Find a Little Faith*, by its very title, is inevitably a spiritual song and matches Cliff's and Olivia's oeuvres perfectly.

The gentle steel-string guitar is played over sustained synthesiser chords leading into Olivia's vocal line which she relinquishes to Cliff before they sing in harmony. The beauty of the song is in the simplicity and arrangement of the accompaniment and the vocals, which are exquisite in the musical intervals performed, but this is elevated further by an unexpected key change into the last verse.

Track Specification
Composed by Amy Sky

Musicians		*Recording Details*	
Ryan Dan	backing vocals	Producer	Amy Sky
Greg Johnson	guitar, bass, programming	Engineered by	Vic Florencia
Olivia Newton-John	vocals, backing vocals	Recording location	Crompton Songs Studio, Miami, Florida, USA, Blackfoot South, Toronto, Canada and The Concrete Jungle, Toronto, Canada
Cliff Richard	vocals, backing vocals		
Unknown	drums, percussion		
		Recording date	31st January 2008 and 2nd February 2008

♫ Finders Keepers

From the film soundtrack album of **Finders Keepers** *and from the album* **Cliff in Japan**

The premise of the film ***Finders Keepers*** is the inadvertent dropping of an unexploded bomb near a small Spanish town where Cliff Richard and the Shadows (as themselves) are scheduled to play. The film's title song is performed during the opening sequence, with the five musicians performing while travelling on top of a steam train carriage carrying some form of vegetation through tunnels and the Spanish countryside. Soon, as the song and titles draw to a close, the engine's driver spots them and chases after the group, who throw their instruments off the train and jump – this is particularly judicious as they notice a sign proclaiming 'San Carlos', which by happy coincidence is where they were heading.

Recorded in just one take at the first main session for the soundtrack, this take and edit was used for both the mono and stereo recordings but with different mixes for the separation of audio channels. In previous films, a separate recording was made of the songs but, for the most part, in *Finders Keepers*, the soundtrack version was used in the film with the band lip-synching and miming. *Finders Keepers*, as a song, was not released as a single but was used as the B-side of a song from ***Cinderella*** (performed later that year in London), ***In the Country***, for which the mono version only was used.

With an obvious Spanish influence in the rhythm and guitar lines, the exuberant theme song is a perfect introduction to the film. Although the title refers to the bomb that they are searching for in the plot, in the song it is about finding the girl of Cliff's dreams. At the height of their compositional powers, the Shadows all contributed to the song, which features a typically strong Cliff vocal matched by the beauty of the vocal harmonies from Hank Marvin, Bruce Welch and John Rostill, including a replica of the hooting a train whistle, matching the film's starting sequence. With a female backing group (uncredited) on the Japan concert, and released on ***Cliff in Japan***, some of the magic is therefore lost.

Track Specification
Composed by Hank Marvin, Bruce Welch, Brian Bennett and John Rostill

1. Finders Keepers

Musicians		*Recording Details*	
Brian Bennett	drums, percussion	Producer	Norrie Paramor
Hank Marvin	backing vocals, guitar	Engineered by	Malcolm Addey, Peter Vince and Richard Lush
Cliff Richard	vocals	Recording location	Abbey Road Studio 2, St. John's Wood, London
John Rostill	backing vocals, bass	Recording date	26th April 1966
Bruce Welch	backing vocals, rhythm guitar		

2. Cliff in Japan

Musicians		*Recording Details*	
Norrie Paramor Orchestra	orchestra	Producer	Norrie Paramor
Norrie Paramor	arranger, conductor	Engineered by	Unknown
Cliff Richard	vocals	Recording location	Shibuya Public Hall, Tokyo, Japan
Unknown	backing vocals	Recording date	18th October 1967

♫ Fire and Rain

From the album **Help It Along**

The origins of the meaning of the spiritual song *Fire and Rain* were unclear since the composer James Taylor himself had given differing accounts in a number of interviews, including references to his enforced stay in a mental institution and the experiences of the treatments he had received there (electric and hydro shock therapy respectively in the title), suggestions that it was in reference to the sudden death of his long-time friend Suzanne Schnerr, and that it was connected to his struggle with fame and fortune as a singer-songwriter and his relationship and marriage to Carly Simon. Later on, he confirmed that it had elements of all three. *Fire and Rain* was a minor hit for him when it was released as his first single and reached number forty-two on the UK charts in November 1970. Since then, it has been regularly covered by a wide variety of artists including Willie Nelson, Nana Mouskouri, the Isley Brothers, John Denver, Bobby Darrin, Cher, Tony Orlando, Dido, Davy Jones and Rick Wakeman among many others.

A favourite of Cliff Richard's within its genre, *Fire and Rain* was one of the many songs related to the Christian religion chosen by Cliff to perform at the studio-based concerts for the charity album ***Help It Along***. The album was recorded in seven sessions over three days at the London-based Morgan Studios and issued in aid of the Tear Fund, of which Cliff is a patron. Note that the sleeve notes for the album suggest that the track is called *Fine and Rain* but this is an error. A simple guitar introduction gives way to the orchestra and Cliff's quiet vocal line, which slowly builds up throughout the track, with a sympathetic arrangement of the James Taylor song.

Track Specification

Composed by James Taylor

Musicians

Terry Britten	guitar
Barrie Guard	arranger, conductor, percussion
Cliff Hall	keyboards
Jean Hawker	backing vocals
Anna Peacock	backing vocals
Kevin Peek	guitar
Cliff Richard	vocals
Trevor Spencer	drums, percussion
Alan Tarney	bass
Unknown	orchestra

Recording Details

Producer	David MacKay
Engineered by	Roger Quested
Recording location	Morgan Studios, London
Recording date	24th, 25th and 26th September 1973

♫ Fireside Song

From the albums **The 31st of February Street** *and* **Japan Tour '74**

One of six songs that Cliff Richard wrote for his 1974 album ***The 31st of February Street***, *Fireside Song* was recorded at the second of four main sessions for the album in February 1974 and the resultant edit was a splice of two unknown takes. The song was subsequently released on the collection of Cliff's self-compositions, ***My Songs***, in 2003.

Strummed chords on the acoustic guitar introduce the song and for a while, this is all that accompanies Cliff before a shimmering electronic keyboard and solo violin join in. Soon, the entire performance slows and Cliff is left with the guitar before the songs builds back up once more.

For the Japan tour in 1974, the guitar is given a wowing electronic sound to it during the introduction, while Cliff's vocals are as competent as they are on the original album. He introduces the song with a gag about singing his own songs that falls flat with the audience but it is a revelation to hear him perform a song that is relatively unfamiliar.

Track Specification

Composed by Cliff Richard

1. The 31st of February Street

Musicians

Barrie Guard	arranger, conductor, percussion
Cliff Hall	keyboards
Kevin Peek	acoustic guitar
Cliff Richard	vocals
Unknown	orchestra

Recording Details

Producer	David MacKay
Engineered by	Tony Clark and Mike Jarrett
Recording location	Abbey Road Studio 2, St. John's Wood, London
Recording date	12th February 1974

2. Japan Tour '74

Musicians

Barrie Guard	arranger, conductor
Cliff Hall	piano
Brian Lewis	guitar
Kevin Peak	acoustic guitar
Cliff Richard	vocals
Shambles Symphonet	orchestra
Trevor Spencer	drums, percussion
Alan Tarney	bass
Bruce Welch	rhythm guitar

Recording Details

Producer	Toshiba EMI (no individual detailed)
Engineered by	Toshiba EMI (no individual detailed)
Recording location	Shinjuku Koseinenkin, Tokyo, Japan
Recording date	7th-8th October 1974

♫ First Date
From the album **Now You See Me, Now You Don't**

Cliff Richard had started an association with Aleksander John (indeed helping him out on his album) back in 1974 and John provided two songs for Cliff's ***Now You See Me... Now You Don't*** album, the first of which was *First Date*. John went on to record his version of this song live for the Greenbelt Festival in 1983.
The introduction to *First Date* is a synthesiser sequence that replicates a piccolo trumpet before the traditional guitars, bass and drums come crashing in. The pace and energy of the song are inexorable, while Cliff's own backing vocals add another dimension to the song. There is a slight resonance of ***Little Town*** in the track's structure but this is more to do with the choice of instruments and vocal arrangement than any particular musical motif.

Track Specification
Composed by Aleksander John and N. Battle

Musicians		*Recording Details*	
Graham Jarvis	cymbals, tom-toms	Producer	Cliff Richard and Craig Pruess
Mart Jenner	electric guitars	Engineered by	Keith Bessey and Steve Cook
Craig Pruess	arranger, piano, synthesisers, electronic percussion, sequencers	Recording location	Strawberry Studios South, Surrey
Cliff Richard	vocals, backing vocals	Recording date	29th March and 2nd-5th April 1982

♫ First Easter, The – The Empty Tomb
From the album **About That Man**

The final Bible reading on Cliff Richard's ***About That Man*** album tells the story of Jesus Christ's rise to life after being crucified to death on the cross. Taken from the books of Luke, chapter 24, verses 1 to 12, John, chapter 20, verses 19 to 20, Luke again, chapter 24, verses 44 to 48 and finally Matthew, chapter 28, verses 18 to 20, Cliff tells the story with passion and characterises the story to make the track meaningful and interesting in this oft-told story from the Bible. It was almost certainly recorded in one continuous take to avoid interrupting the pace of Cliff's delivery.

Track Specification
From the King James Bible

Musicians		*Recording Details*	
Cliff Richard	vocals	Producer	Norrie Paramor
		Engineered by	Richard Lush
		Recording location	Abbey Road Studio 2, St. John's Wood, London
		Recording date	20th February 1970

♫ First Lesson in Love
From the album **Listen to Cliff!**

The second of five original songs to be recorded for ***Listen to Cliff!***, *First Lesson in Love* was written by Bruce Welch and his friend from the Chesternuts days, Pete Chester. In the liner notes for ***The Rock 'n' Roll Years 1958-1963***, the anthology of early material and rarities, it is suggested that Bruce co-wrote the song with Hank Marvin but this is incorrect.
First Lesson in Love was recorded in mono and stereo with the same take and edit being used but with different mixes for the respective aural requirements. The track was included on the ***Listen to Cliff! No. 2*** EP as well as being the penultimate song on the first side of the parent album. The mono album version became the B-side of a South African single issue of ***What'd I Say?***
Jet Harris leads the tune with an eloquent and running bass line with Hank picking out a pretty little counter-melody. The happiness that is imbued in the song comes out in the chief melody and in Cliff's eloquent clarity of vocals. There are a few clever little techniques used to increase and maintain the interest such as bending notes on the guitar and in Cliff's lead vocal and the modulation to unexpected keys.

Track Specification
Composed by Peter Chester and Bruce Welch

Musicians		*Recording Details*	
Jet Harris	bass	Producer	Norrie Paramor
Hank Marvin	guitar	Engineered by	Malcolm Addey
Tony Meehan	drums, percussion	Recording location	Abbey Road Studio 2, St. John's Wood, London
Cliff Richard	vocals	Recording date	13th October 1960
Bruce Welch	rhythm guitar		

♫ Flying Machine
***54th UK single** and from the albums* **Cliff "Live" in Japan '72** *and* **Japan Tour '74**

After the change in musical direction of ***Silvery Rain***, Cliff Richard compounded it by issuing *Flying Machine* as his fifty-fourth British single. Also recorded by little-known acts Wayne Rhoden, Byron Lee and Teddy Magnus, Cliff's version included the Swedish writer George Hultgreen on the recorder accompanying the vocal line, which creates a fluttering sound that emulates a flying motion.

The only song recorded at the session, *Flying Machine* was backed with ***Pigeon*** and issued as a single on the Columbia label (catalogue number DB 8797) on 25th June 1971 and reached thirty-seven in the UK singles charts, making it the worst performing record of Cliff's career – and helping to cement the gleeful critics' opinion that Cliff's star was on the wane, although it reached the top in countries such as Malaysia and Denmark. The issued single was in mono only, although a stereo version was released in Holland (catalogue number 5C006-04846). The stereo mix was included on the 1972 collection ***The Best of Cliff Vol. 2*** and ***The Singles Collection*** in 2002.
The slightly awkward recorder solo that often threatens to go sharp or squeak on occasion is counterpointed by a rhythm on the guitar that plays chords on the off-beat. The guitar ensemble performance during the chorus has echoes of Cliff's work with the Shadows, while he employs a falsetto in places that makes the overall track an exciting original piece of work, admittedly of its time, that deserved to have had a better placing the charts.
The recorder is replaced by a guitar during the Japanese concert and is taken at a slightly faster pace on ***Cliff "Live" in Japan '72***, which is also enhanced by the backing vocals of Olivia Newton-John, who can be clearly heard embellishing her part, and Pat Carroll.

Track Specification
Composed by George Hultgreen

1. Single

Musicians		*Recording Details*	
George Hultgreen	recorder	Producer	Norrie Paramor
Norrie Paramor Orchestra	orchestra	Engineered by	Unknown
Norrie Paramor	arranger, conductor	Recording location	Abbey Road Studio 3, St. John's Wood, London
Cliff Richard	vocals	Recording date	20th March 1971
Unknown	backing vocals		

2. Cliff "Live" in Japan '72

Musicians		*Recording Details*	
Brian Bennett	drums, percussion	Producer	Norrie Paramor
Pat Carroll	backing vocals	Engineered by	Unknown
John Farrar	bass	Recording location	Kosei Nenkin Hall, Tokyo, Japan
Alan Hawkshaw	piano	Recording date	22nd-23rd September 1972
Hank Marvin	guitar		
Olivia Newton-John	backing vocals		
Cliff Richard	vocals		
Bruce Welch	rhythm guitar		

♫ Fly Me to the Moon

From the albums **Love Is Forever** *and* **Kinda Latin**

Originally entitled *In Other Words* (which appears as a bracketed subtitle on the ***Kinda Latin*** album), the song was written in 1954. It took a few years for *Fly Me to the Moon* to subvert the official title, after its first line gained popularity. The first recorded version was by Kaye Ballard in 1954 and has since become a crooning standard made fashionable by Frank Sinatra, whose recording had Count Basie on the piano with an arrangement by Quincy Jones. In the UK, the song has never charted but several artists have covered it including Julie London, Tony Bennett, The Sandpipers and Diana Krall.
Cliff recorded two very different versions, with the first being recorded in late 1961 (but remaining unreleased until 1965's ***Love Is Forever*** album), which is a lush orchestral version with pizzicato guitar accompaniment and a very restrained and gentle vocal line, while the second, recorded for *Kinda Latin*, has a calypso style rhythm to it. The *Love Is Forever* version uses the same take for the mono and stereo edits but with different mixes for the channels and appears on the ***Love Is Forever*** EP. The *Kinda Latin* version was recorded at the middle session of three for the album in October 1965 and the sixth and final take and edit were used for both the mono and stereo recordings with different mixes for the channel separation.
At this period of recording, Cliff tended to over-emphasize the American 'r' sound, which seems at odds with the anglicized pronunciation of the other consonants and vowels. However, other than the perfect timbre of his voice, it also helps to cement a particular style and sound in people's minds. The *Kinda Latin* version is a slight move away from the album's concept since it is more Caribbean than Latin but it fits well with the rest of the album and is a strong opener to the second side. There is an uncredited vocal group who only appear very occasionally; this is likely to the Mike Sammes Singers but this is unconfirmed.

Track Specification
Composed by Bart Howard

1. Love Is Forever

Musicians		*Recording Details*	
Norrie Paramor Orchestra	orchestra	Producer	Norrie Paramor
Norrie Paramor	conductor	Engineered by	Malcolm Addey
Cliff Richard	vocals	Recording location	Abbey Road Studio 2, St. John's Wood, London
		Recording date	11th December 1961

2. *Kinda Latin*

Musicians		*Recording Details*	
Reg Guest	arranger, conductor	Producer	Norrie Paramor
Reg Guest Orchestra	orchestra	Engineered by	Peter Bown
Cliff Richard	vocals	Recording location	Abbey Road Studio 2, St. John's Wood, London
Unknown	backing vocals	Recording date	7th October 1965

♬ Fooled by a Feeling

From the album **Drifting** *(Sheila Walsh)*

Cliff Richard had a dual career as a producer by working with fellow Christian musicians such as Bryn Haworth, Garth Hewitt and Network 3, but his most influential efforts came with singer Sheila Walsh. The first of her albums to be recorded took place over the latter part of 1982 and into 1983 and was released as ***Drifting*** (or *War of Love* in the US). One of the songs on the track listing was a new song by Jamie Owens-Collins called *Fooled by a Feeling*.
The rhythm is created in a jerky instrumentation kept on track by the drums and percussion. The melody is not instantly memorable but the performance is greatly improved by the multi-layered vocal contributions from Cliff. The synthesiser accompaniment seems to use a similar motif to that found in ***A Little in Love***.

Track Specification
Composed by Jamie Owens-Collins

Musicians		*Recording Details*	
Clem Clemson	electric guitar	Producer	Cliff Richard and Craig Pruess
Graham Jarvis	drums, percussion	Engineered by	Keith Bessey
Craig Pruess	arranger, synthesiser	Recording location	Riverside Studios, London, Strawberry Studios, London, Ramp Studios, London and/or Sonoptics Studios, London
Cliff Richard	backing vocals	Recording date	September 1982-January 1983
Sheila Walsh	vocals		

♬ For Emily, Wherever I May Find Her

From the album **Sincerely Cliff Richard**

From the Simon and Garfunkel album *Parsley, Sage, Rosemary and Thyme*, composer Paul Simon has said that *For Emily, Wherever I May Find Her* is a song about belief rather than a real or imaginary girl. Although not released as a single – in fact, it was the B-side of *A Hazy Shade of Winter* – it has nevertheless become a much-loved song by and has led to it being covered by several artists including David Essex, Rocky Nelson, Paul Desmond and Glenn Yarborough among others.
Cliff Richard recorded the song at his last session of 1967, alongside another Paul Simon composition, ***Cloudy***. Cliff had long admired Simon's compositions and had already recorded two others (***Homeward Bound*** and ***Red Rubber Ball***) and the recording of *For Emily, Wherever I May Find Her* cemented his association with Simon's music. Although it was recorded in 1967, it wouldn't be issued until the release of the ***Sincerely Cliff*** album two years later in 1969.
Cliff successfully sings quite complex songs written by Simon and they suit his voice well. There is an uncredited backing vocalist on the track, who also sings a quite complex melody line over the instrumentation. Supported by the reeded instruments, Cliff creates one of the best tracks from the album.

Track Specification
Composed by Paul Simon

Musicians		*Recording Details*	
Mike Leander	arranger, conductor	Producer	Norrie Paramor
Mike Leander Orchestra	orchestra	Engineered by	Peter Vince
Cliff Richard	vocals	Recording location	Abbey Road Studio 2, St. John's Wood, London
Unknown	backing vocals	Recording date	11th October 1967

♬ Forever

From the album **Always Guaranteed**

Since Cliff Richard was heavily involved in evening performances in his role as The Rock Star in ***Time – the Musical***, the approach taken by Alan Tarney to the composition and recording of ***Always Guaranteed***, suited him since he was able to come in during the day and lay down his vocal track without having to worry about the instrumentation, which was also provided by Tarney. Often Tarney would enter the studio with a little musical idea – or just as often none at all – play on a guitar, constructing a song and then recording the basic instrumental track before Cliff came to the studios.
For *Forever*, the dominant accompaniment is the synthesiser, while Cliff sings at both ends of his vocal register, and frequently employs the falsetto for which he is justly famous. There are backing vocals but these are limited.

Track Specification
Composed by Alan Tarney

Musicians		*Recording Details*	
Cliff Richard	vocals, backing vocals	Producer	Alan Tarney
Alan Tarney	backing vocals, guitars, bass, keyboards, drum and percussion programming	Engineered by	Gerry Kitchingham and Keith Bessey
		Recording location	R. G. Jones Studios, Wimbledon, London
		Recording date	13th October-November 1986

♫ Forever Kind of Love, A

From the EP **Forever Kind of Love**

Forever associated with the man who primarily made the song famous, Bobby Vee, his version was a number thirteen UK singles hit in October 1962, which means that the version recorded by Cliff Richard and the Shadows predated that release by almost three months in terms of the chronology of events.

The first of three songs to be recorded in the session (along with two tracks for the 1965's album issue ***Cliff Richard***), *A Forever Kind of Love* took eleven takes to complete, with that final take and edit used for the mono and stereo recordings but with different mixes for the audio channels. Until the release in 1989 of ***The EP Collection: Ballads and Love Songs***, the track was a major rarity, although that album itself is now difficult to find either in vinyl, cassette or CD. However, the track was also included on 1997's anthology ***The Rock 'n' Roll Years 1958-1963***, on which liner notes it is indicated that it is the first time the song has been released in CD format but this is incorrect.

Cliff's version is more upbeat than Vee's recording with a foot-tapping beat kept moving by the Shadows' instrumentation. The introduction features Cliff singing a slower few lines accompanied by Hank Marvin's guitar. There is a strong backing section, which is uncredited and is quite possibly the Mike Sammes Singers (since it doesn't sound like Hank or Bruce Welch on vocal duties), but the session notes make no reference to those vocalists. It is a very different version from the familiar drawling one recorded by Bobby Vee and it is all the better for that.

Track Specification

Composed by Gerry Goffin and Jack Keller

Musicians

Brian Bennett	drums, percussion
Brian 'Licorice' Locking	bass
Hank Marvin	guitar
Norrie Paramor Orchestra	orchestra
Norrie Paramor	arranger, conductor
Cliff Richard	vocals
Unknown	backing vocals
Bruce Welch	rhythm guitar

Recording Details

Producer	Norrie Paramor
Engineered by	Peter Bown
Recording location	Abbey Road Studio 2, St. John's Wood, London
Recording date	12th July 1962

♫ Forever You Will Be Mine

From the album **Stronger**

The penultimate track to be written and produced by Alan Tarney for Cliff Richard's ***Stronger*** album followed the same approach to recording that had begun on the ***Always Guaranteed*** album. Tarney would take time in the studio, creating the song and getting the basic track down on tape before Cliff arrtived to add his vocals. *Forever You Will Be Mine* was one of the six tracks to be presented by compères Mike Read and Cliff to an invited audience of two thousand fans at the London Palladium on 3rd April 1989. Once the results of the poll were received, *Forever You Will Be Mine* was positioned at the bottom of the list in sixth place behind ***Lean on You***.

The melody begins in an almost childlike way as Cliff relays the story of remembering how he feels about a person through the lyrics. The vocal performance has some staccato elements to it, while the accompaniment is kept generally sparse and light. The backing vocals lift the song further, particularly when used across the separate stereo channels.

Track Specification

Composed by Alan Tarney

Musicians

Cliff Richard	vocals, backing vocals
Alan Tarney	arranger, backing vocals, synthesisers, drum and percussion sequencers

Recording Details

Producer	Alan Tarney
Engineered by	Gerry Kitchingham and Ben Robbins
Recording location	R. G. Jones Studios, Wimbledon, London
Mixed by	John Hudson and Noel Rafferty
Mixing location	Mayfair Studios, London
Recording date	27th February 1989, 9th March 1989, 13th-17th March 1989 and 22nd-23rd March 1989

♫ Forgive Me

Unissued track

In early 1969, Tyne Tees Television commissioned a series of six playlets for their religious broadcast slot called *Life with Johnny*, featuring Cliff Richard in the title role as each episode updated a well-known parable told by Jesus in the Bible. Records are unclear on most of the episodes although *Johnny Come Home* and *Johnny Faces Facts* are complete, *Johnny and the Good Samaritan* is partially available, while the remainder are unavailable in either records or film form.

The songs performed had some relevance to the modernized parable being acted out and, in all, there were usually five songs per episode. *Forgive Me*, recorded at the Abbey Road studios with a putative album tie-in project in mind that didn't materialize, appeared in one of *Johnny on the Rocks*, *Johnny and the Blind Rage* or *Johnny in Love*. The end credits of the episode stated that all songs were original and written in collaboration between Cliff, the Settlers and the programme's writer David Winter. The instrumentation and performance details are unknown.

Track Specification
Composed by Cliff Richard, David Winter, Cindy Kent, Mike Jones, John Fyffe and Geoffrey Srodzinski

Musicians		*Recording Details*	
John Fyffe	backing vocals, guitar	Producer	Norrie Paramor
Cindy Kent	backing vocals	Engineered by	Peter Vince
Mike Jones	backing vocals, guitar	Recording location	Abbey Road Studio 3, St. John's Wood, London
Cliff Richard	vocals	Recording date	8th January 1969
Geoffrey Srodzinski	backing vocals, bass		

♫ For Life
From the album **Something's Goin' On**

Co-written by Cliff Richard's long-term friend, Chris Eaton, *For Life* is a liltingly gentle ballad that is spiritual and thoughtful in equal measure. Cliff has suggested in interview that it is a paradoxically difficult song to sing since it is performed almost entirely in the upper register, making Cliff's throat sore. However, a simple technique was employed to get around it: the melody and accompaniment were transposed down a semi-tone, relieving the pressure on the vocal cords. The song gave its name to an album that was essentially a reissue of the parent album, ***Something's Goin' On***, with the four extra tracks that were issued at the same time on B-sides and through Cliff's website: ***Slow Down, How Many Sleeps?, She's All Mine*** and ***Diamonds on a Chain***. The song was also incorporated into Cliff's ***Love... The Album*** in 2007. Most noteworthy, however, is that this track features the guitar performance of Duane Eddy.
The flowing keyboard accompaniment starts this emotionally spectacular song that is underpinned by a stark guitar line. Cliff's vocals are suitably anguished and this increases throughout the song as the dramas and accompaniment builds up. Cliff is called upon to stretch his vocal capabilities moving from his lower register up to the top and beyond into falsetto.

Track Specification
Composed by Chris Eaton and Bobby Huff

Musicians		*Recording Details*	
George Cocchini	electric guitar	Producer	Monroe Jones
Duane Eddy	guitar	Engineered by	Jim Dineen
Mark Hill	bass	Recording location	The Bennett House, Nashville, Tennessee, USA and The Hideout, Franklin, Tennessee, USA
Ken Lewis	percussion		
Michael Mellett	backing vocals	Recording date	2003-2004
Dan Needham	drums, percussion		
Cliff Richard	vocals, backing vocals		
Jeff Roach	keyboards		

♫ Forty Days (to Come Back Home)
From the albums **21 Today** *and* **The Rock 'n' Roll Years 1958-1963**

A Chuck Berry song that has been covered by relatively less well-known artists such as Dean Carter, Bob Wills, Ronnie Hawkins and Jerry Jaye, *Forty Days (to Come Back Home)* took five takes to get right during the session, the last one of which was taken and edited for mono and stereo purposes, although the mix for the channels was different. In the early sixties, Cliff Richard and the Shadows had a show on Radio Luxembourg and would regularly play *Forty Days (to Come Back Home)* as one of their favourites. One such performance was added to ***The Rock 'n' Roll Years 1958-1963***, along with three other tracks from the programme, but has only appeared in mono form (radio of the day had not progressed to FM).
An *a capella* introduction gives way to a storming accompaniment featuring Hank Marvin's guitar in a harmonising melody and an intricate bass line and tocking percussion helping Bruce Welch's rhythm guitar to drive the song along. Cliff's vocals, as usual, are assured and the backing vocals created by the Shadows exemplify the closely-knit harmonies that would become their trademark. The Radio Luxembourg version is introduced by Cliff with a gag about the traffic on the way to the studio taking forty days and the performance is generally more exuberant than the studio original.

Track Specification
Composed by Chuck Berry

1. 21 Today

Musicians		*Recording Details*	
Jet Harris	backing vocals, bass	Producer	Norrie Paramor
Hank Marvin	backing vocals, guitar	Engineered by	Malcolm Addey
Tony Meehan	drums, percussion	Recording location	Abbey Road Studio 2, St. John's Wood, London
Cliff Richard	vocals, hand claps	Recording date	4th July 1961
Bruce Welch	backing vocals, rhythm guitar		

2. The Rock 'n' Roll Years 1958-1963

Musicians		*Recording Details*	
Jet Harris	backing vocals, bass	Producer	Unknown
Hank Marvin	backing vocals, guitar	Engineered by	Unknown
Tony Meehan	drums, percussion	Recording location	Radio Luxembourg Studios, London
Cliff Richard	vocals, hand claps	Recording date	1961
Bruce Welch	backing vocals, rhythm guitar		

♫ For You, For Me
From the EP **Holiday Carnival**

Written by Shadows guitarist Bruce Welch with lyrical help from Cliff Richard, the song was recorded in April 1962 although not released until the issue of the ***Holiday Carnival*** EP. This session and song are both noteworthy for being the first to feature new Shadows drummer Brian Bennett in their line-up. Owing to Tony Meehan's tardiness and generation of disruption in the studio and concerts as a consequence, they decided to sack him and bring in Bennett.

The seventh and final take and edit was used for the mono and stereo recordings but with different mixes for the audio channels. A rarity since the release of its parent EP, it was included on the track listing of the 1970 Music for Pleasure album *All My Love*, itself now a rarity. Finally, it was added to the EP section of the compendium album ***...And They Said It Wouldn't Last! (My 50 Years in Music)***.

A typical Shadows-based song but with swooping strings and uncredited female backing vocals (performing very much in the spirit of ***Theme for a Dream***), Cliff sings his own composition with gusto, while the Shadows keep up their foot-tapping rhythm underneath.

Track Specification
Composed by Bruce Welch and Cliff Richard

Musicians

Brian Bennett	drums, percussion
Jet Harris	bass
Norrie Paramor Strings	orchestra
Hank Marvin	guitar
Norrie Paramor	arranger, conductor
Cliff Richard	vocals
Unknown	female backing vocals
Bruce Welch	rhythm guitar

Recording Details

Producer	Norrie Paramor
Engineered by	Malcolm Addey
Recording location	Abbey Road Studio 2, St. John's Wood, London
Recording date	4th April 1962

♫ Fragen
From the album **Hier Ist Cliff**

Cliff Richard recorded his first German language album at the end of 1968 in spite of having a long pedigree in the singles market with German songs. For the album, *Hier Ist Cliff*, instead of reissuing his previous singles and B-sides, he recorded completely new material, which were translations of songs plundered either from ***Two a Penny*** or ***Established 1958***. *Fragen* was one such, being a translation of the final song from the ***Two a Penny*** film, ***Questions*** (the German title is a direct translation). During the sixties, it had been a strategy to record new vocals and overdub them on a previously recorded backing track. Where Cliff's foreign language songs were concerned, this usually meant recording translated vocals and adding them to the original English backing track. However, for *Hier Ist Cliff*, all of the tracks were recorded anew. Released only in stereo, the rarity of the track was diminished when it was included on Cliff's foreign language German compilation album ***On the Continent*** in 1997. It was subsequently released in the UK on the 2005 remaster of ***Take Me High*** as a bonus track.

Replicating the harp introduction, Norrie Paramor has recreated the sound of the original soundtrack, while Cliff sings the song with impassioned bewilderment as per the meaning the lyrics, which are searching for some sort of answer and requesting God to reveal himself if he exists.

Track Specification
Composed by Cliff Richard and Jim Collier; German lyrics by Carl Ulrich Blecher

Musicians

Norrie Paramor Orchestra	orchestra
Norrie Paramor	arranger, director
Cliff Richard	vocals

Recording Details

Producer	Norrie Paramor
Engineered by	Peter Vince
Recording location	Abbey Road Studio 2, St. John's Wood, London
Recording date	20th November 1968

♫ Free
B-side of **Human Work of Art**

Cliff Richard regularly performed songs on stage that he had never and perhaps would never attempt to record in the studio. During the *Access All Areas* tour in 1992, many of the songs were recorded but were only released as B-sides to singles issued from ***Cliff Richard - The Album***. One such was *Free*, written by Judy Mackenzie, a Christian singer and songwriter, who had composed and recorded principally in the seventies.

This version by Cliff was accompanied by Paul Moessl on keyboards and the result was issued on the second of the dual CD single release of ***Human Work of Art*** and, in 1998, was added to the track listing of the compilation album, ***Yesterday, Today, Forever***. An edited version, cutting the spoken preamble, appears on the faith and inspiration section of the celebratory package ***...And They Said It Wouldn't Last! (My 50 Years in Music)***, released in 2008.

Supported by Paul Moessl on the keyboards, Cliff sings the song with passion and belief as the drama is built up through the verses and into the chorus. As with almost everything Cliff sings, the vocals are perfectly expressed and pitched and it is surprising that he never saw fit to make a studio recording of this powerful song.

Track Specification
Composed by Judy Mackenzie

Musicians	
Paul Moessl	keyboards
Cliff Richard	vocals, guitar

Recording Details	
Producer	Keith Bessey
Engineered by	Keith Bessey
Recording location	Wembley Arena, London
Recording date	27th-29th November 1992

♬ Free My Soul

From the album **Green Light**

Recorded at the third session for the ***Green Light*** album project, *Free My Soul* was completed in four takes and is one of the few tracks not to require additional overdubs at a later session.

A song performed at a walking pace is initiated by a guitar solo introduction before a modern rock rhythm is set up by the rest of the instrumentation under Cliff's lead vocal. There are surprising key changes that elevate the song in interest, while the backing vocals, normally a common element during this period of his recording career are kept to a minimum.

Track Specification
Composed by Terry Britten

Musicians	
Brian Bennett	drums, percussion
Terry Britten	guitar
Stuart Calver	backing vocals
Alan Jones	bass
Duncan MacKay	keyboards
Alan Parker	guitar
John Perry	backing vocals
Tim Renwick	guitar
Cliff Richard	vocals
Tony Rivers	backing vocals
Trevor Spencer	drums, percussion
Alan Tarney	backing vocals, guitar, bass, keyboards
Graham Todd	keyboards

Recording Details	
Producer	Bruce Welch
Engineered by	Tony Clark and Haydn Bendall
Recording location	Abbey Road Studio 3, St. John's Wood, London
Recording date	11th January 1978

♬ Frenesi

From the album **When in Spain** *(Spanish version) and from the EP* **Cliff's Palladium Successes** *(English version)*

Although *Frenesi* is now a jazz standard, it was originally written by Alberto Dominguez as a piece of Spanish music to be performed on the marimba in 1940. Artie Shaw recorded the first popular version when it appeared as the B-side of his *Adios Mariquita Linda* that same year. Translated directly as *Frenzy*, it has been covered by a number of artists including Tommy Dorsey, Harry James, Frank Sinatra, Glenn Miller, Woody Herman, Linda Ronstadt and Dave Brubeck among others.

Cliff Richard's version was recorded at the EMI Studios based in Barcelona, along with three other songs at the same session. The fifth and final edit was used for the mono and stereo recordings but with different mixes for the audio channel requirements. An English version was also recorded, probably using the same backing track as the ***When in Spain*** session, and which appeared on the ***Cliff's Palladium Successes*** EP the following year but only in mono. There is no record of the studio personnel or dates for the English version, which was a considerable rarity (the EP didn't chart) until the issue on CD (still in mono) of the French ***All My Love*** compilation album and later on the celebratory ***...And They Said It Wouldn't Last! (My 50 Years in Music)*** boxed set in 2008.

Possibly with one ear on the future recording of the English version, the instrumentation is allocated to the right stereo channel and Cliff's vocals to the left. The shuffling rhythm keeps the toes tapping while Hank Marvin's guitar solo and Norrie Paramor's slightly out-of-tune piano (after Russ Conway and Winnie Atwell) add an extra dimension to this cha-cha track.

As with many songs recorded in a different language but with the same backing track, there is very little difference to experience, except for the English language lyrics. In addition, Cliff's vocal line is given an echo in the English version that is unmatched by the backing track making it an odd listening experience.

Track Specification

1. When in Spain (Spanish version)
Composed by Alberto Dominguez and Ray Charles

Musicians	
Brian Bennett	drums, percussion
Brian 'Licorice' Locking	bass
Hank Marvin	guitar
Norrie Paramor	piano
Cliff Richard	vocals
Bruce Welch	rhythm guitar

Recording Details	
Producer	Norrie Paramor
Engineered by	Malcolm Addey
Recording location	EMI Studios, Barcelona
Recording date	28th April 1963

2. *Cliff's Palladium Successes EP (English version)*

Composed by Alberto Dominguez and Ray Charles; English lyrics by S.K. Russell

Musicians	
Brian Bennett	drums, percussion
Brian 'Licorice' Locking	bass
Hank Marvin	guitar
Norrie Paramor	piano
Cliff Richard	vocals
Bruce Welch	rhythm guitar

Recording Details	
Producer	Norrie Paramor (backing track) and Unknown (vocals)
Engineered by	Malcolm Addey (backing track) and Unknown (vocals)
Recording location	EMI Studios, Barcelona (backing track) and Abbey Road Studio 2, St. John's Wood (vocals)
Recording date	28th April 1963 (backing track) and early 1964 (vocals)

♫ Friends

From the pantomime cast recording album of **Aladdin and His Wonderful Lamp**

Recorded in Studio three at Abbey Road rather than their familiar Studio two, *Friends* features Cliff Richard and the Shadows performing one of the eighteen tracks the Shadows had written for the pantomime show of ***Aladdin and His Wonderful Lamp***. The only track to be recorded at the session – the last itself for the cast album and the final session for Cliff in 1964 – the fifth and final take and edit was used for the mono and stereo recordings but with different mixes for the separate channels. The mono recording and edit was also released on the EP ***Cliff's Hits from Aladdin and His Wonderful Lamp***.
Starting off as a typical musical number, *Friends* develops into an esoteric little number that employs a honky tonk piano plinking away in the background and roundly-produced brass that evokes the period of the twenties or thirties, musically speaking. Unusually employing his lower register on occasions, Cliff sings the song with gusto as he reaffirms that he is good friends with his mates.

Track Specification

Composed by Hank Marvin, Bruce Welch, Brian Bennett and John Rostill

Musicians	
Brian Bennett	drums, percussion
Hank Marvin	guitar
Mike Sammes Singers	backing vocals
Norrie Paramor Orchestra	orchestra
Norrie Paramor	arranger, conductor
Cliff Richard	vocals
John Rostill	bass
Unknown	honky tonk piano
Bruce Welch	rhythm guitar

Recording Details	
Producer	Norrie Paramor
Engineered by	Malcolm Addey and Ken Scott
Recording location	Abbey Road Studio 3, St. John's Wood, London
Recording date	21st October 1964

♫ From a Distance

***112th UK single** and from the album* **Silver Celebration**

Written in 1985 by Julie Gold, *From a Distance* was not initially picked up for recording because Gold was working as a secretary at the time. However, through a friend, *From a Distance* was finally recorded in 1987 by Nanci Griffith for her *Lone Star State of Mind* album. Although Cliff Richard's version is perhaps the most familiar to UK inhabitants, in the US it is very firmly Bette Midler who made the song popular. Her version was recorded in 1990 and released at the same time as Cliff's single in October of that year, although he was first when performed it as the closing song to ***The Event***, his two-day celebration performances at Wembley Stadium in June 1989. Midler's song went to number two in the Billboard Hot 100 and number six in the UK - outstripping Cliff's by five positions.
Almost a year and a half after the concert, Cliff's version was released, backed by the principal B-side ***Lindsay Jane II***, on the EMI label (catalogue number EM 155) and reached number eleven in the UK singles charts. In addition to the seven-inch single, there were other formats released: a seven-inch picture disc single (catalogue number EMPD 155); a twelve-inch single (12EM 155); and a CD single release (EMCD 155). The picture disc had the live version of ***I Could Easily Fall*** as its B-side, while the twelve-inch and CD singles had *Lindsay Jane II* and the live version of ***Wired for Sound*** (then not released on the parent album). There was also a vinyl and CD album boxed sets that included six exclusive prints, a giant poster with lyrics to the song and an engraved one-sided vinyl single of ***Miss You Nights*** recorded for a German television programme. The accompanying promotional video of *From a Distance* is of the sequence in concert where he performs the song on an elevated platform that went out across the crowds.
The song clearly has a lot of post-production overdubs since Cliff can be heard providing his own backing vocals. The single version fades earlier than the album version, while the track that appears on ***...And They Said I Wouldn't Last! (My 50 Years in Music)*** fades up later and fades ten seconds or so earlier.
The song is highly dramatic and is a perfect example of how Cliff's vocals, great on their own, can blend so well with a harmonized group of backing vocalists. This is no more evident than in the introduction. The explosion of the synthesisers push the song onwards and it is unsurprising that, what with the purpose of the evening plus the importance of the lyrics, that he should have become emotional at the end. *From a Distance* is a perfect piece of pop – some critics would say bombastic but that adds to its charm – that doubles up as a song with a religious message.

Cliff revisited the song for a performance at the Wembley Conference Centre, when he was accompanied by the All Souls Orchestra, with whom he had recorded three titles titles for *The Kendrick Collection* earlier on in 1989. The resultant recording was subsequently issued alongside those of the other performers at the concert on the charity album *Silver Celebration*.

Track Specification
Composed by Julie Gold

1. Single

Musicians		*Recording Details*	
John Clark	guitar	Producer	Cliff Richard
Sonia Jones-Morgan	backing vocals	Engineered by	Keith Bessey and Mick McKenna
Steve Lauri	guitar	Recording location	Rolling Stones Mobile Studio, Wembley Stadium, Wembley, North-west London
Peter May	drums, percussion	Recording date	16th-17th June 1989
Paul Moessl	keyboards		
Tessa Niles	backing vocals		
Alan Park	keyboards		
Provox:			
Peter Howarth	backing vocals		
Mick Mullins	backing vocals		
Keith Murrell	backing vocals		
Cliff Richard	vocals		
Steve Stroud	bass		

2. Silver Celebration

Musicians		*Recording Details*	
All Souls Orchestra	orchestra	Producer	Langham Arts
John Clark	backing vocals, guitar	Engineered by	Unknown
Pete May	drums, percussion	Recording location	Wembley Conference Centre, Wembley, North-west London
Alan Park	keyboards	Recording date	21st October 1997
Cliff Richard	vocals		
Steve Stroud	backing vocals, bass		
Unknown	conductor		

♫ From This Day On
Unissued track

From This Day On was written by popular musical composers Alan Jay Lerner and Frederick Loewe for the 1947 Broadway hit *Brigadoon*, which was the story of a mysterious village that appears every one hundred years while the villagers experience the passage of each century as one night. The plot of the book and its musical counterpart is loosely based on a German story by Friedrich Gerstäcker, where a German town is cursed to appear once a century. With the proximity of the war fresh in everyone's minds, Lerner transferred the action to Scotland. The musical play was made into a film in 1954 and also featured *From This Day On*.
The song was one of three recorded by Cliff Richard at his final session of 1962 in between Christmas and New Year, along with the single ***It's All in the Game*** and ***I Only Have Eyes for You***. However, unlike those two tracks, after recording eight takes, the song has not yet been released, although whether this is to do with dissatisfaction with the result or lack of space on following EPs and albums is not documented.

Track Specification
Composed by Alan Jay Lerner and Frederick Loewe

Musicians		*Recording Details*	
Mike Sammes Singers	backing vocals	Producer	Norrie Paramor
Norrie Paramor Orchestra	orchestra	Engineered by	Malcolm Addey
Norrie Paramor	arranger, conductor	Recording location	Abbey Road Studio 2, St. John's Wood, London
Cliff Richard	vocals	Recording date	28th December 1962

♫ Front Page
From the album **Silver**

Cliff Richard had had a long association with fellow Christian gospel singer Aleksander John and, by the time he recorded ***Silver*** in 1983, John was providing a number of songs for him to record including *Front Page*. The song was positioned on the first side of the album, which was also the first of Cliff's albums to be simultaneously released on CD. The track was left off the reissue of the album in 1992, when elements of both *Silver* and ***Rock 'n' Roll Silver*** were combined, leaving a number of tracks out as a consequence (for space limitation reasons and to fit in the two CD release format of Cliff's back catalogue). It was subsequently restored to its rightful place on the track listing of the remastered *Silver* in 2002.
The rhythm owes much to the synthesized disco material of the period, as does a lot of the drum pad and synthesiser that is so obvious on the track. The mid-section features a short string arrangement that is almost in unison, while Cliff creates his own backing vocals, which is often fed through a vocoder.

Track Specification

Composed by Aleksander John and N. Battle

Musicians

Martyn Ford	conductor
Martyn Ford Orchestra	orchestra
Clive Anstee	'cello
Jim Archer	violin
Andy Babynchuk	violin
Bill Benham	violin
Norris Bosworth	viola
Daniel Daggers	viola
Liz Edwards	violin
Will Gibson	violin
Timothy Good	violin
Chris Hirons	violin
Paul Kegg	'cello
Benjamin Kennard	'cello
John Kitchen	violin
Martin Loveday	'cello
Peter Oxer	violin
Geoff Palmer	violin
Eddie Roberts	violin
Jonathan Strange	violin
Chris Wellington	viola
Simon Whistler	viola
David Woodcock	violin
Gavin Wright	violin
Craig Pruess	arranger, keyboards, synthesiser
Cliff Richard	vocals, backing vocals

Recording Details

Producer	Craig Pruess
Engineered by	Keith Bessey
Recording location	Strawberry Studios South, Surrey (main track) and Henry Wood Hall, Glasgow (strings)
Recording date	19th May 1983, 3rd June 1983 and/or 16th June 1983 (main track) and July and/or August 1983 (strings)

♬ Galadriel (Spirit of Starlight)

B-side of **True Love Ways**

Galadriel was a character in a number of J. R. R. Tolkien's middle earth novels, notable because of the shimmering light from her golden hair. Picking up on these elements, Hank Marvin and John Farrar wrote a song for their self-titled 1973 album. For the time, it was breaking new ground with the use of vocoders and experimenting with changing keys and time signatures.

Cliff Richard added *Galadriel (Spirit of Starlight)* to the set list of his 1982 Royal Albert Hall concert with the London Philharmonic Orchestra, which was recorded and released on the album ***Dressed for the Occasion***. It was one of a small number of songs that he has released live versions of without creating a studio version. From the tracks recorded, Cliff released his version of Buddy Holly's ***True Love Ways*** as a single, with *Galadriel (Spirit of Starlight)* used for its B-side.

While the original used electronic effects, Cliff's version is recreated using effective arrangements for the muted brass and fluttering woodwind and pizzicato strings of the London Philharmonic Orchestra. The chorus then becomes expansive as the ensemble cast of backing vocalists, rock band and orchestra join in the ebullient expression of the lyrics, before quietening down once more into the verse.

Track Specification

Composed by Hank Marvin and John Farrar

Musicians

Stuart Calver	backing vocals
David Cooke	synthesiser
Steve Gray	piano
Mark Griffiths	bass
Tony Harding	backing vocals
Richard Hewson	arranger, conductor
Graham Jarvis	drums, percussion
London Philharmonic Orchestra	orchestra
John Perry	backing vocals
Cliff Richard	vocals
Tony Rivers	backing vocals

Recording Details

Producer	Cliff Richard and Richard Hewson
Engineered by	John Kurlander
Mixed by	Keith Bessey
Recording location	Royal Albert Hall, London
Mixed at	Strawberry Studios South, Surrey
Recording date	23rd November 1982

♬ Gambling Song, The

From the album **Heathcliff Live**

Another new song featuring Cliff Richard appears in the live stage show while not on the teaser album ***Songs from Heathcliff***. Heathcliff (Cliff) is now living at Wuthering Heights with the drunken Hindley (Jimmy Johnston), having failed in his attempt to win Cathy (Helen Hobson) away from the dull Edgar Linton (Darryl Knock). He had returned from his travels gathering riches along the way and had given Isabella Linton (Sara Haggerty) a silk scarf, thereby leaving her to misconstrue his romantic intentions. Hindley and Heathcliff regularly clash and even fight with each other's money at a gambling den, finally using Wuthering Heights as collateral on the outcome of a fixed boxing match - resulting in the drunken Hindley trying to kill Heathcliff as Heathcliff beats him up and forces him to become a servant. The song is sung principally by Knock with a style that is reminiscent of the late sixties and early seventies stage musicals.

The upbeat synthesiser track has echoes of the work Cliff was recording in the eighties, while the ensemble singing is everything expected from a musical with a strong ear for the harmonies. Cliff and Jimmy Johnston sing the song with gusto but, unfortunately, it isn't the best song from the album until it steps up to the chorus, where a key change creates a complete change in rhythm and outlook.

Track Specification

Composed by John Farrar and Tim Rice

Musicians

Sean Callery	orchestrator, orchestra
David Combes	backing vocals
John Clark	guitar
Elements:	
Geoff David	backing vocals
Chris Holland	backing vocals
Sonia Jones	backing vocals
Niki Kitt	backing vocals
Suzanne Parry	backing vocals

Recording Details

Producer	John Farrar
Engineered by	Keith Bessey, John Pearson and Tom Tranter
Recording location	Earl's Court Hall 2, London and/or The Academy, National Indoor Arena, Birmingham, England
Recording date	October 1996

Keith Hayman	keyboards
Jimmy Johnston	spoken vocals, vocals
Peter May	drums, percussion
Bob Noble	keyboards
Alan Park	keyboards
John Perry	backing vocals
Cliff Richard	spoken vocals, vocals
Steve Stroud	bass
Kevin Townend	orchestration
Unknown	orchestra
Mick Wilson	backing vocals

♫ Game, The

From the film soundtrack album of **Take Me High**

For some reason, the ***Take Me High*** soundtrack album is not in the same sequence as that for the film's narrative, possibly for optimal space reasons on the original vinyl release. *The Game* actually appears between ***Life*** and ***Brumburger Duet*** in the film but is brought in earlier between ***Driving*** and *Brumburger Duet* on the album.

Having soured a deal for his rival Hugo Flaxman (Anthony Andrews) and relinquished the money for other projects, Tim Matthews (Cliff Richard) is alone on his houseboat, playing his guitar and singing this song, wondering why he is doing what he is doing and what impact he is having on the world, exemplified by such lyrics as "nothing's changed since I went out". Meanwhile, Sarah (Debbie Watling) is cooking her prototype Brumburger and, at the end of the song, Tim's phone rings and Sarah simply says "Brumburger."

The Game was recorded at a number of sessions taking place in May of 1973 and it took just three takes to complete. Recorded in Studio 3 at the Abbey Road complex rather than the familiar Studio 2, there is some suggestion that the songs recorded at these sessions might have only been backing tracks with vocals overdubbed in September; however, the song details here will state May until or unless further information becomes available.

The picked chords on the guitar introduce the song leading into Cliff's vocals, which are complex in terms of the musical intervals reached but he makes the performance appear easy. When the chorus appears, the basic orchestral accompaniment is brought in and transfers back to the guitar, which (if the film is to be believed) may possibly be Cliff himself, although this is unconfirmed.

Track Specification

Composed by Tony Cole

Musicians

David MacKay Orchestra	orchestra
David MacKay	arranger, conductor
Cliff Richard	vocals

Recording Details

Producer	David MacKay
Engineered by	Tony Clark and Mike Jarrett
Recording location	Abbey Road Studio 3, St. John's Wood, London
Recording date	27th-28th May 1973

♫ Gee But It's Lonesome

Unissued track

During the recording sessions for the EP supporting the *Expresso Bongo* film (Cliff Richard's second excursion into celluloid), a Phil Everly track was recorded but remains unissued. In *The Complete Recording Sessions 1958-1990* by Peter Lewry and Nigel Goodall, the title is written as *Gee But It's Lonesome*, although the Everly song, a 1959 hit for Pat Boone, was actually entitled *Gee But It's Lonely* – it is possible that the lyrics and therefore the title were subsequently changed.

The song was a number two hit in the UK for Boone and, for this reason, it would have been a suitable choice for Cliff to record. However, for whatever reason, the track remains unissued.

Track Specification

Composed by Phil Everly

Musicians

Norrie Paramor Orchestra	orchestra
Norrie Paramor	arranger, conductor
Cliff Richard	vocals

Recording Details

Producer	Norrie Paramor
Engineered by	Malcolm Addey
Recording location	Abbey Road Studio 2, St. John's Wood, London
Recording date	1959

♫ Gee Whiz It's You

13th UK single *and CD B-side of* **All I Have to Do Is Dream/Miss You Nights** *and from the album* **Reunited** *and unissued live track*

Unusually for the times when singles and album tracks were kept apart, *Gee Whiz It's You* was released as a single, even though it started life as an album track (although it would take almost a year before it was finally issued). Using the tenth take from the session at which it was recorded, both the mono and stereo versions are the same with different edits and mixes; the mono version is a few seconds longer revealing more of the lead guitar part by Hank Marvin.

Appearing also on the associated ***Me and My Shadows No. 3*** EP, this was the Cliff single that never was in Britain and is the first time that a foreign single release became a hit in the domestic market. Released in Europe by popular demand as a

single backed with ***I Cannot Find a True Love*** on the Columbia label (catalogue number 45-DC 756), it soon came to the attention of fans in Britain, who created such demand for it that the pressing of the single was imported and thus sufficient sales pushed the record to number four when it was finally 'released' in Cliff's native country in March 1961.
Another Shadows-related composition, the jangling guitar and happy tenor undermine the lyrics, which are of reassessment of loss and negative feelings towards the singer's love interest, but underlying everything is a message of hope and optimism. The ensemble nature of the band comes to the fore in the song's rendition and is clearly the strongest track on the album and therefore hardly surprising that the fans should press for it to be released as a single.
As part of a BBC documentary about Cliff, a number of live tracks were recorded at the Hammersmith Odeon and Manchester Apollo to accompany the broadcast. Some tracks were licensed for release at the time resulting in the ***Daddy's Home*** single, while others remained with the BBC. Thirteen years later, Cliff spent some time remixing and cleaning up the section featuring the duets with Phil Everly that resulted in the release of the double A-sided ***All I Have to Do Is Dream*** and a remixed version of ***Miss You Nights***. While the seven-inch single release was restricted to just those tracks, the first of the dual CD single version had two additional tracks, both featuring Cliff and Everly together, ***When Will I Be Loved?*** and ***Tribute to the Legends Medley***, of which *Gee Whiz It's You* formed part – which is a slight conceit or perhaps justified arrogance. Everly joined Cliff for the medley in three songs but left just before Cliff enters into *Gee Whiz It's You*. It is a straightforward rendition of the song and fits well with the other luminaries in the medley. The guitar solo is a close approximation to what Hank would have done on stage but it is also tangibly different enough to make it a modern take.
The song was incorporated into another medley – the ***Oldies Medley*** – for the 2003 world tour, which was filmed and recorded, although the CD album of the *World Tour Live* did not include the medley on its track listing.
Because of the performance energy and the representation of their early career, *Gee Whiz It's You* was chosen by Cliff and the Shadows for a re-recording on the track listing of the ***Reunited*** album, and was performed in concert on the subsequent promotional tour. The performance is smoother than the original but has lost none of its energy.

Track Specification
Composed by Hank Marvin and Ian Samwell

1. Single

Jet Harris	bass
Hank Marvin	guitar
Tony Meehan	drums, percussion
Cliff Richard	vocals
Bruce Welch	rhythm guitar

Recording Details

Producer	Norrie Paramor
Engineered by	Malcolm Addey and Norman Smith (mono) and Peter Bown and Alan Kane (stereo)
Recording location	Abbey Road Studio 2, St. John's Wood, London
Recording date	17th March 1960

2. CD B-side (All I Have to Do Is Dream)
Musicians

Stuart Calver	backing vocals
John Clark	guitar
Mark Griffiths	bass
Graham Jarvis	drums, percussion
Martin Jenner	guitar
Alan Park	keyboards
John Perry	backing vocals
Cliff Richard	vocals
Tony Rivers	backing vocals
Graham Todd	keyboards

Recording Details

Producer	Cliff Richard
Engineered by	Unknown
Recording location	Hammersmith Odeon, London
Remixed at	R. G. Jones Studio, London
Recording date	1st May 1981 (live track) and 7th September 1994 (remix)

3. Unissued track (World Tour Live)
Musicians

Anthony Clark	backing vocals, guitar
John Clark	guitar
Dave Cooke	keyboards
Pete May	drums, percussion
Alan Park	keyboards
Cliff Richard	vocals, guitar
Steve Stroud	bass

Recording Details

Producer	Keith Bessey
Engineered by	Keith Bessey
Recording location	The Mission Winery, Napier, New Zealand
Recording date	22nd February 2003

4. Reunited
Musicians

Brian Bennett	drums, percussion
Mark Griffiths	bass
Hank Marvin	backing vocals, guitar
Cliff Richard	vocals, backing vocals
Bruce Welch	backing vocals, rhythm guitar

Recording Details

Producer	Warren Bennett (co-ordination)
Engineered by	James Collins (Honeyhill Studios), Ethan Carlson (Middle Ear Studios), Les Williams (Nivram Studios) and Keith Bessey (mixing and mastering)
Recording location	Middle Ear Studios, Miami, Florida, USA (Cliff's vocals), Nivram Studios, Perth, Western Australia (Hank's guitars and vocals) and Honeyhill Studios, Hertfordshire, England (all other vocals and instruments)
Recording date	Early 2009

♬ Geh' Deinen Weg Nicht So Allein

From the album **Hier Ist Cliff**

Recorded at the first session of four designated for laying down German language songs for Cliff Richard's first German album, ***Hier Ist Cliff***, *Geh' Deinen Weg Nicht So Allein* (literally *Don't Go Your Own Way So Alone*) is a translated version of the ***Established 1958*** track ***The Dreams I Dream***. The last of three songs completed at the session, only the stereo version has been released and, although a rarity for many years, it was reissued on CD in the ***On the Continent*** in 1997.
With an arrangement that focuses on the brass, Cliff sings with appeal and a slight vibrato that would become his successful trademark in later years. The female backing vocalists are unknown (possibly the Breakaways but not confirmed) but, when singing prominently on their own, sound as if they are struggling with the German pronunciation. However, it is an excellent version of the song that sounds completely different from the English single.

Track Specification

Composed by Hank Marvin; German lyrics by Carl Ulrich Blecher

Musicians

Norrie Paramor Orchestra	orchestra
Norrie Paramor	arranger, director
Cliff Richard	vocals
Unknown	backing vocals

Recording Details

Producer	Norrie Paramor
Engineered by	Peter Vince
Recording location	Abbey Road Studio 2, St. John's Wood, London
Recording date	31st October 1968

♬ Get Back

From the album **Japan Tour '74**

One of the Beatles' finest rock and roll records, it was principally written by Paul McCartney and featured Billy Preston on keyboards and appeared as the closing track of the last Beatles album, *Let It Be*, in 1970. The song was released as a single and, as with most of the band's output, it went to number one in most countries. Rod Stewart had a number eleven hit with his version in May 1976, while the Beatles singles were all being re-released. It has also been variously covered by Elvis Presley, Ike and Tina Turner, Amen Corner (their single version was unsuccessful as they disbanded at the time of release), Status Quo, Take That, Al Green and it has also been parodied by the Rutles as *Get Up and Go*.
Cliff Richard regularly performed songs in concert that he has never recorded in the studio. For the Japan tour in 1974, *Get Back* was one such song. The band are clearly having a great time performing the complex rock song, while Cliff's lead vocals are as impassioned as McCartney's were although he avoids the spoken middle eight from the Beatles' version. There is a solo electric piano performance by Barrie Guard, who was otherwise the conductor on several other tracks.

Track Specification

Composed by John Lennon and Paul McCartney

Musicians

Barrie Guard	electric piano
Cliff Hall	piano
Brian Lewis	backing vocals, guitar
Kevin Peak	acoustic guitar
Cliff Richard	vocals
Trevor Spencer	drums, percussion
Alan Tarney	backing vocals, bass
Bruce Welch	backing vocals, rhythm guitar

Recording Details

Producer	Toshiba EMI (no individual detailed)
Engineered by	Toshiba EMI (no individual detailed)
Recording location	Shinjuku Koseinenkin, Tokyo, Japan
Recording date	7th-8th October 1974

♬ Get on Board, Little Children

From the album **Good News**

Another spiritual, *Get on Board, Little Children* was used as a teaching aid, since most of the American black population during the slave years often had no access to education. With memorable song, the elders spread the teachings of the Christian religion and it has been recorded by the St. John's Children's Choir, Jack Teagarden and Shirley Temple.
Recorded at Cliff Richard's first main session for the ***Good News*** religious album, *Get on Board, Little Children* was completed in three takes and was the third of four songs to be recorded at that session.
With a bass line and brass introduction that owes much to the Motown sound, the Shadows are on top form on this track, while Cliff once again shows off his versatility at tackling any type of subject matter. There is an uncredited backing vocal group, which is kept back in the mix allowing the instrumentation to take precedence behind Cliff's lead vocal line.

Track Specification

Composed by Traditional, arranged by Mike Leander

Musicians

Brian Bennett	drums, percussion
Mike Leander	arranger, conductor
Hank Marvin	guitar
Mike Leander Orchestra	orchestra
Cliff Richard	vocals
John Rostill	bass
Unknown	backing vocals
Bruce Welch	rhythm guitar

Recording Details

Producer	Norrie Paramor
Engineered by	Peter Vince and Mike Stone
Recording location	Abbey Road Studio 2, St. John's Wood, London
Recording date	27th April 1967

♫ Gettin' the Feelin'

Unissued track

Gettin' the Feelin' was written by Cliff Richard's then backing vocalist, Tony Rivers, and was recorded during the sessions for the ***Green Light*** album. However, although it was the first song attempted, it was stopped after the first take (although later vocal overdubs indicate that it was ready for release) and has never been issued. Because of the lack of information on the musicians on the track, those known to be involved in the sessions at the time are added to the track specification.

Track Specification

Composed by Tony Rivers

Musicians

Brian Bennett	drums, percussion
Terry Britten	guitar
Stuart Calver	backing vocals
Richard Hewson	arranger, conductor
Alan Jones	bass
Duncan MacKay	keyboards
Alan Parker	guitar
John Perry	backing vocals
Tim Renwick	guitar
Cliff Richard	vocals
Tony Rivers	backing vocals
Trevor Spencer	drums, percussion
Alan Tarney	backing vocals, guitar, bass, keyboards
Graham Todd	keyboards
Unknown	orchestra

Recording Details

Producer	Bruce Welch
Engineered by	Tony Clark and Haydn Bendall
Recording location	Abbey Road Studio 3, St. John's Wood, London
Recording date	14th January 1978 and 11th February 1978

♫ Girl Can't Help It, The

From the albums **Tracks 'n' Grooves**, **Cliff "Live" in Japan '72** *and* **From a Distance ***** The Event**

The title track of the 1956 film *The Girl Can't Help It*, it was most famously recorded by Little Richard and released as a single in December of that year, reaching number forty-nine in the US Billboard charts and number nine in the UK charts in March 1957. It has since been covered by a number of artists including the Animals, the Everly Brothers, Jive Bunny (sampling Little Richard's version), Mick Ronson, Bobby Vee and Conway Twitty among others.

Cliff Richard recorded his version at the final session of 1967, although it would be held back until the release of the ***Tracks 'n' Grooves*** album in 1970. As a result of this decision, only the stereo version has ever been issued although, at the time of recording, a mono formatted edit would have been recorded.

Cliff's voice appears further back in the edit than the instrumentation and this creates a perplexing listening experience. The slow-paced song is perfect for Cliff's voice and he uses all parts of his register. The middle section includes an organ solo and, when Cliff returns, he has a very strident and uncredited female backing vocalist accompanying him.

For his Far Eastern tour in 1972, Cliff incorporated *The Girl Can't Help It* into a ***Rock Medley*** that plays tribute to the stars of the fifties when he was just starting out: *The Girl Can't Help It*, ***Great Balls of Fire***, ***Lucille***, ***Jailhouse Rock***, ***Good Old Rock 'n' Roll*** and ***Do You Wanna Dance***.

Subsequently, Cliff resurrected the song for inclusion in the *Oh Boy! Set* section of his event at Wembley Stadium, which he performed with the help of the Dallas Boys, the reformed British vocal group who had backed him on the *Oh Boy!* television show in the late fifties. The performance is pure rock and roll and Cliff is in his element singing this kind of song. The Dallas Boys provide the backing vocals, although the arrangement doesn't tend to move from a unison singing of the song's title.

Track Specification

Composed by Bobby Troup

1. Tracks 'n' Grooves

Musicians

Mike Leander	arranger, conductor
Mike Leander Orchestra	orchestra
Cliff Richard	vocals
Unknown	backing vocals

Recording Details

Producer	Norrie Paramor
Engineered by	Peter Vince
Recording location	Abbey Road Studio 2, St. John's Wood, London
Recording date	11th October 1967

2. Cliff "Live" in Japan '72

Musicians

Brian Bennett	drums, percussion
Pat Carroll	backing vocals
John Farrar	bass
Alan Hawkshaw	piano
Hank Marvin	guitar
Olivia Newton-John	backing vocals
Cliff Richard	vocals
Bruce Welch	rhythm guitar

Recording Details

Producer	Norrie Paramor
Engineered by	Unknown
Recording location	Kosei Nenkin Hall, Tokyo, Japan
Recording date	22nd-23rd September 1972

3. From a Distance ** The Event***

Musicians		*Recording Details*	
Dallas Boys:		Producer	Cliff Richard
Nicky Clarke	backing vocals	Engineered by	Keith Bessey and Mick McKenna
Leon Fisk	backing vocals	Recording location	Rolling Stones Mobile Studio, Wembley Stadium, Wembley, North-west London
Stan Jones	backing vocals	Recording date	16th-17th June 1989
Joe Smith	backing vocals		
Bob Wragg	backing vocals		
Oh Boy! Band	rock 'n' roll band		
Cliff Richard	vocals		

♫ Girl from Ipanema, The

From the album **Kinda Latin**

In the original Portuguese, *The Girl from Ipanema* was entitled *Garota de Ipanema* and, although the most famous version and the only recording to have a hit with it in the UK (reaching number twenty-nine in August 1964) was credited solely to Stan Getz, it is probably far more famously associated with the female singer Astrud Gilberto, who provided the vocals on the single. Written in 1962 and recorded by Pery Ribeiro the same year, it was first performed by co-writer Antônio Carlos Jobim on the *Andy Williams Show* in America three years later. It has been covered by a huge variety of artists such as Jonny Blue, James Last, Oscar Peterson, Lena Horne, Cariocas de Rio, Edgar Cruz, John Holt, Vic Damone, Elaine Elias, Spike Milligan, Sitti Navarro and Andy Williams among a multitude of others.

The first song to be completed from the first of three October 1965 sessions for Cliff Richard's album ***Kinda Latin***, the sixth and final take and edit of *The Girl from Ipanema* were used for the mono and stereo recordings but with different mixes for the separation in the audio channels.

It would be very easy to create a cover that matched the arrangement popularized by Astrud Gilberto, but the arrangement for Cliff's version is more laidback and languid and Cliff's vocals are more sustained than the clipped tones of the original. He also imbues some of the notes with a vibrato that only add interest to the song.

Track Specification

Composed by Antônio Carlos Jobim and Vinícius De Moraes; English lyrics Norman Gimbel

Musicians		*Recording Details*	
Bernard Ebbinghouse Orchestra	orchestra	Producer	Norrie Paramor
Bernard Ebbinghouse	arranger, conductor	Engineered by	Peter Bown
Cliff Richard	vocals	Recording location	Abbey Road Studio 2, St. John's Wood, London
		Recording date	4th October 1965

♫ Girl in Every Port, A

From the film soundtrack album of **Wonderful Life**

The group of seven friends led by Johnny (portrayed by Cliff Richard) have been kicked off the cruise liner on which they were working because they had caused the ship to run aground; the angry captain then cast them adrift in a rubber dinghy leaving them to fend for themselves. Eventually, they reach port in a Spanish-speaking part of the world and, as Johnny ties the boat up to the moorings, he observes the shapely legs of a pretty girl walking past on the promenade above (they belong to Jenny (Susan Hampshire), the eventual love interest in the film) and, although the other six friends complain about being tired, Johnny says one word (the now sexist term 'birds', meaning 'girls') and a speeded up sequence of film see all of them scrambling out of the dinghy and up the steps. The currently unknown Jenny hires a camel taxi, while the boys get into two horse-drawn carts and attempt to follow her, ending up with finding a Scotsman in a kilt as a visual gag. This song allows the entourage to perorm a dance routine (something that they had been reticent to do in earlier films) and it appears that they had a lot of fun doing it, too.

Recorded at two sessions – the first with the orchestra only and the second to dub the vocals on (including the Mike Sammes Singers in place of the actors and the Shadows in the film) – in the book *The Complete Recording Sessions 1958-1990*, authors Peter Lewry and Nigel Goodall indicate that the final edit of the vocal overdub is a splice of two takes but there is no detail as to which ones. The orchestral session broke the track into three parts, with the known information that the second and third takes of the first and second parts respectively were used while there is no information available regarding the take for the third. The second of three tracks recorded to supply the vocals on the orchestral backing, the same combined takes and edits from the two sessions were used for the mono and stereo recordings but with different mixes for the audio channels. The track was also released on the track listing of the ***Wonderful Life No. 2*** EP, while the film version of the song was probably recorded in the first three months of 1964 but has not been released in any other commercial format; it features a very similar arrangement, although the orchestral segments are extended to allow for the dialogue in the film.

The song is a typical British film musical song that is there for the screen spectacular rather than the music *per se*, since the song is not particularly memorable. Played with gusto and designed to accompany the dance sequences during this part of the film's plot, it has an extended instrumental interlude. Cliff performs the song with aplomb but it is certainly with an ear for the dance rhythm that it was composed.

Track Specification
Composed by Peter Myers and Ronald Cass

Musicians		*Recording Details*	
Associated British Studio Orchestra	orchestra	Producer	Bob Barratt (orchestra) and Norrie Paramor (vocals)
Stanley Black	conductor	Engineered by	Malcolm Addey and Alan Kane (orchestra) and Malcolm Addey and Richard Langham (vocals)
Mike Sammes Singers	backing vocals	Recording location	Abbey Road Studio 2, St. John's Wood, London (orchestra and vocals)
Cliff Richard	vocals	Recording date	20th May 1964 (orchestra) and 26th May 1964 (vocals)

♫ Girl Like You, A

***14th UK single** and from the albums* **...And They Said It Wouldn't Last! (My 50 Years in Music)** *and* **Reunited – Special Edition**

Cliff Richard and the Shadows' fourteenth single was written by the man who had given The Shadows their first independent hit with ***Apache*** the previous year, Jerry Lordan. According to Cliff, *A Girl Like You* was the easiest to record in terms of not waiving any minor mistakes and it was the firm favourite of his father, who, although he had died prior to the single's release, believed that this was by far the best song the band had recorded up to that point. Covered by The Hunters, which wasn't a hit, it was originally slated for recording at the session on 27th September 1960 (from which no material would be used) but it was actually delayed until the late January session.

Three versions of the song were used for the mono, stereo and mock stereo, which all used the same take and edit but with different mixes for the single and stereo channels. The mock stereo version took the mono edit and mixed it slightly differently. *A Girl Like You* was released backed with ***Now's the Time to Fall in Love*** on the Columbia label (catalogue number 45-DB 4667) on 16th June 1961, reaching the number three spot in the UK singles charts. The second take was issued as part of the anthology ***...And They Said It Wouldn't Last! (My 50 Fifty Years in Music)***, which features studio chatter and a different arrangement and lengthier guitar solo from Hank Marvin.

The song trips along at a medium walking pace as Cliff's vocals describe the joy experienced upon unexpectedly finding a girl that he can spend his life with. Some of the lyrics and rhymes are simplistic but this adds to the charm of the song rather than being a source of embarrassment. Hank Marvin's guitar is performed with staccato proficiency that mirrors the skipping heartbeat of someone in love before becoming beautifully indulgent in the middle eight. The ensemble musicianship is strongest here than on many earlier songs and is a clear step on the road to the classic band sound.

When Cliff and the Shadows reunited in 2009 to celebrate fifty years in music, they re-recorded twenty-six tracks from their early material. One of the familiar tracks was *A Girl Like You*, which was not issued on the basic ***Reunited*** album; instead it appeared on a three-track CD that was packaged as a special edition with the original album. On this version, Cliff employs stronger vibrato and the recording is sharper but it is a strong replica of the original.

Track Specification
Composed by Jerry Lordan

1. Single

Musicians		*Recording Details*	
Jet Harris	bass	Producer	Norrie Paramor
Hank Marvin	guitar	Engineered by	Malcolm Addey
Tony Meehan	drums, percussion	Recording location	Abbey Road Studio 2, St. John's Wood, London
Cliff Richard	vocals	Recording date	28th January 1961
Bruce Welch	rhythm guitar		

2. ...And They Said It Wouldn't Last! (My 50 Years in Music)

Musicians		*Recording Details*	
Jet Harris	bass	Producer	Norrie Paramor
Hank Marvin	guitar	Engineered by	Malcolm Addey
Tony Meehan	drums, percussion	Recording location	Abbey Road Studio 2, St. John's Wood, London
Cliff Richard	vocals	Recording date	28th January 1961
Bruce Welch	rhythm guitar		

3. Reunited – Special Edition

Musicians		*Recording Details*	
Brian Bennett	drums, percussion	Producer	Warren Bennett (co-ordination)
Warren Bennett	keyboards	Engineered by	James Collins (Honeyhill Studios), Ethan Carlson (Middle Ear Studios), Les Williams (Nivram Studios) and Keith Bessey (mixing and mastering)
Mark Griffiths	bass		
Hank Marvin	backing vocals, guitar		
Cliff Richard	vocals, backing vocals		
Bruce Welch	backing vocals, rhythm guitar	Recording location	Middle Ear Studios, Miami, Florida, USA (Cliff's vocals), Nivram Studios, Perth, Western Australia (Hank's guitars and vocals) and Honeyhill Studios, Hertfordshire, England (all other vocals and instruments)
		Recording date	Early 2009

♫ Girl on the Bus

From the album **Established 1958**

Recorded at a double session that likely included a number of Shadows tracks for the ***Established 1958*** album, *Girl on the Bus* was completed in three takes and was the only Cliff Richard song to be completed that day, although initial attempts at ***Don't Forget to Catch Me*** and ***What's Behind the Eyes of Mary?*** were also tried.

The song, written solely by John Rostill, who Cliff recognized as a major tunesmith, has a country style of arrangement, and there is a beautiful melody matched by the violin and steel guitar that creates a slow hoe-down effect. Cliff imbues the lyrics with emotion as he tells the story of losing the girl he fancies as he only ever sees her on a bus, although there is a bit of advertising for the now defunct BOAC airline in the final line.

In late 1968, Cliff recorded a number of German translations of songs that appeared on *Established 1958* and ***Two a Penny***, one of which was *Girl on the Bus* which was translated into the plot-stealing ***Story Ohne Happy-End***.

Track Specification

Composed by John Rostill

Musicians

Brian Bennett	drums, percussion
Mike Leander	arranger, conductor
Hank Marvin	guitar
Mike Leander Orchestra	orchestra
Cliff Richard	vocals
John Rostill	bass
Bruce Welch	rhythm guitar

Recording Details

Producer	Norrie Paramor
Engineered by	Peter Vince
Recording location	Abbey Road Studio 2, St. John's Wood, London
Recording date	29th May 1968

♫ Girls Back Home, The

From the album **Rock Dreams** *(The Brian Bennett Band)*

Although recording sessions for Cliff Richard were fewer in 1977 than in any previous years for his own material, he did help other artists out. The first was Brian Bennett for a track on the first album by the Brian Bennett Band, *Rock Dreams*, called *The Girls Back Home*. Written by Brian and his son Warren, the song was chosen for release as a single, backed with *Jonty Jump*, on the DJM label (catalogue number DJS 10791) in July 1977, although it didn't enter into the UK charts.

Tony Rivers takes the lead vocals on the track, which is quirkily led by the synthesisers and a running bass line. The backing vocals are more evident than on the band's version of ***C'mon Everybody***, although Cliff's involvement in this is difficult to pick out, which possibly assists with ensemble feel. The song has a nostalgic air to it but is also of its time with a Rubettes sound to the recording and it is a surprise that it didn't receive more airplay as a consequence, although the country was then falling in thrall to the punk rock movement and this would have seemed staid in comparison.

Track Specification

Composed by Brian Bennett and Warren Bennett

Musicians

Brian Bennett	drums, percussion
Stuart Calver	backing vocals
Alan Hawkshaw	keyboards
Les Hurtle	bass
Alan Parkes	guitar
John Perry	backing vocals
Cliff Richard	backing vocals
Tony Rivers	vocals

Recording Details

Producer	Brian Bennett
Engineered by	Dick Plant
Recording location	Honey Hill Studios, Hertfordshire
Recording date	April 1977

♫ Girl von Nebenan, Das

From the album **Ich Träume Deine Träume**

Das Girl von Nebenan was one of the eleven songs completed by Cliff Richard over the marathon two-day, four-session recording in November 1970 for his second album *Ich Träume Deine Träume*. An original German song that has never been recorded in an English equivalent by Cliff, it was the third of five songs completed on the first day. *Das Girl von Nebenan* – or *The Girl Next Door* –was also chosen as the B-side of the title track when released as a single in January 1971 and was then included in the boxed set collection, ***On the Continent***, remastered and released in 1997.

With a faint Latin rhythm at the beginning, the song becomes a standard rock beat in the chorus. In spite of this and Cliff's expert vocals, there are too few hooks within the song to become instantly memorable.

Track Specification

Composed by Rosemeier and Jacobi

Musicians

Nick Ingman	arranger, conductor
Norrie Paramor Orchestra	orchestra
Cliff Richard	vocals
Unknown	backing vocals

Recording Details

Producer	Norrie Paramor (backing track and vocals)
Engineered by	Phil McDonald (backing track and vocals)
Recording location	Cologne, Germany (backing track) and Abbey Road Studio 2, St. John's Wood, London (vocals)
Recording date	November 1970 (backing track) and 24th November 1970 (vocals)

♫ Girl Wie Du, Ein

German single

For Cliff Richard's tenth German language single, *Ein Girl Wie Du* was picked. Even though it translates as ***A Girl Like You***, it is not the same song as the Jerry Lordan-written hit from 1961 of the same name. In fact it is a translation of ***Words*** (an unreleased English version of which existed until it was included on 2008's ***...And They Said I Wouldn't Last! (My 50 Years in Music)***) arranged and conducted by Mike Leander and was recorded simultaneously with the vocals. It is unclear whether the backing track for the German version was used for the English recording or if they are entirely separate – the English version, though, was recorded a couple of weeks later. The liner notes for the album suggest that the composer is unknown; however, it is known from the German release that the English version of *Words* was written by Peter Poll.

Backed with a translated version of ***Visions*** (***Bilder von Dir***), which underwent similar new orchestral treatment and also recorded at the same session, *Ein Girl Wie Du* was released as a single on the international Columbia label (catalogue number C-23510) in June 1967, reaching number twenty-three in the German singles charts. Originally only issued in the mono format as a single (as was Columbia's practice at the time), the stereo version was eventually released on the foreign language collation of Cliff's tracks ***On the Continent*** in 1997.

A plodding bass and full backing vocal chorus introduce the song, which is an incredibly beautiful song that has been unavailable for forty years. The backing vocalists are uncredited and there is no information available as to who they might be, but Cliff's vocal is very strong on this track and he appears to have no trouble with the German pronunciation.

Track Specification

Composed by Peter Poll; German lyrics by Hans Meizer

Musicians

Mike Leander Orchestra	orchestra
Mike Leander	arranger, conductor
Cliff Richard	vocals
Unknown	backing vocals

Recording Details

Producer	Norrie Paramor
Engineered by	Peter Vince
Recording location	Abbey Road Studio 2, St. John's Wood, London
Recording date	25th April 1967

♫ Girl, You'll Be a Woman Soon

B-side of **I'll Come Running** *and from the albums* **Live at the Talk of the Town** *and* **World Tour Live**

Written and recorded by Neil Diamond, *Girl, You'll Be a Woman Soon* was released as a single by him in 1967, reaching number ten in the US singles charts and it appears on his album *Just for You*. It was revived in 1994 by Urge Overkill, who recorded a version that was subsequently melded into the soundtrack of Quentin Tarantino's *Pulp Fiction*, reaching number thirty-seven in the UK charts in November 1994. A number of other artists have interpreted the song including David Essex, Third World, Jackie Edwards, the Countdown Singers, the Starlite Singers and Hugo Montenegro.

Cliff Richard recorded his version during the last of three sessions for the 1968 Eurovision Song Contest candidates and it was chosen to back Cliff's forty-second UK single, ***I'll Love You Forever Today***, which was taken from the minimal soundtrack of the film ***Two a Penny***. The title was also chosen to back the release of the Italian and French versions of ***Congratulations***, ***Il Mondo et Tondo*** and ***Ah! Quelle Histoire***, respectively.

A rolling bass and a single backing vocalist introduce the song before Cliff gasps after the first instrumental rendition and goes on to enunciate the rapid lyrics well in the fast-paced song. The chorus slows the pace a little before returning to the frenetic rush of the verses. The wowing guitar is very much of the period, while the uncredited backing vocalists sing their harmonies well against Cliff's lead – they are quite possibly the Ladybirds, who were involved during these sessions.

Thirty-five years later, Cliff resurrected the song for his world tour in support of his then new album ***Wanted***. The New Zealand show was recorded for a DVD release in 2003, while the following year saw a selection of the songs included on the complementary CD album *World Tour Live*, and the choice included *Girl, You'll Be a Woman Soon*. The blipping bass and strong percussion underneath the synthesiser introduce a faster-paced but reasonably reproduction of the original.

Track Specification

Composed by Neil Diamond

1. B-side (I'll Come Running)

Musicians

Mike Leander	arranger, conductor
Mike Leander Orchestra	orchestra
Cliff Richard	vocals
Unknown	backing vocals

Recording Details

Producer	Norrie Paramor
Engineered by	Peter Vince
Recording location	Abbey Road Studio 2, St. John's Wood, London
Recording date	11th February 1968

2. Live at the Talk of the Town

Musicians

Breakaways:	backing vocals
Vicki Hasemen	
Margo Quantrell	
Jean Ryder	
Norrie Paramor	arranger, conductor
Cliff Richard	vocals
Talk of the Town Orchestra	orchestra

Recording Details

Producer	Norrie Paramor
Engineered by	Peter Vince
Recording location	Talk of the Town Theatre, London
Recording date	30th May 1968

3. World Tour Live

Musicians

Rachel Allen	violin
Elena Bulgakova	violin
Jenni Champion	violin
Anthony Clark	backing vocals, guitar
John Clark	guitar
Dave Cooke	keyboards
Cornelia Didenco	violin
Gina Ferguson	violin
Mike Haughton	saxophone
Peter Howarth	backing vocals, tambourine
Cathy Irons	violin
Pete May	drums, percussion
Mick Mullins	backing vocals
Keith Murrell	backing vocals
Alan Park	keyboards
Hee-Jung Park	violin
Cliff Richard	vocals
Eva Schwanen-Lilley	violin
Steve Stroud	bass

Recording Details

Producer	Keith Bessey
Engineered by	Keith Bessey
Recording location	The Mission Winery, Napier, New Zealand
Recording date	22nd February 2003

♫ Give a Little Bit More

From the album **I'm No Hero**

Give a Little Bit More was the first of two songs not written by Alan Tarney for Cliff Richard's ***I'm No Hero*** album and it was released as a single only in the US; elsewhere, it was the closing track of the first side of the original vinyl release. Backed with the shared B-side for ***A Little in Love***, the non-album track ***Keep on Looking***, *Give a Little Bit More* was released on the EMI America label (catalogue number EMI 8076) in May 1981, and it rose to number thirty-nine in the US Billboard charts. To support the single, too, a promotional disc was released with an edited version of the track as the A-side and the album track on the reverse, also on the EMI America label (catalogue number EMISPRO 9616).

Not to be confused with ***Never Say Die (Give a Little Bit More)*** a few years later, *Give a Little Bit More* is another synthesiser-driven track that is notable for its use of blended vocals, which are Cliff's and Tarney's layered to create a small choir. The beat is relentless and drives the song ever onwards to its conclusion.

Track Specification

Composed by Jonathan Hodge and Andy Hill

Musicians

Michael Boddicker	synthesiser
Nick Glennie-Smith	synthesiser
Cliff Richard	vocals, backing vocals
Trevor Spencer	drums, percussion
Alan Tarney	arranger, backing vocals, bass
Unknown	hand claps

Recording Details

Producer	Alan Tarney
Engineered by	Ashley Howe
Recording location	Riverside Studios, London
Recording date	12th May-27th June 1980

♫ Give Me Back That Old Familiar Feeling

From the albums **The 31st of February Street** *and* **Japan Tour '74**

Writer Bill Graham was originally the bassist with Dean Beard and the Boys and then went on to join Glen Campbell, who recorded his version of *Give Me Back That Old Familiar Feeling* and should not be confused with Cliff Richard's evangelist friend of the same name. *Give Me Back That Old Familiar Feeling* was also covered by Denny Doherty, Dave Dudley, the Whites and Wayne Newton among others (based on the strength of Campbell's version rather than Cliff's).

Cliff recorded the song at a suite of sessions in the middle of February 1974 ostensibly planned for the album ***The 31st of February Street*** on which it appears. *Give Me Back That Old Familiar Feeling* was successfully completed in five takes.

The song begins with a simple guitar motif backing Cliff's lead vocals before the pace picks up in the chorus that has a stomping rhythm familiar to any Eurovision Song Contest fan. With its steel guitar and stentorian bass line, it forges onwards to the end and is one of the best tracks on the album.

Performed during the set list for his 1974 tour of Japan and released on ***Jaan Tour '74***, the album track is pretty faithfully revisited with its stomping chorus and gentle verses, accompanied by strings and the steel guitar.

Track Specification

Composed by Bill C. Graham

1. The 31st of February Street

Musicians

Terry Britten	backing vocals, guitar
Barrie Guard	arranger, conductor, percussion
Cliff Hall	keyboards
Jean Hawker	backing vocals

Recording Details

Producer	David MacKay
Engineered by	Tony Clark and Mike Jarrett
Recording location	Abbey Road Studio 3, St. John's Wood, London
Recording date	11th February 1974

Gordon Huntley	steel guitar
David MacKay	backing vocals
Dave MacRae	keyboards
Anna Peacock	backing vocals
Kevin Peek	acoustic guitar
Cliff Richard	vocals
Trevor Spencer	drums, percussion
Alan Tarney	backing vocals, bass
Unknown	orchestra

2. Japan Tour '74

Musicians

Barrie Guard	arranger, conductor
Cliff Hall	piano
Brian Lewis	backing vocals, steel guitar
Kevin Peak	acoustic guitar
Cliff Richard	vocals
Shambles Symphonet	orchestra
Trevor Spencer	drums, percussion
Alan Tarney	backing vocals, bass
Bruce Welch	backing vocals, rhythm guitar

Recording Details

Producer	Toshiba EMI (no individual detailed)
Engineered by	Toshiba EMI (no individual detailed)
Recording location	Shinjuku Koseinenkin, Tokyo, Japan
Recording date	7th-8th October 1974

♫ Give Me Love Your Way

Unissued track and from the album **Every Face Tells a Story**

After fourteen takes at the first complete session for the song, vocal overdubs were added a week later for the completion of the listing of the album ***Every Face Tells a Story***. The Alan Tarney and Trevor Spencer song was attempted prior to this at the session the day before but was abandoned for an unspecified reason.

The interest in this song is piqued immediately from the start with the curtailed cymbal percussion and the running bass guitar line. When Cliff begins his vocals, the song is already moving at a pace with a foot-tapping rhythm that cannot fail to raise a smile from the listener. But then there is a surprise in the middle eight with the syncopation created in the *a capella* close harmony singing of Cliff and his backing vocal group.

Track Specification

Composed by Alan Tarney and Trevor Spencer

1. Unissued track (Every Face Tells a Story)

Musicians

Brian Bennett	drums, percussion
Terry Britten	guitar
John Perry	backing vocals
Cliff Richard	vocals, backing vocals
Tony Rivers	backing vocals
Alan Tarney	bass
Graham Todd	keyboards

Recording Details

Producer	Bruce Welch
Engineered by	Tony Clark and John Barratt
Recording location	Abbey Road Studio 2, St. John's Wood, London
Recording date	6th September 1976

2. Every Face Tells a Story

Musicians

Brian Bennett	drums, percussion
Terry Britten	guitar
John Perry	backing vocals
Cliff Richard	vocals, backing vocals
Tony Rivers	backing vocals
Alan Tarney	bass
Graham Todd	keyboards

Recording Details

Producer	Bruce Welch
Engineered by	Tony Clark, Mike Jarrett and Alan Rouse
Recording location	Abbey Road Studio 2, St. John's Wood, London
Recording date	7th and 15th September 1976

♫ Glaub' Nur Mir

B-side of **Nur Bei Dir Bin Ich zu Haus**

Cliff Richard was becoming adept at recording in continental languages by the time the mid-sixties came along and this was more than many of his peers tried. Only the Beatles managed to pull off different versions of the songs but, even then, only in the German language. At the end of October 1965, Cliff returned to the studio to record a German single, ***Nur Bei Dir Bin Ich zu Haus***, which was the German equivalent of ***Wind Me Up (Let Me Go)***. Chosen for the B-side was *Glaub' Nur Mir*, which was a translated version of another song recorded in Nashville the previous year, ***On My Word***. The new German vocals were recorded and overdubbed on the original backing track and only released in mono format. The final (unknown) vocal take and edit were applied to the backing track and the result was used for both mono and stereo but with different mixes for the separated audio channels. Until the release of the compilation ***On the Continent*** in 1997, where the stereo version was first issued, the song was a considerable rarity worldwide.

As with all tracks that use previously recorded backing tracks, there is very little to comment, other than Cliff's comfortable vocal line in a foreign language in addition to the overdubbed German backing vocals.

Track Specification
Composed by Chip Taylor; German lyrics by Joachim Relin

Musicians	
Cliff Richard	vocals
Unknown	backing vocals
Unknown	guitar
Unknown	bass
Unknown	piano
Unknown	brass
Unknown	drums, percussion

Recording Details	
Producer	Bob Morgan and Billy Sherrill (backing track), Norrie Paramor (vocals) and Unknown (backing vocals)
Engineered by	Mort Thomason (backing track), Malcolm Addey (vocals) and Unknown (backing vocals)
Recording location	Columbia Studios, Nashville (backing track), Abbey Road Studio 2, St. John's Wood, London (vocals) and Germany (backing vocals)
Recording date	25th August 1964 (backing track), 27th October 1965 (vocals) and October-November 1965 (backing vocals)

♫ Glory of Love, The

From the album **From a Distance ***** The Event**

Cliff Richard is a fully-rounded singer and, although he considers himself a rock 'n' roller at heart, he doesn't limit himself to any specific genre: if the song is good and a joy to sing, he has added it to his repertoire and has often taken it into the studio to record. *The Glory of Love*, though, was only ever recorded as part of the live performance at ***The Event*** at Wembley Stadium in June 1989. The rendition was assisted by his guests, the Kalin Twins, with whom Cliff toured when promoting his first single, ***Move It***, in 1958 and successfully usurping their position at the top of the bill by the end.

The first recording of *The Glory of Love* was by Benny Goodman in 1936, becoming a popular number one hit in the American charts and it was then covered by the Five Keys, Peggy Lee, Eddy Arnold, Tom Rush, Otis Redding and Dean Martin, with Bette Midler recording a version for her 1988 film *Beaches*.

Cliff's version with the Kalin Twins was originally only released on the vinyl LP version of ***From a Distance ***** The Event***, presumably for space considerations on the CD, but when it was remastered in 2005, the album was expanded to two CDs and *The Glory of Love* was restored to its running position in the set list. While the Kalin Twins can sing, their voices sound aged in comparison to the purity and freshness of Cliff's and, although it doesn't detract from the listening, it is a reminder of the different career paths of the artists. In addition, Cliff sings in falsetto over the slow saxophone solo in the middle eight and it is one of the best tracks from the *Oh Boy!* section of the show.

Track Specification
Composed by Billy Hill

Musicians	
Kalin Twins:	
Harold Kalin	backing vocals
Herbie Kalin	backing vocals
Oh Boy! Band	rock 'n' roll band
Cliff Richard	vocals

Recording Details	
Producer	Cliff Richard
Engineered by	Keith Bessey and Mick McKenna
Recording location	Rolling Stones Mobile Studio, Wembley Stadium, Wembley, North-west London
Recording date	16th-17th June 1989

♫ Glück Ist Rosarot, Das

German single

Translating literally as *Luck Is Rose-Red*, Cliff Richard's ninth German language single was recorded in Studio Three at Abbey Road (rather than the familiar home for most of his recordings in Studio Two), but only for his vocals, which were overdubbed on a previously recorded backing track. Since Cliff has not recorded the song in any other language, there is no information on when the backing track was completed and it could possibly have been a track for another artist rather than specifically created for Cliff to apply his vocals over the top.

The final (unknown) take and edit of the vocals of *Das Glück Ist Rosarot* were overdubbed on the backing track and used for both the mono and stereo recordings but with different mixes for the split in audio channels. Initially released in mono format and backed with ***Was Kann Ich Tun***, it was issued on the international Columbia label (catalogue number C-23371) in December 1966 and reached number thirty-five in the German singles charts. A sought-after rarity, the stereo version of the song was finally released on the German boxed set compilation, ***On the Continent***, in 1997.

This upbeat and jaunty number has a distinctive Germanic sound to it. Cliff provides some of his own harmonies, helped along by uncredited backing vocalists and orchestra. Given the exuberance and strong melody, it is a surprise that it failed to get higher in the charts.

Track Specification
Composed by Bert Olden; German lyrics by Joachim Relin

Musicians	
Cliff Richard	vocals, backing vocals
Unknown	backing vocals
Unknown	arranger, conductor
Unknown	orchestra

Recording Details	
Producer	Norrie Paramor
Engineered by	Peter Vince
Recording location	Unknown (backing track) and Abbey Road Studio 3, St. John's Wood, London (vocals)
Recording date	Unknown (backing track) and 10th November 1966 (vocals)

♫ God Rest Ye Merry Gentlemen

From the EP **Carol Singers**

A traditional carol set in a minor key but with a nevertheless perkier attitude, *God Rest Ye Merry Gentlemen* appears to have been written some time before 1760 (the earliest known publication of the Christmas hymn) and may possibly have its roots further back into the medieval period. There is scholoarly debate as to the meaning of the title: it is known that 'rest' takes the meaning of 'keep' or 'remain' rather than 'relax' while 'merry' may take the one-time lost meaning of 'mighty'. If this is correct, then there is a misplaced comma after 'Merry' since it is an instruction rather than an observation.

God Rest Ye Merry Gentlemen has appeared in many Christmas selections on record but a number of popular artists have also covered it, including Julie Andrews, Iron Butterfly, Simon and Garfunkel, Bing Crosby, Jethro Tull, Erasure, Ella Fitzgerald, Nat King Cole, Perry Como, Neil Diamond, Garth Brooks, the Barenaked Ladies, Carly Simon and Chicago among many others.

Cliff Richard recorded his version of the carol without instrumental accompaniment, preferring to record all eight Christmas carols from the session *a capella* with the assistance of the Mastersingers (four Christian teachers of music). Over two sessions on the day, *God Rest Ye Merry Gentlemen* was spliced together from a number of takes with the final edit only being released in mono format on the ***Carol Singers*** EP, with the stereo version being issued twenty-one years later on Cliff's *Carols LP* in 1988.

Initially performed in unison with the backing vocalists, Cliff sings the main melody from the second verse onwards with harmonies cleverly performed by the Mastersingers. Unlike many of the other tracks, Cliff sings with a wry sense of humour rather than straight and reverent and this adds an extra bounce to the proceedings.

Track Specification

Composed by Traditional, arranged by Geoffrey Keating

Musicians

Mastersingers:	backing vocals
John Horrex	
Geoffrey Keating	
George Pratt	
Michael Warrington	
Cliff Richard	vocals

Recording Details

Producer	Norrie Paramor
Engineered by	Peter Vince and John Barrett
Recording location	Abbey Road Studio 2, St. John's Wood, London
Recording date	10th September 1967

♫ Going Away

From the album **The 31st of February Street**

The 31st of February Street was pieced together as a concept album about the emotions of leaving home. However, Raymond Froggatt's two songs (the other being ***The Singer***) were recorded almost two years earlier and it is unclear as to whether either song was intended for the album or whether it was a fortuitous coincidence to add them to the track listing. Both of these songs were recorded at the first session with David MacKay taking over from the retired Norrie Paramor, which also ceded Cliff Richard's first single flop (in chart terms at any rate), ***A Brand New Song***.

All of the songs on the album are about leaving, either in preparation for the activity, or looking back on earlier times having left. *Going Away* therefore fits well with the album's concept. The sparse guitar introduction ushers in Cliff's dulcet voice and this quiet arrangement continues with a lonely violin supporting the main vocal line. The song is not as memorable as others of Froggatt's songs written for Cliff but it serves to add to the emotion of feeling the need to be at home when going away.

Track Specification

Composed by Raymond Froggatt

Musicians

Terry Britten	guitar
David MacKay Orchestra	orchestra
David MacKay	arranger, conductor
Kevin Peek	guitar
Cliff Richard	vocals
Trevor Spencer	drums, percussion
Alan Tarney	bass
Unknown	violin solo

Recording Details

Producer	David MacKay
Engineered by	Peter Vince
Recording location	Abbey Road Studio 3, St. John's Wood, London
Recording date	11th October 1972

♫ Goin' Home

From the album **Small Corners**

Goin' Home was the first song to be completed at the designated sessions for the ***Small Corners*** album, with Cliff Richard temporarily taking over production duties from Bruce Welch. Written by Annie Herring, who had also contributed to ***Hey Whatcha' Say***, the song was completed in three takes with some overdubs being added a couple of weeks later.

Accompanied by piano and an uncredited string orchestra, Cliff's plaintive and emotive vocal line comes in. The most beautiful aspects of the song are the building up of the musical drama that is reverential but also the arrangement of the vocals supporting Cliff.

Track Specification
Composed by Annie Herring
Musicians

Brian Bennett	drums, percussion
Terry Britten	guitar
Stuart Calver	backing vocals
Bryn Haworth	guitar
John Perry	backing vocals
Cliff Richard	vocals
Tony Rivers	backing vocals
Alan Tarney	bass
Graham Todd	piano
Unknown	orchestra
Unknown	conductor

Recording Details

Producer	Cliff Richard
Engineered by	Tony Clark and Haydn Bendall
Recording location	Abbey Road Studio 3, St. John's Wood, London
Recording date	17th January 1977 and 2nd February 1977

♫ Golden

From the promotional disc **Time Machine Tour 2008**

Given that Cliff Richard had been in the music business for fifty years, it was his golden anniversary of release of ***Move It*** back in 1958. To commemorate this, Cliff released a special single, ***Thank You for a Lifetime***, and a rare track, *Golden*, which was only available on the disc that was given out to ticket-holders, if they wanted it, on the *Time Machine* tour in 2008. Written by Chris Eaton, his long-term friend and collaborator, the disc included filmed material in DVD form.
Beginning with a piano accompaniment, this gentle song has Cliff singing a reflective song as he remembers specific (constructed) events in his life. Like *Thank You for a Lifetime*, it is another vote of thanks to his legion of fans, who he describes as 'golden', matching the anniversary.

Track Specification
Composed by Chris Eaton
Musicians

Keith Haymam	keyboards
Cliff Richard	vocals

Recording Details

Producer	Alan Tarney
Engineered by	Alan Tarney
Recording location	Alan Tarney's studio
Recording date	2008

♫ Golden Days Are Over, The

From the albums **Dressed for the Occasion Remaster** *and* **Silver**

Although Terry Britten had not been involved in the recording of the previous couple of Cliff Richard's studio albums, he was still supplying songs for him to record. *The Golden Days Are Over* had not been attempted in the studio at the time of the Royal Albert Hall concert in 1982, although it would become part of the following year's ***Silver*** album. Although it was known that four tracks that had been recorded and remixed in preparation for release had been left off the track listing of ***Dressed for the Occasion***, it was only when a set list from the concert was found at Cliff's offices that *The Golden Days Are Over* was identified as a fifth track. Lodged at the EMI Abbey Road Studios on tape, it was subsequently found and remastered for the 2004 reissue of *Dressed for the Occasion* as a bonus track along with the other four that were already logged.
Although the song was performed with the London Philharmonic Orchestra, the predominant instrumentation is provided by the rock band element of the musicians. The song is highly dramatic and the build up to the mid-section has Cliff's emotional voice belting out the emotion of the lyrics.
It was picked up the following year for inclusion on the track listing of Cliff's twenty-fifth anniversary album, ***Silver***, which was also the first to be released simultaneously in CD format. The song is presented in a straightforward manner with a drumbeat setting the rhythm and accompanied by strummed guitar chords. As the song heads for the chorus, Cliff's voice is fed through a vocoder and the song builds up further with an orchestra added to the mixture.

Track Specification
Composed by Terry Britten and Sue Shifrin

1. Dressed for the Occasion Remaster
Musicians

Stuart Calver	backing vocals
David Cooke	synthesiser
Steve Gray	piano
Mark Griffiths	bass
Tony Harding	backing vocals
Richard Hewson	arranger, conductor
Graham Jarvis	drums, percussion
London Philharmonic Orchestra	orchestra
John Perry	backing vocals
Cliff Richard	vocals
Tony Rivers	backing vocals

Recording Details

Producer	Cliff Richard and Richard Hewson
Engineered by	John Kurlander
Mixed by	Keith Bessey
Recording location	Royal Albert Hall, London
Mixed at	Strawberry Studios South, Surrey
Recording date	23rd November 1982

2. Silver

Musicians

Stuart Calver	backing vocals
John Clark	electric guitar
Martyn Ford	conductor
Mark Griffiths	bass
Graham Jarvis	drums, percussion
Martyn Ford Orchestra	orchestra
Clive Anstee	'cello
Jim Archer	violin
Andy Babynchuk	violin
Martin Baines	French horn
Bill Benham	violin
Norris Bosworth	viola
Daniel Daggers	viola
Liz Edwards	violin
Will Gibson	violin
Timothy Good	violin
James Handy	French horn
Chris Hirons	violin
Paul Kegg	'cello
Benjamin Kennard	'cello
John Kitchen	violin
Martin Loveday	'cello
Peter Oxer	violin
Geoff Palmer	violin
Eddie Roberts	violin
Jonathan Strange	violin
Chris Wellington	viola
Simon Whistler	viola
David Woodcock	violin
Gavin Wright	violin
John Perry	backing vocals
Craig Pruess	arranger, keyboards, synthesiser, electronics
Cliff Richard	vocals, backing vocals
Tony Rivers	backing vocals

Recording Details

Producer	Craig Pruess
Engineered by	Keith Bessey
Recording location	Strawberry Studios South, Surrey (main track) and Henry Wood Hall, Glasgow (strings)
Recording date	19th May 1983, 3rd June 1983 and/or 16th June 1983 (main track) and July and/or August 1983 (strings)

♬ Golden Rule

From the album **Triumph in the Air** *(Sheila Walsh)*

The second song by long-term Cliff Richard songwriter Chris Eaton on Sheila Walsh's second album, ***Triumph in the Air***, featured Cliff only on backing vocals, he having relinquished the production duties to Craig Pruess following the first album, ***Drifting***. It also features the backing vocals of Eaton and former Network 3 members, Annie McCaig and Mo Turner, as well as another upcoming session singer Mark Williamson.

Blipping synthesisers and atonal chords on the keyboard rush this song into the vocals that is pure eighties synthesiser pop. Walsh sings the song with conviction with its quirky rhythm changes. The backing vocals are only occasional but when they are heard, they have Cliff's contribution being the most prominent.

Track Specification

Composed by Chris Eaton

Musicians

Chris Eaton	backing vocals
Rick Fenn	guitar
Annie McCaig	backing vocals
Craig Pruess	arranger, keyboards, electronics
Cliff Richard	backing vocals
Mo Turner	backing vocals
Sheila Walsh	vocals
Mark Williamson	backing vocals

Recording Details

Producer	Craig Pruess, assisted by Keith Bessey
Engineered by	Keith Bessey
Recording location	Cloud 9 Studios, London, Strawberry Studios, London and/or Jacobs Studios, Farnham, Surrey
Recording date	September 1983-January 1984

♬ Gonave, La

From the album **The Rock Connection**

More correctly titled La Gonâve (with the circumflex over the 'a'), it is the largest of the satellite islands surrounding the principal island of Haiti and is positioned approximately northwest of Haiti's capital, Port-au-Prince. The area has always been subject to great poverty and natural disasters and so it was to Haiti that Cliff Richard and his business associate Bill Latham travelled for the first two weeks of April 1984 on behalf of the Tear Fund, a charity organisation with Cliff as an active patron. A bad sufferer of sea-sickness, Cliff had taken some repressant tablets so that they could travel to La Gonâve. As Cliff tells the story, he was leaning against the mast to reduce the rolling effects of the waves underneath the boat and, although he hadn't reached his destination, he was inspired to write the song for the island, with a key and

rhythm dictated by the thrumming of the engine, which he later learned to be A minor. It was recorded at the same session as three other songs that would appear on the Tear Fund film soundtrack, *It's a Small World* (and then on the album of the same name). In 1988, *La Gonave* (without the accent as per the copyright submission) was a bonus track on the CD single release of ***Mistletoe and Wine*** alongside ***Little Town*** and, included in some versions, a Christmas card.
A synthesized choir of deep voices introduces the song that has a slight menace in the structure of keyboard chords and the gently pounding bass on the one note, before Cliff's vocals are brought in. By the chorus, the crashing guitar chords take over and the mood lifts. Cliff provides his own harmony vocals and the blend of the arrangement lifts the song further, and the song proves that Cliff is in denial when stating that he doesn't compose good songs.

Track Specification
Composed by Cliff Richard

Musicians

John Clark	guitar
Mark Griffiths	bass
Graham Jarvis	drums, percussion
Craig Pruess	keyboards, programming
Cliff Richard	vocals, backing vocals

Recording Details

Producer	Cliff Richard and Craig Pruess
Engineered by	Keith Bessey
Recording location	Gallery Studios, Chertsey, Surrey
Recording date	24th June 1984

♫ Goodbye Sam, Das Ist die Liebe

German single

Back into the studios a month and a half after ***Goodbye Sam, Hello Samantha*** was released, Cliff Richard recorded a German language version titled *Goodbye Sam (Das Ist die Liebe)*. Literally translated back into English as *Goodbye Sam (That's Love)*, the song was the only track to be completed that day with recording transferred to the London-based Chappell Studios. Released as a single and backed with ***Kein Zug nach Gretna Green*** on the international Columbia label (catalogue number 1C006-04523) in July 1970, the German market preferred the English original, which reached number eleven, while the German equivalent was not a hit. The song was reissued on the German compilation album *Ich Träume Deine Träume* in 1971 and then was included on the anthology of Cliff's foreign language songs, ***On the Continent***, in 1997.
Beginning with an English rendition of the 'goodbye' and 'hello' sequence, the change of allegiance from mates to girlfriend is managed by using the uncredited male backing vocals on the first word and women on the second to underline the clever lyric. However, the overall arrangement is slightly less punchy than the English original.

Track Specification
Composed by Mitch Murray, Peter Callander and Geoff Stephens; German lyrics by Carl J. Schäublę

Musicians

Mike Vickers Orchestra	orchestra
Cliff Richard	vocals
Unknown	backing vocals
Mike Vickers	arranger, conductor

Recording Details

Producer	Norrie Paramor
Engineered by	Unknown
Recording location	Chappell Studios, London
Recording date	29th June 1970

♫ Goodbye Sam, Hello Samantha

***50th UK single** and from the album* **Cliff "Live" in Japan '72**

On first listening to a demo sent to his office, Cliff Richard recalls that he really didn't like the song and it was only when his then manager, Peter Gormley, was adamant that it would be a hit that he took time to listen to it more intently and understood what it was that Gormley liked in it. Given heavily negative criticism on release, including BBC radio disc jockey Terry Wogan who said it wasn't Cliff's best song, *Goodbye Sam, Hello Samantha* was nevertheless voted the seventh best British song of the year in an NME poll. Part of its appeal is the jaunty melody but mainly it is the juxtaposition of boys' and girls' names as the song develops into life-changing love ballad, where he gives up seeing friends for girls.
Recorded as the first of three songs at the session that also saw the next single, ***I Ain't Got Time Any More***, and its B-side, ***Monday Comes Too Soon***, also completed, *Goodbye Sam, Hello Samantha* was released as Cliff's fiftieth single, backed with Hank Marvin's ***You Never Can Tell***, on the Columbia label (catalogue number DB 8685) on 29th May 1970 and reached number six in the UK singles charts. It was his best showing for almost a year but would be his last top ten single for almost three years, when ***Power to All Our Friends*** was released. The song was later included on the track listing of 1972's ***The Best of Cliff Vol. 2*** and again on 1977's ***40 Golden Greats***.
The ingenuity of the song comes from the arrangement, which relies on the strongest rhythm being on the off-beats boosted by uncredited hand-claps. Essentially a love song that is sung towards his male friends as he transitions to a swathe of beautiful girls to occupy his time – the goodbye to his male friend and hello to the female friend with very close names – it is underpinned by the male vocalists singing 'goodbye' and the females singing 'hello' to underpin the lyrics.
Two months later, a German language version, ***Goodbye Sam (Das Ist die Liebe)*** (or literally *Goodbye Sam (That's Love)*) was recorded and issued in Germany alongside the English language version. Curiously, the German version failed to chart while the English one reached the number eleven spot in the German singles charts.
With the then recent release as a single, it featured on the set list of ***Cliff "Live" in Japan '72***. Accompanied by the audience clapping along to the jaunty upbeat rhythm, the original female and male backing vocals are both here provided by the beautiful voices of Olivia Newton-John and Pat Carroll.

Track Specification
Composed by Mitch Murray, Peter Callander and Geoff Stephens

1. Single

Musicians		*Recording Details*	
Mike Vickers Orchestra	orchestra	Producer	Norrie Paramor
Cliff Richard	vocals, backing vocals	Engineered by	Unknown
Unknown	backing vocals	Recording location	Abbey Road Studio 3, St. John's Wood, London
Unknown	hand-claps	Recording date	12th March 1970
Mike Vickers	arranger, conductor		

2. Cliff "Live" in Japan '72

Musicians		*Recording Details*	
Brian Bennett	drums, percussion	Producer	Norrie Paramor
Pat Carroll	backing vocals	Engineered by	Unknown
John Farrar	bass	Recording location	Kosei Nenkin Hall, Tokyo, Japan
Alan Hawkshaw	piano	Recording date	22nd-23rd September 1972
Hank Marvin	guitar		
Olivia Newton-John	backing vocals		
Cliff Richard	vocals		
Bruce Welch	rhythm guitar		

♬ Goodbye to All the Heroes

From the album **I'm Grateful** *(Garth Hewitt)*

In between two sets of sessions for his album project, ***Rock 'n' Roll Juvenile***, Cliff Richard took time out to support other projects and lent his backing vocals to three songs by Garth Hewitt for his album ***I'm Grateful***. With three producers, one of whom took the role of keyboard-player for the tracks, the entire album was completed quickly in the summer of 1978. Hewitt plays the harmonica in the introduction before singing an excellently measured lead vocal that builds up slowly in the drama as further instrumentation joins the swell. This is further increased by the addition of the surprising backing vocals, which, along with the organ playing sustained chords, become almost reverential. The track sounds like a mixture of Donovan and Bob Dylan but with a more contemporary feel to the ensemble performance.

Track Specification
Composed by Garth Hewitt

Musicians		*Recording Details*	
Rod Edwards	piano, organ, string synthesiser	Producer	Jon Miller, Rod Edwards and Roger Hand
Mike Giles	drums, percussion	Engineered by	Roger T. Wake
Garth Hewitt	vocals, acoustic guitar, harmonica	Recording location	Redan Recorders, London
Mo McCafferty	backing vocals	Recording date	August 1978
Annie McCaig	backing vocals		
John G. Perry	bass		
Cliff Richard	backing vocals		
Shirlie Roden	backing vocals		
Bob Weston	guitar		

♬ Good Golly Miss Molly

From the albums **Don't Stop Me Now!** *and* **From a Distance ***** The Event** *and unissued live tracks*

Co-writer Robert Blackwell originally produced two versions of *Good Golly Miss Molly* as singles. The first released was by The Valiants, which was even faster-paced than the far more familiar version, which was the second single by Little Richard. Richard's vocals and frenetic piano-playing are two of the hooks in what has now become a timeless slice of rock and roll that would also go on to become part of the standard set performed by Jerry Lee Lewis. Other acts have covered *Good Golly Miss Molly* including Mitch Ryder and the Detroit Wheels, Bruce Springsteen and the E Street Band, Credence Clearwater Revival and Dolly Parton's slightly amended version, *Good Golly Miss Dolly*.

The version recorded by Cliff Richard for his ***Don't Stop Me Now!*** album was completed at the last session designated for the album at the beginning of February 1967. The third and final take and edit were used for the mono and stereo recordings.

For those familiar with Little Richard's version, it is quite strange to hear this song given an orchestral treatment. Cliff is clearly enjoying his performance with his yelps replicating Richard's original. The orchestra is uncredited (it may conceivably be Mike Leander because of the style of arrangement), while the uncredited female vocals are quite possibly the Breakaways, who were involved in a number of his recordings of the period. However, there is scant information available from the sessions for this information to be accurate.

Since *Don't Stop Me Now!* had only just been released before the Far East tour at the end of 1967, *Good Golly Miss Molly* was included on the set list to promote the album. The resultant live album from the Tokyo concert included most of the tracks but left this one off, possibly for space considerations, although it remains unissued even on the CD reissue.

Included in the second part of ***The Event*** at Wembley Stadium in June 1989, *Good Golly Miss Molly* was only released on the vinyl issue of ***From a Distance ***** The Event*** but was restored to its correct running position on the remastered issue

of the album in 2005. This version has wailing guitars and a slow-paced introduction but then the rocking rhythm is picked up with Cliff backed by the harmonies of the backing singers.
In 1990, a festival-style concert was held in the grounds of Knebworth House and featured Cliff and the Shadows reunited once again. Their forty-five minute set was broadcast in its entirety on BBC radio but only two tracks were added to the *Knebworth – The Album,* in aid of the Nordoff-Robbins Music Therapy Centre charity, while a third track was included on the resultant DVD in the shape of *Good Golly Miss Molly* and has not been issued in any other format. The rockabilly piano and extraordinary guitar solo take over the middle eight before the vocals are brought back in almost *a capella*.

Track Specification
Composed by Robert Blackwell and John Marascalco

1. Don't Stop Me Now!

Musicians		*Recording Details*	
Cliff Richard	vocals	Producer	Norrie Paramor
Unknown	backing vocals	Engineered by	Peter Vincent and Richard Lush
Unknown	arranger, conductor	Recording location	Abbey Road Studio 2, St. John's Wood, London
Unknown	orchestra	Recording date	5th February 1967

2. Unissued track (Cliff in Japan)

Musicians		*Recording Details*	
Norrie Paramor Orchestra	orchestra	Producer	Norrie Paramor
Norrie Paramor	arranger, conductor	Engineered by	Unknown
Cliff Richard	vocals	Recording location	Shibuya Public Hall, Tokyo, Japan
Unknown	backing vocals	Recording date	18th October 1967

3. From a Distance *** The Event**

Musicians		*Recording Details*	
John Clark	guitar	Producer	Cliff Richard
Sonia Jones-Morgan	backing vocals	Engineered by	Keith Bessey and Mick McKenna
Steve Lauri	guitar	Recording location	Rolling Stones Mobile Studio, Wembley Stadium, Wembley, North-west London
Peter May	drums, percussion	Recording date	16th-17th June 1989
Paul Moessl	keyboards		
Tessa Niles	backing vocals		
Alan Park	keyboards		
Provox:			
Peter Howarth	backing vocals		
Mick Mullins	backing vocals		
Keith Murrell	backing vocals		
Cliff Richard	vocals		
Steve Stroud	bass		

4. Unissued (Knebworth - The Album)

Musicians		*Recording Details*	
Ray Beavis	saxophone	Producer	Chris Kimsey and Steve Smith
Brian Bennett	drums, percussion	Engineered by	Unknown
John Earle	saxophone	Recording location	Knebworth House, Hertfordshire, England
Chris Gower	trombone	Recording date	30th June 1990
Mark Griffiths	bass		
Cliff Hall	keyboards		
Dick Hanson	trumpet		
Peter Howarth	backing vocals		
Hank Marvin	backing vocals, guitar		
Paul Moessl	keyboards		
Mick Mullins	backing vocals		
Keith Murrell	backing vocals		
Cliff Richard	vocals		
Bruce Welch	backing vocals, guitar		

♬ Good News
From the album **Good News**

The title track from Cliff Richard's first spiritually inspirational album, ***Good News***, was recorded at the final session for the album. The song ***Words*** was recorded at that same session, although it was unissued at the time only later given an airing in 2008. Although Mike Leander (who had arranged the music and conducted his own orchestra on earlier Cliff tracks) arranged the traditional Christian song, it would appear that it was the Norrie Paramor Orchestra who were present at the studio (as confirmed in Nigel Goodall's and Peter Lewry's book *The Complete Recordings 1958-1990*).
Arranged with a foot-tapping beat created principally by the bass line, Cliff sings with ebullience in a song that tells the joy of letting Christ into his life. There is a female backing vocal group, which is most likely to be the Breakaways since they were working with Cliff during this period, although records don't appear to exist to confirm this point.

Track Specification
Composed by Traditional, arranged by Mike Leander

Musicians		*Recording Details*	
Norrie Paramor Orchestra	orchestra	Producer	Norrie Paramor
Mike Leander	arranger, conductor	Engineered by	Peter Vince and Mike Stone
Cliff Richard	vocals	Recording location	Abbey Road Studio 2, St. John's Wood, London
Unknown	backing vocals	Recording date	13th May 1967

♫ Good Old Rock 'n' Roll
From the album **Cliff "Live" in Japan '72**

A 1969 hit for the Dave Clark Five which reached number nine later in that year, it has not been covered much by other artists, although Cliff Richard picked it up for his rock and roll medley for the 1972 Japanese tour. Cliff incorporated *Good Old Rock 'n' Roll* into a ***Rock Medley*** that plays tribute to the stars of the fifties when he was just starting out: ***The Girl Can't Help It, Great Balls of Fire, Lucille, Jailhouse Rock***, *Good Old Rock 'n' Roll* and ***Do You Wanna Dance***.

Track Specification
Composed by Roy Michaels, Bob Smith, Michael Equine, Charlie Chin and Larry Packer

Musicians		*Recording Details*	
Brian Bennett	drums, percussion	Producer	Norrie Paramor
Pat Carroll	backing vocals	Engineered by	Unknown
John Farrar	bass	Recording location	Kosei Nenkin Hall, Tokyo, Japan
Alan Hawkshaw	piano	Recording date	22nd-23rd September 1972
Hank Marvin	guitar		
Olivia Newton-John	backing vocals		
Cliff Richard	vocals		
Bruce Welch	rhythm guitar		

♫ Good on the Sally Army
Single by **Allan Shiers** *and from the album* **Small Corners**

Before he recorded his cover for the ***Small Corners*** album, Cliff Richard took up the production for a single by its composer Allan Shiers. Backed with ***School Days*** (also a Cliff production), it was released as a single on the EMI label (catalogue number EMI 2345) in September 1975 but made no impression on the charts. It is a significant rarity in Cliff's history and little information is available on its recording nor on those involved on either side of the studio glass.

According to the Salvation Army Newsletter from around 2004, *Good on the Sally Army* was inspired by help that Shiers received as a charity volunteer in Calcutta. Looking after a group of a hundred boys, he found he was frequently running short of food and, when this happened, he would often go to a Salvation Army centre volunteer, Major Dudley Gardener, who also ran a soup kitchen and was always happy to provide food. When Shiers returned to Britain, he wrote *Good on the Sally Army* to express his thanks to Major Gardener and the Salvation Army for the uncompromising help received.

Naturally, the song was an obvious choice for inclusion on Cliff's next religious album, *Small Corners*, when it was the penultimate song to be completed at the last of three sessions for the album, when it was basically completed in two takes, with further overdubs added almost two weeks later. When Cliff released ***Yes He Lives***, also from the album, as a single, *Good on the Sally Army* was chosen as the B-side.

The synthesiser opens the track as it shimmers between the stereo channels and leads into Cliff's vocal line. The second verse features an organ that gives it a strongly ecclesiastical feel before giving way to the standard band instrumentation. The mid-section features a cleverly arranged vocal section that could be from a hymn, such is the impression, and it employs the stereo to great effect with each of the three backing singers to the left, front and right aural points.

Track Specification
Composed by Allan Shiers

1. Single (Allan Shiers)

Musicians		*Recording Details*	
Allan Shiers	vocals	Producer	Cliff Richard
Unknown	other instrumentation	Engineered by	Unknown
		Recording location	Unknown
		Recording date	July or August 1975

2. Small Corners

Musicians		*Recording Details*	
Brian Bennett	drums, percussion	Producer	Cliff Richard
Terry Britten	guitar	Engineered by	Tony Clark and Haydn Bendall
Stuart Calver	backing vocals	Recording location	Abbey Road Studio 3, St. John's Wood, London
Bryn Haworth	guitar	Recording date	19th and 31st January 1977
John Perry	backing vocals		
Cliff Richard	vocals		
Tony Rivers	backing vocals		
Alan Tarney	bass		
Graham Todd	keyboards		

♫ Good Times (Better Times)

45th UK single and from the album **Cliff Live in Korea**

Written by the long-term friend of Cliff Richard and the Shadows, Jerry Lordan, along with Roger Cook and Roger Greenaway, who had provided other songs for Cliff and others to record (including one of the contenders for the UK entry to the 1968 Eurovision Song Contest), *Good Times (Better Times)* showed perhaps more than any other track of the time the direction Cliff's music would take into the seventies and is often cited as evidence of the decline in Cliff's output. Interestingly, the song is referred to with the bracketed suffix in the *Guinness Book of British Hit Singles* although it only appears as *Good Times* on the original single release label.

Since some critics saw *Good Times (Better Times)* as the start of the rot in Cliff's music until his renaissance in the latter half of the seventies, and that it was compounded by the appearance of the lack of innovation in many of the tracks he was recording, some commentators were moved to ask why, pleasant enough though the songs that he was releasing may be, the public should care about his music any more, which is a strong indictment. The answer came when it was released as a single, backed with ***Occasional Rain*** on the Columbia label (catalogue number DB 8548) on 21st February 1969, reaching a respectable number twelve in the UK charts. The single, as was the company's policy at the time, was only released in mono format with the stereo version only being released three and a half years later on the compilation album ***The Best of Cliff Vol. 2***.

The arrangement of the tune is very much of the sound that Cliff had adopted as he left the sixties and entered the seventies. And while there is nothing particularly new about it, it is certainly a pleasant song that has Cliff singing with light and shade in his volume. The backing vocal group, uncredited but with no further information available, sings in a joyful way to echo Cliff's lead vocal and helps to make it sound like a number from a theatrical musical of the period.

With the recent release as a single, it became part of the set list for Cliff's tour with the Shadows in the Far East in 1969, with a recording made for the Korean market only. The ultra-rare album, *Cliff Live in Korea*, was only ever issued in mono and has yet to be reissued in any other format.

Track Specification

Composed by Jerry Lordan, Roger Cook and Roger Greenaway

1. Single

Musicians		*Recording Details*	
Mike Vickers Orchestra	orchestra	Producer	Norrie Paramor
Cliff Richard	vocals	Engineered by	Peter Vince
Unknown	backing vocals	Recording location	IBC Studios, London
Mike Vickers	arranger, conductor	Recording date	31st January 1969

2. Cliff Live in Korea

Musicians		*Recording Details*	
Brian Bennett	drums, percussion	Producer	Unknown
Alan Hawkshaw	keyboards	Engineered by	Unknown
Hank Marvin	backing vocals, guitar	Recording location	Citizen Hall, Seoul, South Korea
Cliff Richard	vocals	Recording date	16th October 1969
John Rostill	backing vocals, bass		
Bruce Welch	backing vocals, rhythm guitar		

♫ Good Vibrations

From the album **Party at the Palace**

In 1966, the world of popular music was undergoing a groundswell of change, precipitated by the desire to experiment and the rapid change in recording technology that allowed the musicians to effect the results. Naturally there were leaders in the field and, in the UK, the charge was led by the Beatles and, in America, by the Beach Boys. Eschewing the bubblegum pop songs that had established the Beach Boys sound, Brian Wilson began work on the seminal *Pet Sounds*, which employed technically complex recrding techniques and musical composition that was instantly appealing and innovative. *Good Vibrations* was originally written by him and Tony Asher but, after spending time in the studio creating the demo track by building up the sound in layers and pinning the sections together, it was Mike Love who then provided the new lyrics. The song was revisited for *Smile* in 2004 with a suggestion to use Asher's original lyrics but this was abandoned in favour of the familiar words. When the original was released in the UK, it became an instant number one and was the first chart-topper for the band. Psychic TV reached number sixty-five in September 1986 with their version, while Wilson took his solo version to number thirty in 2004, when it was released alongside the completed *Smile*.

A favourite for many artists, it was picked for inclusion in the set of songs performed at the concert at Buckingham House in June 2002 to honour the fiftieth anniversary of Queen Elizabeth II's accession to the throne. With Wilson and his band at the forefront, he was also joined by Cliff Richard, ex-Spice Girl Emma Bunton and the girl group Atomic Kitten. The live version was recorded and released on the *Party at the Palace* album.

Unfortunately, Brian Wilson sounds quite frail in the performance, although the energy of the composition still comes through in the instrumentation and grouped backing vocals, which feature Cliff (although he is not that discernible in the combined collection of voices).

Track Specification
Composed by Brian Wilson and Mike Love

Musicians

Atomic Kitten:	backing vocals
Jenny Frost	
Liz McLarnon	
Natasha Hamilton	
Scott Bennett	backing vocals, keyboards
Emma Bunton	backing vocals
Mike D'Amico	drums, percussion
Jeff Foskett	backing vocals, guitar
Probyn Gregory	backing vocals, guitar
Jim Hines	drums, percussion
Bob Lizik	bass
Paul Mertens	saxophone
Taylor Mills	backing vocals
Cliff Richard	backing vocals
Royal Academy of Music Symphony Orchestra	orchestra
Darian Sahanaja	backing vocals, keyboards
Nick Walusko	guitar
Brian Wilson	vocals, keyboards

Recording Details

Producer	Giles Martin
Engineered by	Andy Rose
Recording location	Buckingham Palace, London
Mixed by	Paul Hicks (Abbey Road) and John Hudson and Greg Jackman (Mayfair)
Mixed at	Abbey Road Studios, St. John's Wood, London and Mayfair Studios, London
Recording date	3rd June 2002

♫ Gospel Medley

From the album **Japan Tour '74**

For Cliff's tours, he often created a medley of a number of songs that he hadn't sung elsewhere in the set list. For his 1974 tour of Japan, he sang a medley of the songs that helped him get the Christian message to the audience:

a) ***Jesus***
b) ***Amazing Grace***
c) ***Jesus Is My Kind of People***

The entries for those songs carry the information on the recording details and musicians.

♫ Got a Funny Feeling

B-side of **When the Girl in Your Arms Is the Girl in Your Heart** *and from the albums* **The Rock 'n' Roll Years 1958-1963**, **Cliff Richard at the Movies 1959-1974**, **The Young Ones – The Remaster** *and* **Live at the ABC Kingston 1962**

The first song to feature Cliff Richard in the film ***The Young Ones*** was effectively the start of the plot; the first song, *Friday Night*, played over the opening titles, was merely to show it was Friday night, people were paid and the youngsters wanted to get to the dance at Simpkin's Youth Club, where Nicky Black (played by Cliff) was performing backed by the Shadows (although they didn't have an overt name in the film). The song goes down well but the enjoyment is brought up short by law firm clerk Ernest (Richard O'Sullivan) announcing that property magnate Hamilton Black (unknown to all to be Nicky's father) has bought the club and wants to knock it down to build a large skyscraper.

The last of three songs to be recorded at the 19th April session for the soundtrack album, the seventh and final take was accepted for the mono and stereo edits but with different mixes for the audio channels. Released as the B-side of the first single from the film, ***When the Girl in Your Arms Is the Girl in Your Heart***, *Got a Funny Feeling* also appeared on the track listing of the ***Hits from The Young Ones*** EP. In the early sixties, Cliff and the Shadows had their own Radio Luxembourg slot; although most of the material they recorded live has yet to be released, four tracks were issued on ***The Rock 'n' Roll Years 1958-1963*** – since the station only broadcast in AM (FM was a few years away), this track is only available in mono.

For the US, the film was renamed to *Wonderful to Be Young* at the request of the distributors, Paramount Pictures. Burt Bacharach and Hal David were conscripted to write a song based on that title, which was subsequently recorded and issued as a single some months after the release of the film in America. For the B-side, a new version of *Got a Funny Feeling* was recorded at the same session intended for release as the B-side, although the original was eventually used instead. Unissued for many years, take thirty of this later recording was subsequently released on the ***Cliff Richard at the Movies 1959-1974*** compendium and it was then edited to the first minute and a half for a promotional cassette called *Cliff Richard at Tower* to mark his appearance in-store on 22nd July 1996. A further take with minor instrumental variations was included as a bonus track on ***The Young Ones – The Remaster***. Both of these different tracks have only ever been released in stereo.

With a simple bass and rhythm section comprising guitar and drums, *Got a Funny Feeling* is good old-fashioned rock and roll style of song. Norrie Paramor's piano tinkles away in the background underneath Cliff's vocal line. The middle eight features a simple guitar melody before control is passed back to Cliff. Overall, it shows Hank Marvin and Bruce Welch to be highly competent songwriters. The version from the Radio Luxembourg show focuses more on the interplay between guitars and the bass, as well as a new guitar middle eight bridge, while the later version has no piano or backing vocals and is closer to the original film version (which was recorded on 23rd May 1961 but remains unissued in any other format).

In subsequent concerts to support and promote the film, Cliff and the Shadows incorporated a selection of songs into a medley of songs from *The Young Ones*, one of which was *Got a Funny Feeling*. For the ABC Kingston concert, this was recorded but remained unreleased until the 2002 album ***Live at the ABC Kingston 1962***, which was only issued in stereo.

Track Specification
Composed by Hank Marvin and Bruce Welch

1. B-side (When the Girl in Your Arms (Is the Girl in Your Heart))

Musicians

Jet Harris	bass
Hank Marvin	guitar
Tony Meehan	drums, percussion
Norrie Paramor	piano
Cliff Richard	vocals
Bruce Welch	rhythm guitar

Recording Details

Producer	Norrie Paramor
Engineered by	Malcolm Addey and Norman Smith
Recording location	Abbey Road Studio 2, St. John's Wood, London
Recording date	19th April 1961

2. The Rock 'n' Roll Years 1958-1963 (Radio Luxembourg performance)

Musicians

Jet Harris	backing vocals, bass
Hank Marvin	backing vocals, guitar
Tony Meehan	drums, percussion
Cliff Richard	vocals, hand claps
Bruce Welch	backing vocals, rhythm guitar

Recording Details

Producer	Unknown
Engineered by	Unknown
Recording location	Radio Luxembourg Studios, London
Recording date	1961

3. Live at the ABC Kingston 1962

Musicians

Brian Bennett	drums, percussion
Jet Harris	backing vocals, bass
Hank Marvin	backing vocals, guitar
Cliff Richard	vocals, hand claps
Bruce Welch	backing vocals, rhythm guitar

Recording Details

Producer	Norrie Paramor
Engineered by	Malcolm Addey and Ken Townsend
Recording location	ABC Theatre, Kingston, Surrey
Recording date	7th March 1962

4. Cliff Richard at the Movies 1959-1974

Musicians

Brian Bennett	drums, percussion
Brian 'Licorice' Locking	bass
Hank Marvin	guitar
Cliff Richard	vocals
Bruce Welch	rhythm guitar

Recording Details

Producer	Norrie Paramor
Engineered by	Malcolm Addey
Recording location	Abbey Road Studio 1, St. John's Wood, London
Recording date	11th August 1962

5. The Young Ones – The Remaster

Musicians

Brian Bennett	drums, percussion
Brian 'Licorice' Locking	bass
Hank Marvin	guitar
Cliff Richard	vocals
Bruce Welch	rhythm guitar

Recording Details

Producer	Norrie Paramor
Engineered by	Malcolm Addey
Recording location	Abbey Road Studio 1, St. John's Wood, London
Recording date	11th August 1962

♫ Go Where I Send Thee

From the album **Good News**

Often titled *Children Go Where I Send Thee*, this is a spiritual song from the Deep South of America. The succession of numbers counting upwards refer to elements of biblical stories; so, one is for the baby (Jesus), three the wise men, five the gospel preachers, ten the commandments and so on. The song was devised as a way of spreading the Christian word in black communities where education was not paramount (or, indeed, allowed in some circumstances) thereby requiring a medium for getting messages across. It is a popular song to be covered by artists wanting gospel or religious material to record, including the most popular by Peter, Paul and Mary, the Kingston Trio, Johnny Cash and Tennessee Ernie Ford.
The final song to be recorded at the particular session for Cliff Richard's first religious album, ***Good News***, it was arranged for Cliff by Mike Leander and successfully completed in three takes.
The uncredited backing vocals are probably provided by the Breakaways, although there is insufficient information to confirm this. The organ that plays sustained chords throughout shimmers in this fast-paced spiritual that is performed with a lot of fun by Cliff. The problem with religious songs is that they can be very sombre (and hence rather dull for most listeners), but this is not the case on this track, which is one of the best on the track listing.

Track Specification
Composed by Traditional, arranged by Mike Leander

Musicians

Brian Bennett	drums, percussion
Hank Marvin	guitar
Cliff Richard	vocals
John Rostill	bass
Unknown	hand-claps
Unknown	female backing vocals
Unknown	organ
Unknown	brass
Bruce Welch	rhythm guitar

Recording Details

Producer	Norrie Paramor
Engineered by	Peter Vince and Mike Stone
Recording location	Abbey Road Studio 2, St. John's Wood, London
Recording date	27th April 1967

♫ Great Balls of Fire

From the albums **Cliff "Live" in Japan '72** *and* **Something Special** *and the CD B-side of* **All I Have to Do Is Dream/Miss You Nights**

Recorded later on by the likes of the Electric Light Orchestra, The Misfits and Dolly Parton, among others, *Great Balls of Fire* is very much the song that is best associated with Jerry Lee Lewis. Lewis recorded it in October 1957 and it was released a month later on the Sun Records label (the then home of the likes of Elvis Presley and Johnny Cash). It was Lewis's first major single success, when it reached number two in the Billboard singles charts and number one in the UK. The Lewis legacy would continue when a biopic of the singer starring Dennis Quaid was released in 1989, using the song as the title of the film.

Used several times in the screenplay for *Gone with the Wind* by the character Scarlett O'Hara, the phrase is derived mostly from its use as an utterance to convey frustration, surprise, fear or anger particularly in the southern states of the US (where Lewis grew up). Many Christian communities see it as blasphemous since they consider the start of the phrase to be a thinly veiled use of the word 'God'.

For his Far Eastern tour in 1972, Cliff Richard incorporated *Great Balls of Fire* into a ***Rock Medley*** that plays tribute to the stars of the fifties when he was just starting out: ***The Girl Can't Help It***, *Great Balls of Fire*, ***Lucille***, ***Jailhouse Rock***, ***Good Old Rock 'n' Roll*** and ***Do You Wanna Dance***.

For a BBC documentary on Cliff being recorded in 1981, a number of live tracks were filmed at the Hammersmith Odeon in west London and the Manchester Apollo, some of which were licensed for release from the corporation at the time (culminating in the single release of ***Daddy's Home*** and its B-side). Others, including the section of duets with Phil Everly, were not licensed for release until thirteen years later when ***All I Have to Do Is Dream*** was issued as a double A-side with a remixed version of ***Miss You Nights***. While the vinyl single was limited to those two tracks the first of a dual CD single release incorporated two additional tracks: ***When Will I Be Loved?*** and the ***Tribute to the Legends Medley***, of which *Great Balls of Fire* formed part. Both tracks featured Phil Everly duetting with Cliff, although Everly only joined him on stage in the middle of the medley after *Great Balls of Fire* in order to sing ***Lucille*** and other songs. Still as energetic as anything that Jerry Lee Lewis managed on stage, it is improved with the purity of Cliff's voice against the raucousness of Lewis's original version.

Later in 1998, Cliff revisited *Great Balls of Fire* as part of his set for the performance in aid of the charity NASS (the National Asylum Support Service) at the Brighton Centre, accompanying himself on the guitar, which was issued on the charity album *Something Special*.

Track Specification
Composed by Jerry Lee Lewis

1. Cliff "Live" in Japan '72

Musicians		*Recording Details*	
Brian Bennett	drums, percussion	Producer	Norrie Paramor
Pat Carroll	backing vocals	Engineered by	Unknown
John Farrar	bass	Recording location	Kosei Nenkin Hall, Tokyo, Japan
Alan Hawkshaw	piano	Recording date	22nd-23rd September 1972
Hank Marvin	guitar		
Olivia Newton-John	backing vocals		
Cliff Richard	vocals		
Bruce Welch	rhythm guitar		

2. CD B-side (All I Have to Do Is Dream)

Musicians		*Recording Details*	
John Clark	guitar	Producer	Cliff Richard
Mark Griffiths	bass	Engineered by	Unknown
Graham Jarvis	drums, percussion	Recording location	Hammersmith Odeon, London
Martin Jenner	guitar	Remixed at	R. G. Jones Studio, Wimbledon, London
Alan Park	keyboards	Recording date	1st May 1981 (live track) and 7th September 1994 (remix)
Cliff Richard	vocals		
Graham Todd	keyboards		

3. Something Special

Musicians		*Recording Details*	
Cliff Richard	vocals, guitar	Producer	Paul Raynor-Brown
		Engineered by	Julius Warren
		Recording location	Brighton Centre, Brighton
		Recording date	7th June 1998

♫ Green Light

74th UK single *and from the album* **Dressed for the Occasion**

When Cliff Richard first heard Alan Tarney's demo of his new song *Green Light*, he became infatuated with it, believing it to be fabulous, which has gone on record as a quote. So enamoured with it was Cliff that it played a major part in his eighties tours and was also included as one of the track listing bonus tracks for ***The Hit List*** in 1994, which had been designed to showcase his thirty-five top five hits across as many years, in spite of its low placing in the UK singles charts.

The song has occasionally been referred to as *Searching for a Green Light* (reflecting the first line of the chorus), which was possibly a working title, and sometimes with the parentheses around the first three words of the title (refer to the entry in *The Complete Recording Sessions 1958-1990* for one such example).
The single version was edited down from the album track, cutting out a few notes from the guitar introduction in the process; in all other respects the edit is the same as that heard on the album. *Green Light* was recorded in one take with some overdubs added at a session just over a week later. Backed with ***Imagine Love***, *Green Light* was issued as a single on the EMI label (catalogue number EMI 2920) on 16th February 1979. Although it only hit the lowly placing of number fifty-seven in the UK charts, it broke a run of three singles which had flopped in chart success terms and it was the only one of the three singles issued from the ***Green Light*** album project to chart. However, Tarney's follow-up, ***We Don't Talk Anymore***, more than made up for all of these perceived failures.
Developing the sound first created on ***I'm Nearly Famous***, Bruce Welch helps Cliff on to another album of songs that show him to be a continuing musical force to be reckoned with. The electronically altered guitar and use of the synthesisers brings Cliff's material right up to date and *Green Light* is one of the best album tracks. The unsurprising highlight is the arrangement of his voice supported by the backing vocalists, which had become a sort of trademark for Bruce's productions.
The dramatic introduction to the song on ***Dressed for the Occasion*** is created by the percussion of the orchestra before Cliff's voice is brought in with a slight delayed echo on his performance.
Although *Green Light* was performed on the World Tour of 2003, the song was performed by the three backing vocalists as a part of a medley with ***Devil Woman*** and ***Carrie*** by the backing vocalists.

Track Specification
Composed by Alan Tarney

1. *Single*

Musicians

Brian Bennett	drums, percussion
Terry Britten	guitar
Stuart Calver	backing vocals
Alan Jones	bass
Duncan MacKay	keyboards
Alan Parker	guitar
John Perry	backing vocals
Tim Renwick	guitar
Cliff Richard	vocals
Tony Rivers	backing vocals
Trevor Spencer	drums, percussion
Alan Tarney	backing vocals, guitar, bass, keyboards
Graham Todd	keyboards

Recording Details

Producer	Bruce Welch
Engineered by	Tony Clark and Haydn Bendall
Recording location	Abbey Road Studio 3, St. John's Wood, London
Recording date	17th and 25th April 1978

2. Dressed for the Occasion

Musicians

Stuart Calver	backing vocals
David Cooke	synthesiser
Steve Gray	piano
Mark Griffiths	bass
Tony Harding	backing vocals
Richard Hewson	arranger, conductor
Graham Jarvis	drums, percussion
London Philharmonic Orchestra	orchestra
John Perry	backing vocals
Cliff Richard	vocals
Tony Rivers	backing vocals

Recording Details

Producer	Cliff Richard and Richard Hewson
Engineered by	John Kurlander
Mixed by	Keith Bessey
Recording location	Royal Albert Hall, London
Mixed at	Strawberry Studios South, Surrey
Recording date	23rd November 1982

♫ Grief Never Grows Old
***Single by* One World Project**

In the early hours of 26th December 2004, a massive megathrust earthquake was triggered off the west coast of Sumatra, Indonesia. The resultant tidal wave, or tsunami, killed almost 230,000 people around the Indian Ocean and was one of the biggest disasters to afflict the region in recent times. Coming at a time of peace and festive cheer for large portions of the world at Christmas time, the pictures of death and destruction beamed into living rooms was particularly poignant.
Mike Read, some time DJ, television presenter, composer and friend of Cliff Richard, was one of those watching and felt it was necessary to take some action. Contacting his various music friends, he built up an impressive list of musicians who wanted to be involved in a charity project. This sort of approach to charity recordings owes much to Bob Geldof and Midge Ure, who created the blueprint with ***Do They Know It's Christmas?*** in 1984 – ironically repeating it for the twentieth anniversary for Christmas 2004. The principal stars would sing a line or two each and then break into a chorus that involved everybody singing in unison. This was the process that Read followed for his own composition *Grief Never*

Grows Old. What was different for him was the huge logistical operation to get everyone's contribution together. Wanting to work fast and get the single out earning money for charity, the contributors had to record their snippets in America, the UK and Ireland and then have them sent into a co-ordination point to be mixed and spliced together.
The resultant track was issued as a single, backed with an orchestral and a choral version of the song (neither of which additional tracks featured Cliff Richard, who had a principal role in the recording of the main track), on the specially created One World Records label (catalogue number OWR1) on 24th January 2005 and reached number four in the UK singles charts. All proceeds and profits were directed to the Disasters Emergency Committee, an umbrella group comprising thirteen charities including the Red Cross, Help the Aged, Islamic Relief, Oxfam, Merlin and Christian Aid.
For those familiar with the Betjeman project (that yielded ***November Night***), the style of the song has the signature of Mike Read's composition. As with all charity records it is now *de rigueur* to give a line or two to each singer, and Cliff performs most of the second verse alongside Barry Gibb (who had worked with Cliff on the ***Something's Goin' On*** album at the same time). This is the case here, although the strength of the performance comes in the backing vocals. The rhythm and ponderous instrumentation perfectly match the sadness of the tragedy, the charities for which this project was supporting.

Track Specification
Composed by Mike Read

Musicians

Jon Anderson	vocals
Sam Blue	backing vocals
Teri Bryant	percussion
Gerry Buckley	backing vocals
Dewey Bunnell	vocals
Céline Cherry	backing vocals
Jon Cristos	vocals
Jeffrey Foskett	vocals
Boy George	vocals
Barry Gibb	vocals
Robin Gibb	vocals
Kenney Jones	percussion
Randall Kirsch	vocals
Hank Linderman	nylon guitar
Gary Moore	electric guitar
Cliff Richard	vocals
Darren Sell	keyboards
Davey Spillane	Uillean pipes
Paul von Mertens	saxophone, bass harmonica
Rick Wakeman	synthesiser
Russell Watson	vocals
Brian Wilson	vocals
Steve Winwood	vocals
Bill Wyman	bass

Recording Details

Producer	Steve Levine (overall track), John Farrar and Peter Wolf (Cliff's vocals), Barry Gibb (Barry Gibb's vocals), Brian Wilson (Brian Wilson's vocals) and Unknown (all other recordings)
Engineered by	Brett Thorngren (Barry Gibb's vocals), Paul Ruest (Boy George vocals), Hank Linderman (Brian Wilson vocals), John Emenaker (Jon Anderson's vocals) and Unknown (all other recordings)
Recording location	Peter Wolf's Studio, Malibu, Los Angeles (Cliff's vocals), Middle Ear Studios, Miami, Florida (Barry Gibb's vocals), The Argot Network, New York City (Boy George's vocals), Brian Wilson's Studio, California (Brian Wilson's vocals), Parsons Green Studio, Culver City, California (Dewey Bunnell's, Jeffrey Foskett's and Randall Kirsch's vocals), Unknown studio, Los Angeles (Jon Anderson's vocals), Steve Levine Studios, Fulham, London (Steve Winwood's, Robin Gibb's, Russell Watson's, Bill Wyman's, Rick Wakeman's, Kenney Jones's, Gary Moore's, Sam Blue's and Céline Cherry's contributions), Unknown studio, Chicago, Illinois (Paul von Mertens' sax and harmonica), Sherman Oaks Studio, California (Gerry Buckley's backing vocals), Burrenstone Studios, Ireland (Davy Spillane's pipes) and West Orange Studio, Preston, Lancashire (Jon Cristos's vocals)
Recording date	January 2005

♫ Growing Up to Be a Child

From the album **Triumph in the Air** *(Sheila Walsh)*

Another song by Graham Kendrick on Sheila Walsh's second album, ***Triumph in the Air***, *Growing Up to Be a Child* featured Cliff Richard on backing vocals as did a handful of other songs on the album. Released as a single, backed with ***Drifting*** album track ***Private Life***, on the DJM Records label (catalogue number DJS 10) in December 1983, *Growing Up to Be a Child* made no impression on the charts.
Squeaking synthesisers and a quirky percussion ease this track into existence and it is transformed into a slow-paced love song by Sheila Walsh's lead vocal, which is performed with an edgy reverence that has flavours of Olivia Newton-John's style of performance. The backing vocals are kept subdued behind the performance and the saxophone solo and then come into their own in the second half of the song.

Track Specification
Composed by Graham Kendrick

Musicians

Mel Collins	saxophone
Graham Jarvis	drums, percussion
Craig Pruess	arranger, keyboards, electronics, percussion
Cliff Richard	backing vocals
Sheila Walsh	vocals

Recording Details

Producer	Craig Pruess, assisted by Keith Bessey
Engineered by	Keith Bessey
Recording location	Cloud 9 Studios, London, Strawberry Studios, London and/or Jacobs Studios, Farnham, Surrey
Recording date	September 1983-January 1984

♫ Gut, Daß Es Freunde Gibt

German single

Just a few short days after the British public had chosen ***Power to All Our Friends*** to be the representative song for the UK at the 1973 Eurovision Song Contest, Cliff Richard was back in the studios to record hastily translated versions for release in Germany, France and Spain (though curiously not Italy). First up was the German version, *Gut, Daß Es Freunde Gibt* (translated roughly as *It's Good that It Gives You Friends*), which was completed at the first recording session for Cliff in 1973. In all cases, the new vocal line (including the backing vocals) was overdubbed on the original backing track, which had been recorded for the English version at the end of December 1972.

The British public had overwhelmingly voted for *Power to All Our Friends*, with ***Come Back Billie Jo*** coming a long way behind in second place. The British single version was released with *Come Back Billie Jo* as its B-side and so it was for the German single release, although *Come Back Billie Jo* remained in English. Released as a single on the EMI label (catalogue number 1C 006-05315) in April 1973, *Gut, Daß Es Freunde Gibt* failed to chart while its English counterpart reached number four. The song was eventually released on the compendium of Cliff's foreign language recordings, ***On the Continent***, in 1997.

Following the same dramatic build-up, the song is obviously very similar (but paradoxically unfamiliar) to the English version. The backing vocals are employed much more than the original and, in many instances, sounds like Cliff singing along as his own backing chorus. This is unconfirmed and it is assumed that the original band was involved as well.

Track Specification

Composed by Guy Fletcher and Doug Flett; German lyrics by Michael Kunze

Musicians		*Recording Details*	
Terry Britten	backing vocals, guitar	Producer	David MacKay (backing track and vocals)
David MacKay Orchestra	orchestra	Engineered by	Peter Vince (backing track and vocals)
David MacKay	backing vocals, arranger, conductor	Recording location	Abbey Road Studio (backing track) and Abbey Road Studio 2 (vocals), St. John's Wood, London
Kevin Peek	guitar		
Cliff Richard	vocals, backing vocals	Recording date	28th December 1972 (backing track) and 21st March 1973 (vocals)
Trevor Spencer	backing vocals, drums, percussion		
Alan Tarney	backing vocals, bass		

♫ Gypsy Bundle

From the albums **Songs from Heathcliff** *and* **Heathcliff Live**

The third song from the ***Songs from Heathcliff***, *Gypsy Bundle* is the part of the musical that looks to Heathcliff's early life when he was found on the streets of Liverpool and was reluctantly taken in by the Earnshaws, where he first meets his kindred spirit Cathy and burning antipathy from her brother Hindley, in whose family Heathcliff was brought up. The *Gypsy Bundle* of the title is the image of the young Heathcliff wrapped up in filthy rags. Following on from ***The Sleep of the Good*** following Cathy's funeral, in between the misery Heathcliff (Cliff Richard) feels for the departed Cathy and the *Gypsy Bundle*, Heathcliff mentions that from the first time he saw her, he had worshipped her, thus initiating the story of his life and how his name was chosen to mirror the heathland in the country environs and the despicable reaction from the people in the street towards him. The song continues to run through the early life until Heathcliff and Cathy become adults and the continuing mistreatment of him, particularly at the hands of Hindley Earnshaw (played by Darryl Knock). The song was performed by Jimmy Johnston (playing the senior Earnshaw) in the stage show, although it was Cliff who performed it on the ***Songs from Heathcliff***.

The upbeat song belies the growing negative emotions expressed by the characters as Heathcliff is taken into the bosom of the Earnshaw family. The staccato performances on the instruments are matched by the flowing backing vocals supporting Cliff's lead vocal. This replicated in the live performance as the lead is spread between the performers playing the main characters. The principal lead is played by Jimmy Johnston as Earnshaw Senior.

A promotional edit of the studio track with the initial one and a half minutes was released on a cassette marking Cliff's appearance at the Tower Records store in London on 22nd July 1996, which was called *Cliff Richard at Tower*.

Track Specification

Composed by John Farrar and Tim Rice

1. Songs from Heathcliff

Musicians		*Recording Details*	
Sean Callery	orchestrator, synclavier, keyboards	Producer	John Farrar
Liz Constantino	backing vocals	Engineered by	Chris Fogel, Eric Rudd and Joe Schiff (Moonee Ponds Studio), Darren Goodwin and Guy Massey (Abbey Road Studios) and James Collins and Caroline Daniel (CTS Studios)
Linda Dalziel	backing vocals		
John Farrar	backing vocals, guitar, synclavier		
Steve Kipner	backing vocals		
Clif Magness	backing vocals	Recording location	Moonee Ponds Studio, Los Angeles, Abbey Road Studios, St. John's Wood, London and CTS Studios, Wembley, London
Kristina Nichols	backing vocals		
Cliff Richard	vocals		
Bob Sabellico	drum programming	Mixed by	Chris Fogel
Heather Sabellico	backing vocals	Mixed at	Moonee Ponds Studio, Los Angeles
Michael Thompson	guitar	Recording date	February-April 1994 and May-August 1995

2. *Heathcliff Live*

Musicians

Sean Callery	orchestrator, conductor
David Combes	backing vocals
John Clark	guitar
Elements:	
Geoff David	backing vocals
Chris Holland	backing vocals
Sonia Jones	backing vocals
Niki Kitt	backing vocals
Suzanne Parry	backing vocals
Keith Hayman	keyboards
Helen Hobson	spoken vocals
Jimmy Johnston	spoken vocals, vocals
Peter May	drums, percussion
Bob Noble	keyboards
Alan Park	keyboards
John Perry	backing vocals
Cliff Richard	spoken vocals, backing vocals
Steve Stroud	bass
Kevin Townend	orchestration
Unknown	orchestra
Mick Wilson	backing vocals

Recording Details

Producer	John Farrar
Engineered by	Keith Bessey, John Pearson and Tom Tranter
Recording location	Earl's Court Hall 2 and/or The Academy, National Indoor Arena, Birmingham, England
Recording date	October 1996

♫ Had to Be

***124th UK single** and B-side of* **Had to Be** *and from the albums* **Heathcliff Live**

Had to Be comprises the third duet performed on record to that date in their careers by Cliff Richard and Olivia Newton-John and it is taken from the ***Songs from Heathcliff*** studio album. The song appears at the point in the story of ***Heathcliff*** that describes how the two lovers dispiritedly parted with inevitable finality because Cathy (Olivia) found Heathcliff (Cliff) to be too controlling of her destiny, while Heathcliff thinks that she is a flibbertigibbet who tries consistently to hurt him.

For the recording, Cliff and Olivia decided not to discuss the approach to their performance individually and together on the song, rather preferring to get into the spirit of the characters and take it from there, feeding off each other's musical reactions to the other. The duet was performed at the 1995 *Royal Variety Show* where Cliff was a toplining act and, when the song started, it was assumed he would be singing it solo. Therefore, when Olivia came on stage as a surprise guest, the reception was rapturous after which it was decided to release the track as a single.

The track was the first of Cliff's singles not to be issued in the now far less popular vinyl format and therefore to be only issued in CD format. *Had to Be* was backed with a live version of the same song taken from one of Cliff's promotional performances at the Sheffield Arena in December 1994, which was used as a trial run for much of the material that had been written to date, alongside the first duet the pair had recorded of ***Don't Move Away*** (originally one of the B-side songs to Cliff's 1971 single ***Sunny Honey Girl***). The whole package was released on the EMI label (catalogue number CDEM 410) on 27th November 1995 and reached number twenty-two, in spite of predictions that the song was going to be that year's Christmas number one. A special edition disc (same catalogue number) was also released that had a number of postcard-sized pictures and an interview while two different promotional discs with just the track on it (catalogue number CDEMDJ 410) was issued with the choice of a picture of either Cliff or Olivia on it.

In the stage show, Cathy (played by Helen Hobson) has split up with Heathcliff and run to her new friend, Edgar Linton (Darryl Knock), who is moneyed and intellectually superior – and therefore more appealing to her young mind – than Heathcliff. Unlike studio recording on the ***Songs from Heathcliff*** album and the single, it is sung as a trio in the stage show, primarily between Linton and Cathy with a brooding Heathcliff (Cliff) counterpointing the middle verse and chorus with his dark jealous thoughts about the pairing. The strident mid-section by Hobson (and Olivia in the original) is Cathy's attack on Heathcliff for running Edgar Linton down and for being pettily envious. There is an additional verse and chorus over and above the original, which is sung by Knock to Hobson to try to convince her character to finally forget about Heathcliff and be with him, which she does by accepting Linton's betrothal of marriage, laughing hurtfully at Heathcliff in the process.

One of the best compositions created by John Farrar for the musical, *Had to Be* is sung gently and longingly by Cliff and more stridently by Olivia – which is a change from her usual gentle vocal approach. Cliff provides some of his own backing vocals although these are overlapping vocal passages more than intended harmonies for the lead; a position, which is resolved by the inclusion of a third person in the stage show. Olivia joins in halfway through the song, which was why it was a surprise for the Royal Variety Performance audience when she made her entrance. The build-up brightens with her introduction but it closes down and is made more confidential as they began to sing their vocal lines against each other. During the triumvirate of vocalists' performances in the live version, the accompaniment is kept simple and similar to the studio version. With this arrangement and the stagecraft, it is easy to see what Tim Rice had in mind when writing the lyrics as the focus changes from one character to the next and round again. The video to promote the single featured Olivia and Cliff walking along a narrow corridor quavering under what appears to be water as they get together and sing the lyrics meaningfully to each other.

Track Specification

Composed by John Farrar and Tim Rice

1. B-side (Had to Be)

Musicians

John Clark	guitar
Mike Haughton	woodwinds
Peter May	drums, percussion
Paul Moessl	keyboards
Bob Noble	keyboards
Cliff Richard	vocals
Steve Stroud	bass

Recording Details

Producer	Keith Bessey
Engineered by	Keith Bessey
Recording location	Sheffield Arena, Sheffield
Recording date	December 1994

2. *Single*

Musicians	
Sean Callery	orchestrator, synclavier, keyboards
Tommy Emmanuel	acoustic guitar
John Farrar	guitar, synclavier
Olivia Newton-John	vocals
Cliff Richard	vocals, backing vocals
Bob Sabellico	drum programming
Lee Sklar	bass
Michael Thompson	guitar

Recording Details	
Producer	John Farrar
Engineered by	Chris Fogel, Eric Rudd and Joe Schiff (Moonee Ponds Studio), Darren Goodwin and Guy Massey (Abbey Road Studios) and James Collins and Caroline Daniel (CTS Studios)
Recording location	Moonee Ponds Studio, Los Angeles, Abbey Road Studios, St. John's Wood, London and CTS Studios, Wembley, London
Mixed by	Allen Sides and Chris Fogel
Mixed at	Moonee Ponds Studio, Los Angeles
Recording date	February-April 1994 and May-August 1995

3. *Heathcliff Live*

Musicians	
Sean Callery	orchestrator, orchestra
John Clark	guitar
Keith Hayman	keyboards
Helen Hobson	vocals
Darryl Knock	vocals
Peter May	drums, percussion
Bob Noble	keyboards
Alan Park	keyboards
Cliff Richard	vocals
Steve Stroud	bass
Kevin Townend	orchestration
Unknown	orchestra

Recording Details	
Producer	John Farrar
Engineered by	Keith Bessey, John Pearson and Tom Tranter
Recording location	The Academy, National Indoor Arena, Birmingham, England
Recording date	17th-18th October 1996

♫ Handle My Heart with Love

From the album **Cliff Richard - The Album**

The penultimate track on the first vinyl side of ***Cliff Richard - The Album*** is a simple and straightforward love song that talks of the effect that a lover has and the power she holds to keep the heart intact without breaking it. The song begins with a synthesiser and a saxophone motif that leads into Cliff's vocals. Predomoninantly, it is the electric piano that accompanies him for the first verse before it builds up to the chorus with backing vocals and further instrumentation. Cliff's vibrato is used to great effect on the track on both the lead and backing vocals.

Track Specification

Composed by Daniels and Thomson

Musicians	
Pete Beachill	trombone
Dave Bishop	saxophones
John Bradbury	violin
Simon Gardener	trumpet
Richard Hewson	arranger, conductor
Peter Howarth	backing vocals
Peter May	drums, percussion
Paul Moessl	arranger, drum programming, keyboards
Keith Murrell	backing vocals
Tessa Niles	backing vocals
Cliff Richard	vocals, backing vocals
Steve Stroud	bass
Jamie Talbot	saxophone
Unknown	orchestra (other strings)
Gary Wallis	percussion
Judith Walmsley	backing vocals
David Woodcock	violin

Recording Details	
Producer	Paul Moessl and Cliff Richard
Engineered by	Gerry Kitchingham and Ben Robbins
Recording location	R. G. Jones Studios, Wimbledon, London
Recording date	25th-31st May 1992, 8th June 1992 (backing track) and 29th May 1992 (vocals)

♫ (You Keep Me) Hangin' On

*62nd **UK single** and from the album* **Japan Tour '74**

Covered by artists such as the Loose Diamonds, Ann Peebles, Ruthie Foster, Joe Simon, Michael Jerome Browne and Billy Vera, it was John Rowles' version that impressed Cliff Richard enough to record it. One of four songs attempted at the first February session and one of three eventually issued, the song was completed in six takes and was the start of Cliff's seventies dalliance with the country music genre, once again proving his mettle as an all-round musician and singer.

Backed with ***Love Is Here***, *(You Keep Me) Hangin' On* was issued as the only single in 1974 – the first year that Cliff had not had more than three singles released – on the EMI label (catalogue number EMI 2150) on 26th April 1974, reaching number thirteen in the UK charts. It was subsequently included on the ***40 Golden Greats*** hits package in 1977 and released again on the 2002 boxed set ***The Singles Collection***.

Cliff's vocal line is given an amount of reverberating echo as he is backed by a honky tonk piano, steel guitar and tinkling percussion, all of which gives the performance a strong country feel. It is a different genre for Cliff to inveigle himself into but, as with most styles of music, he more than adequately carries it off.
Almost immediately after recording the English version, Cliff returned to the studio to record a German translation of the song and its B-side, titled ***Es Gehören Zwei zum Glücklichsein*** and ***Liebeslied*** respectively. Both are available on the foreign language compilation set ***On the Continent***.
The version that appears on the set list of the 1974 Japanese tour features strings for the first time in the set as well as a steel guitar although this is an electric guitar played with a steel slide on the finger.

Track Specification
Composed by Buddy Mize and Ira Allen

1. Single

Musicians

Terry Britten	backing vocals, guitar
Barrie Guard	arranger, conductor, percussion
Cliff Hall	piano
Jean Hawker	backing vocals
Gordon Huntley	steel guitar
David MacKay	backing vocals
Anna Peacock	backing vocals
Kevin Peek	acoustic guitar
Cliff Richard	vocals
Trevor Spencer	drums, percussion
Alan Tarney	backing vocals, bass
Unknown	orchestra

Recording Details

Producer	David MacKay
Engineered by	Tony Clark and Mike Jarrett
Recording location	Abbey Road Studio 3, St. John's Wood, London
Recording date	11th February 1974

2. Japan Tour '74

Musicians

Barrie Guard	arranger, conductor
Cliff Hall	piano
Brian Lewis	backing vocals, guitar, steel guitar
Kevin Peak	acoustic guitar
Cliff Richard	vocals
Shambles Symphonet	orchestra
Trevor Spencer	drums, percussion
Alan Tarney	backing vocals, bass
Bruce Welch	backing vocals, rhythm guitar

Recording Details

Producer	Toshiba EMI (no individual detailed)
Engineered by	Toshiba EMI (no individual detailed)
Recording location	Shinjuku Koseinenkin, Tokyo, Japan
Recording date	7th-8th October 1974

♫ Hang on to a Dream

From the albums **Don't Stop Me Now!** *and* **Cliff in Japan**

Tim Hardin's only UK single reached number fifty for one week at the beginning of 1967. Subsequently, it was recorded by Roger Chapman, Fleetwood Mac, Peter Frampton, Nazareth, Emerson, Lake and Palmer (and Keith Emerson's erstwhile band The Nice), Echo and the Bunnymen and Rod Stewart. Although it didn't chart highly for the writer of the song, it was obviously a popular choice for covering by bands at the end of the sixties and into the seventies.
For this reason, it was the choice of Norrie Paramor to add it to the list of songs for Cliff Richard to record for his next album, ***Don't Stop Me Now!***. One of four songs recorded for the album at the session, and the third to be completed, it took four takes to be completed and it was this final take and edit that was used for the mono and stereo recordings. Note that there are scant records from the session so, other than Cliff's vocals, the musicians who took part are unknown.
Hang on to a Dream is a pretty little song that is accompanied by an uncredited orchestra – at the time, Cliff recorded with the orchestras of Paramor, Mike Leander and Bernard Ebbinghouse, so it is therefore quite likely that the musicians are from one of them – and he instils the love song with much emotion that elevates the song to one of the best on the album.

Track Specification
Composed by Tim Hardin

1. Don't Stop Me Now!

Musicians

Cliff Richard	vocals
Unknown	arranger, conductor
Unknown	orchestra

Recording Details

Producer	Norrie Paramor
Engineered by	Peter Vince and Richard Lush
Recording location	Abbey Road Studio 2, St. John's Wood, London
Recording date	15th January 1967

2. Cliff in Japan

Musicians

Norrie Paramor Orchestra	orchestra
Norrie Paramor	arranger, conductor
Cliff Richard	vocals

Recording Details

Producer	Norrie Paramor
Engineered by	Unknown
Recording location	Shibuya Public Hall, Tokyo, Japan
Recording date	18th October 1967

♫ Hang Up Your Rock and Roll Shoes

From the album **The Rock 'n' Roll Years 1958-1963**

The title of this song as expressed on the track listing of ***The Rock 'n' Roll Years 1958-1963*** is incorrect in two respects: first, it should be '*Hang Up* My *Rock*' and, second and less of an issue, is that it is often entitled with an abbreviated 'and' to '*Rock* 'n' *Roll Shoes*'. This is proven simply by listening to Cliff Richard's enunciation of the lyrics, let alone the publication of the song as performed by other artists. However, since it is the published title for the only version by Cliff Richard, the erratum is deliberately carried forward into this entry.
Written by Chuck Willis, who also had a minor US hit with it, it was primarily covered by Jerry Lee Lewis (who performed the most familiar version in his concerts) and Carl Perkins, although other covers have included artists such as John Cafferty and the Beaver Brown Band, The Catalinas, Rumble King, the Equals and Ryan Foret.
The recording of *Hang Up Your Rock and Roll Shoes* was the debut performance by Cliff and the Shadows in France and was broadcast live on the Europe 1 station. The song had also been a regular track on the band's show on Radio Luxembourg in the early sixties, *Me and My Shadows*, and subsequently issued on ***The Rock 'n' Roll Years 1958-1963***. Cliff is in his element with this rock and roll song that is appreciated by the audience who clapped along with it. With whoops and finger-clicks, Cliff is supported ably by the Shadows, who provide a rhythm section only, although they break out into a short bridge with a simple melody on lead guitar.

Track Specification
Composed by Chuck Willis

Musicians

Brian Bennett	drums, percussion
Brian 'Licorice' Locking	bass
Hank Marvin	guitar
Cliff Richard	vocals, finger-clicks
Bruce Welch	rhythm guitar

Recording Details

Producer	Unknown
Engineered by	Unknown
Recording location	Olympia Theatre, Paris
Recording date	14th May 1963

♫ Hank's Medley

From the album **Live at the Talk of the Town**

For Cliff's earlier tours in particular, he often created a medley of his familiar songs that he hadn't sung elsewhere in the set list. For his 1968 concerts at the Talk of the Town theatre in London, which were recorded and released as ***Live at the Talk of the Town*** album, he performed five songs together:

a) ***London's Not Too Far***
b) ***The Dreams I Dream***
c) ***The Day I Met Marie***

The entries for those carry the information on the recording details and musicians.

♫ Happy Birthday to You

From the album **21 Today** *and commercial birthday card*

The Hill sisters, Patti and Mildred, from Kentucky were kindergarten school teachers and they were keen to develop different teaching methods, particularly with reference to the area of manners. One of their most enduring creations started life in 1893 as an easily memorable tune with which the children could greet their teachers and each other: *Good Morning to All*. By 1912, the song had been adapted to become the more familiar *Happy Birthday to You* or, more commonly, *Happy Birthday*. The *Guinness Book of Records* identifies the composition as the most recognisable song in the English language and it is a bone of contention that, theoretically at any rate, every birthday party (and especially the rendition on video film of the events) should pay an amount to the performing rights society, since it is still under copyright (currently owned by Warner Chappell). However, its administration is impossible and would be prohibitively expensive.
Since ***21 Today*** was recorded to mark Cliff Richard's coming of age on 14th October 1961, the choice of singing *Happy Birthday to You* was an apposite one with which to open the album. Appropriately, there were twenty-one takes recorded of the song with the mono and stereo versions used on the LPs employing the final take and edit but with different mixes for the audio channels of the respective format. The album suggests that the artists were Cliff Richard and the Shadows and Friends, although there is limited information as to who these friends might be, although it is likely to include the multitude of studio personnel drafted in to give the track a party atmosphere.
With an introduction sounds like it could break into ***Apache***, the first verse is archetypal Shadows, which is then lowered in volume as a party kicks off with jokes and ribald repartee, which includes unknown female voices as well as the band ribbing Cliff about his age.
In 2008, Balladeer Ltd. licensed a recording of Cliff singing *Happy Birthday to You* accompanied by his guitar and completing it with a joyous "Have a great day now!" This was placed in a microchip and small speaker that operates as the card is opened. The song is performed in a rocked up version that shuffles along mesmerically. The front of the card shows Cliff opening a bottle of champagne – the same publicity shot that was used for his fiftieth anniversary celebrations, while inside he is smiling with crossed fingers and a fire extinguisher behind a cake with several bright candles. There is no information available regarding where it was recorded and who else was involved.

Track Specification
Composed by Mildred Hill and Patti Hill

1. 21 Today

Musicians		*Recording Details*	
Jet Harris	spoken vocals, bass	Producer	Norrie Paramor
Hank Marvin	spoken vocals, guitar	Engineered by	Malcolm Addey and Norman Smith
Tony Meehan	spoken vocals, drums, percussion	Recording location	Abbey Road Studio 2, St. John's Wood, London
Cliff Richard	spoken vocals	Recording date	28th July 1961
Unknown	spoken vocals		
Bruce Welch	spoken vocals, rhythm guitar		

2. Birthday card

Musicians		*Recording Details*	
Cliff Richard	vocals, spoken vocals, guitar	Producer	Unknown
		Engineered by	Unknown
		Recording location	Unknown
		Recording date	2008

♫ Happy Like a Bell (Ding Dong)

Single by **Cherry Wainer**

Cherry Wainer was a South African ex-patriot, born into a theatrical family, who came to London in the fifties to work as the resident organist at the Windmill Theatre. From this involvement, she worked on the *Oh Boy!* television programmes, through which she befriended Cliff Richard. A member of Lord Rockingham's XI, who had a massive number one hit in 1958 with the novelty song ***Hoots Mon***, it wasn't long before Wainer secured her own recording contract. Initially recording tunes for the Pye label, such as *Itchy Twitchy Feeling*, *Valencia* and *Spanish Marching Song*, she then had releases on the Top Rank, Columbia and Honey Hit labels. For the Columbia release, she turned to her friend Cliff.

Happy Like a Bell (Ding Dong) is the first sole writing credit attributable to Cliff (he had previously had a co-writing credit for ***I Love You So*** with Jet Harris and Ian Samwell). Initially, the song's title seems to be odd, since it is an unfamiliar phrase; however, depending on the pitch and musical interval of the 'ding' and 'dong', it can inspire a feeling of happiness and this is probably what Cliff was attempting to achieve.

There is scant information regarding the recording and the personnel, although research has identified the involvement of Cliff providing backing vocals (the 'ding dong') and chimes, while Bruce Welch is also in a supporting role playing the rhythm guitar. Although the studio information is unavailable, it is quite possible that, since Cliff was involved, it was the partnership of Norrie Paramor and Malcolm Addey in production and engineering roles respectively with the recording taking place at Abbey Road Studios. However, until this is confirmed, the track specification will state it to be unknown.

The single, backed with Wainer's version of the Motown classic *Money (That's What I Want)* – with no known involvement from Cliff– was released in late 1960 on the Columbia label (catalogue number 45-DB 4528). In spite of its rich pedigree and the popularity of Cliff and the Shadows, the single was commercially unsuccessful and is now a considerable rarity.

Track Specification
Composed by Cliff Richard

Musicians		*Recording Details*	
Cliff Richard	backing vocals, chimes	Producer	Unknown
Unknown	other instrumentation	Engineered by	Unknown
Cherry Wainer	vocals, organ	Recording location	Unknown
Bruce Welch	rhythm guitar	Recording date	late 1960

♫ Happy World

Unissued track

In early 1969, Tyne Tees Television commissioned a series of six playlets for their religious broadcast slot called *Life with Johnny*, featuring Cliff Richard in the title role as each episode updated a well-known parable told by Jesus. Records are unclear on most episodes although two episodes are complete, one is partially available, while the rest aren't.

The songs performed had some relevance to the parable being performed and, in all, there were five songs per episode. *Happy World*, recorded at the Abbey Road studios with a putative album tie-in project in mind that didn't materialize, appeared in one of *Johnny on the Rocks*, *Johnny and the Blind Rage* or *Johnny in Love*. The end credits of the episode stated that all songs were original and written in collaboration between Cliff, the Settlers and the programme's writer David Winter. The instrumentation and performance details are unknown.

Track Specification
Composed by Cliff Richard, David Winter, Cindy Kent, Mike Jones, John Fyffe and Geoffrey Srodzinski

Musicians		*Recording Details*	
John Fyffe	backing vocals, guitar	Producer	Norrie Paramor
Cindy Kent	backing vocals	Engineered by	Peter Vince
Mike Jones	backing vocals, guitar	Recording location	Abbey Road Studio 3, St. John's Wood, London
Cliff Richard	vocals	Recording date	11th January 1969
Geoffrey Srodzinski	backing vocals, bass		

♫ Have a Little Talk with Myself

From the album **Cliff "Live" in Japan '72**

Ray Stevens had had a certain amount of success in Britain with his *Everything Is Beautiful* and the quirky *Bridget the Midget* in 1970 and 1971 respectively and so it seemed reasonable to include one of his songs in Cliff Richard's tours of the time. *Have a Little Talk with Myself* is a humorous way of saying that he needs to sort something out but personally rather than having an external influence. Recorded by its author, it was also given another interpretation in the same period by Sammy Davis, Jr. It is one of a handful of songs that Cliff recorded live but he never attempted a studio version.
The wowing and clucking guitar by Hank Marvin and the rocking piano by Alan Hawkshaw are the prominent instruments in this ensemble piece that sees Cliff taking pleasure in singing a song that is an unusual one for his oeuvre.

Track Specification
Composed by Ray Stevens
Musicians

Brian Bennett	drums, percussion
Pat Carroll	backing vocals
John Farrar	bass
Alan Hawkshaw	piano
Hank Marvin	guitar
Olivia Newton-John	backing vocals
Cliff Richard	vocals
Bruce Welch	rhythm guitar

Recording Details

Producer	Norrie Paramor
Engineered by	Unknown
Recording location	Kosei Nenkin Hall, Tokyo, Japan
Recording date	22nd-23rd September 1972

♫ Have a Smile for Everyone You Meet

From the film soundtrack album of **The Young Ones**

Part of the ***Vaudeville Routine*** section of the film ***The Young Ones***, it featured Nicky Black (Cliff Richard) accompanied by eight girls on the stage providing backing vocals. It leads into a spoken joke before it segues into *Tinkle Tinkle Tinkle.*
The entire sequence was recorded in one session along with the segments of ***What D'You Know, We've Got a Show***. Several takes were recorded of each of the sections of the *Vaudeville Routine*, with the same takes chosen for the stereo and mono edits, but with different mixes for the audio channel requirements. The film version of the sequence was recorded later on the year (probably in the same month) but has not been formally released in any other commercial format.

Track Specification
Composed by Bert Rule, J. Keim Cunningham and Paul Brennan
Musicians

Associated British Studio Orchestra	orchestra
Stanley Black	conductor
Mike Sammes Singers	vocals, backing vocals
Cliff Richard	vocals

Recording Details

Producer	Norrie Paramor
Engineered by	Malcolm Addey and Alan Kane
Recording location	Abbey Road Studio 2, St. John's Wood, London
Recording date	9th August 1961

♫ Have I Told You Lately that I Love You?

From the album **Love is Forever**

Not to be confused with the song written by Van Morrison for his 1989 single and album, Scotty Wiseman's title of *Have I Told You Lately that I Love You?* has been covered by a large group of artists over the years including Skeeter Davis, George Faith, Bing Crosby, Richard Clayderman, Willie Nelson, Elvis Presley, Eddy Arnold, Kenny Rogers, Eddie Cochran, the Andrews Sisters, Gene Autry, Floyd Cramer, Billy Fury, Rick Nelson, Jim Reeves, Tex Ritter and Roger Whittaker among many others.
Cliff Richard's version of the song was one of six to be completed at a dual session at the Portuguese studios in May 1965. The final (unknown) take and edit were used for both the mono and stereo recordings but with different mixes for the separate audio channels.
With a vibe similar to *Crying Time, Have I Told You Lately that I Love You?* is an upbeat and very jaunty little song in spite of the lyrical assertion that he is missing her, although the love he feels makes up for this sadness of his loneliness. The backing vocals overwhelm on occasions but this type of ballad is perfectly suited to Cliff's vocals.

Track Specification
Composed by Scott Wiseman
Musicians

Brian Bennett	drums, percussion
Hank Marvin	guitar
Mike Sammes Singers	backing vocals
Norrie Paramor Orchestra	orchestra
Norrie Paramor	arranger, conductor
Cliff Richard	vocals
John Rostill	bass
Unknown	piano
Bruce Welch	rhythm guitar

Recording Details

Producer	Norrie Paramor
Engineered by	Unknown
Recording location	Estudios Valentim de Carvalho, Lisbon, Portugal
Recording date	10th May 1965

♫ Have Yourself a Merry Little Christmas

From the albums **Together with Cliff Richard** *and* **Cliff at Christmas**

Credited to Hugh Martin and Ralph Blane, the former stated in a 2006 interview that while Blane had encouraged him to write the song, there was no input from him otherwise. It was first performed by Judy Garland in the 1944 musical *Meet Me in St. Louis* and it features at the point on Christmas Eve where Esther (Garland) sings to her young sister Tootsie (Margaret O'Brien) because they are scheduled to move from their much-loved St. Louis home to New York for their father's business. The lyrics are deliberately despondent and, despite resistance, Martin eventually relented to pressure from Frank Sinatra to sanitize it for his more upbeat seasonal album *A Jolly Christmas* in 1957 – it is largely this version that has had the most covers with other artists following Sinatra's lead. The variety of acts to cover the song is enormous and includes Christina Aguilera, Delta Goodrem, Anne Murray, Katie Melua, Garth Brooks, the Calico Consort, Ella Fitzgerald, Connie Francis, Glen Campbell, Lena Horne, Linda Ronstadt, Twisted Sister, the Jackson 5, Perry Como, Vic Damone, Carly Simon, James Taylor, Bob Dylan, Barbra Streisand and Luther Vandross to name but a very few.

Cliff Richard recorded his version in the early summer of 1991 – a curious anachronism forced by recording and release schedules – and it appeared as the first track on the album release in November 1991.

Introduced by drum sequencers and a piano, the pace picks up as the bass line keeps the rhythm moving. Cliff provides his own backing vocals and there is frequently an echo placed on his lead. The standard approach to the performance is to take it at a very sedentary pace as if stepping through treacle. Cliff's version makes it a completely different affair with the emphasis on merry, thereby doing away with the original intent of the film version.

In 2003, the original track was revisited for the album ***Cliff at Christmas*** and, while using the basic track recorded for the first album, there is additional percussion in the introduction, additional keyboard throughout the song and slight reverb echo added to the backing vocals as well as mixing the strings further forward in the final product. In all other respects the song is the same.

Track Specification

Composed by Hugh Martin and Ralph Blane

1. Together with Cliff Richard

Musicians

Dave Bishop	tenor saxophone
John Clark	guitar
Paul Dunne	guitar
Dave Cunliffe	violin
Andrew Greasley	violin
Mark Griffiths	bass
Peter May	drums, percussion
Paul Moessl	drum programming, keyboards
Cliff Richard	arranger, vocals, backing vocals
Frank Ricotti	drums, percussion
Steve Stroud	bass

Recording Details

Producer	Cliff Richard and Paul Moessl
Engineered by	Gerry Kitchingham, Andrew Greasley and Ben Robbins
Recording location	R. G. Jones Studios, Wimbledon, London
Recording date	24th June 1991 to July 1991

2. Cliff at Christmas

Musicians

Dave Bishop	tenor saxophone
John Clark	guitar
Paul Dunne	guitar
Dave Cunliffe	violin
Andrew Greasley	violin
Mark Griffiths	bass
Peter May	drums, percussion
Paul Moessl	drum programming, keyboards
Cliff Richard	arranger, vocals, backing vocals
Frank Ricotti	drums, percussion
Steve Stroud	bass

Recording Details

Producer	Cliff Richard and Paul Moessl (original track) and Unknown (additional instrumentation)
Engineered by	Gerry Kitchingham, Andrew Greasley and Ben Robbins (original track) and Unknown (additional instrumentation)
Recording location	R. G. Jones Studios, Wimbledon, London (original track) and Unknown (additional instrumentation)
Recording date	24th June 1991 to July 1991 (original track) and 2003 (additional instrumentation)

♫ Havin' Fun

From the pantomime cast recording album of **Aladdin and His Wonderful Lamp**

The final track from the cast recording of ***Aladdin and His Wonderful Lamp*** was one of four tracks recorded for the album in a double session that day. The final song to be recorded by Cliff Richard at its session, the last (unknown) take and edit was used for both mono and stereo recordings but with different mixes for the separate audio channels. Released on the track listing of the mono-only EP ***Cliff's Hits from Aladdin and His Wonderful Lamp***, the stereo version was issued on the stereo release of the long-player. The song was also released in Malaysia as a single, where it reached number two in 1965.

The Shadows enjoyed using nursery rhyme and children's story imagery in their songs and they employed this to great effect in *Havin' Fun*, which uses the stories of the Grand Old Duke of York, Hey Diddle Diddle, Old Mother Hubbard, Little Miss Muffet and how the characters are having the fun of the title. Employing the beautiful harmonies that Cliff, Hank Marvin, Bruce Welch and John Rostill successfully produced as their sound, it is an upbeat and foot-tapping rock and roll tune that is perfectly performed by Cliff.

Track Specification
Composed by Hank Marvin, Bruce Welch, Brian Bennett and John Rostill

Musicians		*Recording Details*	
Brian Bennett	drums, percussion	Producer	Norrie Paramor
Hank Marvin	backing vocals, guitar	Engineered by	Malcolm Addey and Ken Scott
Cliff Richard	vocals	Recording location	Abbey Road Studio 2, St. John's Wood, London
John Rostill	backing vocals, bass	Recording date	15th October 1964
Bruce Welch	backing vocals, rhythm guitar		

♫ Healing Love

***121st UK single** and from the album* **Cliff Richard - The Album**

The fifth and final single to be released from ***Cliff Richard - The Album*** is essentially a collaboration between Cliff Richard and eighties New Romantic pop singer Nik Kershaw. Backed with two songs – ***Carrie***, which was a revisited and updated version that appeared on the album ***My Kinda Life***, and a non-album track, ***Yesterday's Memories*** – as its B-side, *Healing Love* was issued on the EMI label (catalogue number EM 294) on 6th December 1993 and reached number nineteen in the UK singles charts. The seven-inch release was essentially a remix and edit of the album version which featured only Kershaw, keyboardist Richard Cottle and Cliff on the vocal lines and has never been released in any other format. At the same time, a CD single was issued (catalogue number CDEM 294), including the new version of *Carrie* and the single versions of ***Daddy's Home*** and ***Some People***, and a boxed set CD version (CDEMS 294), featuring an extended version of the Harding and Curnow mix of *Healing Love* alongside *Yesterday's Memories* and *Some People*. A promotional CD was also issued (CDEMDJ 294) of the track on its own.

Healing Love is an upbeat and rhythmic tune that is played principally on the percussion and keyboards. Cliff enjoys singing this song and it provides a perfect example of the blend of his vocals against his own backing vocals, particularly in the strong chorus. For the promotional video, Cliff sings the song with an atmospheric candle-lit scene that cuts to an ostentatious stage set replete with backing singers and dancers.

Track Specification
Composed by Nik Kershaw and Denis Morgan

1. Cliff Richard - The Album

Musicians		*Recording Details*	
Richard Cottle	keyboards	Producer	Paul Moessl, Nik Kershaw and Cliff Richard
John Clark	guitar	Engineered by	Stuart Bruce
Nik Kershaw	arranger, backing vocals, guitar programming	Recording location	Nomis Studios, London and Abbey Road Studios, St. Johns Wood, London (remix)
Peter May	drums, percussion	Recording date	October 1992 and 6th July 1993 (remix)
Paul Moessl	drum programming, keyboards		
Cliff Richard	vocals, backing vocals		

2. Single (seven-inch Harding and Curnow mix)

Musicians		*Recording Details*	
Richard Cottle	keyboards	Producer	Paul Moessl, Nik Kershaw and Cliff Richard
Nik Kershaw	arranger, backing vocals, guitar programming	Engineered by	Stuart Bruce
		Remixed by	Phil Harding and Ian Curnow
Cliff Richard	vocals, backing vocals	Recording location	Nomis Studios, London and Abbey Road Studios, St. Johns Wood, London (remix)
		Recording date	October 1992 and 6th July 1993 (remix)

3. Single (CD Harding and Curnow mix)

Musicians		*Recording Details*	
Richard Cottle	keyboards	Producer	Paul Moessl, Nik Kershaw and Cliff Richard
Nik Kershaw	arranger, backing vocals, guitar programming	Engineered by	Stuart Bruce
		Remixed by	Phil Harding and Ian Curnow
Cliff Richard	vocals, backing vocals	Recording location	Nomis Studios, London and Abbey Road Studios, St. John's Wood, London (remix)
		Recording date	October 1992 and 6th July 1993 (remix)

♫ Heartbeat

From the albums **Don't Stop Me Now!** *and* **Heartbeat** *(Hank Marvin)*

Perhaps one of the most familiar Buddy Holly songs – especially in the UK, where it was recorded as the theme tune for the TV series of the same name (taking place in the sixties, it followed the ups and downs of life in and around a small police station in the Yorkshire Dales, using sixties music as the musical backdrop) – *Heartbeat* was originally released by Holly a month before his fatal flight in February 1959, and it reached number thirty in the UK charts and number eighty-two in the Billboard listings. Re-issued again the UK in April 1960, it reached the same position once again in the UK.

Since then, a variety of artists and groups have recorded their own versions, including Connie Francis, The Hollies, Bobby Vee, Showaddywaddy, Denny Laine, Humble Pie and Herman's Hermits. The aforementioned theme tune to the UK TV series sung by Nick Berry, who played the principal lead, reached number two.

Cliff Richard's version was recorded at the first session of 1967 and was the final track to be completed that day. The fourth and final take and edit were used for the mono and stereo recordings, although the instrumentation is unknown as there is no available record for it so is therefore marked as unknown.

Cliff went through a period of heavy use of orchestral backing in the latter years of the sixties. This has a double-edged effect of making the cover versions sound fresh, while the whole album of similarly treated material begins to sound the same. However, Cliff's version is sung with passion and the uncredited arrangement is a clever updated take on a very familiar song.

In the nineties, Hank Marvin was regularly creating albums of covers with his own special magic. A few tracks on his *Heartbeat* album featured Cliff on backing vocals and these included the album's title track. Featuring Brian Bennett and his son Warren as well as Cliff's long-term bassist Mark Griffiths, the track was recorded some time in 1992 or 1993 – records are unavailable to be more precise – and regularly shows up on compilation albums of Hank's material. With a stronger, faster beat than the original, Hank brings in the melody that is instantly familiar both from Buddy Holly and the signature performance. Cliff sings the word 'heartbeat' in the chorus and then 'dooh's along to the rest of the chorus. This is highly effective since he is not singing the whole song but is deployed at the important parts of the track.

Track Specification
Composed by Bob Montgomery and Norman Petty

1. Don't Stop Me Now!

Musicians

Cliff Richard	vocals
Unknown	arranger, conductor
Unknown	orchestra

Recording Details

Producer	Norrie Paramor
Engineered by	Peter Vince and Richard Lush
Recording location	Abbey Road Studio 2, St. John's Wood, London
Recording date	15th January 1967

2. Heartbeat

Musicians

Brian Bennett	drums, percussion
Warren Bennett	keyboards
Mark Griffiths	bass
Hank Marvin	guitar
Cliff Richard	backing vocals

Recording Details

Producer	Hank Marvin and Brian Bennett
Engineered by	Dick Plant
Recording location	Honeyhill Studios, Hertfordshire
Recording date	1992-1993

♫ Heartbreak Hotel

Unreleased live track

Recorded as an original song in January 1956 by Elvis Presley, *Heartbreak Hotel* was really Presley's breakthrough single around the world, where it reached number one in many national singles charts. Presley received a co-writer credit, not because he was involved in its creation but because of what he did with it in the studio. His producer was unsure that it was the right song to record and RCA were understandably nervous since the song was so different in performance to the material he had created at Sun Records. Nevertheless, he worked at the song and performed it on television; the excitement it generated was enough for record executives to accept that Presley really knew what he was doing.

It has been covered by a number of other artists, including Merle Haggard, Paul McCartney, Guns n' Roses, Connie Francis, The Animals, Adam Faith, Fats Domino, Tanya Tucker and Tom Jones among many others. According to Cliff Richard's autobiography, ***My Life, My Way***, it was hearing the first line or two through an open car window that had him and his mates transfixed. They spent ages listening to a variety of radio stations until they heard the song performed again to find out who and what it was. It was also included as part of Cliff Richard and the Drifters' repertoire for their short residency at the Clacton-on-Sea Butlin's Holiday Camp in August 1958. Anything that had been recorded by Presley was a premium and many bands attempted to cover his songs. One of the nights was recorded on a two-track tape machine by Stan Edwards and some of those recordings made it on to the rarities retrospective, *The Rock 'n' Roll Years 1958-1963*. Other tracks were in too poor a condition to be considered for commercial release. The fate of *Heartbreak Hotel* was that it was chosen for inclusion in the listings of that album. Because of the limited recording capabilities, the only version of this live recording remains in mono only.

Cliff's version from the set is the closest he gets to mimicking Presley's vocal style but, at the same time, he also makes it very much an original interpretation. The lead guitar solo is a little too slow against the speed of the song and the transition through the chords sounds nervous and stuttering in the middle eight. However, Cliff's assured performance is delivered with aplomb and is a remarkable insight into what as to come over his extensive career.

Track Specification
Composed by Mae Axton, Tommy Durden and Elvis Presley

Musicians

Cliff Richard	vocals, guitar
Ian Samwell	guitar
Terry Smart	drums, percussion

Recording Details

Producer	Unknown
Engineered by	Stan Edwards
Recording location	Rock 'n' Roll Ballroom, Butlin's Holiday Camp, Clacton-on-Sea, Essex
Recording date	August 1958

♫ Heart User

***94th UK single** (seven- and twelve-inch formats)*

Written by Terry Britten and Sue Shifrin, who had provided three songs for Cliff Richard's ***Silver*** album in 1983 as well as his last single in America, ***Never Say Die (Give a Little Bit More)***, *Heart User* is documented as Cliff's favourite track from the 1984 album, ***The Rock Connection***. Appearing as the opening track, *Heart User* was also released as a single, backed with non-album track ***I Will Follow You***, on the EMI label (catalogue number EMI RICH 2) on 21st January 1985, but only achieved the highest placing of forty-six in the UK singles charts. A twelve-inch version (catalogue number 12RICH 2) was issued with an extended version of the song, while there was also a seven-inch release that incorporated poster sleeve.

As was the vogue for this period, *Heart User* uses a lot of synthesiser keyboards. The song, telling the story of a woman who has affairs and flings the men aside in her wake and the effect this causes on the emotions, is unusual for Cliff at the time but he carries off the vocals with considered assuredness. If there is to be a problem found with it, it is that the song isn't particularly memorable with too few hooks to be a strong single.

Track Specification

Composed by Terry Britten and Sue Shifrin

1. Single (seven-inch)

Musicians

John Clark	guitar
Dave Cooke	keyboards
Mark Griffiths	bass
Alan Park	keyboards
Cliff Richard	vocals, backing vocals
Stuart Tosh	drums, percussion

Recording Details

Producer	Cliff Richard and Keith Bessey
Engineered by	Keith Bessey
Recording location	Strawberry Studios South, Surrey
Recording date	30th July 1984-3rd August 1984

2. Single (twelve-inch)

Musicians

John Clark	guitar
Dave Cooke	keyboards
Mark Griffiths	bass
Alan Park	keyboards
Cliff Richard	vocals, backing vocals
Stuart Tosh	drums, percussion

Recording Details

Producer	Cliff Richard and Keith Bessey
Engineered by	Keith Bessey
Recording location	Strawberry Studios South, Surrey
Recording date	30th July 1984-3rd August 1984

♫ Heart Will Break, A

From the album **I'm No Hero**

The penultimate song on Cliff Richard's ***I'm No Hero*** album is from the prolific pen of songwriting duo Alan Tarney and Trevor Spencer, who both appear in the band on the track. Tarney had begun to dominate Cliff's studio sessions in the late seventies and into the eighties and here, as with the entire album, he also takes over arrangement and production duties. The rhythm created on the drums is almost tribal in its structure and, for once on the album, the predominant instrument is the guitar rather than the omnipresent synthesiser. The backing vocals are by Cliff and Tarney and are built up in layers in order to sound more like a larger choir of singers.

Track Specification

Composed by Alan Tarney and Trevor Spencer

Musicians

Michael Boddicker	synthesiser
Nick Glennie-Smith	synthesiser
Cliff Richard	vocals, backing vocals
Trevor Spencer	drums, percussion
Alan Tarney	arranger, backing vocals, guitar, bass

Recording Details

Producer	Alan Tarney
Engineered by	Ashley Howe
Recording location	Riverside Studios, London
Recording date	12th May-27th June 1980

♫ Help

Unissued track

Appearing in the updated parable of the Good Samaritan episode of *Life with Johnny* with Cliff Richard in the lead role, there are several songs that are performed to indicate that Johnny and his girlfriend (played by Cindy Kent) are in trouble with no money to get home, in spite of asking for assistance from a number of sources. *Help* is one such song, which is performed as a dance with hitch-hiking elements to it.

The song is performed pretty much straight but breaks into a quirky three-four time signature on the second and fourth lines, while at the end, Cliff improvises the lyrics as was his wont during this period of his career. Recorded at the Abbey Road studios along with all of the other songs from the series, the possible tie-in album didn't materialize and the song has not been issued to date. The end credits indicate that all songs are original and written by the collaboration of the Settlers, Cliff and screenwriter David Winter. Clearly this is not the case here, since it is actually a cover of the Beatles song, although this is not stated in the credits for this episode.

Taken from the Beatles second film of the same name (and with an exclamation mark afterwards on that version), it was the band's eighth successive British number one in 1965 and was subsequently taken into the charts by Tina Turner, who made number forty in February 1984 and Bananarama and LaNaNeeNeeNooNoo (Dawn French and Jennifer Saunders in spectacularly silly form) who reached number three for the Comic Relief charity with an upbeat version in March 1989 and curious dance sequence to mirror the proper moves of Bananarama.

Track Specification
Composed by John Lennon and Paul McCartney

Musicians

John Fyffe	backing vocals, guitar
Cindy Kent	backing vocals
Mike Jones	backing vocals, guitar
Cliff Richard	vocals, finger-clicks
Geoffrey Srodzinski	backing vocals, bass
Unknown	organ
Unknown	drums, percussion

Recording Details

Producer	Norrie Paramor
Engineered by	Peter Vince
Recording location	Abbey Road Studio 3, St. John's Wood, London
Recording date	2nd-3rd December 1968

♫ Help It Along

***60th UK single** (double A-side) and from the album* **Help It Along**

Cliff Richard's favourite song of the six contenders for the 1973 Eurovision Song Contest to represent the UK, *Help It Along*, was the final song performed on the *Cilla* show (hosted by his friend Cilla Black) on Saturday nights in the early weeks of the year. The subsequent postal vote revealed that ***Power to All Our Friends*** had outstripped the other songs resoundingly (with 51.8% of the polled votes), while *Help It Along* came third (10.5%) behind ***Come Back Billie Jo*** (14.1%) and ahead of ***Tomorrow Rising*** (9%).

The track was recorded along with the other five contending songs across two days at the end of December 1972, with *Help It Along* being completed as the first song at the second session alongside its nearest contest rival *Tomorrow Rising* and the winner *Power to All Our Friends*.

It was customary for the winning title and the second-placed song to be released as a single with the remaining songs being released as an EP. However, in this case, all four remaining songs were released as a maxi-single with *The Guinness Book of British Hit Singles* identifying *Help It Along* as a double A-side (literally in this case) with *Tomorrow Rising* on one side. Backed with ***The Days of Love*** and ***Ashes to Ashes***, *Help It Along* and *Tomorrow Rising* were released as a joint single on the EMI label (catalogue number EMI 2022) on 27th April 1973, reaching its highest point of twenty-nine on the first week of entry into the charts. It remained a rarity even in its original form until it was added to the track listing of 1998's *1970s* album.

Introduced by a short oboe piece leading into a violin, *Help It Along* is a beautiful song that is a little out of place in a song contest like Eurovision, which appears to have its own musical rules. Cliff enjoys singing this song as it builds up during the verses and completing with the repetitious song title, with an unusual showing of Cliff's bass register at the very end.

Giving its name to the charity album released in aid of the Tear Fund, *Help It Along* was chosen as a suitably uplifting and meaningful song for the set of studio-bound concerts recorded in seven sessions over three days, particularly since it was a favourite of Cliff's. The arrangement created for the album improves on the Eurovision candidate original, with Cliff imbuing the lyrics with more meaning supported by the straightforward instrumentation and the subdued backing vocals.

Track Specification
Composed by Christopher Neil

1. Single

Musicians

Terry Britten	backing vocals, guitar
David MacKay Orchestra	orchestra
David MacKay	backing vocals, arranger, conductor
Kevin Peek	guitar
Cliff Richard	vocals
Trevor Spencer	backing vocals, drums, percussion
Alan Tarney	backing vocals, bass

Recording Details

Producer	David MacKay
Engineered by	Peter Vince
Recording location	Abbey Road Studio, St. John's Wood, London
Recording date	28th December 1972

2. Help It Along

Musicians

Terry Britten	guitar
Barrie Guard	arranger, conductor, percussion
Cliff Hall	keyboards
Jean Hawker	backing vocals
Anna Peacock	backing vocals
Kevin Peek	guitar
Cliff Richard	vocals
Trevor Spencer	drums, percussion
Alan Tarney	bass
Unknown	orchestra

Recording Details

Producer	David MacKay
Engineered by	Roger Quested
Recording location	Morgan Studios, London
Recording date	24th, 25th and 26th September 1973

♫ Here (So Doggone Blue)

From the album **I'm No Hero**

Written, co-performed, arranged and produced by the pridgious talents of Alan Tarney, *Here (So Doggone Blue)* continues the dominance of Tarney on Cliff Richard's recordings in the studio and it appears as the penultimate track on side one of the original vinyl release of ***I'm No Hero***.

Less frenetic than the previous track, ***A Little in Love***, *Here (So Doggone Blue)* still predominantly comprises the use of synthesisers with a drum and percussion base driving the rhythm along. Cliff's and Tarney's vocals blend well in the layering that Tarney engineered to create the semblance of a small choir behind Cliff's lead that is quite reminiscent of the sound that the Bee Gees were producing around the time. In the penultimate verse, however, Cliff provides a single line harmony that is highly effective and lifts the song as it draws to its conclusion.

Track Specification

Composed by Alan Tarney

Musicians

Michael Boddicker	synthesiser
Nick Glennie-Smith	synthesiser
Cliff Richard	vocals, backing vocals
Trevor Spencer	drums, percussion
Alan Tarney	arranger, backing vocals, bass

Recording Details

Producer	Alan Tarney
Engineered by	Ashley Howe
Recording location	Riverside Studios, London
Recording date	12th May-27th June 1980

♫ Here Comes Summer

From the album **Cliff Sings**

The fourth of eight tracks on the *Cliff Sings* album to feature backing by the Drifters (who would go on to change their names of the Shadows prior to the record's release to avoid confusion with the pre-existing American group of the same name), *Here Comes Summer* was a number one hit in the UK for its writer Jerry Keller in the late summer of 1959 and remains his only chart entry to date. It was also recorded by the Dave Clark Five eleven years later in the summer of July 1970 but only reached number forty-four on that occasion.

Since the original single was riding high at the time of the recording sessions for *Cliff Sings*, it made an obvious choice for inclusion in the track listing of the album in order to capitalize on its popularity.

The mono version – used on the *Cliff Sings* album and the mono version of the *Cliff Sings No. 1* EP – and the stereo version – used on the stereo release of the EP– were derived from the same take but given different mixes for the extra audio channel. Accomplished and smooth, Cliff is clearly in his element singing songs like this. The running bass line and the easy rhythm guitar keep the song moving forwards with a twinkling Hank Marvin solo guitar playing subtly alongside the ensemble cast.

Track Specification

Composed by Jerry Keller

Musicians

Jet Harris	bass
Hank Marvin	guitar
Tony Meehan	drums, percussion
Cliff Richard	vocals
Bruce Welch	rhythm guitar

Recording Details

Producer	Norrie Paramor
Engineered by	Malcolm Addey and Alan Kane (mono) and Stuart Eltham and Norman Smith (stereo)
Recording location	Abbey Road Studio 2, St. John's Wood, London
Recording date	7th September 1959

♫ He's Everything to Me

From the album **His Land**

The final song that featured Cliff Richard in the ***His Land*** project is the second of two duets that he performed with American Cliff Barrows. The song was recorded in Israel, where the location filming was done for the associated film of the same name, and the vocals were overdubbed on a pre-recorded orchestral track that was recorded in Hollywood. There is no information on precise session dates other than that they took place in late 1969.

The song is performed in the final half of the film with Cliff Barrows and Cliff having flown to Galilee and now engaging a group of people sitting around the fire and receiving a warm round of applause upon completion. Performing with just a guitar (played by Cliff (Richard)) and the two voices, *He's Everything to Me* is a short, simple but effective song to match the message of the overall film. The two men's voices combine well, although Cliff Richard's voice is obviously the superlative of the two. With only a guitar accompaniment, the simplicity enhances the beauty of the song.

Track Specification

Composed by Ralph Carmichael

Musicians

Cliff Barrows	vocals
Cliff Richard	vocals, guitar

Recording Details

Producer	Lee Gillette
Engineered by	Unknown
Recording location	Capitol Records, Hollywood, USA (orchestra) and Israel (vocals)
Recording date	Late 1969

♫ He's the One

From the album **Did He Jump... Or Was He Pushed?** *(Garth Hewitt)*

Cliff Richard flexed his strong production talents to produce fellow Christian Garth Hewitt's second solo album, ***Did He Jump... Or Was He Pushed?***, on which *He's the One* appears.
A bouncing rock ballad that verges on the country genre, Hewitt sings the song with conviction, while Cliff supplies backing vocals using his upper register. Pleasant though the song is, it is not the best song on the album but then there is significant competition to be found elsewhere on the track listing.

Track Specification
Composed by Garth Hewitt

Musicians		*Recording Details*	
Garth Hewitt	vocals, guitar	Producer	Cliff Richard
Graham Jarvis	drums, percussion	Engineered by	Tony Clark and Haydn Bendall
Mike Moran	guitar, keyboards	Recording location	Odyssey Studios, London
Jo Partridge	guitar	Recording date	1979
Cliff Richard	backing vocals, guitar		
Dave Wintour	bass		

♫ Hey Doctor Man

From the pantomime cast recording album of **Cinderella**

The final song of the Shadows' version of the classic ***Cinderella*** rags to riches story, *Hey Doctor Man* is actually an observational love song with Cliff Richard complaining of jelly knees and a thumping in his chest and a host of other potentially worrying symptoms associated with love. The song was slated for recording at two sessions for the soundtrack album: the first was at the initial session where, after five takes, the recording was abandoned; it was picked up just over a month later when a further six takes were tried with the sixth and final take and edit being used for the mono and stereo recordings. The song was also issued on the mono-only release of the ***Cinderella*** EP in the middle of 1967.
Another brilliant Shadows composition, Cliff and the Shadows produce their quintessential sound, based around intricate their vocal harmonies. The upbeat rhythm leads into this quirky little love song and, when Cliff sings on his own, the joyful optimism he exudes comes through his portrayal of someone befuddled by love. There is a harmonica that is played (presumably by one of the Shadows, although this is unconfirmed), before the song rushes onwards to its completion. Audiences would have piled out of the Palladium with a grin etched on their faces as a result of this last performance.

Track Specification
Composed by Hank Marvin, Bruce Welch, Brian Bennett and John Rostill

1. Unissued track (Cinderella)

Musicians		*Recording Details*	
Brian Bennett	drums, percussion	Producer	Norrie Paramor
Hank Marvin	backing vocals, guitar	Engineered by	Peter Vince and Richard Lush
Cliff Richard	vocals	Recording location	Abbey Road Studio 2, St. John's Wood, London
John Rostill	backing vocals, bass	Recording date	14th October 1966
Unknown	harmonica		
Bruce Welch	backing vocals, rhythm guitar		

2. Cinderella

Musicians		*Recording Details*	
Brian Bennett	drums, percussion	Producer	Norrie Paramor
Hank Marvin	backing vocals, guitar	Engineered by	Peter Vince and Richard Lush
Cliff Richard	vocals	Recording location	Abbey Road Studio 3, St. John's Wood, London
John Rostill	backing vocals, bass	Recording date	16th November 1966
Unknown	harmony		
Bruce Welch	backing vocals, rhythm guitar		

♫ Hey Jude

From the album **Party at the Park**

Abandoning the received wisdom from the ignorant and patronizing record companies that popular songs needed to be no more than two or three minutes because of the attention span of the audience, the Beatles went for it with *Hey Jude*, which comes in at over six minutes of playing time and was the longest song to reach number one at the time. In 1967, John Lennon had started divorce proceedings against his first wife Cynthia in order to be with Yoko Ono. Paul McCartney recognized the sadness in the young Julian, their son, and wrote a song (*Hey Jules* originally) to comfort him. It transmogrified into *Hey Jude* and is a brilliant piece of sixties pop as it builds up from a lone voice accompanied by piano chords into something extraordinary and big, with the long sing-along trail-out at the end. When it was released as a single in the UK, it became the band's fifteenth number one and firmly cemented them in the annals of music history.
Because of the lengthy outro of the song and the simple melody that supports it, it is a perfect closer to any concert and, whenever McCartney has guested at such events, it is usually *Hey Jude* that is chosen for the assembled group to sing

along with on stage, often involving the audience. So it was when it was employed to close the Buckingham Palace pop concert in June 2002 for Queen Elizabeth II's fiftieth anniversary of her accession to the throne. Driven by McCartney after the completion of ***All You Need Is Love***, other guests including Cliff Richard appeared on the stage to assist in the vocals, although he is not obvious in the mix. As with *All You Need Is Love*, there is a pleasing sing-along element that unites everybody as the song slowly builds up and it was a perfect and dramatic closer for that reason to the Party at the Palace.

Track Specification
Composed by John Lennon and Paul McCartney

Musicians		*Recording Details*	
Rusty Anderson	guitar	Producer	Giles Martin
Sam Brown	backing vocals	Engineered by	Andy Rose
Margo Buchanan	backing vocals	Recording location	Buckingham Palace, London
Joe Cocker	vocals	Mixed by	Paul Hicks (Abbey Road) and John Hudson and Greg Jackman (Mayfair)
Phil Collins	drums, percussion		
Ray Cooper	percussion	Mixed at	Abbey Road Studios, St. John's Wood, London and Mayfair Studios, London
Claudia Fontaine	backing vocals		
Abe Laboriel Jr.	drums, percussion	Recording date	3rd June 2002
Ladysmith Black Mambazo	backing vocals		
Paul McCartney	vocals, piano		
Pino Palladino	bass		
Phil Palmer	guitar		
Brian Ray	guitar		
Cliff Richard	backing vocals		
Eric Robison	saxophone		
Royal Academy of Music Symphony Orchestra	orchestra		
Rod Stewart	vocals		
Wix Wickens	keyboards		

♫ Hey Mister
B-side of **Lean on You**

Written and recorded during the ***Stronger*** album sessions by Alan Tarney and Cliff Richard adding his vocals later, *Hey Mister* was not included on the album but became the B-side of the third single from the project, ***Lean on You***, appearing on all variants of the single. A bit of a rarity, it was eventually included as a bonus track on the 2004 remaster of *Stronger*.
The quirky introduction on Tarney's synthesisers leads into Cliff's angry vocals, which are a selection of railing diatribes about things going on in the world, such as progress and revolution, with the 'mister' of the title being applied to the particular word he is unhappy with and there is an echo applied to his voice which tails away on some of the lyrics. Cliff then moves on to what he loves such as Muddy Waters, Paul Simon and Elvis Presley singing to him and then requests the deejay to play old rock and roll era records to cheer him up.

Track Specification
Composed by Alan Tarney

Musicians		*Recording Details*	
Cliff Richard	vocals, backing vocals	Producer	Alan Tarney
Alan Tarney	arranger, synthesisers, drum and percussion sequencers	Engineered by	Gerry Kitchingham and Ben Robbins
		Recording location	R. G. Jones Studios, Wimbledon, London
		Mixed by	John Hudson and Noel Rafferty
		Mixing location	Mayfair Studios, London
		Recording date	27th February 1989, 9th March 1989, 13th-17th March 1989 and 22nd-23rd March 1989

♫ Hey Mr. Dream Maker
Unissued track and ***68th UK single***

Hey Mr. Dream Maker was originally written for Bruce Welch's then fiancée, Olivia Newton-John, for her 1976 album *Don't Stop Believin'*. Subsequently it was picked up and recorded by country music star Dottie West and also incorporated into the recording sessions for Cliff Richard's album ***Every Face Tells a Story***. Two attempts were made to finish the song, with it being abandoned after five takes in the first session and completing it in two takes on the second. The song is often referred to simply as *Mr. Dream Maker* or *Hey Mr. Dreammaker* and a few other variants without punctuation; however, *Hey Mr. Dream Maker* is the title that appears on the album's track listing and so it is used here in this entry.
Hey Mr. Dream Maker was picked for release as Cliff's sixty-eighth single and was the first of three to be issued from the album project. Backed with ***No-one Waits***, which was recorded as part of the albums sessions but didn't appear on the final track listing, and released on the EMI label (catalogue number EMI 2559) on 6th November 1976, it reached number thirty-one in the British singles charts.
The running arpeggios on the guitar introduce this song that shows off Cliff's developed vibrato employed to great effect and this helps to imbue the song with the sadness from the lyrics, while the backing vocals are in strong evidence in the choruses blending with the lead as the pace picks up with the frustration because the girl of his life is no longer with him.

Track Specification
Composed by Alan Tarney and Bruce Welch

1. *Unissued track (Every Face Tells a Story)*

Musicians

Brian Bennett	drums, percussion
Terry Britten	guitar
John Perry	backing vocals
Cliff Richard	vocals
Frank Ricotti	percussion
Tony Rivers	backing vocals
Alan Tarney	bass
Graham Todd	keyboards

Recording Details

Producer	Bruce Welch
Engineered by	Tony Clark, Haydn Bendall and Alan Rouse
Recording location	Abbey Road Studio 2, St. John's Wood, London
Recording date	9th September 1976

2. *Single*

Musicians

Brian Bennett	drums, percussion
Terry Britten	guitar
John Perry	backing vocals
Cliff Richard	vocals
Frank Ricotti	percussion
Tony Rivers	backing vocals
Alan Tarney	bass
Graham Todd	keyboards

Recording Details

Producer	Bruce Welch
Engineered by	Tony Clark and Alan Rouse
Recording location	Abbey Road Studio 2, St. John's Wood, London
Recording date	18th September 1976

♫ Hey Whatcha' Say

From the album **Small Corners**

Covered by a small group of artistes, such as 2nd Chapter of Acts, Phil Keaggy and A Band Called David, *Hey Whatcha' Say* was recorded by Cliff Richard for his 1978 ***Small Corners*** album, where it was satisfactorily stopped after three sessions and finalized with overdubs almost two weeks later. EMI France decided to release ***Why Should the Devil Have All the Good Music?*** in early 1978 as a single, and *Hey Whatcha' Say* was picked as the B-side.
The frenetic pace is driven by the bass, piano and the percussion and it creates an urgency that is matched in Cliff's almost breathy approach to the song that talks of the feeling of letting God into his life. The chorus takes a moment to gather the thoughts with a slower tempo, but this is soon abandoned as the guitar solo leads into the faster next verse.

Track Specification
Composed by Annie Herring, Matthew Ward and Nelly Ward

Musicians

Brian Bennett	drums, percussion
Terry Britten	guitar
Stuart Calver	backing vocals
Bryn Haworth	guitar
John Perry	backing vocals
Cliff Richard	vocals
Tony Rivers	backing vocals
Alan Tarney	bass
Graham Todd	keyboards

Recording Details

Producer	Cliff Richard
Engineered by	Tony Clark and Haydn Bendall
Recording location	Abbey Road Studio 3, St. John's Wood, London
Recording date	19th and 31st January 1977

♫ High Class Baby

2nd UK single

In an era when British music acts were rarely encouraged to record any original material, preferring to draw on the perceived importance and success of American tunes as covers, it is quite remarkable that Cliff Richard and the Drifters were allowed to record songs written by a member of the band. In part, this was perhaps due to the unexpected and phenomenal success of ***Move It***, which had previously reached number two in the UK singles chart. And so it fell to the writer of that song, the Drifters' guitarist Ian Samwell, to provide not only the A-side to the next single, *High Class Baby*, but also its flip-side ***My Feet Hit the Ground***.
The problem with this and the next few songs that were recorded and issued as B-sides or main singles was that *Move It* proved to a happy accident, rather than an opening into a well of British rock and roll creativity. That's not to suggest that *High Class Baby* and other tracks were bad particularly, but that the writers such as Samwell had no experience at writing rock and roll tunes and, largely, they were heavily influenced by the music being issued by Elvis Presley, Jerry Lee Lewis, Chuck Berry and others from the other side of the Atlantic. Indeed, Cliff has mentioned in a number of interviews that he thinks his subsequent singles after *Move It* were not as good as they could have been because they were recording at a time when British acts were forced into doing covers, or with songwriters employed specifically for that task. To have a member of the act writing the material was actually quite strange for the times.
Nevertheless, *High Class Baby* was recorded along with its B-side in a session just over two months after the first Cliff single was released. As with *Move It*, it is likely that Norrie Paramor wanted to play safe and use session musicians such as Ernie Shears and Frank Clarke. However, records of those playing in the session are unavailable other than for Cliff's

vocals. The song is a straightforward piece of rock and roll that employed Samwell's propensity to drive the rhythm with a restated bass note, either on instruments or using vocals, as is the case here where the backing singers repeat the song title in each chorus. The opening verse is clearly influenced by Elvis Presley and Little Richard with a slow introduction vocal mirrored by the bass guitar before it picks up speed and the song races through to the end.

The lyrics attempt to show the disparity between the members of the class system that was alive and well still at the end of the fifties. It is a quite illuminating social commentary in its right with mention of champagne and caviar and other items unobtainable then by the general populace as being the differentiators of the various echelons of class in Britain. Although Cliff asserts that he likes the girl, it is clear that she is too 'high class' for him with his preference to be involved in dancing and rocking to a rock and roll band – something that the upper classes considered to be very common.

The single was issued on the Columbia label in two formats: seven-inch single (catalogue number 45-DB 4203) and ten-inch 78 r.p.m. (catalogue number DB 4203). Released in November 1958, *High Class Baby* enjoyed a strong UK chart run, eventually settling at the highest position of number seven and staying in the singles chart for a relatively short period of ten weeks. In 1980, a compilation of Cliff's early rock and roll output was released called *Rock On with Cliff* and this was the first time that *High Class Baby* (in mono) and its flip-side had been issued since the single was deleted after its chart run. It has since appeared on anthologies covering Cliff's early rock and roll period with different versions issued as occasional rarities. For Cliff's 100th single (***The Best of Me***), the twelve-inch and CD single versions of the release included this track (perhaps incongruously given the import of the achievement being celebrated by the main release) as a bonus.

Track Specification
Composed by Ian Samwell

Musicians

Cliff Richard	vocals
Unknown	guitar
Unknown	bass
Unknown	drums, percussion
Unknown	male backing vocals

Recording Details

Producer	Norrie Paramor
Engineered by	Malcolm Addey
Recording location	Abbey Road Studio 2, St. John's Wood, London
Recording date	3rd October 1958

♬ Higher Ground

From the albums **Help It Along** *and* **Japan Tour '74**

A traditional religious song, *Higher Ground* was arranged by producer David MacKay for Cliff Richard to perform at his quasi-concerts at the Morgan Studios based in London. *Higher Ground* was one of seventeen songs recorded in a marathon seven sessions over three days, one of thirteen songs eventually issued and one of twelve to be released on the track listing of ***Help It Along***, which was sold in aid of the Tear Fund charity.

The piano introduction leads into Cliff's lead vocals before the orchestra and the other instruments join him. Slowly, the musical tension is built up and by the second verse, there is an evangelical tinge to proceedings with a gospel-like backing vocals added into the mix, before it returns to the quietness of the beginning.

Added to his set list in Japan in 1974 and issued on the associated live album, the build-up of instrumentation and exquisite musical tension follows that of the original album. Cliff employs a vibrato that he has not used to any great degree on any of the earlier tracks and it is well-served on this song, imbuing the lyrics with further emotion.

Track Specification
Composed by Traditional

1. Help It Along

Musicians

Terry Britten	guitar
Barrie Guard	arranger, conductor, percussion
Cliff Hall	keyboards
Jean Hawker	backing vocals
Anna Peacock	backing vocals
Kevin Peek	guitar
Cliff Richard	vocals
Trevor Spencer	drums, percussion
Alan Tarney	bass
Unknown	orchestra

Recording Details

Producer	David MacKay
Engineered by	Roger Quested
Recording location	Morgan Studios, London
Recording date	24th, 25th and 26th September 1973

2. Japan Tour '74

Musicians

Barrie Guard	arranger, conductor, electric piano
Cliff Hall	piano
Brian Lewis	guitar
Kevin Peak	acoustic guitar
Cliff Richard	vocals
Shambles Symphonet	orchestra
Trevor Spencer	drums, percussion
Alan Tarney	bass
Bruce Welch	rhythm guitar

Recording Details

Producer	Toshiba EMI (no individual detailed)
Engineered by	Toshiba EMI (no individual detailed)
Recording location	Shinjuku Koseinenkin, Tokyo, Japan
Recording date	7th-8th October 1974

♫ High 'n' Dry

B-side of **Congratulations**

For each Saturday night over six weeks in the early part of 1968, Cliff Richard sang one of the contender songs for the UK entry to that year's Eurovision Song Contest which was to be held on 6th April at the Royal Albert Hall. With a public vote to choose the winner, *High 'n' Dry* received 12.4% of the votes but still came second to ***Congratulations***, which polled a massive 69%. Written by Roger Cook and Roger Greenaway, who contemporaneously performed as popular duo David and Jonathan, *High 'n' Dry* is actually a rather spiteful piece with the lyrics laughing at a former lover's romantic demise all set to a jaunty tune. As was the custom, the song that came second was chosen as the B-side of the winner, *High 'n' Dry* was paired with *Congratulations*, and gave Cliff his first number one for three years. The song has only been released in mono format with the exception of the stereo version appearing on the German 1968 compilation *Congratulations und 13 Weitere Hits*, and the mono version was made more widely available in 2007 when it was included as a bonus track on the remastered ***Established 1958*** album. The session featured Shadows Bruce Welch and Hank Marvin on backing vocals and bassist John Paul Jones, who would go on to form Led Zeppelin later in that same year.
The undisputed winner was *Congratulations*, but on first listen there is definitely much to commend *High 'n' Dry*, which also uses the same stuttering orchestral introduction. However, although it is sung in an upbeat and happy-go-lucky way, it is actually a quite mean-spirited and gloating song that tells the story of how an ex-lover who treated him badly and then she has the same treatment directed at her by another man. The lyrics revel in her discomfort and the fact that she has been left high and dry and can only be left to cry. The juxtaposition of the bouncy accompaniment and the lyrics is strange and, for this, it is good that it didn't win. Cliff is joined by Bruce and Hank (and a few of the Mike Sammes Singers), while the classic ending, it sounds like a pure Shadows vocal composition helped along by their inclusion.

Track Specification
Composed by Roger Cook and Roger Greenaway
Musicians

Bernard Ebbinghouse Orchestra	orchestra
Bernard Ebbinghouse	conductor
John Paul Jones	bass
Hank Marvin	backing vocals
Mike Sammes Singers	backing vocals
Norrie Paramor	arranger
Cliff Richard	vocals
Bruce Welch	backing vocals

Recording Details

Producer	Norrie Paramor
Engineered by	Peter Vince
Recording location	Abbey Road Studio 2, St. John's Wood, London
Recording date	2nd February 1968

♫ High School Confidential

From the album **Oh Boy!**

Written for the film of the same name, released by Republic Pictures, *High School Confidential* was composed and performed by Jerry Lee Lewis at the start and end of the film during the titles, while sitting on the back of a truck flatbed. It became his third hit single in 1958 but is not one of his most famous releases; at least, certainly not in the UK.
Nevertheless, because it was Lewis and his star was in the ascendency in the late fifties, it made sense that one of his songs would be used in the *Oh Boy!* television show repertoire. Because of the success of the show, it was decided that an official album should be released. Cliff Richard became an *Oh Boy!* regular, often performing covers and some original material.
The backing track and Cliff's vocals were recorded on separate days and, instead of using the Drifters as his backing, the musicians performing were from the Oh Boy! Band. There is no record of who the individual players are, however, and so will be highlighted as unknown in this entry.
The energy that Cliff produces is evident, even if he hasn't got the dangerous nature that Lewis brought to a performance. There is a competent uncredited piano sequence in the middle eight replicating some of Lewis's most familiar moves and, although the album was re-released in the late seventies, it wasn't until the issue of the rarities album *The Rock and Roll Years 1958-1963* that it saw release in digital format.

Track Specification
Composed by Jerry Lee Lewis and Ron Hargrave
Musicians

Oh Boy! Band	guitars, stand-up bass, piano, drums, percussion
Cliff Richard	vocals

Recording Details

Producer	Harry Robinson (backing track) and Norrie Paramor (vocals)
Engineered by	Norman Newell (backing track) and Malcolm Addey (vocals)
Recording location	Abbey Road Studio 2, St. John's Wood, London
Recording date	19th October 1958 (backing track) and 21st October 1958 (vocals)

♫ His Land

From the album **His Land** *(two different tracks)*

Following on from the parochial success of his first film for the Billy Graham Organisation, ***Two a Penny***, Cliff Richard was invited to take part in the 1970 film ***His Land***, which has not had wide release since it is more of a documentary than it is a plot-filled action film. The tracks involving Cliff were recorded in Israel, where the film was also shot on location, while the orchestra track was recorded at the Hollywood studios of Capitol Records. The celebratory collation of Cliff's life, ***...And They Said It Wouldn't Last! (My 50 Years in Music)***, includes the film's title track, stating that it was added to represent the less watched films from his career and suggesting that the track chosen was the opening song but this is an error, since it is actually the reprise performed later in the film, which is shorter.

The opening sequence of the film has Cliff on a viewing promenade high above an Israeli city. He lifts kids up to the rail, interacts with other spectators who are gathered at the viewing promontory or looking through the tourist telescope at the city below. The action moves to a street scene with Cliff walking along, back to the promontory, on to a ship in the harbour, atop a ruined building and finally at the shore's edge, which are all highly powerful visuals matched against the adulatory lyrics of the song. The foot-tapping nature of the song is not necessarily what is considered appropriate for a religious song but it corresponds perfectly what is being sung in the lyrics. Of course, Cliff is perfect in his performance and the ensemble piece sounds very much like the expected opening number to the archetypal film score.

A reprise of the film's opening title track that Cliff made with the Billy Graham Organisation, the second version of *His Land* is shorter than the first with the chorus, a unique verse not used in the first version followed by another chorus and this subsequent recording opened up the second side of the original vinyl version of the album. The track was recorded some time in late 1969 (records are not clear as to exact dates for any of the songs on the soundtrack) with Cliff overdubbing his vocals on an orchestral track already recorded at the Capitol Records studios in California.

The shorter version starts with an aerial view across Jerusalem, cutting to Cliff in a vineyard, where he is carrying a crate of grapes as the song builds up to its climactic crescendo. As with the first instance, it is a straight copy of the ebullient opening section of the song before it slows down and ending on a sustained chord. Although the versions are very similar in construction and arrangement, they are given two separate entries in this book because of the addition of the extra verse in the second track.

Track Specification
Composed by Ralph Carmichael

1. His Land (first track)

Musicians		*Recording Details*	
Ralph Carmichael	arranger, conductor	Producer	Lee Gillette
Ralph Carmichael Chorus	chorus	Engineered by	Unknown
Ralph Carmichael Orchestra	orchestra	Recording location	Capitol Records, Hollywood, USA (orchestra) and Israel (vocals)
Cliff Richard	vocals	Recording date	Late 1969

2. His Land (sixth track reprise)

Musicians		*Recording Details*	
Ralph Carmichael	arranger, conductor	Producer	Lee Gillette
Ralph Carmichael Chorus	chorus	Engineered by	Unknown
Ralph Carmichael Orchestra	orchestra	Recording location	Capitol Records, Hollywood, USA (orchestra) and Israel (vocals)
Cliff Richard	vocals	Recording date	Late 1969

♫ His Latest Flame

From the album **Japan Tour '74**

His Latest Flame was one of twenty-five songs written by the writing team of Doc Pomus and Mort Shuman for Elvis Presley. Reaching number four in the American charts and, as a double A-side with *Little Sister*, number one in the UK, under its correct title of *(Marie's the Name) His Latest Flame*. It has been covered by a number of artists across different genres, including Del Shannon, The Smiths, the Scorpions and Brian May among others.

Cliff Richard regularly performed songs in concert that were popular or resonated in some other way but that he had never recorded in the studio – in the case of the 1974 tour of Japan, this included *His Latest Flame* as part of the ***Rock Medley*** that honoured the musicians that Cliff admired: *His Latest Flame*, ***Chantilly Lace, Bony Maronie, Do You Wanna Dance?, Crocodile Rock*** and *Do You Wanna Dance?* repeated to complete the medley. The foot-tapping pace of the band is led by the percussion and running bass with a strong electric guitar playing staccato chords. Eschewing the predilection of Presley to throttle back and shake his voice as he performed, the song suits Cliff's voice well and, in many respects, it is unfortunate for fans that he has never recorded a studio version.

Track Specification
Composed by Doc Pomus and Mort Shuman

Musicians		*Recording Details*	
Cliff Hall	piano	Producer	Toshiba EMI (no individual detailed)
Brian Lewis	guitar	Engineered by	Toshiba EMI (no individual detailed)
Kevin Peak	acoustic guitar	Recording location	Shinjuku Koseinenkin, Tokyo, Japan
Cliff Richard	vocals	Recording date	7th–8th October 1974
Trevor Spencer	drums, percussion		
Alan Tarney	bass		
Bruce Welch	rhythm guitar		

♫ Hit Medley (1)
From the album **Cliff "Live" in Japan '72**

For most of Cliff's tours, particularly in the early days, he often created a medley or two of his familiar songs, hits or songs that had some particular meaning to him that he hadn't sung elsewhere in the set list. For his 1972 tour of the Far East with the Shadows, Olivia Newton-John and Pat Carroll, he created a medley of the songs that were popular releases originally involving the Shadows backing him, which was then released as *Hit Medley* on the live album, ***Cliff "Live" in Japan '72***:

a) ***Living Doll***
b) ***Bachelor Boy***
c) ***The Young Ones***

The entries for those songs carry the information on the recording details and musicians.

♫ Hit Medley (2)
From the album **Japan Tour '74**

In the sixties and seventies, in particular, Cliff regularly performed medleys of his familiar songs. For his 1974 tour of Japan, he created a medley of the songs that were popular releases, which was released on the live album ***Japan Tour '74***:

a) ***Congratulations***
b) ***In the Country***
c) ***Dancing Shoes***
d) ***The Day I Met Marie***
e) ***On the Beach***
f) ***Sing a Song of Freedom***

The entries for those songs carry the information on the recording details and musicians.

♫ Hold On (1)
B-side of **Wired for Sound**

Recorded during part of the sessions for Cliff Richard's ***I'm No Hero*** album, *Hold On* was not issued on the album, in spite of the track listing's shortness. Indeed, although two other non-album tracks were issued as the B-sides for singles, *Hold On* was held back for a year until it was used as the B-side for the first and eponymous single from the next album project, ***Wired for Sound***. It remained a relative rarity until it was included as a bonus track on the 2001 reissue of ***Wired for Sound***. Cliff's lead vocals are given a lot of reverberation so that the echo is a beat behind the main vocal. Cliff and Tarney provide the backing vocals together, while the dominant instrumentation relies on the synthesiser and an arpeggiated guitar.

Track Specification
Composed by Alan Tarney

Musicians		*Recording Details*	
Michael Boddicker	synthesiser	Producer	Alan Tarney
Nick Glennie-Smith	synthesiser	Engineered by	Ashley Howe
Cliff Richard	vocals, backing vocals	Recording location	Riverside Studios, London
Trevor Spencer	drums, percussion	Recording date	12th May-27th June 1980
Alan Tarney	arranger, backing vocals, guitar, bass		

♫ Hold On (2)
From the album **Silver**

Not to be confused with the B-side of ***Wired for Sound***, this track also titled *Hold On* is a completely different song. A little confusingly, though, both songs were recorded within three years of each other. Written by one of Cliff Richard's most prolific songwriters, Terry Britten, it was arranged by producer Craig Pruess for the twenty-fifth anniversary album, ***Silver***, which was the first of his albums to be simultaneously released in CD format alongside the traditional vinyl.

A cool rhythm is initiated on the keyboards as the sparse accompaniment greets Cliff's introductory vocal line. It then slowly builds up to the chorus, which breaks open with Cliff providing his own backing vocal section accompanied by the percussion and a tinkling synthesiser. In the middle eight, there is a saxophone solo by seasoned session man Mel Collins, before it quietens down to the final chorus section, which completes with a perfect harmonized rallentando.

Track Specification
Composed by Terry Britten and Sue Shifrin

Musicians		*Recording Details*	
Mel Collins	saxophone	Producer	Craig Pruess
Graham Jarvis	drums, percussion	Engineered by	Keith Bessey
Craig Pruess	arranger, keyboards, synthesiser	Recording location	Strawberry Studios South, Surrey
Cliff Richard	vocals, backing vocals	Recording date	19th May 1983, 3rd June 1983 and/or 16th June 1983

♫ Hold Us Together

From the album **Cliff Richard - The Album**

The second of two tracks written by Cliff Richard and Paul Moessl, *Hold Us Together* was the first track to be completed for the ***Cliff Richard – The Album*** project. The track was subsequently released on the track listing of the compilation of Cliff's compositions, ***My Songs***.

The fluttering synthesiser keyboards and the drumbeat keep the rhythm of this love song moving ever onwards. The backing vocals are augmented by the female contingent in addition to Cliff's own backing.

Track Specification

Composed by Cliff Richard and Paul Moessl

Musicians

John Bradbury	violin
John Clark	guitar
Richard Hewson	arranger, conductor
Peter Howarth	backing vocals
Peter May	drums, percussion
Paul Moessl	arranger, drum programming, keyboards
Keith Murrell	backing vocals
Tessa Niles	backing vocals
Cliff Richard	vocals, backing vocals
Steve Stroud	bass
Unknown	orchestra (other strings)
Judith Walmsley	backing vocals
David Woodcock	violin

Recording Details

Producer	Paul Moessl and Cliff Richard
Engineered by	Gerry Kitchingham and Ben Robbins
Recording location	R. G. Jones Studios, Wimbledon, London
Recording date	25th-31st May 1992, 8th June 1992 (backing track) and 25th May 1992 (vocals)

♫ Holly and the Ivy, The

From the EP **Christmas EP**

One of the most favourite of Christmas songs, *The Holly and the Ivy* is a carol that has far fewer Christian messages than most, since it has references to nature and the season throughout rather than talking of the redemption of man through the birth of Christ. The holly and ivy motifs in the carol are the most frequently used items in Christmas decorations through the years since the fifteenth century thereby cementing the leaves firmly in the mind when talking about the celebratory feast. In transition to the Christian festivities, it refers back to the prior pagan festival, where holly was revered by druids.

Cliff Richard completed his ***Carol Singers*** EP sessions with *The Holly and the Ivy* but initially it remained unissued as a track. Recorded *a capella* with a Christian group of music teachers calling themselves the Mastersingers providing harmonies to Cliff's lead vocal, *The Holly and the Ivy* was completed in eight takes, the only song with complete takes in the final edit; all of the other carols were spliced from multiple takes. Although a mono version would have been recorded, it was finally released only in stereo on 1991's ***Christmas EP*** that was issued alongside the single release of ***We Should Be Together***. It was later reissued, again in stereo format only, on the rarity compilation ***...And They Said It Wouldn't Last! (My 50 Years in Music)*** in 2008.

Singing *a capella* is notoriously difficult as pitching problems cannot be covered by instrumentation. But Cliff and the Mastersingers do a superlative job of keeping everything in tune, despite some complex harmonies during the verses. The exposure of Cliff's pure vocal is a brilliant listening experience and shows off his versatility as a musical performer.

Track Specification

Composed by Traditional

Musicians

Mastersingers:	backing vocals
John Horrex	
Geoffrey Keating	
George Pratt	
Michael Warrington	
Cliff Richard	vocals

Recording Details

Producer	Norrie Paramor
Engineered by	Peter Vince and John Barrett
Recording location	Abbey Road Studio 2, St. John's Wood, London
Recording date	10th September 1967

♫ Home

From the film soundtrack album of **Wonderful Life**

With the seven friends – Johnny (Cliff Richard), Jerry (Melvyn Hayes), Edward (Richard O'Sullivan) and the four unnamed musicians (the Shadows) – cast adrift for causing a cruise liner making it run aground, they reach land and desperately try to find work on the many boats in the port but their captain has already spread the word and no-one wants to give them a job. A customer at the café suggests that they might wish to go in search of bananas to pick and sell and so they embark on a journey across endless desert. Suddenly, Jerry things that he can hear the fog-horn of a ship and races off in that direction claiming he can see it. Eventually, Johnny and Edward confirm that they can see this mirage too and that they are feeling homesick. The film switches to the deck of a small boat motoring up the grey waters of the River Thames and they perform a dance routine with landmark monuments such as the Battersea Power Station and the Houses of Parliament in the background. The lyrics mention quintessentially English things such as fish and chips eaten out of

newspaper, the London tube, dancing until the mods and rockers square up to a fight (very much in the news at the time), a cockney knees-up and so on. As they reach the climax of the song, they fall backwards as if into the river but then the scene cuts back to the desert as the threesome roll backwards down the sand-dunes.
Unusually, Richard O'Sullivan and Melvyn Hayes perform the dance routine with Cliff Richard – the earlier films tended to have them sitting or standing in the background or stiffly moving about with the music – and, while Cliff is clearly a natural dancer, both of the others do a creditable job in supporting him.
One of four tracks recorded for the soundtrack at the session, the same (unknown) take and edit were used for the mono and stereo recordings but with different mixes for the purpose of the audio channels. The soundtrack version was also included on the ***Hits from Wonderful Life*** EP listing. The film version was probably recorded in the first three months of 1964, although the location and personnel are unknown, and it has yet to be released in any other commercial format. There are several differences between these two recordings: there are extended orchestral sequences, some lyric changes and the introduction is different; in addition, of course, the film version incorporates both Melvyn Hayes and Richard O'Sullivan supporting Cliff's lead vocals.
Members of the Mike Sammes Singers sing the parts that Hayes and O'Sullivan played in the film version and they are occasionally not in unison nor are they completely in time. The song improves immeasurably when Cliff is given the chance to take the lead but this is, unfortunately, not that often.

Track Specification
Composed by Peter Myers and Ronald Cass

Musicians

Associated British Studio Orchestra	orchestra
Stanley Black	conductor
Mike Sammes Singers	backing vocals
Cliff Richard	vocals

Recording Details

Producer	Norrie Paramor
Engineered by	Malcolm Addey
Recording location	Abbey Road Studio 2, St. John's Wood, London
Recording date	22nd April 1964

♫ Homeward Bound

From the album **Don't Stop Me Now!**

Popular myth tells the story that *Homeward Bound* was written by Paul Simon at Widnes railway station in Cheshire while travelling around England in 1965. While the basics of the story are true, Simon has stated that he can't remember exactly where he was other than it was a station in the north of England. But myth has now been established as popular music folklore and so it prevails as Widnes. This paean to homesickness describes Simon's longing for his then girlfriend and also America. He and his partner Art Garfunkel recorded *Homeward Bound* in December 1965 and it was subsequently released as their first single, reaching number nine in April 1966. As was the procedure at the time, as soon as a song was issued there was a rush to cover it; however, the Quiet Five only managed to get to forty-four a few months later in April. Several other artists have covered *Homeward Bound* including Peter and Gordon, Cher, the King's Singers, Richard Barnes, Petula Clark, Ronan Keating, Glen Campbell, Willie Nelson and Mel Tormé.
Cliff Richard's version was included on his album ***Don't Stop Me Now!***, where it closed the first side of the original vinyl. Recorded at a session in October 1966 (in between other sessions for the ***Cinderella*** cast recording), it was the first of four songs to be completed. Splicing takes one and seven together, the final edit was used for both mono and stereo recordings. The song starts with a desolate arpeggiated string section accompanied by a mournful brass solo. As Cliff enters the chorus, the pace picks up with the optimism driven by of the thought of reaching home. There is an occasional backing vocal, which sounds like Hank Marvin or possibly Cliff himself providing his own backing but this is inconclusive.

Track Specification
Composed by Paul Simon

Musicians

Mike Leander Orchestra	orchestra
Mike Leander	arranger, conductor
Cliff Richard	vocals
Unknown	backing vocals

Recording Details

Producer	Norrie Paramor
Engineered by	Peter Vincent and Richard Lush
Recording location	Abbey Road Studio 2, St. John's Wood, London
Recording date	19th October 1966

♫ (There's a) Honky Tonk Angel

64th UK single *and from the album* **...And They Said It Wouldn't Last! (My 50 Years in Music)**

For Cliff Richard's sixty-fourth UK single, it was Cliff who orchestrated his third chart flop and second single flop in a row (after ***It's Only Me You've Left Behind***), because *(There's a) Honky Tonk Angel* was one of his most controversial recordings ever. Some cynics suggest that Cliff knew what the subject matter was all about – including Bruce Welch (one of the producers of the song) in a number of interviews – and that it was merely a ploy to get his name into the papers and on television, given that his career seemed to be floundering at the time, if taken purely on comparative chart success.
In a number of interviews at the time, Cliff confirmed that he didn't know what a honky tonk was, other than it being something American where you could by a drink (rather than the seedy dives they really are), nor that a honky tonk angel was, by association, a prostitute working the bars for punters. Believing the lyrics to be a lovely story about a young American woman with a penchant for country music, Cliff says that he was alerted to the true meaning while in America

by one of his fans. Being a committed Christian, he didn't want to be seen to be endorsing prostitution, even though it was pointed out that several biblical tracts confirmed that it was acceptable to acknowledge their existence. The problem for Cliff was that the media always strained to find anything about this clean-living musician (often an oxymoron) that they fell on this story with glee. Cliff then took steps to ensure the single was pulled and demanded that the advance copies be returned from radio stations and from that point refused to sing the song. Many might say that no-one could be so astonishingly naïve but the media dynamite and furore that would have ensued, barracking him for Christian beliefs and singing the song, however ignorant this opinion might be, made it the only option. It did, however, achieve what the cynics were also deriding him for: there was a frisson of excitement engendered about Cliff's name once again.
Recorded by Elvis Presley and a few country singers in the US, Cliff's version was issued as a single, backed with ***Wouldn't You Know It (Got Myself a Girl)***, on the EMI label (catalogue number EMI 2344) on 5th September 1975. Because of the decision to pull the single, only around one thousand copies were sold (now a high priced rarity in its original format) and therefore guaranteed that *(There's a) Honky Tonk Angel* was a chart flop. Cliff was true to his word and has never performed it since. Talking heads on documentaries still deride him and make sly references to his naïvety and it would have been consigned to history had it not been remastered, along with its B-side, and reissued on the 2001 release of ***I'm Nearly Famous*** as a bonus track. A different take, with more of a country feel than even the original was issued on the rarities CD of the celebratory ***...And They Said It Wouldn't Last! (My 50 Years in Music)*** boxed set. Time heals.
Although there is a haunting steel guitar playing underneath the performance, the prominent instruments are the rhythm steel-string guitar, the piano and the swooping strings. But what makes this song stand out particularly is the arrangement of the backing vocals, for which Bruce particularly should be noted for his ear for vocal harmony and it is this that he brought to Cliff's work during his time as producer.

Track Specification
Composed by Troy Seals and Denny Rice

1. Single
Musicians

Terry Britten	backing vocals, guitar
Nick Ingman	arranger, conductor
Dave MacRae	piano
Nick Ingman Orchestra	orchestra
Cliff Richard	vocals, backing vocals
Trevor Spencer	drums, percussion
Alan Tarney	backing vocals, bass

Recording Details

Producer	Hank Marvin, Bruce Welch and John Farrar
Engineered by	Roger Quested
Recording location	Morgan Studios, London
Recording date	20th June 1974

2. ...And They Said It Wouldn't Last! (My 50 Years in Music)
Musicians

Terry Britten	backing vocals, guitar
Nick Ingman	arranger, conductor
Dave MacRae	piano
Nick Ingman Orchestra	orchestra
Cliff Richard	vocals
Trevor Spencer	drums, percussion
Alan Tarney	backing vocals, bass

Recording Details

Producer	Hank Marvin, Bruce Welch and John Farrar
Engineered by	Roger Quested
Recording location	Morgan Studios, London
Recording date	20th June 1974

♫ Hope, Faith and You
B-side of **The Miracle**

Not released in any other format, *Hope, Faith and You,* recorded after the sessions for the ***Real as I Wanna Be*** album by Cliff Richard, was chosen as a B-side item for the first disc of the dual CD release of the second and final single to be released from the project, ***The Miracle***. There is no information on the musicians or the recording location available.
The introduction features a lamenting piano before Cliff's vocal is brought in, with a large amount of reverberating echo behind it. There is an uncredited string section that plays in support that adds a lush set of harmonies underneath the impassioned lyrics performed by Cliff.

Track Specification
Composed by Phil Campbell
Musicians

Cliff Richard	vocals
Unknown	piano
Unknown	string orchestra

Recording Details

Producer	Keith Bessey
Engineered by	Keith Bessey
Recording location	Unknown
Recording date	1998

♫ Hot Shot
76th UK single *and from the album* **My Kinda Life**

The product of the fertile collaboration between Terry Britten and B. A. Robertson, *Hot Shot* was recorded in two parts, with the backing track laid down in Paris and the vocal overdubs back in the English studios. Because of the huge success of Cliff Richard's prior single ***We Don't Talk Anymore***, the follow-up was always going to be hard and judged much more harshly against it. *Hot Shot* was backed with ***Walking in the Light***, a non-album track, and released as a single on the EMI label (catalogue number EMI 5003) on 19th October 1979, and reached number forty-six in the UK singles charts. The track was also featured on the track listing of ***Rock 'n' Roll Juvenile***.

The driving beat is created by the saxophone ensemble and the song fits Cliff's vocals well. He supplies his own backing vocals with help from co-producer Britten and Madeleine Bell, who provides a different dimension to the vocal arrangement, which drops into three-four time in the middle eight before resuming the common time of the main piece. The driving beat of the song makes it a suitable song for the open road – a homegrown version of the American road songs.

Cliff revisited the song for a rearrangement to be included on the ***My Kinda Life*** album, which took the original track and embellished it with more electronic instrumentation and guitar work. The tempo is also very slightly slower, although this may be unintentional and the product of the process. There is also a noticeable guitar solo added during the instrumental bridge, while the track fades ten seconds or so later than the original, although this may, too, be a result of the repackaging rather than intention for the new album.

Track Specification
Composed by Terry Britten and B. A. Robertson

1. *Single*

Musicians

Madeleine Bell	backing vocals
Terry Britten	backing vocals, guitar
Mel Collins	saxophone
Martin Drover	saxophone
Herbie Flowers	bass
Graham Jarvis	drums, percussion
Bill Livesy	keyboards
Chris Mercer	saxophone
Cliff Richard	vocals, backing vocals

Recording Details

Producer	Cliff Richard and Terry Britten
Engineered by	Tony Clark and Haydn Bendall
Recording location	Pathé Marconi, Paris, France (backing track) and Abbey Road Studio, St. John's Wood, London (vocals)
Recording date	7th-12th January 1979 (backing track) and 17th February 1979 (vocals)

2. *My Kinda Life*

Musicians

John Clark	guitar
Madeleine Bell	backing vocals
Terry Britten	backing vocals, guitar
Mel Collins	saxophone
Martin Drover	saxophone
Herbie Flowers	bass
Graham Jarvis	drums, percussion
Bill Livesy	keyboards
Chris Mercer	saxophone
Paul Moessl	drum sequencing, synthesisers
Cliff Richard	vocals, backing vocals

Recording Details

Producer	Cliff Richard and Terry Britten (original track) and Cliff Richard and Paul Moessl (new instrumentation)
Engineered by	Tony Clark and Haydn Bendall (original track) and Gerry Kitchingham and Ben Robbins (new instrumentation)
Recording location	Pathé Marconi, Paris, France (backing track) and Abbey Road Studio, St. John's Wood, London (vocals) and R. G. Jones Studios, Wimbledon, London (new instrumentation)
Recording date	7th-12th January 1979 (backing track) and 17th February 1979 (vocals) and 20th-23rd April 1992 (new instrumentation)

♫ Hound Dog

Unreleased live track

Of course, *Hound Dog* is one of the songs that are forever associated with the rip-roaring and raucous vocal version created by Elvis Presley. Written by the perennially golden pairing of Leiber and Stoller, it was originally recorded by the largely unfamiliar Willie Mae 'Big Mama' Thornton back in 1952, before Presley's version became the best-known on its release in July 1956. It went on to top the US singles charts and was given a release too in Britain. It has been covered by such luminaries as Robert Palmer, Eric Clapton, The Everly Brothers, Jeff Beck and James Taylor.

In the August of 1958, Cliff Richard and the Drifters, which consisted of Cliff, Terry Smart and Ian Samwell in a pared-down line-up, took up a short residency at the Butlin's Holiday Camp based at Clacton-on-Sea. Here they performed the standard covers that were expected of rock and roll outfits performing in Britain at the time.

On one of the nights, a man by the name of Stan Edwards recorded their show on a two-track tape machine. While some of the recordings made it on to the rarities retrospective, ***The Rock 'n' Roll Years 1958-1963***, others were in too poor a condition for use commercially. This was the fate of *Hound Dog* and a number of other tracks recorded that night.

Track Specification
Composed by Jerry Leiber and Mike Stoller

Musicians

Cliff Richard	vocals, guitar
Ian Samwell	guitar
Terry Smart	drums, percussion

Recording Details

Producer	Unknown
Engineered by	Stan Edwards
Recording location	Rock 'n' Roll Ballroom, Butlin's Holiday Camp, Clacton-on-Sea, Essex
Recording date	August 1958

♫ House without Windows
From the album **Cliff Richard**

Recorded by Roy Orbison, the Bee Gees and Gene Pitney, *House without Windows* was one of five songs to be completed at the final Cliff Richard session before he travelled to Nashville and New York in the summer of 1964. The same (unknown) take and edit were used for the mono and stereo recordings but with different mixes for the separated channels.

The drama of the track is underpinned by the grumbling bass and piano, matched with the militaristic snare drum as Cliff moves through the key changes and then reverting back to the original pace and arrangement of the chord structure. This type of song is perfect for his voice since Cliff is able to provide the necessary light and shade to elicit the importance of song's lyrics.

Track Specification

Composed by Frederick Tobias and Lee Pockriss

Musicians

Mike Sammes Singers	backing vocals
Norrie Paramor Orchestra	orchestra
Norrie Paramor	arranger, conductor
Cliff Richard	vocals

Recording Details

Producer	Norrie Paramor
Engineered by	Malcolm Addey
Recording location	Abbey Road Studio 2, St. John's Wood, London
Recording date	24th July 1964

♫ How Did She Get Here?
From the album **Something's Goin' On**

Cliff Richard travelled to America to record his first album of original material, ***Something's Goin' On***, for over five years and commissioned American songwriters to provide the songs and American personnel to work with him in the studio. One of the resultant songs was the plaintive *How Did She Get Here?*

Synthesised chords usher in the percussion and guitar underpinning Cliff's anguished vocals. In comparison to a few of the other tracks on the album, Cliff's vocals are stretched but he meets the challenge head-on and achieves the feat of making such a vocally difficult song one of simplicity and beauty.

Track Specification

Composed by Darrell Brown, Garry Burr and Steve Mandile

Musicians

Greg Bieck	programming
Trey Bruce	programming
Pat Buchanan	guitar
Lisa Cochran	backing vocals
J. T. Corenflos	guitar
Tony Harrell	keyboards
Wes Hightower	backing vocals
Greg Morrow	drums, percussion
Nashville String Machine	strings
Alison Prestwood	bass
Cliff Richard	vocals, backing vocals
Michael Spriggs	guitar
Kristin Wilkinson	arranger, conductor

Recording Details

Producer	Trey Bruce
Engineered by	David Buchanan (vocals and instruments) and Terry Christian (strings)
Recording location	Omnisound Recording Studios, Nashville, Tennessee, USA, Sound Stage Studios, Nashville, Tennessee, USA and Pocket Studio, Franklin, Tennessee, USA (vocals and instruments) and Starstruck Studios, Nashville, Tennessee, USA (strings)
Recording date	2003-2004

♫ How Long Is Forever?
From the album **32 Minutes and 17 Seconds with Cliff Richard**

The first track on the ***32 Minutes and 17 Seconds with Cliff Richard*** to feature an orchestra rather than the backing of the Shadows, *How Long Is Forever?* was successfully completed within three takes, the final one being used for the mono and stereo edits but with different mixes for the audio channel requirements.

With pizzicato guitar, swooping strings and gentle drums as the principal instrumentation, Cliff Richard's vocals are perfectly matched to the love song that is another message of how much he loves the girl in his life.

Track Specification

Composed by Chas McDevitt and Shirley Douglas

Musicians

Norrie Paramor Orchestra	orchestra
Norrie Paramor	conductor, piano
Cliff Richard	vocals

Recording Details

Producer	Norrie Paramor
Engineered by	Malcolm Addey
Recording location	Abbey Road Studio 2, St. John's Wood, London
Recording date	5th December 1961

♫ How Many Sleeps?
B-side of **Somethin' Is Goin' On**

Recorded at the same time as ***I Cannot Give You My Love***, which was also co-written by Barry Gibb, and featuring one of the last recordings of Maurice Gibb before his death, *How Many Sleeps?* was chosen as the B-side of ***Somethin' Is Goin' On***, the first single from the ***Something's Goin' On*** album sessions, although not included on the listing of that original album. It was later added to track listing of ***For Life***, which was essentially the original album with four additional tracks.

The song title is a question of an easy measure for a child to judge length of time and the song talks of the love Cliff feels for a child he will be leaving for some time. The harmonica and electronic keyboards create a lullaby state as Cliff's gentle vocals come in. The ensemble piece have all the hallmarks of a Barry Gibb production and, with his voice added to Cliff's lead, this song did not derserve to be tucked away on a B-side; it is an extraordinarily beautiful and emotional song.

Track Specification
Composed by Dave Stuart English and Barry Gibb

Musicians

Barry Gibb	backing vocals, rhythm guitar
Maurice Gibb	keyboards
Alan Kendall	guitar
Gustavo Lescano	harmonica
George Perry	bass
Cliff Richard	vocals
Hal Roland	keyboards
Steve Rucker	drums, percussion

Recording Details

Producer	Barry Gibb
Engineered by	John Merchant
Recording location	Middle Ear Studios, Miami, Florida, USA
Recording date	January and November 2003

♫ How to Handle a Woman

Unissued track

For some time, Cliff Richard hadn't recorded any material from the established musicals. However, in 1983, as he was preparing for his twenty-fifth anniversary celebrations and album ***Silver***, he was recording an original single and B-side written by Mike Batt (***Please Don't Fall in Love*** an ***Too Close to Heaven***). At that same session, he tried *How to Handle a Woman*, taken from the 1960 musical *Camelot*, which follows the legend of King Arthur, Guinevere and Sir Lancelot. An introspective song that investigates what needs to be done in order to satisfy a woman – to which the answer is 'love her' – it has been recorded by Batt for his 1989 *Stage Heroes* album, Johnny Mathis, Richard Harris, Perry Como, Richard Burton (the original King Arthur) and Hugo Montenegro. Cliff's version has not been issued and there is scant information on on the performers, apart from Cliff; therefore this entry includes all musicians known to have been present at the sessions.

Track Specification
Composed by Alan Jay Lerner and Frederick Loewe

Musicians

Mike Batt	arranger, conductor, backing vocals, keyboards
Tony Carr	percussion
Ray Cooper	percussion
Graham Jarvis	drums, percussion
Frank McDonald	bass
Alan Park	guitar
Cliff Richard	vocals
Ray Russell	guitar
Unknown:	orchestra
Clive Anstee	'cello
Howard Ball	violin
Michael Brittain	double bass
Michael Cookson	viola
Paul Frowde	violin
Barry Griffiths	violin
Pat Halling	violin
Maurice Isaacs	violin
Raymond Keenlyside	violin
Paul Kegg	'cello
Tom Kelly	clarinet
Laurie Lewis	violin
Geoff Palmer	violin
Anthony Pleeth	'cello
David Randall	violin
Ian Rhodes	violin
Eddie Roberts	violin
John Ronayne	violin
Basil Smart	violin
Jonathan Snowdon	flute
Derek Solomans	violin
Michael Winfield	oboe

Recording Details

Producer	Mike Batt
Engineered by	Steve Churchyard (main track) and Dick Lewsey (strings)
Recording location	AIR Studio 2, London (main track) and C.T.S. Wembley (strings)
Recording date	21st–23rd March 1983 (main track) and 21st March (strings)

♫ How Wonderful to Know

From the album **21 Today**

The first track on the ***21 Today*** album not to include the Shadows but an orchestra and backing singing group, *How Wonderful to Know* was most famously recorded by Teddy Johnson and Pearl Carr, who hit number twenty-three with it in April 1961; Johnson and Carr had famously represented the UK at the 1959 Eurovision Song Contest with *Sing Little Birdie*.

How Wonderful to Know was also recorded by Andy Williams, the Stanley Black Orchestra, Caterina Valente and Max Bygraves, although none had a singles chart hit with the result. The liner notes for all of Cliff's releases featuring this song detail Salvatore D'Esposito and Kermit Goell as co-writers but research has identified that there was a third writer, Domenico Titomanglio, and, although not on those liner notes, he is added to track listing in this book.
The third and final take of this first song from Cliff's orchestral session was used for both the mono and stereo edits, although the audio channels required different mixes.
With a crashing orchestral and vocal introduction, the pace quietens a little as Cliff's vocals come in. This style of song is well-suited to his voice and the arrangement of the tune is masterfully subtle, with swooping strings and understated 'ooh'ing vocals occasionally in the background.

Track Specification
Composed by Salvatore D'Esposito, Kermit Goell and Domenico Titomanglio

Musicians		*Recording Details*	
Mike Sammes Singers	backing vocals	Producer	Norrie Paramor
Norrie Paramor Orchestra	orchestra	Engineered by	Malcolm Addey
Norrie Paramor	arranger, conductor	Recording location	Abbey Road Studio 2, St. John's Wood, London
Cliff Richard	vocals	Recording date	30th January 1961

♫ Human Work of Art

***118th UK single** and from the album* **Cliff Richard - The Album**

With an outward swivel of his hips, *Human Work of Art* was one of the songs that received the greatest rapturous response from the audience when performed in one of Cliff Richard's concerts. A different take and edit from the album were used for the seven-inch single release with slightly different lyrics and instrumentation at the end, which fades earlier in the fourth chorus. The album version was released on the CD single, while the seven-inch version also appeared on the second of the dual CD single release. Backed principally with non-album track ***Ragged***, *Human Work of Art* was the third of five singles to be released from the project and was issued on the EMI label (catalogue number EM 267) on 1st June 1993 and reached number twenty-four in the UK charts. At this time, Cliff's CD singles generally were released in two parts with some different tracks: the first disc (catalogue number CDEMS 267 on 1st June 1993) featured the revisited track from ***My Kinda Life***, ***Never Even Thought***, alongside a live version of ***Move It*** recorded at Wembley Arena during the *Access All Areas* tour in 1992; the second disc (CDEM 267 on the same date) included the seven-inch edit, and the original B-side, *Ragged*, as well ***Free*** from the *Access All Areas* tour, and the revisited version of ***Devil Woman*** from *My Kinda Life*.
Initiated by a saxophone solo, *Human Work of Art* is a sophisticated reverential love song. The beauty of the song is encapsulated in the lyrics, while the accompaniment elevates the enjoyment further. The rhythm in the electronica is kept moving by the running bass line, while the close harmonies of the backing vocals create further elegance and beauty.
In the promotional video for the song, Cliff sings the song in a leather jacket, interspersed with cut shots of Cuban dancers, and all the time being photographed by a number of cameras.

Track Specification
Composed by Mick Leeson and Peter Vale

1. Single

Musicians		*Recording Details*	
Dave Bishop	saxophone	Producer	Paul Moessl and Cliff Richard
John Clark	guitar	Engineered by	Gerry Kitchingham and Ben Robbins
Peter Howarth	backing vocals	Recording location	R. G. Jones Studios, Wimbledon, London
Peter May	drums, percussion	Recording date	25th-31st May 1992, 8th June 1992 (backing track) and 11th July 1992 (vocals)
Paul Moessl	arranger, drum programming, keyboards		
Keith Murrell	backing vocals		
Tessa Niles	backing vocals		
Cliff Richard	vocals, backing vocals		
Steve Stroud	bass		
Judith Walmsley	backing vocals		

2. Cliff Richard - The Album

Musicians		*Recording Details*	
Dave Bishop	saxophone	Producer	Paul Moessl and Cliff Richard
John Clark	guitar	Engineered by	Gerry Kitchingham and Ben Robbins
Peter Howarth	backing vocals	Recording location	R. G. Jones Studios, Wimbledon, London
Peter May	drums, percussion	Recording date	25th-31st May 1992, 8th June 1992 (backing track) and 11th July 1992 (vocals)
Paul Moessl	arranger, drum programming, keyboards		
Keith Murrell	backing vocals		
Tessa Niles	backing vocals		
Cliff Richard	vocals, backing vocals		
Steve Stroud	bass		
Judith Walmsley	backing vocals		

♫ Hunt, The

From the pantomime cast recording album of **Cinderella**

Recorded at one of the several sessions for the ***Cinderella*** pantomime cast recording in November 1966, the eighth and final take was used for the mono and stereo recordings but with different mixes for the needs of the separate audio channels.

With an extraordinary racing rhythm created by Bruce Welch on the guitar, the arrangement and its performance evoke images of running through fields and woodland. Cliff sings the song with his standard ease and it is elevated further when the harmonies appear between him and the singing Shadows. Presumably a sort of fox-hunt, the song ends with the sounding of horns after a lot of spirited yelping by the band to imitate dogs.

Track Specification

Composed by Hank Marvin, Bruce Welch, Brian Bennett and John Rostill

Musicians

Brian Bennett	yelps, drums, percussion
Hank Marvin	backing vocals, yelps, guitar
Mike Sammes Singers	backing vocals
Norrie Paramor Orchestra	orchestra
Norrie Paramor	arranger, conductor
Cliff Richard	vocals
John Rostill	backing vocals, yelps, bass
Bruce Welch	backing vocals, yelps, rhythm guitar

Recording Details

Producer	Norrie Paramor
Engineered by	Peter Vince and Richard Lush
Recording location	Abbey Road Studio 2, St. John's Wood, London
Recording date	11th November 1966

I - I - I - I - I - I - I - I - I - I - I - I - I - I - I - I - I - I - I - I - I - I

♫ I (Who Have Nothing)

From the album **...And They Said It Wouldn't Last! (My 50 Years in Music)**

Originally an Italian song with the title *Uno Dei Tanti*, the dramatic song had English lyrics added by Elvis Presley's principal writing team of Jerry Leiber and Mike Stoller. The best-known British version is probably by Shirley Bassey, who reached number six in October 1963, while fellow Welshman Tom Jones had a number sixteen hit in 1970 (later naming the associated album after the song) and this was followed by Sylvester who hit number forty-six in April 1979. A number of other artists have recorded it, including Katherine Jenkins, Neil Diamond, Roberta Flack, Gladys Knight, Status Quo, Liza Minnelli, Joe Cocker, Petula Clark, the Righteous Brothers and Luther Vandross among many others.
Cliff Richard recorded his version at the Chappell Studios alongside another song, ***'Cause I Believe in Loving***, neither of which was released at the time, until they were both included on the track listing of the 'lost and found' section of the celebratory anthology ***...And They Said It Wouldn't Last! (My 50 Years in Music)*** in 2008. Little detail is available on the session including the other musicians besides Cliff, and will be updated should further research unearth the information.
A classical guitar plays a Spanish rhythm to introduce the song before Cliff takes up his impassioned vocals accompanied by an orchestra. While nowhere as grand as Tom Jones's or Shirley Bassey's interpretation, Cliff imbues the song with a level of drama that perfectly matches the emotion of the song and his vibrato is used to great effect on the sustained notes.

Track Specification
Composed by Carlo Donida and Giulio Radetti; English lyrics by Jerry Leiber and Mike Stoller

Musicians

Cliff Richard	vocals
Unknown	arranger, conductor
Unknown	orchestra

Recording Details

Producer	Norrie Paramor
Engineered by	Unknown
Recording location	Chappell Studios, London
Recording date	5th March 1971

♫ I Ain't Got Time Any More

51st UK single

The rate at which Cliff Richard was issuing singles had slowed significantly by the end of the sixties and *I Ain't Got Time Anymore* was the third and final one to be released in 1970. It also continued the general decline in average chart placings and Cliff, now focusing on his television shows for the BBC, was not perhaps looking at the material that was being released in his name. Written by Mike Leander and Eddie Seago, who had composed his Japanese hit ***Early in the Morning***, *I Ain't Got Time Anymore* was recorded at the same session that produced its B-side, ***Monday Comes Too Soon***, and the previous single ***Goodbye Sam, Hello Samantha***. Released on the Columbia label (catalogue number DB 8708) on 21st August 1970, it reached number twenty-one in the UK. The song was then included on 1972's ***The Best of Cliff Vol. 2***.
Although released in stereo in most markets, a mono version was issued with the same B-side for the Dutch market on the international Columbia label (catalogue number 5C006-04564); this version has never been released in any other format.
A sad introduction is played on a guitar picking out the chords, as Cliff's emotional lead vocal is brought in as he steps down the octave, with a suitably sparse orchestral backing. The chorus features uncredited backing vocalists who underpin the sense of grief he feels at losing the girl of his dreams.

Track Specification
Composed by Mike Leander and Eddie Seago

Musicians

Mike Vickers Orchestra	orchestra
Cliff Richard	vocals
Unknown	backing vocals
Mike Vickers	arranger, conductor

Recording Details

Producer	Norrie Paramor
Engineered by	Unknown
Recording location	Abbey Road Studio 3, St. John's Wood, London
Recording date	12th March 1970

♫ I Can Hear Love

Single by **Garth Hewitt** *and B-side of* **Come Out Fighting** *(Garth Hewitt)*

Continuing his production association with fellow Christian singer, Garth Hewitt, Cliff Richard looked after the recording of Hewitt's 1980 single and B-side. *I Can Hear Love* was written by Alan Tarney, who was instrumental in much of Cliff's eighties recordings, and was backed with ***Come Out Fighting*** when it was issued as a single on the Pye label (catalogue number 7P 172) in 1980 – curiously, it was also released as the B-side of *Come Out Fighting* on the same label. Neither releases managed to enter the charts. Information on exact dates, other musicians and the technical details are unavailable.

The rocking beat of the song is introduced on the bass and drums leading into Hewitt's vocal line. Cliff supplies backing vocals during the choruses and their voices blend well, creating lovely harmonies. The predominant instrument is an insistent synthesiser and this is deployed in the bridges between verses and chorus.

Track Specification
Composed by Alan Tarney

Musicians

Garth Hewitt	vocals
Cliff Richard	backing vocals
Unknown	guitar
Unknown	bass
Unknown	keyboards
Unknown	drums, percussion

Recording Details

Producer	Cliff Richard
Engineered by	Unknown
Recording location	Unknown
Recording date	1980

♬ I Cannot Find a True Love
From the album **Me and My Shadows**

Another Ian Samwell composition, the fourth take of *I Cannot Find a True Love* was chosen for release as the third track on the ***Me and My Shadows*** album. Although the mono and stereo versions of the releases were of the same take, the edit and mixing process foreshortened the mono version by three or four seconds, cutting out some shouting at the end. When ***Gee Whiz It's You*** was released as a single in the March of 1961, this album track was chosen as its B-side and also appeared on the mono version of the ***Me and My Shadows No. 1*** EP.
Initiated by Cliff Richard's *a capella* vocal, it slowly builds up the story of his desperate search for love all around the world (one of Samwell's techniques of mentioning locations in other countries, particularly in the core lands of music). After a rip-roaring verse and chorus, Cliff brings the song to a stop and returns to the slow *a capella* of the introduction before kicking off the pacey verse again. The bass line is swift and the drums and percussion are in greater evidence than was often the case, with Hank Marvin's and Bruce Welch's guitar work rushing the song headlong into its conclusion.

Track Specification
Composed by Ian Samwell

Musicians

Jet Harris	bass
Hank Marvin	guitar
Tony Meehan	drums, percussion
Cliff Richard	vocals
Bruce Welch	rhythm guitar

Recording Details

Producer	Norrie Paramor
Engineered by	Malcolm Addey and Norman Smith (mono) and Peter Bown and Alan Kane (stereo)
Recording location	Abbey Road Studio 2, St. John's Wood, London
Recording date	30th March 1960

♬ I Cannot Give You My Love
135th UK single and *from the album* **Something's Goin' On** *and German promotional single remix*

One of the last recordings with Maurice Gibb on keyboards before his untimely death during a routine hospital operation, *I Cannot Give You My Love* is an archetypal Bee Gees number that also features its co-writer Barry on vocals, guitar and on the production desk. The only song not to be recorded in Tennessee for Cliff Richard's album ***Something's Goin' On***, the track was severely edited from the album version for release as a single: the introduction is shortened by a bar, while the end of the second verse and the instrumentation leading to the third is cut, the third chorus is cut completely, while additional lyrics can be found at the end of the fourth verse and the end is shortened by almost half a minute. Backed with non-album track, ***She's All Mine***, the album version of the main track and the promotional video for ***Somethin' Is Goin' On***, it was issued on the Decca label (catalogue number 475 661-1) on 13th December 2004 to a relatively lukewarm reception from the critics whose only meaningful albeit snide comment in support of the song was that it wasn't another saccharine Christmas-related release. In spite of this, the song achieved a highest chart placing of number thirteen in the UK. A German promotional disc (Edel label, catalogue number 01264385EREP) with the album and single versions was also released, with the track remixed and additional guitar and keyboard overdubbed on the original.
The arrangement of the instrumentation, the vocals, and the composition is pure Barry Gibb and it is one of the strongest songs on Cliff's album. He sings the lyrics with emotional passion and Gibb himself sings along in unison on the chorus. Their voices blend well in this song that is full of regret but blatant honesty of feeling and forces Cliff to expertly use a lot of his vocal range.

Track Specification
Composed by Ashley Gibb and Barry Gibb

1. Single

Musicians

Matt Bonelli	bass
Doug Emery	keyboards
Barry Gibb	backing vocals, rhythm guitar
Maurice Gibb	keyboards
Cliff Richard	vocals

Recording Details

Producer	Barry Gibb
Engineered by	John Merchant
Recording location	Middle Ear Studios, Miami, Florida, USA
Recording date	January and November 2003

2. Something's Goin' On

Musicians		*Recording Details*	
Matt Bonelli	bass	Producer	Barry Gibb
Doug Emery	keyboards	Engineered by	John Merchant
Barry Gibb	backing vocals, rhythm guitar	Recording location	Middle Ear Studios, Miami, Florida, USA
Maurice Gibb	keyboards	Recording date	January and November 2003
Cliff Richard	vocals		

3. German promotional disc

Musicians		*Recording Details*	
Matt Bonelli	bass	Producer	Barry Gibb
Doug Emery	keyboards	Engineered by	John Merchant
Barry Gibb	backing vocals, rhythm guitar	Recording location	Middle Ear Studios, Miami, Florida, USA
Maurice Gibb	keyboards	Remixed by	Unknown
Cliff Richard	vocals	Recording date	January and November 2003

♫ I Can't Ask for Anything More than You

67th UK single

With Bruce Welch now taking the production duties on his own after a run of songs co-produced by him, Hank Marvin and John Farrar, *I Can't Ask for Anything More than You* was the first of two songs (along with ***Devil Woman***) to be recorded for the new Cliff Richard album, ***I'm Nearly Famous***. Both tracks were released as singles, although *I Can't Anything More than You* would have to wait for both *Devil Woman* and ***Miss You Nights*** to be released first.

The first of the two songs to be recorded at a dual session with the backing track (take three) being laid down on the first day with the vocal overdubs on the second (unknown take), the song was issued as a single, backed with album track ***Junior Cowboy***, on the EMI label (catalogue number EMI 2499) on 31st July 1976 and it reached number seventeen in the UK charts, completing a run of three top twenty singles for the year. It was released in the US and even broke into the Billboard charts, levelling out at number eighty. Curiously, the song is referred to on the album and in much reference material as *I Can't Ask for Any More than You*, whereas the *Guinness Book of British Hit Singles* refers to it as the released single title of *I Can't Ask for Anything More than You*, which actually fits the lyrics and it is this, by official preference, that is used in this book. The song was the first track on the *I'm Nearly Famous* album and of course was issued on CD when the ***40 Golden Greats*** album was issued in 1989 and again when the parent album was reissued in 1993 as a bonus track.

I Can't Ask for Anything More than You is a prime example of Bruce's innovative ideas for Cliff, encouraging him to perform primarily in falsetto, giving the song a completely different feel to anything else he had recorded. The beauty of the song is less about the instruments and more about the attention that had been given to the backing vocals supporting Cliff, the arrangement of which was created by Tony Rivers.

Track Specification

Composed by Ken Gold and Michael Denne

Musicians		*Recording Details*	
Terry Britten	guitar	Producer	Bruce Welch
Clem Cattini	drums, percussion	Engineered by	Tony Clark and John Barrett
Tony Harding	backing vocals	Recording location	Abbey Road Studio 2, St. John's Wood, London
John Perry	backing vocals	Recording date	8th and 9th September 1975
Cliff Richard	vocals		
Tony Rivers	backing vocals, vocal arranger		
Alan Tarney	bass		
Graham Todd	keyboards		
Bruce Welch	arranger		
Unknown	hand claps		

♫ Ich Kann Treu Sein

B-side of **Man Gratuliert Mir**

As was common for Cliff Richard in the sixties, he spent some time in the studios recording translated versions of English songs he had previously recorded or occasionally original material. One of the songs laid down at the September sessions was *Ich Kann Treu Sein* (literally, *I Can Be Faithful*, which is not quite the same intent as the original), a translated version of Cliff's English hit, Neil Diamond's ***I'll Come Running***. It was recorded at the same session as a number of foreign language tracks and overdubbed on an orchestral track laid down the day before.

Ich Kann Treu Sein was chosen as the B-side of the German language recording of ***Man Gratuliert Mir*** (the German translation of Cliff's 1968 Eurovision entry ***Congratulations***) issued the following year. Originally only released in mono, as was the practice by Columbia at the time for singles and EPs, *Ich Kann Treu Sein* was eventually issued in stereo first on the German compilation album *Congratulations und 13 Weitere Hits* in 1968 and then as part of the track listing of the foreign language song compilation ***On the Continent*** in 1997.

The accompaniment is very close to the English original, including the ubiquitous harpsichord, although the bass guitar is mixed further forward in the German version. Cliff sings naturally in the German language and he is supported by an uncredited backing group, also singing in German.

Track Specification
Composed by Neil Diamond; German lyrics by F. Maat

Musicians	
Bernard Ebbinghouse Orchestra	orchestra
Bernard Ebbinghouse	arranger, conductor
Cliff Richard	vocals
Unknown	backing vocals

Recording Details	
Producer	Norrie Paramor (backing track and vocals)
Engineered by	Peter Vince (backing track and vocals)
Recording location	Abbey Road Studio 2, St. John's Wood, London (backing track and vocals)
Recording date	27th September 1967 (backing track) and 28th September 1967 (vocals)

♬ Ich Träume Deine Träume

From the album **Ich Träume Deine Träume**

In late November 1970 over a period of two days and four sessions, Cliff Richard recorded songs for the follow-up to his first German album (*Hier Ist Cliff*), *Ich Träume Deine Träume*. The title track was the last of six completed at the second session. The process was simplified by recording the orchestra earlier allowing the focus to be solely on Cliff's vocals. *Ich Träume Deine Träume* – literally *I Dream Your Dreams* – is an English composition but with German lyrics, although Cliff has never recorded the English equivalent. Backed with ***Das Girl von Nebenan***, *Ich Träume Deine Träume* was released in Germany on the international Columbia label (catalogue number 1C 006-04706) in January 1971 but made no impression on the German chart. The track was later incorporated on the track listing of Cliff's foreign tracks, ***On the Continent***.

A traditional ballad that sounds familiar on initial listening because of its similarity in the opening phrase to Vicky Leandros's winning 1972 Eurovision Song Contest entry, Cliff carries off the song with his usual candour in spite of the difficulty of enunciating some of the German words and he employs a brief falsetto in the final rendition of the chorus. An uncredited backing vocal group supports him but they are subtly and appropriately understated.

Track Specification
Composed by Volauvent and Kurt Hertha

Musicians	
Bernard Ebbinghouse	arranger, conductor
Norrie Paramor Orchestra	orchestra
Cliff Richard	vocals
Unknown	backing vocals

Recording Details	
Producer	Norrie Paramor (backing track and vocals)
Engineered by	Phil McDonald (backing track and vocals)
Recording location	Cologne, Germany (backing track) and Abbey Road Studio 2, St. John's Wood, London (vocals)
Recording date	November 1970 (backing track) and 25th November 1970 (vocals)

♬ I Could Be Persuaded

From the album **Angels and Outlaws Vol. 1** *(The Bellamy Brothers)*

The Bellamy Brothers, comprising David and Homer, had their most successful period in the late seventies and into the eighties. Perhaps their most famous song is *Let Your Love Flow* or the witty *If I Said You Had a Beautiful Body* but they are still recording and performing. In 2004, they recorded an album that featured duets with other stars including Neil Diamond and Cliff Richard, with the latter performing on *I Could Be Persuaded*, although this was not released until 2009 on *The Anthology, Vol. 1* and only available in download format.

Driven by the expected country rock guitars in the introduction, Cliff provides layered backing vocals before taking the lead vocal for the first verse, while the Bellamy Brothers join in on harmonies. The quirky song features a lot of Cliff's lead vocals, while the organ accompaniment and guitars give the track the desired country rock feel and the bridges between the verses and choruses feature a blistering saxophone solo. Cliff uses many facets of his vocal range including the falsetto and this is a great song for driving along to and deserves greater distribution than is currently the case.

Track Specification
Composed by David Bellamy, Homer Bellamy and Don Schlitz

Musicians	
David Bellamy	vocals, keyboards
Homer Bellamy	vocals, guitar
Cliff Richard	vocals, backing vocals
Unknown	bass
Unknown	drums, percussion
Unknown	saxophone

Recording Details	
Producer	Unknown
Engineered by	Unknown
Recording location	Unknown
Recording date	2004

♬ I Could Easily Fall (in Love with You)

28th ***UK single****, unissued live tracks, B-side of* **From a Distance** *(seven-inch picture disc) and from the albums* **Hank Plays Cliff** *(Hank Marvin),* **Summer Holiday** *(Darren Day) and* **Reunited**

At the end of 1964, Cliff Richard and the Shadows embarked on that curiously British phenomenon the pantomime, which had seen something of a resurgence since the beginning of the decade because they now often featured famous chart acts. The Shadows were conscripted to write the music for the London Palladium show, which is based on ***Aladdin and His Wonderful Lamp***. Directed to write from the show, all four members of the band created two in *I Could Easily Fall (in Love with You)* for Cliff and *Genie with the Light Brown Lamp* (a play on the son *Jeannie with the Light Brown Hair*) for themselves.

Some reference material, such as the official chart books, call the song *I Could Easily Fall* (i.e. without the parenthesized phrase). However, since the track listing of *Aladdin and His Wonderful Lamp* has the bracketed part in the title, that is what is used in this entry.
The show started just before Christmas in 1964 but *I Could Easily Fall (in Love with You)* was already in the charts and was a useful piece of pantomime marketing. Recorded at a double session that produced four tracks for the cast recording of the show, the seventh and final take and edit were used for the mono and stereo recordings but with different mixes for the separate audio channels. Backed with ***I'm in Love with You***, also from the show, the single was released on the Columbia label (catalogue number DB 7420) on 27th November 1964 and reached number six in the UK singles charts. The single was only released in mono and this was also included on the mono only EP ***Cliff's Hits from Aladdin and His Wonderful Lamp***. The stereo version was issued on the cast recording and regularly appears on compilations of Cliff's hits.
The power-house that is Bruce Welch's rhythm guitar is matched by Hank Marvin's lead guitar and Brian Bennett's straightforward drumming. The song is punctuated by slightly off-tempo handclaps, which are uncredited but likely to be Cliff. This form of song sees Cliff in his singing element and there are good examples here of the harmonies that became the Shadows sound that was developed in the early sixties.
In April 1965, Cliff was back at Abbey Road overdubbing German lyrics on to the base track. With a translation provided by Carl Ulrich Blecher, it was released as a single with a new title of ***Es War Keine So Wunderbar Wie Du***, although it was the English version that charted reaching number five in Germany, while the German version didn't get anywhere.
Resurrected once again for the *Live & Guaranteed 1988!* tour, it was one of the songs that were recorded and filmed for the video but neither the video nor the accompanying CD released with the 1995 reissue had the song on the track listing. It was also performed at Cliff's thirtieth anniversary event at Wembley Stadium but was not initially released on the track listing of ***From a Distance ***** The Event***: instead, it was issued as the B-side of the picture disc version of the ***From a Distance*** single before it was restored on the 2005 remaster of the parent album. This compensates for the almost criminal reduction in the tracks by the Shadows on the first release. Cliff clearly enjoys singing these songs from that period of his career and his lead is almost casual while still being electric.
In 1995, Hank recorded his next solo album, *Hank Plays Cliff*, which featured his reinterpretations of Cliff's hits, fourof which featured Cliff vocals, including *I Could Easily Fall (in Love with You)*. The introduction is a complete surprise in this arrangement, which has an almost calypso or reggae styling to it, while Cliff provides the wordless backing vocals in multiple layers in the introduction to each verse. The tinkling percussion creates another dimension to the track that is true to the original but brought up to date in its treatment. Cliff resumes the vocals for the entire last minute of the track.
The following year, Cliff recorded harmonies to four tracks on Darren Day's *Summer Holiday*, which was an album of songs performed in the touring show based around Cliff's hits; one of these was *I Could Easily Fall (in Love with You)*. Cliff supplies the non-lyric backing vocals in a multi-tracked creation introducing each verse, as well as singing the harmony to Day's performance of the song title. The problem with many of the songs on the album is that they sound lifeless; although Day is a pleasant enough singer and his pitch is as good as Cliff's, there lacks some of the energy of the original.
As part of the ***Oldies Medley*** performed at Cliff's 2003 world tour, *I Could Easily Fall (in Love with You)* was filmed and issued on DVD, but the complementary CD album, *World Tour Live*, elected not to include the medley on its track listing.
For Cliff's fiftieth anniversary celebrations, he went back into the studio with the Shadows – at least for the purposes of the album – and re-recorded a number of his most famous numbers, which included *I Could Easily Fall (in Love with You)*, before taking the show on the road later in 2009. Taken at a slightly faster pace than the original, this track emphasises the bass line, while the vocal arrangement is quintessentially what Cliff and the Shadows do so well together.

Track Specification
Composed by Hank Marvin, Bruce Welch, Brian Bennett and John Rostill

1. Single

Musicians		*Recording Details*	
Brian Bennett	drums, percussion	Producer	Norrie Paramor
Hank Marvin	backing vocals, guitar	Engineered by	Malcolm Addey and Ken Scott
Cliff Richard	vocals	Recording location	Abbey Road Studio 2, St. John's Wood, London
John Rostill	bass	Recording date	15th October 1964
Unknown	hand claps		
Bruce Welch	backing vocals, rhythm guitar		

2. Unissued track (Live & Guaranteed 1988!)

Musicians		*Recording Details*	
John Clark	guitar	Producer	Unknown
Rosemarie Ford	backing vocals	Engineered by	Unknown
Mark Griffiths	bass	Recording location	Fyens Forum, Odense, Denmark
Peter Howarth	backing vocals	Recording date	22nd May 1988
Steve Lauri	guitar		
Paul Moessl	keyboards		
Mick Mullins	backing vocals		
Alan Park	keyboards		
Cliff Richard	vocals		
Henry Spinetti	drums, percussion		

3. B-side (From a Distance – picture disc)

Musicians

John Clark	guitar
Sonia Jones-Morgan	backing vocals
Steve Lauri	guitar
Peter May	drums, percussion
Paul Moessl	keyboards
Tessa Niles	backing vocals
Alan Park	keyboards
Provox:	
Peter Howarth	backing vocals
Mick Mullins	backing vocals
Keith Murrell	backing vocals
Cliff Richard	vocals
Steve Stroud	bass

Recording Details

Producer	Cliff Richard
Engineered by	Keith Bessey and Mick McKenna
Recording location	Rolling Stones Mobile Studio, Wembley Stadium, Wembley, North-west London
Recording date	16th-17th June 1989

4. Hank Plays Cliff

Musicians

Warren Bennett	arranger, keyboards
Hank Marvin	electric guitar
Cliff Richard	backing vocals
Trevor Spencer	drums, percussion
Gary Taylor	bass, percussion

Recording Details

Producer	Hank Marvin
Engineered by	Les Williams (Planet Sound Studios) and Dick Plant (Honeyhill Studios)
Recording location	Planet Sound Studios, Subiaco, Perth, Australia (instruments) and Honeyhill Studios, Hertfordshire (vocals)
Recording date	1995

5. Summer Holiday (Darren Day)

Musicians

Darren Day	vocals
Mark Griffiths	lead guitar
Cliff Richard	backing vocals
Warren Bennett	arranger, guitar, bass, piano, drums, percussion

Recording Details

Producer	Brian Bennett
Engineered by	Dick Plant
Recording location	Honeyhill Studios, Hertfordshire, England
Recording date	1996

6. Unissued track (World Tour Live)

Musicians

Anthony Clark	backing vocals, guitar
John Clark	guitar
Dave Cooke	keyboards
Pete May	drums, percussion
Alan Park	keyboards
Cliff Richard	vocals, guitar
Steve Stroud	bass

Recording Details

Producer	Keith Bessey
Engineered by	Keith Bessey
Recording location	The Mission Winery, Napier, New Zealand
Recording date	22nd February 2003

7. Reunited

Musicians

Brian Bennett	drums, percussion
Mark Griffiths	bass
Hank Marvin	backing vocals, guitar
Cliff Richard	vocals, backing vocals
Bruce Welch	backing vocals, rhythm guitar

Recording Details

Producer	Warren Bennett (co-ordination)
Engineered by	James Collins (Honeyhill Studios), Ethan Carlson (Middle Ear Studios), Les Williams (Nivram Studios) and Keith Bessey (mixing and mastering)
Recording location	Middle Ear Studios, Miami, Florida, USA (Cliff's vocals), Nivram Studios, Perth, Western Australia (Hank's guitars and vocals) and Honeyhill Studios, Hertfordshire, England (all other vocals and instruments)
Recording date	Early 2009

♫ I'd Just Be Fool Enough

From the album **Tracks 'n' Grooves**

Often referred to with asuffix in parentheses, *I'd Just Be Fool Enough (to Fall)*, the song was made famous by Johnny Cash in 1960 and it has subsequently been recorded by artists such as the Browns, Carl Smith, Faron Young, Don Gibson, Stu Philips and the writer himself, Melvin Endsley.

Cliff Richard recorded his version (and released it without using the bracketed suffix; hence it's inclusion in that form here) at the same session that produced another song destined for the album ***Tracks 'n' Grooves*** three years later and has only ever been released in stereo format (although a mono version would have been recorded at the juncture of this session given that this was the standard approach at the time of the recording session).

Although it's not a very familiar song, the country treatment by Mike Leander is something that Cliff does extremely well and this is entirely evident on this track. The female backing group is uncredited but is likely to be the Breakaways with whom he was regularly working during this period both in the studio and on tour.

Track Specification
Composed by Melvin Endsley
Musicians

Mike Leander Orchestra	orchestra
Mike Leander	arranger, conductor
Cliff Richard	vocals
Unknown	backing vocals

Recording Details

Producer	Norrie Paramor
Engineered by	Peter Vince
Recording location	Abbey Road Studio 2, St. John's Wood, London
Recording date	1st June 1967

♫ Idle Gossip

From the album **Listen to Cliff!**

Covered by a few artists including Lita Roza, Milt Buckner, Sarah Vaughan and Jackie Paris, as far as the British singles charts were concerned, it was Perry Como who was the most success with *Idle Gossip*, hitting the number three slot as his third charting single in 1954.
For Cliff Richard's version that was released on the ***Listen to Cliff!*** studio album and and also on the associated ***Listen to Cliff! No. 2*** EP, the mono and stereo recordings used the same take (the last of five from the session) but used different mixes for the purposes of the aural channelling. Although principally an orchestral backing, The Shadows' drummer Tony Meehan was employed to assist with the rhythm requirements of the song.
The swooping orchestral strings and mellow brass are heard in the introduction to this love ballad that talks of how people will talk about inconsequential things but when it comes to love, the gossips are speaking the truth. Tony Meehan's drumming is very subtle in the mix, while the focus is very clearly – and appropriately – on Cliff's pristinely produced vocals.

Track Specification
Composed by Floyd Huddleston and Joseph Meyer
Musicians

Tony Meehan	drums, percussion
Norrie Paramor Orchestra	orchestra
Norrie Paramor	arranger, conductor
Cliff Richard	vocals

Recording Details

Producer	Norrie Paramor
Engineered by	Malcolm Addey and Norman Smith
Recording location	Abbey Road Studio 2, St. John's Wood, London
Recording date	17th November 1960

♫ I Do Not Love You Isabella

From the albums **Songs from Heathcliff** *and* **Heathcliff Live**

For the song *I Do Not Love You Isabella* from the ***Heathcliff*** musical, the four main characters are Heathcliff (played by Cliff Richard), Isabella Linton (played by promoted backing vocalist Kristina Nichols on the ***Songs from Heathcliff*** album and Sara Haggerty in the stage musical version of ***Heathcliff*** and subsequently released on a live album), Edgar (Darryl Knock in the stage show but any vocals performed by Cliff on the studio album) and Cathy (Olivia Newton-John on the album and Helen Hobson in the show). At the point in the narrative where *I Do Not Love You Isabella* is performed, Isabella is trying to convince Cathy to let Heathcliff be free to love her since Cathy is married to Isabella's brother Edgar. Cathy ridicules her sister-in-law as she revels in telling Heathcliff what Isabella is thinking. Heathcliff drives another wedge between himself and Cathy by pointing out that Isabella is Edgar's only heir for the moment (the married couple being childless) and begins his scheme to marry Isabella in order to get back at Cathy and win a point or two from Edgar. *I Do Not Love You Isabella* begins in the church at Heathcliff's and Isabella's wedding ceremony. The song is sung in confidence towards the audience, while Cathy warns Isabella that Heathcliff doesn't love her but she is blinded by her belief in her own love for him. Next Edgar and Cathy give their view of the couple, while Heathcliff continues his quiet vituperation towards his intended wife. She tries to please him and he upsets her by meanly tipping wine down her wedding dress.
Cliff has said in interview that this song was a real departure for him since, while he often sung of love, it was about falling in love, being in love, wanting love from someone who couldn't give it or the effects of falling out of love but, until the musical, he had never sung such a penurious song that specifically stated that there was no love and indeed the relationship was nothing more than manipulative convenience (although ***High 'n' Dry*** does come close).
The original studio album recording of the song and an instrumental version were used as a B-side track to the release of ***The Wedding***, which featured a new studio recording version of the song sung by Cliff and Helen Hobson but using the original backing track. The tune for *I Do Not Love You Isabella* is embellished and reused for the closing montage song ***Nightmare (A Time for Absolution)***, which sees all of Heathcliff's adversaries blaming him for what has become of Cathy and the poison he has injected into her and the various relationships she had touched.
As is expected at any church-based ceremony, the organ features prominently and continues to play out over this arrogant march featuring Cliff singing spitefully, before handing over to Olivia and Kristina Nicholls at which point accompaniment becomes smoother and more gentle. Once Cliff returns, the staccato string chords strike up once more and so on throughout the song. By the end, there is a twinkling flute as well as a harpsichord that creates an almost dancelike atmosphere.
The live version has a spoken dialogue interaction between Cathy and Isabella watched by Heathcliff. The strength of the staccato chords is more impressive in the live version as Cliff builds up the sneering arrogance and sheer hatred in the lyrics as he tries to get the audience to side with him.

Track Specification
Composed by John Farrar and Tim Rice

1. Single

Musicians

Sean Callery	orchestrator, synclavier, keyboards
Liz Constantino	backing vocals
Linda Dalziel	backing vocals
John Farrar	backing vocals, guitar, synclavier
Steve Kipner	backing vocals
Clif Magness	backing vocals
Olivia Newton-John	vocals
Kristina Nichols	vocals
Cliff Richard	vocals
Michael Thompson	guitar

Recording Details

Producer	John Farrar
Engineered by	Chris Fogel, Eric Rudd and Joe Schiff (Moonee Ponds Studio), Darren Goodwin and Guy Massey (Abbey Road Studios) and James Collins and Caroline Daniel (CTS Studios)
Recording location	Moonee Ponds Studio, Los Angeles, Abbey Road Studios, St. John's Wood, London and CTS Studios, Wembley, London
Mixed by	Allen Sides and Chris Fogel
Mixed at	Moonee Ponds Studio, Los Angeles
Recording date	February-April 1994 and May-August 1995

2. Heathcliff Live

Musicians

Sean Callery	orchestrator, orchestra
David Combes	backing vocals
John Clark	guitar
Elements:	
Geoff David	backing vocals
Chris Holland	backing vocals
Sonia Jones	backing vocals
Niki Kitt	backing vocals
Suzanne Parry	backing vocals
Keith Hayman	keyboards
Sara Haggerty	spoken vocals, vocals
Helen Hobson	spoken vocals, vocals
Darryl Knock	vocals
Peter May	drums, percussion
Bob Noble	keyboards
Alan Park	keyboards
John Perry	backing vocals
Cliff Richard	spoken vocals, vocals
Steve Stroud	bass
Kevin Townend	orchestration
Unknown	orchestra
Mick Wilson	backing vocals

Recording Details

Producer	John Farrar
Engineered by	Keith Bessey, John Pearson and Tom Tranter
Recording location	Earl's Court Hall 2, London and/or The Academy, National Indoor Arena, Birmingham, England
Recording date	October 1996

♫ I Don't Know

From the album **Me and My Shadows**

The final Ian Samwell composition of six on ***Me and My Shadows*** also appears on the ***Me and My Shadows No. 3*** EP. The mono and stereo versions are the same take (the sixteenth from the session, making it one of the most numerous along with ***I Love You So*** from the same album) but with different edits for the stereo channel needs.

Unsurprisingly, there are echos of ***Fall in Love with You,*** given the writer, but the difference comes with the tambourine and simple guitar lines. The song is a bemused story of how a girl feels for him and the song title's utterance is wittily stated. The middle eight bridge features a Hank Marvin guitar solo, using augmented intervals to express the confusion.

Track Specification
Composed by Ian Samwell

Musicians

Jet Harris	bass
Hank Marvin	guitar
Tony Meehan	tambourine
Cliff Richard	vocals
Bruce Welch	rhythm guitar

Recording Details

Producer	Norrie Paramor
Engineered by	Malcolm Addey and Norman Smith (mono) and Peter Bown and Alan Kane (stereo)
Recording location	Abbey Road Studio 2, St. John's Wood, London
Recording date	15th March 1960

♫ I Don't Know Why (I Just Do)

From the album **Cliff Sings**

The first of the second batch of songs from the ***Cliff Sings*** album to be accompanied by the Norrie Paramor Orchestra rather than the Drifters included this song from 1931. There were several versions recorded at this time with the most prominent being those by Russ Columbo, Wayne King, Kate Smith and Bennie Krueger's Orchestra. Fifteen years later in 1956, it was revived by Tommy Dorsey and his orchestra, as well as a version by Frank Sinatra. Yet another version was released in 1973 by Andy and David Williams (relations of the more famously titled Andy) but it only reached the lower echelons of the top forty in the UK singles charts.Other artists to have recorded the song include The Calico Consort, The Andrews Sisters, Hoagy Carmichael, Jimmie Davis, Annette Hanshaw and the Erroll Garner Trio among others.

As with all the tracks on the album, *I Don't Know Why (I Just Do)* was only released in mono format for the album while being released in both mono and stereo for a series of EPs. The same take was used in this case, although there was a different edit used for the stereo channelling. This track was included on the ***Cliff Sings No. 4*** EP.

With a luscious string accompaniment arranged and conducted by producer Norrie Paramor, Cliff Richard shows his capabilities as a singer of ballads (while not quite earning the disingenuous epithet of 'crooner') as well as rock and roll styles. The gentle song talks about a bewildering love he has for a girl, who doesn't seem willing to reciprocate.

Track Specification

Composed by Roy Turk and Fred E. Ahlert

Musicians

Norrie Paramor Orchestra	orchestra
Norrie Paramor	arranger, conductor
Cliff Richard	vocals

Recording Details

Producer	Norrie Paramor
Engineered by	Malcolm Addey and Alan Kane (mono) and Stuart Eltham and Norman Smith (stereo)
Recording location	Abbey Road Studio 2, St. John's Wood, London
Recording date	10th September 1959

♫ I Don't Wanna Lose You

From the album **Something's Goin' On**

Written by old friend Chris Eaton, *I Don't Wanna Lose You* was featured as the penultimate track on Cliff Richard's 2004 album ***Something's Goin' On***. The track was, as with the remainder of the album, recorded entirely in America and like the large proportion of the tracks, completed at studios in and around Nashville.

It is medium-paced ballad that looks at a possibly failing relationship. The keyboards and guitar arrangements are perfect for the anguished notes of Cliff's performance. Echo has been added to his lead vocal which continues as the song builds to the key change towards the end. The backing vocal arrangement is kept simple but is nonetheless effect for all that.

Track Specification

Composed by John Hartley and Chris Eaton

Musicians

Greg Bieck	programming
Trey Bruce	programming
Pat Buchanan	guitar
Lisa Cochran	backing vocals
J. T. Corenflos	guitar
Tony Harrell	keyboards
Wes Hightower	backing vocals
Greg Morrow	drums, percussion
Alison Prestwood	bass
Cliff Richard	vocals, backing vocals
Michael Spriggs	guitar

Recording Details

Producer	Trey Bruce
Engineered by	David Buchanan
Recording location	Omnisound Recording Studios, Nashville, Tennessee, USA, Sound Stage Studios, Nashville, Tennessee, USA and Pocket Studio, Franklin, Tennessee, USA
Recording date	2003-2004

♫ I Don't Wanna Love You

From the album **Cliff Richard**

Recorded by Ricky Nelson in 1964, *I Don't Wanna Love You* was one of the many songs coming out of the compositional partnership of Barry Mann and Cynthia Weil in the sixties. Picked up by Cliff Richard for release on his ***Cliff Richard*** album in 1965, it was one of the clutch of songs recorded during his American sojourn in August 1964, with a suite of sessions in Nashville and New York. The final (unknown) take and edit was used for the mono and stereo recordings but with different mixes for the requirements of the separate audio channels.

With assistance from the Jordanaires, the guitar and bass keep the song moving onwards. Cliff keeps his vocal line measured throughout and matches with the harmonies provided by the backing vocals. The chord sequences throughout are interesting and unexpected, even when there is an inevitable key change.

Track Specification

Composed by Barry Mann and Cynthia Weil

Musicians

Jordanaires	backing vocals
Cliff Richard	vocals
Unknown	guitar
Unknown	bass
Unknown	flute
Unknown	drums, percussion

Recording Details

Producer	Bob Morgan and Billy Sherrill
Engineered by	Mort Thomason
Recording location	Columbia Studios, Nashville
Recording date	24th August 1964

♫ If Ever I Would Leave You

From the albums **Live at the Talk of the Town**, **Cliff Live in Korea** *and* **Hobson's Choice** *(Helen Hobson)*

Taken from the Lerner and Loewe musical *Camelot*, which was first performed in 1960 and converted into a film in 1967, *If Ever I Would Leave You* is sung by the Sir Lancelot character as he assesses the English land and the seasons, concluding that he can never leave. Recorded and covered by a number of artists, these have included Bobby Vinton, Aretha Franklin,

Shirley Bassey, Tom Jones, Russ Conway, Sonny Rollins, Robert Goulet, Percy Faith, Harry Secombe, Andy Williams, the Bachelors, Vic Damone, Mike Batt, Stan Getz, the Lettermen and Roger Whittaker.

Cliff Richard has never recorded a studio version of this song or ***Something Good***, both of which songs were performed during his Talk of the Town concerts, with *Something Good* segueing into *If Ever I Would Leave You*. Slightly more upbeat than its partner song, Cliff sings this song with emotion and it shows off his versatility well.

Repeating the exercise the following year for his tour of Korea, Cliff got back together again with the Shadows. The song was presented in a similar way to the Talk of the Town performance alongside *Something Good*. Released in mono on the very rare *Cliff Live in Korea* album in 1970, the track has never been reissued in any other format.

In 1995, Cliff was heavily involved in the stage production of his pet project, ***Heathcliff***. His chosen leading lady, playing Cathy, was Helen Hobson, with whom he had a minor hit with ***The Wedding***. In that same year, Hobson recorded her first solo album, *Hobson's Choice*, which featured another track that Cliff specially recorded with her: *If Ever I Would Leave You*. Introduced with a violin and a piano, Cliff's vocals are the first to be heard. Hobson sings the next set of vocals as the backing instrumentation slowly builds up their crescendo. The pace picks up in the mid-section, which has Cliff and Hobson singing in harmony for the first time and this is effective, although Hobson's vocal is a little strident without vibrato. The middle eight features the string quartet and piano performing a faster paced tempo before a rallentando resolves to the pair's vocals, which finish in unison apart from the last three notes, which end in delicious music intervals.

Track Specification
Composed by Alan Jay Lerner and Frederick Loewe

1. Live at the Talk of the Town

Musicians		*Recording Details*	
Norrie Paramor	arranger, conductor	Producer	Norrie Paramor
Cliff Richard	vocals	Engineered by	Peter Vince
Talk of the Town Orchestra	orchestra	Recording location	Talk of the Town Theatre, London
		Recording date	30th May 1968

2. Cliff Live in Korea

Musicians		*Recording Details*	
Brian Bennett	drums, percussion	Producer	Unknown
Alan Hawkshaw	keyboards	Engineered by	Unknown
Hank Marvin	guitar	Recording location	Citizen Hall, Seoul, South Korea
Cliff Richard	vocals	Recording date	16th October 1969
John Rostill	bass		
Bruce Welch	rhythm guitar		

3. Hobson's Choice

Musicians		*Recording Details*	
Paul Bateman	arranger, piano	Producer	Beryl Korman
Helen Hobson	vocals	Engineered by	John Timperley
Cliff Richard	vocals	Recording location	Copthorne Studios, Maidenhead, England
Unknown	strings	Recording date	23rd July 1996

♫ If I Do

From the album **...And They Said It Would Never Last! (My 50 Years in Music)**

One of three songs attempted at the session, *If I Do* was the first but was deemed unworthy to release at the time (along with ***Note in a Bottle*** which was also abandoned at the same session). It was subsequently released as a major rarity on the 2008 celebratory boxed set ***...And They Said It Would Never Last! (My 50 Years in Music)***.

The presentation of this song is almost childlike with its staccato strings and thumping bass supported by twinkling instruments in the woodwind and keyboards. The lyrics talk of unicorns and dragons and this adds to the childlike charm. No doubt, had it been issued, Cliff's critics would have been swift to denigrate the song but it is curiously beautiful. There are uncredited backing vocalists in the mix but there is no information as to who they might be.

Track Specification
Composed by Unknown

Musicians		*Recording Details*	
Norrie Paramor Orchestra	orchestra	Producer	Norrie Paramor
Norrie Paramor	conductor	Engineered by	Peter Vince
Cliff Richard	vocals	Recording location	Abbey Road Studio 1, St. John's Wood, London
Unknown	backing vocals	Recording date	24th October 1968

♫ If I Give My Heart to You

From the EP **Look in My Eyes Maria**

Written in 1954, the famous version of *If I Give My Heart to You* was by Doris Day later on that year, when it reached number four in the US. At the same time a version was recorded by Denise Lor, which also charted but only reached number fourteen. Anne Shelton was pressed into recording a version for the UK market, but it wasn't successful in chart terms, losing out to Doris Day's single, which reached number four in the British singles charts. Competing with that for chart prominence was yet another version by Joan Regan, which beat Doris Day's version by just one placing, finishing as it did at the number three spot. Since then, it has been covered by a wide variety of artists, including Solomon Burke, Nat King Cole, Duke Ellington, Acker Bilk, Kitty Kallen, Ken Dodd and Bobby Vinton among others.

In the book *The Complete Recording Sessions 1958-1990* by Peter Lewry and Nigel Goodall, the song is not mentioned anywhere in the listings but it was later found to be part of the final London session before Cliff Richard went to Nashville and New York in summer 1964. One of five songs to be completed on that day, the same (unknown) take and edit were used for the mono and stereo recordings but with different mixes for the separate audio channels. It was only ever released in mono on the ***Look in My Eyes Maria*** EP and it would take another twenty-five years for the stereo version to be issued on the 1989 collation of EP tracks, ***The EP Collection: Ballads and Love Songs***, which is itself now a rarity.

Pizzicato violins and thrumming piano with swooping strings and 'doo-ing' backing vocals from the female section of the Mike Sammes Singers (later joined by the male section), Cliff sings with assured ease when the verse begins. There is an over-reliance on a thudding bass guitar and the backing vocals on occasion but it is a beautiful rendition for all that.

Track Specification
Composed by Jimmie Crane, Jimmy Brewster and Al Jacobs

Musicians

Mike Sammes Singers	backing vocals
Norrie Paramor Orchestra	orchestra
Norrie Paramor	conductor
Cliff Richard	vocals

Recording Details

Producer	Norrie Paramor
Engineered by	Malcolm Addey
Recording location	Abbey Road Studio 2, St. John's Wood, London
Recording date	24th July 1964

♫ If It Were Up to Me

From the albums **Progression** *(Vincenzo La Scola) and* **Vita Mia** *(Vincenzo La Scola)*

The two versions of the song that appear on Vincenzo La Scola's albums *Progression* and *Vita Mia* are essentially the same vocal take but with a different mix of the backing track. The *Vita Mia* version is stronger on guitars, while *Progression* prefers to accentuate the keyboards and piano. Vincenzo La Scola, the Italian tenor, had joined Cliff Richard on the final track of his ***Real as I Wanna Be*** in 1998, ***Vita Mia***, and the opera singer returned the invitation to Cliff to appear on tracks recorded for these two albums. The song, like *Vita Mia*, was written by Peter and Michelle Wolf, who had been so heavily involved in the production and performance of Cliff's album, and it is quite possible that the track was recorded during the sessions that produced the *Vita Mia* duet.

Cliff initiates the song with his non-lyric singing leading into the first verse. The performance is strong although it doesn't quite have the same impact and power as *Vita Mia*. Cliff's and La Scola's blend extraordinarily well given the types of singing the pair are normally performing but this simply adds to the beauty of the ensemble performance.

Track Specification
Composed by Peter Wolf and Michelle Wolf

1. Progression

Musicians

Vincenzo La Scola	vocals
Ian Hughes	arranger, conductor
Steve Lukather	guitar
Cliff Richard	vocals
Unknown	keyboards
Unknown	orchestra
Michelle Wolf	backing vocals

Recording Details

Producer	Peter Wolf
Engineered by	Unknown
Recording location	Little America Recording Studios, Weiler, Austria
Recording date	1997 or 1998

2. Vita Mia

Musicians

Vincenzo La Scola	vocals
Ian Hughes	arranger, conductor
Steve Lukather	guitar
Cliff Richard	vocals
Unknown	keyboards
Unknown	orchestra
Michelle Wolf	backing vocals

Recording Details

Producer	Peter Wolf
Engineered by	Unknown
Recording location	Little America Recording Studios, Weiler, Austria
Recording date	1997 or 1998

♫ I Found a Rose

From the album **Love Is Forever**

One of the twenty-one songs composed by the writing partnership Sid Tepper and Roy Bennett for Cliff Richard to record, *I Found a Rose* was the first of three songs completed at the session (the other two were released on the ***Holiday Carnival*** EP) but would have to wait over two years before being included on the track listing for 1965's ***Love Is Forever*** album. The fourth and final take an edit were used for the mono and stereo recordings but with different mixes dictated by the requirements of the audio channels.

With a slight Latin flavour to the rhythm, the song begins with a guitar and percussion lead-in before Cliff's gentle vocal arrives accompanied by orchestra instrumentation and the languid backing vocals by Mike Sammes Singers. There are key changes throughout, which elevate the interest in the song but it is Cliff's abilities as a performer that are showcased principally on this track.

Track Specification
Composed by Sid Tepper and Roy C. Bennett

Musicians		*Recording Details*	
Mike Sammes Singers	backing vocals	Producer	Norrie Paramor
Norrie Paramor Orchestra	orchestra	Engineered by	Malcolm Addey and Peter Vince
Norrie Paramor	arranger, conductor	Recording location	Abbey Road Studio 2, St. John's Wood, London
Cliff Richard	vocals	Recording date	12th December 1962

♫ If Our Dreams Came True

From the pantomime cast recording album of **Cinderella**

Often referred to as *Wouldn't It Be Nice (If Our Dreams Came True)?*, the track listing of the ***Cinderella*** album only refers to it as the bracketed part. Recorded at one of the specific sessions for the soundtrack album, *If Our Dreams Came True* is a duet between Cliff Richard and his *Cinderella* co-star Jackie Lee. The seventh and final take and edit were used for the mono and stereo recordings.

With the unusual addition of a harpsichord to support the vocal line, this is a strong duet between Jackie Lee and Cliff. As expected, the Shadows have composed another quirky little song. Cliff acts throughout as if he were on stage and that instils the drama from the stage to the cast recording.

Track Specification
Composed by Hank Marvin, Bruce Welch, Brian Bennett and John Rostill

Musicians		*Recording Details*	
Jackie Lee	vocals	Producer	Norrie Paramor
Norrie Paramor Orchestra	orchestra	Engineered by	Peter Vince and Richard Lush
Norrie Paramor	arranger, conductor	Recording location	Abbey Road Studio 2, St. John's Wood, London
Cliff Richard	vocals	Recording date	11th November 1966

♫ If You're Not the One

From the album **Love... The Album**

Daniel Bedingfield's second number one, *If You're Not the One*, was his third single and as issued in 2002. Since the success of that release, the song has been covered by a number of artists including Michael Ball, G4's Jonathan Ansell and *X Factor* winner Shayne Ward.

Cliff Richard recorded the song as one of five new tracks to be included among a selection of well-loved love songs during career for his ***Love... The Album***. The musicians are unknown and these will be updated when research reveals the details.

A great rendition of the original, with Cliff singing the gentle vocals in a conspiratorial manner, in much the same way as Bedingfield does in his version. Cliff also copies the falsetto chorus and improves on the original in the process. He sings most of his own backing vocals and this assists in elevating the track further.

Track Specification
Composed by Daniel Bedingfield

Musicians		*Recording Details*	
Cliff Richard	vocals, backing vocals	Producer	Michael Omartian
Unknown	backing vocals	Engineered by	Terry Christian
Unknown	guitar	Recording location	Sound Kitchen, Franklin, Tennessee, USA, Sound House, Franklin, Tennessee, USA and/or Blue Wave Studios, Bayley's Plantation, St. Phillip, Barbados
Unknown	bass		
Unknown	keyboards		
Unknown	programming		
		Recording date	2007

♫ If You Walked Away

Unissued track and from the album **I'm Nearly Famous**

Recorded by several artists including the Hollies' Allan Clarke, Yvonne Elliman, Nonoy Zuniga, Walter Jackson, Daryl Braithwaite and the writer himself, David Pomeranz, Cliff Richard recorded his version for the penultimate track on the album ***I'm Nearly Famous***. There was an initial attempt to complete it at the first session on 1st December 1975 but it was abandoned after an unspecified number of takes and retried the following day, successfully completing it in five takes. Additional vocal overdubs were recorded at the session six days later.

The tender performance exploits Cliff's vibrato to perfect effect as he is supported by the sustained bass, the orchestral strings and the backing vocals. Like many of his songs, the song can be read as a standard love song but can be imbued with religious connotations. Cliff sings the song with reverential energy but it is the combined arrangement and production by Bruce Welch that takes the honours in providing one of the best and most understated songs on the album.

Track Specification
Composed by David Pomeranz

1. Unissued track (I'm Nearly Famous)

Musicians		*Recording Details*	
Terry Britten	guitar	Producer	Bruce Welch
Clem Cattini	drums, percussion	Engineered by	Tony Clark and John Barrett
Tony Harding	backing vocals	Recording location	Abbey Road Studio 3, St. John's Wood, London
Richard Hewson	arranger, conductor	Recording date	1st December 1975
John Perry	backing vocals		
Cliff Richard	vocals		
Tony Rivers	backing vocals		
Alan Tarney	bass		
Graham Todd	keyboards		
Unknown	orchestra		

2. I'm Nearly Famous

Musicians		*Recording Details*	
Terry Britten	guitar	Producer	Bruce Welch
Clem Cattini	drums, percussion	Engineered by	Tony Clark and John Barrett
Tony Harding	backing vocals	Recording location	Abbey Road Studio 3, St. John's Wood, London
Richard Hewson	arranger, conductor	Recording date	2nd and 8th December 1975
John Perry	backing vocals		
Cliff Richard	vocals		
Tony Rivers	backing vocals		
Alan Tarney	bass		
Graham Todd	keyboards		
Unknown	orchestra		

♫ I Get the Feelin'

B-side of **I'll Come Running**

A brace of Neil Diamond songs was released as Cliff Richard's thirty-eighth single in 1967 with *I Get the Feelin'* issued as ***I'll Come Running***'s B-side. Although Neil Diamond was already famous as both composer and performer, Cliff's single only reached number twenty-six, which, much to the critics' sense of *Schadenfreude*, was the worst performing single since he started in 1958. Recorded at the same session as its A-side, *I Get the Feelin'* was the second song of four to be completed. Originally, only the mono version was released (all Columbia singles at the time were only released in mono). The same mono version was added to the 2007 French compilation *Congratulations to Cliff*, while it took around forty years for the stereo version to be released in 2008 on the celebratory ***...And They Said It Wouldn't Last! (My 50 Years in Music)***.
As with its A-side, Mike Leander's arrangement includes a harpsichord in the accompaniment and it also includes a number of *rallentandos* that add energy to the impassioned performance by Cliff, while there is also an uncredited female backing vocal group, which is most likely to the Breakaways, who also possibly appeared on the main single song.

Track Specification
Composed by Neil Diamond

Musicians		*Recording Details*	
Mike Leander Orchestra	orchestra	Producer	Norrie Paramor
Mike Leander	arranger, conductor	Engineered by	Unknown
Cliff Richard	vocals	Recording location	Abbey Road Studio 2, St. John's Wood, London
Unknown	female backing vocals	Recording date	24th April 1967

♫ I Got a Feeling

From the album **Cliff**

I Got a Feeling had been a minor hit in the UK for Ricky Nelson in November 1958, when it reached number twenty-seven. Because of Nelson's teen idol profile, it was reasonable to select this song for the set list of the 'live' recording by Cliff Richard and the Drifters at Abbey Road Studios in front of an invited audience of fans, screaming their way throughout. The love song has been covered by a few artists including The Collins Kids and Johnny Tillotson as well as Cliff and the Drifters for what would become the fourth track on the album *Cliff*. The performance allows an almost virtuoso performance on lead guitar and bass by Hank Marvin and Jet Harris underpinning Cliff's perfect vocals.
This 'live' version of the song was included on Cliff's first EP, ***Cliff No. 1***.

Track Specification
Composed by Thomas Baker-Knight

Musicians		*Recording Details*	
Jet Harris	bass	Producer	Norrie Paramor
Hank Marvin	guitar	Engineered by	Peter Bown and Stuart Eltham
Tony Meehan	drums, percussion	Recording location	Abbey Road Studio 2, St. John's Wood, London
Cliff Richard	vocals	Recording date	9th February 1958
Bruce Welch	rhythm guitar		

♬ I Got a Woman

Unreleased live track and from the album **Live at the ABC Kingston 1962**

Written and recorded by Ray Charles, he released it as a single in 1954, backed with *Come Back Baby*, and became his first number one in the US. The song is based on and inspired by a gospel hymn (*Jesus Is All the World to Me*), which Charles heard on the radio while travelling with his band. It has since been covered by all manner of artists, including the Beatles, Johnny Cash, Jamie Cullum, The Monkees, Booker T. and the M.G.s, Elvis Presley and Bryan Adams.

In August 1958, it was the turn of Cliff Richard and the Drifters, who were about to enjoy much success with their first single, ***Move It***, scheduled for release later that month. The band, consisting of Cliff, Terry Smart and Ian Samwell, took up a short residency at the Butlin's Holiday Camp based at Clacton-on-Sea on the Essex coast. A technician called Stan Edwards recorded their performance one night on a two-track tape machine and, while some of the recordings made it on to the rarities retrospective, ***The Rock 'n' Roll Years 1958-1963***, some of the songs were in too poor a condition for commercial release. One such recording was the Cliff and the Drifters' version of *I Got a Woman.*

I Got a Woman is one of the few tracks that Cliff Richard (with the Shadows in this event) performed on stage but did not record in the studio. Performed live at the ABC Theatre in Kingston, the track was released first on the compilation album ***The Rock 'n' Roll Years 1958-1963***, before the entire concert was issued on the 2003 CD ***Live at the ABC Kingston 1962***, although this was in stereo only. It was also released as a bonus track on the ***Let Me Be the One*** CD single in 2002.

Crashing chords introduce the song as Cliff sings the first line slowly and enunciates the 't' of 'alright', before taking off into a rip-roaring version of the song that is accompanied by the clapping of the ABC audience. Brian Bennett, in particular, works hard keeping the rhythm frothing on the drums. Cliff asks the band to take the sound down and makes a couple of gags including the pin-drop (again Bennett on percussion) before the performance is ratcheted up to full volume much to the appreciation of the screaming audience.

Track Specification

Composed by Ray Charles

1. *Unissued track (Butlin's)*

Musicians		*Recording Details*	
Cliff Richard	vocals, guitar	Producer	Unknown
Ian Samwell	guitar	Engineered by	Stan Edwards
Terry Smart	drums, percussion	Recording location	Rock 'n' Roll Ballroom, Butlin's Holiday Camp, Clacton-on-Sea, Essex
		Recording date	August 1958

2. *Live at the ABC Kingston 1962*

Musicians		*Recording Details*	
Brian Bennett	drums, percussion	Producer	Norrie Paramor
Jet Harris	bass	Engineered by	Malcolm Addey and Ken Townsend
Hank Marvin	guitar	Recording location	ABC Theatre, Kingston, Surrey
Cliff Richard	vocals	Recording date	7th March 1962
Bruce Welch	rhythm guitar		

♬ I Gotta Know

From the album **Cliff Sings** *and the* **Cliff Sings No. 1 EP**

The third recording of eight featuring The Drifters (who would be renamed The Shadows by the time the album was released) backing Cliff Richard on his first real studio album, ***Cliff Sings***, was of a song made famous by a number of recording artists, including Wanda Jackson, Elvis Presley, co-writer Paul Evans and Bobby Vee.

Two versions of the song recorded by Cliff and the Shadows were released to the public: the mono version from the first recording session and released on the *Cliff Sings* album and the mono ***Cliff Sings No. 1*** EP, while the stereo version, itself driven from a later unknown mono take, was only released on the stereo version of the EP. The stereo version has subsequently been released on ***The Rock 'n' Roll Years 1958-1963*** compendium, while the mono version was re-released with the CD version of the album in 1992. The stereo remaster of the mono track was subsequently released with the remastered version of the entire album in 2001.

The stereo EP version differs from the mono version in its faster pace and the different backing, particularly in Hank Marvin's guitar line. The song is a foot-tapping piece rock 'n' roll and is a beseeching love-song. It is one of the first tracks that display Hank's trademark guitar sound, including the use of the tremolo arm and bending the notes he is playing.

Track Specification

Composed by Matt Williams and Paul Evans

1. *Cliff Sings*

Musicians		*Recording Details*	
Jet Harris	bass	Producer	Norrie Paramor
Hank Marvin	guitar	Engineered by	Malcolm Addey and David Lloyd (mono) and Peter Bown and Stuart Eltham (stereo)
Tony Meehan	drums, percussion		
Cliff Richard	vocals	Recording location	Abbey Road Studio 2, St. John's Wood, London
Bruce Welch	rhythm guitar	Recording date	26th July 1959

2. Cliff Sings No. 1 EP (stereo)

Musicians		*Recording Details*	
Jet Harris	bass	Producer	Norrie Paramor
Hank Marvin	guitar	Engineered by	Malcolm Addey and Alan Kane (mono) and Peter Bown and Norman Smith (stereo)
Tony Meehan	drums, percussion	Recording location	Abbey Road Studio 2, St. John's Wood, London
Cliff Richard	vocals	Recording date	6th September 1959
Bruce Welch	rhythm guitar		

♫ I Honestly Love You

From the album **World Tour Live**

Cliff Richard had been instrumental in bringing Olivia Newton-John to the attention of the world through his regular use of her in his television shows as well as the film *The Case*. She branched out on her own, was affianced to Bruce Welch and had a number of country-style hits. She recorded a number of ballads, including *I Honestly Love You*, which reached number twenty-two at the end of 1974, her last single for over two years. But it sealed her career in the US when the song reached number one selling over two million copies. It was re-released there in 1977, and a new version was issued in 1998 reaching sixty-seven on the Billboard Hot 100. It has also been recorded by one of the writers, Peter Allen, as well as Andy Williams, Glen Campbell, Kaleidoscope, Mantovani, Ray Conniff, Deniece Williams and Bobby Vinton.
Cliff regularly performed songs on stage that he had never attempted in the studio and, for the 2003 world tour, he included his version of *I Honestly Love You* was included on the set list. The New Zealand leg of the tour was filmed for DVD release later in the year and fourteen of the tracks were chosen, including this one, for the track listing of the CD album *World Tour Live* released the following year. His voice is very well suited to the song, which starts with strings and electronic piano. Behind him, pictures of Cliff and Olivia together and separately from the seventies float across the electronic screen. While an homage to Olivia, Cliff also manages to create a version that is also very personal.

Track Specification

Composed by Peter Allen and Jeff Barry

Musicians		*Recording Details*	
Rachel Allen	violin	Producer	Keith Bessey
Elena Bulgakova	violin	Engineered by	Keith Bessey
Jenni Champion	violin	Recording location	The Mission Winery, Napier, New Zealand
Anthony Clark	backing vocals, guitar	Recording date	22nd February 2003
John Clark	guitar		
Dave Cooke	keyboards		
Cornelia Didenco	violin		
Gina Ferguson	violin		
Mike Haughton	flute		
Peter Howarth	backing vocals		
Cathy Irons	violin		
Pete May	drums, percussion		
Mick Mullins	backing vocals		
Keith Murrell	backing vocals		
Alan Park	keyboards		
Hee-Jung Park	violin		
Cliff Richard	vocals		
Eva Schwanen-Lilley	violin		
Steve Stroud	bass		

♫ I Just Don't Have the Heart

Misnomer or **Just Don't Have the Heart**

Cliff Richard's single with the Stock, Aitken and Waterman triumvirate of eighties producers is often incorrectly stated as *I Just Don't Have the Heart*. On the track listing of ***Stronger***, it is correctly identified as ***Just Don't Have the Heart***, which is the title that is clearly given to it on the handwritten page of the lyrics omposed at the time.

♫ Il Faut Chanter la Vie

French single

As soon as the results were announced that Cliff Richard would be singing ***Power to All Our Friends*** to represent the UK in the 1973 Eurovision Song Contest by a large margin, the song was hastily translated into German, French and Spanish for Cliff to record just a few days later. The German song was recorded in one session while the other two languages were recorded two days later. Overdubbing his new vocals in addition to the backing vocals on the backing track that had already been recorded for the British version back at the end of December 1972, Cliff's French version was the first to be completed at the session.
Il Faut Chanter la Vie (translated as *Have to Sing about Life* – a departure from the original meaning) was released as a single in France backed with the untranslated ***Come Back Billie Jo*** (in common with all language versions injcluding English), which had come a distant second to *Power to All Our Friends*, on the EMI label (catalogue number 2C 006-05324) in April

1973 after the Contest was finished, although it failed to register on the French charts. The song, a major rarity, was eventually included on the track listing ***On the Continent*** in 1997, which featured all of Cliff's foreign language songs.

As with the German version, the backing vocals are completely new and, while they are more in evidence than the original version, it is clear that Cliff is involved in providing his own harmonies alongside other voices, assumed to be the original band.

Track Specification

Composed by Guy Fletcher and Doug Flett; French lyrics by Michel Jourdan

Musicians	
Terry Britten	backing vocals, guitar
David MacKay Orchestra	orchestra
David MacKay	backing vocals, arranger, conductor
Kevin Peek	guitar
Cliff Richard	vocals, backing vocals
Trevor Spencer	backing vocals, drums, percussion
Alan Tarney	backing vocals, bass

Recording Details	
Producer	David MacKay (backing track and vocals)
Engineered by	Peter Vince (backing track and vocals)
Recording location	Abbey Road Studio (backing track) and Abbey Road Studio 3 (vocals), St. John's Wood, London
Recording date	28th December 1972 (backing track) and 23rd March 1973 (vocals)

♫ I Live for You

From the album **Listen to Cliff!**

The fourth of five original tracks composed for inclusion on the album ***Listen to Cliff!***, *I Live for You* was co-written by Shadows guitarist Hank Marvin and erstwhile Chesternuts bandmate and friend Pete Chester. The first of the album's songs to be recorded a long time back at the beginning of spring 1960, it is likely that it was not intended specifically for the album but, as it was in the vaults, it was added to the track listing.

The mono and stereo versions used the same take and edit (the eleventh from that April Fools' Day session) with separate mixes to manage the requirements of the differing aural channels.

The twanging guitar is typical of Hank's work and it introduces a typical love song imploring a girl to help mend a broken heart. The guitar makes another appearance in the middle eight bridge, while the susurration of Tony Meehan's drums and the quiet thudding of Jet Harris's bass serve to keep the song moving forward. In addition to the set-up, there is an uncredited xylophone played throughout, twinkling away to counterpoint the vocal melody and the lead guitar harmonisation.

Track Specification

Composed by Hank Marvin and Peter Chester

Musicians	
Jet Harris	bass
Hank Marvin	guitar
Tony Meehan	drums, percussion
Cliff Richard	vocals
Unknown	xylophone
Bruce Welch	rhythm guitar

Recording Details	
Producer	Norrie Paramor and John Schroeder
Engineered by	Malcolm Addey and Norman Smith (mono) and Peter Bown and Alan Kane (stereo)
Recording location	Abbey Road Studio 2, St. John's Wood, London
Recording date	1st April 1960

♫ I'll Be Back

From the album **Don't Stop Me Now!**

By the mid-sixties the world domination by the Beatles was inexorable, but curiously Cliff Richard resisted the temptation to do many covers of their work. *I'll Be Back* was one of the very few exceptions, which would be added to his ***Don't Stop Me Now!*** album in 1967. Taken from the soundtrack of the Beatles' first film venture, *A Hard Day's Night*, it is unusual in a pop song because it changes from major to minor keys and back again. Because of this and the strong melody, it was chosen by George Martin to close the soundtrack album, since he believed that it should go out on a high. The song has been covered by a curious selection of artists including Frankie and the Fashions, Golden Earring, the Buckinghams, Bounty Killer, Lydia Gray, Joshua Rifkin, Roger Nichols and Johnny Rivers among others.

Cliff's version was recorded at a session where it was the only song successfully completed. The third and final take and edit were used for the mono and stereo recordings. The Beatles were masters at clever harmonies and surprising key changes and this is obvious particularly in this song, which is introduced by a stuttering brass band. Cliff's recording is a strong study of the song but, unfortunately, there are no backing vocals, even though Bruce Welch and Hank Marvin turned up for that day's sessions to apply their close harmonies to one or two other tracks; instead the harmonies are left to the instrumentation and, for this reason, the track is lacking some of the original spirit.

Track Specification

Composed by John Lennon and Paul McCartney

Musicians	
Bernard Ebbinghouse Orchestra	orchestra
Bernard Ebbinghouse	arranger, conductor
Cliff Richard	vocals

Recording Details	
Producer	Norrie Paramor
Engineered by	Peter Vincent and Richard Lush
Recording location	Abbey Road Studio 2, St. John's Wood, London
Recording date	19th September 1966

♫ I'll Be Waiting

Unissued track

I'll Be Waiting was the second of two tracks to be recorded at the session on 1st May 1962 but is one of the very few Cliff Richard recordings that have yet to be released; whether the track was incomplete, abandoned in favour of other tracks or agreed nt to be fit for commercial release is unclear.

Information is scant on the composition, including its writer, but it is noteworthy because it is, chronologically speaking, the last Cliff track, commercially released or otherwise, to feature Jet Harris on bass guitar. Tony Meehan had left at the end of 1961 because of his tardiness and resultant disruptive influence to be replaced by Brian Bennett. Now Hank Marvin and Bruce Welch were getting irritated by Harris's attitude and drinking and so he was summarily sacked to be replaced in very short shrift (just four days later for the next session to start recording for the ***Summer Holiday*** soundtrack) by Brian 'Licorice' Locking. Locking used to be a member of Marty Wilde's Wildcats and obtained his nickname from his preferred instrument of the clarinet (American south jazz slang dictated that it was a 'licorice stick', hence the American spelling). Jet Harris and Tony Meehan then joined forces to become a rival guitar- and drum-based instrumental group to The Shadows.

Track Specification

Composed by Unknown

Musicians		*Recording Details*	
Jet Harris	bass	Producer	Norrie Paramor
Hank Marvin	guitar	Engineered by	Malcolm Addey
Brian Bennett	drums, percussion	Recording location	Abbey Road Studio 2, St. John's Wood, London
Cliff Richard	vocals	Recording date	1st May 1962
Bruce Welch	rhythm guitar		

♫ I'll Come Running

38th UK single *and from the albums* **The Best of Cliff** *and* **Cliff in Japan**

Also recorded by its writer Neil Diamond and subsequently by the Murder City Devils, *I'll Come Running* became Cliff Richard's thirty-eighth single release in the UK, with the help of Mike Leander's arrangement and his orchestra. The chorus is uncredited and unknown since there is scant information on the session and is highlighted as such in the entry. The first of four songs to be recorded on the day, along with its eventual B-side ***I Get the Feelin'*** (also written by Diamond), an unknown number of takes saw its completion. Released on the Columbia label (catalogue number DB 8210) on 2nd June 1967, it became Cliff's then worst performing song in the charts when it only managed to reach number twenty-six. The single version was only issued in the mono format, while both the mono and stereo versions appeared on the respective albums of ***The Best of Cliff*** two years later. This stereo version uses the same backing track but employs a different (unknown) vocal take recorded at the same session; the takes are very similar except with slightly different minor inflections on certain words on the first verse.

With the unusual employment of a harpsichord to accompany the song, the melody and arrangement are sympathetic enough to be significantly different from Neil Diamond's but still to give it enough to be clearly one of his compositions. Cliff sings with passion and emotion in this love song and it includes an early example of his use of falsetto at the end of the song. The uncredited backing group may possibly the Breakaways, purely from the sound they produce and because they were regularly recording and touring with Cliff at the time of this session. The same group may also be involved in the live Japan track but this is also undocumented.

Track Specification

Composed by Neil Diamond

1. Single

Musicians		*Recording Details*	
Mike Leander Orchestra	orchestra	Producer	Norrie Paramor
Mike Leander	arranger, conductor	Engineered by	Unknown
Cliff Richard	vocals	Recording location	Abbey Road Studio 2, St. John's Wood, London
Unknown	female backing vocals	Recording date	24th April 1967

2. The Best of Cliff

Musicians		*Recording Details*	
Mike Leander Orchestra	orchestra	Producer	Norrie Paramor
Mike Leander	arranger, conductor	Engineered by	Unknown
Cliff Richard	vocals	Recording location	Abbey Road Studio 2, St. John's Wood, London
Unknown	female backing vocals	Recording date	24th April 1967

3. Cliff in Japan

Musicians		*Recording Details*	
Norrie Paramor Orchestra	orchestra	Producer	Norrie Paramor
Norrie Paramor	arranger, conductor	Engineered by	Unknown
Cliff Richard	vocals	Recording location	Shibuya Public Hall, Tokyo, Japan
Unknown	backing vocals	Recording date	18th October 1967

♫ I'll Love You Forever Today
42nd UK single

The importance of the music in Cliff Richard's dark 1967 film, ***Two a Penny***, is incidental to the drama unfolding on the screen (similar in this respect to ***Serious Charge*** eight years previously). There is casual mention of Jamie Hopkins (played by Cliff) wanting to become a singer (allowing him to perform ***Twist and Shout*** in a pub scene) but it is clear that he is only after easy money rather than being driven by the ned to perform. Having been involved in getting his girlfriend Carol (Ann Holloway) thrown out of the house by her mother, when he was found in her bedroom (although nothing happened), Carol seeks solace in a church. She is locked out and then begins to recite the Lord's Prayer in the open air. Finally, she is found by Jamie, who takes her back home and introduces her to his mother, convincing her that Carol is fine. Over this entire sequence, *I'll Love You Forever Today* is played out with its cynical lyrics stating that love forces one to be tied down and the title shows that he believes love to be short-term, to be shrugged off once he has got what he wants.
In the title sequence, the song, written by Cliff and Jim Collier, is referenced as *Love You Forever Today*; however, the subsequent single release and inclusion on the ***Two a Penny*** album has the additional prefix of *I'll*. Recorded in the same session as all of the songs featured in the film, *I'll Love You Forever Today* was backed with Neil Diamond's ***Girl, You'll Be a Woman Soon***, and was issued on the Columbia label (catalogue number DB 8437) on 21st June 1968 but in mono only – the predilection of Columbia at the time was to reserve the stereo output for albums. The song appeared in that format two months later with the release of the *Two a Penny* album. The single reached number twenty-seven in the UK charts, which, at the time, was the worst placing of a Cliff single since the beginning of his career nine years earlier, and was in stark contrast to the success of his previous hit, which was ***Congratulations*** at number one. However, the song is a personal one because of the important message he wanted to deliver through the film and the single helped to publicize it.
The slinky brass accompaniment to this quite beautiful if cynical love song ushers in Cliff's gentle vocal line. A much underrated single and song from Cliff's introspective period, it is very easy to deride it on the back of a religious project. However, it is clearly something that was a passion for Cliff and this comes through in his performance of the song, while it is the perfect complement the action on the silver screen.
All four of the *Two a Penny* tracks were translated into German for inclusion on Cliff's first German album, *Hier Ist Cliff*, with *I'll Love You Forever Today* becoming ***Die Liebe Ist Immer Nur Heute***. This particular track was also recorded in French in 1973 for *When in France – Chante en Français* released in 1975, where Cliff's vocals were overdubbed on the original backing track and titled ***Je T'Aime pour Toujours Ce Jour***.

Track Specification
Composed by Cliff Richard and Jim Collier

Musicians	
Mike Leander	arranger, conductor
Mike Leander Orchestra	orchestra
Cliff Richard	vocals
Bruce Welch	rhythm guitar

Recording Details	
Producer	Norrie Paramor
Engineered by	Peter Vince
Recording location	Abbey Road Studio 2, St. John's Wood, London
Recording date	1st July 1967

♫ I'll Make It All up to You
From the album **Tracks 'n' Grooves**

A minor hit in the US for Jerry Lee Lewis in the late fifties, *I'll Make It All up to You* has also been covered by Mickey Gilley, Gerry and the Pacemakers and Preacher Jack among others. Cliff Richard recorded this song in 1967, although it was held back from release until the 1970 album ***Tracks 'n' Grooves***. It is the first track recorded by Cliff that has only ever been released in stereo since mono had been largely abandoned by the end of the sixties (although a mono edit of *I'll Make It All up to You* was created at the time of its recording – this remains unreleased).
The omnipresent harpsichord in Mike Leander's arrangements of Cliff's songs from the period makes its appearance here in the introduction to the song. The andante pace of the song matches the mood of the lyrics, which tells of an infringement on a love affair. There is a female backing chorus, about whom there is no information, although it is quite likely to be the Breakaways, who were regularly involved in Cliff recordings and tours during this period.

Track Specification
Composed by Charlie Rich

Musicians	
Mike Leander Orchestra	orchestra
Mike Leander	arranger, conductor
Cliff Richard	vocals
Unknown	backing vocals

Recording Details	
Producer	Norrie Paramor
Engineered by	Unknown
Recording location	Abbey Road Studio 2, St. John's Wood, London
Recording date	24th April 1967

♫ I'll Mend Your Broken Heart
From the album **Phil Everly** *(Phil Everly)*

Having collaborated in concert on some Everly Brothers tracks in 1981, Phil Everly contacted Cliff Richard in the late summer of 1982 with a suggestion that they should record some material together. At the Eden Studios in October of that year, the pair recorded what would become Cliff's eighty-sixth UK single, ***She Means Nothing to Me***, and another track,

I'll Mend Your Broken Heart, which was initially only released on Everly's self-titled album the following year. Featuring a number of well-known session musicians, the track also had Dire Straits front man Mark Knopfler playing guitar. When the album that featured a remixed version of *She Means Nothing to Me*, ***The Rock Connection***, was remastered and reissued in 2004, *I'll Mend Your Broken Heart* was added as a bonus track.
The shimmering guitars and prominence of Everly's voice make the track sound like an Everly Brothers original, so effective is Cliff in blending his voice with Phil Everly. Although Cliff sings alongside him, it is Everly's vocal that can be heard throughout. The middle eight features a gentle guitar solo, before the vocals are brought back in. There are several key changes that keep the interest moving on throughout.

Track Specification
Composed by Stewart Blandamer

Musicians	
Billy Bremner	guitar, acoustic guitar, tremolo guitar
Stuart Coleman	bass, percussion
Phil Everly	vocals
Mickey Gee	rhythm guitar
Mark Knopfler	guitar, rhythm guitar
Cliff Richard	vocals, backing vocals
Terry Williams	drums, percussion
Pete Wingfield	piano

Recording Details	
Producer	Stuart Coleman
Engineered by	Rod Houison and Neill King
Recording location	Eden Studios, London
Recording date	5th October 1982

♬ I'll See You in My Dreams
From the EP **Dream**

A hugely popular song when it was published in 1924, *I'll See You in My Dreams* was chosen as the title song for a film biography of writer Gus Kahn's life. It has also appeared in the Ginger Rogers 1940 film, *Kitty Foyle*, as well as making a brief appearance in a Tom and Jerry cartoon. It was recorded first by co-writer Isham Jones, and it has since been recorded by a variety of artists including Pat Boone (reaching number twenty-seven in the UK singles charts in February 1962), Louis Armstrong, Doris Day, Django Reinhardt, Chet Atkins, Tommy Dorsey, Ella Fitzgerald and Teddy Wilson.
The last of three tracks to be recorded for the ***Dream*** EP (the first such release to incorporate new material not otherwise available by Cliff Richard in any other format) from the early May 1961 session, the final and thirteenth take was used for the mono and stereo edits but with different mixes to meet the respective audio channel requirements. Until the release of a 2000 French compilation album and then the fiftieth anniversary celebration album ***...And They Said It Wouldn't Last! (My 50 Years in Music)***, the track had remained unavailable and was much sought after by fans and collectors.
With a similar approach to ***All I Do Is Dream of You*** from the same EP, there is a late night swing club feel about the performance of *I'll See You in My Dreams*, with Jet Harris playing a double bass rather than a electric equivalent and Tony Meehan playing his drums with brushes, while both Hank Marvin and Bruce Welch play rhythm guitar chords. Cliff's vocals are as competent as ever they were and are well suited to this style of song, even though he felt he was more of a rock and roller.

Track Specification
Composed by Gus Kahn and Isham Jones

Musicians	
Jet Harris	double bass
Hank Marvin	guitar
Tony Meehan	drums, percussion
Cliff Richard	vocals
Bruce Welch	rhythm guitar

Recording Details	
Producer	Norrie Paramor
Engineered by	Malcolm Addey
Recording location	Abbey Road Studio 2, St. John's Wood, London
Recording date	4th May 1961

♬ I'll String Along with You
From the album **Cliff Sings**

For Cliff Richard's second LP, albeit the first true studio album, the tracks on each side were divided between backing from the Norrie Paramor Orchestra and The Drifters (as they were called at the time of recording but, with the successful release of ***Living Doll*** in the US and the subsequent promotional tour, soon to change their name to avoid confusion with the pre-existing American vocal group performing under that name and so became the Shadows). The first song in the former category was *I'll String Along with You*, which was originally published in 1934 and comes from the film *Calamity Jane* although it was also used extensively in the film *Mrs. Henderson Presents* during the audition of the showgirls scene. It has been extensively covered by the likes of Louis Armstrong, Chas & Dave, Nat King Cole, Ray Noble, André Previn, Dana and Dick Powell.
The crooning song fits very well with Cliff's voice and *I'll String Along with You* was the first song to be recorded that was intended to show off Cliff's vocal capabilities and to broaden his appeal to a wider audience with different material. The original track was recorded in mono (for release on the album *Cliff Sings* and the mono issue of ***Cliff Richard Sings No. 3*** EP) but that track was remixed for stereo and released on the stereo version of the EP. Both versions have since been made available on CD respective reissues of the album.

Track Specification
Composed by Al Dubin and Harry Warren
Musicians

Norrie Paramor Orchestra	orchestra
Norrie Paramor	arranger, conductor
Cliff Richard	vocals

Recording Details

Producer	Norrie Paramor
Engineered by	Malcolm Addey and Alan Kane (mono) and Stuart Eltham and Norman Smith (stereo)
Recording location	Abbey Road Studio 2, St. John's Wood, London
Recording date	9th September 1959

♬ I'll Try

From the album **Oh Boy!**

One of Conway Twitty's most enduring country hits in the US, *I'll Try* has appeared on many of Twitty's albums, collections and anthologies. With such a provenance, the song was picked for inclusion in the set recorded by Cliff Richard for the official album to accompany the popular music television show, *Oh Boy!*, the popular music television programme that helped to launch Cliff's career.

Cliff had become a regular favourite on the show, where he performed covers of popular songs and also sang some original material. The backing track and Cliff's vocals were recorded on separate days for the album and, instead of using the Drifters as his backing group, the musicians were taken up from the Oh Boy! Band, while the harmony vocals were provided by The Dallas Boys, all of whom are known from the session. There is no record of who the individual instrumental performers in the band are, however, and so will be highlighted as unknown in this entry.

The slower pace of the song in contrast to those that had gone before such as *Rockin' Robin* not only shows Cliff's effectiveness as a balladeer but also as a rock and roller. His pitch-perfect and emotive vocals manage to supersede the rather lacklustre backing vocals provided by the Dallas Boys.

Although the album was re-released in the late seventies, it wasn't until the issue of the rarities album ***The Rock and Roll Years 1958-1963*** that it saw release in digital format.

Track Specification
Composed by Jack Nance and Conway Twitty
Musicians

Dallas Boys:	
Nicky Clarke	backing vocals
Leon Fisk	backing vocals
Stan Jones	backing vocals
Joe Smith	backing vocals
Bob Wragg	backing vocals
Oh Boy! Band	guitars, stand-up bass, piano, drums, percussion
Cliff Richard	vocals

Recording Details

Producer	Harry Robinson (backing track) and Norrie Paramor (vocals)
Engineered by	Norman Newell (backing track) and Malcolm Addey (vocals)
Recording location	Abbey Road Studio 2, St. John's Wood, London
Recording date	19th October 1958 (backing track) and 21st October 1958 (vocals)

♬ I'll Walk Alone

From the album **Love Is Forever**

Written and published in the year before the end of the Second World War, *I'll Walk Alone*'s lyrics reflect the enforced separation of couples as the men were conscripted to fight in foreign lands and leaving their loved ones at home. This song is slightly different from many that were recorded at the time as it describes the emotions from the point of view of the lover forced to stay at home worrying about the safety of the partner fighting. Perhaps the best known version, certainly in the US, is by Dinah Shore, who sang the song in the 1944 film *Follow the Boys*, and achieved a number one chart hit with it. Also covered by Martha Tilton, by the time the fifties arrived, it had started to be covered by male singers, including Ricky Nelson – while this may not seem peculiar today with women in the armed forces, at the time it was very odd since it was the women who were left behind and, given that the song is from the point of view of the lover staying at home, it would have appeared sexually incongruous.

Cliff Richard followed the increasing trend for male singers to perform the song when, for his album ***Love Is Forever***, he took Nelson's example and recorded his version at the session in June 1965, which resulted in four songs for the album. The final (unknown) take and edit of *I'll Walk Alone* were used for the mono and stereo recordings but with different mixes for the needs of the separation of the audio channels.

While some critics might rail against Cliff's choice of material to record – usually preferring their performers to fit with a particular style or genre – he is clearly an expert at singing the gentle love ballad, and this is strongly evident on *I'll Walk Alone*, which uses a bass and gentle drum to evoke the idea of walking at a slow pace.

Track Specification
Composed by Sammy Cahn and Jule Styne
Musicians

Norrie Paramor Orchestra	orchestra
Cliff Richard	vocals
Ken Woodman	arranger, conductor

Recording Details

Producer	Norrie Paramor
Engineered by	Unknown
Recording location	Abbey Road Studio 2, St. John's Wood, London
Recording date	10th June 1965

♫ I Love
From the album **Small Corners**

Chosen for Cliff Richard's religious album project, ***Small Corners***, which he also produced, *I Love* was recorded at the end of the last session for the album, completed in three takes, with extra overdubs applied almost five months later.
As if ***Why Should the Devil Have All the God Music?*** weren't enough to provide a self-referential answer, its following album track, *I Love*, assists further with providing one to that question. The song talks of mundane everyday occurrences (brown bread toast in bed, old ladies screwing up their faces at babies, friends knocking on the door) and the pleasure to be obtained from it: essentially the joy of living and letting Christ into his life. Cliff completes the song with a semi-sung, part-talking section as he picks out the meaningful lyrics from the entire song.

Track Specification
Composed by Alwyn Wall and Malcolm Wild

Musicians		*Recording Details*	
Brian Bennett	drums, percussion	Producer	Cliff Richard
Terry Britten	guitar	Engineered by	Tony Clark and Haydn Bendall
Bryn Haworth	guitar	Recording location	Abbey Road Studio 3, St. John's Wood, London
Cliff Richard	vocals, backing vocals	Recording date	19th January 1977 and 3rd June 1977
Alan Tarney	bass		
Graham Todd	keyboards		

♫ I Love You
11th UK single *and from the albums* **The Rock 'n' Roll Years 1958-1963**, **...And They Said It Wouldn't Last! (My 50 Years in Music)** *and* **Reunited – Special Edition** *and B-side of* **This New Year**

I Love You and its B-side, ***'D' in Love***, were recorded at the same session and it is a favourite of the band, partly because of its quirky instrumental harmonies and the simple expression of love. The stereo and mono versions are from the fourteenth take with different edits and mixes for the aural formats. The second take was released on the rarity anthology ***The Rock 'n' Roll Years 1958-1963*** and features the first take crumbling, a mistake in the lyrics and no vocal backing. A further take (the tenth) was issued on ***...And They Said It Wouldn't Last! (My 50 Years in Music)*** with no reverberation or echo on Cliff's voice or vocal backing.
The song was issued, backed with *'D' in Love*, on the Columbia label (catalogue number 45-DB 4547) on 25th November 1960 and reached number one in the UK, staying for two weeks. Notably, it was also Cliff's first Christmas number one, although it is often forgotten by compilers who focus on his later Christmas-related songs. Cliff has been quoted as saying that he often forgets that this song was a number one and it is left off Cliff's hits collections, possibly for that reason.
The song is more country than rock and roll and features a gently plodding rhythm guitar and bass line that underlines the simple rhymes and melody that is incredibly catchy. Rather than using Bruce Welch or Hank Marvin for the backing vocals, Cliff uses his own voice to harmonize on the repetition of the song title. A happy-go-lucky song that expresses the *joie de vivre* felt when in love, it uses simple ideas and lyrics to define the breadth of his love for the girl to whom he is singing the song. The middle eight bridge features a brilliantly enigmatic guitar solo from Hank and it is so hook-laden that it is unsurprising that it should turn out to be a massive hit around Europe for them.
Almost exactly thirty-one years after recording the original song, Cliff performed the song on the popular lunchtime BBC magazine show, *Pebble Mill at One*, accompanying himself on the guitar. Unusually, the recording was licensed from the BBC and included as a bonus track on the CD version of the ***This New Year*** single issued in late December 1991.
When the Shadows reformed with Cliff in 2009 to record an album and embark on a tour to promote it, they decided to re-record material that was associated with them as well as three other songs from the period. One of the chosen songs was *I Love You*, which, although not issued on the basic album, it was packaged on to a three-track bonus disc that was released as a special edition of the album. One of the only tracks not to be performed in a similar style to the original, *I Love You* is introduced by a strong rhythm section, before the familiar bouncing guitar comes in.

Track Specification
Composed by Bruce Welch

1. Single

Musicians		*Recording Details*	
Jet Harris	bass	Producer	Norrie Paramor
Hank Marvin	guitar	Engineered by	Malcolm Addey and Norman Smith
Tony Meehan	drums, percussion	Recording location	Abbey Road Studio 2, St. John's Wood, London
Cliff Richard	vocals, backing vocals	Recording date	9th September 1960
Bruce Welch	rhythm guitar		

2. The Rock 'n' Roll Years 1958-1963

Musicians		*Recording Details*	
Jet Harris	bass	Producer	Norrie Paramor
Hank Marvin	guitar	Engineered by	Malcolm Addey and Norman Smith
Tony Meehan	drums, percussion	Recording location	Abbey Road Studio 2, St. John's Wood, London
Cliff Richard	vocals	Recording date	9th September 1960
Bruce Welch	rhythm guitar		

3. ...And They Said It Wouldn't Last! (My 50 Years in Music)

Musicians		*Recording Details*	
Jet Harris	bass	Producer	Norrie Paramor
Hank Marvin	guitar	Engineered by	Malcolm Addey and Norman Smith
Tony Meehan	drums, percussion	Recording location	Abbey Road Studio 2, St. John's Wood, London
Cliff Richard	vocals	Recording date	9th September 1960
Bruce Welch	rhythm guitar		

4. B-side (This New Year)

Musicians		*Recording Details*	
Cliff Richard	vocals, guitar	Producer	Unknown
		Engineered by	Unknown
		Recording location	Pebble Mill Television Studios, Birmingham
		Recording date	7th September 1991

5. Reunited – Special Edition

Musicians		*Recording Details*	
Brian Bennett	arranger (strings), drums, percussion	Producer	Warren Bennett (co-ordination)
Warren Bennett	arranger (strings), keyboards	Engineered by	James Collins (Honeyhill Studios), Ethan Carlson (Middle Ear Studios), Les Williams (Nivram Studios) and Keith Bessey (mixing and mastering)
Mark Berrow	violin		
Dave Daniels	cello		
Mark Griffiths	bass	Recording location	Middle Ear Studios, Miami, Florida, USA (Cliff's vocals), Nivram Studios, Perth, Western Australia (Hank's guitars and vocals) and Honeyhill Studios, Hertfordshire, England (all other vocals and instruments)
Bogustan Kostecki	violin		
Martin Loveday	cello		
Hank Marvin	backing vocals, guitar		
Perry Montague-Mason	violin		
Cliff Richard	vocals, backing vocals	Recording date	Early 2009
Emlyn Singleton	violin		
Chris Tombling	violin		
Kevin Townsend	arranger (strings), conductor		
Bruce Welch	backing vocals, rhythm guitar		
Warren Zeilinski	violin		

♫ I Love You, I Need You

Single by **Patti Brook**

With brother Terry and sister Jean, Patti Brook formed a family vocal group that won a regional television talent contest and, under the wing of earlier winner Emile Ford found an agent with the Lew Grade and Bernard Delfont organisation and worked on several recordings for Pye Records. In the early sixties, the group worked as the support act for The Shadows but, shortly afterwards, the group disbanded. Patti continued to work with Cliff Richard and the Shadows on tour, as well as joining Frankie Vaughan, Ford and Lonnie Donegan for their tours. In 1962, Cliff wrote *I Love You, I Need You* specifically for Patti to record, although he was originally advised to use a pseudonym to avoid rumour of romance. She left the tour circuit in 1964 to take up a vocal residency with the Graham Warner Band at the Mecca Ballroom based in Bradford in Yorkshire and then to get married and start a family.

I Love You, I Need You was backed with a cover of the Kitty Wells song *Unloved, Unwanted* and issued on the Pye label (catalogue number 7N.15422) in March 1962 but didn't chart. The single is now a considerable rarity in its original format, although the label confirms that Cliff didn't opt for a pseudonym. Little information is available regarding the personnel and the studio location but it is likely to be the London-based Pye studios, although it is known that Cliff had no involvement. The song has since appeared on the genre compilations *Teen Dreams 25* and *Here Come the Girls 8*.

Track Specification

Composed by Cliff Richard

Musicians		*Recording Details*	
Patti Brook	vocals	Producer	Unknown
Unknown	all instrumentation	Engineered by	Unknown
		Recording location	Unknown
		Recording date	early 1962

♫ I Love You So

From the album **Me and My Shadows** *(mono and stereo)*

Particularly notable on this track buried in the middle of the second side of the ***Me and My Shadows*** album is the first instance of Cliff Richard writing credit (he would later write ***Happy Like a Bell (Ding Dong)*** for his friend Cherry Wainer, which is the first instance of a *sole* Cliff writing credit). The mono and stereo versions are the sixteenth take from the session, although the mono version has an extended guitar solo taken from the middle eight bridge which was added at a separate session, of which no detail is available but only involved Hank Marvin in the overdubs. The song appears on the ***Me and My Shadows No. 3*** EP. There is a severely edited version, losing about a minute from the end, that appears on the 2001 2-on-1 version of the album alongside ***Listen to Cliff!***.

A pretty little love song (with no explanation required from the title), the instrumentation is kept simple with guitars, bass and austere finger-bell device as the only percussion. There is no guitar solo as such but merely a general progression through a sequence of chords. It is very different from the rest of the album in its structure as there are diminuendos and sforzando sections that help to underline the tenor and meaning of the lyrics.

Track Specification
Composed by Ian Samwell, Jet Harris and Cliff Richard

1. Me and My Shadows (mono issue)

Musicians	
Jet Harris	bass
Hank Marvin	guitar
Tony Meehan	bells
Cliff Richard	vocals
Bruce Welch	rhythm guitar

Recording Details	
Producer	Norrie Paramor
Engineered by	Malcolm Addey and Norman Smith
Recording location	Abbey Road Studio 2, St. John's Wood, London
Recording date	17th March 1960 (basic track) and Unknown (guitar overdubs)

2. Me and My Shadows (stereo issue)

Musicians	
Jet Harris	bass
Hank Marvin	guitar
Tony Meehan	bells
Cliff Richard	vocals
Bruce Welch	rhythm guitar

Recording Details	
Producer	Norrie Paramor
Engineered by	Peter Bown and Alan Kane (stereo)
Recording location	Abbey Road Studio 2, St. John's Wood, London
Recording date	17th March 1960

♫ I Love You the Way You Are

From the album **...And They Said It Wouldn't Last! (My 50 Years in Music)**

Written and recorded by American fifties singer Bobby Vinton, *I Love You the Way You Are* was one of the four songs slated for recording at the penultimate Cliff Richard session of 1965 in the middle of November. The final take and edit was abandoned at the time and remained unissued for another forty-three years until the mono format version was released on the track listing of the celebratory album ***...And They Said It Wouldn't Last! (My 50 Years in Music)***. There is likely to exist a stereo version that was recorded simultaneously, given that most tracks of the period were edited in both formats, although records of its survival are unavailable and the recording has not been found to date.
With a jaunty rhythm set by the bobbing bass and the echoing harp chords, it is surprising that this ebullient performance by Cliff was never released at the time. While there was stronger material that was issued, there were also several songs that were not as good. There is a guitar solo in the instrumental break, which is not as accomplished as it would have been were it Hank Marvin.

Track Specification
Composed by Bobby Vinton

Musicians	
Bernard Ebbinghouse Orchestra	orchestra
Bernard Ebbinghouse	arranger, conductor
Mike Sammes Singers	backing vocals
Cliff Richard	vocals

Recording Details	
Producer	Norrie Paramor
Engineered by	Malcolm Addey
Recording location	Abbey Road Studio 2, St. John's Wood, London
Recording date	17th November 1965

♫ I'm Afraid to Go Home

B-side of **The Twelfth of Never**

Made famous by Brian Hyland, who had a hit with the song in the US, *I'm Afraid to Go Home* has also been covered by a number of artists including Gene Pitney. It was chosen as the B-side for the single release of Cliff Richard's version of ***The Twelfth of Never*** and was the last of five songs to be completed in its session. The unknown take and edit was used for the mono and stereo recordings but with different mixes to cater for the requirements of the separate audio channels. Although it was also included on the ***Why Don't They Understand?*** EP, it would be over thirty-five years before this rare track was released in another medium when, in 2001, it was part of the French CD album *I Could Easily Fall* and then it was added to the track listing of the celebratory ***...And They Said It Wouldn't Last! (My 50 Years in Music)*** in 2008.
Cliff's voice is given a lot of echo and, while it starts slow enough, it picks up the pace in the middle section. There is a rolling piano accompaniment as well as a harmonica (both uncredited specifically) while there is a strong drum and guitar section, too, although this not the Shadows. Cliff performs well and it is a shame that the song wasn't given greater coverage at the time of release because it is a little gem among his recording oeuvre.

Track Specification
Composed by Gary Geld and Peter Udell

Musicians	
Mike Sammes Singers	backing vocals
Norrie Paramor Orchestra	orchestra
Norrie Paramor	conductor
Cliff Richard	vocals

Recording Details	
Producer	Norrie Paramor
Engineered by	Malcolm Addey
Recording location	Abbey Road Studio 2, St. John's Wood, London
Recording date	24th July 1964

♬ Imagina un Giorno

Italian single

In the sixties, Cliff Richard regularly recorded German versions of his hits and original material for single release in Germany, but had thus far restricted the practice to that tongue, although he had recorded EPs and albums in French, Spanish and Italian. Breaking the mould was *Imagina un Giorno* – literally *Imagine a Day* – a translation of his thirty-ninth British single, Hank Marvin's ***The Day I Met Marie***. Both the German and Italian vocals were recorded at the same session and overdubbed on an orchestral track that had been recorded the day before to allow the focus on recording Cliff's voice. *Imagina un Giorno* was issued, backed with ***Oh, No, No*** (an Italian translation of ***I Get the Feelin'***, also recorded at that same session), on the international Columbia label (catalogue number SCMQ-7075) in October 1967. Originally only released in mono, as was the practice by Columbia at the time for singles and EPs, Imagina *un Giorno* was eventually issued in stereo as part of the track listing of the foreign language song compilation ***On the Continent*** in 1997.
Singing in the Italian language provides the song with a musical lilt that doesn't exist in the English or German versions, which makes the brass band chorus sounds incongruous against it. There is a female backing group that is uncredited but may be the same as those singing in the German version, which are also uncredited.

Track Specification
Composed by Hank Marvin; Italian lyrics by Vito Pallavicini

Musicians

Bernard Ebbinghouse Orchestra	orchestra
Bernard Ebbinghouse	arranger, conductor
Cliff Richard	vocals
Unknown	backing vocals

Recording Details

Producer	Norrie Paramor (backing track and vocals)
Engineered by	Peter Vince (backing track and vocals)
Recording location	Abbey Road Studio 2, St. John's Wood, London (backing track and vocals)
Recording date	27th September 1967 (backing track) and 28th September 1967 (vocals)

♬ Imagine

From the albums **Beginnings** *(Cilla Black) and* **Beginnings (2009)** *(Cilla Black)*

After the acrimonious and embittered break-up of the Beatles was made official in April 1970, each of the members of the band went off to work on their own solo projects: John Lennon created what many regard to be a seminal seventies album in *Imagine*. Although the album was issued in 1971, it wasn't until 1975 when the title song was released as a single, shooting straight up the charts and giving Lennon his only solo number one before his death; unsurprisingly, in the wake of his murder in New York, the song was reissued and on a wave of emotion and new appreciation of the song, it hit number one once more. Randy Crawford also released a version at the same time but this only hit number sixty. The message of the song, accompanied by a plaintive sequence of rich piano chords, is simple: whatever your religion, whatever your principles, live in peace and help one another rather than accruing unnecessary chattels and possessions. Some Christians read it as a personal attack because of the line "Imagine there's no heaven..." In some ways this is valid because organized religion has, other than man's cruelty to man, been the cause of much of the world's woes and strife, which was the point Lennon was trying to make, but, in essence, the song is a straightforward message of love and tolerance to the listener. It has been covered a number of times over the years including by Dolly Parton, Eva Cassidy, Avril Lavigne, Madonna, Diana Ross, Liza Minnelli and Joan Baez among several others.
Having recorded together for the first time on ***That's What Friends Are For***, Cliff Richard joined Cilla Black on a new recording of *Imagine* for her album *Beginnings*. As with the original, the song is driven by the plaintive rolling piano motif, and joined by strings and the guitar supporting Black's gentle vocals, which she performs with an attitude akin to wonder. Cliff provides a lovely backing vocal arrangement with layered recordings of his voice as the drama of the song gradually builds. There are other backing vocals perceptibly present but these are kept in the background.
In 2009, for the reissue of Black's album, there was a new mix created that essentially limits the instrumentation and allows the vocals to stand out more obviously. The beauty of Cliff's backing vocals is made more focused and this remix is considerably better than the original, which was strong enough to begin with.

Track Specification
Composed by John Lennon

1. Beginnings

Musicians

Lavine Andrade	viola
David Arch	piano, keyboards
Richard Ashton	French horn
Robert Bailey	cello
Cilla Black	vocals
Adrian Bradbury	cello
Mary Carewe	backing vocals
Lance Ellington	backing vocals
Dai Emanuel	violin
Paul Gardham	French horn
Mick Green	guitars

Recording Details

Producer	Ted Carfrae
Engineered by	Chris West and Mark Bishop
Recording location	Westside Studios, North Yorkshire and State of the Ark, Richmond, Surrey
Recording date	2002 or 2003

Rushen Gunes	viola
Jonathan Hill	violin
Ian Humphries	violin
Stephen Hussey	violin
Fridrik "Frizzy" Karlsson	acoustic and rhythm guitars
Julian Leaper	violin
Pan Hon Lee	violin
Oliver Lewis	violin
Mae McKenna	backing vocals
Don McVay	viola
Steve Pearce	bass
Cliff Richard	backing vocals
Frank Ricotti	percussion
Ralph Salmins	drums, percussion
Stephen Shakeshaft	viola
Celia Sheen	violin
Richard Steggall	French horn
David Towse	violin
Paul Wiley	violin

2. Beginnings (2009)

Musicians

Lavine Andrade	viola
David Arch	piano
Richard Ashton	French horn
Robert Bailey	cello
Cilla Black	vocals
Adrian Bradbury	cello
Mary Carewe	backing vocals
Lance Ellington	backing vocals
Dai Emanuel	violin
Paul Gardham	French horn
Mick Green	guitars
Rushen Gunes	viola
Jonathan Hill	violin
Ian Humphries	violin
Stephen Hussey	violin
Fridrik "Frizzy" Karlsson	acoustic and rhythm guitars
Julian Leaper	violin
Pan Hon Lee	violin
Oliver Lewis	violin
Mae McKenna	backing vocals
Don McVay	viola
Steve Pearce	bass
Cliff Richard	backing vocals
Ralph Salmins	drums, percussion
Stephen Shakeshaft	viola
Celia Sheen	violin
Richard Steggall	French horn
David Towse	violin
Paul Wiley	violin

Recording Details

Producer	Ted Carfrae
Engineered by	Chris West and Mark Bishop
Recording location	Westside Studios, North Yorkshire and State of the Ark, Richmond, Surrey
Recording date	2002 or 2003

♫ Imagine Love

B-side of **Green Light**

Co-written by Cliff Richard's long-term composer Alan Tarney in collaboration with old Cliff and the Shadows friend Jerry Lordan, *Imagine Love* was recorded at Cliff's penultimate full session of 1977. When the eponymous third and final track from the ***Green Light*** project was issued as a single, *Imagine Love* was unearthed and used as its B-side. Although there were high hopes for it, the single didn't sell well, making its B-side a significant rarity, which was rectified by its inclusion as a bonus track on 2002's remastered and reissued version of *Green Light*.

A medium- to fast-paced song, it relies on the guitar and bass to drive the rhythm onwards as Cliff sings his main vocal line. As the recording features his own backing vocals, the blend therefore is brilliant against his main vocal line and this lifts the song into something more special than to be tucked away on a B-side without any other exposure.

Track Specification

Composed by Alan Tarney and Jerry Lordan

Musicians

Terry Britten	guitar
Alan Hawkshaw	keyboards
Cliff Richard	vocals, backing vocals.
Trevor Spencer	drums, percussion
Alan Tarney	backing vocals, bass

Recording Details

Producer	Bruce Welch
Engineered by	Tony Clark
Recording location	Abbey Road Studio 2, St. John's Wood, London
Recording date	11th July 1977

♫ I'm Gonna Get You

From the album **Me and My Shadows**

A somewhat curious collaboration of Shadows Jet Harris and Hank Marvin with erstwhile bandmate and progenitor of many of Cliff Richard's early hits (including the seminal ***Move It***) and B-sides, Ian Samwell, *I'm Gonna Get You* is the first track on the third album by the group, ***Me and My Shadows***.

The tenth take from the 1960 session on 30th March was eventually used and it harks back to those early days with a strong rock and roll riff, with Cliff's vocals being raucous but also paradoxically subdued. The song is the story of the assertion that he is going to get the girl he is driven towards and focused on. There is an unusual bass sequence throughout (perhaps not unusual since the bassist was one of the co-writers). A strong song as an opener to the album, *I'm Gonna Get You* would have been a suitable B-side if there had been no other contenders.

Track Specification

Composed by Jet Harris, Hank Marvin and Ian Samwell

Musicians

Jet Harris	bass
Hank Marvin	guitar
Tony Meehan	drums, percussion
Cliff Richard	vocals
Bruce Welch	rhythm guitar

Recording Details

Producer	Norrie Paramor
Engineered by	Malcolm Addey and Norman Smith (mono) and Peter Bown and Alan Kane (stereo)
Recording location	Abbey Road Studio 2, St. John's Wood, London
Recording date	30th March 1960

♫ I'm in Love with You

From the pantomime cast recording album of **Aladdin and His Wonderful Lamp**

One of the eighteen songs composed by the combined talents of all of the Shadows for the pantomime show ***Aladdin and His Wonderful Lamp***, *I'm in Love with You* was issued as the B-side of the only Cliff Richard single to be issued from the enterprise, ***I Could Easily Fall (in Love with You)***: a second single, *Genie with the Light Brown Lamp*, was also released but was, of course, a Shadows instrumental. One of four songs for the cast recording album to be completed at the double recording session, the fifth and final take and edit was used for the mono and stereo recordings but with different mixes for the separate audio channels. Only released in mono form with the single, the stereo version was also issued on the associated stereo issue of cast recording album.

I'm in Love with You is a perfectly beautiful love song with a lovely string arrangement behind the lead vocal that is accompanied highly competently by the Shadows. Cliff's vocal is as to be expected from this type of song, which also features Hank Marvin and Bruce Welch on backing vocals right at the start and in the last few bars.

Track Specification

Composed by Hank Marvin, Bruce Welch, Brian Bennett and John Rostill

Musicians

Brian Bennett	drums, percussion
Hank Marvin	backing vocals, guitar
Mike Sammes Singers	backing vocals
Norrie Paramor Orchestra	orchestra
Norrie Paramor	arranger, conductor
Cliff Richard	vocals
John Rostill	bass
Bruce Welch	backing vocals, rhythm guitar

Recording Details

Producer	Norrie Paramor
Engineered by	Malcolm Addey and Ken Scott
Recording location	Abbey Road Studio 2, St. John's Wood, London
Recording date	15th October 1964

♫ I'm in the Mood for Love

From the EP **Love Songs**

Written and published in 1935, *I'm in the Mood for Love* was included in the film *Every Night at Eight* that same year and the following year it was resurrected for *The Pinch Singer*. Since then, it has become a major standard for singers from a wide variety of genres, including Ella Fitzgerald, Louis Armstrong, Dorothy Squires, Brenda Lee, Pat Boone, the actor Jerry Lewis, Ray Coniff, Rosemary Clooney, Acker Bilk, Liberace, Frankie Laine, Vera Lynn, Doris Day, James Taylor, Ringo Starr, Nat King Cole, Rod Stewart, Etta James, Mae West, Georgie Fame and the Blue Flames, Quincy Jones, Amy Winehouse, Fats Domino and Sheena Easton among many others. The song has had two assaults on the UK singles charts: in December 1990, it reached number fifty-eight when released by Trinidadian act Lord Tanamo and again in February 2001, when Jools Holland and Jamiroquai took their single to number twenty-nine.

Cliff Richard's version was one of three songs destined for EP release (on the ***Holiday Carnival***, ***Why Don't They Understand?*** and ***Love Songs*** EPs) at the session. The fourth and final take and edit were used for the mono and stereo recordings but with different mixes for the requirements of the audio channels. It was a considerable rarity having never been released in any other format until forty-five years later when it was included on the French CD compilation *All My Love* and then again a few months later on ***...And They Said It Wouldn't Last! (My 50 Years in Music)***.

With the first verse gently introduced with a guitar backing, Cliff sings with with his substantial ability. There is a slight echo on his vocal and the backing vocals occasionally are mixed too loudly in the edit but the arrangement of the strings and the occasional key change help to engage the listener throughout.

Track Specification
Composed by Jimmy McHugh and Dorothy Fields

Musicians

Mike Sammes Singers	backing vocals
Norrie Paramor Orchestra	orchestra
Norrie Paramor	arranger, conductor
Cliff Richard	vocals

Recording Details

Producer	Norrie Paramor
Engineered by	Malcolm Addey and Peter Vince
Recording location	Abbey Road Studio 2, St. John's Wood, London
Recording date	6th December 1962

♫ I'm Looking out the Window

17th UK single

Found by producer Norrie Paramor for his protégé Cliff Richard, *I'm Looking out the Window* was recorded in a session that produced songs for an album (**32 *Minutes and 7 Seconds***), an EP (***Love Songs***), an unissued track (***In Other Words***) and this A-side. Unlike many of his prior singles, *I'm Looking out the Window* is a true ballad.

Backed with ***Do You Wanna Dance?***, it was released as a single on the Columbia label (catalogue number 45-DB 4828) on the 4th May 1962 and it reached number two in the UK singles chart – held off the top by Elvis Presley's *Good Luck Charm*. Although not released as a double A-side, there was such interest and demand for *Do You Wanna Dance?* from the public that it reached number ten itself. There were stereo, mono and mock stereo (derived from the mono) edits with different mixes for the audio channels, which used the second of only two takes needed to complete the song. It was subsequently included along with its B-side on the ***Cliff Hits*** EP.

The guitar and drum are the principal instruments and, although the session notes indicate it is an orchestra (there are sustained strings on the second verse onwards), it could just as easily have been the Shadows providing the backing. There are male and female backing vocals subtly harmonizing with Cliff's languid lead vocal, which are uncredited although they are likely to be the Mike Sammes Singers, who were regular session singers for Cliff during this period.

Track Specification
Composed by John Jacob Niles

Musicians

Norrie Paramor Orchestra	orchestra
Norrie Paramor	conductor
Cliff Richard	vocals
Unknown	backing vocals

Recording Details

Producer	Norrie Paramor
Engineered by	Malcolm Addey
Recording location	Abbey Road Studio 2, St. John's Wood, London
Recording date	11th December 1961

♫ I'm Nearly Famous

From the album **I'm Nearly Famous**

The boisterous titular track from the rejuvenated sound of Cliff Richard's album, ***I'm Nearly Famous***, was found by Bruce Welch for Cliff to record. Finished at the same December 1975 session that saw the next album's title song, ***Every Face Tells a Story***, attempted but abandoned. *I'm Nearly Famous* was recorded in two sessions: first, the backing track realized in two takes; second, nine days later, the vocal overdubs. The song refers to what many new or struggling musicians can relate, since it has several references to the process an artist has to go through to achieve the success they are desperate for.

I'm Nearly Famous starts with an archetypal rock and roll guitar introduction and it sees Cliff firmly back on familiar ground with a surprisingly rocking track that imbues the lyrics with the energy and optimism of someone starting out on the music and recording career path. Cliff's lead vocal is engineered back in the mix while the backing vocals are relatively subdued compared with the other tracks. The guitar interlude in the middle eight is a virtuoso performance.

Track Specification
Composed by Michael Allison and Peter Sills

Musicians

Terry Britten	guitar
Clem Cattini	drums, percussion
Tony Harding	backing vocals
John Perry	backing vocals
Cliff Richard	vocals, backing vocals
Tony Rivers	backing vocals
Alan Tarney	bass
Graham Todd	keyboards
Unknown	saxophone

Recording Details

Producer	Bruce Welch
Engineered by	Tony Clark and John Barrett
Recording location	Abbey Road Studio 3, St. John's Wood, London
Recording date	2nd and 11th December 1975

♫ I'm No Hero

From the album **I'm No Hero**

The title track from Cliff Richard's first album of the eighties, ***I'm No Hero***, was written by the prolific partnership of Alan Tarney and Trevor Spencer. It was one of eight songs from the album involving producer Tarney as composer, proving his increasing dominance in the studio in steering Cliff's recording career throughout the eighties.

With a beat that borrows much from ***My Kinda Life***, the title track is unusual at the time in that it required Cliff to use his entire vocal range. The backing vocals are provided by Tarney and Cliff and built up in layers to sound more like a choir. The fuzzed synthesiser gives the song another interesting hook as do the unusual chord sequences used throughout.

Track Specification
Composed by Alan Tarney and Trevor Spencer

Musicians	
Michael Boddicker	synthesiser
Nick Glennie-Smith	synthesiser
Cliff Richard	vocals, backing vocals
Trevor Spencer	drums, percussion
Alan Tarney	arranger, backing vocals, guitar, bass
Unknown	hand claps

Recording Details	
Producer	Alan Tarney
Engineered by	Ashley Howe
Recording location	Riverside Studios, London
Recording date	12th May-27th June 1980

♫ I'm Not Getting Married
From the album **Sincerely Cliff Richard**

Albert Hammond was an up-and-coming *tour de force* on the sixties American music scene and it is one of his joint compositions, the prophetically titled *I'm Not Getting Married* as far as Cliff Richard's life turned out, that was chosen for eventual inclusion on the ***Sincerely Cliff Richard*** album. Although recorded in January at one of the few sessions that Cliff didn't record at Abbey Road in the first twenty years of his career, it wouldn't be released for another ten months until the issue of the album in 1969.

This jaunty song, which includes a happy whistle, tells of the story of a girl wanting to get married but he refuses. In spite of lines confirming that she is crying and he is causing hurt, the jaunty nature is sustained. But the sting comes in the story's tail when he tries to come back to her but finds she's married someone else. There is a strange pronunciation of the word married (Marr-I-edd) throughout but the quirkiness of the song makes it stand out from the rest of the album tracks.

At the end of November 1970, Cliff was in the studios for four sessions across two days recording material for his second German language album, which included a version of *I'm Not Getting Married*, which was translated to ***Zum Heiraten Bin Ich Kein Typ*** (or *I'm Not the Kind for Marriage*).

Track Specification
Composed by Albert Hammond and Mike Hazelwood

Musicians	
Mike Vickers Orchestra	orchestra
Cliff Richard	vocals
Mike Vickers	arranger, conductor
Unknown	whistling
Unknown	backing vocals

Recording Details	
Producer	Norrie Paramor
Engineered by	Peter Vince
Recording location	IBC Studios, London
Recording date	31st January 1969

♫ I'm on My Way
From the album **32 Minutes and 17 Seconds with Cliff Richard**

The third and final offering by the long-serving compositional team of Sid Tepper and Roy Bennett for the ***32 Minutes and 17 Seconds with Cliff Richard*** album, *I'm on My Way* was the second of two songs to be recorded for the album in the first studio session of 1962. The mono and stereo recordings employ the same take and edit but different mixes are used to meet the requirements of the audio channels.

A guitar introduction (neither Hank Marvin nor Bruce Welch according to the session notes) provides the tenor for this gentle love song that only has female backing singers, a double bass and a piano (which is probably Norrie Paramor) in addition to accompany Cliff's gentle lead vocal, until the end when strings conclude the track by changing the key dramatically and pleasantly.

Track Specification
Composed by Sid Tepper and Roy C. Bennett

Musicians	
Mike Sammes Singers	backing vocals
Norrie Paramor Orchestra	orchestra
Norrie Paramor	arranger, conductor
Cliff Richard	vocals

Recording Details	
Producer	Norrie Paramor
Engineered by	Malcolm Addey
Recording location	Abbey Road Studio 2, St. John's Wood, London
Recording date	18th January 1962

♫ I'm the Lonely One
24th UK single *and from the album* **Reunited – Special Edition**

At the time of Cliff Richard and the Shadows' single release of *I'm the Lonely One*, the critics were somewhat divided. In the north of England, Merseybeat with the Beatles very much at the vanguard was storming charts all over the world, so while one group of critics lauded Cliff and the Shadows for holding their own with the latest song, another faction claimed they were clinging to past glories and even trying to borrow the Merseybeat sound as their own, effectively accusing them of bandwagon-jumping – a charge that Hank Marvin vehemently denied at the time.

Written by Viscounts member Gordon Mills, *I'm the Lonely One* was recorded at the final Cliff session of 1963 in the late November. The session was noteworthy for being the first Cliff recording session to include new Shadows bassist John Rostill, brought in to replace Brian Locking, who had decided to focus more of his time on the Jehovah's Witness religion (and, indeed, who had given Cliff the impetus for his eventual religious conversion a few years later). The last of two songs to be recorded at the session along with its B-side (***Watch What You Do with My Baby***), the same (unknown) take and edit was used for the mono and stereo recordings but with different mixes for the requirements of the audio channels. Released on the Columbia label (catalogue number DB 7203) on 24th January 1963, the record reached number eight in the UK singles charts, a creditable showing contrary to some of the critics' beliefs. It also made a brief entry into the American Billboard chart when it hit number ninety-two.

Some sources suggest that Bruce Welch was not present at the session but there is clearly a rhythm guitar in the mix along with an uncredited piano performance (which would either be Hank Marvin or Norrie Paramor). In addition, there is a standard Shadows vocal harmonisation on the chorus so it is unlikely that he wasn't present. The song is a foot-tapping song that belies the tenor of the message in the lyrics, which tell of a man missing his lover after leaving her for his own emotional gain. There is the usual guitar line from Hank, with a strong rhythm section creation by the rolling bass, the piano and the percussion in addition to the disputed rhythm guitar playing in ensemble force.

A version of the song was recorded in German - ***Zuviel Allein*** (*Too Much Alone* literally) - using the backing track recorded at the session for the English language release and overdubbing Cliff's new lead vocal and a German vocal group for the backing vocals. The song was released in mono only with ***Sag 'No' zu Ihm*** (a German version of ***Don't Talk to Him***) on the Columbia label (catalogue number C-22707) in April 1964 but failed to chart. Both songs were rarities until their stereo versions were incorporated on the 1997 CD boxed set ***On the Continent***.

In 2009, the Shadows and Cliff got back together once again and re-recorded twenty-six tracks from their early days, which included *I'm the Lonely One*. This track was not on the main album but was issued on a three-track CD that accompanied the album packaged as a special edition release. The performance is tighter and crisper than the original but in all other respects this recording is faithful to the original version.

Track Specification
Composed by Gordon Mills

1. Single

Musicians		*Recording Details*	
Brian Bennett	drums, percussion	Producer	Norrie Paramor
Hank Marvin	backing vocals, guitar	Engineered by	Malcolm Addey
Cliff Richard	vocals	Recording location	Abbey Road Studio 2, St. John's Wood, London
John Rostill	bass	Recording date	23rd November 1963
Unknown	hand claps		
Unknown	piano		
Bruce Welch	backing vocals, rhythm guitar		

2. Reunited - Special Edition

Musicians		*Recording Details*	
Brian Bennett	drums, percussion	Producer	Warren Bennett (co-ordination)
Warren Bennett	piano	Engineered by	James Collins (Honeyhill Studios), Ethan Carlson (Middle Ear Studios), Les Williams (Nivram Studios) and Keith Bessey (mixing and mastering)
Mark Griffiths	bass		
Hank Marvin	backing vocals, guitar		
Cliff Richard	vocals, backing vocals		
Bruce Welch	backing vocals, rhythm guitar	Recording location	Middle Ear Studios, Miami, Florida, USA (Cliff's vocals), Nivram Studios, Perth, Western Australia (Hank's guitars and vocals) and Honeyhill Studios, Hertfordshire, England (all other vocals and instruments)
		Recording date	Early 2009

♬ I'm Walkin'
From the album **Cliff Sings**

The final contribution as backing band by The Drifters to the ***Cliff Sings*** album was Fats Domino's *I'm Walkin'*. By the time of the album's release, The Drifters had metamorphosed into The Shadows - same personnel, different name - in order to avoid confusion with the American vocal group. Although it was their last song for the album, it wasn't the last recordings they made as The Drifters with Cliff (that accolade falls to the ***Expresso Bongo*** EP sessions). Domino recorded and released *I'm Walkin'* in 1957 and, in the UK, it reached number nineteen, while attaining the number one spot in the US R&B Best Sellers chart. It has subsequently been covered by a huge variety of artists including the Baha Men, Penny Marshall, Jerry Lee Lewis, Ricky Nelson, Harry Connick Jr., Carl Perkins and Sandy Nelson.

The tracks of the album, released in mono only, were all issued on a series of EPs in both mono and stereo versions. The same take was used for *I'm Walkin'*, although a different edit was used for the stereo channelling. The stereo EP version was eventually released on ***The Rock 'n' Roll Years 1958-1963*** album in 1997.

In many ways, Cliff's version is superior to Fats Domino's and this is because of the cleaner instrumentation supporting his vocal line. The Shadows were firmly in their stride as a backing band and the bass riff is subtle in keeping the sense of plodding forwards, while Tony Meehan's gentle drumming uses a metal brush on the drums. Once again, Hank Marvin's guitar-playing comes to the fore in the solo in the middle eight before Cliff returns to complete the song.

Track Specification
Composed by Antoine 'Fats' Domino and Dave Bartholomew

Musicians	
Jet Harris	bass
Hank Marvin	guitar
Tony Meehan	drums, percussion
Cliff Richard	vocals
Bruce Welch	rhythm guitar

Recording Details	
Producer	Norrie Paramor
Engineered by	Malcolm Addey and Alan Kane (mono) and Stuart Eltham and Norman Smith (stereo)
Recording location	Abbey Road Studio 2, St. John's Wood, London
Recording date	8th September 1959

♫ I'm Walkin' the Blues

From the album **32 Minutes and 17 Seconds with Cliff Richard**

One of three contributions by the songwriting team of Sid Tepper and Roy Bennett to the ***32 Minutes and 17 Seconds with Cliff Richard*** album, *I'm Walkin' the Blues* was recorded in the second studio session of 1962. The track was also the first to feature new Shadows member Brian Bennett on drums, who replaced Tony Meehan as he had at the beginning of the year. His appearance came as a result of an internal argument within The Shadows about Meehan's tardiness and regular failure to turn up for parts of concerts; this was principally, with the benefit of hindsight, due to his comparative youth and inability to overcome the rigours and requirements of touring.

The mono and stereo recordings of *I'm Walkin' the Blues* used the same take (the sixth from the session) and edit but the audio channel requirements dictated different mixes. The song also appears on the ***Time for Cliff and the Shadows*** EP, while the stereo release has Cliff's vocals mixed into the right channel and the instrumentation is predominantly in the left.

A typical Tepper and Bennett rock and roll ballad, *I'm Walkin' the Blues* is a perfect example of the Cliff and the Shadows sound that had been developing over the previous three or four years. With a beat that is a fast walking pace and a rhythm kept principally by the ascending and descending bass line, the middle eight provides Hank Marvin with the chance to play a beautiful guitar solo arrangement of the melody. A key change forces the final verse and, in spite of the message that Cliff is feeling somewhat depressed as expressed in the title, the whole performance is upbeat and spirited enough to belie that.

Track Specification
Composed by Sid Tepper and Roy C. Bennett

Musicians	
Brian Bennett	drums, percussion
Jet Harris	bass
Hank Marvin	guitar
Cliff Richard	vocals
Bruce Welch	rhythm guitar

Recording Details	
Producer	Norrie Paramor
Engineered by	Malcolm Addey
Recording location	Abbey Road Studio 2, St. John's Wood, London
Recording date	4th April 1962

♫ I'm Willing to Learn

From the album **Me and My Shadows**

The mono and stereo versions of *I'm Willing to Learn* are different takes, although the differences are far more subtle than those found on ***We Have It Made*** and ***Choppin' 'n' Changin'***, all of which stereo versions were recorded on 24th June 1960. There is scant information as to when the mono version was recorded but the rendering is certainly different enough to assume that it may have been a different session or possibly the same but a different take from the stereo, the seventh of which was used. The song also appeared on the respective mono and stereo issues of the ***Me and My Shadows No. 3*** EP.

A love song beseeching a girl to teach him the process of loving, the clucking guitar is typical of many of the songs of the period and fits in with Cliff Richard's style of the period perfectly. There is more use of the lower register of Cliff's vocal performance than is prevalent in many of his other songs.

Track Specification
Composed by Fred Wise and Ben Weisman

1. Me and My Shadows (mono issue)

Musicians	
Jet Harris	bass
Hank Marvin	guitar
Tony Meehan	drums, percussion
Cliff Richard	vocals
Bruce Welch	rhythm guitar

Recording Details	
Producer	Norrie Paramor
Engineered by	Malcolm Addey and Norman Smith
Recording location	Abbey Road Studio 2, St. John's Wood, London
Recording date	Unknown but possibly 24th June 1960

2. Me and My Shadows (stereo issue)

Musicians	
Jet Harris	bass
Hank Marvin	guitar
Tony Meehan	drums, percussion
Cliff Richard	vocals
Bruce Welch	rhythm guitar

Recording Details	
Producer	Norrie Paramor
Engineered by	Peter Bown and Alan Kane
Recording location	Abbey Road Studio 2, St. John's Wood, London
Recording date	24th June 1960

♫ Indian Sun

From the album **The Dalit Drum** *(Various)*

One of the few new studio recordings that Cliff Richard made at the beginning of the new millennium other than for his ***Wanted*** album, *Indian Sun* transported him back to the country of his birth. He performed it in a concert there and followed this by going into the studio to record the version that was subsequently issued on the now rare album *The Dalit Drum*. Written by the man partly responsible for ***The Millennium Prayer*** and a long-term friend and associate of Cliff's, Paul Field, it also brought him back together with Dave Cooke. There is scant information readily available on the personnel involved in the recording other than the tablas-player, Arju Pararajasingam.

The gentle song is supported by a picked guitar as the primary instrument. Cliff sings the song with a bewildered anguish supporting the meaning the lyrics of how a girl can know what her future is and the compassion required for those living in poverty. The gentle backing vocals play under his vocal lead and, although the melody is not immediately memorable, the track is nevertheless still a beautiful performance.

Track Specification

Composed by Paul Field

Musicians

Arju Pararajasingam	tablas
Cliff Richard	vocals
Unknown	backing vocals
Unknown	guitar
Unknown	bass
Unknown	keyboards
Unknown	drums, percussion

Recording Details

Producer	Paul Field
Engineered by	Dave Cooke (vocals) and Trevor Michael (instrumentation)
Recording location	ICC Studios, Eastbourne
Recording date	June 2001

♫ Indifference

Unissued track

The first of two songs (the other being ***Rain Cloud***) to be attempted at the session on the last day of June 1970, neither track was issued and, to date, no plans have been made to do so. There is no information available from the session regarding the engineer and the other musicians besides Cliff Richard, but these will be updated should further research highlight the requisite details.

Track Specification

Composed by Unknown

Musicians

Cliff Richard	vocals
Unknown	all instrumentation

Recording Details

Producer	Norrie Paramor
Engineered by	Unknown
Recording location	Abbey Road Studio 2, St. John's Wood, London
Recording date	30th June 1970

♫ I Need Love

From the album **Cliff Richard - The Album**

Another saxophone-drenched song from Cliff Richard's ***Cliff Richard - The Album***, his first studio album for three years and the first release of the nineties, *I Need Love* shows Cliff's unerring ability to evolve with the times and produce sophisticated material that is relevant to the era in which it was recorded.

Driven by twittering keyboards and a straightforward bass, the introduction leads into Cliff's impassioned vocals, imbuing the needy lyrics with the requisite emotion. Cliff provides his own backing vocals and the blend of the harmonies elevates the song further from the standard output.

Track Specification

Composed by John Wilson

Musicians

Chris 'Snake' Davies	saxophone
John Clark	guitar
Peter May	drums, percussion
Paul Moessl	keyboards
Steve Pigott	arranger, bass, keyboards
Cliff Richard	vocals, backing vocals

Recording Details

Producer	Bruce Welch and Cliff Richard
Engineered by	Keith Bessey
Recording location	Westside Studios, North Yorkshire
Recording date	7th-8th June 1992

♫ In Other Words

Unissued track

Although sources conflict, according to the book *The Complete Recording Sessions 1958-1990*, the song *In Other Words* was recorded at the same session as ***Love Letters, I'm Looking out the Window*** and ***Who Are We to Say?***. There is scant information on the composer so no further history can be divined, although Cliff Richard did try eight takes to record the song before it was abandoned.

Track Specification
Composed by Bruce Welch
Musicians

Norrie Paramor Orchestra	orchestra
Norrie Paramor	arranger, conductor
Cliff Richard	vocals

Recording Details

Producer	Norrie Paramor
Engineered by	Malcolm Addey
Recording location	Abbey Road Studio 2, St. John's Wood, London
Recording date	11th December 1961

♫ In the Bleak Midwinter

From the EP **Carol Singers**

Christina Rossetti's poem was written around 1872 but published posthumously in 1904 in a collection of her poems. In 1906, with a musical setting by Gustav Holst, it was published as the familiar carol in *The English Hymnal*. It has had numerous outings in recorded form, mainly by choirs but mainstream artists such as Cyndi Lauper, the Moody Blues, Steeleye Span, Sarah Brightman, Olivia Newton-John and Chris Squire and others have put their indelible mark on it.

Cliff Richard recorded his version for release on the ***Carol Singers*** EP at one of two sessions, with *In the Bleak Midwinter* being the second song to be completed. Singing *a capella* with the Mastersingers (a Christian group of music teachers) providing the vocal harmonies, the final edit was a splice of multiple unknown takes. The result was only issued in mono on the EP (as was the dictate of Columbia at the time, reserving stereo output to albums only) although a stereo version was recorded and mixed but only released on the *Carols LP* in 1988 to capitalize on Cliff's ***Mistletoe and Wine*** success.

The clever arrangement for the *a capella* voices allows Cliff to take the lead vocal, which he performs with straight, pitch-perfect reverence and with a restraint that is rarely heard in his other recordings of the period and this proves that he has many facets as a singer.

Track Specification
Composed by Christina Rossetti and Gustav Holst
Musicians

Mastersingers:	backing vocals
John Horrex	
Geoffrey Keating	
George Pratt	
Michael Warrington	
Cliff Richard	vocals

Recording Details

Producer	Norrie Paramor
Engineered by	Peter Vince and John Barrett
Recording location	Abbey Road Studio 2, St. John's Wood, London
Recording date	10th September 1967

♫ In the Country

Unissued tracks, 36th ***UK single*** *and from the albums* **Cliff Live in Korea**, **Japan Tour '74**, **From a Distance ***** The Event**, **Hank Plays Cliff** *(Hank Marvin)*, **Summer Holiday** *(Darren Day) and* **Reunited**

With the ***Cinderella*** pantomime script requiring a song to describe a day in the country, it fell to the Shadows to write one that did just that. As with the previous pantomime, ***Aladdin and His Wonderful Lamp***, from 1965, there was only one obvious choice for a single release from the show and *In the Country* as it. With its inventive approach to percussion and harmonies, it stands out from the other tracks on the album. The song has been covered by an esoteric collection of artists including Pinky and Perky (the marionette pigs with squeaky voices from British children's television), the Farmers Boys (who reached number forty-four in the UK with their version in August 1984) and the Shadows on their final tours.

Cliff Richard and the Shadows made two attempts to complete the recording of *In the Country*: the first was on 11th November, where an unspecified number of takes were unsuccessfully recorded. Back in the studio five days later, another four takes saw the song completed. The fourth and final take and edit were used for the mono and stereo recordings but with different mixes for the audio channels. The single release was in mono format only, while the stereo and mono versions appeared on the respective formats of the parent album. *In the Country* was issued as a single, backed with the eponymous track from that summer's film ***Finders Keepers***, on the Columbia label (catalogue number DB 8094) on 2nd December 1966 to support the start of the pantomime shows a fortnight or so later. Successful in a run of top ten singles, the song reached number six in the UK singles charts and has been a fixture of hit compilations since.

Four points set this song apart from the others in the show: the lyrical intelligence, the close harmony vocals prized on any record, the expert percussion (particularly after the middle eight bridge) and John Rostill's intricate running bass line. The beauty lies within its melodic simplicity that swaps between the light and shade of introspection and ebullient optimism.

The live version recorded in Tokyo was left off the resultant ***Cliff in Japan*** album and the same fate awaited the medley, of which the song formed part along with ***The Young Ones***, ***Lucky Lips*** and ***Living Doll***, performed at the Talk of the Town shows recorded and released as another live album. Both tracks remain unissued to date. For the Korean market only, the 1969 Seoul concert was recorded with a reunion of sorts with the Shadows, where the song was included in the ***Shadows Medley***: *The Young Ones*, *Living Doll* and *In the Country*. The 1974 Japanese tour had the ***Hit Medley*** that featured a number of his sixties hits: ***Congratulations***, *In the Country*, ***Dancing Shoes***, ***The Day I Met Marie***, ***On the Beach*** and ***Sing a Song of Freedom***. For this latter medley, the instrumentation is left to the band although there is a skim of strings underneath, while the vocalists break off and sing *a capella* in the mid-section.

It is extraordinary that only two of the eight tracks featuring the Shadows have been released from the ***From a Distance ***** The Event*** performances, particularly in light of the influence of the group on Cliff's career. More curious is the fact that, while all of the other unissued tracks were restored on the 2005 album remaster, none of the remaining six Shadows tracks were. Originally, only *The Young Ones* was issued on the vinyl and CD album, with *In the Country* only appearing on the vinyl release, rectified by the 2005 CD reissue. This version is faithful to the original with the vocals of Cliff, Hank and Bruce blending together and this makes it unfortunate that the other Shadows tracks were not re-released.

In 1995, Hank Marvin revisited a number of Cliff's familiar hits for his *Hank Plays Cliff* album, with four tracks – including *In the Country* – featuring Cliff on vocals. Cliff sings the non-lyrical introduction to each verse, with his own harmonies layered on top. The synthesized brass bring a sophistication to the track that was musically clever already but it is Cliff's contribution and Hank's familiar guitar sound that make the track one of the best on this album.

The following year, the album to support *Summer Holiday*, the touring show based around Cliff's hits starring Darren Day, was recorded with Cliff giving his vocals to four of the tracks. *In the Country* also appeared in the final track remix, ***The Summer Holiday Megamix***. Cliff provides the multi-layered, non-lyric vocal introductions to each of the verses and Day's voice is pleasant enough but it doesn't have the same timbre or energy that is generated by the man he is emulating.

One of the favourites in Cliff and the Shadows' back catalogue, it was performed at the Knebworth gig and recorded by the BBC, although that remains unissued. It was inevitable then that this would be chosen for the ***Reunited*** album in 2009. One of the best features other than the close harmony vocal effects is the brilliant rhythm guitar played by Bruce.

Track Specification

Composed by Hank Marvin, Bruce Welch, Brian Bennett and John Rostill

1. Unissued track (single)

Musicians

Brian Bennett	drums, percussion
Hank Marvin	backing vocals, guitar
Cliff Richard	vocals
John Rostill	backing vocals, bass
Bruce Welch	backing vocals, rhythm guitar

Recording Details

Producer	Norrie Paramor
Engineered by	Peter Vince and Richard Lush
Recording location	Abbey Road Studio 2, St. John's Wood, London
Recording date	11th November 1966

2. Single

Musicians

Brian Bennett	drums, percussion
Hank Marvin	backing vocals, guitar
Cliff Richard	vocals
John Rostill	backing vocals, bass
Bruce Welch	backing vocals, rhythm guitar

Recording Details

Producer	Norrie Paramor
Engineered by	Peter Vince and Richard Lush
Recording location	Abbey Road Studio 3, St. John's Wood, London
Recording date	16th November 1966

3. Unissued track (Cliff in Japan)

Musicians

Norrie Paramor Orchestra	orchestra
Norrie Paramor	arranger, conductor
Cliff Richard	vocals
Unknown	backing vocals

Recording Details

Producer	Norrie Paramor
Engineered by	Unknown
Recording location	Shibuya Public Hall, Tokyo, Japan
Recording date	18th October 1967

4. Unissued track (Live at the Talk of the Town)

Musicians

Breakaways:	backing vocals
Vicki Hasemen	
Margo Quantrell	
Jean Ryder	
Norrie Paramor	arranger, conductor
Cliff Richard	vocals
Talk of the Town Orchestra	orchestra

Recording Details

Producer	Norrie Paramor
Engineered by	Peter Vince
Recording location	Talk of the Town Theatre, London
Recording date	30th May 1968

5. Cliff Live in Korea

Musicians

Brian Bennett	drums, percussion
Alan Hawkshaw	keyboards
Hank Marvin	backing vocals, guitar
Cliff Richard	vocals
John Rostill	backing vocals, bass
Bruce Welch	backing vocals, rhythm guitar

Recording Details

Producer	Unknown
Engineered by	Unknown
Recording location	Citizen Hall, Seoul, South Korea
Recording date	16th October 1969

6. Japan Tour '74

Musicians

Barrie Guard	arranger, conductor, piano
Cliff Hall	piano
Brian Lewis	backing vocals, guitar
Kevin Peak	acoustic guitar
Cliff Richard	vocals
Shambles Symphonet	orchestra
Trevor Spencer	drums, percussion
Alan Tarney	backing vocals, bass
Bruce Welch	backing vocals, rhythm guitar

Recording Details

Producer	Toshiba EMI (no individual detailed)
Engineered by	Toshiba EMI (no individual detailed)
Recording location	Shinjuku Koseinenkin, Tokyo, Japan
Recording date	7th-8th October 1974

7. Unissued track (Live & Guaranteed 1988!)

Musicians	
John Clark	guitar
Rosemarie Ford	backing vocals
Mark Griffiths	bass
Peter Howarth	backing vocals
Steve Lauri	guitar
Paul Moessl	keyboards
Mick Mullins	backing vocals
Alan Park	keyboards
Cliff Richard	vocals
Henry Spinetti	drums, percussion

Recording Details	
Producer	Unknown
Engineered by	Unknown
Recording location	Fyens Forum, Odense, Denmark
Recording date	22nd May 1988

8. From a Distance *** The Event**

Musicians	
Ray Beavis	saxophone
Brian Bennett	drums, percussion
Mark Griffiths	bass
Cliff Hall	keyboards
Hank Marvin	backing vocals, guitar
Cliff Richard	vocals
Bruce Welch	backing vocals, rhythm guitar

Recording Details	
Producer	Cliff Richard
Engineered by	Keith Bessey and Mick McKenna
Recording location	Rolling Stones Mobile Studio, Wembley Stadium, Wembley, North-west London
Recording date	16th–17th June 1989

9. Unissued (Knebworth - The Album)

Musicians	
Ray Beavis	saxophone
Brian Bennett	drums, percussion
John Earle	saxophone
Chris Gower	trombone
Mark Griffiths	bass
Cliff Hall	keyboards
Dick Hanson	trumpet
Peter Howarth	backing vocals
Hank Marvin	backing vocals, guitar
Paul Moessl	keyboards
Mick Mullins	backing vocals
Keith Murrell	backing vocals
Cliff Richard	vocals
Bruce Welch	backing vocals, guitar

Recording Details	
Producer	Chris Kimsey and Steve Smith
Engineered by	Unknown
Recording location	Knebworth House, Hertfordshire, England
Recording date	30th June 1990

10. Hank Plays Cliff

Musicians	
Warren Bennett	arranger, keyboards, sampled bass
Hank Marvin	electric guitar
Cliff Richard	backing vocals
Gary Ridge	percussion
Trevor Spencer	drums, percussion

Recording Details	
Producer	Hank Marvin
Engineered by	Les Williams (Planet Sound Studios) and Dick Plant (Honeyhill Studios)
Recording location	Planet Sound Studios, Subiaco, Perth, Australia (instruments) and Honeyhill Studios, Hertfordshire (vocals)
Recording date	1995

11. Summer Holiday (Darren Day)

Musicians	
Darren Day	vocals
Mark Griffiths	lead guitar
Cliff Richard	backing vocals
Warren Bennett	arranger, backing vocals, guitar, bass, drums, percussion

Recording Details	
Producer	Brian Bennett
Engineered by	Dick Plant
Recording location	Honeyhill Studios, Hertfordshire, England
Recording date	1996

12. Reunited

Musicians	
Brian Bennett	drums, percussion
Mark Griffiths	bass
Hank Marvin	backing vocals, guitar
Cliff Richard	vocals, backing vocals
Bruce Welch	backing vocals, rhythm guitar

Recording Details	
Producer	Warren Bennett (co-ordination)
Engineered by	James Collins (Honeyhill Studios), Ethan Carlson (Middle Ear Studios), Les Williams (Nivram Studios) and Keith Bessey (mixing and mastering)
Recording location	Middle Ear Studios, Miami, Florida, USA (Cliff's vocals), Nivram Studios, Perth, Western Australia (Hank's guitars and vocals) and Honeyhill Studios, Hertfordshire, England (all other vocals and instruments)
Recording date	Early 2009

♫ In the Night

From the album **I'm No Hero**

The second of two songs not written or co-written by producer and contributor Alan Tarney for Cliff Richard's first album of the eighties ***I'm No Hero***, *In the Night* was placed as the opening track on the second side of the original vinyl version of the album.
The song conforms to the rest of the album with its predominant focus on synthesisers, although there is a stronger chugging bass on *In the Night* that keeps the rhythm and momentum moving onwards. The vocals are supplied by both Cliff and Tarney with a small layering effect to make it sound like a group.

Track Specification
Composed by Rod Bowkett

Musicians		*Recording Details*	
Michael Boddicker	synthesiser	Producer	Alan Tarney
Nick Glennie-Smith	synthesiser	Engineered by	Ashley Howe
Cliff Richard	vocals, backing vocals	Recording location	Riverside Studios, London
Trevor Spencer	drums, percussion	Recording date	12th May-27th June 1980
Alan Tarney	arranger, backing vocals, bass		

♫ In the Past

From the album **Sincerely Cliff Richard**

Originally recorded as one of the vocal tracks on the Shadows' 1965 album *Shadow Music*, *In the Past* was picked up by Cliff Richard and recorded in the middle of 1968. However, as with many of the tracks featured on ***Sincerely Cliff Richard***, they were collected for a number of months rather than necessarily being destined for one album or another, so it would be another fifteen months before the track was released. Recorded at a session at the relatively unfamiliar Chappell Studios, rather than the Abbey Road Studio complex that had been home to most of Cliff's recordings since the start of his career, *In the Past* was the second track to be completed.
A harp and simmering strings introduce the song, with a lugubrious piano and percussion as Cliff comes in. A very different piece of music from the Shadows' version, it exemplifies Cliff's talents and versatility as a singer, as he performs it with an emotional passion. An unknown and uncredited female vocal group provides the backing with the possibility that this might be either the Breakaways or the Ladybirds, both of whom recorded with Cliff during this period.

Track Specification
Composed by Mick Cahill

Musicians		*Recording Details*	
Mike Leander	arranger, conductor	Producer	Norrie Paramor
Mike Leander Orchestra	orchestra	Engineered by	Peter Vince
Cliff Richard	vocals	Recording location	Chappell Studios, London
Unknown	backing vocals	Recording date	2nd July 1968

♫ In the Stars

From the film soundtrack album of **Wonderful Life**

A duet in the ***Wonderful Life*** film but a solo on its soundtrack, *In the Stars* is the romantic interlude in the film where Johnny (Cliff Richard) and Jenny (Susan Hampshire) are getting to know each other better after working on the set of a disastrous film. Jenny has been concerned about the yashmak she is forced to wear as it interferes with her acting, while the friends decide to make a short film featuring Johnny and Jenny when the set has closed down after a day's filming. Jenny points out that she's only good when she's singing and so they run across the sand-dunes singing this duet to each other and, with swooping orchestral backing, they stand together singing at the top of a dune, as it cuts back to the projection theatre, where they are all watching the rushes (with Hank Marvin dabbing his eye with a corner of the handkerchief) and they all agree the scene is very good – with the singing and without the yashmak. The song is replayed for a short time when playing the completed secondary film later on, although this is not included in the soundtrack.
In the Stars was the first in the can of four songs to be recorded at the session, with. the same (unknown) take and edit used for the mono and stereo recordings with different mixes to meet the needs of the audio channels and it appears on the track listing of the ***Wonderful Life No. 2*** EP. The version used in the film was probably recorded in the first three months of 1964, although, other than Cliff and Susan Hampshire, the musicians, studio personnel and location are not readily available and has not been released in any format other than the film. The film version is very different from that on the soundtrack, principally because the soundtrack features Cliff singing on his own while the film version is treated as a duet with Susan Hampshire (unlike the previous two films, the leading lady didn't require having her voice dubbed). However, the orchestral arrangement is pretty similar, although some sections are extended.
Although there is a guitar introduction, it is solely an orchestral accompaniment for the song rather than employing the Shadows. What disappoints with the film is that there are few opportunities for Cliff and the Shadows to perform together and the remaining songs are not that memorable. This is particularly the case with *In the Stars*, which tries too hard to be the romantic interlude in the film. Cliff carries off his vocal part well but the odd orchestration underneath it, while visually appealing on the film, is not particularly strong material to listen to on a soundtrack.

Track Specification
Composed by Peter Myers and Ronald Cass

Musicians

Associated British Studio Orchestra	orchestra
Stanley Black	conductor
Cliff Richard	vocals

Recording Details

Producer	Norrie Paramor
Engineered by	Malcolm Addey
Recording location	Abbey Road Studio 2, St. John's Wood, London
Recording date	22nd April 1964

♫ Into Each Life Some Rain Must Fall

From the film soundtrack album of **Finders Keepers**

Written in 1944 and first performed as a duet by the Ink Spots and Ella Fitzgerald that same year, *Into Each Life Some Rain Must Fall* has been covered by several artists including Lou Rawls, Frankie Avalon, Rosemary Clooney, Kaye Starr, Don Estelle, the Platters, Charlie Barnet and Smokey Robinson.

Into Each Life Some Rain Must Fall was one of the songs chosen to be recorded at the dual Portugal sessions by Cliff Richard in May 1965. Ostensibly recording material for his upcoming albums ***Love Is Forever*** and ***Kinda Latin***, the song was held back for over a year until it was added as a bonus track to the soundtrack of ***Finders Keepers***. The final (unknown) take and edit were used for the mono and stereo recordings but with different mixes for the separate audio channels.

The upbeat song is at odds with the tenor of the lyrics, which complain of things going wrong, although there are inevitable notes of optimism. Cliff performs with comfortable ease and is ably supported as usual by the Shadows. There is an uncredited orchestra, likely to the Norrie Paramor Orchestra since they are employed on other tracks of the period, and an uncredited backing vocal group, likely to the Mike Sammes Singers for similar reasons.

Track Specification
Composed by Allan Roberts and Doris Fisher

Musicians

Brian Bennett	drums, percussion
Hank Marvin	guitar
Cliff Richard	vocals
John Rostill	bass
Unknown	backing vocals
Unknown	orchestra
Bruce Welch	rhythm guitar

Recording Details

Producer	Norrie Paramor
Engineered by	Unknown
Recording location	Estudios Valentim de Carvalho, Lisbon, Portugal
Recording date	10th May 1965

♫ I Only Came to Say Goodbye

From the album **Cliff Richard**

Recorded in the same session that produced the international hit ***Constantly***, *I Only Came to Say Goodbye* was one of the many songs that were recorded by Cliff Richard but were held back a few months until the release of his 1965 eponymous album. The song was also included on the track listing of the ***Angel*** EP, which was released later that year. The same (unknown) take and edit were used for the mono and stereo recordings but with different mixes for the audio channels.

With a somewhat predictable melody, *I Only Came to Say Goodbye* is elevated by an understated orchestral arrangement by Norrie Paramor and, of course, Cliff's vocal line that has a slight vibrato developing on the sustained notes – this would become one of his trademarks later in his career.

Track Specification
Composed by Gwen Guthrie and Patrick Grant

Musicians

Brian Bennett	drums, percussion
Norrie Paramor Orchestra	orchestra
Norrie Paramor	arranger, conductor
Cliff Richard	vocals

Recording Details

Producer	Norrie Paramor
Engineered by	Malcolm Addey
Recording location	Abbey Road Studio 2, St. John's Wood, London
Recording date	17th November 1963

♫ I Only Have Eyes for You

From the EP **Love Songs**

Originally written for the 1934 film *Dames, I Only Have Eyes for You* was first a major hit for Ben Selvin in the US that same year. It has since been recorded by a number of artists such as the Flamingos in 1959 (which featured in the film *American Graffiti* in 1973), Peggy Lee, Al Jolson, Ella Fitzgerald, Elaine Paige, Frank Sinatra with the Count Basie Orchestra, Rosemary Clooney, Bette Midler and Jamie Cullum. Sung by one of the penguin characters in *Happy Feet* and lending its name to a episode of *Buffy and the Vampire Slayer, I Only Have Eyes for You* was also a major contemporary hit for Art Garfunkel with his first solo single, when it reached number eighteen in the US Billboard Charts and number one in the UK singles charts for two weeks at the end of October 1975.

Recorded at the final session of 1962 in between Christmas and the New Year, the sixth and final take and edit were used for the mono and stereo recordings but with different mixes for the audio channels. Until the release of 1989's ***The EP Collection: Ballads and Love Songs***, the track was a considerable rarity, although that album is now itself a sought after rarity by fans and musicologists alike.

A song arranged with a slight Latin dance rhythm, *I Only Have Eyes for You* features a lovely string arrangement, which includes a harp and a guitar, by Norrie Paramor, while Cliff carries off his lead vocal lines with quiet and gentle composure. The backing vocals occasionally appear a little obsequious but overall, it is a strong cover of a familiar song.

Track Specification
Composed by Al Dubin and Harry Warren

Musicians		*Recording Details*	
Mike Sammes Singers	backing vocals	Producer	Norrie Paramor
Norrie Paramor Orchestra	orchestra	Engineered by	Malcolm Addey
Norrie Paramor	arranger, conductor	Recording location	Abbey Road Studio 2, St. John's Wood, London
Cliff Richard	vocals	Recording date	28th December 1962

♬ I Only Know I Love You

B-side of ***Constantly*** *(Italy only)*

Like many popular music songs, particularly in the sixties, the source material came from translated continental favourites. Such was the case with *I Only Know I Love You*, which was an Italian ditty entitled ***'Na Voce, 'Na Chitarra, E'o Poco 'E Luna*** (literally translated as *A Voice, a Guitar and a Little Moonlight*, but with a dialect applied with the missing letters from the title). Written by two Italians, to which the English version had new lyrics applied by Al Stillman, *I Only Know I Love You* was recorded by a few artists including Johnny Desmond, the Four Aces and Mantovani.

Cliff Richard recorded the English version at the same session that produced another Italian conversion ***Constantly***, and for which single it would provide the B-side but only in mono Italy in mono; all other territories were issued with ***True, True Lovin'*** as the B-side. Confusingly, the Italian B-side was translated back to the original title of *'Na Voce, 'Na Chitarra, E'o Poco 'E Luna*, although it is very definitely the English lyric version that was released – to add further to the confusion, Cliff did record a version of *'Na Voce, 'Na Chitarra, E'o Poco 'E Luna* during the ***When in Rome*** sessions but it was never released. According to Peter Lewry's and Nigel Goodall's book *The Complete Recording Sessions 1958-1990*, *I Only Know I Love You* was unissued – of course, this is true in a parochial sense in the UK but is not in worldwide terms, where it was a rarity for non-Italian fans until it was released for the first time in stereo on the *Congratulations to Cliff* French compilation and then in 2008 on the rarity compendium ***...And They Said It Wouldn't Last! (My 50 Years in Music)***. The same (unknown) take and edit were used for the mono and stereo recordings but with different mixes for the audio channels.

The song is typical of much of the material that Cliff was recording during this period and, although pleasant enough with its militaristic drums and staccato instrumentation backed with sustained orchestral string and horn chords, would never have been strong enough to stand as an A-side. Nevertheless, Cliff's vocals are as ever measured and the occasionally complex melody requires him to stretch his range, which he carries off with almost nonchalant ease.

Track Specification
Composed by Carlo Alberto Rossi and Ugo Calise; English translation by Al Stillman

Musicians		*Recording Details*	
Brian Bennett	drums, percussion	Producer	Norrie Paramor
Norrie Paramor Orchestra	orchestra	Engineered by	Malcolm Addey
Norrie Paramor	arranger, conductor	Recording location	Abbey Road Studio 2, St. John's Wood, London
Cliff Richard	vocals	Recording date	17th November 1963

♬ I Only Live to Love You

Filipino single

I Only Live to Love You was recorded by Cliff Richard at the same session as produced ***All My Love***, both of which were covered at the same time by his friend, Cilla Black. With Cilla taking *I Only Live to Love You* to number twenty-six in December 1967, Cliff's version was passed over for release in favour of *All of My Love*, perhaps for this reason. *The Complete Recording Sessions 1958-1990* suggests that Cliff's track had never been released but this is incorrect, since it was released in the Far East in late 1967, with the only known version being the Filipino release backed with ***It'll Be Me*** (Cliff's eighteenth British single from 1962) on the Parlophone label (catalogue number PAL-60771), although it didn't register in the Filipino singles charts. Only ever released in mono format, the track was an extreme rarity until it was included on the 2007 French compilation *Congratulations to Cliff*, which covers material from the 1967 and 1968 period.

In the same vein as ***All My Love***, *I Only Live to Love You* is a pretty love song that has a banjo-like arpeggiated accompaniment throughout before the drama is picked up and there is a full orchestral backing with the Mike Sammes Singers providing backing vocals. In Cliff's hands, a song that could have fallen on the wrong side of saccharine becomes a lovely well-developed musical experience.

Track Specification
Composed by Norman Newell and Giancarlo Colonello

Musicians		*Recording Details*	
Bernard Ebbinghouse Orchestra	orchestra	Producer	Norrie Paramor
Bernard Ebbinghouse	arranger, conductor	Engineered by	Peter Vince
Mike Sammes Singers	backing vocals	Recording location	Abbey Road Studio 2, St. John's Wood, London
Cliff Richard	vocals	Recording date	5th October 1967

♫ Isabella (Reprise)

From the album **Heathcliff Live**

Heathcliff (Cliff Richard) has taken his bride Isabella (Sara Haggerty) and married her, in spite of the conceit that he only married her to anger her brother Edgar Linton (Darryl Knock) who is married to Heathcliff's only love Cathy (Helen Hobson). At the ceremony, he has brutally forced Isabella to marry him in spite of the doubts expressed by Edgar and Cathy regarding his motives and has upset her by tipping wine down the front of her dress. He follows her to the bedroom and begins to insult her and slaps her across the face. She realizes too late what is happening. The reprise of the wedding ceremony song is sung in a minor key as Heathcliff viciously tells her that holds her to her vow and reminds her that the baby she is carrying is his and this leads to the song ***Choosing When It's Too Late***.
Cliff clearly relishes the performance during this song since it is so much at odds with his public persona, allowing him to act in an unexpected way. Sara Haggerty performs a slower version of the song that was performed during the wedding ceremony and Cliff joins in with the church organ playing in a minor key before it segues into the next track.

Track Specification

Composed by John Farrar and Tim Rice

Musicians

Sean Callery	orchestrator, orchestra
Keith Hayman	keyboards
Sara Haggerty	spoken vocals, vocals
Peter May	drums, percussion
Bob Noble	keyboards
Alan Park	keyboards
Cliff Richard	spoken vocals, vocals
Kevin Townend	orchestration
Unknown	orchestra

Recording Details

Producer	John Farrar
Engineered by	Keith Bessey, John Pearson and Tom Tranter
Recording location	Earl's Court Hall 2, London and/or The Academy, National Indoor Arena, Birmingham, England
Recording date	October 1996

♫ I Saw Her Standing There

From the album **Don't Stop Me Now!**

With the Beatles' domination of the world's pop music and charts, it would have been easy to cover a lot of their material to capitalize on their appeal. However, Cliff Richard avoided the temptation and *I Saw Her Standing There* is one a very few exceptions to his apparently unwritten rule. One of the first songs recorded by the Beatles, it opened their debut album *Please Please Me* and it was chosen as the B-side of *I Want to Hold Your Hand* in the US. Principally Paul McCartney's song, it was conceived when driving home from a gig on Merseyside. Since then it has been covered by several artists including David Cassidy, Little Richard, the Pink Fairies, Jerry Garcia, Gilberto Puente, the Crickets, Gerry and the Pacemakers, Laurence Juber, Anthony Newley, Stan Webb and the Tubes. It has had UK chart success twice: first by Elton John (with John Lennon and the Muscle Shoals Horns) released in March 1981 in memory of the murdered Lennon and reached number forty; the second was more lightweight with Tiffany taking her version to number eight in 1988.
Cliff recorded his version at a session in late September 1966 and it was the last of four songs attempted and one of only two to be satisfactorily completed, with the sixth and final take and edit were used for the mono and stereo recordings.
One of the few tracks from the ***Don't Stop Me Now!*** album to feature Cliff and the Shadows, this is a treat for fans. Mike Leander's strong arrangement makes it a quite different prospect from the original, while the passion with which it is sung, matched with a racing rhythm (including an uncredited piano) and syncopated hand-claps, makes it one of the strongest songs on the album. Noteworthy, too, is one of the first examples of Cliff using the falsetto register.

Track Specification

Composed by John Lennon and Paul McCartney

Musicians

Brian Bennett	drums, percussion
Mike Leander	arranger, conductor
Hank Marvin	guitar
Mike Leander Orchestra	orchestra
Cliff Richard	vocals
John Rostill	bass
Unknown	female backing vocals
Unknown	hand-claps
Unknown	piano
Bruce Welch	rhythm guitar

Recording Details

Producer	Norrie Paramor
Engineered by	Peter Vince and Richard Lush
Recording location	Abbey Road Studio 2, St. John's Wood, London
Recording date	21st September 1966

♫ Is There an Answer?

Unissued track

In early 1969, Tyne Tees Television commissioned a series of six playlets for their religious broadcast slot under the title *Life with Johnny*, featuring Cliff Richard in the title role. Each episode updated a well-known parable told by Jesus in the Bible. Records are unclear on most of the episodes although *Johnny Come Home* and *Johnny Faces Facts* are complete, *Johnny and the Good Samaritan* is partially available, while the remainder are unavailable in either records or film form.

The songs performed had some relevance to the parable being performed and, in all, there were five songs per episode. *Is There an Answer?*, recorded at the Abbey Road studios with a putative album tie-in project in mind that didn't materialize, appeared in one of *Johnny on the Rocks, Johnny and the Blind Rage* or *Johnny in Love*. The end credits of the episode stated that all songs were original and written in collaboration between Cliff, the Settlers and the programme's writer David Winter. The instrumentation and performance details are unknown.

Track Specification
Composed by Cliff Richard, David Winter, Cindy Kent, Mike Jones, John Fyffe and Geoffrey Srodzinski

Musicians		*Recording Details*	
John Fyffe	backing vocals, guitar	Producer	Norrie Paramor
Cindy Kent	backing vocals	Engineered by	Peter Vince
Mike Jones	backing vocals, guitar	Recording location	Abbey Road Studio 3, St. John's Wood, London
Cliff Richard	vocals	Recording date	24th March 1969
Geoffrey Srodzinski	backing vocals, bass		

♬ I Still Believe in You
117th UK single

The first of five singles to be released from ***Cliff Richard - The Album*** was also recorded separately from much of the rest of the project. With Dave Arch on piano, too, rather than Paul Moessl as on other tracks, another difference was that the song was not remixed for the various formats of single release. Backed with a non-album track, ***Bulange Downpour***, *I Still Believe in You* was issued on the EMI label (catalogue number EM 255) on 23rd November 1992 and reached number seven in the UK charts. The same as the album track, it was also issued on the dual CD single release: the first CD single part was issued on the same day as the seven-inch counterpart (catalogue number CDEMS 255) and featured the same B-side plus an additional non-album track, ***There's No Power in Pity***; the second release (CDEM 255) on 30th November 1992 had two different tracks in addition to the main title – ***Ocean Deep***, the late-surfacing single from 1984, and ***Remember***, a French language version of ***When Two Worlds Drift Apart***, previously released as a single in and found on the album ***My Kinda Life***. The promotional video for the single release was filmed almost three weeks earlier on 3rd November.
The piano and an uncredited oboe are the chief instruments during the early stages of the introduction, joined by strings and an echo behind Cliff's lead vocals. The musical intervals that Cliff has to sing are carried off with the nonchalant self-assuredness of the seasoned singer that he is. The song is a beautiful love ballad that is kept simple yet significantly powerful in the drama that ripples throughout.

Track Specification
Composed by David Pomeranz and Dean Pitchford

Musicians		*Recording Details*	
Dave Arch	piano	Producer	Paul Moessl and Cliff Richard
John Bradbury	violin	Engineered by	Mike Ross-Trevor
Richard Hewson	arranger, conductor	Recording location	The Hit Factory, London
Cliff Richard	vocals	Recording date	14th September 1992
Unknown	orchestra (other strings)		
Unknown	oboe		
David Woodcock	violin		

♬ I Still Send Her Flowers
Unissued track

At the last but one session of 1965, Cliff Richard recorded four songs: initially, only one was released as a single, the haunting ***Visions***. Another, ***Closer to Kathy***, was held back for two or three years until the tie-in album for the film ***Two a Penny*** was being prepared. The third was unissued until it appeared on the album ***...And They Said It Wouldn't Last! (My 50 Years in Music)***, Bobby Vinton's ***I Love You the Way You Are***. The fourth, *I Still Send Her Flowers*, remains unissued in any form and there is scant information available either on the recording or the origins of the song.

Track Specification
Composed by Unknown

Musicians		*Recording Details*	
Bernard Ebbinghouse Orchestra	orchestra	Producer	Norrie Paramor
Bernard Ebbinghouse	arranger, conductor	Engineered by	Malcolm Addey
Mike Sammes Singers	backing vocals	Recording location	Abbey Road Studio 2, St. John's Wood, London
Cliff Richard	vocals	Recording date	17th November 1965

♬ It Came upon a Midnight Clear
From the album **...And They Said It Wouldn't Last! (My 50 Years in Music)**

As with most hymns and carols, *It Came upon a Midnight Clear* started its life as a religious poem, and was written in 1849 by pastor from Massachusetts, Edmund Sears. Most familiar of its musical settings in the US is the one chosen by Cliff Richard for his recording of the track, that set to *Carol* written by Richard Willis, composed in 1850, while most common in the UK is the alternative melody called *Noel* adapted from a traditional English melody by Arthur Sullivan in 1874. With

any number of choirs and choral societies performing the carol, it has also been covered by mainstream acts such as Hall and Oates (who had a US hit with their version) and Pat Boone, among many others.
Cliff Richard recorded a version of the song with the *Carol* melody at two sessions that saw eight Christmas carols attempted across the day. Performed *a capella,* joining him as the only other musicians on the track was a Christian group of music teachers providing the harmonies. The first track to be attempted, *It Came Upon a Midnight Clear* remained unissued for forty-one years, until it was added to the track listing of rarities on the ***...And They Said It Wouldn't Last! (My 50 Years in Music)*** album but only in the mono format.
In this version, the collected singers sing incorrectly '*the* midnight clear'. Singing *a capella* is extremely difficult to accomplish without bringing the pitch flat or pushing it sharp in over-compensation, but this group provides a perfectly pitched carol that is best when Cliff is singing with harmonized vocals behind him.

Track Specification
Composed by Edmund Sears and Richard Storrs Willis

Musicians

Mastersingers:	backing vocals
John Horrex	
Geoffrey Keating	
George Pratt	
Michael Warrington	
Cliff Richard	vocals

Recording Details

Producer	Norrie Paramor
Engineered by	Peter Vince and John Barrett
Recording location	Abbey Road Studio 2, St. John's Wood, London
Recording date	10th September 1967

♫ It Has to Be You, It Has to Be Me

From the album **Now You See Me, Now You Don't**

Written by Dave Cooke and Paul Field, who were regular writing collaborators and also involved in the two singles by Network 3 (produced by Cliff Richard – ***Last Train Home*** and ***Dangerous Game***), *It Has to Be You, It Has to Be Me* is another song on the ***Now You See Me... Now You Don't*** album that is a religious song masquerading as pop. This style of rendering songs is something in which Cliff excels.
The emphasis is firmly on jittery synthesisers as the song's introduction kicks off at a hectic pace. Cliff's vocals are mixed to front off the track and it gives the song a confidential atmosphere as the lyrics indicate that everyone needs to pull together to make it work. Cliff supplies his own backing vocals and this is highly effective in the chorus.

Track Specification
Composed by Dave Cooke and Paul Field

Musicians

Paul Hart	violin
Graham Jarvis	drums, percussion
Craig Pruess	piano, synthesisers, sequencers, electronic percussion
Cliff Richard	vocals, backing vocals
Bill Roberts	electric guitar

Recording Details

Producer	Cliff Richard and Craig Pruess
Engineered by	John Walker and Steve Cook
Recording location	Strawberry Studios South, Surrey
Recording date	4th-15th January 1982

♫ It Is No Secret

From the album **Good News**

Hell-raising, hard-drinking actor and occasional songwriter Stuart Hamblen appeared in many films in the thirties and forties, particularly westerns often playing roughneck characters. Simultaneously, he ran a radio show on the west coast of America. In 1952, he underwent a religious conversion following his attendance of a crusade run by Billy Graham. Giving up alcohol and thereafter pushing the temperance message, Hamblen gave up his radio show and acting to go into Christian broadcasting, styling himself as the Cowboy Church of the Air. Money ceased to be so readily available and there is a legend, possibly entirely apocryphal, that John Wayne told him his financial worries started with his conversion and wondered what Christianity gave him to which Hamblen allegedly answered: "It's no secret." Wayne then suggested that he wrote a song based on that. However, with its subtitle of *(What God Can Do)*, it is far more likely to have been inspired by relevant passages from the Bible.
Sometimes incorrectly referred to as *It's No Secret*, the song is a popular one amongst gospel singers and has been covered by Hamblen himself, Engelbert Humperdinck, Jo Stafford, Lonnie Donegan, Andy Griffith, Daniel O'Donnell, Pat Boone, Jim Reeves, Roy Clark, Elvis Presley and Slim Whitman.
Cliff Richard's cover of *It Is No Secret* was included on his first religious album ***Good News*** and was recorded at one of the designated sessions that resulted in completing four songs for the album. Splicing takes one and five together, *It Is No Secret* was the penultimate song to be completed that day.
With literal lyric interpretation, the track starts with a tubular bell before Cliff's vocal line comes in accompanied only by a guitar. The next verse is given the full gospel treatment with a tinkling piano and a full backing vocal chorus, both of which are uncredited. The vocalists sound like the Mike Sammes Singers, but this has yet to be confirmed. Cliff is clearly enjoying the opportunity to give his interpretation on the numerous religious songs on the album; however, it is not brow-beating nor is it tub-thumping, since his perfect pitch and general performance make it stand out as a song.

Track Specification
Composed by Carl Stuart Hamblen

Musicians	
Bernard Ebbinghouse Orchestra	orchestra
Bernard Ebbinghouse	arranger, conductor
Cliff Richard	vocals
Unknown	backing vocals
Unknown	piano

Recording Details	
Producer	Norrie Paramor
Engineered by	Peter Vince and Mike Stone
Recording location	Abbey Road Studio 2, St. John's Wood, London
Recording date	3rd May 1967

♫ It Just Happened That Way

Single by **Brian James**

Although Cliff Richard doesn't appear on this track, he has a writing credit (along with erstwhile Shadows Jet Harris and Ian Samwell). Brian James recorded Barry Mann's *Come Back Silly Girl* in early 1968 and chose this song to back the single release on Olga records (catalogue number OLE 005) in March 1968, issued in mono only, but the single didn't chart.

Track Specification
Composed by Ian Samwell, Jet Harris and Cliff Richard

Musicians	
Brian James	vocals
Unknown	instrumentation

Recording Details	
Producer	Ron Randall
Engineered by	Unknown
Recording location	Unknown
Recording date	February 1968

♫ It'll Be Me

***18th UK single** and from the albums* **The Rock 'n' Roll Years 1958-1963**, **Rock 'n' Roll Silver** *and* **Reunited** *and unissued live tracks*

A foot-stamping, piano-wrecking rock and roller that was originally an album track for Jerry Lee Lewis in the US, Cliff Richard and the Shadows are the only act to have taken *It'll Be Me* into the UK singles charts. Popular as a cover song for rock and roll artists among other genres, it has also been recorded by the likes of Bobby Vee, Ian Gillan, Gerry and the Pacemakers, Michael Bloomfield, Linda Thompson, The Move, Lindisfarne, Tom Jones, Mott the Hoople and Chicken Shack.

For Cliff's version, the song was recorded in a session of tracks destined for the ***32 Minutes and 17 Seconds with Cliff Richard*** album (on which this song appeared as the opener). The mono and stereo edits used the same take but different mixes were applied for the audio channels. It was chosen as Cliff's eighteenth single and, backed with a non-album track, ***Since I Lost You***, it was issued on the Columbia label (catalogue number 45-DB 4886) on 31st August 1962 and reached number two in the British singles chart, stopped from reaching the top by *She's Not You* by Elvis Presley. The track was also released on the ***Cliff's Hits*** EP and regularly appears on collections of his hits.

Acknowledged as one of Cliff's favourite tracks because of the truly rock and roll performance with the blistering piano and raucous vocals, *It'll Be Me* was the first of his singles to be recorded without either of former Shadows Jet Harris and Tony Meehan, who had both left by the middle of 1962 to be replaced by Brian Locking and Brian Bennett respectively. The piano on the recording is not uncredited but there is a possibility that it might have either been producer Norrie Paramor or Hank Marvin – this will be updated should further research confirm the data.

After a run of ballads and home-grown rock and roll tunes, *It'll Be Me* saw Cliff back to the American style of the genre. His voice is mixed further back in the ensemble which includes an instrumental guitar bridge as well as the rumbling piano and the running bass backed with steady pace of the drums and percussion. The song ends with Cliff's repetition of the title and an improvised sequence on the drums.

The version of *It'll Be Me* from the album ***The Rock 'n' Roll Years 1958-1963*** was broadcast live from the Paris Olympia Theatre on the French radio station Europe 1 in what marked the debut performance in France by Cliff and the Shadows. The introduction to the song confirms that it is Hank playing the piano on this version of the song (lending credence to the possibility that he played the instrument on the single). The mix of the track misses most of the instrumentation with Cliff's vocals very prominent, picking up a minor error where he almost sings the wrong word in the first verse.

It'll Be Me was revisited by Cliff's band at the time of recording his twenty-fifth anniversary album ***Rock 'n' Roll Silver***. Dubbed with the name Thunder, the group arranged and produced the song, recording a very different version from the one released twenty-one years earlier. During this period, Cliff had sung new arrangements of ***Dynamite*** and ***Please Don't Tease***, which were also very different in pace and style; so it is with *It'll Be Me*, which is taken at a slower pace and some of the instrumentation is changed but otherwise, it is not so far removed from the original version.

In spite of the restoration of all other unreleased tracks to the 2005 remaster of ***From a Distance ***** The Event***, like their performance at Knebworth that was recorded but not released, *It'll Be Me* was one of six Cliff and the Shadows performances to remain unissued. All of the Shadows-backed tracks were left out of the associated video package.

Inevitably when Cliff rejoined with the Shadows for his 2009 tour, the accompanying album of re-recorded items from their early association, ***Reunited***, inevitably contained a number of their singles, including *It'll Be Me*. The song is taken at a slightly slower pace and the arrangement sounds quite different to the arrangement of the original with its inclusion of the bank of saxophones, while still managing to remain faithful to the original.

Track Specification
Composed by Jack Clement

1. Single

Musicians

Brian Bennett	drums, percussion
Brian 'Licorice' Locking	bass
Hank Marvin	guitar
Cliff Richard	vocals
Unknown	piano
Bruce Welch	rhythm guitar

Recording Details

Producer	Norrie Paramor
Engineered by	Malcolm Addey
Recording location	Abbey Road Studio 2, St. John's Wood, London
Recording date	17th May 1962

2. The Rock 'n' Roll Years 1958-1963

Musicians

Brian Bennett	drums, percussion
Brian 'Licorice' Locking	bass
Hank Marvin	piano
Cliff Richard	vocals
Bruce Welch	guitar

Recording Details

Producer	Unknown
Engineered by	Unknown
Recording location	Olympia Theatre, Paris
Recording date	14th May 1963

3. Rock 'n' Roll Silver

Musicians

Stuart Calver	backing vocals
Dave Cooke	keyboards
John Clark	electric guitar
Mark Griffiths	bass
Graham Jarvis	drums, percussion
Mart Jenner	guitar
John Perry	backing vocals
Alan Park	keyboards
Cliff Richard	vocals, backing vocals
Tony Rivers	backing vocals
Thunder	arranger

Recording Details

Producer	Thunder
Engineered by	Keith Bessey
Recording location	Strawberry Studios South, Surrey
Recording date	9th-18th May 1983

4. Unissued track (From a Distance ** The Event)***

Musicians

Ray Beavis	saxophone
Brian Bennett	drums, percussion
Mark Griffiths	bass
Cliff Hall	keyboards
Hank Marvin	backing vocals, guitar
Cliff Richard	vocals
Bruce Welch	backing vocals, rhythm guitar

Recording Details

Producer	Cliff Richard
Engineered by	Keith Bessey and Mick McKenna
Recording location	Rolling Stones Mobile Studio, Wembley Stadium, Wembley, North-west London
Recording date	16th-17th June 1989

5. Unissued (Knebworth - The Album)

Musicians

Ray Beavis	saxophone
Brian Bennett	drums, percussion
John Earle	saxophone
Chris Gower	trombone
Mark Griffiths	bass
Cliff Hall	keyboards
Dick Hanson	trumpet
Peter Howarth	backing vocals
Hank Marvin	backing vocals, guitar
Paul Moessl	keyboards
Mick Mullins	backing vocals
Keith Murrell	backing vocals
Cliff Richard	vocals
Bruce Welch	backing vocals, guitar

Recording Details

Producer	Chris Kimsey and Steve Smith
Engineered by	Unknown
Recording location	Knebworth House, Hertfordshire, England
Recording date	30th June 1990

6. Reunited

Musicians

Brian Bennett	drums, percussion
Warren Bennett	arranger (saxophones), piano
Dave Bishop	saxophone
Mark Griffiths	bass
Hank Marvin	backing vocals, guitar
Cliff Richard	vocals, backing vocals
Jamie Talbot	saxophone
Phillip D. Todd	saxophone
Kevin Townsend	arranger (strings), conductor
Bruce Welch	backing vocals, rhythm guitar

Recording Details

Producer	Warren Bennett (co-ordination)
Engineered by	James Collins (Honeyhill Studios), Ethan Carlson (Middle Ear Studios), Les Williams (Nivram Studios) and Keith Bessey (mixing and mastering)
Recording location	Middle Ear Studios, Miami, Florida, USA (Cliff's vocals), Nivram Studios, Perth, Western Australia (Hank's guitars and vocals) and Honeyhill Studios, Hertfordshire, England (all other vocals and instruments)
Recording date	Early 2009

♫ It'll Be Me Babe

From the album **Every Face Tells a Story**

Subsequently recorded by the Shadows, Cliff Richard turned to old friend Hank Marvin for another song to record for the ***Every Face Tells a Story*** album and chose *It'll Be Me, Babe,* which was co-written by John Farrar. Recorded at one of the early sessions for the album, it was completed in three takes, with a few vocal overdubs added a week later.

Bruce Welch often played with the stereo channels on the synthesiser chords, letting the sound swim and shimmer between left and right. The song employs this technique as well as clucking guitars and the inevitable close harmonies of the backing vocalists, including Cliff, who also uses his falsetto range and also supplies his own backing vocals.

Track Specification

Composed by Hank Marvin and John Farrar

Musicians

Brian Bennett	drums, percussion
Terry Britten	guitar
John Perry	backing vocals
Cliff Richard	vocals, backing vocals
Frank Ricotti	percussion
Tony Rivers	backing vocals
Alan Tarney	bass
Graham Todd	keyboards

Recording Details

Producer	Bruce Welch
Engineered by	Peter Vince, Tony Clark, Mike Jarrett and Alan Rouse
Recording location	Abbey Road Studio 2, St. John's Wood, London
Recording date	8th and 15th September 1976

♫ It Only Goes to Show

From the album **Sail Away** *(Dave Pope)*

Cliff Richard spent time in the spring of 1978 away from his own projects, producing an album for Dave Pope, in between overdub sessions for his own ***Green Light*** album. The opening track on the resultant album, ***Sail Away***, was *It Only Goes to Show.* The album has no credits for the musicians so the track listing has no information apart from the vocals.

Pope's voice is gently husky but it fits the style of song, which is mid-period disco with an ear for a strong melody and could have come from any of Cliff's albums. Cliff's and the uncredited singers' vocals are gentle and it sounds like a Bee Gees arrangement. There is a classical guitar solo in the mid-section that then leads back to the verse and chorus structure.

Track Specification

Composed by John Daniels

Musicians

Dave Pope	vocals
Cliff Richard	backing vocals
Unknown	backing vocals
Unknown	guitar
Unknown	bass
Unknown	keyboards
Unknown	drums, percussion

Recording Details

Producer	Cliff Richard
Engineered by	Tony Clark
Recording location	Morgan Studios, London
Recording date	April 1978

♫ It's a Boy

From the talking book **Quail's Quest - It's a Boy** *(Various)*

The unusual book of *Quail's Quest - It's a Boy* is a story of three quails who witness the first Christmas and the birth of Jesus Christ in Bethlehem and it tells the story of the Nativity from the point of view of the three small birds. It was subsequently made into a cartoon film featuring the vocal talents of Stephen Berkoff and Joe Pasquale. Both versions had the title song *It's a Boy* performed by Cliff Richard. Written by Mick Gisbey and Simon Goodall, the song was recorded specifically for the talking book, while the film used the same vocal take with some additions but the choir on the original is removed and Cliff is backed by guitar and orchestra only. This latter version has not been issued in any audio format to date. The talking book CD was released in October 2003 just before Cliff released his latest Christmas song, ***Santa's List***, which was a dual CD release and the second disc had *It's a Boy* as a B-side item.

The song starts with sleighbell percussion before the string section of the orchestra comes in alongside Cliff's vocals, which he performs in a straightforward way to match the simple melody. The drama is created by the uncredited choir singing their harmonies as the track builds up throughout its execution. The beauty of the song and the story of the Nativity are perfect and complement the seasonal aspect perfectly.

Track Specification

Composed by Mick Gisbey and Simon Goodall

Musicians

City of Prague Philharmonic Orchestra	orchestra
Keith Getty	arranger, conductor
Simon Goodall	acoustic guitar
Andy Green	drum pads, percussion
Cliff Richard	vocals, backing vocals
Unknown	choir

Recording Details

Producer	Simon Goodall
Engineered by	Keith Bessey (Metropolis) and Yan Holsner (Smetchky)
Recording location	Metropolis Studios, London (non-orchestra and vocals) and Smetchky Studios, Prague, Czech Republic (orchestra)
Recording date	2002 or 2003

♫ It's All for You

From the album **Don't Hide Your Heart**

The final track to feature Sheila Walsh's mentor's backing vocals on her third album ***Don't Hide Your Heart***, *It's All for You* was one of the very few studio recordings that involved Cliff Richard during 1985 and 1986.

The gentle song is brought in by a light synthesiser sequence, while Walsh sings with almost breathy wonder as she bows in reverence towards the object of her affection: the dual possibility of a lover or God. The suave backing vocals are slipped into the end of the second chorus and prove the magic of Cliff's vocal capabilities.

Track Specification
Composed by Graham Kendrick

Musicians

Graham Jarvis	cymbals
Craig Pruess	keyboards, electronics
Cliff Richard	backing vocals
Sheila Walsh	vocals

Recording Details

Producer	Craig Pruess and Keith Bessey
Engineered by	Keith Bessey
Recording location	Gallery Studios, Chertsey, Surrey
Recording date	November 1984-February 1985

♫ It's All in the Game

22nd ***UK single*** *and from the albums* **The Rock 'n' Roll Years 1958-1963**, **Cliff in Japan** *and* **Cliff Live in Korea**

Starting its life as an instrumental piece of music called *Melody in A Major* in 1911 written by Charles Dawes, who was a prominent bank president in his native Chicago as well as being an amateur musician, when he composed the melody. Later, after a musician friend took it to publisher and it became a popular tune, it was referred to as *Dawes's Melody*, following him into politics when he was chosen as the running mate for Calvin Coolidge's presidency. Accordingly, the tune was played wherever he went and it became somewhat of an albatross to Dawes as he grew to hate it. In the spring of 1951, Dawes died and songwriter Carl Sigman chose the melody (firmly in the public's mind because of the funeral) to which he could apply a set of lyrics he had written and it became *It's All in the Game*. That same year, it was recorded by Sammy Kaye, Dinah Shore and Tommy Edwards among others, with Edwards's version becoming the most popular. In 1958, Edwards recorded it again, but in stereo, and it reached number one in the US Billboard charts in the autumn of that year; it also hit number one in the UK where it stayed for three weeks in November 1958. Other than Cliff Richard's version, there was one other that entered the charts by the Four Tops and reached number five in June 1970. It has since been covered by a number of acts including Nat King Cole, Louis Armstrong, Andy Williams, Johnny Mathis, Merle Haggard, Van Morrison, George Benson, Neil Sedaka, Cass Elliott, Barry Manilow and Engelbert Humperdinck among many others.

Recorded by Cliff as one of three songs at his final session of 1962, it required only three takes to complete the recording with the third and final one being used for the mono and stereo recordings with different mixes for the audio channels. Also featured on the ***Cliff's Lucky Lips*** EP, *It's All in the Game* was issued, backed with ***Your Eyes Tell on You*** on the Columbia label (catalogue number DB-7089) on 16th August 1963. The single stopped short of topping the UK singles charts, stalling at number two and being held off the top by *She Loves You* by The Beatles (heralding their stratospheric rise in popularity in the UK and around the world and showing that Cliff still had the ability to fight them in the charts). Cliff's version of the song also featured in the US Billboard charts, where it reached the creditable position of twenty-five. One of the other two takes (possibly the second) was released on the 1997 anthology ***The Rock 'n' Roll Years 1958-1963***, which is almost exactly the same as the released single version but with a different mix that increases the prominence of the piano. Bruce Welch was largely responsible for Cliff's renaissance in the seventies, of course, with his production and keen ear for a commercial tune but, even back in 1963, his future capabilities were showing themselves for it was he who suggested that the song be released as a single (as he would later on the next year with ***The Twelfth of Never***).

The harp and humming backing vocals introduce the song that features a twinkling piano accompaniment behind Cliff's vocals, which is played by Norrie Paramor. The arrangement and the relaxed vocals make *It's All in the Game* the song a superb example of Cliff's balladeering.

Although it was a major hit in the UK, for some reason *It's All in the Game* from Cliff's Japanese tour in 1967 was left off the track listing of the British version of ***Cliff in Japan***, although it was included on the Japanese release. The situation was restored with the remastered version in 2007. The live track has only ever been released in stereo although, given that the album as issued in both mono and stereo, it is reasonable to presume that a mono edit also exists of the recording. The version recorded for the *Cliff Live in Korea* album is rarer still since it was only released for the Korean market and in mono format only.

Track Specification
Composed by Charles Dawes and Carl Sigman

1. Single

Musicians

Mike Sammes Singers	backing vocals
Norrie Paramor Orchestra	orchestra
Norrie Paramor	arranger, conductor, piano
Cliff Richard	vocals

Recording Details

Producer	Norrie Paramor
Engineered by	Malcolm Addey
Recording location	Abbey Road Studio 2, St. John's Wood, London
Recording date	28th December 1962

2. The Rock 'n' Roll Years 1958-1963

Musicians		Recording Details	
Mike Sammes Singers	backing vocals	Producer	Norrie Paramor
Norrie Paramor Orchestra	orchestra	Engineered by	Malcolm Addey
Norrie Paramor	arranger, conductor, piano	Recording location	Abbey Road Studio 2, St. John's Wood, London
Cliff Richard	vocals	Recording date	28th December 1962

3. Cliff in Japan

Musicians		Recording Details	
Norrie Paramor Orchestra	orchestra	Producer	Norrie Paramor
Norrie Paramor	arranger, conductor	Engineered by	Unknown
Cliff Richard	vocals	Recording location	Shibuya Public Hall, Tokyo, Japan
		Recording date	18th October 1967

4. Cliff Live in Korea

Musicians		Recording Details	
Brian Bennett	drums, percussion	Producer	Unknown
Alan Hawkshaw	keyboards	Engineered by	Unknown
Hank Marvin	guitar	Recording location	Citizen Hall, Seoul, South Korea
Cliff Richard	vocals	Recording date	16th October 1969
John Rostill	bass		
Bruce Welch	rhythm guitar		

♫ It's All Over

*Unissued track, **37th UK single** and from the album* **The Best of Cliff**

For such a beautiful song, written by Don Everly ostensibly for recording with his brother Phil, it is surprising that it has not been covered by more artists. The song that talks of the stunned emotion after a relationship breaks apart was covered by Don Gibson, but wasn't released as a single by the Everlys; instead it was buried in the track listing of their 1966 album *In Our Image*. At the time, Cliff Richard raved about the album and *It's All Over* in particular, forcing the decision not only to record it but to issue it as a single.

The first attempt to record it was abandoned after seven takes at the session on 20th September but it was picked back up in the session almost three weeks later, where several songs were retried and completed. The final (unknown) take was used for the mono and stereo recordings but with different mixes for the needs of the separate audio channels. Initially only released in mono single format, the stereo version was eventually released two years later on the ***Best of Cliff*** compilation (as was the mono on the respective LP format). The stereo version has an extended intro played on guitar and it is this version that appears on all future compilations of Cliff's hits.

Backed with ***Why Wasn't I Born Rich?*** from the Christmas 1966 London Palladium pantomime ***Cinderella***, *It's All Over* became Cliff's thirty-seventh UK single. Issued on the Columbia label (catalogue number DB 8150) on 11th March 1967, it reached number nine in the British singles charts.

With a sad beauty permeating the gentle guitar, bass and harp accompaniment, *It's All Over* is elevated further by the achingly beautiful oboe duet that is performed in the instrumental break. The song laments the break-up of a relationship and the impact such a calamity has. The compassion that Cliff puts into his performance perfectly matches the tenor of the lyrics and, musically at any rate, is one of the best songs that he has recorded.

Track Specification
Composed by Don Everly

1. Unissued track

Musicians		Recording Details	
Bernard Ebbinghouse Orchestra	orchestra	Producer	Norrie Paramor
Bernard Ebbinghouse	arranger, conductor	Engineered by	Peter Vince and Richard Lush
Mike Sammes Singers	female backing vocals	Recording location	Abbey Road Studio 2, St. John's Wood, London
Cliff Richard	vocals	Recording date	20th September 1966

2. Single (mono issue)

Musicians		Recording Details	
Bernard Ebbinghouse Orchestra	orchestra	Producer	Norrie Paramor
Bernard Ebbinghouse	arranger, conductor	Engineered by	Peter Vince and Richard Lush
Mike Sammes Singers	female backing vocals	Recording location	Abbey Road Studio 2, St. John's Wood, London
Cliff Richard	vocals	Recording date	11th October 1966

3. The Best of Cliff (stereo issue)

Musicians		Recording Details	
Bernard Ebbinghouse Orchestra	orchestra	Producer	Norrie Paramor
Bernard Ebbinghouse	arranger, conductor	Engineered by	Peter Vince and Richard Lush
Mike Sammes Singers	female backing vocals	Recording location	Abbey Road Studio 2, St. John's Wood, London
Cliff Richard	vocals	Recording date	11th October 1966

♬ It's Alright Now

Misnomer track (**I'm Nearly Famous**)

When Cliff Richard's ***I'm Nearly Famous*** album was released in the US on Elton John's Rocket Records label, the closing track, ***Alright, It's Alright,*** was incorrectly titled *It's Alright Now.*

♬ It's in Every One of Us

Ninety-sixth single (seven- and twelve-inch versions) and from the album **Dave Clark's Time – The Album**

In 1985, Cliff Richard took the role of The Rock Singer in Dave Clark's stage musical, ***Time,*** performing several shows at London's Dominion Theatre. The principal role is one of a popular singer who is brought before a group of alien judges to represent humankind and the Earth and to account for the atrocities that occur around the world. Throughout the musical, the Rock Singer has to justify his and the planet's existence to avoid it being removed from the solar system. It is quite clearly an allegory for the religious faith with a Supreme Being or God in charge of humanity's destiny. At the end, having won them over, the Rock Singer is introspective as he points out that it is entirely within every person in the world to be peaceful and nice to each other for a change, as he is returned back to the stage in front of the crowd for whom he was originally performing ***Born to Rock 'n' Roll*** at the beginning. The resultant song is, of course, *It's in Every One of Us.*

The recording features Cliff's standard band from that period and Craig Pruess and Keith Bessey on production. The album version differs from the single in that the single doesn't have the sound effects of audience applause and cheers, which masks the *a capella* performance at the start of the first verse, and this is also cut. Backed with an instrumental *Alone* (which doesn't appear on the album or feature Cliff either), making it the first single released by Cliff to have a wholly instrumental B-side, *It's in Every One of Us* was the second single to be issued from the project, released on the EMI label (catalogue number EMI 5537) on 25th November 1985 and reached number forty-five in the British singles charts. Simultaneously, it was released with an extended version of the lead track in addition to the seven-inch songs (catalogue number 12EMI 5337), as well as a choral version, which cuts the instrumentation on the second verse and is an *a capella* rendition with Cliff backed by the choir. Finally, for 2002's ***The Singles Collection,*** the album featured an undubbed version of the song without the audience sound effects, which is essentially the LP version.

With Cliff singing *a capella* initially in the first verse and imbuing the lyrics with his strong vibrato, the song can double as a life-affirmation or a reverential faith song. Cliff sings the beautiful song with a sense of relief (the overlords in the play have reprieved the Earth and humankind due to his intervention). Slowly the song builds up in the drama and the vocal arrangement creates a blissful performance in a song that is forgotten but a worthy inclusion in Cliff's musical career.

The promotional video features a simple set-up of Cliff sitting in a darkened studio as the camera slowly moves around him. After the first verse, the studio gradually lights up to reveal the expectant faces of an audience watching him.

Track Specification
Composed by David Pomeranz

1. Single (seven-inch)

Musicians

John Clark	guitar
Full Company	backing vocals
Graham Jarvis	drums, percussion
Martin Loveday	strings
Andy Pask	bass
Craig Pruess	keyboards
Cliff Richard	vocals
Gavin Wright	strings

Recording Details

Producer	Craig Pruess and Keith Bessey
Engineered by	Keith Bessey
Recording location	Rock City Sound Studios, Shepperton and Gallery Studios, Chertsey, Surrey
Recording date	10th-11th June 1985

2. Single (twelve-inch - extended)

Musicians

John Clark	guitar
Full Company	backing vocals
Graham Jarvis	drums, percussion
Martin Loveday	strings
Andy Pask	bass
Craig Pruess	keyboards
Cliff Richard	vocals
Gavin Wright	strings

Recording Details

Producer	Craig Pruess and Keith Bessey
Engineered by	Keith Bessey
Recording location	Rock City Sound Studios, Shepperton and Gallery Studios, Chertsey, Surrey
Recording date	10th-11th June 1985

3. Single (twelve-inch - choral)

Musicians

John Clark	guitar
Full Company	backing vocals
Graham Jarvis	drums, percussion
Martin Loveday	strings
Andy Pask	bass
Craig Pruess	keyboards
Cliff Richard	vocals
Gavin Wright	strings

Recording Details

Producer	Craig Pruess and Keith Bessey
Engineered by	Keith Bessey
Recording location	Rock City Sound Studios, Shepperton and Gallery Studios, Chertsey, Surrey
Recording date	10th-11th June 1985

4. *Dave Clark's Time – The Album*

Musicians		*Recording Details*	
John Clark	guitar	Producer	Craig Pruess and Keith Bessey
Full Company	backing vocals	Engineered by	Keith Bessey
Graham Jarvis	drums, percussion	Recording location	Rock City Sound Studios, Shepperton and Gallery Studios, Chertsey, Surrey
Martin Loveday	strings	Recording date	10th-11th June 1985
Andy Pask	bass		
Craig Pruess	keyboards		
Cliff Richard	vocals		
Unknown	sound effects		
Gavin Wright	strings		

♬ It's Lonely When the Lights Go On

B-side of **Drifting**

Chosen as the B-side of the only charting single by Cliff Richard's protégée Sheila Walsh, the eponymous track from the album ***Drifting***, *It's Lonely When the Lights Go On* was also positioned as the penultimate track on the second side of the vinyl release of the parent album.

Introduced by a soft piano melody, Walsh sings this love song with gentle wonderment and a voice cracking with emotion on occasions. Cliff's vocals are multi-layered and are introduced in the second chorus. The song obviously talks of loneliness but it has a dual meaning either feeling safe with God but also at the apparent death of a lover. The simplicity of the piece is brilliant and the vocal arrangement over the piano is beautiful.

Track Specification

Composed by Costa Coulouris and John Woodfield

Musicians		*Recording Details*	
Craig Pruess	arranger, piano	Producer	Cliff Richard and Craig Pruess
Cliff Richard	backing vocals	Engineered by	Keith Bessey
Sheila Walsh	vocals	Recording location	Riverside Studios, London, Strawberry Studios, London, Ramp Studios, London and/or Sonoptics Studios, London
		Recording date	September 1982-January 1983

♬ It's My Party

From the album **From a Distance ***** The Event**

Depending on the generation, *It's My Party* is either most familiar in the version recorded by American singer Lesley Gore, who had a number nine UK hit in July 1963, or Barbara Gaskin and Dave Stewart's updated cover that reached number one in October 1981. It has also been widely covered by such artists as the Chiffons, Bryan Ferry and the Ventures.

The song was originally about the sadness of a teenage girl who is the centre of attention because it's her party but also because another girl has turned up wearing her boyfriend's ring. For this, it would seem an odd choice for Cliff Richard to sing as part of the ***Oh Boy! Medley***, which opened ***The Event*** at Wembley in 1989. However, the principal vocals were taken by the Vernons Girls and supported by Cliff, the Dallas Boys and the Kalin Twins.

Track Specification

Composed by Herb Weiner, John Gluck Jr. and Wally Gold

Musicians		*Recording Details*	
Dallas Boys:		Producer	Cliff Richard
Nicky Clarke	backing vocals	Engineered by	Keith Bessey and Mick McKenna
Leon Fisk	backing vocals	Recording location	Rolling Stones Mobile Studio, Wembley Stadium, Wembley, North-west London
Stan Jones	backing vocals	Recording date	16th-17th June 1989
Joe Smith	backing vocals		
Bob Wragg	backing vocals		
Kalin Twins:			
Harold Kalin	backing vocals		
Herbie Kalin	backing vocals		
Oh Boy! Band	rock 'n' roll band		
Cliff Richard	vocals		
Vernons Girls:			
Lyn Cornell	backing vocals		
Maureen Kennedy	backing vocals		
Frances Lee	backing vocals		
Jean Owen	backing vocals		

♬ It's Not for Me to Say

From the album **Cliff Richard**

Composed for the 1957 film *Lizzie* and sung by Johnny Mathis, his single reached number five in the US Billboard charts in that year. Although it hasn't featured in the UK charts, the song has been covered by several artists including Nat King Cole, Paul Anka, Barry Manilow, Billie Holiday, Connie Francis, Kitty Kallen and Ray Coniff among many others.

Cliff Richard's version of *It's Not for Me to Say*, eventually released the following year on the self-titled album ***Cliff Richard***, was part of a session that saw a number of tracks being overdubbed in English from the ***When in Spain*** sessions also destined for that same album. This track, however, doesn't feature the Shadows and the fourth and final take and edit was used for the mono and stereo recordings but with different mixes for the separate audio channels.
The saccharine combination of strings and the backing vocals give way to the lightness of touch that Cliff brings to the lead vocal. The beauty of the song lies in the slight vibrato that he brings to the sustained notes and this is something that would become a trademark in later years.

Track Specification
Composed by Al Stillman and Robert Allen

Musicians

Mike Sammes Singers	backing vocals
Norrie Paramor Orchestra	orchestra
Norrie Paramor	arranger, conductor
Cliff Richard	vocals

Recording Details

Producer	Norrie Paramor
Engineered by	Malcolm Addey
Recording location	Abbey Road Studio 2, St. John's Wood, London
Recording date	17th July 1964

♫ It's No Use Pretending

Unissued tracks and from the album **I'm Nearly Famous**

Sourced by new producer Bruce Welch for Cliff Richard's new album, ***I'm Nearly Famous***, there were two prior attempts to finish the song: the first for the backing track (sixth take) and the next day for the vocal overdubs (unknown take). The first unissued track was abandoned after one take, while the next attempt was stopped after the fourth.
The piano is very much in evidence in the right-hand track of the mix, with the bass guitar coming in and taking over the dominance of the supporting instrumentation. But, once again, it is the backing vocal arrangement that elevates the song that brings out the sing-along quality that makes the non-lyric start to the chorus.

Track Specification
Composed by Michael Allison and Peter Sills

1. Unissued track (I'm Nearly Famous)

Musicians

Terry Britten	guitar
Clem Cattini	drums, percussion
Tony Harding	backing vocals
John Perry	backing vocals
Cliff Richard	vocals
Tony Rivers	backing vocals
Alan Tarney	bass
Graham Todd	keyboards
Unknown	hand claps

Recording Details

Producer	Bruce Welch
Engineered by	Tony Clark and John Barrett
Recording location	Abbey Road Studio 3, St. John's Wood, London
Recording date	2nd December 1975

2. Unissued track (I'm Nearly Famous)

Musicians

Terry Britten	guitar
Clem Cattini	drums, percussion
Tony Harding	backing vocals
John Perry	backing vocals
Cliff Richard	vocals
Tony Rivers	backing vocals
Alan Tarney	bass
Graham Todd	keyboards
Unknown	hand claps

Recording Details

Producer	Bruce Welch
Engineered by	Tony Clark and John Barrett
Recording location	Abbey Road Studio 3, St. John's Wood, London
Recording date	3rd December 1975

3. I'm Nearly Famous

Musicians

Terry Britten	guitar
Clem Cattini	drums, percussion
Tony Harding	backing vocals
John Perry	backing vocals
Cliff Richard	vocals
Tony Rivers	backing vocals
Alan Tarney	bass
Graham Todd	keyboards
Unknown	hand claps

Recording Details

Producer	Bruce Welch
Engineered by	Tony Clark and John Barrett
Recording location	Abbey Road Studio 3, St. John's Wood, London
Recording date	10th and 11th December 1975

♫ It's Only Make-Believe

Unissued track

Although the recording has yet to be unearthed, if it indeed exists, the paperwork for the *Cliff* album sessions indicate that *It's Only Make-Believe* was slated for recording. As Peter Lewry and Nigel Goodall mention in the liner notes of ***The Rock 'n' Roll Years 1958-1963***, there exists sheet music of the song with the legend "as recorded by Cliff Richard". However, no

further attempts to record the song were made. Because it is a ballad, like the released ***Donna*** and ***Danny*** from the same album, it is possible that the Mike Sammes Singers were also employed on this track as backing singers. To this end, it is highlighted in italics to indicate that it is unconfirmed in the track specification below.
The song was first released in 1958 by one of its co-writers Conway Twitty and it reached number one in both the UK and US singles charts. As was the vogue of the time, the lyrics describe the thoughts of a man suffering from unrequited love and because the chord progression and yearning vocals, it is a strongly dramatic, almost melodramatic, performance that builds up to the climactic denouement. Of the many people who have recorded the song, the most familiar are probably Connie Francis, Billy Fury, Glen Campbell, The Hollies and Floyd Cramer.

Track Specification
Composed by Conway Twitty and Jack Nance

Musicians

Jet Harris	bass
Hank Marvin	guitar
Tony Meehan	drums, percussion
Mike Sammes Singers	*backing vocals*
Cliff Richard	vocals
Bruce Welch	rhythm guitar

Recording Details

Producer	Norrie Paramor
Engineered by	Peter Bown and Stuart Eltham
Recording location	Abbey Road Studio 2, St. John's Wood, London
Recording date	9th February 1959

♫ It's Only Me You've Left Behind
63rd UK single

By the beginning of 1975, Cliff Richard was beginning a kind of renaissance. For a few years, the quality of material he was recording was generally fallow with only a few gems percolating through. However, with his television series and the critical mauling he was receiving, many considered him to be no longer relevant to the music scene. But Cliff was and remains a consummate performer, where the music is the important part and his reinvention was noticeable from the mid-seventies onwards to when he would become cool once more. First out of the traps was one of three singles to be released that year: *It's Only Me You've Left Behind*. Marvin, Welch and Farrar had been regular guests on his television show and they took over the production duties of his singles and the B-sides and, in the case of this song, also provided the composition.
Critically, the song was very well received and had a lot of radio airplay as well as interest on popular television shows, including *Top of the Pops* (in the days when they exposed one or two new singles each week). The song was recorded at the first session in 1975 and the first of the two on the day; the one in the morning with the next in the evening, with studios two and three at Abbey Road being used, although which saw the completion of the song is not clear. *It's Only Me You've Left Behind* was released, backed with ***You're the One***, on the EMI label (catalogue number EMI 2279) on 14th March 1975. Despite the high hopes, the quality of the song and its exposure, it failed to chart becoming Cliff's second single to do so (the first being ***A Brand New Song***). A significant rarity for many years, it was eventually remastered and reissued on the 2001 release of ***I'm Nearly Famous***, followed by its inclusion the following year on ***The Singles Collection***.
The emphasis is firmly on the synthesisers for the song with clever use of stereo for the backing vocals, spread as they are as if singing directly to the sides of the listener. The melody and the harmony are what would be expected from a song involved Hank and Bruce as well as the quirky hand-clap percussion providing a decent aural hook and this, more than anything else, makes it such a surprise that the song was not a commercial hit.

Track Specification
Composed by Hank Marvin and John Farrar

Musicians

Terry Britten	guitar
Clem Cattini	drums, percussion
Tony Harding	backing vocals
John Perry	backing vocals
Cliff Richard	vocals
Tony Rivers	backing vocals
Alan Tarney	bass
Graham Todd	keyboards
Unknown	hand claps

Recording Details

Producer	Hank Marvin, Bruce Welch and John Farrar
Engineered by	Tony Clark
Recording location	Abbey Road Studio 2 and 3, St. John's Wood, London
Recording date	27th January 1975

♫ It's Only Money
From the film soundtrack album of **Take Me High**

Played out over the opening titles, *It's Only Money* is the song that provides the principal message for the film ***Take Me High***: money is not important and it doesn't buy you happiness. The title snappily summarizes this philosophy before opening the film up to drum it home. During the sequence of the key players, Cliff Richard is filmed singing the song in tight profile, with close-ups of his eyes and mouth, but with no other background interference. One of the best songs on the soundtrack, it could easily have ceded its title to be used as the film's title rather than the more bewildering *Take Me High*. The main phrase "don't let it go to your head" is synthesized and played out menacingly later in the film as Tim Matthews (played by Cliff) enters the London offices of Furness Orlando merchant bankers where he is a senior employee.

Recorded over a series of four sessions across two days at the end of May 1973, most of the soundtrack for the film was completed here, with *It's Only Money* being finished in just two takes. The short synthesized reprise section doesn't appear on the soundtrack album and was probably generated from the main recording rather than being separately recorded.
The glissando electric guitar and thumping percussion and bass introduce the song that gives way to an acoustic guitar to accompany Cliff's ebullient vocal line. Slowing into each verse and building up into the chorus, Cliff also provides his own backing vocals as the song continues inexorably onwards to the plinking percussion that completes the song, perhaps to representation the plinking of money onto a counter.

Track Specification
Composed by Tony Cole
Musicians

David MacKay Orchestra	orchestra
David MacKay	arranger, conductor
Cliff Richard	vocals, backing vocals

Recording Details

Producer	David MacKay
Engineered by	Tony Clark and Mike Jarrett
Recording location	Abbey Road Studio 3, St. John's Wood, London
Recording date	26th May 1973

♫ It's You (1)

From the album **Listen to Cliff!**

The final track on the ***Listen to Cliff!*** album, *It's You*, is also the last of the five original songs to be included in the track listing. It was written, as were three others of those songs, by Shadows rhythm guitarist Bruce Welch and old friend and former Chesternuts bandmate Pete Chester.
The stereo and mono versions of *It's You* use the same take and edit (the fifth and final from that session, although the liner notes of ***The Rock 'n' Roll Years 1958-1963*** imply that there are more sitting in the EMI vaults) but the mixes are different in order to furnish the needs of the differing aural channels.
Another love song that tells the story of a boy waiting by the telephone for his lover to call, the recording employs uncredited strings to accompany the performance. These threaten to overwhelm at points and, in some ways, it would have been better to record the song with just the Shadows supporting, who here are reduced to providing a unison rhythm on their instruments, with only the occasional trademark tremolo twang from Hank Marvin.

Track Specification
Composed by Bruce Welch and Peter Chester
Musicians

Jet Harris	bass
Hank Marvin	guitar
Tony Meehan	drums, percussion
Cliff Richard	vocals
Unknown	strings
Bruce Welch	rhythm guitar

Recording Details

Producer	Norrie Paramor
Engineered by	Malcolm Addey and Norman Smith
Recording location	Abbey Road Studio 2, St. John's Wood, London
Recording date	26th July 1960

♫ It's You (2)

From the album **Sail Away** *(Dave Pope)*

The second song to be written by Chris Eaton for Dave Pope's ***Sail Away*** album, which was produced by Cliff Richard with whom Eaton would have a growing association over the next decade and a half, *It's You* was recorded in the spring of 1978. However, there is scant information available on the musicians involved since even the album sleeve fails to credit them; as such, they will be annotated as unknown until further information is found to identify them.
A synthesiser theme brings in the song and continues to support Pope's lead vocal that is occasionally sung in falsetto, a technique that Cliff himself had exploited in his recent recordings. Cliff supplies part of the backing vocals as the song swaps between a gentle expression in the verse and the upbeat rhythm of the chorus.

Track Specification
Composed by Chris Eaton
Musicians

Dave Pope	vocals
Cliff Richard	backing vocals
Unknown	backing vocals
Unknown	guitar
Unknown	bass
Unknown	keyboards
Unknown	drums, percussion

Recording Details

Producer	Cliff Richard
Engineered by	Tony Clark
Recording location	Morgan Studios, London
Recording date	April 1978

♫ I've Got Confidence

Unissued track

Recorded by Elvis Presley, the Downings, the Imperials and Dennis O'Daniel as well as its author, *I've Got Confidence* was on the set list of the seven-session studio-bound concerts for the ***Help It Along*** charity album but, although it was recorded, it was one of five tracks that remain unissued from the eighteen that were in the can over the three days.

Track Specification
Composed by Andréa Crouch

Musicians		*Recording Details*	
Terry Britten	guitar	Producer	David MacKay
Barrie Guard	arranger, conductor, percussion	Engineered by	Roger Quested
Cliff Hall	keyboards	Recording location	Morgan Studios, London
Jean Hawker	backing vocals	Recording date	24th, 25th and 26th September 1973
Anna Peacock	backing vocals		
Kevin Peek	guitar		
Cliff Richard	vocals		
Trevor Spencer	drums, percussion		
Alan Tarney	bass		
Unknown	orchestra		

♬ I've Got News for You

From the album **Small Corners**

Also recorded by its writer Randy Stonehill, Cliff Richard chose *I've Got News for You* for the track listing of his 1978 religious album ***Small Corners***. Recorded at the first of three major sessions set aside for the album, it was completed in just one take with overdubs recorded and added the following week.
Starting with a fuzzed guitar way back in the mix, slowly the instrumentation is brought up in volume just as Cliff's vocal line starts. Unusually for a song, it begins with the chorus, and, while the verses are kept subdued, the chorus uses the beauty of the close harmonies of the backing vocalists supporting Cliff.

Track Specification
Composed by Randy Stonehill

Musicians		*Recording Details*	
Brian Bennett	drums, percussion	Producer	Cliff Richard
Terry Britten	guitar	Engineered by	Tony Clark and Haydn Bendall
Stuart Calver	backing vocals	Recording location	Abbey Road Studio 3, St. John's Wood, London
Bryn Haworth	guitar	Recording date	17th and 26th January 1977
John Perry	backing vocals		
Cliff Richard	vocals		
Tony Rivers	backing vocals		
Alan Tarney	bass		
Graham Todd	piano		

♬ I've Said Too Many Things

From the pantomime cast recording album of **Aladdin and His Wonderful Lamp**

The second of three tracks recorded for the cast album of the Shadows compositions for the pantomime, ***Aladdin and His Wonderful Lamp***, *I've Said Too Many Things* was completed in four takes. The final take and edit was used for the mono and stereo recordings but with different mixes for the separate audio channel requirements.
With a syncopated rhythm in the orchestra, driving the song on with a sort of subdued urgency, Cliff performs the song with aplomb and gives it the necessary light and shade in terms of the volume produced, including the mid-section where he is almost in a whisper.

Track Specification
Composed by Hank Marvin, Bruce Welch, Brian Bennett and John Rostill

Musicians		*Recording Details*	
Norrie Paramor Orchestra	orchestra	Producer	Norrie Paramor
Norrie Paramor	arranger, conductor	Engineered by	Malcolm Addey and Ken Scott
Cliff Richard	vocals	Recording location	Abbey Road Studio 2, St. John's Wood, London
		Recording date	17th October 1964

♬ I Wake Up Cryin'

From the album **32 Minutes and 17 Seconds with Cliff Richard**

The first of three songs completed in the session for the album ***32 Minutes and 17 Seconds with Cliff Richard*** (the fourth song, ***Do You Remember?*** was abandoned and revisited for the soundtrack to the film ***Wonderful Life***, although one these takes appeared on the remastered soundtrack CD), *I Wake Up Cryin'* was the final track on the second side of the album. The fourth and final take and edit from the session was used for the mono and stereo recordings but with different mixes for the audio channel requirements. At the beginning of December 1961, the music press erroneously announced that *I'll* [sic] *Wake Up Cryin'* would be the chosen B-side for the release of the single ***The Young Ones*** instead of ***We Say Yeah***, which was also from the film soundtrack.
As with many orchestral tracks, there are drums, guitars and bass but these are not provided by the Shadows. The sadness of the song's lyrics exudes from Cliff's vocals and, with pizzicato strings and backing vocals supporting him, it is a perfect example of Cliff's balladeering side of his career.

Track Specification
Composed by Burt Bacharach and Hal David

Musicians		*Recording Details*	
Mike Sammes Singers	backing vocals	Producer	Norrie Paramor
Norrie Paramor Orchestra	orchestra	Engineered by	Malcolm Addey and Norman Smith
Norrie Paramor	arranger, conductor	Recording location	Abbey Road Studio 2, St. John's Wood, London
Cliff Richard	vocals	Recording date	4th December 1961

♫ I Want You to Know
From the album **Listen to Cliff!** *(mono and stereo versions)*

Written and recorded by Fats Domino, although not a hit in the UK, the song was also covered by the Everly Brothers and The Malibus amongst a few others.

The mono and stereo cover versions for the ***Listen to Cliff!*** album were different takes, although it's unclear which of the thirty-eight recorded was used from the marathon session that also saw multiple takes of ***Unchained Melody*** and ***What'd I Say?*** from the same album. Interestingly, the session notes indicate that the recording of these three tracks were remakes. The mono version starts with a short instrumental, while the stereo begins with vocals; other differences are less obvious.

Back on familiar ground with this cover of a rock 'n' roll song, Cliff Richard is in his element singing along to the chugging ensemble guitar accompaniment. There is a perfect guitar solo by Hank Marvin in the middle eight, while Cliff times the rocking notes from one bar to another perfectly.

Track Specification
Composed by Dave Bartholomew and Fats Domino

1. Listen to Cliff! (mono version)

Musicians		*Recording Details*	
Jet Harris	bass	Producer	Norrie Paramor
Hank Marvin	guitar	Engineered by	Malcolm Addey and David Lloyd
Tony Meehan	drums, percussion	Recording location	Abbey Road Studio 2, St. John's Wood, London
Cliff Richard	vocals	Recording date	4th March 1961
Bruce Welch	rhythm guitar		

2. Listen to Cliff! (stereo version)

Musicians		*Recording Details*	
Jet Harris	bass	Producer	Norrie Paramor
Hank Marvin	guitar	Engineered by	Malcolm Addey and David Lloyd
Tony Meehan	drums, percussion	Recording location	Abbey Road Studio 2, St. John's Wood, London
Cliff Richard	vocals	Recording date	4th March 1961
Bruce Welch	rhythm guitar		

♫ I Was Only Fooling Myself
B-side of **Sunny Honey Girl**

Recorded at the same session that made up the maxi-single release – the A-side ***Sunny Honey Girl*** and the second B-side ***Don't Move Away,*** which is a duet with Olivia Newton-John. The second of the three tracks to be completed, with the fourth and last take being used in the final edit, it features Brian Bennett in his dual role as arranger and conductor. *I Was Only Fooling Myself* was a considerable rarity since it had not been released in any other format until it was included on the rare B-side section of the anthology ***...And They Said It Wouldn't Last! (My 50 Years in Music)***.

Starting with an *andante* synthesiser and harmonica introduction in a minor key that ushers in a country feel to the song, Cliff sings of unrequited love for a girl from an early age, going through the motions of meeting the family and so on as new paramours plan to do but not quite reaching the expected conclusion. The middle eight moves into an optimistic major key but this is short-lived as it returns to the minor key for the final verse and chorus.

Track Specification
Composed by Campbell

Musicians		*Recording Details*	
Brian Bennett	arranger, conductor	Producer	Norrie Paramor
Brian Bennett Orchestra	orchestra	Engineered by	Peter Vince and Richard Lush
Cliff Richard	vocals	Recording location	Abbey Road Studio 2, St. John's Wood, London
		Recording date	16th November 1970

♫ I Will Always Love You
From the album **Heartbeat** *(Hank Marvin)*

Written in 1973 by Dolly Parton and released as a single the following year, it wasn't until 1992 when Whitney Houston's version was the principal song on her film, *The Bodyguard*, that the song received wider and critical acclaim. Parton re-recorded the song for the soundtrack of her 1982 film, *The Best Little Whorehouse in Texas*, and reached number one in the country charts with it. But it was Linda Ronstadt's 1975 version that inspired Houston to record it and her single stayed at the number one spot in the UK charts for ten weeks. It has also created chart entries for Sarah Washington and Rik Waller.

In the early nineties, Hank Marvin was working on his next album, *Heartbeat*, and he asked Cliff Richard to provide some vocals to support his familiar guitar work on four tracks, one of which was *I Will Always Love You*. Hank's signature guitar line is eminently recognizable on this track as he plays the first verse and leads into the chorus. With a lot of tremolo and reverb, the second verse features an acoustic guitar, which takes over before the next chorus. Cliff's vocals are gently deployed after the dramatic pause and the restarting of the chorus with a key change. They are almost indistinguishable in the mix against the synthesisers until the end when they are brought to the forefront.

Track Specification
Composed by Dolly Parton

Musicians		*Recording Details*	
Brian Bennett	drums, percussion	Producer	Hank Marvin and Brian Bennett
Warren Bennett	keyboards	Engineered by	Dick Plant
Mark Griffiths	bass	Recording location	Honeyhill Studios, Hertfordshire
Alan Hawkshaw	piano	Recording date	1992-1993
Hank Marvin	guitar		
Cliff Richard	backing vocals		
Trevor Spencer	drums, percussion		

♬ I Will Arise and Go

Unissued track

I Will Arise and Go appears in the *Life with Johnny* episode entitled *Johnny Come Home* (the updated prodigal son parable), with Cliff Richard in the title role. Johnny has had enough of life in the north-east (the choice of setting made by Tyne Tees Television), and has accepted money from his father to travel to London, leaving his girlfriend at home while staying with erstwhile girlfriend Michelle (Una Stubbs). Soon he admits that he is broke and none of his dreams has transpired. He talks to his girlfriend on the phone and admits that he wants to come home but can't face what his father will say. She advises him to come home anyway and to think about his words. The song is played out as he prepares for the journey.
The lyrics focus on saying to his father that he has sinned, he got it wrong having made his choice and that there must be an answer. Gospel-like in its execution, this is more about the biblical parable than the Johnny storyline. Recorded at Abbey Road along with all of the songs used in the series with the Settlers, possibly with an album tie-in plan that was never executed, *I Will Arise and Go* was an original song that the end credits from the show suggested are written by Cliff in collaboration with the Settlers and the screenwriter David Winter.

Track Specification
Composed by Cliff Richard, David Winter, Cindy Kent, Mike Jones, John Fyffe and Geoffrey Srodzinski

Musicians		*Recording Details*	
John Fyffe	backing vocals, guitar	Producer	Norrie Paramor
Cindy Kent	backing vocals	Engineered by	Peter Vince
Mike Jones	backing vocals, guitar	Recording location	Abbey Road Studio 3, St. John's Wood, London
Cliff Richard	vocals	Recording date	11th January 1969
Geoffrey Srodzinski	backing vocals, bass		
Unknown	organ		
Unknown	drums, percussion		

♬ I Will Follow You

B-side of **Heart User** *and from the album* **Mission England Volume 2**

Recorded at a session that saw three other songs recorded for a Tear Fund charity project featuring Cliff Richard, *I Will Follow You* was written by Cliff and appeared as the B-side of **Heart User** from the album ***The Rock Connection***, although the track was not included on the listing, but was added to the album ***It's a Small World*** a few months later in 1985.
A synthesiser sequence introduces the song and leads into Cliff performing the bewildered lyrics, once again suggesting that everyone should be more compassionate and think about others. The quirky percussive rhythm is instigated in the chorus, which also features Cliff on his own backing vocals.
With just a guitar and his vocals, Cliff performed the song at a charity event at the Bramall Lane Stadium, the home to the Sheffield United football club. The result was recorded and released as a charity album, although much of the recording information is not readily available. His guitar work is very good and this aspect of his performances is often forgotten in the face of surrounding himself with great musicians such as Hank Marvin.

Track Specification
Composed by Cliff Richard

1. B-side (Heart User)

Musicians		*Recording Details*	
John Clark	guitar	Producer	Cliff Richard and Craig Pruess
Mark Griffiths	bass	Engineered by	Keith Bessey
Graham Jarvis	drums, percussion	Recording location	Gallery Studios, Chertsey, Surrey
Craig Pruess	keyboards, programming	Recording date	24th June 1984
Cliff Richard	vocals, backing vocals		

2. ***Mission England Volume 2***

Musicians

Cliff Richard	vocals, guitar

Recording Details

Producer	Unknown
Engineered by	Unknown
Recording location	Bramall Lane Stadium, Sheffield
Recording date	28th June 1985

♫ I Will Not Be a Mistake

From the album **Something's Goin' On**

The achingly melancholic and beautiful *I Will Not Be a Mistake* was one of the many songs commissioned for Cliff Richard's ***Something's Goin' On*** album in 2004 and recorded in Nashville, Tennessee.

The intricate guitar introduction leads into Cliff's impassioned performance of a song of breaking up and the analysis of what it means, resulting in the statement of the song's title. The use of the solo cello to support the simple accompaniment is an effective way of underpinning the sadness and emotion rippling through the lyrics.

Track Specification

Composed by Will Robinson, Helen Darling and Gary Burr

Musicians

John Howard	bass
Steve Mandile	electric guitar, classical guitar, acoustic guitar, keyboards
Cliff Richard	vocals
Chuck Tilley	drums, percussion
Jonathan Yudkin	cello

Recording Details

Producer	Dan Huff and Steve Mandile
Engineered by	Steve Mandile
Recording location	Big One Three Studio, Nashville, Tennessee, USA
Recording date	2003-2004

♫ I Wish We'd All Been Ready

From the album **Small Corners** *and unissued live track*

One of the songs by Larry Norman on the ***Small Corners*** album, *I Wish We'd All Been Ready* has also been covered by Chriss Feller, Good News Circle, Pat Boone, dc Talk, Spanky and Our Gang and Gene Viale among others.

For Cliff Richard's religious album of 1978, *I Wish We'd All Been Ready* was recorded as the first song of the final full session for the album and completed in four takes, with additional overdubs applied just over a week later. When it was added to the Faith and Inspiration section of the ***...And They Said It Wouldn't Last! (My 50 Years in Music)*** album, the track was edited slightly so that it goes directly into the piano. In all other respects, the track is the same and doesn't warrant its own track listing entry.

Tape of instrumentation is played backwards and faded up into a plaintive piano introduction, which then features Tony Rivers supplying an ethereal backing vocal. Cliff's simple vocal line is imbued with sadness and regret as matched to the lyrics.

It was incorporated as the third in a religious ***Medley*** during the *Live & Guaranteed 1988!* tour, and, while the Danish concert was recorded and filmed, none of the songs has been issued on CD to date.

Track Specification

Composed by Larry Norman

1. ***Small Corners***

Musicians

Brian Bennett	drums, percussion
Terry Britten	guitar
Stuart Calver	backing vocals
Bryn Haworth	guitar
John Perry	backing vocals
Cliff Richard	vocals
Tony Rivers	backing vocals
Alan Tarney	bass
Graham Todd	piano

Recording Details

Producer	Cliff Richard
Engineered by	Tony Clark and Haydn Bendall
Recording location	Abbey Road Studio 3, St. John's Wood, London
Recording date	19th and 27th January 1977

2. ***Unissued track (Live & Guaranteed 1988!)***

Musicians

John Clark	guitar
Rosemarie Ford	backing vocals
Mark Griffiths	bass
Peter Howarth	backing vocals
Steve Lauri	guitar
Paul Moessl	keyboards
Mick Mullins	backing vocals
Alan Park	keyboards
Cliff Richard	vocals
Henry Spinetti	drums, percussion

Recording Details

Producer	Unknown
Engineered by	Unknown
Recording location	Fyens Forum, Odense, Denmark
Recording date	22nd May 1988

♫ I Wish You'd Change Your Mind

From the album **I'm Nearly Famous**

Terry Britten was by now firmly ensconced with Cliff Richard in his recordings and tours as his guitarist, whilst also creating a number of memorable songs for him to record. One of these was *I Wish You'd Change Your Mind*, which was destined for the ***I'm Nearly Famous*** album. There was a false start with the recording with an attempt made at a session for the album on 1st December 1975, which was abandoned after four takes. The second was more successful with the song being captured in six takes and some overdubs being added a week later.

Employing the guitar harmonics, the plaintive cry from Cliff to a lover to stay so that they can talk (or sing) is performed over a slight reggae style rhythm with the emphasis on the off-beat. The mid-section of the song picks up in a major key as the lyrics suggest hope that her mind will be changed before reverting to the minor key. The backing vocals are gentle but persuasive and mark much of the material on the album.

Track Specification

Composed by Terry Britten

1. Unissued track (I'm Nearly Famous)

Musicians		*Recording Details*	
Terry Britten	guitar	Producer	Bruce Welch
Clem Cattini	drums, percussion	Engineered by	Tony Clark and John Barrett
Tony Harding	backing vocals	Recording location	Abbey Road Studio 3, St. John's Wood, London
John Perry	backing vocals	Recording date	1st December 1975
Cliff Richard	vocals		
Tony Rivers	backing vocals		
Alan Tarney	bass		
Graham Todd	keyboards		

2. I'm Nearly Famous

Musicians		*Recording Details*	
Terry Britten	guitar	Producer	Bruce Welch
Clem Cattini	drums, percussion	Engineered by	Tony Clark and John Barrett
Tony Harding	backing vocals	Recording location	Abbey Road Studio 3, St. John's Wood, London
John Perry	backing vocals	Recording date	4th December 1975 (basic track) and 12th December 1975 (overdubs)
Cliff Richard	vocals		
Tony Rivers	backing vocals		
Alan Tarney	bass		
Graham Todd	keyboards		

♫ I Wonder

B-side of **Lucky Lips**

Recorded alongside its A-side, ***Lucky Lips***, at the first recording session of 1963, *I Wonder* is a joint composition by Cliff Richard and Shadows guitarist Hank Marvin. Recorded in nine takes, the final take and edit was used for the mono and stereo recordings but with different mixes for the audio channels. Also released on the ***Cliff's Lucky Lips*** EP, the track remained a rarity until it was issued on the 1998 compilation *1960s* CD and later on the celebratory anthology ***...And They Said It Wouldn't Last! (My 50 Years in Music)***.

The stereo mix separates the Shadows to the right channel along with uncredited female backing vocals likely to be the Mike Sammes Singers, who were regularly used in Cliff recordings of this period, and the orchestra to the left with Cliff in the centre. The structure of the chief melody is quite complex for a pop song but Cliff's abilities as a musician are more than enough of a match as he pitches the notes perfectly.

Track Specification

Composed by Hank Marvin and Cliff Richard

Musicians		*Recording Details*	
Brian Bennett	drums, percussion	Producer	Norrie Paramor
Brian 'Licorice' Locking	bass	Engineered by	Malcolm Addey
Hank Marvin	guitar	Recording location	Abbey Road Studio 2, St. John's Wood, London
Norrie Paramor Orchestra	orchestra	Recording date	8th March 1963
Norrie Paramor	arranger, conductor		
Cliff Richard	vocals		
Unknown	female backing vocals		
Bruce Welch	rhythm guitar		

THE CLIFF RICHARD RECORDING CATALOGUE

J - J - J - J - J - J - J - J - J - J - J - J - J - J - J - J - J - J - J - J - J - J - J

♫ Jailhouse Rock

From the albums **The Rock 'n' Roll Years 1958-1963** *and* **Cliff "Live" in Japan '72**

A number one single for Elvis Presley, *Jailhouse Rock* was derived from the title of the film soundtrack and is one of Presley's most successful and enduring songs. Written by the songwriting dynamism of Leiber and Stoller, it featured a trawl through a number of different names of supposed prisoners, some of whom were real people. The term 'sad sack' in the lyrics goes back to the Second World War, where US soldiers used the term to mean 'loser'; indeed, this phrase is now used in Britain today, largely due to the inculcation of US television fare and culture spread. One of the problems with the track is that it is a love song; unfortunately, being an all-male prison, there are therefore perhaps unintended references to homosexuality with flirting between the prisoners (as indicated in the lyrics of the song), which caused some minor blustering concern at the time of its release.

It has been covered by a number of other artists, including ZZ Top, Jerry Lee Lewis, Twisted Sister, The Animals, Merle Haggard, Queen and Carl Perkins among many others. It was also on the repertoire for Cliff Richard and the Drifters' short residency at the Butlin's Holiday Camp in Clacton-on-Sea in August 1958. Anything that was recorded by Presley was at a premium and many bands attempted to cover his songs. On one night, Stan Edwards recorded their concerts on a two-track tape machine. Some of those recordings were released on ***The Rock 'n' Roll Years 1958-1963***, while others were in too poor a condition for commercial release. The judicious fate of *Jailhouse Rock* was that it was chosen for inclusion in the listings of that album. Because of the limited recording capabilities, this recording remains in mono.

Cliff's version tries to replicate the sliding chord introduction and thumping drum accompaniment of the original. Although Cliff's vocals are highly competent, his youth plays against him slightly, since it sounds too fresh-faced against the earthy almost sultry original performance by Presley. However, it shows that Cliff is comfortable in his abilities as a performer and that he has his own style that he was nurturing.

For his Far Eastern tour in 1972, Cliff incorporated *Jailhouse Rock* into a ***Rock Medley*** that plays tribute to the stars of the fifties when he was just starting out: ***The Girl Can't Help It, Great Balls of Fire, Lucille,*** *Jailhouse Rock*, ***Good Old Rock 'n' Roll*** and ***Do You Wanna Dance***.

Track Specification

Composed by Jerry Leiber and Mike Stoller

1. The Rock 'n' Roll Years 1958-1963

Musicians		*Recording Details*	
Cliff Richard	vocals, guitar	Producer	Unknown
Ian Samwell	guitar	Engineered by	Stan Edwards
Terry Smart	drums, percussion	Recording location	Rock 'n' Roll Ballroom, Butlin's Holiday Camp, Clacton-on-Sea, Essex
		Recording date	August 1958

2. Cliff "Live" in Japan '72

Musicians		*Recording Details*	
Brian Bennett	drums, percussion	Producer	Norrie Paramor
Pat Carroll	backing vocals	Engineered by	Unknown
John Farrar	bass	Recording location	Kosei Nenkin Hall, Tokyo, Japan
Alan Hawkshaw	piano	Recording date	22nd-23rd September 1972
Hank Marvin	guitar		
Olivia Newton-John	backing vocals		
Cliff Richard	vocals		
Bruce Welch	rhythm guitar		

♫ J'Attendrai

From the EP **When in France**

The popular French song *J'Attendrai* (literally *I Will Wait*) was first recorded in French by Rina Ketty in 1938, although it was originally an Italian song called *Tornerai* (or the different aspect of the lyrics, *You Will Return*), which was written by Dino Olivieri in 1933 with Italian lyrics by Nino Rastelli. Because of the timing of the French song's release, it has become symbolic of the start of the Second World War and the German Occupation of France. It has since been covered in its French guise by a number of artists including the Baguette Quartette, Dalida, Aimable, Pearl Django, Marie Colbert, Ismail Reinhardt, Gary Potter, Django's Moustache, Jack Lentier and Tino Rossi among many others.

One of six songs recorded during the Cliff Richard and the Shadows summer season tenure at the Jubilee Hall in Blackpool, *J'Attendrai* was attempted in the first session, although remained unissued. It was tried again with a nominal remake the next day along with the ***Don't Talk to Him*** B-side, ***Say You're Mine***. Completed in ten takes, *J'Attendrai* has only been released in mono format and is one of the few foreign language songs by Cliff not to be re-recorded with English lyrics. Like its ***When in France*** EP counterparts, *J'Attendrai* was a rarity until it was released on a Belgian 1975 LP, *When in France... Chante en Français*, and appeared on CD for the first time on ***The EP Collection: Ballads and Love Songs***.
With an almost country feel to the presentation that is reminiscent of ***Travellin' Light***, *J'Attendrai* is a quintessential Cliff and the Shadows track. In the instrumental break (enhancing the illusion further but managing to still sound quintessentially French), there is an uncredited harmonica solo rather than the expected and standard guitar.

Track Specification
Composed by Dino Olivieri; French translation by Louis Poterat

Musicians

Brian Bennett	drums, percussion
Brian 'Licorice' Locking	bass
Hank Marvin	guitar
Cliff Richard	vocals
Unknown	harmonica
Bruce Welch	rhythm guitar

Recording Details

Producer	Norrie Paramor
Engineered by	Malcolm Addey and Jimmy Johnson
Recording location	Abbey Road Studio 2, St. John's Wood, London
Recording date	6th August 1963

♫ Jerusalem, Jerusalem

From the album **His Land**

As part of a documentary style film involving Cliff Richard about the life of Jesus and modern Israeli life entitled ***His Land***, Cliff recorded seven songs. One of them was *Jerusalem, Jerusalem* that was performed after the opening titles. There is little information about the recording itself except that it occurred towards the end of 1969 and Cliff overdubbed his vocal on the previously recorded orchestral take (completed in Hollywood without Cliff's involvement).
The subtly gentle song plays as Cliff looks out across a sunset panorama of a desert settlement outside Jerusalem. The song builds in intensity as the camera picks out key locations and buildings in the city before it segues into the narration about the Sabbath and the Saturday nightlife. Cliff performs the song with gentle emotion and passion, while the arrangement evokes the music of the region and includes a number of unexpected cadences and musical intervals.

Track Specification
Composed by Naomi Shemer and Norman Newell

Musicians

Ralph Carmichael	arranger, conductor
Ralph Carmichael Chorus	backing vocals
Ralph Carmichael Orchestra	orchestra
Cliff Richard	vocals

Recording Details

Producer	Lee Gillette
Engineered by	Unknown
Recording location	Capitol Records, Hollywood, USA (orchestra) and Israel (vocals)
Recording date	Late 1969

♫ Je Suis Formidable

From the album **When in France – Chante en Français**

Cliff Richard had spent time in October 1968 recording translations of his songs for his first German language album, *Hier Ist Cliff*, but with all new material. In February 1969, he returned to the studio to record some titles for his first French language album *When in France – Chante en Français*, although, this time, the tracks were made up from his previous French songs as well as a small number of new recordings. Of this latter group, *Je Suis Formidable* (translated as *I Am Strong*) was the French translation of the film title song, ***Two a Penny***. As with those German tracks, rather than use the backing track from the English version, an entirely new version was recorded on 21st February.
Two songs were completed at the session – the other being a translation of ***Questions*** (also from the film) – and *Je Suis Formidable* has only ever been released in stereo. The album and the songs within it were rarities outside France until all of Cliff's foreign language songs were collated and included on the album ***On the Continent*** in 1997. Cliff is designated as the sole writer of the song (certainly he was of the English original); however, it is unlikely, as with the German translation of the same song, that he provided the French lyrics but no information is available to identify the translator.
As with all the versions of this song, they sound very similar, largely due to Norrie Paramor's success in recreating the sound used on the film. Cliff sings with the same arrogance that is asked for by the lyrics and the song sounds very strong in the French language, although he does make some pronunciation errors (one obvious example is the enunciation of *sans* as *sands* instead of *so'*) but this doesn't detract from the listening experience (except possibly for the French listener!).

Track Specification
Composed by Cliff Richard; French lyrics by Unknown

Musicians

Norrie Paramor Orchestra	orchestra
Norrie Paramor	arranger, conductor
Cliff Richard	vocals

Recording Details

Producer	Norrie Paramor
Engineered by	Peter Vince
Recording location	Abbey Road Studio 3, St. John's Wood, London
Recording date	21st February 1969

♫ Jesus

56th UK single** and from the albums **Help It Along** and **Japan Tour '74

For Cliff Richard's fifty-sixth UK single, it was perhaps curious to some commentatrs who had been following his career and private life that it had taken so long for him to release a religious song as a single, particularly one so overtly Christian as *Jesus*. But, as Cliff explained at the time, he was loath to release a religious song simply because he was a Christian – indeed, the critics would have launched themselves at him were that the case – and, if he was to do it, he wanted to wait until the right song came along. In the studio, much time was spent on effects and techniques to ensure it was perfect and Cliff confirms that he was very happy with the result.

The song was issued as a single, backed with another non-album track (as was common policy with the label at the time), ***Mr. Cloud***, on the Columbia label (catalogue number DB 8864) on 26th February 1972, reaching number thirty-five in the British singles charts. Although not his worst showing to date – that accolade contemporaneously lay with ***Flying Machine*** – the single was the least successful in terms on units sold. Released in stereo in many parts of the world, a mono version was issued in Australia. The stereo version was added to the track listing of ***The Best of Cliff Vol. 2*** and later on the *The Singles Collection* released in 2002.

With a contemporary beat and a backing vocal treated electronically, the song is gently brought in as Cliff begins his imploring message of adulation to Jesus. What is clever about the song is that the drama slowly builds up, with its foot-tapping rhythm, its fuzzy guitar solos and evangelical backing vocals, which are uncredited, all of which sound as if it could have been taken from a musical play or film. Disregarding the lyrics and the religious intent, the song actually stands out on its own and it is perhaps the track's content that played against it in terms of sales. Almost forty years on, the recording still sounds fresh and innovative and this point is largely lost to many critics because of its content.

Naturally, given the message and tenor of the song, it was an obvious choice for the studio-bound concerts in front of a small audience at the Morgan Studios, in aid of the Tear Fund charity, of which Cliff is a patron. These concerts resulted in the recording ***Help It Along*** and this version of *Jesus* is very similar to the original single version with the gradual build-up to the almost evangelical conclusion.

It was subsequently incorporated into the ***Gospel Medley*** section of his tour of Japan in 1974: *Jesus*, ***Amazing Grace*** and ***Jesus Is My Kind of People***. As the introduction is started on the piano and drums with the accompaniment of the backing vocalists, Cliff introduces the section professing his Christianity and his desire to sing songs since to do otherwise would be wrong. The performance of *Jesus* is close to the original and suddenly stops in its ebullient performance as the strings are initiated for the segue into the unaccompanied *Amazing Grace*.

Track Specification

Composed by Pierre Darjean and Michel Hamburger

1. Single

Musicians

Nick Ingman	arranger, conductor
Nick Ingman Orchestra	orchestra
Cliff Richard	vocals
Unknown	backing vocals

Recording Details

Producer	Norrie Paramor
Engineered by	Peter Vince
Recording location	Abbey Road Studio 2, St. John's Wood, London
Recording date	14th December 1972

2. Help It Along

Musicians

Terry Britten	guitar
Barrie Guard	arranger, conductor, percussion
Cliff Hall	keyboards
Jean Hawker	backing vocals
Anna Peacock	backing vocals
Kevin Peek	guitar
Cliff Richard	vocals
Trevor Spencer	drums, percussion
Alan Tarney	bass
Unknown	orchestra

Recording Details

Producer	David MacKay
Engineered by	Roger Quested
Recording location	Morgan Studios, London
Recording date	24th, 25th and 26th September 1973

3. Japan Tour '74

Musicians

Barrie Guard	arranger, conductor
Cliff Hall	piano
Brian Lewis	backing vocals, guitar
Kevin Peak	acoustic guitar
Cliff Richard	vocals
Shambles Symphonet	orchestra
Trevor Spencer	drums, percussion
Alan Tarney	backing vocals, bass
Bruce Welch	backing vocals, rhythm guitar

Recording Details

Producer	Toshiba EMI (no individual detailed)
Engineered by	Toshiba EMI (no individual detailed)
Recording location	Shinjuku Koseinenkin, Tokyo, Japan
Recording date	7th-8th October 1974

♫ Jesus Addresses the Crowd on the Hill-Side

From the album **About That Man**

Cliff Richard released an album of religious material called ***About That Man***, which was ostensibly a sequence of biblical readings interspersed with a small handful of songs. On this track, from the book of Matthew chapter five, verses 1 to 17, 21 to 28 and 38 to 48, chapter six, verses 19 to 34, chapter seven, verses 1 to 8, chapter 13 to 14 and verses 24 to 29, it tells the story of the sermon on the mount. Cliff reads the tracts well and brings the message over from the story without bombast and it is likely that the recording was completed in one continuous take.

Track Specification

From the King James Bible

Musicians		*Recording Details*	
Cliff Richard	vocals	Producer	Norrie Paramor
		Engineered by	Richard Lush
		Recording location	Abbey Road Studio 2, St. John's Wood, London
		Recording date	20th February 1970

♫ Jesus, Call Your Lambs

From the album **Don't Hide Your Heart** *(Sheila Walsh)*

The first duet by Cliff Richard and his protégée Sheila Walsh since their single ***Drifting*** two years earlier was recorded for Walsh's third album, *Don't Hide Your Heart*. Cliff did very little recording in 1985, owing to his commitment to the musical play ***Time***, but found time to be involved in providing principally backing vocals for this album project as well as the duet vocals on *Jesus Call Your Lambs*. Released on vinyl only as part of the parent album, it was included on the track listing of the American CD collection, *Compact Favorites* in 1988.

Walsh begins the song before handing over to Cliff for his part of the duet. The accompaniment is gentle and seemingly out of pace with the vocals, but this picks up as they enter the chorus, which features Walsh singing at the top of her range.

Track Specification

Composed by Teri de Sario

Musicians		*Recording Details*	
Dave Mattacks	cymbals	Producer	Craig Pruess and Keith Bessey
Craig Pruess	synthesiser, piano, brass, percussion	Engineered by	Keith Bessey
Cliff Richard	vocals	Recording location	Gallery Studios, Chertsey, Surrey or Riverside Studios, London
Sheila Walsh	vocals	Recording date	November 1984-February 1985

♫ Jesus Is Betrayed and Arrested

From the album **About That Man**

For Cliff Richard's religious album, ***About That Man***, he recorded a sequence of biblical readings with the first vinyl side describing Christ's birth and founding of the religion, and the second the lead-up to his crucifixion and resurrection. In this track that tells the story of Jesus being betrayed by Judas Iscariot just before his arrest and eventual execution by crucifixion, Cliff reads from the book of Luke, chapter twenty-two, verses 1 to 6, the book of John, chapter thirteen, verses 1 to 19 and the book of Luke, chapter twenty-two, verses 33 to 34, 39 to 51 and 54 to 62. Cliff reads the tract well and brings the well-known Christian stories to life; it was probably recorded in one continuous take since Cliff's rhythm in telling the story appears unimpeded.

Track Specification

From the King James Bible

Musicians		*Recording Details*	
Cliff Richard	vocals	Producer	Norrie Paramor
		Engineered by	Richard Lush
		Recording location	Abbey Road Studio 2, St. John's Wood, London
		Recording date	20th February 1970

♫ Jesus Is My Kind of People

From the albums **Live at Spree** *and* **Japan Tour '74**

Principally made famous by Etta James for her version, *Jesus Is My Kind of People* has also been covered by its composer Jim Weatherly as well as Ray Price and Freddie Hart. It was chosen by Cliff Richard for his studio-bound concerts in the Morgan Studios in front of a small audience although it was not released as part of the ***Help It Along*** charity album project. The recording was eventually issued as a track on the Christian music charity album *Live at Spree* later in 1974.

It was subsequently incorporated into the ***Gospel Medley*** section of his tour of Japan: ***Jesus***, ***Amazing Grace*** and *Jesus Is My Kind of People*. Having had the powerfully sentimental *a capella* rendition of *Amazing Grace* the piano comes in to initiate the jazz-like rhythm of *Jesus Is My Kind of People*, which Cliff begins to sing accompanied by the band providing a variety of jammed twiddles on their instruments and backing him vocally.

Track Specification
Composed by Jim Weatherly

1. Live at Spree

Musicians	
Terry Britten	guitar
Barrie Guard	arranger, conductor, percussion
Cliff Hall	keyboards
Jean Hawker	backing vocals
Anna Peacock	backing vocals
Kevin Peek	guitar
Cliff Richard	vocals
Trevor Spencer	drums, percussion
Alan Tarney	bass
Unknown	orchestra

Recording Details	
Producer	David MacKay
Engineered by	Roger Quested
Recording location	Morgan Studios, London
Recording date	24th, 25th and 26th September 1973

2. Japan Tour '74

Musicians	
Cliff Hall	piano
Brian Lewis	backing vocals, guitar
Kevin Peak	acoustic guitar
Cliff Richard	vocals
Trevor Spencer	drums, percussion
Alan Tarney	backing vocals, bass
Bruce Welch	backing vocals, rhythm guitar

Recording Details	
Producer	Toshiba EMI (no individual detailed)
Engineered by	Toshiba EMI (no individual detailed)
Recording location	Shinjuku Koseinenkin, Tokyo, Japan
Recording date	7th-8th October 1974

♫ Jesus Loves You

From the album **Help It Along**

Written by Cliff Richard, the only recording he made of *Jesus Loves You* was during the studio-bound concert in a set of seven sessions over three days in front of a small, politely appreciative audience. One of the thirteen songs released of the seventeen recorded, it was included on the charity album ***Help It Along*** in aid of the Tear Fund.

The Festivals of Light and of Jesus had occurred in the previous two years allowing young people to express their love of Jesus and this inspired Cliff to write the song. With a quiet accompaniment, the track slowly builds up with a foot-tapping rhythm before reverting to the solemnity of the chorus backed with simple instrumentation and backing vocals.

Track Specification
Composed by Cliff Richard

Musicians	
Terry Britten	guitar
Barrie Guard	arranger, conductor, percussion
Cliff Hall	keyboards
Jean Hawker	backing vocals
Anna Peacock	backing vocals
Kevin Peek	guitar
Cliff Richard	vocals
Trevor Spencer	drums, percussion
Alan Tarney	bass
Unknown	orchestra

Recording Details	
Producer	David MacKay
Engineered by	Roger Quested
Recording location	Morgan Studios, London
Recording date	24th, 25th and 26th September 1973

♫ Jesus Recruits His Helpers and Heals the Sick

From the album **About That Man**

Recording a truly religious album must have been daunting for Cliff Richard but ***About That Man*** is an excellent album even though it is principally readings from the Bible. On this particular track, from the book of Mark, chapter one, verse 12, to chapter two, verse 12, Cliff tells the story of Jesus gathering his disciples and one of the most famous stories of Jesus healing the sick. Recorded almost certainly in one take, Cliff reads with passion and imbues it with suitable meaning.

Track Specification
From the King James Bible

Musicians	
Cliff Richard	vocals

Recording Details	
Producer	Norrie Paramor
Engineered by	Richard Lush
Recording location	Abbey Road Studio 2, St. John's Wood, London
Recording date	20th February 1970

♫ Je T'Aime pour Toujours Ce Jour

From the album **When in France – Chante en Français**

Recorded at the last Cliff Richard session of 1973 and specifically for the French language album, *When in France – Chante en Français*, *Je T'Aime pour Toujours Ce Jour* (which translates as *I Love You Forever This Day*) is a translation of the single from the ***Two a Penny*** film, ***I'll Love You Forever Today***. There has been speculation as to whether it was a new recording or the backing track from the original English version with French vocal overdubs. The available documentation does not provide such information, neither does it offer the name of the translator – indeed, the compilation ***On the Continent*** specifically identifies only the original composers but this is unlikely, partly due to the passage of time but mainly because of the lack of fluency in the language. To answer the question of the backing track, by playing the English and French versions simultaneously reveals that the orchestral nuances are exactly the same, while some of the perceived differences are explained by the improved clarity of the mastering; to suggest that it is an original orchestral recording for the French version is impossible since there would be minor but tell-tale differences in the orchestration and instrumentation.

Track Specification
Composed by Cliff Richard and Jim Collier; French lyrics by Unknown

Musicians

Norrie Paramor Orchestra	orchestra
Norrie Paramor	arranger, director
Cliff Richard	vocals

Recording Details

Producer	Norrie Paramor (backing track) and David MacKay (vocals)
Engineered by	Peter Vince (backing track) and Roger Quested (vocals)
Recording location	Abbey Road Studio 2, St. John's Wood, London (backing track) and Morgan Studios, London (vocals)
Recording date	20th November 1968 (backing track) and 28th November 1973 (vocals)

♫ Joanna

B-side of **Stronger than That** *and from the album* **From a Distance ***** The Event Remaster**

During the recording of the ***Stronger*** album, it was a possibility that *Joanna* would be chosen as a single. However, in a poll taken from two thousand invited fans to listen to six of the new tracks at the London Palladium on 3rd April 1989, *Joanna* came in fourth place, even though it came ahead of the first single release, ***Lean on You***. However, *Joanna* was picked as the B-side for all the variants of the fourth single release from the project, ***Stronger than That***. In 1992, *Joanna* was also issued as a track on the French release of ***Remember*** (a translated version of ***When Two Worlds Drift Apart***).
The gentle love song is a reminiscence of a childhood sweetheart and how their relationship fell apart. One of the best parts of the song is the vocal arrangement, which features Cliff harmonizing with himself alongside his usual backing singers. A saxophone solo provides extra sadness to the performance in the middle eight.
Since Cliff had just released the album *Stronger* by the time he performed at Wembley Stadium, it is unsurprising that several of the songs would appear on the set list. However, due to space considerations, *Joanna* was removed from the track listing of the original ***From a Distance ***** The Event*** album in 1990 but was restored when the album was remastered in 2005. After the exuberance of ***Shake, Rattle and Roll***, this live version of *Joanna* creates a pleasant contrast not the least because of the reliance on the electronic instruments against the predecessor's guitar-led performance.

Track Specification
Composed by Chris Eaton

1. B-side (Stronger than That)

Musicians

Keith Bessey	drum and percussion programming
Dave Bishop	saxophone
John Clark	guitar
Paul Moessl	arranger
Mick Mullins	backing vocals
Keith Murrell	backing vocals
Cliff Richard	vocals, backing vocals
Unknown	synthesiser

Recording Details

Producer	Cliff Richard
Engineered by	Gerry Kitchingham and Ben Robbins
Recording location	R. G. Jones Studios, Wimbledon, London
Recording date	27th February 1989, 9th March 1989, 13th-17th March 1989 and 22nd-23rd March 1989

2. From a Distance ** The Event***

Musicians

Ray Beavis	saxophone
John Clark	guitar
Sonia Jones-Morgan	backing vocals
Steve Lauri	guitar
Peter May	drums, percussion
Paul Moessl	keyboards
Tessa Niles	backing vocals
Alan Park	keyboards
Provox:	
Peter Howarth	backing vocals
Mick Mullins	backing vocals
Keith Murrell	backing vocals
Cliff Richard	vocals
Steve Stroud	bass

Recording Details

Producer	Cliff Richard
Engineered by	Keith Bessey and Mick McKenna
Recording location	Rolling Stones Mobile Studio, Wembley Stadium, Wembley, North-west London
Recording date	16th-17th June 1989

♫ Johnny

Unissued track

In 1969, Tyne Tees Television ran a series of six episodes called *Life with Johnny* starring Cliff Richard in the lead role of Johnny, with each one revisiting and modernizing a famous parable as told by Jesus in the Bible. These were:

a) *Johnny Come Home*
b) *Johnny Faces Facts*
c) *Johnny and the Good Samaritan*
d) *Johnny on the Rocks*
e) *Johnny and the Blind Rage*
f) *Johnny in Love*

Accompanied by the Settlers and other actors and dancers, each programme was introduced by *Johnny*, which informed the viewer what Johnny was like and that, while he believed in war and cancer, he still was looking for an answer (a rather poor rhyme), asking whether there is a God and finding doors closed and so he goes on searching.

Cliff's performance is played out on a dark stage with the four members of the Settlers playing two guitars, a stand-up bass and a tambourine, although a synthesized organ (possibly Norrie Paramor, who often played keyboards on Cliff's recordings) can be clearly heard. Recorded at one of five sessions at Abbey Road for the programme, the song has never been issued, although the original intention was to release the songs on an album. *Johnny* is a gospel song, played out in a rock rhythm that, while foot-tapping and with strong harmonies from the Settlers, it succeeds in getting the message across to the audience. It is unclear precisely who wrote the song but the programme credits Cliff, the programme's writer David Winter and all of the Settlers for the original songs and so this is replicated here – this assumption is supported by the credits for ***Where Is That Man?*** from the album ***About That Man***.

Track Specification

Composed by Cliff Richard, David Winter, Cindy Kent, Mike Jones, John Fyffe and Geoffrey Srodzinski

Musicians		*Recording Details*	
John Fyffe	backing vocals, guitar	Producer	Norrie Paramor
Cindy Kent	backing vocals, tambourine	Engineered by	Peter Vince
Mike Jones	backing vocals, guitar	Recording location	Abbey Road Studio 3, St. John's Wood, London
Cliff Richard	vocals	Recording date	8th January 1969
Geoffrey Srodzinski	backing vocals, double bass		
Unknown	organ		

♫ Johnny, Wake Up to Reality

Unissued track

Appearing in the episode entitled *Johnny Faces Facts* in the religious television series *Life with Johnny*, the song *Johnny, Wake Up to Reality* comes in the narrative where Johnny (Cliff Richard) has told everyone how wrong they are and what is right without looking inwards (updating the parable of the speck and plank). He visits the vicar, who has been preaching on late-night television, at the insistence of his girlfriend who is fed up with his attitude. The vicar tells Johnny that he switched the television off too early and that there was more to his message on loneliness and that he could help with answering letters or visiting the community and perhaps thinking about God. Johnny goes to a mirror and sings this song as he realizes that he has got things wrong, that he should face reality, talk about Jesus and finding the path to truth.

The backing vocalists (the Settlers) are in silhouette behind him, while the song is played out in straightforward two-two time with powerful augmented musical intervals underpinning the confusion the character is feeling. It was recorded at Abbey Road over a period of two days, possibly with a view to EMI releasing a tie-in album to the Tyne Tees Television series; however, if that was the case, the project was abandoned. The final rolling credits stipulate that the original songs were written in partnership by Cliff, the programme's writer David Winter and the four members of the Settlers – a fact borne out by the credits on ***About That Man***, which featured a re-recording of ***Where Is That Man?*** in the track listing.

Track Specification

Composed by Cliff Richard, David Winter, Cindy Kent, Mike Jones, John Fyffe and Geoffrey Srodzinski

Musicians		*Recording Details*	
John Fyffe	backing vocals, guitar	Producer	Norrie Paramor
Cindy Kent	backing vocals, tambourine	Engineered by	Peter Vince
Mike Jones	backing vocals, guitar	Recording location	Abbey Road Studio 3, St. John's Wood, London
Cliff Richard	vocals	Recording date	8th January 1969
Geoffrey Srodzinski	backing vocals, double bass		
Unknown	drums, percussion		

♫ John the Baptist Points out Jesus

From the album **About That Man**

On Cliff Richard's religious album, ***About That Man***, he performs six songs interspersed with his readings of the biblical stories that tell the story of the rise of Christ. Cliff expresses the story of John the Baptist well and imbues the reading of the section from the book of John, chapter one, verses 19 to 51 with much passion. The recording was almost certainly completed in one take as the rhythm of Cliff's reading is uninterrupted throughout.

Track Specification
From the King James Bible

Musicians

Cliff Richard	vocals

Recording Details

Producer	Norrie Paramor
Engineered by	Richard Lush
Recording location	Abbey Road Studio 2, St. John's Wood, London
Recording date	20th February 1970

♬ Join the Band

From the film soundtrack album of **Take Me High**

Having successfully received the financial contract from Sir Harry Cunningham (Hugh Griffith) for the renovation of a part of Birmingham City Centre and having sold the idea of financing the Brumburger restaurant and beating his rival Hugo Flaxman (Anthony Andrews) into the bargain, Tim Matthews (Cliff Richard) and girlfriend Sarah (Debbie Watling) are keen to get the publicity for their burger venture moving. Cunningham suggests they make a big splash and the action cuts to a huge parade through the city centre streets with majorettes, banners, brass bands and a cavalcade of cars moving slowly through the cheering public. Tim gets out of the car and on to a motorbike to get to the front of the march and walks back, talking to the majorettes, banging a bass drum and then almost falling out as he gets back in the car.

There is a large brass band introduction that doesn't appear on the soundtrack album, although both were recorded at the same session in September 1973.

Hand claps and staccato chords in the orchestra initiate the song that emulates a marching band, before relinquishing control to a more typical rock style of song. The rhythm and metre regularly change very slightly, matching the action on the screen and simply states that everyone should join him on the quest for good fast food.

Track Specification
Composed by Tony Cole

Musicians

David MacKay Orchestra	orchestra
David MacKay	arranger, conductor
Cliff Richard	vocals, backing vocals
Unknown	hand claps
Unknown	backing vocals

Recording Details

Producer	David MacKay
Engineered by	Tony Clark and Mike Jarrett
Recording location	Abbey Road Studio 3, St. John's Wood, London
Recording date	3rd September 1973

♬ Joseph

From the album **Small Corners**

Recorded during the sessions for the mainstream album ***Every Face Tells a Story***, *Joseph*'s release was deferred to the follow-up religious album ***Small Corners*** in 1978 where it appeared as the opener to the second side of the vinyl album. Although the album is nominally produced by Cliff Richard, of course the prior album was controlled by Bruce Welch and he therefore gets the correct credit for this song not given on the album release. The song was the first to be attempted at the session and it was completed in seven takes, notwithstanding some overdubs recorded a week later.

Interestingly, since *Joseph* had already been recorded with Bruce heading the production, there is a difference between the techniques he uses and those of Cliff on the rest of the album. There is an echo behind Cliff's vocal, while the song subtly changes pace occasionally and this adds to the track's interest. There is a sense of foreboding mixed with excitement of what is to be found with the man called Joseph. Cliff supplies his own backing vocals in addition to the other vocalists.

Track Specification
Composed by Terry Britten

Musicians

Brian Bennett	drums, percussion
Terry Britten	guitar
John Perry	backing vocals
Cliff Richard	vocals
Tony Rivers	backing vocals
Alan Tarney	bass
Graham Todd	keyboards

Recording Details

Producer	Bruce Welch
Engineered by	Peter Vince, Tony Clark, Mike Jarrett and Alan Rouse
Recording location	Abbey Road Studio 2, St. John's Wood, London
Recording date	8th and 15th September 1976

♬ Jovenes, Los

From the album **40 Aniversario: La Ayuda de la Amistad** *(Los Mustang)*

When Cliff Richard made the film *The Young Ones*, the popularity of the title track ensured many a cover of the song. In Spain, it was the Shadows-like group Los Mustang who picked it up and had a parochial hit. To celebrate their forty years in show business in the late nineties, they re-recorded *The Young Ones* under the Spanish title *Los Jovenes* (a literal translation) and invited Cliff to supply the Spanish lead vocals which he duly did. The track was released on the album *40 Aniversario: La Ayuda de la Amistad*, which featured a number of the songs made popular by Los Mustang.

The instrumentation is pretty faithful to the original, while Cliff introduces the song with a falsetto non-lyric before entering into the Spanish lyrics, supported by the backing vocals of band member Santi Carulla Hernandez, who then takes over the lead vocal. The guitar solo is not as mellow as that played by Hank Marvin in the original but it fits well with this version. Cliff sings layered backing vocals leading up to the end, which has a lengthier instrumental play-out than the English version.

Track Specification
Composed by Sid Tepper and Roy C. Bennett; Spanish lyrics by Unknown

Musicians

Marco Rossi Ezquerra	guitar
Santi Carulla Hernandez	vocals, backing vocals
Antonio Mercade Marsal	rhythm guitar
Miguell Navarro	drums, percussion
Cliff Richard	vocals, backing vocals
Antonio Mier Roura	bass

Recording Details

Producer	Los Mustang (backing track) and Keith Bessey (Cliff's vocals)
Engineered by	Unknown (backing track) and Keith Bessey (Cliff's vocals)
Recording location	Barcelona, Spain (backing track) and R. G. Jones Studios, Wimbledon, London (Cliff's vocals)
Recording date	1999

♫ Joy of Living, The
49th UK single

Recorded at Cliff Richard's first session of 1970, the recording of ***The Joy of Living*** was moved to the Advision Studios for no accounted reason and it was the only song slated to be recorded on the day. Backed with two songs – ***Leave My Woman Alone*** (a Cliff solo) and *Boogatoo* (a Hank Marvin instrumental) – *The Joy of Living* was credited to Cliff and Hank and issued as a single on the Columbia label (catalogue number DB 8657) on 6th February 1970 reaching number twenty-five in the UK charts in March 1970. It saw the continuing decline in Cliff's chart successes, which is unfortunate since it is actually a fine song co-written by Hank and Paul Ferris, who had written Cliff's earlier hit ***Visions***. Columbia had changed its policy in releasing singles in mono only to stereo only; there is an exception with this single when it was released in Holland in mono only (catalogue number 5C00604347) in February 1970 and this edit remains a significant rarity. The single was included on the album ***The Best of Cliff Vol.*** 2 in 1972 and later on *The Hits in Between* in 1998. It was remastered and added as a bonus track on the 2004 reissue of the ***Sincerely Cliff Richard*** album.

The song is essentially a cynical look at modern Britain and its progress – motorways, cars, etc. – all expressed in lyrics and bouncing beat that attempts to spread a veneer of comfort over the top, while still making comment about the impact that progress has had. Hank uses wowing and fuzzed guitar effects, while the tambourine and thundering piano in the chorus drive the song forwards (the progression into a polluted future). Although the uncredited female backing vocalists are a little obsequious with their warbling enunciation they are used to great effect in the overall ensemble piece.

Track Specification
Composed by Hank Marvin and Paul Ferris

Musicians

Hank Marvin	vocals, backing vocals, guitar
Mike Vickers Orchestra	orchestra
Cliff Richard	vocals
Unknown	backing vocals
Mike Vickers	arranger, conductor

Recording Details

Producer	Norrie Paramor
Engineered by	Unknown
Recording location	Advision Studios, London
Recording date	7th January 1970

♫ Junior Cowboy
B-side of **I Can't Ask for Anything More Than You**

Michael Allison and Peter Sills were responsible for a few tracks on ***I'm Nearly Famous***, including the title track and *Junior Cowboy*. Bruce Welch's ear for a good commercial tune and quality material ensured that Cliff Richard was on the verge of a renaissance. There was an initial attempt to record the song on 3rd December 1975, which was abandoned after a number of takes, before the backing track was completed in eleven takes the next day with the vocals overdubbed a few days later. *Junior Cowboy* was chosen as the B-side for Cliff's sixty-seventh UK single, ***I Can't Ask for Anything More Than You***.

The guitar introduction is only bettered by Alan Tarney's intricate bass line as it leads into Cliff's vocals, while the rhythm is kept moving forward in this pseudo-country style of song, which features a steel guitar to add to the atmosphere. The backing vocals, when they appear, also mark the song out as something special.

Track Specification
Composed by Michael Allison and Peter Sills

1. Unissued track (I'm Nearly Famous)

Musicians

Terry Britten	guitar
Clem Cattini	drums, percussion
Tony Harding	backing vocals
John Perry	backing vocals
Cliff Richard	vocals
Tony Rivers	backing vocals
Alan Tarney	bass
Graham Todd	keyboards
Unknown	hand claps

Recording Details

Producer	Bruce Welch
Engineered by	Tony Clark and John Barrett
Recording location	Abbey Road Studio 3, St. John's Wood, London
Recording date	3rd December 1975

2. *I'm Nearly Famous*

Musicians

Terry Britten	guitar
Clem Cattini	drums, percussion
Tony Harding	backing vocals
John Perry	backing vocals
Cliff Richard	vocals
Tony Rivers	backing vocals
Alan Tarney	bass
Graham Todd	keyboards
Unknown	hand claps

Recording Details

Producer	Bruce Welch
Engineered by	Tony Clark and John Barrett
Recording location	Abbey Road Studio 3, St. John's Wood, London
Recording date	4th and 8th December 1975

♫ Just a Closer Walk with Thee

From the album **Good News**

A traditional gospel song, *Just a Closer Walk with Thee* is often performed simply as an instrumental, particularly when it appears as part of the dirge at traditional New Orleans jazz funerals (see the opening sequence to the *Live and Let Die* film for such an example). The composer of the tune and the author of the lyrics, possibly the same person, are unknown or they preferred to remain anonymous and, as such, the track is often designated as being traditional. The song increased in popularity and was performed particularly during the Depression in America in the early thirties among the African-American church communities. The first recording of *Just a Closer Walk with Thee* was made in 1941 by the Selah Jubilee Singers, followed in quick succession as a solo by Rosetta Thorpe. It has since been covered, either with the long title or the shortened version of *A Closer Walk*, by Elvis Presley, Red Foley, Tennessee Ernie Ford, Pat Boone, Little Richard, the Seekers, Willie Nelson, Van Morrison, Crystal Gayle, Charley Pride, Tammy Wynette, Joan Baez and Gladys Knight and the Pips among many others. Although it wasn't a chart hit in the UK, a number of versions have been successful in the US.

Recorded in six takes at a session that saw five songs attempted and four completed, Cliff Richard's version of *Just a Closer Walk with Thee* was arranged by Bernard Ebbinghouse, who also conducted the orchestra, and closed the first side of the vinyl version of his ***Good Times*** album.

Given a country make-over with a cod American accent provided by the uncredited backing vocalists (possibly the Mike Sammes Singers as they were regular session singers for Cliff), the jaunty song is a great opener to the second side of the ***Good News*** album. Cliff shows his versatility once again as he performs this song, imbuing the lyrics with emotion and showing off a lovely vibrato on the sustained notes.

Track Specification

Composed by Traditional, arranged by Bernard Ebbinghouse

Musicians

Bernard Ebbinghouse Orchestra	orchestra
Bernard Ebbinghouse	arranger, conductor
Cliff Richard	vocals
Unknown	backing vocals

Recording Details

Producer	Norrie Paramor
Engineered by	Peter Vince and Mike Stone
Recording location	Abbey Road Studio 2, St. John's Wood, London
Recording date	3rd May 1967

♫ Just a Little Bit Too Late

B-side of **On My Word**

A Hank Marvin composition that was chosen for the B-side of ***On My Word*** (the single that was recorded eight months previously in the US during Cliff Richard's recording sojourn in Nashville and New York), it was one of two songs to be attempted at the session, which was the first for Cliff Richard in 1965 – the other song ***Whatcha Gonna Do About It?*** remains unissued. The final (unknown) take and edit were used for both the mono and stereo recordings but with different mixes for the needs of the separate audio channels. Originally released in mono only as the B-side, this mix of the the song was a considerable rarity until it was re-issued for the first time on the 2001 French compilation *I Could Easily Fall*. The stereo version was finally given a release on the celebratory compilation ***...And They Said It Wouldn't Last! (My 50 Years in Music)*** album in 2008.

With the lead guitar and bass in unison with each other, the song is introduced by these instruments before the perfect blending of the Shadows vocals complementing Cliff's lead lifts the song to another level. The stereo mix of the song spreads the instrumentation across the channels. The song is a typical Hank Marvin song of the period; strong on melody, harmony and rhythm.

Track Specification

Composed by Hank Marvin

Musicians

Brian Bennett	drums, percussion
Hank Marvin	backing vocals, guitar
Cliff Richard	vocals
John Rostill	backing vocals, bass
Bruce Welch	backing vocals, rhythm guitar

Recording Details

Producer	Norrie Paramor
Engineered by	Unknown
Recording location	Abbey Road Studio 2, St. John's Wood, London
Recording date	4th April 1965

♫ Just another Guy

B-side of **The Minute You're Gone**

Written by Neil Diamond while he was a jobbing composer in the sixties and before his own solo performing career took off, *Just another Guy* has not been covered by many artists and was chosen for Cliff Richard to record during his Nashville sessions for Columbia in the August of 1964. The final (unknown) take was used for the release of the song, which has only ever been released in mono format, although there exists the possibility that a stereo version was mixed, since this was the general practice at the time – this is unconfirmed and there is no record of such a recording. Chosen as the B-side of the international hit ***The Minute You're Gone***, which was also recorded during Cliff's American sojourn, *Just another Guy* was a relative rarity until it was included on the rare B-sides section of the celebratory package ***...And They Said It Would Never Last! (My 50 Years in Music)*** in 2008.

The upbeat rhythm of the song belies the sorry tale portrayed in the lyrics that talks of being ignored by the object of his affections. There are some backing vocals but these are pretty much limited to the mid-section, although they are subtly used in the final verse too. There are hand-claps as well as standard drums, in addition to the standard instrumentation for a Nashville country song.

Track Specification

Composed by Neil Diamond

Musicians

Jordanaires	backing vocals
Cliff Richard	vocals
Unknown	hand claps
Unknown	guitar
Unknown	bass
Unknown	piano
Unknown	violin
Unknown	drums, percussion

Recording Details

Producer	Bob Morgan and Billy Sherrill
Engineered by	Mort Thomason
Recording location	Columbia Studios, Nashville
Recording date	25th August 1964

♫ Just Don't Have the Heart

107th UK single *(seven-inch, extended version, remixed version and B-side of* **Just Don't Have the Heart***) and from the album* **From a Distance ***** The Event Remaster**

At the Ivor Novello Awards in early 1989, so the story goes, Cliff Richard happened to be sitting on the next table to the triumvirate of extraordinarily successful eighties producers, Mike Stock, Matt Aitken and Pete Waterman. Under Stock, Aitken and Waterman (or SAW), they had enjoyed significant success with ex-*Neighbours* actors Kylie Minogue and Jason Donovan, as well as Bananarama and Hazel Dean among several others. They were present at the awards because they had been nominated for a songwriting award for *Never Gonna Give You Up* by one of their protégés, Rick Astley. As the story goes, Cliff leaned across and suggested that if they had another song of that quality that they should give him a call. Cliff was hot property at the time and so the producers fell over themselves to get the opportunity to write and record a bespoke song that became *Just Don't Have the Heart*. The song is often wrongly written as *I Just Don't Have the Heart* – note that the original paper with the lyrics written out does not have the 'I' at the beginning, while variants of the subsequent release sometimes incorporate it. Following a similar approach to recording as Alan Tarney employed on the rest of the ***Stronger*** album, the three writers went into the studio and began to compose the song, slowly building up the backing track before bringing Cliff in for two days to complete his vocal line.

Part of the recording includes a sample of Cliff's vocal warm-up routine, which was initially bewildering to him but, once he'd heard it, he agreed to keep the effect in because it sounded very different from a lot of other records at the time and agreed that it enhanced the production of the track. Backed with non-album song ***Wide Open Space***, *Just Don't Have the Heart* was issued as the second of four singles from the project on the EMI label (catalogue number EM 101) on 14th August 1989 and the song reached number three in the UK charts. Alongside this release, a remixed version was created that extended the playing time by over a minute and a half and was added to the twelve-inch (catalogue number 12EM 101), the twelve-inch with a poster sleeve (12EMP 101) and the CD (CDEM 101) single releases. A further remixed version by Dave Ford was issued on a special twelve-inch version (12EMX 101) that later appeared on the rare B-sides compilation of the celebratory ***...And They Said It Wouldn't Last! (My 50 Years in Music)*** album in 2008. Finally, an instrumental version with Cliff on backing vocals only was issued on all three twelve-inch formats and the CD single, which was later included as a bonus track on the 2004 remaster of the *Stronger* album.

Introduced by the *a capella* backing vocals alongside Cliff singing part of the chorus, the electronic beat and keyboards are pure Stock, Aitken and Waterman, and the arrangement of the accompaniment is a key signature of much of what they produced. In some ways, Cliff's voice is too good for manufactured pop such as this but, in other respects, it helps to elevate what might have been mediocre in another lesser singer's hands.

Although Cliff performed the song at his thirtieth anniversary concerts at Wembley Stadium, with Stock, Aitken and Waterman also providing backing vocals, the track was left off the original album release of ***From a Distance ***** The Event*** in 1995, probably for space considerations, but was restored to the right running sequence on the two-CD remaster of the album in 2005. With the emphasis on synthesisers and electronic keyboards, the song is a strong and faithful rendition of the original studio version of the song.

Track Specification
Composed by Mike Stock, Matt Aitken and Pete Waterman

1. Single

Musicians	
Matt Aitken	keyboards, sequencers
A. Linn	drums, percussion
Mae McKenna	backing vocals
Cliff Richard	vocals, backing vocals
Mike Stock	keyboards, sequencers
Miriam Stockley	backing vocals

Recording Details	
Producer	Mike Stock, Matt Aitken and Pete Waterman
Engineered by	Karen Hewitt and Yoyo
Mixed by	Phil Harding
Recording location	PWL Studios, London
Recording date	20th January-7th February 1989 (backing track) and 8th-9th February 1989 (vocals)

2. Single (twelve-inch and CD extended)

Musicians	
Matt Aitken	keyboards, sequencers
A. Linn	drums, percussion
Mae McKenna	backing vocals
Cliff Richard	vocals, backing vocals
Mike Stock	keyboards, sequencers
Miriam Stockley	backing vocals

Recording Details	
Producer	Mike Stock, Matt Aitken and Pete Waterman
Engineered by	Karen Hewitt and Yoyo
Mixed by	Phil Harding
Recording location	PWL Studios, London
Recording date	20th January-7th February 1989 (backing track) and 8th-9th February 1989 (vocals)

3. Single (twelve-inch remixed)

Musicians	
Matt Aitken	keyboards, sequencers
A. Linn	drums, percussion
Mae McKenna	backing vocals
Cliff Richard	vocals, backing vocals
Mike Stock	keyboards, sequencers
Miriam Stockley	backing vocals

Recording Details	
Producer	Mike Stock, Matt Aitken and Pete Waterman
Engineered by	Karen Hewitt and Yoyo
Mixed by	Phil Harding
Remixed by	Dave Ford
Recording location	PWL Studios, London
Recording date	20th January-7th February 1989 (backing track) and 8th-9th February 1989 (vocals)

4. B-side (Just Don't Have the Heart – twelve-inch and CD)

Musicians	
Matt Aitken	keyboards, sequencers
A. Linn	drums, percussion
Mae McKenna	backing vocals
Cliff Richard	backing vocals
Mike Stock	keyboards, sequencers
Miriam Stockley	backing vocals

Recording Details	
Producer	Mike Stock, Matt Aitken and Pete Waterman
Engineered by	Karen Hewitt and Yoyo
Mixed by	Phil Harding
Recording location	PWL Studios, London
Recording date	20th January-7th February 1989 (backing track) and 8th-9th February 1989 (vocals)

5. From a Distance ** The Event Remaster***

Musicians	
Matt Aitken	backing vocals
John Clark	guitar
Sonia Jones-Morgan	backing vocals
Steve Lauri	guitar
Peter May	drums, percussion
Paul Moessl	keyboards
Tessa Niles	backing vocals
Alan Park	keyboards
Provox:	
Peter Howarth	backing vocals
Mick Mullins	backing vocals
Keith Murrell	backing vocals
Cliff Richard	vocals
Mike Stock	backing vocals
Steve Stroud	bass
Pete Waterman	backing vocals

Recording Details	
Producer	Cliff Richard
Engineered by	Keith Bessey and Mick McKenna
Recording location	Rolling Stones Mobile Studio, Wembley Stadium, Wembley, North-west London
Recording date	16th-17th June 1989

♫ Just Don't Say Goodbye

B-side of **The Miracle**

In 1997 onwards, Cliff Richard was in the studio working on his new album, ***Real as I Wanna Be***, which was yet another departure in style over his career and featured new musicians and producer in Peter Wolf. As with many of his recording ventures, Cliff recorded a lot of material that never made it on to the track listing of the album and so it was with *Just Don't Say Goodbye*. This song was written by Tommy Lee James and Robin Lerner, who had also conjured up the evocatively titled ***Climbing up Mount Everest***, which made its way on to the album, but *Just Don't Say Goodbye* was left off *Real as I Wanna Be* and remained unissued until the single release of ***The Miracle*** was being prepared. As with many of Cliff's singles in the nineties, they were released on a dual CD disc with different material on each. *Just Don't Say Goodbye* was added to the second of these discs alongside a live version of ***Move It*** from Cliff's fortieth anniversary concert. Unfortunately, there is scant information on the musicians and personnel involved, although the assumption that he recorded it during the album sessions means that those musicians who were present are added to this entry.

Track Specification

Composed by Tommy Lee James and Robin Lerner

Musicians

Vinnie Colaiuta	drums, percussion
Paul Jackson Jr.	guitar, sitar
Cliff Richard	vocals, backing vocals
Michelle Wolf	backing vocals
Peter Wolf	arranger, bass, keyboards, synclavier, percussion

Recording Details

Producer	Peter Wolf
Engineered by	Christian Leitgeb, Chris Heil, Paul Erickson and/or Keith Bessey
Recording location	Little America Recording Studios, Weiler, Austria, Ocean Recording Studios, Burbank, California, USA, Arco Recording Studios, Munich, Germany, R. G. Jones Recording Studios, Wimbledon, London, England and/or The Pierce Room, London, England
Recording date	1997 or 1998

♫ Keep Me Warm
From the album **Stronger**

The closing track on Cliff Richard's ***Stronger*** album was written and produced by Alan Tarney, using the same method they had employed during the recording of the prior album, ***Always Guaranteed***, with Tarney creating a basic musical idea and building on it in the studio before Cliff added his vocals and one such song was *Keep Me Warm*.
A medium-paced ballad, *Keep Me Warm* is reported speech of a girl who is in a relationship. Cliff sings the song almost confidentially in the verses but this brightens and warms up in the chorus, which features backing vocals by Cliff himself.

Track Specification
Composed by Alan Tarney

Musicians

Cliff Richard	vocals, backing vocals
Alan Tarney	arranger, synthesisers, drum and percussion sequencers

Recording Details

Producer	Alan Tarney
Engineered by	Gerry Kitchingham and Ben Robbins
Recording location	R. G. Jones Studios, Wimbledon, London
Mixed by	John Hudson and Noel Rafferty
Mixing location	Mayfair Studios, London
Recording date	27th February 1989, 9th March 1989, 13th-17th March 1989 and 22nd-23rd March 1989

♫ Keep Me Where Love Is
From the album **His Land**

The penultimate song involving Cliff Richard in ***His Land*** was recorded in Israel during filming for the documentary about the life and locations of Christ's good deeds. The vocals were overdubbed on an orchestral track pre-recorded in Hollywood but there is no precise information regarding the session dates other than that being in late 1969. Although pleasant enough with its syrupy strings and guitar accompaniment, there is not much in terms of musical hooks. Cliff performs the song with conviction but with a stronger melody would have helped elevate this song.

Track Specification
Composed by Jim Collier and Ralph Carmichael

Musicians

Ralph Carmichael	arranger, conductor
Ralph Carmichael Chorus	backing vocals
Ralph Carmichael Orchestra	orchestra
Cliff Richard	vocals

Recording Details

Producer	Lee Gillette
Engineered by	Unknown
Recording location	Capitol Records, Hollywood, USA (orchestra) and Israel (vocals)
Recording date	Late 1969

♫ Keep on Looking
B-side of **A Little in Love** *and* **Give a Little Bit More** *(US only)*

Recorded at the last of Cliff Richard's sessions for the ***I'm No Hero*** album, *Keep on Looking* was not included on the album in spite of the track listing running to only ten numbers, making it the shortest Cliff album to date. Instead, the dominance of Alan Tarney on Cliff's eighties recordings was continued with his own song and it was released as the B-side of the second single issued from the album, ***A Little in Love***. For some reason, a third track, ***Give a Little Bit More***, was released as a single in the US only and again *Keep on Looking* was chosen as the B-side, while it was ***Everyman***, another album track, that was used as the B-side of the US release of *A Little in Love*. It would take another twenty years before the track was finally reissued in a different format when it was incorporated as a bonus track on the 2001 remaster of *I'm No Hero*.
As with most of the album tracks, *Keep on Looking* is a synthesiser-driven track with slight echoes of *A Little in Love*. A fast-paced rock song, the lead vocals are underpinned by a chugging bass, percussion and layered backing vocals.

Track Specification
Composed by Alan Tarney

Musicians

Michael Boddicker	synthesiser
Nick Glennie-Smith	synthesiser
Cliff Richard	vocals, backing vocals
Trevor Spencer	drums, percussion
Alan Tarney	arranger, backing vocals, guitar, bass

Recording Details

Producer	Alan Tarney
Engineered by	Ashley Howe
Recording location	Riverside Studios, London
Recording date	8th July 1980

♫ Kein Zug Nach Gretna Green

B-side of **Goodbye Sam (Das Ist die Liebe)**

Written as an English song by Bert Olden and titled simply *Gretna Green*, Cliff Richard translating stalwart Kurt Hertha provided lyrics for Cliff to record in the German language. Little is known about the original English version – indeed, it was one of the small handful of songs that Cliff recorded in a foreign language but which had no English counterpart and it is certain that Cliff didn't record any other version than in the German language.

With a German title of *Kein Zug Nach Gretna Green* (literally translating to *No Train to Gretna Green*), the song refers to the village in Dumfries and Galloway on the Scottish border with England, where for just over a hundred years, young English couples used to elope in order to get married because of the local laws were more lax and allowed marriage that would otherwise have been stopped in England. Although this law revoked and updated in 1856, the notion of Gretna Geen being a centre for clandestine marriages still pervades in romantic folklore and therefore transported into this song, which talks about wanting to get married but having no transport to get to the village.

Kein Zug Nach Gretna Green was chosen as the B-side of the German language single ***Goodbye Sam (Das Ist die Liebe)***, which was itself a translation of Cliff's fiftieth single, ***Goodbye Sam, Hello Samantha***. It was recorded with two other German songs at the Chappell Studios in London, displaced from Abbey Road possibly due to refurbishment of the complex, and it was released in stereo only. Included on the German compilation album *Ich Träume Deine Träume* album in 1971, it was a major rarity for twenty-six years until it was included on the anthology of Cliff's foreign language recordings, ***On the Continent***.

On first listening, the musically sharp (uncredited) female backing vocalists and the stumbling entry with too many words to scan for the rhythm makes the listener uncertain whether to continue listening but it is worth doing so a second or third time because there is much to commend it and, in particular, Cliff's emotional lead vocals. The overall arrangement has strong flavours of Adam Faith's sixties single *Message to Martha* at certain points before breaking away into its own musical path.

Track Specification

Composed by Bert Olden; German lyrics by Kurt Hertha

Musicians

Mike Vickers Orchestra	orchestra
Cliff Richard	vocals
Unknown	backing vocals
Mike Vickers	arranger, conductor

Recording Details

Producer	Norrie Paramor
Engineered by	Unknown
Recording location	Chappell Studios, London
Recording date	21st January 1970

♫ King Creole

From the album **Oh Boy!**

Towards the latter part of the fifties, after Elvis Presley's initial rush of success and being at the vanguard of the change of popular music with his approach to rock and roll, he went on to consolidate his abilities as an entertainer by appearing in a number of films such as ***Jailhouse Rock***, ***Love Me Tender***, *G. I. Blues* and *King Creole*, precipitating an extraordinary career of thirty-three films in just over twelve years. One of the most defining of his particular genre was his performance as teenager Danny Fisher, who has to take the decision to give up on education in order to support his father. Inevitably, Fisher becomes embroiled in trouble and is only saved from being thrown in jail after a barkeeper gives him a job as a singer. But then trouble from the past catches up with Fisher, when a gangster insists that Fisher sings at his bar, using the charms of a girl to assist in the decision-making process. Adapted from a Harold Robbins' novel, the title song was released as a single and reached number two for Presley in the latter part of 1958.

The dark rumbling of the song and vocal presentation expresses some of the themes identified in the film and perfectly matched the persona that Presley was cultivating at the time. Because of the success of the song, it was dutifully picked up by many artists for covering, although it has only been recorded by a handful of acts, usually in tribute to Presley, such as Miaow, Ronnie McDowell, the Hollywood Sound Orchestra, Link Wray and Veeti Velvet. It was also chosen as part of the set that Cliff Richard performed on the *Oh Boy!* official album and it fits neatly with his energetic performance of it. Cliff does a very passable interpretation of the song, although it is very slightly marred by the backing vocals, which are not always in tune and are provided by the Oh Boy! Band rather than the Drifters.

Track Specification

Composed by Jerry Leiber and Mike Stoller

Musicians

Dallas Boys:	
Nicky Clarke	backing vocals
Leon Fisk	backing vocals
Stan Jones	backing vocals
Joe Smith	backing vocals
Bob Wragg	backing vocals
Oh Boy! Band	guitars, stand-up bass, piano, drums, percussion, tambourine
Cliff Richard	vocals

Recording Details

Producer	Harry Robinson (backing track) and Norrie Paramor (vocals)
Engineered by	Norman Newell (backing track) and Malcolm Addey (vocals)
Recording location	Abbey Road Studio 2, St. John's Wood, London
Recording date	19th October 1958 (backing track) and 21st October 1958 (vocals)

♬ King of Love My Shepherd Is, The

From the album **Good News**

Another track from Cliff Richard's ***Good News*** album that is a favourite with church congregations, *The King of Love My Shepherd Is* follows the ***23rd Psalm*** by using the imagery of God and Jesus in a shepherd's role herding their flock towards a life of righteousness. It has been covered by a number or gospel-based acts and was recorded by Cliff at the same session as *23rd Psalm*, his version arranged by producer Norrie Paramor, and he completed the track on the fourth take.

The second side of the album has the more traditional religious hymns and songs and a case in point is this familiar hymn, which has a gentle arrangement in singular instruments and backing vocals. As with other hymns on the record, the vocalists are given free rein on one of the verses, which sounds incongruous against the purity of Cliff's voice. This group is uncredited but is quite possibly the Mike Sammes Singers, given the quavering soprano voices, which was one of their perhaps unfortunate features.

Track Specification

Composed by Traditional, arranged by Norrie Paramor

Musicians

Norrie Paramor Orchestra	orchestra
Norrie Paramor	arranger, conductor
Cliff Richard	vocals
Unknown	backing vocals

Recording Details

Producer	Norrie Paramor
Engineered by	Peter Vince and Mike Stone
Recording location	Abbey Road Studio 2, St. John's Wood, London
Recording date	4th May 1967

♬ King's Place, The

From the pantomime cast recording album of **Cinderella**

Recorded at the third session designated for completing the ***Cinderella*** pantomime cast recording, *The King's Place* was the first song to be recorded and only required two takes. That second and final take and edit was used for the mono and stereo recordings.

A rock and roll style rhythm is set up in the introduction, with clipped accents from the Mike Sammes Singers setting the scene for the grandeur of the king's castle and the dance party as it breaks off into a waltz before returning back to the original rhythm. The guitar throughout is fuzzed, while Cliff's vocals can't easily be distinguished from the others particularly.

Track Specification

Composed by Hank Marvin, Bruce Welch, Brian Bennett and John Rostill

Musicians

Brian Bennett	drums, percussion
Hank Marvin	guitar
Mike Sammes Singers	backing vocals
Norrie Paramor Orchestra	orchestra
Norrie Paramor	arranger, conductor
Cliff Richard	vocals
John Rostill	bass
Bruce Welch	rhythm guitar

Recording Details

Producer	Norrie Paramor
Engineered by	Peter Vince and Richard Lush
Recording location	Abbey Road Studio 2, St. John's Wood, London
Recording date	9th November 1966

♬ Kiss

From the album **Cliff Richard**

Originally recorded in the Spanish language version for Cliff Richard's ***When in Spain*** album, the song ***Tus Besos*** took the subtitle of *Kiss*. At the end of January of 1965, Cliff recorded the English lyric vocals for many of the Spanish tunes he had recorded almost two years previously. One of these was *Kiss*, with the English translation provided by Haven Gillespie. The English version was recorded in three steps: first taking the original instrumentation track (note that this therefore features Brian Locking on bass rather than his replacement John Rostill) recorded in Barcelona, a separate session to add the strings and then the final session in 1965 to add Cliff's new vocal. The final combined take and edit was used for the mono and stereo recordings but with different mixes for the purposes of the audio channels.

For the stereo issue, while Cliff's vocal is pretty much centralized, the Shadows' instrumentation is all in the right channel, with the orchestra in the left, and this makes it an unbalanced listening experience for the most part and is a lazy approach to the use of stereo. There is little to distinguish the two versions, with the obvious note of Cliff's pitch-perfect vocals.

Track Specification

Composed by Lionel Newman; English lyrics by Haven Gillespie

Musicians

Brian Bennett	drums, percussion
Brian 'Licorice' Locking	bass
Hank Marvin	guitar
Norrie Paramor Strings	orchestra
Norrie Paramor	arranger, conductor
Cliff Richard	vocals
Bruce Welch	rhythm guitar

Recording Details

Producer	Norrie Paramor
Engineered by	Malcolm Addey
Recording location	EMI Studios, Barcelona (backing track) and Abbey Road Studio 2 (strings and vocal)
Recording date	28th April 1963 (backing track), 14th May 1963 (strings) and 31st January 1965 (vocal)

♫ Kisses Sweeter Than Wine

Unissued track

With a somewhat tortuous provenance, generated as it was from an Irish folk song and then added to by a variety of people along the way, even the credited composers don't exist as people: both appear to be the pseudonyms for the same person, Howard Richmond, as a way of extracting maximum royalties.

The song was originally recorded by Jimmie Rodgers in 1957, when it reached number three in the US singles charts. As was the practice in the fifties and early sixties, British acts often picked up successful American songs, covered them and went on to have parochial success with it. In this case, it was Frankie Vaughan who picked up the option and he reached number eight in early 1958, while Rodgers' version went one better peaking at number seven at the same time. Later covers include Marlene Dietrich, foreign language versions by Nana Mouskouri, an album version by Peter, Paul and Mary and others by Andy Williams and Alex Harvey.

Frankie Vaughan was a firm favourite with the British public in the late fifties and early sixties, so it was appropriate that it might be chosen for the 'live' set list for the *Cliff* album recordings. However, it is unclear whether it was actually recorded since no tapes exist from the sessions; there is only production paperwork to indicate that it was only slated for recording. However, the assumption is made that it was recorded but remains unissued and, based on the musicians and the studio personel present at the session, these are highlighted in the track listing below until further information can be divined on its existence.

Track Specification

Composed by Paul Campbell and Joel Newman

Musicians

Jet Harris	bass
Hank Marvin	guitar
Tony Meehan	drums, percussion
Cliff Richard	vocals
Bruce Welch	rhythm guitar

Recording Details

Producer	Norrie Paramor
Engineered by	Peter Bown and Stuart Eltham
Recording location	Abbey Road Studio 2, St. John's Wood, London
Recording date	10th February 1959

♫ Kleine Taube

B-side of **Wenn Du Lachst, Lacht das Glück**

With the scheduled release of Cliff Richard's next German single, ***Wenn Du Lachst, Lacht das Glück***, it was decided to record an entirely new song rather than plunder the track listing of his recently released German language album, *Ich Träume Deine Träume* from which the A-side was drawn. ***Flying Machine*** had been released as a single at about this time with a Guy Fletcher and Doug Flett song on its B-side called ***Pigeon***. With new lyrics in German and a retitle of *Kleine Taube* (or a close translation with *Little Pigeon*), the song was recorded at a separate session with Brian Bennett taking on the orchestral arrangement and conducting duties. Originally released in stereo, *Kleine Taube* was a major rarity until it was included on the compendium of Cliff's foreign language recordings, ***On the Continent***, in 1997.

The arrangement is very similar to the English version, although the uncredited backing vocals are mixed further forward and, surprisingly, the choruses sound far less Teutonic than the *Pigeon* version. Cliff sings well in different languages and successfully carries out the performance here in German.

Track Specification

Composed by Guy Fletcher and Doug Flett; German lyrics by Michael Kunze

Musicians

Brian Bennett	arranger, conductor
Brian Bennett Orchestra	orchestra
Cliff Richard	vocals
Unknown	backing vocals

Recording Details

Producer	Norrie Paramor
Engineered by	Peter Vince
Recording location	Abbey Road Studio 2, St. John's Wood, London
Recording date	23rd August 1971

♫ Lady Came from Baltimore, The

From the albums **Live at the Talk of the Town** *and* **Cliff Live in Korea**

Covered by a number of folk and country luminaries over the years such as Bobby Darin, Johnny Cash, Joan Baez, Ian Campbell, Tim Hardin himself, Rick Nelson and Scott Walker, the English version of *The Lady Came from Baltimore* has never been recorded in the studio by Cliff Richard, although he did record a French language version (***La Ballade de Baltimore***) in 1971, which was not credited to Hardin; this is a contentious point since comparison of the tracks clearly highlights the similarity in melody.

However, during his concerts, Cliff often took to performing songs that might be familiar to the audience but not necessarily recorded by him. One such song was *The Lady Came from Baltimore*, a version of which was captured during his concert at the Talk of the Town in May 1968, which was recorded and released as a live album.

Cliff sings this song quietly accompanying himself on the guitar, which helps to show his all-round abilities and talents as a musician. He is a highly competent guitarist and this is a facet of his versatility that is generally forgotten by many critics particularly as Cliff had then lived in the shadow of the brilliance of Hank Marvin for the first ten years of his career. It is a shame for fans that Cliff didn't see fit to record the song in a studio because it is a beautiful song that fits his voice perfectly, although his ability to record live tracks that are almost tudio quality has no equal.

An ultra-rare album was made of the 1969 Seoul concert, which featured this song and with accompaniment from the temporarily reformed Shadows, and released in mono and for the Korean market only, *Cliff Live in Korea*.

Track Specification

Composed by Tim Hardin

__1. Live at the Talk of the Town__

Musicians		*Recording Details*	
Cliff Richard	vocals, guitar	Producer	Norrie Paramor
		Engineered by	Peter Vince
		Recording location	Talk of the Town Theatre, London
		Recording date	30th May 1968

__2. Cliff Live in Korea__

Musicians		*Recording Details*	
Brian Bennett	drums, percussion	Producer	Unknown
Alan Hawkshaw	keyboards	Engineered by	Unknown
Hank Marvin	guitar	Recording location	Citizen Hall, Seoul, South Korea
Cliff Richard	vocals	Recording date	16th October 1969
John Rostill	bass		
Bruce Welch	rhythm guitar		

♫ La La La La La

Unissued track and from the EP **La La La La La** *and the albums* **Cliff in Japan**, **Live at the Talk of the Town** *and* **Cliff Live in Korea**

Covered by Martin LaSalles and Stevie Wonder, the simplistically titled *La La La La La* gave its name to the Cliff Richard EP on which the title song appeared with two others from the same session and another from a session three or so weeks before. *La La La La La* was first attempted at this earlier session but abandoned after two takes, deferring further attempts to the next available session. All three of these vocal songs were recorded at the same session with the final (unknown) take and edit used for the mono and stereo recordings but with different mixes for the separate audio channels. Initially only released in mono on the EP, *La La La La La* first appeared in stereo when included on the German compilation *Congratulations und 13 Weitere Hits* album in 1968. It was subsequently released on CD on the French compilation *All My Love* and then on the rare EP track section of the celebratory ***...And They Said It Wouldn't Last! (My 50 Years in Music)***, both released in 2008.

The song is introduced by crashing orchestral chords and slightly out-of-tune female backing vocals. As might be expected, there are very few lyrics with most of them being variants of the simple title. It's an interesting choice for a recording but Cliff seems to be enjoying the experience.

This is backed up by its regular appearance on his tours and concerts at the back end of the sixties and on the live recordings issued of the period, where it allowed easy audience interaction. The rarest is the mono only version that was issued on the Korean-only *Cliff Live in Korea* album that saw Cliff briefly reunited with the Shadows.

Track Specification
Composed by Clarence Paul

1. Unissued track (La La La La La EP)

Musicians	
Mike Leander	arranger, conductor
Mike Leander Orchestra	orchestra
Cliff Richard	vocals
Unknown	female backing vocals

Recording Details	
Producer	Norrie Paramor
Engineered by	Peter Vincent and Richard Lush
Recording location	Abbey Road Studio 2, St. John's Wood, London
Recording date	21st September 1966

2. La La La La La EP

Musicians	
Bernard Ebbinghouse Orchestra	orchestra
Bernard Ebbinghouse	arranger, conductor
Cliff Richard	vocals
Unknown	female backing vocals

Recording Details	
Producer	Norrie Paramor
Engineered by	Peter Vincent and Richard Lush
Recording location	Abbey Road Studio 2, St. John's Wood, London
Recording date	11th October 1966

3. Cliff in Japan

Musicians	
Norrie Paramor Orchestra	orchestra
Norrie Paramor	arranger, conductor
Cliff Richard	vocals
Unknown	backing vocals

Recording Details	
Producer	Norrie Paramor
Engineered by	Unknown
Recording location	Shibuya Public Hall, Tokyo, Japan
Recording date	18th October 1967

4. Live at the Talk of the Town

Musicians	
Breakaways:	backing vocals
Vicki Hasemen	
Margo Quantrell	
Jean Ryder	
Norrie Paramor	arranger, conductor
Cliff Richard	vocals
Talk of the Town Orchestra	orchestra

Recording Details	
Producer	Norrie Paramor
Engineered by	Peter Vince
Recording location	Talk of the Town Theatre, London
Recording date	30th May 1968

5. Cliff Live in Korea

Musicians	
Brian Bennett	drums, percussion
Alan Hawkshaw	keyboards
Hank Marvin	backing vocals, guitar
Cliff Richard	vocals
John Rostill	backing vocals, bass
Bruce Welch	backing vocals, rhythm guitar

Recording Details	
Producer	Unknown
Engineered by	Unknown
Recording location	Citizen Hall, Seoul, South Korea
Recording date	16th October 1969

♫ La La La Song

From the film soundtrack album of **Finders Keepers**

At the point in the narrative where *La La La Song* is performed, Cliff Richard (playing himself in the 1966 film ***Finders Keepers***) has walked back to the village with Emelia (Vivianne Ventura) and wants to get to know her better. As he leans in to kiss her as they are sitting on the edge of the fountain in the village square, they realize they are being observed by a group of children. Cliff starts singing this song to amuse them and dances with a few of older ones as the song progresses. At the end, as he sings that he must go, the children move away, waving and repeating the song title before Cliff finally manages to kiss Emelia.

Recorded in one take at the sessions set aside for the film's soundtrack, the same edit was used for the mono and stereo recordings but with different mixes for the audio channel separation. Unusually, the soundtrack song was used on the film (rather than recording another version on the sound stage) with Cliff and the children lip-synching to the recording. The song was chosen as the B-side of the only single released from the project, ***Time Drags By***.

The deliberately simplistic melody is sweet and Cliff's vocals are accompanied by a shuffling rhythm and Spanish guitar lines. The boys and girls performing the backing vocals are, by the nature of children, not quite in tune but this only serves to add to the overall charm of the track.

Track Specification
Composed by Hank Marvin, Bruce Welch, Brian Bennett and John Rostill

Musicians	
Brian Bennett	drums, percussion
Corona Boys and Girls	vocals, backing vocals
Hank Marvin	guitar
Cliff Richard	vocals
John Rostill	bass
Bruce Welch	rhythm guitar

Recording Details	
Producer	Norrie Paramor
Engineered by	Peter Vince and Richard Lush
Recording location	Abbey Road Studio 3, St. John's Wood, London
Recording date	28th April 1966

♫ Lamp of Love

From the album **Me and My Shadows**

The writing team of Sid Tepper and Roy Bennett was no stranger to Cliff Richard's recordings having provided a few tracks for B-sides and albums already prior to the composition of *Lamp of Love*. Appearing as the final track on the first side of the ***Me and My Shadows*** album and also on the associated EP ***Me and My Shadows No. 2***, the track was recorded in both stereo and mono using the same take and edit (the fifth from the 30th March session) but with different mixes for the sake of the needs of the stereo.

Another rock and roller from the album, it has the traditional bass run for a rock and roll song with a rip-roaring guitar and toe-tapping rhythm created by the drums and percussion. The middle eight has Hank Marvin showing off his talents with a little use of the tremolo arm for good measure, before Cliff returns with the final verse and ending it firmly with a 'yeah, yeah!'

Track Specification

Composed by Sid Tepper and Roy Bennett

Musicians		*Recording Details*	
Jet Harris	bass	Producer	Norrie Paramor
Hank Marvin	guitar	Engineered by	Malcolm Addey and Norman Smith (mono) and Peter Bown and Alan Kane (stereo)
Tony Meehan	drums, percussion		
Cliff Richard	vocals	Recording location	Abbey Road Studio 2, St. John's Wood, London
Bruce Welch	rhythm guitar	Recording date	30th March 1960

♫ Language of Love

From the albums **Rock 'n' Roll Juvenile** *and* **My Kinda Life**

This is the final song on the ***Rock 'n' Roll Juvenile*** album that was written by co-producer Terry Britten and, in this case, the sixth in collaboration with Scottish singer and songwriter B. A. Robertson. With Cliff Richard taking co-production duties, *Language of Love* was recorded in two parts, with the first completing the backing track and the second the vocal overdubs a couple of weeks or so later.

Featuring the talents of Peter Skellern on the piano and Mellotron (creating the memorable synthesized choir and piano solo in the middle eight section), the driving beat of the song fits perfectly with the rock and roll concept of the album, while the backing vocals are perfectly pitched to elevate the song further. Cliff's lead vocals are suitably raucous and strained for this style of song and it becomes one of the key tracks from the project.

Revisited as part of the ***My Kinda Life*** album project in 1992, Cliff and Paul Moessl took the original recording and embellished it with extra drums, percussion, guitars and keyboards throughout. The final chorus is cut effecting a fade-out of fifteen seconds or so earlier than the album original.

Track Specification

Composed by Terry Britten and B. A. Robertson

1. Rock 'n' Roll Juvenile

Musicians		*Recording Details*	
Terry Britten	backing vocals, guitar	Producer	Cliff Richard and Terry Britten
Stuart Calver	backing vocals	Engineered by	Tony Clark and Haydn Bendall
Herbie Flowers	bass	Recording location	Pathé Marconi, Paris, France (backing track) and Abbey Road Studio, St. John's Wood, London (vocals)
Tristan Fry	percussion		
Graham Jarvis	drums, percussion		
Bill Livesy	keyboards	Recording date	7th-12th January 1979 (backing track) and 27th January 1979 (vocals)
John Perry	backing vocals		
Cliff Richard	vocals, backing vocals		
Tony Rivers	backing vocals		
Peter Skellern	Mellotron, piano		

2. My Kinda Life

Musicians		*Recording Details*	
Terry Britten	backing vocals, guitar	Producer	Cliff Richard and Terry Britten (original track) and Cliff Richard and Paul Moessl (new instrumentation)
Stuart Calver	backing vocals		
John Clark	guitar		
Herbie Flowers	bass	Engineered by	Tony Clark and Haydn Bendall (original track) and Gerry Kitchingham and Ben Robbins (new instrumentation)
Tristan Fry	percussion		
Graham Jarvis	drums, percussion		
Bill Livesy	keyboards	Recording location	Pathé Marconi, Paris, France (backing track) and Abbey Road Studio, St. John's Wood, London (vocals) and R. G. Jones Studios, Wimbledon, London (new instrumentation)
Paul Moessl	drum sequencers, synthesisers		
John Perry	backing vocals		
Cliff Richard	vocals		
Tony Rivers	backing vocals	Recording date	7th-12th January 1979 (backing track) and 17th February 1979 (vocals) and 20th-23rd April 1992 (new instrumentation)
Peter Skellern	Mellotron, piano		

♫ Larger Design

B-side of **Can't Keep This Feeling In**

Recorded during the ***Real as I Wanna Be*** album sessions, *Larger Design* was unreleased until it as incorporated as the B-side of the first of a dual CD disc release of Cliff Richard's first single from the project, ***Can't Keep This Feeling In***.

The song is bouncier in structure and performance than the dance-orientated track listing available on the album. Cliff performs the song with his usual style and assuredness, while the accompaniment relies less on the percussion and bass than other songs of the period. A neat little song, it is a shame that *Larger Design* wasn't given a wider distribution than a B-side track.

Track Specification

Composed by Peter Wolf and Michelle Wolf

Musicians

Vinnie Colaiuta	drums, percussion
Paul Jackson Jr.	guitar
Cliff Richard	vocals, backing vocals
Michelle Wolf	backing vocals
Peter Wolf	arranger, bass, keyboards, synclavier, percussion

Recording Details

Producer	Peter Wolf
Engineered by	Christian Leitgeb, Chris Heil, Paul Erickson and/or Keith Bessey
Recording location	Little America Recording Studios, Weiler, Austria, Ocean Recording Studios, Burbank, California, USA, Arco Recording Studios, Munich, Germany, R. G. Jones Recording Studios, Wimbledon, London, England and/or The Pierce Room, London, England
Recording date	1997 or 1998

♫ Laß Uns Schnell Vergessen

From the album **Ich Träume Deine Träume**

Originally an Everly Bothers song, ***Don't Ask Me to Be Friends*** had been recorded by Cliff Richard for his ***Tracks 'n' Grooves*** album. Clif then recorded the German translation, *Laß Uns Schnell Vergessen*, for his second German album, *Ich Träume Deine Träume*. *Laß Uns Schnell Vergessen* –translated as *Let Us Quickly Forget* – was recorded in the first of four sessions over two days in November 1970, which was made easier by the orchestral backing tracks being recorded prior to the event. The song was reissued on the anthology of Cliff's foreign language recordings, ***On the Continent***, in 1997.

A beautiful rendition, the guitars gently usher in the song as Cliff's vocals, and his backing vocals, tenderly tell the story of a relationship break-up where the girl has suggested that they remain just friends. There are uncredited harmonies from a female group but these are used sparingly. The middle eight has a cello solo which underlines the song's sadness.

Track Specification

Composed by Gerry Goffin, Jack Keller and Bert Olden

Musicians

Bernard Ebbinghouse	arranger, conductor
Norrie Paramor Orchestra	orchestra
Cliff Richard	vocals, backing vocals
Unknown	backing vocals

Recording Details

Producer	Norrie Paramor (backing track and vocals)
Engineered by	Phil McDonald (backing track and vocals)
Recording location	Cologne, Germany (backing track) and Abbey Road Studio 2, St. John's Wood, London (vocals)
Recording date	November 1970 (backing track) and 24th November 1970 (vocals)

♫ Last Train Home

Single by **Network 3**

Previously known as Nutshell, Network 3 was a Christian folk group who had been recording since 1976. Changing their name and with only original member Paul Field remaining, they recorded two singles with Cliff Richard producing. *Last Train Home* was backed with ***Lifeline*** and issued on the EMI label (catalogue number EMI 5120) in January 1981, although it failed to register in the charts. There is scant information available on the recording sessions and these are highlighted as unknown until further information is found and recorded. The follow-up, ***Dangerous Game***, suffered the same fate.

The song begins with a strong rhythm that emulates a train running over track. The sound is very much of its period and the vocal blending of the singers is excellent. The guitar solo in the middle eight reminds the listener of the song's rock roots, while the driving relentless beat and the vocals are what lift the record from the mundane. With Cliff providing backing vocals, too, and the quality of the enterprise, it is surprising the song made such a poor impact on record-buyers.

Track Specification

Composed by Paul Field and Dave Cooke

Musicians

Paul Field	vocals
Mo McCafferty	vocals
Annie McCaig	vocals
Cliff Richard	backing vocals
Unknown	guitar
Unknown	bass
Unknown	keyboards
Unknown	drums, percussion

Recording Details

Producer	Cliff Richard
Engineered by	Unknown
Recording location	Unknown
Recording date	1980

♫ Lawdy Miss Clawdy

Private demo (subsequently released on ***The Rock and Roll Years 1958-1963***)

Lawdy Miss Clawdy is a firm rock and roll staple that started out as a single recorded by its composer Lloyd Price in late 1952 in New Orleans. It has since been covered by many artists over the years, although probably the most familiar renditions are those by Elvis Presley and Little Richard both released in 1956. The Beatles, Led Zeppelin, Joe Cocker and Fats Domino have also tried their hand at covering song along with many other contemporary artists.
The song is a rip-roaring eight-bar blues number that expresses the surprise at the antics of a presupposed prim and proper young girl and how much she lets her inhibitions go when in the company of the singer. The first word is a southern American expression referring to God (as in Lord) and has been spelled with an 'aw' to avoid upsetting the fiercely religious Bible Belt states.
Because of the influence of Elvis Presley and Little Richard on the popular music in Britain, it was a predictable choice for the young Harry Webb and a group of his friends, when they went into the studio in the HMV record shop in London's Oxford Street to record a demo of this and Jerry Lee Lewis's hit ***Breathless***. Given ten pounds by Webb's parents – a huge relative sum in those days just after the period of post-war austerity – the group entered the studio and pressed these songs, which had only been heard by the group, friends, family and music executives at the bigger record companies in order to secure a recording contract. This latter group included Columbia's Norrie Paramor, who signed Cliff Richard and the Drifters on the strength of the demos recorded at HMV. They remained unavailable for almost forty years, when Cliff agreed to include them on an anthology of his early years in music – ***The Rock and Roll Years 1958-1963***. A 78 r.p.m. pressing (no catalogue number) of *Lawdy Miss Clawdy*, backed with *Breathless* was issued with special edition releases of this album.
Whereas the original version of the song and Presley's and Little Richard's covers were driven by a piano chord sequence, on this recording, it was underpinned by guitars and was expressed in a laidback way rather than being raucous. However, it is very clear from the recording that Cliff had a huge talent even at the tender age of seventeen. The drum rhythms sound very much as if it is beaten out on a box rather than a specific percussion instrument.
Although the allocation of instruments and personnel of the band are known, there is no information on the studio personnel and this will notated as unknown until further research unearths pertinent names.

Track Specification
Composed by Lloyd Price

Musicians		*Recording Details*	
Norman Mitham	guitar	Producer	Unknown
Ken Pavey	guitar	Engineered by	Unknown
Cliff Richard	vocals, guitar	Recording location	HMV Record Shop, First Floor studio, Oxford Street, London
Ian Samwell	guitar		
Terry Smart	drums, percussion	Recording date	Early summer, 1958 (possibly July)

♫ Lay All Your Love on Me

B-side of **Somewhere Over the Rainbow/What a Wonderful World** *and unissued live track*

According to some sources, *Lay All Your Love on Me* was originally titled *Yarafat* (possibly as a working title). It was recorded by ABBA for their 1980 album *Super Trouper* and composed to capitalize on the disco craze of the period (even though this was already on the wane). Not intended to be a single, it wasn't until the following year that it was released following a surge in popularity generated by a remixed version and the subsequent single release reached number seven in the UK charts. Covered by the Information Society who had an American hit with it and Helloween, who released it as a single in Japan, it has also been recorded by artists such as Brotherhood of Man, Steps, the A*Teens and Erasure, for their *ABBA-esque* EP, which was a British number one.
Cliff Richard chose the song for inclusion on ***Wanted***, his first album on a different label since EMI summarily dropped him at the end of the nineties. It featured on the four-track promotional disc for the album, with the suggestion that all the tracks were taken from the album. However, *Lay All Your Love on Me* did not appear on the track listing and was only commercially released as the B-side of the first single release from the project, ***Somewhere over the Rainbow/What a Wonderful World***. The promotional disc version is the same as the B-side track but has almost a minute's worth of music excised from the middle of it, cutting from the end of the first instrumental break to the start of the second.
The song is performed with echo behind Cliff's lead vocal, in a stretched out introduction that includes a change of lyrics to say that tennis is his only vice, replete with suitable sound effects. At this point, the pace picks up to match that of the original. The song begs for strong backing vocals and these are added during the choruses, while the end of each of them is brought back down to the arpeggiated chords on the synthesiser behind the slow-paced verses.
To support the album's release, Cliff went on tour around the world in 2003 and the set list featured tracks from the album, songs not performed before and oldies revisited. In addition, he added *Lay All Your Love on Me* to the set list. The New Zealand concert was filmed for a DVD release later in the year and, in 2004, the associated CD album, *World Tour Live*, featured a small subset of the tracks. Even though *Lay All Your Love on Me* was not released in any other format than the promotional CD and the B-side, it was decided not to release it on the album's track listing. The live performance includes the production of a set of tennis balls to illustrate Cliff's only vice from the changed lyrics.

Track Specification
Composed by Benny Andersson and Björn Ulvaeus

1. B-side (Somewhere Over the Rainbow/What a Wonderful World)

Musicians

John Brant	additional programming
Anthony Clark	backing vocals
Cliff Richard	vocals, backing vocals
Alan Tarney	arranger, backing vocals, keyboards, programming

Recording Details

Producer	Alan Tarney
Engineered by	John Brant and Gerry Kitchingham
Recording location	Wilmer Studios, London
Recording date	January-April 2001

2. Unissued track (World Tour Live)

Musicians

Rachel Allen	violin
Elena Bulgakova	violin
Jenni Champion	violin
Anthony Clark	backing vocals, guitar
John Clark	guitar
Dave Cooke	keyboards
Cornelia Didenco	violin
Gina Ferguson	violin
Peter Howarth	backing vocals
Cathy Irons	violin
Pete May	drums, percussion
Mick Mullins	backing vocals
Keith Murrell	backing vocals
Alan Park	keyboards
Hee-Jung Park	violin
Cliff Richard	vocals
Eva Schwanen-Lilley	violin
Steve Stroud	bass

Recording Details

Producer	Keith Bessey
Engineered by	Keith Bessey
Recording location	The Mission Winery, Napier, New Zealand
Recording date	22nd February 2003

♫ Lean on You

***108th UK single** and from the album* **My Kinda Life**

Another Alan Tarney composition, *Lean on You* was the third of four singles to be released from the ***Stronger*** album project. Cliff Richard had worked with Tarney on the massively successful ***Always Guaranteed*** album and wanted to repeat the success with the follow-up release. Once recording for the album was complete, with Mike Read as a compère, Cliff hosted an afternoon at the London Palladium for two thousand fans to listen to six of the tracks destined for the new album: *Lean on You* came fifth in the poll just above ***Forever You Will Be Mine*** and behind ***Joanna***.

Backed with non-album track, ***Hey Mister***, *Lean on You* was released on the EMI label (catalogue number EM 105) on 2nd October 1989 and reached number seventeen in the UK charts. In addition to the standard seven-inch single, a shaped picture disc was issued (catalogue number EMPD 105), and an extended version of *Lean on You*, coming at over three minutes longer, was added to the twelve-inch (12EM 105) and CD (CDEM 105) singles. Filmed in sepia tones, the promotional video features multiple profiles of Cliff with cutaways to life in an Indian village with a woman herding sheep and goats, children playing and so on.

With an atmosphere that wouldn't have been out of place on the previous album, ***Always Guaranteed***, *Lean on You* is one of those songs that doubles as a love song (for a human) as well as being a semi-religious track. Cliff sings the lead vocal in an almost breathy anticipation of the chorus that lists out the qualities of caring and sharing. Cliff and Tarney provide the backing vocals and these are restricted to the chorus, while there is a short guitar solo in the middle eight.

For the ***My Kinda Life*** album in 1992, Cliff and Paul Moessl revisited a number of tracks from the last half of the seventies and into the eighties and, taking the original track, would rework with occasional additional instrumentation and vocals. On the version of *Lean on You*, no additional musical input was recorded, although the introduction is edited down to three repetitions of the riff, and improves the backing vocals by adding them elsewhere on the track but cuts the second verse and the guitar solo for some unexplained reason. The track also fades earlier than the original but this may not have been intentional but rather a product of the remixing process.

Track Specification
Composed by Alan Tarney

1. Single

Musicians

Cliff Richard	vocals, backing vocals
Alan Tarney	arranger, backing vocals, synthesisers, drum and percussion sequencers

Recording Details

Producer	Alan Tarney
Engineered by	Gerry Kitchingham and Ben Robbins
Recording location	R. G. Jones Studios, Wimbledon, London
Mixed by	John Hudson and Noel Rafferty
Mixing location	Mayfair Studios, London
Recording date	27th February 1989, 9th March 1989, 13th-17th March 1989 and 22nd-23rd March 1989

2. *My Kinda Life*

Musicians

Cliff Richard	vocals, backing vocals
Alan Tarney	arranger, backing vocals, synthesisers, drum and percussion sequencers

Recording Details

Producer	Alan Tarney (original track) and Cliff Richard and Paul Moessl (new instrumentation and vocal)
Engineered by	Gerry Kitchingham and Ben Robbins (original track and remix)
Recording location	R. G. Jones Studios, Wimbledon, London (original track and remix)
Recording date	27th February 1989, 9th March 1989, 13th-17th March 1989 and 22nd-23rd March 1989 (original track) and 20th-23rd April 1992 (remix)

♫ Learning How to Rock 'n' Roll

From the album **The Rock Connection**

As if Cliff Richard needed any guidance in how to rock and roll! There seems to be some confusion as to whether the composer is Drew or Zoë McCulloch, although most sources, where a first name is given, choose Zoë - it is this that is used for the track listing below. *Learning How to Rock 'n' Roll* was recorded as part of suite of sessions for the album ***The Rock Connection*** in the early summer of 1984.

Learning How to Rock 'n' Roll is the first and only track on the album that moves away from synthesized sounds and instead reserves the prominent instrument to a boogie-woogie piano dancing in the background, giving anything that Jerry Lee Lewis used to do good competition, and the chugging bass and guitar, which leads to a short solo on both instruments in the passages between chorus and verse. The pace is inexorable and Cliff is clearly enjoying the chance to sing a perfect rock and roll tune. He supplies the backing vocals throughout and this lends the whole track a nostalgic feel.

Track Specification

Composed by Zoë McCulloch

Musicians

John Clark	guitar
Dave Cooke	keyboards
Mark Griffiths	bass
Alan Park	keyboards
Cliff Richard	vocals, backing vocals
Stuart Tosh	drums, percussion

Recording Details

Producer	Cliff Richard and Keith Bessey
Engineered by	Keith Bessey
Recording location	Strawberry Studios South, Surrey
Recording date	30th July 1984-3rd August 1984

♫ Leave My Woman Alone

B-side of **The Joy of Living**

Written and recorded by Ray Charles, no version has been a hit in the UK, although a number of artists have interpreted their own covers including Bobby Darin, Peter and Gordon, Dave Edmunds, Lonnie Donegan, the Everly Brothers, Johnny Winter and the Kingston Trio.

Cliff Richard's version was recorded some sixteen months prior to its release before being chosen as the B-side of his forty-ninth single, ***The Joy of Living***. By this time, Columba had changed its policy and now only released singles in stereo in most territories. The one exception for this single was the release in Holland, which was in mono, and which is now a significant rarity. With the remastering of the ***Tracks 'n' Grooves*** album in 2004, the stereo version of *Leave My Woman Alone* was added to the listing as a bonus track. The song bursts into life with pumping strings and a banjo playing furiously against the brass and raucous tambourine, which drives the rhythm of the track, as Cliff warns that he has something to say and everyone should listen and he is clearly enjoying the time to express the ebullient soul song's lyrics.

Track Specification

Composed by Ray Charles

Musicians

Norrie Paramor Orchestra	orchestra
Norrie Paramor	arranger, conductor
Cliff Richard	vocals

Recording Details

Producer	Norrie Paramor
Engineered by	Peter Vince
Recording location	Abbey Road Studio 2, St. John's Wood, London
Recording date	10th October 1968

♫ Leaving, The

From the album **The 31st of February Street**

Also recorded by its author Chris Sedgwick for his album *Singer Sang the Song, The Leaving* was included in the track listing of Cliff Richard's first concept album (about being way from home) and was recorded in seven takes as the first song to be completed at the February session for the album ***The 31st of February Street***. Later, EMI decided to pair the song to a radio promotional disc of ***Nothing to Remind Me***, where it appeared as the B-side.

An electric piano introduction segues into a rattling arpeggiated sequence of guitar chords as Cliff begins the sad song that talks of the girl he loves wanting to move out of his life and how he feels about it. The steel guitar makes its first appearance in the second verse helping to engender the country music feel of the performance.

Track Specification
Composed by Chris Sedgwick

Musicians		*Recording Details*	
Terry Britten	guitar	Producer	David MacKay
Cliff Hall	electric piano	Engineered by	Tony Clark and Mike Jarrett
Gordon Huntley	steel guitar	Recording location	Abbey Road Studio 2, St. John's Wood, London
Kevin Peek	acoustic guitar	Recording date	13th February 1974
Cliff Richard	vocals, backing vocals		
Trevor Spencer	drums, percussion		
Alan Tarney	bass		

♫ Left Out Again

From the album **Me and My Shadows**

Written by erstwhile bandmate Pete Chester (from the Chesternuts days), *Left Out Again* was recorded in both mono and stereo using the same take (the fifth from the session) and edited bt with a different mix for the needs of playing it in stereo. The song also appeared on the associated ***Me and My Shadows No. 2*** EP with a severely edited version of the same take, shortened by twenty seconds, appearing on the 2001 reissue of the 2 on 1 version of ***Me and My Shadows***.
An andante song that is introduced by Tony Meehan's drums and Hank Marvin's straightforward rock and roll guitar riff (fifth, third, tonic and supertonic in the scale). It's a sad song of lost love (a common feature of many of Cliff's songs in the early days) and the augmented musical intervals cleverly express the anguish experienced by the singer. While not the best song on the album, *Left out Again* is nevertheless pleasant enough to listen to.

Track Specification
Composed by Pete Chester

Musicians		*Recording Details*	
Jet Harris	bass	Producer	Norrie Paramor
Hank Marvin	guitar	Engineered by	Malcolm Addey and Norman Smith (mono) and Peter Bown and Alan Kane (stereo)
Tony Meehan	drums, percussion		
Cliff Richard	vocals	Recording location	Abbey Road Studio 2, St. John's Wood, London
Bruce Welch	rhythm guitar	Recording date	16th March 1960

♫ Legata ad un Granelo di Sabbia

From the album **When in Rome**

Recorded and covered by artists such as Batistococo, the co-writer Nico Fidenco, Paulo di Sabatino, Jimmy Fontana, Delcio Tavares and Fred Rovella, *Legata ad un Granelo di Sabbio* (literally translated as *Tied to a Little Grain of Sand* but often simply reduced to *A Little Grain of Sand*) was one of the Italian original songs chosen for Cliff Richard to record for his album ***When in Rome***. It is also one of the few foreign language songs for which Cliff never recorded an English equivalent. Cliff admits he found Italian hardest of all the continental languages and his vocals were recorded with phonetic annotation of the lyrics for him to sing. In May 1965, the vocals were overdubbed on an orchestral track recorded the previous October, prepared for a time when he was busy with touring, filming and his pantomime show. The third and final orchestral take and edit was applied to the unknown vocal take and edit and has only ever been released in the mono format.
Performed in a slow four-four beat, Cliff's voice is well suited not only to this time of ballad but in its enunciation of the Italian language, which he also later confirmed that, in spite of its difficulty, he enjoyed singing in best of the four European languages he regularly recorded in throughout the sixties.

Track Specification
Composed by Giovanni Marchetti and Nico Fidenco

Musicians		*Recording Details*	
Norrie Paramor Orchestra	orchestra	Producer	John Lee and M. DiPonti (backing track) and Norrie Paramor (vocals)
Norrie Paramor	arranger, conductor		
Cliff Richard	vocals	Engineered by	Malcolm Addey
		Recording location	EMI Studios, Milan (backing track) and Estudios Valentim, De Carvalho, Lisbon (vocals)
		Recording date	2nd-3rd October 1964 (backing track) and 13th-14th May 1965 (vocals)

♫ Lessons in Love

From the film soundtrack album of **The Young Ones** *and from the albums* **Cliff Richard at the Movies**, **The Rock 'n' Roll Years 1958-1963** *and* **Live at the ABC Kingston 1962**

The lilting love song *Lessons in Love* appears in ***The Young Ones*** film after Nicky Black (played by Cliff Richard) confirms that the members of the Simpkin's Youth Club have got the Countess Theatre booked in order to stage their show and he offers to sing the song that he 'wrote' for the show. Exhorting Bruce to play the chords (with Jet Harris thumbing the bass line), he sings the first few verses directly to Toni Crowthier (his girlfriend played by Carole Gray), who then joins him in duet for the final verse and chorus (the performance is dubbed by Grazina Frame). A shrewd manager, meanwhile, who has overheard the excitement regarding the publicity for the show sees an opportunity for his ward, singing star Dorinder

Morrell (played by Sonya Cordeau), to reignite her career. Pushy as ever, they come into the club and disrupt proceedings as all the members become star-struck. Eventually, the manager states that Dorinder should be the one to perform the song with Nicky and Toni reluctantly agrees as this will help the show even more. Dorinder performs a rendition of the song (which is not on the soundtrack) and attempts to kiss Nicky but he is reluctant. Once the manager intervenes, Nicky relaxes a little bit, making Toni jealous as she rushes outside and performs *No-One for Me but Nicky*.
The soundtrack album version of the song was first attempted at the end of the session on 28th July 1961 but none of those ten takes has been issued. Thirty-six takes were tried at the next session two weeks later with the mono and stereo edits using the same take, albeit with different mixes for the stereo channels. In 1996, the film version, recorded some time later (probably in the August), was issued on the compilation ***Cliff Richard at the Movies 1959-1974***, while an undubbed version (that is, without the orchestra) was released on ***The Rock 'n' Roll Years 1958-1963***, but neither version features the duet with Grazina Frame, nor the solo by Sonya Cordeau.
Lessons in Love is a beautiful little love song that is performed gently by Cliff singing and humming quietly, accompanied by the subdued instrumentation of the Shadows, with Hank Marvin's harmony line on the guitar matching the vocal melody. The bass, rhythm and percussion drive the song inexorably on towards the end. On the sustained notes, Cliff sings the note clearly without tremolo and, while several singers would have difficulty maintaining the pitch and making the tone listenable to, he manages the feat with almost nonchalant ease.
In subsequent concerts to support and promote the film, Cliff and the Shadows incorporated a selection of songs into a medley, one of which was *Lessons in Love*. For the ABC Kingston concert, this was recorded but remained unreleased until the 2002 album ***Live at the ABC Kingston 1962***, which was issued in stereo only, although a mono version would almost certainly have been recorded.

Track Specification
Composed by Sy Soloway and Shirley Wolfe

1. The Young Ones

Musicians		*Recording Details*	
Jet Harris	bass	Producer	Norrie Paramor
Hank Marvin	guitar	Engineered by	Malcolm Addey and David Lloyd
Tony Meehan	drums, percussion	Recording location	Abbey Road Studio 2, St. John's Wood, London
Cliff Richard	vocals	Recording date	11th August 1961
Bruce Welch	rhythm guitar		

2. The Rock 'n' Roll Years 1958-1963

Musicians		*Recording Details*	
Jet Harris	bass	Producer	Norrie Paramor
Cliff Richard	vocals	Engineered by	Malcolm Addey
Bruce Welch	rhythm guitar	Recording location	Abbey Road Studio 2, St. John's Wood, London
		Recording date	1961

3. Cliff Richard at the Movies 1959-1974

Musicians		*Recording Details*	
Associated British Studio Orchestra	orchestra	Producer	Norrie Paramor
Stanley Black	conductor	Engineered by	Malcolm Addey
Jet Harris	bass	Recording location	Abbey Road Studio 2, St. John's Wood, London
Cliff Richard	vocals	Recording date	1961
Bruce Welch	rhythm guitar		

4. Live at the ABC Kingston 1962

Musicians		*Recording Details*	
Brian Bennett	drums, percussion	Producer	Norrie Paramor
Jet Harris	backing vocals, bass	Engineered by	Malcolm Addey and Ken Townsend
Hank Marvin	backing vocals, guitar	Recording location	ABC Theatre, Kingston, Surrey
Cliff Richard	vocals, hand claps	Recording date	7th March 1962
Bruce Welch	backing vocals, rhythm guitar		

♫ Let It Be Me

From the albums **Centre Stage – The Very Best of Elaine Paige** *(Elaine Paige) and* **(2)** *(Olivia Newton-John)*

A French song published in 1955 under the title *Je T'Appartiens* (or *I Belong*) that was recorded by Gilbert Bécaud, *Let It Be Me* had English lyrics added in 1957 and this was recorded by Jill Corey who released it as a single. But the most popular English version is by the Everly Brothers, who released a single in 1960 and reached number thirteen in the UK charts in the March of that year. Four years later, Americans Betty Everett and Jerry Butler tried to repeat that success but to no avail and it has since been covered by a variety of artists including Bobbie Gentry, the Shadows, Leslie Gore, Glen Campbell, David Hasselhoff, Pat Boone, Roberta Flack, Andy Gibb, Tom Jones, Brenda Lee and many others.
Until working with Olivia Newton-John, Cliff Richard has never recorded the song in the studio and it is only the duet he performed with Elaine Paige during the 1999 *Live in the Park* concerts that had been released – even then, it can only be found on the video of his performance and Paige's own album ***Centre Stage – The Very Best of Elaine Paige***. With a

principal accompaniment created on a synthesiser, Cliff and Paige sing their vocals in harmony from the start. Paige's voice can be strong on occasions but here it blends well with Cliff's as they carry off the rendition with great conviction.
In 2004, Olivia Newton-John released her curiously titled *(2)* album, which had just eleven tracks when released in most countries. However, a specially recorded duet with Cliff of *Let It Be Me* was added to the track listing of the UK release, although this version of the album is very difficult to source. Cliff takes the lead with a developed vocal arrangement supported by the piano and strong percussion-based rhythm. Olivia sings the next verse supported by Cliff, giving way to a guitar solo in the middle eight. The performance is a modern take and arrangement on the song and, as always, Cliff's and Olivia's voices blend well together and, given their maturity in years, there is an additional beauty created in the performance of the lyrics.

Track Specification
Composed by Gilbert Bécaud and Pierre Delanoë; English lyrics by Mann Curtis

1. Centre Stage – The Very Best of Elaine Paige

Musicians

Elaine Paige	vocals
Cliff Richard	vocals
Unknown	arranger, conductor
Unknown	keyboards
Unknown	bass
Unknown	drums, percussion

Recording Details

Producer	Unknown
Engineered by	Unknown
Recording location	Hyde Park, London
Recording date	July 1999

2. (2)

Musicians

Olivia Newton-John	vocals
Cliff Richard	vocals
Unknown	guitar
Unknown	bass
Unknown	piano
Unknown	drums, percussion

Recording Details

Producer	Andy Timmons
Engineered by	Unknown
Recording location	Unknown
Recording date	2003 or 2004

♫ Let It Snow

From the album **Cliff at Christmas**

A favourite of crooners everywhere and overused in ubiquitous Christmas advertising and television and radio programming idents because of its seasonal imagery in just the title, *Let It Snow* – originally *Let It Snow! Let It Snow! Let It Snow!* – was written in 1945 and first recorded by Vaughan Monroe. It has since been covered by a wide variety of artists including Ella Fitzgerald, Bing Crosby, Jessica Simpson, Twisted Sister and Mika, although it is probably Dean Martin's version that is the most well-known. In spite of the familiarity of the song, it has never been released as a single in the UK.
Cliff Richard decided to cover the song for his second album of Christmas songs, ***Cliff at Christmas***. It is quite possible that the timing of the recordings meant that it was completed in the early sessions for his next studio album ***Something's Goin' On***, particularly given the similar musicians and studio personnel.
Sleighbells aplenty with staccato piano chords and a female backing group singing the song title lead into Cliff's almost crooning version of the song. The jazzy accompaniment and the vocal arrangements make the song a perfect Christmas song by Cliff.

Track Specification
Composed by Sammy Cahn and Jule Styne

Musicians

Mike Brignardello	bass
Rachel Gaines	backing vocals
John Hammond	drums, percussion
Jerry McPherson	guitar
Michael Mellett	backing vocals
Nashville String Machine	strings
Amanda Omartian	backing vocals
Michael Omartian	keyboards
Cliff Richard	vocals
Kara Tualatai	backing vocals

Recording Details

Producer	Michael Omartian
Engineered by	Terry Christian, David Streit and J. C. Monterrosa
Recording location	Sound House, Brentwood, Tennessee, USA, The Blue Room, Nashville, Tennessee, USA and Tennessee Sound Kitchen, Franklin, Tennessee, USA
Recording date	2003

♫ Let Me Be the One

131st UK single *and unissued live track*

Chris Eaton had provided Cliff Richard with a number of quasi-religious songs or popular songs with religious or spiritual messages – the pinnacle was perhaps ***Saviour's Day*** – and, with EMI (temporarily as it turned out) severing Cliff's contract in the new millennium, he was determined to create an album that would sell well in spite of the erstwhile record company's attitude. The fourth track on that ***Wanted*** album became the second and final single from the project and was one of the very few original songs to be recorded.

Backed with ***I Gotta Woman*** (which is a live track taken from the ***Live at the ABC Kingston 1962*** album that was released contemporaneously by EMI) and two new live tracks from the 2001 Royal Albert Hall concerts, ***This Can't Be Love*** and ***My Funny Valentine***, *Let Me Be the One* was issued as a CD single on Cliff's new label, Papillon Records (catalogue number CLIFFCD2) on 1st April 2002 and reached number twenty-nine in the UK singles charts. A promotional copy (catalogue number BTRAD 20) featuring just the track was also released simultaneously to the media.
A slinky beat is created in the percussion that is maintained through it, matched by sustained synthesiser chords, which is joined by Cliff's *sotto voce* performance, which has a slight echo placed on it in the mix. In the chorus, the instrumentation is built up and augmented by guitars and a beautiful arrangement for the backing vocals. One of the best tracks on the album, *Let Me Be the One* deserved a better chart placing than it received, although it can be pointed out that this was a creditable chart performance given the change in direction of popular music and the influence of manufactured soloists and bands through reality talent shows.
Although both singles (*Let Me Be the One* and ***Somewhere Over the Rainbow/What a Wonderful World***) were on the set list of the tour to promote the album and while both were filmed and recorded for the DVD version of *World Tour Live* in 2003, the CD album version issued the following year did not include it on the track listing.

Track Specification
Composed by Chris Eaton

1. Single

Musicians		*Recording Details*	
John Brant	additional programming	Producer	Alan Tarney
Anthony Clark	backing vocals	Engineered by	John Brant and Gerry Kitchingham
John Clark	guitar	Recording location	Wilmer Studios, London
Cliff Richard	vocals, backing vocals	Recording date	January-April 2001
Alan Tarney	arranger, backing vocals, keyboards, programming		

2. Unissued track (World Tour Live)

Musicians		*Recording Details*	
Rachel Allen	violin	Producer	Keith Bessey
Elena Bulgakova	violin	Engineered by	Keith Bessey
Jenni Champion	violin	Recording location	The Mission Winery, Napier, New Zealand
Anthony Clark	backing vocals, guitar	Recording date	22nd February 2003
John Clark	guitar		
Dave Cooke	keyboards		
Cornelia Didenco	violin		
Gina Ferguson	violin		
Mike Haughton	saxophone		
Peter Howarth	backing vocals		
Cathy Irons	violin		
Pete May	drums, percussion		
Mick Mullins	backing vocals		
Keith Murrell	backing vocals		
Alan Park	keyboards		
Hee-Jung Park	violin		
Cliff Richard	vocals		
Eva Schwanen-Lilley	violin		
Steve Stroud	bass		

♫ Let's Go Out
From the album **Did He Jump... Or Was He Pushed?** *(Garth Hewitt)*

Garth Hewitt started his second solo album, ***Did He Jump... Or Was He Pushed?***, with Cliff Richard taking over production duties and incorporated a number of musicians from Cliff's own album sessions, as well as using the same engineer of recent years, Tony Clark.
Cliff's backing vocals are created in layers and performed *a capella* from the start echoing the lyrics performed by Hewitt. For the first verse, a reggae beat is featured with Jo Partridge playing, almost incongruously, a mandolin. The chorus returns with a heavier rock beat before the next verse returns to the reggae. The beauty of the song is in the changing rhythms but the extraordinarily lush vocal arrangements.

Track Specification
Composed by Garth Hewitt

Musicians		*Recording Details*	
Garth Hewitt	vocals, guitar	Producer	Cliff Richard
Graham Jarvis	drums, percussion	Engineered by	Tony Clark and Haydn Bendall
Adrian Lee	synthesiser	Recording location	Odyssey Studios, London
Mike Moran	guitar, keyboards	Recording date	1979
Jo Partridge	guitar, mandolin		
Cliff Richard	backing vocals, guitar		
Dave Wintour	bass		

♫ Let's Have a Party

From the album **From a Distance ***** The Event**

Originally recorded by Elvis Presley for his film *Loving You*, it was also covered by Wanda Jackson, who reached number thirty-two in the UK singles charts, and should not be confused with the ragtime piano medley performed by Winifred Atwell. It has been covered by several artists including the Firebirds, Robert Plant, the Spencer Davis Group and Mud.

Cliff Richard chose the Jessie Mae Robinson song to perform in the opening ***Oh Boy! Medley*** at ***The Event*** to celebrate his then thirty years in showbusiness that took place at the former Wembley Stadium. Singing along with the Dallas Boys and the Kalin Twins, Cliff carries off this rock and roll favourite with his usual aplomb.

Track Specification

Composed by Jessie Mae Robinson

Musicians

Dallas Boys:	
Nicky Clarke	backing vocals
Leon Fisk	backing vocals
Stan Jones	backing vocals
Joe Smith	backing vocals
Bob Wragg	backing vocals
Kalin Twins:	
Harold Kalin	backing vocals
Herbie Kalin	backing vocals
Oh Boy! Band	rock 'n' roll band
Cliff Richard	vocals

Recording Details

Producer	Cliff Richard
Engineered by	Keith Bessey and Mick McKenna
Recording location	Rolling Stones Mobile Studio, Wembley Stadium, Wembley, North-west London
Recording date	16th-17th June 1989

♫ Let's Make a Memory

From the albums **32 Minutes and 17 Seconds with Cliff Richard** *and* **Cliff in Japan**

Although it was only an album track on ***32 Minutes and 17 Seconds with Cliff Richard***, *Let's Make a Memory* was used elsewhere in the world: it formed the B-side (still in English) of the German single ***Rote Lippen Soll Man Küssen*** (the German translated version of ***Lucky Lips***); and it was released as a single in Japan backed with ***It's All in the Game*** on the Odeon label (catalogue number OR-1011) reaching number two in that country's charts; again, it was issued in Holland, backing with ***Big News*** also on the Columbia label (catalogue number CH 3031) in 1963 with the A-side hitting number twenty in the charts in the Netherlands. The eighth and final take and edit was used for mono and stereo recordings with different mixes for the audio channels and *Let's Make a Memory* was the final track on the first side of the *32 Minutes and 17 Seconds with Cliff Richard* album.

The track is performed with such exuberance with its swooping strings and the ever-present backing vocalists that it could easily come from a film musical soundtrack. There is a guitar and drum accompaniment alongside the orchestra but the session notes do not state that the Shadows were involved and, besides, the sound is not familiar enough to be the band backing Cliff.

At the end of Cliff's tours, he regularly performed medleys of songs that hadn't been sung earlier in the show. Because of the recent release of the song as a single in the Far East, for the tour of the region, recorded for the ***Cliff in Japan*** album, *Let's Make a Memory* kicked off the selection that included five songs from the period of the films ***The Young Ones*** and ***Summer Holiday***: ***The Young Ones***, ***Lucky Lips***, ***Summer Holiday*** and ***We Say Yeah***, all to an orchestral accompaniment.

Track Specification

Composed by Bill Crompton

1. 32 Minutes and 17 Seconds with Cliff Richard

Musicians

Mike Sammes Singers	backing vocals
Norrie Paramor Orchestra	orchestra
Norrie Paramor	arranger, conductor
Cliff Richard	vocals

Recording Details

Producer	Norrie Paramor
Engineered by	Malcolm Addey and Norman Smith
Recording location	Abbey Road Studio 2, St. John's Wood, London
Recording date	4th December 1961

2. Cliff in Japan

Musicians

Norrie Paramor Orchestra	orchestra
Norrie Paramor	arranger, conductor
Cliff Richard	vocals
Unknown	backing vocals

Recording Details

Producer	Norrie Paramor
Engineered by	Unknown
Recording location	Shibuya Public Hall, Tokyo, Japan
Recording date	18th October 1967

♫ Let's Stick Together

Original acetate subsequently released on **The Rock 'n' Roll Years 1958-1963**

In *The Complete Chronicle* published in 1995 by Mike Read, Peter Lewry and Nigel Goodall, it was highlighted that an acetate had surfaced on the market that had two tracks: ***Who's Gonna Take You Home?*** and *Let's Stick Together*. However, the authors also go on to say that the sessions for recording the songs are also untraceable since no records exist, although it is believed that they were recorded at some point in 1959.

Let's Stick Together also struggles with information on its provenance. It is not, as reported elsewhere, the Wilbert Harrison song (a hit in the mid-sixties) that was later covered by Bryan Ferry in the seventies. The lyrics and music appear to be original rather than a cover although records of the composer and the performers (other than Cliff Richard, of course) are also unavailable. To this end, the entry for this song simply catalogues this information as unknown until further research unearths more details. The track and its acetate stablemate was eventually released as two of the tracks on the collation of early rock and roll songs and rarities ***The Rock 'n' Roll Years 1958-1963***, which was released in 1997.
Is some respects, Cliff's song is somewhat simplistic in structure, supported by an electric guitar and a group of male backing vocals on later choruses (which may or may not be Hank Marvin and the Drifters) and has many links with the up-tempo gospel style of music being recorded by the likes of Elvis Presley. But it is a catchy little song that would have found a market somewhere if it had been developed. The recording sounds as if it was an impromptu set-up in between takes. The seven-inch acetate was presumably smuggled out of EMI (assuming this was where it was recorded) and kept in someone's collection before surfacing later and fortunately being made more widely available to the public. Cliff's vocal capabilities are clearly maturing as is his innate sense of humour sparkling under the lyrics and the overall performance.

Track Specification
Composed by Unknown

Musicians

Cliff Richard	vocals
Unknown	backing vocals
Unknown	guitar

Recording Details

Producer	Unknown
Engineered by	Unknown
Recording location	Unknown
Recording date	1959

♫ Letter, The
From the album **...And They Said It Wouldn't Last! (My 50 Years in Music)**

Made famous in the late summer of 1967 by the US group the Box Tops, who reached number one in the US Billboard and number five in the UK charts, *The Letter* has also been covered by the A-Teens, Al Green, Eva Cassidy, Del Shannon, Bachman-Turner Overdrive, the Shadows, Dionne Warwick, Melanie, Bobby Darin, Lou Rawls, the Beach Boys and Seasick Steve among others. It has hit the UK charts three times other in adition to the Box Tops: the Mindbenders took their cover to number forty-two at the same time; Joe Cocker recorded a version that reached number thirty-nine in July 1970; and Amii Stewart released a version that also reached number thirty-nine in January 1980.
Cliff Richard recorded a version that was similar in style to the Box Tops at the session that provided tracks for three albums (***Sincerely Cliff Richard, Tracks 'n' Grooves*** and ***Two a Penny***) and would not have been out of place on any of those track listings. However, for whatever reason it remained unissued until it was released on the *Lost and Found* section of the celebratory rarity album ***...And They Said It Wouldn't Last! (My 50 Years in Music)*** in 2008, although its release was pre-empted by a couple of weeks with a tie-in promotion of Cliff's hits given away free with the *Mail on Sunday* newspaper in the UK. The track has only ever made an appearance in mono format, although a stereo version would probably have been created simultaneously, although there are no records of this.
The arrangement owes much to the original, with its stark instrumentation giving way in the chorus to a lush accompaniment. There are backing vocals throughout the track but these are uncredited and are quite possibly the Mike Sammes Singers, who were regularly recording with Cliff at the time. Cliff's version isn't quite as raw as that by the Box Tops, but it is an excellent version nevertheless and a surprise that it has not been released prior to the rarity issue.

Track Specification
Composed by Wayne Carson Thompson

Musicians

Mike Leander	arranger, conductor
Mike Leander Orchestra	orchestra
Cliff Richard	vocals
Unknown	backing vocals

Recording Details

Producer	Norrie Paramor
Engineered by	Peter Vince
Recording location	Abbey Road Studio 2, St. John's Wood, London
Recording date	11th October 1967

♫ Let There Be Love
From the album **Two's Company**

Written in the late thirties, with the first known recording made by Van Alexander and His Orchestra in 1939, *Let There Be Love* was published, according to the song's copyright, the following year. The best known version, though, is by the silken tones of Nat King Cole, who reached number eleven in the UK charts in July 1962. A number of other artists have covered it including Rosemary Clooney, Peggy Lee, Shirley Bassey, Westlife, Tony Bennett, Oscar Peterson, Sammy Davis Jr. and Natalie Cole (singing in duet on the original recording made by her father).
Following in this method, Cliff Richard sang a duet on the cover originally recorded by Matt Monro. Monro, a UK crooner, had died in 1985 and it was agreed with the Monro estate that Cliff could take the original multi-track recording from Monro's 1973 album *The Other Side of the Stars*, and overdub his vocals. The result works very well, mixed and co-ordinated by Keith Bessey, although the original musician and recording staff details are not readily available.
One of the original crooners from the sixties and seventies, Matt Monro sings this song as if it were written with him in mind. Cliff's section of vocals fits in well and the interpolation is seamless and fresh.

Track Specification
Composed by Lionel Rand and Ian Grant

Musicians

Matt Monro	vocals
Cliff Richard	vocals
Unknown	arranger, conductor
Unknown	orchestra

Recording Details

Producer	Unknown (Matt Monroe vocals and backing track) and Keith Bessey (Cliff's vocals)
Engineered by	Unknown (Matt Monroe vocals and backing track) and Keith Bessey (Cliff's vocals)
Recording location	Unknown (Matt Monroe vocals and backing track) and Unknown (Cliff's vocals)
Recording date	1973 Unknown (Matt Monroe vocals and backing track) and 2006 (Cliff's vocals)

♫ Let Us Take You for a Ride

From the film soundtrack album of **Summer Holiday**

In ***Summer Holiday***, Don (played by Cliff Richard) and his three London Transport mechanic friends have taken a converted bus on the road to Athens for a holiday, when they come across an antiquated jalopy driven very slowly in the centre of the road by three girls (Una Stubbs, Jacqueline Daryl and Pamela Hart). Trying to explain to them as they draw alongside that they need to move over, an oncoming truck causes Don to drive into a post and the girls into a field. Going to help them, the boys find that the car won't start and this frustrates Stubbs's character to the point that she pulls off the steering wheel. They suggest that the three girls should join them, taking their baggage and trying to get them on to the bus. The girls, having none of this, take it all back to the car and so on, resulting in a dance routine in the middle of the road before the girls get back into their car and manage to get the car moving, without steering capability, across the incline of the field and into anther tree. From here, the girls become initially reluctant travelling companions.

One of the five soundtrack songs laid down in the session, *Let Us Take You For a Ride* used the same take and edit for the mono and stereo recordings but with different mixes for the audio channels. The version of the song used in the film was recorded later in the year at Elstree Studios but has not, as yet, been released in any other commercial format.

Prominent use of woodwind and percussion evoke mechanical operation to match the lyrics describing why the car won't work, before going into an up tempo orchestral section with Cliff and the Mike Sammes Singers imploring the girls to join them. Some of these additional vocals aren't quite in time but this doesn't detract from the overall performance. There is an extended mid-section for the orchestra before it returns to the main theme, which is played out in short cannon form.

Track Specification
Composed by Peter Myers and Ronald Cass

Musicians

Associated British Studio Orchestra	orchestra
Stanley Black	conductor
Mike Sammes Singers	vocals, backing vocals
Cliff Richard	vocals

Recording Details

Producer	Norrie Paramor
Engineered by	Malcolm Addey and Richard Langham
Recording location	Abbey Road Studio 2, St. John's Wood, London
Recording date	26th August 1962

♫ Liebe Ist Immer Nur Heute, Die

From the album **Hier Ist Cliff**

Recorded at the second of four sessions for Cliff Richard's first German language album, *Hier Ist Cliff, Die Liebe Ist Immer Nur Heute* (translated as *Love Is Only for Today*) is a translation of his single, ***I'll Love You Forever Today***. It is a completely new recording rather than using the original backing and overdubbing Cliff's German vocals. The song was released on the album in stereo only and remained a rarity until it was included on the ***On the Continent*** compilation album in 1997.

As with the other concerted tracks from the film, Norrie Paramor has successfully recreated the sound of the original with just a few minor differences, apart from Cliff singing comfortably in the German language.

Track Specification
Composed by Cliff Richard and Jim Collier; German lyrics by Kurt Hertha

Musicians

Norrie Paramor Orchestra	orchestra
Norrie Paramor	arranger, director
Cliff Richard	vocals

Recording Details

Producer	Norrie Paramor
Engineered by	Peter Vince
Recording location	Abbey Road Studio 2, St. John's Wood, London
Recording date	20th November 1968

♫ Lieben Kann Man Einmal Nur

B-side of **Du, Du Gefällst Mir So**

Recorded at the same session as the single's A-side, ***Du, Du Gefällst Mir So***, *Lieben Kann Man Einmal Nur* is a German original song. The session was moved from Abbey Road to the Chappell Studios, possibly owing to refurbishment at the main studios. *Lieben Kann Man Einmal Nur* (literally *You Can Only Be in Love Once*) was released in stereo only and remained a rarity until it was included on the track listing of ***On the Continent*** in 1997. Cliff employs a lot of vibrato to great effect on some of the sustained notes and also provides his own backing vocals for the most part although there is an uncredited vocal group involved. Ridden with appropriate angst, this style of ballad suits Cliff's vocals exceptionally well.

Track Specification
Composed by Last; German lyrics by Joachim Relin

Musicians		*Recording Details*	
Mike Vickers Orchestra	orchestra	Producer	Norrie Paramor
Cliff Richard	vocals, backing vocals	Engineered by	Unknown
Unknown	backing vocals	Recording location	Chappell Studios, London
Mike Vickers	arranger, conductor	Recording date	21st January 1970

♫ Liebeslied

B-side of **Es Gehören Zwei zum Glücklichsein**

In June 1974, Cliff Richard recorded his final German language single, ***Es Gehören Zwei zum Glücklichsein***, which was a German version of Cliff's single ***(You Keep Me) Hangin' On***. Recorded at the Morgan Studios, *Liebeslied* – translated back to English simply as *Love Song* – it is a translation of that single's original B-side, ***Love Is Here***. The performance is a completely new recording rather than using the backing track of the original English version and overdubbing the new vocals. The song was reissued on the foreign language compilation ***On the Continent*** album in 1997.

Taken at a faster pace than the original, the rhythm guitar, electric piano and steel guitar are strongly in evidence, although the session notes indicate that it is solely an orchestra in attendance. Nevertheless, the arrangement underpins the meaning of the lyrics, which show his joy at falling in love after a long while. Cliff provides his own backing vocals in the middle eight.

Track Specification
Composed by Petrina Lordan and Dave Franklin; German lyrics by Bert Olden

Musicians		*Recording Details*	
Nick Ingman	conductor, arranger	Producer	David MacKay
Nick Ingman Orchestra	orchestra	Engineered by	Roger Quested
Cliff Richard	vocals, backing vocals	Recording location	Morgan Studios, London
		Recording date	24th June 1974

♫ Lies and Kisses

From the EP **Take Four**

One of the songs recorded in New York during Cliff Richard's recording sojourn in America in August 1964, *Lies and Kisses* was originally only issued in mono format on the ***Take Four*** EP. The seventh and final take and edit were used for the mono and stereo issues but with different mixes for the separate audio channels. The song remained a considerable rarity for over forty years until it was reissued on the French album, *All My Love*, in 2008, also in mono. The stereo version was released later that same year on the celebratory ***...And They Said It Wouldn't Last! (My 50 Years in Music)***.

Although the song deals with disloyalty and infidelity, the overall rhythm and arrangement is incongruously upbeat and jaunty, as it swoops through a number of key changes. Enhanced by the tripping drum and bouncing bass line, Cliff is in his element singing this style of song that would have had a broader appeal beyond a track on an EP.

Track Specification
Composed by H. Hunter, D. Heard and B. Boulanger

Musicians		*Recording Details*	
Stan Applebaum	conductor	Producer	Bob Morgan
Cliff Richard	vocals	Engineered by	Frank Laico
Unknown	backing vocals	Recording location	Columbia Studios, New York
Unknown	guitar	Recording date	19th August 1964
Unknown	bass		
Unknown	piano		
Unknown	orchestra		
Unknown	drums, percussion		

♫ Life

From the film soundtrack album of **Take Me High**

For some reason, the initial tracks from the ***Take me High*** film soundtrack are presented in a different order from the sequence in which they appear in the film. And *Life* is pitched as the fourth song rather than the sixth as it appears in the film's narrative. However, from a listening perspective, although the songs have evidently been created to support the storyline, it is not obvious that they are out of sequence.

One other oddity is that the song is simplified and performed at a more melancholic pace with basic guitar-led instrumentation prior to launching into the full-blown version in the film but this doesn't appear on the soundtrack. In this section of the film, Tim Matthews (played by Cliff Richard) has been transferred to Birmingham and he has decided to buy a houseboat to live on the canal. He is visited by Sarah (Debbie Watling), whose parents sold him the boat and whose restaurant Tim was instrumental in closing by disallowing further loans and funding. Sarah remembers the boat from her youth and, as she wanders around looking at the changes he has made, the sad version of the song sung in a minor key and at half speed is played, which doesn't appear on the soundtrack album.

After a few potentially awkward glances, Sarah then throttles up the engine and shows Tim how to get the boat going. As they travel slowly down the canal, there is a montage of the pair as they talk, laugh and joke, principally showing the initial stages of them falling in love. Tim then jumps off the boat and runs up the towpath to the burger stand to buy two cans of drink and two limp burgers. Both chomp into the bun and grimace, throwing the meat into the water suggesting that anyone who provides a decent burger in Birmingham would have it made. Note that this was in the days before McDonalds created its stranglehold on the country's fast food burger business. Throughout all this activity, the faster-paced version of the song that appears on the soundtrack is performed.
This briskly-paced ballad suits Cliff's voice and features an uncredited backing vocal group during the chorus. The driving guitar motif and the throbbing bass help to drive the song forwards and underpins the joy of living exuding from the lyrics and the action on the screen before building up to climactic 'Life!'.

Track Specification
Composed by Tony Cole

Musicians

David MacKay Orchestra	orchestra
David MacKay	arranger, conductor
Cliff Richard	vocals
Unknown	backing vocals

Recording Details

Producer	David MacKay
Engineered by	Tony Clark and Mike Jarrett
Recording location	Abbey Road Studio 3, St. John's Wood, London
Recording date	26th-27th May 1973

♫ Lifeline

B-side of **Last Train Home** *(Network 3)*

Continuing his dual career as a producer for other – often Christian-based – acts, Cliff Richard recorded four tracks with Network 3, who had just changed their names from Nutshell. Scant information is available on the recording sessions and this detail is highlighted as unknown until further information surfaces. *Lifeline* was chosen as the B-side of the group's first single under their new name, ***Last Train Home***.
Setting off in a rhythm that follows directly on from the rolling train beat that was created for the A-side, the song is similarly of the musical period. Cliff's backing vocals are in more evidence on this track than on the A-side but, even with the strength of the foot-tapping rhythm and the blending of all the vocals, there is something lacklustre about the ensemble performance.

Track Specification
Composed by A. Park and D. McCulloch

Musicians

Paul Field	vocals
Mo McCafferty	vocals
Annie McCaig	vocals
Cliff Richard	backing vocals
Unknown	guitar
Unknown	bass
Unknown	keyboards
Unknown	drums, percussion

Recording Details

Producer	Cliff Richard
Engineered by	Unknown
Recording location	Unknown
Recording date	1980

♫ Light across the World

From the album **Don't Hide Your Heart** *(Sheila Walsh)*

In the early eighties, Cliff Richard produced two unfortunately unsuccessful singles for the Christian vocal group Network 3 (***Last Train Home*** and ***Dangerous Game***). Network 3 comprised Paul Field, who co-wrote *Light across the World*, Mo McCafferty (later Turner) and Annie McCaig (both of whom appeared as backing vocalists on this track from Sheila Walsh's third album, ***Don't Hide Your Heart***). Cliff also produced Walsh's first album but limited himself to providing backing vocals here, which also included singer Mark Williamson and long-term Cliff collaborator Chris Eaton.
A high energy beat is established on the electronic music gadgetry by Craig Pruess. The frenetic vocal line by Walsh drives the performance slightly sharp on occasions but the backing vocal arrangement featuring Cliff, discernible amongst the group as an individual while still blending successfully, helps to maintain the overall tuning control.

Track Specification
Composed by Paul Field and Dave Cooke

Musicians

Chris Eaton	backing vocals
Rick Fenn	acoustic guitar, electric guitar
Annie McCaig	backing vocals
Dave Mattacks	cymbals
Craig Pruess	keyboards, electronics
Cliff Richard	backing vocals
Mo Turner	backing vocals
Sheila Walsh	vocals
Mark Williamson	backing vocals

Recording Details

Producer	Craig Pruess and Keith Bessey
Engineered by	Keith Bessey
Recording location	Gallery Studios, Chertsey, Surrey
Recording date	November 1984-February 1985

♫ Like Strangers

From the albums **Wanted** *and* **World Tour Live**

Most famously, Boudleaux Bryant's *Like Strangers* was recorded by the Everly Brothers, even lending its title to the name of the album that featured it in 1960. Their single reached number eleven in the UK charts in December 1960 and it has been covered by only a few artists including Gail Davies, Emmylou Harris and the Wilsons.

Cliff Richard, of course, had successfully released two singles as duets with Phil Everly and regularly covered songs that had been made famous by the brothers in concert. Occasionally he made studio recordings of them, too, and this was the case with *Like Strangers*, which was part of the first post-EMI album ***Wanted*** in 2001.

Gentle sustained chords are punctuated by a reverberating synthesiser note in this emotionally evocative song that Cliff sings with passion. Although it is a sad song, the rhythm is effective and keeps the song moving forward. As with much in the album's track listing, it is the backing vocal harmonies that assist in augmenting the beauty of the track further.

For the supporting tour, Cliff performed a number of the *Wanted* album tracks, including *Like Strangers*. The New Zealand leg was filmed for the DVD released in 2003. The next year, the *World Tour Live* CD issued a selection of the songs, including *Like Strangers*. A faithful adaptation from the original album, the backing strings replicate Tarney's synthesisers.

Track Specification

Composed by Boudleaux Bryant

1. Wanted

Musicians

John Brant	additional programming
Anthony Clark	backing vocals
Cliff Richard	vocals, backing vocals
Alan Tarney	arranger, backing vocals, keyboards, programming

Recording Details

Producer	Alan Tarney
Engineered by	John Brant and Gerry Kitchingham
Recording location	Wilmer Studios, London
Recording date	January-April 2001

2. World Tour Live

Musicians

Rachel Allen	violin
Elena Bulgakova	violin
Jenni Champion	violin
Anthony Clark	backing vocals, guitar
John Clark	guitar
Dave Cooke	keyboards
Cornelia Didenco	violin
Gina Ferguson	violin
Peter Howarth	backing vocals
Cathy Irons	violin
Pete May	drums, percussion
Mick Mullins	backing vocals
Keith Murrell	backing vocals
Alan Park	keyboards
Hee-Jung Park	violin
Cliff Richard	vocals
Eva Schwanen-Lilley	violin
Steve Stroud	bass

Recording Details

Producer	Keith Bessey
Engineered by	Keith Bessey
Recording location	The Mission Winery, Napier, New Zealand
Recording date	22nd February 2003

♫ Lindsay Jane

B-side of **The Best of Me**

Recorded during the ***Stronger*** album sessions, Cliff Richard's self-penned *Lindsay Jane* was inspired by the daughter of his friends although it is, in fact, about a boat. The notes on the ***The Best of Me*** single, for which *Lindsay Jane* was the B-side (alongside the original ***Move It***) in all its variants, states "Love and thanks to the Mason family and the Mediterranean" and it is the latter reference that gave Cliff the idea to write the song while on his first boat-based holiday - the heat, the pitch blackness of the sea at night and the speed of the boat were all elements that inspired the song. It was later issued on the compilation of Cliff Richard compositions, ***My Songs***, and later as a bonus track on the *Stronger* remaster in 2004.

With water effects, perhaps of oars hitting the water or waves crashing on the shore, the gentle beat rocks as if carried on the gentle swell of the sea. The accompaniment is well arranged and performed by Paul Moessl and the combination evokes the image engendered within the lyrics. The beauty of Cliff's backing vocals blending with the lead melody proves once again that Cliff composes lovely songs that are often hidden away on the B-side of single releases.

Track Specification

Composed by Cliff Richard

Musicians

Paul Moessl	arranger, synthesisers, drum and percussion programming
Cliff Richard	vocals, backing vocals

Recording Details

Producer	Cliff Richard
Engineered by	Gerry Kitchingham and Ben Robbins
Recording location	R. G. Jones Studios, Wimbledon, London
Recording date	27th February 1989, 9th March 1989, 13th-17th March 1989 and 22nd-23rd March 1989

♫ Lindsay Jane II

B-side of **From a Distance**

Often mistyped as *Lyndsay Jane II*, the second song to be inspired by a friend's child and her boat was recorded at a separate session after the massive concerts at the Wembley Stadium for Cliff Richard's thirtieth anniversary celebrations, before being chosen as the principal B-side of his single from ***The Event, From a Distance***. To date, it has not been released in any other format.

This song has a strong beat created on the drums and bobbling synthesiser. Cliff sings the song with a bristling energy and supports the melody with his own backing vocals. There are some melodic nods towards the original ***Lindsay Jane*** song and this ties the two episodic songs together. There is a guitar solo in the middle eight underneath the vocal arrangement, while Cliff mentions ***Miss You Nights*** in the lyrics.

Track Specification

Composed by Cliff Richard

Musicians

John Clark	guitar
Pete Howarth	backing vocals
Paul Moessl	keyboards, synthesisers, drum and percussion programming
Mick Mullins	backing vocals
Keith Murrell	backing vocals
Tessa Niles	backing vocals
Cliff Richard	vocals, backing vocals

Recording Details

Producer	Cliff Richard and Paul Moessl
Engineered by	Gerry Kitchingham and Ben Robbins
Recording location	R. G. Jones Studios, Wimbledon, London
Recording date	16th-18th July 1990 and 20th-23rd July 1990

♫ Little Bitty Pretty One

From the album **Rock 'n' Roll Silver**

Written in 1957, *Little Bitty Pretty One* was originally recorded by Bobby Day and then popularized in the US by Thurston Harris who reached number six there, but he is relatively unknown in the UK. More familiar covers have been recorded by Clyde McPhatter (late of the Drifters fame), Frankie Lymon and the Teenagers, the Jackson Five, the Doobie Brothers, Frankie Avalon, the Dave Clark Five, Lindisfarne and host of other acts, although none has made it into the official British singles charts.

But for Cliff Richard, it was Clyde McPhatter's version that resonated and, when his band Thunder, a name that was coined by Cliff himself, chose the track listing for his twenty-fifth anniversary celebration album, ***Rock 'n' Roll Silver***, *Little Bitty Pretty One* was an obvious one for inclusion.

With strummed bass line, the song slowly builds up with a choral line that opens up with additional instruments. Cliff's lead vocals are perfect for this type of song that moves inexorably forward. One of the unexpected highlights of the album, it is unfortunate that this was not released as a single, because there is a complexity that paradoxically is created by the simplicity of the melody and the arrangement that has been developed for this recording.

Track Specification

Composed by Robert Byrd

Musicians

Stuart Calver	backing vocals
Dave Cooke	keyboards
John Clark	electric guitar
Mark Griffiths	bass
Graham Jarvis	drums, percussion
Mart Jenner	guitar
John Perry	backing vocals
Alan Park	keyboards
Cliff Richard	vocals, backing vocals
Tony Rivers	backing vocals
Thunder	arranger

Recording Details

Producer	Thunder
Engineered by	Keith Bessey
Recording location	Strawberry Studios South, Surrey
Recording date	9th-18th May 1983

♫ Little Imagination, A

From the film soundtrack album of **Wonderful Life** *and from the album* **Cliff Richard at the Movies 1959-1974**

After feeling homesick (performed in the prior song ***Home***), Johnny Craig (portrayed by Cliff Richard in ***Wonderful Life***) suddenly notices a girl in Arabic dress shouting for help on a runaway camel. Johnny chases after her and grabs the rope attached to the camel's bridle and is dragged through the sand until the camel comes to rest. It appears that this was done solely for a movie that is being filmed and, after impressing the director Douglas (Walter Slezak), he is offered a job as the leading man's stunt double. He agrees as long as his six friends can also be given jobs – Jerry (Melvyn Hayes) and Edward (Richard O'Sullivan) as tea-boys and the Shadows as the film's musicians (playing cellos, bongos, violins and flutes).

Later, by the harbour, Johnny enters the café with his script and sits down at a table next to a girl who appears to be reading the same lines from her script. She introduces herself as Jenny (Susan Hampshire). They agree to share the same table after he recognizes her as the girl on the runaway camel and also the girl he had attempted to follow earlier at the

port. She is a little depressed because she thinks she is useless as an actress, to which Johnny responds that she just needs to use a little imagination to get into the role better, thereby kicking off the song *A Little Imagination*, where the pair runs through a sequence of familiar filmic clichés: on the deck of a boat cruising to Australia, a Viennese waltz in a large ballroom replete with coiffeured white wigs, a square dance, a cockney dance, into a regal ballroom, a beach party and then with Jenny standing on rocks at the water's edge while Johnny plays an extravagant concerto on a grand piano on the beach, a hula dance, Spanish flamenco, American majorette march, and completed by a swift recall of everything they had imagined with snippets from each of these sequences. At the end of the song, Jenny says she should be going and blinks at Johnny, who disappears. With a knowing smile she looks at the camera, blinks again and she disappears.
One of four tracks recorded at the first session for the soundtrack, *A Little Imagination* was the second song to be completed. The same take and edit was used for the mono and stereo recordings but with different mixes for the audio channels and it was incorporated on the track listing for the ***Wonderful Life No. 2*** EP. An edited version without the orchestral bridge (during the imagined scene sequences) appeared on the ***Cliff Richard at the Movies 1959-1974*** album, making it considerably shorter coming in at just over a minute. The film version was probably recorded during the first three months of 1964, although there is no available record of the musicians and studio personnel and it has not been released in any other commercial format – although there is very little difference in the vocal part, the instrumental bridge performed during the imagined scenes is significantly extended over the soundtrack version.
The problem with the film soundtrack is that it relies too much on traditional British film musical numbers that, while performed perfectly by Cliff, miss the energy that would be provided by having the Shadows backing him. *A Little Imagination* is a case in point, which is composed purely for the dance sequence more than it is for the tune. While this is fine visually, it is far less so when listening to it on a soundtrack album.

Track Specification
Composed by Peter Myers and Ronald Cass

1. *Wonderful Life*

Musicians		*Recording Details*	
Associated British Studio Orchestra	orchestra	Producer	Norrie Paramor
Stanley Black	conductor	Engineered by	Malcolm Addey
Cliff Richard	vocals	Recording location	Abbey Road Studio 2, St. John's Wood, London
		Recording date	22nd April 1964

2. *Cliff Richard at the Movies 1959-1974*

Musicians		*Recording Details*	
Associated British Studio Orchestra	orchestra	Producer	Norrie Paramor
Stanley Black	conductor	Engineered by	Malcolm Addey
Cliff Richard	vocals	Recording location	Abbey Road Studio 2, St. John's Wood, London
		Recording date	22nd April 1964

♬ Little in Love, A

***80th UK single** and unissued live track*

With Alan Tarney at the production helm and also intrinsically involved in the performance and composition, Cliff Richard recorded his eightieth UK single as part of the ***I'm No Hero*** sessions, on which album *A Little in Love* also appears. Issued as a single with a non-album track, ***Keep on Looking***, as its B-side, it was released on the EMI label (catalogue number EMI 5123) on 12th January 1981 and reached number fifteen in the UK charts. The single edit version is shorter than that on the album with the first chorus being cut after the key change.
For the second time in his career, Cliff had greater success with the song in the US (the first was ***Dreamin'***), where it soared to the number eleven position in the Billboard charts and was one of three songs simultaneously in the charts there, alongside the duet with Olivia Newton-John, ***Suddenly***, and *Dreamin'* (also taken from the *I'm No Hero* album). Since *Keep on Looking* was the B-side of the US-only single release of ***Give a Little Bit More***, for the US issue of *A Little in Love*, it was album track ***Everyman*** that was incorporated as the B-side.
A Little in Love was one of the first Cliff singles to have a specially shot promotional video, directed by David Mallett, for airing on television shows and the MTV phenomenon that was just around the corner. In it, Cliff can be seen performing the song as he walks around the interior rooms and external gardens of the manor house at Farningham in Kent. Recorded on 27th January just two weeks after the single's release, this is a different approach to promotion, showing Cliff to be at the forefront of musical changes.
As was common of the period and particularly for the track listing of the *I'm No Hero* album, *A Little in Love* is driven by the predominant synthesiser bass matched with a steady drum and percussion, and although there is a guitar in the mix, this isn't the main feature thereby showing the direction that Cliff's music was moving at the start of the new decade. What also works well is the blending and layering of Cliff's and Tarney's vocals behind Cliff's lead, which occasionally tries out the by now familiar falsetto setting.
As part of the 1988 *Live & Guaranteed 1988!* tour, the Danish leg was filmed for video release, although only half of the set list was eventually issued. A later reissue of the video incorporated a CD of those previously released live tracks; however, *A Little in Love* was one of the tracks that remain unissued.

Track Specification
Composed by Alan Tarney

1. Single

Musicians	
Michael Boddicker	synthesiser
Nick Glennie-Smith	synthesiser
Cliff Richard	vocals, backing vocals
Trevor Spencer	drums, percussion
Alan Tarney	arranger, backing vocals, bass

Recording Details	
Producer	Alan Tarney
Engineered by	Ashley Howe
Recording location	Riverside Studios, London
Recording date	12th May-27th June 1980

2. Unissued track (Live & Guaranteed 1988!)

Musicians	
John Clark	guitar
Rosemarie Ford	backing vocals
Mark Griffiths	bass
Peter Howarth	backing vocals
Steve Lauri	guitar
Paul Moessl	keyboards
Mick Mullins	backing vocals
Alan Park	keyboards
Cliff Richard	vocals
Henry Spinetti	drums, percussion

Recording Details	
Producer	Unknown
Engineered by	Unknown
Recording location	Fyens Forum, Odense, Denmark
Recording date	22nd May 1988

♫ Little Mistreater

From the album **Cliff Richard - The Album**

The saxophone-driven song *Little Mistreater* shows Cliff Richard keeping pace with the times and musical style changes when picking songs for ***Cliff Richard - The Album***, which was his first studio album of the nineties. With fourteen songs destined for the album's track listing, *Little Mistreater* is an eminently suitable closer to the first side of the original vinyl release of the album.

Providing his own backing vocals, Cliff performs this quite sophisticated but slightly angry piece with suitable emotion and the ensemble piece is driven along by the quirky rhythm section and the inevitable bank of saxophones. The song is, as the title suggests, about a girl who is leading him on and then discusses the feelings he has and his reaction to them and her. The melody and the backing vocal harmonies are what make this song, both of which are strong and it is one of the best tracks on the album.

Track Specification
Composed by John Wilson, Steve Piggott and Alan Gorrie

Musicians	
Dave Bishop	saxophones
John Clark	guitar
Peter May	drums, percussion
Paul Moessl	arranger, drum programming, keyboards
Steve Pigott	synthesised bass
Cliff Richard	vocals, backing vocals
Jamie Talbot	saxophone

Recording Details	
Producer	Bruce Welch and Cliff Richard
Engineered by	Keith Bessey
Recording location	Westside Studios, North Yorkshire
Recording date	7th-8th June 1992

♫ Little Rag Doll

From the EP **Congratulations**

Written by Mike Leander, whose orchestra had appeared on many a Cliff Richard recording in the recent years prior to the recording, *Little Rag Doll* was one of the six chosen contenders for the 1968 UK entry into the Eurovision Song Contest. With its French atmosphere (with the predominant accordion sound) and its jaunty rhythm, *Little Rag Doll* could have fitted in perfectly in what was a continental song contest (before it became so political) but it was up against the colossus that was ***Congratulations***. Cliff sang one song each week on the *Cilla Black Show* and then the vote was opened up to the public. With the winner polling 69% of the vote, the remaining share was not great and looks relatively poor but *Little Rag Doll* came fifth, polling 4.2% of the vote and just missed out on the next highest position to ***The Sound of the Candyman's Trumpet***, which received 4.6%. The track was recorded on its own (the other contender tracks had been recorded in two earlier sessions) in the middle of February 1968 and, although the other losing tracks have only ever been released in mono format (primarily on the associated ***Congratulations*** EP), with the exception of the 1968 German compilation *Congratulations und 13 Weitere Hits*, *Little Rag Doll* has been released in stereo on the EP compilation in 1989 ***The EP Collection: Ballads and Love Songs*** before mono version was added as a bonus track to the remastered version of the live album, ***Live at the Talk of the Town*** in 2007.

With an accordion introduction and a staccato tuba, the French-cum-German feel that this induces would have been a popular choice with Cliff's continental cousins, although whether it would have fared better than *Congratulations* is unlikely. Nevertheless, it is a quirky little love song that swings along and is well sung by Cliff.

Track Specification
Composed by Mike Leander
Musicians

Ladybirds	backing vocals
Marian Davies	
Gloria George	
Maggie Stredder	
Mike Leander	arranger, conductor
Mike Leander Orchestra	orchestra
Cliff Richard	vocals

Recording Details

Producer	Norrie Paramor
Engineered by	Peter Vince
Recording location	Abbey Road Studio 2, St. John's Wood, London
Recording date	11th February 1968

♫ Little Things Mean a Lot

From the album **Cliff Sings**

On Cliff Richard's ***Cliff Sings*** album, the tracks were divided between accompaniment by the Drifters and support from Norrie Paramor's orchestra. One of the eight songs featuring accompaniment by the orchestra, *Little Things Mean a Lot* was written in 1953 and first recorded by Kitty Kallen, who had the best known version of it when it reached number one in both the American Billboard charts and the UK charts in 1954. Alma Cogan tried her luck with her version a few months later but only managed to reach number eleven. It has also been covered by Cilla Black, Harry James, Jayne Mansfield, Liberace, Julie London and Jimmy Young.

All of the tracks on the *Cliff Sings* album were originally only released in mono in LP format. At the same time, each song was given a release in the EP format in both mono and stereo. For *Little Things Mean a Lot*, the same studio take was used but edited slightly differently for the stereo version for the best use of the dual listening channels. The song was one of four released on the ***Cliff Sings No. 4*** EP.

A slow-paced love ballad, Cliff's gentle vocal line is accompanied by a sussurating drum, swooping strings and keyboards. It is a testament to Cliff's singing ability that he is able to tackle what is essentially a technically difficult song to sing in terms of the placing of notes.

Track Specification
Composed by Carl Stutz and Edith Lindeman
Musicians

Norrie Paramor Orchestra	orchestra
Norrie Paramor	arranger, conductor
Cliff Richard	vocals

Recording Details

Producer	Norrie Paramor
Engineered by	Malcolm Addey and Alan Kane (mono) and Stuart Eltham and Norman Smith (stereo)
Recording location	Abbey Road Studio 2, St. John's Wood, London
Recording date	9th September 1959

♫ Little Town

85th UK single *and from the albums* **Dressed for the Occasion Remaster** *and* **Together with Cliff Richard** *and unissued live track*

For the final single release from the album, ***Now You See Me... Now You Don't***, *Little Town* was the closer to the first side of the original vinyl release. Chris Eaton took the familiar words from the poem by the Philadelphia priest Phillips Brooks and eschewed the temptation to do a simple arrangement of the familiar setting to music of ***Little Town of Bethlehem***. Instead, he created a highly dramatic, brass- and percussion-driven that required a full orchestra made up almost entirely of brass instruments.

The song was recorded by Cliff in early 1982 and, backed with two non-album tracks recorded during the sessions for the album, ***You, Me and Jesus*** and ***Love and a Helping Hand***, *Little Town* was issued as a single on the EMI label (catalogue number EMI 5348) on 15th November 1982 and just missed getting into the top ten settling as it did at number eleven and became Cliff's first seasonally pertinent single. In addition, a picture disc was issued at the same time (catalogue number EMIP 5348) but that isn't the end of the story of *Little Town*. Included on a number of compilations, notably ***Carols*** and ***Private Collection***, *Little Town* was added as a bonus track on the twelve-inch and CD versions of the ***Mistletoe and Wine*** single in 1988, while the original was revisited for the ***Together with Cliff Richard*** album, when the instrumentation was changed, with the most noticeable being the replacement of Craig Pruess's piano with Paul Moessl's synthesiser. The version that appears on the celebratory ***...And They Said It Wouldn't Last! (My 50 Years in Music)*** album in 2008 is the same as the original single version but with the end being edited to arrive some twelve seconds earlier.

The original promotional video features Cliff in a studio dressed to look like a winter scene; throughout most of it, he is sitting on the ground but stands up just before the falsetto solo by Nigel Perrin, who also features briefly, before the camera pans upwards and Cliff is revealed to be in a glass snow-shaker.

The chiming bells, the rolling drums and the piano chords indicate that what is to follow is going to be dramatic. True enough, the quietness of each of the verses, which feature Cliff singing his own backing vocals, build up into the memorable chorus. It would be very easy to use elements of the familiar music from the carol, but Eaton and Brooks have successfully built up something very different but still seasonally celebratory. The brass and tubular bells playing in the mid-section pile on the effect further before quietening down for Nigel Perrin to sing his lead as Cliff comes in and leads into a section of the nursery rhyme *Twinkle, Twinkle Little Star*, which is a reverent reference to the guiding star of Bethlehem from the Nativity story.

Since it had been a very recent single release at the time of pulling together the set list, *Little Town* was included on the Royal Albert Hall concert at the end of November, which was recorded and released as ***Dressed for the Occasion***. However, it was left off the final album track listing possibly due to space considerations and, if so, to make way for new material not previously recorded in the studio such as ***Softly as I Leave You*** and ***Treasure of Love***. As with this and the four other tracks that were previously unissued, the 2004 remaster of the parent album carried all of these tracks as bonus items, since they had already been prepared and mixed for release – this allowed them to slot in the running order without difficulty. Because of the dramatically orchestral nature of the original, it is unsurprising that the London Philharmonic backing Cliff in concert should be so effective in their rendition. The song is introduced by Cliff wishing the audience a merry Christmas and being the first to do so. Tony Rivers takes over the Nigel Perrin solo for the performance that is a perfect ending to the special occasion. As Cliff takes his bows, the orchestra reprise the orchestral instrumental section as the vocalists repeat the end section from Rivers' solo.

Little Town completed the ***Christmas Medley***, which was performed at the end of Cliff's concerts during his world tour to support the release of ***Wanted***. By February 2003, when the New Zealand concert was filmed for DVD release, although it was still performed, it was distinctly unseasonal by this point and was missed off the track listing of the associated *World Tour Live* CD album in 2004.

Track Specification
Composed by Phillips Brooks and Chris Eaton

1. Single

Musicians

Martyn Ford	conductor
Graham Jarvis	drums, percussion
Martyn Ford Orchestra	orchestra
Ian Anderson	double bass
Dave Arnold	tympani, chimes
Paul Beer	tenor trombone
Roger Brenner	tenor trombone
Michael Brittain	double bass
Jeff Bryant	French horn
Paul Cosh	trumpet
Robin Davies	French horn
Phillip Eastop	French horn
Mark Emney	trumpet
Simon Ferguson	trumpet
Michael Hext	tenor trombone
Ted Hobart	trumpet
John Iveson	tenor trombone
Michael Laird	trumpet
Chris Larkin	French horn
Chris Laurence	double bass
Geoff Perkins	bass trombone
John Pigneevy	French horn
Dave Purser	tenor trombone
John Rooke	French horn
Gerry Ruddock	trumpet
Steve Saunders	bass trombone
Crispian Steele-Perkins	trumpet
David Whitson	tenor trombone
John Wilbraham	trumpet
Nigel Perrin	vocal arranger, vocals, backing vocals
Craig Pruess	orchestral arranger, piano, synthesisers, sequencers, electronic percussion, sleigh bells
Cliff Richard	vocals, backing vocals
Tony Rivers	backing vocals

Recording Details

Producer	Cliff Richard and Craig Pruess
Engineered by	John Walker, Steve Cook and John Kurlander
Recording location	Strawberry Studios South, Surrey and Abbey Road Studios, St. John's Wood, London (orchestra)
Recording date	4th-15th January 1982 and 25th-26th March 1982 (orchestra)

2. Dressed for the Occasion Remaster

Musicians

Stuart Calver	backing vocals
David Cooke	synthesiser
Steve Gray	piano
Mark Griffiths	bass
Tony Harding	backing vocals
Richard Hewson	arranger, conductor
Graham Jarvis	drums, percussion
London Philharmonic Orchestra	orchestra
John Perry	backing vocals
Cliff Richard	vocals
Tony Rivers	backing vocals

Recording Details

Producer	Cliff Richard and Richard Hewson
Engineered by	John Kurlander
Mixed by	Keith Bessey
Recording location	Royal Albert Hall, London
Mixed at	Strawberry Studios South, Surrey
Recording date	23rd November 1982

3. *Together with Cliff Richard*

Musicians

Martyn Ford	conductor
Graham Jarvis	drums, percussion
Martyn Ford Orchestra	orchestra
Ian Anderson	double bass
Dave Arnold	tympani, chimes
Paul Beer	tenor trombone
Roger Brenner	tenor trombone
Michael Brittain	double bass
Jeff Bryant	French horn
Paul Cosh	trumpet
Robin Davies	French horn
Phillip Eastop	French horn
Mark Emney	trumpet
Simon Ferguson	trumpet
Michael Hext	tenor trombone
Ted Hobart	trumpet
John Iveson	tenor trombone
Michael Laird	trumpet
Chris Larkin	French horn
Chris Laurence	double bass
Geoff Perkins	bass trombone
John Pigneevy	French horn
Dave Purser	tenor trombone
John Rooke	French horn
Gerry Ruddock	trumpet
Steve Saunders	bass trombone
Crispian Steele-Perkins	trumpet
David Whitson	tenor trombone
John Wilbraham	trumpet
Paul Moessl	keyboards
Nigel Perrin	vocal arranger, vocals, backing vocals
Craig Pruess	orchestral arranger, synthesisers, sequencers, electronic percussion, sleigh bells
Cliff Richard	vocals, backing vocals
Tony Rivers	backing vocals

Recording Details

Producer	Cliff Richard and Craig Pruess
Engineered by	John Walker, Steve Cook and John Kurlander
Recording location	Strawberry Studios South, Surrey and Abbey Road Studios, St. John's Wood, London (orchestra)
Recording date	4th-15th January 1982 and 25th-26th March 1982 (orchestra)

4. *Unissued track (World Tour Live)*

Musicians

Rachel Allen	violin
Elena Bulgakova	violin
Jenni Champion	violin
Anthony Clark	backing vocals, guitar
John Clark	guitar
Dave Cooke	keyboards
Cornelia Didenco	violin
Gina Ferguson	violin
Mike Haughton	flute, saxophone
Peter Howarth	backing vocals
Cathy Irons	violin
Pete May	drums, percussion
Mick Mullins	backing vocals
Keith Murrell	backing vocals
Alan Park	keyboards
Hee-Jung Park	violin
Cliff Richard	vocals
Eva Schwanen-Lilley	violin
Steve Stroud	bass

Recording Details

Producer	Keith Bessey
Engineered by	Keith Bessey
Recording location	The Mission Winery, Napier, New Zealand
Recording date	22nd February 2003

♫ Little Town of Bethlehem

From the EP **Carol Singers**

Inspired by a visit to the Holy Lands and the Church of the Nativity in Bethlehem, a priest by the name of Phillips Brooks from Philadelphia wrote the poem about Christ's birthplace in 1868, while the organist at his church, Lewis Redner, added the music, which was entitled *St. Louis*. This musical version is the most common in the US, while it is the *Forest Green* melody, which was later adapted by Ralph Vaughan Williams, which is used more often in Britain. Since *O Little Town of Bethlehem* is so redolent of everything that is Christmas, both in the celebratory and religious contexts, it is a popular tune to record and a variety of artists have covered the carol including Elvis Presley, Amy Grant, Julie Andrews, Jim Reeves, Bob Dylan, Andy Williams and Tammy Wynette, among others.

Cliff Richard recorded a version of the carol, which was based on the *St. Louis* tune and released on the ***Carol Singers*** EP. With the help of a Christian group of music teachers, one of whom, Geoffrey Keating, provided the *a capella* arrangement, Cliff produced a brilliantly evocative version of the Christmas carol. Fifteen years later, Cliff would go on to record another version, to a different music setting, but this time calling it ***Little Town***. It should be noted that the *Carol Singers* carol is missing the usual prefix of '*O*'. *Little Town of Bethlehem* was recorded at the second of two sessions on the same day for the EP, with the final edit being constructed from splices from multiple takes. It was only released in the mono format of the EP – Columbia's decision at the time was to reserve stereo releases for albums only – although the stereo version was then included on the 1988 *Carols LP* album.

Track Specification

Composed by Phillips Brooks and Lewis H. Redner, arranged by Geoffrey Keating

Musicians

Mastersingers:	backing vocals
John Horrex	
Geoffrey Keating	
George Pratt	
Michael Warrington	
Cliff Richard	vocals

Recording Details

Producer	Norrie Paramor
Engineered by	Peter Vince and John Barrett
Recording location	Abbey Road Studio 2, St. John's Wood, London
Recording date	10th September 1967

♫ Live-in World

Single by **The Anti-Heroin Project**

In 1986, one of the biggest growing social problems was drug addiction and this was particularly the case in the younger generation. While there were governmental measures put in place, it was really left to charities to bear the brunt of the management of the problem. In 1984, the extraordinary success of Band Aid and the ***Do They Know It's Christmas?*** single followed by the Live Aid phenomenon mean that many stars tried to repeat the triumph by following the same formula, often with very poor results.

Usually, it also used the same format of big stars singing one line each. Charley Foskett, a well-known producer, musician and composer came up with the idea of the Anti-Heroin Project, which would not only produce a single but also come up with a complete album. While most stars wouldn't be able to sustain their involvement in a complete album for charity, it meant that other tracks on the album were duets, trios, solos and other amalgamations of the people involved – so important did the then Conservative government consider this work with the anti-drugs campaign to be that David Mellor, a junior minister at the Home Office, asked him to be his right-hand man on the drugs problem, a position that Foskett declined.

The final result of the recording project was a thirty-track album, *It's a Live-in World*, roughly half of which Foskett wrote, as well as the huge ensemble cast created for the single, *Live-in World*. In a typical copy, too, of the Band Aid video, the Anti-Heroin Project showed the singers individually for the lines and together for the chorus interspersed with scenes from Phoenix House, the charity organisation that would benefit from the royalties to be received from the single's and album's sales and which was set up originally in America to help adults and youths through the trauma of overcoming addiction to drugs and alcohol.

While the song was catchy enough and highly redolent of the eighties synthesized sound, and even though the most spirited performance came from Cliff Richard himself as can be seen in the video – Robin Gibb, Holly Johnson, Bonnie Tyler, Fish and others are obviously committed but it is Cliff's falsetto and almost manic gestures that steal the show as well as the absolute clarity of his vocals – the single failed to ignite that much interest at the time. The problem was two-fold: first, the record-buying public were emotionally tired after a succession of good charity works (including the now biennial Comic Relief telethon supported in 1986 by the new version of ***Living Doll***, which was a comedic collaboration featuring Cliff and Hank Marvin) and yet another charity record left many cold; second, and more important, was that the success of Band Aid, Live Aid and Comic Relief was that the heartstrings could be easily tugged with the sight of people and specifically of children dying – the problem with the Anti-Heroin Project (much as the same with the contemporaneous Just Say No campaign) was that those affected, as they appeared in the video, were a little helpless but looked healthy and therefore not as warranting of sympathy. Very laudable though the project was, it failed to garner the same sort of publicity and the project was, commercially speaking, unsuccessful.

Recorded in the September of 1986 with a huge cast from the popular acts and television stars of the day, *Live-in World*, backed with *Something Better* (a track featuring Precious Wilson, Kim Wilde, Daryl Pandy and Bobby Whitlock), the song was released as a single on the EMI label (with its own catalogue number sequence AHP 1) on 20th October 1986 but failed to reach anywhere in the charts. Simultaneously, a twelve-inch single release was issued (catalogue number 12 AHP 1) with the same tracks as the seven-inch (although not extended or remixed) but including non-LP track *On the Street* by comedian Lenny Henry on the first side and LP track *You Know It Makes Sense* by Ringo Starr on the B-side.

Cliff's contribution to his one-liners stands out because of the voice (as do other artists) and he employs a falsetto that distinguishes him further. The song is pleasant enough but it is too earnest and self-absorbed to have the impact that *Do They Know It's Christmas?* had. Having said that, there is much to commend it and, in particular, the enthusiastic participation of the musicians and the vocal harmony arrangements.

Track Specification

Composed by Charley Foskett

Musicians

Jeremy Alsop	bass
Gary Barnacle	tenor saxophone
Tony Beard	drums, percussion
Gordon Bonnar	vocals
Elkie Brooks	vocals
Mel Collins	saxophone
Hazell Dean	vocals
Jim Diamond	vocals
Adrian Edmondson	vocals
Vince Edwards	backing vocals
Tommy Eyre	keyboards
Phil Fearon	vocals
Sheila Ferguson	vocals
Lauren Field	backing vocals
Finchley Children's Choir	choir
Fish	vocals
Brinsley Ford	vocals
Bobby G	vocals
Barbara Gaskin	vocals
Robin Gibb	vocals
Steve Harley	vocals
Roy Harper	vocals
Hamie Hayman	vocals
Helena	vocals
Nick Heyward	vocals
Chas Hodges	vocals
Holly Johnson	vocals
Chris Layhe	vocals
Julian Littman	backing vocals
Nik Kershaw	vocals
Eddie MacDonald	vocals
John McCoy	vocals
Ian McNabb	vocals
Gillian Mason	backing vocals
Rik Mayall	vocals
Dutch Michaels	vocals
Hayley Mills	vocals
Mike Nolan	vocals
Hazel O'Connor	vocals
Bill Oddie	vocals
Genesis P. Orridge	vocals
Daryl Pandy	vocals
John Parr	vocals
Paula	vocals
Dave Peacock	vocals
Mike Peters	vocals
Nigel Planer	vocals
Shelley Preston	vocals
Jimmy Pursey	vocals
Cliff Richard	vocals
Kate Robbins	vocals
Christopher Ryan	vocals
Chris Sharrock	vocals
Sinitta	vocals
Don Snow	keyboards
Zak Starkey	vocals
Edwin Starr	vocals
Dave Stewart	vocals, keyboards
Poly Styrene	vocals
Suggs	vocals
Bobby Tench	backing vocals
John Thirkle	trumpet
Thompson Twins:	vocals
Tom Bailey	
Alannah Currie	
Joe Leeway	
Peter Thoms	trombone
Luke Tunney	trumpet
Bonnie Tyler	vocals
Dave Wakeling	vocals
Tom Watt	vocals
Lizzy Welch	backing vocals
Bobby Whitlock	vocals
Kim Wilde	vocals
Precious Wilson	vocals
Drummie Zeb	vocals

Recording Details

Producer	Charley Foskett
Engineered by	Tony Clark and Darren Goodwin
Recording location	Universal Studios, Los Angeles, Olympic Studios, London, Powerplant Studios, London, C. T. S., Wembley and Abbey Road Studios, St. John's Wood, London
Recording date	7th September 1986

♫ Living Doll

5th and 97th UK singles, live B-side of **Living Doll** *CD single (Holland only) and live B-side of* **Peace in Our Time** *(CD), from the soundtrack album to the film* **The Young Ones** *and from the albums* **Cliff in Japan**, **Cliff Live in Korea**, **Cliff "Live" in Japan '72**, **Utterly Utterly Live!**, **Something Special**, **Respect** *and* **Reunited** *and unissued live tracks*

After a momentous year for Cliff Richard and the Drifters, where the group had had four singles and an album released, it was topped off by his involvement in the film *Serious Charge*, a gritty drama directed by Terence Young, who would direct a number of the James Bond films in the sixties. Originally a theatre play written by Philip King, *Serious Charge* was adapted for the silver screen by Mickey Delamar and Guy Elmes. It was updated a little for the film and Cliff was asked to play the musician in it, largely to capitalize on his popularity but also, as Cliff suggests, it was because he was cheap and, indeed, would have done the role for nothing just to be in a movie. That's quite self-effacing but has an element of truth – it worked for both film distributor and music star because the one's publicity fed off the other's.

Serious Charge follows the story of a newly-appointed and single vicar, Reverend Howard Phillips (played by Anthony Quayle), who, as part of looking after his parish, sets up a youth club to stop the local teenagers dissolving into delinquency. He also promises the magistrates to look after Larry Thompson and the welfare of his younger brother, Curley (played by Cliff with an impossible quiff). Leading a gang of teenagers into mischief, including breaking into a swimming pool, graffiti and getting his girlfriend pregnant, Thompson doesn't live up to his responsibilities and refuses to acknowledge his forthcoming paternity, leading his girlfriend in a highly emotional state as she steps in front of a bus and is killed. Phillips accuses Thompson of being in part responsible for her death and, in spiteful revenge, Thompson accuses Phillips of molesting him. The people of the town refuse to rally to the vicar's defence and, instead, it is left to him to clear his name of the serious charge of the title. This was really gritty stuff for the period and more so with the clean-cut image that Cliff Richard had effortlessly nurtured since arriving on the scene the revious year. Nevertheless, he sings three songs in the film, which triggered fans to request that *Living Doll* be released as a single.

But there was a problem: Cliff and the Drifters' producer, Norrie Paramor, had guided the band's career to date and, with the release of the film and the contractual obligation of a single release from it without his control, he was determined to forestall any single's success. This he did, after realizing that *Living Doll* was the most popular track with fans, by issuing the Cliff and the Drifters single ***Livin' Lovin' Doll***, obviously intending to cause confusion by the similarly named tracks. *Livin' Lovin' Doll* was released but it only barely scraped into the top twenty and, by comparison with the previous singles, a bit of a failure. Meanwhile, there was an inexorability about *Living Doll* that meant that it was going to be released.

In the film, Cliff sings this rock and roll song while lounging in the coffee bar with a number of girls draped around him. In truth, the song isn't present for that long as the focus of the scene and it soon becomes a background musical number for the next scene with the sound muted for the dialogue.

Lionel Bart was very much ascending the path to glory with a number of music hits behind him. While the film's main score was written by Leighton Lewis, Bart was commissioned to write the tunes that would be sung by Cliff in the film. *Living Doll* was a fast-paced song in common time and, as Cliff has stated in interview, wasn't particularly well-liked because it had the feel of a rock and roll pastiche rather than something that was attuned to the original American sound. In addition to this concern, Cliff and the band were clear that rock and roll simply wasn't selling in the volumes of the popular music category. If they wanted to break out of perception, they would need to get the parents on side with their music, since, as he eruditely pointed out, they were the ones with the money and the fingers on the purse strings.

Before the film version of the song could be released, it was decided that they would try something different. On tour of the northern cities in the UK, Bruce Welch was sitting with his guitar on the steps of the Sheffield City Hall when he suggested that maybe what was needed to improve the song was to keep it in common time but to slow it down and to give it a country and western style make-over, demonstrating what he meant on his guitar. It was agreed and, although none of the band and particularly Welch, took a writing or an arrangement credit for it, the slower, more laidback version was recorded and released.

Issued on the Columbia label (catalogue numbers DB 4306 (78 r.p.m. format) and 45-DB 4306 (seven-inch version)) on 10th July 1959 and backed with a completely different recording of ***Apron Strings*** from the one issued on the *Cliff* album, *Living Doll* became Cliff Richard's first number one in the UK, staying there for a remarkable six weeks. Contrary to perception, which states that Cliff has only had a very few hits in the US starting with ***Devil Woman*** in 1976, *Living Doll* was also the first of his songs to be released in the US, where it reached a very respectable number thirty. Cliff bemoans the fact that, when he was over in the US he had very little support from his record company in spite of this achievement and wonders if that created an issue with his ongoing ability to completely break through into the US market, although it is true that the structure is very different from the UK. This single also marked the last time that the band recorded as The Drifters, because of the success of the single in the US, where there was already an established vocal group of the same name, who had been performing and recording since 1953. To avoid confusion, on the assumption that future Cliff and the Drifters records would take off, and to pre-empt any possible litigation, the band opted to change their name to the Shadows, a suggestion made by bassist Jet Harris.

The song is now one of the most famous of Cliff's back catalogue and has one of the most immediately recognizable introductions, created by Hank Marvin as he steps down through a scale before Cliff's vocals enter. It is a love song and is a list of the things that he finds attractive about his current girlfriend but with a warning that no-one will take her away from him because he'll hide her from view: in some respects, this is quite a dark sentiment but is more than made up for by the ensemble playing of the band right through to the incidental notation at the end on Hank's guitar. One of the highlights, apart from Cliff's accomplished vocals, is the gentle guitar solo in the middle eight, giving Hank a chance to stand in the limelight. Like Cliff, his career exploded as a result of this recording because it showed he could do something completely different from standard rock and roll. The Shadows would embark on their parallel career as instrumentalists the following year with ***Apache***, although there had been attempts to release two singles under The Drifters name.

A small reprise of the song's first two lines was included in the ***Vaudeville Routine*** section of ***The Young Ones*** film, interspersed into the ***What D'You Know, We've Got a Show*** narrative. At this point in the film, the youth club members have taken over the tumbledown theatre and spontaneously pulled together a song, dance and comedy show with the help of dusty props, scenery and wardrobe. The version on the album used the stereo and mono edits of the final take but with different mixes for the audio channels.

It was the habit in Cliff's shows for him to string a few familiar songs together in a medley. This he did for his Talk of the Town shows in May 1968 with four songs linked together: *The Young Ones*, ***Lucky Lips***, *Living Doll* and ***In the Country***. However, this medley was not released on the resultant album and remains unissued to date. Later, another medley was recorded and released in mono only for the ultra-rare album *Cliff Live in Korea*, where it formed part of the ***Shadows Medley***: *The Young Ones*, *Living Doll* and *In the Country*, while for ***Cliff "Live" in Japan '72***, it was part of the ***Hit Medley***: *Living Doll*, *Bachelor Boy* and *The Young Ones*. And for the ***Cliff "Live" in Japan '72*** album, it was performed in its entirety where the focus is firmly on Hank Marvin's guitar behind Cliff's lead vocals.

Following the stupendous and unexpected success of the Band Aid single ***Do They Know It's Christmas?*** in 1984 as a response to the famine in Ethiopia, Richard Curtis and Alexander Mendis followed this in 1985 with *Comic Relief*, the name of the charity itself being a suitable pun. Every other year, there continues to a be live telethon to raise money and, every year including those in between the telethons, there is an associated, often humorous, single released. Rather than using the one-line-a-musician approach of most charity singles, it is usually one or two artists who perform something that is out of public character. In 1985, it was Cliff's turn assisted by the four main cast members of *The Young Ones*, a cult anarchic situation comedy that took its title from Cliff's film because of lead character Rick's supposed adulation of the singer. The humour is brought about by Cliff playing the song straight as if he has been brought to the studio under false pretences, wincing at the flatness of the backing vocals and so on. As Cliff sings gamely on clutching the headphones to his ears the comedians lark about, with Rik Mayall almost apoplectic at meeting his idol. The back wall disappears in the middle eight to reveal a smiling Hank Marvin playing the instrumental break before returning to the beleaguered Cliff singing the final verse before being clubbed over the head with rubber mallets and falling off his chair. The mix version features a spoken vocal segment by the comedians as the music fades up and then continues as the single version, with extra sound effects. Many saw the project as the cast of *The Young Ones* betraying their revolutionary intentions by performing with a 'dinosaur' of convention, while others saw Cliff and his playful sense of humour in a different light and he regained the 'cool' tag once more– whichever is correct, the point wasn't about the public's perceptions of the artists; rather the project was to raise money to assist the charities in famine-stretched countries of Africa as well as Britain. And it worked.

Produced by the man who had worked on ***She Means Nothing to Me***, Stuart Colman, the recording of the new vocals and the background antics only took twenty minutes, although mixing took a further six weeks to perfect the final product. The video was recorded on 30th January 1986, the day after the studio recording had been basically finished. The new version of *Living Doll* was backed with *(All the Little Flowers Are) Happy*, a sequence of comedy by *The Young Ones* but not featuring Cliff or Hank. It was issued as a single on the WEA Records label (catalogue number YZ 65) on 8th March 1986 and quickly reached number one in the UK charts, displacing Diana Ross's *Chain Reaction* and being removed from the top spot by George Michael's *A Different Corner* after three weeks. It was also simultaneously released as a picture disc single (catalogue number YZ 65P) and a CD single in certain markets such as Holland (this time on the EMI label, catalogue number 7243 8 85325 2 5). An extended mix was also included in the twelve-inch single (less than subtly subtitled *The Disco Funk Get Up and Get Down Go to the Lavatory Mix* – a common theme in the television series), which was also issued on the WEA Records label (catalogue number YZ 65T). The success of the record not only helped charity but it also ensured that Cliff was only one of three artists to achieve number one with two different versions of the same song, while also obtaining the record of being the only artist to have recorded number one singles in each of four decades. As part of the whole project, Cliff reprised the song at the Shaftesbury Theatre over a number of nights in early April 1986. One of the performances was recorded and issued on the *Utterly Utterly Live!* album (which took its title from Rik Mayall's utterances in character). There is a lengthy skit to introduce the song with audience participation leading into Cliff's introduction, after pretending that he is not turning up and has been replaced by television presenter John Craven. Cliff introduces the song and they perform it much as it appears on the single. Instead of Hank appearing, there is a fuzzy and out-of-tune guitar solo, possibly played by one of the comedians, although this is unclear.

The original was a regular feature on Cliff's tours, and a version was filmed and recorded during the *Live & Guaranteed 1988!* set that was issued on the video and then re-released alongside a CD. In Holland, *Living Doll* was released as a single again on 30th March 1998 (EMI label; catalogue number 7243 8 85325 2 5) and this featured the *Live & Guaranteed 1988!* live version of the song as one of its B-side elements. In spite of the restoration of all other previously unreleased tracks to the 2005 remaster of ***From a Distance ***** The Event***, *Living Doll* was one of six Cliff and the Shadows performances to remain unissued. Similarly, the Knebworth performance has also yet to be released.

A new live version was released on the second of the dual CD single release of ***Peace in Our Time***. This rendition was recorded at the *Access All Areas* tour in 1992 at Wembley Arena and features Cliff accompanying himself on guitar as part of the opening set that also included ***That's Alright, Mama***, which was also made available on the first CD release of the same single.
By now a perennial favourite by the end of the nineties as a result of the cachet it received from the Comic Relief single and in spite of Cliff's early concern that he was getting tired of it, he was happy to perform it to the expectant audiences. It therefore was included in his set, accompanied by his own guitar-playing, at a Brighton performance in aid of the NASS charity (National Asylum Support Service), which was subsequently released on the *Something Special* album.
In 2002, Queen Elizabeth II enjoyed her golden jubilee to celebrate fifty years since her accession to the throne. To celebrate, a number of activities were planned including a suite of concerts in the grounds of Buckingham Palace, one of which focused on popular music with Cliff representing almost the entirety of her rein. One of the songs, *Living Doll*, was recorded and released on the DVD of the *Party at the Palace* but, as yet, has not been issued in any audio format.
A cover version by Scandinavian group, the Olsen Brothers, also featured Cliff on backing vocals, which he provided while recording his part of the duet ***Look Up, Look Down*** for the brothers' *Respect* album, although the track listing for the album refers to the track with a missing 'g': *Livin' Doll*. The extraordinary introduction is heavy on the bass and percussion and is several miles away from the countrified arrangement of the familiar original single. But it lends itself well to this treatment, which has the Olsen Brothers singing in harmony through the verses and choruses. The guitar solo is in place but arranged very differently from Hank's version: again, this works well in this setting. Cliff's vocals come in at the end with the new lyrics "I know I'll never be lonely, I've got the one and only".
When Cliff was organizing his 2009 tour, it was decided to reunite with the Shadows once more to celebrate fifty years in showbusiness the previous year. To accompany the concerts, the band recorded the ***Reunited*** album, which featured a number of re-recordings of material from their first ten years together, including, inevitably, *Living Doll*, in its single setting rather than the film version or the Comic Relief set-up (although there are one or two nods towards that version). The song is now so familiar that to do anything different with it would be deemed sacrilege. Indeed, this version is a faithful replica down to the brilliant guitar solo, although Hank now plays it in thirds rather than as a simple melody.

Track Specification
Composed by Lionel Bart

1. Single (Cliff and the Shadows)

Musicians

Jet Harris	bass
Hank Marvin	guitar
Tony Meehan	drums, percussion
Cliff Richard	vocals
Bruce Welch	rhythm guitar

Recording Details

Producer	Norrie Paramor
Engineered by	Peter Bown and Stuart Eltham
Recording location	Abbey Road Studio 2, St. John's Wood, London
Recording date	28th April 1959

2. The Young Ones

Musicians

Associated British Studio Orchestra	orchestra
Stanley Black	conductor
Cliff Richard	vocals

Recording Details

Producer	Norrie Paramor
Engineered by	Malcolm Addey and Alan Kane
Recording location	Abbey Road Studio 2, St. John's Wood, London
Recording date	9th August 1961

3. Cliff in Japan

Musicians

Norrie Paramor Orchestra	orchestra
Norrie Paramor	arranger, conductor
Cliff Richard	vocals
Unknown	backing vocals

Recording Details

Producer	Norrie Paramor
Engineered by	Unknown
Recording location	Shibuya Public Hall, Tokyo, Japan
Recording date	18th October 1967

4. Unissued track (Live at the Talk of the Town)

Musicians

Breakaways: Vicki Hasemen, Margo Quantrell, Jean Ryder	backing vocals
Norrie Paramor	arranger, conductor
Cliff Richard	vocals
Talk of the Town Orchestra	orchestra

Recording Details

Producer	Norrie Paramor
Engineered by	Peter Vince
Recording location	Talk of the Town Theatre, London
Recording date	30th May 1968

5. Cliff Live in Korea

Musicians

Brian Bennett	drums, percussion
Alan Hawkshaw	keyboards
Hank Marvin	guitar
Cliff Richard	vocals
John Rostill	bass
Bruce Welch	rhythm guitar

Recording Details

Producer	Unknown
Engineered by	Unknown
Recording location	Citizen Hall, Seoul, South Korea
Recording date	16th October 1969

6. *Cliff "Live" in Japan '72*

Musicians		*Recording Details*	
Brian Bennett	drums, percussion	Producer	Norrie Paramor
John Farrar	bass	Engineered by	Unknown
Alan Hawkshaw	piano	Recording location	Kosei Nenkin Hall, Tokyo, Japan
Hank Marvin	guitar	Recording date	22nd-23rd September 1972
Cliff Richard	vocals		
Bruce Welch	rhythm guitar		

7. *Single (The Young Ones)*

Musicians		*Recording Details*	
Stuart Colman	bass	Producer	Stuart Colman
Adrian Edmondson	vocals	Engineered by	Carb Kanelle and Damien Asker-Brown
Hank Marvin	lead guitar	Recording location	Master Rock Studios, London
Rik Mayall	vocals	Recording date	29th January 1986
Nigel Planer	vocals		
Tim Renwick	guitar		
Cliff Richard	vocals		
Christopher Ryan	vocals		
Howard Tibble	drums, percussion		
Pete Wingfield	keyboards		

8. *Single (The Young Ones – The Disco Funk Get Up Get Down Go to the Lavatory Mix)*

Musicians		*Recording Details*	
Stuart Colman	bass	Producer	Stuart Colman
Adrian Edmondson	spoken vocals, vocals	Engineered by	Carb Kanelle and Damien Asker-Brown
Hank Marvin	lead guitar	Recording location	Master Rock Studios, London
Rik Mayall	spoken vocals, vocals	Recording date	29th January 1986
Nigel Planer	spoken vocals, vocals		
Tim Renwick	guitar		
Cliff Richard	spoken vocals, vocals		
Christopher Ryan	spoken vocals, vocals		
Howard Tibble	drums, percussion		
Pete Wingfield	keyboards		

9. *Utterly Utterly Live!*

Musicians		*Recording Details*	
Adrian Edmondson	vocals	Producer	Stuart Colman and Geoffrey Perkins
Rik Mayall	vocals	Engineered by	Paul Vinall, Bob Krashaar and André Jacquemin
Nigel Planer	vocals	Recording location	Shaftesbury Theatre, London
Cliff Richard	vocals	Recording date	4th, 5th or 6th April 1986
Christopher Ryan	vocals		
Midge Ure	backing vocals (unconfirmed)		
Unknown	drums, percussion		
Unknown	guitar		
Unknown	bass		
Unknown	keyboards		

10. *Live & Guaranteed 1988!*

Musicians		*Recording Details*	
John Clark	guitar	Producer	Unknown
Rosemarie Ford	backing vocals	Engineered by	Unknown
Mark Griffiths	bass	Recording location	Fyens Forum, Odense, Denmark
Peter Howarth	backing vocals	Recording date	22nd May 1988
Steve Lauri	guitar		
Paul Moessl	keyboards		
Mick Mullins	backing vocals		
Alan Park	keyboards		
Cliff Richard	vocals		
Henry Spinetti	drums, percussion		

11. *Unissued track (From a Distance *** The Event)***

Musicians		*Recording Details*	
Ray Beavis	saxophone	Producer	Cliff Richard
Brian Bennett	drums, percussion	Engineered by	Keith Bessey and Mick McKenna
Mark Griffiths	bass	Recording location	Rolling Stones Mobile Studio, Wembley Stadium, Wembley, North-west London
Cliff Hall	keyboards		
Hank Marvin	guitar	Recording date	16th-17th June 1989
Cliff Richard	vocals		
Bruce Welch	rhythm guitar		

12. Unissued (Knebworth - The Album)

Musicians

Ray Beavis	saxophone
Brian Bennett	drums, percussion
John Earle	saxophone
Chris Gower	trombone
Mark Griffiths	bass
Cliff Hall	keyboards
Dick Hanson	trumpet
Peter Howarth	backing vocals
Hank Marvin	backing vocals, guitar
Paul Moessl	keyboards
Mick Mullins	backing vocals
Keith Murrell	backing vocals
Cliff Richard	vocals
Bruce Welch	backing vocals, guitar

Recording Details

Producer	Chris Kimsey and Steve Smith
Engineered by	Unknown
Recording location	Knebworth House, Hertfordshire, England
Recording date	30th June 1990

13. B-side (Peace in Our Time)

Musicians

Cliff Richard	vocals, guitar

Recording Details

Producer	Keith Bessey
Engineered by	Keith Bessey
Recording location	Wembley Arena, London
Recording date	27th-29th November 1992

14. Something Special

Musicians

Cliff Richard	vocals, guitar

Recording Details

Producer	Paul Raynor-Brown
Engineered by	Julius Warren
Recording location	Brighton Centre, Brighton
Recording date	7th June 1998

15. Unissued track (Party at the Palace)

Musicians

Sam Brown	backing vocals
Margo Buchanan	backing vocals
Phil Collins	drums, percussion
Ray Cooper	percussion
Claudia Fontaine	backing vocals
Pino Palladino	bass
Phil Palmer	guitar
Cliff Richard	vocals
Wix Wickens	keyboards

Recording Details

Producer	Giles Martin
Engineered by	Andy Rose
Recording location	Buckingham Palace, London
Mixed by	Paul Hicks (Abbey Road) and John Hudson and Greg Jackman (Mayfair)
Mixed at	Abbey Road Studios, St. John's Wood, London and Mayfair Studios, London
Recording date	3rd June 2002

16. Respect (Olsen Brothers)

Musicians

Jacob Andersen	percussion
Bjarke Falgren	violin
Poul Halberg	guitar
Chris Kreutzfeldt	additional drums, percussion
Stig Kreutzfeldt	arranger, guitar, bass, keyboards, programming
Noller	additional drums, percussion
Jørgen Olsen	vocals
Niels Olsen	vocals
Cliff Richard	backing vocals

Recording Details

Producer	Stig Kreutzfeldt
Engineered by	Unknown
Recording location	Badcat Studio, Copenhagen, Denmark (Olsen vocals and instruments) and Tinman Studio, Portugal (Cliff's vocals)
Recording date	9th-10th June 2008 (Cliff's vocals) and 2008 (remaining track)

17. Reunited

Musicians

Brian Bennett	drums, percussion
Mark Griffiths	bass
Hank Marvin	guitar
Cliff Richard	vocals
Bruce Welch	rhythm guitar

Recording Details

Producer	Warren Bennett (co-ordination)
Engineered by	James Collins (Honeyhill Studios), Ethan Carlson (Middle Ear Studios), Les Williams (Nivram Studios) and Keith Bessey (mixing and mastering)
Recording location	Middle Ear Studios, Miami, Florida, USA (Cliff's vocals), Nivram Studios, Perth, Western Australia (Hank's guitars and vocals) and Honeyhill Studios, Hertfordshire, England (all other vocals and instruments)
Recording date	Early 2009

♫ Living in Harmony

***57th UK single** and from the album **Cliff "Live" in Japan '72** and unissued track*

Written by Alan Tarney and Trevor Spencer, who would both be instrumental in Cliff's later career, *Living in Harmony* was originally recorded by Olivia Newton-John for her 1972 *Olivia* album. Although Cliff liked the song, he was reluctant to record it himself because he was unsure of the arrangement for his style of singing. Persuaded by manager Peter Gormley to go ahead with it, the arrangement was reworked producing something that Cliff was happy with. However, critics weren't particularly keen on the result and used it is a further example of Cliff's fading star. Recorded in studio three at Abbey Road as the only song from the session, *Living in Harmony* was backed with ***Empty Chairs*** (which had been recorded over two months earlier) and released as a single on the Columbia label (catalogue number DB 8917) on 28th July 1972 and it reached number twelve in the UK charts - one of his strongest showings for some time and the pinnacle of a musically poor year that only saw three singles released and two chart. *Living in Harmony* also marked the last time that Norrie Paramor worked on a Cliff single before his retirement, handing control over to new producer Dave McKay.

Although the song was a strong one that performed well as a charting single, for some reason, EMI didn't see fit to issue it on any 'best of...' compilations until it was eventually released on 1998 compilation *The Hits In Between* and again four years later on *The Singles Collection*.

With a group of kazoos almost taunting Cliff in the introduction, the progression through the song features him accompanying himself on backing vocals in addition to an uncredited choral group. Very much of its time, the countrified violin accompanied as well as the slow repetition of the opening phrase that gradually accelerates (such as can also be found in ***Congratulations***) all provide suitable hooks to make this song memorable and an amusing gem.

Picked up on the 1972 Japan tour as it had just been released as a single, kazoos are back with Hank Marvin providing the introduction and it continues with an intricate piano accompaniment and subdued backing vocals from Olivia Newton-John and Pat Carroll. The *a capella* section and subsequent accelerando is introduced by Cliff whispering "Wait for it!"

It was recorded on the 1974 Japanese tour set list but missed off the subsequent album, ***Japan Tour '74***, in spite of its recent success.

Track Specification
Composed by Alan Tarney and Trevor Spencer

1. Single

Musicians		*Recording Details*	
Nick Ingman	arranger, conductor	Producer	Norrie Paramor
Nick Ingman Orchestra	orchestra	Engineered by	Unknown
Cliff Richard	vocals, backing vocals	Recording location	Abbey Road Studio 3, St. John's Wood, London
Unknown	backing vocals	Recording date	4th July 1972

2. Cliff "Live" in Japan '72

Musicians		*Recording Details*	
Brian Bennett	drums, percussion	Producer	Norrie Paramor
Pat Carroll	backing vocals	Engineered by	Unknown
John Farrar	bass	Recording location	Kosei Nenkin Hall, Tokyo, Japan
Alan Hawkshaw	piano	Recording date	22nd-23rd September 1972
Hank Marvin	kazoo, guitar		
Olivia Newton-John	backing vocals		
Cliff Richard	vocals		
Bruce Welch	rhythm guitar		

3. Unissued track (Japan Tour '74)

Musicians		*Recording Details*	
Barrie Guard	arranger, conductor, piano	Producer	Toshiba EMI (no individual detailed)
Cliff Hall	piano	Engineered by	Toshiba EMI (no individual detailed)
Brian Lewis	backing vocals, guitar	Recording location	Shinjuku Koseinenkin, Tokyo, Japan
Kevin Peak	acoustic guitar	Recording date	7th-8th October 1974
Cliff Richard	vocals		
Shambles Symphonet	orchestra		
Trevor Spencer	drums, percussion		
Alan Tarney	backing vocals, bass		
Bruce Welch	backing vocals, rhythm guitar		

♫ Livin' Lovin' Doll

3rd UK single

Cliff's third single marked a few changes. First, in comparison with the recording of the previous two singles, it was the first time that the Drifters were allowed by Norrie Paramor to back Cliff Richard fully in the studio. This was almost wholly due to the fact that Ian Samwell had been replaced by Hank Marvin and Bruce Welch, and Jet Harris had been added as the Drifters' bassist (using an electric bass rather than the double bass), while Terry Smart remained with the group and brought a professional edge that meant session musicians (other than orchestral arrangements) were no longer required. And, third, it was the first single not to make it into the top ten, stalling as it did at number twenty. At the time,

this slow decline in chart success would have perhaps marked a lesser talent as being on the wane but there was something magical that was now experienced with the ensemble performance of Cliff with his permanent group.
It wasn't straightforward for Marvin, however, because, once again, Ernie Shear was originally allocated the job of playing lead guitar but, as he recalls in interview, Cliff wasn't happy with the set up and it was he who convinced Norrie Paramor to give Marvin a try. There was something in his guitar technique that finally convinced Paramor and, from that point on, there was no question that the Drifters and then the metamorphosed Shadows should not be Cliff's backing group.
At the time of recording *Livin' Lovin' Doll*, Cliff Richard was involved with his first film project, *Serious Charge*, in which he played the singing brother of a ne'er-do-well, who accuses the new vicar of molestation to spite him for manslaughter charges levelled at him in turn by the vicar. Cliff performs a number of songs in his role, including a fast-paced version of ***Living Doll***. Part of the film contract for Cliff dictated that there should be an associated single release to assist with the publicity; however, Paramor wasn't happy with this arrangement and, in an attempt to derail those plans, he insisted that Cliff and the Drifters should record *Livin' Lovin' Doll* earlier than the *Living Doll* single that was planned. It can be no coincidence that the titles are so similar but what Paramor hadn't bargained for was that *Livin' Lovin' Doll* was the poorer song, particularly as a follow-up to the relatively disappointing ***High Class Baby***. In the event, Bruce Welch suggested slowing *Living Doll*'s tempo down and making it more like a country song, thereby giving Cliff a new direction musically speaking and his first number one.
Livin' Lovin' Doll is somewhat derivative of the rock and roll genre, although the guitar-playing and rhythm is a lot cleaner than in previous singles and B-sides, showing Hank's mastery of the instrument, particularly in the middle eight guitar solo. The tight ensemble performance lift the song from something could have been quite dull on a track that is a love song that uses clichés to describe the singer's feelings. Although it is a strong vocal performance by Cliff, it is mixed quite far back in the recording. For all these reasons, it's understandable that the single was not as popular as earlier offerings.
The single was released in January 1959, backed with ***Steady with You*** recorded a few days later, on the Columbia label (catalogue numbers DB 4249 (78 r.p.m. version) and 45-DB 4249 (seven-inch single version)) and has appeared on a number of compilations covering Cliff's early years.

Track Specification
Composed by Johnny May and Jim Gustard

Musicians

Jet Harris	bass
Hank Marvin	guitar
Cliff Richard	vocals
Terry Smart	drums, percussion
Bruce Welch	rhythm guitar

Recording Details

Producer	Norrie Paramor
Engineered by	Peter Bown and Stuart Eltham
Recording location	Abbey Road Studio 2, St. John's Wood, London
Recording date	14th November 1958

♫ Locked Inside Your Prison

From the album **Silver**

Recorded as part of the sessions that resulted in the dual album release of ***Silver*** and ***Rock 'n' Roll Silver*** issued by Cliff Richard to celebrate his twenty-fifth anniversary in the music business, *Locked Inside Your Prison* appeared on the *Silver* portion of the album, which was also the first long-player to be simultaneously released in CD format.
Introduced by synthesized percussion, Cliff's backing vocals are electronically altered to appear in the different stereo channels. The oppressive beat that creates the claustrophobia of a prison opens up to a broad synthesized orchestra as he pleads for freedom, which then leads into an interesting saxophone solo before returning control to the claustrophobia of the first verse.

Track Specification
Composed by Bob Heatlie

Musicians

Mel Collins	saxophone
Craig Pruess	arranger, keyboards, synthesiser
Cliff Richard	vocals, backing vocals

Recording Details

Producer	Craig Pruess
Engineered by	Keith Bessey
Recording location	Strawberry Studios South, Surrey
Recording date	19th May 1983, 3rd June 1983 and/or 16th June 1983

♫ London Ist Nicht Weit

German single

Originally a Hank Marvin recording that was released as a single by him in January 1968, ***London's Not Too Far*** was recorded in English by Cliff Richard and the Shadows at a session on 8th March 1968 that was then released on ***Sincerely Cliff Richard*** the next year. The following week, Cliff recorded two German language tracks including a translated version retitled to *London Ist Nicht Weit* (a straightforward translation from the English); however, there is some confusion as to which musicians appear on the track with a suggestion that it may well be the same backing track as appears for the English version – certainly, both tracks sound similar, although the German version is slightly faster in performance. In the liner notes of ***On the Continent***, the album of all Cliff's foreign language recordings, the implication is clear that there are differences, while the book *The Complete Recording Sessions 1958-1990* indicates that it was a completely fresh recording.

Backed with the German song ***Mrs Emily Jones***, *London Ist Nicht Weit* was released as a single in Germany on the international Columbia label (catalogue number C-23777) in August 1968 but failed to make any impression on the parochial charts. Originally released in mono, as was Columbia's policy at the time for singles, the track and its B-side were major rarities for collectors until the stereo version was released on the aforementioned *On the Continent* album.
The German recording of the song seems to lose something from the English original, although it is a perfectly good version of the song. The arrangement by Mike Leander matches anything he has done before for Cliff, while Cliff imbues the lyrics with the sadness of the situation of the runaway girl.

Track Specification
Composed by Hank Marvin; German lyrics by Hans Bradtke

Musicians

Breakaways:	backing vocals
Vicki Hasemen	
Margo Quantrell	
Jean Ryder	
Mike Leander	arranger, conductor
Mike Leander Orchestra	orchestra
Cliff Richard	vocals

Recording Details

Producer	Norrie Paramor
Engineered by	Peter Vince
Recording location	Abbey Road Studio 2, St. John's Wood, London
Recording date	15th March 1968

♬ London's Not Too Far

From the albums **Sincerely Cliff Richard** *and* **Live at the Talk of the Town**

Recorded in March 1968 by Cliff Richard, *London's Not Too Far* was not released for another two years until ***Sincerely Cliff Richard***, although Cliff started performing the song at his concerts including the show from the Talk of the Town. Hank had already issued the song as a solo single at the start of the year (although backed by the Shadows) and, although not a hit, it was reasonably familiar by the time Cliff recorded it and used it in his performances – indeed, he made a German language single released as ***London Ist Nicht Weit***, which may have used the backing track from the English recording.
The staccato, shimmering strings and the brass melody in the introduction evoke a somewhat stereotypical picture of a northern English town. The song tells the story of a girl preparing to leave home and run away to London to meet a man she has seen on television. The clever story has a sting in its tale tugging on the heart-strings when the final line reveals she's just five years old. Cliff packs his vocal line with emotion and he uses his increasing vibrato to great effect.
For his concerts, Cliff performed the song as part of Hank's Medley: *London's Not Too Far*, ***The Dreams I Dream*** and ***The Day I Met Marie***, with the latter being the only Cliff original.

Track Specification
Composed by Hank Marvin

1. Sincerely Cliff Richard

Musicians

Breakaways:	backing vocals
Vicki Hasemen	
Margo Quantrell	
Jean Ryder	
Brian Bennett	drums, percussion
Hank Marvin	guitar
Cliff Richard	vocals
John Rostill	bass
Bruce Welch	rhythm guitar

Recording Details

Producer	Norrie Paramor
Engineered by	Peter Vince
Recording location	Abbey Road Studio 2, St. John's Wood, London
Recording date	8th March 1968

2. Live at the Talk of the Town

Musicians

Breakaways:	backing vocals
Vicki Hasemen	
Margo Quantrell	
Jean Ryder	
Norrie Paramor	arranger, conductor
Cliff Richard	vocals
Talk of the Town Orchestra	orchestra

Recording Details

Producer	Norrie Paramor
Engineered by	Peter Vince
Recording location	Talk of the Town Theatre, London
Recording date	30th May 1968

♬ Lonely Girl

From the album **Two a Penny**

Continuing his renewed interest in songwriting, Cliff Richard worked with orchestral arranger and conductor Mike Leander on *Lonely Girl*, which eventually appeared on the ***Two a Penny*** album as one of the filler tracks, since it didn't appear on the soundtrack. Recorded along with another Cliff and Mike Lander composition, ***(And Me) I'm on the Outside Now***, at the second session of the day, it was the first song to be completed.
The song is a very bittersweet tune that has some exquisitely beautiful musical intervals that Cliff makes the most of during his vocal lines. Mike Leander's arrangement for the orchestra increases the sense of sadness for the lonely girl of the title that is matched by the single backing vocal from the Breakaways.

Track Specification
Composed by Cliff Richard and Mike Leander
Musicians

Breakaways:	backing vocals
Vicki Hasemen	
Margo Quantrell	
Jean Ryder	
Mike Leander	arranger, conductor
Mike Leander Orchestra	orchestra
Cliff Richard	vocals

Recording Details

Producer	Norrie Paramor
Engineered by	Peter Vince
Recording location	Abbey Road Studio 2, St. John's Wood, London
Recording date	8th March 1968

♫ Long Ago (and Far Away)
From the album **Love Is Forever**

Written for the soundtrack of the musical *Cover Girl* in 1944 starring Gene Kelly and Rita Hayworth, *Long Ago (and Far Away)* was composed by Jerome Kern and lyricist Ira Gershwin. Published that same year and selling large numbers of sheet music, the first recording of it to chart was by Dick Haymes and Helen Forrest, who reached number two in the US Billboard charts. This was quickly followed by Jo Stafford a couple of months later, reaching number six, and Bing Crosby a month later who reached number five. Finally Perry Como reached number eight with his rendition released at the same time. Although it has never charted in the UK, it has been covered by a number of popular artists including Engelbert Humperdinck, Kiri Te Kanawa, Oscar Peterson, Stan Kenton, Chet Baker, Percy Faith, Judy Garland, Pat Boone, Doris Day, Bobby Darin, Lesley Garrett, Frank Sinatra, Marni Nixon, Rod Stewart and Mantovani among several others.
Cliff Richard's recording was completed at a session that secured a total of four tracks for the upcoming ***Love Is Forever*** album. The final (unknown) take and edit was used for both the mono and stereo recordings but with differing mixes to cater for the requirements of the audio channels. Although the orchestra used was the Norrie Paramor Orchestra, Norrie Paramor remained in the producer's chair while Ken Woodman took over the arrangement and conducting.
With staccato chords on the strings, twinkling pianos and thudding bass, Cliff carries off the rather unmemorable song well. It has a lot of promise but doesn't seem to go anywhere.

Track Specification
Composed by Jerome Kern and Ira Gershwin
Musicians

Norrie Paramor Orchestra	orchestra
Cliff Richard	vocals
Ken Woodman	arranger, conductor

Recording Details

Producer	Norrie Paramor
Engineered by	Unknown
Recording location	Abbey Road Studio 2, St. John's Wood, London
Recording date	10th June 1965

♫ Long Long Time
From the album **The 31st of February Street**

Covered by a number of artists including Andy Williams, Gene Ammons, Alannah Myles, Spectrum, Carl Wayne, Jerry Jeff Walker, Mindy McCready, Lyn Anderson, Melanie and Linda Ronstadt, Cliff Richard recorded his version for the concept album ***The 31st of February Street***. Recorded at four main sessions for the album in February 1974, *Long Long Time* was completed in eight takes.
The song is initiated with a guitar and string section that builds up to a choir backing Cliff's lead vocals while the simple harp, flutes and arpeggiated guitar continue onwards in this pretty and brilliantly emotive song. The guitar introductions to each verse and chorus sound similar to the guitar work from ***(You Keep Me) Hangin' On*** but there the similarity ends.

Track Specification
Composed by Gary White
Musicians

Terry Britten	backing vocals, guitar
Barrie Guard	arranger, conductor
Jean Hawker	backing vocals
Gordon Huntley	steel guitar
David MacKay	backing vocals
Anna Peacock	backing vocals
Kevin Peek	acoustic guitar
Cliff Richard	vocals
Alan Tarney	backing vocals, bass
Unknown	orchestra

Recording Details

Producer	David MacKay
Engineered by	Tony Clark and Mike Jarrett
Recording location	Abbey Road Studio 2, St. John's Wood, London
Recording date	13th and 14th February 1974

♫ Long Tall Sally
CD B-side of **All I Have to Do Is Dream/Miss You Nights**

Co-written by Little Richard under his real name of Richard Penniman, *Long Tall Sally* was actually recorded and released by Pat Boone before Richard's more familiar version was issued. Boone reached number eighteen in the summer of 1956, while Richard would have to wait until February 1957 to get to number three in the British charts, in spite of his recording it the year before. The converse was true in the US, where Richard's version was released just before Boone's but still made more of an impression on the parochial charts. Since then, it has been recorded by such luminaries as the Beatles, Elvis Presley, the Kinks, Jerry Lee Lewis, the Scorpions and Heart.

As part of a BBC documentary about Cliff Richard, a number of live tracks were recorded at the Hammersmith Odeon and Manchester Apollo to accompany the broadcast. Some tracks were licensed for release at the time resulting in the ***Daddy's Home*** single, while others remained with the BBC. Thirteen years afterwards, the section featuring the duets with Phil Everly, Cliff spent time remixing and cleaning up the product that emerged in the release of the double A-sided ***All I Have to Do Is Dream*** and a remixed version of ***Miss You Nights***. While the seven-inch single release was restricted to just those tracks, the first of the dual CD single discs had two additional tracks, both featuring Cliff and Everly together, ***When Will I Be Loved?*** and ***Tribute to the Legends Medley***, of which *Long Tall Sally* formed part. It is interesting to note that, while Cliff often performed songs that he had not recorded in the studios, it is curious that his only released attempt at *Long Tall Sally* was as part of a medley.

Cliff leads into the song with the first line before being joined by Everly. The jaunty rocker plays out well with a saxophone solo played by Howie Casey, before relinquishing control back to the singers.

Track Specification

Composed by Enotris Johnson, Richard Penniman and Robert Blackwell

Musicians

Howie Casey	saxophone
John Clark	guitar
Phil Everly	vocals
Mark Griffiths	bass
Graham Jarvis	drums, percussion
Martin Jenner	guitar
Alan Park	keyboards
Cliff Richard	vocals
Graham Todd	keyboards

Recording Details

Producer	Cliff Richard
Engineered by	Unknown
Recording location	Hammersmith Odeon, London
Remixed at	R. G. Jones Studio, London
Recording date	1st May 1981 (live track) and 7th September 1994 (remix)

♫ Long Way Home, The

Unissued track

Recorded at the first session on 10th June 1968 after the final session to feature Cliff Richard and the Shadows together (until ***Reunited***), *The Long Way Home* was one of four songs attempted at the session but was not satisfactorily completed. The first song of the day, *The Long Way Home* remains unissued and there are no details available regarding the composer(s). There is a possibility that there is a backing vocal group (that may be female only) since they were involved in other recordings at the time this was recorded, but there is no paperwork to confirm this.

Track Specification

Composed by Unknown

Musicians

Mike Leander	conductor
Mike Leander Orchestra	orchestra
Cliff Richard	vocals

Recording Details

Producer	Norrie Paramor
Engineered by	Peter Vince
Recording location	Abbey Road Studio 3, St. John's Wood, London
Recording date	1st July 1968

♫ Look Before You Love

B-side of **The Time in Between**

Recorded at a double session at studios in Portugal, *Look Before You Love* was chosen as the B-side of Cliff Richard's thirty-first single, ***The Time in Between***. The final (unknown) take and edit was used for both the mono and stereo recordings but with different mixes for the separate audio channels. The B-side, like its A-side, was only released in mono format, as it was on the track listing of the ***Wind Me Up*** EP. It would be over forty years later that this rare song would be reissued, in stereo format this time, on the celebratory anthology ***...And They Said It Wouldn't Last! (My 50 Years in Music)***.

The performance is as polished as would be expected from Cliff and the Shadows and, although it is a pleasant enough song with a Spanish feel, it is not overly memorable. There is a tambourine that is shaken and tapped on the second beat of each bar and the blending of the vocal harmonies are, as always, spot on.

Track Specification

Composed by Chris Arnold, Geoff Morrow and David Martin

Musicians

Brian Bennett	drums, percussion
Hank Marvin	backing vocals, guitar
Norrie Paramor Orchestra	orchestra
Norrie Paramor	arranger, conductor
Cliff Richard	vocals, tambourine
John Rostill	backing vocals, bass
Unknown	piano
Bruce Welch	backing vocals, rhythm guitar

Recording Details

Producer	Norrie Paramor
Engineered by	Unknown
Recording location	Estudios Valentim de Carvalho, Lisbon, Portugal
Recording date	10th May 1965

♫ Look Don't Touch

From the album **Cliff Richard at the Movies 1959-1974**

The penultimate song to be recorded that featured Brian Locking on bass before he left the Shadows to focus on his religion, *Look Don't Touch* was originally intended to be included on the soundtrack of the ***Wonderful Life*** film but, for some undocumented reason, was rejected. It was kept in the EMI vaults for over thirty years until it was given a release as part of the film anthology CD set ***Cliff Richard at the Movies 1959-1974***. Only ever released in mono format, it was the only song recorded at that session with an unknown take used for eventual release, although it is likely that a stereo version would have been mixed. It has since appeared on the remastered version of the film soundtrack album.

It would have been a welcome addition to a lacklustre soundtrack that relied too heavily on the orchestral dance numbers. Here the bass line is intricate and Hank Marvin's witty guitar line, coupled with the rhythm section is an aural gem that would have stood up well if it had been released as a single in its own right. Cliff performs with accustomed ease, particularly in the sections where the instrumentation stops dramatically to underline the lyrics.

Track Specification

Composed by Unknown

Musicians

Brian Bennett	drums, percussion
Brian 'Licorice' Locking	bass
Hank Marvin	guitar
Cliff Richard	vocals
Bruce Welch	rhythm guitar

Recording Details

Producer	Norrie Paramor
Engineered by	Malcolm Addey
Recording location	Abbey Road Studio 3, St. John's Wood, London
Recording date	8th November 1963

♫ Look Homeward Angel

From the album **Love Is Forever**

Made famous by Johnny Ray, who reached number seven in the UK singles charts in February 1957, *Look Homeward Angel* has also been covered by artists such as Ray Conniff, the Fortunes and the Blue Things.

Cliff Richard recorded his version for the ***Love Is Forever*** album, a year or so before it was issued, in a session that yielded much for that album and its predecessor ***Cliff Richard***. Recorded in only two takes, that final take and edit was used for the mono and stereo recordings but with different mixes for the separate audio channel needs.

The piano-driven version by Cliff relies a lot on the backing vocals, which detracts occasionally from the beauty of the song. Cliff's vocals are natural and, with a slight vibrato on the sustained notes, he imbues the meaning of the lyrics with light and shade, by incorporating forte and piano sections as the song demands. This ability to understand the musical needs of the song he is singing sets Cliff apart from many of his contemporaries and also explains his longevity in the music business.

Track Specification

Composed by Wally Gold

Musicians

Mike Sammes Singers	backing vocals
Norrie Paramor Orchestra	orchestra
Norrie Paramor	arranger, conductor
Cliff Richard	vocals

Recording Details

Producer	Norrie Paramor
Engineered by	Malcolm Addey
Recording location	Abbey Road Studio 2, St. John's Wood, London
Recording date	17th July 1964

♫ Look in My Eyes Maria

From the EP **Look in My Eyes Maria**

Another song from the huge cannon of the writing partnership of Burt Bacharach and Hal David, *Look in My Eyes Maria* was one of the songs chosen for Cliff Richard to record during his American sojourn, where he had a succession of recording sessions at the Columbia studios in Nashville and New York. Giving its name to the title of an EP as well, the song was originally only released in mono format. However, twenty-five years later, the stereo version was issued on the See For Miles compilation ***The EP Collection: Ballads and Love Songs***. The seventh and final take and edit were used for the mono and stereo recordings but with different mixes for the separate audio channels. The song is a much sought-after rarity in both mono and stereo formats.

An archetypal Bacharach and David song, *Look in My Eyes Maria* relies on the orchestral brass arrangement underneath Cliff's anguished vocals for its quintessential hooks. A love song that beseeches his lover Maria to look into his eyes to see the truth of his words, the quirky percussion and arrangement make this a song that would have had broader appeal than the EP.

Track Specification

Composed by Burt Bacharach and Hal David

Musicians

Cliff Richard	vocals
Gary Sherman	conductor
Unknown	orchestra

Recording Details

Producer	Bob Morgan
Engineered by	Frank Laico
Recording location	Columbia Studios, New York
Recording date	21st August 1964

♫ Look of Love, The

From the album **Cliff "Live" in Japan '72**

The Look of Love was written by Burt Bacharach and Hal David for Dusty Springfield to sing on the soundtrack of *Casino Royale* and was inspired by Ursula Andress's character's seduction of Peter Sellers' character. The song received an Oscar nomination and reached the top forty in America, while it wasn't released in the UK. The song was later used in the 1997 Bond-genre spoof *Austin Powers: International Man of Mystery*, this time sung by Susanna Hoffs. Other covers include Jack Jones, Shirley Bassey, Diana Krall, Isaac Hayes, Marvin Gaye, Nina Simone and Grover Washington, Jr., among others.
Cliff Richard's version of *The Look of Love* was one of a handful that he performed in concert and on television but never recorded in the studio. For the Japan tour in September 1972, it was performed as a medley with ***Walk on By***, something that was tried by Cliff and Cilla Black on her 1969 television show and released on a DVD of clips in 2009. In Japan, though, Olivia Newton-John and Pat Carroll stepped up to take over the lead vocals, while Cliff sang harmonies before taking the lead himself. The resultant vocals are exquisite and the three voices meld together perfectly.

Track Specification
Composed by Burt Bacharach and Hal David

Musicians

Brian Bennett	drums, percussion
Pat Carroll	backing vocals
John Farrar	bass
Alan Hawkshaw	piano
Hank Marvin	guitar
Olivia Newton-John	backing vocals
Cliff Richard	vocals
Bruce Welch	rhythm guitar

Recording Details

Producer	Norrie Paramor
Engineered by	Unknown
Recording location	Kosei Nenkin Hall, Tokyo, Japan
Recording date	22nd-23rd September 1972

♫ Look Up, Look Down

From the album **Respect** *(The Olsen Brothers) and unreleased track*

The Olsen Brothers, big in Scandinavia but less well-known in Britain, invited Cliff Richard to sing a duet of a new song, *Look Up, Look Down*, which was recorded for their 2008 album *Respect*.
Fluttering percussion introduces what is a foot-stomping rock song and the brothers and Cliff share the lead vocals, joining together in the chorus. A missing gem in Cliff's wide recording career, it deserves broader distribution than this foreign album. The arrangement's pace and ingenuity with Cliff's energy makes the song the best on the album.
At the same time as recording the duet, Cliff recorded a solo version; that is, with the Olsen Brothers' providing backing vocals only and Cliff taking the lead. It was reportedly for an upcoming album but this has yet to be issued.

Track Specification
Composed by Jørgen Olsen and Stig Kreutzfeldt

1. Respect (Olsen Brothers)

Musicians

Jacob Andersen	percussion
Nicolai Bøgelund	trombone
Bjarke Falgren	violin
Poul Halberg	guitar
Chris Kreutzfeldt	drums, percussion
Stig Kreutzfeldt	arranger, backing vocals, guitar, bass, keyboards
Jørgen Olsen	vocals
Niels Olsen	vocals
Cliff Richard	vocals, backing vocals
Jimmi Riise	tenor saxophone
Jette Schandorf	bass
Lars Vissing	trumpet

Recording Details

Producer	Stig Kreutzfeldt
Engineered by	Unknown
Recording location	Badcat Studio, Copenhagen, Denmark (Olsen vocals and instruments) and Tinman Studio, Portugal (Cliff's vocals)
Recording date	9th-10th June 2008 (Cliff's vocals) and 2008 (remaining track)

2. Unissued track (Respect sessions)

Musicians

Jacob Andersen	percussion
Nicolai Bøgelund	trombone
Bjarke Falgren	violin
Poul Halberg	guitar
Chris Kreutzfeldt	drums, percussion
Stig Kreutzfeldt	arranger, backing vocals, guitar, bass, keyboards
Jørgen Olsen	backing vocals
Niels Olsen	backing vocals
Cliff Richard	vocals
Jimmi Riise	tenor saxophone
Jette Schandorf	bass
Lars Vissing	trumpet

Recording Details

Producer	Stig Kreutzfeldt
Engineered by	Unknown
Recording location	Badcat Studio, Copenhagen, Denmark (Olsen vocals and instruments) and Tinman Studio, Portugal (Cliff's vocals)
Recording date	9th-10th June 2008 (Cliff's vocals) and 2008 (remaining track)

♫ Lord, I Love You

From the album **Sail Away** *(Dave Pope)*

With Cliff Richard at the helm of Dave Pope's ***Sail Away*** album sessions, it is perhaps inevitable that at least one Cliff composition would be included. Recorded in the spring of 1978 just as work was concluding on the ***Green Light*** album, the reference material including the sleeve does not give any information regarding the musicians involved. As such, until further research identifies them, they will be annotated as unknown in the track specification.
The song would later be sung in concert by Cliff but, to date, he has not recorded a studio version under his own name. A sophisticated guitar solo introduces the song as Pope's voice takes over with an evocative yearning expressing the meaning of the lyrics. The verse is lifted by the fast walking pace of the percussion undercurrent, while the middle eight guitar solo is reminiscent of early seventies Cliff material. Unusually there are no backing vocals on this track.

Track Specification
Composed by Cliff Richard

Musicians	
Dave Pope	vocals
Unknown	guitar
Unknown	bass
Unknown	keyboards
Unknown	drums, percussion

Recording Details	
Producer	Cliff Richard
Engineered by	Tony Clark
Recording location	Morgan Studios, London
Recording date	April 1978

♫ Lord, I Miss the Rain

From the album **Sail Away** *(Dave Pope)*

John Daniels wrote a large percentage of the songs that appear on Dave Pope's album ***Sail Away,*** which was produced by Cliff Richard, including *Lord, I Miss the Rain*. The reference material available and album sleeve provide no information on the musicians involved in the sessions; as a consequence, these are annotated as unknown in the track specification for this entry until further information has been sought.
The instrumental arrangement behind Pope's impassioned vocals features quirky synthesisers, aggressive guitar chords and a tinkling piano. The backing vocals add an interesting dimension to the performance.

Track Specification
Composed by John Daniels

Musicians	
Dave Pope	vocals
Cliff Richard	backing vocals
Unknown	backing vocals
Unknown	guitar
Unknown	bass
Unknown	piano
Unknown	keyboards
Unknown	drums, percussion

Recording Details	
Producer	Cliff Richard
Engineered by	Tony Clark
Recording location	Morgan Studios, London
Recording date	April 1978

♫ Lord's Prayer, The

From the album **Hopes & Dreams** *(Various)*

The Lord's Prayer is probably the most famous and well-known prayer (in competition with Grace) in the Christian religion, which simply reveres the Christian God, asking Him for forgiveness and for the ability to deal with other's transgressions as well as ensuring there is sufficient to feed the supplicant. Taken directly from the Bible, it was realized that the tune that is most often associated with the oncoming New Year, *Auld Lang Syne*, otherwise referred to as *Roud*, could be used to sing the prayer (albeit with a little manipulation).
Cliff Richard recorded the song for an album entitled *Hopes & Dreams* and it was his only involvement with that project but this quickly took on a life of its own. With a little more arrangement, it was transmogrified into ***The Millennium Prayer***, which Cliff would also record the following year and take the song to number one.

Track Specification
Composed by Traditional; arranged by Paul Field and Stephen Deal

Musicians	
Pete Desmond	arranger, conductor
Cliff Richard	vocals
Unknown	orchestra

Recording Details	
Producer	Paul Field
Engineered by	Gerry Kitchingham
Recording location	R. G. Jones Studios, Wimbledon, London
Recording date	10th June 1998

♫ Lost in a Lonely World

From the album **Wired for Sound**

Chris Eaton would go on to have a long association with writing catchy religious songs for Cliff Richard to record after the start of the eighties. He submitted five songs for Cliff to consider during the ***Wired for Sound*** album preparations and had two chosen: *Lost in a Lonely World* and ***Summer Rain***, which follows immediately in the album's track listing.

One of the few songs on the album to have an additional musician, here John Clark on guitar, which is heard right from the outset in amongst the electronica performed by Tarney, it has Cliff's lead vocals with a strong echo added to it. Cliff and Tarney also supply the backing vocals to this bouncing, foot-tapping gem hidden in the middle of the track listing.

Track Specification
Composed by Chris Eaton

Musicians		*Recording Details*	
John Clark	guitar	Producer	Alan Tarney
Graham Jarvis	drums, percussion	Engineered by	Michael Boddicker and Ian Little
Cliff Richard	vocals, backing vocals	Recording location	Gallery Studios, Chertsey, Surrey
Alan Tarney	arranger, backing vocals, guitar, bass, keyboards	Recording date	27th May-9th July 1981

♫ Love

From the EP **Expresso Bongo**

One of the three songs performed by Cliff Richard and the Shadows in the film *Expresso Bongo* (excluding the Shadows instrumental *Bongo Blues*), it was issued in both mono and stereo for the film's EP. The take used is the same for both formats, although the mixes are necessarily different for the purpose of optimal stereophonic sound. The film explores a satire based on the music industry, where a promoter finds a teenage singer (Cliff as Bongo Herbert) and exploits him using cynical ploys to guarantee hit records. *Love* appears in the film just as Herbert's career is taking off. The track was issued on the *Cliff at the Movies* album and then on ***...And They Said It Wouldn't Last (My Fifty Years in Music)*** compilation.

The version on the film has a lengthy introduction by the Shadows, while the recorded version for the EP has Cliff singing almost immediately. In the film, too, it is Cliff who is seen playing the bongos, playing in character to the name chosen for him by the promoter: there are bongos on this EP track but there is no information readily available as to whether it is Cliff, Tony Meehan or some other musician playing them, since there are also drums and percussion accompanying the performance. This will be highlighted as unknown until further information becomes available.

The song is a fast-paced piece of rock and roll with a great guitar performance from Hank Marvin (using his tremolo arm to great effect) with a running bass line by Jet Harris, which shows his competence and how under-rated he was as a musician. Cliff's vocals are on comfortable territory and there are echoes of his earlier hits in the performance while still making the song into something that sounds unique at a time when the market was saturated with copycat sounds.

Track Specification
Composed by Norrie Paramor and Bunny Lewis

Musicians		*Recording Details*	
Jet Harris	bass	Producer	Norrie Paramor
Hank Marvin	guitar	Engineered by	Malcolm Addey and Alan Kane (mono) and Stuart Eltham and Norman Smith (stereo)
Tony Meehan	drums, percussion		
Cliff Richard	vocals	Recording location	Abbey Road Studio 2, St. John's Wood, London
Unknown	bongos	Recording date	8th September 1959
Bruce Welch	rhythm guitar		

♫ Love and a Helping Hand

B-side of **Little Town**

Keeping it simple with just vocals and keyboards, Cliff Richard recorded his own song at a separate session from the ***Now You See Me... Now You Don't*** album sessions. The third single from that album project was ***Little Town*** and, rather than having one B-side, two were used making it a maxi-single. *Love and a Helping Hand* – which the single states as being taken from the film *Cliff in Kenya* – and ***You, Me and Jesus*** were released on the B-side with both songs providing the same sort of message in the lyrics. The track didn't have to wait long to be reissued (unlike many of Cliff's non-album B-sides), since it was picked up for re-release on LP and CD on the ***Walking in the Light*** album, and subsequently being issued as a bonus track on the 2002 remaster of *Now You See Me... Now You Don't*.

This is an extraordinarily beautiful song that is expressed emotionally by Cliff with a lead vocal imbued with his vibrato as well as the strong harmonized vocals, which he also supplies. As the song moves forward, there are some surprising chord changes, and then there is a sequence of Cliff singing against himself in a kind of rondo. Given that Cliff denigrates is own songwriting capabilities, if there is any evidence required how incorrect this assertion is, this song stands up as the certainty of what he can produce.

Track Specification
Composed by Cliff Richard

Musicians		*Recording Details*	
Craig Pruess	keyboards	Producer	Cliff Richard and Craig Pruess
Cliff Richard	vocals, backing vocals	Engineered by	Keith Bessey
Unknown	guitar	Recording location	Abbey Road Studios, St. John's Wood, London
		Recording date	June 1982

♫ Love Is Enough
B-side of **Miss You Nights**

Recorded by its writer Tim Moore as well as being covered by Becky Hobbs, Cliff Richard recorded the song at the first of his sessions of 1975, with his friends Hank Marvin, Bruce Welch and John Farrar on production duties. The first of two songs to be finished that day (the other being ***It's Only Me You've Left Behind***), further vocal overdubs were added a couple of weeks later. It would be a further ten months before it was released as the B-side of ***Miss You Nights***, which was reissued later in 1982 in the same format. The song was not released in any other format until it appeared as a bonus track on the remastered CD album ***I'm Nearly Famous*** in 2001.

Introduced with the piano and the harmonics on the guitar frets, Cliff's vocals are then supported by uncredited strings. A mark of the songs he recorded in this period is the backing vocals, which are mostly attributable to Bruce, who took this into his later production of Cliff's albums. The beauty of the song is understated and Cliff carries off the performance with his standard self-assuredness.

Track Specification

Composed by Tim Moore

Musicians

Terry Britten	guitar
Clem Cattini	drums, percussion
Tony Harding	backing vocals
John Perry	backing vocals
Cliff Richard	vocals
Tony Rivers	backing vocals
Alan Tarney	bass
Graham Todd	piano
Unknown	conductor
Unknown	orchestra

Recording Details

Producer	Hank Marvin, Bruce Welch and John Farrar
Engineered by	Tony Clark
Recording location	Abbey Road Studio 2 and 3, St. John's Wood, London
Recording date	27th January and 7th February 1975

♫ Love Is Here
B-side of **(You Keep Me) Hangin' On**

Co-written by Petrina Lordan – who had also co-written ***Love, Truth and Emily Stone*** for Cliff Richard – *Love Is Here* was recorded as part of the four-day sessions planned for completing most of Cliff's album ***The 31st of February Street*** in mid-February 1974. Taking six takes to complete the recording, *Love Is Here* was chosen as the B-side of the only 1974 single released by Cliff, ***(You Keep Me) Hangin' On)***. Only available in its B-side format for many years, it was eventually reissued as a bonus track on the remastered album *The 31st of February Street* in 2004.

Following on from the country styling of its A-side, *Love Is Here* follows in similar style with steel guitars and piano accompanying the lead vocal line by Cliff. The upbeat nature makes it a quirky gem from Cliff's back catalogue.

Almost immediately after the release of the single, Cliff returned to the Morgan Studios to record a German version of *Love Is Here*, translated to ***Liebeslied***, to back the German version of its A-side, ***Es Gehören Zwei zum Glücklichsein***.

Track Specification

Composed by Petrina Lordan and John Franklin

Musicians

Terry Britten	guitar
Barrie Guard	arranger, conductor, percussion
Cliff Hall	piano
Gordon Huntley	steel guitar
Dave MacRae	keyboards
Kevin Peek	acoustic guitar
Cliff Richard	vocals
Trevor Spencer	drums, percussion
Alan Tarney	bass
Unknown	orchestra

Recording Details

Producer	David MacKay
Engineered by	Tony Clark and Mike Jarrett
Recording location	Abbey Road Studio 2, St. John's Wood, London
Recording date	13th and 14th February 1974

♫ Love Is Like a Crescendo
From the album **...And They Said It Wouldn't Last! (My 50 Years in Music)**

At a number of 1969's recording sessions, several tracks that would have fitted easily on to the various albums released at the time (***Sincerely Cliff Richard*** and ***Tracks 'n' Grooves*** being two) were recorded but weren't issued. One of these was *Love Is Like a Crescendo*, written by Manfred Mann lead singer Mike d'Abo, recorded in late September but remaining in the EMI vaults for thirty-nine years, when it was included on the lost and found section of the celebratory album ***...And They Said It Wouldn't Last! (My 50 Years in Music)*** in 2008.

This jaunty song is introduced by a bouncy orchestral arrangement, while the lyrics are somewhat obtuse in suggesting that love gets stronger and is there similar to a crescendo; however, to be nitpicking, the musical annotation of a crescendo refers to sound and how it gets louder over a passage of time and therefore becomes meaningless in this context. Cliff performs the song with his usual gusto on such songs and it is a shame that it has taken so long to release it; it would have made an interesting B-side of one of singles of the period.

Track Specification
Composed by Mike d'Abo

Musicians		*Recording Details*	
Nick Ingman	arranger, conductor	Producer	Norrie Paramor
Nick Ingman Orchestra	orchestra	Engineered by	Peter Vince
Cliff Richard	vocals	Recording location	Abbey Road Studio 2, St. John's Wood, London
Unknown	backing vocals	Recording date	22nd September 1969

♫ Love Is More than Words
Unissued track

The final session of 1968 and the first 1969 saw Cliff Richard record songs for the Tyne Tees Television religious series *Life with Johnny*, which was a modern retelling of the parables, with Cliff in the title role. In *Johnny and the Good Samaritan*, he is out on the town with his girlfriend (played by Cindy Kent) but runs out of money and tries to convince strangers to help him get home. They argue and she tells him not to make empty promises and to mean what he says.
A slow love song with strong harmonies between the lead vocals, the song was one of the many recorded at Abbey Road, possibly with a view to releasing a tie-in album to the series that never materialized. The song was written, according to the end credits, by Cliff Richard, David Winter, the programme's writer, and the Settlers.

Track Specification
Composed by Cliff Richard, David Winter, Cindy Kent, Mike Jones, John Fyffe and Geoffrey Srodzinski

Musicians		*Recording Details*	
John Fyffe	backing vocals, guitar	Producer	Norrie Paramor
Cindy Kent	vocals	Engineered by	Peter Vince
Mike Jones	backing vocals, guitar	Recording location	Abbey Road Studio 3, St. John's Wood, London
Cliff Richard	vocals	Recording date	2nd-3rd December 1968
Geoffrey Srodzinski	backing vocals		
Unknown	organ		

♫ Love Is the Strongest Emotion
From the album **Cliff Richard - The Album**

The second track on Cliff Richard's first studio album of the nineties, ***Cliff Richard - The Album***, features a solo from backing vocalist Judith Walmsley who was regularly featured in Cliff's supporting tours of the period.
Electric pianos and sampled finger-clicks create the introduction to the sophisticated love ballad that builds up to the chorus with Cliff singing at the top of his range. The bass and percussion are at the forefront of the mix, alongside the staccato guitars. The mid-section featuring the duet with Walmsley is an effective break from the rest of the song, which is restarted with a ring of a high-pitched bell.

Track Specification
Composed by Mick Leeson and Peter Vale

Musicians		*Recording Details*	
Dave Bishop	saxophone	Producer	Paul Moessl and Cliff Richard
John Clark	guitar	Engineered by	Gerry Kitchingham and Ben Robbins
Peter Howarth	backing vocals	Recording location	R. G. Jones Studios, Wimbledon, London
Peter May	drums, percussion	Recording date	25th-31st May 1992, 8th June 1992 (backing track) and 7th July 1992 (vocals)
Paul Moessl	arranger, drum programming, keyboards		
Keith Murrell	backing vocals		
Tessa Niles	backing vocals		
Cliff Richard	vocals, backing vocals		
Steve Stroud	bass		
Jamie Talbot	saxophone		
Judith Walmsley	vocals, backing vocals		

♫ Love Letters
From the EP **Love Songs**

Written for the 1945 film of the same name, *Love Letters* (performed without the lyrics) was nominated for the Academy Award for Best Song and was first recorded by Dick Haymes, who took it to number eleven in the US singles charts. In the UK, three artists have charted with the song: Kitty Lester (achieving a number four hit in April 1962 with her first single); Elvis Presley (who reached number six in July 1966); and Alison Moyet (number four in December 1987 with a video featuring the antics of comediennes and close friends Jennifer Saunders and Dawn French). In addition, a number of artists have also covered the song including Cilla Black, Sandie Shaw, Jack Jones, Etta James, Jason Donovan, Sinéad O'Connor, Fox, Joe Walsh and there was a duet by Elton John and Bonnie Raitt.
Cliff's version was recorded in just two takes and was the first song in the can from the session and the stereo and mono edits are the same but have different mixes for the audio channels. Until the 1989 EP collection by See For Miles, the track was a major rarity, although the album itself is now a rarity. The song was subsequently issued on the 1998 *1960s* album.

The gentle shuffling brushes on the drums are punctuated by strident strings, which become smoother and shimmering underneath Cliff's vocals. The arrangement is perhaps slower than the familiar versions that have hit the charts and Cliff tends to over-emphasize the American 'r' but this is a minor distraction from an excellent cover version of the song.

Track Specification
Composed by Victor Young and Eddie Heyman

Musicians

Norrie Paramor Orchestra	orchestra
Norrie Paramor	conductor
Cliff Richard	vocals

Recording Details

Producer	Norrie Paramor
Engineered by	Malcolm Addey
Recording location	Abbey Road Studio 2, St. John's Wood, London
Recording date	11th December 1961

♫ Love Me Tender

From the album **Wanted**

Written for Elvis Presley's debut film of the same name, it was the first single to exceed one million in advance sales in the US. Since it was Presley's first film, it was the only time that he didn't get top billing in the publicity. However, it was on the strength of the song that forced a title change: originally, intended to be *The Reno Brothers*, it was altered to *Love Me Tender* to capitalize on the publicity generated by the song's advance sales. Taking place in the American Civil War, it tells the story of the Reno family with Presley playing Clint Reno, who stayed home while his brothers went off to fight. He marries his brother's fiancée after being incorrectly informed that he had died. The film is less about the conflict's historical influence than about the emotional tensions created by this sequence of events, culminating in Clint's death in a gun duel with his brother. The single release reached number eleven in the UK charts in the first few weeks of 1957.

As Presley was a formative influence on the young Cliff Richard back in the fifties, it is inevitable that he should regularly perform his material both on record and in concert. When Cliff was choosing the tracks for his first album since leaving EMI, ***Wanted***, he picked two Presley songs for inclusion, *Love Me Tender* and ***All Shook Up***, both from the same era in his idol's career. The song was included on the promotional sampler for the *Wanted* album and featured a version that is eight seconds longer than appears on the album.

With an arrangement for the keyboards similar to ***Somewhere Over the Rainbow/What a Wonderful World***, this beautiful version cries out for a strong backing vocal accompaniment and adaptation and it doesn't disappoint. Once again, Cliff's lead vocal is kept quiet and considered almost confidential as warranted by the lyrics. But the top marks go to the excellent vocal arrangement.

Track Specification
Composed by Elvis Presley and Vera Matson

Musicians

John Brant	additional programming
Anthony Clark	backing vocals
Cliff Richard	vocals, backing vocals
Alan Tarney	arranger, backing vocals, keyboards, programming

Recording Details

Producer	Alan Tarney
Engineered by	John Brant and Gerry Kitchingham
Recording location	Wilmer Studios, London
Recording date	January-April 2001

♫ Love Never Gives Up

From the album **10th Way of Life Rally** *(Various)*

As a committed Christian, Cliff Richard regularly performed at gospel sessions or fronted large rallies such as the Way of Life, which took place at the Empire Pool (now the Arena) at Wembley. In April, 1975, he performed three songs: *Love Never Gives Up*, ***Why Me?*** and ***Didn't He?*** All three were recorded but only the first was issued on the album *10th Way of Life Rally* to raise funds for charity. The album is a rarity and many of the details regarding the recording are unknown.

Track Specification
Composed by Cliff Richard

Musicians

Cliff Richard	vocals
Unknown	other instrumentation

Recording Details

Producer	Unknown
Engineered by	Unknown
Recording location	Empire Pool, Wembley, Middlesex
Recording date	19th April 1975

♫ Love of My Life

From the album **...And They Said It Wouldn't Last! (My 50 Years in Music)**

In June 1974, Cliff Richard entered the Morgan Studios in London to record a new single (released to much controversy as ***(There's a) Honky Tonk Angel***). At the same time, he recorded two other tracks, *Love of My Life* and ***Song of Yesterday***, which were not only unissued but had been forgotten entirely (Nigel Goodall's and Peter Lewry's book *The Complete Recording Sessions 1958-1990* doesn't mention them and the liner notes for ***...And They Said It Would Last! (My 50 Years in Music)*** indicate that the songs only came to light as they were researching the content of that celebratory album). Placed on the rarities section of that album with just cause, both missing tracks were issued for the first time in 2008.

At this time in Cliff's career, many of his recordings featured an electric piano accompanying the band and possibly a string quartet and this track is no exception. Cliff provides his own melody line harmonies while the other vocals provide a choral sound underneath proceedings. There is a steel guitar that lends the song a country feel that was also dominant in recordings from this period.

Track Specification
Composed by Unknown
Musicians

Terry Britten	backing vocals, guitar
Gordon Huntley	steel guitar
Nick Ingman	arranger, conductor
Dave MacRae	electric piano
Nick Ingman Orchestra	orchestra
Cliff Richard	vocals, backing vocals
Trevor Spencer	drums, percussion
Alan Tarney	backing vocals, bass

Recording Details

Producer	Hank Marvin, Bruce Welch and John Farrar
Engineered by	Roger Quested
Recording location	Morgan Studios, London
Recording date	20th June 1974

♫ Love On (Shine On)
B-side of **Devil Woman**

Recorded a the first session for Cliff Richard in 1976, *Love On (Shine On)* is a quasi-religious song that was completed in three takes, with vocal overdubs added the following day (which was the norm for Bruce Welch's early recordings with Cliff). Chosen as the B-side for the ***Devil Woman*** single, it was reissued in the same format in 1982, with the first instance on CD being the *1970s* album in 1998. It was later added as a bonus track on the remastered album ***I'm Nearly Famous***, the liner notes of which incorrectly state that the production team was Hank Marvin, Bruce and John Farrar. Although these three did look after some of Cliff's recordings in late 1974 and into 1975, by mid-1975, it was Bruce who took up the sole producer credit. This is confirmed by the entry in *The Complete Recording Sessions 1958-1990* book.
A guitar introduction is joined by a shimmering synthesiser, which oscillates between the stereo channels. Cliff's choruses are joined by a simple backing vocal arrangement that creates its own beauty. The instrumentation is kept subdued in clear reverence of the subject matter, until the middle eight where the pace and volume is picked up leading into a guitar solo and this joyous change is perpetuated until multi-layered backing vocals return to bring in the end of the track.

Track Specification
Composed by Cliff Richard
Musicians

Terry Britten	guitar
Clem Cattini	drums, percussion
Tony Harding	backing vocals
John Perry	backing vocals
Cliff Richard	vocals
Tony Rivers	backing vocals
Alan Tarney	bass
Graham Todd	keyboards

Recording Details

Producer	Bruce Welch
Engineered by	Tony Clark and John Barrett
Recording location	Abbey Road Studio 3, St. John's Wood, London
Recording date	25th and 26th March 1976

♫ Lover
From the album **Listen to Cliff!**

The second of three Richard Rodgers musical compositions on the ***Listen to Cliff!*** album, *Lover* first appeared as part of the 1932 romantic musical film, *Love Me Tonight*, which starred Jeanette McDonald and Maurice Chevalier – the film was generally agreed to be remarkable in its departure from stage-sounding musical quality and injecting a touch of realism in its structure and film-making techniques. Of note is the instrumental recording of *Lover* by Les Paul in 1948, which is considered to be the first multi-track recording, and it has also been covered by a huge variety of artists including Steve Allen, Louis Armstrong, Brenda Lee, Dudley Moore, The Supremes, Frank Sinatra, Duane Eddy, Tony Bennett, Ella Fitzgerald, Bert Kaempfert, Liberace, Jimmy Dorsey, Peggy Lee, Charlie Parker and Paul Whiteman, among many others.
The mono and stereo versions are from the same take (the last of eight recorded during the session) and only differ in the mix used for the channel requirements and was also included in the track listing for ***Listen to Cliff! No. 1*** EP.
The latin-esque beats performed on the bongo drums and other percussion expand out to the full blown orchestral block chords in the brass and woodwind, making Cliff's version of the song sound like the full musical production number it is. The melody line is technically difficult to pitch correctly but Cliff carries off the challenge with aplomb.

Track Specification
Composed by Richard Rodgers and Lorenz Hart
Musicians

Bernard Ebbinghouse Orchestra	orchestra
Bernard Ebbinghouse	arranger, conductor
Cliff Richard	vocals

Recording Details

Producer	Norrie Paramor
Engineered by	Malcolm Addey and David Lloyd
Recording location	Abbey Road Studio 2, St. John's Wood, London
Recording date	11th January 1961

♫ Lovers

Unissued track and from the album **I'm Nearly Famous**

With Bruce Welch now on board as Cliff Richard's new producer, Cliff was receiving a much improved quality of material than he had been recording in recent years. A prior attempt was made to record *Lovers*, when it was abandoned after six takes, while the next attempt was broken across two sessions, with the first reserved for the backing track, completed in eight takes, and the next four days later for the vocal overdubs.

After the upbeat foot-stomper that was the title track of ***I'm Nearly Famous***, Cliff sings *Lovers*, which is a very sad song of two people falling apart after the initial flush of love. The beauty of the song is supported by flowing strings arranged by Richard Hewson and latterly the chorale of backing vocals, which is a signature of Bruce Welch's production that Cliff would take into later recordings.

Track Specification

Composed by Mickey Newbury

1. Unissued track (I'm Nearly Famous)

Musicians	
Terry Britten	guitar
Clem Cattini	drums, percussion
Tony Harding	backing vocals
Richard Hewson	arranger, conductor
John Perry	backing vocals
Cliff Richard	vocals
Tony Rivers	backing vocals
Alan Tarney	bass
Graham Todd	piano
Unknown	orchestra

Recording Details	
Producer	Bruce Welch
Engineered by	Tony Clark and John Barrett
Recording location	Abbey Road Studio 3, St. John's Wood, London
Recording date	3rd December 1975

2. I'm Nearly Famous

Musicians	
Terry Britten	guitar
Clem Cattini	drums, percussion
Tony Harding	backing vocals
Richard Hewson	arranger, conductor
John Perry	backing vocals
Cliff Richard	vocals
Tony Rivers	backing vocals
Alan Tarney	bass
Graham Todd	piano
Unknown	orchestra

Recording Details	
Producer	Bruce Welch
Engineered by	Tony Clark and John Barrett
Recording location	Abbey Road Studio 3, St. John's Wood, London
Recording date	4th and 8th December 1975

♫ Lovers and Friends

From the album **The Rock Connection**

Rod Trott and Jon Sweet had almost bludgeoned Cliff Richard into listening to their ***Ocean Deep*** which he recorded for the ***Silver*** album and was then issued as a single (eventually) in its own right. With the following album, ***The Rock Connection***, they provided the track that would appear third on the album's first side. It was Cliff's preferred choice for a single release in place of ***Shooting from the Heart***, although it didn't happen, an some commentators suggest that, had Cliff got his way, the associated album would have fared better in the album charts as a direct result of the publicity.

As with many of the songs on *The Rock Connection*, *Lovers and Friends* adopts synthesisers, which were very much in vogue during this period of New Wave and New Romantics, but there is also strength garnered from the chugging bass and guitars. Cliff provides his own backing vocals in the choruses and this elevates his performance further.

Track Specification

Composed by Rod Trott and Jon Sweet

Musicians	
John Clark	guitar
Dave Cooke	keyboards
Mark Griffiths	bass
Alan Park	keyboards
Cliff Richard	vocals, backing vocals
Stuart Tosh	drums, percussion

Recording Details	
Producer	Cliff Richard and Keith Bessey
Engineered by	Keith Bessey
Recording location	Strawberry Studios South, Surrey
Recording date	30th July 1984-3rd August 1984

♫ Love Song

From the album **Sail Away** *(Dave Pope)*

The late Lesley Duncan was a prolific backing singer in the seventies, including working with Elton John and Graeme Edge of the Moody Blues, among others. She wrote *Love Song* and although solely credited to her on the *Sail Away* album, other sources often cite Elton John and Bernie Taupin in the credits. Recorded by a number of artists including Dobie and Olivia Newton-John, Duncan recorded her version for her first solo album, *Sing Children Sing*, in 1971.

In the spring 1978, Cliff Richard took up the production of the album Dave Pope's ***Sail Away*** in between the completion and overdub sessions for his upcoming ***Green Light*** album. The sleeve and other reference material makes no mention of the musicians involved; the track specification will annotate these as unknown until further research reveals the names. Pope's breathy, husky vocals match the song perfectly and reflect on the version recorded by Olivia. The sadness of the song is drawn out in the sustained arrangement of the accompaniment, while the backing vocals are lush with Cliff's being discernible but blending well.

Track Specification
Composed by Lesley Duncan

Musicians		*Recording Details*	
Dave Pope	vocals	Producer	Cliff Richard
Cliff Richard	backing vocals	Engineered by	Tony Clark
Unknown	backing vocals	Recording location	Morgan Studios, London
Unknown	guitar	Recording date	April 1978
Unknown	bass		
Unknown	keyboards		
Unknown	drums, percussion		

♫ Love's Salvation

From the album **Cliff Richard - The Album**

The first of two songs on ***Cliff Richard - The Album*** written by Cliff Richard in partnership with music director and keyboardist Paul Moessl – the other being ***Hold Us Together*** – *Love's Salvation* is a strong brass- and percussion-driven track. The foot-tapping rhythm drives the song onwards, while Cliff's vocals are echoed on the end of each verse, which swings around the stereo channels. Cliff supplies his own backing vocals and he is occasionally enjoyed by the female vocalists making up his backing group.

Track Specification
Composed by Cliff Richard and Paul Moessl

Musicians		*Recording Details*	
Pete Beachill	trombone	Producer	Paul Moessl and Cliff Richard
Dave Bishop	saxophones	Engineered by	Gerry Kitchingham and Ben Robbins
John Bradbury	violin	Recording location	R. G. Jones Studios, Wimbledon, London
John Clark	guitar	Recording date	25th–31st May 1992, 8th June 1992 (backing track) and 6th August 1992 (vocals)
Simon Gardener	trumpet		
Richard Hewson	arranger, conductor		
Peter May	drums, percussion		
Paul Moessl	arranger, drum programming, keyboards		
Tessa Niles	backing vocals		
Cliff Richard	vocals, backing vocals		
Steve Stroud	bass		
Jamie Talbot	saxophone		
Unknown	orchestra (other strings)		
Judith Walmsley	backing vocals		
David Woodcock	violin		

♫ Love Stealer

From the album **Silver**

Recorded first by Ian Lloyd for his 1979 *Goose Bumps* album, *Love Stealer* was then covered by Uriah Heep on their 1980 *Conquest* album, and also by lesser-known acts Brownsville Station and Hello. In 1983, Cliff Richard recorded his version as part of the ***Silver*** sessions and it appeared as the closing track on that first album, which was also released simultaneously in CD format for the first time.
The threatening percussion at the start of the song builds up the premise of the foreboding nature of the song. Cliff's vocals are fed through a vocoder occasionally, with the lead in to the chorus being a simulation of a megaphone as Cliff calls for the police (including a brief, quiet 'nine, nine, nine' of the UK's emergency number uttered in the second chorus).

Track Specification
Composed by Phil Wainman and Richard Myhill

Musicians		*Recording Details*	
Stuart Calver	backing vocals	Producer	Craig Pruess
John Clark	electric guitar	Engineered by	Keith Bessey
Mark Griffiths	bass	Recording location	Strawberry Studios South, Surrey
Graham Jarvis	drums, percussion	Recording date	19th May 1983, 3rd June 1983 and/or 16th June 1983
John Perry	backing vocals		
Craig Pruess	arranger, keyboards, synthesiser, electronics		
Cliff Richard	vocals, backing vocals		
Tony Rivers	backing vocals		

♫ Love That Knows No End

From the albums **Sopotja** *(Aleksander Mežek) and* **Tracks** *(Aleksander Mežek)*

Cliff Richard first worked with Aleksander Mežek back in 1974, when he sang on *Days Go By* (when Mežek was operating under his then stage name of Aleksander John) and he continued to join voices variously over the next thirty-odd years. The last studio recording the pair completed together was *Love That Knows No End*, which appeared on Mežek's album *Sopotja* and was subsequently issued on a compilation album called *Tracks*, using a different backing track that has more of a focus on the keyboards and less emphasis on the guitars and piano. Both albums are available in Croatia but are expensive rarities in other countries.

Track Specification

Composed by Aleksander Mežek

1. Sopotja

Musicians

Aleksander Mežek	vocals
Cliff Richard	vocals
Unknown	guitar
Unknown	bass
Unknown	keyboards
Unknown	drums, percussion

Recording Details

Producer	Aleksander Mežek
Engineered by	Unknown
Recording location	Launderette and Concept Mastering Studio, London
Recording date	2000 or 2001

2. Tracks

Musicians

Richard Cardwell	piano
Aleksander Mežek	vocals
Sarah Ozelle	backing vocals
Cliff Richard	vocals
Unknown	guitar
Unknown	bass
Unknown	keyboards
Unknown	drums, percussion

Recording Details

Producer	Aleksander Mežek and Dave Goodes
Engineered by	Unknown
Recording location	Launderette and Concept Mastering Studio, London
Recording date	2000 or 2001 (vocals) and 2003 (backing track)

♫ Love, Truth and Emily Stone

From the album **Tracks 'n' Grooves**

The rumour-mill was grinding swiftly in September 1969 that Cliff Richard's next single was going to be *Love, Truth and Emily Stone*, helped by the release of a one-sided promotional disc on the Columbia label (catalogue number SPSRS 332). For whatever reason, any such plan was abandoned and that promotional disc is now a rarity (for what it is rather than the track *per se*, which is the same as appears on the ***Tracks n' Grooves*** album). Written by Hank Marvin and Petrina Lordan, wife of Jerry, who had been instrumental in creating a number of Shadows and Cliff hits, the only version of the song was eventually released on the album in 1970. As is expected from Cliff, the lead vocal is well performed and imbued with an ease that many performers would have difficulty bringing across. The emotion of the song is occasionally thwarted by the uncredited warbling of a female backing chorus.

Track Specification

Composed by Hank Marvin and Petrina Lordan

Musicians

Mike Vickers Orchestra	orchestra
Cliff Richard	vocals
Unknown	female backing vocals
Mike Vickers	arranger, conductor

Recording Details

Producer	Norrie Paramor
Engineered by	Peter Vince
Recording location	Abbey Road Studio 2, St. John's Wood, London
Recording date	29th July 1969

♫ Love Ya

B-side of **My Pretty One**

After completing his run in the ***Time- The Musical*** at London's Dominion Theatre, Cliff Richard was able to concentrate more on finishing the ***Always Guaranteed*** album, which he had recorded during spare moments during the theatre run. The following spring, he recorded a number of new songs, one of which was *Love Ya*, a track that he wrote himself. The song was recorded at the small studio that Cliff had in his Cliff Richard Organisation offices based in Esher in Surrey.

Love Ya was chosen as the B-side of the first single from the album project, ***My Pretty One***, and featured on all the variants of the single release. It first appeared in CD format on the track listing of 1998's *1980s* album and later appeared on ***My Songs***, a collection of songs that Cliff had either written or had a hand in composing, and was later incorporated as one of the eight bonus tracks on the remaster of the *Always Guaranteed* album in 2004.

The synthesiser performance on the song is of the period and sounds like much of the material that appeared on ***Stronger*** and beyond into the early nineties. Cliff sings his own backing vocals in close harmony, usually in thirds that create an additional and natural beauty. While Cliff suggests that he is incapable of writing a good song, *Love Ya* is strong enough to match a lot of what else he was recording at the time, written by designated songwriters.

Track Specification
Composed by Cliff Richard

Musicians		*Recording Details*	
John Clark	guitar, bass	Producer	Cliff Richard
Alan Park	keyboards, drum and percussion programming	Engineered by	Keith Bessey
Cliff Richard	vocals, backing vocals	Recording location	C. R. O. Studios, Esher, Surrey
		Recording date	April 1987

♫ Loving You

Unissued track

During 1977, Cliff Richard recorded very little material for his own album and single projects, although he was involved in recording with other people, such as the Brian Bennett Band, and producing a set of songs for South Africa-based singer and actor Richard Loring. One of these tracks by Loring was *Loving You*; unfortunately, there is scant information on those musicians and studio personnel involved and who wrote it (of all the songs with the same name, there are no pointers to identify precisely which one).

Track Specification
Composed by Unknown

Musicians		*Recording Details*	
Richard Loring	vocals	Producer	Cliff Richard
Unknown	other instrumentation	Engineered by	Unknown
		Recording location	Abbey Road Studios, St. John's Wood, London
		Recording date	August 1977

♫ Lucie

From the album **I Love You, Goodbye** *(Barratt Waugh)*

Performed by French pianist Richard Clayderman and its writer Pascal Obispo, Cliff Richard's long-term musical friend and ex-band member Barratt Waugh chose *Lucie* for his solo album *I Love You, Goodbye*. The album was released on Cliff's own short-lived label Blacknight in the late nineties and *Lucie* was one of two tracks, along with ***Songbird***, to feature Cliff on backing vocals.

A gentle piano introduction leads into another falsetto-driven performance by Waugh. In the second part of the verse, the piano is joined by a string arrangement. The backing vocal arrangement is brought in during the second verse as the start of the quiet percussion. The arrangement of these vocals is kept simple and sporadic throughout, since Waugh harmonizes principally with himself during the verses. Cliff's voice is discernible in the group and it adds sophistication to the very pleasant performance of the love song.

Track Specification
Composed by Pascal Obispo and Lionel Florence; English lyrics by Jeremy Sams

Musicians		*Recording Details*	
John Cameron	arranger, conductor	Producer	John Cameron
Mitch Dalton	guitar	Engineered by	Gerry Kitchingham
Harold Fisher	drums, percussion	Recording location	R. G. Jones Studios, Wimbledon, London
Pat Halling	orchestra leader, violin	Recording date	February 1999
Dave Hartley	piano		
Peter Howarth	backing vocals		
Paul Keogh	guitar		
Caroline Lavelle	cello		
Keith Murrell	backing vocals		
Jacqueline Norrie	violin		
Andy Pask	bass		
Steve Pearce	bass		
Tony Pleeth	cello		
Jocelyn Pook	viola		
Cliff Richard	backing vocals		
Julia Singleton	violin		
Barratt Waugh	vocals, backing vocals		

♫ Lucille

From the albums **Cliff "Live" in Japan '72** *and* **My Kinda Life** *and CD B-side of* **All I Have to Do Is Dream/Miss You Nights** *and B-side of* **Never Say Die (Give a Little Bit More)**

The Beatles, along with many acts (including Cliff Richard) in the sixties, regularly performed songs that had been recorded by established American performers. *Lucille* was just one such song and, having been taken into the British charts to number ten by Little Richard in June 1957, it was quickly picked up and adopted by the fledgling Quarry Men (the precursor to the Beatles) once Paul McCartney had joined and he provided the lead vocals in their live performances. Once the Beatles embarked on their stratospheric fame, they regularly included Little Richard's signature song on their radio and television shows of the early sixties.

For his Far Eastern tour in 1972, Cliff incorporated *Lucille* into a ***Rock Medley*** that pays tribute to the stars of the fifties when he was just starting out in his music career: ***The Girl Can't Help It, Great Balls of Fire***, *Lucille*, ***Jailhouse Rock, Good Old Rock 'n' Roll*** and ***Do You Wanna Dance***.
As part of a BBC documentary about Cliff, a number of live performances were recorded at the Hammersmith Odeon and Manchester Apollo to accompany the broadcast. Some tracks were licensed for release at the time and this resulted in the ***Daddy's Home*** single, while others were held back by the BBC. Thirteen years afterwards, the section that included the duets with Phil Everly was licensed from the corporation, and Cliff spent some time remixing and cleaning up the product that eventually surfaced in the release of the double A-sided single of ***All I Have to Do Is Dream*** (with Everly) and a remixed version of ***Miss You Nights***. While the seven-inch single release was restricted to just those tracks, the first of the dual CD single discs had two additional tracks, both featuring Cliff and Everly together, ***When Will I Be Loved?*** and ***Tribute to the Legends Medley***, the latter of which *Lucille* formed part. Everly joined Cliff on stage for the start of *Lucille*, which was the third in the sequence of songs. Taking it at a slow pace, similar to the Everly Brothers version, Everly's and Cliff's vocals blend well, while they take turns at certain points to take the lead, otherwise singing in unison. The song excerpt is quite short before leading into ***Long Tall Sally***.
Since Cliff was regularly performing the song live either in medley or as the whole song in its own, his band – dubbed Thunder by Cliff – chose it for recording during the sessions for ***Rock 'n' Roll Silver***, arranging and producing it as a sort of collective. This version was used as the B-side on both the seven-inch and twelve-inch formats of Cliff's eighty-ninth British single ***Never Say Die (Give a Little Bit More)***, a track taken from the associated album ***Silver***. The almost suspicious introduction on staccato bass and percussion brings in Cliff's vocal in close harmony with the backing vocals. Slowly, the drama builds up for the chorus, which is a straightforward rendition before closing back down for the verse. The wailing synthesiser solo in the middle eight adds to the freshness of the arrangement of a song that would have otherwise been over-familiar.
In 1992, the original album track was taken and embellished for inclusion on the ***My Kinda Life*** album, with additional guitars and keyboards throughout and extra echo created behind some of Cliff's vocal lines. This version was chosen as the B-side of the French single release of ***Remember***.

Track Specification
Composed by Albert Collins and Richard Penniman

1. Cliff "Live" in Japan '72

Musicians		*Recording Details*	
Brian Bennett	drums, percussion	Producer	Norrie Paramor
Pat Carroll	backing vocals	Engineered by	Unknown
John Farrar	bass	Recording location	Kosei Nenkin Hall, Tokyo, Japan
Alan Hawkshaw	piano	Recording date	22nd-23rd September 1972
Hank Marvin	guitar		
Olivia Newton-John	backing vocals		
Cliff Richard	vocals		
Bruce Welch	rhythm guitar		

2. CD B-side (All I Have to Do Is Dream)

Musicians		*Recording Details*	
Howie Casey	saxophone	Producer	Cliff Richard
John Clark	guitar	Engineered by	Unknown
Phil Everly	vocals	Recording location	Hammersmith Odeon, London
Mark Griffiths	bass	Remixed at	R. G. Jones Studio, London
Graham Jarvis	drums, percussion	Recording date	1st May 1981 (live track) and 7th September 1994 (remix)
Martin Jenner	guitar		
Alan Park	keyboards		
Cliff Richard	vocals		
Graham Todd	keyboards		

3. B-side (Never Say Die (Give a Little Bit More))

Musicians		*Recording Details*	
Stuart Calver	backing vocals	Producer	Thunder
Dave Cooke	keyboards	Engineered by	Keith Bessey
John Clark	electric guitar	Recording location	Strawberry Studios South, Surrey
Mark Griffiths	bass	Recording date	9th-18th May 1983
Graham Jarvis	drums, percussion		
Mart Jenner	guitar		
John Perry	backing vocals		
Alan Park	keyboards		
Cliff Richard	vocals, backing vocals		
Tony Rivers	backing vocals		
Thunder	arranger		

4. My Kinda Life

Musicians		*Recording Details*	
Stuart Calver	backing vocals	Producer	Thunder (original track) and Cliff Richard and Paul Moessl (new instrumentation)
Dave Cooke	keyboards	Engineered by	Keith Bessey (original track) and Gerry Kitchingham and Ben Robbins (new instrumentation)
John Clark	electric guitar (original and new)	Recording location	Strawberry Studios South, Surrey (original track) and R. G. Jones Studios, Wimbledon, London (new instrumentation)
Mark Griffiths	bass	Recording date	9th-18th May 1983 (original track) and 20th-23rd April 1992 (new instrumentation)
Graham Jarvis	drums, percussion		
Mart Jenner	guitar		
Paul Moessl	drum sequencers, synthesisers		
John Perry	backing vocals		
Alan Park	keyboards		
Cliff Richard	vocals		
Tony Rivers	backing vocals		
Thunder	arranger		

♫ Lucky Lips

***21st UK single** and from the albums **Cliff in Japan** and **Reunited** and unissued live tracks*

Written by Elvis Presley's favourite rock and roll writers, Jerry Leiber and Mike Stoller, *Lucky Lips* was first recorded by Ruth Brown in 1957. It was also covered by Alma Cogan (as a B-side), the Hotshots, Laurie London and Gale Storm, but it was Cliff Richard's version was by far the most successful.

Recorded, along with its B-side ***I Wonder***, at the first session in 1963 after Cliff found Ruth Brown's version on a compendium album release and realized its commercial potential, *Lucky Lips* was completed in just six takes. That sixth take and edit was used for the mono and stereo recordings but with different mixes for the audio channels. It was released on the Columbia label (catalogue number DB 7034; the first Cliff Richard single to be issued without the 45- prefix and on seven-inch vinyl only) on 27th April 1963, reaching number four in the UK singles charts, and it also made it into the US Billboard charts stopping at sixty-two. Cliff later recorded a new version in the German language (translated by Hans Bradtke) called ***Rote Lippen Soll Man Küssen***, which reached number one in Germany - as did the English version contemporaneously. Naturally, the English version appeared on the track listing of the ***Cliff's Lucky Lips*** EP.

Lucky Lips is a superlative example of the classic harmonies that the combination of Cliff's lead vocals matched with Hank Marvin, Bruce Welch and John Rostill produce - and is most obvious in the final chords of the songs (itself a trademark of this line-up's vocal harmonisation). The bass line is prominent throughout and the ensemble of the rhythm section drives the song forwards. Ostensibly a love song that talks about the luck with the ladies derived from Cliff's lips from birth through to a mature adult, it includes a gambling reference of kissing the chips to guarantee a win. Noteworthy is Brian Locking's bass line and the understated piano in the mix, which is uncredited and is possibly producer Norrie Paramor.

A number two in Japan on single release, it was part of a medley of five songs that was performed at the end of the concert that was recorded for ***Cliff in Japan***, backed entirely by orchestral instruments: ***Let's Make a Memory***, ***The Young Ones***, *Lucky Lips*, ***Summer Holiday*** and ***We Say Yeah***. For his concert at the Talk of the Town the following year, Cliff also performed a similar medley, this time with a running order of *The Young Ones*, *Lucky Lips*, ***Living Doll*** and ***In the Country***. This time, however, the medley was not released on the live album and remains unissued.

Another unreleased live track was found from the *Live & Guaranteed 1988!* tour, which was recorded and filmed ostensibly for video release. It was then reissued in 1995 with a CD accompaniment but neither the video nor the CD had *Lucky Lips* on the track listing.

The song was one of the many chosen by Cliff and the Shadows to re-record for their ***Reunited*** album, which was released in 2009 and promoted on an accompanying tour. Introduced by the close harmonies, it is clear that this version is going to be similar to the original, although there is an improved energy running throughout.

Track Specification
Composed by Jerry Leiber and Mike Stoller

1. Single

Musicians		*Recording Details*	
Brian Bennett	drums, percussion	Producer	Norrie Paramor
Brian 'Licorice' Locking	bass	Engineered by	Malcolm Addey
Hank Marvin	guitar	Recording location	Abbey Road Studio 2, St. John's Wood, London
Norrie Paramor Orchestra	orchestra	Recording date	8th March 1963
Norrie Paramor	arranger, conductor		
Cliff Richard	vocals		
Unknown	piano		
Bruce Welch	rhythm guitar		

2. Cliff in Japan

Musicians		*Recording Details*	
Norrie Paramor Orchestra	orchestra	Producer	Norrie Paramor
Norrie Paramor	arranger, conductor	Engineered by	Unknown
Cliff Richard	vocals	Recording location	Shibuya Public Hall, Tokyo, Japan
Unknown	backing vocals	Recording date	18th October 1967

3. Unissued track (Live at the Talk of the Town)

Musicians		*Recording Details*	
Breakaways:	backing vocals	Producer	Norrie Paramor
Vicki Hasemen		Engineered by	Peter Vince
Margo Quantrell		Recording location	Talk of the Town Theatre, London
Jean Ryder		Recording date	30th May 1968
Norrie Paramor	arranger, conductor		
Cliff Richard	vocals		
Talk of the Town Orchestra	orchestra		

4. Unissued track (Live & Guaranteed 1988!)

Musicians		*Recording Details*	
John Clark	guitar	Producer	Unknown
Rosemarie Ford	backing vocals	Engineered by	Unknown
Mark Griffiths	bass	Recording location	Fyens Forum, Odense, Denmark
Peter Howarth	backing vocals	Recording date	22nd May 1988
Steve Lauri	guitar		
Paul Moessl	keyboards		
Mick Mullins	backing vocals		
Alan Park	keyboards		
Cliff Richard	vocals		
Henry Spinetti	drums, percussion		

5. Reunited

Musicians		*Recording Details*	
Brian Bennett	drums, percussion	Producer	Warren Bennett (co-ordination)
Warren Bennett	piano	Engineered by	James Collins (Honeyhill Studios), Ethan Carlson (Middle Ear Studios), Les Williams (Nivram Studios) and Keith Bessey (mixing and mastering)
Mark Griffiths	bass	Recording location	Middle Ear Studios, Miami, Florida, USA (Cliff's vocals), Nivram Studios, Perth, Western Australia (Hank's guitars and vocals) and Honeyhill Studios, Hertfordshire, England (all other vocals and instruments)
Hank Marvin	backing vocals, guitar	Recording date	Early 2009
Cliff Richard	vocals, backing vocals		
Bruce Welch	backing vocals, rhythm guitar		

♫ Luxury Liner

From the album **Keep the Ball Rolling** *(Bryn Haworth)*

The second track on Bryn Haworth's *Keep the Ball Rolling* album to feature Cliff Richard on backing vocals (the other being ***Standing on the Rock***), *Luxury Liner* was also written by Haworth, who had previously worked with Cliff on his ***Small Corners*** album and with Garth Hewitt on his Cliff-produced album ***Did He Jump... Or Was He Pushed?***. The album track *City Boy*, not featuring Cliff, was released as a single in 1979 on the A&M label and *Luxury Liner* was chosen for its B-side – the single, however, failed to make an impression on the charts.

The backing vocals, featuring Cliff providing layers of harmony, are present from the start in this sophisticated and rhythmic song that was very much of its era. The song is always lifted when Cliff's vocals are brought in, largely because, while Haworth's lead vocals are pleasant enough, they have little power. But this changes in the middle eight as the guitar becomes more prominent and the lead and backing vocals begin to play off each other.

Track Specification

Composed by Bryn Haworth

Musicians		*Recording Details*	
Bryn Haworth	vocals, guitar	Producer	Jon Astley and Doug Bennet
Dave Markee	bass	Engineered by	Jon Astley, Doug Bennet and Laurence Burrage
Simon Morton	percussion	Recording location	Olympic Studios, Chelsea, London
Cliff Richard	backing vocals	Recording date	1979
Henry Spinetti	drums, percussion		
Pete Wingfield	keyboards		

♫ Mad About You

From the film soundtrack EP of **Serious Charge**

Recorded for the film soundtrack EP of *Serious Charge* at the same session as the other two songs, ***Living Doll*** (the eventual single version) and ***No Turning Back***, *Mad About You* was one of the three songs written specifically for Cliff Richard and the Drifters for his appearance in the film. Cliff took the part of the musical brother of a gang-leading tearaway; the brother was partly responsible for killing his pregnant girlfriend (a social problem destined to make her an outcast in less enlightened times) a crime for which the new vicar accuses him and then he counter-accuses with a charge of molestation.
Although billed as part of the film soundtrack, the songs are not actually a central feature to the action. Two versions of the song were recorded, one for the film track and the other, represented here as it was recorded for disc release, for the ***Serious Charge*** EP. It has since been re-released on the ***...And They Said It Would Never Last (My Fifty Years in Music)*** rarities compilation album as well as the *At the Movies 1959-1974* anthology of tunes from the various films featuring Cliff.
The song is written in a Bo Diddley hambone fashion (a musical style formed by slapping the body to create a rhythm and a type of dance). Unlike the speeded up version of *Living Doll*, this song sounds more authentically American, particularly with Cliff's lugubrious vocals, Hank Marvin's guitar solos and the rest of the band's ensemble rhythm creation.
Although this was the last song to be recorded and to be released under The Drifters name (being the final song of the *Serious Charge* EP sessions), it wasn't the last recording to be made while they were still the Drifters: that accolade falls to the final ***Cliff Sings*** sessions in October, at which point, the band went to America to support the release of *Living Doll* and changed the name to the Shadows to avoid confusion with the black soul band who had been performing and recording for over half a decade there.

Track Specification
Composed by Lionel Bart

Musicians		*Recording Details*	
Jet Harris	bass	Producer	Norrie Paramor
Hank Marvin	guitar	Engineered by	Peter Bown and Stuart Eltham
Tony Meehan	drums, percussion	Recording location	Abbey Road Studio 2, St. John's Wood, London
Cliff Richard	vocals	Recording date	28th April 1959
Bruce Welch	rhythm guitar		

♫ Magic Is the Moonlight

From the album **Cliff Richard**

With a subtitle of *Magic Is the Moonlight*, ***Te Quiero Dijiste*** is the original title of this Spanish tune. The song has been covered by a number of artists including Nat King Cole, Xiomara Alfaro, Barbarito Diez, Alfredo Kraus, Ana Maria Gonzalez, Chico O'Farril, the Orquesta Romantica del Casino de Hawana, Edmundo Ros and Rigo Tovar.
Cliff Richard recorded his English version which was then overdubbed on the Spanish backing track recorded the previous year for the ***When in Spain*** album. The final (unknown) take and edit were overdubbed on the earlier track and used for the mono and stereo recordings but with different mixes for the audio channels and a narrow stereo mix was used for the 1992 CD reissue of the album ***Cliff Richard.*** Those earlier sessions in Barcelona featured Brian Locking as the Shadows' bassist and therefore he appears here as a result, even though he was replaced later in 1963 by John Rostill.
Being a recording with a new vocal line, the stereo version – as was the frequent practice in those early days of the medium – the vocal is pushed to one channel (Cliff sings in the left on this song) while the instrumental accompaniment is channelled into the other (Norrie Paramor's piano and the Shadows appear in the right here). There is not much difference, other than the language, between the two recordings but Cliff imbues the lyrics with something special that is resident in the timbre of his voice.

Track Specification
Composed by Mariá Grever and Charles Pasquale

Musicians		*Recording Details*	
Brian Bennett	drums, percussion	Producer	Norrie Paramor (backing track and vocals)
Brian 'Licorice' Locking	bass	Engineered by	Malcolm Addey (backing track and vocals)
Hank Marvin	guitar	Recording location	EMI Studios, Barcelona (backing track) and Abbey Road Studio 2, St. John's Wood, London (vocals)
Norrie Paramor	piano		
Cliff Richard	vocals		
Bruce Welch	rhythm guitar	Recording date	30th April 1963 (backing track) and 17th July 1964 (vocals)

♫ Make Ev'ry Day a Carnival Day

From the pantomime cast recording album of **Aladdin and His Wonderful Lamp**

For the Christmas 1964 pantomime performed at the London Palladium, ***Aladdin and His Wonderful Lamp***, which featured Cliff Richard and the Shadows, the Shadows wrote all eighteen tracks, some of which were instrumental, others vocal. One of the vocal tracks was *Make Ev'ry Day a Carnival Day*, which was recorded at a session that produced three tracks for the cast recording album. The final edit was on a splice of the fifth and sixth takes and was used for both the mono and stereo recordings but with different mixes for the audio channels.

With a Latin feel and a bossa nova rhythm and an unexpectedly complex structure, Cliff sings the song with gusto, calling all his reserves to sing at the top of his vocal register. Accompanied by the syncopated orchestra and running bass line, the song cannot help but raise a smile.

Track Specification

Composed by Hank Marvin, Bruce Welch, Brian Bennett and John Rostill

Musicians

Norrie Paramor Orchestra	orchestra
Norrie Paramor	arranger, conductor
Cliff Richard	vocals

Recording Details

Producer	Norrie Paramor
Engineered by	Malcolm Addey and Ken Scott
Recording location	Abbey Road Studio 2, St. John's Wood, London
Recording date	17th October 1964

♫ Make It Easy on Yourself

From the album **Japan Tour '74**

One of the many songs coming out of the successful collaboration and writing partnership of Burt Bacharach and Hal David, *Make It Easy on Yourself* was composed in 1962 with the intention that Dionne Warwick should record it. Instead, it was given to the now comparatively lesser-known Jerry Butler, who took it to number eighteen in the American R&B singles charts. However, it was the Walker Brothers' cover version that has become the most well-known, reaching number one in several countries including the UK. Several years later, Dionne Warwick eventually recorded the track in 1970 and it has also been recorded by a number of artists such as Glen Campbell, Rick Astley, Connie Francis, Jackie Trent, Cilla Black, Long John Baldry, the Four Seasons, the Isley Brothers and the Three Degrees.

Cliff Richard had a habit of including a number of songs in his concerts that he hadn't and wouldn't record in the studio, purely because they were great to sing or moved him in some way. One such was a Walker Brothers medley of *Make It Easy on Yourself* and ***The Sun Ain't Gonna Shine Any More*** that was included in his Japan tour in 1974, which was subsequently released on the album ***Japan Tour '74*** in 1975 (in Japan only) and then as part of the ***...And They Said It Wouldn't Last! (My 50 Years in Music)***, although a separate CD was issued in 2010.

All of the vocalists employ a falsetto to introduce the song before Cliff picks up the lead vocal principally accompanied by a liquid electric guitar, piano and strings. While the original had the lugubrious lead vocals of Scott Walker, Cliff's version is lighter and the arrangement here makes it a very different track. It picks up the tempo as it segues into *The Sun Ain't Gonna Shine Any More*. After a couple of verses of that song, the pace slackens again and the song segues back into *Make It Easy on Yourself*, this time with the piano very much in evidence before the orchestral strings take over. The performance finishes on a repetition of the title of *The Sun Ain't Gonna Shine Any More*.

Track Specification

Composed by Burt Bacharach and Hal David

Musicians

Barrie Guard	arranger, conductor
Cliff Hall	piano
Brian Lewis	backing vocals, guitar
Kevin Peak	acoustic guitar
Cliff Richard	vocals
Shambles Symphonet	orchestra
Trevor Spencer	drums, percussion
Alan Tarney	backing vocals, bass
Bruce Welch	backing vocals, rhythm guitar

Recording Details

Producer	Toshiba EMI (no individual detailed)
Engineered by	Toshiba EMI (no individual detailed)
Recording location	Shinjuku Koseinenkin, Tokyo, Japan
Recording date	7th-8th October 1974

♫ Makin' History

From the album **Rock 'n' Roll Silver**

Written by Cliff Richard's then bassist Mark Griffiths, *Makin' History* was the first song to appear on Cliff's twenty-fifth anniversary album, ***Rock 'n' Roll Silver***. The track was arranged and produced by Thunder, which is the name Cliff gave to the group of musicians who treated these sessions as a sort of co-operative. When the album was first released on CD in 1992, possibly for reasons of space, the track was not incorporated on the *Rock 'n' Roll Silver* disc but instead was the final track on ***The Rock Connection*** disc which was the second album on the two-disc reissue.

The gentleness of the introductory vocal belies the pace that is set up for the rest of the song. With a rockabilly rhythm, the focus is on the guitar and relentless drums in the verse, while the synthesisers are brought into greater use during the choruses. Cliff carries out the vocals with his customary nonchalance and he also supplies some of the backing vocals.

Track Specification
Composed by Mark Griffiths and Graham Lyle

Musicians

Stuart Calver	backing vocals
Mel Collins	saxophone
Dave Cooke	keyboards
John Clark	electric guitar
Mark Griffiths	bass
Graham Jarvis	drums, percussion
Mart Jenner	guitar
John Perry	backing vocals
Alan Park	keyboards
Cliff Richard	vocals, backing vocals
Tony Rivers	backing vocals
Thunder	arranger

Recording Details

Producer	Thunder
Engineered by	Keith Bessey
Recording location	Strawberry Studios South, Surrey
Recording date	9th-18th May 1983

♫ Man Gratuliert Mir

German single

With the huge popularity of Cliff Richard's ***Congratulations*** at the 1968 Eurovision Song Contest, in spite of it coming second to the unmemorable Spanish entry *La La La*, it was inevitable that Cliff should be requested to record a German language version – even though, in an ironic twist, it was the German vote on the night that forced Cliff to lose by just one point. Three days after the contest, which was staged at the Royal Albert Hall on 6th April, Cliff entered the studios to record the hastily translated version of the song.

It is often stated that the original orchestral track or the British recording of *Congratulations* was used for the foreign language recordings with the translated lyrics overdubbed on top. However, this is incorrect: the German *Man Gratuliert Mir* (*One Congratulates Me*, literally, although this changes the focus of the message's recipient) was an original recording with the orchestral backing track from that session used on the subsequent recordings in Spanish, French and Italian.

Man Gratuliert Mir was issued as a single, backed with ***Ich Kann Treu Sein***, on the international Columbia label (catalogue number C-23776) in April 1968, although it wasn't a chart hit; however, the English version did reach number one. Released in mono only and a significant rarity for many years, the stereo version was issued on the foreign language song compilation ***On the Continent*** in 1997.

The mix and edit concentrates on the guitar line more than the other instrumentation in comparison with the English version but in all other respects the song is a faithful copy of the original, with the exception of Cliff and the backing vocalists (uncredited but possibly the Breakaways because they were involved in the original) singing along with the accelerando at the end (as happens on all of the foreign language versions but not the English original).

Track Specification
Composed by Bill Martin and Phil Coulter; German lyrics by Fleming and Lambert

Musicians

Norrie Paramor Orchestra	orchestra
Norrie Paramor	arranger, conductor
Cliff Richard	vocals
Unknown	backing vocals
Unknown	hand claps

Recording Details

Producer	Norrie Paramor
Engineered by	Peter Vince
Recording location	Abbey Road Studio 2, St. John's Wood, London
Recording date	9th April 1968

♫ Mann Neben Dir, Der

From the album **Ich Träume Deine Träume**

After the success of his first German language album, *Hier Ist Cliff*, in Germany, Cliff Richard was back in the studios for four sessions over two days in late November 1970, applying his vocal overdubs on pre-recorded orchestral backing tracks. *Der Mann Neben Dir* – or *The Man Next to You* – was the penultimate song to be recorded on the last day and is a German translation of *Baby, Don't You Know Anymore*, which has not been covered to date in its English incarnation by Cliff. As well as its appearance on the long-player album, *Ich Träume Deine Träume*, the track was also collated on to the 1997 foreign language compilation, ***On the Continent***.

The gentleness of the song is accompanied by arpeggiated guitar chords and muted brass. Cliff carries off the vocals with his customary confidence, in spite of *Der Mann Neben Dir* not being the best track on the album.

Track Specification
Composed by Westlake; German lyrics by Joachim Relin

Musicians

Norrie Paramor Orchestra	orchestra
Cliff Richard	vocals
Unknown	backing vocals
Mike Vickers	arranger, conductor

Recording Details

Producer	Norrie Paramor (backing track and vocals)
Engineered by	Phil McDonald (backing track and vocals)
Recording location	Cologne, Germany (backing track) and Abbey Road Studio 2, St. John's Wood, London (vocals)
Recording date	November 1970 (backing track) and 25th November 1970 (vocals)

♫ Maria

From the EP **Look in My Eyes Maria**

Taken from the phenomenally successful 1957 Broadway show, *West Side Story* with the music of Leonard Bernstein and lyrics of Stephen Sondheim, and which was later filmed and released using the same title, *Maria* is a song that is sung by the desperate suitor of the central female lead, Maria. In the narrative, Maria is the sister of Bernardo, who is one of the gang-leaders and a rival of Tony, with whom she falls in love. The story is, of course, loosely based on Shakespeare's tragedy *Romeo and Juliet* but with a contemporary setting of gang warfare in New York. *Maria* is one of the most famous arias from the show and has become a crooning standard as a consequence. It has been covered by a large number of artists including José Carreras, Oscar Peterson, Marvin Gaye, Johnny Mathis, Vic Damone, Sarah Vaughan, Placido Domingo and the Fortunes among several others but it was only P. J. Proby who achieved a UK hit when his version rose to number eight in December 1965.

Recorded at the only session in June 1964, Cliff Richard's cover of *Maria* was destined for the track listing of the ***Look in My Eyes Maria*** EP. The last of three songs to be completed, the released take and edit were spliced from takes seven and eight and used for the mono and stereo recordings but with different mixes for the separate audio channels. Other than the EP, which was only released in mono indicating that the stereo version was intended for album release, it would take almost twenty-five years for the song to be reissued in a different format, when the stereo mix was included on 1989's ***The EP Collection: Ballads and Love Songs***, which itself has become somewhat of a sought after rarity.

Cliff's version is introduced by the orchestral swirls in the strings until his lead vocal is accompanied by percussion a piano and a staccato guitar. His vocal line is given a lot of echo that doesn't quite match the comparative dryness of the instrumentation.

Track Specification

Composed by Leonard Bernstein and Stephen Sondheim

Musicians

Norrie Paramor Orchestra	orchestra
Norrie Paramor	arranger, conductor
Cliff Richard	vocals

Recording Details

Producer	Norrie Paramor
Engineered by	Malcolm Addey
Recording location	Abbey Road Studio 2, St. John's Wood, London
Recording date	23rd June 1964

♫ Maria Ninguém

From the album **When in Rome**

Originally recorded by Cliff Richard in Spanish under the title *Maria No Mas* (or the literal translation of *Maria No More*) for his ***When in Spain*** album, he re-recorded Italian vocals under the Portuguese title ***Maria Ninguém*** (literally translated as *Maria No-one*, thereby following the same interpretation as the Spanish version). However, the English subtitle (and version with English lyrics) is called *Maria's Her Name*, which is slightly different from the intended message that the girl Maria is not part of the singer's life. Under its Italian lyrics but Portuguese title, it was covered by a number of artists including Brigitte Bardot, João Gilberto, Carlos Lyra, Phil Woods, Astrud Gilberto, Silvio Francesco and Jim Hall.

Cliff's *Maria No Mas* was the final track to be recorded for the *When in Spain* album at its own session at the EMI Studios in Barcelona after four days of intensive recording. That original backing track by the Shadows was simplified and reused for the Italian version of the song, with Cliff's new vocals overdubbed at a May session in 1965, which was over two years after the first version was recorded. The unknown take and edit was overdubbed on the backing track and has only ever been released in mono format. Note that Brian Locking therefore appears on this track, even though he was replaced by John Rostill at the end of 1963.

Against the orchestral tracks on the album, it is refreshing to hear a song featuring the Shadows accompanying Cliff's vocal. There are some key changes in the verses and in the instrumental middle eight, while Cliff is clearly enjoying the singing of the song. Unlike its Spanish counterpart there are no backing vocals or strings.

Track Specification

Composed by Carlos Lyra; Italian lyrics by Mogol

Musicians

Brian Bennett	drums, percussion
Brian 'Licorice' Locking	bass
Hank Marvin	guitar
Cliff Richard	vocals
Bruce Welch	rhythm guitar

Recording Details

Producer	Norrie Paramor (backing track vocals)
Engineered by	Malcolm Addey (backing track and vocals)
Recording location	EMI Studios, Barcelona (backing track) and Estudios Valentim de Carvalho, Lisbon (vocals)
Recording date	1st May 1963 (backing track) and 14th May 1965 (vocals)

♫ Marianne

43rd ***UK single*** *and from the album* **Hier Ist Cliff**

With English lyrics provided by actor Bill Owen (who was later best known for his portrayal as the scruffy Compo in the long-running situation comedy *Last of the Summer Wine*), although some sources also credit Mike Sammes for the arrangement, *Marianne* is an original Italian song of the same name. Sung in the original language by writer Sergio Endrigo, it was the Italian entry for the 1968 Eurovision Song Contest and, therefore, one of Cliff Richard's direct

competitors when he performed ***Congratulations*** for the UK. Endrigo finished in tenth position (out of seventeen participating countries) far behind Cliff's placing of second.
Marianne was issued as Cliff's forty-third UK single, backed with ***Mr. Nice*** (recorded at the session the day before), on the Columbia label (catalogue number DB 8476) on 20th September 1968 and reached number twenty-two in the British singles charts. As was Columbia policy at the time, singles were released in mono; both the A- and B-sides were released in mono, therefore, and the stereo version of *Marianne* wouldn't appear until it was included on the track listing of ***The Best of Cliff Vol. 2*** in 1972.
The original song is a pleading love song to the titular character wondering why, given his love for her, she never stays and wondering what she is doing. With a lovely oboe and gentle string accompaniment, Cliff sings this simple appealing love song with much emotion. The chorus includes a full orchestra and the uncredited female backing vocals (which is likely to be the Breakaways but this is unconfirmed), before returning to the simplicity of the beginning. There is a piano instrumental interlude that fits perfectly with the structure of the rest of the song. It is, overall, a beautiful performance that deserved to get a better placing in the charts.
The song was chosen for inclusion on Cliff's first German language album, *Hier Ist Cliff*, and was recorded at the first of four sessions slated for completing the album's tracks. Rather than using the English backing track and overdubbing the German vocals, a completely new recording was made. The German version has only ever been released in stereo and was a major rarity until it was issued on the foreign language compilation ***On the Continent*** in 1997. Repeating the same harp, oboe and (uncredited) female backing vocal introduction, the pace is slightly faster than the English original.

Track Specification

1. Single
Composed by Sergio Endrigo; English lyrics by Bill Owen

Musicians		*Recording Details*	
Mike Leander	arranger, conductor	Producer	Norrie Paramor
Mike Leander Orchestra	orchestra	Engineered by	Peter Vince
Cliff Richard	vocals	Recording location	Chappell Studios, London
Unknown	backing vocals	Recording date	2nd July 1968

2. Hier Ist Cliff
Composed by Sergio Endrigo; English lyrics by Kurt Feltz

Musicians		*Recording Details*	
Norrie Paramor Orchestra	orchestra	Producer	Norrie Paramor
Norrie Paramor	arranger, director	Engineered by	Peter Vince
Cliff Richard	vocals	Recording location	Abbey Road Studio 2, St. John's Wood, London
Unknown	backing vocals	Recording date	31st October 1968

♫ Maria No Mas
From the album **When in Spain**

Recorded again under the Portuguese title ***Maria Ninguém*** but in the Italian language for Cliff Richard's ***When in Rome*** album, the same backing track was used as for the ***When in Spain*** sessions but with the Italian vocals overdubbed. *Maria No Mas* (or the literal translation of *Maria No More*) was the final track to be recorded for the Spanish album at its own session at the EMI Studios in Barcelona after four days of intensive recording. The eleventh and final take and edit were used for the mono and stereo recordings but with different mixes for the audio channels and is a favourite of Cliff's from the album's sessions.
Although the backing instrumentation by the Shadows is split across the stereo channels, Cliff's vocals are placed in the left only. The Spanish rhythm is kept up by Bruce Welch's stentorian chord structure as Hank Marvin performs a complex accompanying melody on Spanish guitar under Cliff's lead vocal line. The backing vocals (Cliff and Bruce overdubbed at a later session) are sparse but add an extra dimension to the end of the chorus.

Track Specification
Composed by Carlos Lyra and M. Salina

Musicians		*Recording Details*	
Brian Bennett	drums, percussion	Producer	Norrie Paramor
Brian 'Licorice' Locking	bass	Engineered by	Malcolm Addey
Hank Marvin	guitar	Recording location	EMI Studios, Barcelona (main) and Abbey Road Studio 2 (backing vocals)
Cliff Richard	vocals, backing vocals		
Bruce Welch	backing vocals, rhythm guitar	Recording date	1st May 1963 (main recording) and 28th May 1963 (backing vocals)

♫ Marked with Death
From the albums **Songs from Heathcliff** *and* **Heathcliff Live**

Having run away from Heathcliff (Cliff Richard) and her dull but domineering husband Edgar (Darryl Knock in the stage show) on to the beloved but stormy moors, Cathy (Olivia Newton-John on the studio album ***Songs from Heathcliff*** and Helen Hobson in the stage show) is having trouble with her pregnancy. In pain, it is Heathcliff for whom she calls, and she tells him that he has killed her. The duet is performed between the couple on the moors as Heathcliff tells Cathy that she is the architect of her broken heart and not him as they embrace. They tell each other how much they love each other but they know that she is dying. Desperately, Heathcliff carries her back across the moors to try to save her but to no avail as he cries in grief for her passing. He urges her not to leave him and to be with him forever, segueing neatly into the final song from the studio album, ***Be with Me Always***.

A piano introduction ushers in this sad and gently reflective and regretful song. Cliff sings the song with restrained emotion while Olivia is almost breathless as she makes her admissions of love. The church-like organ is present again as Cathy's death comes near and while they gently admonish each other. The live version is introduced by whistling wind and the soliloquy by Helen Hobson, interrupted by Cliff as he finds her dying on the moors. The gentleness of the keyboard accompaniment belies the turbulent emotion that is felt in the song.

Track Specification
Composed by John Farrar and Tim Rice

1. Songs from Heathcliff

Musicians	
Sean Callery	orchestrator, synclavier, keyboards
John Farrar	guitar, synclavier
Olivia Newton-John	vocals
Cliff Richard	vocals
Bob Sabellico	drum programming
Michael Thompson	guitar

Recording Details	
Producer	John Farrar
Engineered by	Chris Fogel, Eric Rudd and Joe Schiff (Moonee Ponds Studio), Darren Goodwin and Guy Massey (Abbey Road Studios) and James Collins and Caroline Daniel (CTS Studios)
Recording location	Moonee Ponds Studio, Los Angeles, Abbey Road Studios, St. John's Wood, London and CTS Studios, Wembley, London
Mixed by	Chris Fogel
Mixed at	Moonee Ponds Studio, Los Angeles
Recording date	February-April 1994 and May-August 1995

2. Heathcliff Live

Musicians	
Sean Callery	orchestrator, orchestra
John Clark	guitar
Keith Hayman	keyboards
Helen Hobson	spoken vocals, vocals
Peter May	drums, percussion
Bob Noble	keyboards
Alan Park	keyboards
Cliff Richard	spoken vocals, vocals
Steve Stroud	bass
Kevin Townend	orchestration
Unknown	orchestra

Recording Details	
Producer	John Farrar
Engineered by	Keith Bessey, John Pearson and Tom Tranter
Recording location	Earl's Court Hall 2, London and/or The Academy, National Indoor Arena, Birmingham, England
Recording date	October 1996

♫ Marmaduke

Unissued live track and B-side of **Mistletoe and Wine**

When the Shadows temporarily disbanded in the late sixties, Hank Marvin and Bruce Welch joined forces with Australian John Farrar to form the somewhat unimaginatively titled group Marvin, Welch & Farrar. They produced two albums before Bruce left and Hank and John released one further album together. In the first guise, *Marmaduke*, written by as then unknown writing duo of Alan Tarney and Trevor Spencer, was released in 1972 as the group's final single, although it failed to make any impact on the UK singles charts. There is some controversy regarding the composers: on the original album and single release by Marvin, Welch and Farrar, it was assigned to Tarney and Spencer but, in later years, the name of Mervyn began to crop up as a joint composer although no first name could be found. In fact, this is incorrect and should remain as a sole Tarney and Spencer composition with the publisher being Mervyn Music Ltd. – the name has somehow been added to the writer list in error in some standard and online publications.

Cliff Richard took up the song to perform sixteen years later for his *Live & Guaranteed 1988!* tour. The Danish leg was filmed and recorded for VHS release, which was then reissued with a CD album accompanying it. However, on neither formats was the live version of *Marmaduke* released.

Cliff took the song into the studio a couple of months later and recorded it alongside another eventual B-side, ***All the Time You Need***, and it was chosen as the principal B-side for all the format variants of single release of ***Mistletoe and Wine***. Unusually, other than those releases, it never found its way on to any other format until it was included as a bonus track on the 2004 remaster of the ***Stronger*** album. Cliff's version is far heavier than the Marvin, Welch & Farrar version, with a fuzzed guitar driving the counterpointed melody. The bouncy rhythm is reminiscent of a Status Quo performance and it is matched by the impassioned and occasionally raucous vocals over the running guitar lines. The arrangement of the vocals is one of the most extraordinary parts of the song, particularly in the middle eight when the backing vocalists join Cliff in an *a capella* rendition as they sing about the train, with the whistle portrayed by the guitar. The song deserved broader exposure and many would be surprised by the rocky nature of the song from a period when synthesisers were the standard instrument of choice.

Track Specification
Composed by Alan Tarney and Trevor Spencer

1. Unissued track (Live & Guaranteed 1988!)

Musicians

John Clark	guitar
Rosemarie Ford	backing vocals
Mark Griffiths	bass
Peter Howarth	backing vocals
Steve Lauri	guitar
Paul Moessl	keyboards
Mick Mullins	backing vocals
Alan Park	keyboards
Cliff Richard	vocals
Henry Spinetti	drums, percussion

Recording Details

Producer	Unknown
Engineered by	Unknown
Recording location	Fyens Forum, Odense, Denmark
Recording date	22nd May 1988

2. B-side (Mistletoe and Wine)

Musicians

John Clark	guitar
Mark Griffiths	bass
Peter Howarth	backing vocals
Steve Lauri	guitar
Paul Moessl	synthesisers
Mick Mullins	backing vocals
Keith Murrell	backing vocals
Alan Park	piano
Cliff Richard	vocals
Henry Spinetti	drums, percussion

Recording Details

Producer	Cliff Richard
Engineered by	Gerry Kitchingham and Ben Robbins
Recording location	R. G. Jones Studios, Wimbledon, London
Recording date	August 1988

♬ Mary's Boy Child
From the album **Cliff at Christmas**

Because of the religious motifs and approximation to the Nativity story, *Mary's Boy Child*, written in 1956, is now often sung as a modern-day Christmas carol. First recorded by Harry Belafonte, who reached number one with his single at Christmas 1957, it was also a number twenty-six hit for Nina and Frederick in 1959, while Boney M melded *Oh My Lord* to it and successfully created a Christmas number one in 1978. Since then, a host of artists have covered it including Bryn Terfel, the Calico Consort, Charlotte Church, Jim Reeves, the Lettermen, Nat King Cole, Roger Whittaker, the Three Degrees, Harry Connick Jr. and John Denver among several others.

Having recorded Christmas material in 1991 for the album ***Together with Cliff Richard***, Cliff Richard wanted to update the track listing and add new material to accompany the release of his next single ***Santa's List*** in 2003. Having already sung a duet with Helmut Lotti, ***Danny Boy***, for the latter's solo album, Lotti was invited to join Cliff on his own version of *Mary's Boy Child*. The song later appeared as a B-side item on the second disc of the dual CD single release of *Santa's List*. At the same time, the track was issued on a promotional disc with only the one track for media use only on the EMI label (catalogue number CLIFF 300).

Creating a reggae beat with a gospel choir built up behind Cliff's lead vocals, his cover has echoes of both Belafonte's and Boney M's versions but improves on both. In this performance, Lotti's vocal line sounds very similar to Cliff's in timbre and on occasions it is quite difficult to tell them apart until they have sung their chosen sections for a long period.

Track Specification
Composed by Jester Hairston

Musicians

Pete Beachill	trombone
Katie Beadle	backing vocals
Stuart Brooks	trumpet
Lizzie Deane	backing vocals
Mike Drinkwater	keyboards
Mike Haughton	saxophone
Helmut Lotti	vocals
Ian Mack	backing vocals, programming
Stuart Mack	backing vocals, guitar, keyboards
Dave Nettleton	guitar
Cliff Richard	vocals

Recording Details

Producer	Brothers Mack
Engineered by	Tim Earnes
Recording location	Metropolis Studios, London
Recording date	2003

♬ Mary What You Gonna Call That Pretty Little Baby?
From the album **Good News**

Taken from the Broadway musical *Black Nativity*, the lengthily titled *Mary What You Gonna Call That Pretty Little Baby?* is a spiritual-cum-gospel song that was included on the track listing of Cliff Richard's first religious song album, ***Good News***. Recorded at the session on 27th April, it was completed in five takes.

Reminiscent of a song from one of the many theatrical musicals from the period, Mike Leander's orchestral arrangement tends to overwhelm the performance by the Shadows. In addition, the shrill backing vocals detract from the beauty of Cliff's performance; these are provided by an uncredited group but are likely to be the Mike Sammes Singers.

Track Specification
Composed by Richard King, arranged by Mike Leander

Musicians

Brian Bennett	drums, percussion
Mike Leander	arranger, conductor
Hank Marvin	guitar
Mike Leander Orchestra	orchestra
Cliff Richard	vocals
John Rostill	bass
Unknown	backing vocals
Bruce Welch	rhythm guitar

Recording Details

Producer	Norrie Paramor
Engineered by	Peter Vince and Mike Stone
Recording location	Abbey Road Studio 2, St. John's Wood, London
Recording date	27th April 1967

♫ Matter of Moments, A

From the film soundtrack album of **Wonderful Land**

Another romantic interlude in the ***Wonderful Land*** film as Johnny (Cliff Richard) professes his love for Jenny (Susan Hampshire). She is suspicious that he has been absent but he can't tell her that he has been working on a dual film for fear of upsetting her. But he confirms that he is here now with her and that he loves her. They are up a mountainside, sitting on a rug. They get up and take a walk as he starts singing, they take a horse and cart and then make their way back down the mountainside, finishing with a tender kiss.

The tender ballad, written by Bruce Welch, is notable in that it is the last chronological appearance of bassist Brian Locking on a Cliff Richard recording. He was to be replaced by John Rostill (who also appears in the film) so that he could concentrate on his religious activities. For the only track to be recorded in that session, the same (unknown) take and edit were used for the mono and stereo recordings but with different mixes to cater for the requirements of the separate audio channels. One of Cliff's favourite ballads, *A Matter of Moments* was chosen as the B-side of the only single from the project, ***On the Beach***, and also appears on the track listing of the ***Wonderful Life No. 2*** EP. The film version is very similar to the soundtrack version with the exception of the more overt orchestral backing. This unreleased version was probably recorded in the first three months of 1964, although the musicians (other than Cliff and the Shadows), the studio personnel and recording location are unavailable.

Bruce is a much under-rated tunesmith and has a great ear for a strong melody and this is clear in his composition for the film. Beginning with his rhythm guitar supporting his harmonies against Hank Marvin's, Cliff's vocals come in with this reflective little ballad-cum-love-song. The bridge section is particularly beautiful with its augmented musical intervals.

Track Specification
Composed by Bruce Welch

Musicians

Brian Bennett	drums, percussion
Brian 'Licorice' Locking	bass
Hank Marvin	backing vocals, guitar
Norrie Paramor Orchestra	orchestra
Norrie Paramor	arranger, conductor
Cliff Richard	vocals
Bruce Welch	backing vocals, rhythm guitar

Recording Details

Producer	Norrie Paramor
Engineered by	Malcolm Addey
Recording location	Abbey Road Studio 2, St. John's Wood, London
Recording date	10th November 1963

♫ Maybe Someday

From the album **Dressed for the Occasion**

Cliff Richard regularly performed songs on stage that he hadn't recorded in the studio and, while he used to perform a large amount of material from his hits and recent albums, the ***Dressed for the Occasion*** concert at the Royal Albert Hall featured a significant number of such songs, one of which was *Maybe Someday*.

The dance-like arrangement introduced on the strings of the London Philharmonic Orchestra ushers in Cliff's lead vocal line. What this performance shows is not only his ability to sing any type of melodic song but also his ability to pitch the notes perfectly. The song is performed entirely with the orchestra with none of the supporting vocalists or the rock band musicians.

Track Specification
Composed by Dean Klevatt and Karel Fialka

Musicians

Richard Hewson	arranger, conductor
London Philharmonic Orchestra	orchestra
Cliff Richard	vocals

Recording Details

Producer	Cliff Richard and Richard Hewson
Engineered by	John Kurlander
Mixed by	Keith Bessey
Recording location	Royal Albert Hall, London
Mixed at	Strawberry Studios South, Surrey
Recording date	23rd November 1982

♬ May God Be with You
Unissued track

Published in 1953 in its original Spanish form of ***Vaya con Dios***, the song is often subtitled *May God Be with You*, although it more accurately translates as the slightly different *Go with God*. It was first recorded by Les Paul and Mary Ford in late 1953, earning them a US Billboard number one and a UK number seven with their only British release. Twenty years later in December 1973, Millican and Nesbitt successfully reached number twenty in the UK chart. It has also been covered by many different artists including Desi Arnaz, Bing Crosby, Chet Atkins, the Drifters, Gene Autrey, Julio Iglesias, Kitty Kallen, Mel Tormé, Nana Mouskouri, Julie London, Al Martino, Roger Whittaker and Tony Orlando and Dawn.
Cliff Richard recorded the Spanish version for his album ***When in Spain*** in 1963 and, at the end of January 1965, he re-recorded the vocals in English of many of the songs from those sessions in Barcelona and they were overdubbed on the original instrumental backing track for release on his upcoming ***Cliff Richard*** album. For whatever reason, however, this track was not included on the track listing and remains unissued to date.

Track Specification
Composed by Larry Russell, Inez James and Buddy Pepper

Musicians

Brian Bennett	drums, percussion
Brian 'Licorice' Locking	bass
Hank Marvin	guitar
Norrie Paramor Strings	orchestra
Norrie Paramor	arranger, conductor
Cliff Richard	vocals
Bruce Welch	rhythm guitar

Recording Details

Producer	Norrie Paramor
Engineered by	Malcolm Addey
Recording location	EMI Studios, Barcelona (backing track) and Abbey Road Studio 2 (strings and vocals)
Recording date	30th April 1963 (backing track), 14th May 1963 (strings) and 31st January 1965 (vocals)

♬ May the Good Lord Bless and Keep You
From the album **Good News**

Originally published in 1950, *May the Good Lord Bless and Keep You* was used as the theme song to *The Big Show* fronted by actress Tallulah Bankhead and she employed her huskily deep spoken vocals over the instrumental melody. It was then picked up by Kate Smith, who used it to close her television show in the US. Now a standard, the intent of the wishes in the song makes it a beloved tune, particularly to close a show and bid the audiences goodbye and farewell, and it has been covered by artists such as Bing Crosby, Eddy Arnold, the Andrews Sisters, the Jordanaires, Gene Autry, Perry Como, Nat King Cole, Frankie Laine, Jim Reeves, Katherine Jenkins, Tammy Wynette and Ernest Tubb among others.
Used as the closing song to Cliff Richard's first album of religious songs, ***Good News***, *May the Good Lord Bless and Keep You* was issued with a splice of the first and third takes and was also the final song to be recorded at the session. A fitting title to complete the album, Cliff's accomplished vocal style lift a song that could easily become tedious and, in his professional hands, the song is a beautiful thing to listen to. There is an uncredited backing vocal group, who sing in a subdued way behind a few of his verses and in the instrumental break.

Track Specification
Composed by Meredith Willson

Musicians

Bernard Ebbinghouse Orchestra	orchestra
Bernard Ebbinghouse	arranger, conductor
Cliff Richard	vocals
Unknown	backing vocals

Recording Details

Producer	Norrie Paramor
Engineered by	Peter Vince and Mike Stone
Recording location	Abbey Road Studio 2, St. John's Wood, London
Recording date	3rd May 1967

♬ Me and My Shadows – Reprise
From the album **The Rock 'n' Roll Years 1958-1963**

Taking the Al Jolson favourite, *Me and My Shadow*, and pluralizing the second word for the pun that would be used as the title of an album and several EPs, it was also used as the title of Cliff Richard and the Shadows' regular radio slot from 1959-1962 on Radio Luxembourg, where the slightly updated lyrics were recorded live topping and tailing the show.
The song in its original form was a popular Al Jolson song from 1927 and, although Jolson has a writing credit, he was the performer, who often added his name to the credits of the songs he sang for the money; however, he may have made a small contribution in order to warrant the co-composer credit. It has been recorded by a number of artists including Elkie Brooks, Judy Garland, Liberace, Vic Damone, Perry Como, Nat Shilkret, Lou Rawls, Peggy Lee and Robbie Williams with Jonathan Wilkes, although it is Frank Sinatra and Sammy Davis Jr. who had the UK singles hit in December 1962, reaching number twenty with a change of lyrics referencing John and Bobby Kennedy.
Although most of the material Cliff and the Shadows recorded live for the radio show has not been released, four tracks were added to ***The Rock 'n' Roll Years 1958-1963*** including *Me and My Shadows – Reprise*, which comes from the show's end. Since the radio station only broadcast in the one-channel AM, this track is only available in mono.
The arrangement of the song is very different from the familiar treatment it is usually given, with rock and roll syncopation and a faster tempo applied. While the announcer signs the show off with the Ever Ready batteries sponsor ident after Cliff sings the first verse only, the Shadows are given free rein to jam an instrumental before the track fades.

Track Specification
Composed by Al Jolson, Billy Rose and Dave Dreyer; updated title and lyrics by Cliff Richard and the Shadows

Musicians		*Recording Details*	
Jet Harris	bass	Producer	Unknown
Hank Marvin	guitar	Engineered by	Unknown
Tony Meehan	drums, percussion	Recording location	Radio Luxembourg Studios, London
Cliff Richard	vocals	Recording date	1961
Bruce Welch	rhythm guitar		

♫ Mean Streak
4th UK single

After the relative poor chart showing of Cliff Richard and the Drifters' third single, ***Livin' Lovin' Doll,*** due to the political machinations against the upcoming mooted single from *Serious Charge,* **Living Doll,** it was back to a tried and tested formula for the fourth single. Both ***Move It*** and ***High Class Baby*** had been written by then Drifters guitarist Ian Samwell and so it was that *Mean Streak* was chosen, which he co-wrote with Joseph Seener. It worked to an extent because the single just made it into the top ten, nestling at number ten as its highest achievement.
The song is a familiar sound, this time bolstered by having new Shadows guitarist Hank Marvin on lead. *Mean Streak* was recorded at the same session as *Livin' Lovin' Doll,* where Cliff had to fight for Hank to play lead guitar and was proven to be correct that, while the session musicians were competent, they didn't have the same verve or understanding of the music he was trying to record. The song is a straightforward rock and roll tune that talks about a relationship that is heading for the rocks because the girl is mean and he can't cope with the emotions that induces. The guitar solos help embellish Cliff's vocal performance and continue to show the future ensemble expertise that the band would develop.
Backed with ***Never Mind,*** which would be given its own chart placing a week after *Mean Streak* entered the singles charts, it was issued on the Columbia label (catalogue numbers DB 4290 (78 r.p.m. format) and 45-DB 4290 (seven-inch single format)) in April 1959. Since then, it has regularly appeared on a number of collations of Cliff's early work.

Track Specification
Composed by Ian Samwell and Joseph Seener

Musicians		*Recording Details*	
Jet Harris	bass	Producer	Norrie Paramor
Hank Marvin	guitar	Engineered by	Peter Bown and Stuart Eltham
Cliff Richard	vocals	Recording location	Abbey Road Studio 2, St. John's Wood, London
Terry Smart	drums, percussion	Recording date	14th November 1958
Bruce Welch	rhythm guitar		

♫ Mean Woman Blues
From the album **Cliff Sings**

Of the sixteen songs presented on Cliff Richard's second album, half were backed by the Norrie Paramor Orchestra; the remainder was supported by The Drifters, as they were then still called although they had undergone a name change to The Shadows by the time of the album release to avoid confusion with the pre-existing American vocal group of the same name, once ***Living Doll*** had become a success in the US. *Mean Woman Blues* fell into the latter category and was one of the songs from the soundtrack of the Elvis Presley film *Loving You,* which had then been recently released. It was later recorded by Roy Orbison as a double A-side track with *Blue Bayou* and reached number five in the Billboard charts and number three in the UK charts in late 1963. The song has also been covered by the Spencer Davis Group, Jerry Lee Lewis, Dion, and Carl Perkins along with many others over the years.
As with many of the tracks on the album, *Mean Woman Blues* was also released in the EP format, with the mono edit being the same as the album version while the stereo version took the same take but edited it slightly differently for the channel separation with a later fade-out than the mono release, providing a few more seconds of Hank Marvin's guitar line: this extended version was later issued on ***The Rock 'n' Roll Years 1958-1963***.
A plaintive guitar introduction leads into Cliff humming before a rip-roaring version of the song is initiated. Although Cliff confirms that Elvis was his idol, there is no propensity to make this recording a complete imitation of Presley's original, although there are the occasional nods in that direction particularly with the end of each couplet where Cliff enunciates the trademark 'uh-huh-huh'. The middle eight has the Shadows in full throttle and giving some idea of what their future instrumental career would be like. But this is firmly an ensemble piece with the band's musicianship ably supporting Cliff's raucous rock and roll vocal line.

Track Specification
Composed by Claude DeMetrius

Musicians		*Recording Details*	
Jet Harris	bass	Producer	Norrie Paramor
Hank Marvin	guitar	Engineered by	Malcolm Addey and Alan Kane (mono) and Stuart Eltham and Norman Smith (stereo)
Tony Meehan	drums, percussion		
Cliff Richard	vocals	Recording location	Abbey Road Studio 2, St. John's Wood, London
Bruce Welch	rhythm guitar	Recording date	7th September 1959

♫ Meditation
From the album **Kinda Latin**

Originally a Portuguese song – with the compositional title *Meditação – Meditation* is a bossa nova standard that has been covered by Frank Sinatra, Chet Atkins, Jack Jones, Brad Prevedoros, Count Basie, the writer of the song Antônio Carlos Jobim, Salena Jones and Andy Williams amongst many others and should not be confused with the jazz title of the same name written by Duke Ellington.
Meditation was recorded by Cliff Richard with an orchestral backing in just one take at the first of three sessions in October 1965 for Cliff's ***Kinda Latin*** album. The final song to be completed on the day, that sole take and edit were used for both the mono and stereo recordings but with different mixes according to the needs of the audio channels.
Introduced by syncopated percussion played quietly (in the left channel), Cliff brings his vocal gently in and adds the occasional vibrato on the sustained notes. He is in his element with this style of song because he instinctively knows when to inculcate the necessary light and shade as dictated by the accompaniment and the requirements of the lyrics.

Track Specification
Composed by Antônio Carlos Jobim and Newton Mendonça; English lyrics Norman Gimbel

Musicians		*Recording Details*	
Bernard Ebbinghouse Orchestra	orchestra	Producer	Norrie Paramor
Bernard Ebbinghouse	arranger, conductor	Engineered by	Peter Bown
Cliff Richard	vocals	Recording location	Abbey Road Studio 2, St. John's Wood, London
		Recording date	4th October 1965

♫ Medley (1)
From the album **Cliff in Japan**

On many of Cliff's tours, he would sing a number of specific and familiar songs arranged together as a medley particularly those that he hadn't sung elsewhere in the set list. For his 1967 tour of Japan, which was recorded and released as ***Cliff in Japan,*** he performed five songs together from songs that were popular in that country:

a) ***Let's Make a Memory***
b) ***The Young Ones***
c) ***Lucky Lips***
d) ***Summer Holiday***
e) ***We Say Yeah***

The entries for those carry the information on the recording details and musicians.

♫ Medley (2)
Unissued live track

Medleys of songs were a general feature of Cliff's tours, and he chose familiar songs that he hadn't sung elsewhere in the set list. For his 1968 concerts from the Talk of the Town theatre, he created a medley of his popular songs:

a) ***The Young Ones***
b) ***Lucky Lips***
c) ***Living Doll***
d) ***In the Country***

Although this medley was not included on the final release, the entries for those carry the information on the recording details and musicians.

♫ Medley (3)
Unissued live track

For Cliff's tours, he usually created a medley of his favourite religious songs that he hadn't sung elsewhere in the set list. For the *Live & Guaranteed 1988!* tour, which was filmed and recorded for release on video and then a subsequent CD in 1995, he created a medley of his popular religious-based songs:

a) ***UFO***
b) ***Thief in the Night***
c) ***I Wish We'd All Been Ready***

Although this medley was not included on the final edit, the entries for those carry the information on the recording details and musicians.

♫ Medley (4)
From the album **From a Distance ***** The Event**

To close out the *Oh Boy! Set* that opened ***The Event*** to celebrate Cliff Richard's thirty years in show business, it finished as it started with a medley of songs from the rock 'n' roll era when Cliff started his career. Assisted by the Dallas Boys and the Vernons Girls (both vocal groups who backed him on the *Oh Boy!* television programme) and the Kalin Twins (whom

Cliff superseded to get top billing when they toured with Cliff as support when ***Move It*** was originally released), the medley featured:

a) ***Book of Love***
b) ***Blue Moon***
c) ***Do You Wanna Dance?***
d) ***Chantilly Lace***
e) ***At the Hop***
f) ***Rock 'n' Roll Is Here to Stay***

The section ends with Cliff singing the final line from ***Teddy Bear***, although this is not credited on any of the releases associated with the event and, for this reason, the title is not included in the medley here either.
The entries for those tracks in the medley as well as the nod towards *Teddy Bear* all carry the information on the recording details and musicians.

♬ Me Lo Dijo Adela

From the album **When in Spain**

Subtitled ***Sweet and Gentle***, *Me Lo Dijo Adela* literally translates as *Say It to Me Sweetly*. The Spanish language version has been covered by a number of artists (principally Latin-based) including Bobby Capó, Orquesta América, Tito Rodriguez and Chico O'Farrill among others.
On 31st January 1965, Cliff Richard recorded the English version with the lyrics being overdubbed on to this base track recorded in Barcelona for the ***When in Spain*** album's Spanish language version of *Me Lo Dijo Adela*. The last of three songs to be recorded at the session, the seventh and final take and edit were used for the mono and stereo recordings but with different mixes for the audio channel requirements.
Over the period of the early sixties, the Shadows experimented with Spanish music, either written by members of the band or by others, and *Me Lo Dijo Adela* shows how they perfected the technique of the Spanish rhythms, particularly with Bruce Welch's stentorian rhythm guitar chords and Hank Marvin's adept solo lines. Cliff's vocals show that he really enjoys the experience of singing the song. There is an uncredited piano on the track, which is likely to be Norrie Paramor and, although a few tracks on the parent album separate the stereo pleasingly, here it forces Cliff into the left channel and everything else into the right.

Track Specification
Composed by Otilio Portal

Musicians		*Recording Details*	
Brian Bennett	drums, percussion	Producer	Norrie Paramor
Brian 'Licorice' Locking	bass	Engineered by	Malcolm Addey
Hank Marvin	guitar	Recording location	EMI Studios, Barcelona
Cliff Richard	vocals	Recording date	30th April 1963
Unknown	piano		
Bruce Welch	rhythm guitar		

♬ Melting into One

Unissued track

For the twentieth anniversary of Cliff Richard and the Shadows working in music and showbusiness together and separately, a set of concerts was put on at the London Palladium in March 1978. The result was televised (and subsequently released on video) and the performances produced an associated album. The track listings of both video and album differ to some degree, while there was a collection of songs that were not included on either. On the liner notes for the remastered version of ***Thank You Very Much*** in 2004, it was stated that one of those songs was *Melting into One*, although there is no information regarding the song, its writer or even its genre. It is included here for completeness and will be updated when further information is unearthed regarding its provenance.

Track Specification
Composed by Unknown

Musicians		*Recording Details*	
Terry Britten	guitar	Producer	Bruce Welch
Stuart Calver	backing vocals	Engineered by	Tony Clark
Clem Cattini	drums, percussion	Recording location	London Palladium, London
Dave Christopher	guitar	Recording date	4th March 1978
Mo Foster	bass		
Graham Jarvis	drums, percussion		
Graham Murray	guitar		
John Perry	backing vocals		
Cliff Richard	vocals		
Tony Rivers	backing vocals		
Graham Todd	keyboards		

♫ Memories

From the album **I'm Grateful** *(Garth Hewitt)*

Although Cliff Richard was otherwise busy with recording his next album ***Rock 'n' Roll Juvenile*** in the latter part of 1978 and into 1979, he found time to help out his friend Garth Hewitt by singing backing vocals on three tracks for his album, *I'm Grateful*, including Hewitt's self-penned song *Memories*, on which Cliff is also credited with handclaps. The song was subsequently reissued on CD in 2003 when it was included on the album *30 Songs Spanning 30 Years 1973-2003*.
An excellent harmonica introduction supported by stilted guitar chords leads into Hewitt's vocals, which have a trembling vibrato that creates an extra emotion. With a country feel to the performance that has echoes of *Hickory Holler's Tramp*, the backing vocals add further to the ensemble piece and Cliff's contribution is by the strongest.

Track Specification
Composed by Garth Hewitt

Musicians

B. J. Cole	steel guitar
Rod Edwards	backing vocals, hand claps, piano
Mike Giles	drums, percussion
Roger Hand	backing vocals, hand claps
Garth Hewitt	vocals, acoustic guitar, harmonica
John G. Perry	bass
Cliff Richard	backing vocals, hand claps
Bob Weston	guitar

Recording Details

Producer	Jon Miller, Rod Edwards and Roger Hand
Engineered by	Roger T. Wake
Recording location	Redan Recorders, London
Recording date	August 1978

♫ Memories Linger On

From the album **Listen to Cliff!**

The third of five original songs written for inclusion on ***Listen to Cliff!***, *Memories Linger On* was composed by Shadows rhythm guitarist Bruce Welch and long-term collaborator and friend Peter Chester from the early days of their career.
The mono and stereo versions of *Memories Linger On* used the tenth take and edit but employed different mixes to achieve the requirements of the separate aural channels. It was one of the few tracks that were not also released in EP format.
An andante sad song looking back on a love that has died, it is a quite familiar Cliff and the Shadows style of song, with the exception that there are saccharine swelling strings echoing each of the four lines of the verse. While not the best song on the album, it is an interesting exercise in displaying Cliff's vocal talents as well as providing a showcase for Bruce's songwriting abilities.

Track Specification
Composed by Peter Chester and Bruce Welch

Musicians

Jet Harris	bass
Hank Marvin	guitar
Tony Meehan	drums, percussion
Cliff Richard	vocals
Unknown	strings
Bruce Welch	rhythm guitar

Recording Details

Producer	Norrie Paramor
Engineered by	Malcolm Addey and Norman Smith
Recording location	Abbey Road Studio 2, St. John's Wood, London
Recording date	26th July 1960

♫ Mer, La

From the EP **When in France**

Allegedly written in ten minutes on SNCF toilet paper while on a train travelling from Paris to Narbonne by Charles Trenet, an often uncredited Leo Chauliac assisted with the melody later on. Completed in 1943, the song was not recorded until 1946 by Trenet himself, becoming a classic that appears in many a balladeers' repertoire. English words were written by Jack Lawrence, renaming it to *Beyond the Sea* with the most famous recording being for Bobby Darrin in 1959, who reached number eight in the UK charts in February 1960, and it charted again when released by George Benson in April 1985 when it only reached number sixty. In its original French title form, it has also been covered by a wide variety of artists including Alain Barriere, Guy Bonnet, Acker Bilk, Miguel Bosé, Richard Hayman and many others.
Cliff Richard and the Shadows also recorded the French language version during their summer season at Blackpool and it was one of the few for which an English cover was not recorded. Completed during three sessions over five days that resulted in the four tracks for the ***When in France*** EP, on which this track appears, a song for the ***Wonderful Life*** film soundtrack and a B-side, *La Mer* was recorded in eight takes and only released in mono format. It would take another twelve years for it to be released in any other format, when it was issued on the Belgian album *When in France... Chante en Français*. It was first released on CD as part of the 1989 See For Miles compilation ***The EP Collection: Ballads and Love Songs*** and has since appeared on other albums including ***On the Continent***.
Introduced by a cymbal crash crescendo, there are uncredited backing vocals (possibly the Mike Sammes Singers who were prevalent at the time on Cliff's recordings, which means they might have been overdubbed at a later date) before Cliff's assured vocal line comes in, requiring him to use his bass register frequently. Towards the end, there is a louche piano accompaniment, which is also uncredited but quite possibly Norrie Paramor. Hank Marvin's guitar and the supportive chords from Bruce Welch make this a forgotten but quintessential Cliff and the Shadows track.

Track Specification
Composed by Charles Trenet and Leo Chauliac

Musicians		*Recording Details*	
Brian Bennett	drums, percussion	Producer	Norrie Paramor
Brian 'Licorice' Locking	bass	Engineered by	Malcolm Addey and Jimmy Johnson
Hank Marvin	backing vocals, guitar	Recording location	Jubilee Hall, Blackpool
Cliff Richard	vocals	Recording date	5th August 1963
Unknown	backing vocals		
Unknown	piano		
Bruce Welch	backing vocals, rhythm guitar		

♫ Michelle

Unissued track subsequently released on **...And They Said It Wouldn't Last! (My 50 Years in Music)**

Michelle was intended to be an album track and either space or dissatisfaction prevented being on either ***Listen to Cliff*** or ***21 Today*** both released during this period. Three takes were recorded of the song before it was abandoned, remaining in the vaults until the issue of the rarity selection ***...And They Said It Wouldn't Last! (My 50 Years in Music)***.

The composer is not on the studio notes so remains unknown until further research unearths the information about this slow-paced love ballad aimed at the eponymous girl. Although the music is competently performed and Cliff's vocals are as exemplary as ever, the song feels a little lacklustre, although it is good to hear this hitherto hidden song from Cliff's history. The repetition of the title name is a little grating while the accompaniment appears to be recorded further back in the mix than was familiar for the band.

Track Specification
Composed by Unknown

Musicians		*Recording Details*	
Jet Harris	bass	Producer	Norrie Paramor
Hank Marvin	guitar	Engineered by	Malcolm Addey
Tony Meehan	drums, percussion	Recording location	Abbey Road Studio 2, St. John's Wood, London
Cliff Richard	vocals	Recording date	20th September 1960
Bruce Welch	rhythm guitar		

♫ Midnight Blue

From the film soundtrack album of **Take Me High**

The first song to be part of the narrative of the ***Take Me High*** film, *Midnight Blue* is presented in a country music style and the strains of the introductory bars are heard after Tim Matthews (played by Cliff Richard) is chucked out of the flat he shares with his girlfriend after revealing he is going to America for work purposes. He tries to mollify her with a present of a food mixer (at the time, this was a much desired luxury regularly given away on television game shows as the top prize and it was considered to be such because it was new, expensive and therefore aspirational). As he stands on the steps, the door is open and the box the mixer came in is thrown out. Placing the mixer into the box, Tim walks to a passing cement lorry and expertly throws the box into the truck's hod. After that, his black Mini Cooper is seen parked on a stretch of grass as he sits through the sunroof to sing the song. Then he sits inside and takes out a glass and a bottle of champagne from the glove-box and shoots the cork up through the sunroof and sips at the liquid. He checks his stubbly beard and begins to shave before finally taking out the BOAC airline tickets for his impending removal to America.

The song was the final one of three to be recorded at a session in late May 1973 and was completed in ten takes. There is a suggestion in Peter Lewry's and Nigel Goodall's *The Complete Recording Sessions 1958-1990* that these sessions may have only been for the backing tracks with vocals added in sessions over three days at the beginning of September; however, other sources seem to confirm that the vocals were applied at the same time as the backing track. For the moment, this entry will reflect that latter position until it can be confirmed or denied that the vocals were subsequently overdubbed.

An altogether gentler track to match the mood of the narrative, a piano and slide guitar introduce the evocative song that suits Cliff's vocal abilities perfectly. Presented at an andante pace, the song requires Cliff to use his lower register on occasions, while the middle eight features a honky tonk style piano solo, until the climax is reached with a rallentando.

Track Specification
Composed by Tony Cole

Musicians		*Recording Details*	
David MacKay Orchestra	orchestra	Producer	David MacKay
David MacKay	arranger, conductor	Engineered by	Tony Clark and Mike Jarrett
Cliff Richard	vocals	Recording location	Abbey Road Studio 3, St. John's Wood, London
		Recording date	28th May 1973

♫ Mighty Lonely Man, A

From the album **21 Today**

A Mighty Lonely Man was part of a marathon session that saw six songs recorded. The fifth and final take of this song was used for the stereo and mono edits but with different mixes for the audio channel requirements.

Swooping strings and a plinking guitar help Cliff to build up the emotion in this song that celebrates finding a girl at long last. It is reminiscent of the Elvis Presley ballads of the period and into the decade; however, the song is not that memorable, even though it tries hard with its variety of techniques to draw the listener in with key changes, light and shade in volume and so on.

Track Specification
Composed by Eddie Curtis

Musicians		*Recording Details*	
Mike Sammes Singers	backing vocals	Producer	Norrie Paramor
Norrie Paramor Orchestra	orchestra	Engineered by	Malcolm Addey
Norrie Paramor	arranger, conductor	Recording location	Abbey Road Studio 2, St. John's Wood, London
Cliff Richard	vocals	Recording date	30th January 1961

♬ Milk Cow Blues

Unreleased live track

In the August of 1958, with Cliff Richard and the Drifters about to enjoy much success with their first single, ***Move It***, which was scheduled for release at the end of the month, the band, which consisted of Cliff, Terry Smart and Ian Samwell in a pared-down line-up, took up a short residency at the Butlin's Holiday Camp based at Clacton-on-Sea on the Essex coast. Here they performed the standard covers that were expected of rock and roll outfits in Britain at the time.

On one night, a man called Stan Edwards took the opportunity to record one of their performances on a two-track tape machine. While some of the recordings made it on to the rarities retrospective, *The Rock 'n' Roll Years 1958-1963*, others of the songs were in poor condition to the point that they were unusable in a commercial release. This was the fate of *Milk Cow Blues* and a number of other tracks recorded that night.

Milk Cow Blues was a staple song in any performer's repertoire from the forties onwards and has been covered several times by artists such as Eddie Cochran, Rick Nelson, Elvis Presley, Glen Campbell and Willy Nelson among many others. Written by slide guitarist and singer Kokomo Arnold, it was one of his biggest hits when he recorded his version in the latter part of the thirties.

Track Specification
Composed by Kokomo Arnold

Musicians		*Recording Details*	
Cliff Richard	vocals, guitar	Producer	Unknown
Ian Samwell	guitar	Engineered by	Stan Edwards
Terry Smart	drums, percussion	Recording location	Rock 'n' Roll Ballroom, Butlin's Holiday Camp, Clacton-on-Sea, Essex
		Recording date	August 1958

♬ Millennium Prayer, The

129th UK single *and B-sides to* **The Millennium Prayer** *and* **Somewhere over the Rainbow/Wonderful World** *and from the album* **Songs of Praise – Songs from the Holy Land** *(Various) and unissued live track*

The vituperative criticism of Cliff Richard continued unabated when he recorded and released *The Millennium Prayer* in 1999. There were the snide asides that he was only interested in obtaining a Christmas number one while others sniggered that he had created a Christmas turkey. In reality, the performance of the song as a single defied all logic since there was very little airplay but it successfully sold almost a million copies in the UK alone and went to number one in a number of countries around the world.

Notwithstanding that, technically at least, the millennium actually started on 1st January 2001 rather than when all the digits flipped over from 1999 to 2000, what was realized was that, as far as the millennium celebrations were concerned, Christianity was being marginalized in spite it being the UK's principal religion. Paul Field and Stephen Deal were asked to come up with an hour's worth of material to help reverse this and they devised the concept album *Hopes & Dreams*. They knew they needed something to round off the music with something memorable and optimistic and it was reportedly Deal's wife who suggested that they should use the Lord's Prayer or *Auld Lang Syne*. Initially, the idea sounded crazy but Field took the notion home, sat down at the piano and began singing the starting lines of the prayer to the tune. With some minor lyric changes to make it scan better, he had it completed. Cliff was asked to record it for the album, which he did under ***The Lord's Prayer***, before returning to it in 1999 and retitling it ***The Millennium Prayer***.

The Lord's Prayer is probably the most famous and well-known prayer (in competition with Grace) in the Christian religion, which simply reveres the Christian God, asking Him for forgiveness and ability to deal with other's transgressions as well as ensuring there is sufficient to feed the supplicant. Taken directly from the Bible, it was realized that the tune that is most often associated with the oncoming New Year, *Auld Lang Syne* (otherwise referred to as *Roud*), could be used to sing the prayer albeit with a little manipulation.

Backed with another newly-recorded track, ***Two Worlds***, and sold in support of the Children's Promise charity, *The Millennium Prayer* was released as a single on the Papillon label (catalogue number PROMISECD01) on 15th November 1999. It reached number one in the UK on 4th December, displacing *King of My Castle* by the long-forgotten Wamdue Project, stayed in the top spot for three weeks, before being outsold by Westlife's covers of Abba's *I Have a Dream* doubled with Terry Jacks' *Seasons in the Sun*, thus making that the official Christmas and Millennium number one. An instrumental version (with just the backing vocals and without the lead) appeared on the Dutch release of the single (Roadrunner label, catalogue number RR 2125-3) issued on 29th November 1999, while this instrumental was also factored into the package of the US single release, which went under the title ***The Prayer (for the New Year)*** which was issued on the Sparrow Records label (catalogue number SPD 1811) on 21st November 2000 (in preparation for the true millennium change-over?). Finally, an *a capella* version was released as the B-side of ***Somewhere over the Rainbow/Wonderful World***, and it was claimed incorrectly to be included on the track listing of *The 50th Anniversary Album*. The promotional video featured Cliff in a white shirt and black trousers in front of a filmic backdrop showing the poor and ill children around the world - it was kept simple in part because of the budget given that he had just moved record labels from EMI to Papillon.

The bass drum keeps the song rhythmically on track, while Cliff's reverential vocals, packed with his trademark vibrato, slowly builds up the song as he makes the first pass through the Prayer. An orchestra and backing vocals (both of whom are uncredited) add extra layers to the second pass, as Cliff sings a harmonized version of the main melody including rising perfectly into falsetto for an octave leap. The middle eight has a trumpet solo which gives way to the choir supported by percussion as Cliff rejoins as the song reaches its climax and quietens as they sing "Amen" to the fade out.

On 2nd January 2000, the BBC broadcast a special *Songs of Praise* (their long-running religious television programme) that featured much of the *Hopes & Dreams* album and Cliff resurrected his very recent number one hit, *The Millennium Prayer*. The track was included on the now rare BBC album release, *Songs of Praise – Songs from the Holy Land* in April 2000.

An *a capella* version was recorded and released as the B-side of the second CD single disc of ***Somewhere over the Rainbow/What a Wonderful World*** in 2001. Ostensibly, it is the same basic melody line but with the drama created by the backing vocals. Cliff takes the lead with echo added in the first pass, while the choir joins in for the second run through the prayer. To begin with, it sounds sterile and empty but slowly, it intensifies.

In spite of the lack of seasonality by the time Cliff's tour came around to New Zealand in 2003, he still performed a ***Christmas Medley*** and followed it up with *A Millennium Prayer* to finish the concert (not as festive admittedly as the others but still associated with the season). This show was filmed for DVD release but the track was not included on the associated CD album, *World Tour Live*, in 2004.

Track Specification

1. Single
Composed by Traditional; arranged by Paul Field and Stephen Deal

Musicians		*Recording Details*	
David Arch	orchestral arranger, conductor	Producer	Nigel Wright
Paul Field	backing vocals	Engineered by	Unknown
Cliff Richard	vocals, backing vocals	Recording location	Skratch Studios, London and Whitfield Street Studios, London
Anne Skates	vocal arranger, backing vocals		
Unknown	backing vocals	Recording date	August 1999
Unknown	orchestra		
Unknown	trumpet solo		

2. B-side (The Millennium Prayer – instrumental (The Netherlands only))
Composed by Traditional; arranged by Paul Field and Stephen Deal

Musicians		*Recording Details*	
David Arch	orchestral arranger, conductor	Producer	Nigel Wright
Paul Field	backing vocals	Engineered by	Unknown
Cliff Richard	backing vocals	Recording location	Skratch Studios, London and Whitfield Street Studios, London
Anne Skates	vocal arranger, backing vocals		
Unknown	backing vocals	Recording date	August 1999
Unknown	orchestra		

3. B-side (Somewhere Over the Rainbow/Wonderful World)
Composed by Traditional; arranged by Anne Skates, Nigel Wright and Cliff Richard

Musicians		*Recording Details*	
Paul Field	backing vocals	Producer	Nigel Wright
Cliff Richard	vocals, backing vocals	Engineered by	Unknown
Anne Skates	vocal arranger, backing vocals	Recording location	Skratch Studios, London and Whitfield Street Studios, London
Nigel Wright	backing vocals		
		Recording date	August 1999

4. Songs of Praise – Songs from the Holy Land
Composed by Traditional; arranged by Paul Field and Stephen Deal

Musicians		*Recording Details*	
Hopes & Dreams Choir	backing vocals	Producer	Robert Prizeman
Cliff Richard	vocals	Engineered by	Unknown
Unknown	orchestra	Recording location	Cardiff Millennium Stadium, Cardiff, Wales
		Recording date	2nd January 2000

5. Unissued track (World Tour Live)
Composed by Traditional; arranged by Paul Field and Stephen Deal

Musicians		*Recording Details*	
Rachel Allen	violin	Producer	Keith Bessey
Elena Bulgakova	violin	Engineered by	Keith Bessey
Jenni Champion	violin	Recording location	The Mission Winery, Napier, New Zealand
Anthony Clark	backing vocals, guitar	Recording date	22nd February 2003
John Clark	guitar		
Dave Cooke	keyboards		
Cornelia Didenco	violin		
Gina Ferguson	violin		
Mike Haughton	saxophone		
Peter Howarth	backing vocals		
Cathy Irons	violin		
Pete May	drums, percussion		
Mick Mullins	backing vocals		
Keith Murrell	backing vocals		
Alan Park	keyboards		
Hee-Jung Park	violin		
Cliff Richard	vocals		
Eva Schwanen-Lilley	violin		
Steve Stroud	bass		

♫ Minute You're Gone, The

***29th UK single** and from the albums **Cliff in Japan**, **Cliff "Live" in Japan '72** and **Live in Japan** and unissued track*

Sonny James had recorded the Jimmy Gately tune *The Minute You're Gone* for his album of the same name in late 1963, and released it in early 1964. It has also been recorded by Al Martino, Gerry and the Pacemakers and Daniel O'Donnell, but it is probably James's version that inspired Cliff Richard to record it at the final Nashville session in the August of 1964.
The session musicians are unknown, although it was revealed to Cliff during the recording that four of them were from Elvis Presley's backing band, The Jordanaires, which made the recording sessions in Nashville more special for him, even though he didn't meet his idol. Although the eventual single and the song's appearance on the ***Angel*** EP were only in mono, the stereo version was first released on the compilation album ***The Best of Cliff*** and the final (unknown) take and edit were used for both the mono and stereo recordings but with different mixes for the separate audio channel requirements. Released as a single backed with ***Just Another Guy***, *The Minute You're Gone* was issued on the Columbia label (catalogue number DB 7496) on 5th March 1965. It reached the number one spot in several countries including the UK where it stayed for only one week before being displaced by the Beatles' *Ticket to Ride*. The single also marks the end of a remarkable run of top ten hits stretching back to ***A Voice in the Wilderness*** in January 1960; the following single, ***On My Word***, stalled at number twelve, thereby narrowly missing out on being the twenty-fourth successive top ten single – meanwhile, *The Minute You're Gone* was Cliff's eighth number one in just six years. The song has since featured on many compilations of Cliff's hits and remains a favourite of Cliff's from the sixties for the memories it evokes.
From the introductory *a capella* statement of the song title through the typical country instrumentation of tinkling piano and slide guitar to the *a capella* completion of the song, Cliff's apparent change in direction to the Nashville country sound serves him well and his voice fits perfectly with the song. The backing vocalists on the ***Cliff in Japan*** version may be the Breakaways, who appeared on tour with Cliff at the end of the decade but this not documented.
In April 1965, Cliff overdubbed German vocals on the original Nashville track for his sixth German language single, ***Es War Keine So Wunderbar Wie Du***. With lyrics provided by Kurt Hertha, ***Es Könnte Schon Morgen Sein*** was the B-side of the single, although it didn't chart.
Although the English original was recorded without the Shadows, they joined him on the song during the ***Thank You Very Much*** concert in 1978. The track was not released on either the video or the album and remains unissued. Prior to this, Bruce Welch and Hank Marvin played on the ***Cliff "Live" in Japan '72*** album, which also featured the perfect backing vocals of Olivia Newton-John and Pat Carroll, which come into their own when singing the second chorus on their own.

Track Specification
Composed by Jimmy Gately

1. Single

Musicians		*Recording Details*	
Jordanaires	male backing vocals	Producer	Bob Morgan and Billy Sherrill
Cliff Richard	vocals	Engineered by	Mort Thomason
Unknown	female backing vocals	Recording location	Columbia Studios, Nashville
Unknown	guitar	Recording date	25th August 1964
Unknown	slide guitar		
Unknown	bass		
Unknown	piano		
Unknown	violin		
Unknown	drums, percussion		

2. *Cliff in Japan*

Musicians		*Recording Details*	
Norrie Paramor Orchestra	orchestra	Producer	Norrie Paramor
Norrie Paramor	arranger, conductor	Engineered by	Unknown
Cliff Richard	vocals	Recording location	Shibuya Public Hall, Tokyo, Japan
Unknown	backing vocals	Recording date	18th October 1967

3. *Cliff "Live" in Japan '72*

Musicians		*Recording Details*	
Brian Bennett	drums, percussion	Producer	Norrie Paramor
Pat Carroll	backing vocals	Engineered by	Unknown
John Farrar	bass	Recording location	Kosei Nenkin Hall, Tokyo, Japan
Alan Hawkshaw	piano	Recording date	22nd-23rd September 1972
Hank Marvin	guitar		
Olivia Newton-John	backing vocals		
Cliff Richard	vocals		
Bruce Welch	rhythm guitar		

4. *Thank You Very Much*

Musicians		*Recording Details*	
Brian Bennett	drums, percussion	Producer	Bruce Welch
Alan Jones	bass	Engineered by	Tony Clark
Cliff Hall	keyboards	Recording location	London Palladium, London
Hank Marvin	guitar	Recording date	4th March 1978
Cliff Richard	vocals		
Bruce Welch	rhythm guitar		

♬ Miracle, The

128th UK single

Carefully constructed to be both religious (as in the title *The Miracle*) and with a contemporary feel to it, Cliff Richard's penultimate song on the ***Real as I Wanna Be*** album is credited to three people in the track listing but only one (misspelled) in the lyric sheet. However, the co-writing credits are correctly stated in the track specification of this entry. The dual CD issue of the final single release from the album featured non-album track ***Hope, Faith and You*** and a live version of ***The Twelfth of Never*** from the fortieth anniversary concert as the B-side of the first disc, while the second included non-album track ***Just Don't Say Goodbye*** and a further live anniversary track, ***Move It***. The single was issued on the Blacknight subsidiary (catalogue number CDEM 546) on 28th July 1999 and reached number twenty-three in the UK. Introduced by guitar and electric piano in staccato syncopation, the surprise comes when the vocals arrive, since they are largely *a capella*. Although the message is powerful and the performance is impassioned by Cliff, it is an unusual choice as a single, given the wealth of stronger material available elsewhere on the album, such as ***Vita Mia***.

Track Specification

Composed by Brenda Lee Eager, Zoë Fox and Terry Wollman

Musicians		*Recording Details*	
Vinnie Colaiuta	drums, percussion	Producer	Peter Wolf
Lynn Davis	backing vocals	Engineered by	Christian Leitgeb, Chris Heil, Paul Erickson and/or Keith Bessey
Kevin Dorsey	backing vocals	Recording location	Little America Recording Studios, Weiler, Austria
Siedah Garrett	backing vocals	Recording date	March-April 1996 and November 1997
James Ingram	backing vocals		
Paul Jackson Jr.	guitar		
Phil Perry	backing vocals		
Cliff Richard	vocals, backing vocals		
Michelle Wolf	backing vocals		
Peter Wolf	arranger, bass, keyboards, percussion		

♬ Miss You Nights

65th UK single** and special single (**From a Distance**) from the albums **Thank You Very Much**, **Dressed for the Occasion**, **Live and Guaranteed 1988!**, **From a Distance ** The Event Remaster**, **Centre Stage – The Very Best of Elaine Paige** (Elaine Paige) and **G4 & Friends** (G4) and B-side of **We Should Be Together** and **Scarlet Ribbons** and special track on the promotional **The Whole Story***

Perhaps, with the exception of ***Move It, Devil Woman*** and ***We Don't Talk Anymore***, the most important song that Cliff Richard has ever committed to tape, *Miss You Nights* was recorded over two sessions with the eleventh take being used from the first and some overdubs added at the second. Bruce Welch had taken over as Cliff's producer and, with his fine ear for quality songs and strong melodies, he was looking out for songs for Cliff. On a trip to Los Angeles, he met Lionel Conway, who was the head of Island Records and who had provided some of the songs composed by the writers at Island as demos on a cassette. Bruce wasn't enamoured with any of them particularly but, on returning to London, he happened to turn the cassette over and found a full recording of *Miss You Nights* performed by Dave Townsend for a mooted Island Records album that had been shelved and instantly knew that he had found a hit for Cliff. Ironically, for all the air miles clocked up, Townsend was actually a British songwriter and singer so was closer to home than the journey expended.

As it turned out, Cliff so loved the song that it has never been off his concert set list and, indeed, when he launched his perfume range in the new millennium, it was inevitable that it would be a suitable name for it. Although it is inextricably linked to Cliff and most of his songs have not been touched by other artists, *Miss You Nights* has been covered by Carl Wayne, 1976 Eurovision winners Brotherhood of Man, Acker Bilk, Art Garfunkel, Marie Osmond, the Nolan Sisters, double Eurovision winner Johnny Logan, Bunny Melody, Rupert Parker, Demis Roussos, Smokie and Rick Springfield, but, most famously, it was Westlife who took the song back into the charts in April 2003, when they released it as part of a double A-side with *Tonight*, reaching number three. Although they reached a higher position than Cliff, this is more a statement on the state of the charts and the dearth of decent material being released alongside.

Cliff released his sixty-fifth single, backed with ***Love Is Enough***, on the EMI label (catalogue number EMI 2376) on 14th November 1975, and reached number fifteen in the UK singles charts. It was reissued in the same format and the same catalogue number in 1982 but didn't re-enter the charts. Next, it was released as a double A-side with the Phil Everly duet, ***All I Have to Do Is Dream***, on the EMI label (catalogue number EM 359 (seven-inch single) and CDEMS 359 (CD single)) on 28th November 1992; this time it reached number fourteen in the UK charts. A favourite of hits anthology compilers, the song was also included on the album ***The Hit List***, which was a collection of all those songs that had reached the top five, and added purely because it was Cliff's favourite song. The CD single, as with many of Cliff's releases in the nineties, was a double disc issue, with a second bonus disc released a week later with another selection of songs on it.

For the listener who is now so familiar with the song, it is difficult to look back to the release of the ***I'm Nearly Famous*** album, on which *Miss You Nights* appeared, and the single and understand how refreshing the song was after a few years of what many considered to be substandard material. What sets it apart is the simple string and piano accompaniment and the beautifully arranged backing vocals, which are a mark of Bruce's production. Here more than any other song of the period, Cliff's effective vibrato can be heard and the ensemble result ensures that this song is a jewel in Cliff's oeuvre.

It became a favourite in many a concert and it was one of the songs performed by Cliff and his band during the ***Thank You Very Much*** reunion concerts with the Shadows (giving them a rest off-stage). The song loses something by being performed on an electric piano but the strength of the song and Cliff's performance overcomes such limitations.

Included in the ***Dressed for the Occasion*** set list with the backing of the London Philharmonic Orchestra, there are more frills and twiddles in Richard Hewson's arrangement, but essentially it is the same as the original with the string and woodwind accompaniment behind the close harmony vocals and the piano.

In November 1984, a Sydney concert was filmed for video release and *Miss You Nights* was subsequently transferred and remixed for issue on the B-side of Cliff's single ***We Should Be Together***, and the ***Scarlet Ribbons*** Dutch-only single release. Similarly, the *Live & Guaranteed 1988!* tour was transposed to CD with the video reissue in 1995 and included *Miss You Nights* with a lengthy section of Cliff taking a photograph with a group of fans, which doesn't work well in audio only.

Cliff next chose *Miss You Nights* to represent the latter half of his career in the *Cliff's Set* section of the Wembley Stadium concerts in 1989. However, for space reasons, the song was not included on the track listing of the album ***From a Distance ***** The Event*** in 1990, although it was successfully restored as part of the remaster in 2005. The electric piano and close harmony vocals are all intact and this version confirms the beauty of the track in a live setting. When ***From a Distance*** was issued as a single, there was a special boxed set version that included a one-sided seven-inch vinyl single (catalogue number CRTBX 31) of Cliff singing *Miss You Nights a capella* accompanied by Cora Cross Corona, which was taken from a performance recorded for the German television programme, *ARD Wunschkonzert*, and is now a considerable rarity. The thirty-strong male voice choir provides the harmonies in hummed or non-language sounds but, in addition, there is Cliff's standard backing vocal group singing along with the harmonies of the English lyrics from the second chorus onwards. During the performance, Cliff, wearing a diamante-studded white suit, is flanked by two groups of fifteen male singers dressed in dark suits. The song's quality is proven in that it can be treated so differently from the original.

Another live version performed in Hyde Park had Cliff duetting with Elaine Paige and was released on her compilation album, *Centre Stage – The Very Best of Elaine Paige*, although it was originally released on the Cliff video *Live in the Park*. This arrangement is very similar to the original with the piano and string arrangement and Cliff sings in harmony against Paige's principal melody. Paige's voice can tend to be a little piercing but, here, her vocals blend well with Cliff's.

In 2000, a new mix of the original song by DMC was released on the promotional disc for *The Whole Story*, which was another compilation of Cliff's hits over his extraordinary forty years in the business. This version has not been released commercially in any other format to date.

In April 2003, Westlife released their version of *Miss You Nights*, thereby raising the profile of the song to a new generation (and genre of music-lovers). With this manufactured pop sound and the huge popularity of reality television talent shows, it was inevitable that one of the participants would want to record a version. However, G4, so named as the four-man close harmony group had studied music at the Guildhall School of Music and Drama, were very different. Not only were they hugely talented as singers but they also did their own arrangements rather than blandly copying originals. Inevitably, the group failed to win the 2004 *X Factor* show but they were runners-up and, before they split in 2007, they had had far more success than the actual winner Steve Brookstein. Their 2005 album, *G4 & Friends*, included reworkings of several familiar songs with the original artists participating. Cliff was invited to appear on *Miss You Nights*, which also appeared on his 2006 album ***Two's Company – The Duets***. The arrangement is familiar with the strings, here led by the cello, and the ubiquitous piano. Jonathan Ansell is the principal vocalist of the group and he shares the lead with Cliff, while the other three assist with the backing vocals.

Track Specification
Composed by Dave Townsend

1. Single

Musicians	
Tony Harding	backing vocals
Richard Hewson	arranger, conductor
John Perry	backing vocals
Cliff Richard	vocals
Tony Rivers	backing vocals
Graham Todd	piano
Unknown	orchestra

Recording Details	
Producer	Bruce Welch
Engineered by	Tony Clark and John Barrett
Recording location	Abbey Road Studio 2 and 3, St. John's Wood, London
Recording date	9th September 1975 and 11th December 1975

2. Thank You Very Much

Musicians	
Stuart Calver	backing vocals
Mo Foster	bass
John Perry	backing vocals
Cliff Richard	vocals
Tony Rivers	backing vocals
Graham Todd	keyboards

Recording Details	
Producer	Bruce Welch
Engineered by	Tony Clark, remixed by Peter Vince
Recording location	London Palladium, London
Remix location	Abbey Road Studios, St. John's Wood, London
Recording date	4th March 1978

3. Dressed for the Occasion

Musicians	
Stuart Calver	backing vocals
Steve Gray	piano
Tony Harding	backing vocals
Richard Hewson	arranger, conductor
London Philharmonic Orchestra	orchestra
John Perry	backing vocals
Cliff Richard	vocals
Tony Rivers	backing vocals

Recording Details	
Producer	Cliff Richard and Richard Hewson
Engineered by	John Kurlander
Mixed by	Keith Bessey
Recording location	Royal Albert Hall, London
Mixed at	Strawberry Studios South, Surrey
Recording date	23rd November 1982

4. B-side (*We Should Be Together* and *Scarlet Ribbons*)

Musicians	
Stuart Calver	backing vocals
John Clark	guitar
Dave Cooke	keyboards
Mark Griffiths	bass
Graham Jarvis	drums, percussion
Mart Jenner	guitar
Alan Park	keyboards
John Perry	backing vocals
Cliff Richard	vocals
Tony Rivers	backing vocals

Recording Details	
Producer	Cliff Richard
Engineered by	Unknown
Recording location	Entertainment Centre, Sydney, Australia
Recording date	9th or 10th November1984

5. Live & Guaranteed 1988!

Musicians	
John Clark	guitar
Rosemarie Ford	backing vocals
Mark Griffiths	bass
Peter Howarth	backing vocals
Steve Lauri	guitar
Paul Moessl	keyboards
Mick Mullins	backing vocals
Alan Park	keyboards
Cliff Richard	vocals
Henry Spinetti	drums, percussion

Recording Details	
Producer	Unknown
Engineered by	Unknown
Recording location	Fyens Forum, Odense, Denmark
Recording date	22nd May 1988

6. From a Distance ** The Event Remaster***

Musicians	
John Clark	guitar
Sonia Jones-Morgan	backing vocals
Steve Lauri	guitar
Peter May	drums, percussion
Paul Moessl	keyboards
Tessa Niles	backing vocals
Alan Park	keyboards
Provox:	
Peter Howarth	backing vocals
Mick Mullins	backing vocals
Keith Murrell	backing vocals
Cliff Richard	vocals
Steve Stroud	bass

Recording Details	
Producer	Cliff Richard
Engineered by	Keith Bessey and Mick McKenna
Recording location	Rolling Stones Mobile Studio, Wembley Stadium, Wembley, North-west London
Recording date	16th-17th June 1989

7. Special single (From a Distance boxed set)

Musicians		*Recording Details*	
Coro Cross Corona	backing vocals	Producer	Unknown
Peter Howarth	backing vocals	Engineered by	Unknown
Mick Mullins	backing vocals	Recording location	Germany
Keith Murrell	backing vocals	Recording date	5th-9th July 1989
Cliff Richard	vocals		

8. Centre Stage – The Very Best of Elaine Paige

Musicians		*Recording Details*	
Elaine Paige	vocals	Producer	Unknown
Cliff Richard	vocals	Engineered by	Unknown
Unknown	backing vocals	Recording location	Hyde Park, London
Unknown	piano	Recording date	July 1999
Unknown	arranger, conductor		
Unknown	orchestra		

9. The Whole Story (promotional disc – DMC mix)

Musicians		*Recording Details*	
Terry Britten	guitar	Producer	Bruce Welch (original track) and DMC (remix)
Clem Cattini	drums, percussion	Engineered by	Tony Clark and John Barrett (original track) and DMC (remix)
Tony Harding	backing vocals	Recording location	Abbey Road Studio 2 and 3, St. John's Wood, London
Richard Hewson	arranger, conductor	Remixed by	DMC
John Perry	backing vocals	Remix location	Unknown
Cliff Richard	vocals	Recording date	9th September 1975 and 11th December 1975 (original track) and 2000 (remix)
Tony Rivers	backing vocals		
Alan Tarney	bass		
Graham Todd	keyboards		
Unknown	orchestra		

10. G4 & Friends

Musicians		*Recording Details*	
G4:		Producer	Graham Stack and Matt Furmidge
Jonathan Ansell	arranger (vocals), vocals	Engineered by	Nial Acott, Steve Price, James Stone and Mat Bartram
Michael Christie	arranger (vocals), backing vocals	Recording location	Unknown
Matthew Stiff	arranger (vocals), backing vocals	Recording date	2005
Ben Thapa	arranger (vocals), backing vocals		
London Session Orchestra	orchestra		
Cliff Masterson	arranger (orchestra), conductor, piano		
John Parricelli	guitar		
Cliff Richard	vocals		

♫ Mistletoe and Wine

***105th UK single** and unissued live track*

Of the many things that hound Cliff Richard by the prurient press and sneering critics is the number of Christmas songs that he has recorded. In fact, by the time *Mistletoe and Wine* had been released, there had only been the ***Carol Singers*** EP contents and a new musical setting of ***Little Town***. Later on, of course, he would record a couple of albums and release other singles but it is inauspicious that this is one of the principal 'facts' that many now trot out about this singer.

Mistletoe and Wine, though, came as a surprise. Having hooked up with the young Paul Moessl to become Cliff's new music director, his first task was to oversee the direction of the recording of a Christmas single at the height of summer. The song had all of the elements of a classic Christmas song with a bit of Eurovision style thrown in for good measure, which may go some way to understanding its popularity. Also recorded by Paul Brooks, Dawn and the Bachelors and sampled by Jive Bunny and the Mastermixers, Cliff's version was backed with a studio recording of ***Marmaduke*** and released as a single on the EMI label (catalogue number EM 78) on 21st November 1988 and reached number one in the UK singles charts, displacing Robin Beck's Coca-Cola jingle *The First Time* and being removed after three weeks by the saccharine *Especially for You* by Kylie Minogue and Jason Donovan. Contemporaneously, there were other formats for the single: the same A-side but with ***True Love Ways*** as the B-side (catalogue number EMS 78); the same single but with a poster sleeve (EMP 78); a twelve-inch single with *Little Town* as an additional track (12EM 78); another twelve-inch version with an advent calendar sleeve (EMX 78); and a CD single with *Little Town* and ***La Gonave*** as extra tracks (CDEM 78). The single version differed from the version that appeared on the ***Private Collection*** album with ten seconds of the introductory synthesiser that appears on the album lopped off for no readily apparent reason. It was this latter version that appeared as a bonus track on the 1991 ***Christmas EP***, the ***We Should Be Together*** CD single also in 1991 and on the first of the dual CD single release of ***Santa's List*** in 2003. The original (slightly edited) version of the song reached number sixty-eight on 29th December 2007 purely on download sales – the first Cliff Richard single to enter the charts based on the newly-incorporated download sales. The associated promotional video features Cliff surrounded by children, marching band soldiers, a snowman and a lot of snow. All of them are suitably dressed in thick coats and scarves, gloves and hats as they rock along with the music. The final segment features James Rainbird singing the clear boy vocals as Cliff looks on.

Starting with a tinkling music-box arrangement of the main theme, Cliff's vocals begin and the song slowly builds up with drums, strings, brass and even sleighbells. Now quintessentially a Christmas song, *Mistletoe and Wine* is greatly enhanced by the vocal arrangement, which features Cliff firmly placed in the mêlée.
The song was revisited by German singer Claudia Jung for her *Winterträume* album and included Cliff duetting with her. The track was slightly retitled on the album's listing with a prefix of ***Weihnachtszeit – Mistletoe and Wine***, with the German word meaning *Christmas Time* after the utterance in the first phrase in the performance.
In spite of the lack of seasonality – in February 2003 – Cliff still sang a ***Christmas Medley*** of his hits from the festive period as part of his world tour. The New Zealand concert was filmed and released on DVD while the associated *World Tour Live* CD album in 2004 missed this medley off the track listing.

Track Specification
Composed by Keith Strachan, Leslie Stewart and Jeremy Paul

1. Single

Musicians

Barry Castle	horns arranger
Mark Griffiths	bass
Peter Howarth	backing vocals
Paul Moessl	non-orchestral arranger, conductor, keyboards, synthesiser, drum and percussion programming
Sonia Morgan	backing vocals
Mick Mullins	backing vocals
Keith Murrell	backing vocals
James Rainbird	chorister vocals
Cliff Richard	vocals
Jack Rothstein	string arranger
Unknown	horns
Unknown	strings

Recording Details

Producer	Cliff Richard
Engineered by	Gerry Kitchingham and Ben Robbins
Recording location	R. G. Jones Studios, Wimbledon, London
Recording date	6th-10th June 1988 (vocals and basic track) and 12th-13th July 1988 (orchestra)

2. Unissued track (World Tour Live)

Musicians

Rachel Allen	violin
Elena Bulgakova	violin
Jenni Champion	violin
Anthony Clark	backing vocals, guitar
John Clark	guitar
Dave Cooke	keyboards
Cornelia Didenco	violin
Gina Ferguson	violin
Peter Howarth	backing vocals
Cathy Irons	violin
Pete May	drums, percussion
Mick Mullins	backing vocals
Keith Murrell	backing vocals
Alan Park	keyboards
Hee-Jung Park	violin
Cliff Richard	vocals
Eva Schwanen-Lilley	violin
Steve Stroud	bass

Recording Details

Producer	Keith Bessey
Engineered by	Keith Bessey
Recording location	The Mission Winery, Napier, New Zealand
Recording date	22nd February 2003

♬ Misunderstood Man, A

***123rd UK single** and from the albums* **Songs from Heathcliff** *and* **Heathcliff Live**

Cliff Richard had long had the desire to play the role of Heathcliff from Emily Brontë's novel, *Wuthering Heights*, since his schooldays. With his own drive, enthusiasm and money to back the project, he brought John Farrar in to compose the music and lyricist Tim Rice for his clever wordplay. *A Misunderstood Man* is the first song in the musical is and Rice uses it to set the scene, not by giving the plot away, but rather setting up a defence as if Heathcliff were before a judge and jury. Essentially, the lyrics state that the whole musical play will bring in elements for the audience to decide whether the flawed character is the devil incarnate for his actions are merely the misunderstood man of the title. Note that the original album has the indefinite article in the title, while the single releases and therefore the associated resources drop it.
The first single to be released from the project, *Misunderstood Man* (as per the release material) was backed with an instrumental version of the song (without Cliff's involvement) on the EMI label (catalogue number EM 394) on 9th October 1995 and reached number nineteen in the UK charts. The album and seven-inch single versions differ with the keyboard introduction reduced, most of the piano in the introduction excised and the second half of the instrumental bridge removed. Notably, *Misunderstood Man* was the last of his singles to be released in vinyl seven-inch format. Alongside this, the CD single (catalogue number CDEM 394) featured the album version, the seven-inch version and the instrumental track. Additionally, a promotional CD (CDEMDJ 394) was issued with the seven-inch version of the song the only track.

The song follows the guitar and synthesiser overture as the stage show opens. Heathcliff (Cliff) walks on to the stage and, with an almost menacing air, he looks from the corners of his eyes rather than moving his head, assertively challenging the audience to decide what type of man he is. A lugubrious synthesiser chord introduces the track as the piano and keyboards are brought in, providing an interesting transition through the chord sequences. Cliff sings with passion, requiring him to sing at the extents of his natural vocal register. The pace picks up as he nears the end of the song juggling the options on which the listener must decide. The live version is a recreation of the studio version with few differences. Gordon Giltrap, who figured highly as the solo guitarist in the live shows, recorded a medley of *A Misunderstood Man* with ***Be with Me Always*** for his *Troubadour* album, simply titled ***A Misunderstood Man/Be with Me Always***, which featured Cliff on backing vocals.

Track Specification
Composed by Tim Rice and John Farrar

1. Songs from Heathcliff

Musicians	
Sean Callery	orchestrator, synclavier, keyboards
Liz Constantino	backing vocals
Linda Dalziel	backing vocals
John Farrar	backing vocals, guitar, synclavier
Steve Kipner	backing vocals
Clif Magness	backing vocals
Kristina Nichols	backing vocals
Cliff Richard	vocals
Bob Sabellico	drum programming
Michael Thompson	guitar

Recording Details	
Producer	John Farrar
Engineered by	Chris Fogel, Eric Rudd and Joe Schiff (Moonee Ponds Studio), Darren Goodwin and Guy Massey (Abbey Road Studios) and James Collins and Caroline Daniel (CTS Studios)
Recording location	Moonee Ponds Studio, Los Angeles, Abbey Road Studios, St. John's Wood, London and CTS Studios, Wembley, London
Mixed by	Allen Sides and Chris Fogel
Mixed at	Moonee Ponds Studio, Los Angeles
Recording date	February-April 1994 and May-August 1995

2. Single

Musicians	
Sean Callery	orchestrator, synclavier, keyboards
Liz Constantino	backing vocals
Linda Dalziel	backing vocals
John Farrar	backing vocals, guitar, synclavier
Steve Kipner	backing vocals
Clif Magness	backing vocals
Kristina Nichols	backing vocals
Cliff Richard	vocals
Bob Sabellico	drum programming
Michael Thompson	guitar

Recording Details	
Producer	John Farrar
Engineered by	Chris Fogel, Eric Rudd and Joe Schiff (Moonee Ponds Studio), Darren Goodwin and Guy Massey (Abbey Road Studios) and James Collins and Caroline Daniel (CTS Studios)
Recording location	Moonee Ponds Studio, Los Angeles, Abbey Road Studios, St. John's Wood, London and CTS Studios, Wembley, London
Mixed by	Allen Sides and Chris Fogel
Mixed at	Moonee Ponds Studio, Los Angeles
Recording date	February-April 1994 and May-August 1995

3. Heathcliff Live

Musicians	
Sean Callery	orchestrator, conductor
John Clark	guitar
Elements:	
Geoff David	backing vocals
Chris Holland	backing vocals
Sonia Jones	backing vocals
Niki Kitt	backing vocals
Suzanne Parry	backing vocals
Keith Hayman	keyboards
Peter May	drums, percussion
Bob Noble	keyboards
Alan Park	keyboards
Cliff Richard	vocals
Steve Stroud	bass
Kevin Townend	orchestration
Unknown	orchestra

Recording Details	
Producer	John Farrar
Engineered by	Keith Bessey, John Pearson and Tom Tranter
Recording location	The Academy, National Indoor Arena, Birmingham, England
Recording date	17th-18th October 1996

♫ Misunderstood Man (Reprise), A
From the album **Heathcliff Live**

As the musical started, so it ends. Having been through the story from Heathcliff's (Cliff Richard) standpoint, from his youthful obsession with Cathy (Helen Hobson), the antipathy he holds for her brother Hindley (Jimmy Johnston), her marriage to Edgar Linton (Darryl Knock) and his own deceitful marriage to Isabella Linton (Sara Haggerty), his foreign trips to gain wealth and then the death of his beloved Cathy in childbirth, the audience is invited once more to make a judgment about the man: devil incarnate or a misunderstood man. Each main player stands in a line and moves forward to say what they think, before Heathcliff and Cathy return to the stage and sing in duet. The cast members assert that he is the devil while the women deny it and prefer to think of him as misunderstood, before all agree he is callously evil.

Track Specification
Composed by Tim Rice and John Farrar

Musicians

Sean Callery	orchestrator, orchestra
David Combes	backing vocals
John Clark	guitar
Elements:	
Geoff David	backing vocals
Chris Holland	backing vocals
Sonia Jones	backing vocals
Niki Kitt	backing vocals
Suzanne Parry	backing vocals
Gordon Giltrap	backing vocals
Keith Hayman	keyboards
Sara Haggerty	vocals
Helen Hobson	vocals
Jimmy Johnston	vocals
Darryl Knock	vocals
Peter May	drums, percussion
Bob Noble	keyboards
Alan Park	keyboards
John Perry	backing vocals
Cliff Richard	vocals
Steve Stroud	bass
Kevin Townend	orchestration
Unknown	orchestra
Mick Wilson	backing vocals

Recording Details

Producer	John Farrar
Engineered by	Keith Bessey, John Pearson and Tom Tranter
Recording location	Earl's Court Hall 2, London and/or The Academy, National Indoor Arena, Birmingham, England
Recording date	October 1996

♫ Misunderstood Man, A/Be with Me Always

From the album **Troubadour** *(Gordon Giltrap)*

Gordon Giltrap was one of the featured musicians in Cliff Richard's musical ***Heathcliff***, playing as he did solo guitar in the overtures to the first and second acts. A couple of years later, Giltrap recorded his solo album, *Troubadour*, and featured ***I Do Not Love You Isabella*** and a medley of two of the other songs that Cliff had released as singles: ***A Misunderstood Man*** and ***Be with Me Always***. This latter medley also featured Cliff on non-lyric vocals (hence the removal of Tim Rice as composer in the track specififcation), although the obvious focus is Giltrap's virtuoso performance on the guitar. This is supported by the strings and French horn as the familiar melody is played out, although the arrangement sounds quite distinctly different from some of the expected elements of the original as it segues into the *Be with Me Always* segment. Cliff's vocal contribution is multi-layered and only used very sparingly throughout the track but most obviously during the latter half. The arrangement then gently switches back to *A Misunderstood Man* to complete the track. An interesting variation on what had become a very familiar couple of tracks, particularly for fans.

Track Specification
Composed by John Farrar

Musicians

Mike Brittain	double bass
Dirk Campbell	Uillean pipes
Andy Findon	flute
Gordon Giltrap	guitars
Paul Kegg	cello
Boguslav Kostecki	violin
Peter Lale	viola
Chris Laurence	double bass
Frank Lloyd	French horn
David Nolan	violin
Tony Pleeth	cello
Maciej Rakowski	violin
Cliff Richard	vocals, backing vocals
George Robertson	viola
Jack Rothstein	violin

Recording Details

Producer	Gordon Giltrap
Engineered by	Gerry O'Riordan and Cameron McBride
Recording location	Snake Ranch Studios, London
Mixed by	Iain Hodge
Mixing location	Vestry Hall, London College of Music, London
Recording date	1997 or 1998

♫ Mobile Alabama School Leaving Hullaballoo

From the album **...And They Said It Wouldn't Last! (My 50 Years in Music)**

Recorded by Cliff Richard at his final full session of 1977, the heavily rocking *Mobile Alabama School Leaving Hullabaloo* was written by Chris East, who had penned Cliff's hit earlier that year, ***My Kinda Life***. And this may have been the reason for not releasing this at the time because, while the song is bouncy and catchy enough, it has very strong echoes of the other song. It was the final track to be recorded at the session and remained unissued until it was included on the lost and found section of the celebratory ***...And They Said It Wouldn't Last! (My 50 Years in Music)*** album in 2008. It was then released as the B-side of Cliff's fiftieth anniversary single, ***Thank You for a Lifetime***.

With its quacking guitar structure and the rhythm, Cliff sings *Mobile Aabama School Leaving Hullabaloo* in a similar style to the aforementioned *My Kinda Life* with a rough edge to his voice. The thumping bass drives the song relentlessly onwards and into middle eight section, which features a strong guitar solo that also includes part of the chorus from ***Move It*** in amongst the lyrics. The foot-stomping beat and the energy with which Cliff sings it makes it a surprising song to be left in the EMI vaults rarhr thasn pushing it out on an album or even possibly as a single.

Track Specification
Composed by Chris East

Musicians		*Recording Details*	
Terry Britten	guitar	Producer	Bruce Welch
Alan Hawkshaw	keyboards	Engineered by	Tony Clark
Cliff Richard	vocals, backing vocals	Recording location	Abbey Road Studio 2, St. John's Wood, London
Trevor Spencer	drums, percussion	Recording date	11th July 1977
Alan Tarney	backing vocals, bass		

♬ Monday Comes Too Soon
B-side of **I Ain't Got Time Anymore**

Co-written by Hank Marvin and the man who had provided a number of hits for both Cliff Richard and the Shadows separately, Jerry Lordan, *Monday Comes Too Soon* was recorded at the same session as its A-side, ***I Ain't Got Time Anymore*** and the prior single ***Goodbye Sam, Hello Samantha***. *Monday Comes Too Soon* was the last of the three tracks to be completed and, as with the other two songs, it features the orchestra and arrangement of Mike Vickers, late of Manfred Mann and contemporaneously working on a number of projects including recording a single with his wife Sue for Threshold Records. Released in stereo, *Monday Comes Too Soon* was given a mono edit release in Holland. Until the release of ***...And They Said It Wouldn't Last! (My 50 Years in Music)*** in 2008, the track had not been issued in any other format and had remained a rarity for fans and collectors alike to that point.
Certainly a feeling that many workers experience, particularly after a good weekend, is that the Monday morning back to work blues are not great, but throw in the possibility of breaking up from a lover and Cliff successfully injects the necessary emotional grief into the song. The final sustained note employs his natural vibrato and this also helps to drive home some of the anxiety within the song's lyrics.

Track Specification
Composed by Hank Marvin and Jerry Lordan

Musicians		*Recording Details*	
Mike Vickers Orchestra	orchestra	Producer	Norrie Paramor
Cliff Richard	vocals	Engineered by	Unknown
Unknown	backing vocals	Recording location	Abbey Road Studio 3, St. John's Wood, London
Mike Vickers	arranger, conductor	Recording date	12th March 1970

♬ Monday Thru' Friday
From the albums **Rock 'n' Roll Juvenile** *and* **My Kinda Life**

Eschewing the services of Bruce Welch as producer after three highly commercial albums, Cliff Richard co-produced the ***Rock 'n' Roll Juvenile*** album with the help of the writer of *Monday Thru' Friday*, Terry Britten, who had enjoyed a long association with Cliff throughout the seventies. The spelling of 'through' and its usage is very American since the British equivalent is simply 'to' but that fits with the necessarily American feel of the rock and roll concept of the album. The backing track was recorded in Paris along with all of the album's songs, with vocals added seven months later back in the UK on familiar ground of the Abbey Road Studios.
The rock and roll feel to the ***Rock 'n' Roll Juvenile*** album is strongly initiated in this first track with a grooving guitar introduction. Cliff's vocals are engineered quite a way back in the mix as if he is cooped up and this works well to indicate the claustrophobia of working throughout the week wishing Saturday would arrive in order to rock and roll.
The version that appeared on 1992's ***My Kinda Life*** built on the original track by adding extra guitars in order to freshen the sound. The fade-out is also some five seconds longer, although this may have only been the product of the remixing process than of deliberate intent.

Track Specification
Composed by Terry Britten

1. Rock 'n' Roll Juvenile

Musicians		*Recording Details*	
Terry Britten	backing vocals, guitar	Producer	Cliff Richard and Terry Britten
Lance Dixon	synthesiser	Engineered by	Tony Clark and Haydn Bendall
Herbie Flowers	bass	Recording location	Pathé Marconi, Paris, France (backing track) and Abbey Road Studio, St. John's Wood, London (vocals)
Graham Jarvis	drums, percussion	Recording date	18th-20th July 1978 (backing track) and 10th February 1979 (vocals)
Cliff Richard	vocals, backing vocals		

2. My Kinda Life

Musicians

Terry Britten	backing vocals, guitar
John Clark	guitar
Lance Dixon	synthesiser
Herbie Flowers	bass
Graham Jarvis	drums, percussion
Cliff Richard	vocals, backing vocals

Recording Details

Producer	Cliff Richard and Terry Britten (original track) and Cliff Richard and Paul Moessl (new instrumentation)
Engineered by	Tony Clark and Haydn Bendall (original track) and Gerry Kitchingham and Ben Robbins (new instrumentation)
Recording location	Pathé Marconi, Paris, France (backing track) and Abbey Road Studio, St. John's Wood, London (vocals) and R. G. Jones Studios, Wimbledon, London (new instrumentation)
Recording date	18th-20th July 1978 (backing track) and 10th February 1979 (vocals) and 20th-23rd April 1992 (new instrumentation)

♬ Mondo et Tondo, Il

Italian single

Cliff Richard's entry into the 1968 Eurovision Song Contest, ***Congratulations***, was performed at the Royal Albert Hall on 6th April, and was an immediate post-contest favourite in spite of coming second to Spain's unmemorable *La La La* after some dubious voting at the last minute. It was inevitable that the song would be translated for Cliff to record foreign language versions and so it came to be with German, French, Spanish and Italian versions hastily translated and Clif's convened sessions to record them.

There are publications that suggest the backing tracks for each of these use the same track recorded for the English version on 3rd February 1968 with Cliff's new vocals overdubbed but this is incorrect. In fact, the German version (***Man Gratuliert Mir***) was recorded three days after the contest complete with upgraded orchestral backing and harmony vocals. Two weeks later, the Spanish and French versions were recorded but they used the German backing track from 9th April, as did the Italian version ten days later, all with Cliff's new vocals and the unknown backing vocals overdubbed. *Il Mondo et Tondo* (translated as *The World Is Round*, a departure from the original lyrics) was issued as a single with the English B-side ***Girl, You'll Be a Woman Soon*** on the Columbia label (catalogue number SCMQ-7099) in May 1968. Originally released in mono format, as per Columbia's singles policy at the time, and a rarity for collectors, the stereo version was eventually released thirty-nine years later on the compilation of Cliff's foreign language recordings, ***On the Continent***.

The version is a faithful copy of the English original with the exception that the mix favours the dancing guitar line and Cliff and the uncredited female backing vocalists (possibly the Breakaways but unconfirmed) singing along with the accelerando at the end of the song.

Track Specification

Composed by Bill Martin and Phil Coulter; Italian lyrics by Diano

Musicians

Norrie Paramor Orchestra	orchestra
Norrie Paramor	arranger, conductor
Cliff Richard	vocals
Unknown	backing vocals
Unknown	hand claps

Recording Details

Producer	Norrie Paramor (backing track and vocals)
Engineered by	Peter Vince (backing track and vocals)
Recording location	Abbey Road Studio 2 (backing track and vocals), St. John's Wood, London
Recording date	9th April 1968 (backing track) and 3rd May 1968 (vocals)

♬ Money Honey

Unreleased live track subsequently issued on **The Rock 'n' Roll Years 1958-1963**

Released in September 1953, *Money Honey* was the first hit for the Drifters (the American vocal group, of course, rather than Cliff Richard's original backing band). However, for many music listeners, it is probably Elvis Presley's cover version in 1956, which is the most familiar when it featured on his ***Heartbreak Hotel*** EP and which reached number 76 in the Billboard singles chart. The song is a slow-paced rock and roll song that talks of the singer's need for money and that being the sole thing he wants from his girl if they are to stay together.

Since Cliff was an avid Elvis Presley fan, who admired the American singer's music and performance style, it is hardly surprising that the song was also on the repertoire for Cliff and the Drifters' short residency at the Butlin's Holiday Camp based in Clacton-on-Sea in August 1958. On one of the nights, their set was recorded by Stan Edwards and, while some of those recordings made it on to the rarities retrospective, ***The Rock 'n' Roll Years 1958-1963***, others were in too poor a condition to be considered for commercial release. *Money Honey* was one chosen for inclusion in the listings of that album but, because of the limited recording capabilities, the only version of this live recording remains in mono only.

Cliff's version focuses on the guitar accompaniment as a rhythm tool rather than as a lead. On this tune, a harmonica is played very occasionally, and it's likely that Ian Samwell would have taken those duties while Terry Smart played percussion; it is the harmonica that takes the lead in the middle eight. Cliff's performance is very assured and is delivered with an aplomb that most seventeen-year-olds would not be accustomed to but it shows what a natural entertainer he was even at that young age.

Track Specification
Composed by Jesse Stone

Musicians		*Recording Details*	
Cliff Richard	vocals, guitar	Producer	Unknown
Ian Samwell	guitar, harmonica	Engineered by	Stan Edwards
Terry Smart	drums, percussion	Recording location	Rock 'n' Roll Ballroom, Butlin's Holiday Camp, Clacton-on-Sea, Essex
		Recording date	August 1958

♬ Moonlight Bay
From the EP **Holiday Carnival**

The popular song *Moonlight Bay* was originally published in 1912 and has become a standard song for performance, particularly in the close harmony style of the barbershop quartets of the twenties. Taken as the title of the film starring Doris Day who also covered the tune, the song has been recorded by a variety of artists, including Tommy Dorsey, Bing Crosby, Guy Lombardo, the American Quartet, Gene Kelly, the Drifters, Harry James, the Chordettes, Glenn Miller, Billy Vaughn and Frank Sinatra, among many others.
One of three EP tracks (for the ***Holiday Carnival*** and ***Love Is Forever*** releases) to be recorded at the session, the third and final take and edit of *Moonlight Bay* was used for the mono and stereo recordings but with different mixes for the requirements of the audio channels. The EP track was a rarity until the release of the compendium album ***The EP Collection: Ballads and Love Songs***, which has itself become a rarity.
With a calypso feel and an upbeat rhythm, Cliff is in his element with this form of song. Unfortunately, the backing vocals detract from the performance. The guitars, bass and drums sound suspiciously like the Shadows although the session notes and other sources indicate that it is the work of the Norrie Paramor Orchestra.

Track Specification
Composed by Edward Madden and Percy Wenrich

Musicians		*Recording Details*	
Mike Sammes Singers	backing vocals	Producer	Norrie Paramor
Norrie Paramor Orchestra	orchestra	Engineered by	Malcolm Addey and Peter Vince
Norrie Paramor	arranger, conductor	Recording location	Abbey Road Studio 2, St. John's Wood, London
Cliff Richard	vocals	Recording date	12th December 1962
Unknown	guitars		
Unknown	drums		

♬ Moon River
From the album **Wanted** *and unissued live track*

One of the most familiar film-based songs, *Moon River* was written for the Audrey Hepburn vehicle *Breakfast at Tiffany's* in 1961 and went on to win the Academy Award for the Best Song as well as a Grammy for the Record of the Year in 1962. Sung by Hepburn in the film, it was performed by Andy Williams at the 1962 Oscar ceremony and featured as one of his album tracks, even naming his production company after the song, although he never released it as a single. In fact, the most popular version was by South African singer Danny Williams, who hit number one with it in 1961, while the original soundtrack version by Henry Mancini and his chorus only reached number forty-four. Lyricist Johnny Mercer has indicated in interview that the term "Huckleberry friend" is meaningless but was such a delicious phrase to say as well as conjuring up nostalgic albeit false memories of childhood, possibly created by Mark Twain's *The Adventures of Tom Sawyer*.
It was a suitable song of choice for Cliff Richard to add to the track listing of ***Wanted***, his first post-EMI album, which primarily featured a host of well-known songs. Working with Alan Tarney for the first time since ***Stronger*** in 1989, they created a version that is unique while recognizing the influence of the original.
A lush sequence of chords ushers in the song with a guitar accompaniment, which is reduced to sustained keyboard chords during the verse, which then picks up the rhythm and lush accompaniment once more for the chorus. In the second verse, Cliff's vocal is given some atmospheric echo. Curiously, there is very little in the way of backing vocals other than the echo. *Moon River* is one of the best and most emotional of the songs on the album.
The song was on the set list for the tour supporting the release of the album. The New Zealand leg was filmed and recorded for DVD release later in 2003 but, the following year, a CD album of a selection of the songs was also issued, although *Moon River* was not on the track listing.

Track Specification
Composed by Henry Mancini and Johnny Mercer

1. Wanted

Musicians		*Recording Details*	
John Brant	additional programming	Producer	Alan Tarney
Cliff Richard	vocals	Engineered by	John Brant and Gerry Kitchingham
Alan Tarney	arranger, guitar, keyboards, programming	Recording location	Wilmer Studios, London
		Recording date	January-April 2001

2. *Unissued track (World Tour Live)*

Musicians	
Rachel Allen	violin
Elena Bulgakova	violin
Jenni Champion	violin
Anthony Clark	backing vocals, guitar
John Clark	guitar
Dave Cooke	keyboards
Cornelia Didenco	violin
Gina Ferguson	violin
Peter Howarth	backing vocals
Cathy Irons	violin
Pete May	drums, percussion
Mick Mullins	backing vocals
Keith Murrell	backing vocals
Alan Park	keyboards
Hee-Jung Park	violin
Cliff Richard	vocals
Eva Schwanen-Lilley	violin
Steve Stroud	bass

Recording Details	
Producer	Keith Bessey
Engineered by	Keith Bessey
Recording location	The Mission Winery, Napier, New Zealand
Recording date	22nd February 2003

♬ More to Life

114th UK single

After the success of slightly preposterous television drama series such as *Howard's Way*, which were created on the back of the glamorous US series such as *Dallas* and *Dynasty*, the BBC commissioned a series based around horse-racing and specifically the training of such. Broadcast in the prestige Sunday evening slot on BBC1, the first series ran for thirteen episodes. Although it was a reasonable success with around six million viewers, the BBC decided to put the second series in the evening slot on Wednesday, running for only ten episodes. The series had been updated, making it a continuing drama format rather than a specific story per episode. The second series was left on an unresolved cliff-hanger because, having changed the programme and its slot, viewers were driven way and further series were cancelled. Starring Mark Greenstreet, Susannah York, David McCallum, Neil Nisbet and Floyd Bevan in the principal roles, the theme tune was written by Simon May and Mike Read.

Simon May was the resident BBC theme writer for a number of years and had already given the memorable tunes for *EastEnders*, *Howard's Way* and *Eldorado*, while Mike Read was a BBC radio and television presenter, who was close friends with Cliff Richard and co-writer of *The Complete Chronicle*, which incorrectly states that the series was aired on independent channel, ITV, although it is correctly stated as the BBC earlier in the same section.

More to Life was recorded over three days in June 1991 at the R. G. Jones Studios in Wimbledon and, backed with *Mo's Theme* (an instrumental by May and Read from the series), was issued as a single on the EMI label (catalogue label EM 205) on 2nd September 1991 and reached number twenty-three in the UK charts. It was also released on the CD version of the single (catalogue number CDEM 205) and appeared on the associated *Trainer* vinyl LP and CD. Later it was included on the compilation albums *The Winner* and *Yesterday, Today, Forever* – albeit incorrectly titled ***There's More to Life*** – before being included as a bonus track on the remastered ***Small Corners*** album in 2007.

The chugging guitar introduction emulates the freedom of a horse running in the countryside. The song fits Cliff's vocals well, although the melody is not immediately memorable and takes a few listens to hear and understand its nuances. Cliff performs his own backing vocals on the recording and these sections where they appear are the best part, as usual, along with John Clark's guitar solo in the middle eight.

Track Specification

Composed by Simon May and Mike Read

Musicians	
John Clark	guitar
Paul Dunne	guitar
Andrew Greasley	violin
Peter May	drums, percussion
Paul Moessl	programming, keyboards
Cliff Richard	vocals, backing vocals
Steve Stroud	bass

Recording Details	
Producer	Cliff Richard and Paul Moessl
Engineered by	Gerry Kitchingham, Andrew Greasley and Ben Robbins
Recording location	R. G. Jones Studios, Wimbledon, London
Recording date	10th-13th June 1991

♬ Move It

1st and 138th UK single** and from the albums* **Cliff, Don't Stop Me Now!, Cliff in Japan, Cliff Live in Korea, Live in Japan 1972, Thank You Very Much, Rock 'n' Roll Silver, Live and Guaranteed, From a Distance ** The Event, Knebworth** *(unreleased),* **Hank Plays Cliff, Hank Plays Live, Party at the Palace, World Tour Live, Two's Company** *and* **Reunited** *and B-side of the singles* **Human Work of Art** *and* **The Miracle** *and unissued live tracks*

The story of *Move It* is an extraordinary one for its time and one that was critical for the burgeoning British music scene at the end of the decade. During the fifties and even into the early sixties, British music acts very rarely recorded home-grown original material and, only then, it was usually a song delivered by a tunesmith specifically employed to churn out possible hits in places like Tin Pan Alley.

Cliff Richard and the Drifters had been signed to the Columbia label under the production auspices of Norrie Paramor on the strength of two covers that the band had recorded privately: ***Lawdy Miss Clawdy*** and Jerry Lee Lewis's then recent hit, ***Breathless***. It would therefore seem logical that, since Cliff and the Drifters sold themselves as a rock and roll band and rock and roll was wholly an American invention, the first choice of single should be a cover of an American song, the somewhat gawky ***Schoolboy Crush***.
Move It (originally with an exclamation point) was written by Ian Samwell, the Drifters' then guitarist, on the top deck of a bus taking him to Cliff's house for one of their rehearsals. At the same session that recorded *Schoolboy Crush*, for want of any other material, *Move It*, rehearsed and prepared, was agreed to be recorded for the B-side. However, since Paramor did not trust the talents of many of the band members, particularly Ian Samwell, except for Terry Smart's drumming, the other instrumentation was handed over to established session musicians such as Ernie Shears, who was responsible for the perfectly-paced introductory guitar riff, and Frank Clarke on stand-up bass. So the first recording of the song was less of a Cliff Richard and the Drifters track but a Cliff solo effort backed by a disparate group of musicians working by the hour.
With both of the songs recorded and mastered, the next step in the evolution of *Move It* was how it was decided to flip the disc to make *Schoolboy Crush* the B-side. There is a series of stories regarding how this came about but the most likely are that powerful television producer Jack Goode (who, at the time, oversaw the popular music programmes such as *Oh Boy!*) insisted that he would only plug *Move It*, while at the same time Paramor had taken the masters home and played the results to his daughter, who raved about the original song but was nonplussed by *Schoolboy Crush*. The former story version is given greater credence by its confirmation in Cliff's autobiography, ***My Life, My Way***, in which he describes it being the obstinate support of Goode who was responsible for pushing the song as an A-side, although the story of Paramor's daughter has a certain romantic aspect to it. Whatever the case, *Move It* was eventually promoted to the A-side and released on the Columbia label (two formats: 7-inch single (catalogue number 45-DB 4178) and 10-inch 78 r.p.m. (catalogue number DB 4178)) on 29th August 1958.
The single was an instant hit and moved swiftly up the charts to the number two spot in the UK, held off from the top by Connie Francis's double A-side of *Carolina Moon* and *Stupid Cupid*. Incidentally, the number one disc prior to that was *When* by the Kalin Twins from the US, who were touring Britain and who had invited Cliff and the Drifters to support them. On the strength of the single's performance and the band's energy against the Twins' more sedentary approach, the tour promoters reversed the headlining act to be Cliff and the Drifters supported by The Kalin Twins, and their music career in Britain was blighted (although they returned for an appearance at ***From a Distance ***** The Event***).
Naturally, the song was given an airing at the 'live' recording in front of an invited audience that became the album ***Cliff***. It was then resurrected for his ***Don't Stop Me Now!*** album released in 1967, where a highly unusual and quite phenomenal fifty-four takes and false starts were attempted before the song was successfully completed; this last take and edit were used for the mono and stereo recordings. The familiar guitar riff intro has been replaced by a rolling brass band and drum combination. The arrangement includes a variation on the main melody and a female backing chorus, driven by an insistent twanging guitar and a beaten tambourine and is Cliff Richard upgrading his first hit with a very late-sixties, curiously non-rock and roll feel. Because of the musical status of the original, while interesting to listen to this arrangement, it was very much of its time and later performances reverted back to the standard guitar riff introduction. There is an uncredited orchestra and female backing vocal section on this quintessentially sixties version, which may be Mike Leander, Norrie Paramor or Bernard Ebbinghouse, and the Breakaways respectively, since they were all recording with Cliff around this period.
A key song for Cliff's tours, the few live albums released, such as ***Cliff in Japan*** (with a purely orchestral accompaniment), *Cliff Live in Korea*, ***Cliff "Live" in Japan '72*** (a piano-thumping, guitar-fired frenzy of a version that is worth getting hold of in place of any other versions), ***Thank You Very Much***, *Hank Plays Live* and *From a Distance ***** The Event* (featuring former Shadows Jet Harris and Tony Meehan working with Cliff for the first time since 1961), have all included live versions of the song, some as the original, some pared down and some at a slower, drier pace, but all to great reaction from the assembled audiences. With the guitar riff reinstated and the instrumentation played by a specially selected band that Cliff elected to call Thunder, Cliff re-recorded the song for his 1983 album ***Rock 'n' Roll Silver***. The introduction is played on a heavier guitar, which is also used in the middle eight before it is quietened down to an audience participation section where phrases are repeated – these were the early days of large venue performances and most acts were doing this sort of routine to interact with the fans. The introductory guitar riff is repeated at a slowing pace to end the track. It was also recorded as part of the documentary on Cliff by the BBC in 1981, from which the single ***Daddy's Home*** was successfully licensed for release but, to date, that version of *Move It* has yet to find a release format.
Yet another version of the song was recorded at some point in 1972 for the Cliff and Tim Brooke-Taylor television film vehicle, *The Case*. However, the film was only released for television and, as of the date of publication of this book, the soundtrack has yet to be released.
The song was performed in the second set of the *From a Distance ***** The Event* in 1989 although it didn't feature any of the Shadows current line-up. Instead Jet Harris and Tony Meehan were invited on the stage to perform with Cliff and his backing band. This time there were no different arrangements; simply a straightforward performance, with only some audience participation in the middle eight, of the song Cliff had made famous thirty years previously.
A live version of the song, taken from a recording of the *Access All Areas* tour in 1992 was featured as a B-side track on the first of a dual CD single release of ***Human Work of Art***. Several other tracks from the concerts were also released as B-sides

of singles from ***Cliff Richard - The Album*** project, including the only released version of ***That's Alright, Mama***, which, like *Move It*, had Cliff accompanying himself on steel-string guitar.

In 1995, Drifters' and Shadows' lead guitarist Hank Marvin released the next in his *Hank Plays...* series, this time looking at Cliff's immense back catalogue for the content. With Cliff guesting on some vocals and backing vocals, it seemed appropriate that, since Hank hadn't played on the original recording but had become so instrumental (if the pun can be pardoned) in Cliff's career to resurrect the song for this album with Cliff on lead vocals – the first verse though is performed by Hank on guitar before handing over to Cliff for the full vocal version, replete with echo. What is more extraordinary is that the composer, Ian Samwell, was asked to provide a second verse (the original repeats the only verse and the chorus). The effect was to bring a much more sultry and almost greasy side to the song with images created by the words 'fireflies', 'bullfrogs croaking' and 'the Mississippi heat', a reference to the area of the United States that is held to be the cradle of country music and rock and roll, and New Orleans, the home of traditional jazz. Hank takes the tune much more languidly than the original production as he plays the introduction and main theme as a guitar solo, before drums pick the pace up for Cliff's vocals accompanied by the answering call of Hank's guitar. It is a brilliant rendition that has been expertly arranged by Warren Bennett, son of Shadows' long-term drummer, Brian.

For Cliff's fortieth anniversary concerts in the summer and autumn of 1998 he performed a number of hits but only two were released from the live recordings made, one of which was *Move It* and this was chosen to accompany the second disc of the dual CD single release of ***The Miracle*** in 1999.

On 3rd June 2002, the country celebrated Queen Elizabeth's Diamond Jubilee, and there was a massive music extravaganza organized to take place in the grounds of Buckingham Palace. Sir Cliff Richard was invited to do a set and, rather than work on his own, he performed in this instance with Queen guitarist Brian May and the then biggest pop group S Club 7. The resident vocal group provide backing vocals and include the new words of "let's dance to a rock 'n' roll band", and members of S Club 7 take turns on the lead vocals from Cliff. The performance, incidentally, marked the final appearance of band member Paul Cattermole with the group, before they downsized to the simpler S Club.

For Cliff's duets album, *Two's Company*, released in 2006, a new recording was made, again with Brian May but also with Brian Bennett on drums. Cliff himself played rhythm guitar, while the trademark wailing of May's lead guitar and Brian Bennett's driving drums and thumping percussion keeps the song moving ever onwards but at a slower, more sultry pace than the original. The middle eight is an *a capella* repetition of the song title and this version, as had become standard since Samwell had created the second verse for *Hank Plays Cliff*, includes the additional lyrics. This recording of the song was also issued as a double A-side single with ***21st Century Christmas*** on the EMI label as a seven-inch vinyl record (catalogue number CLIFFX217) and CD with the songs reversed (00946 3799312 5) on 11th December 2006, and it reached number two in the UK charts, showing the power of the song even after almost fifty years.

A live version of the song was included on the *World Tour Live* set list, which was recorded live in Napier, New Zealand. This performance also includes the additional backing vocals created for the *Party at the Palace*, with the "jump, clap, stamp your feet" and its variations that have subsequently been dropped in live sets.

By 2008, Cliff has successfully completed fifty years at the top of the music business and, to celebrate, he reunited with the Shadows once again for a tour and an album the following year, which featured a number of re-recordings including *Move It*. This time, of course, although with the same driving guitar and bass rhythm of the original, the new lyrics were added to the recording making the track something very special.

Ian Samwell has stated that the song was inspired by a music paper article that seemed to predict and relish the death throes of rock and roll – wishful thinking by fretful parents and authority figures of the time. It was merely a response to that with mention of ballads and calypsos leaving him unmoved but good, traditional country music being the best fillip for jaded musical tastes. The additional lyrics almost forty years later underline these thoughts admirably. The original song is a milestone in British pop history with many musicologists such as Paul Gambaccini citing it as the first true British rock and roll single. What is more extraordinary is that rock and roll has dated but, with the syncopated time signatures introducing the song, it still sounds fresh over fifty years later and that is a considerable achievement.

Track Specification
Composed by Ian Samwell

1. Single

Musicians		*Recording Details*	
Frank Clarke	bass	Producer	Norrie Paramor
Cliff Richard	vocals	Engineered by	Malcolm Addey
Ernie Shear	guitar	Recording location	Abbey Road Studio 2, St. John's Wood, London
Terry Smart	drums, percussion	Recording date	24th July 1958

2. Cliff

Musicians		*Recording Details*	
Jet Harris	bass	Producer	Norrie Paramor
Hank Marvin	guitar	Engineered by	Malcolm Addey
Tony Meehan	drums, percussion	Recording location	Abbey Road Studio 2, St. John's Wood, London
Cliff Richard	vocals	Recording date	9th February 1959
Bruce Welch	rhythm guitar		

3. *Don't Stop Me Now!*

Musicians

Cliff Richard	vocals
Unknown	guitar
Unknown	bass
Unknown	drums, percussion
Unknown	female backing vocals
Unknown	orchestra

Recording Details

Producer	Norrie Paramor
Engineered by	Peter Vince and Richard Lush
Recording location	Abbey Road Studio 2, St. John's Wood, London
Recording date	5th February 1967

4. *Cliff in Japan*

Musicians

Norrie Paramor Orchestra	orchestra
Norrie Paramor	conductor
Cliff Richard	vocals
Unknown	backing vocals

Recording Details

Producer	Norrie Paramor
Engineered by	Unknown
Recording location	Shibuya Public Hall, Tokyo, Japan
Recording date	18th October 1967

5. *Cliff Live in Korea*

Musicians

Brian Bennett	drums, percussion
Alan Hawkshaw	keyboards
Hank Marvin	guitar
Cliff Richard	vocals
John Rostill	bass
Bruce Welch	rhythm guitar

Recording Details

Producer	Unknown
Engineered by	Unknown
Recording location	Citizen Hall, Seoul, South Korea
Recording date	16th October 1969

6. *Cliff "Live" in Japan '72*

Musicians

Brian Bennett	drums, percussion
John Farrar	bass
Alan Hawkshaw	keyboards
Hank Marvin	guitar
Cliff Richard	vocals

Recording Details

Producer	Unknown
Engineered by	Unknown
Recording location	Kosei Nenkin Hall, Tokyo, Japan
Recording date	22nd and 23rd October 1972

7. *Thank You Very Much*

Musicians

Brian Bennett	drums, percussion
Alan Jones	bass
Cliff Hall	keyboards
Hank Marvin	guitar
Cliff Richard	vocals
Bruce Welch	rhythm guitar

Recording Details

Producer	Bruce Welch
Engineered by	Tony Clark, remixed by Peter Vince
Recording location	London Palladium, London
Remix location	Abbey Road Studios, St. John's Wood, London
Recording date	4th March 1978

8. *Unissued track (BBC documentary)*

Musicians

Stuart Calver	backing vocals
Howie Casey	saxophone, trumpet, trombone
John Clark	guitar
Mark Griffiths	bass
Graham Jarvis	drums, percussion
Martin Jenner	guitar
Alan Park	keyboards
John Perry	backing vocals
Cliff Richard	vocals
Tony Rivers	backing vocals
Graham Todd	keyboards

Recording Details

Producer	Cliff Richard
Engineered by	Unknown
Recording location	Hammersmith Odeon, London
Recording date	1st May 1981

9. *Rock 'n' Roll Silver*

Musicians

Stu Calver	backing vocals
John Clark	guitar
Dave Cooke	keyboards
Mark Griffiths	bass
Graham Jarvis	drums, percussion
Mart Jenner	guitar
Alan Park	keyboards
John Perry	backing vocals
Cliff Richard	vocals
Tony Rivers	backing vocals

Recording Details

Producer	Thunder
Engineered by	Keith Bessey
Recording location	Strawberry Studios South, Surrey
Recording date	9th-18th May 1983

10. Live and Guaranteed 1988! (unreleased)

Musicians

John Clark	guitar
Rosemary Ford	backing vocals
Mark Griffiths	bass
Peter Howarth	backing vocals
Steve Lauri	guitar
Paul Moessl	keyboards
Mick Mullins	backing vocals
Alan Park	keyboards
Cliff Richard	vocals
Henry Spinetti	drums, percussion

Recording Details

Producer	Unknown
Engineered by	Unknown
Recording location	Fyens Forum, Odense, Denmark
Recording date	22nd May 1988

11. From a Distance ** The Event***

Musicians

John Clark	guitar
Jet Harris	bass
Sonia Jones-Morgan	backing vocals
Steve Lauri	guitar
Tony Meehan	drums, percussion
Paul Moessl	keyboards
Tessa Niles	backing vocals
Alan Park	keyboards
Provox:	
Peter Howarth	backing vocals
Mick Mullins	backing vocals
Keith Murrell	backing vocals
Cliff Richard	vocals

Recording Details

Producer	Cliff Richard
Engineered by	Keith Bessey and Mick McKenna
Recording location	Rolling Stones Mobile Studio, Wembley Stadium, Wembley, North-west London
Recording date	16th-17th June 1989

12. Unissued (Knebworth - The Album)

Musicians

Ray Beavis	saxophone
Brian Bennett	drums, percussion
John Earle	saxophone
Chris Gower	trombone
Mark Griffiths	bass
Cliff Hall	keyboards
Dick Hanson	trumpet
Peter Howarth	backing vocals
Hank Marvin	backing vocals, guitar
Paul Moessl	keyboards
Mick Mullins	backing vocals
Keith Murrell	backing vocals
Cliff Richard	vocals
Bruce Welch	backing vocals, guitar

Recording Details

Producer	Chris Kimsey and Steve Smith
Engineered by	Unknown
Recording location	Knebworth House, Hertfordshire, England
Recording date	30th June 1990

13. B-side (Human Work of Art)

Musicians

Cliff Richard	vocals, guitar

Recording Details

Producer	Keith Bessey
Engineered by	Keith Bessey
Recording location	Wembley Arena, Wembley, North London
Recording date	27th, 28th or 29th November 1992

14. Hank Plays Cliff

Musicians

Warren Bennett	arranger, keyboards
Ben Marvin	guitar
Hank Marvin	acoustic guitar, electric guitar
Cliff Richard	vocals, backing vocals
Gary Ridge	percussion
Trevor Spencer	drums, percussion
Gary Taylor	bass

Recording Details

Producer	Hank Marvin
Engineered by	Les Williams (Planet Sound Studios) and Dick Plant (Honeyhill Studios)
Recording location	Planet Sound Studios, Subiaco, Perth, Australia (instruments) and Honeyhill Studios, Hertfordshire (vocals)
Recording date	1995

15. Hank Plays Live

Musicians

Warren Bennett	arranger, keyboards
Mark Griffiths	bass
Ben Marvin	guitar
Hank Marvin	guitar
Pete May	drums, percussion
Cliff Richard	vocals

Recording Details

Producer	Hank Marvin
Engineered by	Unknown
Recording location	Birmingham Symphony Hall, Birmingham
Recording date	15th December 1995

16. B-side (The Miracle)

Musicians		*Recording Details*	
Cliff Richard	vocals	Producer	Keith Bessey
Unknown	backing vocals	Engineered by	Keith Bessey
Unknown	all instruments	Recording location	Royal Albert Hall, London
		Recording date	September 1998

17. Party at the Palace

Musicians		*Recording Details*	
Sam Brown	backing vocals	Producer	Giles Martin
Margo Buchanan	backing vocals	Engineered by	Andy Rose
Phil Collins	drums, percussion	Recording location	Buckingham Palace, London
Ray Cooper	percussion	Mixed by	Paul Hicks (Abbey Road) and John Hudson and Greg Jackman (Mayfair)
Claudia Fontaine	backing vocals		
Brian May	guitar	Mixed at	Abbey Road Studios, St. John's Wood, London and Mayfair Studios, London
Pino Palladino	bass		
Phil Palmer	guitar	Recording date	3rd June 2002
Cliff Richard	vocals		
Eric Robison	saxophone		
S Club 7:	vocals, backing vocals		
Tina Barrett			
Paul Cattermole			
Jon Lee			
Bradley McIntosh			
Jo O'Meara			
Hannah Spearritt			
Rachel Stevens			
Wix Wickens	keyboards		

18. World Tour Live

Musicians		*Recording Details*	
Anthony Clark	backing vocals, guitar	Producer	Keith Bessey
John Clark	guitar	Engineered by	Keith Bessey
Dave Cooke	keyboards	Recording location	The Mission Winery, Napier, New Zealand
Peter Howarth	backing vocals	Recording date	22nd February 2003
Pete May	drums, percussion		
Mick Mullins	backing vocals		
Keith Murrell	backing vocals		
Alan Park	keyboards		
Cliff Richard	vocals		
Steve Stroud	bass		

19. Two's Company

Musicians		*Recording Details*	
Brian Bennett	drums, percussion	Producer	Brian Bennett and Brian May
Mo Foster	bass	Engineered by	Justin Shirley Smith, assisted by Richard Lancaster
Brian May	guitar		
Cliff Richard	vocals, guitar	Recording location	Abbey Road Studio 2, St. John's Wood, London
		Recording date	2006

20. Reunited

Musicians		*Recording Details*	
Brian Bennett	drums, percussion	Producer	Warren Bennett (co-ordination)
Mark Griffiths	bass	Engineered by	James Collins (Honeyhill), Ethan Carlson (Middle Ear), Les Williams (Nivram) and Keith Bessey (mixing and mastering)
Hank Marvin	guitar		
Cliff Richard	vocals		
Bruce Welch	rhythm guitar	Recording location	Middle Ear Studios, Miami, Florida, USA (Cliff's vocals), Nivram Studios, Perth, Western Australia (Hank's guitars and vocals) and Honeyhill Studios, Hertfordshire, England (all other vocals and instruments)
		Recording date	Early 2009

♫ Moving In
B-side of **Carrie**

Rather than issuing a ***Rock 'n' Roll Juvenile*** album track to back ***Carrie***, Cliff Richard wrote a song later in the year which was used instead. There was some turn-over of the backing backing him for the session, too. The track was reissued on vinyl LP and CD in 1985 on *It's a Small World* and later as a bonus track on the 2001 remaster of *Rock 'n' Roll Juvenile*.
The introduction features a guitar that leads into a piano as Cliff begins to sing replete with studio reverb added to his track. Effectively, Cliff provides his own backing vocals and this makes the performance special since it is a known fact that similar vocal performances will always blend perfectly. The synthesized strings on the keyboards add a lilting sweetness to the ensemble but it is the vocals and guitar that are the key performances on the track.

Track Specification
Composed by Cliff Richard

Musicians		*Recording Details*	
Clem Cattini	drums, percussion	Producer	Cliff Richard
George Ford	bass	Engineered by	Unknown
Mart Jenner	guitars	Recording location	Abbey Road Studio 3, St. John's Wood, London
Adrian Lee	keyboards	Recording date	26th October 1979
Cliff Richard	vocals, backing vocals		
Graham Todd	keyboards		

♫ Mrs. Emily Jones

B-side of **London Ist Nicht Weit**

Although the title is in English, and is sung in English whenever it appears in the lyrics, Cliff Richard's version of the song is in German, although no English equivalent has been recorded by him. As was common for Cliff in the sixties, he spent time in the studios recording translated versions of English songs or original material. One of the songs laid down at the September sessions was *Mrs Emily Jones*, which is a translated version of the song of the same name. It was recorded at the same session as a number of foreign language tracks.

Mrs Emily Jones was chosen as the B-side of the German language recording of ***London Ist Nicht Weit*** (the translation of a Hank Marvin composition, ***London's Not Too Far***). Originally only released in mono, as was the practice by Columbia at the time for singles and EPs, *Mrs. Emily Jones* was eventually issued in stereo as part of the track listing of the foreign language song compilation ***On the Continent*** in 1997.

Performed with a country and western feel to it, Cliff is backed throughout by an uncredited female backing group and he appears to be enjoying the performance of this slinky love song.

Track Specification
Composed by Carson Parks; German lyrics by Fleming

Musicians		*Recording Details*	
Bernard Ebbinghouse Orchestra	orchestra	Producer	Norrie Paramor
Bernard Ebbinghouse	arranger, conductor	Engineered by	Peter Vince
Norrie Paramor	unknown	Recording location	Abbey Road Studio 2, St. John's Wood, London
Cliff Richard	vocals	Recording date	28th September 1967
Unknown	backing vocals		

♫ Mrs. Robinson

From the album **Heartbeat** *(Hank Marvin)*

Witten by Paul Simon and performed with his singing partner Art Garfunkel, *Mrs. Robinson* featured in the 1967 film *The Graduate* starring Dustin Hoffman in the title role and Anne Bancroft as the older woman seducer. In reality it was only the chorus that was a regularly repeated motif on the soundtrack whenever there was something going on between the two main characters. Simon then built up the song and recorded it for the debut Simon and Garfunkel album, *Bookends*, the following year. The single, when it was released, reached number one in the Billboard charts in the US and number four in the UK singles charts (followed by the EP which reached number nine a few months later). Such is the power of the song and the film it supported that it has been much parodied in other films such as *Wayne's World* and *American Pie*. There is also a lengthy section of a *Simpsons* episode devoted to an updated lyric version as Grampa Simpson tries to stop his new love marrying someone else. More up to date, when the wife of the then Northern Ireland First Minister, Iris Robinson, was found to be having an affair with the adult son of a family friend, there was an immediate Facebook campaign to get *Mrs. Robinson* back into the charts and up to number one on downloads – but the attempt failed. Over the years, it has been covered by several artists including Ray Conniff, Chet Atkins, the Lemonheads (a number nineteen in December 1992), Percy Faith, the Korgis and Booker T. and the MGs among a number of others.

In the early nineties, Hank Marvin released a number of albums under his own name with newly arranged covers of well-known songs. For the album *Heartbeat*, Cliff Richard helped out on vocals on four tracks including *Mrs. Robinson*, which also featured Brian Bennett on drums. Beginning with an acoustic guitar introduction, Cliff provides the non-lyric vocal opening that replicates the introduction performed by Simon and Garfunkel but leaves the melody to Hank's signature guitar line. In the middle eight bridge, Cliff sings "somebody loves you, more than you'll ever know" but then hands back the control to Hank's guitar. He then repeats the non-lyric opening before singing the song title followed by "here's to you". This is repeated as the track heads to the end and Cliff repeats the specific lyrics until the song fades out.

Track Specification
Composed by Paul Simon

Musicians		*Recording Details*	
Brian Bennett	drums, percussion	Producer	Hank Marvin and Brian Bennett
Warren Bennett	keyboards	Engineered by	Dick Plant
Mark Griffiths	bass	Recording location	Honeyhill Studios, Hertfordshire
Hank Marvin	guitar	Recording date	1992-1993
Cliff Richard	vocals, backing vocals		

♫ Mr. Businessman

From the album **Help It Along**

Written and recorded by Ray Stevens in 1971 and covered by Marmalade, there is some confusion over the spelling of the title. The original album sleeve for ***Help It Along*** suggests *Mr. Businessman*, while the label states *Mr. Business Man*. From an understanding point, both are acceptable; however, Stevens' original dictates that it is the former and it is this that is used in this entry.

Cliff Richard chose the song, deftly batting away suggestion that it was a deliberate attack on businessmen *per se*, for his studio-bound suite of concert sessions in front of a small audience at the Morgan Studios, which were recorded over seven sessions in three days. *Mr. Businessman* was one of the twelve (of the seventeen recorded) to be released on the charity album *Help It Along* in aid of the Tear Fund. Staccato piano chords start the song before the instrumentation joins in, creating an ebullient song that keeps the toes tapping.

Track Specification

Composed by Ray Stevens

Musicians	
Terry Britten	guitar
Barrie Guard	arranger, conductor, percussion
Cliff Hall	keyboards
Jean Hawker	backing vocals
Anna Peacock	backing vocals
Kevin Peek	guitar
Cliff Richard	vocals
Trevor Spencer	drums, percussion
Alan Tarney	bass
Unknown	orchestra

Recording Details	
Producer	David MacKay
Engineered by	Roger Quested
Recording location	Morgan Studios, London
Recording date	24th, 25th and 26th September 1973

♫ Mr. Cloud

B-side of **Jesus**

Guy Fletcher and Doug Flett continued their increasing dominance as writers of material for Cliff Richard to record with the sad but beautiful song *Mr. Cloud*. The only completed song from a late April session, the song features the orchestral arrangement of Shadows drummer Brian Bennett. The track was chosen as the B-side of Cliff's first religious single, ***Jesus***, and, issued in most markets in stereo, there was a mono version released in Australia at the same time. The stereo version was included on the rare B-sides section of the 2008 collation ***...And They Said It Wouldn't Last! (My 50 Years in Music)***.

An extraordinarily beautiful in deconstruction, it is enhanced by the thumping bass guitar underneath the flowing melody assisted by Cliff's own backing vocals. In many ways, the song would have made a perfect single purely because of the lyrical motion and the passion with which Cliff sings. The horns and thrumming bass keep the song moving onwards. Perfect.

Track Specification

Composed by Guy Fletcher and Doug Flett

Musicians	
Brian Bennett	arranger, conductor
Brian Bennett Orchestra	orchestra
Cliff Richard	vocals, backing vocals
Unknown	backing vocals

Recording Details	
Producer	Norrie Paramor
Engineered by	Unknown
Recording location	Abbey Road Studios, St. John's Wood, London
Recording date	28th April 1971

♫ Mr. Nice

B-side of **Marianne**

The first song by Terry Britten, who would be so instrumental in Cliff Richard's seventies renaissance, to be recorded by Cliff, *Mr. Nice* was one of four songs tried and three completed at the session. Chosen as the B-side of Cliff's forty-third UK single, ***Marianne***, *Mr. Nice* has only ever been released in mono. For a while, it was a rarity since it was only available on copies of the single, *Mr. Nice* was released as a bonus track on the 2007 remaster of the album that had been contemporaneously released in 1968, ***Established 1958***.

The staccato piano and accompanying rich brass introduces the song, which has a brass interlude that sounds vaguely ecclesiastical in its structure and intensity, while *Mr. Nice* is the first example of a Cliff recording that includes the Mellotron, which was a favourite amongst bands performing classical rock or pomp rock, such as the Moody Blues. There is a vocal backing group, but they are uncredited and no information is available about them.

Track Specification

Composed by Terry Britten

Musicians	
Mike Leander	conductor
Mike Leander Orchestra	orchestra
Cliff Richard	vocals
Unknown	backing vocals

Recording Details	
Producer	Norrie Paramor
Engineered by	Peter Vince
Recording location	Abbey Road Studio 3, St. John's Wood, London
Recording date	1st July 1968

♫ Mr. Niemand

From the album **Hier Ist Cliff**

Cliff Richard recorded his first German language album at the end of 1968 in spite of having a long pedigree in the German singles market. For the album, *Hier Ist Cliff,* instead of reissuing his previous singles and B-sides, he recorded completely new material, which were translations of songs plundered either from ***Two a Penny*** or ***Established 1958***. *Mr. Niemand* was one such and was a translation of the ***Two a Penny*** title theme. The original lyrics suggested arrogantly that he was not like anyone else but one of a kind, desperately trying to force himself above the rest of the population but not ultimately achieving it – so *Two a Penny* was retitled *Mr. Niemand,* which translates back to *Mr. Nobody.* The German lyrics are uncredited and it is highly unlikely that Cliff provided them himself; given that Kurt Hertha and Carl Ulrich Blecher wrote lyrics for a number of other tracks, it is quite possible that it was one of them who wrote the *Mr. Niemand* lyrics.

During the earlier part of the sixties, it had been a strategy to record new vocals and overdub them on a previously recorded backing track. Where Cliff's foreign language songs were concerned, this usually meant recording translated vocals and adding over the original English backing track. However, for *Hier Ist Cliff,* all of the tracks were recorded anew.

Released only in stereo, the rarity of the track was diminished when it was included on Cliff's foreign language compilation ***On the Continent*** in 1997.

With a backing track that sounds almost exactly the same as that used on the film soundtrack but with subtle differences, Cliff performs the song in German as he did the English version, with a certain amount of optimistic arrogance as the lyrics demand. In the final section, Cliff reverts back to the English lyrics.

Track Specification

Composed by Cliff Richard; German lyrics by Unknown

Musicians

Norrie Paramor Orchestra	orchestra
Norrie Paramor	arranger, director
Cliff Richard	vocals

Recording Details

Producer	Norrie Paramor
Engineered by	Peter Vince
Recording location	Abbey Road Studio 2, St. John's Wood, London
Recording date	27th November 1968

♫ Muddy Water

Unissued track

Recorded by Jim McCann and Rick Shea, *Muddy Water* was including in the recording sessions for the ***Green Light*** album project by Cliff Richard. It was the second of two songs attempted at the third session but stopped after two takes although additional overdubs were recorded exactly a month later (this presumably indicates that the track was successfully completed but not deemed worthy of release at any stage). Because it is unclear what the arrangement of the song is, the known musicians to be involved in the sessions are added to the track specification in their entirety.

Track Specification

Composed by Joe Babcock

Musicians

Brian Bennett	drums, percussion
Terry Britten	guitar
Stuart Calver	backing vocals
Richard Hewson	arranger, conductor
Alan Jones	bass
Duncan MacKay	keyboards
Alan Parker	guitar
John Perry	backing vocals
Tim Renwick	guitar
Cliff Richard	vocals
Tony Rivers	backing vocals
Trevor Spencer	drums, percussion
Alan Tarney	backing vocals, guitar, bass, keyboards
Graham Todd	keyboards
Unknown	orchestra

Recording Details

Producer	Bruce Welch
Engineered by	Tony Clark and Haydn Bendall
Recording location	Abbey Road Studio 3, St. John's Wood, London
Recording date	11th January 1978 and 11th February 1978

♫ Mumblin' Mosie

B-side of **Theme for a Dream**

From the same session as its A-side, ***Theme for a Dream***, *Mumblin' Mosie* was only available in back copies of the single until the release of the anthology of early material ***Rock On with Cliff Richard*** which was compiled and issued in the early eighties. It was also included in the track listing of the rarities compilation albums ***The Rock 'n' Roll Years 1958-1963*** and ***...And They Said It Wouldn't Last! (My 50 Years in Music)***. The mono and stereo versions are based on the same studio take but with different mixes for the stereo channelling.

The accompaniment is mixed further back than Cliff's lead vocals, which give way to the singing Shadows taking over the chorus while Cliff giggles and talks the lyrics. It is presented in the hambone style of rhythm (used to great effect in ***Willie and the Hand Jive***) and it is a surprise that compilers hadn't seen fit to release the song earlier.

Track Specification
Composed by Johnny Otis

Musicians		*Recording Details*	
Jet Harris	backing vocals, bass	Producer	Norrie Paramor
Tommy Kamara	bongos	Engineered by	Malcolm Addey
Hank Marvin	backing vocals, guitar	Recording location	Abbey Road Studio 2, St. John's Wood, London
Tony Meehan	drums, percussion	Recording date	28th January 1961
Cliff Richard	vocals		
Bruce Welch	backing vocals, rhythm guitar		

♬ Must Be Love

From the album **Every Face Tells a Story**

Another Terry Britten song written for Cliff Richard to record for his ***Every Face Tells a Story*** album, *Must Be Love* was recorded in thirteen takes at the first of its sessions, while vocal overdubs were added eight days later at the next.
The lazy beat is initiated in the guitars and the cymbals, as the other instruments come in. Cliff's vocals are engineered quite a way back in the mix with a little echo, while the backing vocals also feature heavily and are a mark of Bruce Welch's approach to production of Cliff's tracks.

Track Specification
Composed by Terry Britten

Musicians		*Recording Details*	
Brian Bennett	drums, percussion	Producer	Bruce Welch
Terry Britten	guitar	Engineered by	Tony Clark, Haydn Bendall and Alan Rouse
John Perry	backing vocals	Recording location	Abbey Road Studio 2, St. John's Wood, London
Cliff Richard	vocals, backing vocals	Recording date	9th and 17th September 1976
Frank Ricotti	percussion		
Tony Rivers	backing vocals		
Alan Tarney	bass		
Graham Todd	keyboards		

♬ My Babe

From the albums **Cliff** *and* **Don't Stop Me Now!**

Willie Dixon's tune is a blues song that is based on a traditional gospel song, *This Train (Is Bound for Glory)*, and follows the technique that Ray Charles began with ***I Got a Woman*** (itself based on the gospel song *Jesus Is All the World to Me*). It was specifically written as a single for Little Walter and was released in the US in 1955, reaching number one in the charts. Many artists have covered the song including Bo Diddley, Chuck Berry, Ricky Nelson (the famous version in the UK), the Steve Miller Band, Ike and Tina Turner and, of course, Cliff Richard's rock and roll idol, Elvis Presley. It was for the latter reason and Nelson's single success that this song was included in the 'live' set recorded at Abbey Road in front of an invited guest list of fans and which became Cliff and the Drifters' first long-player (simply entitled ***Cliff***).
With the screaming of the female fans drowning out the beginning, it gets into its stride with a strong but subtle guitar lead by Hank Marvin. During the guitar solo in the middle eight and on into the next verse, Cliff performs hand claps to assist with the rhythm; something which seems to drive the girls in the small audience wild.
This 'live' version of the song was included on the ***Cliff No. 1*** EP and it was subsequently resurrected and given an orchestral treatment for the album ***Don't Stop Me Now!***. Recorded at a session with unknown musicians, *My Babe* was completed in three takes with that third and final take and edit being used for both the mono and stereo recordings.
As with many of the tracks on *Don't Stop Me Now!*, the musician details are unknown, so the orchestra remains uncredited, although it is likely to one of Mike Leander, Norrie Paramor or Bernard Ebbinghouse. There is also a female backing group, but information is scant on this too; however, it is highly likely that it is the Breakaways providing the vocals since they were recording and touring regularly with Cliff during this period.

Track Specification
Composed by Willie Dixon

1. Cliff

Musicians		*Recording Details*	
Jet Harris	bass	Producer	Norrie Paramor
Hank Marvin	guitar	Engineered by	Peter Bown and Stuart Eltham
Tony Meehan	drums, percussion	Recording location	Abbey Road Studio 2, St. John's Wood, London
Cliff Richard	vocals, hand-claps	Recording date	9th February 1959
Bruce Welch	rhythm guitar		

2. Don't Stop Me Now!

Musicians		*Recording Details*	
Cliff Richard	vocals	Producer	Norrie Paramor
Unknown	female backing vocals	Engineered by	Peter Vincent and Richard Lush
Unknown	arranger, conductor	Recording location	Abbey Road Studio 2, St. John's Wood, London
Unknown	orchestra	Recording date	5th February 1967

♫ My Blue Heaven

From the albums **21 Today** *and* **Live at the ABC Kingston 1962**

Published in 1927, *My Blue Heaven* was popularized by Gene Austin the following year. It has since been covered by a variety of esoteric artists including the Boston Pops Orchestra, the Calico Consort, Doris Day, Bing Crosby, Eddie Fisher, Erroll Garner, Fats Domino (who had a hit in the US with it), Frank Ifield, Glenn Miller, Slim Whitman, Bobby Vinton, The Smashing Pumpkins, Marty Robbins and Frank Sinatra (who had a number thirty-three UK single in the spring of 1961).
Six takes were recorded for the ***21 Today*** album, with the final one being used for the mono and stereo edits with separate mixes for the needs of the audio channels. The live version that appears on ***Live at the ABC Kingston 1962*** was released finally in 2003 but this only appeared in stereo, although it is probable that a mono mix also exists given the date.
Cliff Richard and the Shadows have produced another version of a song that has so much mental baggage that it is quite hard for the listener not to be jaded; but here, the arrangement is subtly placed around a running bass line and the tinkling cymbals and drums with a rhythm performed in a cha-cha style. The instrumental interlude also allows Hank Marvin free rein to jam on the main melody, which takes the song in an altogether different direction, before settling back to the simplicity of the introductory section.

Track Specification
Composed by George Whiting and Walter Donaldson

1. 21 Today

Musicians		*Recording Details*	
Jet Harris	bass	Producer	Norrie Paramor
Hank Marvin	guitar	Engineered by	Malcolm Addey and Norman Smith
Tony Meehan	drums, percussion	Recording location	Abbey Road Studio 2, St. John's Wood, London
Norrie Paramor	piano	Recording date	19th April 1961
Cliff Richard	vocals		
Bruce Welch	rhythm guitar		

2. Live at the ABC Kingston 1962

Musicians		*Recording Details*	
Brian Bennett	drums, percussion	Producer	Norrie Paramor
Jet Harris	backing vocals, bass	Engineered by	Malcolm Addey and Ken Townsend
Hank Marvin	backing vocals, guitar	Recording location	ABC Theatre, Kingston, Surrey
Cliff Richard	vocals, hand claps	Recording date	7th March 1962
Bruce Welch	backing vocals, rhythm guitar		

♫ My Coloring Book

From the album **Love Is Forever**

Recorded by a varied range of artists, *My Coloring Book* [sic – note that this is an American song, hence the missing 'u' in 'coloring'] has been covered by Barbra Streisand, Perry Como, Kitty Kallen, Skeeter Davis, Julie London, Aretha Franklin, Jane Morgan, Dusty Springfield, Andy Williams, Nana Mouskouri, Agnetha Fältskog (who released it as a single for her comeback recording in the new millennium), Brenda Lee and Chris Farlowe among many others.
My Coloring Book was recorded by Cliff Richard for the ***Love Is Forever*** album and its similarly named counterpart EP at the session that resulted in three songs being completed. The sixth and final take and edit were used for the mono and stereo recordings but with different mixes for the separate needs of the audio channels.
Cliff sings the song very gently imbuing it with light and shade to reflect the tenor of the lyrics. The croaking at the beginning of certain lines help to inculcate the meaning of the song with emotion and this is where Cliff is particularly clever in his approach to performance, setting him apart from his contemporaries.

Track Specification
Composed by John Kander and Fred Ebb

Musicians		*Recording Details*	
Mike Sammes Singers	backing vocals	Producer	Norrie Paramor
Norrie Paramor Orchestra	orchestra	Engineered by	Malcolm Addey
Norrie Paramor	arranger, conductor	Recording location	Abbey Road Studio 2, St. John's Wood, London
Cliff Richard	vocals	Recording date	23rd June 1964

♫ My Feet Hit the Ground

B-side of **High Class Baby**

Recorded at the same session as the A-side single of which *My Feet Hit the Ground* was the flip, ***High Class Baby***, it was a remarkable achievement for the Drifters' guitarist Ian Samwell, who not only co-wrote this tune, but the A-side and its prior single, ***Move It***, too. This was unusual, simply because it was recorded in an era when conventional popular musical wisdom dictated that American music was far superior and that, in order to get a hit record, it really had to be a cover of an American tune. To have original songs written by a member of the band making the recording was extraordinary.
However, although *Move It* was a classic British rock and roll record, the following singles and B-sides were relatively poor, largely, as Cliff has intimated in interview, because they were just not familiar enough with writing rock and roll

music. In fact, there are clear influences of Elvis Presley, Little Richard, Buddy Holly and others in the composition of the later Samwell songs and, for *My Feet Hit the Ground*, it has exactly the same musical motif as heard on *High Class Baby*, even using the words 'high class' in the first line. Indeed, playing the two songs back to back, it initially sounds like there is only a brief pause in the recording of the same song.

Nevertheless, although not as powerful as Cliff's first single, as a B-side, *My Feet Hit the Ground* is still far better than *Move It*'s B-side, ***Schoolboy Crush***. The song is a rocking love song that talks about the feelings experienced when his love is not around and the effect that she has on him when she is present, interspersed with a strong guitar-led middle eight.

Norrie Paramor, the track's producer, always preferred to use session musicians on such recordings and it is likely that he used Ernie Shears and Frank Clarke from the *Move It* session on guitar and stand-up bass (the latter instrument clearly heard in this recording). However, records of those involved don't extend to the musicians for this particular session, other than Cliff's main vocals and so will remain stated as unknown until further research identifies the relevant information.

In February 1980, the track was released for the first time since the single was deleted in the late fifties on the *Rock On with Cliff* compilation that covered the first few months of Cliff's rock and roll recording career and has since been included on a couple of other anthologies released in CD format.

Track Specification

Composed by Ian Samwell and Joseph Seener

Musicians		*Recording Details*	
Cliff Richard	vocals	Producer	Norrie Paramor
Unknown	guitar	Engineered by	Malcolm Addey
Unknown	bass	Recording location	Abbey Road Studio 2, St. John's Wood, London
Unknown	drums, percussion	Recording date	3rd October 1958
Unknown	male backing vocals		

♫ My Foolish Heart

From the album **Love Is Forever**

Written as the theme song to the film of the same name released in 1949, *My Foolish Heart* was a considerable success in spite of the excoriation heaped on the film in general by critics and went on to be nominated for an Academy Award. Only a hit in the US with Gordon Jenkins reaching the top ten and Billy Eckstine hitting number six and becoming the most commercially successful in the process, *My Foolish Heart* has been covered by a wide variety of artists including Tom Jones, Nelson Riddle, Astrud Gilberto, Mel Tormé, Frank Sinatra, Tony Bennett, Oscar Peterson and Carmen McRae among many others.

My Foolish Heart was one of four songs recorded by Cliff Richard for his upcoming album ***Love Is Forever*** at the June 1965 recording session. The final (unknown) take and edit were used for the mono and stereo recordings but with different mixes for the requirements of the audio channel separation.

Cliff is in his element in this type of song, proving his worth as an able singer of any genre that focuses on melody and harmony. The song itself is not particularly memorable with few hooks but Cliff's efforts significantly elevate it.

Track Specification

Composed by Victor Young and Ned Washington

Musicians		*Recording Details*	
Norrie Paramor Orchestra	orchestra	Producer	Norrie Paramor
Cliff Richard	vocals	Engineered by	Unknown
Ken Woodman	arranger, conductor	Recording location	Abbey Road Studio 2, St. John's Wood, London
		Recording date	10th June 1965

♫ My Funny Valentine

B-side of **Let Me Be the One**

One of the more memorable tunes to be written by Richard Rodgers and Lorenz Hart for the 1937 musical *Babes in Arms*, *My Funny Valentine* became a jazz standard after popular versions recorded by Frank Sinatra, Chet Baker and Miles Davis sold well and it has since covered hundreds of artists, including Ella Fitzgerald, Jimmy Giuffre and Nico.

Coupled with another Rodgers and Hart song, ***This Can't Be Love***, as a sort of medley Cliff Richard performed the songs at his 2001 concerts at the Royal Albert Hall in London. These were recorded and included as B-side items for the second and final single to be released from the ***Wanted*** project, ***Let Me Be the One***, alongside the live version of ***I Gotta Woman*** from the 1962 Kingston concert album.

Track Specification

Composed by Richard Rodgers and Lorenz Hart

Musicians		*Recording Details*	
Cliff Richard	vocals	Producer	Unknown
Unknown	all instrumentation	Engineered by	Unknown
		Recording location	Royal Albert Hall, London
		Recording date	May 2001

♬ My Head Goes Around

From the album **Tracks 'n' Grooves**

Songwriter Geoff Goddard was the sole composer for Joe Meek's one-flat, one-producer record label RGM in the sixties and he wrote a number of classic sixties tunes, including *Just Like Eddie, Johnny Remember Me, Son This Is She* and *Wild Wind* among others and also took an uncredited role in the phenomenal success of the Tornados' *Telstar* on which he played the keyboard.

Less known but with all the spirit of those types of songs is *My Head Goes Around,* which Cliff Richard recorded for his ***Tracks 'n' Grooves*** album. This quirky number is performed with a degree of knowing humour by Cliff and would not appear out of place on the Eurovision Song Contest with its screaming brass, upbeat lyric and rhythm as well as the unexpected key change in the middle eight.

Track Specification

Composed by Geoff Goddard

Musicians

Mike Vickers Orchestra	orchestra
Cliff Richard	vocals
Unknown	backing vocals
Mike Vickers	arranger, conductor

Recording Details

Producer	Norrie Paramor
Engineered by	Peter Vince
Recording location	Abbey Road Studio 2, St. John's Wood, London
Recording date	22nd April 1969

♬ My Heart Is an Open Book

From the EP **Take Four**

Covered by a number of artists including Carl Dobkins, Jr., Dean Martin and Luther Henderson and his Orchestra, *My Heart Is an Open Book* was recorded by Cliff Richard during the suite of sessions at the Columbia studios based in New York and Nashville during his American sojourn in summer 1964. The song was recorded during the New York sessions and the eighth and final take and edit were used for the mono and stereo recordings but with different mixes for the divided audio channels. Released on the ***Take Four*** EP but only in mono, it would take another twenty-five years before the stereo version was issued on the similarly rare compilation album ***The EP Collection: Ballads and Love Songs*** in 1989. It has not been released in any other format.

The gentle but upbeat song that relies on brass and backing vocals (all uncredited) sees Cliff in his element singing a love song that deals with the affirmation of love by opening himself up to her so that she can see everything about him. A jealous person has told lies about him and it is this message that seems at odds with the jaunty rhythm of the performance.

Track Specification

Composed by Lee Pockriss and Hal David

Musicians

Stan Applebaum	conductor
Cliff Richard	vocals
Unknown	backing vocals
Unknown	guitar
Unknown	bass
Unknown	orchestra
Unknown	drums, percussion

Recording Details

Producer	Bob Morgan
Engineered by	Frank Laico
Recording location	Columbia Studios, New York
Recording date	19th August 1964

♬ (All of a Sudden) My Heart Sings

From the album **Love Is Forever**

Recorded by Duke Ellington, Spike Jones, Carole Carr, the King Sisters, Joya Sherrill and Charles Trenet, it was Paul Anka who had the most success with it when his single version reached number ten in the UK singles charts in early 1959. The song is often misnamed as simply *My Heart Sings* or without the brackets.

Cliff Richard's version, which was destined for the ***Love Is Forever*** album that was released the year after the session that yielded it, was recorded at a session that yielded many tracks for that album and its predecessor ***Cliff Richard***. Splicing takes five and seven together, that combination and edit were used for the mono and stereo recordings but with different mixes for the needs of the separate audio channels.

Cliff's performance is strong with a slight vibrato and cracks of emotion at certain points on the lyrical content. In addition, he uses the vocal glissandi that imbue it further with greater emotion. There are a few tempo changes as the rendition is played out in triplets before moving into the broader song accompanied by the backing vocals and the strings and piano.

Track Specification

Composed by Harold Rome, Henry Herpin and Jean-Marie Blanvillain

Musicians

Mike Sammes Singers	backing vocals
Norrie Paramor Orchestra	orchestra
Norrie Paramor	arranger, conductor
Cliff Richard	vocals

Recording Details

Producer	Norrie Paramor
Engineered by	Malcolm Addey
Recording location	Abbey Road Studio 2, St. John's Wood, London
Recording date	17th July 1964

♫ My Kinda Life
69th UK single and from the album **My Kinda Life**

Cliff Richard recorded his sixty-ninth single in the first session of 1977 and it was added as the first track of the album ***Every Face Tells a Story*** almost as an afterthought, given that the previous sessions had taken place in September 1976. With a new slimmed down band, too, *My Kinda Life* was the next step in Cliff's musical rehabilitation in terms of chart success and general popularity. Later Cliff would record ***Mobile Alabama School-Leaving Hulabalooo***, also written by Chris East but not released at the time possibly because of he similarity of the sound created on it.

My Kinda Life was issued as a single, backed with non-album track ***Nothing Left for Me to Say***, on the EMI label (catalogue number EMI 2589) on 16th February 1977 and reached number fifteen in the UK charts. The single version was edited from the album track, fading earlier and shortening it by nineteen seconds.

My Kinda Life is a foot-tapping rock song with Cliff performing a rough vocal making the performance sound raw. Bruce Welch makes clever use of the stereo for the instrumentation supporting the vocal line. The guitars are the principal instruments to be heard and Cliff provides many of his own backing vocals.

Giving its name to the 1992 album that took seventies and eighties tracks and embellished them with new mixes, instrumentation or vocals, *My Kinda Life* completed the track listing and had additional guitars. The original sounded more country while the new version had a harder edge. The track also fades out some ten seconds earlier than the single.

Track Specification
Composed by Chris East

1. Single

Musicians		*Recording Details*	
Alan Hawkshaw	keyboards	Producer	Bruce Welch
Alan Jones	bass	Engineered by	Tony Clark
John Perry	backing vocals	Recording location	Abbey Road Studio 2, St. John's Wood, London
Roger Pope	drums, percussion	Recording date	10th January 1977
Cliff Richard	vocals, backing vocals		
Tony Rivers	backing vocals		
Mo Witham	guitar		

2. My Kinda Life

Musicians		*Recording Details*	
John Clark	guitar	Producer	Bruce Welch (original track) and Cliff Richard and Paul Moessl (new instrumentation)
Alan Hawkshaw	keyboards		
Alan Jones	bass	Engineered by	Tony Clark (original track) and Gerry Kitchingham and Ben Robbins (new instrumentation)
John Perry	backing vocals		
Roger Pope	drums, percussion		
Cliff Richard	vocals, backing vocals	Recording location	Abbey Road Studio 2, St. John's Wood, London (original track) and R. G. Jones Studios, Wimbledon, London (new instrumentation)
Tony Rivers	backing vocals		
Mo Witham	guitar		
		Recording date	10th January 1977 (original track) and 20th-23rd April 1992 (new instrumentation)

♫ My Life, My Way
From the album **My Life, My Way**

As part of Cliff Richard's fiftieth anniversary celebrations in 2008, he published an autobiography assertively entitled ***My Life, My Way***. This was then taken, abridged and recorded by Cliff and released on two CDs as a talking book and it takes the listener through his early life, his relationship with his father, his love of music and with a fuller focus on his Christianity and life with God. Recorded in 2009, the studio personnel, location and dates are unknown. It is clear from the fades that there were separate recordings but it is unknown how many takes or sessions were required.

Track Specification
Written by Cliff Richard; abridged by Yvonne Antrobus

Musicians		*Recording Details*	
Cliff Richard	spoken vocals	Producer	Strathmore Publishing
		Engineered by	Unknown
		Recording location	Unknown
		Recording date	2009

♫ My Love
From the album **Vita Mia** *(Vincenzo La Scola)*

After Cliff Richard had recorded ***Vita Mia*** with Vincenzo La Scola for his album ***Real as I Wanna Be***, the tenor invited Cliff to join him on two duets for his album, *Vita Mia*. The first was ***If It Were Up to Me*** and the second was *My Love*.

As with *If It Were up to Me*, Cliff initiates the Stevie Wonder song with some non-lyrical vocals leading into the first verse. Cliff's and La Scola's voices blend very well together in spite of their differing musical backgrounds and the drama is intensified with the backing chorus who sing behind the harmonized duet.

Track Specification
Composed by Stevie Wonder

Musicians	
Vincenzo La Scola	vocals
Cliff Richard	vocals
Unknown	backing vocals
Unknown	guitar
Unknown	synthesiser
Unknown	drums, percussion
Unknown	conductor
Unknown	orchestra

Recording Details	
Producer	Nigel Wright
Engineered by	Unknown
Recording location	Whitfield Street Studios, London, Olympic Studios, London, Sarm West Studios, London and/or Skratch Studios, Surrey
Recording date	1997 or 1998

♫ My Luck Won't Change

From the album **Rock 'n' Roll Juvenile**

Written by Terry Britten and new chart force B. A. Robertson, who had had a major hit with *Bang Bang* at the beginning of 1979, *My Luck Won't Change* was recorded in two sections by Cliff Richard: the first saw the completion of the backing track at the EMI studios in Paris, while the next added vocal overdubs to finalize the track a month or so later.

The gentle vocal introduction belies the foot-stomping rock and roll beat that is picked up by the guitars, bass and keyboards. Cliff is clearly in his element here and the song suits his voice well. The ethereal backing vocals with the addition of Madeleine Bell inject some of the mystery created by the rationalisation of being the target of fate.

Track Specification
Composed by Terry Britten and B. A. Robertson

Musicians	
Madeleine Bell	backing vocals
Terry Britten	backing vocals, guitar
Mel Collins	saxophone
Martin Drover	trumpet
Herbie Flowers	bass
Graham Jarvis	drums, percussion
Bill Livesy	keyboards
Chris Mercer	saxophone
Cliff Richard	vocals, backing vocals

Recording Details	
Producer	Cliff Richard and Terry Britten
Engineered by	Tony Clark and Haydn Bendall
Recording location	Pathé Marconi, Paris, France (backing track) and Abbey Road Studio, St. John's Wood, London (vocals)
Recording date	7th-12th January 1979 (backing track) and 17th February 1979 (vocals)

♫ My Pretty One

101st UK single *(seven- and twelve-inch) and unissued live track*

The first of four singles to be released from the ***Always Guaranteed*** project was slowly developed by Alan Tarney in the studio before Cliff Richard came into the studio to record his vocal lines. Since Cliff was working at the Dominion Theatre in his Rock Star role in ***Time – the Musical***, this approach worked well as it made optimal use of his availability.

Backed with non-album track ***Love Ya***, *My Pretty One* was released as a single on the EMI label (catalogue number EM 4) on 8th June 1987 and reached number six in the UK singles charts. In addition, it was issued in a gatefold sleeve (catalogue number EMG 4) and an extended version was incorporated on the twelve-inch vinyl release (12EM 4), with an ancillary poster sleeve on some releases (12EMP 4). When the follow-up single, ***Some People***, was issued, the promotional video for *My Pretty One* was published alongside *Some People* on a CD video. In October 2009, the track was included as a bonus track on the ***When I Need You*** single. The accompanying video, filmed at the Albert Wharf in London on 7th May 1987, featured a barren landscape as Cliff sings the song while a girl dances in silhouette against a large full moon. She drops a glass box, which he picks up, falling into a trap and ending up in a representation of hell replete with devil-hooded dancers. He opens the box and escapes, finishing with putting a ring on the recumbent girl's finger and waking her up.

Of all the songs on the album, *My Pretty One*, is the most musical in its arrangement with its lilting arpeggios in the synthesiser backed up with strong percussion and sustained synthesised chords. During the chorus, Cliff underlines certain phrases by singing two or three of the words and these appear in the right stereo channel.

Track Specification
Composed by Alan Tarney

1. Single (seven-inch)

Musicians	
Cliff Richard	vocals, backing vocals
Alan Tarney	guitars, bass, keyboards, drum and percussion programming

Recording Details	
Producer	Alan Tarney
Engineered by	Gerry Kitchingham and Keith Bessey
Recording location	R. G. Jones Studios, Wimbledon, London
Recording date	13th October-November 1986

2. Single (twelve-inch extended)

Musicians	
Cliff Richard	vocals, backing vocals
Alan Tarney	guitars, bass, keyboards, drum and percussion programming

Recording Details	
Producer	Alan Tarney
Engineered by	Gerry Kitchingham and Keith Bessey
Recording location	R. G. Jones Studios, Wimbledon, London
Recording date	13th October-November 1986

3. *Unissued track (Live & Guaranteed 1988!)*

Musicians		*Recording Details*	
John Clark	guitar	Producer	Unknown
Rosemarie Ford	backing vocals	Engineered by	Unknown
Mark Griffiths	bass	Recording location	Fyens Forum, Odense, Denmark
Peter Howarth	backing vocals	Recording date	22nd May 1988
Steve Lauri	guitar		
Paul Moessl	keyboards		
Mick Mullins	backing vocals		
Alan Park	keyboards		
Cliff Richard	vocals		
Henry Spinetti	drums, percussion		

♬ Mystery

From the album **Drifting** *(Sheila Walsh)*

Paul Field had been a member of Christian vocal group, Network 3, for whom Cliff Richard produced two singles (***Last Train Home*** and ***Dangerous Game***) and, with Dave Cooke, wrote a number of songs for Cliff's album ***Now You See Me... Now You Don't***. It is therefore unsurprising that they would be commissioned to write a song, *Mystery*, for Cliff's protégée Sheila Walsh's first album, ***Drifting***. The song was issued on CD for the first time on the 1988 US album *Compact Favorites*. With an introductory melody that has echoes of *Dancing Queen* by ABBA, the song takes a different direction as Walsh sings the song in the upper register of her voice for the chorus. Cliff supplies backing vocals that work well with Walsh's lead vocals and Mel Collins provides a beautiful saxophone solo.

Track Specification

Composed by Dave Cooke and Paul Field

Musicians		*Recording Details*	
Clem Clemson	electric guitar	Producer	Cliff Richard and Craig Pruess
Mel Collins	saxophone	Engineered by	Keith Bessey
Graham Jarvis	drums, percussion	Recording location	Riverside Studios, London, Strawberry Studios, London, Ramp Studios, London and/or Sonoptics Studios, London
Craig Pruess	arranger, synthesiser, percussion		
Cliff Richard	backing vocals		
Sheila Walsh	vocals	Recording date	September 1982-January 1983

♬ My Way

From the album **Cliff "Live" in Japan '72**

Composed in 1967, *My Way* started life as a French song entitled *Comme d'Habitude* (or *As Usual*). Paul Anka, the American singer and composer heard the song and negotiated its rights. In a 2007 interview, he said that he thought it wasn't a great song but that it had something and he reworked the lyrics for Frank Sinatra. Sinatra was sick of the showbusiness treadmill and wanted to retire but this song changed his mind. Anka adjusted the melody slightly and added completely new, unrelated English lyrics. Sinatra recorded it in December 1968 and it reached number twenty-seven in the US, while in the UK, it had eight chart re-entries and reached a high of number five and amassed a total of 122 weeks on the chart. It was reissued in April 1994 but reached only number forty-five. Now a karaoke favourite, it has also been in the UK charts for Dorothy Squires (number twenty-five in August 1970), Elvis Presley (number nine four months after his death), the Sex Pistols (number seven in July 1978 with a punked version as part of a double A-side) and Shane McGowan (number twenty-nine in April 1996). *My Way* has been recorded by hundreds of different artists in many different styles.

Cliff Richard regularly performed songs that he would not record in the studio and *My Way* was one such example. Most were never released as live recordings but several were, particularly for those live recordings in Japan, where his material and covers were hugely popular. It made sense to add *My Way* to the set list in 1972 since it had been such a phenomena worldwide success for Sinatra across the previous two years. So popular was Cliff's version that it was released as a Japanese single, backed with ***The Look of Love*** and ***Walk on By*** also from the same concert on the Orion label (catalogue number EOR-10260) in January 1973, although it didn't chart.

The piano and guitar introduction ushers in Cliff's perfect rendition of the song, which seems misplaced in the set list given the opening lyrics of the end nearing. Olivia Newton-John's and Pat Carroll's backing vocals are kept deliberately subtle in comparison with other tracks on the album, growing as the drama builds in Cliff's lead vocal.

Track Specification

Composed by Claude François and Jacques Revaux; English lyrics by Paul Anka

Musicians		*Recording Details*	
Brian Bennett	drums, percussion	Producer	Norrie Paramor
Pat Carroll	backing vocals	Engineered by	Unknown
John Farrar	bass	Recording location	Kosei Nenkin Hall, Tokyo, Japan
Alan Hawkshaw	piano	Recording date	22nd-23rd September 1972
Hank Marvin	guitar		
Olivia Newton-John	backing vocals		
Cliff Richard	vocals		
Bruce Welch	rhythm guitar		

THE CLIFF RICHARD RECORDING CATALOGUE

N - N - N - N - N - N - N - N - N - N - N - N - N - N - N - N - N

♫ 'Na Voce, 'Na Chitarra, e'o Poco 'e Luna

Unissued track

With the release of Cliff Richard's ***Constantly*** (often subtitled with *L'Edera*) in Italy, Columbia chose a completely different song for the B-side from that released in all other territories (***True, True Lovin'***); instead, they chose ***I Only Know I Love You***. Confusingly, although this was an English translation of an original Italian song (like *Constantly*), and it was released in the English language, Columbia decided to issue it with its Italian title of *'Na Voce, 'Na Chitarra, E'o Poco 'E Luna* (literally translated as *A Voice, a Guitar and a Little Moonlight*).
To add more to the entangled story, Cliff did record a version of *'Na Voce, 'Na Chitarra, E'o Poco 'E Luna* in Italian during the ***When in Rome*** sessions but it was never released. It would have been Cliff's recorded Italian vocals overdubbed on the original English version of the song's backing track and would therefore be very similar to its English counterpart.

Track Specification

Composed by Carlo Alberto Rossi and Ugo Calise

Musicians

Brian Bennett	drums, percussion
Norrie Paramor Orchestra	orchestra
Norrie Paramor	arranger, conductor
Cliff Richard	vocals

Recording Details

Producer	Norrie Paramor (backing track and vocals)
Engineered by	Malcolm Addey (backing track and vocals)
Recording location	Abbey Road Studio 2, St. John's Wood, London (backing track) and Estudios Valentim De Carvalho, Lisbon, Portugal (vocals)
Recording date	17th November 1963 (backing track) and 13th-14th May 1965 (vocals)

♫ Neben Dir Wird's Keine Geben

From the album **Ich Träume Deine Träume**

For Cliff Richard's second German language album, ***Ich Träume Deine Träume***, which was released in 1971 in Germany only, he was almost camped out in the Abbey Road Studio complex over two days and four sessions to complete all the material, which was made easier by having the backing track recorded earlier so that the focus could be on the vocals. *Neben Dir Wird's Keine Geben* – translated loosely as *No-one Compares with You* – was the third song to be finished on the first day and it was subsequently included on the foreign language compilation, ***On the Continent***, in 1997. It is a German translation of Cliff's Japanese hit ***Early in the Morning***, which was, in turn, taken from his ***Tracks 'n' Grooves*** album.
Staccato string chords and accompanying percussion bring in the track, while the bouncing rhythm is suitably replicated from the English original. The uncredited backing vocals are a little too much and tend to overwhelm the ensemble but they also help to evoke the musical memories of the period, where stage musical songs were all the fashion.

Track Specification

Composed by Mike Leander and Eddie Seago; German lyrics by Raschek

Musicians

Norrie Paramor Orchestra	orchestra
Cliff Richard	vocals
Unknown	backing vocals
Mike Vickers	arranger, conductor

Recording Details

Producer	Norrie Paramor (backing track and vocals)
Engineered by	Phil McDonald (backing track and vocals)
Recording location	Cologne, Germany (backing track) and Abbey Road Studio 2, St. John's Wood, London (vocals)
Recording date	November 1970 (backing track) and 25th November 1970 (vocals)

♫ Needing a Friend

B-side of **Can't Take the Hurt Anymore**

Self-penned by Cliff Richard with Gary help from Isherwood, *Needing a Friend* was recorded almost a year before the completion of the associated album project ***Green Light***. Finished at the final session for Cliff of 1977, it was the second of three songs to be tried, alongside the previously unreleased ***Mobile Alabama School Leaving Hullabaloo*** and *Needing a Friend*'s eventual A-side, ***Can't Take the Hurt Anymore***. Because that single was a commercial flop, the B-side became a considerable rarity that was only resolved by its inclusion on the *1970s* compilation album and then as a bonus on the 2002 remaster of *Green Light*.
With a dominant electric piano introducing the song, a real piano joins in with the rest of the instrumentation. Cliff provides his own backing vocals performed in thirds on the chorus, while Alan Tarney builds up a choir of his own voice for the remainder of the backing vocals. Thirty years on, the track still sounds surprisingly fresh.

Track Specification
Composed by Cliff Richard and Gary Isherwood

Musicians		*Recording Details*	
Terry Britten	guitar	Producer	Bruce Welch
Alan Hawkshaw	keyboards	Engineered by	Tony Clark
Cliff Richard	vocals, backing vocals	Recording location	Abbey Road Studio 3, St. John's Wood, London
Trevor Spencer	drums, percussion	Recording date	11th July 1977
Alan Tarney	backing vocals, bass		

♫ Nel Blu Dipinto di Blu
From the album **When in Rome**

Starting life as the Italian entry for the 1958 Eurovision Song Contest, *Nel Blu Dipinto di Blu* (literally *In the Blue Painted Blue*) was performed by its writer Domenico Modugno. It came third (from a field of ten countries) after a technical hitch where some countries hadn't seen the original performance meant that Modugno sang it again at the end of the Contest. Taking on a life of its own, English lyrics were added by Mitchell Parish and retitled to *Volare*, after the repetition in the refrain. The following year it won prizes at the first Grammy Awards ceremony after Modugno successfully took the song to the number one spot in the US Billboard charts. It has since been covered by a variety of artists including Gracie Fields (who changed the lyrics to fit her performance), Louis Armstrong, the Platters, Chet Atkins, Trini Lopez, Connie Francis, Petula Clark, Engelbert Humperdinck, Russell Watson, G4, Barry White, Al Martino, the Gipsy Kings, Luciano Pavarotti and David Bowie among many others. In the UK, Modugno reached number ten in September 1958, while comedian Charlie Drake had a hit at the same time reaching number twenty-eight. Dean Martin's recording is perhaps the most famous reaching number two in the late summer of 1958, while Mario Marini and His Quartet reached number two later on that same year with Bobby Rydell only managing number twenty-two two years later.

Cliff Richard's version was sung in the original Italian and, unlike many of his foreign language recordings, was not subsequently recorded into an English equivalent. One of several tracks for the ***When in Rome*** album recorded at the Lisbon studio sessions, Cliff's vocals were overdubbed on pre-recorded orchestral tracks from seven months beforehand. The final (unknown) take and edit of the vocal recording was overdubbed on the fifth and final orchestral take and edit and issued in mono format only and was also included on the EP ***Hits from When in Rome***. There is some confusion over the studio personnel involved in the recording: while Malcolm Addey might have been involved in the vocal tracks, it is unlikely that he was engineering the orchestral backing track.

Cliff performs the song with a bright wit that is matched by the amusing orchestral accompaniment. Although he had to spend a lot of time mastering the phonetic description of the lyrics, Italian suits Cliff's voice well.

Track Specification
Composed by Domenico Modugno and Franco Migliacci

Musicians		*Recording Details*	
Norrie Paramor Orchestra	orchestra	Producer	John Lee and M. DiPonti (backing track) and Norrie Paramor (vocals)
Norrie Paramor	arranger, conductor	Engineered by	Malcolm Addey
Cliff Richard	vocals	Recording location	EMI Studios, Milan (backing track) and Estudios Valentim De Carvalho, Lisbon (vocals)
		Recording date	2nd-3rd October 1964 (backing track) and 14th May 1965 (vocals)

♫ Never Be Anyone Else But You
Unissued track and from the album **Rock 'n' Roll Silver**

Originally a 1959 Ricky Nelson hit, which reached number fourteen in the UK charts in the summer, *Never Be Anyone Else But You* has also been covered by Edison Lighthouse, Emmylou Harris, Daniel O'Donnell and a number of others.

Before Cliff Richard recorded his version of the song for the ***Rock 'n' Roll Silver*** album, he was involved in producing the track for Guernsey singer and actor Richard Loring, ostensibly for release in South Africa, although it was one of three tracks not released by EMI from the sessions. The song was chosen by Cliff's band, which he named Thunder and who arranged and produced the album as a collective, for the *Rock 'n' Roll Silver* twenty-fifth anniversary album.

As the song starts gently, it seems to be a completely different song, although this is rectified once Cliff's vocals come in – which includes a complex pitching of musical intervals – and it becomes clear how special this arrangement is. Cliff provides his own backing vocals alongside the other singers and this assists with the perfect close harmony blending.

Track Specification
Composed by Thomas Baker Knight

<u>1. Unissued track (Richard Loring)</u>

Musicians		*Recording Details*	
Richard Loring	vocals	Producer	Cliff Richard
Unknown	other instrumentation	Engineered by	Unknown
		Recording location	Abbey Road Studios, St. John's Wood, London
		Recording date	August 1977

2. Rock 'n' Roll Silver

Musicians

Stuart Calver	backing vocals
Dave Cooke	keyboards
John Clark	electric guitar
Mark Griffiths	bass
Graham Jarvis	drums, percussion
Mart Jenner	guitar
John Perry	backing vocals
Alan Park	keyboards
Cliff Richard	vocals, backing vocals
Tony Rivers	backing vocals
Thunder	arranger

Recording Details

Producer	Thunder
Engineered by	Keith Bessey
Recording location	Strawberry Studios South, Surrey
Recording date	9th-18th May 1983

♫ Never Even Thought

From the albums **Green Light** *and* **My Kinda Life**

Written by singer and songwriter Murray Head, *Never Even Thought* was also recorded by him and then separately by Colin Blunstone (for his 1978 album of the same name). Completed in one take at the fourth session for Cliff Richard's ***Green Light*** album project, additional overdubs were recorded just over a month later.

Keeping it simple with a guitar and synthesized harpsichord introduction, the fragility in the meaning of the lyrics are expertly handled by Cliff as he sings about finding love. The beauty of the track is enhanced by the addition of a string accompaniment. The second verse takes on a syncopated rhythm change before the next picks up the original.

Revisiting the track in 1992 for the album ***My Kinda Life***, Cliff and music director Paul Moessl took the original recording and pretty much changed it by adding new guitars and keyboards, giving it a much funkier rhythm and there are additional vocals by Cliff that are not on the original. This updated version of the song was added as an extra track on the first of the dual CD discs of the single release of ***Human Work of Art***.

Track Specification

Composed by Murray Head

1. Green Light

Musicians

Brian Bennett	drums, percussion
Terry Britten	guitar
Stuart Calver	backing vocals
Richard Hewson	arranger, conductor
Alan Jones	bass
Duncan MacKay	keyboards
Alan Parker	guitar
John Perry	backing vocals
Tim Renwick	guitar
Cliff Richard	vocals
Tony Rivers	backing vocals
Trevor Spencer	drums, percussion
Alan Tarney	backing vocals, guitar, bass, keyboards
Graham Todd	keyboards
Unknown	orchestra

Recording Details

Producer	Bruce Welch
Engineered by	Tony Clark and Haydn Bendall
Recording location	Abbey Road Studio 3, St. John's Wood, London
Recording date	12th January 1978 and 19th February 1978

2. My Kinda Life

Musicians

Brian Bennett	drums, percussion
Terry Britten	guitar
Stuart Calver	backing vocals
John Clark	guitar
Richard Hewson	arranger, conductor
Alan Jones	bass
Duncan MacKay	keyboards
Paul Moessl	drum sequencers, synthesisers
Alan Parker	guitar
John Perry	backing vocals
Tim Renwick	guitar
Cliff Richard	vocals
Tony Rivers	backing vocals
Trevor Spencer	drums, percussion
Alan Tarney	backing vocals, guitar, bass, keyboards
Graham Todd	keyboards
Unknown	orchestra

Recording Details

Producer	Bruce Welch (original track) and Cliff Richard and Paul Moessl (new instrumentation)
Engineered by	Tony Clark and Hayden Bendall (original track) and Gerry Kitchingham and Ben Robbins (new instrumentation and vocal)
Recording location	Abbey Road Studio 3, St. John's Wood, London (original track) and R. G. Jones Studios, Wimbledon, London (new instrumentation and vocal)
Recording date	12th January 1978 and 19th February 1978 (original track), 1st-2nd February 1992 (new vocal) and 20th-23rd April 1992 (new instrumentation)

♫ Never Knew What Love Could Do

From the EP **La La La La La**

One of the songs from the increasingly prolific Shadows in the mid-sixties, *Never Knew What Love Could Do* was recorded at the same session as the first attempt to record ***La La La La La***, the song that gave its title to the EP on which both songs appear. The fifth and final take and edit were used for the mono and stereo recordings but with different mixes for the separate audio channels. Originally only released in mono format for the EP, *Never Knew What Love Could Do* was reissued in stereo two years later on the German album *Congratulations und 13 Weitere Hits* and languished in relative obscurity until it was included on the French CD compilation *All My Love* in 2008. In the same year, an edited version (fading out ten or so seconds earlier) was also included on ***...And They Said It Wouldn't Last! (My 50 Years in Music)***.

With a melody that could have been part of the ***Finders Keepers*** soundtrack, this is a quintessential Cliff and the Shadows track, with its memorable melody but also the brilliant close harmony vocals that they produced so well together. However, the arrangement, with a raw guitar and lead vocal, means that it is a very different beast from other recordings.

Track Specification

Composed by Hank Marvin, Brian Bennett and John Rostill

Musicians

Brian Bennett	drums, percussion
Mike Leander	arranger, conductor
Hank Marvin	backing vocals, guitar
Mike Leander Orchestra	orchestra
Cliff Richard	vocals
John Rostill	backing vocals, bass
Bruce Welch	backing vocals, rhythm guitar

Recording Details

Producer	Norrie Paramor
Engineered by	Peter Vince and Richard Lush
Recording location	Abbey Road Studio 2, St. John's Wood, London
Recording date	21st September 1966

♫ Never Let Go

120th UK single

The fourth of five singles to be lifted from ***Cliff Richard - The Album***, *Never Let Go* was Cliff Richard's one hundred and twentieth single release in thirty-five years in the business. Backed with ***Congratulations***, it was issued on the EMI label (catalogue number EM 281) on 20th September 1993 and reached number thirty-two in the UK singles charts. There was only one CD disc in that format release (catalogue number CDEM 281), although there was a boxed set (CDEMS 281), both of which included ***The Young Ones*** and ***You Got Me Wondering***, the latter being a revisited version released on the album ***My Kinda Life***. There was also a promotional CD single released (CDEMDJ 281) that had only the one track on it. *Never Let Go* was subsequently included as an extra track on the 2007 single ***When I Need You*** and its promotional video that accompanied the song's release was filmed on 28th September 1993 at the Black Island Studios in London.

The use of the saxophone exemplifies much of the material on the album and it is used here to introduce the song but gives way to the swimming synthesiser keyboards supporting Cliff's lead vocals. The beat picks up in the chorus as Cliff is joined by the backing vocalists and the rest of the instrumentation before quietening down once more for the next verse. Cliff's lead vocal is impassioned and makes great use of his upper range as he sings to a girl wanting her to refuse to let him go and to stay with him. Once again, like ***I Still Believe in You***, the featured vocalist (this time uncredited) is Judith Walmsley, who takes a descant vocal on the trail-out of the song.

Track Specification

Composed by John Wilson and Alan Gorrie

Musicians

Dave Bishop	saxophone
John Clark	guitar
Peter Howarth	backing vocals
Peter May	drums, percussion
Paul Moessl	arranger, drum programming, keyboards
Keith Murrell	backing vocals
Tessa Niles	backing vocals
Cliff Richard	vocals, backing vocals
Steve Stroud	bass
Judith Walmsley	vocals, backing vocals

Recording Details

Producer	Paul Moessl and Cliff Richard
Engineered by	Gerry Kitchingham and Ben Robbins
Recording location	R. G. Jones Studios, Wimbledon, London
Recording date	May-June 1992

♫ Never Mind

B-side of **Mean Streak** *and from the album* **...And They Said It Wouldn't Last (My Fifty Years in Music)**

Cliff Richard's fourth single, ***Mean Streak***, was a return to formula after the relatively disastrous foray with ***Livin' Lovin' Doll***, by using a rock and roll song written by Ian Samwell who had also penned the first two singles. The previous single had just scraped into number twenty in the UK singles charts and was only chosen because of Norrie Paramor's decision to try to block the release of ***Living Doll*** from the soundtrack of *Serious Charge*, Cliff's first film project.

Never Mind, another Samwell song, was chosen for B-side of *Mean Streak* and it was completed first in its session. A week after *Mean Streak* hit the charts, fans started listening to and requesting the B-side. Unusually, therefore, for its time, the

two songs were in the chart at different placings without being an official double A-side release. The disc was released in April 1959 on the Columbia label (catalogue numbers DB 4290 (78 r.p.m. format) and 45-DB 4290 (seven-inch single format)). While *Mean Streak* hit the number ten spot, unsurprisingly for a B-side, *Never Mind* only reached number twenty-one: not bad for a song not officially released as the chief single. It has been released in different formats over the years on compilations of Cliff's early work but a different take was issued on ***...And They Said It Wouldn't Last (My Fifty Years in Music)***, which is essentially the same track that appeared as the B-side but with a slightly enhanced guitar solo from Hank Marvin brought further forward in the mix. This version was the tenth take from the session.
The song, though, is quite similar to the A-side, although it is presented at a faster pace than *Mean Streak*. One of the problems that Cliff admitted in interview in later years is that the strength of the songs after ***Move It*** wasn't that great, in part because bands then were unused to writing material since it was common practice to cover American material. However, that denigrates Cliff's energetic vocal performance and the initiation of the trademark twanging style that Hank Marvin brought to his playing. In juxtaposition to the A-side, which talks of splitting up if the girl doesn't stop being so mean, *Never Mind* takes the opposite stance of wanting to stay together in spite of her quite obvious human failings.
This track is also noteworthy for being the first single release (albeit a B-side) to feature Tony Meehan, who replaced Terry Smart on drums, leading to the first enduring and formal line-up of what would quickly become The Shadows.

Track Specification
Composed by Ian Samwell

1. B-side (Mean Streak)

Musicians		*Recording Details*	
Jet Harris	bass	Producer	Norrie Paramor
Hank Marvin	guitar	Engineered by	Peter Bown and Stuart Eltham
Tony Meehan	drums, percussion	Recording location	Abbey Road Studio 2, St. John's Wood, London
Cliff Richard	vocals	Recording date	9th March 1959
Bruce Welch	rhythm guitar		

2. ...And They Said It Wouldn't Last (My Fifty Years in Music)

Musicians		*Recording Details*	
Jet Harris	bass	Producer	Norrie Paramor
Hank Marvin	guitar	Engineered by	Peter Bown and Stuart Eltham
Tony Meehan	drums, percussion	Recording location	Abbey Road Studio 2, St. John's Wood, London
Cliff Richard	vocals	Recording date	9th March 1959
Bruce Welch	rhythm guitar		

♬ Never Say Die (Give a Little Bit More)

89th UK single *(seven-inch and twelve-inch versions)*

A statement of disambiguation for the track released as Cliff Richard's eighty-ninth UK single (and the last to chart in the US for him to date): ***Give a Little Bit More***, which was recorded for the ***I'm No Hero*** album (and coincidentally was released as a single only in the US) is not the same as the song that was recorded during the ***Silver*** album sessions, in spite of the fact that it is frequently referred to as the part of the title within the parentheses – one has to wonder whether the Americans were confused by this thinking they were experiencing a reissue of their earlier single.
Backed with a new arrangement of ***Lucille***, from the album ***Rock 'n' Roll Silver***, *Never Say Die (Give a Little Bit More)* was issued as a single on the EMI label (catalogue number EMI 5415) on 22nd August 1983 and reached number fifteen in the British charts. The American release saw Cliff hit the Billboard charts for the final time to date reaching number seventy-three. It was the first Cliff single issued as a twelve-inch single (12EMI 5415) with the same B-side and an extended mix of the A-side. The associated promotional video, filmed on 19th July 1983, features Cliff as a taxi-driver in a mystery story that swaps between police station, prison and other locations such as a fish and chip shop where the news story is used as wrapping while the authorities search for someone matching a pen drawing of the perpetrator. This is the first of Cliff's videos to be a full production with dancers as well as a narrative that matches the lyrics – a mini-film, in fact.
With a disco rhythm that feels fresh and nostalgic simultaneously, Cliff shares the backing vocals with the song's writer Terry Britten. The mid-section is part-whispered, part-sung and would not be out of place on a Michael Jackson album from the period.

Track Specification
Composed by Terry Britten and Sue Shifrin

1. Single (seven-inch)

Musicians		*Recording Details*	
Ronnie Asprey	saxophone	Producer	Terry Britten
Michael Boddicker	keyboards	Engineered by	John Hudson
Terry Britten	arranger, backing vocals, guitar	Recording location	Mayfair Recording Studios, London
Martin Drover	trumpet	Recording date	21st–22nd May 1983
Mark Griffiths	bass		
Graham Jarvis	drums, percussion		
Cliff Richard	vocals, backing vocals		

2. *Single (twelve-inch)*

Musicians

Ronnie Asprey	saxophone
Michael Boddicker	keyboards
Terry Britten	arranger, backing vocals, guitar
Martin Drover	trumpet
Mark Griffiths	bass
Graham Jarvis	drums, percussion
Cliff Richard	vocals

Recording Details

Producer	Terry Britten
Engineered by	John Hudson
Recording location	Mayfair Recording Studios, London
Recording date	21st-22nd May 1983

♫ New 23rd, The

From the album **His Land**

Of the 150 psalms in the Bible, the twenty-third is the most familiar, given that it is often sung at funerals, particularly with the most familiar setting to the *Crimond*, which was composed by Jessie Seymour Irvine. Written, according to religious lore, by King David, it describes his God as a shepherd leading his bewildered sheep through danger with protection, though famine with abundance and so on. It was recorded for Cliff Richard's first religious album, ***Good News***. For the film ***His Land***, which featured Cliff performing songs in Israel as part of a documentary, Ralph Carmichael composed a new setting of the psalm with an orchestral backing recorded in Hollywood and Cliff adding his vocal line in Israel. Unfortunately, there are few records of precise dates other than they took place towards the end of 1969.

Walking down the side of a hill as he sings, Cliff comes to a grove that has a herd of goats, where he pauses momentarily before getting into a large boat and rowing into the middle of the lake. The song completes with exquisite adulation for the song's subject and segues into Cliff Barrows and Cliff talking about the importance of Bethlehem to the Christian faith. Cliff performs the psalm with passion and also provides his own close harmony vocals accompanied by a haunting string section and harmonica. The backing chorus is understated and adds much to the important meaning of the lyrics.

Track Specification

Composed by Ralph Carmichael

Musicians

Ralph Carmichael	arranger, conductor
Ralph Carmichael Chorus	backing vocals
Ralph Carmichael Orchestra	orchestra
Cliff Richard	vocals, backing vocals

Recording Details

Producer	Lee Gillette
Engineered by	Unknown
Recording location	Capitol Records, Hollywood, USA (orchestra) and Israel (vocals)
Recording date	Late 1969

♫ Next Time, The

***19th UK single** and from the albums* **Summer Holiday – Special Edition**, **The Rock 'n' Roll Years 1958-1963** *and* **Reunited** *and unissued live tracks*

In ***Summer Holiday***, having escaped from angry Yugoslavian peasants after a misunderstanding led them to believe that Don Preston (Cliff Richard) was marrying one of the village daughters, the bus speeds its way to Athens, drawing up in the city centre, where the travelling boys and girls are mobbed by an excited crowd. A suited man in a bowler hat and stiff English accent explains that everyone is so excited to see a London bus travelling the continent and shows them the front page of the *Daily Mail*. Turning to the inside page, there is a full spread on the disappearance of American heiress Barbara Winters (Lauri Peters) with whom Don has fallen in love, and reveals her to be their travelling companion. With her mother shouting instructions to the police, Don and his friends are arrested for kidnap and he feels betrayed. While the others settle into a hotel room, Don walks up to the Acropolis and sings *The Next Time*, which allows him to bemoan the fact that he will fall in love again except that he is still so in love with Barbara.

One of two songs recorded at the studio session (the second, ***Quarter to Three***, has not been issued), the ninth and final take and edit was used for the mono and stereo recordings but with different mixes for the audio channels. Also released on the track listing of the ***Hits from Summer Holiday*** EP, *The Next Time* was issued, backed with ***Bachelor Boy***, on the Columbia label (45-DB 4950) on 6th December 1962 and reached number one, where it stayed for three weeks. Initially, *Bachelor Boy* was marked as the B-side but, from the second week at number one, both songs were listed as a double A-side after requests from fans. Cliff's film version was recorded later in the year at Elstree Studios and, while a different recording, the arrangement and performance remain very similar, and it appears on the ***Summer Holiday –Special Edition*** album as a bonus track. On the same album, too, was released a rehearsal take (probably the third) that was lyrically different and slower and without the orchestra or piano. Finally from the film sessions, a further take was issued on the anthology ***The Rock 'n' Roll Years 1958-1963***, which is the released single but without the orchestral and piano overdubs.

The slinky instrumentation on guitars, drums and piano underpin the negative emotions expressed in the lyrics, which talk about forgetting the current love and moving on eventually to a new one. The beauty of Norrie Paramor's arrangement and piano accompaniment perfectly match Cliff's sad vocal line.

On the set list for Cliff's 1967 Far East tour, ***Cliff in Japan*** was issued but without the performance of *The Next Time*, which remains unissued. Similarly, this was the case for the recorded concerts two years later that resulted in ***Japan Tour '74***.

The Next Time was one of the re-recording choices for ***Reunited***, the album that saw Cliff back with the Shadows. It was also performed during the associated tour to promote the album. The piano and electric guitar are more mellifluous than in the original and Cliff imbues the lyrics with more vibrato but in all other respects it is faithful to the first recording.

Track Specification
Composed by Buddy Kaye and Philip Springer

1. Single

Musicians

Brian Bennett	drums, percussion
Brian 'Licorice' Locking	bass
Hank Marvin	guitar
Norrie Paramor Strings	orchestra
Norrie Paramor	arranger, conductor, piano
Cliff Richard	vocals
Bruce Welch	rhythm guitar

Recording Details

Producer	Norrie Paramor
Engineered by	Malcolm Addey
Recording location	Abbey Road Studio 2, St. John's Wood, London
Recording date	10th May 1962

2. Summer Holiday – Special Edition (1)

Musicians

Brian Bennett	drums, percussion
Brian 'Licorice' Locking	bass
Hank Marvin	guitar
Norrie Paramor Strings	orchestra
Norrie Paramor	arranger, conductor, piano
Cliff Richard	vocals
Bruce Welch	rhythm guitar

Recording Details

Producer	Norrie Paramor
Engineered by	Unknown
Recording location	Elstree Studios, Hertfordshire
Recording date	1962

3. Summer Holiday – Special Edition (2)

Musicians

Brian Bennett	drums, percussion
Brian 'Licorice' Locking	bass
Hank Marvin	guitar
Cliff Richard	vocals
Bruce Welch	rhythm guitar

Recording Details

Producer	Norrie Paramor
Engineered by	Malcolm Addey
Recording location	Abbey Road Studio 2, St. John's Wood, London
Recording date	10th May 1962

4. The Rock 'n' Roll Years 1958-1963

Musicians

Brian Bennett	drums, percussion
Brian 'Licorice' Locking	bass
Hank Marvin	guitar
Cliff Richard	vocals
Bruce Welch	rhythm guitar

Recording Details

Producer	Norrie Paramor
Engineered by	Malcolm Addey
Recording location	Abbey Road Studio 2, St. John's Wood, London
Recording date	10th May 1962

5. Unissued track (Cliff in Japan)

Musicians

Norrie Paramor Orchestra	orchestra
Norrie Paramor	arranger, conductor
Cliff Richard	vocals

Recording Details

Producer	Norrie Paramor
Engineered by	Unknown
Recording location	Shibuya Public Hall, Tokyo, Japan
Recording date	18th October 1967

6. Unissued track (Japan Tour '74)

Musicians

Barrie Guard	arranger, conductor
Cliff Hall	piano
Brian Lewis	guitar
Kevin Peak	acoustic guitar
Cliff Richard	vocals
Shambles Symphonet	orchestra
Trevor Spencer	drums, percussion
Alan Tarney	bass
Bruce Welch	rhythm guitar

Recording Details

Producer	Toshiba EMI (no individual detailed)
Engineered by	Toshiba EMI (no individual detailed)
Recording location	Shinjuku Koseinenkin, Tokyo, Japan
Recording date	7th-8th October 1974

7. Reunited

Musicians

Brian Bennett	arranger (strings), drums, percussion
Warren Bennett	arranger (strings), piano
Mark Berrow	violin
Dave Daniels	cello
Mark Griffiths	bass
Bogustan Kostecki	violin
Martin Loveday	cello
Hank Marvin	backing vocals, guitar
Perry Montague-Mason	violin
Cliff Richard	vocals, backing vocals
Emlyn Singleton	violin
Chris Tombling	violin
Kevin Townsend	arranger (strings), conductor
Bruce Welch	backing vocals, rhythm guitar
Warren Zeilinski	violin

Recording Details

Producer	Warren Bennett (co-ordination)
Engineered by	James Collins (Honeyhill Studios), Ethan Carlson (Middle Ear Studios), Les Williams (Nivram Studios) and Keith Bessey (mixing and mastering)
Recording location	Middle Ear Studios, Miami, Florida, USA (Cliff's vocals), Nivram Studios, Perth, Western Australia (Hank's guitars and vocals) and Honeyhill Studios, Hertfordshire, England (all other vocals and instruments)
Recording date	Early 2009

♫ Night, The

B-side of **Wind Me Up (Let Me Go)**

In 1982, EMI issued a boxed set of twelve of Cliff Richard's singles in special picture sleeves, as a celebration of his upcoming twenty-five years in the music business, which included an errant B-side coupled with ***Wind Me Up (Let Me Go)***. The correct track is the Hank Marvin and Cliff Richard collaboration *The Night* but, for some reason, the boxed set version of the single was coupled with ***The Night Is So Lonely*** which was released on the track listing of his 1961 album ***21 Today***; it was even titled *The Night* on the label, although it is quite easy to see where the confusion might have arisen. The problem was noticed quickly and unsold boxed sets recalled, with subsequent sets being released correctly with *The Night* as the B-side. Those first few sets that were sold with the incorrect B-side are now valuable rarities.
The only song to be recorded at the session in 1965, *The Night* was initially only released in mono format. The final (unknown) take and edit were used for the mono and stereo recordings but with different mixes for the separation in audio channels. Also released on the ***Wind Me Up*** EP, *The Night* was a rarity in its own right until it was included in that boxed set and it made its first appearance on CD on the 1998 UK issue of *1960s*. The stereo version as only released as part of the celebratory rarity collection ***...And They Said It Wouldn't Last! (My 50 Years in Music)*** in 2008.
Talking of troubled thoughts exhibited during the night with relief found in the morning, there is a lovely middle eight section that cleverly uses key modulation in the vocal harmonies, which are evident throughout and show off that perfect Cliff and the Shadows sound. Hank Marvin's guitar lead is mixed forward in the edit and sounds more rounded than many of his recordings. It is a hidden gem from Cliff's oeuvre, both as a writer and as a performer.

Track Specification
Composed by Hank Marvin and Cliff Richard

Musicians

Brian Bennett	drums, percussion
Hank Marvin	backing vocals, guitar
Cliff Richard	vocals
John Rostill	backing vocals, bass
Unknown	tambourine
Bruce Welch	backing vocals, rhythm guitar

Recording Details

Producer	Norrie Paramor
Engineered by	Peter Bown
Recording location	Abbey Road Studio 2, St. John's Wood, London
Recording date	5th October 1965

♫ Night Is So Lonely, The

From the album **21 Today**

The penultimate track on the first side of Cliff Richard's birthday celebration album, ***21 Today***, was co-written by one of his peers, Gene Vincent. Also recorded by Vincent, but not a UK singles hit, the style of song fits well with the album. In the recording session at the beginning of July 1961, *The Night Is So Lonely* was the final song to be recorded. The fifth and final take was used for the stereo and mono edits, although the audio requirements directed different mixes. The track was incorporated on the track listing of the ***Cliff Richard No. 2*** EP and it was also incorrectly issued in 1982 as the B-side of ***Wind Me Up (Let Me Go)*** as part of the boxed set of twelve singles released by EMI for Cliff's twenty-fifth anniversary in music. After unsold sets were recalled, the problem was rectified when reissued correctly with ***The Night*** but the first sets sold with the incorrect B-side are now a considerable rarity.
Cliff's rendition is unusual with the Shadows performing backing vocals against the hammering and staccato instrumentation. The pitching is critical to its success in what is a technically complex song to sing but the band plays it with assuredness and it is sung with a heartwarming nonchalance.

Track Specification
Composed by Clifton Simmons and Gene Vincent

Musicians

Jet Harris	backing vocals, bass
Hank Marvin	backing vocals, guitar
Tony Meehan	drums, percussion
Cliff Richard	vocals
Bruce Welch	backing vocals, rhythm guitar

Recording Details

Producer	Norrie Paramor
Engineered by	Malcolm Addey
Recording location	Abbey Road Studio 2, St. John's Wood, London
Recording date	4th July 1961

♫ Nightmare, The (A Time for Absolution)

From the album **Heathcliff Live**

With the death in childbirth of Cathy (Helen Hobson) on his conscience, Heathcliff (Cliff Richard) sets about trying to find a reason for why his love for her was doomed. So maddened in grief, he lies with Cathy's coffin and even tries taking the lid off. The theme from ***I Do Not Love You Isabella*** is used for the song as each of the characters return to him in his nightmare blaming him in turn, while he tries to protect his memories and version of events. First it is Cathy's brother Hindley (Jimmy Johnston), then Heathcliff's wife Isabella (Sara Haggerty), Cathy's husband Edgar (Darryl Knock) and then the dead Cathy herself in the montage.
Sometimes without the parenthesised subtitle, the performance has the same plodding arrogance and the church organ running underneath the performance. Although using the same music as that used in the wedding ceremony, the pace is slower and more lugubrious mirroring the conflicting emotions felt in the narrative.

Track Specification
Composed by John Farrar and Tim Rice

Musicians	
Sean Callery	orchestrator, orchestra
David Combes	backing vocals
John Clark	guitar
Elements:	
Geoff David	backing vocals
Chris Holland	backing vocals
Sonia Jones	backing vocals
Niki Kitt	backing vocals
Suzanne Parry	backing vocals
Gordon Giltrap	vocals, guitar
Keith Hayman	keyboards
Sara Haggerty	vocals
Helen Hobson	vocals
Jimmy Johnston	vocals
Darryl Knock	vocals
Peter May	drums, percussion
Bob Noble	keyboards
Alan Park	keyboards
John Perry	backing vocals
Cliff Richard	spoken vocals, vocals
Steve Stroud	bass
Kevin Townend	orchestration
Unknown	orchestra
Mick Wilson	backing vocals

Recording Details	
Producer	John Farrar
Engineered by	Keith Bessey, John Pearson and Tom Tranter
Recording location	Earl's Court Hall 2, London and/or The Academy, National Indoor Arena, Birmingham, England
Recording date	October 1996

♫ Nine Times out of Ten

***10th UK single** and from the albums* **The Rock and Roll Years 1958-1963, ...And They Said It Wouldn't Last! (My 50 Years in Music)** *and* **Reunited**

In the middle of 1960, around two hundred Cliff Richard fan club members were invited to Abbey Road to listen to a selection of twelve tracks that Cliff and the Shadows had recorded with the purpose of deciding which of them were the strongest and, therefore, which would be best served to be released as singles. The favourites in the poll were clearly *Nine Times out of Ten*, ***Please Don't Tease*** and ***Gee Whiz It's You***, with the most popular (*Please Don't Tease*) being released as their ninth single and which reached the coveted position of number one in the UK singles charts.
The second favourite was *Nine Times out of Ten*, a racing Otis Blackwell number that showed off Bruce Welch's skills as a rhythm guitarist and Hank Marvin's in the lead. The song was covered by esoteric bands such as Kim and the Hurmio and Danny Dean and the Homewreckers but it was Cliff and the Shadows version that captured the record-buying public's imagination. Backed with ***Thinking of Our Love***, *Nine Times out of Ten* was released on 16th September 1960 on the Columbia label (catalogue number 45-DB 4506) and reached number three in the UK singles charts. The single set a then record for British singles in the number of advance sales, which were in the order of 180,000.
A regular visitor on anthologies of Cliff's work, two other studio versions have been released first on ***The Rock 'n' Roll Years 1958-1963*** (which includes studio chatter and jamming on instruments with Cliff's request for another take (making it a separate entry in the track listing), the eleventh, which was used for the single and this take is the first true stereo version that's available) and ***...And They Said It Wouldn't Last! (My 50 Years in Music)*** (the sixth take and, while basically the same arrangement as that of the final single release take, it has subtle differences in the performance).
Cliff stated in an early seventies interview that there is definitely an Elvis Presley vibe about this track (of which he is very proud) and that his vocal performance pushes hard to be raucous, becoming one of the strongest rock and roll style records that they recorded in the sixties. The racing drums by Tony Meehan and the thrumming guitars and bass line from the others drive the song relentlessly forward. There are many hooks throughout the song, musically speaking, as well as the pause with Cliff uttering 'well!' The only slight jarring aspect of the song is the failing rhyme of 'it ain't no use' with 'stubborn as a doggone mule' but this is a minor distraction from a very strong song otherwise. Hank Marvin is given free rein in the middle eight providing a lengthy guitar solo before Cliff returns with the concluding verse and chorus.
In 2009, for Cliff's tour of the UK and then the world, the Shadows got back together with him in order to promote an album of re-recorded material from the early days, ***Reunited***, which included *Nine Times out of Ten*. The arrangement is crisper and the rhythm just as driving as the original but it is successfully close to the first recording.

Track Specification
Composed by Waldense Hall and Otis Blackwell

1. Single

Musicians	
Jet Harris	bass
Hank Marvin	guitar
Tony Meehan	drums, percussion
Cliff Richard	vocals
Bruce Welch	rhythm guitar

Recording Details	
Producer	Norrie Paramor
Engineered by	Malcolm Addey and Norman Smith (mono) and Peter Bown and Alan Kane (stereo)
Recording location	Abbey Road Studio 2, St. John's Wood, London
Recording date	15th March 1960

2. The Rock and Roll Years 1958-1963

Musicians		*Recording Details*	
Jet Harris	bass	Producer	Norrie Paramor
Hank Marvin	guitar	Engineered by	Malcolm Addey and Norman Smith (mono) and Peter Bown and Alan Kane (stereo)
Tony Meehan	drums, percussion	Recording location	Abbey Road Studio 2, St. John's Wood, London
Cliff Richard	spoken vocals, vocals	Recording date	15th March 1960
Bruce Welch	rhythm guitar		

3. ...And They Said It Wouldn't Last! (My 50 Years in Music)

Musicians		*Recording Details*	
Jet Harris	bass	Producer	Norrie Paramor
Hank Marvin	guitar	Engineered by	Malcolm Addey and Norman Smith (mono) and Peter Bown and Alan Kane (stereo)
Tony Meehan	drums, percussion	Recording location	Abbey Road Studio 2, St. John's Wood, London
Cliff Richard	vocals	Recording date	15th March 1960
Bruce Welch	rhythm guitar		

4. Reunited

Musicians		*Recording Details*	
Brian Bennett	drums, percussion	Producer	Warren Bennett (co-ordination)
Mark Griffiths	bass	Engineered by	James Collins (Honeyhill Studios), Ethan Carlson (Middle Ear Studios), Les Williams (Nivram Studios) and Keith Bessey (mixing and mastering)
Hank Marvin	guitar	Recording location	Middle Ear Studios, Miami, Florida, USA (Cliff's vocals), Nivram Studios, Perth, Western Australia (Hank's guitars and vocals) and Honeyhill Studios, Hertfordshire, England (all other vocals and instruments)
Cliff Richard	vocals, backing vocals	Recording date	Early 2009
Bruce Welch	rhythm guitar		

♬ No Alibi

From the album **Triumph in the Air** *(Sheila Walsh)*

Two members of Network 3, with whom Cliff Richard worked, Mo Turner and Annie McCaig, joined him on providing backing vocals for *No Alibi* from Sheila Walsh's second album, ***Triumph in the Air***.

The quirky rhythm is established in the keyboards and electronic percussion, leading into a spoken section that is supported by occasional backing vocals, through which Cliff's contribution can be clearly discerned. The blipping rhythm and the slight Scottish brogue make this one of the most enjoyable tracks on the album.

Track Specification

Composed by Graham Kendrick

Musicians		*Recording Details*	
Judd Lander	harmonica	Producer	Craig Pruess, assisted by Keith Bessey
Annie McCaig	backing vocals	Engineered by	Keith Bessey
Craig Pruess	arranger, keyboards, electronics	Recording location	Cloud 9 Studios, London, Strawberry Studios, London and/or Jacobs Studios, Farnham, Surrey
Cliff Richard	backing vocals	Recording date	September 1983-January 1984
Mo Turner	backing vocals		
Sheila Walsh	spoken vocals, vocals		
Mark Williamson	backing vocals		

♬ No Matter What

From the album **The 31st of February Street**

Written by Ken Ashby for Cliff Richard to record for his ***The 31st of February Street*** album, the song was the first to be completed at the final session in February 1974 for the album (along with the album's opening and closing title tracks).

The pretty little song is introduced by an arpeggiated guitar and electric piano and Cliff sings a technically difficult melody line as the quietness segues into a more upbeat and fuller chorus with its steel guitar and percussion accompaniment before returning to the quieter and more reflective pace of the verse. Although the male vocalists back Cliff with wordless sounds, Cliff provides his own backing vocals matching the main melody line and lyrics.

Track Specification

Composed by Ken Ashby

Musicians		*Recording Details*	
Terry Britten	backing vocals, guitar	Producer	David MacKay
Cliff Hall	keyboards	Engineered by	Tony Clark and Mike Jarrett
Gordon Huntley	steel guitar	Recording location	Abbey Road Studio 2, St. John's Wood, London
David MacKay	backing vocals	Recording date	25th February 1974
Dave MacRae	keyboards		
Kevin Peek	acoustic guitar		
Cliff Richard	vocals, backing vocals		
Trevor Spencer	drums, percussion		
Alan Tarney	backing vocals, bass		

♫ No Name, No Fame

From the album **...And They Said It Wouldn't Last! (My 50 Years in Music)**

In 1969, several tracks were recorded that would have fitted on the various albums released at the time (***Sincerely Cliff Richard*** and ***Tracks 'n' Grooves***, for example) but weren't issued. One of these was *No Name, No Fame*, which has no writing credits available and was recorded in early May but remained unissued for thirty-nine years, when it was included on the lost and found section of***...And They Said It Wouldn't Last! (My 50 Years in Music)*** in 2008.

A love song that reflects on the man who has the hand of the woman he loves, the song is driven onwards by Mike Vickers' arrangement accompanying Cliff's gentle expostulation of the lyrics. There is an uncredited female backing vocal group, which doesn't add much to ensemble piece.

Track Specification

Composed by Unknown

Musicians		*Recording Details*	
Mike Vickers Orchestra	orchestra	Producer	Norrie Paramor
Cliff Richard	vocals	Engineered by	Peter Vince
Unknown	backing vocals	Recording location	Abbey Road Studio 2, St. John's Wood, London
Mike Vickers	arranger, conductor	Recording date	2nd May 1969

♫ Non Dimenticare Chi Ti Ama

Italian single

In the last few months of 1968 and the first of 1969, Cliff Richard recorded a number of foreign language versions of his songs from previous albums and recent singles. At the end of February of 1969, he recorded an Italian single version of his UK hit ***Don't Forget to Catch Me***, called *Non Dimenticare Chi Ti Ama* (or, back into English, *Don't Forget Who Loves You*). Backed with ***Chi Lo Sà*** (a translation of Cliff's 1964 hit ***On the Beach***), *Non Dimenticare Chi Ti Ama* was released as a single on the Columbia label (catalogue number 3C 006 04056) in April 1969 in Italy, and was only released in mono format. The stereo version was released on the 1977 *When in Rome* compilation and then on the ***On the Continent*** boxed set in 1997.

In the Italian language and in Cliff's safe hands, the performance sounds improved on the original, with the exception that the Shadows vocal harmonies are missing, which are replaced by a backing vocal group who are uncredited and are pleasant enough but are subdued.

Track Specification

Composed by Hank Marvin, Bruce Welch and Brian Bennett; Italian lyrics by Cassia

Musicians		*Recording Details*	
Norrie Paramor Orchestra	orchestra	Producer	Norrie Paramor
Norrie Paramor	arranger, conductor	Engineered by	Peter Vince
Cliff Richard	vocals	Recording location	Abbey Road Studios, St. John's Wood, London
Unknown	backing vocals	Recording date	24th February 1969

♫ Non l'Ascoltare

From the album **When in Rome**

For Cliff Richard's ***When in Rome*** album, most of the tracks had already been recorded in either English or Spanish. The backing tracks were then used from those older sessions and Cliff's new Italian vocals were overdubbed. So it was with ***Don't Talk to Him***, his 1963 single, which was translated from Cliff's original lyrics to Italian by Giuseppe Cassia and retitled *Non l'Ascoltare* (literally *Don't Listen to Him* – the same end result but using the ears instead of the tongue). The backing track recorded by the Shadows in October 1963 featured bassist Brian Locking who was to be replaced by John Rostill; since the backing track appears from that time, it is a new recording of the vocals backed with a former band member. The unknown take and edit of Cliff's new vocals were applied to the backing track and released in mono format.

As with all of the foreign language versions of the song that use the English or original backing track, there is often little to distinguish the versions and this is the case here. Cliff sounds very much at home with the Italian language in spite of the difficulties he had learning how to enunciate the words but, instead of the Shadows beautifully harmonizing backing vocals, there is an uncredited Italian male group singing the echo at the end of each couplet: this sounds distinctly odd since the overdub is mixed further forward than anything else.

Track Specification

Composed by Bruce Welch and Cliff Richard; Italian lyrics by Giuseppe Cassia

Musicians		*Recording Details*	
Brian Bennett	drums, percussion	Producer	Norrie Paramor (backing track and vocals) and Unknown (backing vocals)
Brian 'Licorice' Locking	bass		
Hank Marvin	guitar	Engineered by	Malcolm Addey (backing track and vocals) and Unknown (backing vocals)
Cliff Richard	vocals		
Unknown	backing vocals	Recording location	Abbey Road Studio 3, St. John's Wood, London (backing track), Estudios Valentim de Carvalho, Lisbon (vocals) and Italy (backing vocals)
Bruce Welch	rhythm guitar		
		Recording date	13th October 1963 (backing track), 14th May 1965 (vocals) and May 1965 (backing vocals)

♬ No-One Seems to Care

Unissued track

Cliff Richard played the title role in the religious series *Life with Johnny*, which were modern settings of biblical parables. Johnny is having trouble relying on other people and, after running out of money, struggles to get home with his girlfriend (played by Cindy Kent) and sings this song, which makes a melodrama out of his situation belying his worries.
A slow-paced song with close harmony vocals provided by the Settlers, the song would not be out of place on any Cliff album from the period. Recorded at the Abbey Road studios possibly for an abandoned tie-in album project, the song remains unissued, as do all the songs from the series. The end credits indicate that all the songs are original and written by Cliff, the screenwriter David Winter and the Settlers in collaboration.

Track Specification
Composed by Cliff Richard, David Winter, Cindy Kent, Mike Jones, John Fyffe and Geoffrey Srodzinski

Musicians

John Fyffe	backing vocals, guitar
Cindy Kent	backing vocals
Mike Jones	backing vocals, guitar
Cliff Richard	vocals, finger-clicks
Geoffrey Srodzinski	backing vocals, bass
Unknown	drums, percussion

Recording Details

Producer	Norrie Paramor
Engineered by	Peter Vince
Recording location	Abbey Road Studio 3, St. John's Wood, London
Recording date	2nd-3rd December 1968

♬ No-One Waits

B-side of **Hey Mr. Dream Maker**

Recorded with no requirement for vocal overdubs unlike the rest of the project, *No-One Waits* was co-written by Cliff Richard and completed in four takes at one of the last sessions for ***Every Face Tells a Story***, although it wasn't included on the track listing. The song was then chosen to back the first of three singles from the album, ***Hey Mr. Dream Maker***. As it never appeared on the album, it was subsequently reissued twenty-two years later for the first time on the *1970s* album before being included as a bonus track on the remastered *Every Face Tells a Story* album in 2002.
Performed on a guitar behind Cliff's gentle vocal line, *No-One Waits* gives way to a clever close harmony vocal section, with Cliff at the centre and the other voices individually in the right and left channels. It is this that sets the song apart from others and is a perfect example of Cliff's overall musicianship. As the vocals build up, Bruce Welch adds fading effects to add to the drama. It is possible that it is Cliff accompanying himself on the guitar but this is uncorroborated.

Track Specification
Composed by Cliff Richard and Gary Isherwood

Musicians

Terry Britten	guitar
John Perry	backing vocals
Cliff Richard	vocals
Tony Rivers	backing vocals

Recording Details

Producer	Bruce Welch
Engineered by	Tony Clark and Alan Rouse
Recording location	Abbey Road Studio 2, St. John's Wood, London
Recording date	17th September 1976

♬ No Particular Place to Go

From the album **World Tour Live**

Written and recorded for Chuck Berry's 1964 album *St. Louis to Liverpool*, it was subsequently issued as a single, reaching number ten in the US Billboard Hot 100 and number three in the UK charts. *No Particular Place to Go* is a wry observation on the calamitous state of a date that is affected by a faulty seatbelt and it has been covered by a number of artists including Bonnie Bramlett, George Thorogood, the Toy Dolls, Jerry Lee Lewis, Mos Def and the Troggs, among others.
Cliff often performs songs in concert not attempted in the studio and he included this song on his 2003 world tour. The New Zealand show was filmed for DVD release and, in 2004, it was decided to issue a complementary CD album also called *World Tour Live*. Several DVD tracks were not included, but *No Particular Place to Go* was added to the track listing.
Cliff's version is a slightly slower pace than Berry's original but he performs it with his customary ease, with a lovely vocal harmony section as the key changes lead into the middle eight guitar solo.

Track Specification
Composed by Chuck Berry

Musicians

Anthony Clark	backing vocals, guitar
John Clark	guitar
Dave Cooke	keyboards
Mike Haughton	saxophone
Peter Howarth	backing vocals
Pete May	drums, percussion
Mick Mullins	backing vocals
Keith Murrell	backing vocals
Alan Park	keyboards
Cliff Richard	vocals
Steve Stroud	bass

Recording Details

Producer	Keith Bessey
Engineered by	Keith Bessey
Recording location	The Mission Winery, Napier, New Zealand
Recording date	22nd February 2003

♫ Not Afraid to Rock 'n' Roll

From the album **Did He Jump... Or Was He Pushed?** *(Garth Hewitt)*

In 1979, Cliff Richard continued his secondary career as a producer by working on fellow Christian Garth Hewitt's second album, ***Did He Jump... Or Was He Pushed?***. The opening song was, like the rest of the track listing, written by Hewitt and features a number of musicians who had been involved in Cliff's own recordings.

The liner notes suggest that Cliff and Hewitt play acoustic guitar but the specific tracks are not made clear and the instrument is assigned to both musicians. The perfect piece of seventies rock has an extraordinary energy and pace to it that keeps going on to the end. Cliff supplies backing vocals which are occasionally in falsetto.

Track Specification

Composed by Garth Hewitt

Musicians		*Recording Details*	
Garth Hewitt	vocals, guitar	Producer	Cliff Richard
Graham Jarvis	drums, percussion	Engineered by	Tony Clark and Haydn Bendall
Mike Moran	guitar, keyboards	Recording location	Odyssey Studios, London
Jo Partridge	guitar	Recording date	1979
Cliff Richard	backing vocals, guitar		
Dave Wintour	bass		

♫ Note in a Bottle

From the album **...And They Said It Wouldn't Last! (My 50 Years in Music)**

Recorded at a session that saw only the B-side track ***You Never Can Tell*** completed and subsequently released, *Note in a Bottle* along with another unissued song ***If I Do*** from that same session were kept back from release, possibly because there was stronger material that had been recorded and was available for release at the time. Neither of the two unissued songs has any record of the composers and both were eventually released in stereo only on the lost and found collection on ***...And They Said It Wouldn't Last! (My 50 Years in Music)*** in 2008, although mono versions would almost certainly have been created at the time of recording, since the mixes had been finished.

Strong on the bass line, *Note in a Bottle* talks about the singer trying to desperately find any woman that he can by sending an imploring note stuffed into a bottle, while expressing who and what he is in the hope that a girl will pick it up and get in contact with him. The quirky accompaniment is occasionally out of time with Cliff's lead vocals, possibly a reason for holding it back, and there is an uncredited backing group included that adds to the ensemble piece. However, it is a well-crafted song that is unfortunate to have been languishing in the vaults at EMI for so long.

Track Specification

Composed by Unknown

Musicians		*Recording Details*	
Norrie Paramor Orchestra	orchestra	Producer	Norrie Paramor
Norrie Paramor	conductor	Engineered by	Peter Vince
Cliff Richard	vocals	Recording location	Abbey Road Studio 1, St. John's Wood, London
Unknown	backing vocals	Recording date	24th October 1968

♫ Nothing Left for Me to Say

B-side of **My Kinda Life** *and* **Don't Turn the Light Out** *(US only)*

In the seventies, Cliff Richard was becoming quite a prolific composer, and one of his songs, *Nothing Left for Me to Say* was recorded during the many sessions set aside for the ***Every Face Tells a Story*** album, although it wasn't included on the finalized track listing. It was chosen for the B-side of the second of three singles from the project, ***My Kinda Life***. In the US, it was decided to release another album track as a single, ***Don't Turn the Light Out*** and again *Nothing Left for Me to Say* was included as its B-side. The track appeared on the 1985 album *From the Heart* but it wasn't until 1998 that it was released in CD form for the first time on the *1970s* compilation album. Subsequently it was added as a bonus track on the remastered issue of *Every Face Tells a Story* in 2002.

Nothing Left for Me to Say has a nostalgic feel to it in the arrangement of the introductory instrumentation, with the keyboards and guitar alongside the running bass line. The melody is pretty and this is enhanced by the backing vocal arrangement that is deployed throughout the song, and which occasionally Cliff also makes a contribution.

Track Specification

Composed by Cliff Richard

Musicians		*Recording Details*	
Brian Bennett	drums, percussion	Producer	Bruce Welch
Terry Britten	guitar	Engineered by	Peter Vince and Haydn Bendall
John Perry	backing vocals	Recording location	Abbey Road Studio 2, St. John's Wood, London
Cliff Richard	vocals, backing vocals	Recording date	22nd September 1976
Tony Rivers	backing vocals		
Alan Tarney	bass		
Graham Todd	keyboards		

♫ Nothing's Impossible

From the film soundtrack album of **The Young Ones**

After the bombshell news that the hitherto secret father of Nicky Black (played by Cliff Richard) intended to pull down the youth club and build a skyscraper in its place, Nicky's girlfriend, Toni Crowthier (Carole Gray), feels despondent about the future. With understandable family loyalty, Nicky tries to protect his father by finding optimistic reasons for what he is doing and suggests that something will come up and all will be well. This leads directly into a dance routine involving Nicky and Toni in the darkened street as they sing the duet *Nothing's Impossible* together, which uses historical references such as climbing Everest and sending a man into space to underline the fact that these were deemed impossible but were achieved (a bit of a stretch from those accolades to saving a local youth club, naturally, but this is feel-good musical). In the process, several rather odd film tricks are tried (now looking antiquated in terms of the special effects), with Cliff swinging at the perpendicular angle around a Belisha beacon, both of them jumping over a high wrought iron fence from a standing start, spurring flowers to spontaneously grow so he can pick one to give to her and Cliff jumping backwards into a wall and disappearing after saying goodnight to her – all of this seems at odds with the rest of the film.
Carole Gray didn't perform any of her singing vocals and these were dubbed by Grazina Frame separately five days after Cliff recorded his vocals. Further edits and overdubs may have been carried out on the Elstree Sound Stage where the film was being primarily recorded. Take four of Cliff's vocals was used from his session and the eventual overdubbed version was used as the basis for both the mono and stereo edits but with different mixes for the audio channels. The version on the commercially released album was different from that on the film, which was recorded at a separate time in 1961, although no information on the precise date is available and has not been released in any commercial aural format.
Away from the rock and roll tunes elsewhere, the introduction to the song with woodwind, muted brass and xylophone is the old school style of musical film and just draws short of jarring in juxtaposition with the more contemporary tunes in the film. Nevertheless, Cliff's vocals are gentle and accomplished, while Grazina Frame's lines are a little too piercing for absolute comfort, although the harmonizing sections work well.

Track Specification
Composed by Peter Myers and Ronald Cass

Musicians

Associated British Studio Orchestra	orchestra
Stanley Black	conductor
Grazina Frame	vocals
Cliff Richard	vocals

Recording Details

Producer	Norrie Paramor
Engineered by	Malcolm Addey and Alan Kane
Recording location	Abbey Road Studio 2, St. John's Wood, London
Recording date	9th August 1961 (backing track and Cliff's vocals) and 14th August 1961 (Grazina's vocals)

♫ Nothing to Remind Me

From the album **The 31st of February Street** *and unissued track*

Cliff Richard wrote six of the songs that appear on the album ***The 31st of February Street***, one of which was *Nothing to Remind Me*, which Cliff believed at the time to be the best song he had written. Recorded at the first of four main sessions for the album throughout February 1974, the song was the last song to be completed. Occasionally, EMI would release promotional discs for the radio stations in order to support the upcoming album release and *Nothing to Remind Me* was issued with ***The Leaving*** as its B-side on the EMI label (catalogue number PSR 368) in October 1974 in the original edits found on the album. In the first CD reissue of the album, *Nothing to Remind Me* was left off the track listing, although not the CD – this seems to have been an error, since the inlay card specifies its presence, while the reverse of the CD shows that the track is missing. With the remaster and reissue of the album in 2004, it was restored to its rightful position on the listing, and it was released on the ***My Songs*** collection of Cliff-authored songs the previous year.
The song begins with guitars, clucking and playing chords in a minor key, while Cliff's vocal line builds up and quietens down to the repetition. The middle eight features a more upbeat rhythm and a major key promoting the idea of optimism among all the gloom of there being nothing to remind him of a relationship with a girl.
The song was included on the set list of the Japanese tour later on in 1974 and, although the concerts on 7th and 8th October were recorded, *Nothing to Remind Me* and three other songs were not released and remain unissued.

Track Specification
Composed by Cliff Richard

1. The 31st of February Street

Musicians

Terry Britten	guitar
Barrie Guard	arranger, conductor, percussion
Cliff Hall	keyboards
Dave MacRae	keyboards
Kevin Peek	acoustic guitar
Cliff Richard	vocals
Trevor Spencer	drums, percussion
Alan Tarney	bass
Unknown	orchestra

Recording Details

Producer	David MacKay
Engineered by	Tony Clark and Mike Jarrett
Recording location	Abbey Road Studio 3, St. John's Wood, London
Recording date	11th February 1974

2. *Unissued track (Japan Tour '74)*

Musicians

Barrie Guard	arranger, conductor
Cliff Hall	piano
Brian Lewis	backing vocals, guitar
Kevin Peak	acoustic guitar
Cliff Richard	vocals
Shambles Symphonet	orchestra
Trevor Spencer	drums, percussion
Alan Tarney	backing vocals, bass
Bruce Welch	backing vocals, rhythm guitar

Recording Details

Producer	Toshiba EMI (no individual detailed)
Engineered by	Toshiba EMI (no individual detailed)
Recording location	Shinjuku Koseinenkin, Tokyo, Japan
Recording date	7th-8th October 1974

♪ Nothin' Shakin' (But the Leaves on the Trees)

Unissued track

First released as a single by one of its co-writers, Eddie Fontaine, it wasn't a hit in the UK; however, it was later picked up by other artists who performed or recorded their own versions including Dr. Feelgood, the Beatles and Billy Fury.

Since Fury's popularity as riding high at the time of the ***Cliff*** album recordings, it made sense to add this title to the 'live' set list. However, it is unclear whether it was actually recorded since no tapes appear to exist from the sessions; there are only the announcements to indicate that it was slated for recording. For completeness, it is included here based on the assumption that it was recorded but has simply been lost.

Track Specification

Composed by Eddie Fontaine, Cirino Colacrai, Diane Lambert and John Gluck Jr.

Musicians

Jet Harris	bass
Hank Marvin	guitar
Tony Meehan	drums, percussion
Cliff Richard	vocals
Bruce Welch	rhythm guitar

Recording Details

Producer	Norrie Paramor
Engineered by	Peter Bown and Stuart Eltham
Recording location	Abbey Road Studio 2, St. John's Wood, London
Recording date	9th or 10th February 1959

♪ Not the Way It Should Be

From the album **Established 1958**

As with all of the ***Established 1958*** tracks, *Not the Way It Should Be* was written by the Shadows. Its recording was a sad event, if only in retrospect, since this was the last time Cliff Richard and the Shadows would be in the studio at the same (even their 2009 ***Reunited*** album was recorded in different venues and then mixed together) and it was the beginning of the end of the Shadows for a while as each member went off to concentrate on their own projects.

A piano is the only instrument to accompany Cliff's impassioned performance of a song that talks of a disintegrating relationship. The other instruments are brought in as are the trademark harmony vocals, with the Shadows performing in falsetto and Cliff included as his own backing vocalist. This is a perfect gem from the band that was itself disintegrating.

Taking many songs from *Established 1958*, they were translated into German for the album *Hier Ist Cliff* and *Not the Way It Should Be* was given the title ***Stell' Mich Deinen Eltern Vor*** (or *Introduce Me to Your Parents*, which changes the meaning).

Track Specification

Composed by Hank Marvin and Brian Bennett

Musicians

Brian Bennett	drums, percussion
Hank Marvin	backing vocals, guitar, piano
Cliff Richard	vocals, backing vocals
John Rostill	backing vocals, bass
Bruce Welch	backing vocals, rhythm guitar

Recording Details

Producer	Norrie Paramor
Engineered by	Peter Vince
Recording location	Abbey Road Studio 2, St. John's Wood, London
Recording date	10th June 1968

♪ No Turning Back

From the EP **Serious Charge**

One of three songs written by Lionel Bart, along with ***Living Doll*** and ***Mad About You***, specifically for Cliff Richard to sing in his first film role in ***Serious Charge*** in 1959, *No Turning Back* wasn't intended to be a focal point of the film's narrative (about a new vicar trying to take charge of an unruly boy, who is partly responsible for the death of his pregnant girlfriend and then, out of spite, counter-accuses the vicar of molesting him). Indeed, the music only plays an incidental part, which suggests that it was interpolated into the screenplay to capitalize on Cliff's burgeoning fame.

Two versions were recorded of *No Turning* Back: the first for the film itself and the other, represented here as the track released in disc form on the ***Serious Charge*** EP selection and was also released on the *At the Movies 1959-1963* anthology of Cliff's music in the film world. It can also be found on ***The Rock 'n' Roll Years 1958-1963*** album.

Written in a slinky and dark bossa nova style, it is one of the best examples of the sound that Cliff and the Drifters had developed together. Cliff's vocals are naturally assured, although he is clearly trying to emulate Elvis Presley at some points. There is a lovely Hank Marvin solo in the middle eight of this short track, but it is Jet Harris's bass line that is the main point of note.

Track Specification
Composed by Lionel Bart

Musicians		*Recording Details*	
Jet Harris	bass	Producer	Norrie Paramor
Hank Marvin	guitar	Engineered by	Peter Bown and Stuart Eltham
Tony Meehan	drums, percussion	Recording location	Abbey Road Studio 2, St. John's Wood, London
Cliff Richard	vocals	Recording date	28th April 1959
Bruce Welch	rhythm guitar		

♬ November Night
From the album **Words and Music** *(Mike Read)*

In the late eighties, BBC radio DJ and television presenter (and later Cliff Richard chronicler) Mike Read followed his ambition to pursue a career in music. Read had always loved the works of the late Poet Laureate Sir John Betjeman and, obtaining agreement from his estate, set a number of his poems to music and asked several music luminaries to contribute to the resultant album, *Poetry in Motion*, such as Justin Hayward singing *Tregardock* and Annie Haslam performing *Hunter Trials*. A decade later, Read worked on other Betjeman poems and followed the original album with a second disc of material, again asking different musicians to contribute to the reworked *Poetry in Motion* album, which was retitled *Words and Music*. In this second round, Cliff was invited to perform *November Night*.

While Betjeman tended to be tongue-in-cheek and knowing in much of his writing, he was also a powerfully evocative poet, able to conjure up images of the subject he was writing about with suitable adjectives and flowing language. So it is with *November Night*, which is also quintessentially British in some of the subjects it tackles. Written in 1952 with the clumsy title of *Verses turned in aid of A Public Subscription (1952) Towards the Restoration of the Church of St. Katherine, Chiselhampton, Oxon.*, Read rightly chose a new title for his interpretation, taking two of the words from the first line, which creates the atmosphere of a wet, chilly (typical) November evening at a church awaiting the start of Evensong, the plaintive bell tolling calling the parishioners, the choirboys faces lit by the warming light of candles and so on.

Read is an underrated composer and this is obvious on the tracks on the album and particularly on *November Night*, which exudes nostalgia in the simple but instantly memorable melody, while the arrangement of the instrumentation, particularly the picked guitars, and backing vocals is quite extraordinary supporting Cliff's lead vocal.

Track Specification
Composed by Sir John Betjeman and Mike Read

Musicians		*Recording Details*	
Peter Boita	drums, percussion	Producer	Jon Sweet
Herbie Flowers	bass	Engineered by	Gerry Kitchingham and John 'Magic Tea' Brant
Gary Forse	keyboards, piano	Recording location	R. G. Jones Studios, Wimbledon, London and Powersong Studios, Somerset
Cliff Richard	vocals, backing vocals		
Tony Rivers	backing vocals	Recording date	1997 or 1998
Anthony Thompson	backing vocals		
Tom Toomey	guitar		

♬ Nowhere Man
Unissued track

In early 1969, Tyne Tees Television commissioned a series of six playlets for their religious broadcast slot called *Life with Johnny*, featuring Cliff Richard in the title role as each episode modernized a well-known parable told by Jesus in the Bible. Records are unclear on most of the episodes although *Johnny Come Home* and *Johnny Faces Facts* are complete, *Johnny and the Good Samaritan* is partially available, while the remainder are unavailable in either records or film form.

The songs performed had some relevance to the parable being performed and, on average, there were five songs per episode. *Nowhere Man*, recorded at the Abbey Road studios with a putative album tie-in project in mind that didn't materialize, appeared in one of *Johnny on the Rocks*, *Johnny and the Blind Rage* or *Johnny in Love*. The end credits of the episode stated that all songs were original and written in collaboration between Cliff, the Settlers and the programme's writer David Winter. However, two Beatles songs were used: *Nowhere Man* and ***Help*** (from *Johnny and the Good Samaritan*) which are not credited as such.

Taken from *Rubber Soul*, *Nowhere Man* was primarily written by John Lennon with support from Paul McCartney and was released as a single in America reaching number three in the charts there. The Settlers themselves recorded a version three years before Cliff's Abbey Road sessions, while the Smashing Pumpkins, Randy Travis, Jeff Lynne, the Carpenters and others have all released covers.

Track Specification
Composed by John Lennon and Paul McCartney

Musicians		*Recording Details*	
John Fyffe	backing vocals, guitar	Producer	Norrie Paramor
Cindy Kent	backing vocals	Engineered by	Peter Vince
Mike Jones	backing vocals, guitar	Recording location	Abbey Road Studio 3, St. John's Wood, London
Cliff Richard	vocals	Recording date	11th January 1969
Geoffrey Srodzinski	backing vocals, bass		

♫ Now I've Done It

Unissued track

In early 1969, Tyne Tees Television commissioned a series called *Life with Johnny*, featuring Cliff Richard in the title role. Each episode was an updated modern setting of six biblical parables told by Jesus and was set for broadcast in the early evening religious slot. Records are unclear on most episodes, although *Johnny Come Home* and *Johnny Faces Facts* are complete, *Johnny and the Good Samaritan* is partially available, while the remainder are unavailable.

The songs performed had some relevance to the parable being played out and there were on average five songs per episode. *Now I've Done It*, recorded at the Abbey Road studios with a putative album tie-in project in mind that didn't materialize, appeared in one of the *Johnny on the Rocks*, *Johnny and the Blind Rage* or *Johnny in Love* episodes. The end credits stated that all songs were original and written in collaboration between Cliff, the Settlers and the programme's writer David Winter. The instrumentation and performance details are unknown. There is some suggestion that the full title of the song is *Now I've Gone and Done It* but the information in records is unclear.

Track Specification

Composed by Cliff Richard, David Winter, Cindy Kent, Mike Jones, John Fyffe and Geoffrey Srodzinski

Musicians		*Recording Details*	
John Fyffe	backing vocals, guitar	Producer	Norrie Paramor
Cindy Kent	backing vocals	Engineered by	Peter Vince
Mike Jones	backing vocals, guitar	Recording location	Abbey Road Studio 3, St. John's Wood, London
Cliff Richard	vocals	Recording date	8th January 1969
Geoffrey Srodzinski	backing vocals, bass		

♫ Now's the Time to Fall in Love

Unissued track, B-side of **A Girl Like You** *and from the album* **...And They Said It Wouldn't Last! (My 50 Years in Music)**

There were two sessions covering the recording of *Now's the Time to Fall in Love*, which was written by Bruce Welch and erstwhile Chesternuts bandmate Pete Chester. The first on 28th July 1960 was abandoned, while the version that was used for the single from the 20th September session is in fact a splice of takes 41 and 42. The resultant spliced edit was used for both mono and stereo and mixed differently for the aural channels.

Until the release of the French compilation *Congratulations to Cliff*, where it was a bonus track, the song remained unissued other than as the B-side of ***A Girl Like You***. That album suggests that it is an alternative version from the B-side but it is, in fact, exactly the same. There is an additional version on ***The Rock 'n' Roll Years 1958-1963*** anthology but this is simply the full 42nd take, and includes studio banter and the attempt at the song that was used in the splice before it falls apart. There is, however, a different unknown take that appears on***...And They Said It Wouldn't Last! (My 50 Years in Music)***, which is the same arrangement as the released version but with different lyrics here and there and an earlier fade.

The introduction features Hank Marvin, Bruce Welch and Jet Harris in vocal harmony before Cliff Richard's lead vocal enters and is a brilliant early exemplar of their vocal harmonisation. The pace is punishing and occasionally the instruments do sound out of kilter with each other but, given that they had already done over forty takes, it is hardly surprising if there were some timing problems (hence the splicing together of takes, it is suspected). The song is a typical love song and relies heavily on drums, the driving bass line as well as the delicious vocal harmonies to set this B-side apart from a lot of the others.

Track Specification

Composed by Bruce Welch and Pete Chester

1. Unissued track

Musicians		*Recording Details*	
Jet Harris	backing vocals, bass	Producer	Norrie Paramor
Hank Marvin	backing vocals, guitar	Engineered by	Malcolm Addey
Tony Meehan	drums, percussion	Recording location	Abbey Road Studio 2, St. John's Wood, London
Cliff Richard	vocals	Recording date	20th September 1960
Bruce Welch	backing vocals, rhythm guitar		

2. B-side (A Girl Like You)

Musicians		*Recording Details*	
Jet Harris	bass	Producer	Norrie Paramor
Hank Marvin	guitar	Engineered by	Malcolm Addey
Tony Meehan	drums, percussion	Recording location	Abbey Road Studio 2, St. John's Wood, London
Cliff Richard	vocals	Recording date	20th September 1960
Bruce Welch	rhythm guitar		

3. ...And They Said It Wouldn't Last! (My 50 Years in Music)

Musicians		*Recording Details*	
Jet Harris	bass	Producer	Norrie Paramor
Hank Marvin	guitar	Engineered by	Malcolm Addey
Tony Meehan	drums, percussion	Recording location	Abbey Road Studio 2, St. John's Wood, London
Cliff Richard	vocals	Recording date	20th September 1960
Bruce Welch	rhythm guitar		

♫ Now That You Know Me

Unissued track

From the ***Now You See Me... Now You Don't*** sessions, there were five tracks that were attempted but that have notbeen issued, including *Now That You Know Me*. This entry assumes all the musicians and staff known to be present at the session were involved in the recording.

Track Specification

Composed by Unknown

Musicians		*Recording Details*	
Mel Collins	saxophone	Producer	Cliff Richard and Craig Pruess
Mark Griffiths	bass	Engineered by	John Walker and Steve Cook
Graham Jarvis	drums, percussion	Recording location	Strawberry Studios South, Surrey
Mart Jenner	electric guitar	Recording date	4th-15th January 1982
Craig Pruess	piano, synthesisers, sequencers, electronic percussion		
Cliff Richard	vocals, backing vocals		
Bill Roberts	electric guitar		

♫ Now You See Me, Now You Don't

From the album **Now You See Me, Now You Don't**

In 1974, Cliff Richard appeared on stage with Aleksander John and assisted with his recording. When recording ***Now You See Me... Now You Don't*** in 1982, Cliff recorded two of John's songs, one of which was used for the album's title.
A fast-paced rocking beat is established by synthesisers, giving way to staccato chords from the assembled musicians. Cliff's voice is mixed quite far back while also supplying his own harmonies that are very effective in the choruses.

Track Specification

Composed by Aleksander John and Steve Turner

Musicians		*Recording Details*	
John Clark	electric guitar	Producer	Cliff Richard and Craig Pruess
Mel Collins	saxophone	Engineered by	Keith Bessey and Steve Cook
Graham Jarvis	drums, percussion	Recording location	Strawberry Studios South, Surrey
Mart Jenner	electric guitar	Recording date	29th March and 2nd-5th April 1982
Andy Pask	bass		
Craig Pruess	arranger, piano, synthesisers, sequencers, electronic percussion		
Cliff Richard	vocals, backing vocals		

♫ Nur Bei Dir Bin Ich zu Haus

German single

As had become the habit with many of Cliff Richard's English language hits, they were translated into German for specific release in Germany. *Nur Bei Dir Bin Ich Zu Haus* is a German translation of his number two hit ***Wind Me Up (Let Me Go)***, although the new title literally translates into English as *Only with You Am I at Home*. The original backing track from the English release was reused with overdubs of Cliff's German vocals. Released as a single, backed with ***Glaub' Nur Mir*** (a German version of ***On My Word***), on the international Columbia label (catalogue number C-23103) in November 1965, the song reached number twenty-one in the German charts. The final (unknown) vocal take and edit were overdubbed on the original backing track and used for the mono and stereo recordings but with different mixes for the needs of the audio channels. Originally, the single was released in mono format only and was a considerable rarity until the stereo version of the single and its B-side were released on the German compilation of all Cliff's foreign recordings, ***On the Continent***.
The backing track is slower than the English equivalent for some inexplicable reason, which makes it feel as if the turntable has been restrained. However, Cliff's vocal performance is imbued with the same emotion as the English single version. There is a new backing vocal track, which is uncredited, that has been added but it fits very well with the original backing track.

Track Specification

Composed by John Talley and Bob Montgomery; German lyrics by Ralph Maria Siegel

Musicians		*Recording Details*	
Cliff Richard	vocals	Producer	Bob Morgan and Billy Sherrill (backing track), Norrie Paramor (vocals) and Unknown (backing vocals)
Unknown	backing vocals		
Unknown	guitar		
Unknown	bass	Engineered by	Mort Thomason (backing track), Malcolm Addey (vocals) and Unknown (backing vocals)
Unknown	orchestra		
Unknown	drums, percussion	Recording location	Columbia Studios, Nashville (backing track), Abbey Road Studio 2, St. John's Wood, London (vocals) and Germany (backing vocals)
		Recording date	24th August 1964 (backing track), 27th October 1965 (vocals) and October-November 1965 (backing vocals)

♫ Nur mit Dir

B-side of **Das Ist die Frage Aller Fragen**

Using the instrumentation track from the original English recording of the only single to be released from the ***Wonderful Life*** film, ***On the Beach,*** for the German translation *Nur mit Dir* (literally *Only with You*), Cliff Richard added the German lyric vocals separately at a session in October 1964. Intended as a B-side of ***Das Ist die Frage Aller Fragen*** (the German version of ***Spanish Harlem***), the writing credit for Cliff remains, even though his English lyrics are obviously not used; this is because the German translation is based on his work. Also, note that the bassist featured is Brian Locking, although it had been almost a year since he had left the Shadows to be replaced by John Rostill in order to concentrate on his religious activities.

The translation by Hans Bradtke follows on from his earlier work with Cliff's second German single version of ***Lucky Lips, Rote Lippen Soll Man Küssen.*** A significant rarity in the UK, the song was originally only released in mono format, and record-buyers would have to wait thirty-two years for the stereo version to be released on the foreign language compilation boxed set album ***On the Continent.*** The same combined take and edit were used for the mono and stereo recordings but with different mixes for the separate audio channels.

Since the original backing track from the English recording is used, musically there is little to distinguish the two versions. However, there is an uncredited set of backing vocals (not as some sources would suggest Hank Marvin and Bruce Welch) but are possibly provided by the Botho Lucas Quartet or Chorus, both of which had worked on prior German language recordings of the period by Cliff. The lyrics to *Nur mit Dir* mention *Rote Lippen Soll Man Küssen,* which was a significant hit in Germany for him at the time of its release.

Track Specification

Composed by Hank Marvin, Bruce Welch and Cliff Richard; German lyrics by Hans Bradtke

Musicians

Brian Bennett	drums, percussion
Brian 'Licorice' Locking	bass
Hank Marvin	guitar
Cliff Richard	vocals
Unknown	backing vocals
Bruce Welch	rhythm guitar

Recording Details

Producer	Norrie Paramor (backing track and vocals) and Unknown (backing vocals)
Engineered by	Malcolm Addey (backing track and vocals) and Unknown (backing vocals)
Recording location	Abbey Road Studio 3 (backing track), Abbey Road Studio 2 (vocals), St. John's Wood, London and Germany (backing vocals)
Recording date	5th November 1963 (backing track), 10th October 1964 (vocals) and October 1964 (backing vocals)

♫ Occasional Rain

B-side of **Good Times (Better Times)**

Completed a year before the release of its paired single, ***Good Times (Better Times)***, *Occasional Rain* was recorded at a session that saw two songs finalized by Cliff Richard. Released in mono only, it was a major rarity that was only available on the single until it was added to the rare B-sides section of the album ***...And They Said It Wouldn't Last! (My 50 Years in Music)*** in 2008. The liner notes erroneously state that one of the co-writers was Richard (presumably pointing to Cliff) when it was by two brothers. The error was perpetuated in the *Rare B-Sides* spin-off CD from the main project.

With a sweep of the piano keyboard, leading into uncredited female backing vocalists (possibly the Breakaways but unconfirmed), Cliff performs this song with a strong passion. It isn't the best of his material and verges on the bombastic as Cliff sings in his lower register of expecting rough times in any relationship.

Track Specification

Composed by Simon Richey and Peter Richey

Musicians		*Recording Details*	
Mike Leander	conductor	Producer	Norrie Paramor
Mike Leander Orchestra	orchestra	Engineered by	Peter Vince
Cliff Richard	vocals	Recording location	Abbey Road Studio 2, St. John's Wood, London
Unknown	backing vocals	Recording date	6th July 1968

♫ Ocean Deep

B-side of **Baby You're Dynamite**, ***joint 91st UK single*** *and B-side of* **I Still Believe in You** *(CD single)*

Ocean Deep was specifically written for Cliff Richard by Rod Trott and Jon Sweet, who sent him a cassette with the song tagged with a message that it was "a terrific song", that it was "the best love song of all time" and that "only Cliff could record it". Possibly quite arrogant in their belief, and although Cliff didn't listen to it for a while, when he finally did so, he loved it. It was recorded during the sessions for the dual albums ***Silver*** and ***Rock 'n' Roll Silver***. When ***Baby You're Dynamite*** was set for release, ***Ocean Deep*** was chosen as its B-side. Initially the track was on its own, reached number twenty-seven and slipped out of the top forty after three weeks. However, DJs began to play the B-side and demand pushed the single back into the charts as a double A-side as originally issued on the EMI label (original catalogue number EMI 5457) on 7th May 1984 as the A-side, but this time it only reached number seventy-two for one week on the nineteenth of that month. Later on, in September 1992, *Ocean Deep* was included as a bonus track on the second of the dual CD single discs release of ***I Still Believe in You***. For the German, Dutch and Australian issues of *Baby You're Dynamite*, *Ocean Deep* was rejected in favour of new song ***Back in Vaudeville***, which had been recorded earlier in the year.

Since *Ocean Deep* was never intended to be a single, no video was shot to support its elevated status to A-side, although Cliff regularly performed it in concerts at the time with one of the first laser light shows and dry ice, evoking the feeling of being on a ship on the ocean swallowed up by the mist, as he raised a hand that was then subsumed by the white fog.

The introduction to the song played on keyboards ushers in Cliff's emotive voice that uses his vibrato to great effect. Primarily supported by the orchestra and keyboards, the drama of the song builds up to a rallentando as it enters the explosive chorus.

Track Specification

Composed by Rod Trott and Jon Sweet

Musicians		*Recording Details*	
Stuart Calver	backing vocals	Producer	Craig Pruess
John Clark	12-string guitar	Engineered by	Keith Bessey
Martyn Ford	conductor	Recording location	Strawberry Studios South, Surrey (main track) and Henry Wood Hall, Glasgow (strings)
Mark Griffiths	bass		
Graham Jarvis	drums, percussion	Recording date	19th May 1983, 3rd June 1983 and/or 16th June 1983 (main track) and July and/or August 1983 (strings)
Martyn Ford Orchestra:	orchestra		
Clive Anstee	'cello		
Jim Archer	violin		
Andy Babynchuk	violin		
Martin Baines	French horn		
Bill Benham	violin		
Norris Bosworth	viola		
Daniel Daggers	viola		
Liz Edwards	violin		

Will Gibson	violin
Timothy Good	violin
James Handy	French horn
Chris Hirons	violin
Paul Kegg	'cello
Benjamin Kennard	'cello
John Kitchen	violin
Martin Loveday	'cello
Peter Oxer	violin
Geoff Palmer	violin
Eddie Roberts	violin
Jonathan Strange	violin
Chris Wellington	viola
Simon Whistler	viola
David Woodcock	violin
Gavin Wright	violin
Alan Park	piano
John Perry	backing vocals
Craig Pruess	arranger, vocal loops, synthesiser
Cliff Richard	vocals, backing vocals
Tony Rivers	backing vocals

♬ Oh Boy!

From the album **From a Distance ***** The Event**

Buddy Holly's *Oh Boy!* was one of those songs that are so familiar that it seems impossible not to have been in the charts. In fact, the version that sounds so familiar was by his backing group, the Crickets, which reached number three in the UK charts at the end of 1957, followed by a near *a capella* version by Mud in May 1975 when the late Les Gray took it to number one. But the song changed the cultural map in Britain because it lent its name to the title of a seminal television popular music show that assisted the early career of the likes of Cliff Richard and Marty Wilde. Produced by Jack Good, the series ran from 1958 to 1959 and also featured British vocal groups the Dallas Boys and the Vernons Girls as backing vocalists and a house band that performed all the instrumentation to accompany the singers.

When Cliff was organising ***The Event*** at Wembley Stadium in 1989, he wanted to express the full range of his career, starting off with where he began as Britain's answer to the rock 'n' roll of Elvis Presley. Choosing to reform the Vernons Girls, the Dallas Boys and the Oh Boy! Band, he also contacted the Kalin Twins, whom he had accompanied on tour at the time of ***Move It*** being released and subsequently usurping them on the performing order as his success superseded theirs, and together they performed the opening set of *The Event*. First of the performances was the ***Oh Boy! Medley***, which featured, naturally, *Oh Boy!* as well as a number of other tracks that gave a nod to the formative influences at the time.

Initiated by an announcer that this was how it all started, the Dallas Boys were first on, followed by Cliff, the Vernons Girls and then the Kalin Twins. The audience is in raptures as their hero struts the stage and he executes his allotted sections well. The Kalin Twins sound a little aged while the Vernons Girls are just a little too shrill for perfection.

Track Specification

Composed by Norman Petty, Sonny West and Bill Tilghman

Musicians

Dallas Boys:	
Nicky Clarke	backing vocals
Leon Fisk	backing vocals
Stan Jones	backing vocals
Joe Smith	backing vocals
Bob Wragg	backing vocals
Kalin Twins:	
Harold Kalin	backing vocals
Herbie Kalin	backing vocals
Oh Boy! Band	rock 'n' roll band
Cliff Richard	vocals
Vernons Girls:	
Lyn Cornell	backing vocals
Maureen Kennedy	backing vocals
Frances Lee	backing vocals
Jean Owen	backing vocals

Recording Details

Producer	Cliff Richard
Engineered by	Keith Bessey and Mick McKenna
Recording location	Rolling Stones Mobile Studio, Wembley Stadium, Wembley, North-west London
Recording date	16th-17th June 1989

♬ Oh Boy! Medley

B-side of **Saviour's Day**

For many of Cliff's tours and concerts, he use to bend a number of familiar songs together in a medley that hadn't been sung elsewhere in the set list. In 1989, when he was assembling ***The Event*** over a two-day tenure at the old Wembley Stadium, there were several songs that had been a formative influence and that Cliff wanted to perform, and he succeeded in squeezing a large number of period songs into two medleys, the first being the *Oh Boy! Medley*, which comprised:

a) ***Oh Boy!***
b) ***Whole Lotta Shakin' Goin' On***
c) ***Bird Dog***
d) ***Let's Have a Party***
e) ***It's My Party***
f) ***C'mon Everybody***
g) *Whole Lotta Shakin' Goin' On*

which included two different versions of *Whole Lotta Shakin' Goin' On*. The medley was then chosen as the principal B-side for all the variant formats of the single release of ***Saviour's Day***.
The entries for those carry the information on the recording details and musicians.

♬ Oh No, Don't Let Go

From the album **Wired for Sound**

The third song to be written by Alan Tarney for Cliff Richard's ***Wired for Sound*** album, *Oh No, Don't Let Go* is a departure from the electronica sound of many of the other tracks that were recorded for the project. Of course, the synthesisers are still there but it is the rhythm, which sets this song apart with its Caribbean flavour.
The strange synthesiser and drum introduction leads into a section where Cliff's vocal is matched with the harmonies, created by layering Tarney's and Cliff's voices in order to create a group. In the lines of the verses, Cliff supplies his own gentle harmonies, while the insistent drum rhythm and staccato bass line drive the song breathlessly onwards.

Track Specification
Composed by Alan Tarney

Musicians		*Recording Details*	
Graham Jarvis	drums, percussion	Producer	Alan Tarney
Cliff Richard	vocals, backing vocals	Engineered by	Michael Boddicker and Ian Little
Alan Tarney	arranger, backing vocals, guitar, bass, keyboards	Recording location	Gallery Studios, Chertsey, Surrey
		Recording date	27th May-9th July 1981

♬ Oh, No, No

B-side of **Imagina un Giorno**

Although Cliff Richard regularly recorded in continental languages, often translations of his English hits or album tracks, it had almost always been in German, in which market he was very popular. At the end of 1967, however, he recorded a version of his worldwide hit, ***The Day I Met Marie***, which had been translated into Italian and retitled ***Imagina un Giorno***. This was released as a single in Italy, backed with *Oh, No, No*, which, in turn, was a translation of ***I Get the Feelin'***, which had formed the English B-side of ***I'll Come Running***. The translated vocal lines were recorded and overdubbed on an orchestral track that had been recorded the day before.
Originally only released in mono, as was the practice by Columbia at the time for singles and many EPs, *Oh No, No* was eventually issued in stereo as part of the track listing of the foreign language song compilation ***On the Continent***.
The track is taken at a faster pace than the English original and it does seem at points that Cliff is forced to gabble the lyrics as a result. There is an uncredited female backing group singing in Italian too but there is no readily available information on them.

Track Specification
Composed by Neil Diamond; Italian lyrics by Vito Pallavicini

Musicians		*Recording Details*	
Bernard Ebbinghouse Orchestra	orchestra	Producer	Norrie Paramor (backing track and vocals)
Bernard Ebbinghouse	arranger, conductor	Engineered by	Peter Vince (backing track and vocals)
Cliff Richard	vocals	Recording location	Abbey Road Studio 2, St. John's Wood, London (backing track and vocals)
Unknown	backing vocals	Recording date	27th September 1967 (backing track) and 28th September 1967 (vocals)

♬ Oh Señorita

From the film soundtrack album of **Finders Keepers** *and from the album* **Cliff Richard at the Movies 1959-1974**

In the narrative of ***Finders Keepers***, after the Shadows (playing themselves) have finished performing *My Way* (an extraordinary vocal song not to be confused with the song of the same name made famous by Frank Sinatra), Cliff Richard (also playing himself) rushes in to perform *Oh Señorita*. They walk around the floor of the café-cum-restaurant keeping an eye on the American soldiers because they are have worked out what the military is up to with regards to the missing bomb. The song is sung first to a veiled woman (played by an irascible Peggy Mount) and then a pretty young woman.
This is the only song in the film that differs from the soundtrack version, which was recorded at the dual sessions on 28th April and completed in four takes, the final one of which was used for subsequent issue. The soundtrack version was completed at the first session for the film two days earlier. The tenth and final take and edit were used for the mono and stereo recordings but with different mixes to match the needs of the separate audio channels. In the film, Brian Bennett

plays a tambourine to allow him to walk around the set as the script demanded but in the recording he actually plays full drums and percussion.
For the release of the compilation album ***Cliff Richard at the Movies 1959-1974***, an extended edit was included on the track listing. This took the first part of the soundtrack edit and spliced it with the second part of the film edit that has Ronnie Brody and other unknown cast members performing caricature vocals before it descends into a raucous party-like atmosphere.
Cliff sings this song with an ebullience that befits the foot-tapping beat created on the supporting instruments. It's a love song that tries to get the object of his affection to ignore possible competitors in the game of love. Once again, the singing Shadows provide exquisitely beautiful vocal harmonies, making this song a much under-rated gem from Cliff's back catalogue and film career.

Track Specification
Composed by Hank Marvin, Bruce Welch, Brian Bennett and John Rostill

1. Finders Keepers

Musicians		*Recording Details*	
Brian Bennett	drums, percussion	Producer	Norrie Paramor
Hank Marvin	backing vocals, guitar	Engineered by	Malcolm Addey, Peter Vince and Richard Lush
Cliff Richard	vocals	Recording location	Abbey Road Studio 2, St. John's Wood, London
John Rostill	backing vocals, bass	Recording date	26th April 1966
Bruce Welch	backing vocals, rhythm guitar		

2. Cliff Richard at the Movies 1959-1974

Musicians		*Recording Details*	
Brian Bennett	drums, percussion	Producer	Norrie Paramor (both parts)
Ronnie Brodie	vocals	Engineered by	Malcolm Addey (first part), Peter Vince and Richard Lush (both parts)
Hank Marvin	backing vocals, guitar		
Cliff Richard	vocals	Recording location	Abbey Road Studios 2(first part) and 3 (second part), St. John's Wood, London
John Rostill	backing vocals, bass		
Unknown	other lead vocals	Recording date	26th and 28th April 1966
Bruce Welch	backing vocals, rhythm guitar		

♫ Old Accordion, The
Unreleased track and B-side of **A Brand New Song**

Raymond Frogatt had provided Cliff Richard with an earlier hit with ***Big Ship*** and gave him another beautiful song in *The Old Accordion*. Unfortunately, by far the better song over the choice of A-side (***A Brand New Song***), it sank without trace as that single had the ignominious accolade of being Cliff's first single not to get anywhere in the UK singles charts. Cliff had attempted a recording of the song in the middle of 1970 but none of the three songs from that session was released at the time; it would take another fifteen months before he would try it again, this time with the assistance of Shadows drummer Brian Bennett in control of the arrangement and orchestra.
The original B-side has not been officially reissued (and is therefore a considerable rarity given the poor numbers of sales the single garnered), although a slightly extended version was included on the rare B-sides section of ***...And They Said It Wouldn't Last! (MY 50 Years in Music)*** in 2008, which had an extra repeated line on the run-out but this doesn't warrant a separate entry in the track specification of this entry.
Beginning with a colliery brass band arrangement, a curious juxtaposition is created by the use of a harpsichord against the strummed guitar and shimmering tambourine. The beauty of the song, about a poor man who covets the accordion in a junk-shop and, knowing he can't afford it, goes to sleep and wakes up to find the accordion at the foot of his bed, is greatly enhanced by Cliff's emotive performance and the echoey close harmony backing vocals that he provides himself. An accordion only comes in at the end of the song once it is revealed that the old man has received the instrument. It is unfortunate that the single failed because *The Old Accordion* is one of the absolute gems from Cliff's oeuvre.

Track Specification
Composed by Raymond Froggatt

1. Unissued track

Musicians		*Recording Details*	
Cliff Richard	vocals	Producer	Norrie Paramor
Unknown	orchestra	Engineered by	Unknown
Unknown	arranger, conductor	Recording location	Abbey Road Studio 3, St. John's Wood, London
		Recording date	1st June 1970

2. B-side (A Brand New Song)

Musicians		*Recording Details*	
Brian Bennett	arranger, conductor	Producer	Norrie Paramor
Brian Bennett Orchestra	orchestra	Engineered by	Unknown
Cliff Richard	vocals, backing vocals	Recording location	Abbey Road Studio 1, St. John's Wood, London
		Recording date	9th September 1971

♫ Oldies Medley
Unissued live track

In 2003, Cliff Richard embarked on a world tour to promote his then new album, ***Wanted***. The result was filmed during the show in New Zealand and issued on DVD later that year and included the entire concert. A CD album to complement the film, also titled *World Tour Live*, was released the following year but only included fourteen of the tracks performed. Of the chosen tracks, one of those sidelined was the *Oldies Medley*, which covered:

a) ***Gee Whiz It's You***
b) ***I Could Easily Fall (in Love with You)***

The entries for those songs carry the information on the recording details and musicians.

♫ O Mio Signore
From the album **When in Rome**

Literally *Oh My Lord* in English, *O Mio Signore* has been translated into the song title *The Questions* (which is not to be confused with ***Questions*** from the ***Two a Penny*** film soundtrack). In its original Italian, it has been recorded by one of its co-writers, Eduardo Vianello.
Cliff Richard's version in the original Italian is one of the very few foreign language recordings that he didn't then dub back into English at a later date. The final take and edit of the vocal, recorded in May 1965, was overdubbed on the fourth and final take and edit of the orchestral backing track, which was recorded seven months previously. The song has only ever been released in mono format and there is some confusion over the studio personnel involved in the recording: while Malcolm Addey might have been involved in the vocal sessions, it is unlikely that he engineered the orchestral track.
A fast waltz pace is set by staccato strings, before Cliff's comes in with his vocal line. The overall feel is more Spanish in rhythm than it is Italian but Cliff pulls off the self-confirmed difficult Italian language with great success.

Track Specification
Composed by Eduardo Vianello and Mogol

Musicians

Norrie Paramor Orchestra	orchestra
Norrie Paramor	arranger, conductor
Cliff Richard	vocals

Recording Details

Producer	John Lee and M. DiPonti (backing track) and Norrie Paramor (vocals)
Engineered by	Malcolm Addey
Recording location	EMI Studios, Milan (backing track) and Estudios Valentim De Carvalho, Lisbon (vocals)
Recording date	2nd-3rd October 1964 (backing track) and 13th May 1965 (vocals)

♫ On and On
From the album **Did He Jump... Or Was He Pushed?** *(Garth Hewitt)*

The second track on the ***Did He Jump... Or Was He Pushed?*** album by Garth Hewitt was produced by Cliff Richard and includes a number of musicians from Cliff's late seventies recordings as well as the provision of harmonies by Cliff.
The bouncing nature of the song and the brilliant melody makes it a suitable candidate for a Cliff song of the period. Hewitt produces a lead vocal that is matched with Cliff's obvious and occasional backing vocals. The guitar solo is pure rock and roll and this religious song is wrapped up perfectly in a brilliant piece of music.

Track Specification
Composed by Garth Hewitt

Musicians

Garth Hewitt	vocals
Graham Jarvis	drums, percussion
Adrian Lee	synthesiser
Mike Moran	keyboards
Jo Partridge	guitar
Cliff Richard	backing vocals
Dave Wintour	bass

Recording Details

Producer	Cliff Richard
Engineered by	Tony Clark and Haydn Bendall
Recording location	Odyssey Studios, London
Recording date	1979

♫ Once Again
From the album **Sail Away** *(Dave Pope)*

Towards the end of the ***Green Light*** album sessions, Cliff Richard took up the production duties for ***Sail Away*** by his friend Dave Pope. The third track on the first side of the album was *Once Again* by Herb Pederon. Unfortunately the reference material, including the album sleeve itself, bears no mention of the musicians involved; therefore, these are annotated as unknown in the track specification until further research can identify them.
The focus is on the strident guitar chords with a gentle undercurrent of accompaniment behind Pope's voice which has a slight echo placed on it. The slightly clandestine feel to the verses sounds similar to ***Devil Woman*** in some respects, but this is immediately dispelled by the brightness of the chorus. The backing vocals are very much in evidence on this song, which elevate the joy and freedom displayed in the chorus as he beseeches his captor to set him free.

Track Specification
Composed by Herb Pederon
Musicians

Dave Pope	vocals
Cliff Richard	backing vocals
Unknown	backing vocals
Unknown	guitar
Unknown	bass
Unknown	keyboards
Unknown	drums, percussion

Recording Details

Producer	Cliff Richard
Engineered by	Tony Clark
Recording location	Morgan Studios, London
Recording date	April 1978

♫ Once in a While
From the album **Wired for Sound**

Alan Tarney continued his eighties dominance of Cliff Richard's recordings with the second song that he wrote, produced and performed many of the instruments and backing vocals in the sessions for the ***Wired for Sound*** album. Tarney's continued relationship with Cliff had started in the seventies and it would prove to be a lucrative and musically positive relationship that he held with him.

Alan Tarney's guitar has a particular signature sound to it and this is heard in the introduction to *Once in a While*. The clever use of the synthesiser makes the track sound fresh while the blending of the backing vocals by Cliff and Tarney brighten the performance further.

Track Specification
Composed by Alan Tarney
Musicians

Cliff Richard	vocals, backing vocals
Trevor Spencer	drums, percussion
Alan Tarney	arranger, backing vocals, guitar, bass, keyboards

Recording Details

Producer	Alan Tarney
Engineered by	Michael Boddicker and Ian Little
Recording location	Gallery Studios, Chertsey, Surrey
Recording date	27th May-9th July 1981

♫ Once upon a Time
From the album **Always Guaranteed**

Because Cliff Richard was heavily involved in the matinee and evening performances of ***Time – The Musical*** in London, it meant that any recording for a new album (his first in almost three years) had to be carried out at od times during the day at a location that gave Cliff easy access to London. Working once again with Alan Tarney, who dominated many of his recordings in the seventies and eighties, Cliff would add his vocals to a basic track of a song that had been composed in the studio and had been laid down by Tarney prior to his arrival at the studios. This gave Cliff the freedom to perform at night without having to be bogged down with the complete recording process, particularly since Tarney also provided all of the instrumentation and electronic gadgetry that formed the resultant abum.

The strength of the songs on the *Always Guaranteed* album comes from the freshness emanating from the *ad hoc* approach to the generation of the song but, more important, the focus on the arrangement, particularly with respect to the backing vocals, which are layered from multiple recordings by both Cliff and Tarney.

Track Specification
Composed by Alan Tarney
Musicians

Cliff Richard	vocals, backing vocals
Alan Tarney	backing vocals, guitars, bass, keyboards, drum and percussion programming

Recording Details

Producer	Alan Tarney
Engineered by	Gerry Kitchingham and Keith Bessey
Recording location	R. G. Jones Studios, Wimbledon, London
Recording date	13th October-November 1986

♫ One (Singular Sensation)
From the album **Something Special** *(Various)*

Written in 1975, *A Chorus Line* is a musical play about a choreographer-cum-director who auditions dancers for a forthcoming musical. Asking each person who is auditioning for a role in the chorus line (of the title) to tell him something about themselves leads to a number of issues before culminating in a major song and dance number at the end when he has chosen his members of his dance troupe. The premise is interesting but some critics hated the concept and lambasted Richard Attenborough's lacklustre film version even more. *One (Singular Sensation)* appears towards the end and is generally performed in hushed tones before building up gradually to become one of the most dramatic set-pieces of the musical.

In June 1998, a charity concert was performed at the Brighton Centre in aid of NASS (the National Asylum Support Service) with some of the acts appearing on the resultant *Something Special* album. In the line-up, Cliff Richard headlined with his set of rock and roll songs and his hits which then led into actors, television presenters and sports personalities joining him on stage to perform *One (Singular Sensation)* as the finale. The album is now a considerable rarity and the author has been unable to specify anything about the performance other than those stars taking part.

Track Specification
Composed by Marvin Hamlisch and Edward Kleban

Musicians		*Recording Details*	
Jane Alexander	arranger, conductor	Producer	Paul Raynor-Brown
Lionel Blair	vocals	Engineered by	Julius Warren
June Brown	vocals	Recording location	Brighton Centre, Brighton
Dora Bryan	vocals	Recording date	7th June 1998
Robin Cousins	vocals		
Fiona Dunn	vocals		
Dawn French	vocals		
Amanda Hall	vocals		
Steven Houghton	vocals		
Cliff Richard	vocals		
Melanie Stace	vocals		
Unknown	orchestra		

♬ One Fine Day

Unissued tracks and from the album **Don't Stop Me Now!**

Made famous by the Chiffons with the release of their cover of *One Fine Day* was a number twenty-nine hit in Britain in July 1963. Carole King and Gerry Goffin were reportedly inspired to write the song after listening to the aria *Un Bel Di* from *Madame Butterfly* by Giacomo Puccini. Little Eva, formerly Goffin's and King's maid before they oversaw the recording of her massive hit with *The Locomotion*, was slated to sing the vocals on *One Fine Day* but it was reassigned to girl group the Chiffons, and it fared better than the UK when it reached number five in their native USA. Giving its name to a film starring George Clooney and Michelle Pfeiffer in 1996, the song has been covered by a wide variety of artists including Natalie Merchant, the Crystals, Aaron Neville, Johnny Adams, the Nylons, Rita Coolidge and Carole King herself amongst several others.

Cliff Richard attempted the song in two different sessions, both intended to produce songs for the albums of the period, although it eventually wound up on ***Don't Stop Me Now!***: the first session was on 21st September 1966, when it was abandoned after three takes, while the completed version was recorded three weeks later in October. The final (unknown) take and edit were used for the mono and stereo recordings.

With a rasping saxophone and hand-claps introducing the song, Cliff's version of the familiar track is a paced foot-tapper that fairly crackles along. Cliff is enjoying the performance, which comes through in the recording, and it is a nice arrangement of what is a highly familiar song, of which the original version was sung slightly out of tune.

The song was chosen for inclusion in the ***Help It Along*** charity album project, which was a set of studio-based concerts in front of a small audience, but *One Fine Day* was one of the five tracks that remain unissued. This may have been due to its lyrical tenor not quite fitting in with the rest of the songs performed and released on the album.

Track Specification
Composed by Carole King and Gerry Goffin

1. Unissued track (Don't Stop Me Now!)

Musicians		*Recording Details*	
Bernard Ebbinghouse Orchestra	orchestra	Producer	Norrie Paramor
Bernard Ebbinghouse	arranger, conductor	Engineered by	Peter Vincent and Richard Lush
Cliff Richard	vocals	Recording location	Abbey Road Studio 2, St. John's Wood, London
Unknown	female backing vocals	Recording date	21st September 1966
Unknown	hand claps		

2. Don't Stop Me Now!

Musicians		*Recording Details*	
Bernard Ebbinghouse Orchestra	orchestra	Producer	Norrie Paramor
Bernard Ebbinghouse	arranger, conductor	Engineered by	Peter Vincent and Richard Lush
Cliff Richard	vocals	Recording location	Abbey Road Studio 2, St. John's Wood, London
Unknown	female backing vocals	Recording date	11th October 1966
Unknown	hand claps		

3. Unissued track (Help It Along)

Musicians		*Recording Details*	
Terry Britten	guitar	Producer	David MacKay
Barrie Guard	arranger, conductor, percussion	Engineered by	Roger Quested
Cliff Hall	keyboards	Recording location	Morgan Studios, London
Jean Hawker	backing vocals	Recording date	24th, 25th and 26th September 1973
Anna Peacock	backing vocals		
Kevin Peek	guitar		
Cliff Richard	vocals		
Trevor Spencer	drums, percussion		
Alan Tarney	bass		
Unknown	orchestra		

♫ One Night (1)
From the album **The Rock 'n' Roll Years 1958-1963**

Although a small number of songs have had the accolade of being at number one twice on different issues or re-releases, Elvis Presley's *One Night* can take the record for the greatest span in between, with the first showing at the top spot in late 1958, and the second in early 2005 for the King's would-be 70th birthday. It also has the accolade of being the UK's 1000th number one and has been covered by Fats Domino, Mud, Pérez Prado and Arlo Guthrie, amongst others.

For its time in the late fifties, the song was controversial. The lyrics cover the yearning of a would-be suitor wanting to spend a single night in the bed of the woman of his dreams; this was very salacious in the more prudish times of the mid-twentieth century, although the only concession made to that was to slightly retitle *One Night (of Sin)* by removing the words in parentheses. The attraction of the song comes from the fact that it is generally performed in a highly operatic and therefore dramatic way, which grabs the attention of the listener from the start. There is also a tortuous triple negative in the line "I ain't never did no wrong" that sounds far better in an American accent than a British one.

Because of the Presley connection, it was a suitable addition in the 'live' show recorded over two days at Abbey Road before a selection of fans. However, there had been no record of its recording and it was only when going through tapes that one marked 'out-takes' was found upon which this song was identified. It was subsequently released on the compilation of rarities of Cliff's early years, ***The Rock 'n' Roll Years 1958-1963***, although it has not been added to reissues of the original album to date.

The screams of the girls in the audience occasionally overwhelm the music but this is Cliff at his most raucous, with a rough vocal on the words of the title. The ensemble of the Drifters backing Cliff's strong vocal lead gives some indication of what was to come in their careers: Hank Marvin's solid lead guitar drives the tune along underpinned by the sussurating cymbals played by Tony Meehan and the driving rhythm of the bass and rhythm guitar.

Track Specification
Composed by Dave Bartholomew, Pearl King and Anita Steiman

Musicians

Jet Harris	bass
Hank Marvin	guitar
Tony Meehan	drums, percussion
Cliff Richard	vocals
Bruce Welch	rhythm guitar

Recording Details

Producer	Norrie Paramor
Engineered by	Peter Bown and Stuart Eltham
Recording location	Abbey Road Studio 2, St. John's Wood, London
Recording date	9th or 10th February 1959

♫ One Night (2)
From the album **Always Guaranteed**

After a break of a few years, Alan Tarney resumed work with Cliff Richard on the ***Always Guaranteed*** tracks, which would go on to be Cliff's most successful album. Because Cliff was firmly tied up with performing in ***Time – The Musical*** at the Dominion Theatre in London in the evenings, Tarney would write the song in the studio, lay down the basic track and then Cliff would arrive to do his vocal lines. *One Night* was the opening track on the eventual album.

As with some of the material from the early eighties, *One Night* has Tarney's signature sound. The track is a foot-tapping song that talks of the love for a woman with whom he has yet to have a relationship but wants to be with her for one night to prove his feelings. Cliff and Tarney provide the effective backing vocals in this highly catch piece of mid-eighties pop.

Track Specification
Composed by Alan Tarney

Musicians

Cliff Richard	vocals, backing vocals
Alan Tarney	backing vocals, guitars, bass, keyboards, drum and percussion programming

Recording Details

Producer	Alan Tarney
Engineered by	Gerry Kitchingham and Keith Bessey
Recording location	R. G. Jones Studios, Wimbledon, London
Recording date	13th October-November 1986

♫ One Note Samba
From the album **Kinda Latin**

Another Antônio Carlos Jobim song that Cliff Richard recorded for his ***Kinda Latin*** album, *One Note Samba* was originally a Portuguese song entitled *Samba de Una Nota Só* (which is close enough to the English translation). Recorded by Stan Getz and Charlie Bird, Frank Sinatra, Eydie Gormé, Al Jarreau and Ella Fitzgerald among others, the title is derived from the melody line, which is played, as would be expected, repetitively on one note in a samba rhythm, first played in the dominant and then the tonic before reverting back to the dominant.

One of four songs to be recorded at the third and final October 1965 session for Cliff's album, the fourth and final take and edit of *One Note Samba* were taken for both the mono and stereo recordings bit with different mixes for the audio channel separation.

Another samba (as the title suggests) but repeated on the same note (or its related melodics), Cliff performs it with sch professionalism that the risk of it becoming dull is eliminated. A fitting end to the first side of the parent album, it is worth listening to through headphones for the instrumental nuances accompanying his vocal lead.

Track Specification
Composed by Antônio Carlos Jobim, Jon Hendricks and Newton Mendonça

Musicians		*Recording Details*	
Les Reed Orchestra	orchestra	Producer	Norrie Paramor
Les Reed	arranger, conductor	Engineered by	Peter Bown
Cliff Richard	vocals	Recording location	Abbey Road Studio 3, St. John's Wood, London
		Recording date	22nd October 1965

♫ One Time Lover Man

B-side of **Some People**

Finishing his role in ***Time,*** Cliff Richard was able to focus on new recordings and, during this time he managed to record his vocals for ***Always Guaranteed.*** In spring 1987, he recorded several tracks at the small studio in the basement of his Surrey offices, including *One Time Lover Man,* which he also wrote. It was chosen as the B-side of ***Some People,*** in all of its variants. It would take another eleven years for the song to be issued in CD format when it was included on the *1980s* compilation in 1998 and also as one of the eight bonus tracks added to the 2004 remaster of *Always Guaranteed.*
The structure of the song is sound and is added to by the inclusion of Cliff doubling as his own backing vocalist. While the song is not as memorable as many of his own that he recorded, it is still strong enough and a fine example of the genre that was popular at the time. The mid-section includes a muted guitar solo that is a throwback to his early career.

Track Specification
Composed by Cliff Richard

Musicians		*Recording Details*	
John Clark	guitar, bass	Producer	Cliff Richard
Alan Park	keyboards, drum and percussion programming	Engineered by	Keith Bessey
		Recording location	C. R. O. Studios, Esher, Surrey
Cliff Richard	vocals, backing vocals	Recording date	April 1987

♫ Only Angel

From the album **Cliff Richard - The Album**

Cliff Richard recorded this emotionally-charged song for ***Cliff Richard - The Album*** in 1992. Its slow-paced rhythm and exquisite melody is performed in a minor key supported by an organ and languid guitar sections. The tear-jerker talks of the death of a loved one and Cliff's anguished vocals cannot help but tug at the heartstrings and, during performances to support the album, it was one of the few tracks that instilled reverential quiet in the audiences.

Track Specification
Composed by Williams

Musicians		*Recording Details*	
John Clark	guitar	Producer	Paul Moessl and Cliff Richard
Peter May	drums, percussion	Engineered by	Gerry Kitchingham and Ben Robbins
Paul Moessl	arranger, drum programming, organ, keyboards	Recording location	R. G. Jones Studios, Wimbledon, London
		Recording date	25th-31st May 1992, 8th June 1992 (backing track) and 7th August 1992 (vocals)
Cliff Richard	vocals, backing vocals		
Steve Stroud	bass		

♫ Only Way Out, The

83rd UK single

Also recorded by Julie Anthony in 1988 for her *I Dreamed a Dream* album, *The Only Way Out* was the opening track to Cliff Richard's 1982 album ***Now You See Me... Now You Don't.*** Dispensing with Alan Tarney with whom Cliff had worked on the last two albums, he co-produced it with Craig Pruess.
Backed with ***Under the Influence,*** *The Only Way Out* was issued as the first of three singles from the album on the EMI label (catalogue number EMI 5318) on 2nd July 1982 and reached number ten in the UK and, in the US, number sixty-four. The associated video was a literal interpretation with Cliff running around a maze trying to get out interspersed with him singing on a bench. He didn't play an instrument on the recording, but he is seen playing the acoustic guitar in the video.
While still employing electronic keyboards, after ***Wired for Sound,*** *The Only Way Out* is a return to the basic rock instrumentation with a strong emphasis on the rhythm guitar. Cliff supplies all of the vocals on the track and, as is expected with using the same voice, the blend of the harmonies is near perfection.

Track Specification
Composed by Ray Martinez

Musicians		*Recording Details*	
John Clark	electric guitar, acoustic guitar	Producer	Cliff Richard and Craig Pruess
Dave Cooke	synthesiser	Engineered by	John Walker and Steve Cook
Mark Griffiths	bass	Recording location	Strawberry Studios South, Surrey
Graham Jarvis	drums, percussion	Recording date	4th-15th January 1982
Mart Jenner	electric guitar		
Cliff Richard	vocals, backing vocals		
Graham Todd	piano		

♫ Only You
B-side of **All I Ask of You**

Only You is taken from Andrew Lloyd Webber's musical *Starlight Express*, with lyrics by Richard Stilgoe. The show was first performed in 1984 in London and is basically the story of a little boy's dream when all his toys come to life and how they interact. In 1986, Lloyd Webber invited Cliff Richard to join is then wife Sarah Brightman to record a duet from the forthcoming *The Phantom of the Opera*, ***All I Ask for You***. On the seven-inch release of the song, it was backed with the orchestral overture to the second act, while the same was true of the twelve-inch version, but *Only You* was added as a bonus track. The song was recorded at the same session as the A-side and was a significant rarity until it was included on the Sarah Brightman collection *Love Changes Everything: the Andrew Lloyd Webber Collection, Volume Two* in 2005.
The gentle song is initiated by a guitar motif leading into Cliff's vocals, who hands over vocal control to Brightman, while supplying layered vocals in harmony. The instrumentation is a classic rock band of the period, although the sleeve suggests that is the Royal Philharmonic Orchestra, which is incorrect. A guitar solo is performed in the middle eight, which leads into a buoyant and emotionally-charged section where Brightman and Cliff sing exuberantly in harmony.

Track Specification
Composed by Andrew Lloyd Webber and Richard Stilgoe

Musicians

Sarah Brightman	vocals
Cliff Richard	vocals, backing vocals
Unknown	guitar
Unknown	bass
Unknown	keyboards
Unknown	drums, percussion

Recording Details

Producer	Andrew Lloyd Webber
Engineered by	Martin Levan
Recording location	Abbey Road Studios, St. John's Wood, London
Recording date	6th August 1986

♫ On My Word
30th UK single

Written by young composer Chip Taylor, who would compose the classics *Angel of the Morning* and *Wild Thing* amongst others and return to Nashville in the seventies, *On My Word* was listed for recording by Cliff Richard during his month-long sojourn in America at the Columbia studios sessions in Nashville and New York. There is some discrepancy in recollection as to where the song was recorded – for instance Cliff, in interview, stated that he got a hit out of the New York sessions – but all reference material strongly points to it being recorded in Nashville rather than New York.
The eighth and final take and edit were used for the mono and stereo recordings with different mixes for the needs of the separate audio channels. *On My Word* was released as a single, backed with ***Just a Little Bit Too Late*** (recorded the following year back in London), on the Columbia label (catalogue number DB 7596) on 4th June 1965, reaching number twelve in the charts. It was the first single since the beginning of 1960 that had not been a top ten hit in the UK, breaking a run of a potential twenty-four successive singles hitting that magic top ten. Originally only released in mono, as was its appearance on the ***Angel*** EP, the stereo version was given its first airing four years later on the album ***The Best of Cliff***.
On My Word is a quirky little number that is driven by a shuffling rhythm on the guitar and matched by a responsive brass section and a twinkling piano. Cliff sings the song perfectly, with a touch of anguish in the emotive lyrics that confirm to a lover that he will be faithful whatever the temptations. It really deserved to get a higher position in the charts than it did but it had stiff competition from other quality acts.
In October 1965, Cliff recorded a German vocal line for ***Glaub' Nur Mir***, which was overdubbed on the original backing track of *On My Word*. It was released as the B-side of the German version of ***Wind Me Up (Let Me Go)***, ***Nur Bei Dir Bin Ich zu Haus***, and was originally only to be found in mono, until the release of the compilation ***On the Continent***.

Track Specification
Composed by Chip Taylor

Musicians

Jordanaires	backing vocals
Cliff Richard	vocals
Unknown	female backing vocals
Unknown	guitar
Unknown	bass
Unknown	piano
Unknown	brass
Unknown	drums, percussion

Recording Details

Producer	Bob Morgan and Billy Sherrill
Engineered by	Mort Thomason
Recording location	Columbia Studios, Nashville
Recording date	25th August 1964

♫ On the Beach
26th UK single *and from the film soundtrack album* **Wonderful Life – The Remaster** *and from the albums* **Cliff in Japan**, **Japan Tour '74**, **Knebworth – The Album**, **Summer Holiday** *(Darren Day) and* **Reunited**

The only song in the ***Wonderful Life*** film that stands alone as a sequence in its own right (that is, it can be excised without having to worry about the plot), *On the Beach* comes at the point in the film where the stranded cruise liner stewards and musicians have landed jobs on the set of what is turning out to be a terrible movie being filmed. Jerry (Melvyn Hayes) and Edward (Richard O'Sullivan) are making awful tea and coffee and Jerry suddenly says that he feels depressed.

Meanwhile, Johnny (Cliff Richard) is strumming his guitar playing a quiet first couple of lines of *On the Beach* to Jenny (Susan Hampshire) before getting up and suggesting that he can provide a solution to the depression by singing a song and getting everyone to dance. The Shadows jump to their instruments and the song starts with Jenny and Johnny dancing together on the beach and in the sea before being joined by the whole company. The scene cuts swiftly to the director's office as he expresses his concern about the success (or otherwise) of the movie he is making.

Written by the prolific collaboration of Hank Marvin and Bruce Welch with assistance in the lyrics by Cliff, *On the Beach* was recorded at the same session that provided the film's title song. The eleventh and final take and edit were used for the mono and stereo recordings but with different mixes for the audio channels' needs. Appearing on the ***Hits from Wonderful Life*** EP, *On the Beach* was issued as a single, backed with ***A Matter of Moments*** (also from the film soundtrack), on the Columbia label (catalogue number DB 7305) on 26th June 1964, reaching number seven in the UK singles charts. Although it is John Rostill, the Shadows bassist, who appears in the film, it was actually his predecessor Brian Locking who took the bass guitar on the recording of the soundtrack song. A favourite of Cliff's sisters (of all his huge oeuvre of music to that point), *On the Beach* has also been covered by the Galaxies, while the film version features a brief vocal by Susan Hampshire on the final verse on what is a recording that is otherwise indistinguishable from the soundtrack. That recording has not been released in any other commercial format and was likely to have been recorded in the first three months of 1964, although the studio personnel and recording location are unknown.

On the original stereo version of the record, Cliff can be heard coughing or clearing his throat in the right channel during the first guitar solo interlude. On *Wonderful Life – The Remaster*, it includes the stereo version with that cough is edited out. A further version was released on the album ***Cliff Richard at the Movies 1959-1974***, which has the cough edited out and includes a count-in; in all other respects, it is exactly the same as the originally released version.

Strangely, the instrumentation is restricted to the left channel, the backing vocals are in the right only, and Cliff's lead vocal is kept central, making it as curious listening experience. One of the best songs in the film, *On the Beach* shows the Cliff and Shadows vocal harmony sound that they developed and is a worthy choice as a single to represent the project.

Towards the end of 1964, Cliff overdubbed German vocals on the original English backing track by the Shadows. With a translation by Hans Bradtke (who had previously reworked ***Lucky Lips*** for the German market), ***Nur Mt Dir*** (or *Only with You*) was released as the B-side of the translated version of ***Spanish Harlem*** (***Das Ist die Frage Aller Fragen***) and became a number one hit for him in that country. A new version was recorded in Italian, retitled ***Chi Lo Sà***, in February 1969 and backed the Italian version of ***Don't Forget to Catch Me*** (***Non Dimenticare Chi Ti Ama***) as a single in May of that year.

For the Japanese tour in 1974, Cliff created a ***Hit Medley*** that featured a number of his sixties hits: ***Congratulations***, ***In the Country***, ***Dancing Shoes***, ***The Day I Met Marie***, *On the Beach* and ***Sing a Song of Freedom***. Bruce Welch's voice can be heard backing Cliff during the performance and the song breaks off into an instrumental jam in the mid-section before Cliff's vocals come back in. The segue into the slower *Sing a Song of Freedom* is a little awkward but the musicianship of those involved covers it adequately.

In 1990, the Shadows got back together with Cliff for a short set at a festival taking place in the grounds of Knebworth House. At the time, the full performance was broadcast on the BBC Radio 1 station, although only *On the Beach* and ***Do You Wanna Dance?*** were issued on the track listing of *Knebworth – The Album*, a charity release in aid of the Nordoff-Robbins Music Therapy Centre.

In 1997 and into early 1998, there was a touring play of *Summer Holiday*, which was a musical based around Cliff's hits starring Darren Day. The associated album featured all of the songs from the show and four of the songs also featured Cliff on backing vocals, including *On the Beach*. The track was remixed to form part of ***The Summer Holiday Megamix***. Cliff provides all of the backing vocals previously created by Hank and Bruce, while Darren Day carries the song off pleasantly enough but he doesn't have the innate power that Cliff possesses and imbues into his performances.

The inevitable fondness with which the song is held in the hearts of fans and band alike, it was a sure-fire choice for re-recording on the Cliff and the Shadows new 2009 album, ***Reunited***, and then for subsequent performance in the associated tour. A pretty faithful rendition of the song, the best part, as with the original, is derived from the backing vocals.

Track Specification

Composed by Hank Marvin, Bruce Welch and Cliff Richard

1. Single

Musicians		*Recording Details*	
Brian Bennett	drums, percussion	Producer	Norrie Paramor
Brian 'Licorice' Locking	bass	Engineered by	Malcolm Addey
Hank Marvin	backing vocals, guitar	Recording location	Abbey Road Studio 3, St. John's Wood, London
Cliff Richard	vocals	Recording date	5th November 1963
Bruce Welch	backing vocals, rhythm guitar		

2. Wonderful Life – The Remaster

Musicians		*Recording Details*	
Brian Bennett	drums, percussion	Producer	Norrie Paramor
Brian 'Licorice' Locking	bass	Engineered by	Malcolm Addey
Hank Marvin	backing vocals, guitar	Recording location	Abbey Road Studio 3, St. John's Wood, London
Cliff Richard	vocals	Recording date	5th November 1963
Bruce Welch	backing vocals, rhythm guitar		

3. *Cliff in Japan*

Musicians

Norrie Paramor Orchestra	orchestra
Norrie Paramor	arranger, conductor
Cliff Richard	vocals
Unknown	backing vocals

Recording Details

Producer	Norrie Paramor
Engineered by	Unknown
Recording location	Shibuya Public Hall, Tokyo, Japan
Recording date	18th October 1967

4. *Japan Tour '74*

Musicians

Barrie Guard	arranger, conductor
Cliff Hall	piano
Brian Lewis	backing vocals, guitar
Kevin Peak	acoustic guitar
Cliff Richard	vocals
Shambles Symphonet	orchestra
Trevor Spencer	drums, percussion
Alan Tarney	backing vocals, bass
Bruce Welch	backing vocals, rhythm guitar

Recording Details

Producer	Toshiba EMI (no individual detailed)
Engineered by	Toshiba EMI (no individual detailed)
Recording location	Shinjuku Koseinenkin, Tokyo, Japan
Recording date	7th-8th October 1974

5. *Knebworth - The Album*

Musicians

Ray Beavis	saxophone
Brian Bennett	drums, percussion
John Earle	saxophone
Chris Gower	trombone
Mark Griffiths	bass
Cliff Hall	keyboards
Dick Hanson	trumpet
Peter Howarth	backing vocals
Hank Marvin	backing vocals, guitar
Paul Moessl	keyboards
Mick Mullins	backing vocals
Keith Murrell	backing vocals
Cliff Richard	vocals
Bruce Welch	backing vocals, guitar

Recording Details

Producer	Chris Kimsey and Steve Smith
Engineered by	Unknown
Recording location	Knebworth House, Hertfordshire, England
Recording date	30th June 1990

6. *Summer Holiday (Darren Day)*

Musicians

Darren Day	vocals
Mark Griffiths	lead guitar
Cliff Richard	backing vocals
Warren Bennett	arranger, guitar, bass, drums, percussion

Recording Details

Producer	Brian Bennett
Engineered by	Dick Plant
Recording location	Honeyhill Studios, Hertfordshire, England
Recording date	1996

7. *Reunited*

Musicians

Brian Bennett	drums, percussion
Mark Griffiths	bass
Hank Marvin	backing vocals, guitar
Cliff Richard	vocals, backing vocals
Bruce Welch	backing vocals, rhythm guitar

Recording Details

Producer	Warren Bennett (co-ordination)
Engineered by	James Collins (Honeyhill Studios), Ethan Carlson (Middle Ear Studios), Les Williams (Nivram Studios) and Keith Bessey (mixing and mastering)
Recording location	Middle Ear Studios, Miami, Florida, USA (Cliff's vocals), Nivram Studios, Perth, Western Australia (Hank's guitars and vocals) and Honeyhill Studios, Hertfordshire, England (all other vocals and instruments)
Recording date	Early 2009

♫ Ooh La La

From the album **Established 1958**

Extraordinarily, *Ooh La La* was recorded at a session that fell in the middle of three evening shows at the Talk of the Town in London (later released as ***Live at the Talk of the Town***). The afternoon session also saw the completion of the only single from the project, ***Don't Forget to Catch Me***, and the second failed attempt at ***What's Behind the Eyes of Mary?*** All of the tracks on the ***Established 1958*** album were written by one or more of the Shadows, with John Rostill working alone on *Ooh La La*, which was the final song to be completed.

Another witty song featuring the close harmony vocals of the Shadows and the piano of Hank Marvin, Cliff sings it with is tongue firmly in his cheek. The title is, of course, the clichéd utterance of the French to indicate shock or surprise and so the lyrics reflect this as little stories are told that have a sting in the tale.

Recorded in German for the *Hier Ist Cliff* album, it was given the suffix of ***Ooh La La (Sagte Cäsar zu Cleopatra)*** or *(As Caesar Said to Cleopatra)* retitled from the first few English lyrics.

Track Specification
Composed by John Rostill
Musicians

Brian Bennett	drums, percussion
Hank Marvin	backing vocals, guitar, piano
Cliff Richard	vocals
John Rostill	backing vocals, bass
Bruce Welch	backing vocals, rhythm guitar

Recording Details

Producer	Norrie Paramor
Engineered by	Peter Vince
Recording location	Abbey Road Studio 2, St. John's Wood, London
Recording date	31st May 1968

♫ Ooh La La (Sagte Cäsar zu Cleopatra)
From the album **Hier Ist Cliff**

For Cliff Richard's first German album *Hier Ist Cliff*, many of the tracks were plundered from the then recently released album ***Established 1958*** and translated into German. One of them was ***Ooh La La***, which maintained the title but added the suffix *Sagte Cäsar zu Cleopatra* (literally *As Caesar Said to Cleopatra*). The German song has only been released in stereo and was a major rarity until it was included on the boxed set of ***On the Continent***, featuring Cliff's foreign language songs. Norrie Paramor has successfully recreated the Shadows sound and there is even a male backing group who almost emulate the harmonies of Hank Marvin, Bruce Welch and John Rostill, although there is no information as to who they are. Cliff appears to struggle to get all the lyrics in, possibly because he is enunciating each syllable very carefully.

Track Specification
Composed by John Rostill; German lyrics by Volauvent
Musicians

Norrie Paramor Orchestra	orchestra
Norrie Paramor	arranger, director
Cliff Richard	vocals
Unknown	backing vocals

Recording Details

Producer	Norrie Paramor
Engineered by	Peter Vince
Recording location	Abbey Road Studio 2, St. John's Wood, London
Recording date	27th November 1968

♫ Our Day Will Come
From the album **Kinda Latin**

Made famous by Ruby and the Romantics who had their only UK charting single which reached number thirty-eight in April 1963, *Our Day Will Come* fared better in the US where it was a number one. It has since been recorded by several artists including Frankie Valli, the Carpenters, Doris Day, Christina Aguilera, Brenda Lee, Jamie Cullum, Chris Montez, Billy Fury, Bobby Darin, the Supremes, Bobby Rydell, Julie London and Trini Lopez amongst many others.
The third song to be completed at the first of three ***Kinda Latin*** sessions in October 1965 by Cliff Richard, the fourth and final take and edit of *Our Day Will Come* were used for both the mono and stereo recordings with different mixes for the audio channel separation.
Supported initially by a shimming xylophone and then a guitar, Cliff's careful performance ushers in a slow Latin rhythm. There is more of an echo on this track than others on the album, which adds to the yearning atmosphere in the lyrics.

Track Specification
Composed by Mort Garson and Bob Hilliard
Musicians

Bernard Ebbinghouse Orchestra	orchestra
Bernard Ebbinghouse	arranger, conductor
Cliff Richard	vocals

Recording Details

Producer	Norrie Paramor
Engineered by	Peter Bown
Recording location	Abbey Road Studio 2, St. John's Wood, London
Recording date	4th October 1965

♫ Our Love Could Be So Real
From the album **31st February Street**

For the album ***The 31st of February Street***, Cliff Richard wrote six of the fourteen songs, one of which was *Our Love Could Be So Real*. Recorded at one of the four main album sessions in February 1974, the song was finished in seventeen takes. With strings and a glissando on the bass guitar, the introduction is reminiscent of the Beatles *Come Together*, although this is dispelled after Cliff's vocal is brought in. The gentle verse builds up to a more optimistic and ebullient middle eight but this quietens down into the string accompaniment and this process is continued until the end.

Track Specification
Composed by Cliff Richard
Musicians

Terry Britten	guitar
Barrie Guard	arranger, conductor
Cliff Hall	keyboards
Kevin Peek	acoustic guitar
Cliff Richard	vocals
Trevor Spencer	drums, percussion
Alan Tarney	bass
Unknown	orchestra

Recording Details

Producer	David MacKay
Engineered by	Tony Clark and Mike Jarrett
Recording location	Abbey Road Studio 2, St. John's Wood, London
Recording date	12th and 14th February 1974

♫ Our Story Book

B-side of **The Day I Met Marie**

The last of four songs to be recorded at the 24th April session, *Our Story Book* remained in the vaults a few months until it came time to choose the B-side of Cliff Richard's thirty-ninth single, ***The Day I Met Marie***. Originally only released in mono, as per the custom by companies such as Columbia in the sixties where often albums took precedence for release in stereo as well as mono, although the stereo version was eventually released on the German compilation album, *Congratulations und 13 Weitere Hits*, in 1968. It remained a relative rarity until it was included first on 2007's French compilation *Congratulations to Cliff Richard* and the following year's celebratory compendium ***...And They Said It Wouldn't Last! (My 50 Years in Music)***.
In this period, Mike Leander seemed to enjoy using a harpsichord in his arrangements and it is used effectively in this song, which uses the structure of a novel, plotting and characterisation to talk about the passage of his love affair and how it falls apart. Cliff provides his own backing vocals during the verses, while a female chorus is used elsewhere, although it is unknown who they are (possibly the Breakaways with whom Cliff recorded and toured around this period). The song ends on an unresolved chord sequence, which seems to invite suggestions that there is more yet to tell in this story.

Track Specification
Composed by Lor Crane and Joan Kingsbury
Musicians

Mike Leander Orchestra	orchestra
Mike Leander	arranger, conductor
Cliff Richard	vocals, backing vocals
Unknown	female backing vocals

Recording Details

Producer	Norrie Paramor
Engineered by	Unknown
Recording location	Abbey Road Studio 2, St. John's Wood, London
Recording date	24th April 1967

♫ Outsider

From the album **21 Today**

Composing partnership Sid Tepper and Roy Bennett had already provided Cliff Richard and the Shadows with tracks early on in their career and they composed two for the ***21 Today*** album. However, *Outsider* was originally commissioned as one of three for the upcoming film musical starring Cliff (that would become ***The Young Ones***). Two of those songs, ***The Young Ones*** and ***When the Girl in Your Arms Is the Girl in Your Heart***, made it into the film while the third was recorded but sidelined into this earlier album.
The song was one of six to be recorded at the session with just four takes required to complete it, of which the last was used for the mono and stereo edits but with different mixes required for the audio channels.
The chinking tambourines, backing vocals and strings confirm that this song was intended for a musical. Although Cliff's vocals are as strong as on any other track, there are insufficient hooks to make this song memorable and the repetition of the words by the Mike Sammes Singers in the middle eight bridge feel out of place.

Track Specification
Composed by Sid Tepper and Roy C. Bennett
Musicians

Mike Sammes Singers	backing vocals
Norrie Paramor Orchestra	orchestra
Norrie Paramor	arranger, conductor
Cliff Richard	vocals

Recording Details

Producer	Norrie Paramor
Engineered by	Malcolm Addey
Recording location	Abbey Road Studio 2, St. John's Wood, London
Recording date	30th January 1961

♫ Over in Bethlehem

From the album **His Land**

Recorded for Cliff Richard's religious vehicle for the Billy Graham Organisation, ***His Land***, *Over in Bethlehem* is another song that talks of the genesis of Jesus Christ as the revered Christian figure he is. Unusually for the time, it is a duet, and Cliff sings with Cliff Barrows (who also provided solo tracks for the enterprise) and their vocals were recorded and overdubbed in Israel on an orchestral backing track completed at the Capitol Records studios based in Hollywood. There is no information regarding the precise recording dates other than that they occurred towards the end of 1969.
Over in Bethlehem slowly builds up as the two Cliffs walk alongside a group of children and it is sung gently with the accompaniment of children's voices raised in happiness as they play. The song ends as the pair flies north to Galilee with Barrows narrating once again. The integration of the two Cliffs' voices works well, although it detracts from the performance when Barrows talks in an American accent.

Track Specification
Composed by Ralph Carmichael
Musicians

Cliff Barrows	vocals, backing vocals
Ralph Carmichael	arranger, conductor
Ralph Carmichael Orchestra	orchestra
Cliff Richard	vocals

Recording Details

Producer	Lee Gillette
Engineered by	Unknown
Recording location	Capitol Records, Hollywood, USA (orchestra) and Israel (vocals)
Recording date	Late 1969

♫ Over You

From the album **The Rock Connection**

Over You was one of the several tracks recorded for Cliff Richard's 1984 album ***The Rock Connection*** during a suite of sessions across June, July and August of that year. Written by Dave Cooke and Cliff Richard, the song appeared on the second side of the vinyl version of the album.

A pleasant sequence of chords created on the synthesiser keyboard ushers in Cliff's lead vocal line, which seamlessly builds up to the hook-laden chorus sublimating the song into one of Cliff's great compositions. He provides his own backing vocals to great effect during the chorus, too, and with the blend of these with the lead vocal, it makes the track something special and optimistic as per the title.

Track Specification

Composed by Dave Cooke and Cliff Richard

Musicians

John Clark	guitar
Dave Cooke	keyboards
Mark Griffiths	bass
Alan Park	keyboards
Cliff Richard	vocals, backing vocals
Stuart Tosh	drums, percussion

Recording Details

Producer	Cliff Richard and Keith Bessey
Engineered by	Keith Bessey
Recording location	Strawberry Studios South, Surrey
Recording date	30th July 1984-3rd August 1984

♫ Paella

From the film soundtrack album of **Finders Keepers**

Cliff Richard (playing himself in ***Finders Keepers***) has taken his new Spanish girlfriend Emilia (Vivianne Ventura) back to her grandmother's house on horseback. Dealing with a stroppy goat, Cliff is introduced to the old woman via interpreting the language and remarks on the paella that she is making, bringing a smile to the her face. Then he tells Emilia – in a slightly jarring script device given that she should know about her country's cultural heritage – about the origins of the word paella; that it was made for a beautiful girl and was derived from the contraction of *para ella* (for her). Using dolls to illustrate the lyrics, Emilia joins in the latter part of the song performing a kind of descant over Cliff's vocals. At the end, the grandmother indicates that she has run out of gas and, attempting to open up a new cylinder, Cliff sees that she is hammering the tip of the errant bomb that they have been looking for during the film. He instructs the grandmother boldly not to hit it using the rather crude and crass Englishman abroad lingo 'No basho!'

Paella is, of course, considered to be the national dish of Spain, certainly the coastal southern parts and comprises rice steeped in saffron and a collection of fish and shellfish (including octopus and squid in some parts of the country).

Recorded along with the Shadows' own performances for the film at the same session, both the film and soundtrack versions are the same with Cliff and Vivianne Ventura lip-synching along with the recorded lyrics. However, the descant vocal are uncredited on the album and it is unclear whether this is Ventura or a session vocalist. The final (unknown) soundtrack version take and edit were used or both mono and stereo recordings but with different mixes for the requirements of the separate audio channels.

A curious subject for a song, the Shadows use imagery from the legend to describe the differences in caste between the nobility and the countrymen. A medium-paced waltz, the melody is instantly memorable and Cliff does it justice with his excellent performance.

Track Specification

Composed by Hank Marvin, Bruce Welch, Brian Bennett and John Rostill

Musicians

Brian Bennett	drums, percussion
Hank Marvin	guitar
Cliff Richard	vocals
John Rostill	bass
Unknown	female vocal (possibly Vivianne Ventura)
Bruce Welch	rhythm guitar

Recording Details

Producer	Norrie Paramor
Engineered by	Unknown
Recording location	Abbey Road Studio 2, St. John's Wood, London
Recording date	30th April 1966

♫ Paradise Lost

From the EP **Love Is Forever**

With its title based on John Milton's epic poem written in 1667 about human sinfulness and banishment from Paradise as a consequence, the song *Paradise Lost* was recorded by Cliff Richard for his 1965 album ***Love Is Forever***, although it was recorded at the summer 1964 sessions in America and had to wait for fifteen months before it was finally released. The eleventh and final take and edit were used for the mono and stereo recordings but with different mixes for the requirements of the separate audio channels.

The lugubrious and thumping accompaniment on a broad brass sound and thudding bass make the performance of the song quite dark. The piano and rhythm guitar drive the song onwards but the instrumental break at the middle eight section is dramatic enough almost too operatic in its intensity.

Track Specification

Composed by Estelle Loring and Kaye Rodgers

Musicians

Jordanaires	backing vocals
Cliff Richard	vocals
Unknown	female backing vocals
Unknown	slide guitar
Unknown	guitar
Unknown	bass
Unknown	piano
Unknown	brass
Unknown	drums, percussion

Recording Details

Producer	Bob Morgan and Billy Sherrill
Engineered by	Mort Thomason
Recording location	Columbia Studios, Nashville
Recording date	25th August 1964

♬ Part of Me

Unissued tracks

Not much is known about the provenance of this song, *Part of Me,* although what is in record is that Cliff Richard did make two attempts to record it during two sessions for the ***Every Face Tells a Story*** album. The first was abandoned after the first take, while, four days later, it was stopped again after an unspecified number of takes, possibly because it was the last song and studio time had run out. The full band details are included here in both sessions since it is unclear who was involved.

Track Specification
Composed by Unknown

1. Unissued track (*Every Face Tells a Story*)

Musicians

Brian Bennett	drums, percussion
Terry Britten	guitar
Richard Hewson	arranger, conductor
John Perry	backing vocals
Cliff Richard	vocals
Frank Ricotti	percussion
Tony Rivers	backing vocals
Alan Tarney	bass
Graham Todd	keyboards
Unknown	orchestra

Recording Details

Producer	Bruce Welch
Engineered by	Tony Clark and John Barrett
Recording location	Abbey Road Studio 2, St. John's Wood, London
Recording date	6th September 1976

2. Unissued track (*Every Face Tells a Story*)

Musicians

Brian Bennett	drums, percussion
Terry Britten	guitar
Richard Hewson	arranger, conductor
John Perry	backing vocals
Cliff Richard	vocals
Frank Ricotti	percussion
Tony Rivers	backing vocals
Alan Tarney	bass
Graham Todd	keyboards
Unknown	orchestra

Recording Details

Producer	Bruce Welch
Engineered by	Tony Clark and Alan Rouse
Recording location	Abbey Road Studio 2, St. John's Wood, London
Recording date	10th September 1976

♬ Party Megamix

B-side of **All I Have to Do Is Dream/Miss You Nights**

The *Party Megamix* that appears on the second of the dual CD release of the double A-side ***All I Have to Do Is Dream*** and ***Miss You Nights*** required no new recording but instead was a new mix of certain sections of a selection of Cliff Richard's hits by Steve Moore. Initially created to promote the release of ***The Hit List*** – a compilation of Cliff's sons that had reached the top five over thirty-five years – it was subsequently released on the CD single, featuring the following tracks:

a) ***Do You Wanna Dance***
b) ***Congratulations***
c) ***Power to All Our Friends***
d) ***In the Country***
e) ***Move It***
f) ***On the Beach***
g) ***Gee Whizz It's You***
h) ***I Could Easily Fall (in Love with You)***

The choice across the track listing is good but it is probably a little optimistic to refer to the resultant mix as a *Party Megamix*. No new recording was reqired to develop the combined track.

♬ Peace and Quiet

From the pantomime cast recording album of **Cinderella** *and unissued track*

As with many of the songs on the pantomime cast recording album of ***Cinderella***, there were multiple attempts to complete the recordings. This is true of *Peace and Quiet,* the second song featuring Cliff from the album, which was first attempted early in November but abandoned after five takes. It was picked up again at the session a week later, where five takes were also recorded. The fifth and final take and edit were used for both the mono and stereo recordings but with different mixes required for the audio channel separation. Another version – see ***Peace and Quiet (Reprise)*** – was recorded three days later. The mono version appeared on the ***Cinderella*** EP.

Singing on one note rising through the scale, Cliff sings in the necessarily subdued way to match the title and lyrics. The rhythm is *andante* and the melody instantly memorable as was now expected from the Shadows, who wrote all the material for the show.

Track Specification
Composed by Hank Marvin, Bruce Welch, Brian Bennett and John Rostill

1. Unissued track (Cinderella)

Musicians		*Recording Details*	
Brian Bennett	drums, percussion	Producer	Norrie Paramor
Hank Marvin	guitar	Engineered by	Peter Vince and Richard Lush
Norrie Paramor Orchestra	orchestra	Recording location	Abbey Road Studio 2, St. John's Wood, London
Norrie Paramor	arranger, conductor, piano	Recording date	9th November 1966
Cliff Richard	vocals		
John Rostill	bass		
Bruce Welch	rhythm guitar		

2. Cinderella

Musicians		*Recording Details*	
Brian Bennett	drums, percussion	Producer	Norrie Paramor
Hank Marvin	guitar	Engineered by	Peter Vince and Richard Lush
Norrie Paramor Orchestra	orchestra	Recording location	Abbey Road Studio 3, St. John's Wood, London
Norrie Paramor	arranger, conductor	Recording date	16th November 1966
Cliff Richard	vocals		
John Rostill	bass		
Bruce Welch	rhythm guitar		

♫ Peace and Quiet (Reprise)

From the pantomime cast recording album of **Cinderella**

Sung very early on the ***Cinderella*** pantomime, ***Peace and Quiet*** was later reprised towards the end as Buttons (Cliff Richard) reminds himself of his thoughts from the beginning of the story. Recorded at the last session for the soundtrack album, *Peace and Quiet (Reprise)* was completed in an unknown number of takes.

The final take and edit were used for both the mono and stereo recordings but with different mixes required for the audio channel separation. The original song, featured near the start was successfully recorded three days earlier.

A slightly different arrangement of the song from the first half, this time it features the cleverly worked rhythm that is straight out of the end-of-the-musical, kick-the-feet-out rhythm and its strength lies not only in the memorable melody but in the expert handling of the close harmony vocals.

Track Specification
Composed by Hank Marvin, Bruce Welch, Brian Bennett and John Rostill

Musicians		*Recording Details*	
Brian Bennett	drums, percussion	Producer	Norrie Paramor
Hank Marvin	backing vocals, guitar	Engineered by	Peter Vince and Richard Lush
Cliff Richard	vocals	Recording location	Abbey Road Studio 2, St. John's Wood, London
John Rostill	backing vocals, bass	Recording date	19th November 1966
Bruce Welch	backing vocals, rhythm guitar		

♫ Peace in Our Time

118th UK single *(multiple formats), B-sides to* **Peace in Our Time** *and from the album* **Cliff Richard - The Album**

Originally written and recorded for for the 1988 Seoul Olympics official album by Jennifer Holliday, the American soul-singer and actress, *Peace in Our Time* includes some imagery and oblique references to the colours of the rings, the flame, the games and so on, but, more than that, it is a powerfully spiritual song that talks of knocking walls down but not to build prisons with the stone but heaven on earth instead. Also recorded by Eddie Money, *Peace in Our Time* was picked up by Cliff Richard as the opener to his first studio album of the nineties – ***Cliff Richard - The Album***.

Backed with non-album track, ***Somebody Loves You***, an edited version of the song, which cuts much of the introductory keyboards but adds more over the first verse while excising the vocal middle eight and adding a string accompaniment, was issued as the second of five singles from the project. Released on the EMI label (catalogue number EM 265) on 15th March 1993, it reached number eight in the UK singles charts; a good placing but not as high as Cliff had hoped, believing the song to be worthy of the number one spot. Many of Cliff's singles of the period were released in a two-step sequence for the CD format with different tracks included on each. The second of these CDs was issued on 22nd March (catalogue number CDEM 265) and featured the seven-inch mix as one of its bonus tracks. Other versions of the song were also released: an extended mix was released on the first of the dual CD single (catalogue number CDEMS 265) on 15th March 1993; a gospel mix, appearing on the second CD single, which removes much of the instrumentation and focuses on the vocals (this track was subsequently added as a bonus track on the remastered ***Small Corners*** album in 2007); and an instrumental version which featured on the second CD single disc, but featured no vocals at all and is a unique recording of the song – it has never been released in any other format.

Heavy on the percussion for the introduction, with clanking machinery noises emulating the building process of the wall of the prison, the other instruments are slowly built up along with Cliff's lead vocals. The dark nature of the verse is brightened as the optimistic and upbeat song enters the chorus. The rhythm is kept up relentlessly by the drums, bass and

guitar, while the backing vocals and sustained chords of the synthesisers create reflective harmonies. The ensemble piece ensures this is not only a great album opener but also one of the best tracks on its listing.
The promotional video features Cliff playing the part of a politician talking to an amassed crowd and protected by a phalanx of security guards. As he sings the song, the audience nods and then gets up to dance for the chorus.

Track Specification
Composed by Peter Sinfield and Andy Hill

1. Cliff Richard - The Album

Musicians

John Clark	guitar
Peter Howarth	backing vocals
London Community Gospel Choir	choir
Peter May	drums, percussion
Paul Moessl	arranger, drum programming, keyboards
Keith Murrell	backing vocals
Tessa Niles	backing vocals
Cliff Richard	vocals, backing vocals
Steve Stroud	bass
Judith Walmsley	backing vocals

Recording Details

Producer	Paul Moessl and Cliff Richard
Engineered by	Gerry Kitchingham and Ben Robbins
Recording location	R. G. Jones Studios, Wimbledon, London
Recording date	25th-31st May 1992 and 8th June 1992 (backing track)

2. Single (seven-inch)

Musicians

John Bradbury	violin
John Clark	guitar
Richard Hewson	arranger, conductor
Peter Howarth	backing vocals
London Community Gospel Choir	choir
Peter May	drums, percussion
Paul Moessl	arranger, drum programming, keyboards
Keith Murrell	backing vocals
Tessa Niles	backing vocals
Cliff Richard	vocals, backing vocals
Steve Stroud	bass
Unknown	orchestra (other strings)
Judith Walmsley	backing vocals
David Woodcock	violin

Recording Details

Producer	Paul Moessl and Cliff Richard
Engineered by	Gerry Kitchingham and Ben Robbins
Recording location	R. G. Jones Studios, Wimbledon, London
Recording date	25th-31st May 1992 and 8th June 1992 (backing track)

3. Single (CD)

Musicians

John Clark	guitar
Peter Howarth	backing vocals
London Community Gospel Choir	choir
Peter May	drums, percussion
Paul Moessl	arranger, drum programming, keyboards
Keith Murrell	backing vocals
Tessa Niles	backing vocals
Cliff Richard	vocals, backing vocals
Steve Stroud	bass
Judith Walmsley	backing vocals

Recording Details

Producer	Paul Moessl and Cliff Richard
Engineered by	Gerry Kitchingham and Ben Robbins
Recording location	R. G. Jones Studios, Wimbledon, London
Recording date	25th-31st May 1992 and 8th June 1992 (backing track)

4. B-side (gospel mix - Peace in Our Time)

Musicians

Peter Howarth	backing vocals
London Community Gospel Choir	choir
Peter May	percussion
Paul Moessl	arranger, keyboards
Keith Murrell	backing vocals
Tessa Niles	backing vocals
Cliff Richard	vocals, backing vocals
Steve Stroud	bass
Judith Walmsley	backing vocals

Recording Details

Producer	Paul Moessl and Cliff Richard
Engineered by	Gerry Kitchingham and Ben Robbins
Recording location	R. G. Jones Studios, Wimbledon, London
Recording date	25th-31st May 1992 and 8th June 1992 (backing track)

5. B-side (instrumental version - Peace in Our Time)

Musicians

John Clark	guitar
Peter May	drums, percussion
Paul Moessl	arranger, drum programming, keyboards
Steve Stroud	bass

Recording Details

Producer	Paul Moessl and Cliff Richard
Engineered by	Gerry Kitchingham and Ben Robbins
Recording location	R. G. Jones Studios, Wimbledon, London
Recording date	25th-31st May 1992 and 8th June 1992 (backing track)

♫ Pentecost

Unissued track

Recorded at the session that resulted in three German language songs, *Pentecost* was probably destined for the ***His Land*** film and album project but rejected for some unknown reason. The session took place at the London-based Chappell Studios rather than the usual Abbey Road Studio 2, possibly due to the refurbishment of the studio complex. Unfortunately, there is little information available on either the composer or the track itself; therefore, the basic detail from the session is applied and will be updated should further research unearth relevant information.

Track Specification

Composed by Unknown

Musicians

Mike Vickers Orchestra	orchestra
Cliff Richard	vocals
Mike Vickers	arranger, conductor

Recording Details

Producer	Norrie Paramor
Engineered by	Unknown
Recording location	Chappell Studios, London
Recording date	21st January 1970

♫ Perfidia

From the albums **Cliff Richard** *and* **When in Spain**

The word 'perfidia' is the Spanish for unfaithfulness, treachery or deceit and, in *Perfidia*, refers to a disloyal lover cheating on the singer. Originally published in 1939, it was first a hit for Spanish artist Xavier Cugat the following year. In addition to the dance scene between Ingrid Bergman and Humphrey Bogart in *Casablanca*, it has become a standard and has been covered by a variety of artists including Mel Tormé, Dave Brubeck, Benny Goodman, Ben E. King, the Ventures, Nana Mouskouri, Glenn Miller, Charlie Parker, Tito Puente and Edmundo Ross among many others.

Cliff Richard and the Shadows have recorded three different versions of *Perfidia*: an English language version (for ***Cliff Richard***), a Spanish language version (for ***When in Spain***) and an instrumental version (Shadows only). The English version was recorded as the only track in the session, with the fourth and final take and edit used for the mono and stereo recordings but with different mixes for the audio channels. There is some doubt as to when the backing vocals by the Bruce Welch and Cliff Richard were dubbed for *When in Spain*: the album ***On the Continent*** states that they were applied on 28th May 1963, although the Shadows were enjoying their lengthy Blackpool concert season and it may be that it was 28th April. However, no further detail is available and, until such is found, this entry maintains the stated date.

The racing rhythm guitar and simple melody in the lead guitar are very similar to the Shadows' instrumental version. The backing vocals are in the right channel only and seem to confirm that they might have been overdubbed afterwards. Cliff's vocal line is very easy and assured and the ensemble result of the song is a brilliant testament to their musicianship. The Spanish version is unsurprisingly similar, but with Cliff's vocals in the left channel, the instrumentation in the right and the occasional backing vocals taking centre for some reason, making it a disjointed listening experience in stereo.

Track Specification

1. Cliff Richard (English version)

Composed by Alberto Dominguez; English lyrics by Milton Leeds

Musicians

Brian Bennett	drums, percussion
Brian 'Licorice' Locking	bass
Hank Marvin	backing vocals, guitar
Cliff Richard	vocals
Bruce Welch	backing vocals, rhythm guitar

Recording Details

Producer	Norrie Paramor
Engineered by	Malcolm Addey
Recording location	Abbey Road Studio 2, St. John's Wood, London
Recording date	21st December 1962

2. When in Spain (Spanish version)

Composed by Alberto Dominguez

Musicians

Brian Bennett	drums, percussion
Brian 'Licorice' Locking	bass
Hank Marvin	guitar
Cliff Richard	vocals, backing vocals
Bruce Welch	backing vocals, rhythm guitar

Recording Details

Producer	Norrie Paramor
Engineered by	Malcolm Addey
Recording location	EMI Studios, Barcelona
Recording date	28th April 1963 (main recording) and 28th May 1963 (backing vocals)

♫ Perhaps, Perhaps, Perhaps

From the EP **Cliff's Palladium Successes**

Written in 1947 under the Spanish title of ***Quizás, Quizás, Quizás*** (precisely *Perhaps, Perhaps, Perhaps*), American Joe Davis translated the lyrics and it is this which has become more popular after Doris Day's 1964 version and Nat King Cole's 1958 cover. Other artists to have covered the song include Samantha Fox, Emma Bunton, Geri Halliwell and the Pussycat Dolls. In early 1964, although there are no specific records, Cliff Richard recorded the English lyrics over the backing recorded in 1963 for *Quizás, Quizás, Quizás* from ***When in Spain*** and *Perhaps, Perhaps, Perhaps* was issued on the ***Cliff's Palladium Successes*** EP in mono only. The English version of the song was later issued on the track listing of the French *All My Love* CD and the celebratory ***...And They Said It Wouldn't Last! (My 50 Years in Music)*** – both using the mono version.

The song's performance sounds better in some respects in the Spanish language but that is to denigrate Cliff's recording against the same backing track provided by the Shadows. There appear to be minor differences in the instrumentation and Cliff's vocal has an echo placed over it which is not matched by the backing track, which creates an odd sensation when listening to it.

Track Specification
Composed by Osvaldo Farrés; English lyrics by Joe Davis

Musicians

Brian Bennett	drums, percussion
Brian 'Licorice' Locking	bass
Hank Marvin	guitar
Cliff Richard	vocals
Bruce Welch	rhythm guitar

Recording Details

Producer	Norrie Paramor
Engineered by	Malcolm Addey
Recording location	EMI Studios, Barcelona (backing track) and Unknown (lead vocals)
Recording date	29th April 1963 (backing track) and early 1964 (lead vocals)

♫ Per un Bacio d'Amor

From the album **When in Rome**

Better known by its English equivalent, *Tell Me You're Mine,* and covered in this translation by Vic Damone, Connie Francis and Mindy Carson, *Per un Bacio d'Amor* actually translates more closely to *For a Kiss of Love*. The Italian song was recorded by Cliff Richard in the marathon two-day session in May 1965 at the Lisbon studios and his vocals were overdubbed on a prepared orchestral track recorded seven months earlier. Unusually, *Per un Bacio d'Amor* is one of a very few foreign language songs that Cliff recorded without trying the English language equivalent. The unknown takes and edits of the orchestral and vocal tracks were mixed for release in mono format only.

With a tinkling piano and sustained organ chords played over a waltz rhythm on a brushed drum, Cliff's vocals generate a beautiful little tune. The organ and strings are used in the instrumental break and it is possible to imagine an impromptu dance sequence breaking out in the studio. Not the best song on the album but it is certainly a suitable track to complete it.

Track Specification
Composed by Nino Ravasini and Bertini

Musicians

Norrie Paramor Orchestra	orchestra
Norrie Paramor	arranger, conductor
Cliff Richard	vocals

Recording Details

Producer	John Lee and M. DiPonti (backing track) and Norrie Paramor (vocals)
Engineered by	Malcolm Addey
Recording location	EMI Studios, Milan (backing track) and Estudios Valentim, De Carvalho, Lisbon (vocals)
Recording date	2nd-3rd October 1964 (backing track) and 13th-14th May 1965 (vocals)

♫ Physical Pain

From the album **Did He Jump... Or Was He Pushed?** *(Garth Hewitt)*

As with all the tracks on the ***Did He Jump... Or Was He Pushed?*** album, *Physical Pain* was written by the album's protagonist Garth Hewitt and produced by Cliff Rchard, who also supplied harmony vocals.

The gentle song is full of anguish in this love song with Hewitt performing the lead vocals with a slight vibrato that adds much to the emotion of the lyrics. The beauty of the song is derived from the arrangement of Cliff's multi-layered backing vocals, which are present almost continuously throughout the sung sections.

Track Specification
Composed by Garth Hewitt

Musicians

Garth Hewitt	vocals, guitar
Graham Jarvis	drums, percussion
Mike Moran	guitar, keyboards
Jo Partridge	guitar
Cliff Richard	backing vocals, guitar
Dave Wintour	bass

Recording Details

Producer	Cliff Richard
Engineered by	Tony Clark and Haydn Bendall
Recording location	Odyssey Studios, London
Recording date	1979

♫ Pigeon

B-side of **Flying Machine**

The team of Guy Fletcher and Doug Flett had provided a number of songs for Cliff Richard to record and they continued that pattern with the song *Pigeon,* which was recorded at the first session of 1971, alongside another B-side ***Annabella Umbrella***. The first song to be finished at the session, *Pigeon* was chosen as the B-side of Cliff's fifty-fourth UK single, ***Flying Machine,*** with both tracks being issued in mono only in most markets, although a stereo version was simultaneously released in Holland. The song was a rarity until an edited stereo version that fades out earlier than the B-side track by a few seconds was issued in the rare B-sides section of the celebratory anthology ***...And They Said It Wouldn't Last! (My 50 Years in Music)*** in 2008.

Perhaps a curious subject for a song, *Pigeon* is introduced by a brass arrangement typical of the period, while the chorus is redolent of the oom-pah style of German folk music, which is perhaps why it lent itself so well to the Teutonic treatment when Cliff re-recorded it under the title ***Kleine Taube***. There is much to commend the song, though, with successive key changes adding interest to the song.

Track Specification
Composed by Guy Fletcher and Doug Flett

Musicians	
Nick Ingman	arranger, conductor
Nick Ingman Orchestra	orchestra
Cliff Richard	vocals
Unknown	backing vocals

Recording Details	
Producer	Norrie Paramor
Engineered by	Unknown
Recording location	Chappell Studios, London
Recording date	12th February 1971

♫ Please Don't Fall in Love
90th UK single

In most people's minds, Mike Batt is probably most associated with the Wombles in the mid-seventies and latterly acting as the mentor for his protégée Katie Melua. However, Batt is a fine musician, songwriter and arranger, having written *Bright Eyes* for Art Garfunkel, arranged and conducted an album of orchestrated songs for Justin Hayward (with whom Cliff Richard would later record the charity single ***Everybody's Got a Crisis in Their Lives***) and the stage musical version of Lewis Carroll's *The Hunting of the Snark* (the part of the Bellman being played by Cliff on the soundtrack recording).
Writing *Please Don't Fall in Love* for Cliff, Mike Batt also performed on the recording and produced at a session that also completed the B-side, ***Too Close to Heaven***, and an as yet unissued track ***How to Handle a Woman***. At the session, ever the perfectionist, Batt reportedly put Cliff through his paces working hard to ensure the enunciation was precisely right.
Please Don't Fall in Love was released as a single on the EMI label (catalogue number EMI 5437) on 7th November 1983, reaching number seven in the British singles charts. The song was included on the ***Silver*** track listing, while its B-side was left off, the album and its songs being the first Cliff release to be issued simultaneously on CD. In the promotional video, Cliff is seen talking with a girl on a balcony overlooking a river, cutting to him being alone in his bedroom, and back to memories of what they used to do together, and then to her reading books and taking walks with her new man.
The gentleness and beauty of the song is initiated by the Batt's piano introduction as they are then joined by the orchestra. Cliff sings his backing vocals accompanied by Batt and their voices blend well together. Cliff's lead vocal has an effective vibrato that matches the emotion of the lyrics, which talk of someone not wanting his lover to get together with anyone else. One of the features of Batt's arrangements of sad songs is the use of oboes and he effectively deploys one here.

Track Specification
Composed by Mike Batt

Musicians	
Mike Batt	arranger, conductor, backing vocals, piano
Tony Carr	percussion
Ray Cooper	percussion
Graham Jarvis	drums, percussion
Frank McDonald	bass
Alan Park	guitar
Cliff Richard	vocals, backing vocals
Ray Russell	guitar
Unknown:	orchestra
Clive Anstee	'cello
Howard Ball	violin
Michael Brittain	double bass
Michael Cookson	viola
Paul Frowde	violin
Barry Griffiths	violin
Pat Halling	violin
Maurice Isaacs	violin
Raymond Keenlyside	violin
Paul Kegg	'cello
Tom Kelly	clarinet
Laurie Lewis	violin
Geoff Palmer	violin
Anthony Pleeth	'cello
David Randall	violin
Ian Rhodes	violin
Eddie Roberts	violin
John Ronayne	violin
Basil Smart	violin
Jonathan Snowdon	flute
Derek Solomans	violin
Michael Winfield	oboe

Recording Details	
Producer	Mike Batt
Engineered by	Steve Churchyard (main track) and Dick Lewsey (strings)
Recording location	AIR Studio 2, London (main track) and C.T.S. Wembley (strings)
Recording date	21st-23rd March 1983 (main track) and 21st March (strings)

♫ Please Don't Tease

9th UK single, from the albums **Thank You Very Much** *and* **Reunited** *and B-side of* **Please Remember Me** *and unissued live track*

Around two hundred fan club members were exclusively invited to the Abbey Road Studios with the purpose of choosing the song that would be the ninth single for Cliff Richard and the Shadows: this had echoes of the invited audience for Cliff's first album and both exercises had a clear commercial directive beneath it. However, by engaging the fans it would also allow the eventual release to have some critical and commercial impetus in the record shops and on the radio.

From that session with the fans, the clear favourites from the twelve recordings on offer were *Please Don't Tease*, ***Nine Times out of Ten*** and ***Gee Whiz It's You***. But, in particular, there was overwhelming support for the song by Bruce Welch and erstwhile bandmate Pete Chester and thus *Please Don't Tease* was chose as the ninth single. Backed with ***Where Is My Heart?*** from a later session in March 1960, the single was issued on the Columbia label (catalogue number 45-DB 4479) on 24th June 1960 and reached number one in the UK singles charts staying for one week at the end of July, before being knocked off by ***Shakin' All Over*** by Johnny Kidd and the Pirates. What was extraordinary about *Please Don't Tease* was that it was the first record since Guy Mitchell's version of ***Singing the Blues*** in early 1957 to return to the number one spot, where it stayed for a further two weeks only to be knocked off again but this time by The Shadows' ***Apache*** (which was in the top position for five weeks and was the group's first commercial success in chart terms). The song has become a regular concert favourite and also featured on the set list of the Shadows' own Final Tour in 2004.

Consolidating the sound that was crystallizing with the previous single, ***Fall in Love with You***, Cliff and the Shadows would continue recording songs with that trademark guitar mix and wonderful vocal harmonies – Cliff's, Hank Marvin's and Bruce's blend so very well together and the result is always highly distinctive, although these are not employed on this single. The recording uses a slight reverberation echo on Cliff's vocal line, while Jet Harris's bass line and Bruce's rhythm guitar are brought forward in the mix. Hank is given a chance to show off his skill with a guitar solo in the middle eight and, in the background, Tony Meehan's steady drumming assists in keeping the rhythm. As the title suggests, it is a song about a girl who leads him on and his imprecations to her that she should stop teasing him by running hot and cold.

For the performance of *Please Don't Tease* at the ***Thank You Very Much*** concert in 1978 to celebrate twenty years in the music business, the Shadows were replaced by Cliff's own backing band, giving them a rest after the first part, which included backing Cliff as well as running through a number of their own hits. Given a beat and arrangement that is highly reminiscent of the then recently released ***My Kinda Life***, this version is as refreshing take on what had become very familiar. To follow the Shadows with a song that is from their era is a risky option but it is achieved successfully.

During the ***Green Light*** album sessions, a new version was recorded under Bruce Welch's direction. Completed in five takes with some overdubs added at the session four weeks later, this version of *Please Don't Tease* was chosen as the B-side of the first of three singles to be released from the album, ***Please Remember Me***. Because the song failed in sales and chart terms, the B-side was a major rarity until it was added as a bonus track to the remastered and reissued *Green Light* album in 2002. The recording is essentially a studio version of the arrangement performed during the London Palladium concert but obviously with the benefit of the crispness of the studio.

In spite of the restoration of all other previously unreleased tracks to the 2005 remaster of ***From a Distance ***** The Event***, *Please Don't Tease* was one of six Cliff and the Shadows performances to remain unissued with no information given as to why the decision was taken.

Given the support for the song back in 1960, it was unsurprising that it would be re-recorded by the reformed Cliff and the Shadows for their 2009 album, ***Reunited***, and performed at concerts promoting the release. Faithful to the original, the performance is tighter but still the years roll away when listening to it.

Track Specification

Composed by Bruce Welch and Pete Chester

1. Single

Musicians

Jet Harris	bass
Hank Marvin	guitar
Tony Meehan	drums, percussion
Cliff Richard	vocals
Bruce Welch	rhythm guitar

Recording Details

Producer	Norrie Paramor
Engineered by	Malcolm Addey
Recording location	Abbey Road Studio 2, St. John's Wood, London
Recording date	25th March 1960

2. Thank You Very Much

Musicians

Terry Britten	guitar
Stuart Calver	backing vocals
Clem Cattini	drums, percussion
Dave Christopher	guitar
Mo Foster	bass
Graham Jarvis	drums, percussion
Graham Murray	guitar
John Perry	backing vocals
Cliff Richard	vocals
Tony Rivers	backing vocals
Graham Todd	keyboards

Recording Details

Producer	Bruce Welch
Engineered by	Tony Clark, remixed by Peter Vince
Recording location	London Palladium, London
Remix location	Abbey Road Studios, St. John's Wood, London
Recording date	4th March 1978

3. B-side (Please Remember Me)

Musicians

Brian Bennett	drums, percussion
Terry Britten	guitar
Stuart Calver	backing vocals
Alan Jones	bass
Duncan MacKay	keyboards
Alan Parker	guitar
John Perry	backing vocals
Tim Renwick	guitar
Cliff Richard	vocals, backing vocals
Tony Rivers	backing vocals
Trevor Spencer	drums, percussion
Alan Tarney	backing vocals, guitar, bass, keyboards
Graham Todd	keyboards

Recording Details

Producer	Bruce Welch
Engineered by	Tony Clark and Haydn Bendall
Recording location	Abbey Road Studio 3, St. John's Wood, London
Recording date	14th January 1978 and 10th February 1978

4. Unissued track (From a Distance *** The Event)**

Musicians

Ray Beavis	saxophone
Brian Bennett	drums, percussion
Mark Griffiths	bass
Cliff Hall	keyboards
Hank Marvin	backing vocals, guitar
Cliff Richard	vocals
Bruce Welch	backing vocals, rhythm guitar

Recording Details

Producer	Cliff Richard
Engineered by	Keith Bessey and Mick McKenna
Recording location	Rolling Stones Mobile Studio, Wembley Stadium, Wembley, North-west London
Recording date	16th-17th June 1989

5. Reunited

Musicians

Brian Bennett	drums, percussion
Mark Griffiths	bass
Hank Marvin	backing vocals, guitar
Cliff Richard	vocals, backing vocals
Bruce Welch	backing vocals, rhythm guitar

Recording Details

Producer	Warren Bennett (co-ordination)
Engineered by	James Collins (Honeyhill Studios), Ethan Carlson (Middle Ear Studios), Les Williams (Nivram Studios) and Keith Bessey (mixing and mastering)
Recording location	Middle Ear Studios, Miami, Florida, USA (Cliff's vocals), Nivram Studios, Perth, Western Australia (Hank's guitars and vocals) and Honeyhill Studios, Hertfordshire, England (all other vocals and instruments)
Recording date	Early 2009

♫ Please Remember Me

72nd UK single

Recorded in 1977 by one of its writers, American Dave Loggins, *Please Remember Me* was the lead single to be released from Cliff Richard's ***Green Light*** album project. Recorded in two takes at the second session for the album, a number of overdubs were added at a later session.

Please Remember Me was released as Cliff's seventy-second UK single, backed with ***Please Don't Tease*** (a completely new recording of Cliff's original hit), on the EMI label (catalogue number EMI 2832) on 28th June 1978. It was the second of three successive songs that failed to chart for Cliff and the fifth of his career to date.

Featuring on the ***Green Light*** album, it has a guitar-led accompaniment that picks up the pace after the introduction is completed. The strength of the song is undeniable from its beat and the arrangement of the instruments. But it is the backing vocals that improve the performance further.

Track Specification

Composed by Dave Loggins and Bruce Woodley

Musicians

Brian Bennett	drums, percussion
Terry Britten	guitar
Stuart Calver	backing vocals
Alan Jones	bass
Duncan MacKay	keyboards
Alan Parker	guitar
John Perry	backing vocals
Tim Renwick	guitar
Cliff Richard	vocals, backing vocals
Tony Rivers	backing vocals
Trevor Spencer	drums, percussion
Alan Tarney	backing vocals, guitar, bass, keyboards
Graham Todd	keyboards

Recording Details

Producer	Bruce Welch
Engineered by	Tony Clark and Haydn Bendall
Recording location	Abbey Road Studio 3, St. John's Wood, London
Recording date	10th January 1978 and 7th February 1978

♫ Pointed Toe Shoes

From the album **Cliff Sings**

The second track on the second side of ***Cliff Sings*** is also the second of the final batch of tunes on the album to feature The Drifters in accompaniment. The band was still named as such during the recording sessions but had changed to The Shadows prior to its release to avoid confusion with the pre-existing American group during the promotional US tour for ***Living Doll***. Another Carl Perkins song, recorded by the man himself but not a hit, it was also recorded by Alan Hager. Appearing on the ***Cliff Sings No. 2*** EP, the same take was used but with different mixes for the stereo. With the album released in mono only, it is this version that was pressed for the mono EP. The tinkling percussive cymbals and the archetypal guitar introduction back up another fine rock and roll recording from Cliff Richard. Hank Marvin's guitar solo in the middle eight backed by the rest of the band is pure Shadows and already shows what their instrumental career was going to entail. The song is, as was the practice of the day, quite short coming in at just under two and a half minutes.

Track Specification

Composed by Carl Perkins

Musicians		*Recording Details*	
Jet Harris	bass	Producer	Norrie Paramor
Hank Marvin	guitar	Engineered by	Malcolm Addey and Alan Kane (mono) and Stuart Eltham and Norman Smith (stereo)
Tony Meehan	drums, percussion		
Cliff Richard	vocals	Recording location	Abbey Road Studio 2, St. John's Wood, London
Bruce Welch	rhythm guitar	Recording date	7th September 1959

♫ Poor Boy

From the albums **21 Today** *and* **...And They Said It Wouldn't Last! (My 50 Years in Music)**

The final track on the first side of Cliff Richard's birthday album, ***21 Today***, was the first to be recorded in the session. Several takes were recorded, with a later one being used for both mono and stereo edits, but different mixes for the audio channels. The track was issued on the ***Cliff Richard No. 2*** EP and, for the ***...And They Said It Wouldn't Last! (My 50 Years in Music)*** album, a different take (the thirteenth) was released, but only in mono. There is studio talk at the start of the track and, while the same arrangement as that on the original album, the performance has a number of subtle differences. A showcase here for Bruce Welch's expert rhythm guitar work, the song requires Cliff to work at the middle and top of his register. The rhythm and arrangement sounds similar to *Geronimo* or *Guitar Tango*. Cliff sings occasionally with a jerky vocal tic emulating Buddy Holly and this adds an interesting dimension to the tune.

Track Specification

Composed by Jim McEntire

1. 21 Today

Musicians		*Recording Details*	
Jet Harris	bass	Producer	Norrie Paramor
Hank Marvin	guitar	Engineered by	Malcolm Addey and Norman Smith
Tony Meehan	drums, percussion	Recording location	Abbey Road Studio 2, St. John's Wood, London
Cliff Richard	vocals	Recording date	19th April 1961
Bruce Welch	rhythm guitar		

2. ...And They Said It Wouldn't Last! (My 50 Years in Music)

Musicians		*Recording Details*	
Jet Harris	bass	Producer	Norrie Paramor
Hank Marvin	guitar	Engineered by	Malcolm Addey and Norman Smith
Tony Meehan	drums, percussion	Recording location	Abbey Road Studio 2, St. John's Wood, London
Cliff Richard	vocals	Recording date	19th April 1961
Bruce Welch	rhythm guitar		

♫ Postmark Heaven

From the album **...And They Said It Wouldn't Last! (My 50 Years in Music)**

In 1969, several tracks that would have fitted easily on to the various albums of the period were recorded but not issued. One was *Postmark Heaven*, with unknown writing credits, which remained in the EMI vaults for thirty-nine years, when it was added to the lost and found section of ***...And They Said It Wouldn't Last! (My 50 Years in Music)*** in 2008.
A Latin rhythm is created in the percussion, piano and strings, which is picked up in the vocal line, which Cliff sings with his usual purity and, from the overall ebullience of the track, he is clearly enjoying the experience.

Track Specification

Composed by Unknown

Musicians		*Recording Details*	
Mike Vickers Orchestra	orchestra	Producer	Norrie Paramor
Cliff Richard	vocals	Engineered by	Peter Vince
Mike Vickers	arranger, conductor	Recording location	Abbey Road Studio 2, St. John's Wood, London
		Recording date	22nd September 1969

♫ Poverty

From the pantomime cast recording album **Cinderella**

As the name of the song suggests, *Poverty* underlines the discrepancy of riches between Cinderella, who is forced to drudge for her stepmother and -sisters, and those relatives and the circles they aspire to move in. It comes in the pantomime stage show of ***Cinderella*** (written by the highly prolific Shadows) that was staged at the London Palladium over Christmas 1966 and into the new year. It is at this point that it is observed that Cinderella really has nothing to call her own in this rags to riches story.
Recorded at a session set aside for completing tracks for the soundtrack album, takes nine and ten were spliced together and used or both the mono and stereo recordings but with different mixes for the requirements of the split audio channels. Introduced by the money men (the Mike Sammes Singers), the quirky accompaniment and lyrical cleverness are very reminiscent of a Gilbert and Sullivan operetta.

Track Specification

Composed by Hank Marvin, Bruce Welch, Brian Bennett and John Rostill

Musicians

Brian Bennett	drums, percussion
Hank Marvin	guitar
Mike Sammes Singers	vocals, backing vocals
Norrie Paramor Orchestra	orchestra
Norrie Paramor	arranger, conductor
Cliff Richard	vocals
John Rostill	bass
Bruce Welch	rhythm guitar

Recording Details

Producer	Norrie Paramor
Engineered by	Peter Vince and Richard Lush
Recording location	Abbey Road Studio 2, St. John's Wood, London
Recording date	9th November 1966

♫ Power to All Our Friends

59th UK single *and from the album* **Japan Tour '74**

Having narrowly missed out on winning Eurovision Song Contest title in 1968 with ***Congratulations***, which came second, Cliff Richard was invited to represent the United Kingdom once more in 1973. As with the previous contests, a short list of six songs was sung over a succession of weeks on a Saturday night television variety show – in 1973, Cliff sang each song on *Cilla*, hosted Cilla Black – and it was left to the public to choose by a postal vote. *Congratulations* had polled around three-quarters of the votes and was the clear winner; for *Power to All Our Friends*, while the percentage lead was not so great, it was nevertheless a clear winner. Polling 51.8% of the votes, with its closest rival ***Come Back Billie Jo*** achieving just 14.1%, it was obvious which song would be taken into the contest.
The critics, naturally, hated it in general suggesting the cod radical message wrapped up in a typically Eurovision style song was too much to bear without cringing. While it certainly wasn't the strongest of songs in Cliff's career, it has much to commend it nevertheless. It is triumphantly forthright, and memorable with its key changes, *a capella* sections and foot-stomping rhythmic beats. And it caused controversy, too, although only in the grammatical difference between the girl 'laying' or 'lying' down in Monte Carlo – a common mistake but one that embarrassed the BBC's Billy Cotton enough to request the correct word be used for the live final. Cliff reverted to 'lying' to avoid any potential sexual connotation.
Cliff performed the song on the night as the sixteenth competitor of seventeen on 7th April 1973 (almost exactly five years to the day since his first Eurovision performance) at the Nouveau Théâtre in Luxembourg, and progressively the participating countries' voting panels edged his song further up the ranks, where it finished at number three behind the host country winning with the forgettable *Tu Te Reconnaîtras*. Cliff later complained that he didn't like the winning song, that *Power to All Our Friends* should have won and that his outburst wasn't sour grapes.
However, he was the ultimate winner, since it was his song that sold over a million not only in Europe but elsewhere in the world, such was his popularity as a performer. The song was released as a single, backed with *Come Back Billie Jo*, on the EMI label (catalogue number EMI 2012) on 9th March 1973 and reached its highest position of four in the UK charts on the first week of entry. It was Cliff's first single on the EMI label after the amalgamation of a number of subsidiary labels including his former label Columbia. *Power to All Our Friends*, with a kind of beautiful symmetry, was Cliff's best-performing record in sales terms since *Congratulations* five years earlier and his highest chart placing since ***Goodbye Sam, Hello Samantha*** almost three years previously. Naturally, the song has appeared on any number of compilations of Cliff's hits but it does appear to mark the high tide of poor charting material that critics observed he was now recording, even though this denigrates the number of gems that were released over the period.
From the dramatic *a capella* introduction to the gentle verses and on to the powerful choruses, it is quite clear how *Power to All Our Friends* was the primary choice of the voting British public. It has all the key Eurovision points, such as the light and shade, the thumping bass drum, the raspberry brass, the changes of pace and the slowed climax. Cliff sings songs like these with consummate ease.
Shortly after the song was chosen to represent the UK, Cliff was back in the recording studio at the end of March 1973 to record hastily translated versions of the song for the European market. Curiously, it wasn't recorded in Italian and it was left to Germany (***Gut, Daß Es Freunde Gibt***), France (***Il Faut Chanter la Vie***) and Spain (***Todo el Poder a los Amigos***) to receive a unique version backed in every case with *Come Back Billie Jo*, which was not translated. In each case, the singles were released in the respective countries immediately after the contest was completed.

The Japanese tour in 1974 included *Power to All Our Friends* but it was edited for the CD reissue – presumably for space limitation reasons – where it is faded out almost half a minute earlier than the Japanese vinyl version, removing a lot of the instrumental end of the song. The song is faithfully reproduced here with the *a capella* vocal introduction but its thumping introduction ruins the mood of the foreshortened ***Visions*** which precedes it. Nevertheless, that denigrates a superlative performance of the song that closes the ***Japan Tour '74*** album perfectly.

Track Specification
Composed by Guy Fletcher and Doug Flett

1. Single

Musicians		*Recording Details*	
Terry Britten	backing vocals, guitar	Producer	David MacKay
David MacKay Orchestra	orchestra	Engineered by	Peter Vince
David MacKay	backing vocals, arranger, conductor	Recording location	Abbey Road Studio, St. John's Wood, London
Kevin Peek	guitar	Recording date	28th December 1972
Cliff Richard	vocals		
Trevor Spencer	backing vocals, drums, percussion		
Alan Tarney	backing vocals, bass		

2. Japan Tour '74

Musicians		*Recording Details*	
Barrie Guard	arranger, conductor	Producer	Toshiba EMI (no individual detailed)
Cliff Hall	piano	Engineered by	Toshiba EMI (no individual detailed)
Brian Lewis	backing vocals, guitar	Recording location	Shinjuku Koseinenkin, Tokyo, Japan
Kevin Peak	acoustic guitar	Recording date	7th-8th October 1974
Cliff Richard	vocals		
Shambles Symphonet	orchestra		
Trevor Spencer	drums, percussion		
Alan Tarney	backing vocals, bass		
Bruce Welch	backing vocals, rhythm guitar		

♬ Praise My Soul, the King of Heaven
Unissued track

Another favourite hymn for church congregations in the traditional style, *Praise My Soul, the King of Heaven* has been recorded by acts such as Linda Gentille, the Amen Singers, the Grimethorpe Colliery Band and Lauren Waterworth among others. Cliff Richard also tried recording it for inclusion on his ***Good News*** album but, after three takes, no further work was done and what has been recorded remains unissued.

Track Specification
Composed by Henry Francis Lyte and Benjamin John Goss

Musicians		*Recording Details*	
Norrie Paramor Orchestra	orchestra	Producer	Norrie Paramor
Mike Leander	arranger, conductor	Engineered by	Peter Vince and Mike Stone
Cliff Richard	vocals	Recording location	Abbey Road Studio 2, St. John's Wood, London
		Recording date	4th May 1967

♬ Prayer, The (for the New Year)
American title for **The Millennium Prayer**

When ***The Millennium Prayer*** was released in the US (a year after most other countries), it was retitled – perhaps for obvious reasons – to *The Prayer (for the New Year)*. Backed with an instrumental version of the original, featuring Cliff on backing vocals, and ***Two Worlds***, the single was released on the Sparrow Records label (catalogue number SPD 1811) on 21st November 2000. Pedantry dictates that the Americans got the millennium correct, which started on 1st January 2001.

♬ Prijatelju
From the album **Podarjeno Srcu** *(Aleksander Mežek)*

Cliff Richard has had a long association with Aleksander Mežek going back to his vocal contribution on the title track of the *Days Go By* album in 1974. At that time, Mežek was recording under the name Aleksander John (then using his middle name as a surname for better pronunciation in the English-speaking world). In 1989, Mežek released his *Podarjeno Srcu* album in his native tongue and featured Cliff on two tracks. The first of these (the other being ***Vodna Pot***) was *Prijatelju* (literally *Friend* in Slovenian). The album, which was issued in what was then Yugoslavia, is now a major rarity and, for this reason, the author has been unable to listen to the track to confirm the instrumentation used. Therefore, the track specification incorporates all of the artists known to have been involved in recording the album and will be updated once further information has been made available.
In 1990, however, Cliff returned to the studio with Mežek to record an English duet version of the track, which was closely retitled ***To a Friend***.

Track Specification
Composed by Aleksander Mežek and Eugenija Dumbatze

Musicians	
Ian Bairnson	guitar
Paul Buckmaster	arranger, conductor
Richard Cottle	clarinet, keyboards
Jonathan Du Bose	electric guitar
London Symphony Orchestra	orchestra
Komorni Zbor RTV Ljubljana	choir
Aleksander Mežek	vocals
Davy Paton	bass
Cliff Richard	backing vocals
Jeremy Stacy	drums, percussion
Rick Wakeman	keyboards
Saša Zalepugin	acoustic guitar

Recording Details	
Producer	Aleksander Mežek and Rick Wakeman
Engineered by	Chris Sheldon, John Burns, John Kurlander and/or Russel Bracher
Recording location	Studio House, London, Studio 26 RTV Ljubljana, Yugoslavia, Abbey Road Studio 1, St. John's Wood, London and/or Master Control Studio, Burbank, Los Angeles, California, USA
Recording date	1988 or 1989

♬ Private Life

From the album **Drifting** *(Sheila Walsh)*

Graham Kendrick was responsible for a number of faith-related songs for Cliff Richard to record either in his solo career or in helping with others' projects. So it was with *Private Life*, which Cliff commissioned for his protégée Sheila Walsh's first album, ***Drifting*** (or *War of Love* in the US). The song was chosen as the B-side of ***Growing Up to Be a Child*** in 1983, which was taken from the successor album, ***Triumph in the Air***.
The racing rhythm sets off at a pace, while Walsh's vocal starts electronically enhanced and echoing on the final word of each couplet. Cliff's backing vocals are whispered conspiratorially matching the meaning of the song's title.

Track Specification
Composed by Graham Kendrick

Musicians	
John Clark	electric guitar
Craig Pruess	arranger, synthesiser, percussion
Cliff Richard	backing vocals
Sheila Walsh	vocals

Recording Details	
Producer	Cliff Richard and Craig Pruess
Engineered by	Keith Bessey
Recording location	Riverside Studios, London, Strawberry Studios, London, Ramp Studios, London and/or Sonoptics Studios, London
Recording date	September 1982-January 1983

♬ Psalm 106 Extract

From the album **The Christmas Story**

In 2007, Cliff Richard was invited by Premier Christian Radio to take part in a recording of the story of the Nativity, with Cliff providing the readings interspersed by the relevant carols to punctuate the story further sung by the choristers of Exeter Cathedral. Two extracts from Psalm 106 were recorded, running straight into each other: the first was verses one to five, which is an exhortation to praise God in the fullest way possible and the final two verses (tagged as ***Further Extract Psalm 106***). Cliff reads these verses with a passion and concludes the Christmas story with reverent panache.

Track Specification
Written by Traditional

Musicians	
Cliff Richard	spoken vocals

Recording Details	
Producer	Gordon Lorenz
Engineered by	Richard Scott
Recording location	Exeter Cathedral, Exeter, England
Recording date	2007

♬ Psalm 150

From the album **The Christmas Story**

Cliff Richard recorded a number of readings from the bible, which told the story of the Nativity for the album ***The Christmas Story***, with these being broken up by carols sung by the choristers of Exeter Cathedral. The first track on the album is an ebullient reading of the final psalm in the bible, which is an exhortation to praise god with all kinds of instruments and voices. All six verses of the psalm are read by Cliff and the organ introduction to ***O Come All Ye Faithful*** can be heard underneath the last few words of the reading.

Track Specification
Written by Traditional

Musicians	
Cliff Richard	spoken vocals

Recording Details	
Producer	Gordon Lorenz
Engineered by	Richard Scott
Recording location	Exeter Cathedral, Exeter, England
Recording date	2007

♬ Punch and Judy

From the album **Sincerely Cliff Richard**

One of the first tracks to be recorded for ***Sincerely Cliff Richard,*** it would be held back from release for over a year and a half before the album was ready. Written by Manfred Mann singer, Mike d'Abo, who had also written the long unreleased ***Love Is Like a Crescendo,*** *Punch and Judy* was recorded during the suite of Cliff Richard's sessions or the UK contenders for 1968's Eurovision Song Contest.
The andante bass line plods along underneath a piano accompaniment and Cliff's vocal, which is imbued with emotion in this love song that talks of regret for what his relationship has come to, likening it to the seaside Punch and Judy puppet show. There is an uncredited female vocal group supporting Cliff, but they sound a little dreary and occasionally off the note. However, this doesn't detract from the general enjoyment of the song that closes the album.

Track Specification
Composed by Mike d'Abo

Musicians		*Recording Details*	
Mike Leander	arranger, conductor	Producer	Norrie Paramor
Mike Leander Orchestra	orchestra	Engineered by	Peter Vince
Cliff Richard	vocals	Recording location	Abbey Road Studio 2, St. John's Wood, London
Unknown	backing vocals	Recording date	11th February 1968

♬ Put My Mind at Ease

From the album **Tracks 'n' Grooves**

During 1967, one of Cliff Richard's favourite writers was Neil Diamond, whose laconic melodies suited his voice well. One such song was *Put Your Mind at Ease,* which was recorded on 1st June, although it remained unissued until the release of the ***Tracks 'n' Grooves*** album almost three years later in 1970, where it was only released in stereo although a mono version would have also been recorded at the time of recording as was the practice; however, this has no been given a release.
A typically lush arrangement by Mike Leander focusing on the brass more than any other section sees Cliff enjoying his performance of a melodically complex song to sing. There is a backing vocal group, which is uncredited but likely to be the Breakaways, with whom Cliff was regularly working at the time.

Track Specification
Composed by Neil Diamond

Musicians		*Recording Details*	
Mike Leander Orchestra	orchestra	Producer	Norrie Paramor
Mike Leander	arranger, conductor	Engineered by	Peter Vince
Cliff Richard	vocals	Recording location	Abbey Road Studio 2, St. John's Wood, London
Unknown	backing vocals	Recording date	1st June 1967

Q - Q - Q - Q - Q - Q - Q - Q - Q - Q - Q - Q - Q - Q - Q - Q - Q

♫ Quando, Quando, Quando?

From the album **Kinda Latin**

Although Pat Boone is often credited with writing the English lyrics to the song *Quando, Quando, Quando?* (or *When, When, When?*), there is some doubt as to its veracity. The Songwriters Hall of Fame for instance, credits Ervin Drake, while on the ***Kinda Latin*** liner notes, only the Italian names of Tony Renis and Alberto Testa appear. Of course, Pat Boone had a hit with it (under the Italian title but with English lyrics) reaching number forty-one in the British charts in May 1962 and this adds some credence to the theory that he contributed to the lyrics. Engelbert Humperdinck used to include the song in his act but his cover wasn't released until January 1999, when it hit number forty in the UK charts. It has also been covered by eclectically different artists such as Al Martino, the Drifters, Michael Bublé and Nelly Furtado, Emilio Pericoli, Eddie Calvert, the Hit Crew, Buddy Holly, Montefiore Cocktail and Victor Silvester.

The first song to be recorded in the middle session for Cliff Richard's upcoming album in October 1965, the third and final take and edit of *Quando, Quando, Quando?* were used for mono and stereo but with different mixes for the audio channels. Tom-toms, percussion instruments and muted brass usher in this fast-paced song, which Cliff performs with his usual exuberance. There are uncredited backing vocals occasionally applied and these are likely to be the Mike Sammes Singers although this is unconfirmed. The middle eight features a frenetic trumpet solo before passing the control back to Cliff.

Track Specification

Composed by Tony Renis and Alberto Testa; English lyrics by Pat Boone or Ervin Drake

Musicians		*Recording Details*	
Reg Guest	arranger, conductor	Producer	Norrie Paramor
Reg Guest Orchestra	orchestra	Engineered by	Peter Bown
Cliff Richard	vocals	Recording location	Abbey Road Studio 2, St. John's Wood, London
Unknown	backing vocals	Recording date	7th October 1965

♫ Quarter to Three

Unissued track

In *The Complete Recording Sessions 1958-1990* by Peter Lewry and Nigel Goodall, it is suggested that *Quarter to Three* was recorded by Cliff Richard at the same session as ***The Next Time***, although other sources have excluded it. Certainly the song was performed on Cliff's Radio Luxembourg shows of the period and the Shadows used to perform it without Cliff in concert and it would therefore be likely that Cliff would have tried recording it for a future album, even though it had nothing to do with the ***Summer Holiday*** project being recorded during this period.

Originally, *Quarter to Three* was a song adapted from an instrumental entitled *A Night with Daddy 'G' – Part 1*, which was recorded by The Church Street Five. The updated and retitled version was recorded by Gary U.S. Bonds in a familiar doo-wop style and, in June 1961, the single hit the top of the Billboard charts. Before Bruce Springsteen was a major star, he regularly performed it in his shows and continues to do so. It has also been covered by Chubby Checker, Paul McCartney, Chuck Jackson, the Shadows (at the ABC Kingston concert), Ringo Starr and Bill Wyman among others.

Although the ABC Kingston version by the Shadows was eventually released on the album, the studio attempt (in an unknown number of takes) by Cliff remains unissued.

Track Specification

Composed by Gene Barge, Frank Guida and Joseph Royster; new lyrics and arrangement by Gary Anderson and Gary U.S. Bonds

Musicians		*Recording Details*	
Brian Bennett	drums, percussion	Producer	Norrie Paramor
Brian 'Licorice' Locking	bass	Engineered by	Malcolm Addey
Hank Marvin	guitar	Recording location	Abbey Road Studio 2, St. John's Wood, London
Cliff Richard	vocals	Recording date	10th May 1962
Bruce Welch	rhythm guitar		

♫ ¡Qué Buena Suerte!

Spanish single

Translated as *What Luck!* or *How Lucky!*, the Spanish version of Cliff Richard's ***Congratulations*** was an inevitable graduation from the song's success at the 1968 Eurovision Song Contest, in spite of its second placing one point behind the unmemorable winner, the Spanish *La La La*. There is a suggestion that General Franco organized vote-rigging at the contest, where *Congratulations* had been leading the pack for the evening and then Germany gave full marks to the dull

Spanish song, forcing a win. However, the irony was not lost on Spain when the Spanish record-buyers wanted Cliff's song and it became inevitable that a Spanish language version would be recorded.
At the same session where the French version was laid down, there are published accounts suggesting that the backing track used was the same as that recorded on 3rd February for the English version. However, this is incorrect since the German version, recorded three days after the event, which took place on 6th April at the Royal Albert Hall, was an original with full orchestral backing (and unknown backing singers). It is this backing track that was subsequently used for the French, Italian and Spanish versions. *¡Qué Buena Suerte!* was released as a single on the Columbia label (catalogue number PL 63.198) in May 1968 but in mono only. It was a major rarity for non-Spanish fans until the stereo version was included on the 1997 boxed set of Cliff's foreign language recordings, ***On the Continent***.
The mix focuses on the dancing guitar line, while Cliff sings the first word in English. In all other respects it is a faithful copy musically of the English original, with the exception that Cliff and the female backing vocalists (possibly the Breakaways but unconfirmed) sing along with the accelerando at the end, as they do with all the foreign versions.

Track Specification
Composed by Bill Martin and Phil Coulter; Spanish lyrics by Alpin

Musicians		*Recording Details*	
Norrie Paramor Orchestra	orchestra	Producer	Norrie Paramor (backing track and vocals)
Norrie Paramor	arranger, conductor	Engineered by	Peter Vince (backing track and vocals)
Cliff Richard	vocals	Recording location	Abbey Road Studio 2 (backing track) and Abbey Road Studio 1 (vocals), St. John's Wood, London
Unknown	backing vocals		
Unknown	hand claps	Recording date	9th April 1968 (backing track) and 23rd April 1968 (vocals)

♫ Questions

From the film soundtrack album of **Two a Penny**

One of only four songs to feature on the soundtrack of the film ***Two a Penny*** – the remainder of the album was filled with covers and original songs unconnected with the film project – *Questions* appears at the end of the film as it is played out over Jamie Hopkins's (Cliff Richard) soul-searching while walking through trees and bushes growing on the inside of a ruined London church. To this point, the film has been about what a thoroughly self-centred, arrogant person Hopkins is who leaches off his friends, mother and girlfriend, Carol (Ann Holloway). Carol has been to see Billy Graham at Earl's Court twice and has found something to believe in – Jesus, redemption and God – but Hopkins is ambivalent and close-minded. After a series of exploits that include burglary, fighting, stealing drugs and other more minor crimes, Hopkins begins to question the existence of God and what He might be able to do for Hopkins as an individual. The film ends abruptly at the completion of *Questions*, which is asking all the questions of a man who is soul-searching, cleverly not making it a happy ending – necessarily. It leaves the viewer thinking about the possible outcomes and the messages that are plotted throughout the film.
Recorded in one session along with the other three songs to appear in the film and released on the soundtrack album, it was subsequently issued on the ***Cliff Richard at the Movies 1959-1974*** album with the suggestion that it was the film version – in fact, the film and the soundtrack album versions are exactly the same recording.
The downward progressing bass line and twinkling harp accompanying Cliff's impassioned vocal line introduces an unexpectedly complex song, which expresses the bewildering search for a meaning in life and asking if it can be found in religion. There are some witty lines and this culminates in him beseeching whoever might be listening to be real to him.
All of the *Two a Penny* tracks were translated into German and recorded for Cliff's first German language album, *Hier Ist Cliff*, with *Questions* being given the straightforwardly translated title of ***Fragen***. Four months later in February 1969, Cliff recorded another version, this in French, called ***Relève Mon Défi***, which wasn't released until six years later on the compilation *When in France – Chante en Français*.

Track Specification
Composed by Cliff Richard and Jim Collier

Musicians		*Recording Details*	
Mike Leander	arranger, conductor	Producer	Norrie Paramor
Mike Leander Orchestra	orchestra	Engineered by	Peter Vince
Cliff Richard	vocals	Recording location	Abbey Road Studio 2, St. John's Wood, London
		Recording date	1st July 1967

♫ ¿Quién Será?

From the album **When in Spain**

Written by a Mexican bandleader in 1953 as a mambo dance tune, *¿Quién Será?* translates literally to *Whoever It Will Be*, although it is more popularly known as *Sway*. With English lyrics provided the following year by Norman Gimbel, *Sway* was popularized by Dean Martin, who took the song to number six in the UK singles chart in October 1954, followed six year later by Bobby Rydell who had a number twelve hit in December 1960. It has since been covered and recorded by a number of artists including Björk, the composer Pablo Beltrán Ruiz, Michael Bublé, the Pussycat Dolls, Perez Prado with Rosemary Clooney and Ben E. King.

With an English version (*Sway*) recorded in 1965 using the same backing track as that for the Spanish language version issued on ***When in Spain,*** Cliff Richard first recorded the song at the Barcelona-based EMI Studios in one of the sessions at the end of April 1963. One of four songs completed at that session, the fourteenth and final take and edit were used for the mono and stereo recordings but with different mixes for the audio channels.
The Shadows had perfected the Spanish music sound and often returned to it on their instrumental work and, of course, throughout the film ***Finders, Keepers,*** and this track exemplifies their capabilities. It is unfortunate that the stereo recording forced Cliff's vocals into the left channel with the instrumentation into the right, which makes for a perplexing listening experience. Cliff carries off the song with quiet aplomb ending with a shouted 'Olé!' to complete the album.

Track Specification
Composed by Pablo Beltrán Ruiz
Musicians

Brian Bennett	drums, percussion
Brian 'Licorice' Locking	bass
Hank Marvin	guitar
Cliff Richard	vocals
Bruce Welch	rhythm guitar

Recording Details

Producer	Norrie Paramor
Engineered by	Malcolm Addey
Recording location	EMI Studios, Barcelona
Recording date	29th April 1963

♫ Quiet Nights of Quiet Stars
From the album **Kinda Latin**

Quiet Nights of Quiet Stars has been covered by a variety of artists including Vic Damone, Mario Castro-Neves, Dean Martin, Perry Como, Tony Bennett, Dardanelle, the writer of the song Antônio Carlos Jobim, Ella Fitzgerald, Percy Faith, Andy Williams, Frank Sinatra, Mel Tormé, Jo Stafford and Queen Latifah.
Recorded at the first of three Cliff Richard sessions during October 1965 for his upcoming ***Kinda Latin*** album, *Quiet Nights of Quiet Stars* was the second of three songs to be finished that day. The third and final take and edit were used for both the mono and stereo recordings of the song but with different mixes for the requirements of the separate audio channels.
Cliff performs songs like these brilliantly, with its minimal accompaniment (here a small amount of percussion and a strummed guitar, initially before a single muted horn is brought in matched with oboes and then gradually building), and he excels at keeping the difficult musical intervals pitch perfect. This slow love song is surprisingly gentle and is an interesting addition to the collected theme for the album.

Track Specification
Composed by Antônio Carlos Jobim and Gene Lees
Musicians

Bernard Ebbinghouse Orchestra	orchestra
Bernard Ebbinghouse	arranger, conductor
Cliff Richard	vocals

Recording Details

Producer	Norrie Paramor
Engineered by	Peter Bown
Recording location	Abbey Road Studio 2, St. John's Wood, London
Recording date	4th October 1965

♫ Quizás, Quizás, Quizás
From the album **When in Spain**

Written in 1947, the first successful recording of *Quizás, Quizás, Quizás* (which translates to ***Perhaps, Perhaps, Perhaps***) was two years later by Gordon Jenkins. American Joe Davis translated the lyrics and it is perhaps this version which has become more popular after Doris Day's 1964 version and Nat King Cole's 1958 cover. Other artists to have recorded the song include Trini Lopez, Celia Cruz, Samantha Fox, ex-Spice Girls Emma Bunton and Geri Halliwell with their separate versions, Dennis Brown and the Pussycat Dolls.
In early 1965, Cliff Richard recorded the English lyrics over the backing recorded in 1963 for ***When in Spain*** and *Perhaps, Perhaps, Perhaps* was issued on the ***Cliff's Palladium Successes*** EP. The original Spanish song was recorded as one of four tracks for the album at that session. The thirteenth and final take and edit were used as the mono and stereo recordings but with different mixes for the requirements of the audio channels.
What is unfortunate for the stereo version is that Cliff's vocal is placed in the left with the Shadows instrumentation in the right, which makes for a muddy listening experience. Nevertheless, Hank Marvin's complex solo guitar line, Bruce Welch's rigid chord structure and the militaristic drumming by Brian Bennett perfectly evoke the Spanish music and dance. Cliff's singing is, as expected, strong and his Spanish pronunciation, phonetically written for him, sounds good certainly to the layman's ear.

Track Specification
Composed by Osvaldo Farrés
Musicians

Brian Bennett	drums, percussion
Brian 'Licorice' Locking	bass
Hank Marvin	guitar
Cliff Richard	vocals
Bruce Welch	rhythm guitar

Recording Details

Producer	Norrie Paramor
Engineered by	Malcolm Addey
Recording location	EMI Studios, Barcelona
Recording date	29th April 1963

THE CLIFF RICHARD RECORDING CATALOGUE

R – R – R – R – R – R – R – R – R – R – R – R – R – R – R – R – R – R

♫ Ragged
B-side of **Human Work of Art**

Recorded during the sessions for Cliff's first studio album of the nineties, ***Cliff Richard - The Album***, *Ragged* was not included on the final listing, although it was chosen as the principal B-side of the release of ***Human Work of Art***, featuring on the seven-inch single and the second of the dual CD discs of the single.
Driven by an insistent synthesiser and bass line, Cliff sings the song with passion, while supplying his own backing vocals. He sings in falsetto several times and this adds to the interest of the track; however, in spite of the familiar lyrics of rich man, poor man, beggar-man, thief, it takes a number of listens before the song really grows into something for the listener. The song ends on a short *a capella* section built up from Cliff's multi-layered vocals.

Track Specification
Composed by Rod Trott and Colin Elswood

Musicians

John Clark	guitar
Peter May	drums, percussion
Paul Moessl	arranger, drum programming, keyboards
Cliff Richard	vocals, backing vocals
Steve Stroud	bass

Recording Details

Producer	Paul Moessl and Cliff Richard
Engineered by	Gerry Kitchingham and Ben Robbins
Recording location	R. G. Jones Studios, Wimbledon, London
Recording date	25th-31st May 1992, 8th June 1992 (backing track) and 8th June 1992 (vocals)

♫ Rain Cloud
Unissued track

The second of two songs recorded at the June 1970 session, the other being ***Indifference***, neither that nor *Rain Cloud* has been released nor attempted again. There is scant information from the session and detail such as the writer, the engineer and the other musicians performing alongside Cliff Richard are unknown; should this be found during further research, this entry will be updated accordingly.

Track Specification
Composed by Unknown

Musicians

Cliff Richard	vocals
Unknown	all instrumentation

Recording Details

Producer	Norrie Paramor
Engineered by	Unknown
Recording location	Abbey Road Studio 2, St. John's Wood, London
Recording date	30th June 1970

♫ Rattler
From the album **Two a Penny**

Covered by Herman's Hermits, Judith Durham, Lulu and the Seekers, Cliff Richard recorded his version of *Rattler* at the first of two sessions on 8th March 1968, with the track being the first song completed.
Introduced with hand-claps, possibly by Cliff himself, the rhythm created by the Shadows is reminiscent of a train running along a track in the middle of nowhere. Alongside the Breakaways, Cliff also provides his own backing vocals on the main lines of the song and this adds a brilliant dimension to the performance.

Track Specification
Composed by Bob Woodley

Musicians

Breakaways: Vicki Hasemen, Margo Quantrell, Jean Ryder	backing vocals
Brian Bennett	drums, percussion
Mike Leander	arranger, conductor
Hank Marvin	guitar
Mike Leander Orchestra	orchestra
Cliff Richard	vocals, backing vocals
John Rostill	bass
Unknown	hand claps
Bruce Welch	rhythm guitar

Recording Details

Producer	Norrie Paramor
Engineered by	Peter Vince
Recording location	Abbey Road Studio 2, St. John's Wood, London
Recording date	8th March 1968

♫ Razzle Dazzle

From the albums **Live at the ABC Kingston 1962**, **Cliff Richard** *and* **The Rock 'n' Roll Years 1958-1963**

Before recording the track for the ***Cliff Richard*** album, Cliff Richard and the Shadows regularly performed *Razzle Dazzle* in concert. Most famously recorded by Bill Haley and His Comets (who reached number thirteen in the UK charts in September 1956), while it has been covered by artists such as Jive Bunny (sampling Haley's version), Ella Mae Morse and Tommy Steele. The first live version to be recorded by Cliff and the Shadows was a concert performed at the ABC Theatre in Kingston, Surrey. These tracks remained unreleased until the 2002 stereo CD album ***Live at the ABC Kingston 1962***.
Having honed the song in concert, it was decided to record it in the middle of 1962. Slated for recording along with ***Save My Soul*** at an earlier session, both songs were dropped although *Razzle Dazzle* was revisited in July. The spliced take and edit derived from takes one and four were used for the mono and stereo recordings but with different mixes for the audio channels. The recording would languish in the vaults for almost three years when it was picked up (along with ***Reelin' and Rockin'*** from the session) for the *Cliff Richard* album in 1965 and it was used as the B-side for a non-UK, international single release of ***Angel***. In 1997, the anthology set ***The Rock 'n' Roll Years 1958-1963*** incorporated the same take and edit used on the album but without the Shadows backing vocals and with the studio count-in at the start.
A perfectly-pitched rock and roll song but with the Cliff and Shadows sound applied, *Razzle Dazzle* is a perfect example of what the group could do. With the Shadows returning his call to get ready and go and ending with Cliff speaking the title, *Razzle Dazzle* is a superlative version of this familiar rock and roll track.

Track Specification
Composed by Charles Calhoun

1. Live at the ABC Kingston 1962

Musicians		*Recording Details*	
Brian Bennett	backing vocals, drums, percussion	Producer	Norrie Paramor
Jet Harris	backing vocals, bass	Engineered by	Malcolm Addey and Ken Townsend
Hank Marvin	backing vocals, guitar	Recording location	ABC Theatre, Kingston, Surrey
Cliff Richard	vocals	Recording date	7th March 1962
Bruce Welch	backing vocals, rhythm guitar		

2. Cliff Richard

Musicians		*Recording Details*	
Brian Bennett	backing vocals, drums, percussion	Producer	Norrie Paramor
Brian 'Licorice' Locking	bass	Engineered by	Peter Bown
Hank Marvin	backing vocals, guitar	Recording location	Abbey Road Studio 2, St. John's Wood, London
Cliff Richard	vocals	Recording date	12th July 1962
Bruce Welch	backing vocals, rhythm guitar		

3. The Rock 'n' Roll Years 1958-1963

Musicians		*Recording Details*	
Brian Bennett	drums, percussion	Producer	Norrie Paramor
Brian 'Licorice' Locking	bass	Engineered by	Peter Bown
Hank Marvin	guitar	Recording location	Abbey Road Studio 2, St. John's Wood, London
Cliff Richard	vocals	Recording date	12th July 1962
Bruce Welch	rhythm guitar		

♫ Ready Teddy

From the album **Cliff**

Little Richard had been a growing force in rock and roll in the US since the mid-fifties and his music had successfully crossed the Atlantic to the UK. Although his version of the song *Ready Teddy* wasn't a singles success in the UK, it went on to be covered by the likes of Buddy Holly, Carl Perkins and Elvis Presley (and later by the Beatles and John Lennon). As a consequence of the song's pedigree, it was appropriate and unsurprising that it would be chosen by Cliff Richard and the Drifters to form part of their set of the 'live' recording for the album ***Cliff*** recorded in front of selected invited fans in the studio. The performance appeared on the second of two days and was the first to be recorded in the session. The song was one of a selection incorporated on the ***Cliff No. 2*** EP released in June 1959.
This is Cliff at his best; singing the fast-paced rock and roll tunes with an excellent bass run by Jet Harris, ably supported by the rest of the band. The screaming of the fans is less here than on earlier tracks and it naturally enhances the performance not to have the vocals drowned out.

Track Specification
Composed by John Marascalco and Robert Blackwell

Musicians		*Recording Details*	
Jet Harris	bass	Producer	Norrie Paramor
Hank Marvin	guitar	Engineered by	Peter Bown and Stuart Eltham
Tony Meehan	drums, percussion	Recording location	Abbey Road Studio 2, St. John's Wood, London
Cliff Richard	vocals, hand-claps	Recording date	10th February 1959
Bruce Welch	rhythm guitar		

♬ Real as I Wanna Be

From the album **Real as I Wanna Be**

The title song of Cliff Richard's first studio album for what was almost three years, ***Real as I Wanna Be***, is a surprising departure for the man who is best known for his rock and roll foot-tappers and crystal-clear balladeering. But it also shows what the audience can expect for the rest of the album. A completely new band had been assembled with a new producer and arranger in Peter Wolf, who also wrote many of the album's songs. Cliff was once again the subject of cruel criticism and it was obvious he was no longer considered cool even in an ironic way, but *Real as I Wanna Be* shows his ability to metamorphose to cope with different and changing styles of music.

Using guitar harmonics and muted guitar strings, the introduction leads into the emotive vocal performance by Cliff. Using the upper register of his voice during the chorus and the gentle backing vocals, as well as the bass-heavy accompaniment reveals just how different the album's offerings are intended to be.

Track Specification

Composed by Peter Zizzo

Musicians

Vinnie Colaiuta	drums, percussion
Paul Jackson Jr.	guitar
Cliff Richard	vocals, backing vocals
Michelle Wolf	backing vocals
Peter Wolf	arranger, bass, keyboards, percussion

Recording Details

Producer	Peter Wolf
Engineered by	Christian Leitgeb, Chris Heil, Paul Erickson and/or Keith Bessey
Recording location	Little America Recording Studios, Weiler, Austria, Ocean Recording Studios, Burbank, California, USA, R. G. Jones Recording Studios, Wimbledon, London, England and/or The Pierce Room, London, England
Recording date	1997 or 1998

♬ Really Waltzing

From the film soundtrack album of **Summer Holiday**

Don (portrayed by Cliff Richard) and his coterie of friends – three fellow London Transport mechanics, played by Melvyn Hayes, Teddy Green and Jeremy Bulloch, three girls they picked up along the way after their car conked out and fell apart (played by Una Stubbs, Jacqueline Daryl and Pamela Hart) and the stowaway American heiress Barbara Winters (portrayed by Lauri Peters) – have come to a restaurant to get something to eat and drink. In this scene that results in the performance of *Really Waltzing*, the group introduces the song by talking in rhythmic sentences, a technique that builds up to an impressive dance routine played out on the suspiciously shiny piazza, which is obviously an internal set in a studio. The lyrics suggest that waltzing is really square and they can't believe they are enjoying themselves as Don dances with Barbara. The dancing fizzles out and Don grabs Barbara and takes her off into a side alley to profess his love and to change his opinion on romance and relationships, confirming that he doesn't mind being 'owned', something that he railed against earlier during ***A Swingin' Affair***.

The song was laid down in two sections at the mainly orchestral session. The first part was completed in five takes and the second in nine. Splicing these two parts together, the same combined edit was used for the mono and stereo recordings but with different mixes for the separate audio channels. The film version, recorded at Elstree, is very different from the released soundtrack version, with some of Cliff's vocal lines being taken by other characters, including Lauri Peters (possibly dubbed by Grazina Frame), Una Stubbs, Melvyn Hayes and others and the orchestral interludes for the dancing extended. The film version remains unreleased in any other commercial format to date while the soundtrack album version also appears on the ***More Hits from Summer Holiday*** EP.

A waltz, of course, the song is executed with a slight swinging feel. There are several supporting roles played by the Mike Sammes Singers, with preposterous accents, which detract slightly from the performance, particularly as they are the principal performers in the song, with Cliff only performing the first verse and chorus.

Track Specification

Composed by Peter Myers and Ronald Cass

Musicians

Associated British Studio Orchestra	orchestra
Stanley Black	conductor
Mike Sammes Singers	backing vocals
Cliff Richard	vocals

Recording Details

Producer	Norrie Paramor
Engineered by	Malcolm Addey
Recording location	Abbey Road Studio 2, St. John's Wood, London
Recording date	22nd November 1962

♬ Red Hot and Cooking

B-side of **The Hungry Wind** *(Garth Hewitt)*

Cliff Richard had had a long associated with fellow Christian singer Garth Hewitt, performing on some of his tracks, producing others and recording covers of Hewitt's songs (for example, ***Under the Influence***). The final time that Cliff worked with Hewitt in the studio was on a track that became the B-side of the single *The Hungry Wind* (which was released on the Blue Moon label with a catalogue number of BMS 001). While the A-side didn't involve Cliff, he did lend his harmony vocals to its coupled track, *Red Hot and Cooking*.

Were such an apposite title created for a song, it has to be *Red Hot and Cooking*. Kicking off at an astonishing rock and roll pace, Hewitt sings the song with extraordinary gusto, supported by a phalanx of saxophones and the regular rock and roll instrumentation and, of course, Cliff's backing vocals that add an extra layer of energy on something that is already frenetic in its execution. For this alone, *Red Hot and Cooking* is the superlative track on the release.

Track Specification
Composed by Garth Hewitt

Musicians		*Recording Details*	
Garth Hewitt	vocals	Producer	Tom Blades
Cliff Richard	backing vocals	Engineered by	Unknown
Unknown	guitar	Recording location	Unknown
Unknown	bass	Recording date	1982
Unknown	keyboards		
Unknown	saxophones		
Unknown	drums, percussion		

♫ Red Rubber Ball
From the film soundtrack album of **Two a Penny**

Written by Paul Simon in 1966, Simon suggests that *Red Rubber Ball* was composed in order to get a financial advance from the Seekers, whose member Bruce Woodley assisted with the song. But it was the Cyrkle who had a number two hit in the US that year, and they assert they were offered the song by Simon when the band was supporting Simon and Garfunkel on tour. It has since been covered by Neil Diamond, the Diodes (who claim they covered the song as punk because of Simon's outspoken dislike of the genre), the Seekers, Simon and Garfunkel, Gary Frenay and Mel Tormé among others.
Recorded at a Cliff Richard session in June 1967 that also saw the recording of one of Cliff's favourite songs, ***The Day I Met Marie***, *Red Rubber Ball* was included on the ***Two a Penny*** soundtrack album, although it is not performed anywhere in the film; the film only features four songs and so other songs were added to pad out the track listing rather than issue the songs as an EP.
With an emphasis on the orchestral brass, the principal instrumentation is the guitar, bass and drums and this evokes memories of the Cliff's work with the Shadows. There is a female backing vocal group singing along with Cliff, but these are uncredited and it is possible of them being provided by the Breakaways, who were regularly singing with him at the time. Such ebullient songs as this are well suited to the energy that Cliff clearly enjoys injecting into his songs.

Track Specification
Composed by Paul Simon and Bruce Woodley

Musicians		*Recording Details*	
Mike Leander Orchestra	orchestra	Producer	Norrie Paramor
Mike Leander	arranger, conductor	Engineered by	Peter Vince
Cliff Richard	vocals	Recording location	Abbey Road Studio 2, St. John's Wood, London
Unknown	backing vocals	Recording date	1st June 1967

♫ Reelin' and Rockin'
From the album **Cliff Richard**

A Chuck Berry original that appeared on his album taking its name from the song title, *Reelin' and Rockin'* was recorded by Berry in 1959 but it wasn't released in the UK until February 1973 (his final single to be issued in Britain) where it reached number eighteen. In fact, in chart terms, it was the Dave Clark Five who got there first in March 1965, when their version reached number twenty-five. Since then, it has been covered by many artists including Eddy Clearwater, The Astronauts, the Hollies, Chris Farlowe, Alex Harvey, the Big Three, Gerry and the Pacemakers, Fats Domino and Conway Twitty among many others.
For Cliff Richard's version, it would take almost three years from recording the song (along with ***Razzle Dazzle*** from the same session) for it to be released as part of the track listing of 1965's ***Cliff Richard***. A regular favourite on concert set-lists, the third and final take and edit were used for the mono and stereo recordings but with different mixes for the audio channels.
Introduced by Brian Bennett's drums and joined by the guitars of the other Shadows, *Reelin' and Rockin'* is an upbeat song that, typically of the genre, uses an ascending counting motif, but rather than steps, it uses the time on the clock to indicate the passage of time during a dance. Some lyrics have been changed in Cliff's cover, such as 'the Shads told me they won't play no more' but this helps to make it parochial and a brilliant ensemble piece showing off the musicianship of all.

Track Specification
Composed by Chuck Berry

Musicians		*Recording Details*	
Brian Bennett	drums, percussion	Producer	Norrie Paramor
Brian 'Licorice' Locking	bass	Engineered by	Peter Bown
Hank Marvin	guitar	Recording location	Abbey Road Studio 2, St. John's Wood, London
Cliff Richard	vocals	Recording date	12th July 1962
Bruce Welch	rhythm guitar		

♫ Reflections

B-side of **Throw Down a Line** *and unissued track*

Originally recorded almost a year before the remainder of the ***About That Man*** album, on which this religious song eventually appeared and therefore most likely not originally intended for the album project, *Reflections* was first recorded at a session that also produced a single A-side and a track for the ***Tracks 'n' Grooves*** album. The sporadic nature of Cliff's recordings, where he would enter the studio and simply record what he felt were strong songs and then find suitable avenues for their release, is underlined by the output from the sessions at the time. *Reflections* was chosen for the B-side of Cliff's forty-seventh single – a duet with is writer Hank Marvin – ***Throw Down a Line***. Columbia's policy at the time for singles was to issue them only in mono, since the radio stations had not yet fully converted to the stereo FM in sufficient numbers thus making stereo releases an expensive luxury. *Reflections* was eventually issued in stereo format with the release of the *About That Man* album in the later part of 1970.

Playing a complex guitar accompaniment to his sole vocal line, Cliff sings with much spiritual emotion as he tells the story of letting Jesus into his life and how sinful he is in comparison on a song that was co-written by him and Keith Craddock. It was an obvious choice, too, for the set list of the ***Help It Along*** studio-bound concerts played in front of a small audience. However, this version of the song was not released as part of the charity project and remains in the EMI vaults.

Track Specification
Composed by Cliff Richard and Keith Craddock

1. B-side (Throw Down a Line)

Musicians

Cliff Richard	vocals, guitar

Recording Details

Producer	Norrie Paramor
Engineered by	Peter Vince
Recording location	Abbey Road Studio 2, St. John's Wood, London
Recording date	2nd May 1969

2. Unissued track (Help It Along)

Musicians

Terry Britten	guitar
Barrie Guard	arranger, conductor, percussion
Cliff Hall	keyboards
Jean Hawker	backing vocals
Anna Peacock	backing vocals
Kevin Peek	guitar
Cliff Richard	vocals
Trevor Spencer	drums, percussion
Alan Tarney	bass
Unknown	orchestra

Recording Details

Producer	David MacKay
Engineered by	Roger Quested
Recording location	Morgan Studios, London
Recording date	24th, 25th and 26th September 1973

♫ Relève Mon Défi

From the album **When in France – Chante en Français**

Following on from Cliff Richard's efforts in October 1968 in recording German translations of his songs for his first German language album, *Hier Ist Cliff*, in February 1969 with all new material, he returned to the studio to record some titles in French for his first French language album *When in France – Chante en Français*, although this time the tracks comprised his previous French songs as well as a small number of new recordings. Of this latter group, *Relève Mon Défi* (translated back to English as *Take up My Challenge*, which is close to the original intent) was a French translation of the song ***Questions*** from the film, ***Two a Penny***. As with those German tracks, rather than use the backing track from the English version, an entirely new arrangement was recorded on 21st February 1969.

Two songs were completed at the session – the other being a translation of the title song from *Two a Penny* – and *Relève Mon Défi* has only ever been released in stereo. The French album and the songs within it were rarities outside the country, until all of the foreign language songs were collated and included on the compilation album ***On the Continent*** in 1997. Cliff and the film's director Jim Collier are designated as the writer of the song (which they indeed were of the English original); however, it is unlikely, as with the German translation of the same song, that they provided the French lyrics but no information is available to identify the translator and this highlighted as unknown.

Like the German version, Norrie Paramor has successfully recreated the ambience of the film soundtrack original and Cliff sings it with the same bewildered passion as dictated by the lyrics which are searching for a life meaning and questioning the existence of a god.

Track Specification
Composed by Cliff Richard and Jim Collier; French lyrics by Unknown

Musicians

Norrie Paramor Orchestra	orchestra
Norrie Paramor	arranger, conductor
Cliff Richard	vocals

Recording Details

Producer	Norrie Paramor
Engineered by	Peter Vince
Recording location	Abbey Road Studio 3, St. John's Wood, London
Recording date	21st February 1969

♫ Remember

French single

In 1992, Cliff Richard returned to R. G. Jones Studios – his new preferred base – to record a different kind of album. Rather than recording covers, different versions of his own songs or new material, instead he embellished prior tracks with fresh ideas. This was the case for all tracks with the exception of *Remember*, which was a French translation of ***When Two Worlds Drift Apart***, although the original backing track was used with additional guitars and keyboards dubbed to refresh the sound. And, of course, Cliff sang once again in French (although this was not added to the 1997 compilation of his foreign language recordings, ***On the Continent***). Backed with the upgraded version of ***Lucille***, also from the ***My Kinda Life*** album project, *Remember* was issued as a single on the EMI label (catalogue number 8-80055-7) in 1992 in France only along with a CD version (catalogue number 8-80055-2). *Remember* was subsequently added as a bonus track on the second of the dual CD single releases of ***I Still Believe in You*** in November 1992.

The principal accompaniment is as beautiful as the English original, as would be expected, while the French enunciation supplies a very different and highly pleasant atmosphere. However, the section that begins 'we prefer the greenery' in English is much better lyrically than the French words which translate as having a cigarette and guitar in the hand.

Track Specification

Composed by Peter Sills; French lyrics by Didier Barbelivien

Musicians

John Clark – acoustic guitar
Richard Hewson – arranger, conductor
John Perry – backing vocals
Cliff Richard – vocals, backing vocals
Tony Rivers – backing vocals
Graham Todd – piano
Unknown – orchestra

Recording Details

Producer – Bruce Welch (original track) and Cliff Richard and Paul Moessl (new instrumentation)
Engineered by – Tony Clark, Mike Jarrett and Alan Rouse (original track) and Gerry Kitchingham and Ben Robbins (new instrumentation)
Recording location – Abbey Road Studio 2, St. John's Wood, London (original track) and R. G. Jones Studios, Wimbledon, London (new instrumentation)
Recording date – 8th-9th September 1975 (original track), 1st-2nd February 1992 (new vocals) and 20th-23rd April 1992 (new instrumentation)

♫ Remember Me

103rd UK single *(original and extended) and from the albums* **Live & Guaranteed 1988!** *And* **From a Distance ***** The Event Remaster**

The third single to be released from the ***Always Guaranteed*** project, *Remember Me* was developed in the same way as the other tracks with producer Alan Tarney working on a musical idea and then recording the basic backing track before Cliff Richard arrivedto record his vocal lines in between performances of ***Time – the Musical*** in London. After that, Tarney would continue to work on the instrumentation until he felt it was satisfactory.

Backed with non-album track, ***Another Christmas Day***, *Remember Me* was released on the EMI label (catalogue number EM 31) on 19th October 1987, reaching number thirty-five in the UK singles charts. In tandem with this release, the track was extended and released in twelve-inch format (catalogue number 12EM 31). It was also the first single to be released as a CD single (CDEM 31) on 2nd November 1987. Both the twelve-inch and CD versions incorporated the extended version, the seven-inch B-side and another non-album track, ***Brave New World***, as well as the seven-inch version of ***Some People*** as an extra only on the CD single. The promotional video was filmed on 15th September 1987 and features Cliff walking down a run-down street, observing the girl of his thoughts through a window. He enters a bar and there are frequent dual shots to allow Cliff to sing backing vocals. Eventually, he dances with the girl and kisses her (chastely) on the forehead.

The style of the song is has associations with the early eighties material but with a fresher synthesiser arrangement. Cliff's vocal is imbued with a longing in the verses, which occasionally echoes the last few words before fading. The chorus features Cliff and Tarney on multi-layered backing vocals, which build up the drama into the successive verses.

Remember Me was filmed and recorded on the associated tour and an incomplete version of the song appears on the 1995 reissue of *Live & Guaranteed 1988!*. As a most recent single, it was also added to the *Cliff's Set* part of *The Event* at Wembley Stadium in June 1989 but was initially not part of the track listing of the resultant ***From a Distance ***** The Event*** album release. In 2005, when the album was remastered, the track was dutifully restored to the correct place in the running order. Once again, as with much of the material from the previous two studio albums, the live version of this song is a faithful reproduction of what can be heard on the studio recording, although the backing vocals sound a little tentative; however, Cliff makes up for any such misgivings by the strength of his lead.

Track Specification

Composed by Alan Tarney

1. Single (original)

Musicians

Cliff Richard – vocals, backing vocals
Alan Tarney – backing vocals, guitars, bass, keyboards, drum and percussion programming

Recording Details

Producer – Alan Tarney
Engineered by – Gerry Kitchingham and Keith Bessey
Recording location – R. G. Jones Studios, Wimbledon, London
Recording date – 13th October-November 1986

2. Single (extended)

Musicians

Cliff Richard	vocals, backing vocals
Alan Tarney	backing vocals, guitars, bass, keyboards, drum and percussion programming

Recording Details

Producer	Alan Tarney
Engineered by	Gerry Kitchingham and Keith Bessey
Recording location	R. G. Jones Studios, Wimbledon, London
Recording date	13th October-November 1986

3. Live & Guaranteed 1988!

Musicians

John Clark	guitar
Rosemarie Ford	backing vocals
Mark Griffiths	bass
Peter Howarth	backing vocals
Steve Lauri	guitar
Paul Moessl	keyboards
Mick Mullins	backing vocals
Alan Park	keyboards
Cliff Richard	vocals
Henry Spinetti	drums, percussion

Recording Details

Producer	Unknown
Engineered by	Unknown
Recording location	Fyens Forum, Odense, Denmark
Recording date	22nd May 1988

4. From a Distance ** The Event Remaster***

Musicians

John Clark	guitar
Sonia Jones-Morgan	backing vocals
Steve Lauri	guitar
Peter May	drums, percussion
Paul Moessl	keyboards
Tessa Niles	backing vocals
Alan Park	keyboards
Provox:	
Peter Howarth	backing vocals
Mick Mullins	backing vocals
Keith Murrell	backing vocals
Cliff Richard	vocals
Steve Stroud	bass

Recording Details

Producer	Cliff Richard
Engineered by	Keith Bessey and Mick McKenna
Recording location	Rolling Stones Mobile Studio, Wembley Stadium, Wembley, North-west London
Recording date	16th-17th June 1989

♬ Reunion of the Heart

B-side of **Some People** *(twelve-inch version)*

In the middle of the eighties, Cliff Richard was working in the lead role of the Rock Star in ***Time – The Musical***, performing at the Dominion Theatre in London. In the autumn of 1986, Cliff also recorded the tracks for his then new album ***Always Guaranteed*** when he had spare time away from rehearsals and performances and this resulted in en tracks being completed. By early 1987, he had relinquished his theatrical role and he was able to record a number of tracks at the small studio in the basement of his Cliff Richard Organisation offices in Surrey, one of which was *Reunion of the Heart*. Originally recorded by the Hollies, Cliff's cover was chosen as the B-side of the second single taken from the album project, ***Some People***, but only the twelve-inch version variants; it also appeared in audio form on the *Some People* video CD. *Reunion of the Heart* was released in album CD format for the first time when it was included on the album ***The Winner*** in 1995. It subsequently appeared on a number of other compilations before being included on the track listing of the 2004 remaster of *Always Guaranteed* as one of the eight bonus tracks.

The electric piano chimes the initial chords leading into Cliff's vocal line that is underpinned by a lot of studio reverberation. The chorus features a choir of harmonized vocals, which are all supplied by Cliff and the blend of the arrangement brings something special to the track.

Track Specification

Composed by Maldwyn Pope

Musicians

John Clark	guitar, bass
Alan Park	keyboards, drum and percussion programming
Cliff Richard	vocals, backing vocals

Recording Details

Producer	Cliff Richard
Engineered by	Keith Bessey
Recording location	C. R. O. Studios, Esher, Surrey
Recording date	April 1987

♬ Reunited

From the album **Together** *(Lulu)*

The archetypal love song for those couples who have split up and are either thinking of getting back together again or have resumed their relationship and often incongruously played at weddings, *Reunited* was originally a hit for Peaches and Herb in April 1979 when it reached number four and has since been a regular track on many a love song compilation. Although Peaches and Herb's recording is considered to the quintessential version, *Reunited* has also been covered by artists including Tom Jones, Audrey Landers, Ray Conniff, Bob James, Owen Richards and Toots Thielemans among a few others.

Lulu, who has been in showbusiness for almost as long as Cliff Richard, is a veteran of the Eurovision Song Contest, as Cliff is, and they have both had their own Saturday night television series in the seventies but, in spite of the similarity in their career paths, the two singers had never got around to recording a song together. While Lulu made a chart comeback with *Relight My Fire* with Take That in 1993, Cliff, of course, has never really been that far away from getting songs into the charts, but the experience fired Lulu up to record more material and, in 2002, she invited Cliff to join her on a duet of *Reunited* for her *Together* album. Two years later, the duet was added to the track listing of Cliff's ***Two's Company*** album of duets with different artists.

With a more staccato approach and a heavier bass line to the song than was in the original, Cliff initiates the song, before handing over to Lulu for the second half of the song. Both sing together in close harmony, with Lulu singing the min melody, during the chorus, which slowly builds up its dramatic emotion.

Track Specification

Composed by Dino Fekaris and Freddie Perren

Musicians		*Recording Details*	
Chris Cameron	arranger, conductor	Producer	Chris Porter and Rick Mitra
Lulu	vocals	Engineered by	Chris Porter
Rick Mitra	bass, keyboards, drums, percussion	Recording location	Porterhouse Studios, London (vocals and backing) and Sony Music Studios, London (orchestra)
Phil Palmer	guitar		
Cliff Richard	vocals		
Luke Smith	keyboards	Recording date	2002
Unknown	orchestra		

♬ Right Here Waiting

From the album **Wanted** *and unissued live track*

Cliff Richard had recorded other songs by Richard Marx and it was to Marx's 1989 number two UK hit that he turned when compiling the covers album, ***Wanted***. The ballad was composed for Marx's *Repeat Offender* album and the lyrics were written as an open love letter to his wife, Cynthia, who was away filming in South Africa at the time. It has since been covered by artists such as *X Factor* winner Shayne Ward, Bonnie Tyler, Clay Aiken, Julio Iglesias, Alexander O'Neal, Donny Osmond, John Barrowman, Westlife and Barry Manilow among several others.

The gentle introduction is cleverly juxtaposed against the upbeat rhythm that is generated as Cliff's lead vocal comes in. The arrangement of the song is cleverly articulated and, once again, it is the backing vocals that elevate the song further, to which Cliff also contributes.

Inevitably Cliff took the album on tour and, while in New Zealand, the performance was filmed and recorded for the *World Tour Live* DVD in 2003. A CD album was issued the following year but only with a subset of the songs, and this didn't include *Right Here Waiting*, which remains unissued to date.

Track Specification

Composed by Richard Marx

1. Wanted

Musicians		*Recording Details*	
John Brant	additional programming	Producer	Alan Tarney
Anthony Clark	backing vocals	Engineered by	John Brant and Gerry Kitchingham
Cliff Richard	vocals	Recording location	Wilmer Studios, London
Alan Tarney	arranger, backing vocals, keyboards, programming	Recording date	January-April 2001

2. Unissued track (World Tour Live)

Musicians		*Recording Details*	
Rachel Allen	violin	Producer	Keith Bessey
Elena Bulgakova	violin	Engineered by	Keith Bessey
Jenni Champion	violin	Recording location	The Mission Winery, Napier, New Zealand
Anthony Clark	backing vocals, guitar	Recording date	22nd February 2003
John Clark	guitar		
Dave Cooke	keyboards		
Cornelia Didenco	violin		
Gina Ferguson	violin		
Peter Howarth	backing vocals		
Cathy Irons	violin		
Pete May	drums, percussion		
Mick Mullins	backing vocals		
Keith Murrell	backing vocals		
Alan Park	keyboards		
Hee-Jung Park	violin		
Cliff Richard	vocals		
Eva Schwanen-Lilley	violin		
Steve Stroud	bass		

♫ Rip It Up

CD B-side of **All I Have to Do Is Dream/Miss You Nights**

Perhaps best known in the version recorded by Bill Haley and His Comets, it was actually Little Richard who got into the charts with his version of *Rip It Up* first. Richard's single was issued as his first British release at the end of 1956, but it only stayed in the charts for one week having only reached number thirty. Haley's version was far more popular and it reached the number four position, while Elvis Presley took his cover to number twenty-seven in the early spring of 1957. Other covers include recordings by Gerry and the Pacemakers, Chuck Berry, Jerry Lee Lewis, the Everly Brothers, Buddy Holly, John Lennon, Jimmy Barnes and Roy Orbison among several others.

As part of a BBC documentary about Cliff Richard, a number of live tracks were recorded at the Hammersmith Odeon and Manchester Apollo to accompany the broadcast. Some tracks were licensed for release at the time resulting in the ***Daddy's Home*** single, while others remained with the BBC. Thirteen years afterwards, the section featuring the duets with Phil Everly was remixed and cleaned up by Cliff and this resulted in the release of the double A-sided ***All I Have to Do Is Dream*** and a remixed version of the original ***Miss You Nights***. While the seven-inch single release was restricted to just those tracks, the first of the dual CD single version had two additional tracks, both featuring Cliff and Everly together, ***When Will I Be Loved?*** and ***Tribute to the Legends Medley***, of which *Rip It Up* formed part. It is interesting to note that, while Cliff often performed songs that he had not recorded in the studios, his only released attempt at *Rip It Up* was as part of a medley.

Segueing from *Long Tall Sally*, Phil Everly and Cliff are having a lot of fun in recreating a number of rock and roll classics. In this section there is a riproaring electric piano solo that emulates the best of Jerry Lee Lewis in his prime, while the rest of the band rock soundly in accompaniment.

Track Specification

Composed by Robert Blackwell and John Marascalco

Musicians

Howie Casey	saxophone
John Clark	guitar
Phil Everly	vocals
Mark Griffiths	bass
Graham Jarvis	drums, percussion
Martin Jenner	guitar
Alan Park	keyboards
Cliff Richard	vocals
Graham Todd	keyboards

Recording Details

Producer	Cliff Richard
Engineered by	Unknown
Recording location	Hammersmith Odeon, London
Remixed at	R. G. Jones Studio, London
Recording date	1st May 1981 (live track) and 7th September 1994 (remix)

♫ Rockin' Robin

From the album **Oh Boy!**

Written in 1958, *Rockin' Robin* was a major hit for US one-hit wonder Bobby Day, when he reached number two in the Billboard charts of the same year; it was also a minor hit in the UK, but it stalled at number twenty-nine. It was enough to generate sufficient interest for a number of covers by the likes of Gene Vincent but it wasn't until 1972 when Michael Jackson released his version, which reached number two in the UK charts, that the song came into its own.

Back in 1958, though, Cliff Richard became a regular favourite on Jack Good's *Oh Boy!* show, performing covers and some original material as well as his contemporaneous hits. Because of the success of the television show, it was decided that an album should follow as an official release.

The backing track and Cliff's vocals were recorded on separate days and, instead of using the Drifters as his backing, the musicians were from the Oh Boy! Band. There is no record of who the individual performers are, however, and so will be highlighted as unknown in this entry. The song segues from ***TV Hop*** and it is clear, once again that Cliff's musical talents are enormous. The clarity of the vocal line and pitch-perfect enunciation (something that even the prepubescent Jackson couldn't achieve with occasional flattened notes during the chorus) is somewhat spoiled by the bored sounding 'twiddly-diddly-dee' responses from the Dallas Boys' backing vocalists.

Although the *Oh Boy!* album was re-released in the late seventies, it wasn't until the issue of the rarities album ***The Rock and Roll Years 1958-1963*** that it saw release in digital format.

Track Specification

Composed by Jimmie Thomas

Musicians

Dallas Boys:	
Nicky Clarke	backing vocals
Leon Fisk	backing vocals
Stan Jones	backing vocals
Joe Smith	backing vocals
Bob Wragg	backing vocals
Oh Boy! Band	guitars, stand-up bass, piano, drums, percussion, tambourine
Cliff Richard	vocals

Recording Details

Producer	Harry Robinson (backing track) and Norrie Paramor (vocals)
Engineered by	Norman Newell (backing track) and Malcolm Addey (vocals)
Recording location	Abbey Road Studio 2, St. John's Wood, London
Recording date	19th October 1958 (backing track) and 21st October 1958 (vocals)

♫ Rock Medley (1)

From the album **Cliff "Live" in Japan '72**

Often, Cliff Richard performed medleys of songs that had either inspired him or that time restricted him to singing shortened versions of his hits combined. On his 1972 tour of the Far East with the Shadows, Olivia Newton-John and Pat Carroll, he sang a medley of the songs that were instrumental in affecting his early career in the late fifties and as a tribute to some of those stars popular at the time and at the vanguard of rock and roll:

a) ***The Girl Can't Help It***
b) ***Great Balls of Fire***
c) ***Lucille***
d) ***Jailhouse Rock***
e) ***Good Old Rock 'n' Roll***
f) ***Do You Wanna Dance***

The entries for those songs carry the information on the recording details and musicians.

♫ Rock Medley (2)

From the album **Japan Tour '74**

For Cliff's tours, he frequently performed medleys of his familiar songs or songs that had been a formative influence or inspiration that he hadn't sung elsewhere in the set list. For his 1974 Japanese tour, he created a medley of the songs that were instrumental in affecting his early career in the late fifties and a contemporaneous song from Elton John. It was intended as a tribute to some of those stars popular at the time and at the vanguard of rock and roll:

a) ***His Latest Flame***
b) ***Chantilly Lace***
c) ***Bony Maronie***
d) ***Do You Wanna Dance?***
e) ***Crocodile Rock***
f) ***Do You Wanna Dance?***

The entries for those songs carry the information on the recording details and musicians.

♫ Rock 'n' Roll Is Here to Stay

From the album **From a Distance ***** The Event**

In the fifties, and particularly in America where several important acts were at the vanguard of musical change, rock and roll was seen as an insidious disruption to the 'normal' way of life while many commentators optimistically brushed it aside suggesting that it was only a flash in the pan and normality – such as it was – would be resumed. And then came the defiant song, *Rock 'n' Roll Is Here to Stay* (wonderfully parodied by Monty Python during the resurgence of the genre in the seventies when they generated the title *Rock 'n' Roll Is Here to Stay... Again!*), which helped cement the feelings of the youth at the time and was made popular by Danny and the Juniors, although the song has never been a hit in the British charts. Interest was renewed in the song when it was performed by *Sha Na Na* as a backdrop to the dance competition in the film *Grease*, but it has also been covered by Bobby Vee and has been sampled by Jive Bunny and the Mastermixers.

The defiance of the song's title makes it a suitable choice to complete the final ***Medley*** and the overall *Oh Boy! Set* during Cliff Richard's two-date Wembley Stadium extravaganza to celebrate his thirty years in showbusiness in 1989.

Segueing from ***At the Hop***, Cliff takes the lead vocals through a number of key changes and is supported by the Dallas Boys, the Kalin Twins and the Vernons Girls. The section ends with the final line from Elvis Presley's ***Teddy Bear*** although this is uncredited on the track listing and therefore the medley's description.

Track Specification

Composed by D. Bergen White

Musicians

Dallas Boys:	
Nicky Clarke	backing vocals
Leon Fisk	backing vocals
Stan Jones	backing vocals
Joe Smith	backing vocals
Bob Wragg	backing vocals
Kalin Twins:	
Harold Kalin	backing vocals
Herbie Kalin	backing vocals
Oh Boy! Band	rock 'n' roll band
Cliff Richard	vocals
Vernons Girls:	
Lyn Cornell	backing vocals
Maureen Kennedy	backing vocals
Frances Lee	backing vocals
Jean Owen	backing vocals

Recording Details

Producer	Cliff Richard
Engineered by	Keith Bessey and Mick McKenna
Recording location	Rolling Stones Mobile Studio, Wembley Stadium, Wembley, North-west London
Recording date	16th–17th June 1989

♫ Rock 'n' Roll Juvenile

Unissued tracks and from the album **Rock 'n' Roll Juvenile**

Taken from the eponymous Cliff Richard album, ***Rock 'n' Roll Juvenile***, it was the only track written by Cliff Richard. The song, naturally, gave its name to the album (rather than the other way around) and it closed the first side of the original vinyl album release. Of all the tracks on the listing, *Rock 'n' Roll Juvenile* was the only one that was abandoned at the first session, which took place at the EMI studios in Paris - possibly bypassed due to pressure of the lack of studio time, which was expenive - but it was revisited back in England two weeks later in Abbey Road, where it was finally completed in just four takes.

The militaristic drum accompanied by the guitars establishes *Rock 'n' Roll Juvenile* as a perfect piece of rock and roll that manages to mention Chuck Berry's *Roll over Beethoven* as well as various references to Christian religion, being two aspects of Cliff's life that are very close to his heart. The rolling bass and the screaming guitar solos ensure that this closing track on the album's first side forces the listener to switch the record over.

During Cliff's 1981 UK tour, several tracks were recorded by the BBC as a backdrop to accompany a four-part documentary and, while some of these were eventually licensed for issue and released (including ***Daddy's Home*** and ***All I Have to Do Is Dream*** which became singles from the enterprise), several tracks remained unreleased, including *Rock 'n' Roll Juvenile*.

Track Specification

Composed by Cliff Richard

1. Unissued track (Rock 'n' Roll Juvenile)

Musicians		*Recording Details*	
Terry Britten	guitar	Producer	Cliff Richard and Terry Britten
Stuart Calver	backing vocals	Engineered by	Tony Clark and Haydn Bendall
Herbie Flowers	bass	Recording location	Pathé Marconi, Paris, France
Graham Jarvis	drums, percussion	Recording date	7th-12th January 1979
Bill Livesy	keyboards		
John Perry	backing vocals		
Cliff Richard	vocals		
Tony Rivers	backing vocals		

2. Rock 'n' Roll Juvenile

Musicians		*Recording Details*	
Terry Britten	guitar	Producer	Cliff Richard and Terry Britten
Stuart Calver	backing vocals	Engineered by	Tony Clark and Haydn Bendall
Herbie Flowers	bass	Recording location	Abbey Road Studio 3, St. John's Wood, London
Graham Jarvis	drums, percussion	Recording date	24th January 1979
Bill Livesy	keyboards		
John Perry	backing vocals		
Cliff Richard	vocals		
Tony Rivers	backing vocals		

3. Unissued track (BBC Documentary)

Musicians		*Recording Details*	
Stuart Calver	backing vocals	Producer	Cliff Richard
Howie Casey	saxophone, trumpet, trombone	Engineered by	Unknown
John Clark	guitar	Recording location	Hammersmith Odeon, London
Mark Griffiths	bass	Recording date	1st May 1981
Graham Jarvis	drums, percussion		
Martin Jenner	guitar		
Alan Park	keyboards		
John Perry	backing vocals		
Cliff Richard	vocals		
Tony Rivers	backing vocals		
Graham Todd	keyboards		

♫ Rock that Doesn't Roll, The

Unissued track and from the album **Rock, Scissors et Papier** *(Larry Norman)*

First recorded by its composer and latterly Cliff Richard's friend, the late Larry Norman for his 1976 religious album, *In another Land*, *The Rock that Doesn't Roll* was a feature of Cliff's concerts before he decided to attempt a studio recording of it ostensibly lined up for inclusion on ***Now You See Me... Now You Don't***. *The Rock that Doesn't Roll* was one of five songs recorded at those album sessions that have not, to date, been released in any format.

In 1985, Cliff joined Larry Norman for a duet for a BBC television programme. The track was licensed from the Corporation and released on Norman's 2003 album *Rock, Scissors et Papier*. The stomping beat is set from the outset after Cliff has given the background for his choice of song and introduced Norman to the stage, and they take turns on the leads, while singing together in the chorus. The foot-tapping song is never better than when the pair sings together in harmony.

Track Specification
Composed by Larry Norman

__1. Unissued track (Now You See Me... Now You Don't)__

Musicians

Mel Collins	saxophone
Mark Griffiths	bass
Graham Jarvis	drums, percussion
Mart Jenner	electric guitar
Craig Pruess	piano, synthesisers, sequencers, electronic percussion
Cliff Richard	vocals, backing vocals
Bill Roberts	electric guitar

Recording Details

Producer	Cliff Richard and Craig Pruess
Engineered by	John Walker and Steve Cook
Recording location	Strawberry Studios South, Surrey
Recording date	4th-15th January 1982

__2. Rock, Scissors et Papier__

Musicians

Larry Norman	vocals, guitar
Cliff Richard	vocals
Unknown	guitar
Unknown	bass
Unknown	keyboards
Unknown	drums, percussion

Recording Details

Producer	Unknown
Engineered by	Unknown
Recording location	BBC Television Studios, London
Recording date	7th April 1985

♬ Roll On

From the album **Did He Jump... Or Was He Pushed?** *(Garth Hewitt)*

In 1979, Cliff Richard worked on a number of extracurricular recording projects for other artists including Garth Hewitt. The final song from the ***Did He Jump... Or Was He Pushed?*** album was written by Hewitt and produced by Cliff. *Roll On* was later chosen as the B-side track to the single release of the album's title track, ***Did He Jump?***. The song featured many familiar musicians from Cliff's own recordings and was written by the partnership Elton John and Gary Osborne, and the latter was involved in writing and performing on the phenomenon that was *The War of the Worlds* and *Forever Autumn*, alongside guitarist Jo Partridge, who was present on the recording of this track.

The signature sound of writer Elton John is present in the performance, generated by the piano accompaniment. The second coming of Christ is the subject of the song, which is sung with ebullience by Hewitt, matched by Cliff's excellent backing vocal, making the track an apposite choice for closing what is a great album that few have heard.

Track Specification
Composed by Gary Osborne and Elton John

Musicians

Garth Hewitt	vocals, guitar
Graham Jarvis	drums, percussion
Mike Moran	guitar, keyboards
Jo Partridge	guitar
Cliff Richard	backing vocals, guitar
Dave Wintour	bass

Recording Details

Producer	Cliff Richard
Engineered by	Tony Clark and Haydn Bendall
Recording location	Odyssey Studios, London
Recording date	1979

♬ Rosalie (Come Back to Me)

From the album **The Rock 'n' Roll Years 1958-1963**

Recorded by co-writer Fats Domino as an album track and covered by The Searchers, *Rosalie (Come Back to Me)* was later chosen by Cliff Richard and the Shadows for their regular radio slot. From 1959-1962, the Cliff and the band broadcast on Radio Luxembourg and, although most of the material they recorded live has not been released, four tracks have been issued on ***The Rock 'n' Roll Years 1958-1963*** including the transmitted verson of *Rosalie (Come Back to Me)*; since the radio station only broadcast in AM (the move to FM was yet a few years away), this track is only available in mono.

Introduced as the final song of the night, the performance is a fast-paced rock and roll number, with a rocking but uncredited piano accompaniment (possibly Hank Marvin since there is no guitar lead discernible on the song but this is unconfirmed). Cliff is clearly having fun on the main vocal while the Shadows do a rollicking good accompaniment with flourishes on bass and drums driving the song relentlessly onwards.

Track Specification
Composed by Antoine 'Fats' Domino and Dave Bartholomew

Musicians

Jet Harris	backing vocals, bass
Hank Marvin	backing vocals, guitar
Tony Meehan	drums, percussion
Cliff Richard	vocals
Unknown	piano
Bruce Welch	backing vocals, rhythm guitar

Recording Details

Producer	Unknown
Engineered by	Unknown
Recording location	Radio Luxembourg Studios, London
Recording date	1961

♫ Rote Lippen Soll Man Küssen

German single

A much-covered song in the native tongue in Germany, *Rote Lippen Soll Man Küssen* has been recorded by Gus Bachus, Peter Kraus, Captain Cook und Seine Singenden Saxophone, Günter Geissler, Tommy and, more recently, Declan, and it has even been used for the title of a home-grown 1963 musical film. It is a German translation of ***Lucky Lips***, although the title is literally translated back to English as *Red Lips One Should Kiss*, which is removed slightly from the meaning of the English original, which talks of the success the singer has with kissing the opposite sex because of the lucky lips (and also winning in gambling by kissing the chips for a cheap rhyme).

Cliff Richard's German version was recorded five months after his English version but uses the same Shadows backing track with the new vocals overdubbed, alongside the backing vocals, which are provided by a German chorus and were recorded in Germany on a separate occasion, thus making the recording a three-stage process. The sixth original take of the backing track with an unknown takes and edits of Cliff's new lead vocals and the backing vocals were used as the mono and stereo edits but with different mixes for the audio channels. Backed with the English ***Let's Make a Memory***, *Rote Lippen Soll Man Küssen* was issued on the Columbia label (catalogue number C-22563) in Germany in September 1963. It reached number one shortly after the English version (*Lucky Lips*) had achieved the same status. Until the issue of all Cliff's foreign language songs on the album ***On the Continent***, the song remained a highly-prized rarity.

For those familiar with the English version, the sound of the new backing vocals and Cliff singing in German is quite different but, in all other respects it is a faithful reproduction of the original, even down to the vocal chord harmonisation at the end, which is, however, not a patch on the Shadows original backing Cliff. Cliff recorded a lot of material in German and he seems to be comfortable with the pronunciation of the lyrics on this song.

Track Specification

Composed by Jerry Leiber and Mike Stoller; German translation by Hans Bradtke

Musicians

Brian Bennett	drums, percussion
Botho Lucas Chorus	backing vocals
Brian 'Licorice' Locking	bass
Hank Marvin	guitar
Cliff Richard	vocals
Unknown	hand claps
Unknown	piano
Bruce Welch	rhythm guitar

Recording Details

Producer	Norrie Paramor
Engineered by	Malcolm Addey
Recording location	Abbey Road Studio 2 (backing track) and Abbey Road Studio 3 (lead vocal), St. John's Wood, London and Germany (backing vocals)
Recording date	8th March 1963 (backing track), 11th August 1963 (lead vocal) and August 1963 (backing vocals)

♫ Rovin' Gambler

From the album **Live at the ABC Kingston 1962**

Recorded by Eddy Arnold, Tennessee Ernie Ford, Burl Ives and The Dwyers, *Rovin' Gambler* is one of the few tracks that Cliff Richard (with the Shadows in this event) performed on stage but did not attempt to record in the studio. Performed live at the ABC Theatre in Kingston, the track was held back until it was eventually issued on the 2003 CD ***Live at the ABC Kingston 1962***, although this was in stereo only.

Cliff's version begins with a guitar introduction that is reminiscent of ***Travellin' Light*** in its country feel and the bass line. The lyrics are changed to incorporate Kingston, where the band was performing, and Adam Faith (one of Cliff's contemporary competition) eliciting screams from the girls. The only percussion is provided by Brian Bennett on the tambourine, played enthusiastically against the guitar ensemble. The rhythm is broken into triplets in the final verse while Cliff breaks into recitation on occasions to set the scene for the following verses. The end of the track sets up the introduction to ***Save My Soul***.

Track Specification

Composed by Samuel F. Omar

Musicians

Brian Bennett	tambourine
Jet Harris	bass
Hank Marvin	guitar
Cliff Richard	vocals
Bruce Welch	rhythm guitar

Recording Details

Producer	Norrie Paramor
Engineered by	Malcolm Addey and Ken Townsend
Recording location	ABC Theatre, Kingston, Surrey
Recording date	7th March 1962

♫ Run for Shelter

From the album **...And They Said It Wouldn't Last! (My 50 Years in Music)**

Guy Fletcher and Doug Flett were the composers of the moment for Cliff in the early seventies as he was recording a number of their songs at the time (including a prior single ***Sing a Song of Freedom*** and the later Eurovision Song Contest entry ***Power to All Our Friends***). *Run for Shelter* was recorded at the same session as ***Empty Chairs***, later a B-side of ***Living in Harmony***, but, in spite of its pedigree, it wasn't issued. Given the lean amount of material recorded by Cliff over this time, that comes as a surprise. Nevertheless, this slice of early seventies Cliff was eventually included on the unreleased rarities section of the celebratory compilation ***...And They Said It Wouldn't Last! (My 50 Years in Music)*** in 2008.

Evocative of the style of this period of Cliff's material, *Run for Shelter* features a fuzzed guitar and tinkling piano as the prominent instruments. Cliff sings with a kind of impassioned benevolence as he instructs a friend to find protection with him (or perhaps religion).

Track Specification

Composed by Guy Fletcher and Doug Flett

Musicians

Nick Ingman	arranger, conductor
Nick Ingman Orchestra	orchestra
Cliff Richard	vocals

Recording Details

Producer	Norrie Paramor
Engineered by	Unknown
Recording location	Abbey Road Studio 3, St. John's Wood, London
Recording date	28th April 1972

♫ Run to the Door

From the film soundtrack album of **Finders Keepers**

Covered by Clinton Ford who took the song to number twenty-five in the UK charts in January 1967 with his final charting single, *Run to the Door* was recorded for inclusion on the ***Finders Keepers*** soundtrack album. Although it was not part of the film, the album was short on material prior to release and was padded out with three additional tracks (the other two were ***Into Each Life Some Rain Must Fall*** and ***Where Did the Summer Go?***). *Run to the Door,* featuring an orchestral backing and choral singers, is the best fit of the three additional tracks with the other songs on the album, which was written entirely by all four Shadows for the film soundtrack.

The third and final take and edit from the session was used for the mono and stereo recordings with different mixes for the needs of the separate audio channels.

This is a fun little song that Cliff successfully injects with a little knowing wit and humour. It is introduced by an *a capella* section by the Mike Sammes Singers. A real foot-tapper that is excellently arranged by Bernard Ebbinghouse, it requires Cliff to use his lower register, which is unusual in a lot of the material he had recorded up to this point.

Track Specification

Composed by Thomas Baker-Knight

Musicians

Bernard Ebbinghouse Orchestra	orchestra
Bernard Ebbinghouse	arranger, conductor
Mike Sammes Singers	backing vocals
Cliff Richard	vocals

Recording Details

Producer	Norrie Paramor
Engineered by	Peter Vincent and Richard Lush
Recording location	Abbey Road Studio 2, St. John's Wood, London
Recording date	20th September 1966

♬ Sad Song with a Happy Soul, A

From the album **...And They Said It Would Never Last! (My 50 Years in Music)**

One of three songs that were attempted at the session with none of them being released (although ***The Old Accordion*** and ***I Was Only Fooling Myself*** would be retried successfully at later sessions), Cliff Richard's recording of th quirky *A Sad Song with a Happy Soul* languished in the EMI vaults for thirty-eight years until it was unearthed during the research for the track listing of the celebratory release of the boxed set ***...And They Said It Would Never Last! (My 50 Years in Music)*** anthology in 2008. There is no information available from the sessions, and this includes the nams of the engineer and the other musicians performing on the track besides Cliff. Should this information come to light in later research, it will be updated in this entry.

It is curious that the song was not issued at the time because it is a lovely period piece. It is a love song that Cliff sings well as it is suited to his style and it is typically British with its evocation of preserving the stiff upper lip when things get tough, in this case the disintegration of a relationship. What makes the song so much better are the achingly beautiful diminished intervals between the melody and the supporting instrumental harmonies, while Cliff introduces some raucous emotion into a few of the lyrics.

Track Specification

Composed by Terry Cashman, Gene Pistilli and Tommy West

Musicians

Cliff Richard	vocals
Unknown	guitar
Unknown	bass
Unknown	drums, percussion
Unknown	keyboards

Recording Details

Producer	Norrie Paramor
Engineered by	Unknown
Recording location	Abbey Road Studio 3, St. John's Wood, London
Recording date	1st June 1970

♬ Sag 'No' zu Ihm

B-side of **Zuviel Allein**

Although Cliff Richard is one of the composers of the English language original of ***Don't Talk to Him***, this German translation version is based on his original lyrics and so, for this entry, he remains in the composer detail. *Sag 'No' zu Ihm* (literally translated as *Say 'No' to Him*, thus protecting the original theme of the song), was recorded in three steps: first, taking the original Shadows instrumental recording from the English language version of the song (thereby making this German release one of the final appearances of Brian 'Licorice' Locking as the Shadows bassist on a 'new' record, since he had been replaced by John Rostill in November the previous year), Cliff Richard overdubbed his German vocals at a separate session in March 1964, which also produced the A-side ***Zuviel Allein*** (the German language equivalent of ***I'm the Lonely One***) and then a German vocal group were recorded separately to add their backing vocals. The same takes and edits from the variety of sessions were used to create the mono and stereo recordings but with different mixes catering for the needs of the audio channels, although the song was originally only released in mono format and was a considerable rarity until the stereo release included in the foreign language package ***On the Continent*** in 1997.

As with all the foreign language versions of familiar Cliff hits, there is not much difference between the translated and English originals, which should come as no surprise. On *Sag 'No' zu Ihm*, what goes awry (as with its German A-side) is the backing vocals: the Botho Lucas Quartet, while musically competent, sound sterile, they are no Shadows and the song misses the extra magic that Hank Marvin, Bruce Welch and Cliff bring to the blending of their vocal harmonies. It should be noted that the backing track may well be a different take from the English equivalent, since the ending completes abruptly on a cymbal rather than the succession of guitar chords and drums.

Track Specification

Composed by Bruce Welch and Cliff Richard; German lyrics by Carl Ulrich Blecher

Musicians

Brian Bennett	drums, percussion
Botho Lucas Quartet	backing vocals
Brian 'Licorice' Locking	bass
Hank Marvin	guitar
Cliff Richard	vocals
Bruce Welch	rhythm guitar

Recording Details

Producer	Norrie Paramor
Engineered by	Malcolm Addey
Recording location	Abbey Road Studio 2, St. John's Wood, London (Shadows track and lead vocals) and Germany (backing vocals)
Recording date	13th October 1963 (Shadows track), 20th March 1964 (lead vocals) and March 1964 (backing vocals)

♫ Sail Away

From the album **Sail Away** *(Dave Pope)*

The title song of Dave Pope's solo album, ***Sail Away***, closes the first side of the album was one of a number of tracks recorded and produced by Cliff Richard on Pope's behalf in the spring of 1978. *Sail Away* was written by Chris Eaton, who would be instrumental in Cliff's own recording career in the eighties and into the new millennium. The album sleeve of Pope's album and other reference material provide no information regarding the musicians involved, although they could well be the same band that Cliff was using for his sessions and concerts of the period, and, until further research can identify them, they are annotated as unknown in the track specification of this entry.
The track is introduced by a languid piano solo that leads into Pope's lead vocal, which sounds stronger and less husky than it had on the earlier tracks on the album. The backing vocals are brought in around the mid-point of the song, with Cliff's contribution much in evidence. However, their use is limited with a preference to concentrate on the orchestral string arrangement and the piano accompaniment. The last minute of the song features the rock band, orchestra and a well-arranged backing vocal section repeating "we were lost but now we're found" before ending abruptly on an echoing instrumental chord.

Track Specification
Composed by Chris Eaton

Musicians

Dave Pope	vocals
Cliff Richard	backing vocals
Unknown	backing vocals
Unknown	guitar
Unknown	bass
Unknown	piano
Unknown	drums, percussion
Unknown	arranger, conductor
Unknown	orchestra

Recording Details

Producer	Cliff Richard
Engineered by	Tony Clark
Recording location	Morgan Studios, London
Recording date	April 1978

♫ Sam

From the album **Sincerely Cliff Richard**

The first song to be completed by Cliff Richard at the recording session, this song called *Sam* should not be confused with the single of the same name recorded by Olivia Newton-John in the mid-seventies, which was written by Hank Marvin, John Farrar and Don Black. Cliff's recording was co-written by Pete Callender, who had worked on the English lyrics for Cliff's earlier hit, ***All My Love***.
Using shimmering strings, a racing rhythm section and 'dooh'ing backing vocalists to move the song onwards, the song is a selection of hints and advice given to a man about being with a particular woman and is particularly evocative of the songs that Cliff was recording in the period.

Track Specification
Composed by Mitch Murray and Peter Callender

Musicians

Alan Hawkshaw Orchestra	orchestra
Alan Hawkshaw	arranger, conductor
Mike Sammes Singers	backing vocals
Cliff Richard	vocals

Recording Details

Producer	Norrie Paramor
Engineered by	Peter Vince
Recording location	Abbey Road Studio 2, St. John's Wood, London
Recording date	18th April 1969

♫ Santa's List

***132nd UK single** (original and edit)*

Written by Chris Eaton, who had already given Cliff Richard seasonal hits with ***Little Town*** and ***Saviour's Day***, *Santa's List* was Cliff's strongestattempt to obtain a number of chart firsts: his first number one of the new decade, his latest Christmas number one (thereby cementing his critics' belief that this was now all that he was good for in terms of recorded material), and his continuing record of having a number one in six successive decades. Backed with ***Mistletoe and Wine*** on the first disc of a dual CD release, *Santa's List* was issued on the EMI label (catalogue number SANTA 01) on 8th December 2003 and went on to reach number five in the UK singles charts, just a few sales short of reaching his dream. The second disc (catalogue number SANTA 02) featured ***Mary's Boy Child***, a duet with Helmut Lotti, and ***It's a Boy***, the theme song to the Christmas talking book of the same name released the same year, and it also included the promotional video for the song as well as a slightly edited version of the main track, with a slight remix and additional percussion and several cuts, particularly in the second verse. A promotional disc (CLIFF 200) was also released for the media's use. The promotional video was a film of Cliff performing the song interspersed with scenes of a typical family Christmas including a child writing on his list to Santa that he wants peace on earth.
With an exciting rhythm created on guitars and bass drum, *Santa's List* has echoes of *Saviour's Day* and *The Millennium Prayer*. As the song builds up, Cliff provides his own backing vocals leading into the ebullience of the sing-along chorus. Bells chime and strings swoop behind the glorious excitement of the song as the list of peace and generosity are itemized.

Track Specification
Composed by Chris Eaton and Nick Trevisick

1. Single

Musicians

Chris Cameron	conductor
Alex Charles	backing vocals
David Laudet	backing vocals
Hazel Ferenandez	backing vocals
Peter Gordeno	keyboards
Rick Mitra	drums, percussion
Phil Palmer	guitar
Cliff Richard	vocals, backing vocals
Samantha Scott	backing vocals
Unknown	orchestra
Gavin Wright	violin, leader

Recording Details

Producer	Chris Porter
Engineered by	Chris Porter
Recording location	Sony Studios, London (orchestra) and Porterhouse Studios, London (other instruments and vocals)
Recording date	2003

2. Single (second disc edit)

Musicians

Chris Cameron	conductor
Alex Charles	backing vocals
David Laudet	backing vocals
Hazel Ferenandez	backing vocals
Peter Gordeno	keyboards
Rick Mitra	drums, percussion
Phil Palmer	guitar
Cliff Richard	vocals, backing vocals
Samantha Scott	backing vocals
Unknown	orchestra
Unknown	percussion
Gavin Wright	violin, leader

Recording Details

Producer	Chris Porter
Engineered by	Chris Porter
Recording location	Sony Studios, London (orchestra) and Porterhouse Studios, London (other instruments and vocals)
Recording date	2003

♫ Saturday Night at the Whirl

Unissued track

During the February 1974 sessions for Cliff Richard's album ***The 31st of February Street***, there were three songs that were recorded that have never been released. One of these was *Saturday Night at the Whirl*, which was abandoned after two takes, about which there is scant information on the composer or the musicians playing on them. Until further information is unearthed, the known musicians at the sessions (from the other released tracks completed) are highlighted against the track specification.

Some sources suggest that the correct title of the song might either be *Night at the Whirl* or *Saturday Night at the World*, the latter written by Mason Williams and recorded by Jennifer Warnes in 1969. For the purposes of this book, deference is made to the research carried out by Peter Lewry and Nigel Goodall for their book *The Complete Recording Sessions 1958-1990*, which states the unissued title to be *Saturday Night at the Whirl*.

Track Specification
Composed by Unknown

Musicians

Terry Britten	backing vocals, guitar
Barrie Guard	arranger, conductor, percussion
Cliff Hall	keyboards
Jean Hawker	backing vocals
Gordon Huntley	steel guitar
David MacKay	backing vocals
Dave MacRae	keyboards
Anna Peacock	backing vocals
Kevin Peek	acoustic guitar
Cliff Richard	vocals
Trevor Spencer	drums, percussion
Alan Tarney	backing vocals, bass
Unknown	orchestra

Recording Details

Producer	David MacKay
Engineered by	Tony Clark and Mike Jarrett
Recording location	Abbey Road Studio 2, St. John's Wood, London
Recording date	12th February 1974

♫ Save My Soul

From the album **The Rock 'n' Roll Years 1958-1963**

Written and originally recorded by Jack Scott at the back end of the fifties, *Save My Soul* is one of the few tracks that Cliff Richard (with the Shadows in this event) performed on stage but did not record in the studio. Performed live at the ABC Theatre in Kingston, the track was released first on the compilation album ***The Rock 'n' Roll Years 1958-1963*** in 1997, before the entire concert was issued on the 2003 CD ***Live at the ABC Kingston 1962***, although this was in stereo only.

The introduction to this song is set up in the trail-off from the previous track, ***Rovin' Gambler***, and then is repeated at the beginning of this track on the CD. Cliff's version is performed with rapturous ebullience, supported by a fast-paced guitar ensemble and rattling drums as the audience claps along. Gospel-like with a rock and roll undertow, the final section slips into a dramatic diminuendo that is then picked up in force to the final climax, which is something that Elvis Presley executed so well in his performances of songs similar to this.

Track Specification
Composed by Jack Scott
Musicians

Brian Bennett	drums, percussion
Jet Harris	bass
Hank Marvin	guitar
Cliff Richard	vocals
Bruce Welch	rhythm guitar

Recording Details

Producer	Norrie Paramor
Engineered by	Malcolm Addey and Ken Townsend
Recording location	ABC Theatre, Kingston, Surrey
Recording date	7th March 1962

♫ Save the Last Dance for Me
From the album **Don't Stop Me Now!**

The final track on the ***Don't Stop Me Now!*** album by Cliff Richard is most famously associated with the Drifters (the American vocal group rather than the Shadows' earlier incarnation), who recorded and released it in 1960. Written by the prolific writing collaboration of Doc Pomus and Mort Shuman, the Drifters enjoyed a three-week tenure at the number one spot in the US and hit number two in the UK at the end of 1960 with what was their second single and first top ten success. The lead singer of the Drifters, Ben E. King, re-recorded the song and it was released much later in 1987 (after his sixties single *Stand By Me* was reissued and hit number one on the strength of a successful jeans commercial) but only achieved the number sixty-nine position. It was given another chart run in 1994, when General Saint ignominiously stayed at number seventy-five for just one week. The song has also been variously covered by artists such as Jerry Lee Lewis, Craig Douglas, the Heptones, the Swinging Blue Jeans, Dolly Parton, Bobby Vee, Neil Diamond, Jay and the Americans, Dion and the Belmonts, Tom Jones, the Righteous Brothers, the Troggs and Bobby Vinton among several others.

Recorded at one of the first sessions for the album, Cliff's version of *Save the Last Dance for Me* was one of four tracks completed that day with this song only requiring two takes to be finalized. Cliff has acknowledged liking Mike Leander's arrangements and this was the first session on which he worked with him. The second and final take and edit were used for the mono and stereo recordings.

With a quirky, if a little kitsch, brass arrangement to introduce the song, the song is kept at a steady pace, which is slightly slower than the original. Because of the unusual treatment and Cliff's clear enjoyment of the song matched with the Breakaways providing echoing backing vocals on each verse, it is a sound closer to the album, particularly with the meaning instigated by the lyrics.

Track Specification
Composed by Jerome Pomus and Mort Shuman
Musicians

Breakaways:	backing vocals
Vicki Hasemen	
Margo Quantrell	
Jean Ryder	
Mike Leander Orchestra	orchestra
Mike Leander	arranger, conductor
Cliff Richard	vocals

Recording Details

Producer	Norrie Paramor
Engineered by	Peter Vincent and Richard Lush
Recording location	Abbey Road Studio 2, St. John's Wood, London
Recording date	19th October 1966

♫ Saviour's Day
***113th UK single** and from the album* **Winterträume** *(Claudia Jung) and unissued live track*

Cliff Richard's extraordinary longevity in the music business showed no signs of abating as the nineties dawned. After his massive concerts at Wembley Stadium in June 1989 and a critically well-received album in ***Stronger***, Cliff was selling more records at this stage of his career than in the middle of the sixties. When the ***From a Distance ***** The Event*** album was issued, it added further to his acclaim and it was neatly rounded off with a number one single in *Saviour's Day* at the end of the year. It not only gave him his third Christmas number one in a row (***Mistletoe and Wine*** and ***Do They Know It's Christmas?*** being the first two) but it also gave him the unbeatable accolade of having number ones in five separate decades – from the fifties with the first version of ***Living Doll*** to the nineties with *Saviour's Day*.

Backed with the ***Oh Boy! Medley*** from the Wembley Stadium concerts as its principal B-side, *Saviour's Day* was released as a single on the EMI label (catalogue number XMAS 90) on 26th November 1990 and climbed to number one, displacing *Ice Ice Baby* by Vanilla Ice and staying for one week before being toppled by Iron Maiden's unsubtle *Bring Your Daughter... to the Slaughter* in the first chart of 1991. There were other formats of the single released simultaneously: a seven-inch single in a decade pack (catalogue number XMASP 90); a twelve-inch single (12XMAS 90); and a CD single (CDXMAS 90). Both the twelve-inch and CD singles incorporated an extra track in ***Where You Are***. A promotional disc was also cut for radio play, backed with *Mistletoe and Wine* (XMASDJ 90); in addition, another version shortened by the later fade up and sooner fade down on a promotional release of the ***Together with Cliff Richard*** album. *Saviour's Day* was first released in album form on *From a Distance ***** The Event* as a ploy to push sales, and the following year it appeared on the Christmas album

Together with Cliff Richard. The promotional video was filmed on 25th September 1990 at Durdle Door in Dorset (a rock carved out by nature with a large hole that is named a door). It features Cliff in a long white cotton coat observing a small girl through a window and building up so that everyone in the town follows him to the top of Durdle Door where he leads them in a sing-along to the backing of crashing waves timed in the film to the percussive accompaniment.

The performance of the song is deceptively powerful with a skittering bass and assured percussion running underneath each verse, while the main melody builds up dramatically throughout into the chorus accompanied by synthesized pipes (possibly intended to either be pan-pipes, as many critics suggested that they were the real thing and sneered accordingly, or more likely recorders). In the middle eight, the syncopated drums against the simplicity of the pipe sounds add an extra frisson to a song that already is something quite different in the charts.

In 1995, German singer Claudia Jung invited Cliff to duet on new arrangements of his two most well-known Christmas songs (at that juncture): *Saviour's Day* and ***Mistletoe and Wine***. Both tracks appeared on her Dutch album *Winterträume*. A faithful keyboard arrangement by Frank Busch ushers in the Jung's and Cliff's vocal performances, who sing close harmonies during the choruses, which is highly effective because, as noted in ***Weihnachtszeit***, Jung's voice sounds youthfully innocent, while Cliff's sounds mature and wise and this adds an extra dimension to the performance of the song. Cliff also provides multi-layered backing vocals in response to Jung's vocals. Although similar to the original, it is kept fresh by being just different enough.

Creating a ***Christmas Medley*** from his festive hits, in spite of the lack of seasonality by the time February 2003 came around, Cliff sang the selection of festive hits at the end of the world tour concerts. The New Zealand concert was filmed for DVD release while its companion *World our Live* CD album chose to miss releasing the medley on its track listing.

Track Specification
Composed by Chris Eaton

1. Single

Musicians		*Recording Details*	
John Clark	guitar	Producer	Cliff Richard and Paul Moessl
Pete Howarth	backing vocals	Engineered by	Gerry Kitchingham and Ben Robbins
Paul Moessl	keyboards, synthesisers, drum and percussion programming	Recording location	R. G. Jones Studios, Wimbledon, London
Mick Mullins	backing vocals	Recording date	16th-18th July 1990 and 20th-23rd July 1990
Keith Murrell	backing vocals		
Tessa Niles	backing vocals		
Cliff Richard	vocals, backing vocals		

2. Winterträume

Musicians		*Recording Details*	
Frank Busch	arranger, guitar, keyboards, programming	Producer	Dietmar Kawohl and Hans Singer
Claudia Jung	vocals	Engineered by	Keith Bessey
Cliff Richard	vocals, backing vocals	Recording location	Unknown
		Recording date	1996

3. Unissued track (World Tour Live)

Musicians		*Recording Details*	
Rachel Allen	violin	Producer	Keith Bessey
Elena Bulgakova	violin	Engineered by	Keith Bessey
Jenni Champion	violin	Recording location	The Mission Winery, Napier, New Zealand
Anthony Clark	backing vocals, guitar	Recording date	22nd February 2003
John Clark	guitar		
Dave Cooke	keyboards		
Cornelia Didenco	violin		
Gina Ferguson	violin		
Mike Haughton	flute		
Peter Howarth	backing vocals		
Cathy Irons	violin		
Pete May	drums, percussion		
Mick Mullins	backing vocals		
Keith Murrell	backing vocals		
Alan Park	keyboards		
Hee-Jung Park	violin		
Cliff Richard	vocals		
Eva Schwanen-Lilley	violin		
Steve Stroud	bass		

♫ Say You Don't Mind
From the album **Wired for Sound**

Not to be confused with the Denny Laine-written hit for Colin Blunstone in 1972, *Say You Don't Mind* is an Alan Tarney original written specifically for Cliff Richard's 1981 album ***Wired for Sound***. Tarney's increasing dominance in Cliff's recordings is evident throughout the album, particularly as he wrote most tracks, produced and arranged the album and

performs most of the instruments. The exception here, apart from the drums, is engineer Michael Boddicker performing the piano on this penultimate track in the album's track listing.
The rhythm of *Say You Don't Mind,* the sadness of the lyrics and minor key in which it is predominantly performed slow the pace down after a frenetic album's worth of material, although the drama is built up again as it leads into the mid-section. The freshness of the backing vocals, Tarney and Cliff together but not in the multi-layer format of the other tracks, lift the song further.

Track Specification
Composed by Alan Tarney

Musicians		*Recording Details*	
Michael Boddicker	piano	Producer	Alan Tarney
Graham Jarvis	drums, percussion	Engineered by	Michael Boddicker and Ian Little
Cliff Richard	vocals, backing vocals	Recording location	Gallery Studios, Chertsey, Surrey
Alan Tarney	arranger, backing vocals, guitar, bass, keyboards	Recording date	27th May-9th July 1981

♬ Say You're Mine
B-side of **Don't Talk to Him**

Only released in mono format only, *Say You're Mine* was one of a number of songs recorded in Blackpool during the Cliff Richard and the Shadows summer season in that seaside town (the other five being the entire ***When in France*** EP and a song that would be added to the ***Wonderful Life*** soundtrack).
Written by ex-Shadows drummer Tony Meehan (and an unknown first name for Rodgers), it was the second of two tracks completed on that session. Chosen as the B-side of Cliff's twenty-third UK single, ***Don't Talk to Him*** and then on the track listing of the ***Cliff Sings Don't Talk to Him*** EP, *Say You're Mine* was a real rarity until it was included on the track listing for the French album *Do You Want to Dance with Cliff Richard* and then the rarity collection album ***...And They Said It Wouldn't Last! (My 50 Years in Music)*** and then on a separate CD of ***Rare B-sides 1963-1989*** (which is the same that CD from the first collection).
With an uncredited piano performance – possibly either Hank Marvin,who plays the lead guitar melody here, or Norrie Paramor, which is more likely – the latinesque rhythm created by the percussion and the rhythm guitar and he minor key evokes the anguished emotion in the lyrics. Cliff's vocals are set back in the mix and are perfectly attuned to the tenor of this pleading love song.

Track Specification
Composed by Tony Meehan and Rodgers

Musicians		*Recording Details*	
Brian Bennett	drums, percussion	Producer	Norrie Paramor
Brian 'Licorice' Locking	bass	Engineered by	Malcolm Addey and Jimmy Johnson
Hank Marvin	guitar	Recording location	Jubilee Hall, Blackpool
Cliff Richard	vocals	Recording date	6th August 1963
Unknown	piano		
Bruce Welch	rhythm guitar		

♬ Scarlet Ribbons
From the album **Together with Cliff Richard** *and Dutch single (twelve-inch and CD)*

Many people incorrectly believe *Scarlet Ribbons* to be a traditional folk song but it was, in fact, written and published in 1949. Although not obviously a Christmas song, it appears on many a compilation and seasonal collections because of its story and the happy ending with a sort of religious message that evokes pictures of the festive season. A little girl is overheard by her father praying for scarlet hair ribbons before she goes to sleep. Her father is distraught that he is unable to find any ribbons or any material from which he can make them but is astounded when he looks in on his daughter the next morning to see scarlet ribbon everywhere in her bedroom.
The most familiar version to be recorded was by Harry Belafonte and Millard Thomas when they reached number seventeen in 1957 in the UK. Since then, a number of artists have recorded covers, including Gene Vincent, Jo Stafford, Sinéad O'Connor, Jim Reeves, Roy Orbison, Doris Day, Burl Ives, Val Doonican, Frank Ifield, the Bonzo Dog Doo-Dah Band, Gracie Fields, Bobbie Gentry and Joan Baez among several others.
Cliff Richard's version was recorded in the height of summer 1991 for release on the album ***Together with Cliff Richard*** later that year. Backed with the original recording of ***Miss You Nights***, *Scarlet Ribbons* was released as a single in Holland on the EMI label (catalogue numbers 20 4526 7 (seven-inch), 20 4526 6 (twelve-inch) and 20 4526 2 (CD)) on 14th October 1991; the twelve-inch single also featured an extended mix of the song. *Scarlet Ribbons* was then chosen to be the B-side of ***This New Year***, which was the second and final UK single to be released from the project, while the twelve-inch and CD versions incorporated the Dutch remix version on their track listings.
The arrangement of this familiar song is upbeat and syncopated with the synthesizers playing staccato chords on the offbeat. Meanwhile, Cliff's lead vocals have a slight echo applied. Cliff takes the melody and arranges it for the voice to take in a broader range. He provides his own backing vocals, which elevates the track further.

Track Specification
Composed by Evelyn Danzig and Jack Segal

1. Together with Cliff Richard

Musicians		*Recording Details*	
John Clark	guitar	Producer	Cliff Richard and Paul Moessl
Paul Dunne	guitar	Engineered by	Gerry Kitchingham, Andrew Greasley and Ben Robbins
Mark Griffiths	bass		
Peter May	drums, percussion	Recording location	R. G. Jones Studios, Wimbledon, London
Paul Moessl	drum programming, keyboards	Recording date	24th June 1991 to July 1991
Cliff Richard	arranger, vocals, backing vocals		
Frank Ricotti	drums, percussion		
Steve Stroud	bass		

2. 12-inch and CD singles (Holland)

Musicians		*Recording Details*	
John Clark	guitar	Producer	Cliff Richard and Paul Moessl
Paul Dunne	guitar	Engineered by	Gerry Kitchingham, Andrew Greasley and Ben Robbins
Mark Griffiths	bass		
Peter May	drums, percussion	Recording location	R. G. Jones Studios, Wimbledon, London
Paul Moessl	drum programming, keyboards	Recording date	24th June 1991 to July 1991
Cliff Richard	arranger, vocals, backing vocals		
Frank Ricotti	drums, percussion		
Steve Stroud	bass		

♫ Schön Wie ein Traum

German single

At the beginning of the sixties, Cliff Richard began a parallel singing career of recording songs in the four main non-English European languages that would last almost a decade and a half. Initially, though, the songs he recorded were in German, starting with the single ***Bin Verliebt*** (a version of ***Fall in Love with You***) in 1960 and followed by *Schön Wie Ein Traum*, which was recorded in April 1961. The mono and stereo versions of the song were the same take and edit but with different mixes for the requirements of the audio channels.

Schön Wie Ein Traum – literally translated as *As Beautiful as a Dream* – was a newly recorded version of Cliff's UK number three hit ***Theme for a Dream***. The basic instrumental accompaniment and Cliff's vocals were laid down at the UK session with overdubs performed in Germany (the studio personnel, dates and precise location are unknown) at a later date, although, in spite of being named The Hansen Boys, it was the female contingent of this chorus that was used on this recording. Released as a single in Germany, backed with ***Vreneli***, *Schön Wie Ein Traum* was issued on the Columbia label (catalogue number C 21843) in June 1961. It reached number thirty-three in the German singles charts, while its B-side charted separately, reaching number fifty.

The introduction to this German version is slightly different and slower than the domestic version but, unlike the B-side *Vreneli*, the Shadows' sound is maintained without the additional of extra instruments. The female voices that echo the end of each of the line are more subtle than the English version and, to this point, are a slight improvement.

Track Specification
Composed by Mort Garson and Earl Shuman with German translation by Ralph Maria Siegel

Musicians		*Recording Details*	
The Hansen Boys	female backing vocals	Producer	Norrie Paramor
Jet Harris	bass	Engineered by	Malcolm Addey
Hank Marvin	guitar	Recording location	Abbey Road Studio 2, St. John's Wood, London plus overdubs in unknown location in Germany
Tony Meehan	drums, percussion		
Cliff Richard	vocals	Recording date	10th April 1961
Bruce Welch	rhythm guitar		

♫ Schoolboy Crush

***Mooted first single** and B-side of* **Move It**

The fifties music scene in Britain was limited, with the American produce taking considerable precedence over home-grown fare. With new artists starting up in the wake of the phenomenal success of Bill Haley's rock 'n' roll sound, followed by the stratospheric appeal of the golden tones of Elvis Presley, it was felt by the music men in charge of the recording studios and the big labels that the only money to be made was with American tunes and British compositions being relegated to one-hit wonders and novelty songs.

As a result of this strategy, more often than not, the recording acts of the time were forced to record covers of songs by established American artists, even if they had not been written by them specifically. In the case of *Schoolboy Crush*, it was a song that had been relegated to a minor album track recorded by Bobby Helms.

Norrie Paramor, who had been assigned the task of producing the new signing to the Columbia label at EMI of Cliff Richard and the Drifters, chose this track as a perfect foil for Cliff's image of a young burgeoning heartthrob, who could easily express the words within the song without it appearing odd. It was intended to be released as his first single and,

rather than record another cover for its B-side, the band was allowed to record an original song that had been penned by Drifters guitarist Ian Samwell on the way to a rehearsal session at Cliff's house, ***Move It***.
There are various stories regarding how *Move It* became the A-side instead of *Schoolboy Crush* but the two most credible are: first, the influential television producer Jack Good, then at his career zenith with popular music programmes such as *Oh Boy!*, wanted Cliff to perform *Move It* and not Paramor's choice (in those days, Good held significant sway over the music business and they generally kowtowed to his suggestions or demands); second, and more romantically prosaic and possibly holding greater currency for the truth, Paramor took the masters for both *Schoolboy Crush* and *Move It* home and played them to his teenaged daughter, who then raved about the quality and beauty of the B-side. Whichever is true, it is nevertheless a twist of fate that allowed the far superlative *Move It* to be released in place of the relatively mediocre *Schoolboy Crush*.
The arrangement of the song is outmoded and rather pedestrian for the direction that music was going for the youth of the day, with embarrassing wolf-whistles and a large orchestra supporting what was essentially supposed to be a rock and roll outfit. It harked back to much that was going on in the late forties and early fifties and, although Cliff carries the vocals of with customary ease, the song sounds listless and dull, certainly in comparison to the extraordinary sound and vitality of its flip side. It also only featured a few of the members of Cliff's backing band since Paramor preferred to employ established session musicians rather than the Drifters.
The song was never released as the A-side, with *Move It* winning the coveted position and, apart from being the B-side of Cliff's first single (released as both a seven-inch 45 r.p.m. and ten-inch 78 r.p.m. single), for decades the song was unavailable in any other format and, even then, only in the original mono recording, although it has been since released as part of compendium anthologies of Cliff singles and rarities.

Track Specification
Composed by Ray Gilbert and Aaron Schroeder

Musicians		*Recording Details*	
Mike Sammes Singers	backing vocals	Producer	Norrie Paramour
Norrie Paramour Orchestra	orchestra	Engineered by	Malcolm Addey
Cliff Richard	vocals	Recording location	Abbey Road Studio 2, St. John's Wood, London
		Recording date	24th July 1958

♫ School Days

B-side of **Good on the Sally Army** *(Allan Shiers)*

In mid-1975, Cliff Richard started on his dual career as a producer by working on the single ***Good on the Sally Army*** by Allan Shiers and its B-side *School Days*. The single didn't sell many copies and there is, unfortunately, scant information on the technical and musical people involved or the location of the recording, although it is likely to Abbey Road. Once this information is identified, this entry will be updated accordingly.

Track Specification
Composed by Allan Shiers

Musicians		*Recording Details*	
Allan Shiers	vocals	Producer	Cliff Richard
Unknown	other instrumentation	Engineered by	Unknown
		Recording location	Unknown
		Recording date	July or August 1975

♫ Sci-Fi

From the album **Rock 'n' Roll Juvenile**

The opening track of the second side of the vinyl album ***Rock 'n' Roll Juvenile*** was the sixth to be written by co-producer Terry Britten and the second to be co-written by Scottish writer and performer B. A. Robertson, who was enjoying solo success in the British charts at the time. *Sci-Fi* was recorded in two sections, with the first taking place at the Parisian EMI studios, which provided the backing track for the second session, which was recorded back at Abbey Road, for the complex vocal overdubs.
Opening with an almost ethereal synthesiser track, the rock and roll rhythm is soon transplanted into the proceedings with twinkling effects and vocoders creating a science fiction atmosphere as per the title. The instrumentation is heaving on the guitars and the percussion and the performance is reminiscent of late period Barclay James Harvest.

Track Specification
Composed by Terry Britten and B. A. Robertson

Musicians		*Recording Details*	
Terry Britten	backing vocals, vocoder, Martian voices, guitar, keyboards	Producer	Cliff Richard and Terry Britten
Herbie Flowers	bass	Engineered by	Tony Clark and Haydn Bendall
Graham Jarvis	drums, percussion	Recording location	Pathé Marconi, Paris, France (backing track) and Abbey Road Studio, St. John's Wood, London (vocals)
Cliff Richard	vocals, backing vocals, vocoder, Martian voices	Recording date	18th-20th July 1978 (backing track) and 18th April 1979 (vocals)

♫ Sea Cruise

From the albums **From a Distance ***** The Event** *and* **Reunited**

Cliff Richard performed a number of rock 'n' roll era numbers as part of the opening set to ***The Event*** at Wembley Stadium in 1989 to showcase his own musical heritage and the songs that and inspired him along the way as well as reminding the audience of the other songs apart from his own that were released in that period. One of them was *Sea Cruise* which he performed as a solo. When first written, the song was first covered by Frankie Ford in 1959 using writer Huey Smith's own backing track and was subsequently covered by a number of artists including Status Quo, the Beach Boys, John Fogerty, Herman's Hermits, James Taylor and Johnny Rivers although no version has made it into the British singles charts in spite of its assumed familiarity.

Introduced by the ringing of a bell to indicate the ship taking the singer and listeners on the cruise, Cliff sings in falsetto during the rock and roll instrumentation introduction. Cliff sings the song with such ease and alacrity that it is not easy to understand that some of the notes are difficult to pitch in the musical intervals.

The song was also one of three chosen for recording for the ***Reunited*** album by Cliff and the Shadows in 2009 that wasn't one of their original songs, along with ***Singing the Blues*** and ***C'mon Everybody***. With a group of saxophonists and the clanging of a ship's bell, which would be in close focus on the set's backdrop during the supporting tour, this version is similar to Cliff's live version and is every bit as sophisticated with the backing of the Shadows.

Track Specification

Composed by John Vincent and Huey "Piano" Smith

1. From a Distance ** The Event***

Musicians		*Recording Details*	
Dallas Boys:		Producer	Cliff Richard
Nicky Clarke	backing vocals	Engineered by	Keith Bessey and Mick McKenna
Leon Fisk	backing vocals	Recording location	Rolling Stones Mobile Studio, Wembley Stadium, Wembley, North-west London
Stan Jones	backing vocals	Recording date	16th-17th June 1989
Joe Smith	backing vocals		
Bob Wragg	backing vocals		
Oh Boy! Band	rock 'n' roll band		
Cliff Richard	vocals		

2. Reunited

Musicians		*Recording Details*	
Brian Bennett	drums, percussion	Producer	Warren Bennett (co-ordination)
Warren Bennett	arranger (saxophones), piano	Engineered by	James Collins (Honeyhill Studios), Ethan Carlson (Middle Ear Studios), Les Williams (Nivram Studios) and Keith Bessey (mixing and mastering)
Dave Bishop	saxophone		
Mark Griffiths	bass		
Hank Marvin	guitar		
Cliff Richard	vocals, backing vocals	Recording location	Middle Ear Studios, Miami, Florida, USA (Cliff's vocals), Nivram Studios, Perth, Western Australia (Hank's guitars and vocals) and Honeyhill Studios, Hertfordshire, England (all other vocals and instruments)
Jamie Talbot	saxophone		
Phillip D. Todd	saxophone		
Bruce Welch	rhythm guitar		
		Recording date	Early 2009

♫ Secret Love

From the EP **Love Songs**

By far and away the most familiar version of *Secret Love* is by the singer who first performed it: Doris Day in her role as Calamity Jane in the film 1953 film of the same name. It was recorded in August 1953 and became an instant success reaching number one in the Billboard charts in the US, while in the UK, it was her sixth single release (since the charts were formed two years previously) and it became her first number one, reaching the top spot in April 1954, enjoying an interrupted nine weeks there. Two other versions have made the UK charts: Kathy Kirby (number in four in 1963) and Daniel O'Donnell (number twenty-eight in 1995). Other acts to have recorded the song include Mandy Moore, Cerys Matthews, Allan Sherman (a pastiche called *Secret Code*), Spike Jones, kd lang, Connie Francis, The Moonglows, Billy Stewart and George Michael, among several others.

The first song to be recorded by Cliff Richard at his 5th December 1961 session, *Secret Love* used the same take and edit for the mono and stereo versions but with different mixes for the audio channels. Although it was released on Cliff's US album (*It's All in the Game*), it was only ever available in the UK on the ***Love Songs*** EP, until the 1989 EP compilation release ***The EP Collection: Ballads and Love Songs***, which itself has become a rarity. The song was also released on the 2003 compilation *Cliff Richard Sings the Standards* album.

An oboe accompanied by strings provides the familiar melody as an introduction before Cliff takes up the vocal line. The woodwind, particularly clarinets and flutes, underpin the accompaniment as Cliff carries off a song that is traditionally associated with a female singer. The occasionally complex musical intervals are exercised with alacrity by Cliff and, once again, the performance shows Cliff's capabilities as a singer of any type of melodic song.

Track Specification
Composed by Paul Francis Webster and Sammy Fain

Musicians

Norrie Paramor Orchestra	orchestra
Norrie Paramor	conductor
Cliff Richard	vocals

Recording Details

Producer	Norrie Paramor
Engineered by	Malcolm Addey
Recording location	Abbey Road Studio 2, St. John's Wood, London
Recording date	5th December 1961

♫ Seeing Is Believing
Unissued track

In early 1969, Tyne Tees Television commissioned six playlets for their religious broadcast slot called *Life with Johnny,* featuring Cliff Richard in the role of Johnny as each episode one of Jesus' parables. Records are unclear on most of the episodes although *Johnny Come Home* and *Johnny Faces Facts* are complete, *Johnny and the Good Samaritan* is partially available, while the remainder are unavailable in either records or film form.

The songs had some relevance to the parable and there were usually five songs per episode. *Seeing Is Believing* appeared in one of *Johnny on the Rocks, Johnny and the Blind Rage* or *Johnny in Love.* The end credits of the episode stated that all songs were original and written in collaboration between Cliff, the Settlers and the programme's writer David Winter. The instrumentation and performance details are unknown.

Track Specification
Composed by Cliff Richard, David Winter, Cindy Kent, Mike Jones, John Fyffe and Geoffrey Srodzinski

Musicians

John Fyffe	backing vocals, guitar
Cindy Kent	backing vocals
Mike Jones	backing vocals, guitar
Cliff Richard	vocals
Geoffrey Srodzinski	backing vocals, bass

Recording Details

Producer	Norrie Paramor
Engineered by	Peter Vince
Recording location	Abbey Road Studio 3, St. John's Wood, London
Recording date	11th January 1969

♫ Sentimental Journey
From the album **Listen to Cliff!**

Published in 1944, *Sentimental Journey* was a major hit for the co-writers' own band, Les Brown and His Band of Renown, which starred Doris Day in one of her earliest recordings. The tenor of the lyrics and the gentle swing of the melody matched the optimistic mood at the time it was released since it coincided with the end of the Second World War, and reached number one in the US. It has since been covered by Ella Fitzgerald, Floyd Cramer, Woody Herman, Julie London, Rosemary Clooney, Duke Ellington, Bing Crosby, Ringo Starr, Rita Coolidge and Hank Snow among several others.

Issued on ***Listen to Cliff!***, *Sentimental Journey* was recorded in mono and stereo using the same sixth and final take and edit but with different mixes for the channels. The mono version was added to the CD single of ***What Car?*** in 2005, since Cliff had performed both tracks at the VE Day Remembrance Concert – it's unclear why the stereo version was not used.

With a late-night club feel to the song (belying once again Cliff's age at the time of recording), the orchestral arrangement squeezes in all the expected musical clichés for this style of song, with muted trumpets, crashing brass chords in the chorus and the thudding stand-up bass slapped in the background. As with many of the standards from the forties and fifties, Cliff carries the vocal lead extraordinarily well for one so young and confirms his ability to try something different rather than being pigeon-holed into a particular genre. The gentle swing style in this type of ballad suits his voice well.

Track Specification
Composed by Les Brown, Ben Homer and Bud Green

Musicians

Bernard Ebbinghouse Orchestra	orchestra
Bernard Ebbinghouse	arranger, conductor
Cliff Richard	vocals

Recording Details

Producer	Norrie Paramor
Engineered by	Malcolm Addey and David Lloyd
Recording location	Abbey Road Studio 2, St. John's Wood, London
Recording date	11th January 1961

♫ Seven Days to Our Holiday
From the film soundtrack album of **Summer Holiday**

Recorded at the end of a long session that saw *Orlando's Mime*, the opening title sequence and ***Really Waltzing*** recorded, *Seven Days to Our Holiday* is the first song to appear in the film, ***Summer Holiday***. With Cliff Richard playing a bus garage mechanic called Don, he persuades London Transport (then owners of the bus and underground train system) to lend him an old, red London bus, which he wants to convert into a sort of caravan, with showers, galley and sleeping compartments, so that he and three friends (played by Melvyn Hayes, Jeremy Bulloch and Teddy Green), who all work with him at the London Transport overhaul factory at Aldenham, Hertfordshire, can take it on a two-week holiday to Athens in Greece, tracking their way through many of the major European countries along the way. The interior shots for the sequence were performed at the real garage as the song counts down the number of days before the holiday as the group has so much to do for its preparation: ripping out the seats, putting in doors, plumbing in the sink and shower room, and making sure it is mechanically sound for its arduous journey. It is a great introduction to the film as it sets the

basic premise (the unusual act of taking a converted bus on holiday with a bunch of mates) as well as providing some comedic moments such as the shower exploding water into Hayes's face and the lyric alluding to the kitchen sink given the popular phrase about taking everything. Even though it is four of them who are destined to make the journey, the only slightly unrealistic point in the performance is that everybody in the entire factory appears to be involved in converting the bus and the conversion looks to be being done in working time, essentially implying that the overhaul of other buses is closed down for the seven days prior to the start of the boys' journey.
The same take and edit were used for both the mono and stereo recordings but with different mixes employed for the audio channels. The track was also featured on the listing for the ***More Hits from Summer Holiday*** EP. The film version of the song was recorded later in 1962 at the Elstree Studios but this remains unreleased in any other commercial format.
The orchestral flourishes in the song's introduction show what is to come in terms of the excitement and anticipation of the upcoming holiday. The verses are broken into each section of the countdown as the holiday nears. The Mike Sammes Singers provide the interaction on the soundtrack recording that can be heard by the actors in the film and are a bit too perfect for the rough and ready mechanics in the story.

Track Specification
Composed by Peter Myers and Ronald Cass

Musicians

Associated British Studio Orchestra	orchestra
Stanley Black	conductor
Mike Sammes Singers	vocals, backing vocals
Cliff Richard	vocals

Recording Details

Producer	Norrie Paramor
Engineered by	Malcolm Addey
Recording location	Abbey Road Studio 2, St. John's Wood, London
Recording date	22nd November 1962

♬ Shadows Medley
From the album **Cliff Live in Korea**

Often for Cliff Richard's tours, he developed a medley of familiar songs that hadn't been sung elsewhere in the concert. For his 1969 Korean tour with the Shadows, he sang a medley of songs that were popular with the Shadows backing him:

a) ***The Young Ones***
b) ***Living Doll***
c) ***In the Country***

The entries for those carry the information on the recording details and musicians.

♬ Shake, Rattle and Roll
From the album **From a Distance ***** The Event** *and unissued live track*

A well-loved rock and roll classic that goes back to 1954 when it was written by Jesse Stone under his pseudonym of Charles Calhoun, *Shake, Rattle and Roll* is an archetypal song of the genre that was originally recorded by Big Joe Turner but had its greatest success when it was released by Bill Haley and His Comets. Haley and his group reached number four in December of 1954 in the UK charts with what was their first single and ushering in the rock and roll era to Britain. It has since been covered by Elvis Presley (released as a single in the US), the Swinging Blue Jeans, Fats Domino, the Beatles, Sam Cooke and Huey Lewis and the News among several others.
Although Cliff Richard had performed an entire set of rock and roll classics at his thirtieth anniversary performances at Wembley Stadium, he included *Shake, Rattle and Roll* in the section designated *Cliff's Set* and has yet to record a studio version of it. It is a straightforward mid-paced rock and roll performance that is slower than the original but it is no worse for the different speed and rhythm. This sort of song is Cliff's metier and he clearly enjoys performance the song. In the penultimate chorus, Cliff inviters the audience to sing along while the instrumentation is played at low volume, before picking up again and taking control.

Track Specification
Composed by Charles Calhoun

1. From a Distance ** The Event***

Musicians

John Clark	guitar
Sonia Jones-Morgan	backing vocals
Steve Lauri	guitar
Peter May	drums, percussion
Paul Moessl	keyboards
Tessa Niles	backing vocals
Alan Park	keyboards
Provox:	
Peter Howarth	backing vocals
Mick Mullins	backing vocals
Keith Murrell	backing vocals
Cliff Richard	vocals
Steve Stroud	bass

Recording Details

Producer	Cliff Richard
Engineered by	Keith Bessey and Mick McKenna
Recording location	Rolling Stones Mobile Studio, Wembley Stadium, Wembley, North-west London
Recording date	16th-17th June 1989

2. Unissued (Knebworth - The Album)

Musicians

Ray Beavis	saxophone
Brian Bennett	drums, percussion
John Earle	saxophone
Chris Gower	trombone
Mark Griffiths	bass
Cliff Hall	keyboards
Dick Hanson	trumpet
Peter Howarth	backing vocals
Hank Marvin	backing vocals, guitar
Paul Moessl	keyboards
Mick Mullins	backing vocals
Keith Murrell	backing vocals
Cliff Richard	vocals
Bruce Welch	backing vocals, guitar

Recording Details

Producer	Chris Kimsey and Steve Smith
Engineered by	Unknown
Recording location	Knebworth House, Hertfordshire, England
Recording date	30th June 1990

♫ Shakin' All Over

B-side of **Daddy's Home**

Written by Fred Heath (better known by his stage name of Johnny Kidd), he recorded it with his backing group the Pirates and it reached number one for just one week in July 1960, displacing Cliff Richard and the Shadows' ***Please Don't Tease***. Johnny Kidd and the Pirates were subsequently displaced by *Please Don't Tease* after it rallied for another two weeks at the top spot. It wasn't a major hit, however, outside Europe and it was a cover version by Chad Alan that was successful in North America. It has subsequently been covered by the Flamin' Groovies, Steve Marriott, Van Morrison, Suzi Quatro, Bachman-Turner Overdrive, Dee Dee Ramone, Generation X, Terry Dene, Iggy Pop and the Swinging Blue Jeans.

Cliff regularly performed songs in concert that he had never tried to record in the studio and, in 1981, *Shakin' All Over* was recorded live at a concert at the Hammersmith Odeon for musical material to accompany a four-part BBC documentary about Cliff. Three songs were licensed from the BBC for proposed released, *Shakin' All Over*, ***Daddy's Home*** and ***Stood Up***, although the latter remains unissued to date. When *Daddy's Home* was agreed to be Cliff's eighty-second single release in the UK, *Shakin' All Over* was chosen as its B–side. Quite a rarity for a number of years, the track was eventually reissued as a bonus track on the 2001 remaster of ***Wired for Sound***.

Track Specification

Composed by Fred Heath

Musicians

Stuart Calver	backing vocals
Howie Casey	saxophone, trumpet, trombone
John Clark	guitar
Mark Griffiths	bass
Graham Jarvis	drums, percussion
Martin Jenner	guitar
Alan Park	keyboards
John Perry	backing vocals
Cliff Richard	vocals
Tony Rivers	backing vocals
Graham Todd	keyboards

Recording Details

Producer	Cliff Richard
Engineered by	Unknown
Recording location	Hammersmith Odeon, London
Recording date	1st May 1981

♫ Shame on You

From the album **21 Today**

The final track on the ***21 Today*** album was the third and final home-grown track. Co-written by Hank Marvin and Bruce Welch and someone called Jacobson (research has not unearthed a first name), it was the last of three songs to be recorded in the session with twenty takes, the final one of which was used for the mono and stereo edits but with different mixes to cater for the requirements of the audio channels. According to the liner notes of ***The Rock 'n' Roll Years 1958-1963***, it was suggested that Cliff Richard was a co-writer of the song; however, this is incorrect and should be aligned to the notes for ***Without You*** instead.

Back on comfortable ground, the song is another example of the perfect blend of voices and harmonies between Cliff, Hank and Bruce principally. A strong rock and roll song, it also has the sound that would be the Cliff and the Shads trademark.

Track Specification

Composed by Bruce Welch, Hank Marvin and Jacobson

Musicians

Jet Harris	backing vocals, bass
Hank Marvin	backing vocals, guitar
Tony Meehan	drums, percussion
Cliff Richard	vocals
Bruce Welch	backing vocals, rhythm guitar

Recording Details

Producer	Norrie Paramor
Engineered by	Malcolm Addey
Recording location	Abbey Road Studio 2, St. John's Wood, London
Recording date	11th July 1961

♬ Share a Dream

From the album **Stronger** *and B-side of* **Scarlet Ribbons** *(Holland twelve-inch and CD single only) and unissued tracks*

As with many of the songs he eventually recorded, Cliff Richard liked to try them out in front of an audience before committing them to tape in the studio. Several never made it into the studio but *Share a Dream* was one such that did. Performed during the *Live and Guaranteed 1988!* tour, *Share a Dream* was one of the songs that was recorded and filmed at the Danish concert but never subsequently issued on the subsequent album.

At the time of recording the studio version, Aswad had had a major number two hit earlier in the year with *Don't Turn Around* and were then much sought after for recording gigs. This demand for their involvement included Cliff, who has always been canny about choosing the people he works with. At the time of the release of his 1989 album, ***Stronger***, on which the studio version of *Share a Dream* appeared, there was much discussion and quotes from Aswad's press office that it was their collaboration that was destined to be Cliff's one hundredth single release. The discussion and presumption was moot, partly because ***The Best of Me*** was touted as the hundredth single and mainly because, in fact, ***Slow Rivers*** (a minor hit duet he recorded with Elton John) was Cliff's hundredth single release – *The Best of Me* was still the hundredth *charting* song, however, and the prestige of having been involved in such a historic record would have pushed publicity machines into overdrive.

With a strong reggae beat built into the synthesized bass line, Cliff sings this style of song well, even though it was quite a departure from his familiar material. The backing vocals are in close harmony and, over and above the reggae rhythm, it is this that creates a focus of interest.

A new remix of the track by Ben Robbins was included as a bonus track on the Dutch single release of ***Scarlet Ribbons***, which was issued in October 1991, but only the twelve-inch and CD versions of the release.

The song was performed and recorded at Cliff's thirtieth anniversary celebrations at Wembley Stadium but, rather than use the live version, the studio version was employed with applause dubbed on to the beginning and the live version transposed at the end. For this reason, it has its own track specification, although the song has only ever been released in its studio format only. *Share a Dream* was incorporated on to the ***From a Distance ***** The Event*** vinyl and CD albums in 1990 but was removed from the 2005 remaster (since it wasn't itself from the concert). What happened to the original live recordings is unknown.

Track Specification

Composed by Rod Trott, Jon Sweet and Richard Osborne

1. Unissued track (Live & Guaranteed 1988!)

Musicians		*Recording Details*	
John Clark	guitar	Producer	Unknown
Rosemarie Ford	backing vocals	Engineered by	Unknown
Mark Griffiths	bass	Recording location	Fyens Forum, Odense, Denmark
Peter Howarth	backing vocals	Recording date	22nd May 1988
Steve Lauri	guitar		
Paul Moessl	keyboards		
Mick Mullins	backing vocals		
Alan Park	keyboards		
Cliff Richard	vocals		
Henry Spinetti	drums, percussion		

2. Stronger

Musicians		*Recording Details*	
Brinsley Forde	backing vocals, guitar	Producer	Aswad
Angus Gaye	backing vocals, drums, percussion	Engineered by	Godwin Logie
Cliff Richard	vocals, backing vocals	Recording location	"The Lighthouse Studio", Battery Studios, London
Tony Robinson	bass	Recording date	29th-31st August 1988

3. B-side (Scarlet Ribbons – twelve-inch and CD only)

Musicians		*Recording Details*	
Brinsley Forde	backing vocals, guitar	Producer	Aswad
Angus Gaye	backing vocals, drums, percussion	Engineered by	Godwin Logie
Cliff Richard	vocals	Recording location	"The Lighthouse Studio", Battery Studios, London
Tony Robinson	bass	Recording date	29th-31st August 1988

4. Unissued track (From a Distance ** The Event)***

Musicians		*Recording Details*	
Brinsley Forde	backing vocals, guitar	Producer	Cliff Richard
Angus Gaye	backing vocals, drums, percussion	Engineered by	Keith Bessey and Mick McKenna
Cliff Richard	vocals	Recording location	Rolling Stones Mobile Studio, Wembley Stadium, Wembley, North-west London
Tony Robinson	bass	Recording date	16th-17th June 1989

♫ She Makes Me Feel Like a Man

From the album **Real as I Wanna Be**

The only song to have a writing contribution from Cliff Richard on his album ***Real as I Wanna Be***, *She Makes Me Feel Like a Man* is also archetypal Cliff ballad material and a departure from the electronica-led soul of much else on the album. Presented at a slow waltz speed, the bass introduction leads into the gentle vocal by Cliff as he emotes in this beautifully structured love song. The arrangement of the backing vocals, augmented by additional singers and including Cliff, adds further beauty to the song.

Track Specification

Composed by Peter Wolf, Michelle Wolf and Cliff Richard

Musicians

Lynn Davis	backing vocals
Kevin Dorsey	backing vocals
Michael Landau	guitar
Ricky Lawson	drums, percussion
Phil Perry	backing vocals
Daryyl Phinnessee	backing vocals
Cliff Richard	vocals, backing vocals
Michelle Wolf	backing vocals
Peter Wolf	arranger, bass, keyboards, percussion

Recording Details

Producer	Peter Wolf
Engineered by	Christian Leitgeb, Chris Heil, Paul Erickson and/or Keith Bessey
Recording location	Little America Recording Studios, Weiler, Austria, Ocean Recording Studios, Burbank, California, USA, Arco Recording Studios, Munich, Germany, R. G. Jones Recording Studios, Wimbledon, London, England and/or The Pierce Room, London, England
Recording date	March-April 1996 and November 1997

♫ She Means Nothing to Me

86th UK single *and from the album* **The Rock Connection Remastered**

In 1981, Cliff Richard invited Phil Everly to join him in concert to cover Everly Brothers' hits and a tribute to the rock and roll legends. Although these tracks weren't issued until 1994, with the ***All I Have to Do Is Dream*** single release, Everly remembered the experience and contacted Cliff with the idea that they should collaborate on some original material. When Cliff first heard *She Means Nothing to Me*, written by one of the guitarists in the band, he was enthusiastic and entered the studious in early October 1982. Also playing on the track were other well-known session men as well as the Dire Straits guitarist Mark Knopfler, whose distinctive style can be heard on the track. When Cliff arrived at the Eden Studios, Everly ensured he knew his part and expended effort to make Cliff happy before leaving, after which Everly re-recorded his vocal line again. At the same session, another track was also recorded: ***I'll Mend Your Broken Heart***.

She Means Nothing to Me was backed with *A Man and a Woman*, a Phil Everly only track, and released on the Capitol label (catalogue number CL 276) on 7th February 1983 and it reached number nine in the UK singles charts. Originally, *She Means Nothing to Me* was only available on Everly's album *Phil Everly*, but it was subsequently remixed and added to the ***The Rock Connection*** when it was realized that there was insufficient material to complete the album. This version has Everly's vocals mixed up-front with the guitars mixed differently and, prominently, an end to the track rather than a fade-out. It features Cliff singing the principal melody line and Everly singing descant harmonies, as would have been the case had he been singing with his brother, Don. Both take the lead throughout the song, while Cliff provides backing vocals.

Track Specification

Composed by John David

1. Single

Musicians

Stuart Coleman	reverse lead guitar, bass, six-string bass, percussion
John David	guitar
Phil Everly	vocals
Mickey Gee	rhythm guitar
Rod Houison	percussion
Mark Knopfler	guitar, rhythm guitar
Cliff Richard	vocals, backing vocals
Terry Williams	drums, percussion
Pete Wingfield	electric piano

Recording Details

Producer	Stuart Coleman
Engineered by	Rod Houison and Neill King
Recording location	Eden Studios, London
Recording date	5th October 1982

2. The Rock Connection Remastered

Musicians

Stuart Coleman	reverse lead guitar, bass, six-string bass, percussion
John David	guitar
Phil Everly	vocals
Mickey Gee	rhythm guitar
Rod Houison	percussion
Mark Knopfler	guitar, rhythm guitar
Cliff Richard	vocals, backing vocals
Terry Williams	drums, percussion
Pete Wingfield	electric piano

Recording Details

Producer	Stuart Coleman
Engineered by	Rod Houison and Neill King
Recording location	Eden Studios, London
Recording date	5th October 1982

♫ She Needs Him More than Me

From the pantomime cast recording album of **Cinderella**

She Needs Him More than Me is a typical song at the dying moments of a pantomime where the principal characters appear unable to get together in the mistaken belief that they are better off with someone else. So it was with ***Cinderella,*** which was performed in the winter of 1966 into 1967 at the London Palladium starring Cliff Richard and the Shadows. Recorded at the second designated session for the cast recording of the show, it was the first song in the can. The eighth and final take and edit was used for both the mono and stereo recordings. The mono version also appeared on the ***Cinderella*** EP that was issued in the middle of 1967.

This lovely introspective song is a classic Cliff and the Shadows song that breaks from quiet and thoughtful to a slightly more upbeat ensemble performance, elevated by the classic close harmony vocals. Tinged with regret, it is a perfect song for a pantomime performance.

Track Specification

Composed by Hank Marvin, Bruce Welch, Brian Bennett and John Rostill

Musicians		*Recording Details*	
Brian Bennett	drums, percussion	Producer	Norrie Paramor
Hank Marvin	backing vocals, guitar	Engineered by	Peter Vince and Richard Lush
Cliff Richard	vocals	Recording location	Abbey Road Studio 2, St. John's Wood, London
John Rostill	backing vocals, bass	Recording date	17th October 1966
Bruce Welch	backing vocals, rhythm guitar		

♫ She's a Gypsy

From the album **Green Light** *and unissued live track*

Recorded at the final session (other than for overdubs) for the ***Green Light*** album, *She's a Gypsy* was co-written by John Bryant who had provided a number of titles for the Shadows in the sixties. Completed in one take, further overdubs were added at a session a week later.

Referred to on the album's liner notes as *She's a Gipsy* (using the alternative less popular spelling), the song is a medium-paced love song with a competent rock band supporting Cliff's lead vocal. Again, as with many tracks under Bruce Welch's direction, it is the arrangement of backing vocals then elevate the track into something more special.

Unusually, Cliff included this album track on his 2003 world tour in support of the then newly released album, ***Wanted.*** While he performed a number of tracks from that album, he also resurrected a number of other tracks from his early career. The New Zealand show was recorded for DVD release later in the year and, in 2004, a complementary CD was released with a subset of the tracks heard in the film, which did not include *She's a Gypsy.*

Track Specification

Composed by John Bryant and Dempsey

1. Green Light

Musicians		*Recording Details*	
Brian Bennett	drums, percussion	Producer	Bruce Welch
Terry Britten	guitar	Engineered by	Tony Clark and Haydn Bendall
Stuart Calver	backing vocals	Recording location	Abbey Road Studio 3, St. John's Wood, London
Alan Jones	bass	Recording date	18th and 25th April 1978
Duncan MacKay	keyboards		
Alan Parker	guitar		
John Perry	backing vocals		
Tim Renwick	guitar		
Cliff Richard	vocals		
Tony Rivers	backing vocals		
Trevor Spencer	drums, percussion		
Alan Tarney	backing vocals, guitar, bass, keyboards		
Graham Todd	keyboards		
Unknown	saxophone		

2. Unissued track (World Tour Live)

Musicians		*Recording Details*	
Anthony Clark	backing vocals, guitar	Producer	Keith Bessey
John Clark	guitar	Engineered by	Keith Bessey
Dave Cooke	keyboards	Recording location	The Mission Winery, Napier, New Zealand
Mike Haughton	saxophone	Recording date	22nd February 2003
Peter Howarth	backing vocals		
Pete May	drums, percussion		
Mick Mullins	backing vocals		
Keith Murrell	backing vocals		
Alan Park	keyboards		
Cliff Richard	vocals		
Steve Stroud	bass		

♫ She's All Mine

iTunes download

Co-written by Cliff Richard's old friend Chris Eaton, *She's All Mine* was recorded during the American sessions for Cliff's 2004 album ***Something's Goin' On***. Initially, although it wasn't an official single, it was only released for download on iTunes in October 2004 but was then added as a B-side track to the second single to be released from the album, ***I Cannot Give You My Love***, before being added as one of the four extra tracks of the reissue of the album's new title, ***For Life***.
The introduction to the song sounds like a pomp rock song from the seventies with an up-to-date, contemporary feel to it. The rocking bass, keyboards and guitars are superb, while Cliff's vocals fit the style of the song perfectly as he is pushed to use all elements of his vocal performance capabilities.

Track Specification
Composed by Chris Eaton and Ralph van Manen

Musicians	
Greg Bieck	programming
Trey Bruce	programming
Pat Buchanan	guitar
Lisa Cochran	backing vocals
J. T. Corenflos	guitar
Tony Harrell	keyboards
Wes Hightower	backing vocals
Greg Morrow	drums, percussion
Alison Prestwood	bass
Cliff Richard	vocals, backing vocals
Michael Spriggs	guitar

Recording Details	
Producer	Trey Bruce
Engineered by	David Buchanan
Recording location	Omnisound Recording Studios, Nashville, Tennessee, USA, Sound Stage Studios, Nashville, Tennessee, USA and Pocket Studio, Franklin, Tennessee, USA
Recording date	2003-2004

♫ She's Gone

From the album **Me and My Shadows**

Yet another Shadows-written song appears as the fifth title on the ***Me and My Shadows*** album. Using the seventh take from the session on 17th March 1960, the mono and stereo versions use the same recording but are mixed differently with the mono version also being edited a few seconds shorter than the stereo, thus missing out on a further repetition of the playing out chorus. The song also appeared on the release of the ***Me and My Shadows No. 1*** EP.
A foot-tapping song, it employs a repetitive guitar riff that shows off Hank Marvin's trademark sound that is unmistakable in his performance. The track is another song regarding the lost love of a girl who has left Cliff in the lurch. The middle eight features an extended guitar solo, underpinned by a plodding bass line that gives the impression of walking slowly around the town.

Track Specification
Composed by Hank Marvin and Jet Harris

Musicians	
Jet Harris	bass
Hank Marvin	guitar
Tony Meehan	drums, percussion
Cliff Richard	vocals
Bruce Welch	rhythm guitar

Recording Details	
Producer	Norrie Paramor
Engineered by	Malcolm Addey and Norman Smith (mono) and Peter Bown and Alan Kane (stereo)
Recording location	Abbey Road Studio 2, St. John's Wood, London
Recording date	17th March 1960

♫ She's Leaving You

B-side of **Big Ship**

Written by Shadows drummer Brian Bennett, he also arranged and conducted his own orchestra to accompany Cliff Richard's vocals. The song was chose as the B-side of Cliff's forty-sixth UK single, ***Big Ship***, which had been recorded at a session the week before. This is the first example of Brian's arrangements, which would be a future successful dual career for him. Issued in mono only – Columbia's policy had remained the same for some years in that singles should be released in mono and albums now in stereo only partly because most radio stations were still broadcasting in mono only – *She's Leaving You* was a considerable rarity for many years, until the stereo version was released on the rare B–sides section of the celebratory collection ***...And They Said It Wouldn't Last! (My 50 Years in Music)***.
The sweet string arrangement that swaps between minor and major keys underpins this bittersweet song that is an observation of a couple splitting up. Cliff's vocal is impassioned, as expected, and even cracks slightly during the middle eight; and it is mixed with a slight echo behind it. There is a lovely vocal arrangement in the chorus with uncredited female vocalists (possibly the Breakaways but unconfirmed) before control is passed back to the verse.

Track Specification
Composed by Brian Bennett

Musicians	
Brian Bennett	arranger, conductor
Brian Bennett Orchestra	orchestra
Cliff Richard	vocals
Unknown	backing vocals

Recording Details	
Producer	Norrie Paramor
Engineered by	Peter Vince and Richard Langham
Recording location	Abbey Road Studio 2, St. John's Wood, London
Recording date	30th April 1969

♫ She's So Beautiful

95th UK single (seven- and twelve-inch versions), B-side of **She's So Beautiful** *and from the album* **Dave Clark's Time – The Album**

The first of three singles by Cliff Richard released from the stage musical soundtrack of Dave Clark's ***Time*** was *She's So Beautiful*, which was produced by Stevie Wonder as well as performing all of the instrumentation on it (effectively making it a duet with the great Motown musician). The concept of the stage show is that the Earth and humanity are under trial by alien justice-keepers, who can't understand why human beings treat others and nature in such a shabby way and they call a representative to account. Because of the Rock Singer's obvious popularity at a stadium concert, he is chosen to justify man's actions and protect the Earth. Played by Cliff, he mounts his defence by talking about the sheer beauty and wonder of nature by singing *She's So Beautiful*, which refers to the planet but can also be a standard love song directed at a partner. Stevie Wonder laid down the initial track and, because Cliff didn't want to fly out to Los Angeles, he recorded his part at Abbey Road Studios, sending the result back to Wonder, who then re-recorded everything else to fit in with Cliff's lead.

Backed with a specially mixed version of the song as its B-side, *She's So Beautiful* was released as a single on the EMI label (catalogue number EMI 5531) on 2nd September 1985 and reached number seventeen in the UK charts. At the same time, a twelve-inch single featured an extended version of the song was issued (12EMI 5531) and the seven-inch single was first released on CD on the ***Private Collection*** album in 1988. The single version differs from the album in that the lyric is slightly different at the start and fades out around thirty seconds after the album version. The special mix that appears on the seven-inch B-side is effectively an instrumental version but also features Cliff on backing vocals and fades out around forty-five seconds earlier than the single. This version was extended and appears on the German twelve-inch single release and has several extra seconds before fading out (catalogue number EMI 12EMI 2007996).

The languid synthesiser accompaniment brings the song in, with Cliff performing his anguished, pleading vocals, pointing out all the good points of the earth. It becomes van upbeat and life-affirming song that can double as an observational love song or a human girl or the planet Earth.

The video for the single was filmed in the Lake District and directed by the great Ken Russell over a four-day period from 17th to 21st June 1985. With images of sand running through an hour glass and several clock faces, Cliff is seen in the beautiful Lakeland scenery, bouncing a football-shaped globe. The video also features a number of children as Cliff twizzles the globe like basketball players have a tendency to do.

Track Specification

Composed by Hans Poulsen

__*1. Single (seven-inch)*__

Musicians		*Recording Details*	
Cliff Richard	vocals	Producer	Stevie Wonder
Stevie Wonder	backing vocals, keyboards, drum sequencers	Engineered by	Bob Harlan
		Recording location	Abbey Road Studios, St. John's Wood, London (Cliff Richard) and Wonderland Studios, Los Angeles, California (Stevie Wonder)
		Recording date	20th-21st December 1984 (lead vocals) and 1984 (other musicians)

__*2. B-side (She's So Beautiful (special mix – not Germany))*__

Musicians		*Recording Details*	
Cliff Richard	vocals	Producer	Stevie Wonder
Stevie Wonder	backing vocals, keyboards, drum Sequencers	Engineered by	Bob Harlan
		Recording location	Abbey Road Studios, St. John's Wood, London (Cliff Richard) and Wonderland Studios, Los Angeles, California (Stevie Wonder)
		Recording date	20th-21st December 1984 (lead vocals) and 1984 (other musicians)

__*3. B-side (She's So Beautiful (special mix –Germany))*__

Musicians		*Recording Details*	
Cliff Richard	vocals	Producer	Stevie Wonder
Stevie Wonder	backing vocals, keyboards, drum Sequencers	Engineered by	Bob Harlan
		Recording location	Abbey Road Studios, St. John's Wood, London (Cliff Richard) and Wonderland Studios, Los Angeles, California (Stevie Wonder)
		Recording date	20th-21st December 1984 (lead vocals) and 1984 (other musicians)

__*4. Single (twelve-inch)*__

Musicians		*Recording Details*	
Cliff Richard	vocals	Producer	Stevie Wonder
Stevie Wonder	backing vocals, keyboards, drum Sequencers	Engineered by	Bob Harlan
		Recording location	Abbey Road Studios, St. John's Wood, London (Cliff Richard) and Wonderland Studios, Los Angeles, California (Stevie Wonder)
		Recording date	20th-21st December 1984 (lead vocals) and 1984 (other musicians)

5. *Dave Clark's Time – The Album*

Musicians		*Recording Details*	
Cliff Richard	vocals	Producer	Stevie Wonder
Stevie Wonder	backing vocals, keyboards, drum Sequencers	Engineered by	Bob Harlan
		Recording location	Abbey Road Studios, St. John's Wood, London (Cliff Richard) and Wonderland Studios, Los Angeles, California (Stevie Wonder)
		Recording date	20th-21st December 1984 (lead vocals) and 1984 (other musicians)

♫ Shine, Jesus, Shine

From the album **The Kendrick Collection** *(Graham Kendrick)*

Cliff Richard had long been a fan of Graham Kendrick's religious songs having recorded a number himself and also offered many to his various protégées, including Sheila Walsh. He therefore was an obvious choice to sing a number of his favourites at a session at the All Souls Church in Langham. The final one of three he recorded, *Shine, Jesus, Shine,* is the only track featuring the choir as well as the orchestra.

A gentle piano melody ushers in the song and is joined by running strings and brass as Cliff's lead vocal starts. Cliff sings the initial lines in a clandestine, covered way but this opens up for the chorus, where he is joined by the choir. The song quietens down again as the song enters into the second verse, which slowly builds up once more.

Track Specification

Composed by Graham Kendrick

Musicians		*Recording Details*	
All Souls Choir	choir	Producer	Burt Rhodes
All Souls Orchestra	orchestra	Engineered by	Graham McHutchon
Cliff Richard	vocals	Recording location	All Souls Church, Langham, London
Noël Tredinnick	arranger, conductor	Recording date	2nd February 1989

♫ Ships that Pass in the Night

Unissued track

Written by Terry Britten, *Ships that Pass in the Night* has been covered by Billy J. Kramer and very few others. During the ***Green Light*** album sessions, there were several tracks that were recorded by Cliff Richard but which haven't been issued. One such was *Ships that Pass in the Night,* recorded at the second session for the album and abandoned after one take (whether it was sufficient or not is unclear but this is quite possible as there were vocal overdubs added a month or so later). Because there is scant information on the song and its recording, the known musicians involved in the sessions are added in their entirety in the track specification.

Track Specification

Composed by Terry Britten

Musicians		*Recording Details*	
Brian Bennett	drums, percussion	Producer	Bruce Welch
Terry Britten	guitar	Engineered by	Tony Clark and Haydn Bendall
Stuart Calver	backing vocals	Recording location	Abbey Road Studio 3, St. John's Wood, London
Richard Hewson	arranger, conductor	Recording date	10th January 1978 and 19th February 1978
Alan Jones	bass		
Duncan MacKay	keyboards		
Alan Parker	guitar		
John Perry	backing vocals		
Tim Renwick	guitar		
Cliff Richard	vocals		
Tony Rivers	backing vocals		
Trevor Spencer	drums, percussion		
Alan Tarney	backing vocals, guitar, bass, keyboards		
Graham Todd	keyboards		
Unknown	orchestra		

♫ Shoom Llamma Boom Boom

Unissued track and from the album **Hier Ist Cliff**

Recorded during the sessions for the 1968 Eurovision Song Contest candidates, although it was not one of the original candidates, the version of *Shoom Llamma Boom Boom* was recorded in English but, to date, remains unreleased. In November of that year, the song was revisited for a set of German language songs. Still with the same title but with German lyrics provided by Hans Bradtke (who had worked on translations for previous Cliff Richard recordings), the accompaniment was completely new rather than using the original backing track with new vocals and it was released in stereo only on the German album *Hier Ist Cliff.* The collation of Cliff's foreign language recordings, ***On the Continent***, took the stereo version and added it to its track listing.

The German version is a spirited version that fair moves along with a driving bass and orchestral accompaniment. With its nonsensical title and treatment, it sounds very much as if it could have been a Eurovision song entry. The pace and energy instilled into the song make it an interesting gem missing from the comparative English Cliff Richard oeuvre.

Track Specification

1. Unissued track (English version)
Composed by Roker and Littlewood

Musicians	
John Paul Jones	arranger, bass
Ladybirds	backing vocals
Marian Davies	
Gloria George	
Maggie Stredder	
Norrie Paramor Orchestra	orchestra
Norrie Paramor	conductor
Cliff Richard	vocals

Recording Details	
Producer	Norrie Paramor
Engineered by	Peter Vince
Recording location	Abbey Road Studio 2, St. John's Wood, London
Recording date	3rd February 1968

2. Hier Ist Cliff
Composed by Roker and Littlewood; German lyrics by Hans Bradtke

Musicians	
Norrie Paramor Orchestra	orchestra
Norrie Paramor	arranger, director
Cliff Richard	vocals
Unknown	backing vocals

Recording Details	
Producer	Norrie Paramor
Engineered by	Peter Vince
Recording location	Abbey Road Studio 2, St. John's Wood, London
Recording date	28th November 1968

♫ Shooting from the Heart

93rd UK single

The first of two singles from Cliff Richard's album project, ***The Rock Connection***, was co-written by a long-term Cliff collaborator, Roger Greenaway. Recorded over the early summer of 1984, *Shooting from the Heart* was issued as a single, backed with a non-album track ***Small World*** (recorded for a Tear Fund film project – *It's a Small World*), on the EMI label (catalogue number EMI RICH 1) on 22nd October 1984 and it reached the lowly position of fifty-one in the British singles charts. Simultaneously, a heart-shaped picture disc single (catalogue number RICHP 1) was also issued. In the promotional video, Cliff is seen walking down a street trying to prove his love for a girl who appears to be oblivious to him, as he abjectly fails to give her presents. He takes the part of a salesman called Rick Clifford and tries extreme measures to get to the object of his desires, ending up in hospital, where she comes in with a bunch of flowers.

In comparison to the other songs on the album, *Shooting from the Heart* is a gentle guitar- and piano-led song that is pleasant enough but is not perhaps the best choice for a single release, as is reflected in its chart placing. However, that being said, there is much to commend it, including the gently insistent accompaniment and Cliff's lead vocals blending with the harmonies, which are also provided by him, and these are particularly well-arranged across the stereo channels in the dying moments of the song.

Track Specification
Composed by Richard Giles and Roger Greenaway

Musicians	
John Clark	guitar
Dave Cooke	keyboards
Mark Griffiths	bass
Alan Park	keyboards
Cliff Richard	vocals, backing vocals
Stuart Tosh	drums, percussion

Recording Details	
Producer	Cliff Richard and Keith Bessey
Engineered by	Keith Bessey
Recording location	Strawberry Studios South, Surrey
Recording date	30th July 1984-3rd August 1984

♫ Shooting Star

From the film soundtrack EP of **Thunderbirds Are Go!**

Recorded during the sessions that were planned for the soundtrack of another film ***Finders Keepers***, *Shooting Star* featured in the puppet film of ***Thunderbirds Are Go!*** The premise of the film was that a brand new plane (the Fireball XL5) had been targeted by terrorists and had to be saved by International Rescue, which runs the Thunderbirds craft – the Tracy brothers and their father operate from a small private island and use the film's title as a means to confirm that everything was ready for the mission. At the point of the Cliff Richard's appearance, it is a dream sequence perpetrated by Alan Tracy who is fantasizing about taking Lady Penelope on a date to an outer space restaurant, where Cliff Richard Junior and the Shadows were performing. The song takes in its own dream sequence with the Cliff puppet sliding off a crescent moon and the band standing on the fretboard of a guitar as they perform. The puppets are a good approximation to the real people, although it is sometimes hard to see the likeness from certain angles.

Only ever released in mono format on the ***Thunderbirds Are Go!*** EP (alongside three instrumental tracks by the Shadows), the final (unknown) take and edit were used for the release. Later released as a twelve-inch picture disc in 1992, it was first released on CD four years later on ***Cliff Richard at the Movies 1959-1974***.

With a samba rhythm, *Shooting Star* is a typical song composed by the Shadows with all the expected components of complex drums, string lead guitar melody, staccato bass line and the driving rhythm guitar, although the lyrics are quite warlike and aggressive in order to play a pun on the the common phrase 'shooting star'. It is as a brilliant example of the beauty that Hank Marvin, Bruce Welch, John Rostill and Cliff created with their perfect vocal harmonies.

Track Specification
Composed by Hank Marvin, Brian Bennett and John Rostill

Musicians		*Recording Details*	
Brian Bennett	drums, percussion	Producer	Norrie Paramor
Hank Marvin	backing vocals, guitar	Engineered by	Unknown
Cliff Richard	vocals	Recording location	Olympic Studios, London
John Rostill	backing vocals, bass	Recording date	5th May 1966
Bruce Welch	backing vocals, rhythm guitar		

♫ Shout

From the albums **Don't Stop Me Now!**, **Cliff in Japan**, **Live at the Talk of the Town** *and* **Cliff Live in Korea**

Originally recorded by the writers of the song, the Isley Brothers, it is probably most familiar owing to Lulu's throat-mangling yell at the beginning of the song on the word 'well'. Most recently, it was Louchie Lou and Michie One, a female rap duo from the UK, who had a chart hit when they reached number seven in June 1993 with *Shout* as their first single. But the honours really do go to Lulu, who memorably also hit the number seven spot in May 1964. However, such a popular song will always find acts to cover it, and these include Joey Dee, Screamin' Jay Hawkins, the Chipmunks, Otis Day and the Knights, Tom Petty and the Heartbreakers, the Countdown Singers, the Trammps and Lloyd Williams among many others.

Cliff Richard recorded his version for his ***Don't Stop Me Now!*** album at the second recording session of 1967 in February. The first song to be completed, the eighth and final take and edit were used for the mono and stereo recordings.

Eschewing the familiar raucous Lulu scream at the start of the track, instead Cliff repeats the first line before entering into *Shout* properly. The arrangement is an interesting one, since it is syncopated with staccato instrumentation on the offbeat. As with many of the songs that received the Cliff treatment, *Shout* is made specifically part of his oeuvre rather than a being little more than a straightforward cover.

A regular feature of tours of the period, *Shout* appeared on a number of live recordings with the rarest, in mono only, being from *Cliff Live in Korea*, an album that was released only for the Korean market in March 1970. The backing vocalists on the Japan version may also be the Breakaways but this is not documented.

Track Specification
Composed by O'Kelly Isley, Ronald Isley and Rudolph Isley

1. Don't Stop Me Now!

Musicians		*Recording Details*	
Cliff Richard	vocals	Producer	Norrie Paramor
Unknown	female backing vocals	Engineered by	Peter Vince and Richard Lush
Unknown	arranger, conductor	Recording location	Abbey Road Studio 2, St. John's Wood, London
Unknown	orchestra	Recording date	5th February 1967

2. Cliff in Japan

Musicians		*Recording Details*	
Norrie Paramor Orchestra	orchestra	Producer	Norrie Paramor
Norrie Paramor	arranger, conductor	Engineered by	Unknown
Cliff Richard	vocals	Recording location	Shibuya Public Hall, Tokyo, Japan
Unknown	backing vocals	Recording date	18th October 1967

3. Live at the Talk of the Town

Musicians		*Recording Details*	
Breakaways:	backing vocals	Producer	Norrie Paramor
Vicki Hasemen		Engineered by	Peter Vince
Margo Quantrell		Recording location	Talk of the Town Theatre, London
Jean Ryder		Recording date	30th May 1968
Norrie Paramor	arranger, conductor		
Cliff Richard	vocals		
Talk of the Town Orchestra	orchestra		

4. Cliff Live in Korea

Musicians		*Recording Details*	
Brian Bennett	drums, percussion	Producer	Unknown
Alan Hawkshaw	keyboards	Engineered by	Unknown
Hank Marvin	backing vocals, guitar	Recording location	Citizen Hall, Seoul, South Korea
Cliff Richard	vocals	Recording date	16th October 1969
John Rostill	backing vocals, bass		
Bruce Welch	backing vocals, rhythm guitar		

♫ Shrine on the Second Floor, The
From the EP **Expresso Bongo**

Intended to be a satirical joke from the film ***Expresso Bongo***, *The Shrine on the Second Floor* took on a life of its own outside the film. The plot centred around a manipulative music manager, who was intent on exploiting his 'discovery', Bongo Herbert (played by Cliff Richard), and had succeeded in having a smash hit with the teenage boy's first hit, ***A Voice in the Wilderness***. In order to capitalize on this success, the promoter decides to go with something entirely more saccharine by abusing the relationship between mother and son. However, it had already been made clear that this relationship was extremely rocky but this didn't stop the promoter getting a song together that talks about the deep love for the 'grey-haired Madonna' who had given birth to Herbert on the second floor of the tenement block in which he was living with her. Thus the song was a deliberately crude attempt to eke out all possible emotion.
In public life, once the film was on general release, fans took the song to their hearts and, as a direct result of repeatedly asking for the song by name, the EP accompanying the film entered the UK singles chart and rose to number fourteen in January 1960. Cliff himself was rather baffled by the desire to hear the song out of context purely because it was supposed to be the satirical joke on which much of the premise of the closing section of the film was based. However, the words are quite beautiful even taken away from the film and it is quite easy to see the appeal in hearing Cliff singing what could be construed as a sentimental love song rather than the caustic exploitation of an older lady that it was.
In the film, too, the pathos is hiked up further by – curiously almost as a portent of what was to happen to Cliff's life just a few years later – Bongo Herbert claiming to be a good Christian boy as he addresses the audience in his concert. As the curtains draw back, there is a stage set of an internal view of a church with pews underneath a stained glass window. As the song starts, Herbert is joined by a choir of backing vocalists dressed in surpluses, cassocks and ruffs to drive the cynicism of the marketing ploy right home. In the song that appears on the EP, there is no backing vocal and is a straightforward rendition with Cliff's vocals accompanied by the instrumentation of the Shadows.
As the initial chords are played and Cliff begins his vocal line, it is clear that it is a standard rock and roll ballad, with a stentorian bass line and chunking rhythm guitar rippling underneath with chinking cymbals. The basic tune is memorable while the arrangement is deliberately predictable to underline the tenor of that point in the film. But the overall performance is quite brilliant, emulating some of Elvis Presley's offerings such as *Are You Lonesome Tonight?*, and nowhere near the mediocre result it could have been. Although it remained unreleased outside of the EP (apart from one boxed set collection in the early seventies), it was eventually incorporated on the See For Miles 1989 anthology ***The EP Collection*** and in 1996 on the ***Cliff Richard at the Movies 1959-1974*** album. A short edit of the first minute and a half also appeared on the *Cliff Richard at Tower* promotional cassette given away at his appearance at Tower Records on 22nd July 1996.

Track Specification
Composed by David Heneker, Julian More and Monty Norman

Musicians

Jet Harris	bass
Hank Marvin	guitar
Tony Meehan	drums, percussion
Cliff Richard	vocals
Bruce Welch	rhythm guitar

Recording Details

Producer	Norrie Paramor
Engineered by	Malcolm Addey (mono) and Stuart Eltham and Alan Kane (stereo)
Recording location	Abbey Road Studio 2, St. John's Wood, London
Recording date	19th October 1959

♫ Silent Night
From the albums **Together with Cliff Richard** *and* **Cliff at Christmas**

Quite possibly one of the most familiar and favourite of all Christmas carols, *Silent Night* was written by an Austrian priest (Joseph Mohr providing the German lyrics) and an Austrian headmaster (the melody), with English lyrics being provided by John Freeman Young in 1819 the year after its first performance at the Nikolauskirche in Oberndorf. It has undergone a number of arrangements over the years but the simplicity of the melody and ability to arrange close harmonies to blend with it successfully evokes more than many other songs the traditional images of Christmas. The first person to have a hit in the UK with it was Bing Crosby when he reached number eight in 1952 shortly after the singles charts were first initiated. A punked-up version was released by the Dickies in 1978 reaching number forty-seven, while boy band Bros fared better when they hit number two in 1988. In 1991, two versions were released: first, Simon and Garfunkel had included it on their *Parsley, Sage, Rosemary & Thyme* album but released it over twenty years later and reached number thirty, and, second, Sinéad O'Connor with a hauntingly beautiful *a capella* version that only reached number sixty.
Cliff Richard's version was arranged by him and his music director Paul Moessl. A beautiful arrangement, it also includes a new section in the middle eight as it conjures up the picture of closeness and warmth at home by the Christmas tree cuddling together over a coffee as ***Mistletoe and Wine*** plays on the radio.
The song was revisited during the development of the ***Cliff at Christmas*** album and, while the same original take is used, it has been remixed with some edits and additional instrumentation. The strings are removed from the saxophone solo and the second (traditional) verse, while the song fades earlier than the original *Together with Cliff Richard* version. The beauty of the song comes from the syncopated rhythm imbued into the arrangement throughout, as well as Paul Moessl's clever keyboard arrangements. The new lyrics in the mid-section are performed with a slight echo and are fed through an electronic vocoder. Throughout the final verse, Cliff provides his own close harmony backing vocals.

Track Specification
Composed by Joseph Mohr, Franz Gruber and John Freeman Young; additional lyrics and arrangement by Cliff Richard and Paul Moessl

1. Together with Cliff Richard

Musicians

Dave Bishop	saxophone
Dave Cunliffe	violin
Andrew Greasley	violin
Mark Griffiths	bass
Peter May	drums, percussion
Paul Moessl	drum programming, keyboards
Cliff Richard	arranger, vocals, backing vocals
Frank Ricotti	drums, percussion
Steve Stroud	bass

Recording Details

Producer	Cliff Richard and Paul Moessl
Engineered by	Gerry Kitchingham, Andrew Greasley and Ben Robbins
Recording location	R. G. Jones Studios, Wimbledon, London
Recording date	24th June 1991 to July 1991

2. Cliff at Christmas

Musicians

Dave Bishop	saxophone
Dave Cunliffe	violin
Andrew Greasley	violin
Mark Griffiths	bass
Peter May	drums, percussion
Paul Moessl	drum programming, keyboards
Cliff Richard	arranger, vocals, backing vocals
Frank Ricotti	drums, percussion
Steve Stroud	bass

Recording Details

Producer	Cliff Richard and Paul Moessl (original track) and Unknown (new mix)
Engineered by	Gerry Kitchingham, Andrew Greasley and Ben Robbins (original track) and Unknown (new mix)
Recording location	R. G. Jones Studios, Wimbledon, London (original track) and Unknown (remix)
Recording date	24th June 1991 to July 1991 (original track) and Unknown (remix)

♬ Silhouettes

111th UK single

Silhouettes is a mixture of a sad and then happy love song that initially is a tale of being cuckolded by his girlfriend after the singer sees her shadow in a clinch with another man on the shade that is pulled down over the window, before suddenly turning to optimism when he realizes he is walking past the wrong house and, sure enough, at his girlfriend's house, she is there waiting for him. The idea for the song was inspired by the sight of two silhouettes on a window-shade as co-writer Bob Crewe saw them from a passing train. Doo-wop group The Rays were the first to record it and managed to get to number three in the US Billboard charts in 1957, while Canadian group the Diamonds competed with their version, but only managed to get to number sixty. In the UK, it was another eight years before Herman's Hermits took their cover to number three in the UK charts and five in the US.

But it was the Rays' version that Cliff Richard had on his home jukebox (see also ***Daddy's Home***), inspiring him to include it on the set list of the second part of his marathon performances at Wembley Stadium in June 1989. Released on the ***From a Distance ***** The Event*** album, it was also issued as a single, backed with studio track ***The Winner***, on the EMI label (catalogue number EM 152) on 13th August 1990 and reached number ten in the British singles charts. A number of other single formats were issued: a seven-inch with a picture frame (catalogue number EMS 152); a twelve-inch single version (12EM 152); and a CD single (CDEM 152). Both the twelve-inch and CD versions incorporated another non-live track, ***All the Time You Need***, although this was also incongruously added to the track listing of ***From a Distance ***** The Event***. The promotional video was naturally the video filmed during the performance.

What makes the song so expressive is the vocal arrangement that is kept up throughout the performance. Cliff sings with passion but still manages to keep the lead vocal gentle, evoking the pictures within the lyrics. The key change leads into a saxophone solo, which lifts the song further as Cliff reveals he rings he bell at the stranger's house on the wrong street. Another key change elevates the optimism and energy again leading to the perfect vocal close.

Track Specification
Composed by Frank C. Slay Jr. and Bob Crewe

Musicians

Ray Beavis	saxophone
John Clark	guitar
Sonia Jones-Morgan	backing vocals
Steve Lauri	guitar
Peter May	drums, percussion
Paul Moessl	keyboards
Tessa Niles	backing vocals
Alan Park	keyboards
Provox:	
Peter Howarth	backing vocals
Mick Mullins	backing vocals
Keith Murrell	backing vocals
Cliff Richard	vocals
Steve Stroud	bass

Recording Details

Producer	Cliff Richard
Engineered by	Keith Bessey and Mick McKenna
Recording location	Rolling Stones Mobile Studio, Wembley Stadium, Wembley, North-west London
Recording date	16th-17th June 1989

♫ Silver's Home Tonight

From the album **Silver**

Craig Pruess took over complete production control for Cliff Richard's twenty-fifth anniversary album, ***Silver***, and also co-wrote the first song to appear on it, *Silver's Home Tonight*. It was also therefore the first song to appear on the first album to be issued simultaneously on CD.

One of the best songs on the album, *Silver's Home Tonight* is driven on by simple heavy drum beat with a skittering synthesiser accompaniment. Cliff's voice is engineered further back in the mix, while he also supplies his own backing vocals. The subtlety of the arrangement means that it builds up almost without the listener noticing and then finishes with a very gradual fade-out.

Track Specification

Composed by Craig Pruess and David Reilly

Musicians		*Recording Details*	
John Clark	guitar	Producer	Craig Pruess
Mark Griffiths	bass	Engineered by	Keith Bessey
Graham Jarvis	drums, percussion	Recording location	Strawberry Studios South, Surrey
Craig Pruess	arranger, keyboards, synthesiser	Recording date	19th May 1983, 3rd June 1983 and/or 16th June 1983
Cliff Richard	vocals, backing vocals		

♫ Silvery Rain

53rd UK single *and from the albums* **Cliff "Live" in Japan '72** *and* **Help It Along**

For Cliff Richard's fifty-third single, he chose to record Hank Marvin's restrained environmental protest song, *Silvery Rain*. It was later covered by Hank on the first and eponymous album by Marvin, Welch & Farrar and it was also picked up by Olivia Newton-John for her 1981 album *Physical*. Cliff had already sung some veiled protest songs in recent months but *Silvery Rain* marked a musical departure in many respects and, as Norrie Paramor noted, it was probably this single that launched him slowly into being regarded as an adult performer rather than being targeted at a younger market.

Recorded in November 1970 at a session that saw one other, as yet unreleased track, ***Take a Look Around*** attempted (which might have been the anticipated B-side), *Silvery Rain* was issued as a single, backed with two songs, ***Annabella Umbrella*** and ***Time Flies*** as a maxi-single, on the Columbia label (catalogue number DB 8774) on 26th March 1971 in mono format only, and it reached number twenty-seven in the UK singles charts. The stereo version was included on the album ***The Best of Cliff Vol. 2*** the following year. In chart terms, by that point, *Silvery Rain* equalled Cliff's previously worst performing song, ***I'll Love You Forever Today***, which is unfortunate for a song that has much going for it.

With spooky wind effects and shimmering strings introducing the track, unusually the principal section of the chorus is used first before slowing down for the picked guitar chords in the verses. These are sung with a slight injection of menace before picking up for the optimistic chorus, which is replete with chirping piccolo trumpet. The song slows down once again as the protest element of the song is revisited as a warning about the environmental damage perpetrated by man. Cliff sings the song perfectly and also provides his own backing vocals. In spite of the critical assumptions about Cliff, this song is completely original and sounds new, fresh and interesting even today.

The performance of the song on the ***Cliff "Live" in Japan '72*** is very close to the original but is enhanced by the perfection of Hank Marvin's guitar solo in the accompaniment.

Because of the quasi-religious message within the lyrics that man is messing up God's perfect creation of the planet with his profligacy, *Silvery Rain* was chosen to be recorded as part of the studio-bound concert set list for the ***Help It Along*** charity album project in aid of the Tear Fund. It is closer to the original in its performance with its spooky string introduction and guitar-led verses and dramatic choruses.

Track Specification

Composed by Hank Marvin

1. Single

Musicians		*Recording Details*	
Brian Bennett	arranger, conductor	Producer	Norrie Paramor
Brian Bennett Orchestra	orchestra	Engineered by	Peter Vince and Richard Lush
Cliff Richard	vocals, backing vocals	Recording location	Abbey Road Studio 3, St. John's Wood, London
		Recording date	17th November 1970

2. Cliff "Live" in Japan '72

Musicians		*Recording Details*	
Brian Bennett	drums, percussion	Producer	Norrie Paramor
Pat Carroll	backing vocals	Engineered by	Unknown
John Farrar	bass	Recording location	Kosei Nenkin Hall, Tokyo, Japan
Alan Hawkshaw	piano	Recording date	22nd-23rd September 1972
Hank Marvin	guitar		
Olivia Newton-John	backing vocals		
Cliff Richard	vocals		
Bruce Welch	rhythm guitar		

3. *Help It Along*

Musicians		*Recording Details*	
Terry Britten	guitar	Producer	David MacKay
Barrie Guard	arranger, conductor, percussion	Engineered by	Roger Quested
Cliff Hall	keyboards	Recording location	Morgan Studios, London
Jean Hawker	backing vocals	Recording date	24th, 25th and 26th September 1973
Anna Peacock	backing vocals		
Kevin Peek	guitar		
Cliff Richard	vocals		
Trevor Spencer	drums, percussion		
Alan Tarney	bass		
Unknown	orchestra		

♬ Simplicity

From the album **Something's Goin' On**

Cliff Richard recorded ***Something's Goin' On*** as his first album of original material in over five years, featuring a number of songs commissioned from American writers, which included the slow ballad *Simplicity*. It was recorded at studios across Tennessee, centred on Nashville. The version of the song that appeared on the repackaged album, ***For Life***, is the same song but Cliff's vocals are out of kilter by one beat, although this does not detract from the listening pleasure.

The syncopated, jazz-like rhythm keeps the song on track while Cliff's vocals are anguished in the expression of the lyrics of this love song that tells his partner that he finds loving her easy. The American origins of the song are revealed with the use of the description of the television talking heads as "yada yada".

Track Specification

Composed by Dennis Matkosky, Craig Wiseman and Bob Farrell

Musicians		*Recording Details*	
Ziggie Diaz	programming	Producer	Tommy Sims
DeMarco Johnson	harmonica	Engineered by	Bryan Lenox and Tommy Sims (vocals and instruments) and Ronnie Brookshire (strings)
Ken Lewis	percussion		
Nashville String Machine	strings	Recording location	Uncle Tom's Cabin, Franklin, Tennessee, USA (vocals and instruments) and The Tracking Room, Nashville, Tennessee, USA (strings)
Cliff Richard	vocals		
Richie Pena	programming		
Tommy Sims	guitar, bass, keyboards	Recording date	2003-2004

♬ Since I Don't Have You

From the album **World Tour Live**

In America, the Skyliners were an in-demand doo-wop group and, in 1958, they released their cover of *Since I Don't Have You*. Although not issued in the UK, the song reached number twelve in the Billboard charts. As for Britain, it was in 1979, when Art Garfunkel issued his single, reaching number thirty-eight. Guns 'n' Roses fared better in 1994 when they reached number ten. In addition, *Since I Don' Have You* has been recorded by Patti LaBelle, Manfred Mann, Rick Nelson, Don McLean (who released it in the US and reached number twenty-three in 1981) and the Brian Setzer Orchestra.

Never performed or recorded by Cliff Richard, he chose the song for the ***Doo-Wop Medley*** for his 2003 world tour. The New Zealand show was filmed ostensibly for DVD release later in the year and, in 2004, a complementary CD album was issued on *World Tour Live*. While many DVD tracks were not included, the *Doo-Wop Medley* was added to the track listing. Of the three tracks in the medley, it is the only one that employs the string section, while the backing vocals and Cliff's expert singing of the genre create a perfect slice of doo-wop nostalgia.

Track Specification

Composed by Joe Rock and Jimmy Beaumont

Musicians		*Recording Details*	
Rachel Allen	violin	Producer	Keith Bessey
Elena Bulgakova	violin	Engineered by	Keith Bessey
Jenni Champion	violin	Recording location	The Mission Winery, Napier, New Zealand
Anthony Clark	backing vocals, guitar	Recording date	22nd February 2003
John Clark	guitar		
Dave Cooke	keyboards		
Cornelia Didenco	violin		
Gina Ferguson	violin		
Mike Haughton	flute, saxophone		
Peter Howarth	backing vocals		
Cathy Irons	violin		
Pete May	drums, percussion		
Mick Mullins	backing vocals		
Keith Murrell	backing vocals		
Alan Park	keyboards		
Hee-Jung Park	violin		
Cliff Richard	vocals		
Eva Schwanen-Lilley	violin		
Steve Stroud	bass		

♬ Since I Lost You

B-side of **It'll Be Me** *and from the album* **Congratulations to Cliff**

First attempted at the session on 11th August 1961 but under the title of ***What Is There to Say?***, *Since I Lost You* was the final song to be recorded in the 19th December session, which was also the final recording of 1961. It was also the very last Cliff Richard recording to feature Tony Meehan on drums, who was replaced by Brian Bennett at the beginning of the new year because, in spite of his talent and skills as a drummer, Meehan was forever tardy and disrupted concerts and recordings by turning up late and Hank Marvin and Bruce Welch particularly had had enough.

Since I Lost You took twelve takes to complete successfully with the final one edited for mono only, since it has never been released in any form of stereo. The song was eventually chosen to be the B-side of Cliff's eighteenth single, ***It'll Be Me***, later in 1962 and appears on the ***Cliff's Hits*** EP. It was also chosen as the B-side of the Filipino single release of ***I Only Live to Love You***. On the rarity compilation ***The Rock 'n' Roll Years 1958-1963***, a stereo version was released with the count-in and studio banter. It is assumed it is the same take and edit since it is exactly the same as the mono B-side; the album's liner notes claim it is the B-side but the stereo and studio count-in belie that fact. A further version was released on the 2007 French compilation *Congratulations to Cliff*, which is essentially the same as the original release but without the orchestral and backing vocal overdubs and the first guitar solo is cut at the beginning of the track.

There is an uncredited orchestra and backing chorale, which is likely to be the Norrie Paramor Orchestra and the Mike Sammes Singers respectively, both organisations having been involved in the recordings of the period. The introduction is played on guitars by Bruce and Hank, which is continued throughout the song and, particularly on the non-orchestral version, makes for a simple and heart-wrenching song that talks of how he feels after losing the one he loves.

Track Specification

Composed by Bruce Welch and Hank Marvin

1. B-side (It'll Be Me)

Musicians		*Recording Details*	
Hank Marvin	guitar	Producer	Norrie Paramor
Tony Meehan	drums, percussion	Engineered by	Malcolm Addey
Cliff Richard	vocals	Recording location	Abbey Road Studio 2, St. John's Wood, London
Unknown	backing vocals	Recording date	19th December 1961
Unknown	orchestra		
Unknown	arranger, conductor		
Bruce Welch	rhythm guitar		

2. Congratulations to Cliff

Musicians		*Recording Details*	
Hank Marvin	guitar	Producer	Norrie Paramor
Tony Meehan	drums, percussion	Engineered by	Malcolm Addey
Cliff Richard	vocals	Recording location	Abbey Road Studio 2, St. John's Wood, London
Bruce Welch	rhythm guitar	Recording date	19th December 1961

♬ Sing a Song of Freedom

55th UK single *and from the albums* **Cliff "Live" in Japan '72**, **Help It Along** *and* **Japan Tour '74**

Recorded over two sessions alongside its eventual B-side, ***A Thousand Conversations***, Guy Fletcher and Doug Flett turned out another song for Cliff Richard but, this time, it was on the A-side of the single release. Although seemingly innocuous, the title suggests something of a protest and, for this reason, the song was banned in South Africa at the time because of the politically oppressive apartheid regime leading the country. It also caused controversy when the record was used as a rally song by the Scottish Conservatives but they had to back down after being forced to pay royalties for the privilege.

Backed with *A Thousand Conversations*, *Sing a Song of Freedom* was released as a single on the Columbia label (catalogue number DB 8836) on 29th October 1971, reaching number thirteen in the British singles charts, temporarily reversing a worsening trend in Cliff's chart career. The song was released in stereo in most places but here was a mono version issued for the Australian market. The stereo edit was included on the album ***The Best of Cliff Vol. 2*** the following year and has regularly appeared on compilations ever since.

Typical of Cliff's output at the time, the song starts off quietly, almost reverentially, before building up to something that is highly charged with emotion. The clever arrangement helps the song avoid the trap of appearing too religious and therefore off-putting to some record-buyers and it holds a well-deserved position in the history of Cliff's career.

The Japan tour 1972 performance is similar to the single, as the accompaniment slowly builds up behind Cliff's vocal. What is beneficial is Olivia Newton-John's and Pat Carroll's backing vocals which are an improvement on the original.

The final track on the ***Help It Along*** album, this rendition is close to the original single version both in terms of the arrangement and way that Cliff successfully builds the song up to each of the choruses.

For the Japanese tour in 1974, Cliff created a ***Hit Medley*** that featured a number of his sixties hits: ***Congratulations***, ***In the Country***, ***Dancing Shoes***, ***The Day I Met Marie***, ***On the Beach*** and *Sing a Song of Freedom*. The song was reprised in instrumental form only later in the concert. A faithful rendition of the original single is assisted by the quality of Cliff's vocals and the shimmering strings behind him and the accompaniment of the assembled band. As the song dies down, Cliff asks for the theatre lights to go up so that he can exhort the audience to clap along.

Track Specification
Composed by Guy Fletcher and Doug Flett

1. Single

Musicians

Brian Bennett	arranger, conductor
Brian Bennett Orchestra	orchestra
Cliff Richard	vocals
Unknown	backing vocals
Unknown	hand-claps

Recording Details

Producer	Norrie Paramor
Engineered by	Peter Vince
Recording location	Abbey Road Studio 2, St. John's Wood, London
Recording date	24th August 1971

2. Cliff "Live" in Japan '72

Musicians

Brian Bennett	drums, percussion
Pat Carroll	backing vocals
John Farrar	bass
Alan Hawkshaw	piano
Hank Marvin	guitar
Olivia Newton-John	backing vocals
Cliff Richard	vocals
Bruce Welch	rhythm guitar

Recording Details

Producer	Norrie Paramor
Engineered by	Unknown
Recording location	Kosei Nenkin Hall, Tokyo, Japan
Recording date	22nd-23rd September 1972

3. Help It Along

Musicians

Terry Britten	guitar
Barrie Guard	arranger, conductor, percussion
Cliff Hall	keyboards
Jean Hawker	backing vocals
Anna Peacock	backing vocals
Kevin Peek	guitar
Cliff Richard	vocals
Trevor Spencer	drums, percussion
Alan Tarney	bass
Unknown	hand-claps
Unknown	orchestra

Recording Details

Producer	David MacKay
Engineered by	Roger Quested
Recording location	Morgan Studios, London
Recording date	24th, 25th and 26th September 1973

4. Japan Tour '74 (Hit Medley)

Musicians

Barrie Guard	arranger, conductor, piano
Cliff Hall	piano
Brian Lewis	backing vocals, guitar
Kevin Peak	acoustic guitar
Cliff Richard	vocals
Shambles Symphonet	orchestra
Trevor Spencer	drums, percussion
Alan Tarney	backing vocals, bass
Bruce Welch	backing vocals, rhythm guitar
Unknown	hand claps

Recording Details

Producer	Toshiba EMI (no individual detailed)
Engineered by	Toshiba EMI (no individual detailed)
Recording location	Shinjuku Koseinenkin, Tokyo, Japan
Recording date	7th-8th October 1974

♫ Singer, The

From the album **The 31st of February Street**

The parent album was conceived with the theme of leaving home and reflection on the emotions generated. However, *The Singer* and its fellow album track ***Going Away*** were recorded almost two years before the album's release and it is not obvious whether these two Raymond Froggatt songs were made for the album or had later been found appropriate for the album's concept. Both songs were recorded at the first recording session presided over by David MacKay, who took over from the retired Norrie Paramor, and was the second of three to be recorded, along with ***A Brand New Song***.
Quirkier in its exposition than *Going Away*, the emphasis is on the orchestral strings largely playing pizzicato, with a vocal group that would seal the seventies Cliff Richard sound and a brassy saxophone solo. More memorable, too, it doesn't fit so easily with the concept but this is largely forgotten by the time the listener reaches this penultimate track of the album.

Track Specification
Composed by Raymond Froggatt

Musicians

Terry Britten	backing vocals, guitar
David MacKay Orchestra	orchestra
David MacKay	backing vocals, arranger, conductor
Kevin Peek	guitar
Cliff Richard	vocals
Trevor Spencer	backing vocals, drums, percussion
Alan Tarney	backing vocals, bass
Unknown	saxophone

Recording Details

Producer	David MacKay
Engineered by	Peter Vince
Recording location	Abbey Road Studio 3, St. John's Wood, London
Recording date	11th October 1972

♫ Singing the Blues

141st UK single

Written and published in 1956, the best-known version of *Singing the Blues* was recorded by Guy Mitchell and released as a single in October 1956, reaching number one in the US Billboard charts. In the UK, it was a fight between Mitchell's version and that recorded by Tommy Steele and the Steelmen, who both had a number one almost simultaneously, with Mitchell reaching the top spot on 4th January, Steele on 11th January, and Mitchell back again on the 18th before being knocked off and returning once more on 1st February as a joint number one with Frankie Vaughan's *Garden of Eden*. Dave Edmunds took his version to number twenty-eight in 1980 and Daniel O'Donnell made number twenty-three in 1994. It has also been covered by Marty Robbins (who had an American single with his version), Bill Haley, Black Oak Arkansas, Paul McCartney and Marie Osmond among others.

When Cliff Richard and the Shadows got back together in early 2009 to celebrate fifty years in the music business, they chose a number of their songs to be re-recorded. In addition to choices from their voluminous back catalogue, they also recorded ***C'mon Everybody***, ***Sea Cruise*** and *Singing the Blues*, with the latter being released as the only single from the project. Backed with the re-recording of ***A Voice in the Wilderness***, *Singing the Blues* was issued on the EMI label on seven-inch vinyl, to reflect the early days (catalogue number 50999 687887 7 3) and a CD single (50999 687885 2 0) on 14th September 2009 but, in spite of the publicity, the new material by the band and extensive airplay on Sir Terry Wogan's BBC Radio 2 *Wake Up with Wogan* show, the song only made it to number forty in the UK charts. The download version of the single also incorporated two more songs, ***Dancing Shoes*** and ***We Say Yeah***.

The song is taken at a slower pace than the original and requires Cliff to use more of his upper register throughout than he does on some other tracks. The backing vocals that make the Shadows working with Cliff so great are present throughout, as is the pure artistry of the ensemble piece. Hank plays a guitar solo in the middle eight as it shifts up a key.

Track Specification

Composed by Melvin Endsley

Musicians

Brian Bennett	drums, percussion
Warren Bennett	keyboards
Mark Griffiths	bass
Hank Marvin	backing vocals, guitar
Cliff Richard	vocals, backing vocals
Bruce Welch	backing vocals, rhythm guitar

Recording Details

Producer	Warren Bennett (co-ordination)
Engineered by	James Collins (Honeyhill Studios), Ethan Carlson (Middle Ear Studios), Les Williams (Nivram Studios) and Keith Bessey (mixing and mastering)
Recording location	Middle Ear Studios, Miami, Florida, USA (Cliff's vocals), Nivram Studios, Perth, Western Australia (Hank's guitars and vocals) and Honeyhill Studios, Hertfordshire, England (all other vocals and instruments)
Recording date	Early 2009

♫ Sleep of the Good, The

From the albums **Songs from Heathcliff** *and* **Heathcliff Live** *and B-side of* **The Wedding**

A song of vituperative longing for his beloved Cathy, *The Sleep of the Good* is a bitter love song sung by Heathcliff (Cliff Richard) as he prays for the ability to find peace and to sleep soundly without thinking about her and what they had been through. The song plays out during Heathcliff's anguish over the death of Cathy in childbirth. He has followed the coffin to the graveside and, after the cortege has dispersed, he sings this song to the coffin wishing her onward peace.

A trial run of some of the upcoming show's material was performed in Sheffield at the Arena to a very warm reception. Two of these songs, ***Had to Be*** and *The Sleep of the Good* were recorded and released as B-sides, with the latter featuring on the back of ***The Wedding***, a re-recorded vocal version of ***I Do Not Love You Isabella*** with Helen Hobson.

Synthesised strings and a brass passage introduce the song. Cliff sings the song with emotion and gentility while imbuing it with the sadness the character feels at the death of the girl he loves so deeply. The brief organ lends the piece an air of a church-led service for the funeral. The live version focuses more on the piano as the instrument of choice but in other respects it is the same as that recorded for the original studio album.

The B-side of *The Wedding* features the introductory spoken vocals by Cliff in character but in all other respects there are very few differences between this and what was to be developed in the studio and on stage.

Track Specification

Composed by John Farrar and Tim Rice

1. B-side (The Wedding)

Musicians

John Clark	guitar
Mike Haughton	woodwinds
Peter May	drums, percussion
Paul Moessl	keyboards
Bob Noble	keyboards
Cliff Richard	vocals
Steve Stroud	bass

Recording Details

Producer	Keith Bessey
Engineered by	Keith Bessey
Recording location	Sheffield Arena, Sheffield
Recording date	December 1994

2. *Songs from Heathcliff*

Musicians		*Recording Details*	
Sean Callery	orchestrator, synclavier, keyboards	Producer	John Farrar
John Farrar	guitar, synclavier	Engineered by	Chris Fogel, Eric Rudd and Joe Schiff (Moonee Ponds Studio), Darren Goodwin and Guy Massey (Abbey Road Studios) and James Collins and Caroline Daniel (CTS Studios)
Cliff Richard	vocals	Recording location	Moonee Ponds Studio, Los Angeles, Abbey Road Studios, St. John's Wood, London and CTS Studios, Wembley, London
Bob Sabellico	drum programming	Mixed by	Elliot Scheiner
Michael Thompson	guitar	Mixed at	Moonee Ponds Studio, Los Angeles
		Recording date	February-April 1994 and May-August 1995

3. *Heathcliff Live*

Musicians		*Recording Details*	
Sean Callery	orchestrator, conductor	Producer	John Farrar
John Clark	guitar	Engineered by	Keith Bessey, John Pearson and Tom Tranter
Keith Hayman	keyboards	Recording location	The Academy, National Indoor Arena, Birmingham, England
Peter May	drums, percussion	Recording date	17th-18th October 1996
Bob Noble	keyboards		
Alan Park	keyboards		
Cliff Richard	vocals		
Steve Stroud	bass		
Kevin Townend	orchestration		
Unknown	orchestra		

♫ Sleepwalking

B-side of **Turn! Turn! Turn!** *(Sheila Walsh)*

Graham Kendrick provided songs for many a project involving Cliff Richard in the seventies and eighties and *Sleepwalking* was the latest, written for inclusion on the Sheila Walsh album ***Drifting***. In addition to appearing on the album, *Sleepwalking* was chosen as the B-side for one of the singles to be released from the project, ***Turn! Turn! Turn!***.

The rhythm in the synthesized percussion and harmony line belies the meaning of the song's title and Walsh gamely sings the song, which is not great on melody and is only carried by the strong arrangement and Cliff's layered backing vocals.

Track Specification

Composed by Graham Kendrick

Musicians		*Recording Details*	
Craig Pruess	arranger, synthesiser, percussion	Producer	Cliff Richard and Craig Pruess
Cliff Richard	backing vocals	Engineered by	Keith Bessey
Sheila Walsh	vocals	Recording location	Riverside Studios, London, Strawberry Studios, London, Ramp Studios, London and/or Sonoptics Studios, London
		Recording date	September 1982-January 1983

♫ Slow Down

From the website **www.cliffrichard.org**

Co-written by Cliff Richard's long-term collaborator Chris Eaton, *Slow Down* was recorded at the same sessions that produced tracks for ***Something's Goin' On*** and the ***Santa's List*** single. It was originally only released through Cliff's own website, although it was later added as a bonus on the promotional disc accompanying the release of the project's first single, ***Somethin' Is Goin' On***. It was commercially issued as a B-side item on the ***What Car?*** single release and then on the track listing of ***For Life***, which was essentially the album re-released with four extra tracks including *Slow Down*.

A drum and percussion motif leads into a close harmony section and then into the vocal supported by guitars and bass. Much of what Cliff records relies on clever use of harmonies and *Slow Down* uses this to great effect and it deserved better coverage than being issued from the website (at a time when older fans might have been suspicious about downloads).

Track Specification

Composed by Gary Burr, Chris Eaton and Kenny Greenburg

Musicians		*Recording Details*	
Robert Bailey	backing vocals	Producer	Michael Omartian
Chad Cromwell	drums, percussion	Engineered by	Terry Christian
Chris Eaton	backing vocals	Recording location	Sound House, Brentwood, Tennessee, USA and The Blue Room, Nashville, Tennessee, USA
Da'dra Greathouse	backing vocals	Recording date	2003
Kenny Greenbert	guitar		
Vicki Hampton	backing vocals		
Jerry McPherson	guitar		
Michael Omartian	keyboards		
Cliff Richard	vocals, backing vocals		
Michael Rhodes	bass		
Biff Watson	guitar		

♫ Slow Rivers

100th UK single

Curiously, much is made of ***The Best of Me*** being Cliff Richard's one hundredth single but, in fact, it was this minor duet with Elton John, *Slow Rivers,* which was recorded during John's *Ice on Fire* album sessions in 1984 but not issued until two years later as a single and then as part of the track listing to the follow-up album, ***Leather Jackets***. Backed with an Elton John track, *Billy and the Kids, Slow Rivers* was issued on John's own record label, Rocket Record Company (catalogue number EJS 13), on 21st November 1986 and reached number forty-four in the British singles charts. A picture disc was also released (catalogue number EJSP 13) and twelve-inch (EJS 1312). Although it was added to Cliff's *Private Collection* vinyl LP, it wasn't until the ***Two's Company*** album that a Cliff-related CD incorporated *Slow Rivers*. In the promotional video, John plays the piano across the river from Sydney Opra House while Cliff performs along London's Embankment.
Inevitably for an Elton John track, the predominant instrument is the piano. In the backing vocals is Kiki Dee with whom John had had his then only number one with *Don't Go Breaking My Heart*. Cliff's and John's vocals work well together, even though they are different timbres. The drama of the song is evident in the chorus and, while this isn't absolutely the best of his songs, it is strong enough, which makes the lacklustre response from the buyers so surprising.

Track Specification
Composed by Elton John and Bernie Taupin

Musicians

Kiki Dee	backing vocals
James Newton Howard	string arranger, conductor
Elton John	vocals, piano
Davey Johnstone	guitar
Fred Mandell	keyboards
Charlie Morgan	drums, percussion
Cliff Richard	vocals, backing vocals
Unknown	orchestra
Paul Westwood	bass

Recording Details

Producer	Gus Dudgeon
Engineered by	Stuart Epps (main track) and Graham Dickson (strings)
Recording location	The SOL Studios, Cookham (backing track) and C.T.S., Wembley (strings)
Recording date	15th May 1984 (main track) and 1984 (strings)

♫ Small World

Unissued track and B-side of **Shooting from the Heart**

In early 1969, Tyne Tees Television commissioned a series of six religious playlets called *Life with Johnny,* featuring Cliff Richard playing Johnny with each episode modernising a well-known parable told by Jesus in the Bible. Records are unclear on most of the episodes although *Johnny Come Home* and *Johnny Faces Facts* are complete, *Johnny and the Good Samaritan* is partially available, while the remainder are unavailable in either records or film form.
The songs performed had some relevance to the parable being performed andthere were usually five songs per episode. *Small World* appeared in one of *Johnny on the Rocks, Johnny and the Blind Rage* or *Johnny in Love*. The end credits of the episode stated that all songs were original and written in collaboration between Cliff, the Settlers and the programme's writer David Winter, although is disputed. The instrumentation and performance details are currently unknown.
The song was re-recorded in 1984 as part of a Tear Fund project entitled ***It's a Small World***, although this time the writing credits were only specified as Cliff. Recorded alongside three other songs for the Tear Fund film project, *Small World* was chosen as the B-side of ***Shooting from the Heart*** from the album project ***The Rock Connection***, although *Small World* didn't appear on that album's track listing. It was subsequently released on the vinyl album, cassette and CD versions of ***It's a Small World*** in 1985.
Using synthesized exotic African percussion, this song is almost a sequel to ***Tiny Planet*** which precedes it on the album. Cliff performs the song with his customary ease and provides his own backing vocals. The melody is simple and straightforward but this helps get the important message across of giving to those less fortunate and filling lives with compassion.

Track Specification
Composed by Cliff Richard

1. Unissued track (Life with Johnny)

Musicians

John Fyffe	backing vocals, guitar
Cindy Kent	backing vocals
Mike Jones	backing vocals, guitar
Cliff Richard	vocals
Geoffrey Srodzinski	backing vocals, bass

Recording Details

Producer	Norrie Paramor
Engineered by	Peter Vince
Recording location	Abbey Road Studio 3, St. John's Wood, London
Recording date	24th March 1969

2. B-side (Shooting from the Heart)

Musicians

John Clark	guitar
Mark Griffiths	bass
Graham Jarvis	drums, percussion
Craig Pruess	keyboards, programming
Cliff Richard	vocals, backing vocals

Recording Details

Producer	Cliff Richard and Craig Pruess
Engineered by	Keith Bessey
Recording location	Gallery Studios, Chertsey, Surrey
Recording date	24th June 1984

♫ Snake and the Bookworm, The

From the album **Cliff Sings** *(mono take) and from* **Cliff Sings No. 1 EP** *(stereo take)*

Also recorded by the Coasters, *The Snake and the Bookworm* was one of the set of eight songs featuring The Drifters (soon to become The Shadows by the time of the release) backing Cliff Richard on his first true studio album, ***Cliff Sings***.

The song is a medium-paced jive dance that talks about a nasty boy, who is trying to wheedle his way into the affections of a girl who prefers to study and concentrate on her education – the snake and the bookworm of the title. The almost military precision of Tony Meehan's drumming drives the song along assisted by Hank Marvin's perfect guitar solo.

For most songs on the album, recorded entirely in mono, Norrie Paramor and his engineers took the original master and created a stereo version from it. However, for three tracks, Paramor decided to revisit the tapes and he chose a different take, from the later of three sessions at which the song was recorded, to appear on the ***Cliff Sings No. 1*** stereo EP, which was also recorded in mono but with a stereo mix developed from that. *The Snake and the Bookworm* differs from the mono version (also released on the mono EP) only inasmuch as the Hank's guitar line is performed with altered harmonies. The mono version was made available on CD in 1992 but the stereo version only became available in modern format with the release of ***The Rock 'n' Roll Years 1958-1963***. Subsequently, the original album has been remastered into stereo and a new stereo version of the original mono track is now available.

Track Specification

Composed by Mort Shuman and Jerome Pomus

1. Cliff Sings

Musicians		*Recording Details*	
Jet Harris	bass	Producer	Norrie Paramor
Hank Marvin	guitar	Engineered by	Malcolm Addey and David Lloyd (mono) and Peter Bown and Stuart Eltham (stereo)
Tony Meehan	drums, percussion		
Cliff Richard	vocals	Recording location	Abbey Road Studio 2, St. John's Wood, London
Bruce Welch	rhythm guitar	Recording date	26th July 1959

2. Cliff Sings No. 1 EP

Musicians		*Recording Details*	
Jet Harris	bass	Producer	Norrie Paramor
Hank Marvin	guitar	Engineered by	Malcolm Addey and Alan Kane (mono) and Peter Bown and Norman Smith (stereo)
Tony Meehan	drums, percussion		
Cliff Richard	vocals	Recording location	Abbey Road Studio 2, St. John's Wood, London
Bruce Welch	rhythm guitar	Recording date	6th September 1959

♫ Snowfall on the Sahara

From the album **Real as I Wanna Be**

Continuing his departure from musical expectations, Cliff Richard recorded *Snowfall on the Sahara*: another song written by Peter Wolf, who was also the principal instrumentalist and producer of the parent album, ***Real as I Wanna Be***.

Initiated by a synthesized bass that is intended to sound exotic and parochial to the north African Saharan region, the song evolves into a slow-paced love song that is driven by the percussive beat over the heavy bass line. Cliff performs the song with gentle energy and emotion and he frequently uses a lot of his upper register in the performance. The backing vocals arrangement, moving in unison and thirds in the chorus elevate the beauty further as the track heads for completion.

Track Specification

Composed by Peter Wolf, Natalie Cole and Ina Wolf

Musicians		*Recording Details*	
John Cushon	drums, percussion	Producer	Peter Wolf
Cliff Richard	vocals, backing vocals	Engineered by	Christian Leitgeb, Chris Heil, Paul Erickson and/or Keith Bessey
Jeff Richman	guitar		
Michelle Wolf	backing vocals	Recording location	Little America Recording Studios, Weiler, Austria, Ocean Recording Studios, Burbank, California, USA, Arco Recording Studios, Munich, Germany, R. G. Jones Recording Studios, Wimbledon, London, England and/or The Pierce Room, London, England
Peter Wolf	arranger, bass, keyboards, percussion		
		Recording date	March-April 1996 and November 1997

♫ Softly as I Leave You

From the album **Dressed for the Occasion**

In 1960, Italian singer Mina had major success at the San Remo Music Festival with a song entitled *Piano* (translating from the Italian as *Softly*) and went on to record it as a single later in that year. Hal Shaper added English lyrics in 1961 and retitled it *Softly as I Leave You*. The best known version was by Matt Monro, at least in the UK, when he released it as a single in February 1962 and reached number ten in the UK charts. In the US, although Monroe's version received much airplay, it didn't chart and it was left to Frank Sinatra to record his version two years later, reaching number twenty-seven in the Billboard charts, and it was the song used to accompany the website announcement of the singer's death in 1998.

Artists to cover the song include Bobby Darin, Doris Day, Andy Williams, Elvis Presley, David Whitfield, Shirley Bassey, the Lettermen and Michael Bublé among others.
Cliff Richard regularly performed songs that he enjoyed singing but had not recorded in the studio and so it was for *Softly as I Leave You*, which he sang at the Royal Albert Hall, which was recorded and subsequently released on the ***Dressed for the Occasion*** album.
According to Elvis Presley in his introduction to the song, it is about a man on his deathbed and consumed with sickness. His wife lies next to him on the third day of her vigil and, not wanting to disturb her, while knowing that his time was coming to pass over, wrote on a notepad by his bed *Softly as I Leave You*.
The orchestral woodwind introduce the song, accompanied by the strings as Cliff's strong vibrato ushers in the ballad. The syrupy strings take the song through its various key changes and onwards to the end of the song that features none of the backing singers or the rock band instrumentation.

Track Specification
Composed by Antonia de Vita and Giorgio Calabrese; English lyrics by Hal Shaper

Musicians		*Recording Details*	
Richard Hewson	arranger, conductor	Producer	Cliff Richard and Richard Hewson
London Philharmonic Orchestra	orchestra	Engineered by	John Kurlander
Cliff Richard	vocals	Mixed by	Keith Bessey
		Recording location	Royal Albert Hall, London
		Mixed at	Strawberry Studios South, Surrey
		Recording date	23rd November 1982

♫ So I've Been Told

From the album **32 Minutes and 17 Seconds with Cliff Richard**

The only home-grown original song to be included on the track listing for ***32 Minutes and 17 Seconds with Cliff Richard***, *So I've Been Told* was written by the Shadows' rhythm guitarist Bruce Welch. The mono and stereo recordings used the same take (the tenth from the session) and edit but the audio channel requirements dictated different mixes. The song also appears on the track listing of the associated ***Time for Cliff and the Shadows*** EP.
The gentle guitar introduction leads into the Shadows harmonising the song's title. Cliff's main vocal comes in and is laidback with the languid guitar accompaniment and the vocal accompaniment. In the vocal bridge, the backing vocals are mixed far back and are provided with an echo before the song cycles back to the verse.

Track Specification
Composed by Bruce Welch

Musicians		*Recording Details*	
Jet Harris	backing vocals, bass	Producer	Norrie Paramor
Hank Marvin	backing vocals, guitar	Engineered by	Malcolm Addey
Tony Meehan	drums, percussion	Recording location	Abbey Road Studio 2, St. John's Wood, London
Cliff Richard	vocals	Recording date	18th December 1961
Bruce Welch	backing vocals, rhythm guitar		

♫ Solamente una Vez

From the album **When in Spain**

Subtitled ***You Belong to My Heart*** but literally translated from the Spanish as *Only Once*, *Solamente una Vez* was published in 1944 and first recorded by Bing Crosby and the Charlie Spivak Orchestra. Ray Gilbert was responsible for translating the lyrics into English and it is primarily this version that was covered most by non-Latin musicians, which included Gene Autrey, Engelbert Humperdinck, Roy Hamilton, Gracie Fields, Marty Robbins, the Flamingoes, Elvis Presley and Pérez Prado. Janis and Rick Carnes added further lyrics in 1998, this time taking the closer translation of *Only Once in My Life*.
Cliff Richard later recorded the English song for his ***Cliff Richard*** album, but first it was the Spanish lyric that he recorded at the EMI Studios based in Barcelona. The first of the session, it took thirteen takes to complete the recording. The final take and edit was used for the mono and stereo recordings but with different mixes for the needs of the audio channels.
The problem with the infancy of stereo is that many companies liked to put vocals in one channel (here Cliff's are in the left) and the instrumentation often in the other (the Shadows and Norrie Paramor's piano are in the right). The juxtaposition is confused further when the backing vocals are centred making it a very odd listening experience.

Track Specification
Composed by Augustín Lara

Musicians		*Recording Details*	
Brian Bennett	drums, percussion	Producer	Norrie Paramor
Brian 'Licorice' Locking	bass	Engineered by	Malcolm Addey
Hank Marvin	guitar	Recording location	EMI Studios, Barcelona (main track) and Abbey Road Studio 2, St. John's Wood, London (backing vocals and strings)
Norrie Paramor Strings	orchestra		
Norrie Paramor	arranger, conductor, piano		
Cliff Richard	vocals, backing vocals	Recording date	29th April 1963 (main track), 14th May 1963 (strings) and 28th May 1963 (backing vocals)
Bruce Welch	rhythm guitar, backing vocals		

♫ Solitary Man

Unissued track and from the EP **La La La La La**

For a number of years in the early sixties, Neil Diamond had composed several songs for other artists to record before finding his metier as a performer in his own right. In early 1966, he wrote and recorded his first single, *Solitary Man*, which, although not a hit in the UK, it did reach number fifty-five in the US, but it cemented his profile as a performer as well as a composer. The song was re-released at the end of the sixties, faring better when it reached number fifteen in the US (again not charting in the UK although by now a popular song with his fans). Essentially autobiographical, *Solitary Man* has also been released by others as singles, including Chris Isaak in 1993, Johnny Cash in 2000, and Finnish group HIM in 2004, reaching number two in their local charts and number nine in the UK charts in May 2004. Other than these releases, it has also been covered by artists such as Deep Six, Tracey Grammer, Tor, One Bar Town, Tom Bartsch, Robbie Cooper, Crooked Fingers, Marina Strings, the Sidewinders and B. J. Thomas.

Released originally in mono as part of Cliff Richard's ***La La La La La*** EP, his cover of Solitary Man was issued for the first time in stereo on the German compilation *Congratulations und 13 Weitere Hits* album in 1968. It would take another twenty-one years before being released from obscurity when it appeared on the collection ***The EP Collection: Ballads and Love Songs*** in 1989. Recorded at the same session as two other vocal tracks for the EP, the final (unknown) take and edit of *Solitary Man* were used for both the mono and stereo recordings but with different mixes for the separate audio channel requirements. The song was first attempted at the 19th September session along with EP stable-mate, ***Things We Said Today***, but after an unknown number of takes was abandoned until the session three or so weeks afterwards where it was successfully finalized.

A gentle harp introduces the song that picks up the pace with subdued percussion as Cliff sings a lovely version of the song; his voice has always been well-suited to performing Diamond songs. The performance is elevated by the inclusion of Bruce Welch and Hank Marvin on backing vocals during the choruses, serving to make it a quintessential Cliff track of the period.

Track Specification
Composed by Neil Diamond

__1. Unissued track (La La La La La EP)__

Musicians		*Recording Details*	
Bernard Ebbinghouse Orchestra	orchestra	Producer	Norrie Paramor
Bernard Ebbinghouse	arranger, conductor	Engineered by	Peter Vincent and Richard Lush
Hank Marvin	backing vocals	Recording location	Abbey Road Studio 2, St. John's Wood, London
Cliff Richard	vocals	Recording date	19th September 1966
Bruce Welch	backing vocals		

__2. La La La La La EP__

Musicians		*Recording Details*	
Bernard Ebbinghouse Orchestra	orchestra	Producer	Norrie Paramor
Bernard Ebbinghouse	arranger, conductor	Engineered by	Peter Vincent and Richard Lush
Hank Marvin	backing vocals	Recording location	Abbey Road Studio 2, St. John's Wood, London
Cliff Richard	vocals	Recording date	11th October 1966
Bruce Welch	backing vocals		

♫ So Long

B-side of **With the Eyes of a Child**

In the late sixties, many 'serious' pop music critics had started writing Cliff Richard off as a failing pop artist, exemplified by the lower quality of material he was issuing as singles. In part, they had a point about the songs but, on the other hand, Cliff has never been afraid to embrace the new. *So Long*, chosen as the B-side of his forty-eighth UK single, ***With the Eyes of a Child***, continued his series of recordings with an updated orchestra, this time arranged and conducted by Alan Hawkshaw, who would join the Shadows in the seventies as a sidesman playing the keyboards. As was the wont of Columbia at the time, all singles and their B-sides were released in mono format only since the radio stations were largely broadcasting in that medium too. *So Long* was a rarity for almost forty years until the stereo version was included on the rare B-sides section of the celebratory ***...And They Said It Wouldn't Last! (My 50 Years in Music)*** in 2008.

A single violin plays a solo during the song's introduction before Cliff brings in his gentle vocal. As expected, the beauty of his pure voice is what makes any song special and this is particularly so on this performance, particularly as he also provides his own duet vocal line in the middle of the song. There is an uncredited vocal group also singing on the track but there is no information available on them.

Track Specification
Composed by Chris Arnold, Geoff Morrow and David Martin

Musicians		*Recording Details*	
Alan Hawkshaw Orchestra	orchestra	Producer	Norrie Paramor
Alan Hawkshaw	arranger, conductor	Engineered by	Peter Vince
Cliff Richard	vocals, backing vocals	Recording location	Abbey Road Studio 2, St. John's Wood, London
Unknown	backing vocals	Recording date	18th April 1969

♫ Some Are Lonely

From the album **Out of the Shadows** *(The Shadows) (standard mono and stereo and French mono versions)*

One of the first recording sessions to feature new Shadows drummer Brian Bennett, who was brought in to replace Tony Meehan at the end of 1961, saw a recording of a Cliff Richard original, although he doesn't perform on the record.
The stereo and mono edits used the same take but with different mixes for the audio channel requirements. A different mono version of the song was incorporated on the French issue of the *Out of the Shadows* LP, which is similar in all ways except that the pace is slower – the result is a rarity much sought after by both Shadows and Cliff fans.
The tune is a beautiful melody with a strong bass line and a tinkling triangle and clinking blocks throughout, giving the tune a slightly Latin feel with its syncopation. Bruce Welch performs regular arpeggiated chords underneath Hank Marvin's lead guitar, which is performed with some reverberation and echo.

Track Specification
Composed by Cliff Richard

1. Out of the Shadows (standard version)

Musicians		*Recording Details*	
Brian Bennett	drums, percussion, triangle	Producer	Norrie Paramor
Jet Harris	bass	Engineered by	Malcolm Addey
Hank Marvin	guitar	Recording location	Abbey Road Studios, St. John's Wood, London
Cliff Richard	vocals	Recording date	21st December 1961
Bruce Welch	rhythm guitar		

2. Out of the Shadows (French mono version)

Musicians		*Recording Details*	
Brian Bennett	drums, percussion, triangle	Producer	Norrie Paramor
Jet Harris	bass	Engineered by	Malcolm Addey
Hank Marvin	guitar	Recording location	Abbey Road Studios, St. John's Wood, London
Cliff Richard	vocals	Recording date	21st December 1961
Bruce Welch	rhythm guitar		

♫ Somebody

From the album **Triumph in the Air** *(Sheila Walsh)*

Having been instrumental in producing his protégée Sheila Walsh's first album, ***Drifting***, Cliff Richard decided to limit his involvement in the second, ***Triumph in the Air***, to the provision of backing vocals on a handful of tracks, including *Somebody*, which also included regular Cliff songwriter Chris Eaton and singer Mark Williamson. The song was subsequently released on CD for the first time on the 1985 US-only album *Compact Favorites*.
Setting off at a faster pace than many of the tracks on the album, the feel is very much of its period with synthesisers bleeping and electronic drums pounding behind the real percussion as is Walsh's lead vocal. Cliff's contribution to the harmonies are just discernible in the closed vocal section in the chorus, which has Walsh singing sharp as she acts out the need for somebody to save her.

Track Specification
Composed by Teri de Sario Purse and Bill Purse

Musicians		*Recording Details*	
Chris Eaton	backing vocals	Producer	Craig Pruess, assisted by Keith Bessey
Rick Fenn	guitar	Engineered by	Keith Bessey
Graham Jarvis	drums, percussion	Recording location	Cloud 9 Studios, London, Strawberry Studios, London and/or Jacobs Studios, Farnham, Surrey
Craig Pruess	arranger, keyboards, electronics		
Cliff Richard	backing vocals		
Sheila Walsh	vocals	Recording date	September 1983-January 1984
Mark Williamson	backing vocals		

♫ Somebody Loses

B-side of **Blue Turns to Grey**

One of twenty-one songs from the writing partnership of Sid Tepper and Roy Bennett for Cliff Richard to record in his early career, *Somebody Loses* was recorded at the first session in 1966 along with the eventual A-side ***Blue Turns to Grey***. The final (unknown) take and edit were used for the mono and stereo recordings but with different mixes for the needs of the separate recording channels. Originally only released in mono as part of the single packag, it was a desired rarity until it was initially released in stereo format for the first time on the French *Congratulations to Cliff* collection in 2007 and again as part of the celebratory ***...And They Said It Wouldn't Last! (My 50 Years in Music)*** the following year.
Another song displaying the perfect vocal harmonies created by the band, *Somebvody Loses* is an upbeat song that is optimistic in its message but also gloating in that he has stolen the girl from someone else and, in turn, reflective now he is subject to the same humiliation by someone else. The guitar accompaniment and the strength of Bruce Welch's rhythm drive the song onwards through a few key changes. Cliff's vocals have rarely been bettered and, in many respects, this song would have stood well on its own as a single.

Track Specification
Composed by Sid Tepper and Roy C. Bennett

Musicians		*Recording Details*	
Brian Bennett	drums, percussion	Producer	Norrie Paramor
Hank Marvin	backing vocals, guitar	Engineered by	Unknown
Cliff Richard	vocals	Recording location	Abbey Road Studio 2, St. John's Wood, London
John Rostill	backing vocals, bass	Recording date	17th January 1966
Bruce Welch	backing vocals, rhythm guitar		

♫ Somebody Loves You
B-side of **Peace in Our Time**

Recorded by Cliff Richard at the second set of sessions with Bruce Welch assisting in the production at studios in Yorkshire, *Somebody Loves You* was the principal B-side of ***Peace in Our Time***, appearing on the seven-inch release and the first of the dual CD version of the single.
Driven by synthesisers or organs, there is a synthesized bass section that adds a touch of jazzy class to the song. Cliff sings the song with apparent nonchalance but, although there are some interesting things going on in the song, particularly on the range of vocals and the backing harmonies provided by Cliff, the melody itself is not immediately memorable and this detracts from the overall involvement of the listener.

Track Specification
Composed by John Wilson

Musicians		*Recording Details*	
Paul Moessl	arranger, drum programming, keyboards	Producer	Bruce Welch and Cliff Richard
		Engineered by	Keith Bessey
Steve Pigott	bass, keyboards	Recording location	Westside Studios, North Yorkshire
Cliff Richard	vocals, backing vocals	Recording date	7th-8th June 1992

♫ Somebody Touched Me
From the album **Oh Boy!**

Cliff Richard became a regular favourite on Jack Good's *Oh Boy!* popular music television show, where he used to perform covers and familiar songs and some original material, including his hits of the period. Because of the success of the television show, it was decided that an album should follow as an official release. Originally, Marty Wilde was lined up to perform ***TV Hop*** and *Somebody Touched Me* but, for some reason, couldn't make it to the recordings, at which point Cliff stepped up to the microphone.
Somebody Touched Me was written by a Turkish ex-patriot who had worked with many jazz luminaries during the thirties and forties. It was a big hit in the US for Ruth Brown in the early fifties, while Buddy Knox popularized it again towards the end of that decade. Although neither version nor any other covers made it into the UK singles charts, the fact that it was popular in America was sufficient for its inclusion in the *Oh Boy!* set recorded by Cliff.
The backing track and Cliff's vocals were recorded on separate days and, instead of using the Drifters as his backing, the musicians were from the Oh Boy! Band and the Dallas Boys harmonizing. There is no record of who the individual band performers are, however, and so will be highlighted as unknown in this entry. Cliff's vocals are spot on and show what a burgeoning talent there was awaiting the public. It's unfortunate that the backing vocals by the Dallas Boys don't replicate Cliff's energy as they sound a little lacklustre as if it were a jobbing group waiting to sign off for the day. Nevertheless, it is an interesting document marking Cliff's progression through his teen idol years.
Although the album was re-released in the late seventies, it wasn't until the issue of the rarities album ***The Rock and Roll Years 1958-1963*** that *Somebody Touched Me* saw release in digital format.

Track Specification
Composed by Ahmet Ertegun

Musicians		*Recording Details*	
Dallas Boys:		Producer	Harry Robinson (backing track) and Norrie Paramor (vocals)
Nicky Clarke	backing vocals		
Leon Fisk	backing vocals	Engineered by	Norman Newell (backing track) and Malcolm Addey (vocals)
Stan Jones	backing vocals		
Joe Smith	backing vocals	Recording location	Abbey Road Studio 2, St. John's Wood, London
Bob Wragg	backing vocals	Recording date	19th October 1958 (backing track) and 21st October 1958 (vocals)
Oh Boy! Band	guitars, stand-up bass, piano, saxophone, drums, percussion		
Cliff Richard	vocals		

♫ Someday (You'll Want Me to Want You)
From the album **Love Is Forever**

With covers by Gene Autry, Brenda Lee, Patsy Cline, the Drifters, Tex Ritter, Bobby Vinton, Eddy Arnold, Ray Charles, Jerry Lee Lewis, Rick Nelson, the Mills Brothers, Jim Reeves, Gene Pitney, the Ravens and Gene Vincent, Jodie Sands was the only artist to have a British hit with *Someday (You'll Want Me to Want You)* when she reached number fourteen in

October 1958 with her only charting single. The song has also mistakenly been changed to *Someday (You'll Want Me to Love You)* including some literature on Cliff Richard, and, in this guise, it has been covered by Mickey Gilley, Mina and even comedian Jimmy Tarbuck.
Cliff's version was recorded at a dual session on 10th May 1965 with the Shadows accompanying, which resulted in six completed songs for a variety of future projects. Destined for the upcoming album ***Love Is Forever***, the final take and edit was used for the mono and stereo recordings but with different mixes for the separate audio channels. The song was included on the track listing of the associated ***Love Is Forever*** EP, which was only released in mono format.
One of the two songs that feature the Shadows on the album, the stereo edit forces Cliff's vocal into the right channel and the chugging work of the Shadows into the left, making it a slightly disorienting and muddy listening experience, which is unfortunate, because the song is one of the highlights of the album, with Bruce Welch's understated rhythm chords and Hank Marvin's syncopated lead guitar.

Track Specification
Composed by Jimmie Hodges

Musicians		*Recording Details*	
Brian Bennett	drums, percussion	Producer	Norrie Paramor
Hank Marvin	guitar	Engineered by	Unknown
Cliff Richard	vocals	Recording location	Estudios Valentim de Carvalho, Lisbon, Portugal
John Rostill	bass		
Bruce Welch	rhythm guitar	Recording date	10th May 1965

♬ Some of These Days
From the EP **Holiday Carnival**

Written in 1910 especially for one of America's biggest recording stars, Sophie Tucker (who was known as the 'last of the red-hot mamas'), she released *Some of These Days* to great acclaim the following year. It has been used in a number of films over the years, was a recurrent theme in Jean Paul Sartre's novel *Nausea* and has been recorded by a number of artists including George Benson, Rosemary Clooney, Elkie Brooks, Bix Beiderbecke, Bing Crosby, Louis Armstrong, Stéphane Grapelli, Cab Calloway, Bobby Darrin (and Kevin Spacey in the film biopic of Darrin's life), Les Paul, Benny Goodman, Brenda Lee, Humphrey Lyttelton, the Original Dixieland Jazz Band and Barbra Streisand among many others.
Cliff's cover of *Some of These Days* was recorded in a session that resulted in three EP tracks (two for ***Holiday Carnival*** and one for ***Love Is Forever***). The fourth and final take and edit was used for the mono and stereo recordings but with different mixes for the audio channels. Until the 2000 French album release *Do You Want to Dance with Cliff Richard*, the song remained a rarity and it was also included, edited with five or so seconds taken off the end cutting out the final chorus line, on ***...And They Said It Wouldn't Last! (My 50 Years in Music)***.
With a slow *a capella* introduction of the song's title, the track continues as a bossa nova style of arrangement. Cliff's vocals are well-suited to this kind of tune, although it was over fifty years old at the time of his recording. There are guitars and drums, as with the other tracks created at the session, which sound like the Shadows but the session notes indicate that these are the Norrie Paramor Orchestra and so this entry reflects that.

Track Specification
Composed by Shelton Brooks

Musicians		*Recording Details*	
Mike Sammes Singers	backing vocals	Producer	Norrie Paramor
Norrie Paramor Orchestra	orchestra	Engineered by	Malcolm Addey and Peter Vince
Norrie Paramor	arranger, conductor	Recording location	Abbey Road Studio 2, St. John's Wood, London
Cliff Richard	vocals	Recording date	12th December 1962

♬ Some People
102nd UK single *(seven- and twelve-inch) and from the albums* **Live and Guaranteed 1988!**, **From a Distance ***** The Event** *and* **World Tour Live**

As with the entire ***Always Guaranteed*** album, Alan Tarney wrote all the songs and played all the instruments. Chief engineer Gerry Kitchingham remembered, in interview for the liner notes of the 2004 remaster of the album, that Tarney would often arrive at the studio with nothing ready; instead he would strum a guitar and generate something that might be usable. With *Some People*, this was the process that he followed but was dissatisfied with the result, not believing it to be worth anything nor even if Cliff Richard would record deign to record it. Cliff was, at the time, involved in performing in London in ***Time – The Musical*** and could only appear in the studio during the day and Tarney's approach suited him well. On the day that he was presented with *Some People*, Cliff was astounded that Tarney was so unsure about it and knew it would be the perfect single material.
Issued with non-album track ***One Time Lover Man***, *Some People* was released as the second single from the project on the EMI label (catalogue number EM 18) on 17th August 1987 and reached number three in the UK charts. Simultaneously, it was released in a gatefold sleeve (catalogue number EMG 18), a picture disc (EMP 18) and in extended form on a twelve-inch single, which also included another non-album track ***Reunion of the Heart*** (12EM 18). The extended version simply has some additional instrumentation in the mid-section and at the end. In September 1987, the first CD video was released and featured the promotional video of the song, while the track was also later included on the CD single release of the

next single, ***Remember Me***, as a bonus track on the first Cliff solo single to be released in digital format. Finally, in December 1993, *Some People* in its original single edit was chosen again as a bonus track on the CD single release of ***Healing Love*** from the ***Cliff Richard – The Album*** project.

The song was a favourite of Cliff's, as he regularly performed it with a Chinese visual dance involving helpers at either end of lengths of sheeting, raising them, letting them billow as they were brought down to the floor and repeating the exercise throughout the performance. The associated promotional video saw Cliff in almost agonized performance, with dancers surrounding him, the females made up to look like Marilyn Monroe in white dresses as they walk around an edifice replicating one of Escher's confusing drawings. Then there are actors in *Cabaret*-style theatre, sailors and businessmen, all representing the normality of life and how people love or use one another. Cliff himself walk's along the Escher replica. The video won much respect and awards, thrusting Cliff back into the music forefront once again.

The introduction features a programmed drum that sets the pace that is matched by sustained chords on the synthesiser and Cliff's emoting lead vocal. The drama of the song builds up into the second verse as the key changes and then returns to the original key for the instrumental bridge. Cliff employs a falsetto during this bridge and also supplies backing vocals with Tarney, although these are deliberately limited to slight echoes of key words in the lyrics. The instrumentation is pared down as Cliff drives onwards into the final section. The arrangement of the song is what provides the extraordinary beauty of the song that slowly quietens as it reaches the end, with Cliff's sustained note saturated with the vibrato which had become a kind of musical signature for him.

Some People was included on the set list for ***From a Distance ***** The Event*** and it is a faithful version of the original with the sustained chords on the keyboards and the blipping staccato percussion as well as Cliff's impassioned lead.

Cliff resurrected the song for his 2003 world tour, the New Zealand show of which was filmed and recorded for a DVD release later in the year. In 2004, fourteen of those songs were included on the CD *World Tour Live* to complement the DVD and, among the choices, was the latest version of *Some People*. With the synthesised percussion and sustained keyboard chords, the song is again very close to the original.

Track Specification
Composed by Alan Tarney

1. Single (seven-inch)

Musicians		*Recording Details*	
Cliff Richard	vocals, backing vocals	Producer	Alan Tarney
Alan Tarney	backing vocals, guitars, bass, keyboards, drum and percussion programming	Engineered by	Gerry Kitchingham and Keith Bessey
		Recording location	R. G. Jones Studios, Wimbledon, London
		Recording date	13th October-November 1986

2. Single (twelve-inch extended)

Musicians		*Recording Details*	
Cliff Richard	vocals, backing vocals	Producer	Alan Tarney
Alan Tarney	backing vocals, guitars, bass, keyboards, drum and percussion programming	Engineered by	Gerry Kitchingham and Keith Bessey
		Recording location	R. G. Jones Studios, Wimbledon, London
		Recording date	13th October-November 1986

3. Live & Guaranteed 1988!

Musicians		*Recording Details*	
John Clark	guitar	Producer	Unknown
Rosemarie Ford	backing vocals	Engineered by	Unknown
Mark Griffiths	bass	Recording location	Fyens Forum, Odense, Denmark
Peter Howarth	backing vocals	Recording date	22nd May 1988
Steve Lauri	guitar		
Paul Moessl	keyboards		
Mick Mullins	backing vocals		
Alan Park	keyboards		
Cliff Richard	vocals		
Henry Spinetti	drums, percussion		

4. From a Distance ** The Event***

Musicians		*Recording Details*	
John Clark	guitar	Producer	Cliff Richard
Sonia Jones-Morgan	backing vocals	Engineered by	Keith Bessey and Mick McKenna
Steve Lauri	guitar	Recording location	Rolling Stones Mobile Studio, Wembley Stadium, Wembley, North-west London
Peter May	drums, percussion		
Paul Moessl	keyboards	Recording date	16th-17th June 1989
Tessa Niles	backing vocals		
Alan Park	keyboards		
Provox:			
Peter Howarth	backing vocals		
Mick Mullins	backing vocals		
Keith Murrell	backing vocals		
Cliff Richard	vocals		
Steve Stroud	bass		

5. *World Tour Live*

Musicians	
Rachel Allen	violin
Elena Bulgakova	violin
Jenni Champion	violin
Anthony Clark	backing vocals, guitar
John Clark	guitar
Dave Cooke	keyboards
Cornelia Didenco	violin
Gina Ferguson	violin
Mike Haughton	flute
Peter Howarth	backing vocals
Cathy Irons	violin
Pete May	drums, percussion
Mick Mullins	backing vocals
Keith Murrell	backing vocals
Alan Park	keyboards
Hee-Jung Park	violin
Cliff Richard	vocals
Eva Schwanen-Lilley	violin
Steve Stroud	bass

Recording Details	
Producer	Keith Bessey
Engineered by	Keith Bessey
Recording location	The Mission Winery, Napier, New Zealand
Recording date	22nd February 2003

♬ Something Good

From the albums **Live at the Talk of the Town** *and* **Cliff Live in Korea**

Originally from the musical *The Sound of Music*, the beautiful *Something Good* comes at the point where Maria (played memorably in the film by Julie Andrews) is reviewing her situation and can't believe her luck with the way her life has turned out putting it down to the fact that she must have done something good in her earlier life to reap the reward. Recorded of course by Julie Andrews, *Something Good* has also been covered by artist such as Teri Hansen, Sarah Blasko, Rebecca Luker, Cynthia Dale, Angela Cartwright and Jill Walsh among a number of largely female performers, which is why it seems surprising that Cliff Richard would choose to cover it by including it in his set list for concerts.

Recorded live at the Talk of the Town (and released on the album of the same name), *Something Good* was performed with a segue into ***If Ever I Would Leave You***. Cliff sings the song with minimal accompaniment other than strings and piano and it suits his voice to sing emotional film ballads such as this.

The two songs appeared together on the set list for the Korean tour at the end of 1969. The concert in Seoul with the Shadows accompanying him was recorded and released in mono format only for the Korean market on the album *Cliff Live in Korea*.

Track Specification

Composed by Richard Rodgers and Oscar Hammerstein II

1. *Live at the Talk of the Town*

Musicians	
Norrie Paramor	arranger, conductor
Cliff Richard	vocals
Talk of the Town Orchestra	orchestra

Recording Details	
Producer	Norrie Paramor
Engineered by	Peter Vince
Recording location	Talk of the Town Theatre, London
Recording date	30th May 1968

2. *Cliff Live in Korea*

Musicians	
Brian Bennett	drums, percussion
Alan Hawkshaw	keyboards
Hank Marvin	guitar
Cliff Richard	vocals
John Rostill	bass
Bruce Welch	rhythm guitar

Recording Details	
Producer	Unknown
Engineered by	Unknown
Recording location	Citizen Hall, Seoul, South Korea
Recording date	16th October 1969

♬ Somethin' Is Goin' On

134th UK single

Something's Goin' On was Cliff Richard's first album of original material for over five years and was recorded in and around Nashville with American personnel and musicians performng a number of songs commissioned for the project. The second track on the album is a saxophone-drive, late-night style of song that explores the emotions created by one or the other of a couple embarking on an illicit affair.

Backed with non-album track, ***How Many Sleeps?***, the near title track from the album, *Somethin' Is Goin' On* was issued as the first single from the project and was released on the Decca label (catalogue number 475 619) on 11th October 2004 and reached number nine in the UK singles charts. The promotional video for the song was added to the ***I Cannot Give You My Love*** single later the same year and again on the ***What Car?*** DVD single release the following year. The single version was a shorter edit of the album version with around forty seconds cut from the end as it fades early. Two promotional

discs were released, one with only the single track on it, while another also featured non-album track ***Slow Down***, which had only been issued on Cliff's website at that point, and the album version of *Somethin' Is Goin' On*.
The beautiful guitar picking at the beginning of the song leads into Cliff's falsetto vocal supported by the guitar and stark percussion. The performance is suitably warm and this warmth increases further with the addition of the rest of the instrumentation, particularly the brass, and the syncopation of the accompaniment pushes the song onwards and gives credence to song's title.

Track Specification
Composed by Steve Mandile, David Mullen and Marcus Hummon

Musicians

Jeff Coffin	saxophone
Ziggie Diaz	programming
Mark Douthit	saxophone
Wes Hightower	backing vocals
DeMarco Johnson	harmonica
Ken Lewis	percussion
Doug Moffet	saxophone
Cliff Richard	vocals
Richie Pena	programming
Michael Ripoll	acoustic guitar
Jeff Roach	keyboards
Tommy Sims	arranger, guitar, bass, keyboards
Unknown	orchestra

Recording Details

Producer	Tommy Sims
Engineered by	Bryan Lenox and Tommy Sims (vocals and instruments) and Ronnie Brookshire (strings)
Recording location	Uncle Tom's Cabin, Franklin, Tennessee, USA (vocals and instruments) and The Tracking Room, Nashville, Tennessee, USA (strings)
Recording date	2003-2004

♬ Sometimes Love

From the album **Something's Goin' On**

The 2004 album ***Something's Goin' On*** was Cliff Richard's first album of original material for over five years and was recorded in Tennessee. He commissioned several songs from American writers to give the album a genuine American country feel and employed American musicians and studio personnel. *Sometimes Love* is a grooving song that evokes images of driving on the US highways, while talking about love like a loaded gun, an odd image to associate with Cliff.
The driving bass and guitar combination brings Cliff back full circle to the start of his career while imbuing the song with a contemporary feel. Cliff is in his element singing songs with a rock and roll rhythm and this is a track that would have been a good single.

Track Specification
Composed by Brian White and Don Poythress

Musicians

Trey Bruce	programming
J. T. Corenflos	guitar
Tony Harrell	keyboards
Wes Hightower	backing vocals
Greg Morrow	drums, percussion
Alison Prestwood	bass
Cliff Richard	vocals
Marty Slayton	backing vocals
Michael Spriggs	guitar

Recording Details

Producer	Trey Bruce
Engineered by	David Buchanan
Recording location	Omnisound Recording Studios, Nashville, Tennessee, USA, Sound Stage Studios, Nashville, Tennessee, USA and Pocket Studio, Franklin, Tennessee, USA
Recording date	2003-2004

♬ Somewhere

Unissued track

Taken from the hugely popular and successful 1957 Broadway musical, *West Side Story*, and the subsequent film, the melody is based on a phrase from one of the movements of Beethoven's *Emperor* Piano Concerto. A regular favourite for performance at reality talent competitions such as *The X Factor*, it has been covered by a variety of artists such as Barbra Streisand, Oscar Peterson, Kylie Minogue, Bobby Darin, Devo, Leona Lewis, Phil Collins (whose 1996 cover didn't chart), Il Divo, Julian Lloyd Webber, Charlotte Church and Aretha Franklin among others. Two acts have taken it into the British charts: first was P. J. Proby, reaching number six in 1964 and, second, the Pet Shop Boys reaching number nine in 1997.
Cliff Richard recorded his version at one of the first sessions that was used to record the tracks for the ***Cinderella*** pantomime cast recording but, after five takes, for whatever reason the song was abandoned and, to date, remains unissued.

Track Specification
Composed by Leonard Bernstein and Stephen Sondheim

Musicians

Brian Bennett	drums, percussion
Hank Marvin	guitar
Cliff Richard	vocals
John Rostill	bass
Bruce Welch	rhythm guitar

Recording Details

Producer	Norrie Paramor
Engineered by	Peter Vince and Richard Lush
Recording location	Abbey Road Studio 2, St. John's Wood, London
Recording date	17th October 1966

♫ Somewhere along the Way

From the album **Cliff Sings**

The penultimate song by Cliff Richard on the ***Cliff Sings*** album is also the last but one to feature backing by the Norrie Paramor Orchestra rather than the traditional Drifters (later to change their name to The Shadows prior to the album's release). *Somewhere along the Way* was first recorded by Nat King Cole and released in 1952, reaching number eight in the Billboard charts. It was also Cole's first hit in the UK, where it reached number three in the same year. The song has subsequently been covered extensively by such artists as Tony Bennett, The Platters, Doris Troy, Frank Sinatra, Bobby Vinton, Matt Monro and Dean Martin.

All of the album tracks were released only in mono in the long-player format. However, with the burgeoning interest in stereo from the record-buying public, EMI also undertook to release the entire album on four EPs in both mono and stereo. While the mono EP version of *Somewhere along the Way* is the same as appears on the album, the stereo EP version used the same studio take but was edited slightly differently for the sound-channelling requirements.

Norrie Paramor's luscious and almost saccharine string accompaniment suits Cliff's vocals well. As has been proven on other tracks, Cliff's abilities as a singer are stretched on the ballads section of the album but never to breaking point. Technically speaking, this is a difficult song to sing in terms of pitching the notes but Cliff carries the tune well in the upper and lower registers, showing his comfort with singing in a variety of genres.

Track Specification

Composed by Sammy Gallop and Kurt Adams

Musicians

Norrie Paramor Orchestra	orchestra
Norrie Paramor	arranger, conductor
Cliff Richard	vocals

Recording Details

Producer	Norrie Paramor
Engineered by	Malcolm Addey and Alan Kane (mono) and Stuart Eltham and Norman Smith (stereo)
Recording location	Abbey Road Studio 2, St. John's Wood, London
Recording date	9th September 1959

♫ Somewhere by the Sea

From the album **Established 1958**

Written by the Shadows, as were all the tracks on the ***Established 1958*** album, *Somewhere by the Sea* was recorded in four takes in the penultimate session ever to have Cliff Richard and the Shadows together in one place (even the 2009 ***Reunited*** album was recorded separately and then mixed together). It was the only Cliff song to be recorded at the session and it is likely that the Shadows' instrumentals were recorded during the rest of the time.

Somewhere by the Sea is written with much wit and the quirky performance, which includes an upbeat dance section in the middle eight and a telephone ring and a 'discussion' between Cliff and Bruce Welch (on the other end of the call), makes it a very interesting track. Once again, the Shadows provide their perfect vocal harmonies and this lifts a great song even further.

Track Specification

Composed by Hank Marvin, Bruce Welch, Brian Bennett and John Rostill

Musicians

Brian Bennett	drums, percussion
Hank Marvin	backing vocals, guitar
Cliff Richard	vocals, spoken vocals
John Rostill	backing vocals, bass
Bruce Welch	backing vocals, spoken vocals, rhythm guitar

Recording Details

Producer	Norrie Paramor
Engineered by	Peter Vince
Recording location	Abbey Road Studio 2, St. John's Wood, London
Recording date	5th June 1968

♫ Somewhere Over the Rainbow

From the album **Wanted**

Correctly titled *Over the Rainbow* but often called *Somewhere over the Rainbow*, the song is inextricably linked to Judy Garland's performance as Dorothy Gale in the 1939 film, *The Wizard of Oz*. The song is performed by the MGM Orchestra over the opening credits but it is the gentle, yearning version by Garland that appears in the first few minutes of the action after Dorothy complains to her Auntie Em about an incident with her dog Toto and Miss Gulch who attacked the animal with a rake. Her frustrated aunt won't hear of it and tells her niece to find somewhere where she will stay out of trouble and Dorothy walks off into the farm and sings the song. It is a defining moment in the film since it precipitates her journey to Oz, in order that she finds and understands herself and her world better. It has been covered by Garland's daughter Liza Minnelli, Louis Armstrong, Olivia Newton-John, who recorded a very plaintive and beautiful version as did Eva Cassidy, Chet Atkins, Glen Miller and Kylie Minogue among hundreds of others.

In 1993, Hawaiian ukulele player Israel Kamakawiwo'ole melded *Somewhere over the Rainbow* with Louis Armstrong's ***What a Wonderful World*** (to create ***Somewhere over the Rainbow/What a Wonderful World*** as a complete song). Although it passed unnoticed at the time, even after his death in 1997, the combined song backed by only a ukulele was passed to Cliff Richard by his friend and radio DJ, Graham Dene, in the new millennium and Cliff fell in love with it, recording it for his ***Wanted*** album and releasing it as his first single from the enterprise.

♬ Somewhere Over the Rainbow/What a Wonderful World

130th UK single and unreleased live track

Somewhere Over the Rainbow was familiar to many a film fan as one of the defining moments from the film *The Wizard of Oz* and ***What a Wonderful World*** is one of the most optimistic songs to come out of America during its most troubled period at the end of the sixties and is forever associated with its original recording by Louis Armstrong. But it was Hawaiian ukulele-player Israel Kamakawiwo'ole who saw something musically similar in the two songs and combined them to create one whole. It works successfully as the two songs are segued seamlessly. Kamakawiwo'ole recorded his version in 1993 and it would have sunk with his death in 1997 from weight-related diseases had not Graham Dene, Cliff Richard's friend and respected DJ, passed Cliff a copy and he knew he wanted to record it. Kamakawiwo'ole then reached number sixty-eight entirely through downloads in April 2007, after it had appeared in a successful advertising campaign.
But it was Cliff's more rounded version that showed he was not ready to give up, even though his long-term record company, EMI, had dispensed with his contract. The first song on the ***Wanted*** album, *Somewhere Over the Rainbow/What a Wonderful World* was edited for single use and was released in two formats on the Papillon Records label on 3rd December 2001: the first was a CD/DVD combination (catalogue number Cliff CD 1) with the edited title track, an *a capella* version of ***The Millennium Prayer*** and the promotional video of the single; the second was an audio-only CD (CR CDX 1), which included the single edit of the song and two non-album tracks, ***Lay All Your Love on Me*** and ***(Let's Go) Where There Are Horses***. Proving his erstwhile record label wrong, the single reached number eleven in the UK charts. A promotional sampler (RAINBOW 1 01) with an extended single track with additional percussion at the start, also featured ***Love Me Tender, You've Got a Friend*** and *Lay All Your Love on Me.*
The stunning feature of Cliff's cover is the collective backing vocals that appear throughout and they mark the song as a more lush version than the Hawaiian original and Cliff's vocal is mixed to front of the edit making it confidential. What is obvious is that Cliff is enjoying singing this upbeat tune and taking this enjoyment into the segue to the other song. The promotional video saw Cliff flying over a non-descript city's skyline, and waving to people standing at the windows.
In 2003, during the tour to support the album, Cliff performed the single as part of the set list. This was filmed and released on DVD (*World Tour Live*) the same year while a CD version that took only fourteen of those tracks was released the following year but did not include *Somewhere over the Rainbow/What a Wonderful World.*

Track Specification
Composed by Harold Arlen and E Y "Yip" Harburg; George David Weiss and George Douglas

1. Single

Musicians		*Recording Details*	
John Brant	additional programming	Producer	Alan Tarney
Anthony Clark	backing vocals	Engineered by	John Brant and Gerry Kitchingham
Cliff Richard	vocals, backing vocals	Recording location	Wilmer Studios, London
Alan Tarney	arranger, backing vocals, guitar, keyboards, programming	Recording date	January-April 2001

2. Unissued track (World Tour Live)

Musicians		*Recording Details*	
Rachel Allen	violin	Producer	Keith Bessey
Elena Bulgakova	violin	Engineered by	Keith Bessey
Jenni Champion	violin	Recording location	The Mission Winery, Napier, New Zealand
Anthony Clark	backing vocals, guitar	Recording date	22nd February 2003
John Clark	guitar		
Dave Cooke	keyboards		
Cornelia Didenco	violin		
Gina Ferguson	violin		
Peter Howarth	backing vocals		
Cathy Irons	violin		
Pete May	drums, percussion		
Mick Mullins	backing vocals		
Keith Murrell	backing vocals		
Alan Park	keyboards		
Hee-Jung Park	violin		
Cliff Richard	vocals		
Eva Schwanen-Lilley	violin		
Steve Stroud	bass		

♬ Songbird

From the album **I Love You, Goodbye** *(Barratt Waugh)*

Cliff Richard has had a long association with Barratt Waugh but it was in 2000 that Cliff's own Blacknight label released Waugh's *I Love You, Goodbye* album, which featured Cliff on backing vocals for two tracks: *Songbird* and ***Lucie***. *Songbird* was originally written by Christine McVie for Fleetwood Mac's hugely popular 1977 album *Rumours* and has since been covered by acts such as Eva Cassidy (naming her posthumous album after it), Lena Martell, Pat Benatar, Rita Coolidge, Willie Nelson and Hayley Westenra among others.

The ethnic flute creates an exotic atmosphere accompanied by steel-stringed guitars and percussion, as Barratt Waugh enters with an exquisite falsetto rendition of the song. Cliff's contribution to the backing vocals can be discerned in the second verse and chorus onwards, which are gently placed behind Waugh's emotively high-pitched evocation of the song's lyrics.

Track Specification
Composed by Christine McVie

Musicians

John Cameron	arranger, conductor
Mitch Dalton	guitar
Harold Fisher	drums, percussion
Tristan Fry	percussion
Pat Halling	orchestra leader, violin
Dave Hartley	piano, keyboards
Peter Howarth	backing vocals
Shaila Kanga	harp
Paul Keogh	guitar
Caroline Lavelle	cello
Keith Murrell	backing vocals
Jacqueline Norrie	violin
Andy Pask	bass
Steve Pearce	bass
Tony Pleeth	cello
Jocelyn Pook	viola
Cliff Richard	backing vocals
Frank Ricotti	percussion
Tony Roberts	ethnic flute
Julia Singleton	violin
Barratt Waugh	vocals

Recording Details

Producer	John Cameron
Engineered by	Christopher Dibble
Recording location	C.T.S. Studios, Wembley, London and Lansdowne Studios, London
Recording date	June-July 1999 and February 2000

♫ Song from *Moulin Rouge*, The

Unissued track

Originally composed with French lyrics (written by Jacques Larue), the English translation was added to *The Song from Moulin Rouge* by William Engvick. Although commonly known by the clunky title of *The Song from Moulin Rouge*, it often also goes by the subtitle (occasionally used as its main title) of ***Where Is Your Heart?***, although the film from which it is taken annotates it as *It's April Again* – perhaps the confusion that this created is why it has been referred to as *The Song from [the] Moulin Rouge*, under which title Mantovani reached number in the UK charts in 1953.
It is the recording under *Where Is Your Heart?* that was eventually released by Cliff Richard on the EP ***Look in My Eyes Maria*** which was recorded on 24th July 1964. However, there was a first trial attempt at the session seven days earlier that was nominally identified as *The Song from Moulin Rouge* on the session notes and tape box. Four takes were attempted but none has yet been issued commercially. Those known to be involved in the session are added to the track specification and this will be amended if proven to be incorrect.

Track Specification
Composed by William Engvick and George Auric

Musicians

Mike Sammes Singers	backing vocals
Norrie Paramor Orchestra	orchestra
Norrie Paramor	arranger, conductor
Cliff Richard	vocals

Recording Details

Producer	Norrie Paramor
Engineered by	Malcolm Addey
Recording location	Abbey Road Studio 2, St. John's Wood, London
Recording date	17th July 1964

♫ Song of Yesterday

From the album **...And They Said It Wouldn't Last! (My 50 Years in Music)**

In June 1974, Cliff Richard entered the Morgan Studios in London to record a new single (released to much controversy as ***(There's a) Honky Tonk Angel***). At the same time, he recorded two other tracks, ***Love of My Life*** and *Song of Yesterday*, which were not only unissued but had been forgotten entirely (Nigel Goodall's and Peter Lewry's book *The Complete Recording Sessions 1958-1990* doesn't mention them and the liner notes for ***...And They Said It Would Last! (My 50 Years in Music)*** indicate that the songs only came to light as they were researching the content of that celebratory album). Placed on the rarities section of that album with just cause, both missing tracks were issued for the first time in 2008.
That same album incorrectly credits the song to Bruce Welch and Brian Bennett when it is, in fact, another Shadows pairing Bruce Welch and John Rostill who co-authored it. Originally, the song was recorded by Bruce as a solo B-side of his single *Please Mr. Please*.
As is expected from Bruce, there is a strong melody and harmony, particularly in the vocals. In the period of the recording, there was much use of the steel guitar and electric piano and these are very much in evidence here both in solo and accompaniment. The song has a sing-along feel to it in the main chorus and it is possible to imagine the crowd waving their arms along in rhythm with the song, which is about a reconciliation after the break-up of a relationship.

Track Specification
Composed by Bruce Welch and John Rostill

Musicians

Terry Britten	backing vocals, guitar
Gordon Huntley	steel guitar
Nick Ingman	arranger, conductor
Dave MacRae	electric piano
Nick Ingman Orchestra	orchestra
Cliff Richard	vocals, backing vocals
Trevor Spencer	drums, percussion
Alan Tarney	backing vocals, bass

Recording Details

Producer	Hank Marvin, Bruce Welch and John Farrar
Engineered by	Roger Quested
Recording location	Morgan Studios, London
Recording date	20th June 1974

♫ Sonntag mit Marie, Ein

B-side of **Es Ist Nicht Good, Allein zu Sein**

In the sixties, it was common practice for Cliff Richard to re-record some of his English hits in German. Such was the case with his thirty-ninth British single, ***The Day I Met Marie***, which was not only translated into German (*Ein Sonntag mit Marie* – literally *A Sunday with Marie*) but also Italian (***Imagina un Giorno*** – literally *Imagine a Day*). Both of these new vocal versions were overdubbed at the session on the same orchestral backing track recorded the day before.
Ein Sonntag mit Marie was chosen as the B-side of the original German language recording of ***Es Ist Nicht Gut, Allein zu Sein***. Originally only released in mono, as was the practice by Columbia at the time for singles and EPs, *Ein Sonntag mit Marie* was eventually issued in stereo first on the German compilation album *Congratulations und 13 Weitere Hits* in 1968 and then as part of the track listing of the foreign language song compilation ***On the Continent*** in 1997.
The instrumental backing is subtly different from the English equivalent. What is interesting is that the Teutonic oom-pah band in the chorus sounds even better with the German lyrics. Cliff sings with his usual competence and he is well supported by an uncredited female backing vocal group.

Track Specification
Composed by Hank Marvin; German lyrics by Hans Bradtke

Musicians

Bernard Ebbinghouse Orchestra	orchestra
Bernard Ebbinghouse	arranger, conductor
Cliff Richard	vocals
Unknown	backing vocals

Recording Details

Producer	Norrie Paramor (backing track and vocals)
Engineered by	Peter Vince (backing track and vocals)
Recording location	Abbey Road Studio 2, St. John's Wood, London (backing track and vocals)
Recording date	27th September 1967 (backing track) and 28th September 1967 (vocals)

♫ Son of a Gunn

From the album **R&BA** *(B. A. Robertson)*

In 1979 and 1980, there was a big buzz around relative newcomer B. A. Robertson, who was a regular in the single charts' top ten placings with esoteric songs such as *Bang Bang*, *Knocked It Off* and *To Be or Not to Be*. By 1982, however, interest in his output had begun to wane although he was still writing and recording quirky, interesting tunes with witty and surprising lyrics. Of course, he had worked with Terry Britten on the lyrics for half of the songs found on the second side of Cliff Richard's ***Rock 'n' Roll Juvenile*** album and he had written the words to Alan Tarney's tune that became ***Wired for Sound***; it was therefore timely for Cliff to work with Robertson on one of his works. In 1982, Robertson was working on his next album, *R&BA*, and Cliff was invited to sing the harmony vocals on the track *Son of a Gunn*. Using many of the same musicians that Cliff employed at the time, the track and the album have long since become major rarities. Therefore, it is not currently possible to confirm the instruments used in the recording or to describe the meaning of the lyrics.

Track Specification
Composed by Rick Parfitt and B. A. Robertson

Musicians

Billy Bremner	guitar
William C. Brown	backing vocals
Deborah Carter	backing vocals
Alan Gorrie	bass
Graham Jarvis	drums, percussion
Billy Livesey	keyboards
Memphis Horns:	brass
Ben Cawley	trumpet
Jack Hale	trombone
Andrew Love	alto saxophone, tenor saxophone
Gary Topper	baritone saxophone
Memphis Strings	strings
Cliff Richard	backing vocals
B. A. Robertson	vocals
Vanessa Thomas	backing vocals
Adrian Watt	guitar
Val Young	backing vocals

Recording Details

Producer	B. A. Robertson and Alan Gorrie (vocals and basic track), Carl Marsh (brass) and Mike McNaught (strings)
Engineered by	John Hudson, Brian Tench and Bob Parr (lead vocals and basic track), William C. Brown and Robert Jackson (backing vocals and brass), Geoffrey Calver (strings) and John Hudson (final mix)
Recording location	Mayfair Recording Studios, London (lead vocals and basic track), Ardent Studios, Memphis, Tennessee (backing vocals and brass) and Marcus, London (strings)
Recording date	1982

♫ Son of Thunder

From the album **Now You See Me, Now You Don't**

Cliff Richard built a new band around him when recording of ***Now You See Me... Now You Don't,*** which featured Mart Jenner on guitar. *Son of Thunder* was co-written by him and one of Cliff's backing vocalists John Perry (who is not on the track). While most of the album was recorded at the Strawberry Studios South based in Surrey, an early suite of sessions was carried out in September 1981 at the familiar Abbey Road studio complex. *Son of Thunder* was the first song to be completed for the album project, while another song ***Take Me to the Leader*** remains unissued from the same sessions.
Cliff sings his own backing vocals in this laidback song that instils a lot of echo during the utterance of the song's title. A straightforward piece of pop music, it picks up the pace slightly in the middle eight with Cliff singing his own responses to the lyrics. Some key changes are a surprise because they seem misplaced but on the whole the song is a strong addition.

Track Specification

Composed by Mart Jenner and John Perry

Musicians

Dave Cooke	synthesiser
Graham Jarvis	drums, percussion
Mart Jenner	electric guitar
Craig Pruess	piano, synthesisers, sequencers, electronic percussion
Cliff Richard	vocals, backing vocals
Paul Westwood	bass

Recording Details

Producer	Cliff Richard and Craig Pruess
Engineered by	John Walker and Tony Richards
Recording location	Abbey Road Studio 3, St. John's Wood, London
Recording date	9th–11th September 1981

♫ Sooner or Later

From the album **...And They Said It Wouldn't Last! (My 50 Years in Music)**

Disney's *Song of the South* was cited one of the favourite films from the studio, which as a blend of cartoon and live action, and is based on the Uncle Remus stories by Joel Chandler Harris. First released in 1946, it was last shown in 1986 and is now kept from public view because studio executives fear a backlash for the use of racially insensitive stereotypes in the film. Regardless of the changes in points of view over the years and the rights and wrongs of its content, the film did produce a number of memorable tunes, one of which, ***Zip-a-Dee-Doo-Dah,*** won an Academy Award for Best Song. Another song was *Sooner or Later,* which was sung in the film by Hattie McDaniels, as Aunt Tempy, in one of her last appearances. As she is making a pastry-topped pie, she sings of how Uncle Remus loves her cooking and particularly her gooseberry pie. The song has since been covered by a number of artists including Doris Day, Tony Pastor, Dinah Shore, Barbara Cook (a slower version), Sarah Zahn, Les Brown and His Orchestra and Rosemary Clooney.
At the last session of 1965, Cliff Richard recorded four tracks from Disney films (two each from *Song of the South* and *Mary Poppins*), including *Sooner or Later.* Although they were successfully recorded, they were fated not to be released - indeed, it is unclear what the original intention was for the songs, whether for a film project, release as a Disney-related EP or simply as a suite of songs to be included as B-sides or on an album - until they were included over forty years later on the rarity collation of the celebratory ***...And They Said It Wouldn't Last! (My 50 Years in Music).*** The fourth and final take and edit were used for both mono and stereo recordings, although it has only been released in stereo format.
With a late night jazz bar feel to the arrangement, Cliff sings the song as if it were written for him. It is completely bewildering as to why EMI didn't see fit to release the song on some format or other because Cliff is having immense fun and it is a surprise that he didn't include it on any of his tours since it would have been an instant crowd-pleaser.

Track Specification

Composed by Ray Gilbert and Charles Wolcott

Musicians

Cliff Richard	vocals
Unknown	backing vocals
Unknown	orchestra
Unknown	arranger, conductor

Recording Details

Producer	Norrie Paramor
Engineered by	Malcolm Addey
Recording location	Abbey Road Studio 2, St. John's Wood, London
Recording date	18th November 1965

♫ Sound of the Candyman's Trumpet, The

From the EP **Congratulations**

Also recorded by writer Tony Hazzard and released as a single, *The Sound of the Candyman's Trumpet* was one of six candidates for the UK entry to the 1968 Eurovision Song Contest. Cliff Richard sang one of the contesting songs each week on the *Cilla Black Show* in February and it was then opened up to the public vote. With the final winner, ***Congratulations,*** polling 69% of the votes, it is unsurprising that the other five appear to have such relatively low results. *The Sound of the Candyman's Trumpet* came fourth with 4.6% beating ***Little Rag Doll*** which managed 4.2%. The song has only been released in mono format (the inevitable ***Congratulations*** EP) with the exception of the German 1968 compilation *Congratulations und 13 Weitere Hits;* the mono version was added as a bonus on the 2007 remaster of ***Live at the Talk of the Town*** album. The original recording features the future Led Zeppelin bassist, John Paul Jones, who also arranged the song.
The unusual title may have put some voters off, too, with some confusion as to its meaning. In some parts of the UK, the candyman was the epithet pressed upon local tax officials, while horror aficionados will know the candyman to be a

bogeyman who is called up by mentioning his title three times in succession, and children from a certain age with American influences will know the candyman to be a sweet-seller. It is likely to be the latter meaning, since the first two are too sinister to contemplate for the song contest, with the sound of the trumpet referring to the method of telling buyers of the sweets that the sweet-seller was present – in much the same way as the tinkling tune is still played on ice-cream vans up and down the country.

From the track, Cliff is enjoying singing this curious little song. Although it was not overly popular, it didn't come last either and therefore captured the public's imagination. The Ladybirds join Cliff as backing vocals; they were a splinter group from the Vernons Girls, as were the Breakaways, who regularly recorded and toured with Cliff. The instrumentation accompanying Cliff's vocals is unsurprisingly focused on a solo trumpet line.

Track Specification
Composed by Tony Hazzard

Musicians	
John Paul Jones	arranger, bass
Ladybirds	backing vocals
Marian Davies	
Gloria George	
Maggie Stredder	
Norrie Paramor Orchestra	orchestra
Norrie Paramor	conductor
Cliff Richard	vocals

Recording Details	
Producer	Norrie Paramor
Engineered by	Peter Vince
Recording location	Abbey Road Studio 2, St. John's Wood, London
Recording date	3rd February 1968

♬ Space Oddity

From the album **Heartbeat** *(Hank Marvin)*

In 1969, David Bowie had moved labels from Deram Records to Philips and secured a new producer in Gus Dudgeon. The story goes that a number of well-known producers were approached including George Martin and Tony Visconti, who liked the demos but decided not to take up the offer of working with Bowie. *Space Oddity* was considered a gimmicky single because of the countdown and references to being out in space, particularly because of the excitement generated by the Apollo 11 moon landings in the July of that year. The original recording featured a Stylophone, which was a very new product that allowed a synthesiser keyboard (albeit just under two octaves available) to be in everyone's home at a fraction of the expense of a real keyboard. However, the tone was buzzy and limited in what it could do but, because of its newness, it fitted well with a song about the future. The central character of Major Tom was later revisited in Bowie's songs *Ashes to Ashes* and *Hallo Spaceboy*. The song reached number five in the UK charts in the autumn of 1969 and then number one when it was reissued in 1975.

Hank Marvin has been noted for his covers of popular songs both on solo albums and with the Shadows, making his guitar sound and arrangements integral to his versions and, in the early nineties, he involved Cliff Richard in providing vocals for four tracks on his *Heartbeat* album. On *Space Oddity*, Cliff can be heard softly counting down the time to take-off (indicated by his whispered "lift off") behind the melody while Hank's daughter, Tahlia, provides the main sung vocals on the remainder of the track although these are kept subdued in the mix.

Track Specification
Composed by David Bowie

Musicians	
Brian Bennett	drums, percussion
Warren Bennett	keyboards
Mark Griffiths	bass
Hank Marvin	guitar
Tahlia Marvin	backing vocals
Cliff Richard	countdown vocals

Recording Details	
Producer	Hank Marvin and Brian Bennett
Engineered by	Dick Plant
Recording location	Honeyhill Studios, Hertfordshire
Recording date	1992-1993

♬ Spanish Harlem

From the albums **32 Minutes and 17 Seconds with Cliff Richard** *and* **Cliff in Japan** *and unissued live track*

Based on the premise of the folk story (from different cultures) of a beautiful flower being found in the cracks of a pavement (or sidewalk in American parlance) in a rundown part of town (here the Spanish quarter of Harlem in New York), before being picked, taken home and nurtured, it is an allegory for a love affair. Ben E. King, who made the song famous and spawned several covers, had left the Drifters as their main vocalist in 1961 and had embarked on a solo career: *Spanish Harlem* was his first single to be released and it reached number fifteen in the US Billboard charts, although it didn't chart for him in the UK. However, the first person to have a UK singles chart hit with it was Jimmy Justice with his third and final British single, which reached number twenty in September 1962. Later, it was taken into the charts by Sounds Incorporated (number thirty-five in August 1964) and then Aretha Franklin (number fourteen in October 1971). It has been covered a wide variety of artists, including Leon Russell, the Mamas and the Papas, Neil Diamond, Tom Jones, Percy Faith, Herb Alpert's Tijuana Brass Band, Chet Atkins and Trini Lopez.

For Cliff's album ***32 Minutes and 17 Seconds with Cliff Richard***, the fifth and final take and edit were used for mono and stereo recordings but with different mixes to meet the demands of the audio channels and it also appears on the ***Cliff***

Richard Sings Don't Talk to Him EP. On the anthology release ***The Rock 'n' Roll Years 1958-1963***, there is a 'count-in' version, which is essentially the same take but with the studio banter left in at the start.

Cliff's recording is very similar in arrangement to the Drifters' version and is introduced by deep backing vocals and a xylophone playing staccato performance along with guitars and orchestral strings. Cliff's vocal is perfectly matched to this ballad and the overall performance is made special by his timing and pitching of the notes, although he does tend to over-emphasize the 'r' of the words in an attempt to make it sound American.

In late 1964, Cliff recorded German language vocals for a single release under the translated title of ***Das Ist die Frage Aller Fragen*** (literally *That Is the Question of All Questions*). Combined with ***Nur Mit Dir*** (a translation of ***On the Beach***), it was released in November 1964 alongside the English language issue with both reaching the number one spot in Germany.

Having laid dormant for over twenty years in Cliff's repertoire, *Spanish Harlem* was resurrected for his *Live & Guaranteed 1988!* performances, the Danish leg of which was recorded and filmed for initial video release. The video was subsequently re-released this time with a CD accompaniment featuring some of the songs but unfortunately not including *Spanish Harlem*.

Track Specification

Composed by Jerry Leiber and Phil Spector

1. 32 Minutes and 17 Seconds with Cliff Richard

Musicians		*Recording Details*	
Mike Sammes Singers	backing vocals	Producer	Norrie Paramor
Norrie Paramor Orchestra	orchestra	Engineered by	Malcolm Addey and Norman Smith
Norrie Paramor	arranger, conductor	Recording location	Abbey Road Studio 2, St. John's Wood, London
Cliff Richard	vocals	Recording date	4th December 1961

2. Cliff in Japan

Musicians		*Recording Details*	
Norrie Paramor Orchestra	orchestra	Producer	Norrie Paramor
Norrie Paramor	arranger, conductor	Engineered by	Unknown
Cliff Richard	vocals	Recording location	Shibuya Public Hall, Tokyo, Japan
Unknown	backing vocals	Recording date	18th October 1967

3. Unissued track (Live & Guaranteed 1988!)

Musicians		*Recording Details*	
John Clark	guitar	Producer	Unknown
Rosemarie Ford	backing vocals	Engineered by	Unknown
Mark Griffiths	bass	Recording location	Fyens Forum, Odense, Denmark
Peter Howarth	backing vocals	Recording date	22nd May 1988
Steve Lauri	guitar		
Paul Moessl	keyboards		
Mick Mullins	backing vocals		
Alan Park	keyboards		
Cliff Richard	vocals		
Henry Spinetti	drums, percussion		

♫ Spider Man

From the album **Every Face Tells a Story** *(UK) and promotional B-side* **Every Face Tells a Story (It Never Tells a Lie)**

Another Terry Britten song, *Spider Man* closes the ***Every Face Tells a Story*** album. When the album was being prepared for release, a promotional disc with the title song as the A-side was issued with *Spider Man* and ***You Got Me Wondering*** as joint B-side tracks. The edit for this promotional track was different from the UK album release and subsequently appeared on the US album in this form; the guitar instrumental is cut and a number of the lines of the verses are swapped around for no reported reason. At the end of both versions, Cliff can be heard saying 'What? Me worried?', although there is no information available as to what this comment refers.

As a portent of songs that he would record later in the decade, *Spider Man* is a superlative example. With echoes of ***Devil Woman*** from his previous album, Cliff whispers some lyrics in a menacing way but also uses his lower register far more than had been the case on other tracks. The foreboding message is built up in the instrumentation that supports the main vocal line, which is slightly double-tracked (that is, two versions or the same version used to create the single vocal line).

Track Specification

Composed by Terry Britten

1. Every Face Tells a Story (UK)

Musicians		*Recording Details*	
Brian Bennett	drums, percussion	Producer	Bruce Welch
Terry Britten	guitar	Engineered by	Tony Clark, Mike Jarrett and Alan Rouse
Cliff Richard	vocals	Recording location	Abbey Road Studio 2, St. John's Wood, London
Frank Ricotti	percussion	Recording date	7th and 15th September 1976
Alan Tarney	bass		
Graham Todd	keyboards		

2. Promotional B-side (Every Face Tells a Story (It Never Tells a Lie))

Musicians

Brian Bennett	drums, percussion
Terry Britten	guitar
Cliff Richard	vocals
Frank Ricotti	percussion
Alan Tarney	bass
Graham Todd	keyboards

Recording Details

Producer	Bruce Welch
Engineered by	Tony Clark, Mike Jarrett and Alan Rouse
Recording location	Abbey Road Studio 2, St. John's Wood, London
Recording date	7th and 15th September 1976

♫ Spiel Ohne Grenzen, Ein

B-side of **Gut, Daß Es Freunde Gibt**

In late November 1970 over a period of two days and four sessions, Cliff Richard recorded a number of songs for his follow-up to *Hier Ist Cliff*, his first German language album, *Ich Träume Deine Träume*, which was released in 1971. *Ein Spiel Ohne Grenzen* was the first one of six songs completed at the second session. The process was simplified by recording the orchestral track earlier and this had the benefit of allowing the focus of the session to be solely on Cliff's vocals. *Ein Spiel Ohne Grenzen* – literally translated as *A Game without Boundaries* – is an original German composition and Cliff has never recorded an English equivalent. It was chosen as the B-side of the single ***Gut, Daß Es Freunde Gibt***, which was released in April 1973 (but doesn't appear on the album). Both tracks were later incorporated on the track listing of Cliff's foreign language tracks, ***On the Continent***, released in 1997.

The orchestral accompaniment is evocatively Mediterranean with its twinkling mandolins and bazuki style of performance. As was becoming an increasing – and highly effective – ploy, Cliff provides his own backing vocals. The Greek dance style has throwbacks to his ***Summer Holiday*** film and the unexpected key changes, swapping between major and minor, provide further points of interest to a song that had originally only had limited exposure.

Track Specification

Composed by Volauvent and Kurt Hertha

Musicians

Norrie Paramor Orchestra	orchestra
Norrie Paramor	arranger, conductor
Cliff Richard	vocals, backing vocals

Recording Details

Producer	Norrie Paramor (backing track and vocals)
Engineered by	Phil McDonald (backing track and vocals)
Recording location	Cologne, Germany (backing track) and Abbey Road Studio 2, St. John's Wood, London (vocals)
Recording date	November 1970 (backing track) and 24th November 1970 (vocals)

♫ Spoonful of Sugar, A

From the album **...And They Said It Wouldn't Last! (My 50 Years in Music)**

One of the most phenomenally successful Disney films of all time was *Mary Poppins*, which was based on the story of the magical nanny of the title written by P. L. Travers. Starring Julie Andrews in the eponymous role and Dick van Dyke as her friend Bert, she comes into the lives of two children whose parents are typically Victorian in an Edwardian era and their childhood is suffering as a result. *A Spoonful of Sugar*, one of the most memorable and popular tunes from the cartoon and live action hybrid, started out as an instructional tale that even desultory jobs such as clearing up a bedroom could be fun using the allegory of taking horrible medicine with something nice such as sugar. Originally, it was lyricist Robert Sherman's idea when his children came back from the doctors', having taken their polio vaccine, which in those days was administered on a cube of sugar. Other than Julie Andrews' definitive version, it has also been covered by Kenny Ball, Rosemary Clooney, Harry Connick, Jr., Cheryl Baker, Duke Ellington, Burl Ives and Laurence Juber among others.

At the final recording session executed in 1965, Cliff Richard recorded four Disney songs: two from *Mary Poppins* (*A Spoonful of Sugar* and ***Chim-Chim-Cheree***) and two from *Song of the South* (***Zip-a-Dee-Doo-Dah*** and ***Sooner or Later***). Since *Mary Poppins* had been released the year before, the songs were still fresh in people's minds and made a suitablesubject for the session. However, for unexplained reasons, the four songs remained unreleased for over forty years until the release of the rarity compilation ***...And They Said It Wouldn't Last! (My 50 Years in Music)***. The seventh and final take and edit were used for both mono and stereo recordings, although it has only been released in stereo format.

The problem with Disney-related songs is that for the most part they tended to be twee and saccharine and, therefore, possibly a strange choice for Cliff to cover. However, the arrangement of his cover is jazzed up and given the full swing era treatment, which Cliff performs with considerable success. The orchestra and backing vocalists are unknown but are likely to be the Norrie Paramor Orchestra and the Mike Sammes Singers respectively, since they were involved in many of the recordings at the time.

Track Specification

Composed by Richard M. Sherman and Robert B. Sherman

Musicians

Cliff Richard	vocals
Unknown	backing vocals
Unknown	orchestra
Unknown	arranger, conductor

Recording Details

Producer	Norrie Paramor
Engineered by	Malcolm Addey
Recording location	Abbey Road Studio 2, St. John's Wood, London
Recording date	18th November 1965

♬ Standing on the Rock

From the album **Keep the Ball Rolling** *(Bryn Haworth)*

Written and performed by Bryn Haworth, who had been involved in the ***Small Corners*** album for Cliff Richard, *Standing on the Rock* sees Cliff return the favour by adding his backing vocals to the mix. Cliff also worked on another track from the *Keep the Ball Rolling* album, ***Luxury Liner***, probably recorded at the same session, although records are unavailable to confirm.

A straightforward balladeering rock song of the period, it relies on the guitar and bass to drive the song forward. Haworth's voice is pleasant enough but seems to lack power. This is elevated, however, by Cliff's vocal contribution in the second chorus and onwards for the repetitions after the middle eight and there is a key change that lifts it further. The song takes a few listens to appreciate its subtleties but it doesn't match the raw energy of Garth Hewitt's albums.

Track Specification

Composed by Bryn Haworth

Musicians		*Recording Details*	
Bryn Haworth	vocals, guitar	Producer	Jon Astley and Doug Bennet
Dave Markee	bass	Engineered by	Jon Astley, Doug Bennet and Laurence Burrage
Simon Morton	percussion	Recording location	Olympic Studios, Chelsea, London
Cliff Richard	backing vocals	Recording date	1979
Henry Spinetti	drums, percussion		
Pete Wingfield	keyboards		

♬ Star of Hope

Unissued track

Recorded by Roy Rogers and Sons of the Pioneers, *Star of Hope* was included on the list of songs intended for the track listing of Cliff Richard's first album of religious songs, ***Good News***. However, it was the only one of five songs not to be completed at the session and, after two takes, it was abandoned and remains unissued.

Track Specification

Composed by Traditional

Musicians		*Recording Details*	
Bernard Ebbinghouse Orchestra	orchestra	Producer	Norrie Paramor
Bernard Ebbinghouse	arranger, conductor	Engineered by	Peter Vince and Mike Stone
Cliff Richard	vocals	Recording location	Abbey Road Studio 2, St. John's Wood, London
		Recording date	3rd May 1967

♬ Star Song

Single by **Sheila Walsh**

Star Song was the track that began Cliff Richard's long association with Christian music singer Sheila Walsh and also a regular working relationship with Craig Pruess and Keith Bessey. The song was backed with ***Burn On*** (which had no involvement from Cliff, although he later recorded a version with the All Souls Orchestra) and released as a single on the DJM Records label (catalogue number DJS 10992) in 1981 but failed to chart. A considerable rarity in its original format, it was subsequently reissued on the track listing of the US-only album *War of Love* the following year and the UK-based *Portrait* five years later and finally on CD in the US on the *Compact Favorites* album in 1988.

Walsh's voice fits this gentle style of song well and she is lifted by the arrangement of the backing vocals, which include Cliff in layered recording. Craig Pruess's arrangement changes this track from another religious song to something that is as much a pop song. The beauty of the melody and the vocal accompaniment are the key hooks in this song.

Track Specification

Composed by S. McClung and K. Allen

Musicians		*Recording Details*	
Mart Jenner	guitar	Producer	Cliff Richard and Craig Pruess
Craig Pruess	arranger, synthesiser, piano, brass, percussion	Engineered by	Keith Bessey
		Recording location	Unknown
Cliff Richard	backing vocals	Recording date	1981
Sheila Walsh	vocals		

♬ Start All over Again

From the album **Green Light**

At the time of recording the ***Green Light*** album, Scottish performer B. A. Robertson's singing career was just on the verge of taking off with *Bang Bang* just missing the top spot the following year. Before that, he was a jobbing performer and songwriter and he co-wrote *Start All over Again* with long-term Cliff Richard composer Terry Britten.

A standard drum and keyboard introduction leads into a medium-paced rock ballad that talks of rekindlin a relationship. The beauty of the track's melody is enhanced by the sporadic backing vocal harmonies that generally only appear at the end of the second half of the chorus. The synthesiser is in prominence here, too, lending the song a modern edge.

Track Specification
Composed by Terry Britten and B. A. Robertson

Musicians	
Brian Bennett	drums, percussion
Terry Britten	guitar
Stuart Calver	backing vocals
Alan Jones	bass
Duncan MacKay	keyboards
Alan Parker	guitar
John Perry	backing vocals
Tim Renwick	guitar
Cliff Richard	vocals
Tony Rivers	backing vocals
Trevor Spencer	drums, percussion
Alan Tarney	backing vocals, guitar, bass, keyboards
Graham Todd	keyboards

Recording Details	
Producer	Bruce Welch
Engineered by	Tony Clark and Haydn Bendall
Recording location	Abbey Road Studio 3, St. John's Wood, London
Recording date	14th January 1978 and 15th March 1978

♫ Steady with You
B-side of **Livin' Lovin' Doll**

For Cliff Richard's third single, ***Livin' Lovin' Doll*** was chosen by producer Norrie Paramor in an attempt to derail the popularity amongst fans of the similarly named ***Living Doll*** from the film soundtrack of *Serious Charge*, which was slated as a single release (much to Paramor's annoyance). Aside from the politics surrounding the choice of single, the B-side, *Steady with You*, was a revelation. Once again written by former Drifters guitarist Ian Samwell, as had the first two singles and B-sides, it was a slow-paced ballad rather than the up tempo rockers with which he had previously been associated. In addition, it had the line-up of Hank Marvin, Bruce Welch and Jet Harris now on board as part of the backing band and, after a bit of a trial in the studio against session musicians on the A-side, this was the first recording session that allowed the Drifters to back Cliff fully. Although not quite: in later years, the beautiful harmonies created by Cliff, Hank and Bruce in particular would be one of the band's trademarks. For the recording of *Steady with You*, however, the Mike Sammes Singers were drafted in by Paramor for the backing vocals, making it sound slightly out-moded as a consequence.
The gentle plodding beat suits Cliff's performance and gives him insight as to what his future achievements might be. There is an uncredited tinkling piano, possibly Paramor, gently playing repeated chords but this assists the rhythm. The aforementioned backing vocals are a little obtrusive and could have been better arranged in order to lift the song further.
Other than the original 78 r.p.m. and seven-inch formats, this song was unavailable in any other media until it was included on the rarities compilation boxed set ***The Rock 'n' Roll Years 1958-1963***.

Track Specification
Composed by Ian Samwell

Musicians	
Jet Harris	bass
Hank Marvin	guitar
Mike Sammes Singers	backing vocals
Cliff Richard	vocals
Terry Smart	drums, percussion
Unknown	piano
Bruce Welch	rhythm guitar

Recording Details	
Producer	Norrie Paramor
Engineered by	Peter Bown and Stuart Eltham
Recording location	Abbey Road Studio 2, St. John's Wood, London
Recording date	19th November 1958

♫ Stell' Mich Deinen Eltern Vor
From the album **Hier Ist Cliff**

At the end of 1968, Cliff Richard completed his first fully German language album, *Hier Ist Cliff*, with *Stell' Mich Deinen Eltern Vor* being finished as the first song at the third of four sessions for the album. Literally translated as *Introduce Me to Your Parents* (rather forward in intent and completely different from the English version), the song was yet another plundered from the vocal tracks on the then recent album ***Established 1958, Not the Way That It Should Be***. The stereo album track was a considerable rarity, particularly in non-German territories, until it was reissued on the foreign language compilation album ***On the Continent*** in 1997.
Introduced by arpeggiated chords on a piano, Cliff sings with a slightly anticipatory edge to his voice, as one would possibly expect given the meaning of the translated lyrics. There is a great female backing vocal group accompanying him on the choruses, but there is no information on them, although it is quite possible that it is the Breakaways.

Track Specification
Composed by Hank Marvin and Brian Bennett; German lyrics by Fleming

Musicians	
Norrie Paramor Orchestra	orchestra
Norrie Paramor	arranger, director
Cliff Richard	vocals
Unknown	backing vocals

Recording Details	
Producer	Norrie Paramor
Engineered by	Peter Vince
Recording location	Abbey Road Studio 2, St. John's Wood, London
Recording date	27th November 1968

♫ Sternengold

From the album **Congratulations und 13 Weitere Hits**

A German version of ***All My Love*** with which Cliff Richard had a hit in late 1967, *Sternengold* (literally *Gold Star*) is erroneously credited to Peter Callender as well as Monti Arduini, although Callender did write the English lyrics to the original Italian tune. Commonly, Cliff used to record vocal overdubs in the new language on to the original backing tracks. However, in the last couple of years of the sixties, it was much more likely that he would record songs anew, since the recording techniques were now cheaper. *Sternengold* was a major rarity for many years since it was only released on the German compilation album *Congratulations und 13 Weitere Hits*, until it was included on the track listing of the foreign language compilation ***On the Continent*** in 1997. In both cases, only the stereo version has been released although the time of recording it would have meant that a mono version would also have been created.

In many respects, the arrangement is the same as that on Cliff's original, with xylophones and harps backed up with quiet strings and Cliff sings the song as if German were his first language. The female backing vocalists are uncredited, although it is likely the Breakaways who were involved in ***London Ist Nicht Weit***, also recorded at the same session.

Track Specification

Composed by Monti Arduini; German lyrics by Raschek

Musicians

Breakaways:	backing vocals
Vicki Hasemen	
Margo Quantrell	
Jean Ryder	
Mike Leander	arranger, conductor
Mike Leander Orchestra	orchestra
Cliff Richard	vocals

Recording Details

Producer	Norrie Paramor
Engineered by	Peter Vince
Recording location	Abbey Road Studio 2, St. John's Wood, London
Recording date	15th March 1968

♫ Stimme der Liebe, Die

B-side of **Bin Verliebt**

Initiating a long career of recording translated versions of his songs and original tunes on the continent, Cliff Richard started by recorded a German version of ***Fall in Love with You, Bin Verliebt***, which was released in Germany in early 1961 and reached number forty. Backing that single was *Die Stimme der Liebe* (literally *The Voice of Love*), a translated version of Cliff and the Shadows' sixth single ***A Voice in the Wilderness***, which appeared in the film ***Expresso Bongo***.

Cliff and the Shadows recorded the instrumental line and the lead vocal, while later overdub sessions were executed in Germany (with no information on personnel and location being available) to provide the backing vocals and additional instrumentation, although this decision detracts from the sound that had been developed by the close-knit band. As with its A-side, *Die Stimme der Liebe* was recorded in mono only and was only available in the rare single format until it was included in the boxed CD set ***On the Continent***.

There seems to be a predilection for the early German records to have all the instruments playing the same rhythm from drums to lead guitar. The arrangement of the German is far quirkier than the English original, while the German backing singers don't quite gel as well as the Shadows do. There is a plinking piano in the accompaniment, which helps create a quite different version, while Cliff's schooling in pronunciation is impressive. Although not a patch on the original, it is an interesting record of Cliff's broadening horizons at this stage in his career.

Track Specification

Composed by Norrie Paramor and Jean Nicolas

Musicians

Friedel Berlipp	conductor
Berlipp's Band	additional instruments
The Hansen Boys	backing vocals
Jet Harris	bass
Hank Marvin	guitar
Tony Meehan	drums, percussion
Cliff Richard	vocals
Bruce Welch	rhythm guitar

Recording Details

Producer	Norrie Paramor
Engineered by	Malcolm Addey
Recording location	Abbey Road Studio 2, St. John's Wood, London plus overdubs in unknown location in Germany
Recording date	5th December 1960 and Unknown (overdubs)

♫ Stood Up

Unissued live track

Originally recorded by Ricky Nelson, who released the *Stood Up* as his first single in Britain and reached number twenty-seven in March 1958, it has subsequently been covered by a number of artists including Mike Berry and the Outlaws, the Stray Cats, Sandy Nelson and Dave Grant among others.

Cliff Richard regularly performs songs that he likes but has never taken into the studio. One such was *Stood Up*, which he performed during his 1981 tour, part of which was recorded by the BBC for background material for the four-part documentary on Cliff that was being made. They recorded a dozen or so songs at the Hammersmith Odeon and Manchester Apollo and three songs, *Stood Up*, ***Shakin' All Over*** and ***Daddy's Home***, were immediately licensed for release from the BBC, although *Stood Up* remains unissued.

Track Specification
Composed by Willie Dickerson and Erma Herrold

Musicians	
Stuart Calver	backing vocals
Howie Casey	saxophone, trumpet, trombone
John Clark	guitar
Mark Griffiths	bass
Graham Jarvis	drums, percussion
Martin Jenner	guitar
Alan Park	keyboards
John Perry	backing vocals
Cliff Richard	vocals
Tony Rivers	backing vocals
Graham Todd	keyboards

Recording Details	
Producer	Cliff Richard
Engineered by	Unknown
Recording location	Hammersmith Odeon, London
Recording date	1st May 1981

♫ Story Ohne Happy-End
From the album **Hier Ist Cliff**

By late 1968, Cliff Richard had regularly recorded German language singles but, until the release of *Hier Ist Cliff* the following year, he had not issued a full German album. Pulling together the track listing, rather than choosing previously released singles and B-sides from the previous seven or eight years, new material was sought from recent English releases. One was *Story Ohne Happy-End* (literally and perhaps obviously *Story without a Happy Ending*, somewhat giving it away), which was a translation of John Rostill's ***Girl on the Bus***, which was originally released on the album ***Established 1958***.
Cliff's recording was the last of three for the German album at the session (which included the only single ***Zärtliche Sekunden*** from the project) and has only ever been released in stereo format only. The track was a rarity until it was reissued, also in stereo, on the boxed set ***On the Continent*** in 1997.
With a similar country treatment to the original Shadows accompanied version, the German translation has all the drama and the beautiful musical intervals and passionate performance of the English version.

Track Specification
Composed by John Rostill; German lyrics by Joachim Relin

Musicians	
Norrie Paramor Orchestra	orchestra
Norrie Paramor	arranger, director
Cliff Richard	vocals

Recording Details	
Producer	Norrie Paramor
Engineered by	Peter Vince
Recording location	Abbey Road Studio 2, St. John's Wood, London
Recording date	28th November 1968

♫ Stranger in Town, A
From the film soundtrack album of **Summer Holiday**

Don (played by Cliff Richard) is falling in love with the stowaway the group found on their converted double decker bus, Barbara Winters (Lauri Peters) who reveals herself not to be the boy she was trying to pass herself to be. He sings *A Stranger in Town*, which is an allegory for how everyone feels on embarking on a love affair with the daunting possibilities that entails, with a dance sequence that imagines old, Parisian ladies to be youthful girls, before they transmogrify into ancient harridans intent on battering Don with umbrellas and handbags and eventually they push him into a shallow lake.
Recorded at the start of the second of two sessions on 26th August, four takes were completed, with the final take and edit being used for the mono and stereo recordings but with different mixes for the audio channels. The version used in the film was recorded later in 1962 at the Elstree Studios but has not, to date, been released in any other commercial format. The soundtrack album version appeared on the track listing of the ***More Hits from Summer Holiday*** EP.
An old school style of musical film song, there are not many hooks to be found in *A Stranger in Town*. There is uncredited whistling on the track (possibly Cliff but unlikely), while the orchestral interlude (for the dance sequence) is the intended purpose of the song's existence. The film version was recorded sepasrately but has not been in issued in aural format.

Track Specification
Composed by Peter Myers and Ronald Cass

Musicians	
Associated British Studio Orchestra	orchestra
Stanley Black	conductor
Mike Sammes Singers	backing vocals
Cliff Richard	vocals
Unknown	whistling

Recording Details	
Producer	Norrie Paramor
Engineered by	Malcolm Addey and Richard Langham
Recording location	Abbey Road Studio 2, St. John's Wood, London
Recording date	26th August 1962

♫ Streets of London
Unissued track

First recorded by Ralph McTell for his 1969 *Spiral Staircase* album, it was inspired by his experiences busking around Europe, with particular emphasis on the capital cities of London and Paris. The stories of lonely, elderly, and generally ignored sections of society still resonate now and the simplicity of the chord sequences make it a popular busking favourite mirroring McTell's experiences. It took another five years for McTell to release the song as a single, when it reached number two in the early part of 1975. It was revived in 1982 by the Anti-Nowhere League, who took it to number forty-eight; however, over two hundred other non-charting artists have covered it.

One of them was Cliff Richard, who included it on the set list of his studio-bound charity concert project in front of a small audience, eventually releasing twelve songs on the ***Help It Along*** album in aid of the Tear Fund, although *Streets of London* was one of five songs that remain unissued.

Track Specification
Composed by Ralph McTell

Musicians

Terry Britten	guitar
Barrie Guard	arranger, conductor, percussion
Cliff Hall	keyboards
Jean Hawker	backing vocals
Anna Peacock	backing vocals
Kevin Peek	guitar
Cliff Richard	vocals
Trevor Spencer	drums, percussion
Alan Tarney	bass
Unknown	orchestra

Recording Details

Producer	David MacKay
Engineered by	Roger Quested
Recording location	Morgan Studios, London
Recording date	24th, 25th and 26th September 1973

♫ Stronger than That

110th UK single** (seven-inch, twelve-inch, CD and promo) and from the albums* **Stronger** *and* **From a Distance ** The Event Remaster**

After the stupendous success of ***Always Guaranteed***, Cliff Richard was in a difficult position in how to follow it. One of the first songs to be completed followed exactly the style of working as that prior album, with Alan Tarney developing the germ of a musical idea and building on it in the studio before Cliff added his vocals. The first track on the ***Stronger*** album and its title song, *Stronger than That*, was constructed in this way and, when Cliff and disc jockey Mike Read compèred a session in front of two thousand invited fans at the London Palladium on 3rd April 1989, it was *Stronger than That* that won the poll when they played six new songs from the album.

In spite of that result, *Stronger than That* was not the first single to be released from the project; rather it was the fourth and final one. Backed with ***Joanna***, which had come fourth in that same fan poll, *Stronger than That* was released as a single on the EMI label (catalogue number EM 129) on 12th February 1990 and reached number fourteen in the UK singles charts. The single release differs from the album track in that there is a synthesized horn overdub and this features on all single variants. In addition to the main single release, there was also a seven-inch version that incorporated a set of picture postcards of Cliff (catalogue number EMS 129). The extended version of the song that ran to nearly eight minutes was included on the twelve-inch (12EM 129) and CD (CDEM 129) versions of the single in addition to the original seven-inch version – the extended mix later appeared on the rare B-sides section of the celebratory ***...And They Said It Wouldn't Last! (My 50 Years in Music)*** album in 2008. A further version of the twelve-inch single release was issued with the only difference being a signed photograph of Cliff (12EMP 12). Finally, there was a radio promotion single (EMDJ 129), which was one-sided, and had the third chorus excised and some of the instrumental passages edited down but otherwise it is the same as the original single version with the added horns. The promotional video was filmed at the Shepperton Studios on 4th January 1990 and features a set that looks like a desert gorge with the musicians and dancers performing behind Cliff. Cliff shows his ability as a dancer keeping in time with the professionals and goes through a number of costume changes throughout the video.

As with many of the songs recorded at the time, the predilection was to use synthesisers and sampled vocals that were played and replayed. The first song on the *Stronger* album uses this process with a heavy drumbeat, but there is a strongly chugging guitar running along the accompaniment and Cliff provides his own backing vocals for the track.

As the single and album were released close to the timing of ***The Event*** – Cliff's thirtieth anniversary performances at Wembley Stadium – it was unsurprising that many tracks would be included on the set list. However, for reasons of space, the track was not issued on the eventual album ***From a Distance **** The Event*** in 1990, but was restored in the correct running order on the now two-CD remaster of the album in 2005. The strength of the song shines out in a live setting with the running bass and the chords from the synthesiser and guitar. The backing vocalists sound less tentative than on some other tracks but Cliff sings the song with conviction and makes up for any misgivings in so doing.

Track Specification
Composed by Alan Tarney

1. Single (seven-inch)

Musicians

Cliff Richard	vocals, backing vocals
Alan Tarney	arranger, synthesisers, drum and percussion sequencers, horn synthesisers

Recording Details

Producer	Alan Tarney
Engineered by	Gerry Kitchingham and Ben Robbins
Recording location	R. G. Jones Studios, Wimbledon, London
Recording date	27th February 1989, 9th March 1989, 13th-17th March 1989 and 22nd-23rd March 1989

2. Single (twelve-inch and CD extended version)

Musicians

Cliff Richard	vocals, backing vocals
Alan Tarney	arranger, synthesisers, drum and percussion sequencers, horn synthesisers

Recording Details

Producer	Alan Tarney
Engineered by	Gerry Kitchingham and Ben Robbins
Recording location	R. G. Jones Studios, Wimbledon, London
Recording date	27th February 1989, 9th March 1989, 13th-17th March 1989 and 22nd-23rd March 1989

3. Single (radio edit)

Musicians

Cliff Richard	vocals, backing vocals
Alan Tarney	arranger, synthesisers, drum and percussion sequencers, horn synthesisers

Recording Details

Producer	Alan Tarney
Engineered by	Gerry Kitchingham and Ben Robbins
Recording location	R. G. Jones Studios, Wimbledon, London
Recording date	27th February 1989, 9th March 1989, 13th-17th March 1989 and 22nd-23rd March 1989

4. Stronger

Musicians

Cliff Richard	vocals, backing vocals
Alan Tarney	arranger, synthesisers, drum and percussion sequencers

Recording Details

Producer	Alan Tarney
Engineered by	Gerry Kitchingham and Ben Robbins
Recording location	R. G. Jones Studios, Wimbledon, London
Recording date	27th February 1989, 9th March 1989, 13th-17th March 1989 and 22nd-23rd March 1989

5. From a Distance *** The Event Remaster**

Musicians

John Clark	guitar
Sonia Jones-Morgan	backing vocals
Steve Lauri	guitar
Peter May	drums, percussion
Paul Moessl	keyboards
Tessa Niles	backing vocals
Alan Park	keyboards
Provox:	
Peter Howarth	backing vocals
Mick Mullins	backing vocals
Keith Murrell	backing vocals
Cliff Richard	vocals
Steve Stroud	bass

Recording Details

Producer	Cliff Richard
Engineered by	Keith Bessey and Mick McKenna
Recording location	Rolling Stones Mobile Studio, Wembley Stadium, Wembley, North-west London
Recording date	16th-17th June 1989

♫ Strong Is the Current

B-side of **To a Friend** *(Aleksander Mežek)*

Aleksander Mežek had a long working history with Cliff Richard, starting with *Days Go By* in 1974 and then on to Cliff's own albums in the eighties. In June 1990, shortly before Cliff went back to the studios to record his first number one of the nineties, ***Saviour's Day***, he helped out on the English versions of two tracks for Mežek's vinyl album *Presented to the Heart*, which was released later that year: ***To a Friend*** was a new version of ***Prijatelju***, while ***Strong Is the Current*** was a new version of ***Vodna Pot***; both the Slovenian tracks had been recorded in 1989 for Mežek's album, *Podarjeno Srcu*. In June 1991, ***To a Friend***, a duet between Cliff and Mežek, was released as a single, backed with *Strong Is the Current*, but only in Germany. The track appeared on all formats of the single (seven-inch, twelve-inch and CD) and was reissued on the album CD for the first time in 1998 but then only in Slovenia.

Track Specification

Composed by Aleksander Mežek and Eugenija Dumbatze

Musicians

Ian Bairnson	electric guitar
Richard Cottle	synthesiser
Jonathan Du Bose	electric guitar
Bill Elliott	acoustic guitar
Aleksander Mežek	vocals
Davy Paton	bass
Cliff Richard	backing vocals
Jeremy Stacy	drums, percussion
Rick Wakeman	keyboards
Saša Zalepugin	acoustic guitar

Recording Details

Producer	Aleksander Mežek and Rick Wakeman
Engineered by	Ben Robbins
Recording location	R. G. Jones Studios, Wimbledon, London
Recording date	June 1990

♫ Such Is the Mystery

From the album **I'm Nearly Famous**

Although ***I'm Nearly Famous*** was not intended to be a gospel or spiritual album, it was perhaps inevitable that there would be one of two songs of this ilk. However, although *Such Is the Mystery* is a song about the wonders of God's work, it fits well with the rest of the track listing with Cliff Richard's beseeching vocals making it one of the most impressive tracks on the album. The track was completed in four takes in the first of its two sessions, with the second being used for vocal overdubs. The song is imbued with such meaning that it is regularly included on collections and compilations of Cliff's religious output.

The gentle guitar introduction plays diminished interval chords to support Cliff's vocal line, which is imbued with a sort of quiet passion mixed with reverence for his subject. By the second verse, the bass has been brought in to support the guitar and to underline the strength that Cliff is expressing through the lyrics. The middle eight sees a slow string melody that leads into the third verse and adds to the growing optimism of the song.

Track Specification
Composed by John Dawson Read

Musicians

Terry Britten	guitar
Richard Hewson	arranger, conductor
Cliff Richard	vocals
Alan Tarney	bass
Unknown	orchestra

Recording Details

Producer	Bruce Welch
Engineered by	Tony Clark and John Barrett
Recording location	Abbey Road Studio 3, St. John's Wood, London
Recording date	3rd and 10th December 1975

♫ Suddenly

79th UK single

Olivia Newton-John and John Farrar had both regularly appeared on Cliff Richard's television shows in the seventies and had both followed him in successive years to represent the UK at the Eurovision Song Contest. After this association, both Olivia and John had forged a massively successful career in the USA, with John acting as Olivia's music director, starting with the stratospherically popular film *Grease*. The film starred Olivia in a lead role, while John penned the multi-million selling single *You're the One That I Want*.

Her next film project was *Xanadu*, based on Samuel Coleridge's poem *Kubla Khan*, which starred Olivia as Terpsichorean muse Kira, Michael Beck as dreaming artist Sonny who hankers after fame and Gene Kelly as a construction industry mogul with a former career performing with big bands. Sonny leaves his job but, being forced to return to it after not making money in a recording career, he resumes his artistry painting record covers. He bumps into a roller-skating girl (Kira) who kisses him and he becomes obsessed with finding her, tracing her to an abandoned auditorium. The building becomes the focus of much of the plot as he joins forces with Danny (Kelly) to convert it into a club.

The soundtrack featured music by the Electric Light Orchestra and Olivia Newton-John, with the title song being performed by both (reaching number one in several countries including the UK). *Suddenly*, written and produced by John Farrar, was a duet with Cliff and it is played out in the film as Sonny and Kira skate together in the auditorium as their feelings grow for each other. Allegedly, Michael Beck couldn't or didn't want to sing and Farrar contacted Cliff to become involved in the project, particularly since he had just scored a massive hit with ***We Don't Talk Anymore*** in the US. *Suddenly* was recorded in a studio that Cliff likened to a garage and, it appears, it has been proven that it was owned by the engineer for the session. This caused problems with the background noise and, as Cliff and Olivia sang their vocal lines simultaneously on to a pre-recorded backing track, it is thought that Olivia returned to re-record her vocals at a later date because of the background noise behind her original vocals – this is unconfirmed. In the associated promotional video, Cliff and Olivia are seen sitting on a sofa, lit by soft lighting beside a roaring fire.

Backed with *You Made Me Love You*, a non-album track by Olivia (although the Glenn Miller version is played on record during the film), *Suddenly* was issued as a single on the Jet Records label (catalogue number JET 7002) – and not on the EMI label as stated in the book *The Complete Chronicle* – on 10th October 1980 and reached number fifteen in the UK singles charts. In the US, it fared similarly, reaching number twenty in the Billboard charts. For the only time in his career, Cliff had three songs in the US charts (***Dreamin', A Little in Love*** and *Suddenly*). The song has frequently appeared on a number of compilations for both Cliff and Olivia.

For those who wanted to make something more of the pair's relationship either personally or musically could do no worse than accept this song for the beauty that it is. Cliff's and Olivia's voices blend together very well with Cliff often taking the descant role in the harmonies. The lead vocal is swapped between the two of them and the differentiation is created by a sudden stop in the supporting instrumentation before it resumes with the other singing. There is a clear echo of the vocals underlying the leads, and this is particularly noticeable as the song changes key for the middle eight.

Track Specification
Composed by John Farrar

Musicians

Michael Boddicker	vocoder
John Farrar	guitar, synthesiser
Ed Greene	drums, percussion
Richard Hewson	arranger, conductor
David McDaniel	bass
Olivia Newton-John	vocals
Cliff Richard	vocals
Unknown	orchestra
Jai Winding	electric piano

Recording Details

Producer	John Farrar
Engineered by	David J. Holman
Recording location	Unknown Studio, Los Angeles
Recording date	March 1980

♫ Summer Holiday

20th UK single and from the albums **Summer Holiday – Special Edition**, **Cliff Richard at the Movies 1959-1974**, **Cliff in Japan**, **From a Distance ***** The Event** *and* **Reunited** *and unissued live tracks and B-side of* **Be with Me Always**

One of Cliff Richard's most famous and memorable songs, *Summer Holday* was never particularly liked by the band as they felt it wasn't strong as a song and, in interview, Cliff has stated that it would have been unlikely to be released as single if it weren't for the fact that it was the theme song for the film.

In the film, the four young men (Cliff, Melvyn Hayes, Jeremy Bulloch and Teddy Green) have used their jobs as mechanics at the London Transport bus overhaul garage and their connections with London Transport to convert a bus into a caravan for use as a method to get to Athens in Greece for a summer holiday. Having prepared it, they leave the depot, as the guitar intro and the drums introduce the song that Don (Cliff Richard) sings as he drives the bus. The film version is cut short after just over a minute once the bus has tracked through the south of England and on into France. With waving children, drinking a cup of tea at the wheel, passing the Shadows in French berets riding on bicycles, the bus is slowed down by a group of girls (Una Stubbs, Jacqueline Daryl and Pamela Hart) in an old car taking up the road at which point the tune fades. For this and other external sequences, Cliff actually learnt how to drive a bus.

The song appears three times: in the opening credits, the film section mentioned above and over the end titles. Each of these was recorded later on in the year at the Elstree Studios. Until the release of the special edition of the soundtrack album (opening sequence along with *The Opening*, featuring a brass band) and ***Cliff Richard at the Movies 1959-1974*** (closing title sequence), these film versions had not been released in any other commercial format. Even though the special CD edition of the soundtrack proclaims to include the film version of the song, it is in fact that used over the end titles and, as such, the short version used during the scene described above has yet to be released. The end title version features Hank Marvin, Bruce Welch and Brian 'Licorice' Locking on balalaikas (a nod to the location of the Greek capital of Athens, where the film ends).

Released as a single, backed with another track from the film, ***Dancing Shoes***, on the Columbia label (catalogue number 45-DB 4977, the last of Cliff's singles with Columbia to have the prefix '45-') on 8th February 1963, *Summer Holiday* reached the number one slot in the UK singles charts, where it stayed for two weeks, was temporarily displaced by The Shadows' own *Foot Tapper* (also from the film) before returning for another week at number one. This was to be the last number one to be enjoyed by Cliff Richard with The Shadows as a unit. The track was also released on the ***Hits from Summer Holiday*** EP and has been incorporated on to countless anthologies and collections of Cliff's hits since. The song has also been covered by Jive Bunny and the Mastermixers (although this is a sampled version of the original), the Caribbean Steel Band, Hank Marvin (on his *Hank Plays Cliff* album), Norrie Paramor, Foster and Allen, the Shadows (during their final tour) and Vibha. In addition to the familiar version, the puppet Kevin the Gerbil (part of the Roland Rat franchise) took his version into the charts to number fifty in August 1984.

Summer Holiday had been attempted at an earlier session on 5th April 1962, but it wasn't until the session on 5th May 1962 that the single version (along with its B-side) was completed. Marked as remakes on the EMI session sheets, it took eleven takes before it was satisfactory to all concerned. This take and edit was used for the mono and stereo recordings but with different mixes for the needs of the audio channels. The session is also noteworthy for being the first not to include Jet Harris in the line-up. Brian Bennett had already replaced Tony Meehan at the end of 1961 (owing to tardiness and disruption of performances and recording) and, by the beginning of May 1962, Hank Marvin's and Bruce Welch's issues with Jet and his drinking came to a head, forcing him to leave to be replaced in short shrift (the prior recording session had been only four days earlier) by the bassist from Marty Wilde's Wildcats, Brian 'Licorice' Locking.

The Shadows appear in the left channel, while the orchestra dominates the right and Cliff is at the centre. The song, as has been said, is simplistic and, for that reason, highly memorable for children as well as adults, particularly as the theme to the film. Hank plays a guitar solo in the bridge while Cliff's vocals are as assured as ever.

At the end of his concert in Tokyo as part of the Far East tour that resulted in the live recorded album ***Cliff in Japan***, Cliff formed a medley of popular songs that he had not sung earlier in the show: ***Let's Make a Memory***, ***The Young Ones***, ***Lucky Lips***, *Summer Holiday* and ***We Say Yeah***, all with orchestral accompaniment rather than guitars and drums.

Although Cliff had done a small set with the Shadows in the first section of ***The Event*** at Wembley Stadium, he left *Summer Holiday* to the second part, which he called *Cliff's Set*, performing with his current band. The track was issued only on the vinyl version of the ***From a Distance **** The Event*** album in 1990 but was restored on the now two-CD remaster of the album in 2005. A good sing-along song, Cliff performs the song with a bouncing edge and is joined by the audience throughout. The later Knebworth performance with the Shadows, however, remains unissued to date.

Cliff's love of tennis is well-known and he regularly visits the Wimbledon tournament each year. 1996 was a particularly damp year and, after an extended period of no play due to rain, an official handed Cliff a microphone and asked him to sing to entertain the crowd. With clapping support from a number of female tennis stars behind him, he ran through a number of hits including *Summer Holiday*, which was later licensed from the BBC and released as one of three tracks from that unique event released as the B-side of ***Be with Me Always***.

Given that the song is so much associated with Cliff's image, it was inevitable that a re-recording of *Summer Holiday* would be included on the ***Reunited*** album in 2009, which saw Cliff and the Shadows revisiting a number of songs from their early years and then performing them in concert to promote the album's release. The song is recreated almost perfectly including the strings, although the synthesiser keyboard is included.

Track Specification
Composed by Bruce Welch and Brian Bennett

1. Single

Musicians

Brian Bennett	drums, percussion
Brian 'Licorice' Locking	bass
Hank Marvin	guitar
Norrie Paramor Strings	orchestra
Norrie Paramor	arranger, conductor
Cliff Richard	vocals
Bruce Welch	rhythm guitar

Recording Details

Producer	Norrie Paramor
Engineered by	Malcolm Addey
Recording location	Abbey Road Studio 2, St. John's Wood, London
Recording date	5th May 1962 (main recording) and 19th November 1962 (orchestra)

2. Summer Holiday – Special Edition (opening sequence)

Musicians

Associated British Studio Orchestra	strings
Brian Bennett	drums, percussion
Stanley Black	conductor
Brian 'Licorice' Locking	bass
Hank Marvin	guitar
Norrie Paramor Strings	orchestra
Cliff Richard	vocals
Bruce Welch	rhythm guitar

Recording Details

Producer	Norrie Paramor
Engineered by	Unknown
Recording location	Elstree Studios, Hertfordshire
Recording date	1962

3. Cliff Richard at the Movies 1959-1974 (end title sequence)

Musicians

Brian Bennett	drums, percussion
Stanley Black	conductor
Brian 'Licorice' Locking	bass, balalaika
Hank Marvin	guitar, balalaika
Norrie Paramor Strings	orchestra
Norrie Paramor	arranger, conductor
Cliff Richard	vocals
Bruce Welch	rhythm guitar, balalaika

Recording Details

Producer	Norrie Paramor
Engineered by	Unknown
Recording location	Elstree Studios, Hertfordshire
Recording date	1962

4. Cliff in Japan

Musicians

Norrie Paramor Orchestra	orchestra
Norrie Paramor	arranger, conductor
Cliff Richard	vocals

Recording Details

Producer	Norrie Paramor
Engineered by	Unknown
Recording location	Shibuya Public Hall, Tokyo, Japan
Recording date	18th October 1967

5. Unissued track (Live & Guaranteed 1988!)

Musicians

John Clark	guitar
Rosemarie Ford	backing vocals
Mark Griffiths	bass
Peter Howarth	backing vocals
Steve Lauri	guitar
Paul Moessl	keyboards
Mick Mullins	backing vocals
Alan Park	keyboards
Cliff Richard	vocals
Henry Spinetti	drums, percussion

Recording Details

Producer	Unknown
Engineered by	Unknown
Recording location	Fyens Forum, Odense, Denmark
Recording date	22nd May 1988

6. From a Distance ** The Event Remaster***

Musicians

John Clark	guitar
Sonia Jones-Morgan	backing vocals
Steve Lauri	guitar
Peter May	drums, percussion
Paul Moessl	keyboards
Tessa Niles	backing vocals
Alan Park	keyboards
Provox:	
Peter Howarth	backing vocals
Mick Mullins	backing vocals
Keith Murrell	backing vocals
Cliff Richard	vocals
Steve Stroud	bass

Recording Details

Producer	Cliff Richard
Engineered by	Keith Bessey and Mick McKenna
Recording location	Rolling Stones Mobile Studio, Wembley Stadium, Wembley, North-west London
Recording date	16th-17th June 1989

7. Unissued (Knebworth - The Album)

Musicians	
Ray Beavis	saxophone
Brian Bennett	drums, percussion
John Earle	saxophone
Chris Gower	trombone
Mark Griffiths	bass
Cliff Hall	keyboards
Dick Hanson	trumpet
Peter Howarth	backing vocals
Hank Marvin	backing vocals, guitar
Paul Moessl	keyboards
Mick Mullins	backing vocals
Keith Murrell	backing vocals
Cliff Richard	vocals
Bruce Welch	backing vocals, guitar

Recording Details	
Producer	Chris Kimsey and Steve Smith
Engineered by	Unknown
Recording location	Knebworth House, Hertfordshire, England
Recording date	30th June 1990

8. B-side (Be with Me Always)

Musicians	
Cliff Richard	vocals

Recording Details	
Producer	Unknown
Engineered by	Unknown
Recording location	Wimbledon Lawn Tennis Association
Recording date	3rd July 1996

9. Reunited

Musicians	
Brian Bennett	arranger, drums, percussion
Warren Bennett	arranger, piano, synthesiser
Mark Berrow	violin
Dave Daniels	cello
Mark Griffiths	bass
Bogustan Kostecki	violin
Martin Loveday	cello
Hank Marvin	guitar
Perry Montague-Mason	violin
Cliff Richard	vocals
Emlyn Singleton	violin
Chris Tombling	violin
Kevin Townsend	arranger, conductor
Bruce Welch	rhythm guitar
Warren Zeilinski	violin

Recording Details	
Producer	Warren Bennett (co-ordination)
Engineered by	James Collins (Honeyhill Studios), Ethan Carlson (Middle Ear Studios), Les Williams (Nivram Studios) and Keith Bessey (mixing and mastering)
Recording location	Middle Ear Studios, Miami, Florida, USA (Cliff's vocals), Nivram Studios, Perth, Western Australia (Hank's guitars and vocals) and Honeyhill Studios, Hertfordshire, England (all other vocals and instruments)
Recording date	Early 2009

♬ Summer Holiday Advertising EP

From the album **The Rock 'n' Roll Years 1958-1963**

After the release of ***The Young Ones*** as ***Wonderful to Be Young*** in the US in 1962, the next film ***Summer Holiday*** generated more interest, particularly as there was a growing genre for beautiful young things on celluloid with improbable plots, the first of which was *Beach Party*, starring Frankie Avalon and Annette Funicello wearing very little on a sun-kissed Californian beach. This film was an extraordinary success for the distributors, American International Pictures, and they owned the US distribution rights for *Summer Holiday*. There was a huge publicity drive on the radio with lengthy calls for the nation's teenagers to get to the film, with voice-overs by John Ashley (who starred as Ken in the *Beach Party* films) and an uncredited female voice urging similar. The strange vocabulary used to describe the *Summer Holiday* is at odds with the quintessentially British film that it is. Indeed, the *Beach Party* films are mediocre bubblegum stories and *Summer Holiday* is an ill fit alongside this canon – "If you loved *Beach Party*, you'll love *Summer Holiday*" is one ill-judged comment.

The six breathy radio announcements all featured a snippet of the ***Summer Holiday*** single running behind them, although Cliff Richard and the Shadows had nothing to do with the generation of the advertisements. All six have been edited together and were released on ***The Rock 'n' Roll Years 1958-1963*** album as an EP, although they weren't originally released as such.

Track Specification

Composed by Bruce Welch and Brian Bennett (*Summer Holiday snippet*); Unknown (*voice-over script*)

Musicians	
John Ashley	spoken vocals (*voice-over*)
Brian Bennett	drums, percussion (*song snippet*)
Brian 'Licorice' Locking	bass (*song snippet*)
Hank Marvin	guitar (*song snippet*)
Norrie Paramor Strings	orchestra (*song snippet*)
Norrie Paramor	arranger, conductor (*song snippet*)
Cliff Richard	vocals (*song snippet*)
Unknown	spoken vocals (*voice-over*)
Bruce Welch	rhythm guitar (*song snippet*)

Recording Details	
Producer	Norrie Paramor (*Summer Holiday snippet*); Unknown (*voice-over*)
Engineered by	Malcolm Addey (*Summer Holiday snippet*) ; Unknown (*voice-over*)
Recording location	Abbey Road Studio 2, St. John's Wood, London (*Summer Holiday snippet*) ; Unknown (*voice-over*)
Recording date	5th May 1962 (main) and 19th November 1962 (orchestra) (*Summer Holiday snippet*); 1963 (*voice-over*)

♫ Summer Holiday Medley

Single by **Darren Day**

The touring show, which featured a story based around the early hits of Cliff Richard, starred Darren Day in the lead role, and was called *Summer Holiday* in deference to one of the tracks that is most representative of Cliff's oeuvre by most people. An album of cover material was recorded by Day and a medley was mixed from three of the four tracks that also featured Cliff on backing vocals. These are:

a) ***In the Country***
b) ***On the Beach***
c) ***Do You Wanna Dance?***

On the album, the set was titled ***The Summer Holiday Megamix***, but, backed with Day's versions of ***Summer Holiday*** and ***Bachelor Boy***, the mix was retitled ***Summer Holiday Medley*** and released as a single on the RCA label (catalogue number 7432138444472) in June 1996 and reached the top position of number seventeen in the UK charts. The entries for those included songs carry the information on the recording details and musicians.

♫ Summer Holiday Megamix, The

From the album **Summer Holiday** *(Darren Day)*

In the mid-nineties, Darren Day took the lead role in a touring stage musical that was based around Cliff Richard's hits. The associated album, also called *Summer Holiday*, was recorded in 1996 and featuring Brian Bennett as producer and it had four tracks that included Cliff's backing vocals, while three of those songs were incorporated into the final track to create a 'megamix':

a) ***In the Country***
b) ***On the Beach***
c) ***Do You Wanna Dance?***

The mix was retitled ***Summer Holiday Medley*** and released as a single in June 1996 and reached the top position of number seventeen in the UK charts.

The entries for those included songs carry the information on the recording details and musicians.

♫ Summer Rain

From the album **Wired for Sound**

The second of two songs by Chris Eaton on Cliff Richard's ***Wired for Sound*** album, *Summer Rain* was chosen along with its track listing predecessor, ***Lost in a Lonely World***, from five that Eaton had submitted for Cliff's assessment during the preparation for the album. As with his other song, it is a catchy pop song that actually covers the fact that it has a Christian message and can be treated as a gospel song, which is why it has been included on the several collations of inspirational and faith-related songs released over the years such as *Walking in the Light* and *Rockspell*.

Introduced with an electric sitar, *Summer Rain* is a gentle love song that begs a girl to join with him now that he has realized how much he loves her. The arrangement of the backing vocals is understated but extraordinarily beautiful, helped by the layered texture of Tarney's and Cliff's voices, which blend so well with Cliff's lead.

Track Specification

Composed by Chris Eaton

Musicians

Cliff Richard	vocals, backing vocals
Trevor Spencer	drums, percussion
Alan Tarney	arranger, backing vocals, guitar, electric sitar, bass, keyboards

Recording Details

Producer	Alan Tarney
Engineered by	Michael Boddicker and Ian Little
Recording location	Gallery Studios, Chertsey, Surrey
Recording date	27th May-9th July 1981

♫ Sun Ain't Gonna Shine Anymore, The

From the album **Japan Tour '74**

The most familiar version of *The Sun Ain't Gonna Shine Anymore* is almost certainly that by The Walker Brothers, which was taken to number one in the UK in early 1966. Cher has also had a version in the charts, reaching number twenty-six in August 1996. A number of other artists have also recorded covers of the song, including Neil Diamond, Long John Baldry, David Essex, Jay Black, Frankie Valli and Tight Fit.

Cliff Richard often includes songs in his concerts that he hadn't and wouldn't record in the studio. One such was a Walker Brothers medley of ***Make It Easy on Yourself*** and *The Sun Ain't Gonna Shine Any More* that was included in his Japan tour in 1974, which was subsequently released on the album ***Japan Tour '74*** in 1975 (in Japan only) and then as part of the ***...And They Said It Wouldn't Last! (My 50 Years in Music)*** album before being released separately as a CD album.

Having picked up the pace from Make *It Easy on Yourself*, Cliff leads the vocal ensemble that is the principal focus of the arrangement of the song. The orchestral accompaniment is pared down with a preference for the song to focus on the traditional rock band accompaniment. After two verses, the rhythm slows down and segues back into *Make It Easy on Yourself*. The coupling of the songs completes with a repetition of this song's title, echoed by the backing vocalists.

Track Specification
Composed by Bob Crewe and Bob Gaudio

Musicians	
Barrie Guard	arranger, conductor
Cliff Hall	piano
Brian Lewis	backing vocals, guitar
Kevin Peak	acoustic guitar
Cliff Richard	vocals
Shambles Symphonet	orchestra
Trevor Spencer	drums, percussion
Alan Tarney	backing vocals, bass
Bruce Welch	backing vocals, rhythm guitar

Recording Details	
Producer	Toshiba EMI (no individual detailed)
Engineered by	Toshiba EMI (no individual detailed)
Recording location	Shinjuku Koseinenkin, Tokyo, Japan
Recording date	7th-8th October 1974

♫ Sunny Honey Girl

*52nd **UK single** and from the album* **Cliff "Live" in Japan '72**

Part of a maxi-single combination that saw two songs issued on the B-side, *Sunny Honey Girl* was recorded alongside the other two songs, ***Don't Move Away*** (which is the first of a number of duets with Olivia Newton-John that Cliff Richard has recorded over his career, and who had then been appearing with him on his television show) and ***I Was Only Fooling Myself***, at the same session. The fourth and final take was used for *Sunny Honey Girl* and it was the last song to be completed. The accompaniment featured Shadows drummer Brian Bennett, moving inexorably into his dual career as an arranger and conductor.

Sunny Honey Girl was released as a single with the two B-side songs on the Columbia label (catalogue number DB 8747) on 8th January 1971 and reached the position of just nineteen in the British singles charts. Although it was a pretty little tune with a jaunty arrangement, it was nevertheless another song that attracted negative criticism from the music press, who were now suggesting that Cliff was mainstream and middle of the road and no longer important to the music business. The song was included on the following year's ***The Best of Cliff Vol. 2*** album and has occasionally popped up on other hit compilations with a bent towards the unusual.

An upbeat organ introduces the song, very redolent of the early seventies, while Cliff is accompanied by some gentle uncredited backing vocalists that never threaten to overwhelm but complement his lead vocal. A highly optimistic love song about a girl who has came into his life, it is surprising that the ebullience in the performance didn't successfully push the song higher in the charts.

The version that appears on the ***Cliff "Live" in Japan '72*** album is taken at a slightly faster pace and features Olivia Newton-John's and Pat Carroll's backing vocals in strong prominence, while the combined forces of the instrumentation comfortably drive the song ever onwards.

Track Specification
Composed by Roger Cook, Roger Greenaway, Johnny Goodison and Tony Hiller

1. Single

Musicians	
Brian Bennett	arranger, conductor
Brian Bennett Orchestra	orchestra
Cliff Richard	vocals
Unknown	backing vocals

Recording Details	
Producer	Norrie Paramor
Engineered by	Peter Vince and Richard Lush
Recording location	Abbey Road Studio 2, St. John's Wood, London
Recording date	16th November 1970

2. Cliff "Live" in Japan '72

Musicians	
Brian Bennett	drums, percussion
Pat Carroll	backing vocals
John Farrar	bass
Alan Hawkshaw	piano
Hank Marvin	guitar
Olivia Newton-John	backing vocals
Cliff Richard	vocals
Bruce Welch	rhythm guitar

Recording Details	
Producer	Norrie Paramor
Engineered by	Unknown
Recording location	Kosei Nenkin Hall, Tokyo, Japan
Recording date	22nd-23rd September 1972

♫ Sunset Skies

From the album **Drifting** *(Sheil Walsh)*

Chris Eaton had provided a number of tracks for Cliff Richard to record by the early eighties and would continue to do so into the next decade and beyond. This collaboration made it unsurprising that Cliff would organize a song by Eaton for his protégée Sheila Walsh to record for her first album, ***Drifting*** (or as it was called in the US, *War of Love*).

Twinkling synthesisers initiate this gentle song and Sheila Walsh sings the vocals with conviction that sounds, according to the position in the mix, as if she is singing in duet with herself. The beautiful melody is supported by the synthesiser arrangement and the gentle rhythm created by the bass and drums rhythm section. The chorus sees Cliff providing his harmony vocals in layers, as the speed slows dramatically.

Track Specification
Composed by Chris Eaton
Musicians

Graham Jarvis	drums, percussion
Craig Pruess	arranger, synthesiser
Cliff Richard	backing vocals
Sheila Walsh	vocals

Recording Details

Producer	Cliff Richard and Craig Pruess
Engineered by	Keith Bessey
Recording location	Riverside Studios, London, Strawberry Studios, London, Ramp Studios, London and/or Sonoptics Studios, London
Recording date	September 1982-January 1983

♫ Surrendering

From the album **Triumph in the Air**

The final track on the first side of Sheila Walsh's second album, ***Triumph in the Air,*** was written by Cliff Richard songwriting stalwart Chris Eaton. Although Cliff co-produced her first album, he reduced himself to just providing backing vocals on a handful of tracks for the second, including *Surrendering*, the second such involvement on the album.
A gentle piano introduction leads into Walsh's reverential vocal. The song is more religious in its overall message than those on the previous album but it is still effective as a straightforward piece of eighties balladeering pop. Cliff supplies the backing vocals in the chorus and, unlike other tracks on the album, these are generally kept subdued in the mix.

Track Specification
Composed by Chris Eaton
Musicians

Craig Pruess	arranger, keyboards, electronics
Cliff Richard	backing vocals
Sheila Walsh	vocals

Recording Details

Producer	Craig Pruess, assisted by Keith Bessey
Engineered by	Keith Bessey
Recording location	Cloud 9 Studios, London, Strawberry Studios, Surrey and/or Jacobs Studios, Farnham, Surrey
Recording date	September 1983-January 1984

♫ Sway

From the album **Cliff Richard**

Written by a Mexican bandleader in 1953 as a mambo dance tune, ***¿Quién Será?***, which Cliff Richard recorded for his ***When in Spain*** album, became more popularly known as *Sway*. With English lyrics provided the following year by Norman Gimbel, *Sway* was popularized by Dean Martin, who took the song to number six in the UK singles chart in October 1954, followed six year later by Bobby Rydell who had a number twelve hit in December 1960. It has since been covered and recorded by a number of artists including Björk, the composer Pablo Beltrán Ruiz, Michael Bublé, the Pussycat Dolls, Perez Prado with Rosemary Clooney and Ben E. King among others.
Using the same backing track as that for the song recorded at the *When in Spain* sessions in Barcelona, Cliff Richard recorded overdubbed vocals for a number of previously-recorded Spanish tracks at the same session back in London. Indeed, on *Sway*, the shout of 'Olé!' from the earlier session can still be heard on the trail-out. The same (unknown) vocal take was used overdubbed on the Spanish language take and edit and used for the mono and stereo recordings but with different mixes for the separate needs of the audio channels. Since the original track was recorded in 1963, the Shadows had bassist Brian Locking in their line-up, although he left later that year to be replaced by John Rostill, and therefore it is he who appears on the track rather than John.
As with many stereo tracks recorded in the infancy of the medium and particularly of new vocals were intended to added, the vocal was placed in one channel (Cliff performs in the left on this song) while the instrumentation appears in the other (the Shadows are pushed into the right). This makes the overall listening process a little muddy, although Cliff caries off the performance successfully. This is particularly prominent on the CD release of ***Cliff Richard*** in 1992, which used a narrow stereo mix rather than the split stereo mix for the original LP.

Track Specification
Composed by Pablo Beltrán Ruiz; English lyrics by Norman Gimbel
Musicians

Brian Bennett	drums, percussion
Brian 'Licorice' Locking	bass
Hank Marvin	guitar
Cliff Richard	vocals
Bruce Welch	rhythm guitar

Recording Details

Producer	Norrie Paramor (backing track and vocals)
Engineered by	Malcolm Addey (backing track and vocals)
Recording location	EMI Studios, Barcelona (backing track) and Abbey Road Studio 2, St. John's Wood, London (vocals)
Recording date	29th April 1963 (backing track) and 17th July 1964 (vocals)

♫ Sweet and Gentle

From the EP **Take Four**

Me Lo Dijo Adela (literally *Say It to Me Sweetly* in English) was recorded by Cliff Richard during the 1963 sessions in Barcelona for the album ***When in Spain***. With English lyrics applied by George Thorn and retitled *Sweet and Gentle*, it has been covered by several artists including Eartha Kitt, Stanley Black, Ben E. King, Ray Anthony and Norrie Paramor.

At the end of January 1965, Cliff Richard recorded the English version with the lyrics being overdubbed on to the base track recorded for the Spanish language version of the song, including the backing vocals. Note that the track has Brian Locking on bass since it was recorded in 1963 a few months before he was replaced by John Rostill. Released in mono on the ***Take Four*** EP, it remained a considerable rarity for over forty years until it was included on the track listing of the French release *All My Love* and then the celebratory ***...And They Said It Wouldn't Last! (My 50 Years in Music)*** album both in 2008 (and both still in mono).

There is little to note on the English version over the Spanish original particularly since it uses the same backing track, except to point out that Cliff appears to enjoy performing the English version far more.

Track Specification

Composed by Otilio Portal; English lyrics by George Thorn

Musicians

Brian Bennett	drums, percussion
Brian 'Licorice' Locking	bass
Hank Marvin	guitar
Cliff Richard	vocals, backing vocals
Unknown	piano
Bruce Welch	backing vocals, rhythm guitar

Recording Details

Producer	Norrie Paramor
Engineered by	Malcolm Addey
Recording location	EMI Studios, Barcelona (backing track) and Abbey Road Studio 2 (backing vocals and vocals)
Recording date	30th April 1963 (backing track), 28th May 1963 (backing vocals) and 31st January 1965 (vocals)

♫ Sweet Dreams

Unissued track

Originally a minor hit for Dave Sampson in the UK, when it reached number twenty-nine in the UK charts, *Sweet Dreams* has also been covered by its writer Don Gibson, Chet Atkins, the Everly Brothers, Tammy Wynette, Willie Nelson, Patsy Cline and Roy Orbison among others.

During a recording session that unsuccessfully attempted to record the retitled film song, ***It's Wonderful to Be Young***, for Cliff Richard's first major US film venture (a retitling of ***The Young Ones*** for the American market), he also attempted *Sweet Dreams*, which was abandoned after twelve takes. The song was never been issued or retried in the studio.

Track Specification

Composed by Don Gibson

Musicians

Brian Bennett	drums, percussion
Brian 'Licorice' Locking	bass
Hank Marvin	guitar
Cliff Richard	vocals
Bruce Welch	rhythm guitar

Recording Details

Producer	Norrie Paramor
Engineered by	Malcolm Addey and Peter Vince
Recording location	Abbey Road Studio 2, St. John's Wood, London
Recording date	20th July 1962

♫ Sweet Little Jesus Boy

B-side of **All My Love** *and from the album* **About that Man**

Taking its inspiration from traditional spirituals, *Sweet Little Jesus Boy* is a Christmas song that was written and published in 1934 by Robert MacGimsey. It has been covered by choirs and artists such as Jessye Norman, Booker T. and the MGs, Anne Murray, Kathleen Battle, Mahalia Jackson, Peabo Bryson and Kenny Rogers among others.

Cliff Richard recorded his version during the ***Good News*** album sessions but it was held back from the track listing to form the B-side of ***All My Love***, his fortieth UK single. In part, this was because that single was being released at the lead-up to Christmas in 1967 and, with its Christmas theme, it also takes the honours as being the first truly Christmas-related song recorded by Cliff, kick-starting a perceived new career that was the subject of many witless articles in later years. It was originally released in mono only (as was the wont of Columbia at the time, a company which preferred to reserve its stereo technology for album releases only), remaining a considerable rarity for over forty years until the stereo version was included on the collection ***...And They Said It Wouldn't Last! (My 50 Years in Music)*** in 2008.

Supported by a lush arrangement predominantly on the strings with a brief harp playing alongside, *Sweet Little Jesus Boy* has much to commend it, even though its subject matter may have limited appeal. Cliff sings with a passion in his belief, and he is supported by Pat Clark who produces a perfect soprano descant in the latter half of the song, adding an extra dimension of beauty to the recording. In comparison, the version that appears as the first song on ***About That Man*** features Cliff accompanying himself on the guitar and follows the reading of the Bible tract covering the birth of Jesus.

Track Specification

Composed by Robert MacGimsey

1. B-side (All My Love)

Musicians

Pat Clark	backing vocals
Mike Leander	arranger, conductor
Norrie Paramor Orchestra	orchestra
Cliff Richard	vocals

Recording Details

Producer	Norrie Paramor
Engineered by	Peter Vince and Mike Stone
Recording location	Abbey Road Studio 2, St. John's Wood, London
Recording date	28th April 1967

2. *About That Man*

Musicians

Cliff Richard	vocals, guitar

Recording Details

Producer	Norrie Paramor
Engineered by	Richard Lush
Recording location	Abbey Road Studio 2, St. John's Wood, London
Recording date	20th February 1970

♫ Sweet Lovin' Ways

From the album **...And They Said It Wouldn't Last! (My 50 Years in Music)**

Recorded during the later sessions for the ***Take Me High*** film soundtrack, it is unlikely that *Sweet Loving Ways* was intended for inclusion on the film since that was written in its entirety by Tony Cole. Written by Guy Fletcher and Doug Flett, who were fresh from their success with Cliff Richard at the Eurovision Song Contest in Luxembourg where their ***Power to All Our Friends*** came third but also gave Cliff his highest chart placing for years, *Sweet Lovin' Ways* was left in the vaults until the research for the celebratory album ***...And They Said It Wouldn't Last! (My 50 Years in Music)*** unearthed it.

The driving beat from the running bass line and percussion keeps the song moving. With a requirement for Cliff to use the upper register of his voice for parts of the song, the saxophones and ensemble orchestration and backing vocals make it surprising that the song wasn't released at the time.

Track Specification

Composed by Guy Fletcher and Doug Flett

Musicians

Terry Britten	backing vocals, guitar
David MacKay Orchestra	orchestra
David MacKay	backing vocals, arranger, conductor
Kevin Peek	guitar
Cliff Richard	vocals
Trevor Spencer	backing vocals, drums, percussion
Alan Tarney	backing vocals, bass

Recording Details

Producer	David MacKay
Engineered by	Tony Clark
Recording location	Abbey Road Studio 3, St. John's Wood, London
Recording date	16th August 1973

♫ Swingin' Affair, A

From the film soundtrack album of **Summer Holiday**

American heiress Barbara Winters (played Lauri Peters) has revealed herself to be a beautiful young woman rather than the callow youth she was dressed up to be when stowing away on the bus with Don (Cliff Richard), his friends and the three girls they picked up on the drive through France. Don has strong feelings for her and, although he pushes her heavily for romance, he also states that he doesn't want to be owned and this she finds an upsetting stance, because she loves him passsionately. The pair disembarks from the bus and she storms off to a café with Don following helplessly behind her. He tries to explain what their relationship would be like in the song *A Swingin' Affair*; he picks a flower for her, she smells it but hands it back. Then she takes over the vocals (dubbed by Grazina Frame, who previously worked on ***The Young Ones***) and tries to make Don feel jealous and understand her point of view by picking on the other clientèle and trying to get cosy with them, including placating another angry girlfriend. The ensuing dance routine with a group of suitors ends with Barbara surrounded by five men, who order beer from the waitress as Don slinks away, troubled.

The song was recorded in the second of a double session planned for 26th August and the same take and edit was used for the mono and stereo recordings but with different mixes for the audio channels. The film version of the song was recorded later in the year at Elstree, with very few differences from the studio version, but has not been formally released in any other commercial aural format.

A jazz-like beat is supported by the brushed drums and a twinkling flute that dances over the lead vocals. Cliff once again carries off his vocals, while Grazina Frame tends to perform rather nasally. There is a lovely harmony section between Cliff and Grazina and the whole performance is, as the title suggests, performed with a swinging rhythm.

Track Specification

Composed by Peter Myers and Ronald Cass

Musicians

Associated British Studio Orchestra	orchestra
Stanley Black	conductor
Grazina Frame	vocals
Mike Sammes Singers	backing vocals
Cliff Richard	vocals

Recording Details

Producer	Norrie Paramor
Engineered by	Malcolm Addey and Richard Langham
Recording location	Abbey Road Studio 2, St. John's Wood, London
Recording date	26th August 1962

♬ Take Action

From the album **Sincerely Cliff Richard**

The second of two Terry Britten songs to appear on the ***Sincerely Cliff Richard*** album, *Take Action* features erstawhile Shadows lead guitarist Hank Marvin on the instrument. The final song to be recorded at the session, *Take Action* appears to use a different orchestra from that used on the other two tracks from the session, the B-sides ***She's Leaving You*** and ***Time Flies***.

With Hank guesting on fuzzed guitar, the song is elevated from just being another album track for Cliff Richard. Clearly from the evidence of this track, Cliff enjoys singing Britten's songs and his pure vocals and approach to performance add an extra dimension to the song, helped by including his own backing vocals alongside those already provided by the Mike Sammes Singers.

Track Specification

Composed by Terry Britten

Musicians

Hank Marvin	guitar
Mike Sammes Singers	backing vocals
Mike Vickers Orchestra	orchestra
Cliff Richard	vocals, backing vocals
Mike Vickers	arranger, conductor

Recording Details

Producer	Norrie Paramor
Engineered by	Peter Vince and Richard Langham
Recording location	Abbey Road Studio 2, St. John's Wood, London
Recording date	30th April 1969

♬ Take a Look Around

Unissued track

Recorded in Studio three in the Abbey Road complex rather than number two that had almost become like a second home for Cliff Richard given the number of his earlier songs he had recorded there, *Take a Look Around* was attempted along with the fifty-third single track ***Silvery Rain***, although, unlike the single, the track has never been released. There is no information available on the composer or any other musicians that might have been performing on the song other than those stated; these will be updated should further detail be unearthed in later research.

Track Specification

Composed by Unknown

Musicians

Brian Bennett	arranger, conductor
Brian Bennett Orchestra	orchestra
Cliff Richard	vocals

Recording Details

Producer	Norrie Paramor
Engineered by	Peter Vince and Richard Lush
Recording location	Abbey Road Studio 3, St. John's Wood, London
Recording date	17th November 1970

♬ Take another Look

From the album **I'm No Hero**

Alan Tarney had been involved in recordings by Cliff Richard variously since the end of the sixties, but it was at the end of the seventies and into the eighties that he became integral to Cliff's recording career. *Take another Look* was one of the prime examples of Tarney's increasing dominance because not only did he write it, but he also performed on it and took over the production, which had moved from Abbey Road to the Riverside Studios. *Take another Look* was featured as the first track on the ***I'm No Hero*** album.

There is a distinct signature to Tarney's production and this evident particularly on *Take another Look*. The song is a medium-paced rock song that features both Cliff and Tarney on backing vocals, while the synthesiser, guitar and bass combination provide all that is expected from one of Cliff's album track.

Track Specification

Composed by Alan Tarney

Musicians

Michael Boddicker	synthesiser
Nick Glennie-Smith	synthesiser
Cliff Richard	vocals, backing vocals
Trevor Spencer	drums, percussion
Alan Tarney	arranger, backing vocals, bass

Recording Details

Producer	Alan Tarney
Engineered by	Ashley Howe
Recording location	Riverside Studios, London
Recording date	12th May-27th June 1980

♫ Take Good Care of Her

From the album **Sincerely Cliff Richard**

A minor hit for Adam Wade in June 1961, when his only single reached number thirty-eight in the UK charts and number seven in the US charts, *Take Good Care of Her* was famously covered in the beginning of the seventies by Elvis Presley in a set of prolific recording sessions that saw over one hundred tracks completed and sporadically released over the following years. *Take Good Care of Her* has also been covered by Sonny James, Bobby Helms, Brook Benton, Gene McDaniels, Daniel O'Donnell, Slim Whitman and Johnny Tillotson among others.

Cliff Richard's version of *Take Good Care of Her* was the final song to be completed at a session that included ***Sam***, which was also released on the ***Sincerely Cliff Richard*** album. The track is syrupy song that is sung in unison with the backing vocals at the beginning. It is bittersweet and sung to a girl he adores who has now found someone else. One of the best songs on the album, Cliff instils the necessary emotion into his enunciation of the notes and lyrics.

Track Specification

Composed by Arthur Kent and Ed Warren

Musicians

Alan Hawkshaw Orchestra	orchestra
Alan Hawkshaw	arranger, conductor
Hank Marvin	guitar
Mike Sammes Singers	backing vocals
Cliff Richard	vocals

Recording Details

Producer	Norrie Paramor
Engineered by	Peter Vince
Recording location	Abbey Road Studio 2, St. John's Wood, London
Recording date	18th April 1969

♫ Take Me High

***61st UK single** and from the album* **Japan Tour '74**

Possibly due to timing issues for each side of the original vinyl release (and subsequently the CD) of the soundtrack for ***Take Me High***, many of the songs are presented in a different sequence from that in the narrative of the film; so the title song is placed before ***The Anti-Brotherhood of Man*** and after ***Brumburger Duet*** on the album but is after ***Driving*** and before *The Anti-Brotherhood of Man* in the film; however, this doesn't affect the listening of the album as a separate entity.

In the film, Tim Matthews (Cliff Richard) has concluded his business with Sir Harry Cunningham (Hugh Griffith) and a celebratory lunch is planned, which is to be laid on by his girlfriend Sarah (Debbie Watling), leading towards the Brumburger Restaurant they are setting up. Sarah and Tim walk through fields, swing in slow motion, kiss, pick flowers and row a boat on the lake before finishing with another slow (filmically overdone), tender kiss.

The song was recorded in two parts: the first was the backing track with a basic vocal line followed by the second when the vocal overdubs were added. It was released as the only single from the film project, backed with ***Celestial Houses*** from the ***Help It Along*** album, on the EMI label (catalogue number EMI 2088) on 9th January 1973 and reached number twenty-seven in the UK charts. This is unfortunate since it is a very strong song out of much of the material Cliff had recorded in the first few years of the seventies but its chart placing reflected more what the public believed of his persona and his importance to the music business, since he was reportedly mainstream and even middle of the road.

Acoustic guitars, electric guitars, pianos and bass bring the song in, which is a happy tune full of optimism and comfortable reflection. Cliff is never better than when he has a song with a strong melody and he has one in *Take Me High*, allowing him to also provide the backing vocals. As with many of the songs on the album, there is a slide guitar, which is used to finish the track in a nostalgic way to fit with the screen action.

The electric guitar wows on the introduction in the ***Japan Tour '74*** performance but in all other respects it is a faithful rendition of the original, and Cliff introduces the bass-player (Alan Tarney) as he plays the interlude between the first chorus and the second verse.

Track Specification

Composed by Tony Cole

1. Take Me High

Musicians

David MacKay Orchestra	orchestra
David MacKay	arranger, conductor
Cliff Richard	vocals, backing vocals
Unknown	hand claps

Recording Details

Producer	David MacKay
Engineered by	Tony Clark and Mike Jarrett
Recording location	Abbey Road Studio 3, St. John's Wood, London
Recording date	26th May 1973 (backing track) and 18th September 1973 (vocals)

2. Japan Tour '74

Musicians

Cliff Hall	piano
Brian Lewis	backing vocals, guitar
Kevin Peak	acoustic guitar
Cliff Richard	vocals
Trevor Spencer	drums, percussion
Alan Tarney	backing vocals, bass
Bruce Welch	backing vocals, rhythm guitar

Recording Details

Producer	Toshiba EMI (no individual detailed)
Engineered by	Toshiba EMI (no individual detailed)
Recording location	Shinjuku Koseinenkin, Tokyo, Japan
Recording date	7th-8th October 1974

♫ Take Me to the Leader

Unissued track

Heavy on the religious message, *Take Me to the Leader* was recorded at the first set of sessions for Cliff Richard's ***Now You See Me... Now You Don't*** album in September 1981. Two songs were attempted, but *Take Me to the Leader* has never been issued in any format and those involved in the session are listed in the specification, although this will be updated should further information be uncovered.

Track Specification

Composed by Steve Taylor

Musicians		*Recording Details*	
Dave Cooke	synthesiser	Producer	Cliff Richard and Craig Pruess
Graham Jarvis	drums, percussion	Engineered by	John Walker and Tony Richards
Mart Jenner	electric guitar	Recording location	Abbey Road Studio 3, St. John's Wood, London
Craig Pruess	piano, synthesisers, sequencers, electronic percussion	Recording date	9th-11th September 1981
Cliff Richard	vocals, backing vocals		
Paul Westwood	bass		

♫ Take Me Where I Wanna Go

Unissued track

Another Chris Eaton song recorded during Cliff Richard's album sessions for ***Now You See Me... Now You Don't***, *Take Me Where I Wanna Go* was one of five that have not, to date, been released in any format. Cliff tried these songs out in concert and they went down well and, for this reason, they were included on the list for the recording studio.

Track Specification

Composed by Chris Eaton

Musicians		*Recording Details*	
Mel Collins	saxophone	Producer	Cliff Richard and Craig Pruess
Mark Griffiths	bass	Engineered by	John Walker and Steve Cook
Graham Jarvis	drums, percussion	Recording location	Strawberry Studios South, Surrey
Mart Jenner	electric guitar	Recording date	4th-15th January 1982
Craig Pruess	piano, synthesisers, sequencers, electronic percussion		
Cliff Richard	vocals, backing vocals		
Bill Roberts	electric guitar		

♫ Take My Hand, Precious Lord

From the album **Good News**

A gospel song written and published by the Reverend Thomas A. Dorsey in 1932, it took its melody inspiration from a pre-existing hymn (*Maitland*), written by George Allen, although Allen is rarely credited on any recordings or performances. Written by Dorsey after suffering inconsolation and bereavement following the death of his beloved wife in childbirth and his new-born son the day after, the earliest recorded example of the hymn was in 1938 by Emory Johnson and it has since been translated into numerous languages. A favourite among gospel-singers, it has been successfully covered by a variety of artists including Lonnie Donegan, Ike and Tina Turner, Little Richard, Jim Reeves, Pat Boone, Elvis Presley, Nina Simone, Chet Atkins, Aretha Franklin and Engelbert Humperdinck among many others.

Take My Hand, Precious Lord was the first of five songs attempted at Cliff Richard's first session in May 1967 designated for recording tracks for his album ***Good News***, and it was finally completed by splicing takes one and three together.

Introduced by the warbling vocals of the uncredited backing group, Cliff takes over with a simple instrumental accompaniment in the percussion, bass and woodwind. There is always a danger of turning slow religious songs into a dirge but Cliff's exacting vocals, the vibrato on sustained notes and the passion he obviously feels for the subject matter lifts it up and away from that possibility.

Track Specification

Composed by Thomas A. Dorsey and George N. Allen

Musicians		*Recording Details*	
Bernard Ebbinghouse Orchestra	orchestra	Producer	Norrie Paramor
Bernard Ebbinghouse	arranger, conductor	Engineered by	Peter Vince and Mike Stone
Cliff Richard	vocals	Recording location	Abbey Road Studio 2, St. John's Wood, London
Unknown	backing vocals	Recording date	3rd May 1967

♫ Take Special Care

From the albums **Cliff Richard** *and* **The Rock 'n' Roll Years 1958-1963**

Originally recorded as part of the suite of sessions for the ***32 Minutes and 17 Seconds with Cliff Richard*** album, *Take Special Care* was abandoned after several takes only to be picked up again, but with a slower pace than the first attempted recording, in the May 1962 sessions for the ***Cliff Richard*** album.

One of the takes of the faster version from that first session was released on the 1997 rarity anthology ***The Rock 'n' Roll Years 1958-1963***. The second attempt was recorded in mid-1962 but was not released for a further three years and was the only song to be completed in that session. The thirtieth and final take and edit was used for the mono and stereo recordings but mixed differently for the audio channels. This recording also marks the last commercially released Cliff track with Cliff featuring Jet Harris as bassist; there was another track recorded at the same session (***I'll Be Waiting***) but this remains unissued. There were disagreements within the band not helped by Harris's drinking and Brian 'Licorice' Locking was brought in to replace him at very short notice, since the next session was within four days.
With a vibe from a few of the Shadows own singles, such as *Guitar Tango* and *Geronimo*, *Take Special Care* is a medium-paced song that sees Cliff in his element. The strings and female backing vocals are sometimes a little bit too much and would have been better with just the Shadows performing their accompaniment.
The faster version is almost Spanish in its execution with Bruce Welch's racing chords on the rhythm, while Jet Harris performs a complex bass line run underneath the vocal line. Whether the faster or slower version is better is down to taste but each has something to commend it.

Track Specification
Composed by Bruce Welch and Hank Marvin

1. The Rock 'n' Roll Years 1958-1963

Musicians		*Recording Details*	
Jet Harris	bass	Producer	Norrie Paramor
Hank Marvin	guitar	Engineered by	Malcolm Addey
Tony Meehan	drums, percussion	Recording location	Abbey Road Studio 2, St. John's Wood, London
Cliff Richard	vocals	Recording date	18th December 1961
Bruce Welch	rhythm guitar		

2. Cliff Richard

Musicians		*Recording Details*	
Brian Bennett	drums, percussion	Producer	Norrie Paramor
Jet Harris	bass	Engineered by	Malcolm Addey
Hank Marvin	guitar	Recording location	Abbey Road Studio 2, St. John's Wood, London
Mike Sammes Singers	backing vocals	Recording date	1st May 1962
Norrie Paramor Strings	orchestra		
Norrie Paramor	arranger, conductor		
Cliff Richard	vocals		
Bruce Welch	rhythm guitar		

♫ Taste of Honey, A

From the albums **Live at the Talk of the Town** *and* **Cliff Live in Korea**

Written for the 1960 Broadway play version of *A Taste of Honey* that was first performed in the UK in 1958, the title song was originally intended to be an instrumental. Although Herb Alpert and His Tijuana Brass had the American hit and Acker Bilk took it into the UK charts in January 1963 reaching number sixteen, to most people the definitive version is probably that by the Beatles when it was issued on their debut album *Please Please Me*. It has been covered by a number of other artists including Pat Boone, the Hollies, Patricia Barber, Peggy Lee, Chet Atkins, the Supremes, Lena Horne, the Artwoods, the Temptations, Les Baxter, Bobby Darin, Floyd Cramer, Lionel Hampton, Tom Jones, Julie London, Sarah Vaughan and Roger Whittaker among others.
Although Cliff Richard never recorded the song in the studio, he did take to performing different songs on stage, including *A Taste of Honey* and a version was captured from his performance at the Talk of the Town. This version was a complete departure, too, since it features him playing the solo guitar.
The gentle orchestral accompaniment allows Cliff to play his guitar solo on a classical guitar. Although he is no Hank Marvin, he is obviously a competent guitar player. There are some minor slips, particularly when changing key but these do not detract from the listening pleasure. The track is interesting since it shows Cliff's versatility as a musician but putting an instrument at the forefront rather than his superlative vocals.
Another live version was recorded during Cliff's concert with the Shadows (a sort of reunion for the band) at a concert in Seoul in 1969, this time with Cliff performing the vocals. The ultra-rare resulting album *Cliff Live in Korea* has only ever been issued in mono format and was released for the Korean market only in 1970.

Track Specification
Composed by Ric Marlow and Bobby Scott

1. Live at the Talk of the Town

Musicians		*Recording Details*	
Norrie Paramor	arranger, conductor	Producer	Norrie Paramor
Cliff Richard	guitar	Engineered by	Peter Vince
Talk of the Town Orchestra	orchestra	Recording location	Talk of the Town Theatre, London
		Recording date	30th May 1968

2. ***Cliff Live in Korea***

Musicians

Brian Bennett	drums, percussion
Alan Hawkshaw	keyboards
Hank Marvin	guitar
Cliff Richard	vocals
John Rostill	bass
Bruce Welch	rhythm guitar

Recording Details

Producer	Unknown
Engineered by	Unknown
Recording location	Citizen Hall, Seoul, South Korea
Recording date	16th October 1969

♬ Taxi, Taxi, Take Me to Your Baby

Unissued track

Very little is known about this track or Cliff Richard's recording of this song. A curious title, with the suggestion that the taxi driver should take him to the driver's lover, it may be more correctly titled *Taxi, Taxi, Take Me to* My *Baby*. Whatever the position on the song, it was probably recorded some time in 1964 and 1965 as has been shown by the acetate that was sold at Sotheby's Auction House in London in 1988. As at the time of writing, the song has not been commercially released and notes from the session are unavailable.

Track Specification

Composed by Unknown

Musicians

Cliff Richard	vocals
Unknown	all instrumentation

Recording Details

Producer	Unknown but probably Norrie Paramor
Engineered by	Unknown but probably Malcolm Addey
Recording location	Unknown but probably Abbey Road Studio 2, St. John's Wood, London
Recording date	1964 or 1965

♬ Tea for Two

From the album **21 Today**

Written for the 1925 musical *No, No, Nanette* by Vincent Youmans and Irving Caesar, *Tea for Two* is actually a duet performed in the second act by the two main characters of Nanette and Tom singing a verse in turn, imagining their future together. In 1928, the song was orchestrated by Dimitri Shostakovich in forty-five minutes in order to win a bet set by Nikolai Malko. The tune has been recorded by a variety of different and esoteric acts including Chubby Checker, Dave Brubeck, Julie Andrews, Harpo Marx, Benny Carter, Tony Martin, Benny Goodman, Louis Armstrong, Doris Day, Stéphane Grapelli, the Mantovani Orchestra and Django Reinhardt among many others with the Tommy Dorsey Orchestra starring Warren Covington achieving a UK number three in 1958 with the *Tea for Two Cha-Cha*.

Eight takes were recorded in the first part of the Cliff Richard session that resulted in three songs in the can, with the eighth and final take being used for the stereo and mono edits but with different mixes for the separate audio channels.

A foot-tapping take on the original song sees a rockier version by Cliff and the Shadows. The approach to the performance has a slinky late-night club feel to it with the focus on the running bass line and drums supported by Hank Marvin's muted guitar. It is only in the instrumental middle eight section that gives free rein also to Tony Meehan's drums for a few bars that the familiar cha-cha-cha style is brought in before reverting to the style that introduced it.

Track Specification

Composed by Vincent Youmans and Irving Caesar

Musicians

Jet Harris	bass
Hank Marvin	guitar
Tony Meehan	drums, percussion
Cliff Richard	vocals
Bruce Welch	rhythm guitar

Recording Details

Producer	Norrie Paramor
Engineered by	Malcolm Addey
Recording location	Abbey Road Studio 2, St. John's Wood, London
Recording date	4th July 1961

♬ Teddy Bear

Unissued live track and from the album **Rock 'n' Roll Silver**

Recorded by Pat Boone, Ray Hamilton, Shorty Mitchell, Laurel Aitken and the Residents and sampled by Jive Bunny, it is, of course, one of Elvis Presley's most enduring early hits, when it reached number three in the summer of 1957. More formally titled *(Let Me Be Your) Teddy Bear*, it is referred to in its shortened form on Cliff Richard's ***Rock 'n' Roll Silver*** album. Before recording it in the studio, however, Cliff used to perform it regularly in concert as a tribute to his musical hero. In 1981, it was recorded as part of the BBC documentary on Cliff live at the Hammersmith Odeon in London but, to date, it has yet to be licensed from the corporation for release.

At the time of the sessions for Cliff's twenty-fifth anniversary album ***Rock 'n' Roll Silver***, it was the band who suggested recording it since they were already regularly performing it in concerts as a tribute to Presley. The band was a group of musicians brought together by Cliff and named Thunder and, under that co-operative name, they arranged and produced the song in collaboration. The track was left off the listing of the CD reissue in 1993 but was restored as a bonus track on the remaster of ***The Rock Connection*** released in 2004.

The arrangement of the song for *Rock 'n' Roll Silver* is around half the pace of Elvis's original. At the time, Cliff experimented with new versions of faster rock 'n' roll songs, such as his own ***Dynamite*** and ***Please Don't Tease*** and this is the latest in that line. It is recognizable for the song it is, but the vocal arrangement and the accompaniment given it a completely fresh make-over that works very well.
The final line from the song, in imitation of Elvis Presley's version, is sung by Cliff to complete the ***Medley*** of rock and roll songs and finishes off the rendition of ***Rock 'n' Roll Is Here to Stay***, although *Teddy Bear* is not credited in any of the formats associated with ***From a Distance ***** The Event***.

Track Specification
Composed by Karl Mann and Bernie Lowe

<u>1. Unissued track (BBC Documentary)</u>

Musicians		*Recording Details*	
Stuart Calver	backing vocals	Producer	Cliff Richard
Howie Casey	saxophone, trumpet, trombone	Engineered by	Unknown
John Clark	guitar	Recording location	Hammersmith Odeon, London
Mark Griffiths	bass	Recording date	1st May 1981
Graham Jarvis	drums, percussion		
Martin Jenner	guitar		
Alan Park	keyboards		
John Perry	backing vocals		
Cliff Richard	vocals		
Tony Rivers	backing vocals		
Graham Todd	keyboards		

<u>2. Rock 'n' Roll Silver</u>

Musicians		*Recording Details*	
Stuart Calver	backing vocals	Producer	Thunder
Dave Cooke	keyboards	Engineered by	Keith Bessey
John Clark	electric guitar	Recording location	Strawberry Studios South, Surrey
Mark Griffiths	bass	Recording date	9th-18th May 1983
Graham Jarvis	drums, percussion		
Mart Jenner	guitar		
John Perry	backing vocals		
Alan Park	keyboards		
Cliff Richard	vocals		
Tony Rivers	backing vocals		
Thunder	arranger		

♫ Teenager in Love, A
Unissued track

One of the most important songs to be written in the first wave of rock and roll, *A Teenager in Love* is a paean to the feelings of anxious love felt by pubescent children entering into adulthood and the severe feelings of pain of the first love hitting back unrequited or having done something terrible to cause hurt. It was recorded first by Dion and the Belmonts and released in March 1959. In the UK, the charts had three simultaneous versions running with Dion's original being his first British hit in June of 1959, reaching number twenty-eight, Craig Douglas released at the same time and reaching number thirteen while Marty Wilde had the third version that was by the most successful as it reached number two.
During what was ostensibly a Drifters recording session (for *Driftin'* and *Jet Black*), Cliff Richard managed to put down a vocal version of *A Teenager in Love* but it remained unreleased, possibly because the charts were already littered with a number of versions and the market was therefore too crowded.

Track Specification
Composed by Jerome Pomus and Mort Shuman

Musicians		*Recording Details*	
Jet Harris	bass	Producer	Norrie Paramor
Hank Marvin	guitar	Engineered by	Peter Bown and Stuart Eltham
Tony Meehan	drums, percussion	Recording location	Abbey Road Studio 2, St. John's Wood, London
Cliff Richard	vocals	Recording date	4th May 1959
Bruce Welch	rhythm guitar		

♫ Tell Me
Unissued track and from the album **Me and My Shadows** *(mono and stereo)*

The stereo and mono versions of this ***Me and My Shadows*** track differ in that the mono version has an *a capella* introduction that was recorded separately from the main song. In all other respects the take is the same (the eleventh from the second session; the first attempt at the recording on 25th March remains unissued) and is another Shadows-related composition featuring the burgeoning talents of Bruce Welch and erstwhile Chesternuts bandmate Peter Chester. The song was also released on the associated ***Me and My Shadows No. 3*** EP.

Welch has an ear for a strong melody and arrangement of simple instrumentation to make a greater whole. In this love song that asks a girl to tell the singer how she feels, there is a focus on an intricate bass line while Hank Marvin and Bruce himself content themselves with simple guitar accompaniment. A strong song in the line-up of strong material on the album, it also shows Cliff's capabilities as a singer who makes the process sound simple.

Track Specification
Composed by Pete Chester and Bruce Welch

1. Unissued track (Me and My Shadows)

Musicians	
Jet Harris	bass
Hank Marvin	guitar
Tony Meehan	drums, percussion
Cliff Richard	vocals
Bruce Welch	rhythm guitar

Recording Details	
Producer	Norrie Paramor
Engineered by	Malcolm Addey and Norman Smith (mono) and Peter Bown and Alan Kane (stereo)
Recording location	Abbey Road Studio 2, St. John's Wood, London
Recording date	25th March 1960

2. Me and My Shadows (mono)

Musicians	
Jet Harris	bass
Hank Marvin	guitar
Tony Meehan	drums, percussion
Cliff Richard	vocals
Bruce Welch	rhythm guitar

Recording Details	
Producer	Norrie Paramor
Engineered by	Malcolm Addey and Norman Smith
Recording location	Abbey Road Studio 2, St. John's Wood, London
Recording date	25th March 1960 and 30th March 1960 (*a capella* introduction)

3. Me and My Shadows (stereo)

Musicians	
Jet Harris	bass
Hank Marvin	guitar
Tony Meehan	drums, percussion
Cliff Richard	vocals
Bruce Welch	rhythm guitar

Recording Details	
Producer	Norrie Paramor
Engineered by	Peter Bown and Alan Kane
Recording location	Abbey Road Studio 2, St. John's Wood, London
Recording date	25th March 1960

♫ Temptation

From the album **Listen to Cliff!**

Made famous in Britain by the Everly Brothers, who took the song to number one in the charts in July 1961, prior to this it had been recorded by Bing Crosby, Mario Lanza, Chet Atkins, The Sandpipers, Freddy Cole, the John Kirby Sextet, Perry Como, Les Baxter, Lou Donaldson and Fran Warren among many others.

The version that appears on ***Listen to Cliff!*** was recorded in both mono and stereo, using the same take and edit (the second of only two from the session) and the engineers mixed them differently for the purposes of the differing aural channel needs. It is one of the few tracks from the album that was not released in an associated EP format.

Cliff's version is very different from the then Everly Brothers familiar version. The big band treatment of the song with a Latin dance rhythm (at times replicating the *Bolero* by Ravel) pulsing underneath make it something extraordinary and lifts it from the more sterile versions that are often recorded. Cliff's vocals are clear but with a little bit of guarded menace brought in to underline the point that he is falling for the womanly guile of a girl despite his attempts to resist the lure.

Track Specification
Composed by Nacio Herb Brown and Arthur Freed

Musicians	
Tony Meehan	drums, percussion
Norrie Paramor Orchestra	orchestra
Norrie Paramor	arranger, conductor
Cliff Richard	vocals

Recording Details	
Producer	Norrie Paramor
Engineered by	Malcolm Addey and Norman Smith
Recording location	Abbey Road Studio 2, St. John's Wood, London
Recording date	17th November 1960

♫ Te Quiero Dijiste

From the album **When in Spain**

With a subtitle of ***Magic Is the Moonlight***, *Te Quiero Dijiste* translates literally as *I Want You to Say*. The song has been covered by a number of artists including Nat King Cole, Xiomara Alfaro, Barbarito Diez, Alfredo Kraus, Ana Maria Gonzalez, Chico O'Farrill, the Orquesta Romantica del Casino de Hawana, Edmundo Ros and Rigo Tovar.

Cliff Richard went on to record the English version, using the established subtitle for the track, for his 1965 album ***Cliff Richard***, which had the English vocals overdubbed on the backing track created in Barcelona sessions for the ***When in Spain*** album. For that album, *Te Quiero Dijiste* was the first of these songs completed for the album with the fifteenth and final take and edit being used for the mono and stereo recordings but with different mixes to meet the requirements of the audio channels.

The stereo recording, as with many of the album's tracks, pushes Cliff's vocal into the left channel, while the Shadows appear *in toto* in the right channel –a practice often used in the medium's infancy. Cliff's vocal is as assured as ever, while the Shadows' languid accompaniment is perfect for the song helped along by the short piano solo by Norrie Paramor.

Track Specification
Composed by Mariá Grever and Charles Pasquale

Musicians		*Recording Details*	
Brian Bennett	drums, percussion	Producer	Norrie Paramor
Brian 'Licorice' Locking	bass	Engineered by	Malcolm Addey
Hank Marvin	guitar	Recording location	EMI Studios, Barcelona
Norrie Paramor	piano	Recording date	30th April 1963
Cliff Richard	vocals		
Bruce Welch	rhythm guitar		

♫ Thank You for a Lifetime

140th UK single

Because Cliff had successfully stayed at the top of the music game for fifty years in 2008, he commissioned a song to commemorate that achievement. The result was *Thank You for a Lifetime*, which was a kind of autobiographical trawl through his career as well as a heartfelt nod towards his fans and others who had supported him.

Backed with ***Mobile Alabama School Leaving Hullabaloo***, a track that had been unearthed from the late seventies during research for the celebratory boxed set ***...And They Said It Wouldn't Last! (My 50 Years in Music)***, *Thank You for a Lifetime* was released as a CD single on the EMI label (catalogue number 50999 2 36462 2 3) on 8th September 2008 but was exclusively available for purchase at the now-defunct Woolworths high street chain. In addition, it was accessible for internet download and the combined sales pushed the song to number three in the UK charts. The song was subsequently included as one of the tracks on the ***50th Anniversary Album***. The musicians are unknown at this stage but will be updated once further research reveals the information.

A sustained violin note is met with piano chords underneath Cliff's initial vocals as he reminisces on his early days, which includes sound effects of applause as well as a stylized arrangement of the introductory guitar passage for ***Move It*** to fit with the metre of the song. The beauty of the track comes in the sincerity with which Cliff sings his thanks. There is a lot going on in this track as the different genres of his career are visited and interpolated in between each of the choruses.

Track Specification
Composed by Jez Ashurst, Charlie Grant and Peter Woodroffe

Musicians		*Recording Details*	
Cliff Richard	vocals, backing vocals	Producer	Chris Neil
Unknown	backing vocals	Engineered by	Unknown
Unknown	guitar	Recording location	Unknown
Unknown	bass	Recording date	2008
Un known	piano		
Unknown	keyboards		
Unknown	drums, percussion		
Unknown	saxophone		
Unknown	arranger, conductor		
Unknown	orchestra		

♫ That'll Be the Day

From the album **Cliff**

According to research, the title of the song was inspired by the world-weary repeated phrase by John Wayne's character in the film, *The Searchers*. Buddy Holly and Jerry Allison then took that idea and came up with the up tempo song and used the theme of forthright unlikelihood when applied to relationships; for example, the lover saying goodbye, the lover making him cry and so on. It was recorded in 1956 but wasn't given an issue date. In February 1957, another version was recorded and released on Holly's new label, Brunswick. It reached number one in the US and became an enduring favourite for fans. Indeed, it was used as the title of a film made in 1973, starring David Essex and Ringo Starr, recalling the life and times of men working on the funfairs at the back end of the fifties. The song has since been covered by a wide variety of acts including The Quarrymen (the predecessor band to The Beatles and whose version was released on the *Anthology* series by EMI), Linda Ronstadt and Paul and Barry Ryan amongst others. As a quintessential piece of music marking the times, it was chosen as part of the 'live' set list by Cliff Richard and the Drifters, performing at Abbey Road Studios over two days in February 1959 in front of an invited guest list drawn from the fan base.

Cliff's vocals give a nod towards Holly's style of hiccupping singing, while Hank Marvin's guitar work adequately replicates and enhances the original melody lines.

Track Specification
Composed by Buddy Holly, Jerry Allison and Norman Petty

Musicians		*Recording Details*	
Jet Harris	bass	Producer	Norrie Paramor
Hank Marvin	guitar	Engineered by	Peter Bown and Stuart Eltham
Tony Meehan	drums, percussion	Recording location	Abbey Road Studio 2, St. John's Wood, London
Cliff Richard	vocals	Recording date	10th February 1959
Bruce Welch	rhythm guitar		

♫ That's Alright, Mama

B-side of **Peace in Our Time** *(CD)*

Written in 1946, the original title was *That's All Right Mama,* although this often gets transmuted to *That's Alright Mama,* as was the case for Cliff Richard's live version. It underwent another name change in 1954 when Elvis Presley recorded it as his first single in America, when it was called simply *That's All Right.* At the time, Presley's cover wasn't released in the UK – his first single was *Heartbreak Hotel* – but, as part of the celebrations for what would have been his seventieth birthday, several hits were reissued and the first was *That's All Right,* which reached number three in the UK charts in July 2004. Since it was first recorded, it inspired a number of musicians and it has also been covered by Marty Robbins, the Beatles, Canned Heat, Stray Cats, Paul McCartney, Steve Walsh and Rod Stewart among several others.

As was his wont, Cliff regularly sang songs in concert that he had not recorded and, during his *Access All Areas* tour in 1992, *That's Alright, Mama* opened the set, with Cliff accompanying himself on guitar. The song was later included as an bonus B-side track on the first of two CD singles for ***Peace in Our Time***.

The guitar is played well, although it is not an instrument readily associated with Cliff after years of fronting the Shadows as lead singer and having Hank Marvin perform the solos. Nevertheless, in the mid-section, Cliff plays a quite complex motif on the guitar that fits perfectly with the atmosphere, and is performed with self-assuredness by Cliff.

Track Specification

Composed by Arthur Crudup

Musicians

Cliff Richard	vocals, guitar

Recording Details

Producer	Keith Bessey
Engineered by	Keith Bessey
Recording location	Wembley Arena, London
Recording date	27th-29th November 1992

♫ That's My Desire

From the album **Cliff Sings**

The final track on the ***Cliff Sings*** album features accompaniment by the Norrie Paramor Orchestra rather than the more familiar Drifters sound – a ploy to demonstrate Cliff's versatility and to capitalize on the more mainstream pop hits ***Living Doll*** and ***Travellin' Light***. *That's My Desire* was written in 1931 and recorded by the Sammy Kaye Orchestra and then Frankie Laine, whose version became better known and more popular in the mid-forties. Although these charted in the US, it was before the UK had begun to compile charts (November 1952) and so the song never found an outing there. Other artists to record the song include Louis Armstrong, James Brown, Ella Fitzgerald, Patsy Cline, Buddy Holly, Jerry Lee Lewis, Nat Shilkret, Art Mooney and The Hollies.

All of the tracks on the album were released on four separate EPs. While the album itself was originally released only in mono, the ***Cliff Sings No. 4*** EP was issued in both mono (the same edits as used on the album) and stereo (using the same recording take as the mono but edited slightly differently for best use of the dual listening channels).

Shimmering strings and shuffling drums played with brushes arranged by producer Norrie Paramor support Cliff's vocal line. The brief up tempo middle eight is perhaps the best part of the song, first with a vocal and later with strings only. The technical ability of the performance is difficult but Cliff carries off the execution of it with accustomed alacrity.

Track Specification

Composed by Helmy Kresa and Carroll Loveday

Musicians

Norrie Paramor Orchestra	orchestra
Norrie Paramor	arranger, conductor
Cliff Richard	vocals

Recording Details

Producer	Norrie Paramor
Engineered by	Malcolm Addey and Alan Kane (mono) and Stuart Eltham and Norman Smith (stereo)
Recording location	Abbey Road Studio 2, St. John's Wood, London
Recording date	9th September 1959

♫ That's My Kind of Life

Unissued track

Sung in one of the religious playlets in the series *Life with Johnny, That's My Kind of Love* has often been interpreted incorrectly as ***This Is My Kind of Love***. Appearing in the episode entitled *Johnny Come Home*, featuring Cliff Richard in the title role, Johnny has met up with hedonist good-time girl Michelle (played by his old friend Una Stubbs) and they have moved in together in London, away from his father and girlfriend in the north-east, being profligate with the money his father has given him, spending it on having a good time, minks, good food and so on. It's played over an extended dance routine with repeated scenes of restaurants and shops where he spends cash, as is Michelle for whom he buys presents.

The song, a duet between Johnny and Michelle (with Cindy Kent dubbing the vocals as Una Stubbs lip-synchs) is performed in a slow tempo, underlining the fact that he is not really enjoying his life in spite of the delusion he is setting up for himself and focuses on the theme of spending money. As with all the songs for the six-episode series, *That's My Kind of Life* was recorded at Abbey Road studios possibly with a view to releasing an album tie-in that never materialized. The track has never been released and the end titles of the episode suggest that the song is an original written in collaboration between Cliff, the programme's writer David Winter and the four Settlers.

Track Specification
Composed by Cliff Richard, David Winter, Cindy Kent, Mike Jones, John Fyffe and Geoffrey Srodzinski

Musicians

John Fyffe	backing vocals, guitar
Cindy Kent	vocals
Mike Jones	backing vocals, guitar
Cliff Richard	vocals
Geoffrey Srodzinski	backing vocals
Unknown	organ
Unknown	drums, percussion

Recording Details

Producer	Norrie Paramor
Engineered by	Peter Vince
Recording location	Abbey Road Studio 3, St. John's Wood, London
Recording date	11th January 1969

♫ That's What Friends Are For

From the album **Through the Years** *(Cilla Black)*

Written for Rod Stewart in the 1982 film *Night Shift*, *That's What Friends Are For* is best known for the cover by Dionne Warwick (and Friends), recorded for the American Foundation for AIDS Research with artists such as Elton John, Gladys Knight and Stevie Wonder. Released in 1985, it was an American number one and number sixteen in the UK. Sung as the finale to the 1990 New York AIDS benefit concert, it was later broadcast on television, and raised over $2.5 million.

The title of the song makes it apposite for Cliff Richard and Cilla Black to be their first recording together. They had been friends since the sixties and had appeared on each other's television shows singing a choice of songs together – indeed Cliff sang the contenders for both Eurovision Song Contests on Cilla's shows – but had never been in the studio together. In 1993, to celebrate Cilla's thirtieth anniversary in the music business, they recorded *That's What Friends Are For*, which was released on the *Through the Years* album. Cliff also wrote a glowing testimonial to his friend on the liner notes.

Starting with laid-back saxophones, Black sings the initial lyrics before handing over to Cliff. At the chorus, they sing together in unison as the backing instrumentation and vocal arrangement builds up underneath them, before quietening for the next verse and so on to the end. Cliff sings in falsetto on occasions while Black keeps her vocal line measured.

Track Specification
Composed by Carole Bayer Sager and Burt Bacharach

Musicians

Julie Andrews	bassoon
John Barclay	trumpet
Gary Barnacle	saxophone
Peter Beachill	trombone
Bill Benham	violin
Cilla Black	vocals
Richard Blanshard	backing vocals, saxophone
Belinda Bunt	violin
Nick Busch	French horn
Les Craven	clarinet
Ben Cruft	violin
Chris 'Snake' Davies	saxophone
Andy Findon	flute
David Fuest	clarinet
Roger Garland	violin
Wilf Gibson	violin
Jim Grant	violin
Garfield Jackson	viola
Shaila Kanga	harp
Paul Kegg	cello
Pat Kirnan	violin
Boguslaw Kostecki	violin
Helen Liebmann	cello
Martin Loveday	cello
Jim McLeod	violin
Rita Manning	violin
Perry Montague-Mason	violin
Pete Oxer	violin
Andy Parker	viola
Jane Pickles	flute
John Peneguy	French horn
Tony Pleeth	cello
Maciej Rakowski	violin
Cliff Richard	vocals
Frank Ricotti	percussion
George Robertson	viola
Hugh Seenan	French horn
Charlie Skarbek	backing vocals, keyboards, programs
Bob Smissen	viola
David Theodore	oboe
John Thirkell	trumpet
Derek Watkins	trumpet
Cleveland Watkiss	backing vocals
Barry Wilde	violin
Gavyn Wright	violin

Recording Details

Producer	Charlie Skarbek and Rick Blaskey
Engineered by	Pat Stapley, Mark Chamberlain and Charlie Skarbek
Recording location	Savage Sound Studios, London, Metropolis Studios, London and The Hit Factory, London
Recording date	1993

♫ That's What Love Is

Unissued track

In early 1969, Tyne Tees Television commissioned a series of playlets called *Life with Johnny*, featuring Cliff Richard in the title role as each episode modernizing a Biblical parable. Records are unclear on the episodes but *Johnny Come Home* and *Johnny Faces Facts* are complete, *Johnny and the Good Samaritan* is partially available, while the remainder are unavailable. The songs had some relevance to the parable being acted and usually there were five songs per episode. *That's What Love Is* appeared in one of *Johnny on the Rocks*, *Johnny and the Blind Rage* or *Johnny in Love*. The end credits of the episode stated that all songs were original and written in collaboration between Cliff, the Settlers and the programme's writer David Winter. The instrumentation and performance details are unknown.

Track Specification

Composed by Cliff Richard, David Winter, Cindy Kent, Mike Jones, John Fyffe and Geoffrey Srodzinski

Musicians	
John Fyffe	backing vocals, guitar
Cindy Kent	backing vocals
Mike Jones	backing vocals, guitar
Cliff Richard	vocals
Geoffrey Srodzinski	backing vocals, bass

Recording Details	
Producer	Norrie Paramor
Engineered by	Peter Vince
Recording location	Abbey Road Studio 3, St. John's Wood, London
Recording date	2nd-3rd December 1968

♫ That's Why I Love You

B-side of **When Two Worlds Drift Apart**

Also recorded by Anne Murray in 1972 and Andrew Gold in 1975, Cliff Richard recorded *That's Why I Love You* during one of the sessions for the ***Every Face Tells a Story*** album. It was subsequently chosen as the B-side of the single ***When Two Worlds Drift Apart*** and the song was a major rarity for a number of years until it was included as a bonus track on the remastered and reissued CD version of the album in 2002.

The song is begun on a synthesiser sequence that gives way to a straightforward love song that is elevated by the quirky guitar use on syncopated off-beats as well as the lovely backing vocal arrangement that had become a trademark of Cliff's recordings of the period. The guitars are strongly in evidence in the middle eight solo section before returning to the main vocal, which is generally sung with a kind of innocent air.

Track Specification

Composed by Andrew Gold and Gene Garfin

Musicians	
Brian Bennett	drums, percussion
Terry Britten	guitar
John Perry	backing vocals
Cliff Richard	vocals
Tony Rivers	backing vocals
Alan Tarney	bass
Graham Todd	keyboards

Recording Details	
Producer	Bruce Welch
Engineered by	Peter Vince and Haydn Bendall
Recording location	Abbey Road Studio 2, St. John's Wood, London
Recording date	22nd September 1976

♫ Theme for a Dream

12th UK single

The choice of song for the twelfth single release by Cliff Richard and the Shadows is another unusual one. Although ostensibly a rock and roll act, the band was astute in their choice of songs, since it showed a breadth of talent beyond a particular genre. The first few singles were standard rock and roll fare before there was a change of direction following Cliff's appearance in the film ***Serious Charge*** and his first number one with ***Living Doll***, which had a strong country feel. Then there were gentler ballads like ***Fall in Love with You*** as well as the crooning standards that appeared on ***Cliff Sings***. *Theme for a Dream*, then, saw a further departure from the expected career path that many saw him treading.

With a more pop music feel but not easily fitting into that musical pigeonhole, the tune is a catchy and memorable melody that is gently sung by Cliff. What marks it as different for the time was the addition of the chirping female members of the Mike Sammes Singers singing the response refrains to mirror Cliff's lead. In interview, Cliff has confirmed that, while they liked the song, they were unsure about it. On hearing the playback, they agreed that the additional backing vocals made the song appear quite sophisticated (although sophistication then and now are quite different, of course). In addition to Cliff's version, it has also been covered by the Hunters and Bobby Vee.

Backed with ***Mumblin' Mosie***, *Theme for a Dream* was released on the Columbia label (catalogue number 45-DB 4593) on 24th February 1961 and reached number three in the UK singles chart. Three versions were created: mono, stereo and mock stereo, all of which were derived from the same studio take with different mixes for the stereo channels; the mock stereo version was created from the mono mix. *Theme for a Dream* appears on many compilations featuring Cliff's greatest hits but it was included on the ***Cliff's Hit Parade*** EP at the time.

A gentle guitar introduces Cliff's vocals, which is accompanied by soft staccato guitar, bass and drums as well as the saccharine female backing vocals. It would be interesting to hear the song without the female voices. However, the fans loved it to the point of breaking chart records at that time by having over 200,000 pre-sales orders for the single.

Track Specification

Composed by Mort Garson and Earl Shuman

Musicians		*Recording Details*	
Jet Harris	bass	Producer	Norrie Paramor
Tommy Kamara	bongos	Engineered by	Malcolm Addey
Hank Marvin	guitar	Recording location	Abbey Road Studio 2, St. John's Wood, London
Tony Meehan	drums, percussion	Recording date	28th January 1961
Mike Sammes Singers	backing vocals		
Cliff Richard	vocals		
Bruce Welch	rhythm guitar		

♫ Theme from *A Summer Place*

From the album **Love Is Forever**

As the song's title suggests, this is the main theme from the 1959 film *A Summer Place*, which was a starring vehicle for actress Sandra Dee. For the film, the song was recorded by Hugo Winterhalter, although it has been recorded by Duane Eddy, Julie London, James Last, Chet Atkins, the Tornados, Carmen Cavallaro, the Lettermen (who had a US Billboard number sixteen with it) and Ray Conniff, with Norrie Paramor and his Orchestra taking the melody into the British charts in March 1960, reaching a high of thirty-six. This was followed by Percy Faith, the Canadian orchestral leader, who had a number two single shortly afterwards; he revisited the song twice with a choral version in 1969 and with a disco backbeat in 1976. The Shadows also produced a pastiche on their eponymous album called *Theme from a Filleted Plaice*.

One of four songs recorded at Cliff Richard's June 1965 session for his album ***Love Is Forever***, the final (unknown) take and edit were used for the mono and stereo recordings but with different mixes for the audio channel separation. Shimmering strings and a tinkling piano support Cliff's lead vocals and, as with many songs in this particular genre of gentle balladeering, he carries off the role perfectly.

Track Specification

Composed by Max Steiner and Mack Discant

Musicians		*Recording Details*	
Norrie Paramor Orchestra	orchestra	Producer	Norrie Paramor
Cliff Richard	vocals	Engineered by	Unknown
Ken Woodman	arranger, conductor	Recording location	Abbey Road Studio 2, St. John's Wood, London
		Recording date	10th June 1965

♫ There Is a Green Hill Far Away

Unissued track

A favourite hymn, particularly at Easter time because of its imagery of the place of Christ's cross, it has been covered by a number of choirs including the Huddersfield Choral Society, the Salvation Army Band and Choir, Seaford Chapel Choir and the 103rd Street Gospel Choir, as well acts such as Jenny Jordan Frogley, Mark Small and Rick Wakeman. Cliff Richard's version was intended for his ***Good News*** album but, after four takes, it was abandoned and remains unissued.

Track Specification

Composed by Cecil Frances Alexander

Musicians		*Recording Details*	
Norrie Paramor Orchestra	orchestra	Producer	Norrie Paramor
Mike Leander	arranger, conductor	Engineered by	Peter Vince and Mike Stone
Cliff Richard	vocals	Recording location	Abbey Road Studio 2, St. John's Wood, London
		Recording date	4th May 1967

♫ There's Gotta Be a Way

From the pantomime cast recording album of **Aladdin and His Wonderful Lamp**

One of the eighteen numbers written by all of the Shadows in collaboration for the pantomime version of ***Aladdin and His Wonderful Lamp***, which featured Cliff Richard and the Shadows in performances starting in December 1964 and going on into the new year, *There's Gotta Be a Way* was the first of three songs for the cast album to be completed at the session. The fifth and final take and edit were used for the mono and stereo recordings but with different mixes for the requirements of the divided stereo audio channels.

The almost furtive arrangement in the orchestra underlines the lyrics, where Aladdin has been arrested and thrown into jail and is looking for a way out and requiring the lamp to assist him. With the Shadows' ear for rhythm, *There's Gotta Be a Way* is an interesting little nugget from the show that ends on an unresolved startled muted brass chord.

Track Specification

Composed by Hank B. Marvin, Bruce Welch, Brian Bennett and John Rostill

Musicians		*Recording Details*	
Mike Sammes Singers	backing vocals	Producer	Norrie Paramor
Norrie Paramor Orchestra	orchestra	Engineered by	Malcolm Addey and Ken Scott
Norrie Paramor	arranger, conductor	Recording location	Abbey Road Studio 2, St. John's Wood, London
Cliff Richard	vocals	Recording date	17th October 1964

♫ There's More to Life

Misnomer for **More to Life**

The theme to the nineties BBC racing drama, *Trainer,* was recorded by Cliff Richard and released as a single. Properly titled ***More to Life,*** the track listings of the compilation albums *The Winner* and *Yesterday, Today, Forever* incorrectly suggest it is called *There's More to Life.*

♫ There's No Power in Pity

B-side of **I Still Believe in You** *and from the album* **Silver Celebration**

Like ***Bulange Downpour,*** which Cliff Richard had written after being inspired by the force of nature in a sudden rainstorm while visiting the small Ugandan village of Bulange, *There's No Power in Pity* was also written during that tour of Uganda on behalf of the Tear Fund charity to which he was closely associated. The song was chosen as one of the B-side items on the first disc of the dual CD single release of ***I Still Believe in You.*** Subsequently, it appeared on the track listing of *Yesterday, Today, Forever* and then as a bonus track on the 2007 remaster of the ***Small Corners*** album before being included on the 2008 boxed set ***...And They Said It Wouldn't Last! (My 50 Years in Music).***

With a sound that fits perfectly with the rest of the album, *There's No Power in Pity* is an impassioned song by Cliff that tells all to look towards compassion rather than pity since that is far more effective and powerful. The driving bass is matched by rounded synthesiser chords and once again, adds evidence that Cliff is incorrect in his assertion that he is not a good songwriter.

In 1997, Cliff performed at a concert with the All Souls Orchestra at the Wembley Conference Centre. Certain songs were recorded and released on the *Silver Celebration* album including *There's No Power in Pity.*

Track Specification
Composed by Cliff Richard

1. B-side (I Still Believe in You)

Musicians

John Clark	guitar
Peter May	drums, percussion
Paul Moessl	arranger, drum programming, keyboards
Cliff Richard	vocals, backing vocals
Steve Stroud	bass

Recording Details

Producer	Paul Moessl and Cliff Richard
Engineered by	Gerry Kitchingham and Ben Robbins
Recording location	R. G. Jones Studios, Wimbledon, London
Recording date	25th-31st May 1992, 8th June 1992 (backing track) and 16th July 1992 (vocals)

2. Silver Celebration

Musicians

All Souls Orchestra	orchestra
John Clark	backing vocals, guitar
Pete May	drums, percussion
Alan Park	keyboards
Cliff Richard	vocals
Steve Stroud	backing vocals, bass
Unknown	conductor

Recording Details

Producer	Langham Arts
Engineered by	Unknown
Recording location	Wembley Conference Centre, Wembley, North-west London
Recording date	21st October 1997

♫ There You Go Again

From the album **The 31st of February Street**

Finding his feet as a writer after leaving most of the duties to the Shadows for so many years, a number of Cliff Richard's own songs appear on ***The 31st of February Street*** album, with *There You Go Again* being one of the six in the track listing. It was recorded in eight takes at a suite of sessions in February 1974 for the album.

The initial electric piano gives way to the guitar accompaniment to Cliff's vocals. The gentleness of the song performed in a minor key matches the emotions of the lyrics created by the fact that his girlfriend is looking to leave him and how frustrated he feels by her actions, which he has now come to know.

Track Specification
Composed by Cliff Richard

Musicians

Terry Britten	backing vocals, guitar
Cliff Hall	keyboards
Jean Hawker	backing vocals
David MacKay	backing vocals
Dave MacRae	keyboards
Anna Peacock	backing vocals
Kevin Peek	acoustic guitar
Cliff Richard	vocals
Trevor Spencer	drums, percussion
Alan Tarney	backing vocals, bass

Recording Details

Producer	David MacKay
Engineered by	Tony Clark and Mike Jarrett
Recording location	Abbey Road Studio 2, St. John's Wood, London
Recording date	13th and 14th February 1974

♫ Thief in the Night

From the albums **Now You See Me, Now You Don't, Dressed for the Occasion** *and* **From a Distance ***** The Event** *and unissued live track*

In 1981, Cliff Richard produced singles for Network 3, a Christian music group. The lead singer, Paul Field, went on to forge a solo career and one of the two songs that he provided for him to record on his ***Now You See Me... Now You Don't*** album, *Thief in the Night* is often cited as a favourite song to perform with a Christian message within a catchy pop song.
The keyboard introduction shimmers as it moves between the stereo channels and the swooping motif representing a thief making a getaway flits from left to right and back again. For most of the song, the predominant instrument is the guitar. There are several changes in pace, starting slowly, breaking off and then there is a high energy instrumental piece, which then abruptly changes to a half-pace for Cliff's vocals. Here, too, Cliff supplies his own backing vocals.
As one of his then recent songs, *Thief in the Night* was included on the ***Dressed for the Occasion*** performance with an orchestra backing. The dramatic nature fits well with the expansive sound afforded by a symphony orchestra but Cliff also melded a rock band into it and this works well in replicating the track, particularly in the upbeat, frenetic mid-point.
For the *Live and Guaranteed 1988!* tour, *Thief in the Night* was sung in medley with ***UFO*** and ***I Wish We'd All Been Ready***, but, although recorded and filmed, the ***Medley*** has yet to be issued on CD.
Combined with ***Fighter*** as a sort of medley, Cliff added *Thief in the Night* into his second set at the Wembley Stadium concerts for his thirtieth anniversary celebrations. Segueing from *Fighter* as the instrumentation quietens down, Cliff uses his vibrato to great effect on the song, singing low down in his register and then building up to the song's end by singing an octave higher, helping to create the juxtaposition of the lyrics and the faster paced musical interlude.

Track Specification
Composed by Paul Field

1. Now You See Me... Now You Don't

Musicians

John Clark	electric guitar
Dave Cooke	synthesiser
Mark Griffiths	bass
Graham Jarvis	drums, percussion
Mart Jenner	electric guitar
Craig Pruess	autoharp
Cliff Richard	vocals, backing vocals
Graham Todd	electric piano

Recording Details

Producer	Cliff Richard and Craig Pruess
Engineered by	John Walker and Steve Cook
Recording location	Strawberry Studios South, Surrey
Recording date	4th-15th January 1982

2. Dressed for the Occasion

Musicians

David Cooke	synthesiser
Steve Gray	piano
Mark Griffiths	bass
Richard Hewson	arranger, conductor
Graham Jarvis	drums, percussion
London Philharmonic Orchestra	orchestra
Cliff Richard	vocals

Recording Details

Producer	Cliff Richard and Richard Hewson
Engineered by	John Kurlander
Mixed by	Keith Bessey
Recording location	Royal Albert Hall, London
Mixed at	Strawberry Studios South, Surrey
Recording date	23rd November 1982

3. Unissued track (Live & Guaranteed 1988!)

Musicians

John Clark	guitar
Rosemarie Ford	backing vocals
Mark Griffiths	bass
Peter Howarth	backing vocals
Steve Lauri	guitar
Paul Moessl	keyboards
Mick Mullins	backing vocals
Alan Park	keyboards
Cliff Richard	vocals
Henry Spinetti	drums, percussion

Recording Details

Producer	Unknown
Engineered by	Unknown
Recording location	Fyens Forum, Odense, Denmark
Recording date	22nd May 1988

4. From a Distance ** The Event***

Musicians

John Clark	guitar
Sonia Jones-Morgan	backing vocals
Steve Lauri	guitar
Peter May	drums, percussion
Paul Moessl	keyboards
Tessa Niles	backing vocals
Alan Park	keyboards
Provox:	
Peter Howarth	backing vocals
Mick Mullins	backing vocals
Keith Murrell	backing vocals
Cliff Richard	vocals
Steve Stroud	bass

Recording Details

Producer	Cliff Richard
Engineered by	Keith Bessey and Mick McKenna
Recording location	Rolling Stones Mobile Studio, Wembley Stadium, Wembley, North-west London
Recording date	16th-17th June 1989

♫ Things We Said Today

Unissued track and from the EP **La La La La La**

One of the surprisingly few covers of a Beatles song by Cliff Richard, *Things We Said Today* first appeared on the soundtrack of the Beatles' first film *A Hard Day's Night* and also issued as the B-side of the single of the title song when released in July 1964. Paul McCartney was the principal composer of the song and wrote it in the Caribbean while on holiday with his then girlfriend Jane Asher. The lyrics touch on the regret that he experienced with her as two ambitious people's careers interrupted their relationship. An esoteric set of artists have recorded the song, including Gordon Haskell, Chet Atkins, Barbara Dickson, the Band of the Irish Guards, Kid Creole and the Coconuts, the Iguanas, Paul McCartney (live recordings), the London Jazz Four, the Sandpipers, Salamander Crossing and Rick Wakeman.

Cliff's version was recorded, at the same session as two other vocal tracks for the ***La La La La La*** EP. The first attempt had been tried at the session three or four weeks beforehand. The final (unknown) take and edit of *Things We Said Today* from the session were used for both the mono and stereo recordings but with different mixes for the audio channel requirements. Issued originally in mono on the EP, it was released for the first time in stereo on the German compilation *Congratulations und 13 Weitere Hits* in 1968. It would take another twenty-one years before being released from obscurity when it appeared on the collection ***The EP Collection: Ballads and Love Songs*** in 1989, itself now a considerable rarity.

With a Latin flavour to the arrangement, the song is perfectly suited to Cliff's singing style. It calls on him to stretch the upper vocal range as well as requiring him to keep the pitch as the song is based around a sequence of five basic notes. Hank and Bruce were present at some of the sessions that saw this recording completed and, given the Beatles were also masters of the harmonized vocal, it is a shame that neither Shadow was used to support Cliff here.

Track Specification

Composed by John Lennon and Paul McCartney

1. Unissued track (La La La La La EP)

Musicians

Bernard Ebbinghouse Orchestra	orchestra
Bernard Ebbinghouse	arranger, conductor
Cliff Richard	vocals

Recording Details

Producer	Norrie Paramor
Engineered by	Peter Vincent and Richard Lush
Recording location	Abbey Road Studio 2, St. John's Wood, London
Recording date	19th September 1966

2. La La La La La EP

Musicians

Bernard Ebbinghouse Orchestra	orchestra
Bernard Ebbinghouse	arranger, conductor
Cliff Richard	vocals

Recording Details

Producer	Norrie Paramor
Engineered by	Peter Vincent and Richard Lush
Recording location	Abbey Road Studio 2, St. John's Wood, London
Recording date	11th October 1966

♫ Thinking of Our Love

B-side of **Nine Times out of Ten** *and from the album* **The Rock and Roll Years 1958-1963**

One of twelve tracks that were performed to an invited audience comprising members of the fan club, *Thinking of Our Love* (the first to be written by Bruce Welch and Hank Marvin together) was not as popular as the A-side that it was attached to, ***Nine Times out of Ten***, and a few other songs including ***Please Don't Tease*** and ***Gee Whiz It's You***. The fifth take from the session was used for final release and, to date, that B-side version has not been released in another format, with the exception of the same stereo track being released on ***The Rock 'n' Roll Years 1958-1963*** but with a take confirmation (five) and a count-in before starting. In all other respects, it is the same song as appears on the B-side of the eventual single.

Thinking of Our Love is a pretty love song that shows what Bruice and Hank would be composing over the next few years. It is an archetypal Shadows tune, with Hank's tinkling guitar, Jet Harris's thudding bass and Bruce's subtle rhythmic guitar keeping the pace. A key change in the middle eight keeps the interest high before returning to the original key.

Track Specification

Composed by Bruce Welch and Hank Marvin

1. B-side (Nine Times out of Ten)

Musicians

Jet Harris	bass
Hank Marvin	guitar
Tony Meehan	drums, percussion
Cliff Richard	vocals
Bruce Welch	rhythm guitar

Recording Details

Producer	Norrie Paramor
Engineered by	Malcolm Addey and Norman Smith (mono) and Peter Bown and Alan Kane (stereo)
Recording location	Abbey Road Studio 2, St. John's Wood, London
Recording date	16th March 1960

2. The Rock and Roll Years 1958-1963

Musicians

Jet Harris	bass
Hank Marvin	guitar
Tony Meehan	drums, percussion
Cliff Richard	vocals
Bruce Welch	count-in, rhythm guitar

Recording Details

Producer	Norrie Paramor
Engineered by	Peter Bown and Alan Kane
Recording location	Abbey Road Studio 2, St. John's Wood, London
Recording date	16th March 1960

♫ This Can't Be Love

B-side of **Let Me Be the One**

Written for the 1938 musical *The Boys from Syracuse*, *This Can't Be Love* was also featured in the later film, 1962's *Billy Rose's Jumbo*. The song's witty lyrics turn the traditional love song on its head by talking about a bunch of worrying symptoms that are absent but that are normally present in the more anguished peons to love (one such example professes it can't be love because he feels too well). The Eddy Duchin Orchestra and the Benny Goodman Orchestra had the first hits with the tune later in 1938 while Nat King Cole was the first artist to sing it solo in 1954. It has subsequently been recorded by artists such as Rufus Wainwright, Michel Legrand, Tony Bennett and Cole's daughter Natalie.

Coupled with another Rodgers and Hart song, ***My Funny Valentine***, Cliff Richard performed the songs at his 2001 concerts. These were recorded and included as B-side items for the second and final single to be released from the ***Wanted*** project, ***Let Me Be the One***, alongside the live version of ***I Gotta Woman*** from the 1962 Kingston concert album.

Track Specification

Composed by Richard Rodgers and Lorenz Hart

Musicians		*Recording Details*	
Cliff Richard	vocals	Producer	Unknown
Unknown	all instrumentation	Engineered by	Unknown
		Recording location	Royal Albert Hall, London
		Recording date	May 2001

♫ This Day

Unissued track and from the film soundtrack album of **Finders Keepers**

Performed in an underground cavern with huge stalactites to be negotiated by Cliff Richard (playing himself) as he steers a boat carrying his new love Emilia (Vivianne Ventura) away from the town, they notice the echoes of the chamber and begin to shout words. Suddenly an echoey introduction to *This Day* is heard with the Shadows' instruments and effective vocal percussion before Cliff takes up the vocal and settles next to Emilia, kissing her once the song ends.

Although there is some trickery played in the film on the opening bars, the song is the same as the soundtrack with Cliff lip-synching to the lyrics. In addition Norrie Paramor's Orchestra makes the only orchestral appearance in the film. There was an attempt at recording the song at a session on 27th April 1966 but, after six takes, it was abandoned; to date, none of these has been released. Seven weeks later at the beginning of June, further attempts were made with the final (unknown) take and edit being used for both the mono and stereo recordings but with different mixes for the separate audio channels. With the now familiar vocal harmonies from the singing Shadows introducing the song, the gentle love song is sung with great effect and emotion by Cliff. Incorporating the vocal percussion (shushing) provided by Hank Marvin, there is also a shimmering organ behind the lead vocal, which is probably played by Norrie Paramor but this is not confirmed.

Track Specification

Composed by Hank Marvin, Bruce Welch, Brian Bennett and John Rostill

1. Unissued track (Finders Keepers)

Musicians		*Recording Details*	
Brian Bennett	drums, percussion	Producer	Norrie Paramor
Hank Marvin	backing vocals, vocal percussion, guitar	Engineered by	Peter Vince and Richard Lush
Norrie Paramor Orchestra	orchestra	Recording location	Abbey Road Studio 2, St. John's Wood, London
Norrie Paramor	arranger, conductor	Recording date	27th April 1966
Cliff Richard	vocals		
John Rostill	backing vocals, bass		
Unknown	organ		
Bruce Welch	backing vocals, rhythm guitar		

2. Finders Keepers

Musicians		*Recording Details*	
Brian Bennett	drums, percussion	Producer	Norrie Paramor
Hank Marvin	backing vocals, vocal percussion, guitar	Engineered by	Unknown
Norrie Paramor Orchestra	orchestra	Recording location	Abbey Road Studio 3, St. John's Wood, London
Norrie Paramor	arranger, conductor	Recording date	4th June 1966
Cliff Richard	vocals		
John Rostill	backing vocals, bass		
Unknown	organ		
Bruce Welch	backing vocals, rhythm guitar		

♫ This Is My Kind of Love

Misnomer for **That's My Kind of Life**

Portrayed in the religious playlet in the series *Life with Johnny*, some publications refer to *This Is My Kind of Love*, which is actually ***That's My Kind of Life***. Refer to that entry for the detail.

♬ This Is Our Country

Putative single

According to *The Complete Chronicle* by Peter Lewry, Nigel Goodall and Mike Read, plans were made in July 1992 imediately after the sessions for ***Cliff Richard - The Album*** for Cliff Richard to record a putative single, which had been written by Chris Eaton, called *This Is Our Country*, to commemorate the fortieth anniversary of the reign of Queen Elizabeth II. However, there is no available evidence that this took place or that Cliff has ever recorded the song. If it has been recorded, it naturally remains unissued.

♬ This Love

From the albums **Without Walls** *(Tammy Wynette) and* **The Cooke Files** *(Dave Cooke)*

Written by two long-term writing and recording collaborators of Cliff Richard, Paul Field and Dave Cooke, *This Love* was recorded by Tammy Wynette and Cliff to celebrate Wynette's twenty-five years in the music industry in 1993 and the track appeared on an album of Wynette's duets called *Without Walls* in 1995. In preparation for the session, Wynette met up with Cliff at his home in Surrey before recording the song at the R. G. Jones studios a couple of days later. She stated in interview that the privilege of recording with someone with a voice like Cliff's was enormous and one of the highlights of her career to date.

A gentle combination of a saxophone and keyboards introduces the song that leads into a string and piano accompaniment. The late Tammy Wynette performs first and sings it competently enough but it is left to Cliff to inject just enough dramatic passion into the song, which talks of love and peace and it is ultimately a spiritual song. Cliff's and Wynette's voices blend well when they sing together and they duet in the last few moments of the song, which has a rallentando that seems to have been missed by Wynette being a beat or so behind Cliff's vocals; however, this goes unnoticed because it is effective.

Revisited again for Dave Cooke's own album, *The Cooke Files* that was recorded and released in 1999, *This Love* featured Cliff on the main vocals with Cooke providing all of the instrumentation except the saxophone. This track is supremely rare.

Track Specification

Composed by Dave Cooke and Paul Field

1. Without Walls

Musicians

William Benham	violin
Mark Berrow	violin
Dave Bishop	soprano saxophone
John Brandbury	violin
John Clark	guitar
Benedict Cruft	violin
Michael Desaulles	violin
David Emanuel	violin
Roger Garland	violin
Jim Grant	violin
Jonathan Henley	violin
C. Illrons	violin
Paul Kegg	cello
Peter Lale	viola
Jim McLeod	violin
Peter May	drums, percussion
Paul Moessl	arranger, keyboards, synthesisers
Anthony Pleeth	cello
Jonathan Rees	violin
Cliff Richard	vocals
Frank Ricotti	percussion
George Robertson	viola
John Ronayne	violin
Roger Smith	cello
Jonathan Strange	violin
Robin Wilson	violin
Tammy Wynette	vocals

Recording Details

Producer	Cliff Richard and Paul Moessl
Engineered by	Jeff Balding
Recording location	R. G. Jones Studios, Wimbledon, London
Recording date	30th June (main track) and 1st July 1993 (backing vocals and saxophone)

2. The Cooke Files

Musicians

Dave Cooke	guitars, keyboards, programming
Mike Haughton	soprano saxophone
Cliff Richard	vocals

Recording Details

Producer	Dave Cooke
Engineered by	Dave Cooke and Crispin Retev
Recording location	JMF Studios, Twickenham, London
Recording date	1994 or 1995

♫ This Love You Will Never Forget

From the album **Wanted**

In the new millennium, Cliff Richard had been dropped inexplicably from his long-term record company EMI, perhaps in the belief that he was not the musical force he used to be. To counter this, Cliff endeavoured to prove the decision wrong by recording an album that would take him into the upper section of the charts. The result was ***Wanted***, which was created in partnership with Alan Tarney with whom Cliff hadn't worked meaningfully since ***Stronger*** in 1989. While most of the track listing featured well-known songs, there was also a small selection of tracks that were original compositions, including two by Tarney. With famous lyricist Don Black on board for *This Love You Will Never Forget*, Cliff's recording is a brilliant counterpoint to the hugely familiar songs elsewhere on the album.

The introduction features a choir of close harmonies built up in layers that lead into Cliff's lead vocals. The rhythm is mid-paced and kept moving by the programmed percussion. Although the stark instrumentation adds flavours underneath the vocals, it is the warm and lush vocal arrangement supporting the lead that makers the track what it is.

Track Specification

Composed by Alan Tarney and Don Black

Musicians	
John Brant	additional programming
Anthony Clark	backing vocals
Cliff Richard	vocals, backing vocals
Alan Tarney	arranger, backing vocals, keyboards, programming

Recording Details	
Producer	Alan Tarney
Engineered by	John Brant and Gerry Kitchingham
Recording location	Wilmer Studios, London
Recording date	January-April 2001

♫ This New Year

116th UK single *(all formats)*

Written by long-term Cliff Richard collaborator Chris Eaton, who had provided the 1990 Christmas number one with ***Saviour's Day***, *This New Year* closes the ***Together with Cliff Richard*** album cleverly introducing the other element of festive season: the welcoming of a new year. An edited version of *This New Year* – which had a verse and chorus cut and fades early – was backed with album track ***Scarlet Ribbons*** and issued as a single on the EMI label (catalogue number EMS 218) on 30th December 1991 but only reached number thirty in the UK singles charts. This single featured both the tracks on one side with a Christmas message from Cliff etched into the blank reverse. The twelve-inch (catalogue number 12EMP 218) and CD (CDEM 218) had the unedited album version as the principal track and both included the PWL Remix of ***We Don't Talk Anymore***, the album track version of *Scarlet Ribbons* as well as the remixed version that was created for the Dutch single release of *Scarlet Ribbons*. The CD single had one more track, which was a television studio performance (from the BBC's *Pebble Mill at One* magazine show) of his first Christmas number one, ***I Love You***.

Heavy on drums and synthesiser keyboards, there is a sophisticated rhythm and arrangement that is brought in underneath Cliff's lead vocals. The full backing vocal group is here on the track, while the brass and full instrumentation force the song ever onwards to welcome in the optimistic expectations about the coming year. Cliff uses his falsetto to great effect on the song but the problem is that the melody is not as memorable or as dramatic as other songs composed by Eaton. The promotional video has Cliff sitting atop a snowy roofline as he sings the song as the camera moves around him. For the chorus, he gets up and begins to dance around the set.

Track Specification

Composed by Chris Eaton

1. Single (seven-inch)

Musicians	
John Clark	guitar
Mick Clarke	backing vocals
Paul Dunne	guitar
Dave Cunliffe	violin
Andrew Greasley	violin
Mark Griffiths	bass
Peter Howarth	backing vocals
Mae McKenna	backing vocals
Peter May	drums, percussion
Paul Moessl	drum programming, keyboards
Sonia Morgan	backing vocals
Mick Mullins	backing vocals
Keith Murrell	backing vocals
Tessa Niles	backing vocals
Cliff Richard	arranger, vocals, backing vocals
Frank Ricotti	drums, percussion
Miriam Stockley	backing vocals
Steve Stroud	bass
Anthony Thompson	backing vocals
Derek Watkins	trumpet

Recording Details	
Producer	Cliff Richard and Paul Moessl
Engineered by	Gerry Kitchingham, Andrew Greasley and Ben Robbins
Recording location	R. G. Jones Studios, Wimbledon, London
Recording date	24th June 1991 to July 1991

2. *Single (twelve-inch and CD)*

Musicians

John Clark	guitar
Mick Clarke	backing vocals
Paul Dunne	guitar
Dave Cunliffe	violin
Andrew Greasley	violin
Mark Griffiths	bass
Peter Howarth	backing vocals
Mae McKenna	backing vocals
Peter May	drums, percussion
Paul Moessl	drum programming, keyboards
Sonia Morgan	backing vocals
Mick Mullins	backing vocals
Keith Murrell	backing vocals
Tessa Niles	backing vocals
Cliff Richard	arranger, vocals, backing vocals
Frank Ricotti	drums, percussion
Miriam Stockley	backing vocals
Steve Stroud	bass
Anthony Thompson	backing vocals
Derek Watkins	trumpet

Recording Details

Producer	Cliff Richard and Paul Moessl
Engineered by	Gerry Kitchingham, Andrew Greasley and Ben Robbins
Recording location	R. G. Jones Studios, Wimbledon, London
Recording date	24th June 1991 to July 1991

♫ This Time Now

From the album **Always Guaranteed**

Cliff Richard was a busy man during the recording of his ***Always Guaranteed*** album, which was overseen by long-term collaborator Alan Tarney, since Cliff was working at the Dominion Theatre each night in his Rock Star role in ***Time – the Musical***. Therefore, the Tarney approach of composing something and recording the basic track against which Cliff could record his vocals worked well since he didn't have to wait around in the studio for the instrumentation to be sorted out.

With a vibe similar to that of ***Two Hearts***, *This Time Now* opens with a syncopated drum rhythm that is supported by the synthesized brass chord statements. But the real strength of the song comes from the beautiful backing vocal arrangements, with Cliff primarily supporting his lead, singing in thirds and creating an exquisite set of harmonies.

Track Specification

Composed by Alan Tarney

Musicians

Cliff Richard	vocals, backing vocals
Alan Tarney	backing vocals, guitars, bass, keyboards, drum and percussion programming

Recording Details

Producer	Alan Tarney
Engineered by	Gerry Kitchingham and Keith Bessey
Recording location	R. G. Jones Studios, Wimbledon, London
Recording date	13th October-November 1986

♫ This Was My Special Day

Special single from the pantomime cast recording album **Aladdin and His Wonderful Lamp**

One of eighteen tracks written by the Shadows for ***Aladdin and His Wonderful Lamp***, the 1964 pantomime show starring Cliff Richard and the Shadows, *This Was My Special Day* also featured several of the cast. It was given a special release as a single, which was only available for purchase by those patrons of the show. Backed with *I'm Feeling Oh So Lovely* – which didn't feature Cliff – *This Was My Special Day* was even given a Columbia catalogue number (DB 7435) and was released in mono only on 11th December 1964 (the pantomime's first night) but, because of the limited market and non-standard outlet, didn't sell enough to dent the singles charts nor was it intended to. It should be noted that it is not listed as an official single but is only a marketing device. The eleventh and final take and edit were used for the mono and stereo but with different mixes for the audio channels and was the only song featuring Cliff to be recorded at the session.

In the entry for the session in Peter Lewry's and Nigel Goodall's book, *The Complete Recording Sessions 1958-1990*, it suggests that one of the female singers was film stalwart Una Stubbs, but this is erroneous; rather, it was Faye Fisher who performed the third female solo in the session alongside Audrey Bayley and Joan Palethorpe.

The girl singers introduce the song by singing in unison with some pitching problems at the start. As with all Shadows compositions, the melody is memorable and the orchestral arrangement does sufficient justice to the song. Cliff comes in at just after two minutes and immediately improves the performance, since the female voices don't blend together well.

Track Specification

Composed by Hank B. Marvin, Bruce Welch, Brian Bennett and John Rostill

Musicians

Audrey Bayley	vocals
Faye Fisher	vocals
Mike Sammes Singers	backing vocals
Norrie Paramor Orchestra	orchestra
Joan Palethorpe	vocals
Norrie Paramor	arranger, conductor
Cliff Richard	vocals

Recording Details

Producer	Norrie Paramor
Engineered by	Malcolm Addey and Ken Scott
Recording location	Abbey Road Studio 2, St. John's Wood, London
Recording date	16th October 1964

♫ Thousand Conversations, A

B-side of **Sing a Song of Freedom**

Reverting back to the trusted partnership of Hank Marvin and Bruce Welch for *A Thousand Conversations* for one of Cliff Richard's B-sides in the early seventies, like ***Silvery Rain***, the composers covered the song on their *Marvin, Welch & Farrar* album, while Olivia Newton-John recorded a version of the track for her 1976 album *Don't Stop Believin'*. To complete the Shadows circle Cliff's recording was overseen orchestrally by Brian Bennett, who also arranged the performance. *A Thousand Conversations* was completed at the same session as its A-side ***Sing a Song of Freedom***. Although predominantly released in stereo, a mono version was issued in Australia. For several years, the song was a rarity until it was included on the B-side rarity section of the celebratory ***...And They Said It Wouldn't Last! (My 50 Years in Music)*** album released in 2008.

Sung in a similar style to Hank's original voca with Marvin, Welch & Farrar, the orchestral accompaniment is less sparse than that on their eponymous album. Cliff's voice is a perfect vehicle for singing songs by Marvin and Welch and Brian Bennett's arrangement has a beautiful flute and violin accompaniment to the later verses and choruses that expresses some of the lyrical thoughts perfectly.

Track Specification

Composed by Hank Marvin and Bruce Welch

Musicians

Brian Bennett	arranger, conductor
Brian Bennett Orchestra	orchestra
Cliff Richard	vocals

Recording Details

Producer	Norrie Paramor
Engineered by	Peter Vince
Recording location	Abbey Road Studio 2, St. John's Wood, London
Recording date	24th August 1971

♫ Thousand Miles to Go

From the album **Something's Goin' On**

For Cliff Richard's first album of original material, ***Something's Goin' On***, for over five years, he commissioned American writers to provide him with a selection of songs. As he had in the mid-sixties, he returned to Nashville to record them and this helped give them an American feel in their execution. *Thousand Miles to Go* was assisted in this respect by the mention of place names and the thrumming rhythm that was reminiscent of many of the classic driving songs.

The staccato guitar introduction reveals what is to come as the percussion joins in and then Cliff's effervescent vocal joins in the mix. The foot-stomping rock and roll song is perfect for Cliff's voice and there is something nostalgic about the performance, stirring memories of some of the work he was recording and performing in the later part of the seventies, while simultaneously creating a fresh sound.

Track Specification

Composed by Brian White, Dennis Matkosky and Steve Mandile

Musicians

Tim Akers	organ
John Howard	bass
Jerry McPherson	electric guitar
Steve Mandile	backing vocals, electric guitar, acoustic guitar
Cliff Richard	vocals, backing vocals
Chuck Tilley	drums, percussion

Recording Details

Producer	Dan Huff and Steve Mandile
Engineered by	Ben Fowler and Steve Mandile
Recording location	Ocean Way, Nashville, Tennessee, USA and Big One Three Studio, Nashville, Tennessee, USA
Recording date	2003-2004

♫ Through the Eye of the Needle

From the album **Love Is Forever**

One of two songs written for Cliff Richard by Burt Bacharach and Hal David to record during his American sessions in the summer of 1964 – the other was ***Everyone Needs Someone to Love*** – *Through the Eye of the Needle* was recorded in the same session in New York. The eighth and final take and edit were used for the mono and stereo recordings but with different mixes for the separate audio channels.

Unusually for a Bacharach and David song, there are very few musical hooks in the song, although the harmonizing female backing vocals in addition to the pizzicato strings accompanying Cliff generate some interest. The lyrics, too, are curious as it talks of elephants and mountains and the eye of the needle, which initially distracts as the memory of the Biblical story referring to camels is brought to mind. However, rather than passing through it, it is more about perception given that these huge objects can be easily viewed through something so small. And so it is with love.

Track Specification

Composed by Burt Bacharach and Hal David

Musicians

Cliff Richard	vocals
Gary Sherman	conductor
Unknown	backing vocals
Unknown	orchestra

Recording Details

Producer	Bob Morgan
Engineered by	Frank Laico
Recording location	Columbia Studios, New York
Recording date	21st August 1964

♫ Throw Down a Line

***47th UK single** and from the album* **Cliff Live in Korea**

Written by Hank Marvin in 1968 with Jimi Hendrix in mind, *Throw Down a Line* was rejected for unknown reasons and then producer Mickie Most picked it up to give to Jeff Beck and Rod Stewart to record. Subsequently recorded by the Jeff Beck Group in March 1969 for the band's album *Beck-ola*, an out-take version was included as a bonus track on the remastered version of the album almost thirty-five years later. In May 1969, Cliff Richard recorded his cover as a duet with Hank Marvin, before Hank took the song further and recorded it with John Farrar and Bruce Welch for the debut eponymous album by Marvin, Welch & Farrar.
Recorded with two other songs at the session but with one temporarily unissued (***No Name, No Fame***), *Throw Down a Line* was issued as a single that was credited to Cliff and Hank, who appears here on guitar and vocals. Backed with ***Reflections***, which was Cliff by himself, the single was released on the Columbia label (catalogue number DB 8615) on 6th September 1969. When it reached the number seven position in the UK singles charts, it became Cliff's highest chart position since his number one, ***Congratulations***, a year and a half before. At the time, Cliff's critics were jumping on the variety of bandwagons to decry his musical deliveries, suggesting that he should stick to what he was good at, although he was also being given a tough time when he did that, too. *Throw Down a Line* was a far darker song than many expected from him and this seemed to be at odds with the expected public image. Nevertheless, the fans and the record-buyers seemed to think it was good enough to push it into the top ten. The single, as per Columbia's policy at the time, was released in mono format, with the stereo version finally released three years later on the hit compilation album ***The Best of Cliff Vol.*** 2.
Throw Down a Line shows Hank (and Cliff by association) trying to shed the by then cosy image of the Shadows and to be seen as a serious writer of music. This was what he tried to achieve with Marvin, Welch & Farrar but found that he was forced to play Shadows standards in concert because of the demands of the fans, thereby detracting from his original purpose.
The drums that introduce this dark song and the lugubrious instrumentation, which include squeaks possibly created by the movement of fingers on the steel guitar strings, immediately make *Throw Down a Line* a completely different prospect from anything that Cliff had recorded. Hank Marvin's guitar is fuzzed and it is a welcome addition to something that is so different from their previous offerings, while Cliff sings the song with appropriate emotion and is joined by uncredited backing solos as well as Hank, who takes a duet role in the final verse and chorus. *Throw Down a Line* ends a little suddenly on an unresolved key in the brass, which merely adds to the darkness and unexpected nature of the ensemble piece.
Since it was a recent single release, it appeared on the set list of the Far East tour that saw the Shadows team back up with Cliff (but only because of the money it has been said by more than one of them). The hugely rare *Cliff Live in Korea* album was recorded at one of the concerts in Seoul in mono only and for the Korean market.

Track Specification
Composed by Hank Marvin

1. Single

Musicians		*Recording Details*	
Hank Marvin	vocals, backing vocals, guitar	Producer	Norrie Paramor
Mike Vickers Orchestra	orchestra	Engineered by	Peter Vince
Cliff Richard	vocals	Recording location	Abbey Road Studio 2, St. John's Wood, London
Unknown	backing vocals	Recording date	2nd May 1969
Mike Vickers	arranger, conductor		

2. *Cliff Live in Korea*

Musicians		*Recording Details*	
Brian Bennett	drums, percussion	Producer	Unknown
Alan Hawkshaw	keyboards	Engineered by	Unknown
Hank Marvin	backing vocals, guitar	Recording location	Citizen Hall, Seoul, South Korea
Cliff Richard	vocals	Recording date	16th October 1969
John Rostill	backing vocals, bass		
Bruce Welch	backing vocals, rhythm guitar		

♫ Till I'm Home Again

From the album **Real as I Wanna Be**

The soulful songs continue as the tenth track on Cliff Richard's ***Real as I Wanna Be*** album, *Till I'm Home Again*, expresses the emotion experienced when away from home and loved ones for lengthy periods. Unusually, the track also features a mouth harp and the pure high-pitched whining created by rubbing a finger around the rim of a crystal glass, which works surprisingly well to underline the meaning of the lyric.
More reliant on the guitar than many of the tracks on the album, it also employs greater use of backing vocals missing elsewhere. Cliff sings the song with emotion, although the melody is not immediately memorable and is only the arrangement and his energy that rescues it from being potentially mediocre.

Track Specification
Composed by Andy Hill and Amy Sky

Musicians		*Recording Details*	
Vinnie Colaiuta	drums, percussion	Producer	Peter Wolf
Matthias Jabbs	guitar	Engineered by	Christian Leitgeb, Chris Heil, Paul Erickson and/or Keith Bessey
Paul Jackson Jr.	guitar		
Cliff Richard	vocals, backing vocals	Recording location	Little America Recording Studios, Weiler, Austria, Ocean Recording Studios, Burbank, California, USA, Arco Recording Studios, Munich, Germany, R. G. Jones Recording Studios, Wimbledon, London, England and/or The Pierce Room, London, England
Michelle Wolf	backing vocals		
Peter Wolf	arranger, bass, keyboards, percussion, mouth harp, wine glasses		
		Recording date	March-April 1996 and November 1997

♫ Till Winter Follows Spring

Unissued track

In early 1969, Tyne Tees Television commissioned a series of six playlets for their religious broadcast slot called *Life with Johnny*, featuring Cliff Richard in the title role with each episode a modernized take on parables told by Jesus in the Bible. Records are unclear on most of the episodes although *Johnny Come Home* and *Johnny Faces Facts* are complete, *Johnny and the Good Samaritan* is partially available, while the remainder are unavailable in either records or film form.

The songs performed had some relevance to the parable being performed and, on average, there were five songs per episode. *Till Winter Follows Spring*, recorded at the Abbey Road studios with a putative album tie-in project in mind that didn't materialize, appeared in one of *Johnny on the Rocks*, *Johnny and the Blind Rage* or *Johnny in Love*. The end credits of the episode stated that all songs were original and written in collaboration between Cliff, the Settlers and the programme's writer David Winter. The instrumentation and performance details are unknown.

Track Specification
Composed by Cliff Richard, David Winter, Cindy Kent, Mike Jones, John Fyffe and Geoffrey Srodzinski

Musicians		*Recording Details*	
John Fyffe	backing vocals, guitar	Producer	Norrie Paramor
Cindy Kent	backing vocals	Engineered by	Peter Vince
Mike Jones	backing vocals, guitar	Recording location	Abbey Road Studio 3, St. John's Wood, London
Cliff Richard	vocals	Recording date	11th January 1969
Geoffrey Srodzinski	backing vocals, bass		

♫ Time

From the album **Sincerely Cliff Richard**

Recorded in September 1966 by Cliff Richard, it wasn't released until three years later when it appeared on the track listing of the album ***Sincerely Cliff Richard***. The first song to be completed at the session, the final (unknown) take and edit were used for both the mono and stereo but with different mixes for the needs of the separate audio channels.

With an almost ecclesiastical backing singing group at the beginning of *Time*, the instrumentation comes in for the second verse. Cliff sings the song with perfection and proves again his capabilities as a singer who can turn his voice to any style or genre, although ballads of this nature are a natural fit for his talents.

Track Specification
Composed by Michael Merchant

Musicians		*Recording Details*	
Bernard Ebbinghouse Orchestra	orchestra	Producer	Norrie Paramor
Bernard Ebbinghouse	arranger, conductor	Engineered by	Peter Vince and Richard Lush
Mike Sammes Singers	backing vocals	Recording location	Abbey Road Studio 2, St. John's Wood, London
Cliff Richard	vocals	Recording date	20th September 1966

♫ Time Drags By

35th UK single *and from the album* **Reunited**

A lot of critics had started to write Cliff Richard off as a major force in rock and pop music by the time the film ***Finders Keepers*** was released. However, proof, if it were needed, that this wasn't the case came in the recording of the only single to be released from the soundtrack, *Time Drags By*. Eschewing the standard approach of recording straight into microphones (on to different tracks on the tape), *Time Drags By* was the first time double tracking was used on a Cliff record. Building up a choir of sound, the vocals and backing vocals were developed by recording different harmonies performed by the quartet of Cliff, Hank Marvin, Bruce Welch and John Rostill, effectively producing a choir of eight voices. The harmonies are quite beautiful and languid and the recording is an example of the beauty created by the blending of those voices that were trademark of the type of song recorded by Cliff and his backing band.

In the film, having found the Hotel Bellamar, where Cliff and the Shadows (playing themselves) are scheduled to play and finding it empty (the town has been cleared because of a dropped unexploded bomb somewhere in the vicinity), they loll about in the foyer becoming increasingly bored before beginning this song. Brian Bennett plays the harmonica (although it's unclear whether this is the case on the soundtrack), while John Rostill plays a tambourine. The performance is deliberately lethargic and languid with Cliff and Hank being dragged along the floor (by Brian and John) on their backs before they all lean their heads on the hotel reception desk culminating in the vocal arpeggio that ends the song and they sink to the floor in a torpor. It is reprised in a later scene when Cliff and the band are incarcerated in the wine cellar at the behest of the American base commander after Cliff had confirmed that he knew where the errant bomb was. In this scene, the band use an out of tune piano (actually a pianola as it is revealed later as the self-playing keys that are triggered by the piano roll shows) ostensibly performed by Brian Bennett as they thump out a percussion with hammers and lumps of wood, to cover the noise as they take it in turns to bang out the bars on the window to effect their escape.

In previous films, different versions of songs were recorded for the film, usually on the sound stage, but the version of *Time Drags By* performed in the hotel foyer is the same as that on the soundtrack with the band (including the non-singing Brian Bennett) lip-synching and miming to the recorded song. The cellar version uses the double-tracked vocal recording from the soundtrack and this is overdubbed on the piano backing (uncredited but possibly either Hank Marvin or Norrie Paramor) but there is no record as to when this was mixed and it has not been issued in any commercial aural format to date. The complex song took just four takes to complete with the final take and edit being used for both the mono and stereo recordings but with different mixes for the separation in the audio channels. *Time Drags By* was released as a single, backed with ***La La La Song*** (also from the soundtrack), on the Columbia label (catalogue number DB 8017) on 7th October 1966 but only in mono. The stereo version was issued a month later on the soundtrack album. The single reached the number ten spot in the UK singles charts and, because of its beauty and complexity, the position was a bit of a disappointment to Cliff at the time who had high hopes of it doing a lot better. It regularly features on hit compilations of Cliff's work and was voted the runner-up to *Born Free* in the Film Song of the Year at the annual Ivor Novello Awards.

The listless nature of the song is superbly brought across in the instrumentation, the uncredited harmonica and the strained vocals. As has already been mentioned, the layers of vocal harmonies were built up and mixed together and, since the perfection of the blend of the four singers' voices works well on other tracks, the choir that is created makes *Times Drags By* something incredibly intimate and aurally pleasant.

This harmonic perfection made it a suitable showcase for the timeless blending of Cliff's, Hank's and Bruce's vocals on the re-recording of the song for the 2009 album ***Reunited***, and became one of the best performances during the concerts on the promotional tour. With the guest appearance of Mark Griffiths playing the harmonica, this song more than any others exemplifies the beauty and clever arrangements of Cliff's harmony vocals blending with Hank's and Bruce's.

Track Specification
Composed by Hank Marvin, Bruce Welch, Brian Bennett and John Rostill

1. Single

Musicians		*Recording Details*	
Brian Bennett	drums, percussion	Producer	Norrie Paramor
Hank Marvin	backing vocals, guitar	Engineered by	Malcolm Addey, Peter Vince and Richard Lush
Cliff Richard	vocals, backing vocals	Recording location	Abbey Road Studio 2, St. John's Wood, London
John Rostill	backing vocals, bass	Recording date	26th April 1966
Unknown	harmonica		
Bruce Welch	backing vocals, rhythm guitar		

2. Reunited

Musicians		*Recording Details*	
Brian Bennett	drums, percussion	Producer	Warren Bennett (co-ordination)
Mark Griffiths	bass, harmonica	Engineered by	James Collins (Honeyhill Studios), Ethan Carlson (Middle Ear Studios), Les Williams (Nivram Studios) and Keith Bessey (mixing and mastering)
Hank Marvin	backing vocals, guitar	Recording location	Middle Ear Studios, Miami, Florida, USA (Cliff's vocals), Nivram Studios, Perth, Western Australia (Hank's guitars and vocals) and Honeyhill Studios, Hertfordshire, England (all other vocals and instruments)
Cliff Richard	vocals, backing vocals	Recording date	Early 2009
Bruce Welch	backing vocals, rhythm guitar		

♫ Time Flies

B-side of **Silvery Rain**

Although *Time Flies* was recorded on the last day of April 1969, it wouldn't be released for another two years until it was picked as the B-side of ***Silvery Rain***. Columbia still insisted on released singles only in mono and that included B-sides. With writer Brian Bennett conducting his own orchestra at the session, *Time Flies* was a rarity until it was released in stereo on ***...And They Said It Wouldn't Last! (My 50 Years in Music)*** in 2008. Unusually, *Silvery Rain* boasted two B-sides (almost making it an EP) with *Time Flies* nestling up against ***Annabella Umbrella***, which was recorded in February 1971.

The opening bars have the same music intervals as ***Visions*** but then *Time Flies* becomes quite a different song. Cliff's vocal is mixed up front in the edit and this creates a cosy atmosphere in the performance. Cliff sings the song with the great purity of his vocal line, while a lovely harmony arrangement is created for the uncredited female backing group.

Track Specification
Composed by Brian Bennett and Mike Hawker

Musicians		*Recording Details*	
Brian Bennett	arranger, conductor	Producer	Norrie Paramor
Brian Bennett Orchestra	orchestra	Engineered by	Peter Vince and Richard Langham
Cliff Richard	vocals	Recording location	Abbey Road Studio 2, St. John's Wood, London
Unknown	backing vocals	Recording date	30th April 1969

♫ Time in Between, The

31st UK single

Based on a French song that was written by Georges Aber, Micky Jones and Thomas Brown provided the English lyrics for Cliff Richard and the Shadows to record. One of six songs that the band attempted at the double session on the 10th May 1965 at the Lisbon studios in Portugal, the final take and edit was used for both the mono and stereo recordings but with different mixes catering for the needs of the separate audio channels. Initially, the song was only issued in mono format, as was the policy for Columbia's singles (and more often than not, the EPs) at the time, as the A-side and also on the track listing of the ***Wind Me Up*** EP. The stereo version was eventually released three years later on the compilation ***The Best of Cliff***.

Backed with ***Look Before You Love***, which was also recorded at the same dual sessions, the single was released on the Columbia label (catalogue number DB 7660) on 13th August 1965 but only reached the number twenty-two position in the UK singles chart. This particularly surprised Cliff because he thought it was a great single, although he admitted that the record-buying public knew what they wanted and commerce would be the arbiter of taste. In fact, at that point, it was his worst chart placing in the UK since he started making records seven years previously and this gave the critics some fodder they wanted in order to 'prove' that Cliff's career was on the wane in the face of the huge opposition created by the Beatles and Merseybeat tunes in general. However, this was rectified by the release of ***Wind Me Up (Let Me Go)***, which reached a healthier number two position.

With a bossa nova rhythm and a strong vocal harmony by the three singing Shadows, there is also a synthesized piano brought into the recording. Although the performance is polished and highly competent, it isn't the strongest of songs and is unsurprising that it didn't chart as well as had been hoped by Cliff.

A year later in 1966, a version translated into German was recorded and overdubbed on the original backing track. ***Was Ist Dabei?*** was released as the B-side of ***Du Bist Mein Erster Gedanke*** in the summer but only in mono format. Subsequently, some thirty or so years later, the stereo versions of both were issued on the compilation ***On the Continent***.

Track Specification
Composed by Georges Aber, Micky Jones and Thomas Brown

Musicians		*Recording Details*	
Brian Bennett	drums, percussion	Producer	Norrie Paramor
Hank Marvin	backing vocals, guitar	Engineered by	Unknown
Cliff Richard	vocals	Recording location	Estudios Valentim de Carvalho, Lisbon, Portugal
John Rostill	backing vocals, bass	Recording date	10th May 1965
Unknown	synthesized piano		
Bruce Welch	backing vocals, rhythm guitar		

♫ Tiny Planet

From the album **It's a Small World**

Although the self-penned Cliff Richard song *Tiny Planet* was initially unreleased, it was included on the track listing of the Myrrh vinyl album, ***It's a Small World***, the year after it was recorded. There is scant information on the musicians involved and these are highlighted as unknown on the track specification. The track listing of the album indicates that it was from the film for the Tear Fund charity film, *It's a Small World*. While this is true, it is the same recording from the session rather than a new one created for the film.

The quirky rhythm created on the percussion leads into this quite starkly arranged song. Cliff performs his own backing vocals, which are often presented on the off-beat. The foot-tapping nature of the song belies the message of compassion but also imbues it with a level of optimism. The guitar fires up in the mid-section as the song builds into an almost party-like atmosphere with whistles and shouts. The lyrics make reference to a small world, the title of the song that follows it on the track listing.

Track Specification
Composed by Cliff Richard

Musicians		*Recording Details*	
John Clark	guitar	Producer	Cliff Richard and Craig Pruess
Mark Griffiths	bass	Engineered by	Keith Bessey
Graham Jarvis	drums, percussion	Recording location	Gallery Studios, Chertsey, Surrey
Craig Pruess	keyboards, programming	Recording date	24th June 1984
Cliff Richard	vocals, backing vocals		
Unknown	whistles		

♫ To a Friend

Single by **Aleksander Mežek**

In 1989, Cliff Richard recorded two tracks in the Slovenian language with old friend Aleksander Mežek for his album, *Podarjeno Srcu*: ***Vodna Pot*** and ***Prijatelju***. Just before Cliff went back into the studios to record his first number one of the nineties, ***Saviour's Day***, the month earlier he was working with Mežek on a couple of updated tracks that were released on Mežek's album *Presented to a Heart*. Mežek had reverted to his original surname having worked under the stage name of Aleksander John (his middle name) for the initial years in music, under which moniker he had first recorded with Cliff on his 1974 album *Days Go By* and later on tracks for Cliff's own albums.

Backed with ***Strong Is the Current*** (the English version of *Vodna Pot*), *To a Friend* (the English version of *Prijatelju*) was issued as a single on the Mercury label (catalogue number 878 737-7) in June 1991 but in Germany only. Two other formats were also issued: the twelve-inch (catalogue number 878 737-1) and CD (878 737-2). But it would take another eight years before the album was reissued on CD, but then only in Slovenia.

A very different arrangement to the Slovenian original, the principal vocal is started by Mežek accompanied by a synthesiser passage and strong rhythm created in the drums, percussion and bass line, with a beautiful string arrangement in the orchestra as Cliff's vocal comes in. As with much of his recent work, Cliff also provides the backing vocals for the choruses. Cliff sings with passion and clearly enjoys singing with Mežek.

Track Specification

Composed by Aleksander Mežek and Eugenija Dumbatze

Musicians

Ian Baironson	electric guitar
Paul Buckmaster	arranger, conductor
Richard Cottle	synthesiser
Jonathan Du Bose	electric guitar
Bill Elliott	acoustic guitar
London Symphony Orchestra	orchestra
Aleksander Mežek	vocals
Davy Paton	bass
Cliff Richard	vocals
Jeremy Stacy	drums, percussion
Rick Wakeman	keyboards
Saša Zalepugin	acoustic guitar

Recording Details

Producer	Aleksander Mežek and Rick Wakeman
Engineered by	Ben Robbins
Recording location	R. G. Jones Studios, Wimbledon, London
Recording date	June 1990

♫ Todo el Poder a los Amigos

Spanish single

Within days of confirming that the British public wanted ***Power to All Our Friends*** to be the song to represent the UK at the 1973 Eurovision Song Contest by an overwhelming margin, Cliff Richard returned to the studios for his first sessions of 1973 to record the song translated for the German, French and Spanish markets (although curiously not the Italian). At the second session, the French and Spanish versions were recorded with Cliff overdubbing his new vocals and the updated harmonies on the backing track created for the original English recording made in December 1972.

Todo el Poder a los Amigos – literally *All the Power to the Friends* – was released as a single, backed with the untranslated ***Come Back Billie Jo*** (in common with all versions), which had come a distant second in the public's affection. Issued on the EMI label (catalogue number 1J 006-05340) in April 1973 shortly after the contest was over, the song in either Spanish or English failed to register in the Spanish charts. It was eventually included on the track listing of the compendium of Cliff's foreign language recordings, ***On the Continent***, in 1997.

As with the German and French versions, it is clear that Cliff provides some of his own backing harmonies, while the other voices are assumed to be by the original band. As would be expected, the drama between the quiet verses and the thumping choruses are reiterated in the different languages.

Track Specification

Composed by Guy Fletcher and Doug Flett; French lyrics by Belgrano

Musicians

Terry Britten	backing vocals, guitar
David MacKay Orchestra	orchestra
David MacKay	backing vocals, arranger, conductor
Kevin Peek	guitar
Cliff Richard	vocals, backing vocals
Trevor Spencer	backing vocals, drums, percussion
Alan Tarney	backing vocals, bass

Recording Details

Producer	David MacKay (backing track and vocals)
Engineered by	Peter Vince (backing track and vocals)
Recording location	Abbey Road Studio (backing track) and Abbey Road Studio 3 (vocals), St. John's Wood, London
Recording date	28th December 1972 (backing track) and 23rd March 1973 (vocals)

♫ Tomorrow Rising

60th UK single *(double A-side)*

Over a number of Saturday nights at the beginning of 1973, Cliff Richard appeared on the *Cilla* show to sing each of the shortlisted six contenders for the Song for Europe for the UK entry into that year's Eurovision Song Contest, after which it was opened up to the public postal vote. *Tomorrow Rising*, co-written by Shadows drummer Brian Bennett, was the third

to be performed but it came fourth, polling just 9% of the votes (against the 51.8% of the winner, ***Power to All Our Friends***) just behind ***Help It Along*** (10.5%) and ahead of ***The Days of Love*** (7.6%).
Tomorrow Rising was recorded along with the other five candidates during a two-day session at the end of December 1972, with this song being the last one completed at the second of the sessions that also yielded *Help It Along* and *Power to All Our Friends.*
It was customary for the winner and second-placed song to be combined and released as a single, with the remaining songs issued as an EP; however, in 1973 EMI decided to be different, with *Help It Along* and *Tomorrow Rising* being released as a joint literal double A-side. Backed with both *The Days of Love* and ***Ashes to Ashes*** (the fifth and sixth placed songs), *Help It Along* and *Tomorrow Rising* were released as a single on the EMI label (catalogue number EMI 2022) on 27th April 1973 and they reached a high of number twenty-nine in the first week of chart entry. It was a significant rarity as a track until it was re-released as part of the collection of hits ***The Singles Collection*** in 2002.
Blaring saxophones and quiet orchestration ushers in Cliff's lead vocal. There is a slide guitar effect performed underneath the first verse, while the melodramatic juxtaposition of the chorus against the gentleness of the verses gives the right light and shade for a Eurovision contender but, in spite of that and the pleasant melody, it doesn't quite have the same cachet as the winning entry.

Track Specification
Composed by Mike Hawker and Brian Bennett

Musicians		*Recording Details*	
Terry Britten	backing vocals, guitar	Producer	David MacKay
David MacKay Orchestra	orchestra	Engineered by	Peter Vince
David MacKay	backing vocals, arranger, conductor	Recording location	Abbey Road Studio, St. John's Wood, London
Kevin Peek	guitar	Recording date	28th December 1972
Cliff Richard	vocals		
Trevor Spencer	backing vocals, drums, percussion		
Alan Tarney	backing vocals, bass		

♫ Too Beautiful to Cry
Single by **Craig Pruess**

Craig Pruess worked on Cliff Richard's album ***Now You See Me... Now You Don't*** in 1981 as co-producer and keyboardist as well as his musical director. Cliff returned the favour the following year when he supplied backing vocals to Pruess's single *Too Beautiful to Cry* but not its B-side. Backed with *You Are the One, Too Beautiful to Cry* was issued as a single on the EMI label (catalogue number EMI 5338) in 1982 but didn't register in the charts.

Track Specification
Composed by Catherine Courage

Musicians		*Recording Details*	
Craig Pruess	arranger, vocals, synthesisers	Producer	Craig Pruess and Keith Bessey
Cliff Richard	backing vocals	Engineered by	Keith Bessey
		Recording location	Abbey Road Studios, St. John's Wood, London
		Recording date	1982

♫ Too Close to Heaven
B-side of **Please Don't Fall in Love**

Although ***Please Don't Fall in Love*** was included on the track listing of Cliff Richard's twenty-fifth anniversary album ***Silver*** in 1983, as was common with Cliff's singles, the B-side only appeared in the single format, until it was included as a bonus track on the 2002 remaster of the album. With Mike Batt in the producer's chair, his *Too Close to Heaven* was recorded at a suite of sessions that produced the A-side and a hitherto unissued track, which was a song from the stage musical *Camelot*, ***How to Handle a Woman***.
A single guitar and violin introduce the song. As Cliff sings the first verse, the remainder of the instruments are brought in which is supported by the orchestra that also performed on *Please Don't Fall in Love*. Meanwhile, Cliff supplies his own backing vocals alongside Batt. The song is pretty enough but it feels as if it is trying too hard and becomes bombastic rather than highly effective. Nevertheless, it is strong enough for it to be worthy addition to Cliff's oeuvre and still deserves a wider distribution than being limited to a B-side.

Track Specification
Composed by Mike Batt

Musicians		*Recording Details*	
Mike Batt	arranger, conductor, backing vocals, keyboards	Producer	Mike Batt
Tony Carr	percussion	Engineered by	Steve Churchyard (main track) and Dick Lewsey (strings)
Ray Cooper	percussion	Recording location	AIR Studio 2, London (main track) and C.T.S. Wembley (strings)
Graham Jarvis	drums, percussion	Recording date	21st-23rd March 1983 (main track) and 21st March (strings)
Frank McDonald	bass		
Alan Park	guitar		

Cliff Richard	vocals
Ray Russell	guitar
Unknown:	orchestra
Clive Anstee	'cello
Howard Ball	violin
Michael Brittain	double bass
Michael Cookson	viola
Paul Frowde	violin
Barry Griffiths	violin
Pat Halling	violin
Maurice Isaacs	violin
Raymond Keenlyside	violin
Paul Kegg	'cello
Tom Kelly	clarinet
Laurie Lewis	violin
Geoff Palmer	violin
Anthony Pleeth	'cello
David Randall	violin
Ian Rhodes	violin
Eddie Roberts	violin
John Ronayne	violin
Basil Smart	violin
Jonathan Snowdon	flute
Derek Solomans	violin
Michael Winfield	oboe

♫ Too Late to Say Goodbye

Unissued track

Attempted at the first session for the album ***Every Face Tells a Story***, Cliff Richard tried four takes before the song was abandoned, none of which takes has been issued. The full band details are included here from both sessions.

Track Specification

Composed by David Scott

Musicians

Brian Bennett	drums, percussion
Terry Britten	guitar
Richard Hewson	arranger, conductor
John Perry	backing vocals
Cliff Richard	vocals
Frank Ricotti	percussion
Tony Rivers	backing vocals
Alan Tarney	bass
Graham Todd	keyboards
Unknown	orchestra

Recording Details

Producer	Bruce Welch
Engineered by	Tony Clark and John Barrett
Recording location	Abbey Road Studio 2, St. John's Wood, London
Recording date	6th September 1976

♫ Too Much

From the albums **Cliff** *and* **World Tour Live**

Another Elvis Presley track, *Too Much* was a major hit in the US, reaching number two in the Billboard charts while getting to number six in the UK in 1959. Since then, it has been covered by numerous artists, including contemporaneous stars such as Billy Fury, and later acts such as Robert Gordon, Bernard Hardison and Wanda Jackson. It was a then added to the set list for the 'live' recording or the album ***Cliff*** over two days at Abbey Road studios in front of a selected audience. The track was incorporated on the second Cliff and the Drifters EP, ***Cliff No. 2***.

Once again, Cliff's vocals are assured, while the Drifters' instrumental backing maintains the great ensemble that would be one of the key attractions to the band. The screaming of the girls sometimes threatens to overwhelm and, fifty-and-more years on, what might have seemed a fresh exercise in recording techniques now seems a little pointless.

In 2003, in the set list of the world tour, Cliff sang the ***Elvis Medley*** in which *Too Much* featured along with ***Don't Be Cruel***. The New Zealand show was filmed for DVD release while, in 2004, the complementary *World Tour Live* CD album featured just fourteen of the tracks, which included the medley. The song is performed in a bouncy rhythm with bass and baritone backing vocals and is a Cliff song rather than one of Presley's.

Track Specification

Composed by Lee Rosenberg and Bernard Weinman

1. Cliff

Musicians

Jet Harris	bass
Hank Marvin	guitar
Tony Meehan	drums, percussion
Cliff Richard	vocals
Bruce Welch	rhythm guitar

Recording Details

Producer	Norrie Paramor
Engineered by	Peter Bown and Stuart Eltham
Recording location	Abbey Road Studio 2, St. John's Wood, London
Recording date	10th February 1959

2. World Tour Live

Musicians

Anthony Clark	backing vocals, guitar
John Clark	guitar
Dave Cooke	keyboards
Mike Haughton	saxophone
Peter Howarth	backing vocals
Pete May	drums, percussion
Mick Mullins	backing vocals
Keith Murrell	backing vocals
Alan Park	keyboards
Cliff Richard	vocals, guitar
Steve Stroud	bass

Recording Details

Producer	Keith Bessey
Engineered by	Keith Bessey
Recording location	The Mission Winery, Napier, New Zealand
Recording date	22nd February 2003

♫ To Prove My Love for You

From the album **21 Today**

The third of six songs to be recorded in the late January 1961 session, six takes were attempted for *To Prove My Love for You*. The final take was used for the mono and stereo edits with different mixes for the respective audio channels.

Using a guitar alongside the orchestra and the slightly overbearing backing singers, Cliff sings as assuredly as he does on any of the other tracks on the album. The song is technically difficult to perform but Cliff manages the trick of making even the most complex music seem easy.

Track Specification

Composed by Don Wolf and Ben Raleigh

Musicians

Mike Sammes Singers	backing vocals
Norrie Paramor Orchestra	orchestra
Norrie Paramor	arranger, conductor
Cliff Richard	vocals

Recording Details

Producer	Norrie Paramor
Engineered by	Malcolm Addey
Recording location	Abbey Road Studio 2, St. John's Wood, London
Recording date	30th January 1961

♫ To the Sun

Single by **Pat Carroll**

Written by Alan Tarney and Trevor Spencer, who had also provided several tracks for Cliff Richard, *To the Sun* was recorded as a single by Pat Carroll, who was married to John Farrar and who had been a backing singer with Olivia Newton-John on Cliff's 1972 tour. Backed with *Out of My Mind*, the song was released on the Pye label (catalogue number 7N.25592) in August 1972 but made no impression on the charts. It was later became the B-side of Pat Carroll's final single in 1974, *Curly-Headed Rooster*, in Australia only. There is scant information on the recording but it is quite likely to include Farrar in the mix; in addition to Cliff's backing vocals, it is the first time that David MacKay had worked with Cliff.

Track Specification

Composed by Alan Tarney and Trevor Spencer

Musicians

Pat Carroll	vocals
Cliff Richard	backing vocals
Trevor Spencer	backing vocals, drums, percussion
Alan Tarney	backing vocals, bass
Unknown	other instrumentation

Recording Details

Producer	David MacKay
Engineered by	Unknown
Recording location	Abbey Road Studio 2, St. John's Wood, London
Recording date	mid-1972

♫ Touch of Your Lips, The

From the album **Cliff Sings**

The final track of the first side of ***Cliff Sings*** was a ballad made famous by writer Ray Noble and has since become standard in the repertoire of balladeers and crooners, with Nana Mouskouri, Chet Baker, Nelson Riddle, Oscar Peterson, Tony Bennett, Nat King Cole, Andy Williams and Ted Heath adding their own interpretations. The choice of the song was designed to show Cliff's performance versatility, thereby eschewing the by now familiar backing of the Drifters.

Cliff's interpretation of the song relies on swelling strings and plinking double bass and harps to support his simple and easy vocal style. The song is technically a difficult one to pitch as it runs into the lower and upper register of his voice but Cliff carries it off with aplomb. The same take of the track was used but with a different mix for the mono (on the album and the ***Cliff Sings No. 3*** EP) and stereo (stereo version of the EP) releases.

Track Specification

Composed by Ray Noble

Musicians

Norrie Paramor Orchestra	orchestra
Norrie Paramor	arranger, conductor
Cliff Richard	vocals

Recording Details

Producer	Norrie Paramor
Engineered by	Malcolm Addey and Alan Kane (mono) and Stuart Eltham and Norman Smith (stereo)
Recording location	Abbey Road Studio 2, St. John's Wood, London
Recording date	10th September 1959

♫ Tough Enough

From the album **21 Today**

Cliff Richard and the Drifters regularly chose Johnny Otis songs to perform, the most famous and popular being ***Willie and the Hand-Jive***, and they selected *Tough Enough* for the track listing of Cliff's birthday celebration album, ***21 Today***.
Of the four takes recorded of this song at the late January session, the final one was used for the stereo and mono edits, although different audio mixes were applied for the channels. The song was included on the track listing of the ***Cliff Richard No. 1*** EP.
A great showcase for Hank Marvin's rocking guitar and Cliff's rock and roll vocals, the song fairly drives along in spite of being a relatively slow tempo. A few key changes are employed, while Jet Harris's thumping bass line helps move the song inexorably towards its conclusion.

Track Specification
Composed by Johnny Otis

Musicians

Jerry Furst	bongos
Jet Harris	bass
Hank Marvin	guitar
Tony Meehan	drums, percussion
Cliff Richard	vocals
Bruce Welch	rhythm guitar

Recording Details

Producer	Norrie Paramor
Engineered by	Malcolm Addey
Recording location	Abbey Road Studio 2, St. John's Wood, London
Recording date	28th January 1961

♫ Travellin' Light

6th UK single *and from the albums* **The 31st of February Street, Japan Tour '74** *and* **Reunited**

After the stupendous success of ***Living Doll***, which helped transition Cliff Richard and the Drifters into a more popular music and mainstream genre, the band decided to follow it up with another slow ballad entitled *Travellin' Light*. This single also marks the first time that the new name for the Drifters – the Shadows – was used on an official British release. During the publicity tour of the US for *Living Doll*, it was obvious that there was some confusion about the use of the Drifters moniker since there was already the black soul band recording under that name and having global hits. Jet Harris first suggested the name of the Shadows and it stuck. *Travellin' Light* was written by Sid Tepper and Roy Bennett, who would go on to be instrumental in several of Cliff's hits in the early sixties.
Travellin' Light was released on the Columbia label (catalogue numbers DB 4351 (78 r.p.m. format) and 45-DB 4351 (seven-inch single format)) on 9th October 1959. Like its predecessor, it hit the top of the UK charts, where it stayed for five weeks, cementing Cliff Richard and the newly-born Shadows entertainment status, for now he had proven himself to be able to cover not just rock and roll material but strong ballads as well (in spite of the lyrics to the chorus of ***Move It***!). The B-side, ***Dynamite***, was listed as a separate song for chart compilation reasons and it separately reached number sixteen.
The song is about a man on his way to see his sweetheart, travelling without money and without many possessions to his name. The chief hook, apart from Hank Marvin's guitar is the slow vocal glissando on the end of each of the phrases, giving the song a weary but paradoxically energetic edge. It has been noted that there is some music-sheet shuffling going on, in addition to him opening his mouth, during the guitar introduction, which is Cliff preparing for the first verse.
For the 1974 album, ***The 31st of February Street***, Cliff re-recorded *Travellin' Light* with a different arrangement to fit in with the concept of leaving home and being away and the emotions homesickness induces. It was recorded in eleven takes in a long session for the album in the middle of February 1974. The frenzied string introduction is reminiscent of the Beatles' *Eleanor Rigby*, which gives way to the vocals by Cliff. The accompaniment is odd to anyone familiar with the original song since it sounds so very different and, as a consequence, out of place; however, the listener should persevere because it is the very clever, sparse accompaniment that exemplifies the emotion of being away and coming home again. It was inevitable that this arrangement would be used on his tour in 1974 and it appears on ***Japan Tour '74*** album and takes the audience some time to realize what it is that he is singing.
When Cliff was organizing his tour of 2009, having completed fifty successful years in the music business the previous year, it was mooted that the Shadows should join him, which spawned the album, ***Reunited***, featuring a number of re-recorded songs from their early days together in the fifties and sixties and the track listing included *Travellin' Light*. The recording techniques have obviously improved so the performance sounds crisper. The other point to note is the exquisite backing vocal harmonisation in this version at the introduction.

Track Specification
Composed by Sid Tepper and Roy Bennett

1. Single
Musicians

Jet Harris	bass
Hank Marvin	guitar
Tony Meehan	drums, percussion
Cliff Richard	vocals
Bruce Welch	rhythm guitar

Recording Details

Producer	Norrie Paramor
Engineered by	Peter Bown and Stuart Eltham
Recording location	Abbey Road Studio 2, St. John's Wood, London
Recording date	25th July 1959

2. *The 31st of February Street*

Musicians		*Recording Details*	
Barrie Guard	arranger, conductor	Producer	David MacKay
Cliff Hall	keyboards	Engineered by	Tony Clark and Mike Jarrett
Cliff Richard	vocals	Recording location	Abbey Road Studio 2, St. John's Wood, London
Alan Tarney	bass	Recording date	12th February 1974
Unknown	orchestra		

3. *Japan Tour '74*

Musicians		*Recording Details*	
Barrie Guard	arranger, conductor	Producer	Toshiba EMI (no individual detailed)
Brian Lewis	guitar	Engineered by	Toshiba EMI (no individual Detailed)
Cliff Richard	vocals	Recording location	Shinjuku Koseinenkin, Tokyo, Japan
Shambles Symphonet	orchestra	Recording date	7th-8th October 1974
Alan Tarney	bass		

4. *Reunited*

Musicians		*Recording Details*	
Brian Bennett	drums, percussion	Producer	Warren Bennett (co-ordination)
Mark Griffiths	bass	Engineered by	James Collins (Honeyhill Studios), Ethan Carlson (Middle Ear Studios), Les Williams (Nivram Studios) and Keith Bessey (mixing and mastering)
Hank Marvin	backing vocals, guitar		
Nunzio Mondia	accordion		
Cliff Richard	vocals, backing vocals		
Bruce Welch	backing vocals, rhythm guitar	Recording location	Middle Ear Studios, Miami, Florida, USA (Cliff's vocals), Nivram Studios, Perth, Western Australia (Hank's guitars and vocals) and Honeyhill Studios, Hertfordshire, England (all other vocals and instruments)
		Recording date	Early 2009

♫ Treasure of Love

From the album **Dressed for the Occasion**

Originally a hit for Clyde McPhatter (of the American Drifters fame) as his only solo UK single, when he reached number twenty-seven in the summer of 1956, *Treasure of Love* has been covered by a number of artists including Johnny Burnette, Pat Boone, Tommy Steele, George Jones and B. J. Thomas.

Cliff Richard used to perform songs he liked to sing but had not recorded (and often would never would) in a studio and *Treasure of Love* was one such that was part of the Royal Albert Hall concert from 1982 that was recorded and issued as the album ***Dressed for the Occasion***.

The performance of the song is dominated by pizzicato orchestral strings and the backing vocal harmonies, running underneath the gentleness of Cliff's vocal line. The pace is kept up by the bass and the drums but its strength is drawn from the vocal performances.

Track Specification

Composed by Joe Shapiro and Lou Stallman

Musicians		*Recording Details*	
Stuart Calver	backing vocals	Producer	Cliff Richard and Richard Hewson
Tony Harding	backing vocals	Engineered by	John Kurlander
Richard Hewson	arranger, conductor	Mixed by	Keith Bessey
Graham Jarvis	drums, percussion	Recording location	Royal Albert Hall, London
London Philharmonic Orchestra	orchestra	Mixed at	Strawberry Studios South, Surrey
John Perry	backing vocals	Recording date	23rd November 1982
Cliff Richard	vocals		
Tony Rivers	backing vocals		

♫ Trial of Jesus, His Execution and Death, The

From the album **About that Man**

The penultimate reading on Cliff Richard's religious album, ***About That Man***, tells the story of Pontius Pilate's trial of Jesus Christ, Christ's crucifixion and ultimate death. It comes from the book of Luke, chapter 22, verses 66 to 71, the book of John, chapter 18, verse 28 to chapter 19, verse 19 and the book of Luke, chapter 23, verses 39 to 46 and 56. Cliff's erudition and passionate belief elevate the reading of the tracts from the Bible and the track was probably recorded in one complete and continuous take since Cliff's rhythm and enunciation appear unimpeded.

Track Specification

From the King James Bible

Musicians		*Recording Details*	
Cliff Richard	vocals	Producer	Norrie Paramor
		Engineered by	Richard Lush
		Recording location	Abbey Road Studio 2, St. John's Wood, London
		Recording date	20th February 1970

♫ Tribute to the Legends Medley

CD B-side of **All I Have to Do Is Dream/Miss You Nights**

In 1981, the BBC produced a documentary about Cliff Richard. Part of the broadcast was planned to include footage from concerts at the Hammersmith Odeon in London and the Manchester Apollo. Some tracks were released at the time, which resulted in the top five single ***Daddy's Home*** and its B-side, while the remainder of the dozen or so tracks remained unissued. In 1994, Cliff oversaw the remixing of a set of tracks that featured Phil Everly in duet with him from the same concert. One, ***All I Have to Do Is Dream*** was issued as a double A-side with a remixed version of the original ***Miss You Nights*** single. The vinyl seven-inch only had these two tracks, while the CD release consisted of two CDs issued over the space of a week; the first included two more tracks with Everly, ***When Will I Be Loved?*** and *Tribute to the Legends Medley*, which featured genuflection towards the following famous rock and roll songs by Elvis Presley, Bill Haley, Little Richard, Jerry Lee Lewis and even himself:

a) ***Blue Suede Shoes***
b) ***Great Balls of Fire***
c) ***Lucille***
d) ***Long Tall Sally***
e) ***Rip It Up***
f) ***Gee Whiz It's You***

The entries for those songs carry the information on the recording details and musicians.

♫ True Love Ways

87th UK single

Recorded by Buddy Holly four months before his untimely death, *True Love Ways* was released posthumously as a single and it reached number one in the US charts and number twenty-five in the UK. It has been covered a number of times with three versions charting: first, Peter and Gordon took it to number two in spring 1965; next was Cliff Richard's version; and then David Essex recorded a duet with actress Catherine Zeta-Jones, which made number thirty-eight in December 1994. In addition, it has been recorded by a wide variety of artists, including the Shadows, Elvis Costello, Mickey Gilley, Rick Nelson, Tommy Cash, Alan Price and Bobby Vee among several others.

Cliff recorded his version at the 1982 concert at the Royal Albert Hall in London with the backing of the London Philharmonic Orchestra. It was one of the small list of songs that he had never recorded in the studio (and never has to date). Backed with ***Galadriel (Spirit of Starlight)***, which was also performed at the concert, *True Love Ways* was issued as a single on the EMI label (catalogue number EMI 5385) on 8th April 1983 and went on to reach number eight in the UK chart. Included on the ***Private Collection*** album, it was added as a B-side item to the release of ***Mistletoe and Wine*** and later as a bonus track on the second of the dual CD single release of ***All I Have to Do Is Dream*** in 1994.

The arrangement by Richard Hewson is perfect for an orchestral accompaniment, while Cliff carries off his version of the Holly classic with considered confidence. While many of the tracks that appear on the ***Dressed for the Occasion*** album feature both the orchestra and rock band, it is principally the orchestra that is in evidence on *True Love Ways* in addition to the backing vocals which adds a frisson of extra interest in proceedings.

Track Specification

Composed by Norman Petty and Buddy Holly

Musicians

Stuart Calver	backing vocals
Tony Harding	backing vocals
Richard Hewson	arranger, conductor
Graham Jarvis	drums, percussion
London Philharmonic Orchestra	orchestra
John Perry	backing vocals
Cliff Richard	vocals
Tony Rivers	backing vocals

Recording Details

Producer	Cliff Richard and Richard Hewson
Engineered by	John Kurlander
Mixed by	Keith Bessey
Recording location	Royal Albert Hall, London
Mixed at	Strawberry Studios South, Surrey
Recording date	23rd November 1982

♫ True Love Will Come to You

From the album **Listen to Cliff!** *(mono and stereo versions)*

The first of five original tracks from the ***Listen to Cliff!*** album, *True Love Will Come to You* was written by Shadows guitarist Bruce Welch and former Chesternuts bandmate Pete Chester. The stereo and mono versions are two separate takes (of the six recorded, it is unclear which was used). The mono version features an extended instrumental middle eight that is twice the length of the stereo. The song was also issued on the accompanying ***Listen to Cliff! No. 1*** EP. Both versions have since been released on CD (the stereo on the CD issue of the main album, the mono on ***The Rock 'n' Roll Years 1958-1963***).

Following on from ***Blue Moon***, *True Love Will Come to You* offers a lift in mood. The guitar arpeggios and staccato rendition on the lead guitar counterpointing the main melody, the optimism is perfectly expressed in this song of advice to a person who feels they have lost out in love. The now familiar guitar solo in the middle eight bridge is expertly handled, while the overall composition and the arrangement further confirm Bruce Welch's ability to find or define a brilliantly catchy tune.

Track Specification
Composed by Peter Chester and Bruce Welch

<u>1. Listen to Cliff! (mono version)</u>

Musicians	
Jet Harris	bass
Hank Marvin	guitar
Tony Meehan	drums, percussion
Cliff Richard	vocals
Bruce Welch	rhythm guitar

Recording Details	
Producer	Norrie Paramor
Engineered by	Malcolm Addey
Recording location	Abbey Road Studio 2, St. John's Wood, London
Recording date	13th October 1960

<u>2. Listen to Cliff! (stereo version)</u>

Musicians	
Jet Harris	bass
Hank Marvin	guitar
Tony Meehan	drums, percussion
Cliff Richard	vocals
Bruce Welch	rhythm guitar

Recording Details	
Producer	Norrie Paramor
Engineered by	Malcolm Addey
Recording location	Abbey Road Studio 2, St. John's Wood, London
Recording date	13th October 1960

♫ True, True Lovin'

B-side of **Constantly** *(except Italy)*

Recorded at the first session in 1964 for Cliff Richard and the Shadows, *True, True Lovin'* is another Bruce Welch penned pacey song. Only ever released in mono format, it was chosen as the B-side of the single ***Constantly*** in all territories except Italy, which used *I Only Know I Love You*, for an unknown reason other than it is another Italian tune with translated English lyrics. The first of two songs to be recorded at the session (the other track, ***Just a Little Bit Too Late,*** remains unissued, although it was retried at a session in April the following year and became the B-side of ***On My Word***), *True, True Lovin'* was also released on the ***A Forever Kind of Love*** EP and remained a rarity until it was included on the French compilation album *I Could Easily Fall* in 2001 and then in 2008 in the celebratory boxed set ***...And They Said It Wouldn't Last! (My 50 Years in Music)***. The liner notes on that latter issue for this track state that the A-side peaked at number three in the UK charts – however, the *Guinness Book of British Hit Singles* confirms this to be incorrect, since *Constantly* only reached the number four slot.

With a piano glissando, uncredited but likely to be Norrie Paramor, running down the keyboard, the crashing guitar, bass and drums come in with the brilliant harmonies provided by the melding of Cliff's, Hank Marvin's, Bruce Welch's and John Rostill's voices producing the classic sound from the era. The foot-tapping upbeat song is a love song that ends on an unresolved minor chord.

Track Specification
Composed by Bruce Welch

Musicians	
Brian Bennett	drums, percussion
Hank Marvin	backing vocals, guitar
Cliff Richard	vocals
John Rostill	backing vocals, bass
Unknown	piano
Bruce Welch	backing vocals, rhythm guitar

Recording Details	
Producer	Norrie Paramor
Engineered by	Malcolm Addey
Recording location	Abbey Road Studio 2, St. John's Wood, London
Recording date	26th March 1964

♫ Try a Smile

From the album **Every Face Tells a Story**

Written by John Perry, who was one of Cliff Richard's backing vocalists, *Try a Smile* was recorded at the first session for the ***Every Face Tells a Story*** album in September 1976 and completed in three takes, although vocal overdubs were added at a later session a week later.

After the exuberance of the album's title track, the gentleness of the piano introduction and Cliff's vocals with an added slight echo make a stark contrast. The shift through the sometimes unexpected keys instils the song with further drama and enjoment. The backing vocal harmonies provide another point of listening interest and are a mark of the production by Bruce Welch of the period.

Track Specification
Composed by John Perry

Musicians	
Brian Bennett	drums, percussion
Terry Britten	guitar
John Perry	backing vocals
Cliff Richard	vocals
Frank Ricotti	percussion
Tony Rivers	backing vocals
Alan Tarney	bass
Graham Todd	keyboards

Recording Details	
Producer	Bruce Welch
Engineered by	Tony Clark and John Barrett
Recording location	Abbey Road Studio 2, St. John's Wood, London
Recording date	6th and 14th September 1976

♫ Turn Around

From the album **32 Minutes and 17 Seconds with Cliff Richard**

The second of three contributions by the stalwart writing team of Sid Tepper and Roy Bennett for the ***32 Minutes and 17 Seconds with Cliff Richard*** album, *Turn Around* was the first song to be recorded in 1962. The mono and stereo edits use the same take (the eighth and final one) but apply different mixes for the requirements of the audio channels.

A gentle melody that is subtly complex with its muted horn and arpeggiated orchestral accompaniment, *Turn Around* is another Cliff Richard original that underlines his perfect pitch and singing capabilities. The Mike Sammes Singers provide the backing vocals and they are edited quite far back in the mix so as not to overwhelm the performance.

Track Specification

Composed by Sid Tepper and Roy C. Bennett

Musicians

Mike Sammes Singers	backing vocals
Norrie Paramor Orchestra	orchestra
Norrie Paramor	arranger, conductor
Cliff Richard	vocals

Recording Details

Producer	Norrie Paramor
Engineered by	Malcolm Addey
Recording location	Abbey Road Studio 2, St. John's Wood, London
Recording date	18th January 1962

♫ Turn It into Cash

Unissued track

The second song from the *Johnny Come Home* episode in the Tyne Tees Television series *Life with Johnny*, sets the scene for the modern-day setting of the prodigal son parable, with Cliff Richard playing the title role of Johnny, who has decided to leave employment at his father's hardware shop and to leave his girlfriend Janet at home in order to meet up with slapper Mavis Breeze (played by Una Stubbs), who has changed her name to Michelle to dance at London strip-joints. As Johnny is getting ready to go, he looks back on his working life and the need to turn things into cash with lines like 'hope is good, help is better' and the message that money is most important. At the end of the song, the action moves to his travels to London with £200 from his father, played by former Doctor Who, William Hartnell, in a kind of semi-bewildered way.

All of the songs for the six-episode series were recorded at Abbey Road at the end of 1968 and into 1969, with a possible album tie-in with the show for EMI, although, if this were the case, the project was abandoned. The song is not particularly memorable other than the dark chorus but it pleasant enough with its guitar-led rhythms and straightforward melody. The end titles of the episodes indicated that the songs were original and written by Cliff, the programme's writer David Winter and the four members of the Settlers. There is nothing, apart from two songs (the Beatles' ***Help*** and ***Nowhere Man***), to suggest that this isn't the case; therefore, this song has those credits assigned in this entry.

Track Specification

Composed by Cliff Richard, David Winter, Cindy Kent, Mike Jones, John Fyffe and Geoffrey Srodzinski

Musicians

John Fyffe	backing vocals, guitar
Cindy Kent	backing vocals
Mike Jones	backing vocals, guitar
Cliff Richard	vocals
Geoffrey Srodzinski	backing vocals
Unknown	drums, percussion

Recording Details

Producer	Norrie Paramor
Engineered by	Peter Vince
Recording location	Abbey Road Studio 3, St. John's Wood, London
Recording date	11th January 1969

♫ Turn Me Loose

Unissued television track subsequently released on **The Rock 'n' Roll Years 1958-1963**

Turn Me Loose was written with Elvis Presley in mind but, due to his US Army commitments, he never got the chance to record it. Instead, other artists' covers include Dion, Adam Faith, Frankie Avalon and Fabian, and Manhattan Transfer.

By 1959, Cliff Richard and the Drifters had become an almost permanent fixture on the *Oh Boy!* television programme. Although this book has deliberately avoided listing songs recorded specifically for film and television, this track from an *Oh Boy!* performance was released on the Cliff anthology of his early years, ***The Rock 'n' Roll Years 1958-1963***. Other tracks were obviously recorded but have not been released in aural format.

Cliff's version is typical of his performances of the period, probably while clutching his elbow and trying to curl his lip, all of which sent the girls in the audience into frenzy. The quality of the recording is limited so it is difficult to hear some of the nuances; however, there is an uncredited backing vocal group (not the Drifters), which may be the group that can be heard on the official *Oh Boy!* release and reformed on for ***From a Distance ***** The Event***, the Dallas Boys.

Track Specification

Composed by Mort Shuman and Jerome 'Doc' Pomus

Musicians

Jet Harris	bass
Hank Marvin	guitar
Tony Meehan	drums, percussion
Cliff Richard	vocals
Unknown	backing vocals
Bruce Welch	rhythm guitar

Recording Details

Producer	Unknown
Engineered by	Unknown
Recording location	Hackney Empire, Hackney, London
Recording date	30th May 1959

♫ Turn! Turn! Turn!

Single by **Sheila Walsh**

In 1959, Pete Seeger took the words almost verbatim from the book of Ecclesiastes, from the Old Testament, chapter three, verses one to eight and set them to music. With only slight additions, including the 'Turn! Turn! Turn!' phrase and the 'A time for peace, I swear it's not too late' final line as the only original lyrics, the song's correct full title as *Turn! Turn! Turn! (To Everything There Is a Season)*, although the words in the parentheses and even the exclamation marks are often missed off. The first time the song was recorded was in 1962 by the Limeliters, just beating Seeger to his version, which was released on his album *The Bitter and the Sweet* in the same year. Jim McGuinn (also known as Roger) was one of Seeger's backing musicians and he arranged the song for folk singer Judy Collins to record before taking it to his next group, the Byrds, who recorded what many regard as the seminal and certainly most popular version, reaching number twenty-six in November 1965. The song has been recorded by a number of artists including Chris de Burgh, Mary Hopkin, Dolly Parton, Larry Norman, The Seekers, Nina Simone and Bruce Springsteen among several others.

With its message of peace and love and expressing the point that there is a time for everything and acknowledging when that might be, it made sense to include the song on Sheila Walsh's religious album ***Drifting*** (*War of Love* in the US), which was co-produced by Cliff Richard and Craig Pruess, along with some of the musicians from Cliff's then current band. Backed with ***Sleepwalking***, also an album track, *Turn! Turn! Turn!* was released as a single on the DJM Records label (catalogue number DJS 5) in 1983 but it failed to chart. It was first released on CD on the track listing of the 1988 US album *Compact Favorites*.

The swimming synthesisers and brass effects create an ethereal effect to the track. Cliff provides his unmistakeable backing vocals from the second verse onwards and the ensemble piece crackles with wonderment and energy that sets this version apart from the familiar hit by the Byrds. The middle eight features a guitar solo that lifts the song further as the track careers towards its climax.

Track Specification

Composed by Pete Seeger

Musicians

Clem Clemson	electric guitar
Graham Jarvis	drums, percussion
Craig Pruess	arranger, backing vocals, synthesiser, piano, brass, percussion
Cliff Richard	backing vocals
Sheila Walsh	vocals

Recording Details

Producer	Cliff Richard and Craig Pruess
Engineered by	Keith Bessey
Recording location	Riverside Studios, London, Strawberry Studios, Dorking, Surrey, Ramp Studios, London and/or Sonoptics Studios, London
Recording date	September 1982-January 1983

♫ Tus Besos

From the album **When in Spain**

With a subtitle of ***Kiss*** that would be used for the English language version recorded in January 1965 for the ***Cliff Richard*** album and overdubbed on the ***When in Spain*** basic track, *Tus Besos* literally translates as *Your Kisses*. The third of four songs to be recorded for the album in the Barcelona session at the EMI Studios, the song was completed in twenty-three takes with the final take and edit being used for the mono and stereo recordings but with different mixes for the purposes of the audio channels.

Because the Spanish language was not Cliff's second language, he had the lyrics written down phonetically and worked hard at the pronunciation and, on tracks like *Tus Besos*, this shows since the gentle nature of the performance, ably backed by the Shadows and the string section of Norrie Paramor's orchestra, which was overdubbed at a later date, forces the pronunciation to be perfect or risk ruining the song. Cliff's singing is pitch-perfect here and, in many ways, it is better than the later English version.

Track Specification

Composed by Lionel Newman

Musicians

Brian Bennett	drums, percussion
Brian 'Licorice' Locking	bass
Hank Marvin	guitar
Norrie Paramor Strings	orchestra
Norrie Paramor	arranger, conductor
Cliff Richard	vocals
Bruce Welch	rhythm guitar

Recording Details

Producer	Norrie Paramor
Engineered by	Malcolm Addey
Recording location	EMI Studios, Barcelona (main recording) and Abbey Road Studio 2 (strings)
Recording date	28th April 1963 (main recording) and 14th May 1963 (strings)

♫ Tutti Frutti

From the album **Rock 'n' Roll Silver**

Although forever associated with Little Richard, *Tutti Frutti* has been recorded and regularly performed by diverse acts such as Elton John, Sting, Queen, the Carpetbaggers, Elvis Presley and, incongruously, Pat Boone. For the clean, wholesome image that people have of Boone, it belies the saucy nature of the origins of the song. The song also gave its title to a 1990s drama series featuring an upcoming Robbie Coltrane in the lead role.

During some recording sessions in 1955, where Richard Penniman (soon to become Little Richard) was playing the piano, he was growing frustrated that the recording techniques of the day were unable to pick up the energy of his piano performance. As a result, to get rid of the pent-up frustration, he launched into a frenetic version of a song he had been working on called *Tutti Frutti* although the lyrics were far too rude for the sensitivities of the executives to release as a record. Drafting in Dorothy LaBostrie to clean them up, she did so in fifteen minutes and the song was recorded and released reaching number two in the Billboard charts in the US. However, it only appeared as the B-side of ***Long Tall Sally*** in the UK and the single barely reached the top thirty.
More often than not, the song is credited solely to Penniman (or Little Richard) and LaBostrie but occasionally the name Joe Lubin appears (as it does in this entry). This is because it was common for executives and producers to take a credit in order to obtain monies from the popularity of the song. Who Joe Lubin actually is remains open to question and, for this reason, the name is often dropped from the publishing credits.
The final track to be chosen for Cliff Richard's twenty-fifth anniversary album ***Rock 'n' Roll Silver***, *Tutti Frutti* was arranged and produced by Thunder, which was Cliff's chosen epithet for the hand-picked band performing at the sessions. Interestingly, *Tutti Frutti* was not included on the CD reissue in 1993 of the album (mainly for space limitation reasons), although it was later added as a bonus track on the 2004 remaster of ***The Rock Connection***.
With an extraordinary drum introduction and falsetto pitched yell from Cliff, his energetic version of *Tutti Frutti* is quite close, in many respects, to the original by Little Richard. Rather than a piano solo, there is a fuzzed guitar and then a synthesiser in the breaks and Cliff takes the chance to do his best impression of Little Richard by singing the song raucously. As with much on the album, it is a brilliantly realized nod to Cliff's rock and roll roots.

Track Specification
Composed by Dorothy LaBostrie, Richard Penniman and Joe Lubin

Musicians

Stuart Calver	backing vocals
Dave Cooke	keyboards
John Clark	electric guitar
Mark Griffiths	bass
Graham Jarvis	drums, percussion
Mart Jenner	guitar
John Perry	backing vocals
Alan Park	keyboards
Cliff Richard	vocals, backing vocals
Tony Rivers	backing vocals
Thunder	arranger

Recording Details

Producer	Thunder
Engineered by	Keith Bessey
Recording location	Strawberry Studios South, Surrey
Recording date	9th-18th May 1983

♫ Tu, Tu, Mi Piaci
Unissued track

With the release of Cliff Richard's single ***Constantly***, all territories except Italy had ***True, True Lovin'*** on its B-side. In Italy, it was released with ***I Only Know I Love You*** on the reverse. Both of these English language songs were attempted to be recorded in Italian during the ***When in Rome*** album sessions but both remain unissued. In spite of the authors' assertion in *The Complete Chronicles* that it had been an Italian issue, *Tu, Tu, Mi Piaci* (literally translating to *You, You, My Pleasure*) has never been issued, although this confusion might have arisen from having the title *True, True Lovin'* translated on labels.
Recorded during the two-day suite of sessions at a Portuguese studio based in Lisbon, the backing track from the original English version B-side would have been used for Cliff to overdub his new vocals on.

Track Specification
Composed by Bruce Welch; Italian lyrics by Unknown

Musicians

Brian Bennett	drums, percussion
Hank Marvin	guitar
Cliff Richard	vocals
John Rostill	bass
Bruce Welch	rhythm guitar

Recording Details

Producer	Norrie Paramor (backing track and vocals)
Engineered by	Malcolm Addey (backing track and vocals)
Recording location	Abbey Road Studio 2, St. John's Wood, London (backing track) and Estudios Valentim De Carvalho, Lisbon, Portugal (vocals)
Recording date	26th March 1964 (backing track) and 13th-14th May 1965 (vocals)

♫ TV Hop
From the album **Oh Boy!**

Cliff Richard became a regular favourite on Jack Good's *Oh Boy!* show, performing covers and some original material. Because of the success of the television show, it was decided that an album should follow as an official release. Originally, Marty Wilde was lined up to perform *TV Hop* and ***Somebody Touched Me*** but, for unknown reasons, couldn't make it to the recordings, at which point Cliff stepped up to the microphone.
In 1958, Danny and the Juniors had had a massive hit with ***At the Hop*** (subsequently recorded by Cliff for his ***From a Distance ***** The Event*** CD), and to capitalize on its and the dance style's popularity, *TV Hop* was written. There are

echoes of the Danny and the Juniors hit throughout the performance, short though it as at just over three-quarters of a minute before it segues into ***Rockin' Robin***.

The backing track and Cliff's vocals were recorded on separate days and, instead of using the Drifters as his backing, the musicians were from the Oh Boy! Band and the Dallas Boys. There is no record of who the individual band performers are, however, and so will be highlighted as unknown in this entry.

Although the album was re-released in the late seventies, it wasn't until the release of the rarities album ***The Rock and Roll Years 1958-1963*** that it saw release in digital format.

Track Specification

Composed by Melvin Endsley

Musicians

Dallas Boys:	
Nicky Clarke	backing vocals
Leon Fisk	backing vocals
Stan Jones	backing vocals
Joe Smith	backing vocals
Bob Wragg	backing vocals
Oh Boy! Band	guitars, stand-up bass, piano, drums, percussion
Cliff Richard	vocals

Recording Details

Producer	Harry Robinson (backing track) and Norrie Paramor (vocals)
Engineered by	Norman Newell (backing track) and Malcolm Addey (vocals)
Recording location	Abbey Road Studio 2, St. John's Wood, London
Recording date	19th October 1958 (backing track) and 21st October 1958 (vocals)

♫ Twelfth of Never, The

***27th UK single** and B-side of* **The Miracle**

Not much used in modern times, the term 'the twelfth of never' referred to an indeterminate point of time in the infinite future. It can be used disparagingly but more often it is used to underline more positive emotions such as the endurance and depth of love that one person might feel for another. *The Twelfth of Never* has been covered by a wide variety of artists including Petula Clark, Cher, the Bee Gees, Jeri Brown, Percy Faith, Billy J. Kramer and the Dakotas, Lou Rawls, the Chi-Lites, Johnny Mathis (whose version reached number nine in the US Billboard charts in 1959 and inspired Cliff Richard to record his version of the song and release it as a single), Floyd Cramer, Hank Marvin (on his *Hank Plays Cliff* album), Olivia Newton-John, Nina Simone and Bobby Vinton among many others. In the UK, other than Cliff's single, it has been a hit three times. The first (and most famous depending on the generation) was Donny Osmond, who had a massive number one during his stratospheric success in the early to mid-seventies; the second was Elvis Presley, who had a posthumous number twenty-one hit in collaboration with The Voice in 1995; the last was the Carter Twins, whose only record to hit the charts was their version of this song, which hit number sixty-one in 1997.

Cliff's version was recorded at the only session in the month of June 1964 and was the first of three songs to be completed. Splicing together takes three and four, the combined take and edit was used for the mono and stereo recordings but with different mixes for the requirements of the separate audio channels. Even as early as 1964, Bruce Welch was showing his keen ear for a good commercial song, for it was he who suggested that the song be released as a single. Backed with ***I'm Afraid to Go Home***, *The Twelfth of Never* was issued on the Columbia label (catalogue number DB 7372) on 23rd September 1964, reaching number eight in the UK singles charts. The track was also released in the track listing of the ***Why Don't They Understand?*** EP and regularly appears on compilations of Cliff's hits across the years. For a time, before ***The Day I Met Marie*** usurped it in Cliff's mind, he would regularly cite *The Twelfth of Never* as being his most favourite song that he had recorded to date.

Introduced with a plodding bass, drum and an arpeggiated harp, Cliff's gentle vocal incorporates a glissando between certain notes, which serves to underline the emotion portrayed in the lyrics. Once again, Norrie Paramor's orchestral arrangement is a perfect addition to Cliff's version of this song, which stands out among its contemporaries and followers. The backing vocals employ only the female contingent of the Mike Sammes Singers.

It would take almost thirty-five years for a new version to be released when Cliff revisited the song for his fortieth anniversary concert at the Royal Albert Hall, where he performed the song in duet with Michelle Wolf, who had been instrumental in the recording of the ***Real as I Wanna Be*** album. The live song was one of two released in the CD single package release of ***The Miracle*** in 1999, with *The Twelfth of Never* appearing on the first disc of the dual issue. The other musicians are unknown. Starting with a synthesiser playing an arrangement of the song's accompaniment, Cliff begins his vocal line and then is joined by Michelle Wolf. Their voices coalesce well, although the jamming aspect of the arrangement detracts from the familiar melody, which is fine but a little perplexing on first listen.

Track Specification

Composed by Jerry Livingstone and Paul Francis Webber

1. Single

Musicians

Mike Sammes Singers	backing vocals
Norrie Paramor Orchestra	orchestra
Norrie Paramor	arranger, conductor
Cliff Richard	vocals

Recording Details

Producer	Norrie Paramor
Engineered by	Malcolm Addey
Recording location	Abbey Road Studio 2, St. John's Wood, London
Recording date	23rd June 1964

2. B-side (The Miracle)

Musicians		*Recording Details*	
Cliff Richard	vocals	Producer	Keith Bessey
Unknown	synthesiser	Engineered by	Keith Bessey
Michelle Wolf	vocals	Recording location	Royal Albert Hall, London
		Recording date	September 1998

♫ Twelve Days of Christmas

From the EP **Christmas EP**

Considered to be a traditional English Christmas carol first published in 1780, it is quite like that the *Twelve Days of Christmas* may actually be French in origin. Essentially, the song builds up with a sequence of increasingly grandiose gifts provided from a lover on each of the days from Christmas day onwards, starting with a partridge in a pear tree, through turtle doves, hens, rings, swans, dancers, pipers, lords and ladies. Ripe for parody, it has been rewritten by Allan Sherman (ending in a Japanese transistor radio) and Frank Kelly (who begins with gratitude and then describes the mayhem in the house wrought by the close living of all of these presents). The most famous straight version in the UK is probably by folk group The Spinners.

Cliff Richard recorded a version in 1967 originally destined for the ***Carol Singers*** EP but unreleased at the time. With help from the Mastersingers (comprising Christian friends who were also music teachers) providing vocal harmonies, all of the carols were recorded *a capella*. As a result of the complexities of performing in this way, the final edit was constructed from splicing together multiple takes. Although a mono version was recorded, only the stereo version was eventually released on the ***Christmas EP*** in 1991 to accompany the single release of ***We Should Be Together***. The track was reissued, also in stereo, on the compilation album ***...And They Said It Wouldn't Last! (My 50 Years in Music)*** in 2008.

With a straightforward backing accompaniment, the counter-tenor includes a phrase or two from *Ding Dong Merrily on High*, which works well as a backing to this hugely popular song. Cliff keeps the song moving with a lovely vibrato in his voice. Singing *a capella* is extraordinarily difficult because the tendency is to either drag the tuning flat or, to avoid that, to push it sharp but Cliff and the Mastersingers successfully keep it in pitch. One splice between takes can clearly be heard in between the tenth and eleventh days of Christmas. Each time around, the arrangement supporting the lead vocal is changed keeping the whole carol fresh and a lovely experience to listen to. This is just one of many examples that show off Cliff's versatility as a musician.

Track Specification

Composed by Traditional

Musicians		*Recording Details*	
Mastersingers:	backing vocals	Producer	Norrie Paramor
John Horrex		Engineered by	Peter Vince and John Barrett
Geoffrey Keating		Recording location	Abbey Road Studio 2, St. John's Wood, London
George Pratt		Recording date	10th September 1967
Michael Warrington			
Cliff Richard	vocals		

♫ Twenty Flight Rock

From the albums **The Rock 'n' Roll Years 1958-1963** *and* **Cliff Sings**

Twenty Flight Rock was originally recorded by Eddie Cochrane as part of the soundtrack of the 1956 film *The Girl Can't Help It*. It was a very popular tune with audiences and was subsequently released as a single in 1957. The sole writer is actually Ned Fairchild – in reality, a woman called Nelda Fairchild, the sexism in the music business making it difficult to be a success in some areas – although Cochrane was given a co-composer credit as a way of sorting out various egos. However, Cochrane didn't receive any royalties via the arrangement. It has been covered by a number of artists including The Rolling Stones, Robert Gordon, Dick Rivers and Tiger Army, but one interesting point of information is that the song was the choice of Paul McCartney in his audition to John Lennon to join the Quarrymen (the fore-runner of the Beatles).

It is a typical twelve bar blues style of song and relies on an increasing numerical sequence of counting in the style of the formidable *Rock Around the Clock* as one of its hooks. The driving bass line and shushing percussion drive the momentum of the song through to the end, lending the urgency that the singer has to get to his girlfriend living so high up in the tower block.

The song was on the repertoire for Cliff Richard and the Drifters' short residency at the Butlin's Holiday Camp based in Clacton-on-Sea in August 1958. On one night, Stan Edwards recorded their performances on a two-track tape machine. Some of those recordings made it on to the rarities retrospective, ***The Rock 'n' Roll Years 1958-1963***, while others were in too poor a condition to be considered for commercial release. The Butlin's version of *Twenty Flight Rock* was one of four tracks that made it on to the listing and is performed at a slightly faster pace than can be heard on other versions and particularly the album recording sessions for ***Cliff Sings***. But it is an interesting historical document in that it shows Cliff's assuredness as a singer and performer and, as with all his performances, it is in tune; something that is quite difficult for a seventeen-year-old to achieve regardless of talent. Because of the limited recording capabilities, the only version of this live recording remains in mono only.

The album version of the song was released in both mono and stereo for the ***Cliff Sings No. 2 EP***, and is a beautifully performed if a little clinical in the production with Jet Harris's bass line subtly underpinning the rhythm and producing the sense of walking up and down flights of stairs. Naturally, the vocal talents of Cliff against the assured playing of the guitar solos by Hank Marvin ensure that the track is carried off with aplomb.

Track Specification
Composed by Eddie Cochrane and Ned Fairchild

1. The Rock 'n' Roll Years 1958-1963

Musicians		*Recording Details*	
Cliff Richard	vocals, guitar	Producer	Unknown
Ian Samwell	guitar	Engineered by	Stan Edwards
Terry Smart	drums, percussion	Recording location	Rock 'n' Roll Ballroom, Butlin's Holiday Camp, Clacton-on-Sea, Essex
		Recording date	August 1958

2. Cliff Sings

Musicians		*Recording Details*	
Jet Harris	bass	Producer	Norrie Paramor
Hank Marvin	guitar	Engineered by	Malcolm Addey and Alan Kane (mono) and Stuart Eltham and Norman Smith (stereo)
Tony Meehan	drums, percussion		
Cliff Richard	vocals	Recording location	Abbey Road Studio 2, St. John's Wood, London
Bruce Welch	rhythm guitar	Recording date	7th September 1959

♫ Twist and Shout

From the film soundtrack album of **Two a Penny** *and from the album* **Cliff in Japan**

Most people associate *Twist and Shout* with either the Isley Brothers or the Beatles (or, a couple of generations later the strangely named Chaka Demus and Pliers). However, the first band to record it was the American group the Topnotes in 1961, with Phil Spector on production duties. A year later, writer Bert Berns, disaffected by the original recording, offered it to the Isley Brothers, who created a much better and energetic version. But it is John Lennon's throat-thrashing version on the Beatles' first album (and EP of the same name, *Please Please Me*) that gives the song its raw energy and power. Recorded in one take, Lennon was adamant that it should sound as if he had been smoking, drinking and shouting all night and this is what gives the track its raw edge, helped by the fact that he had a cold coming on during the sessions. Brian Poole and the Tremeloes also recorded it but, prior to that, it was offered to Birmingham-based Gerry Levene and the Avengers, who recorded it but it remains unreleased.

Cliff Richard recorded the song for the soundtrack to his 1967 film ***Two a Penny***, and it was the one of the four that he can be seen performing in the film (the other three original songs – all composed by Cliff himself – feature as a backdrop at certain parts of the action). Jamie Hopkins (Cliff) has delusions about his worth and wants a way to a fast buck and, although he has a good singing voice, can't really be bothered to pursue the dream of becoming a performer. Cynical in its performance at a pub, he grabs the microphone and suggests that the other musicians should play faster. At the end, after polite but desultory applause, he spits "Thank you... fans!" before returning to the bar to his girlfriend.

Twist and Shout was recorded at the same session as the other three songs in the film and issued on the ***Two a Penny*** album (which featured all four songs plus some other material unconnected to the film project). The engineering on the soundtrack version is cleaner than that in the film although it is the same recording to which Cliff lip-synchs.

With a rocking piano and raucous brass accompaniment, Cliff manages to produce a sound that almost equals Lennon's raw version. It takes a little time to get used to hearing the song with an orchestral backing (albeit with a foot-stomping piano and thumping drums) but, as with much that Cliff touched, he managed to make the song a little different from the other versions that were recorded.

In late 1968, Cliff recorded his first all-German album, *Hier Ist Cliff*, taking many of the tracks from *Two a Penny* and ***Established 1958***. One of those was ***Twist Im Blut*** (or *Twist in the Blood*) and was the first track on the album.

Track Specification
Composed by Bert Russell and Phil Medley

1. Two a Penny

Musicians		*Recording Details*	
Mike Leander	arranger, conductor	Producer	Norrie Paramor
Mike Leander Orchestra	orchestra	Engineered by	Peter Vince
Cliff Richard	vocals	Recording location	Abbey Road Studio 2, St. John's Wood, London
Unknown	piano	Recording date	1st July 1967

2. Cliff in Japan

Musicians		*Recording Details*	
Norrie Paramor Orchestra	orchestra	Producer	Norrie Paramor
Norrie Paramor	arranger, conductor	Engineered by	Unknown
Cliff Richard	vocals	Recording location	Shibuya Public Hall, Tokyo, Japan
		Recording date	18th October 1967

♫ Twist im Blut

From the album **Hier Ist Cliff**

Of all the languages in the European community in which Cliff Richard recorded, aside from a couple of albums in Spanish and Italian, it was German that saw him have most success, particularly within that country's singles market. Therefore it seemed strange that it took him until 1968 to record an entire album specifically for release in Germany. With his version of ***Twist and Shout*** being released on the ***Two a Penny*** album the year before and with the sessions plundering the songs from that film's soundtrack and ***Established 1958***, it was an obvious choice for inclusion with a German translation. On that note, the credits for the composition are the same as those for the original, implying that the original writers also provided the translation, but this is unlikely.

For Cliff's recording of *Twist im Blut* (literally translated back into English as *Twist in the Blood*, which is not as grisly as it might sound since it refers to the intrinsic nature of that style of dance to the being), the practice of overdubbing vocals on previous backing tracks had pretty much been abandoned with the orchestral backing for the updated German track being recorded at the same time. Being released on *Hier Ist Cliff* for the German market only in 1969 and also only in stereo (it is unlikely that a mono mix would ave been made so late in the decade), it was a rarity until it was included on the foreign language compendium, ***On the Continent***, in 1997.

The arrangement is very similar to the English original with rousing brass accompaniment and Cliff sings the song with more clarity and less raucousness in German, although there are still the yelps and shouts. As with the English original, the use of the orchestra initially seems at odds with the energy of the song but it works. Cliff uses falsetto at the end of this track, which he would go on to use successfully in his mid-seventies reinvention.

Track Specification

Composed by Bert Russell and Phil Medley

Musicians

Norrie Paramor Orchestra	orchestra
Norrie Paramor	arranger, director
Cliff Richard	vocals

Recording Details

Producer	Norrie Paramor
Engineered by	Peter Vince
Recording location	Abbey Road Studio 2, St. John's Wood, London
Recording date	20th November 1968

♫ Two a Penny

From the film soundtrack album of **Two a Penny**

After the light-hearted frippery of Cliff Richard's previous films in the first half of the sixties, the juxtaposition of the stark nature of the drama of ***Two a Penny*** was quite a contrast. What also made it different was that the focus was firmly on the story – the question of what God can do for an individual against the backdrop of Cliff's cynical character who is only out for himself – rather than the music, echoing his earlier filmic outing in ***Serious Charge***. There are only four songs in the film and their performance are incidental to the script, with the title song, composed by Cliff Richard himself, playing out over the opening titles as the camera follows a cocky Jamie Hopkins (Cliff) strutting through the streets of central London. The thumping drum and sinister chord motif from the opening bars, however, are used throughout the film in the incidental music to underpin the bad things that Hopkins does (taking money from his mother, borrowing money without wanting to repay, burglary, selling drugs and so on).

The *Two a Penny* of the title is a phrase that is often used to mean common or numerous and worthless or throwaway. The lyrics indicate the self-delusion of Cliff's character in his cynical arrogance that he is more important than others and that there is only one of him for which others should be thankful; a dry observation on what is to come in the film's dramatic sequences, in that there truly is only one of him – but not in a good way.

The song was recorded along with the other three tracks featured in the film (the single ***I'll Love You Forever Today***, ***Twist and Shout*** and ***Questions***) and released on the album that also took the film's title (although most of the track listing is padded out with covers and new songs not connected to the film).

Introduced with a menacing drum roll, percussion and thudding bass line and then a guitar solo, Cliff sings assuredly as he boasts about what he is going to become and how special he is. The upbeat accompaniment in the orchestral brass section match the tenor of the lyrics and, as an opener for the album and the film, it is difficult to beat; in many ways, it's surprising that it wasn't released as a single from the film project.

At the back end of 1968, Cliff recorded a set of translated songs from ***Established 1958*** and *Two a Penny* and a few others for his first German language album, *Hier Ist Cliff*, with the song being changed to ***Mr. Niemand*** (or *Mr. Nobody*). In February 1969, Cliff re-entered the studios to record another new version – this time in French, which was released on the 1975 album *When in France – Chante en Français*, called *Je Suis Formidable*.

Track Specification

Composed by Cliff Richard

Musicians

Mike Leander	arranger, conductor
Mike Leander Orchestra	orchestra
Cliff Richard	vocals

Recording Details

Producer	Norrie Paramor
Engineered by	Peter Vince
Recording location	Abbey Road Studio 2, St. John's Wood, London
Recording date	1st July 1967

♫ Two Hearts

104th UK single** and from the albums* **Live and Guaranteed 1988!** *and* **From a Distance ** The Event Remaster**

Since Cliff Richard was working on ***Time – the Musical*** at night, he recorded his vocal tracks for the ***Always Guaranteed*** album during the day. For the first time, the project was not an ensemble piece, too, with Alan Tarney composing the songs more often than not in the studio, recording the basic track and then working with Cliff to record his vocal lines. Given his other pressures, this worked well and produced the most popular album of his career as well as four singles.

The final single was the last track on side one of the original vinyl album and, backed with non-album track ***Yesterday, Today, Forever,*** *Two Hearts* was released as a single on the EMI label (catalogue number EM 42) on 1st February 1988 and reached number thirty-four in the UK charts. Alongside the seven-inch vinyl, there was a heart-shaped picture disc (catalogue number EMP 42), a CD single (CDEM 42) and a twelve-inch vinyl release (12EM 42), the latter two of which featured an extended version of the single (and a Valentine's Day card all in a gatefold sleeve on the twelve-inch) as well as an additional non-album track, ***Wild Geese***. The promotional video was simply Cliff's performance of it recorded in concert, possibly the *Live & Guaranteed 1988!* film, which was also incorporated on the associated CD release in 1995.

What makes this song work so well is the syncopated rhythm underneath Cliff's vocals, which are presented in a slightly clandestine perhaps confidential manner, until the chorus is reached when it becomes brighter. The syncopation forces the incorrect emphasis on some syllables but this doesn't detract from the listening. But, over and above this, it is the arrangement of the vocal harmonies provided by both Cliff and Tarney that make the song an exquisite example of what the pair achieved in the studio for the album and it is a perfect closer to the first side of the album.

Two Hearts was one of the songs in *Cliff's Set* during his two-day thirtieth anniversary performances at Wembley Stadium. Initially, the song was not released on the resultant album ***From a Distance ***** The Event*** in 1990 but was restored when the album was remastered on to two discs in 2005. With some minor differences from the original, this version is slightly more laidback in the instrumentation, although Cliff still sings it with the same kind of confidentiality that was present on the studio recording. The beauty of the vocal arrangements is brought out during the performance.

Track Specification
Composed by Alan Tarney

1. Single (seven-inch)

Musicians		*Recording Details*	
Cliff Richard	vocals, backing vocals	Producer	Alan Tarney
Alan Tarney	backing vocals, guitars, bass, keyboards, drum and percussion programming	Engineered by	Gerry Kitchingham and Keith Bessey
		Recording location	R. G. Jones Studios, Wimbledon, London
		Recording date	13th October-November 1986

2. Single (twelve-inch extended)

Musicians		*Recording Details*	
Cliff Richard	vocals, backing vocals	Producer	Alan Tarney
Alan Tarney	backing vocals, guitars, bass, keyboards, drum and percussion programming	Engineered by	Gerry Kitchingham and Keith Bessey
		Recording location	R. G. Jones Studios, Wimbledon, London
		Recording date	13th October-November 1986

3. Live & Guaranteed 1988!

Musicians		*Recording Details*	
John Clark	guitar	Producer	Unknown
Rosemarie Ford	backing vocals	Engineered by	Unknown
Mark Griffiths	bass	Recording location	Fyens Forum, Odense, Denmark
Peter Howarth	backing vocals	Recording date	22nd May 1988
Steve Lauri	guitar		
Paul Moessl	keyboards		
Mick Mullins	backing vocals		
Alan Park	keyboards		
Cliff Richard	vocals		
Henry Spinetti	drums, percussion		

4. From a Distance ** The Event Remaster***

Musicians		*Recording Details*	
John Clark	guitar	Producer	Cliff Richard
Sonia Jones-Morgan	backing vocals	Engineered by	Keith Bessey and Mick McKenna
Steve Lauri	guitar	Recording location	Rolling Stones Mobile Studio, Wembley Stadium, Wembley, North-west London
Peter May	drums, percussion		
Paul Moessl	keyboards	Recording date	16th-17th June 1989
Tessa Niles	backing vocals		
Alan Park	keyboards		
Provox:			
Peter Howarth	backing vocals		
Mick Mullins	backing vocals		
Keith Murrell	backing vocals		
Cliff Richard	vocals		
Steve Stroud	bass		

♫ Two to the Power of Love

92nd UK single

One of the most extraordinary and unlikely pairings for a duet was when Cliff Richard recorded *Two to the Power of Love* with Janet Jackson, then a seventeen-year-old girl who had been living in the huge shadow of her brothers in the Jackson 5 and particularly the most famous of them, Michael. Ostensibly chosen by Giorgio Moroder for inclusion on her first album, *Dream Street,* the song was picked as a single, which was backed with a Jackson-only track *Rock 'n' Roll,* on the A&M label (catalogue number AM210) on 15th September 1984, although it failed to chart. The twelve-inch single version, also included another Jackson-only track, *Don't Mess Up a Good Thing,* and was also issued simultaneously with the seven-inch version (twelve-inch catalogue number AMX210) on the same date. The parent album was issued on vinyl, cassette and CD at the same time. The song was also performed by Jackson and Jessee Borrego for an episode in the fourth season of the *Fame* television programme in the eighties.

With dense guitars and synthesiser passages, the high-pitched voice of Jackson starts the song off before the duties are taken over by Cliff. The combination of the pair's voices seems to work well, with Cliff singing the harmony line when they sing together but the style of song is at odds with many an expectation.

Track Specification

Composed by Peter Beckett and Stephen A. Kipner

Musicians

Beth Anderson	backing vocals
Arthur Barrow	bass, keyboards
Gary Falcone	backing vocals
Janet Jackson	vocals
Joe Pizzulo	backing vocals
Cliff Richard	vocals
Phil Shenale	keyboards
Richie Zito	guitar

Recording Details

Producer	Giorgio Moroder and Pete Bellotte
Engineered by	Steve Bates and Steve Hodge
Recording location	Advision Studios, London
Recording date	26th April 1984

♫ Two Worlds

B-side of **The Millennium Prayer**

Recorded at the same time as ***The Millennium Prayer****, Two Worlds* was issued as its B-side when the main song was released as a single. The track is a lilting song whose melody has elements of a suitable lullaby. As with everything Cliff sings, he performs it with conviction against the simple orchestral string and keyboard accompaniment. The unknown backing vocals and instrumentation are perfectly arranged behind Cliff's lead vocal, which is gently performed with a perfect vibrato.

Track Specification

Composed by Craig Pruess and Jennifer Lawrence

Musicians

David Arch	orchestral arranger, conductor
Cliff Richard	vocals, backing vocals
Unknown	keyboards
Unknown	bass
Unknown	drums, percussion
Unknown	orchestra

Recording Details

Producer	Nigel Wright
Engineered by	Unknown
Recording location	Skratch Studios, London and Whitfield Street Studios, London
Recording date	August 1999

♬ UFO
Unissued live track

Written by Larry Norman, who had previously worked with Cliff Richard over the previous two decades, *UFO* was the first in a medley performed at the *Live & Guaranteed 1988!* tour. The Danish performance was recorded and filmed for video release but fewer than half of the songs were included on the track listing and, in 1995, it was re-released with an accompanying CD. Once again, neither formats had the ***Medley*** included.

Track Specification
Composed by Larry Norman
Musicians

John Clark	guitar
Rosemarie Ford	backing vocals
Mark Griffiths	bass
Peter Howarth	backing vocals
Steve Lauri	guitar
Paul Moessl	keyboards
Mick Mullins	backing vocals
Alan Park	keyboards
Cliff Richard	vocals
Henry Spinetti	drums, percussion

Recording Details

Producer	Unknown
Engineered by	Unknown
Recording location	Fyens Forum, Odense, Denmark
Recording date	22nd May 1988

♬ Umbarella
From the album **Ich Träume Deine Träume**

A German translation of a later English language B-side by Cliff Richard, ***Annabella Umbrella***, the German version is titled *Umbarella*, which has no direct translation; rather it is a phonetic treatment of the word fitting across four notes with three real syllables as in the English version. The English B-side version was recorded three months later in February 1971, so the German is very much a trial run. *Umbarella* was the first song to be completed in a length two-day set of four sessions, made easier to record so much material by recording the orchestral backing track earlier, conducted by Mike Vickers. The song was destined for Cliff's second German language album, *Ich Träume Deine Träume*, released the following year and was included on the remastered foreign language song compilation, ***On the Continent***, in 1997.
The arrangement follows that of the B-side that was recorded later and Cliff's emotive performance is replicated in this German version, too. The increased pace of the chorus fits perfectly with the traditional German style. There is a prominent harpsichord in the mix, while the uncredited backing vocalists are deliberately kept understated.

Track Specification
Composed by Valerie Avon and Harold Spiro; German lyrics by Neilburg
Musicians

Norrie Paramor Orchestra	orchestra
Cliff Richard	vocals
Unknown	backing vocals
Mike Vickers	arranger, conductor

Recording Details

Producer	Norrie Paramor (backing track and vocals)
Engineered by	Phil McDonald (backing track and vocals)
Recording location	Cologne, Germany (backing track) and Abbey Road Studio 2, St. John's Wood, London (vocals)
Recording date	November 1970 (backing track) and 24th November 1970 (vocals)

♬ Unchained Melody
From the album **Listen to Cliff!** *(European and South African versions)*

By far and away one of the most popular songs of the twentieth century pop scene, particularly after the emotion-riddled version performed by the Righteous Brothers in 1965, the song *Unchained Melody* had a surprisingly modest start in life. A now obscure prison-based film from 1955, in which the central character contemplates a jailbreak against completing his jail sentence, it was called *Unchained*. Alex North and Hy Zaret were employed to score the film and, when it came to the main theme, rather than write potentially crass lyrics to feature the film's title, they instead went for the theme of a man parted for an unexplained reason from his lover and built the imagery of the earth and nature continuing their inexorable path in spite of his sense of loneliness and yearning. With no obvious title coming to mind, they chose to call it simply *Unchained Melody* to describe it exactly as it was. The song was recorded for the film by Todd Duncan and was nominated for an Oscar for best song, although it as eventually beaten by *Love Is a Many-Splendoured Thing*.

Unchained Melody has been recorded by many different acts over the years, including Gene Vincent, Ricky Nelson, Roy Orbison, Elvis Presley, Cyndi Lauper, Roy Hamilton and LeAnn Rimes and continues to be a popular choice of song for the audition stages of reality singing shows such as *The X-Factor* and *American Idol*. In Britain, the song has charted eight times to date: Al Hibbler (number two in 1955), Jimmy Young (number one in 1955, holding off Hibbler's version), Les Baxter (number ten in 1955, the third version to be in the charts simultaneously), Liberace (an instrumental version at number twenty later on in 1955), The Righteous Brothers (number fourteen in 1965 and number one on reissue in 1990 after it had appeared in the clay-pot modelling seen in the Demi Moore and Patrick Swayze film vehicle, *Ghost*), Leo Sayer (a lowly number fifty-four in 1986), Robson and Jerome (number one in 1995 on the back of the actors' performance of it in the television drama *Soldier, Soldier*) and finally Gareth Gates (who came second to Will Young in *Pop Idol* in 2002 and reached number one with the song early that year).
Cliff's version for the ***Listen to Cliff!*** album was finally completed after a marathon session in early March 1961 when thirty-one different takes were recorded before the result was satisfactory. The mono and stereo versions of the recording used the same take and edit but the mix was different for the aural channelling. *Unchained Melody* has appeared on a number of Cliff-related compilations over the years and was also included on the ***Listen to Cliff! No. 2*** EP. A further take with a different, more drawn-out vocal approach from Cliff was taken for the South African release of the album but only in mono and has yet to be released in any other format.
Eschewing the overblown histrionics that have been the copycat versions of the brilliant Righteous Brothers version, Cliff and the Shadows provide a rendition that is reflective and sad, evoking thoughts of the loneliness of the character in the song. The understated guitar solo breaks by Hank Marvin serve to underline the beauty of this version of the song. There is echo applied to Cliff's vocal line and, in the bridge part, accompanied only by a strummed chord, he is singing *a capella*.

Track Specification
Composed by Alex North and Hy Zaret

1. Listen to Cliff! (European version)

Musicians

Jet Harris	bass
Hank Marvin	guitar
Tony Meehan	drums, percussion
Cliff Richard	vocals
Bruce Welch	rhythm guitar

Recording Details

Producer	Norrie Paramor
Engineered by	Malcolm Addey and David Lloyd
Recording location	Abbey Road Studio 2, St. John's Wood, London
Recording date	4th March 1961

2. Listen to Cliff! (South African version)

Musicians

Jet Harris	bass
Hank Marvin	guitar
Tony Meehan	drums, percussion
Cliff Richard	vocals
Bruce Welch	rhythm guitar

Recording Details

Producer	Norrie Paramor
Engineered by	Malcolm Addey and David Lloyd
Recording location	Abbey Road Studio 2, St. John's Wood, London
Recording date	4th March 1961

♫ Under Lock and Key

From the album **Green Light**

Written by Terry Britten, who, along with Alan Tarney, was the principal provider of material for Cliff Richard to record for much of the seventies, *Under Lock and Key* was the first song from the ***Green Light*** album project to be recorded and was completed in two takes with some overdubs added at a session a month and a half later.
The second track from the album, *Under Lock and Key* is heavy on the drums and percussion, with tinkling piano and guitars playing staccato chords underneath Cliff's vocals. Unsurprisingly, the highlight of recording is the vocal arrangement supporting Cliff's lead.

Track Specification
Composed by Terry Britten

Musicians

Brian Bennett	drums, percussion
Terry Britten	guitar
Stuart Calver	backing vocals
Alan Jones	bass
Duncan MacKay	keyboards
Alan Parker	guitar
John Perry	backing vocals
Tim Renwick	guitar
Cliff Richard	vocals
Tony Rivers	backing vocals
Trevor Spencer	drums, percussion
Alan Tarney	backing vocals, guitar, bass, keyboards
Graham Todd	keyboards

Recording Details

Producer	Bruce Welch
Engineered by	Tony Clark and Haydn Bendall
Recording location	Abbey Road Studio 3, St. John's Wood, London
Recording date	9th January 1978 and 21st February 1978

♫ Under the Gun

From the album **Don't Hide Your Heart** *and the B-side of* **My Pretty One** *(12-inch version) and unissued live track*

Cliff Richard's Christian rock protégée Sheila Walsh began recording her third album, ***Don't Hide Your Heart***, in late 1984 and, like the previous album, Cliff only sings backing vocals. With Craig Pruess, a frequent Cliff collaborator, on production and keyboards, *Under the Gun* also featured ex-Roxy Music guitarist Phil Manzanera on guitar.
Essentially a protest song that rails against nuclear bombs and general warfare, it begins with a throbbing bass and synthesiser chord structure. Walsh's voice matches the slightly staccato approach to song, while Cliff's vocals appear gently underneath the arrangement and it is his harmonies that complete the song.
Cliff took the song to perform for himself, which he did in the middle of 1987 when it was included on the set list of his tour that year. This live version of *Under the Gun*, for which there are scant details on the personnel and location, was added as a bonus track on the twelve-inch versions (one with a poster, another without) of the ***My Pretty One*** single that was the first to be released from the ***Always Guaranteed*** project, as well as the ***Some People*** video CD, although in audio form only. It was first included, in album format, on the *Yesterday, Today, Forever* compilation in 1998 before being added as one of the eight bonus tracks on the 2004 remaster of *Always Guaranteed*.
Cliff's version is driven forward by the bass guitar playing one note for much of the song. Cliff hasn't sung an overtly protesting song since ***Silvery Rain*** and, because of his associations, hearing him singing about man's fate in this way sounds curious initially but then it matches his general feelings. The song ends with the throbbing bass dying out and leaving the vocal and backing vocals *a capella*.
During the Danish leg of the *Live & Guaranteed 1988!* tour, the set was filmed and recorded initially for VHS release. In 1995, the video was reissued along with a CD of some of the songs. However, neither the video nor the CD had the live version of *Under the Gun* as part of the track listing.

Track Specification
Composed by James A. Rushing and J. D. Martin

1. Don't Hide Your Heart

Musicians		*Recording Details*	
Phil Manzanera	guitar	Producer	Craig Pruess and Keith Bessey
Dave Mattacks	cymbals	Engineered by	Keith Bessey
Craig Pruess	keyboards, electronics	Recording location	Gallery Studios, Chertsey, Surrey
Cliff Richard	backing vocals	Recording date	November 1984-February 1985
Sheila Walsh	vocals		

2. B-side (My Pretty One)

Musicians		*Recording Details*	
John Clark	guitar	Producer	Cliff Richard
Mark Griffiths	bass	Engineered by	Keith Bessey
Peter Howarth	backing vocals	Recording location	Unknown
Steve Lauri	guitar	Recording date	1987
Paul Moessl	keyboards		
Mick Mullins	backing vocals		
Alan Park	keyboards		
Cliff Richard	vocals		
Henry Spinetti	drums, percussion		

3. Unissued track (Live & Guaranteed 1988!)

Musicians		*Recording Details*	
John Clark	guitar	Producer	Unknown
Rosemarie Ford	backing vocals	Engineered by	Unknown
Mark Griffiths	bass	Recording location	Fyens Forum, Odense, Denmark
Peter Howarth	backing vocals	Recording date	22nd May 1988
Steve Lauri	guitar		
Paul Moessl	keyboards		
Mick Mullins	backing vocals		
Alan Park	keyboards		
Cliff Richard	vocals		
Henry Spinetti	drums, percussion		

♫ Under the Influence

B-side of **The Only Way Out**

Cliff Richard had had a long association working on Garth Hewitt's solo projects as backing vocalist or producer – and often both – and so it was inevitable that he would record some of Hewitt's compositions. *Under the Influence* was recorded as part of the ***Now You See Me... Now You Don't*** album sessions, although it wasn't included on the final track listing. Instead, it was picked as the B-side for the first single to be released from the project, ***The Only Way Out***. Several of Cliff's non-album B-sides had to wait a number of years before being dusted off and reissued in CD format, but *Under the Influence* was re-released in LP and CD form on Cliff's 1984 faith and inspiration collation, *Walking in the Light*, and it was also added as a bonus track on the 2002 remaster of *Now You See Me... Now You Don't*.

Under the Influence is a term that is generally used to describe the deleterious effects of alcohol or drugs but here it is about the effect people have on other individuals, intentionally or otherwise, for at least part of the time and is articularly about the effect of God in his life. The track is a strong song that uses, as its principal hook, Cliff's choir of his own voice layered together, singing the song's title over and over. His lead vocal is mixed to the front and this gives a cosy even confidential feeling to the song that deserved a better initial fate than being demoted to a B-side.

Track Specification
Composed by Garth Hewitt

Musicians

John Clark	electric guitar, acoustic guitar
Dave Cooke	synthesiser
Mark Griffiths	bass
Graham Jarvis	drums, percussion
Mart Jenner	electric guitar
Craig Pruess	synthesisers, sequencers
Cliff Richard	vocals, backing vocals
Graham Todd	piano

Recording Details

Producer	Cliff Richard and Craig Pruess
Engineered by	John Walker and Steve Cook
Recording location	Strawberry Studios South, Surrey
Recording date	4th-15th January 1982

♫ Under Your Spell

From the album **Always Guaranteed**

The first track opening the second side of the vinyl version of the ***Always Guaranteed*** album, *Under Your Spell* was composed in the same way as much of the material recorded at the sessions. Producer Alan Tarney would have a musical idea - or sometimes no idea at all - and develop it on the guitar while in the studio. Working with Gerry Kitchingham, he would then lay down the basic track and build on it until Cliff Richard came in to learn and record his vocal lines before going to London to appear as the Rock Star in ***Time – the Musical*** at the Dominion Theatre. The only slight difference for *Under Your Spell* was that another long-term friend, Chris Eaton, assisted on the keyboards for the track.

Another song that packs in Tarney's electronica gives Cliff freedom to express the lyrics matched by the backing vocal arrangement built up in layers from recordings of Tarney's and Cliff's voice. It is a perfect piece of pop from the period and is one of the stand-out tracks from the project.

Track Specification
Composed by Alan Tarney

Musicians

Chris Eaton	keyboards
Cliff Richard	vocals, backing vocals
Alan Tarney	backing vocals, guitars, bass, keyboards, drum and percussion programming

Recording Details

Producer	Alan Tarney
Engineered by	Gerry Kitchingham and Keith Bessey
Recording location	R. G. Jones Studios, Wimbledon, London
Recording date	13th October-November 1986

♫ United for Evermore

From the album **Real as I Wanna Be**

The fifth track on ***Real as I Wanna Be*** sees Cliff Richard continuing to forge a furrow in a new approach to his music. *United for Evermore* is a much more soulful sound that many fans are used to, although it was precipitated by the tracks on ***Cliff Richard – The Album*** at the start of the decade.

The funky percussive beat keeps the song moving through some beautifully unexpected key changes, while Cliff sings in an emotional way that is supported by the almost unison backing vocals, which are presented in a breathy, anticipatory way.

Track Specification
Composed by Stephen Duberry, John McLaughlin and Dennis Morgan

Musicians

Vinnie Colaiuta	drums, percussion
Paul Jackson Jr.	guitar
Cliff Richard	vocals, backing vocals
Michelle Wolf	backing vocals
Peter Wolf	arranger, bass, keyboards, synclavier, percussion, funky percolator

Recording Details

Producer	Peter Wolf
Engineered by	Christian Leitgeb, Chris Heil, Paul Erickson and/or Keith Bessey
Recording location	Little America Recording Studios, Weiler, Austria, Ocean Recording Studios, Burbank, California, USA, Arco Recording Studios, Munich, Germany, R. G. Jones Recording Studios, Wimbledon, London, England and/or The Pierce Room, London, England
Recording date	March-April 1996 and November 1997

♫ Until the Right One Comes Along

Unissued track

Until the Right One Comes Along was one of three songs attempted at the 27th September session (along with ***First Lesson in Love*** and ***True Love Will Come to You***), none of which was released.

Track Specification
Composed by Unknown

Musicians		*Recording Details*	
Jet Harris	bass	Producer	Norrie Paramor
Hank Marvin	guitar	Engineered by	Malcolm Addey
Tony Meehan	drums, percussion	Recording location	Abbey Road Studio 2, St. John's Wood, London
Cliff Richard	vocals	Recording date	27th September 1960
Bruce Welch	rhythm guitar		

♫ Unto Us a Boy Is Born
From the EP **Carol Singers**

The tract from the Bible covering the birth of Christ is continued with the adulatory "For unto us a child is born", the saviour of mankind for which mortals should give appropriate thanks. It is a much-loved section, too, from Handel's *Messiah*. Occasionally the carol is perfrmed under the title without the prefixed 'for'.
Cliff Richard recorded a version of the traditional carol that was destined for the ***Carol Singers*** EP. It was arranged by Geoffrey Keating, who was one of the Mastersingers, a Christian group of music teachers acquainted with Cliff, and who performed with him on the EP. Singing in *a capella* form, with the teachers providing vocal harmonies to Cliff's lead, the final edit was spliced from multiple takes and initially only released in the mono format of the EP. However, it was reissued in stereo format in 1988 on the ***Carols*** LP, which was issued to build on the success of that Christmas's best-selling number one single ***Mistletoe and Wine***.
Initiated by the Mastersingers, the tune is then repeated by Cliff as a form of canon. Cliff sings the song with a reverence and straightforward performance that proves his abilities as a singer and something that is not regularly heard in other recordings from the period.

Track Specification
Composed by Traditional, arranged by Geoffrey Keating

Musicians		*Recording Details*	
Mastersingers:	backing vocals	Producer	Norrie Paramor
John Horrex		Engineered by	Peter Vince and John Barrett
Geoffrey Keating		Recording location	Abbey Road Studio 2, St. John's Wood, London
George Pratt		Recording date	10th September 1967
Michael Warrington			
Cliff Richard	vocals		

♫ Up in Canada
From the albums **Small Corners** *and* **Thank You Very Much**

One of the best tracks on the ***Small Corners*** album and a nominal favourite of Cliff Richard, *Up in Canada* was one of three songs on the album that was written by his friend Larry Norman. It was recorded at the first of three main sessions for the album, with it being the second song, which was completed in just two takes with additional overdubs recorded a fortnight later.
Staccato guitar chords lead into this quirky foot-tapping song that talks of unexpectedly meeting Jesus on the road while the way to Canada. The extraordinary pace is set up in the guitars that almost duel for prominence. The piano is pure rock and roll that wouldn't be out of place in a Jerry Lee Lewis performance but the strength of the song comes from Cliff's ebullience in his performance as well as the sheer joy to be heard from the ensemble group of musicians supporting his lead.
Up in Canada was on the set list for the twentieth anniversary concert ***Thank You Very Much***, but it was only released on the video that accompanied the project. In 2004, it was restored to the remastered release of the album but, since it was generated from the mono video soundtrack, it appears out of sequence and as a bonus track to avoid possible problems with the listening pleasure against the original stereo release.

Track Specification
Composed by Larry Norman

1. Small Corners

Musicians		*Recording Details*	
Brian Bennett	drums, percussion	Producer	Cliff Richard
Terry Britten	guitar	Engineered by	Tony Clark and Haydn Bendall
Stuart Calver	backing vocals	Recording location	Abbey Road Studio 3, St. John's Wood, London
Bryn Haworth	guitar	Recording date	17th January 1977 and 2nd February 1977
John Perry	backing vocals		
Cliff Richard	vocals		
Tony Rivers	backing vocals		
Alan Tarney	bass		
Graham Todd	piano		
Unknown	hand claps		

2. *Thank You Very Much*

Musicians

Terry Britten	guitar
Stuart Calver	backing vocals
Clem Cattini	drums, percussion
Dave Christopher	guitar
Mo Foster	bass
Graham Jarvis	drums, percussion
Graham Murray	guitar
John Perry	backing vocals
Cliff Richard	vocals
Tony Rivers	backing vocals
Graham Todd	keyboards

Recording Details

Producer	Bruce Welch
Engineered by	Tony Clark
Recording location	London Palladium, London
Recording date	4th March 1978

♫ Up in the World

From the albums **Every Face Tells a Story** *and* **Dressed for the Occasion** *and unissued live track*

Another favourite of Cliff Richard's to sing, the Clifford T. Ward song was also recorded by the underrated talent of the composer. Recorded by Cliff at the penultimate session for the ***Every Face Tells a Story*** album and the last recording session for Cliff in 1976, *Up in the World* was completed in seven takes with no overdubs required.

The gentleness of the song is introduced with strings playing a sequence of descending chords with diminished intervals that are simply exquisite. Cliff is in his element singing songs such as this and, as the tension builds up through the developing arrangement, he uses his vibrato to great effect.

The song was performed at the ***Thank You Very Much*** concerts in 1978, but a small handful, including *Up in the World*, were not included on the original release of the video or album. It was also included in the ***Dressed for the Occasion*** concert and, with Richard Hewson's orchestral arrangement, it is highly effective and more emotional even than the original. As with a number of tracks on the album, Cliff is only accompanied by the London Philharmonic Orchestra.

Track Specification

Composed by Clifford T. Ward

1. *Every Face Tells a Story*

Musicians

Richard Hewson	arranger, conductor
Cliff Richard	vocals
Unknown	orchestra

Recording Details

Producer	Bruce Welch
Engineered by	Tony Clark
Recording location	Abbey Road Studio 2, St. John's Wood, London
Recording date	24th September 1976

2. *Unissued track (Thank You Very Much)*

Musicians

Terry Britten	guitar
Stuart Calver	backing vocals
Clem Cattini	drums, percussion
Dave Christopher	guitar
Mo Foster	bass
Graham Jarvis	drums, percussion
Graham Murray	guitar
John Perry	backing vocals
Cliff Richard	vocals
Tony Rivers	backing vocals
Graham Todd	keyboards

Recording Details

Producer	Bruce Welch
Engineered by	Tony Clark
Recording location	London Palladium, London
Recording date	4th March 1978

3. *Dressed for the Occasion*

Musicians

Richard Hewson	arranger, conductor
London Philharmonic Orchestra	orchestra
Cliff Richard	vocals

Recording Details

Producer	Cliff Richard and Richard Hewson
Engineered by	John Kurlander
Mixed by	Keith Bessey
Recording location	Royal Albert Hall, London
Mixed at	Strawberry Studios South, Surrey
Recording date	23rd November 1982

♫ Up Where We Belong

From the album **Two's Company**

The theme tune from *An Officer and a Gentleman*, starring Richard Gere and Debra Winger, *Up Where We Belong* was sung by Joe Cocker and Jennifer Warnes. Released as a single later that year, it reached number one in the US Billboard Hot 100 in November and number seven in the UK singles charts. The performance received a Golden Globe and an Academy Award for the best song in 1983 and a BAFTA in 1984 and Cocker and Warnes later received a Grammy award for their duet. Co-writer Buffy Sainte-Marie covered the song and it has also been subject to recordings by Richard Clayderman, William Goldstein, Sweet Surrender and the Williams Brothers among others.

Cliff Richard recorded some additional songs in 2006 with favourite performers to pad out the compilation of duets for his ***Two's Company*** album. Choosing *Up Where We Belong* to perform with Anne Murray, who was a popular Canadian singer particularly in the sixties, it matches their combined vocals well. A complex guitar introduction leads into the shuffling rhythm that supports first Murray's and the Cliff's lead vocals. While the original song was ubiquitous at the time the film was released, Murray's and Cliff's version has a successful arrangement that makes it sound fresh and different. The pair's voices work well together although Murray sings in a lower register and Cliff generally in the higher register.

Track Specification

Composed by Will Jennings, Jack Nitzsche and Buffy Sainte-Marie

Musicians

Suzanne Barbieri	backing vocals
Richard Cardwell	keyboards
Mickey Féat	bass
Gavin Harrison	drums, percussion
Jakko M. Jakszyk	backing vocals
Anne Murray	vocals
Phil Palmer	guitar
Cliff Richard	vocals, backing vocals

Recording Details

Producer	Chris Porter
Engineered by	Chris Porter
Recording location	Metropolis Studios, London and Stanley House Studios, west London
Recording date	2006

THE CLIFF RICHARD RECORDING CATALOGUE

V - V - V - V - V - V - V - V - V - V - V - V - V - V - V - V - V

♫ Vaudeville Routine
From the film soundtrack album of **The Young Ones**

In ***The Young Ones*** narrative, having broken into the dilapidated Finsbury Park Empire theatre, the members of the youth club, initially despondent, pick up the props, wardrobe, scenery and lighting and enter into an extensive song and dance routine that features slapstick routines, jokes, songs and dancing. The soundtrack album breaks the sequence up thus:

a) ***Have a Smile for Everyone You Meet***
b) *Tinkle Tinkle Tinkle*
c) *The Eccentric*
d) *Algy the Piccadilly Johnny*
e) ***Captain Ginjah***
f) *Joshuah*
g) ***Where Did You Get That Hat?***
h) ***Living Doll***

The entire sequence was recorded in one session along with the segments of ***What D'You Know, We've Got a Show***. Several takes were recorded of each of the sections of the *Vaudeville Routine*, with the same takes used for the stereo and mono edits, but with different mixes for the audio channel requirements. The film version of the sequence was recorded later on the year (probably in the same month) but has not been formally released in any other commercial format.

♫ Vaya Con Dios
From the album **When in Spain**

Published in 1953, it is often subtitled ***May God Be with You,*** although it more accurately translates as the slightly different *Go with God*. It was first recorded by Les Paul and Mary Ford in late 1953, earning them a US Billboard number one and a UK number seven with their only release in Britain. Twenty years later in December 1973, Millican and Nesbitt successfully reached number twenty in the UK singles chart with their first of two singles. It has also been covered by many different artists including Desi Arnaz, Bing Crosby, Chet Atkins, the Drifters, Gene Autrey, Julio Iglesias, Kitty Kallen, Mel Tormé, Nana Mouskouri, Julie London, Al Martino, Roger Whittaker and Tony Orlando and Dawn.

Cliff Richard has recorded both the Spanish and English versions under their respective titles, with the English lyrics being overdubbed on the top of the backing track recorded in Barcelona at the EMI Studios for the ***When in Spain*** album. The ninth and final take and edit was used for the mono and stereo recordings but with different mixes for the needs of the audio channels.

Vaya Con Dios in Cliff Richard's and the Shadows' capable hands is a beautiful nugget that will inevitably be overlooked since it is performed in a foreign language. Calling on Cliff to sing at all levels of his range, his pitching of the notes and the emotion he injects into the lyrics elevate this version of the song into something special. The string arrangement and Hank Marvin's simple guitar solo are worthy of note too.

Track Specification
Composed by Larry Russell, Inez James and Buddy Pepper

Musicians

Brian Bennett	drums, percussion
Brian 'Licorice' Locking	bass
Hank Marvin	guitar
Norrie Paramor Strings	orchestra
Norrie Paramor	arranger, conductor
Cliff Richard	vocals
Bruce Welch	rhythm guitar

Recording Details

Producer	Norrie Paramor
Engineered by	Malcolm Addey
Recording location	EMI Studios, Barcelona (main) and Abbey Road Studio 2, St. John's Wood, London (strings)
Recording date	30th April 1963 (main recording) and 14th May 1963 (strings)

♫ Venite (O Come All Ye Faithful)
From the album **Together with Cliff Richard**

The most familiar version of the popular Christmas carol, *Oh Come All Ye Faithful*, is set to a tune called *Adeste Fideles* that is attributed to John Francis Wade. Leading up to Christmas, the final verse (talking of the birth of Christ that morning) is often dropped since it is anachronistic, until Christmas morning.

In 1982, Cliff Richard recorded ***Little Town,*** which was the traditional carol of ***O Little Town of Bethlehem*** set to a new tune written by Chris Eaton. For the ***Together with Cliff Richard*** album in 1991, Eaton reworked *Oh Come All Ye Faithful* to

become *Venite (O Come All Ye Faithful)*. 'Venite' is a Latin command that means 'come', while later in the song, more Latin is sung: 'Venite Venite Adoremus Dominum', which means unsurprisingly to 'Come, Come, Adore God'. The song was one of several recorded for the album in the early summer of 1991, a strange sensation recording seasonal material at the mid-part of the year.
Cliff's lead vocal has a slight echo added to it, while the performance sounds cosy and confidential until it opens up in the chorus for the Latin. The accompaniment consists of sustained synthesiser chords and a lovely arrangement of the lead and backing vocals, some of which are provided by Cliff himself. The melody and the sheer joy evident in the performance make this the best track on the album and a worthy candidate for a single if such a choice were sought.

Track Specification
Composed by Traditional and Chris Eaton

Musicians

John Clark	guitar
Mick Clarke	backing vocals
Paul Dunne	guitar
Mark Griffiths	bass
Peter Howarth	backing vocals
Peter May	drums, percussion
Paul Moessl	drum programming, keyboards
Mick Mullins	backing vocals
Keith Murrell	backing vocals
Cliff Richard	arranger, vocals, backing vocals
Frank Ricotti	drums, percussion
Steve Stroud	bass

Recording Details

Producer	Cliff Richard and Paul Moessl
Engineered by	Gerry Kitchingham, Andrew Greasley and Ben Robbins
Recording location	R. G. Jones Studios, Wimbledon, London
Recording date	24th June 1991 to July 1991

♫ Visions

***34th UK single** and from the album* **Cliff in Japan, Live at the Talk of the Town, Cliff Live in Korea** *and* **Japan Tour '74** *and unissued live track*

Often used to finished Cliff Richard's stage set following its single release, *Visions* is a sad song that talks of longing for those left behind or who have gone away – hence a suitable choice to close many a Cliff Richard show. When the song was first submitted to Cliff and his team, they agreed that it should be recorded, while also not being entirely sure it should be a single. It was only after it was completed that it was agreed that it was strong enough to stand on its own in the market. The song was written by an actor Paul Ferris, who was at the time appearing with Harry Secombe and who regularly wrote with another actor Nicky Henson. Curiously, the song has not been picked up by other balladeers.
Recorded at the penultimate session of 1965, the final (unknown) take and edit of *Visions* were used for both the mono and stereo versions but with different mixes for the needs of the separate audio channels. Initially, the single was only released in mono but, three years later, the stereo mix was included on the compilation album ***The Best of Cliff*** in 1969.
Issued as a single, backed with ***What Would I Do (For the Love of a Girl)?***, which was written by Hank Marvin and Bruce Welch, *Visions* was released on the Columbia label (catalogue number DB 7968) on 15th July 1966 and it reached the number seven spot in the UK singles charts. Most critics at the time suggested that it was by far the best song he had recorded for a long time. It has since appeared on the many hit compilations of Cliff's music.
Visions is a very pretty and beautifully arranged song that relies on a bass line, a harp and simple brushed drums to accompany the vocal line. There is a sustained string accompaniment and in Cliff's hands, the performance is exquisite and deservedly gained its chart position as a consequence.
Recorded as part of a number of live concerts that were issued as albums, it is a fitting song to complete shows with the lines "when will we meet again?", and these included the Far East tours and the performance at the Talk of the Town and later resurrected for the 1988 tour supporting the release of ***Always Guaranteed***. One other such concert was the Japanese tour or 1974 when Cliff's vocal line was accompanied by the gentle tweeting of the orchestral strings and the subdued rock band behind him. Unfortunately, the track only lasts for a minute before it mysteriously segues into ***Power to All Our Friends***, thereby losing some of the mood and beauty of the rendition of *Visions*.

Track Specification
Composed by Paul Ferris

1. Single

Musicians

Bernard Ebbinghouse Orchestra	orchestra
Bernard Ebbinghouse	arranger, conductor
Mike Sammes Singers	backing vocals
Cliff Richard	vocals

Recording Details

Producer	Norrie Paramor
Engineered by	Malcolm Addey
Recording location	Abbey Road Studio 2, St. John's Wood, London
Recording date	17th November 1965

2. Cliff in Japan

Musicians

Norrie Paramor Orchestra	orchestra
Norrie Paramor	arranger, conductor
Cliff Richard	vocals
Unknown	backing vocals

Recording Details

Producer	Norrie Paramor
Engineered by	Unknown
Recording location	Shibuya Public Hall, Tokyo, Japan
Recording date	18th October 1967

3. Live at the Talk of the Town

Musicians		*Recording Details*	
Breakaways:	backing vocals	Producer	Norrie Paramor
Vicki Hasemen		Engineered by	Peter Vince
Margo Quantrell		Recording location	Talk of the Town Theatre, London
Jean Ryder		Recording date	30th May 1968
Norrie Paramor	arranger, conductor		
Cliff Richard	vocals		
Talk of the Town Orchestra	orchestra		

4. Cliff Live in Korea

Musicians		*Recording Details*	
Brian Bennett	drums, percussion	Producer	Unknown
Alan Hawkshaw	keyboards	Engineered by	Unknown
Hank Marvin	backing vocals, guitar	Recording location	Citizen Hall, Seoul, South Korea
Cliff Richard	vocals	Recording date	16th October 1969
John Rostill	backing vocals, bass		
Bruce Welch	backing vocals, rhythm guitar		

5. Japan Tour '74

Musicians		*Recording Details*	
Barrie Guard	arranger, conductor	Producer	Toshiba EMI (no individual detailed)
Cliff Hall	piano	Engineered by	Toshiba EMI (no individual detailed)
Brian Lewis	backing vocals, guitar	Recording location	Shinjuku Koseinenkin, Tokyo, Japan
Kevin Peak	acoustic guitar	Recording date	7th-8th October 1974
Cliff Richard	vocals		
Shambles Symphonet	orchestra		
Trevor Spencer	drums, percussion		
Alan Tarney	backing vocals, bass		
Bruce Welch	backing vocals, rhythm guitar		

6. Unissued track (Live & Guaranteed 1988!)

Musicians		*Recording Details*	
John Clark	guitar	Producer	Unknown
Rosemarie Ford	backing vocals	Engineered by	Unknown
Mark Griffiths	bass	Recording location	Fyens Forum, Odense, Denmark
Peter Howarth	backing vocals	Recording date	22nd May 1988
Steve Lauri	guitar		
Paul Moessl	keyboards		
Mick Mullins	backing vocals		
Alan Park	keyboards		
Cliff Richard	vocals		
Henry Spinetti	drums, percussion		

♬ Visit of the Wise Men and the Escape to Egypt, The

From the album **About that Man**

Cliff Richard produced an album that was principally a number of tracks of his readings of parts of the bible fitting around only four songs. The second reading is taken from the book of Matthew, chapter two, verses 1 to 23. Cliff reads the tracts with passion and imbues the story with character and meaning as he unfolds the story of the wise men and Herod's fear of the rumours of the birth of Christ. It was probably completed in one take since there are obvious splices in the track.

Track Specification

From the King James Bible

Musicians		*Recording Details*	
Cliff Richard	vocals	Producer	Norrie Paramor
		Engineered by	Richard Lush
		Recording location	Abbey Road Studio 2, St. John's Wood, London
		Recording date	20th February 1970

♬ Vita Mia

From the album **Real as I Wanna Be**

In the nineties, many popular music artists were involved in the cross-over with opera phenomenon, a genre that was most famously observed by Freddie Mercury's duet with Montserrat Caballé at the beginning of the nineties, *Barcelona*, for the upcoming Olympic Games. Cliff Richard teamed up with tenor Vincenzo La Scola to perform *Vita Mia* (translated as *My Life*), which was written by producer Peter Wolf and backing vocalist Michelle Wolf. Operatic style requires a completely different approach than is required to sing popular music and most examples of the genre have the classically trained artist drowning out the popular singer; however, Cliff holds his own perfectly and pitches his voice brilliantly with La Scola's.

The music is extraordinarily evocative and beautiful, but what makes this song something so noteworthy is the combination of Cliff's pitch-perfect voice and La Scola's classically trained voice, particularly at the pinch-point of extraordinarily high drama when Cliff has to reach for the highest note he has sung without resorting to falsetto. Absolutely beautiful in its execution, the power would have been enough to drive the song into the charts.
The project resulted in Cliff being invited to join La Scola on a couple of tracks from La Scola's album that took its name from this song. There was some talk at the time of releasing this powerful ballad as a single but this was dropped.

Track Specification
Composed by Peter Wolf and Michelle Wolf; Italian lyrics by Zucchero Fornaciari

Musicians

Vincenzo La Scola	vocals
Munich Symphony Orchestra	orchestra
Cliff Richard	vocals
Michelle Wolf	backing vocals
Peter Wolf	arranger, conductor, keyboards

Recording Details

Producer	Peter Wolf
Engineered by	Christian Leitgeb, Chris Heil, Paul Erickson and/or Keith Bessey
Recording location	Little America Recording Studios, Weiler, Austria
Recording date	1997 or 1998

♫ Vodna Pot

From the album **Podarjeno Srcu** *(Aleksander Mežek)*

Aleksander Mežek first worked with Cliff Richard when Cliff supplied his vocal contribution on the title track of the *Days Go By* album in 1974, when Mežek was recording under the name Aleksander John. In 1989, Mežek released his *Podarjeno Srcu* album in his native tongue, which featured Cliff on two tracks. The second of these (the other being ***Prijatelju***) was *Vodna Pot* (which translates from the Slovenian as *Water Path* or *Waterway*). The album, which was issued in what was then Yugoslavia, is now a major rarity and, for this reason, the author has been unable to listen to the track to confirm the instrumentation used. Therefore, the track specification incorporates all of the artists known to have been involved in recording the album and will be updated once further information has been made available.
In 1990, however, Cliff returned to the studio with Mežek to record backing vocals for an English version of the track, which was retitled ***Strong Is the Current***. This became the B-side of the single release of ***To a Friend***, which was the English version of *Prijatelju*.

Track Specification
Composed by Aleksander Mežek and Eugenija Dumbatze

Musicians

Ian Bairnson	guitar
Paul Buckmaster	arranger, conductor
Richard Cottle	clarinet, keyboards
Jonathan Du Bose	electric guitar
London Symphony Orchestra	orchestra
Komorni Zbor RTV Ljubljana	choir
Aleksander Mežek	vocals
Davy Paton	bass
Cliff Richard	backing vocals
Jeremy Stacy	drums, percussion
Rick Wakeman	keyboards
Saša Zalepugin	acoustic guitar

Recording Details

Producer	Aleksander Mežek and Rick Wakeman
Engineered by	Chris Sheldon, John Burns, John Kurlander and/or Russel Bracher
Recording location	Studio House, London, Studio 26 RTV Ljubljana, Yugoslavia, Abbey Road Studio 1, St. John's Wood, London and/or Master Control Studio, Burbank, Los Angeles, California, USA
Recording date	1988 or 1989

♫ Voice in the Wilderness, A

7th UK single *and from the* **Expresso Bongo EP** *and B-side of* **Singing the Blues**

The curiously-titled film ***Expresso Bongo*** was Cliff Richard's second foray into films after ***Serious Charge***. While *Serious Charge* was altogether more gritty (the serious charge of the title being a claim of paedophilia against a benign and helpful priest), *Expresso Bongo* was much more light-hearted, although it was still intended to be a biting satire on the music business and the shallowness of many of the music promoters of the time. Like its predecessor, too, *Expresso Bongo* started its existence as a West End play that was quite popular, given the desire for satire from the audience in the latter days of the fifties and into the sixties. The plot was based around a cynical music agent, who spots a teenage singer (whom he renamed Bongo) in a coffee-house and, using his acumen and contacts forces Bongo's first record (*A Voice in the Wilderness*) to be a smash hit, with a saccharine follow-up (***The Shrine on the Second Floor***) to make his signing more widely acceptable. In the play, the joke was that Bongo Herbert couldn't sing or perform very well. In the film, Cliff took on the role of Herbert but changes were made to avoid potentially damaging his then fledgling recording career by ensuring that Bongo would surprise in that he *could* sing. All the other satirical elements remained, however. And so it was that *A Voice in the Wilderness* was issued in the film as Herbert's first single. The film's title is drawn from the coffee-shop inferences and the speed and agility with which the song becomes a hit as well as the percussion Herbert plays.
As well as being on the film's accompanying EP, *A Voice in the Wilderness* was also released as Cliff Richard and Shadows' seventh single and it was remarkable insofar as it was the last time it was issued in the 78 r.p.m. format as well as seven-inch vinyl. Released on 15th January 1960 on the Columbia label (seven-inch catalogue number 45-DB 4398; 78 r.p.m.

catalogue number DB 4398), the single reached number two in the UK charts, just stopped from being Cliff's third number one in a row by Anthony Newley's *Why?* The associated EP (also called ***Expresso Bongo***) featured the song and three other titles from the film (including one of the Shadows performing the instrumental *Bongo Blues*) and was Cliff's first EP to chart in the UK (see separate section on EPs and *The Shrine on the Second Floor*)).
The song performance in the film is different from those used for the single and the EP. The stereo version of the track has not been edited differently from the same recording take but, instead, it was decided to take the mono recording and make a stereo version from that: in this sense, these versions heard on the EPs are not different. The arrangement for the mono EP version of the song is another take from that used for the single, although there are very few differences to be heard other than slight differences in lyrics (use of the word 'a' instead of 'the' and so on). The stereo version is basically the same as the mono in terms of the vocals and instrumentation but there is a different guitar line played by Hank Marvin tacked on to it (descending scales rather than single notes being played). The same basic recording for mono and stereo was achieved by recording on two different machines at the same time, thereby giving rise to further differences created by playback and recording speeds, although these will generally not be heard by most people.
Having had significant success with the more countrified songs ***Living Doll*** and ***Travellin' Light***, it is no surprise that the gently swinging *A Voice in the Wilderness* should appeal to Cliff's legion of fans. Co-written by producer Norrie Paramor, the love song is appealing to the girl of his dreams in the depths of his angst as he tries to establish what went wrong with their relationship after a fight. What marks this song out particularly is Hank's solo guitar line throughout, using the tremolo dominantly for the first time to add even more pathos to the angst-ridden boy pining for his girlfriend. The vocal line, too, is surprisingly technically complex, particularly on the rising notes at the end of the chorus but Cliff carries it off with such ease as to give the illusion of simplicity.
In the early part of 1961, a version of this song was translated into German, ***Die Stimme der Liebe*** (literally '*The Voice of Love*') and issued as the B-side of ***Bin Verliebt***, which was a translated version of ***Fall in Love with You***.
Cliff and the Shadows reunited in 2009 for his fiftieth anniversary celebrations, re-recording several early songs for the ***Reunited*** album which they then took out on tour. Some tracks were not issued on the album and *A Voice in the Wilderness* instead formed the B-side of ***Singing the Blues***from the project. Although the performance is crisper, it is one of the few tracks that sound as if it is the original– at least until the witty doo-wop backing vocals come in during the chorus.

Track Specification
Composed by Norrie Paramor and Bunny Lewis

1. Expresso Bongo EP (mono and stereo)

Musicians		*Recording Details*	
Jet Harris	bass	Producer	Norrie Paramor
Hank Marvin	guitar	Engineered by	Malcolm Addey
Tony Meehan	drums, percussion	Recording location	Abbey Road Studio 2, St. John's Wood, London
Cliff Richard	vocals	Recording date	8th December 1959
Bruce Welch	rhythm guitar		

2. Single

Musicians		*Recording Details*	
Jet Harris	bass	Producer	Norrie Paramor
Hank Marvin	guitar	Engineered by	Malcolm Addey and Alan Kane
Tony Meehan	drums, percussion	Recording location	Abbey Road Studio 2, St. John's Wood, London
Cliff Richard	vocals	Recording date	20th December 1959
Bruce Welch	rhythm guitar		

3. B-side (Singing the Blues)

Musicians		*Recording Details*	
Brian Bennett	drums, percussion	Producer	Warren Bennett (co-ordination)
Mark Griffiths	bass	Engineered by	James Collins (Honeyhill Studios), Ethan Carlson (Middle Ear Studios), Les Williams (Nivram Studios) and Keith Bessey (mixing and mastering)
Hank Marvin	backing vocals, guitar	Recording location	Middle Ear Studios, Miami, Florida, USA (Cliff's vocals), Nivram Studios, Perth, Western Australia (Hank's guitars and vocals) and Honeyhill Studios, Hertfordshire, England (all other vocals and instruments)
Cliff Richard	vocals, backing vocals	Recording date	Early 2009
Bruce Welch	backing vocals, rhythm guitar		

♫ Vreneli
German single

Vreneli is a colloquial term for gold coins minted in Switzerland from the end of the nineteenth century to just before the Second World War and then for a short period at the end of the forties. The figurine on the face of the coin represents the lady of Liberty or the Confederation of Switzerland, who was called Verena, with the suffix meaning 'little'. Minted in different denominations, they were also called Swiss Misses, and are often seen as the forerunner to today's Euro coin.

The song, *Vreneli,* has only ever been released in mono format and remained a rarity until the release of the 1997 ***On the Continent*** boxed set of CDs featuring all the foreign translation titles from Cliff's career. *Vreneli* was released in Germany initially as the B-side of ***Schön Wie Ein Traum*** (the German translated version of his UK hit ***Theme for a Dream***) before finding a position at number fifty in the German charts in its own right, although adopting the same catalogue number on the Columbia label (C 21843).
With a typical German folk feel to the song that would not be out of place in the Eurovision Song Contest of the period, the instrumentation from the Shadows is quite different from the sound they had developed on their domestic recordings and this is further bolstered by the saxophones and orchestral accompaniment. A swiftly swinging piece of music, Cliff's enunciation of the German is well-placed and it is a surprisingly (but not quite irritatingly) catchy little tune.

Track Specification
Composed by Rudi Lindt, T. Thorn and R. Horn

Musicians

Friedel Berlipp	conductor
Berlipp's Band	additional instruments
The Hansen Boys	backing vocals
Jet Harris	bass
Hank Marvin	guitar
Tony Meehan	drums, percussion
Cliff Richard	vocals
Bruce Welch	rhythm guitar

Recording Details

Producer	Norrie Paramor
Engineered by	Malcolm Addey
Recording location	Abbey Road Studio 2, St. John's Wood, London plus overdubs in unknown location in Germany
Recording date	10th April 1961

♫ Waiting for a Girl Like You
From the album **Love... The Album**

Foreigner had not really enjoyed major chart success when they started out in 1978 but, just three years later, they were riding high in the charts with *I Want to Know What Love Is* (a British number one) and *Waiting for a Girl Like You*, which reached number eight late in December 1981. Included on the soundtrack of dance film *Footloose*, it has also been covered by a variety of artists including Rick Springfield, Paul Anka and Julio Iglesias.

Cliff Richard recorded five new songs to accompany a selection of love songs from as early as the sixties for his album ***Love... The Album***, released in 2007. The first track was *Waiting for a Girl Like You*, the musicians for which are unknown. Creating a grooving rhythm from the beginning, the arrangement becomes more of an homage to the Foreigner original. Cliff sings his own backing vocals and performs the song in a mildly confidential manner that begins to open up in the more explosive choruses.

Track Specification
Composed by Lou Gramm and Mick Jones

Musicians

Cliff Richard	vocals, backing vocals
Unknown	backing vocals
Unknown	guitar
Unknown	bass
Unknown	keyboards, programming
Unknown	drums, percussion
Unknown	strings

Recording Details

Producer	Michael Omartian
Engineered by	Terry Christian
Recording location	Sound Kitchen, Franklin, Tennessee, USA, Sound House, Franklin, Tennessee, USA and/or Blue Wave Studios, Bayley's Plantation, St. Phillip, Barbados
Recording date	2007

♫ Wake Up, Wake Up
From the album **Two a Penny**

Written by the duo that also performed as David and Jonathan, *Wake Up, Wake Up* was the second song to be completed by Cliff Richard at the first of two sessions set aside for that day.

With a cheery trumpet line and a bouncy orchestral accompaniment matched by the Breakaways backing vocals, Cliff sings with ebullience and injects the happy lyrics with high emotion. The upbeat mood of the track sets it apart from many of the tracks on the album, which tend to be introspective and sad.

Track Specification
Composed by Roger Cook and Roger Greenaway

Musicians

Breakaways:	backing vocals
Vicki Hasemen	
Margo Quantrell	
Jean Ryder	
Mike Leander	arranger, conductor
Mike Leander Orchestra	orchestra
Cliff Richard	vocals

Recording Details

Producer	Norrie Paramor
Engineered by	Peter Vince
Recording location	Abbey Road Studio 2, St. John's Wood, London
Recording date	8th March 1968

♫ Walking in the Air
From the album **Cliff at Christmas**

One of the now perennial and ubiquitous songs associated with Christmas, *Walking in the Air* was originally on the soundtrack of the cartoon film version of Raymond Briggs's *The Snowman* from 1982 (commissioned by then new British television company Channel 4 for their first Christmas season) and comes at the part in the narrative where the lonely young boy is taken up into the night sky by the snowman that he has built in the back garden and which has anthropomorphized into his new friend. Originally the song was recorded by a chorister from St. Paul's Cathedral in London, Peter Auty, but it has since become forever associated with boy singer Aled Jones, who took the song to number five at Christmas in 1985. Auty's version, released at the same time, only managed to reach number forty-two. When his version was re-released a couple of years later, it fared better but still only reached number thirty-seven.

When Cliff Richard was compiling his second Christmas music album, ***Cliff at Christmas***, he decided to include a more mature arrangement of *Walking in the Air* as the first wholly new track on the listing. It was recorded during the early sessions for Cliff's next studio album, ***Something's Goin' On***.

A rumbling synthesiser chord is sustained as percussion, the guitar and a piano perform the introductory melody. The problem with many covers is that the expectation is high regarding potential comparisons but the reality is limited because of the original. But Cliff's version is sufficiently different not to draw such differentiations and he creates a contrasting version of the song while keeping it recognizable. He provides his own backing vocals as he relays the story of the Snowman.

Track Specification
Composed by Howard Blake

Musicians	
Mike Brignardello	bass
John Hammond	drums, percussion
Jerry McPherson	guitar
Nashville String Machine	strings
Amanda Omartian	backing vocals
Michael Omartian	keyboards
Cliff Richard	vocals, backing vocals

Recording Details	
Producer	Michael Omartian
Engineered by	Terry Christian, David Streit and J. C. Monterrosa
Recording location	Sound House, Brentwood, Tennessee, USA, The Blue Room, Nashville, Tennessee, USA and Tennessee Sound Kitchen, Franklin, Tennessee, USA
Recording date	2003

♬ Walking in the Light
B-side of **Hot Shot**

Recorded at the same sessions that produced the track listing for the ***Rock 'n' Roll Juvenile*** album, *Walking in the Light* was the first song to be completed at the session that produced the backing track, with a follow-up session nine months later to record the vocal overdubs. Chosen as the B-side of the second single from the album, ***Hot Shot***, the song also gave its title to a collation of gospel-related songs in 1984, on which it also appeared. It was also included as a bonus track on the 2001 reissue of the remastered version of *Rock 'n' Roll Juvenile*.
There is a funky beat to *Walking in the Light* that has a syncopated rhythm to the drums and percussion, alongside the tinkling of the keyboards. The uncredited strings provide a lilting accompaniment, while Cliff's vocals are recorded so that they occasionally overlap each other, therefore requiring a planned number of takes to be edited together. A mature sound for a mature song, it deserved its position as the title track to the compilation album that featured a number of favourite inspirational faith-related tracks.

Track Specification
Composed by Terry Britten

Musicians	
Terry Britten	backing vocals, guitar
Lance Dixon	synthesiser
Herbie Flowers	bass
Graham Jarvis	drums, percussion
Cliff Richard	vocals, backing vocals
Unknown	orchestra
Unknown	conductor

Recording Details	
Producer	Cliff Richard and Terry Britten
Engineered by	Tony Clark and Haydn Bendall
Recording location	Pathé Marconi, Paris, France (backing track) and Abbey Road Studio, St. John's Wood, London (vocals)
Recording date	18th-20th July 1978 (backing track) and 18th April 1979 (vocals)

♬ Walk on By/The Look of Love
From the album **Cliff "Live" in Japan '72**

At the end of 1969, Cliff Richard was a regular feature on Cilla Black's television show, *Cilla*, and they were firm friends. On the show broad cast on 19th February 1969, Cliff and Black performed a duet of ***Walk on By*** and ***The Look of Love*** together. This was something that Cliff would take into his own programmes and on tour, most memorably with Olivia Newton-John and Pat Carrol performing with him on the album ***Cliff "Live" in Japan '72***. The version with Black was later released on a Cilla Black retrospective, *The Definitive Collection (A Life in Music)*, in 2009 as part of a selection of television clips on a supplementary DVD, although the titles were reversed on the track listing.

♬ Walk on By
From the album **Cliff "Live" in Japan '72**

Written by Burt Bacharach and Hal David specifically for Dionne Warwick, it is her version that was released as a single and is the most familiar. It reached number six on the US Billboard charts in the spring of 1964, while reaching number nine in the UK. Other versions charting in Britain are the Stranglers punk version in August 1978, which reached number twenty-one, the Average White Band who reached number forty-nine in August 1979, D Train in May 1982 (number forty-four), Sybil who reached number six in February 1990 and Gabrielle who took it to number seven in February 1997. Over the four and a half decades it has been covered by many tens of artists from a multiplicity of genres.
Cliff Richard's version of *Walk on By* was one of a handful that he performed in concert and on television but never recorded a studio version. For the Japanese tour in September 1972, it was performed as a medley with ***The Look of Love***, but with backing singers Olivia Newton-John and Pat Carroll stepping up to take over the lead vocals, while Cliff reversed roles with them, interspersing a few lines every now and again. The combined harmonies are luscious and beautiful.

Track Specification

Composed by Burt Bacharach and Hal David

Musicians

Brian Bennett	drums, percussion
Pat Carroll	backing vocals
John Farrar	bass
Alan Hawkshaw	piano
Hank Marvin	guitar
Olivia Newton-John	backing vocals
Cliff Richard	vocals
Bruce Welch	rhythm guitar

Recording Details

Producer	Norrie Paramor
Engineered by	Unknown
Recording location	Kosei Nenkin Hall, Tokyo, Japan
Recording date	22nd-23rd September 1972

♬ Washerwoman

From the film soundtrack album of **Finders Keepers**

In ***Finders, Keepers***, Cliff Richard and the Shadows (playing themselves) walk through countryside to find people to whom they can perform. Their original destination of San Carlos is deserted owing to the frantic search for an unexploded bomb inadvertently dropped by the British and Americans. As they come to a clearing, they observe women doing their washing by the lakeside. The Shadows play on a promontory, as Cliff wanders among the women singing his song asking the women where they are staying. He finally settles on Emelia (Vivianne Ventura), who initially thinks that Cliff and the band are bomb engineers rather than itinerant musicians. The scene finishes with Cliff pulling clothes out of her basket.

The first song to be completed in the dual session on that day, *Washerwoman* features guest backing vocalists (as the washerwomen by the lake) from the Mike Sammes Singers, although predominantly the backing vocals are taken by the Shadows supporting Cliff in their inimitable way. The second and final take were used for both the mono and stereo recordings but with different mixes for the separation in audio channels. The soundtrack version of the song was used on the film soundtrack with Cliff, the Shadows and the women actors lip-synching and miming to the music.

Although the subject matter is deliberately geared to the film sequence, *Washerwoman* is, in fact, a love song beseeching the woman of the title to be his and has much to commend it from the instantly memorable melody, the esoteric but witty lyrics, the vocal harmonies and the incorporation of a few grunts from Hank Marvin.

Track Specification

Composed by Hank Marvin, Bruce Welch, Brian Bennett and John Rostill

Musicians

Brian Bennett	drums, percussion
Hank Marvin	backing vocals, grunts, guitar
Mike Sammes Singers	backing vocals
Cliff Richard	vocals
John Rostill	backing vocals, bass
Bruce Welch	backing vocals, rhythm guitar

Recording Details

Producer	Norrie Paramor
Engineered by	Peter Vince and Richard Lush
Recording location	Abbey Road Studio 3, St. John's Wood, London
Recording date	28th April 1966

♬ Was Ist Dabei?

B-side of **Du Bist Mein Erster Gedanke**

For the B-side of the original recording of the German language single ***Du Bist Mein Erster Gedanke***, a translation of Cliff Richard's British number twenty-two hit, ***The Time in Between***, was recorded at a session in the spring of 1966. For *Was Ist Dabei* – literally *What Is with Her?* – Cliff's new vocals were overdubbed on the original backing track from the British single. The final (unknown) vocal take and edit were overdubbed on the backing track and mixed differently for the separate audio channels. Initially issued in mono as part of the single release, the stereo version was eventually released just over thirty years later when it was included on the collection of foreign language recordings ***On the Continent***.

Since it uses the same backing track as the English original, there is not much difference in the overall performance with the exception of the language. Cliff appears comfortable with the German language on this recording and, apart from the natural guttural sounds of the enunciation, it is probably closest of all his German recordings to the original. There are different backing vocals overdubbed on the performance but these are uncredited.

Track Specification

Composed by Georges Aber, Micky Jones and Thomas Brown; German lyrics by Joachim Relin

Musicians

Brian Bennett	drums, percussion
Hank Marvin	guitar
Cliff Richard	vocals
John Rostill	bass
Unknown	backing vocals
Bruce Welch	rhythm guitar

Recording Details

Producer	Norrie Paramor (backing track and vocals) and Unknown (backing vocals)
Engineered by	Unknown (backing track), Peter Vince and Richard Lush (vocals) and Unknown (backing vocals)
Recording location	Estudios Valentim de Carvalho, Lisbon, Portugal (backing track), Abbey Road Studio 3, St. John's Wood, London (vocals) and Germany (backing vocals)
Recording date	10th May 1965 (backing track), 13th May 1966 (vocals) and May 1966 (backing vocals)

♫ Was Kann Ich Tun?

B-side of **Das Glück Ist Rosarot**

Recorded at the same session as its A-side, ***Das Glück Ist Rosarot***, *Was Kann Ich Tun?* – a translation of ***What Would I Do (For the Love of a Girl)?*** – was overdubbed on the original Shadows tracks recorded earlier in May. The final (unknown) take and edit of the vocal track was applied to the backing track and used for both the mono and stereo versions of but with different mixes for the split audio channels. Initially only released in mono, the stereo version of the song was finally released on the German boxed set compilation of all Cliff's foreign language recordings, ***On the Continent***, in 1997.
Using the backing track from the English version means that the versions are very similar, of course, with the exception of the different language, which Cliff carries off with aplomb. There are backing vocals that have been overdubbed but these are uncredited (and are not the Shadows). Before the instrumental break, Cliff breaks into English to say 'hear me now'.

Track Specification

Composed by Bruce Welch and Hank Marvin; German lyrics by Walker

Musicians

Brian Bennett	drums, percussion
Hank Marvin	guitar
Cliff Richard	vocals
John Rostill	bass
Unknown	backing vocals
Bruce Welch	rhythm guitar

Recording Details

Producer	Norrie Paramor (backing track and vocals) and Unknown (backing vocals)
Engineered by	Malcolm Addey, Peter Vince and Richard Lush (backing track), Peter Vince (vocals) and Unknown (backing vocals)
Recording location	Abbey Road Studio 3, St. John's Wood, London (backing track and vocals) and Unknown (backing vocals)
Recording date	22nd May 1966 (backing track), 10th November 1966 (vocals) and November 1966 (backing vocals)

♫ Watch Me Come Alive

From the album **The Chicken Shed Album** *(Various)*

The Chicken Shed Theatre Company – later Chicken Shed and then Chickenshed – was founded in 1974 in Cockfosters, north-east London, in a disused chicken shed. Gaining charity status later on, it was set up to help children of different backgrounds and abilities to gain confidence through performance. Branching into recording in 1997, the company produced an album begun at the end of the nineties and enlisted the help of Cliff Richard on the track *Watch Me Come Alive*. According to the album's liner notes, Cliff appeared at the theatre ready to record with a vocal line and harmonies already worked out and this gave them the encouragement they needed with such a big name tied to the project.
The song is a bouncing foot-tapping song that features Cliff providing a lot of his own backing vocals, while supported by the driving percussion and bass and assisted by some attractive guitar lines. The story talks of Christmas and how he feels at the time. It is a lovely song, well-performed by the ensemble band, and deserves a broader distribution and increased awareness of its existence. The arrangement has a slightly nostalgic air about it while the performance is fully modern.

Track Specification

Composed by Paul Morrall and Jo Collins

Musicians

Giles Brading	backing vocals
Fiona Callan	backing vocals
David Carey	keyboards
Jo Collins	keyboards
Simon Copper	drums, percussion
San Fuster-Burnett	guitars
Francis Haines	keyboards
Liz Kitchen	drums, percussion
Cliff Richard	vocals, backing vocals
Iain Whitmore	backing vocals, bass
Greg Williams	backing vocals

Recording Details

Producer	David Carey, Jo Collins and Francis Haines
Engineered by	Giles Brading, Simon Cooper, Keith Jay and Saul Gillingham
Recording location	Chickenshed Studios, Southgate, London
Recording date	29th September 1999 (Cliff's vocals and initial backing track) and June 2003 (backing track completion)

♫ Watch What You Do with My Baby

B-side of **I'm the Lonely One**

Co-written by one of Elvis Presley's songwriters, Bill Giant, *Watch What You Do with My Baby* has been covered by a few artists including Ginny Arnell and Julie Grant, and was the B-side of Cliff Richard's twenty-fourth single, ***I'm the Lonely One***. Recorded at the final session of 1963, it is particularly noteworthy for the inclusion of a new musician. Since it was the first song of the session, it is also the first Cliff recording to feature new Shadows bassist, John Rostill, brought in to replace Brian Locking, who had recently left the group to focus on his religion. The (unknown) take and edit were used for the recording, which has only been released in mono. It was subsequently issued on the ***Cliff's Palladium Successes*** EP on CD with 2001 *I Could Easily Fall* in 2001 and then on ***...And They Said It Wouldn't Last! (My 50 Years in Music)*** in 2008.
Watch What You Do with My Baby is an unusual track for Cliff to perform in that it is doesn't follow the standard rock and roll or ballad style of approach. Indeed, the timbre of his voice is reminiscent of what he was doing later in the seventies.

There is an uncredited piano (possibly Norrie Paramor or, more unlikely, Hank Marvin) mixed forward and played in the instrumental break in place of the usual guitar. In other respects, it is a typical ensemble performance by the band, particularly when the harmonies are performed on the last lines of each chorus.

Track Specification
Composed by Bill Giant, Bernie Baum and Florence Kaye

Musicians

Brian Bennett	drums, percussion
Hank Marvin	backing vocals, guitar
Cliff Richard	vocals
John Rostill	backing vocals, bass
Unknown	piano
Bruce Welch	backing vocals, rhythm guitar

Recording Details

Producer	Norrie Paramor
Engineered by	Malcolm Addey
Recording location	Abbey Road Studio 2, St. John's Wood, London
Recording date	23rd November 1963

♫ Water Is Wide, The

From the album **Now You See Me, Now You Don't**

In its original Scottish folk-song form from the early seventeenth century, *The Water Is Wide* is also referred to as *O Waly, Waly*. Still popular for performance today, the song refers to the challenges created by being in love or wanting to love. Benjamin Britten arranged the song for voice and piano in 1948, while John Rutter uses the theme for the Third Movement of his *Suite for Strings* composed in 1973 and the melody is often used for the hymn ***When I Survey the Wondrous Cross***. The song has been variously recorded by artists such as Felicity Lott, Steeleye Span, Sarah Brightman, Benjamin Luxon, Enya, Joan Baez, Pete Seeger, Bob Dylan, Eva Cassidy, James Taylor and the Seekers among many others.
For the ***Now You See Me... Now You Don't*** album, Cliff Richard and Craig Pruess worked on their own arrangement and Cliff is on record as saying that the performance of songs like *The Water Is Wide* is easy because it allows the performer to express the requisite emotions.
Cliff's impassioned vocal employs a vibrato, while it is mixed with an echo over the piano and the twiddling synthesisers. The arrangement is simplistically beautiful and lifted by the vocal arrangement, with Cliff supplying his own harmonies.

Track Specification
Composed by Traditional, arranged by Cliff Richard and Craig Pruess

Musicians

Mo Foster	fretless bass
Mart Jenner	electric guitar
Dave Mattacks	drums, percussion
Craig Pruess	synthesisers, sequencers
Cliff Richard	vocals, backing vocals
Peter Skellern	piano

Recording Details

Producer	Cliff Richard and Craig Pruess
Engineered by	John Walker and Tony Richards
Recording location	Abbey Road Studio 2, St. John's Wood, London
Recording date	21st-22nd September 1981

♫ We Being Many

From the album **Nothing but the Best** *(Helen Shapiro)*

Cliff Richard was in the studios in the mid-nineties recording duets with a number of other famous singers: Cilla Black, Tammy Wynette and then Helen Shapiro on *We Being Many*. The musicians featured mostly have a long connection with Cliff and particularly Dave Cooke. The vocals were recorded at the R. G. Jones Studios in one session on 10th January 1995 while the instrumentation and overdubs were carried out elsewhere on unspecified dates the same month. Originally on Shapiro's *Nothing But the Best* album in April 1995, the song was later included on the track listing of the compilation album of faith and inspiration songs, *Yesterday, Today, Forever* in 1998 and *The Gospel Collection* in 2002.
The synthesisers and electric piano introduce the song, initially sung by Helen Shapiro. A spiritual song, with reverential lyrics, Cliff sings the second verse, partly in Hebrew. Their voices blend beautifully in the middle chorus and the reverence is touchingly portrayed. In the third verse, they sing separate melodies before coming together in unison.

Track Specification
Composed by Marty Goetz

Musicians

Bernie Armstrong	backing vocals
Dave Cooke	arranger, keyboards, programming
Cooke Thorp String Ensemble:	
Josie Abbott	cello
Marcus Broome	violin
Penelope Thompson	viola
William Thorp	violin
Sarah Denton	solo violin
Mike Haughton	soprano and alto saxophones
Annie McCaig	backing vocals
Mark Purdy	drums, percussion
Cliff Richard	vocals, backing vocals
Helen Shapiro	vocals
Mark Williamson	backing vocals

Recording Details

Producer	Dave Cooke
Engineered by	Bruce Pont
Recording location	R. G. Jones Studios, Wimbledon, London (vocals), ICC Studios, Eastbourne (instrumentation) and JMF Studios, Twickenham, London (overdubs and final mixing)
Recording date	10th January 1995 (vocals) and January 1995 (instrumentation and overdubs)

♫ Wedding, The

125th UK single

With the phenomenal success of Cliff Richard's interpretative project, ***Heathcliff,*** came the need for a single from the show. Although two songs had already been released from the studio album, ***A Misunderstood Man*** and ***Had to Be,*** with another to be released later, ***Be with Me Always,*** it was decided to record a new version of one of the other songs with Cliff's leading lady playing Cathy, Helen Hobson. However, rather than using live material, or re-recording it in its entirety, the original backing track of ***I Do Not Love You Isabella*** from ***Songs from Heathcliff*** was used and new vocals from Cliff and Hobson dubbed over the top, while completely removing Olivia Newton-John's and Kristina Nichol's original vocal lines.

Backed with a live recording of the preview of one of the musical's songs from a performance back in December 1995, ***The Sleep of the Good,*** and the album original of *I Do Not Love You Isabella* as well as the instrumental version (that is, the backing track), the song was retitled *The Wedding* and released on the EMI label (catalogue number CDEM 422) on 18th March 1996 and reached number forty in the UK singles charts. It was later featured on Helen Hobson's first solo album, *Hobson's Choice,* along with another track that Cliff recorded with her, ***If Ever I Would Leave You.*** For Cliff, it was included on his *1990s* compilation album.

This version is, of course, very similar to the original album version, with the same evocative instrumentation that swaps from arrogant swaggering from the Heathcliff character to the smooth and gentle of Isabella. Once again Cliff takes all the lead male parts while Hobson performs all the female characterisations, which are spread out among the principal characters in the stage show. The synthesized oboe is slightly more in evidence on the updated version and Olivia Newton-John's vocal is more emotional than Hobson's but otherwise *The Wedding* is a strong version of the song.

Track Specification

Composed by John Farrar and Tim Rice

Musicians

Sean Callery	orchestrator, synclavier, keyboards
Liz Constantino	backing vocals
Linda Dalziel	backing vocals
John Farrar	backing vocals, guitar, synclavier
Helen Hobson	vocals
Steve Kipner	backing vocals
Clif Magness	backing vocals
Cliff Richard	vocals
Michael Thompson	guitar

Recording Details

Producer	John Farrar (backing track) and Keith Bessey (new vocals)
Engineered by	Chris Fogel, Eric Rudd and Joe Schiff (Moonee Ponds Studio), Darren Goodwin and Guy Massey (Abbey Road Studios) and James Collins and Caroline Daniel (CTS Studios) (backing track) and Keith Bessey (new vocals)
Recording location	Moonee Ponds Studio, Los Angeles, Abbey Road Studios, St. John's Wood, London and CTS Studios, Wembley, London (backing track) and Abbey Road Studios, St. John's Wood, London (new vocals)
Mixed by	Allen Sides and Chris Fogel (backing track) and Keith Bessey (new vocals)
Mixed at	Moonee Ponds Studio, Los Angeles (backing track) and Abbey Road Studios, St. John's Wood, London (new vocals)
Recording date	February-April 1994 and May-August 1995 (backing track) and 1996 (new vocals)

♫ We Don't Talk Anymore

75th UK single, *German single and from the albums* **Dressed for the Occasion, Live and Guaranteed 1988!, World Tour Live** *and* **From a Distance ***** The Event** *and unissued live track*

Although *We Don't Talk Anymore* remains Cliff Richard's biggest selling single of his career and he enjoys performing the song that catapulted him into being cool once more during the early part of the eighties decade, he still avers that it is for ***Devil Woman*** that he would prefer to be remembered. The history of *We Don't Talk Anymore* was as extraordinary as it was imbued with controversy: extraordinary because it proved that Cliff was still at the forefront of the modern sound and it catapulted him into a completely new phase and image in his career; controversial because, although it sold in stupendous numbers, it was produced by Bruce Welch, who had been sidelined for production of the previous ***Rock 'n' Roll Juvenile*** album and had let it be known how upset he was by that. Because of the popularity of the song EMI pushed hard to add it as the final track on that album, in spite of it being against Cliff's wishes since the musical style didn't fit with the overall effect intended for *Rock 'n' Roll Juvenile* – indeed, Cliff felt that the song had overshadowed the strong material on the album and, while it inevitably increased album sales, it ensured that the two singles that followed, ***Hot Shot*** and ***Carrie,*** had much to prove as a consequence.

We Don't Talk Anymore was originally written by Alan Tarney for an album project with his writing partner Trevor Spencer but, when Welch heard the demo cassette, he wanted to play it to Cliff and his manager, Peter Gormley. Reports state that Cliff was very keen to record it and, at the end of May 1979, after the last sessions for *Rock 'n' Roll Juvenile,* it was completed at the R. G. Jones studios based in Wimbledon in three takes. Marking the last time that Bruce Welch would act as Cliff's producer until a brief stint in the early nineties, it featured Tarney on most of the instruments – something that would be repeated for the ***Always Guaranteed*** album a few years later – supported by Trevor Spencer on drums.

Backed with ***Green Light*** album track ***Count Me Out***, *We Don't Talk Anymore* was released as a single on the EMI label (catalogue number EMI 2975) on 6th July 1979 and, after increased radio play, it reached the number one spot in the UK singles charts on 25th August of that year, deposing the Boomtown Rats *I Don't Like Mondays*, and staying at that position for four weeks until Gary Numan's *Cars* replaced it. It became Cliff's tenth number one and his first for over eleven years since ***Congratulations*** and set him on the record-breaking path of achieving a number one in every decade since the fifties. An extended edit was produced but this was only released on the twelve-inch single version for the Dutch market (EMI label; catalogue number K052Z-07076) also released in July 1979. A promotional version was released in the US on the EMI America label (catalogue number P-8025) in October 1979, which was the album version but faded out around half a minute earlier.

Tinged with some sadness, too, it was at the beginning of September that Cliff's erstwhile producer and mentor Norrie Paramor died after a long illness with cancer and Cliff has said that one of the last things he would have heard was that he was number one again after Paramor's many years of nurturing his protégé through the late fifties and the sixties, and producing his prior number one with ***Congratulations*** in 1968.

We Don't Talk Anymore has been covered by many artists over the years, including Hank Marvin (on his *Hank Plays Cliff* album), Tom Jones and Brotherhood of Man, but none has been a patch on the success of Cliff's original. The single was issued in the US and became Cliff's fourth top forty success when it reached number seven in the Billboard charts. Cliff was also at the forefront of the burgeoning promotional video methodology that has now become *de rigueur* for any single release today. Although it was a simplistic affair with Cliff singing the song to the cameras, it was experimental at the point of the single's release and became the sixth video to be shown when the MTV channel was initiated in Europe at the beginning of August 1981.

The completely different musical feel to the song confirms Cliff's belief that it would interrupt the *Rock 'n' Roll Juvenile* albums flow. Nevertheless, like ***Devil Woman*** and ***Miss You Nights***, it is now almost impossible to imagine the impact of the song when it was first heard. With its driving bass line and structured synthesiser chords with Alan Tarney's choir created from layering his own voice as well as Cliff's falsetto, this song was something completely different for a time that was beginning to fall out of love with punk rock but tie its allegiance to the new wave and new romantics movement that was ushered into the beginning of the eighties with its reliance on synthesisers. Naturally, it also proved that Cliff was once again at the vanguard of musical change and was still a force to be reckoned with.

Inevitably, it was chosen for his Royal Albert Hall appearance with the London Philharmonic Orchestra, which was then released on the ***Dressed for the Occasion*** album as the second track and the string arrangement over the rock band sounds quite different from the original.

In 1990, Cliff was reunited once again with the Shadows to play a short set of his hits and other material at the festival-like event in June 1990 that took place in the grounds of Hertfordshire's Knebworth House (the start of a continuing but relatively short-lived venue for pop concerts). Although the entire thirteen-song performance was broadcast on the radio by the BBC, the charity album of the event, sold in aid of the Nordoff-Robbins Music Therapy Centre, only featured two songs (***On the Beach*** and ***Do You Wanna Dance?***) with an additional two songs also appearing on the DVD (***Good Golly Miss Molly*** and *We Don't Talk Anymore*).

At the same time as the Knebworth concert, a remixed single version of *We Don't Talk Anymore* surfaced, purporting to be a remix of the original ***From a Distance ***** The Event*** performance by the Stock, Aitken and Waterman franchise. However, it is clearly a studio recording with new vocals because the production is too pristine and 'close', although there is no information available on when it was done. This was issued on the original concert album. In December 1990, the seven-inch PWL remix version was issued which was the same as the album version but without the mixed in audience noises (EMI label, catalogue number 006-20 4090 7), and also appeared on the twelve-inch version (006-20 4090 6) and CD (006-20 4090 2). A twelve-inch and CD remix of the remix was also released which simply boosts the drums and loops effects. Finally an edit of this latest remix, which cuts out much of the instrumental introduction and returns to the looping vocal effects at the end, was incorporated on the twelve-inch and CD single issues of ***This New Year*** and later on the ***My Kinda Life*** album both in 1991. The original live performance was reinstated for the 2005 remaster of *From a Distance ***** The Event*. The instrumentation is not as sharp as on many recordings from live shows but Cliff makes up for it with his crisp vocals and exuberance in performing the song to the appreciative Wembley crowd.

A version recorded in New Zealand was subsequently released on the *World Tour Live* DVD in 2003 and then was the first track on the CD album (with a reduced number of tracks) released the following year. The backing vocals act as a kind of reminder for the lyrics coming up, as Cliff sings the song in the familiar arrangement of the live version of the original.

Track Specification
Composed by Alan Tarney

1. Single

Musicians		*Recording Details*	
Cliff Richard	vocals	Producer	Bruce Welch
Trevor Spencer	drums, percussion	Engineered by	Tony Clark
Alan Tarney	backing vocals, guitar, bass, keyboards	Recording location	R. G. Jones Recording Studios, Wimbledon, London
		Recording date	29th May 1979

2. *Dressed for the Occasion*

Musicians	
Stuart Calver	backing vocals
David Cooke	synthesiser
Steve Gray	piano
Mark Griffiths	bass
Tony Harding	backing vocals
Richard Hewson	arranger, conductor
Graham Jarvis	drums, percussion
London Philharmonic Orchestra	orchestra
John Perry	backing vocals
Cliff Richard	vocals
Tony Rivers	backing vocals

Recording Details	
Producer	Cliff Richard and Richard Hewson
Engineered by	John Kurlander
Mixed by	Keith Bessey
Recording location	Royal Albert Hall, London
Mixed at	Strawberry Studios South, Surrey
Recording date	23rd November 1982

3. *Live & Guaranteed 1988!*

Musicians	
John Clark	guitar
Rosemarie Ford	backing vocals
Mark Griffiths	bass
Peter Howarth	backing vocals
Steve Lauri	guitar
Paul Moessl	keyboards
Mick Mullins	backing vocals
Alan Park	keyboards
Cliff Richard	vocals
Henry Spinetti	drums, percussion

Recording Details	
Producer	Unknown
Engineered by	Unknown
Recording location	Fyens Forum, Odense, Denmark
Recording date	22nd May 1988

4. *From a Distance *** The Event***

Musicians	
John Clark	guitar
Sonia Jones-Morgan	backing vocals
Steve Lauri	guitar
Peter May	drums, percussion
Paul Moessl	keyboards
Tessa Niles	backing vocals
Alan Park	keyboards
Provox:	
Peter Howarth	backing vocals
Mick Mullins	backing vocals
Keith Murrell	backing vocals
Cliff Richard	vocals
Steve Stroud	bass

Recording Details	
Producer	Cliff Richard
Engineered by	Keith Bessey and Mick McKenna
Recording location	Rolling Stones Mobile Studio, Wembley Stadium, Wembley, North-west London
Recording date	16th-17th June 1989

5. *Unissued (Knebworth - The Album)*

Musicians	
Brian Bennett	drums, percussion
Mark Griffiths	bass
Cliff Hall	keyboards
Peter Howarth	backing vocals
Hank Marvin	guitar
Paul Moessl	keyboards
Mick Mullins	backing vocals
Keith Murrell	backing vocals
Cliff Richard	vocals
Bruce Welch	guitar

Recording Details	
Producer	Chris Kimsey and Steve Smith
Engineered by	Unknown
Recording location	Knebworth House, Hertfordshire, England
Recording date	30th June 1990

6. *German single (PWL Remix)*

Musicians	
Cliff Richard	vocals
Trevor Spencer	drums, percussion
Alan Tarney	backing vocals, guitar, bass, keyboards

Recording Details	
Producer	Cliff Richard
Engineered by	Keith Bessey
Recording location	Unknown
Remixed by	Phil Harding and Ian Curnow
Remix location	PWL Studios, London
Recording date	1990

7. *World Tour Live*

Musicians	
Rachel Allen	violin
Elena Bulgakova	violin
Jenni Champion	violin
Anthony Clark	backing vocals, guitar
John Clark	guitar
Dave Cooke	keyboards

Recording Details	
Producer	Keith Bessey
Engineered by	Keith Bessey
Recording location	The Mission Winery, Napier, New Zealand
Recording date	22nd February 2003

Cornelia Didenco	violin
Gina Ferguson	violin
Peter Howarth	backing vocals
Cathy Irons	violin
Pete May	drums, percussion
Mick Mullins	backing vocals
Keith Murrell	backing vocals
Alan Park	keyboards
Hee-Jung Park	violin
Cliff Richard	vocals
Eva Schwanen-Lilley	violin
Steve Stroud	bass

♫ We Have It Made

Unissued tracks and from the album **Me and My Shadows** *(mono and stereo versions)*

Although complete records are only available for the stereo recording of *We Have It Made* from the ***Me and My Shadows*** album sessions, it is clear that the mono version was recorded separately (quite possibly at an earlier unspecified date). An acetate and seven-inch of this track were later found but it's unclear whether they are connected to the *Me and My Shadows* sessions or are separate. What is known is that the differences in the mono and stereo versions mean that both are different takes of the song, regardless of the session details. The song also appeared on the associated ***Me and My Shadows No. 2*** EP. The song was attempted twice before in 1959, with sixty-three takes attempted at the second of those sessions; none of these recordings have been issued and it is possible that the aforementioned acetates came from one or other of these sessions.

Hank Marvin's shimmering guitar introduces this song and plays quietly in the background underneath Cliff Richard's gentle vocals. Another love song that celebrates the feelings of a man for a woman he loves, the ambling pace of the song matches perfectly with the lyrics.

Track Specification
Composed by Sugar Hall

1. Unissued track (Me and My Shadows)

Musicians	
Jet Harris	bass
Hank Marvin	guitar
Tony Meehan	drums, percussion
Cliff Richard	vocals
Bruce Welch	rhythm guitar

Recording Details	
Producer	Norrie Paramor
Engineered by	Peter Bown and Stuart Eltham
Recording location	Abbey Road Studio 2, St. John's Wood, London
Recording date	2th May 1959

2. Unissued track (Me and My Shadows)

Musicians	
Jet Harris	bass
Hank Marvin	guitar
Tony Meehan	drums, percussion
Cliff Richard	vocals
Bruce Welch	rhythm guitar

Recording Details	
Producer	Norrie Paramor
Engineered by	Peter Bown and Stuart Eltham
Recording location	Abbey Road Studio 2, St. John's Wood, London
Recording date	26th July 1959

3. Mono recording (Me and My Shadows)

Musicians	
Jet Harris	bass
Hank Marvin	guitar
Tony Meehan	drums, percussion
Cliff Richard	vocals
Bruce Welch	rhythm guitar

Recording Details	
Producer	Norrie Paramor
Engineered by	Malcolm Addey and Norman Smith
Recording location	Abbey Road Studio 2, St. John's Wood, London
Recording date	Unknown but possibly 24th June 1960

4. Stereo recording (Me and My Shadows)

Musicians	
Jet Harris	bass
Hank Marvin	guitar
Tony Meehan	drums, percussion
Cliff Richard	vocals
Bruce Welch	rhythm guitar

Recording Details	
Producer	Norrie Paramor
Engineered by	Malcolm Addey and Norman Smith
Recording location	Abbey Road Studio 2, St. John's Wood, London
Recording date	24th June 1960

♫ Weihnachtszeit – Mistletoe and Wine

From the album **Winterträume** *(Claudia Jung)*

In 1996, Cliff Richard was invited to record new arrangements of two of his best-known Christmas songs, ***Mistletoe and Wine*** and ***Saviour's Day***, with German singer Claudia Jung. The former song was slightly retitled for the *Winterträume* album, with *Weihnachtszeit* prefixed to it (otherwise translated as *Christmas Time*, after the first phrase uttered in the song). The keyboards are imbued with a more twinkling Christmas sound than the original. Claudia Jung sings initially in

German and Cliff in English but both also sing in the other's language. Jung's voice sounds very young against the maturity of Cliff's vocals but this works well given some of the images evoked in the lyrics. At the end, Jung sings the vocals normally sung by the chorister, although Cliff not only sings his original lines but provides backing vocals for her too. In summary, this is a lovely variation and arrangement of the song.

Track Specification
Composed by Keith Strachan, Leslie Stewart and Jeremy Paul; German lyrics by Claudia Jung

Musicians

Paulo Alves	choral vocals
Jane Bogaert	choral vocals
Frank Busch	arranger, guitar, keyboards, programming
Chris De Belle	choral vocals
Freeda Goodlet	choral vocals
Claudia Jung	vocals
Jacky Nemorin	choral vocals
Achim Radloff	arranger
Cliff Richard	vocals, backing vocals
Peter Risavy	choral vocals
Jerry Rix	choral vocals
Kristian Schultze	keyboards

Recording Details

Producer	Dietmar Kawohl and Hans Singer
Engineered by	Keith Bessey
Recording location	Unknown
Recording date	1996

♬ We Kiss in a Shadow

From the album **Listen to Cliff!** *(mono and stereo versions)*

Taken from the Rodgers and Hammerstein 1951 musical *The King and I, We Kiss in a Shadow* is a declaration of love between Tuptim and Lun Tha desperately trying avoid the wrath of the Siamese King (hence kissing in a shadow rather than in public), sung by Reuben Fuentes and Leona Gordon (dubbing for the actors) in the film. The song, often not a duet outside of the film, was also recorded by Perry Como, Vic Damone, Barbra Streisand, Frank Sinatra, Sonny Rollins, June Christy and Doris Day among several others.

The stereo and mono versions recorded for the ***Listen to Cliff!*** album are different takes, although it's unclear which of the seven in the can correspond to which version. *We Kiss in a Shadow* was placed as the penultimate song in the track listing of the second side of the album.

On this album in particular, the choice of songs show the breadth of Cliff Richard's capabilities as a singer, matching songs from musicals and covers of ballads and rock and roll songs. All of them require different techniques in their performance and *We Kiss in a Shadow* is a case in point. With the demands of the emotions to be displayed, it would be easy to pull the tune flat but, instead, Cliff manages a pitch-perfect performance, which requires him to use his lower register far more than he is usually requested to do, while the musical intervals between notes are quite complex, all of which Cliff carries off without it appearing to cause him concern.

Track Specification
Composed by Richard Rodgers and Oscar Hammerstein II

1. Listen to Cliff! (mono version)

Musicians

Tony Meehan	tambourine
Norrie Paramor Orchestra	orchestra
Norrie Paramor	arranger, conductor
Cliff Richard	vocals

Recording Details

Producer	Norrie Paramor
Engineered by	Malcolm Addey and Norman Smith
Recording location	Abbey Road Studio 2, St. John's Wood, London
Recording date	17th November 1961

2. Listen to Cliff! (stereo version)

Musicians

Tony Meehan	tambourine
Norrie Paramor Orchestra	orchestra
Norrie Paramor	arranger, conductor
Cliff Richard	vocals

Recording Details

Producer	Norrie Paramor
Engineered by	Malcolm Addey and Norman Smith
Recording location	Abbey Road Studio 2, St. John's Wood, London
Recording date	17th November 1961

♬ We Love a Movie

From the film soundtrack album of **Wonderful Life**

Having tried to convince the director (Walter Slezak) of the terrible movie being filmed on the sand-dunes that the leading lady, Jenny (Susan Hampshire), should perform without a yashmak, Johnny (Cliff Richard) and his friends are ejected from his office. As they walk through the props store in the same building, the group - which includes Jerry (Melvyn Hayes), Edward (Richard O'Sullivan), Barbara the film's script prompter (Una Stubbs), Jenny and the unnamed musicians (the Shadows) - slowly come to the idea of making a film of their own, filming alongside the real one and interspersing other scenes with songs. They start throwing a few ideas around, including walking in front of a screen with a moving background and a plane, singing this song about how they want to make their own movie. Edward pompously dictates that the group needs to understand the history of film before recording an inch of film and thus begins a sequence featuring the group playing various roles such as Charlie Chaplin and the Keystone Kops, and illustrating the history of the talkies, musicals (with a Noel Coward delivery from Cliff with the Shadows, Hayes and O'Sullivan dressed as women!), gangsters, war films, cowboys and the Marx Brothers as well as Greta Garbo, epics, a pastiche on West End Story and finally Cliff as James Bond and Susan Hampshire as Ursula Andress from *Dr. No*, ending up in kissing in the surf before sending the incongruously placed Keystone Kops on their way as the song finishes.

The sequence features snippets of a number of familiar tunes and was recorded in two stages for the film soundtrack: the orchestral parts were recorded at the start of the first session with the fifth take used, followed by the vocal section six days later in which the fifth take and edit of that was used. The same combined take and edit was used for the mono and stereo recordings but with different mixes to match the audio channel requirements. The song was included on the track listing of the ***Hits from Wonderful Life*** EP, while the version used in the film itself was probably recorded some time during the first three months of 1964. There is a major difference between the soundtrack and film versions: other than the dialogue, the lengthy film history sequence (fourteen minutes) with Richard O'Sullivan's voice-over (which incidentally doesn't match what he saying on screen) does not appear on the soundtrack, although the remainder of the arrangement and performance is similar. The film version has not, to date, been released in any other commercial format.

The problem with many of the tracks on the soundtrack is that they are an aural accompaniment to the action of the caper taking place on the screen and they don't stand well on their own and neither are they especially memorable. Cliff carries off his vocal duties well but there are far better songs (usually with the Shadows) on the album.

Track Specification

Composed by Peter Myers and Ronald Cass

Musicians

Associated British Studio Orchestra	orchestra
Stanley Black	conductor
Mike Sammes Singers	backing vocals
Cliff Richard	vocals

Recording Details

Producer	Bob Barratt (orchestra) and Norrie Paramor (vocals)
Engineered by	Malcolm Addey and Alan Kane (orchestra) and Malcolm Addey and Richard Langham (vocals)
Recording location	Abbey Road Studio 2, St. John's Wood, London (orchestra and vocals)
Recording date	20th May 1964 (orchestra) and 26th May 1964 (vocals)

♫ Wenn Du Lachst, Lacht das Glück

From the album **Ich Träume Deine Träume**

Sally Sunshine was a song recorded by the Everly Brothers, which Cliff Richard then recorded in German, with a completely new title of *Wenn Du Lachst, Lacht das Glück* (which retranslates to *When You Laugh, Laugh with Happiness*). The song was recorded for Cliff's second German language album, *Ich Träume Deine Träume*, which was released in 1971 and it was one of the songs recorded in four sessions over a two-day period in November 1970. *Wenn Du Lachst, Lacht das Glück* was the final song to be recorded on the first day. Backed with ***Kleine Taube*** (the German version of ***Pigeon***) and released as a single on the international Columbia label (catalogue number 1C 006-04903) in October 1971, the song reached number thirty-nine in the German singles charts. The edited single version appears on the 1997 foreign language compilation, ***On the Continent***, while the album edit has not been issued in any other format.

Reliant on brass and a shimmering electric piano, Cliff's lead vocal gradually builds up through the first two verses. Unfortunately, it descends into stereotypical German song style in the chorus accompanied by a harsh uncredited backing vocal group. However, Cliff's vocals are as pure and direct as is expected from any of his recordings.

Track Specification

Composed by Geoff Stephens and L. Reed; German lyrics by Werner

Musicians

Norrie Paramor Orchestra	orchestra
Norrie Paramor	arranger, conductor
Cliff Richard	vocals
Unknown	backing vocals

Recording Details

Producer	Norrie Paramor (backing track and vocals)
Engineered by	Phil McDonald (backing track and vocals)
Recording location	Cologne, Germany (backing track) and Abbey Road Studio 2, St. John's Wood, London (vocals)
Recording date	November 1970 (backing track) and 24th November 1970 (vocals)

♫ We're All One

From the album **Sail Away** *(Dave Pope)*

Written by Bryn Haworth, a friend and one-time guitarist with Cliff Richard's backing band, *We're All One* was recorded in the spring of 1978 with Cliff at the production helm. Chosen to close the album, there is scant information on the musicians involved in the recording and, until this can be rectified with fresh information, they will be annotated as unknown in the track specification. Note that Cliff would also be involved in recording a couple of tracks by Haworth later on.

The rocking beat of the song features Pope's voice performed through an electronic gadget, supported by the guitars, percussion and plodding bass associated with this genre. The backing vocals ebulliently song the chorus, which expresses the joy experienced in the realisation that everyone is the same under God's eyes.

Track Specification
Composed by Bryn Haworth

Musicians		*Recording Details*	
Dave Pope	vocals	Producer	Cliff Richard
Cliff Richard	backing vocals	Engineered by	Tony Clark
Unknown	backing vocals	Recording location	Morgan Studios, London
Unknown	guitar	Recording date	April 1978
Unknown	bass		
Unknown	piano		
Unknown	keyboards		
Unknown	drums, percussion		

♫ Were You There?

Unissued track

Another spiritual from the sessions for Cliff Richard's ***Good News*** religious album, *Were You There?* has been covered by the Calico Consort, Aaron Neville, Marian Anderson, Tennessee Ernie Ford, Mahalia Jackson, Sam Cooke, Martha and the Vandellas, Paul Robeson, Randy Travis, Kate Smith and Larry Williams.

It was the third song to be recorded by Cliff Richard in the 28th April session for the ***Good News*** album, although, after three takes, further attempts were abandoned and the song remains unissued. Pat Clark was present at these sessions but, without access to the recording, it is unclear whether she performs on this song or not.

Track Specification
Composed by Traditional

Musicians		*Recording Details*	
Pat Clark	vocals	Producer	Norrie Paramor
Norrie Paramor Orchestra	orchestra	Engineered by	Peter Vince and Mike Stone
Mike Leander	arranger, conductor	Recording location	Abbey Road Studio 2, St. John's Wood, London
Cliff Richard	vocals	Recording date	28th April 1967

♫ We Say Yeah

B-sides of **The Young Ones** *and* **Singing the Blues** *(download only) and from the albums* **The Rock 'n' Roll Years 1958-1963**, **Live at the ABC Kingston 1962** *and* **Cliff in Japan**

The final full song to be performed in ***The Young Ones***, it is sung by Nicky Black (portrayed by Cliff Richard) with the backing of the Shadows (who have no obviously assigned name as a group in the film), after revealing himself to be the Mystery Singer and giving a short rendition of ***When the Girl in Your Arms (Is the Girl in Your Heart)*** to prove it. During the performance, there are several shots of the audience from between Nicky's jiving legs, through which can also be seen the variety of fruit thrown at Ernest (Richard O'Sullivan) as he tries to quell the anger of the audience when he tells them that the Mystery Singer wouldn't be turning up (Nicky had raced off to help his father back at the Youth Club and in danger of being beaten up before sorting them out, returning to the theatre and doing the aforementioned revelation as the Mystery Singer).

Written by Shadows Bruce Welch and Hank Marvin, with help from the band's then manager Peter Gormley, six takes were recorded in the session for the album version of the song with the final take being used for the mono and stereo edits with different mixes for the audio channels. The film version of the song was recorded later on that year (possibly in August) but remains unreleased in any other commercial format, although an undubbed version (without the backing vocals) was released on ***The Rock 'n' Roll Years 1958-1963***. The differences between the versions are the vocal and guitar lines, while the film version stops short of the guitar solo. The album track was chosen as the B-side of the sixteenth UK single by Cliff Richard, the film's title track, and also features on the ***Hits from the Young Ones*** EP.

The raucous vocal line from Cliff is at deliberate odds with the songs from the rest of the film, confirming his versatility as a performer and singer. The Shadows provide vocal accompaniment (in answer to Cliff's assertion of the song's title) with a rip-roaring bass line underpinning the rhythm. The middle eight sees the Shadows performing a beautifully syncopated variation on the main theme before Cliff returns to run through the nominal members of his family being negative once more. The song finally ends on a pleasantly unresolved interval and a small drum roll.

In subsequent concerts to support and promote the film, Cliff and the Shadows incorporated a selection of songs into their set list, including *We Say Yeah*. For the ABC Kingston concert, this was recorded but remained unreleased until the 2002 album ***Live at the ABC Kingston 1962***, which was released in stereo only and is similar to he film performance.

The end of 1967 saw a tour of the Far East, with one show being recorded in Tokyo for the album ***Cliff in Japan***. The final song in the selection, Cliff created a medley of five songs he had not sung earlier in the show, all to an orchestral accompaniment: ***Let's Make a Memory, The Young Ones, Lucky Lips, Summer Holiday*** and *We Say Yeah*.

In 2009, the fiftieth anniversary celebrations were in full swing and culminated in Cliff and the Shadows coming back together in the studio to record ***Reunited***, which saw much of their popular early material being re-recorded including *We Say Yeah*. Although the song was not issued on any album package, it was released as a B-side item to the download-only version of the only single, ***Singing the Blues***. This version is faithful to the original with its effervescent energy, and the brilliance of the close harmony vocals. Another point of interest is Bruce's stentorian rhythm guitar.

Track Specification
Composed by Peter Gormley, Bruce Welch and Hank Marvin

1. B-side (The Young Ones)

Musicians	
Jet Harris	backing vocals, bass
Hank Marvin	backing vocals, guitar
Tony Meehan	drums, percussion
Cliff Richard	vocals
Bruce Welch	backing vocals, rhythm guitar

Recording Details	
Producer	Norrie Paramor
Engineered by	Malcolm Addey and Norman Smith
Recording location	Abbey Road Studio 2, St. John's Wood, London
Recording date	28th July 1961

2. The Rock 'n' Roll Years 1958-1963

Musicians	
Jet Harris	bass
Hank Marvin	guitar
Tony Meehan	drums, percussion
Cliff Richard	vocals
Bruce Welch	rhythm guitar

Recording Details	
Producer	Norrie Paramor
Engineered by	Unknown
Recording location	Elstree Studios, Hertfordshire
Recording date	August 1961

3. Live at the ABC Kingston 1962

Musicians	
Brian Bennett	drums, percussion
Jet Harris	backing vocals, bass
Hank Marvin	backing vocals, guitar
Cliff Richard	vocals, hand claps
Bruce Welch	backing vocals, rhythm guitar

Recording Details	
Producer	Norrie Paramor
Engineered by	Malcolm Addey and Ken Townsend
Recording location	ABC Theatre, Kingston, Surrey
Recording date	7th March 1962

4. Cliff in Japan

Musicians	
Norrie Paramor Orchestra	orchestra
Norrie Paramor	arranger, conductor
Cliff Richard	vocals
Unknown	backing vocals

Recording Details	
Producer	Norrie Paramor
Engineered by	Unknown
Recording location	Shibuya Public Hall, Tokyo, Japan
Recording date	18th October 1967

5. B-side (Singing the Blues - download)

Musicians	
Brian Bennett	drums, percussion
Mark Griffiths	bass
Hank Marvin	backing vocals, guitar
Cliff Richard	vocals, backing vocals
Bruce Welch	backing vocals, rhythm guitar

Recording Details	
Producer	Warren Bennett (co-ordination)
Engineered by	James Collins (Honeyhill Studios), Ethan Carlson (Middle Ear Studios), Les Williams (Nivram Studios) and Keith Bessey (mixing and mastering)
Recording location	Middle Ear Studios, Miami, Florida, USA (Cliff's vocals), Nivram Studios, Perth, Western Australia (Hank's guitars and vocals) and Honeyhill Studios, Hertfordshire, England (all other vocals and instruments)
Recording date	Early 2009

♫ We Shall Be Changed
From the album **Good News**

With both Cliff Richard and Hank Marvin going through religious conversions at the time (with Hank following Jehovah's Witnesses), it is hardly surprising that the Shadows would appear on some tracks on Cliff's first religious album: ***Good News***. A popular traditional song, here arranged by Mike Leander for the album, it has been covered by a small number of artists including Tampa Lann and the Stars of Faith. The title is inspired Biblical tract from Corinthians, where Paul is talking of the second coming of Christ and the impact it would have on those on Earth who are still living.
One of four recorded together at the session saw *We Shall Be Changed* completed first. Their version was finished in just two takes. Cliff sings this toe-tapping tune with gusto, and is supported by a female gospel choral group, who are uncredited with no further information available on them; these may be the Breakaways since they sound more natural and less shrill than the Mike Sammes Singers, both of whom were regularly recording with Cliff around this period.

Track Specification
Composed by Traditional arranged by Mike Leander

Musicians	
Brian Bennett	drums, percussion
Mike Leander	arranger, conductor
Hank Marvin	guitar
Mike Leander Orchestra	orchestra
Cliff Richard	vocals
John Rostill	bass
Unknown	backing vocals
Bruce Welch	rhythm guitar

Recording Details	
Producer	Norrie Paramor
Engineered by	Peter Vince and Mike Stone
Recording location	Abbey Road Studio 2, St. John's Wood, London
Recording date	27th April 1967

♫ We Should Be Together

***115th UK single** and unissued live track*

Cliff Richard recorded his Christmas album ***Together with Cliff Richard*** in the early weeks of summer in 1991, an anachronism created by the demands of the recording and release schedules to hit the shops in time for Christmas. *We Should Be Together* was written for Cliff to record and was also the first of two singles to be released from the album. Backed with a live version of ***Miss You Nights*** (recorded in Sydney in 1984), it was issued as a single on the EMI label (catalogue number XMASG 91) on 25th November 1991 and reached number ten in the UK singles charts. A souvenir version of the seven-inch single was also released (also with the catalogue number XMASG 91) that came in a white sleeve, in addition to the now requisite CD version (CDXMAS 91) and it was the first of Cliff's singles not to be issued on the twelve-inch format since it had been introduced in the eighties. There had been high hopes that the single would replicate the success of ***Saviour's Day*** the previous year but, apart from the apparent unwillingness of record-buyers, sales were also hit by the death of Freddie Mercury at the time of release and Queen's back catalogue became the focus of many purchases. The song was later issued on the ***Christmas EP*** in early December 1991 and featured ***The Holly and the Ivy*** and ***The Twelve Days of Christmas*** from the 1968 ***Carol Singers EP*** sessions and ***Mistletoe and Wine*** from 1988.

Beginning with an old-style telephone dial and ringing tone, Cliff's lead begins as if heard from the other end of the line. The sophistication of the song is brought out in the gentle guitar and percussion accompaniment and languid strings throughout. In the middle eight, the key changes create a dramatic change during the trumpet solo, which is repeated at the end breaking into a wistful few bars of *A New World Symphony* by Dvořak, evoking memories of the bread advertisement and the sense of togetherness and family. Cliff provides his own backing vocals accompanied by the female voices present on the album. The promotional video features Cliff talking into a phone and represents the distance of loved ones with a North Sea oil rig, cutting to a wife and kids sitting at home in front of a fire and Christmas tree, interspersed with profiles of Cliff.

For Cliff's world tour running into 2003, and in spite of the lack of seasonality by February, he sang a ***Christmas Medley*** of his festive hits. The New Zealand concert was filmed for DVD release while the CD album, ***World Tour Live,*** only had a subset of the songs performed and missed the medley from its track listing.

Track Specification

Composed by Bruce Roberts

1. Single

Musicians

John Clark	guitar
Paul Dunne	guitar
Dave Cunliffe	violin
Andrew Greasley	violin
Mark Griffiths	bass
Mae McKenna	backing vocals
Peter May	drums, percussion
Paul Moessl	drum programming, keyboards
Sonia Morgan	backing vocals
Tessa Niles	backing vocals
Cliff Richard	arranger, vocals, backing vocals
Frank Ricotti	drums, percussion
Steve Stroud	bass
Anthony Thompson	backing vocals
Derek Watkins	cornet

Recording Details

Producer	Cliff Richard and Paul Moessl
Engineered by	Gerry Kitchingham, Andrew Greasley and Ben Robbins
Recording location	R. G. Jones Studios, Wimbledon, London
Recording date	24th June 1991 to July 1991

2. Unissued track (World Tour Live)

Musicians

Rachel Allen	violin
Elena Bulgakova	violin
Jenni Champion	violin
Anthony Clark	backing vocals, guitar
John Clark	guitar
Dave Cooke	keyboards
Cornelia Didenco	violin
Gina Ferguson	violin
Mike Haughton	saxophone
Peter Howarth	backing vocals
Cathy Irons	violin
Pete May	drums, percussion
Mick Mullins	backing vocals
Keith Murrell	backing vocals
Alan Park	keyboards
Hee-Jung Park	violin
Cliff Richard	vocals
Eva Schwanen-Lilley	violin
Steve Stroud	bass

Recording Details

Producer	Keith Bessey
Engineered by	Keith Bessey
Recording location	The Mission Winery, Napier, New Zealand
Recording date	22nd February 2003

♫ We Sure Do

From the album **Did He Jump... Or Was He Pushed?** *(Garth Hewitt)*

Cliff Richard spent time in 1979 being involved in working on projects by fellow Christians Garth Hewitt and Bryn Haworth. For Hewitt's ***Did He Jump.. Or Was He Pushed?*** album, where *We Sure Do* is the penultimate track, Cliff also took up the production duties.

The shuffling percussion and guitar introduction has echoes of ***My Kinda Life***, while Hewitt's vocals are strident in falsetto and in his normal register. With Cliff's falsetto backing vocals, it creates an almost gospel atmosphere to the recording. The track is surprising in its beauty, which keeps its bouncing rhythm moving onwards by subtle use of the accompanying instrumentation. The ensemble piece is a wonderful piece of production of which Cliff can be justifiably proud.

Track Specification

Composed by Garth Hewitt

Musicians

Garth Hewitt	vocals, guitar
Graham Jarvis	drums, percussion
Adrian Lee	synthesiser
Mike Moran	guitar, keyboards
Jo Partridge	guitar
Cliff Richard	backing vocals, guitar
Dave Wintour	bass

Recording Details

Producer	Cliff Richard
Engineered by	Tony Clark and Haydn Bendall
Recording location	Odyssey Studios, London
Recording date	1979

♫ What a Friend We Have in Jesus

From the album **Good News**

What a Friend We Have in Jesus started as a comforting poem written by Joseph Scrivens for his mother while away on a trip abroad in 1855. Although credited as anonymous until the 1880's, it was set to music by Charles Converse in 1868 and has been a firm favourite for evangelical church services since. As an ebullient praise for the spiritual leader of the Christian religion, it has been covered on gospel and religious recordings by a number of artists including Dolly Parton, Pat Boone, Aretha Franklin, Willie Nelson, Sandy Posey, Tennessee Ernie Ford, Aaron Neville, Ray Price and Roy Rogers among several other musicians.

Cliff Richard recorded his version for his first religious album, ***Good News***, in 1967, requiring just two takes to complete the song, which was one of five attempted at the session (only two others were completed and issued, while the other two remain unreleased).

The string arrangement is perfectly sympathetic to the upbeat principal melody, which Cliff carries off with consummate ease and shows his complete versatility in covering any style of song and making it interesting. Cliff is joined by Pat Clark, who sings a descant in the middle and final verse.

Track Specification

Composed by Joseph Scriven and Charles C. Converse

Musicians

Pat Clark	vocals
Norrie Paramor Orchestra	orchestra
Mike Leander	arranger, conductor
Cliff Richard	vocals

Recording Details

Producer	Norrie Paramor
Engineered by	Peter Vince and Mike Stone
Recording location	Abbey Road Studio 2, St. John's Wood, London
Recording date	28th April 1967

♫ What a Silly Thing to Do

From the album **Tracks 'n' Grooves**

Terry Britten, who would be instrumental in Cliff Richard's seventies renaissance, began writing and submitting songs for Cliff to record in 1968. One of those was *What a Silly Thing to Do*, which was recorded at the early July session that also saw another of Britten's compositions recorded, ***Mr. Nice***. However, *What a Silly Thing to Do* would remain unissued for two years until it was added to the track listing of ***Tracks 'n' Grooves***. By this time, Columbia's policy on album releases had changed with albums being released in stereo from 1969 onwards. Given the timing of the session, there would have been a mono edit created of the song, although this has never been issued.

A familiar style of arrangement for songs recorded by Cliff at this time, *What a Silly Thing to Do* becomes quite quirky, matching the song's title, in its changes of rhythm and the use of strange percussion. There is a male backing group on the song but they are uncredited and no further information is available, although it is quite possible that Hank Marvin and Bruce Welch may have joined him in the studio supporting his lead.

Track Specification

Composed by Terry Britten

Musicians

Mike Leander	arranger, conductor
Mike Leander Orchestra	orchestra
Cliff Richard	vocals
Unknown	backing vocals

Recording Details

Producer	Norrie Paramor
Engineered by	Peter Vince
Recording location	Abbey Road Studio 3, St. John's Wood, London
Recording date	1st July 1968

♫ What a Wonderful World

From the album **Wanted**

Written by Bob Thiele (under the pseudonym George Douglas) and George David Weiss in 1968, *What a Wonderful World* was intended to be the antidote to some of the increasingly racial and political problems in late sixties America, where there was a lot of hate being generated by the swell of change away from apartheid as well as the politically charged problems with fighting the losing war in Viet Nam. With its title and references to babies being born with something to look forward to as they grow up and its upbeat rhythms and melody in a major key, the whole package was optimistic. Initially, the song was offered to crooner Tony Bennett who decided not to record it, after which it was given to Louis Armstrong, who successfully created the version by which all others would inevitably be measured. His version reached number one in the UK charts in 1968 becoming the oldest siner to reach the top of the charts, while in 1992, the unlikely pairing of Nick Cave and the Pogues' Shane McGowan had a very minor hit with it reaching number seventy-two. Later, Katie Melua overdubbed her vocals on the recording by the late Eva Cassidy, achieving a number one in 2007.

In 1993, Hawaiian ukulele-player Israel Kamakawiwo'ole recorded his plaintive version of *What a Wonderful World* melded together with ***Somewhere over the Rainbow***. The combined song was almost forgotten, even after his death in 1997, until Cliff Richard's friend and DJ Graham Dene passed a copy of the song to him in the new millennium and Cliff knew he wanted to record ***Somewhere over the Rainbow/What a Wonderful World***.

♫ What Car?

*136th **UK single** and B-side of* **What Car?** *DVD single*

Catching his fiercest critics completely off guard with the third single from ***Something's Going On***, the reviews were begrudging in their support of the song *What Car?*, although they witlessly missed the point by suggesting that he was old enough to be the protagonist's grandfather and that, at the age of sixteen if he had stolen his father's car, he would have been more likely to go to church to confess than to cover it up even though Cliff didn't find his religion until his mid-twenties. The song is a spirited and highly energetic song that reminisces about the time his father left the car-keys out to his classic Comero car and the temptation was too strong not to take it and show off to his girlfriend, ultimately crashing it into a tree. The performance from Cliff is extraordinary, injecting it as he does with the humour of the story and the witty lyrics, as well as the cringing anguish at some of the memories of lying to his father to cover up his crime.

Backed with a non-album track, ***Slow Down***, which was originally only available on Cliff's website before being included on the promotional disc for ***Somethin' Is Goin' On***, and the mono version of ***Sentimental Journey*** (Cliff had performed both this and the single at the VE Remembrance Day concert), from his ***Listen to Cliff!*** album, *What Car?* was issued as a single on the Decca label (catalogue number 475 6943) on 9th May 2005 and reached number twelve in the UK singles charts, which was a surprisingly low result for such a strong song. A DVD version was issued simultaneously, with the audio single, another non-album track, ***Diamonds on a Chain***, the promotional videos for both *What Car?* (recorded at Leeds Castle for the ***Castles in the Air*** performance DVD) and *Somethin' Is Goin' On* as well as the *Make Poverty History* click advertisement. Further a single-track promotion disc was also released.

The clanking guitars, bouncing percussion rhythm and running bass brings this brilliant song to life. The foot-tapping energy of the song drives it onwards as the witty tales unfolds in the lyrics, while Cliff manages to emulate the childish denial of the car's theft. The backing vocals create an inner beauty within the repeated chorus.

Track Specification

Composed by Trey Bruce, Gary Burr and David Mullen

1. Single

Musicians		*Recording Details*	
Trey Bruce	programming	Producer	Trey Bruce
J. T. Corenflos	guitar	Engineered by	David Buchanan
Tony Harrell	keyboards	Recording location	Omnisound Recording Studios, Nashville, Tennessee, USA, Sound Stage Studios, Nashville, Tennessee, USA and Pocket Studio, Franklin, Tennessee, USA
Wes Hightower	backing vocals		
Greg Morrow	drums, percussion		
Alison Prestwood	bass		
Cliff Richard	vocals, backing vocals	Recording date	2003-2004
Marty Slayton	backing vocals		
Michael Spriggs	guitar		

2. B-Side (What Car? DVD single)

Musicians		*Recording Details*	
John Clark	guitar	Producer	Unknown
Keith Hayman	keyboards	Engineered by	Unknown
Peter Howarth	backing vocals, guitar	Recording location	Leeds Castle, Maidstone, Kent
Peter May	drums, percussion	Recording date	25th July 2004
Mick Mullins	backing vocals		
Keith Murrell	backing vocals		
Alan Park	keyboards		
Cliff Richard	vocals		
Steve Stroud	bass		

♫ Whatcha Gonna Do About It?

Unissued track

Ten days after *Whatcha Gonna Do About It?* was attempted but abandoned, Cliff Richard and the Shadows were back in the studio to record ***Boom Boom (That's How My Heart Beats)*** for the ***Take Four*** EP. There is a theory that, given the proximity of the sessions and the prominence of the lyric *Whatcha Gonna Do About It?* in the *Boom Boom (That's How My Heart Beats)* chorus that this is the same song recorded under a different title. There is also a possibility that this is the same song recorded that year by the Small Faces – this has some credence, too, since one of the co-writers of that song was Ian Samwell, who had given Cliff Richard so many of his early hits and B-sides, thus creating the connection to allow the song to be recorded. However, neither theory is proven since there is scant information regarding the song at that recording session, so the definitive answer remains open until further research is unearthed.

Track Specification

Composed by Unknown

Musicians		*Recording Details*	
Brian Bennett	drums, percussion	Producer	Norrie Paramor
Hank Marvin	guitar	Engineered by	Unknown
Cliff Richard	vocals	Recording location	Abbey Road Studio 2, St. John's Wood, London
John Rostill	bass	Recording date	4th April 1965
Bruce Welch	rhythm guitar		

♫ What'd I Say?

Unissued tracks, South African single and from the albums **Listen to Cliff!** *and* **Cliff in Japan**

Starting its life as an impromptu and improvised song at the end of one of Ray Charles's concerts, where the band and he had run through their planned set with time left over, the public reaction was such that he declared that he would record it. Released in the middle of 1959, it was a major hit for Charles in the US, which is surprising giving the prevailing attitude to any sexual innuendo – of which the song is filled. Such an impact did it have that some commentators point to it as the start of soul, with its heavy gospel influences. It was subsequently performed and recorded by a variety of acts including Elvis Presley (in his *Viva Las Vegas* film), The Beatles, Sammy Davis, Jr., Eddie Cochran, Eric Clapton and Jerry Lee Lewis, with the latter being the only artist to take the song into the UK singles charts when it peaked at number ten in the middle of 1961.

It was chosen for the recording of ***Listen to Cliff!*** during the latter part of 1960 and into 1961. It was first attempted at the end of a session on 1st April 1960 but was abandoned after one take. It was resurrected again for the 13th October 1960 afternoon session, where five takes were attempted but remain unissued, but it wasn't until a marathon session on 4th March 1961, when thirty-three takes were tried, that all those involved found a version they were happy with – interestingly, these takes from that session are listed as remakes on the EMI session sheets.

The mono and stereo recordings are taken from the same take and edit but are mixed differently for the separate audio channels. Although not released in the UK, *What'd I Say* was released for the international market, backed with another track from the *Listen to Cliff!* album, ***Blue Moon***, on the Columbia label (catalogue number 45-DC 758) in February 1962 in mono format only. In spite of it being an export single, however, copies were demanded and sold in the UK, although the single didn't chart. A further take was used for the South African version of the album, which was then used for a single that was issued in mono only on the 78 r.p.m. format in South Africa, with ***First Lesson in Love*** as its B-side on the Columbia label (catalogue number DSA 373) in 1961, although it didn't chart; this version was subsequently released on the 1997 anthology ***The Rock 'n' Roll Years 1958-1963***. The mono and stereo versions were also included on the ***Listen to Cliff No. 1*** EP.

Initiated with drums and a strong guitar line and a variety of grunts, Cliff's vocals are brought in. Although a highly competent (and even wryly amusing with the syncopated grunting), his projection is simply not raucous enough to do the song its originally intended justice. Hank Marvin's guitar lines are the familiar sound with a very slight edge to them, with some notes played with a rapid fire technique similar to the way a mandolin is performed. Polished but with a hint of rebelliousness in its style, *What'd I Say?* is a strong opener to the album.

For the live album ***Cliff in Japan***, all of the tracks were accompanied by Norrie Paramor and his orchestra, creating an odd juxtaposition for some of the familiar rock and roll songs without the traditional instrumentation to effect the expected sound.

Track Specification

Composed by Ray Charles

1. Unissued track (Listen to Cliff!)

Musicians		*Recording Details*	
Jet Harris	backing vocals, bass	Producer	Norrie Paramor
Hank Marvin	backing vocals, guitar	Engineered by	Malcolm Addey and J. Schroeder
Tony Meehan	drums, percussion	Recording location	Abbey Road Studio 2, St. John's Wood, London
Cliff Richard	vocals	Recording date	1st April 1960
Bruce Welch	backing vocals, rhythm guitar		

2. Unissued track (Listen to Cliff!)

Musicians		*Recording Details*	
Jet Harris	backing vocals, bass	Producer	Norrie Paramor
Hank Marvin	backing vocals, guitar	Engineered by	Malcolm Addey
Tony Meehan	drums, percussion	Recording location	Abbey Road Studio 2, St. John's Wood, London
Cliff Richard	vocals	Recording date	13th October 1960
Bruce Welch	backing vocals, rhythm guitar		

3. Listen to Cliff!

Musicians		*Recording Details*	
Jet Harris	backing vocals, bass	Producer	Norrie Paramor
Hank Marvin	backing vocals, guitar	Engineered by	Malcolm Addey and David Lloyd
Tony Meehan	drums, percussion	Recording location	Abbey Road Studio 2, St. John's Wood, London
Cliff Richard	vocals	Recording date	4th March 1961
Bruce Welch	backing vocals, rhythm guitar		

4. South African single

Musicians		*Recording Details*	
Jet Harris	backing vocals, bass	Producer	Norrie Paramor
Hank Marvin	backing vocals, guitar	Engineered by	Malcolm Addey and David Lloyd
Tony Meehan	drums, percussion	Recording location	Abbey Road Studio 2, St. John's Wood, London
Cliff Richard	vocals	Recording date	4th March 1961
Bruce Welch	backing vocals, rhythm guitar		

5. Cliff in Japan

Musicians		*Recording Details*	
Norrie Paramor Orchestra	orchestra	Producer	Norrie Paramor
Norrie Paramor	arranger, conductor	Engineered by	Unknown
Cliff Richard	vocals	Recording location	Shibuya Public Hall, Tokyo, Japan
Unknown	backing vocals	Recording date	18th October 1967

♫ What D'You Know, We've Got a Show

From the film soundtrack album of **The Young Ones**

Having broken into the dilapidated Finsbury Park Empire, the substitute for the Countess Theatre bought up by Hamilton Black (Robert Morley) to prevent the youth club show going ahead, the group looks around. Initially despondent because of the dust and decay, they begin to pick up antiquated props and wardrobe, check the lights, curtains and scenery and then sing a song that segues into the ***Vaudeville Routine***. There is a reprise that intersperses one line of ***Living Doll*** at the end of the routine. It is also reprised at the end of the show, this time also featuring Robert Morley.

The recordings for *What D'You Know, We've got a Show* and *Vaudeville Routine* were all completed at the same session, with the stereo and mono edits being the identical take, but with differing mixes for the audio channels. The film version was recorded later in the year (probably also in August) but that version has not had a commercial release outside the film.

The vocal performance is straightforward and familiar to those who enjoy the British film musical genre and, while this is a sort of pastiche of that type of routine, it is also archetypal of the variety shows that were put on in theatres everywhere at the time and had made it successfully on to television with shows like *Sunday Night at the London Palladium.*

Track Specification

Composed by Peter Myers and Ronald Cass

Musicians		*Recording Details*	
Associated British Studio Orchestra	orchestra	Producer	Norrie Paramor
		Engineered by	Malcolm Addey and Alan Kane
Stanley Black	conductor	Recording location	Abbey Road Studio 2, St. John's Wood, London
Mike Sammes Singers	vocals, backing vocals	Recording date	9th August 1961
Cliff Richard	vocals		

♫ What Is There to Say?

Unissued track

The third of three songs recorded for the soundtrack album for the film ***The Young Ones*** (with the theme tune and ***Lessons in Love***), *What Is There to Say?* was abandoned from the project. Eleven takes were recorded in that session but none has been issued in any format. However, although it was not used, the song transmogrified into ***Since I Lost You***, which was recorded at the session on 19th December 1961.

Track Specification

Composed by Bruce Welch and Hank Marvin

Musicians		*Recording Details*	
Jet Harris	bass	Producer	Norrie Paramor
Hank Marvin	guitar	Engineered by	Malcolm Addey and David Lloyd
Tony Meehan	drums, percussion	Recording location	Abbey Road Studio 2, St. John's Wood, London
Cliff Richard	vocals	Recording date	11th August 1961
Bruce Welch	rhythm guitar		

♫ What's Behind the Eyes of Mary?

From the album **Established 1958**

Written by members of the Shadows, as were all of the tracks on ***Established 1958***, here the unusual pairing of Hank Marvin and Brian Bennett, there were three separate attempts to record the *What's Behind the Eyes of Mary?*. The first was on 29th May 1968, although it was abandoned after just one take and this has not been issued. Two days later, it was attempted again but again not completed satisfactorily. This was at the same time as performing in the evening at the Talk of the Town, so possibly there were time constraints involved. The third session a month later was successful. Curiously, the 2nd July session is slated in session comments as an orchestral session and yet, the backing is clearly by the Shadows (as also indicated on the album liner notes). Whether an earlier backing track was used to overdub the vocals or whether, indeed, the Shadows came back into the studio for this one track is uncertain, particularly as the session on 10th June (recording ***Not the Way It Should Be*** also for the album) is designated as the very last session to feature both Cliff Richard and the Shadows performing together at the same session.

A complex guitar and bass line introduce the track, which is a beautifully understated love song as Cliff tries to interpret what the girl called Mary is thinking and how he can make her his. The final Cliff song on the album, it would have been interesting to see what the song would have achieved as a single.

A lot of the *Established 1958* tracks were translated into German for Cliff to record for his first German language album, *Hier Ist Cliff*, with *What's Behind the Eyes of Mary?* being given a new title of ***Deine Augen Träumen Mary*** (or *Your Eyes Are Dreaming of Mary*).

Track Specification

Composed by Hank Marvin and Brian Bennett

1. Unissued track (Established 1958)

Musicians		*Recording Details*	
Brian Bennett	arranger, drums, percussion	Producer	Norrie Paramor
Mike Leander	conductor	Engineered by	Peter Vince
Hank Marvin	guitar	Recording location	Abbey Road Studio 2, St. John's Wood, London
Mike Leander Orchestra	orchestra	Recording date	29th May 1968
Cliff Richard	vocals		
John Rostill	bass		
Bruce Welch	rhythm guitar		

2. Unissued track (Established 1958)

Musicians		*Recording Details*	
Brian Bennett	arranger, drums, percussion	Producer	Norrie Paramor
Mike Leander	conductor	Engineered by	Peter Vince
Hank Marvin	guitar	Recording location	Abbey Road Studio 2, St. John's Wood, London
Mike Leander Orchestra	orchestra	Recording date	31st May 1968
Cliff Richard	vocals		
John Rostill	bass		
Bruce Welch	rhythm guitar		

3. Established 1958

Musicians		*Recording Details*	
Brian Bennett	arranger, drums, percussion	Producer	Norrie Paramor
Mike Leander	conductor	Engineered by	Peter Vince
Hank Marvin	guitar	Recording location	Chappell Studios, London
Mike Leander Orchestra	orchestra	Recording date	2nd July 1968
Cliff Richard	vocals		
John Rostill	bass		
Bruce Welch	rhythm guitar		

♫ What's Love Got to Do with It?

From the album **Wanted** *and unissued live track*

Terry Britten was, of course, instrumental in Cliff Richard's career in the seventies and eighties specifically, writing many a song that helped in Cliff's renaissance of the period. Britten wrote many other songs and one of these was *What's Love Got to Do with It?*, which was most famously recorded by Tina Turner as part of her comeback, and who reached number three with the song in 1984. It was later covered by Warren G featuring Adina Howard, who did even better with it when they reached number two in 1993. In addition, the song has been covered by Buck's Fizz, Tiffany, Gary Tesca and Roger Williams among a few others.

A jazz beat is established on the keyboards and programmed percussion, while Cliff's vocals, backed by his own hamonies, is kept confidential in its enunciation until the chorus, when the performance opens up before closing back down for the next verse. Turner's version verged on the strident but Cliff keeps his cover brilliantly understated.

During the 2003 tour to promote the album, the New Zealand leg was recorded and filmed, ostensibly for a DVD released (featuring dancers dressed in black) later in the year and, although the *World Tour Live* was released the following year on CD, *What's Love Got to Do with It?* was not included on the track listing.

Track Specification
Composed by Terry Britten and Graham Lyle

1. Wanted

Musicians		*Recording Details*	
John Brant	additional programming	Producer	Alan Tarney
Anthony Clark	backing vocals	Engineered by	John Brant and Gerry Kitchingham
Cliff Richard	vocals, backing vocals	Recording location	Wilmer Studios, London
Alan Tarney	arranger, backing vocals, guitar keyboards, programming	Recording date	January-April 2001

2. Unissued track (World Tour Live)

Musicians		*Recording Details*	
Anthony Clark	backing vocals, guitar	Producer	Keith Bessey
John Clark	guitar	Engineered by	Keith Bessey
Dave Cooke	keyboards	Recording location	The Mission Winery, Napier, New Zealand
Peter Howarth	backing vocals	Recording date	22nd February 2003
Pete May	drums, percussion		
Mick Mullins	backing vocals		
Keith Murrell	backing vocals		
Alan Park	keyboards		
Cliff Richard	vocals		
Steve Stroud	bass		

♫ What's More (I Don't Need Her)

B-side of **Don't Forget to Catch Me** *and from the album* **Live at the Talk of the Town**

Written by Guy Fletcher and Doug Flett, who would go on to write a number of Cliff Richard's tracks into the first half of the seventies, *What's More (I Don't Need Her)* was recorded by Cliff at the second of two sessions slated for 8th March 1968. Also covered by Lee Hazlewood, the song was chosen as the B-side of ***Don't Forget to Catch Me*** and has only ever been released in mono (as was the policy at Columbia for singles at the time). A major rarity, given the popularity of the song, it was reissued on CD as a bonus track on the remastered album ***Established 1958*** in 2007.
Although it was resurrected for his Talk of the Town shows, it is unfortunate that this beautiful but sad song about breaking up wasn't given broader release. Cliff sings with emotion and passion and the clever, unexpected musical intervals make it a song worth listening to more than once at a sitting.
Recorded as part of the Talk of the Town concert in 1968, the arrangement and performance are a faithful adaptation of the studio recording and Cliff sings it well.

Track Specification
Composed by Guy Fletcher and Doug Flett

1. B-side (Don't Forget to Catch Me)

Musicians		*Recording Details*	
Breakaways:	backing vocals	Producer	Norrie Paramor
Vicki Hasemen		Engineered by	Peter Vince
Margo Quantrell		Recording location	Abbey Road Studio 2, St. John's Wood, London
Jean Ryder		Recording date	8th March 1968
Mike Leander	arranger, conductor		
Mike Leander Orchestra	orchestra		
Cliff Richard	vocals		

2. Live at the Talk of the Town

Musicians		*Recording Details*	
Breakaways:	backing vocals	Producer	Norrie Paramor
Vicki Hasemen		Engineered by	Peter Vince
Margo Quantrell		Recording location	Talk of the Town Theatre, London
Jean Ryder		Recording date	30th May 1968
Norrie Paramor	arranger, conductor		
Cliff Richard	vocals		
Talk of the Town Orchestra	orchestra		

♫ What've I Gotta Do?

From the film soundtrack album of **Wonderful Life**

The first track to be recorded for the ***Wonderful Life*** film soundtrack, *What've I Gotta Do?* is one of the songs in the dual film within the main film. Johnny (Cliff Richard) has tried to persuade Jenny (Susan Hampshire) to record the other film with him but she is reluctant. Instead, his friends hide cameras and sound equipment in drinks crates on the trolley they serve the beverages from and record the action being filmed for the 'real' film. In it a group of Arab warriors are fighting against the legionnaires, headed up by Johnny's character. Instead of continuing as a fight scene, it transforms into a song and dance number. The filmed action moves into the screen at the projection theatre with the group of friends (now

including Barbara (Una Stubbs) but not Jenny) getting up and picking up the melody and dancing as they eventually troop out of the room, leaving Jerry (Melvyn Hayes) singing to himself before he realizes he's on his own.
Recorded during the Cliff and the Shadows summer season at Blackpool some months earlier, it is another track that features bassist Brian Locking, even though his successor John Rostill appears in the film. The tenth and final take was used for the mono and stereo recordings but with different mixes for the separate audio channels. The song also appeared on the track listing of the ***Wonderful Life No. 1*** EP. The version used in the film misses the second verse and chorus and was probably recorded in the first three months of 1964, although the location and studio personnel are unknown. To date, the film version has not been released in any other commercial format. On the released track, there is an uncredited piano, which is possibly Norrie Paramor or Hanki Marvin although this is unconfirmed.
With a foot-stomping beat that includes the rhythm guitar, the drums, a running bass line and the piano, *What've I Got to Do?* is certainly one of the highlights of the soundtrack. Hank plays a number of guitar solos and he, Cliff and Bruce join forces to sing the perfect harmonies that were their speciality.

Track Specification
Composed by Bruce Welch and Hank Marvin

Musicians		*Recording Details*	
Brian Bennett	drums, percussion	Producer	Norrie Paramor
Brian 'Licorice' Locking	bass	Engineered by	Malcolm Addey and Jimmy Johnson
Hank Marvin	backing vocals, guitar	Recording location	Jubilee Hall, Blackpool
Cliff Richard	vocals	Recording date	9th August 1963
Unknown	piano		
Bruce Welch	backing vocals, rhythm guitar		

♫ What Would I Do (For the Love of a Girl)?

B-side of **Visions**

A Hank Marvin and Bruce Welch collaboration, *What Would I Do (For the Love of a Girl)?* was recorded and released in May 1966 for the B-side of the top ten hit ***Visions***. The final (unknown) take and edit of the song was only ever released in mono format and remained a sought-after rarity until it was included in the track listing as a bonus song on the ***Finders Keepers*** remastered CD album in 2005.
With a typical instrumental accompaniment from the Shadows that is very much of the period, the lead guitar wows a little as each note is played. More frequently as they entered the second half of the decade, the vocal harmonies made more appearances and this is a real blessing because they are never less than perfect and show Bruce Welch's and Hank Marvin's ear for brilliant melody and harmony. The song is upbeat, optimistic and jaunty and the group is clearly enjoying the performance on the record.

Track Specification
Composed by Bruce Welch and Hank Marvin

Musicians		*Recording Details*	
Brian Bennett	drums, percussion	Producer	Norrie Paramor
Hank Marvin	backing vocals, guitar	Engineered by	Malcolm Addey, Peter Vince and Richard Lush
Cliff Richard	vocals	Recording location	Abbey Road Studio 3, St. John's Wood, London
John Rostill	backing vocals, bass	Recording date	22nd May 1966
Bruce Welch	backing vocals, rhythm guitar		

♫ When a Child Is Born

From the album **Cliff at Christmas**

A massive hit for Johnny Mathis at Christmas in 1976, *When a Child Is Born* has also been covered by Brook Benton, Boney M, the Three Degrees, Judy Collins, the Moody Blues and that stalwart of Christmas, Bing Crosby, amongst many others. Because of its Christian message of peace, it was an obvious choice for Cliff Richard to include on his second album of Christmas material, ***Cliff at Christmas***.
The introduction proves that this is not going to be a straight copy of Mathis's famous version. The arrangement has a pseudo-calypso beat running behind it, while Cliff sings the impassioned lyrics, providing his own echoes. As the chorus starts, the main melody is developed into something special before returning to the verse. Eschewing the desire to repeat the excruciating spoken excerpt that Mathis inflicted on his version, instead Cliff sings a wordless bridge to the final verse, which includes new lyrics "Nation shall speak peace unto nation". A worthy addition to Cliff's Christmas canon.

Track Specification
Composed by Ciro Dammaccio and Fred Jay

Musicians		*Recording Details*	
Lizzie Deane	backing vocals	Producer	Brothers Mack
Mike Drinkwater	keyboards	Engineered by	Tim Earnes
Ian Mack	backing vocals, programming	Recording location	Metropolis Studios, London
Stuart Mack	backing vocals, guitar, keyboards	Recording date	2003
Cliff Richard	vocals, backing vocals		
Urban Soul Orchestra	orchestra		

♫ Whenever God Shines His Light

109th UK single

Cliff Richard joined forces with famously taciturn Northern Irish singer Van Morrison to produce one of the strangest duets of Cliff's career, which is a pleasant song that bows in reverence towards Christ. Originally recorded for Morrison's *Avalon Sunset* album that was released in June 1989, *Whenever God Shines His Light* was eventually issued, backed with a Morrison-only track *I'd Love to Write Another Song*, as a single. It was edited slightly so that it fades around half a minute earlier than the album version, and was released on the Polydor label (catalogue number VANS 2) on 27th November 1989 and reached number twenty in the UK singles charts. The same edited version was issued on the CD single (catalogue number VANSCD 2), while the album version was included on the twelve-inch (VANX 2) and the CD. It was later added as an extra track to Van Morrison's 1997 CD single release of *The Healing Game*. A radio promotional single was also issued (VANS2DJ) at the time, which was the same as the seven-inch version of the record. The associated promotional video was filmed at Shepperton Studios on 4th December 1989.

The simple piano introduction is matched with a Caribbean style of percussion on the marimbas. Van Morrison's vocal line is a little more raucous and this shows in comparison to the purity of Cliff's voice, which is also using the falsetto, whereas Morrison tends to strain on the much higher notes in his throat-positioned voice. When they sing together in harmony, the effect is electric and proves what master musicians both men are. The curious rhythm and staccato accompaniment throughout make the song an oddity but it is this very point that raises the interest in it over and above the vocal efforts of the protagonists.

Track Specification

Composed by Van Morrison

Musicians

Clive Culberson	bass
Neil Drinkwater	piano
Dave Early	drums, percussion
Roy Jones	drums, percussion
Carol Kenyon	backing vocals
Katie Kissoon	backing vocals
Arty McGlynn	guitar
Van Morrison	vocals
Steve Pearce	backing vocals
Cliff Richard	vocals
Fiachra Trench	arranger, conductor
Gavin Wright	strings leader
Unknown	orchestra

Recording Details

Producer	Van Morrison
Engineered by	Mick Glossop
Recording location	The Townhouse Studios, London
Recording date	20th February 1989

♫ When I Find You

From the album **Sincerely Cliff Richard**

The penultimate track on the ***Sincerely Cliff Richard*** album was recorded as the last song at the session on 22nd April 1968, featuring an arrangement by Alan Hawkshaw who would go on to act as sidesman to the rejuvenated Shadows in the seventies, playing keyboards.

With a lilt and arrangement that sounds as if the song has come straight out of the Eurovision Song Contest, Cliff sings the song with gusto as he is backed by the circus-like brass band. There is a female backing group, who are not credited but who are also occasionally out of tune, although this doesn't detract from the pleasure created from listening to this happy little song.

Track Specification

Composed by Campbell

Musicians

Alan Hawkshaw	arranger
Mike Vickers Orchestra	orchestra
Cliff Richard	vocals
Mike Vickers	arranger, conductor
Unknown	backing vocals

Recording Details

Producer	Norrie Paramor
Engineered by	Peter Vince
Recording location	Abbey Road Studio 2, St. John's Wood, London
Recording date	22nd April 1969

♫ When I Grow Too Old to Dream

From the EP **Dream**

Made popular by British actress and singer Gracie Fields, *When I Grow Too Old to Dream* was written and published in 1934. Long since regarded as a standard, it was recorded by Nat King Cole, Nelson Eddy, The Cliff Adams Singers, the Everly Brothers, Dave Brubeck, Percy Faith, Dizzy Gillespie, Louis Armstrong, Linda Ronstadt, Phil Coulter, Doris Day, Benny Goodman, Julie London, Charlie Parker and Kiri Te Kanawa among many others.

The final track to be recorded for Cliff Richard's ***Dream*** EP (the first such release to include all new material not otherwise available on any other medium), *When I Grow Too Old to Dream* was the only track to be recorded separately (the other three were completed in one session). The eighth and final take was used for the mono and stereo edits, although different mixes for the audio channels were required. Until the 1989 See For Miles EP compilation album, ***The EP Collection: Ballads and Love Songs***, the track was a considerable rarity for fans and collectors, although the vinyl and CD versions of the album themselves are now much sought-after rarities, too.

All of the tracks on the EP begin with a simple melody played on a classical guitar before entering into the song. Cliff's vocals are sweetly portrayed and lilt between the higher part of his vocal range and the mid-range. The waltz beat is maintained by brushed drums and strummed rhythm guitar while Hank Marvin plays a mandolin-like supporting harmony on the lead guitar. This song, more than most, shows Cliff's capabilities as a singer and his superb range and control.

Track Specification
Composed by Oscar Hammerstein II and Sigmund Romberg

Musicians

Jet Harris	bass
Hank Marvin	guitar
Tony Meehan	drums, percussion
Cliff Richard	vocals
Bruce Welch	rhythm guitar

Recording Details

Producer	Norrie Paramor
Engineered by	Malcolm Addey
Recording location	Abbey Road Studio 2, St. John's Wood, London
Recording date	12th May 1961

♫ When I'm Sixty-Four

From the albums **Live at the Talk of the Town** *and* **Cliff Live in Korea**

Ostensibly written by Paul McCartney with minimal help from John Lennon, it was inspired by his love of music hall mixed with the cosy image of family. To the young fifteen-year-old (when the song was first drafted), the age of sixty-four would have seemed an incredible age away that would never be reached and the song refers to all the things that he thinks he might need at that age: being looked after, grandchildren and so on. Making its appearance on the seminal *Sergeant Pepper's Lonely Hearts Club Band*, it has become a favourite among many performers, among whom the following have recorded it: the Bee Gees, Courtney Pine, Max Bygraves, Bernard Cribbens, Georgie Fame, Frankie Howerd and Cheap Trick. But it was Kenny Ball and His Jazzmen who are the only act to have a hit with it in the British charts when they took it to number forty-three in July 1967 shortly after the Beatles released it in album form.

Cliff Richard has not recorded the song in the studio – and is unlikely to now given his age unless he changes the lyrics – but often added songs in this way to his performance set. His version of *When I'm Sixty-Four* was included in the set list for his performances at the Talk of the Town Theatre in London at the end of May 1968 and subsequently released on the live album.

Cliff sings the song with tongue firmly planted in his cheek, with, for example, a hic when singing about the bottle of wine and sings the Breakaways names for what the grandchildren's names might be. The arrangement is deliberately jauntier than the Beatles version and it has a cabaret feel to it. The final line is repeated three times before completing.

The song also appeared on the 1969 Korean tour, with the Seoul concert being recorded for release in mono only to the Korean market on the ultra-rare album *Cliff Live in Korea*.

Track Specification
Composed by John Lennon and Paul McCartney

1. Live at the Talk of the Town

Musicians

Breakaways:	backing vocals
Vicki Hasemen	
Margo Quantrell	
Jean Ryder	
Norrie Paramor	arranger, conductor
Cliff Richard	vocals
Talk of the Town Orchestra	orchestra
Unknown	hand claps

Recording Details

Producer	Norrie Paramor
Engineered by	Peter Vince
Recording location	Talk of the Town Theatre, London
Recording date	30th May 1968

2. Cliff Live in Korea

Musicians

Brian Bennett	drums, percussion
Alan Hawkshaw	keyboards
Hank Marvin	guitar
Cliff Richard	vocals
John Rostill	bass
Bruce Welch	rhythm guitar

Recording Details

Producer	Unknown
Engineered by	Unknown
Recording location	Citizen Hall, Seoul, South Korea
Recording date	16th October 1969

♫ When I Need You

139th UK single

First recorded in 1976 by one of its writers, Albert Hammond, *When I Need You* was most famous in the UK when Leo Sayer had his first number one with his cover in early 1977. Sayer's single also reached number one in the Billboard Hot 100 in the US. In February 1998, actor Will Mellor had a number five hit, while, in the same year, chanteuse Céline Dion

recorded a version for her *Let's Talk about Love* album, which was issued as a single in September 1998 but only in Brazil. The song has been covered by Luther Vandross, Rod Stewart, Perry Como, Brotherhood of Man, Barry Manilow and Julio Iglesias among others.
In 2007, Cliff Richard recorded his version as one of five new love ballads to be included on a compilation by EMI, ***Love... The Album***, which covered songs from his entire career (although focused on the last twenty-five years or so in particular). *When I Need You* was chosen as the only single from the project. Backed with prior singles ***Never Let Go*** and ***My Pretty One***, it was issued on the EMI label (catalogue number 50999 511452 2 4) on 29th October 2007, preceding the album's release by two weeks, and reached number thirty-eight in the UK charts. The musicians involved are unknown.
Leo Sayer's version is so familiar that it would be easy to create a carbon copy or, worse, a pastiche, but Cliff's adaptation is an homage but is arranged in a successfully different way and, in so doing, creates a brilliant version that is worthy as a single release.

Track Specification
Composed by Carole Bayer Sager and Albert Hammond

Musicians		*Recording Details*	
Cliff Richard	vocals, backing vocals	Producer	Michael Omartian
Unknown	backing vocals	Engineered by	Terry Christian
Unknown	guitar	Recording location	Sound Kitchen, Franklin, Tennessee, USA, Sound House, Franklin, Tennessee, USA and/or Blue Wave Studios, Bayley's Plantation, St. Phillip, Barbados
Unknown	bass		
Unknown	piano		
Unknown	drums, percussion		
Unknown	orchestra	Recording date	2007
Unknown	conductor		

♫ When I Survey the Wondrous Cross

From the albums **Good News**, **Small Corners** *and* **Silver Celebration**

Written by Isaac Watts, the hymn *When I Survey the Wondrous Cross* was first published in 1707 and was seen as an innovation on the style of hymns that had been written to that point that simply set tracts of the Bible to music. Instead, this was more of a poem inspired by sections of the Bible including Galatians in its second verse. The most common version is that set to music by Edward Miller under the title *Rockingham* and it is this that was used by the BBC as the introduction to its Good Friday morning broadcast. A classic representation of what it means to be Christian, *When I Survey the Wondrous Cross* has been recorded and covered by any number of church choirs and choral societies, including the London Philharmonic Choir and the Huddersfield Choral Society, as well as established popular acts such as Tennessee Ernie Ford, the Grimethorpe Colliery Band, John Jones, the Mormon Tabernacle Choir, Kathryn Scott and Rick Wakeman among others.
Recorded at the last April 1967 session for Cliff Richard's religious album ***Good News***, it was the final song in the can and was completed in five takes.
Introduced by the clarity of Pat Clark's harmonies singing wordlessly, the swooping strings support Cliff's able vocal line. He brings something special to a song that could easily have been turned into a dirge, by imbuing the lyrics with passionate meaning.
Tony Rivers, Cliff's backing vocalist in the latter half of the seventies and into the eighties, arranged the hymn again for recording on the ***Small Corners*** album. It was the final song to be completed at the second the three album sessions in January 1977 with some overdubs added at a later session, and *When I Survey the Wondrous Cross* was chosen to close the album. What this shows more eloquently than most of the songs Cliff has recorded is his innate ability to pitch the notes. The close harmony vocals are beautifully portrayed and lift what again could have been a funereal dirge into something that is quite special.
Accompanied only by a cello, Cliff revisited the song in a 1997 concert with the All Souls Orchestra, which was subsequently released on the album *Silver Celebration*.

Track Specification
Composed by Isaac Watts and Edward Miller

1. Good News

Musicians		*Recording Details*	
Pat Clark	vocals	Producer	Norrie Paramor
Norrie Paramor Orchestra	orchestra	Engineered by	Peter Vince and Mike Stone
Norrie Paramor	arranger, conductor	Recording location	Abbey Road Studio 2, St. John's Wood, London
Cliff Richard	vocals	Recording date	28th April 1967

2. Small Corners

Musicians		*Recording Details*	
Stuart Calver	backing vocals	Producer	Cliff Richard
John Perry	backing vocals	Engineered by	Tony Clark, Haydn Bendall and Alan Rouse
Cliff Richard	vocals	Recording location	Abbey Road Studio 3, St. John's Wood, London
Tony Rivers	arranger, backing vocals	Recording date	18th January 1977 and 4th February 1977

3. Silver Celebration

Musicians	
Cliff Richard	vocals
Robin Thompson-Clarke	cello

Recording Details	
Producer	Langham Arts
Engineered by	Unknown
Recording location	Wembley Conference Centre, Wembley, North-west London
Recording date	21st October 1997

♫ When My Dream Boat Comes Home

From the album **32 Minutes and 17 Seconds with Cliff Richard**

Written in the mid-thirties, *When My Dream Boat Comes Home* became a ready jazz standard and was covered by contemporaneous artists and later acts including Bing Crosby, Red Allen, Arnett Cobb, Count Basie, Eddy Howard, Guy Lombardo, the Blue Note Six, Fats Domino (who had the biggest hit with it in the US), Coleman Hawkins, Brenda Lee, Kay Starr and Elvis Presley among several others.

The first of three songs to be completed for the 17th May 1962 session for the ***32 Minutes and 17 Seconds with Cliff Richard*** album, the same take and edit was used for the mono and stereo recordings with differing mixes for the requirements of the audio channels. The song also appeared on the ***Time for Cliff and the Shadows*** EP and is the first track on the second side of the original vinyl version of the album.

Beginning with the instrumentation appearing in the left stereo channel, Cliff's lead vocal comes in soon after in the right channel – this was the early days of stereo techniques and this tended to be the chosen approach to it for a lot of popular recordings – nevertheless it provides a peculiar experience when listening through headphones. There is an uncredited piano performance in the mix (likely to be either Hank Marvin or Norrie Paramor) that helps the overall rhythm, which is kept steady by Brian Bennett's drumming.

Track Specification

Composed by Clifford Friend and David Franklin

Musicians	
Brian Bennett	drums, percussion
Brian 'Licorice' Locking	bass
Hank Marvin	guitar
Cliff Richard	vocals
Unknown	piano
Bruce Welch	rhythm guitar

Recording Details	
Producer	Norrie Paramor
Engineered by	Malcolm Addey
Recording location	Abbey Road Studio 2, St. John's Wood, London
Recording date	17th May 1962

♫ When the Girl in Your Arms (Is the Girl in Your Heart)

15th UK single *and from the album* **Live at the ABC Kingston 1962**

When Sid Tepper and Roy Bennett were contracted to write material for the soundtrack to ***The Young Ones***, they submitted three songs: *When the Girl in Your Arms (Is the Girl in Your Heart)*, the title song ***The Young Ones*** *and* ***Outsider***. Only the last one wasn't used, although it was still recorded and formed part of the track listing to Cliff Richard's ***21 Today*** album. *When the Girl in Your Arms (Is the Girl in Your Heart)* was covered by Connie Francis, who had a reasonable hit with it in the US, with the obligatory change in lyrics and gender emphasis, and which caused a contretemps between the singers since Connie's version was issued before the release of Cliff's film; something that he saw, according to the liner notes of the remastered version of ***The Young Ones*** album, as rather unethical. Later in the seventies, in interview, Cliff confessed that he didn't really like the song and, although he had had much pressure from fans to perform it, was highly reluctant to do so. This was not the case, of course, when the single and film was released and it needed to be publicized: it became one of the set list tracks for the concert recorded live at the ABC Theatre in Kingston, Surrey in March 1962, subsequently released in its entirety on a 2003 stereo CD.

In the film, having located a new but now secret venue for the show that the Simpkin's Youth Club members are putting on in order to pay the £1,500 necessary to extend the lease on their hut for five years and having successfully confirmed that it was viable to put on such a show, Nicky Black (played by Cliff) recognizes the need for publicity. Suddenly animated, he asks them all if they know where to get hold of a tape recorder and a radio transmitter. Later, in a small corner of the clubhouse, with look-outs posted on the door, Nicky performs *When the Girl in Your Arms (Is the Girl in Your Heart)* into a microphone and directly towards his girlfriend Toni Crowthier (Carole Gray), while being accompanied acoustically by the Shadows (who do not have an overt name in the film). On completion of the song, the transmitter is carried concealed on a fruit and vegetable market barrow and the song and Toni's introduction is irregularly played disrupting the ITV (an advertisement for the long-gone Strand cigarettes brand) and BBC (Richard Baker reading a news item about the ITV disruption) programme output. Cutting to an increasingly exasperated Home Office official who calls out the detector vans and Scotland Yard to go to various locations (including the BBC and Scotland Yard itself) to locate the source of the transmitter, there are other scenes of a girls school dormitory (incongruously with a television allowed especially after lights out) with dreamy-eyed girls and then cutting to a bridge foursome playing a rubber with one of them cheating as the other old ladies are mesmerised by the voice. The broadcast is heard several times through the latter part of the film, culminating with the stage performance as Nicky Black. He had helped his monstrous father (Robert Morley) take on the villains intent on beating him up and then he had returned to the theatre to perform in front of the increasingly restless crowd calling for the Mystery Singer, revealing himself to be the Mystery Singer as the curtain draws back. This staged version only performs the first couple of lines accompanied by the Shadows and then quickly segues into ***We Say Yeah***.

Backed with ***Got a Funny Feeling*** from the film's soundtrack album, *When the Girl in Your Arms (Is the Girl in Your Heart)* was released as a single on the Columbia label (catalogue number 45-DB 4716) on the 6th October 1961, reaching the number three spot in the UK singles chart. It was also included on the track listing of the ***Cliff's Hit Parade*** EP. The first song to be recorded for the film at the end of a session that produced five songs for *21 Today*, *When the Girl in Your Arms (Is the Girl in Your Heart)* used the same take for the mono and stereo edits but with different mixes for the audio channels. There is a mock stereo version also available, which is built on the mono edit. The film version was recorded later in the year (probably in August) but, as yet, has not been released in any other commercial format.

Although Cliff didn't particularly like the song enough to perform it that often, it fits well his vocals. The accompaniment of gentle humming harmonies, strummed guitars and uncredited strings and piano, all make the song the perfect vehicle for the intention of the storyline: that a great singer could melt the hearts of many a woman listening to it.

Track Specification
Composed by Sid Tepper and Roy C. Bennett

__*1. Single*__

Musicians		*Recording Details*	
Jet Harris	bass	Producer	Norrie Paramor
Hank Marvin	guitar	Engineered by	Malcolm Addey
Tony Meehan	drums, percussion	Recording location	Abbey Road Studio 2, St. John's Wood, London
Mike Sammes Singers	backing vocals	Recording date	30th January 1961
Cliff Richard	vocals		
Unknown	piano		
Unknown	strings		
Bruce Welch	rhythm guitar		

__*2. Live at the ABC Kingston 1962*__

Musicians		*Recording Details*	
Brian Bennett	drums, percussion	Producer	Norrie Paramor
Jet Harris	backing vocals, bass	Engineered by	Malcolm Addey and Ken Townsend
Hank Marvin	backing vocals, guitar	Recording location	ABC Theatre, Kingston, Surrey
Cliff Richard	vocals, hand claps	Recording date	7th March 1962
Bruce Welch	backing vocals, rhythm guitar		

♫ When Two Worlds Drift Apart

70th UK single

Written by the man responsible for four tracks on the ***I'm Nearly Famous*** album and two on the new ***Every Face Tells a Story*** album, Peter Sills created this sad and introspective song that discusses the effects of a soured relationship breaking up. Also recorded by Ruthie Henshall, Cliff Richard's version appeared on the *Every Face Tells a Story* album and was chosen as the third single from that project and became Cliff's seventieth UK single release. Backed with ***That's Why I Love You***, which was recorded during the album sessions but not included on the track listing, *When Two Worlds Drift Apart* was released on the EMI label (catalogue number EMI 2633) on 27th June 1977, reaching only forty-six in the UK charts, which was a surprise for such a beautiful and strong song. As a result, *When Two Worlds Drift Apart* was Cliff's worst performing charting single of his career to that point.

This beautiful song is introduced on the piano and stays with Cliff's vocals. Cliff sings with a vibrato that he began to use increasingly during this period. The second verse is joined by gentle strings and this helps build up the drama expressed in the lyrics, which reaches its zenith in the middle eight when the close harmony backing vocals drop into triplets before returning back to the orchestra and piano. This time a plaintive oboe is employed to add further sad emotion to underpin the story of a relationship break-up.

In 1992, while compiling a new album, ***My Kinda Life***, Cliff and music director Paul Moessl revisited a number of previously recorded tracks, took those original recordings and added new instrumentation and vocals. In the case of *When Two Worlds Drift Apart*, new guitars and keyboards were overdubbed, while the lyrics were translated into French and the song retitled to ***Remember*** after the repeated lyric that appears in the latter chorus. It was released as a single in France and added as an extra track on the CD single release of ***I Still Believe in You***.

Track Specification
Composed by Peter Sills

Musicians		*Recording Details*	
Richard Hewson	arranger, conductor	Producer	Bruce Welch
John Perry	backing vocals	Engineered by	Tony Clark, Mike Jarrett and Alan Rouse
Cliff Richard	vocals, backing vocals	Recording location	Abbey Road Studio 2, St. John's Wood, London
Tony Rivers	backing vocals	Recording date	7th and 13th September 1976
Graham Todd	piano		
Unknown	orchestra		

♫ When Will I Be Loved?

CD B-side of **All I Have to Do Is Dream/Miss You Nights**

A bigger hit for the Everly Brothers in the UK, where it reached number four, than in the US, where it reached number eight, *When Will I Be Loved?* was recorded in late 1959 and issued in the middle of 1960. It was most famously covered by Linda Ronstadt when, in 1975, she reached number two in the US Billboard charts, but it has also been recorded by a number of artists including Amanda Broom (a live performance in an episode of *Magnum P.I.*), Tanya Tucker, Sandy Posey and Jamison Belushi among several others.

In 1981, the BBC were filming a four-part documentary about Cliff Richard and, as part of the production, the corporation recorded live performances of a number of tracks at London's Hammersmith Odeon and the Manchester Apollo. Some of these were licensed for release at the time and resulted in the single ***Daddy's Home***. Thirteen years later, the section of the concert that featured duets with Phil Everly were also licensed and remixed, with ***All I Have to Do Is Dream*** being issued as a double A-side single with a remixed version ***Miss You Nights***. While it was only those tracks that appeared on the vinyl seven-inch version of the single, additional songs were added to a two-part CD single version with *When Will I Be Loved?* and ***Tribute to the Legends Medley*** from the same live show being included on the first disc.

As with *All I Have to Do Is Dream*, Cliff takes the principal melody while Everly performs the higher harmonies as he did when in partnership with his brother, Don. There is more scope on the song for instrumental virtuoso performances, with a guitar break in the mid-section, but it is the perfect blending of the men's vocals that works so well.

Track Specification

Composed by Phil Everly

Musicians

John Clark	guitar
Phil Everly	vocals
Mark Griffiths	bass
Graham Jarvis	drums, percussion
Martin Jenner	guitar
Alan Park	keyboards
Cliff Richard	vocals
Graham Todd	keyboards

Recording Details

Producer	Cliff Richard
Engineered by	Unknown
Recording location	Hammersmith Odeon, London
Remixed at	R. G. Jones Studio, Wimbledon, London
Recording date	1st May 1981 (live track) and 7th September 1994 (remix)

♫ When You Are There

From the album **...And They Said It Wouldn't Last! (My 50 Years in Music)**

At a number of 1969's recording sessions, several tracks that would have fitted easily on to the various albums released at the time (for example, ***Sincerely Cliff Richard*** and ***Tracks 'n' Grooves***) were recorded by Cliff Richard but weren't issued. One of these was *When You Are There*, with unknown writing credits, recorded in late September but remaining in the EMI vaults for thirty-nine years, when it was finally included on the lost and found section of the celebratory album ***...And They Said It Wouldn't Last! (My 50 Years in Music)*** in 2008.

The orchestral arrangement typifies songs from this period for Cliff, but it is elevated by the strength and purity of his vocal line, which is pitched perfectly in its emotive passages. When Cliff enters the main section of each chorus, it sounds like he is either double-tracked or singing in unison with himself by overdubbing. The string and brass passages in the bigger moments are a little overdone but this is nevertheless a brilliant song that strangely was not released at the time when it would have at least made a good B-side or album track.

Track Specification

Composed by Unknown

Musicians

Mike Vickers Orchestra	orchestra
Cliff Richard	vocals
Mike Vickers	arranger, conductor

Recording Details

Producer	Norrie Paramor
Engineered by	Peter Vince
Recording location	Abbey Road Studio 2, St. John's Wood, London
Recording date	22nd September 1969

♫ When You Say Nothing at All

From the album **Love... The Album**

First recorded by country star, Keith Whitley, who took it to the top of the US country charts in December 1988, Alison Krauss followed it by making it an American top ten hit in 1995 but it was, for Britain, Ronan Keating who had the most familiar version, having gone solo from Boyzone, with his first single and it reached number one in the late summer of 1999. Since Whitley's recording, it has also been covered by a variety of artists including Foster and Allen, Cheryl Christine, Engelbert Humperdinck, Frances Black, Déjà Vu and Kathy Phillips among others.

When You Say Nothing at All was one of five new songs recorded by Cliff to add to a compilation of his love ballad favourites from across his career for the 2007 album ***Love... The Album***. The musicians involved are unknown.

The beauty of Cliff's version is created through the use of the flowing piano, the violin solo and an accordion accompaniment playing quietly underneath everything, but more than anything else, it is Cliff's own layered backing vocals that provide the interest in the performance and make it so much improved on the original and the covers.

Track Specification
Composed by Don Schlitz and Paul Overstreet

Musicians	
Cliff Richard	vocals, backing vocals
Unknown	piano
Unknown	guitar
Unknown	bass
Unknown	drums, percussion
Unknown	violin
Unknown	accordion
Unknown	strings

Recording Details	
Producer	Michael Omartian
Engineered by	Terry Christian
Recording location	Sound Kitchen, Franklin, Tennessee, USA, Sound House, Franklin, Tennessee, USA and/or Blue Wave Studios, Bayley's Plantation, St. Phillip, Barbados
Recording date	2007

♫ When You Thought of Me

From the albums **Songs from Heathcliff** *and* **Heathcliff Live**

The closing song of the first act of ***Heathcliff*** features Heathcliff (Cliff Richard) reflecting on what has happened so far. Cathy (Helen Hobson) is having doubts about her impending marriage to the rich but rather dull Edgar Linton (Darryl Knock). Heathcliff overhears her confessing her love for him, Heathcliff, on the moors but will stay with Linton for the stability and the financial security, after which Heathcliff travels the world, vowing to make his own fortune and to exact his revenge on those who hate him. This he does by trading for and brutally taking valuable metals and gemstones from the indigenous peoples of the lands he visits. A lengthy segue from *The Journey* into *When You Thought of Me* builds up to the point where Heathcliff is sitting on his own in fine clothes and revewing his journey but all the while thinking of Cathy back at home with Edgar. By the end of the song, he justifies his appalling actions by saying it was all for her and that he is coming back to her.

Drum-led from the start with tinkling synthesiser motifs, *When You Thought of Me* has an upbeat rhythm that drives relentlessly onwards. There are some complex musical intervals, which Cliff carries off perfectly supported by the female backing vocalists. This is replicated almost faithfully in the stage version, although Cliff imbues the song with more emotion whilst he is performing.

Track Specification
Composed by John Farrar and Tim Rice

1. Songs from Heathcliff

Musicians	
Sean Callery	orchestrator, synclavier, keyboards
Liz Constantino	backing vocals
Linda Dalziel	backing vocals
John Farrar	guitar, synclavier
Gary Grant	trumpet
Jerry Hey	horn arranger, trumpet
Dan Higgins	saxophone
John 'Juke' Logan	harmonica
Kristina Nichols	backing vocals
Bill Reichenbach	trombone
Cliff Richard	vocals
Bob Sabellico	drum programming
Michael Thompson	guitar

Recording Details	
Producer	John Farrar
Engineered by	Chris Fogel, Eric Rudd and Joe Schiff (Moonee Ponds Studio), Darren Goodwin and Guy Massey (Abbey Road Studios) and James Collins and Caroline Daniel (CTS Studios)
Recording location	Moonee Ponds Studio, Los Angeles, Abbey Road Studios, St. John's Wood, London and CTS Studios, Wembley, London
Mixed by	Chris Fogel
Mixed at	Moonee Ponds Studio, Los Angeles
Recording date	February-April 1994 and May-August 1995

2. Heathcliff Live

Musicians	
Sean Callery	orchestrator, orchestra
David Combes	backing vocals
John Clark	guitar
Elements:	
Geoff David	backing vocals
Chris Holland	backing vocals
Sonia Jones	backing vocals
Niki Kitt	backing vocals
Suzanne Parry	backing vocals
Keith Hayman	keyboards
Peter May	drums, percussion
Bob Noble	keyboards
Alan Park	keyboards
John Perry	backing vocals
Cliff Richard	vocals
Steve Stroud	bass
Kevin Townend	orchestration
Unknown	orchestra
Mick Wilson	backing vocals

Recording Details	
Producer	John Farrar
Engineered by	Keith Bessey, John Pearson and Tom Tranter
Recording location	Earl's Court Hall 2, London and/or The Academy, National Indoor Arena, Birmingham, England
Recording date	October 1996

♫ When You Thought of Me (Reprise)

From the album **Heathcliff Live**

In the ***Heathcliff*** stage show, there is a guitar overture performed by Gordon Giltrap accompanying dancers as the second act starts. Heathcliff (Cliff Richard) has been away to make his fortune by whatever violent means in foreign lands and, at the end of the first act had reflected on his journey with ***When You Thought of Me***, justifying his actions as being Cathy's fault because she is marrying Edgar Linton but is still in love with him. To tie the two acts together, the song is reprised from the midpoint as Heathcliff returns to England and seeks out Cathy to attempt to impress her with his new-found wealth and therefore social standing. The performance is unsurprisingly similar to the full-length song that completed the first act, replete with the arrangement and backing vocal accompaniment.

Track Specification

Composed by John Farrar and Tim Rice

Musicians

Sean Callery	orchestrator, orchestra
David Combes	backing vocals
John Clark	guitar
Elements:	
Geoff David	backing vocals
Chris Holland	backing vocals
Sonia Jones	backing vocals
Niki Kitt	backing vocals
Suzanne Parry	backing vocals
Keith Hayman	keyboards
Peter May	drums, percussion
Bob Noble	keyboards
Alan Park	keyboards
John Perry	backing vocals
Cliff Richard	vocals
Steve Stroud	bass
Kevin Townend	orchestration
Unknown	orchestra
Mick Wilson	backing vocals

Recording Details

Producer	John Farrar
Engineered by	Keith Bessey, John Pearson and Tom Tranter
Recording location	Earl's Court Hall 2, London and/or The Academy, National Indoor Arena, Birmingham, England
Recording date	October 1996

♫ When You Walk in the Room

From the album **Wanted**

Written and originally recorded by Jackie de Shannon in 1963, *When You Walk in the Room* is a frustrated love song that talks of the emotions experienced from being near a person who she can't tell how she feels. De Shannon's version was not a hit in the UK, since it was released as the B-side of her *Till You Say You'll Be Mine* single. Once the Searchers had released their arrangement, De Shannon's single was flipped, possibly to capitalize on the UK group's success and the song became a small US hit. The Searchers had already had a major hit with *Needles and Pins*, another De Shannon composition, and their follow-up with *When You Walk in the Room* reached number five in the UK charts and number thirty-five in the US. It hit number thirty-eight in 1978 for Child, while Paul Carrack achieved number forty-eight when he released it as his first single in 1987 and Status Quo reached number thirty-four in November 1995. In 2004, ABBA lead singer Agnetha Fältskog returned to music from self-imposed seclusion in Sweden with her album *My Colouring Book*, which included *When You Walk in the Room* and was subsequently released as the second single from the enterprise, reaching number thirty-four.

Cliff Richard chose the song to close the first album he had recorded since parting company with his long-term record company EMI, ***Wanted***, which featured mainly covers of hugely famous tracks in addition to three original songs. This track has more of a throwback feel to the early eighties but doesn't suffer for that because of the freshness and energy with which it is imbued, particularly from the joy that is apparent in Cliff's voice. The synthesiser performances rattle between the stereo channels, while Cliff's lead is matched by the perfect harmonies of the backing vocals.

Track Specification

Composed by Jackie De Shannon

Musicians

John Brant	additional programming
Anthony Clark	backing vocals
Cliff Richard	vocals, backing vocals
Alan Tarney	arranger, backing vocals, keyboards, programming

Recording Details

Producer	Alan Tarney
Engineered by	John Brant and Gerry Kitchingham
Recording location	Wilmer Studios, London
Recording date	January-April 2001

♫ Where Did the Summer Go?

From the album **Finders Keepers**

Where Did the Summer Go? is one of three tracks that were added to the original soundtrack album of the film ***Finders Keepers***, since the material for the film (written entirely by the Shadows) brought the running time too short (the other two are ***Into Each Life Some Rain Must Fall*** and ***Run to the Door***).

Recorded in just two takes backed with orchestra and backing singers, this final take and edit were used for both the mono and stereo recordings but with different mixes for the requirements of the separate audio channels.
A saccharine and wistful that Cliff sings well, in spite of the over-reliance of the backing vocals provided by the Mike Sammes Singers. *Where Did the Summer Go?* is interesting in that it was at the vanguard of similar material that would be Cliff's choice as he entered the seventies.

Track Specification
Composed by Gary Geld and Peter Udell

Musicians

Bernard Ebbinghouse Orchestra	orchestra
Bernard Ebbinghouse	arranger, conductor
Mike Sammes Singers	backing vocals
Cliff Richard	vocals

Recording Details

Producer	Norrie Paramor
Engineered by	Peter Vincent and Richard Lush
Recording location	Abbey Road Studio 2, St. John's Wood, London
Recording date	20th September 1966

♫ Where Did You Get That Hat?

From the film soundtrack album of **The Young Ones**

Drawing the ***Vaudeville Routine*** section of ***The Young Ones*** almost to a close is this well-known music-hall ditty, featuring Nicky Black (portrayed by Cliff Richard) in a preposterously tall turban-like hat with a long plumed feather stuck vertically in the base. This segues into an energetic dance routine without Cliff, who returns for the reprise of ***What D'You Know, We've Got a Show***.
The entire sequence was recorded in one session along with the segments of *What D'You Know, We've Got a Show*. Several takes were recorded of each of the sections of the *Vaudeville Routine*, with the same takes chosen stereo and mono edits, but with different mixes for the audio channel requirements. The film version of the sequence was recorded later on the year (probably in the same month) but has not been formally released in any other commercial format.

Track Specification
Composed by James Rolmaz

Musicians

Associated British Studio Orchestra	orchestra
Stanley Black	conductor
Mike Sammes Singers	vocals, backing vocals
Cliff Richard	vocals

Recording Details

Producer	Norrie Paramor
Engineered by	Malcolm Addey and Alan Kane
Recording location	Abbey Road Studio 2, St. John's Wood, London
Recording date	9th August 1961

♫ Where Do We Go from Here?

84th UK single

The first of three songs to be written by Chris Eaton and recorded by Cliff Richard as part of the ***Now You See Me... Now You Don't*** album, *Where Do We Go From Here?* was the second single to be released from the project. Backed with ***Discovering***, which was another Eaton song, *Where Do We Go From Here?* was issued as a single on the EMI label (catalogue number EMI 5341) on 10th September 1982. Not as catchy as ***The Only Way Out*** or as instantly memorable as ***Little Town***, it was perhaps unwise to settle on this song as a single, since it was Cliff's worst chart-placing in his career (of those singles that had charted to date) when it stalled at number sixty. The associated promotional video, recorded in London on 8th September 1982, was essentially a film of him and a band in the recording studio. However, there are also backing singers and Craig Pruess on the keyboards, while there is also someone seen at the production mixing desk.
The thumping bass and electric piano introduce this rocking number that breaks into a syncopated rhythm after the first verse and chorus. Cliff supplies his own backing vocals and generally sings in thirds, a device which lifts the energy of the piece further.

Track Specification
Composed by Chris Eaton

Musicians

Mel Collins	saxophone
Mark Griffiths	bass
Graham Jarvis	drums, percussion
Mart Jenner	electric guitar
Craig Pruess	piano, synthesisers, sequencers, electronic percussion
Cliff Richard	vocals, backing vocals
Bill Roberts	electric guitar

Recording Details

Producer	Cliff Richard and Craig Pruess
Engineered by	John Walker and Steve Cook
Recording location	Strawberry Studios South, Surrey
Recording date	4th-15th January 1982

♫ Where Is My Heart?

B-side of **Please Don't Tease**

Although a stereo version of *Where Is My Heart?* was recorded, it has never been released and, to date, only the mono version is available. Chosen as the B-side of the ninth single, ***Please Don't Tease***, it as one of twelve songs played to an invited group of around two hundred members of the fan club to assist in choosing which of them would be released as singles. Less popular than the A-side and a few other tracks, it was then chosen for the B-side of the first single out of the decision-making process. Until the release of the rarity anthology ***The Rock 'n' Roll Years 1958-1963***, *Where Is My Heart?* had only been available on the original pressing of the single.

It was the right decision by those fan club judges because, although *Where Is My Heart?* is not a poor song, there was definitely stronger material created from that session. Telling the story of a heart lost to love, Cliff's echoing voice is backed strongly by Bruce Welch's rhythm guitar and Hank Marvin's lead guitar line, the latter of which is also given a brief airing in the middle eight (essentially the melody from the first couple of lines from the song). A standard rock and roll love ballad, *Where Is My Heart?* doesn't stretch the band and there are far fewer hooks than the songs chosen for the next few A-sides.

Track Specification

Composed by Sid Tepper and Roy C. Bennett

Musicians	
Jet Harris	bass
Hank Marvin	guitar
Tony Meehan	drums, percussion
Cliff Richard	vocals
Bruce Welch	rhythm guitar

Recording Details	
Producer	Norrie Paramor
Engineered by	Malcolm Addey and Norman Smith (mono) and Peter Bown and Alan Kane (stereo)
Recording location	Abbey Road Studio 2, St. John's Wood, London
Recording date	30th March 1960

♬ Where Is That Man?

Unissued track and from the album **About that Man**

In early 1969, Cliff Richard recorded six episodes for the religious broadcasting arm of Tyne Tees Television in a series called *Life with Johnny*, which reset parables into contemporaneous Britain. In the episode called *Johnny Faces Facts*, the playlet ended with a duet between Settlers singer Cindy Kent and Cliff on guitar, on slightly raised dais either side of a plain white cross all picked out in bright spotlight.

On the recording sheets and other notes on the sessions, the song is titled *Where is* the *Man?*, but this is incorrect since it was re-recorded and released on the later album ***About That Man*** (the third and final take was used from that session). In the television episode, the song is sung gently initially by Cindy Kent for the first verse, before Cliff joins her accompanying them on a simple guitar line as the programme fades out to run the credits.

For the album version, Cliff not only accompanies himself on the guitar but on backing vocals too, adding an extra dimension to the song. With much vibrato, the lustrous harmonies created lift the song to something approaching adulatory of the son of God.

Track Specification

Composed by Cliff Richard, David Winter, Cindy Kent, Mike Jones, John Fyffe and Geoffrey Srodzinski

1. Unissued track (Life with Johnny)

Musicians	
Cindy Kent	vocals
Cliff Richard	vocals, guitar

Recording Details	
Producer	Norrie Paramor
Engineered by	Peter Vince
Recording location	Abbey Road Studio 3, St. John's Wood, London
Recording date	8th January 1969

2. About That Man

Musicians	
Cliff Richard	vocals, backing vocals, guitar

Recording Details	
Producer	Norrie Paramor
Engineered by	Richard Lush
Recording location	Abbey Road Studio 2, St. John's Wood, London
Recording date	20th February 1970

♬ Where Is The Man?

Incorrect title from **Life with Johnny**

In the session notes for the recordings made for the Tyne Tees Television series *Life with Johnny*, the song ***Where Is That Man?*** is titled *Where Is* the *Man?*. However, it is clear that it is exactly the same song as *Where Is* That *Man?*, which was re-recorded and formed part of the ***About That Man*** album. See entry for *Where Is That Man?*.

♬ Where Is Your Heart?

From the EP **Look in My Eyes Maria**

With a few artists covering the song, including Percy Faith (reaching number one in the Billboard charts in 1953), Fred Lipsius, Gene Pitney, Beegie Adair and Bobby Creed, *Where Is Your Heart?* was a minor standard in the late fifties and early sixties and is taken from the English version of the song from the 1952 film *Moulin Rouge*. Although it is popularly known as *Where Is Your Heart?*, the film annotates it as *It's April Again* instead. Sometimes also called ***The Song from (the) Moulin Rouge***, it was Mantovani who had the biggest hit with it under that title reaching the top of the UK charts in 1953 (and also charting in the US).

Although it was recorded for the ***Look in My Eyes Maria*** EP, Cliff Richard's version titled *Where Is Your Heart?* was recorded at the start of the session that saw five songs completed; a week before, the version titled *The Song from Moulin Rouge* (according to the session notes and tape box) had been attempted but abandoned after four takes. The same unknown take and edit from the later session was used for the mono and stereo recordings but with different mixes for the separate audio channels. Until 2008, when it was issued on the French *All My Love* CD album and also the celebratory ***...And They Said It Wouldn't Last! (My 50 Years in Music)***, the track was a considerable rarity for almost forty-five years.
Introduced by the Mike Sammes Singers singing the song's title Cliff takes up the lead vocal as he is accompanied by shimmering strings, a tinkling piano and a drum and bass guitar. It is a lovely love song although the backing vocals tend to overwhelm at certain points.

Track Specification
Composed by George Auric and William Engvick

Musicians

Mike Sammes Singers	backing vocals
Norrie Paramor Orchestra	orchestra
Norrie Paramor	arranger, conductor
Cliff Richard	vocals

Recording Details

Producer	Norrie Paramor
Engineered by	Malcolm Addey
Recording location	Abbey Road Studio 2, St. John's Wood, London
Recording date	24th July 1964

♫ Where the Four Winds Blow
From the EP **Why Don't They Understand?**

The final song of three in a session that produced three tracks for three EPs (***Holiday Carnival***, ***Love Songs*** and ***Why Don't They Understand?***), *Where the Four Winds Blow* was completed in two takes with the second take and edit being used for the mono and stereo recordings but with different mixes for the needs of the audio channels. Until the release of the song on ***The EP Collection: Ballads and Love Songs*** in 1989, *Where the Four Winds Blow* was a collector's item, although that album is now itself difficult to get hold of.
Expressed in a minor key, the introduction is performed on a hand-thumped drum and arpeggiated guitar. Although the Shadows are not noted to be involved, the guitar does have the band's familiarity to it. The gentle performance in Cliff's lead vocal line is matched by the backing vocals and it has a cowboy country song feel to the overall presentation.

Track Specification
Composed by Ruth Batchelor and Bob Roberts

Musicians

Mike Sammes Singers	backing vocals
Norrie Paramor Orchestra	orchestra
Norrie Paramor	arranger, conductor
Cliff Richard	vocals
Unknown	guitar
Unknown	drums

Recording Details

Producer	Norrie Paramor
Engineered by	Malcolm Addey and Peter Vince
Recording location	Abbey Road Studio 2, St. John's Wood, London
Recording date	6th December 1962

(Let's Go) Where There Are Horses
B-side of **Somewhere Over the Rainbow/What a Wonderful World**

Cliff Richard's critical star appeared to be on the wane by the end of the nineties with sneering comments and sniggering at leaving him off playlists, not helped by what many considered to be disastrous final number one in ***The Millennium Prayer***, which completely flew in the face of the evidence and logic, and he was also dropped from his long-term record label, EMI. In the new millennium, to counter this, Cliff endeavoured to prove the decision wrong by recording an album that would take him into the top section of the charts. The result was ***Wanted***, which featured well-known songs, as well as a small selection of songs that were original compositions, including two by Alan Tarney, one of which was co-written by famous lyricist Don Black (***This Love You Will Never Forget***). Other songs were recorded but were left off the final track listing, including ***Lay All Your Love on Me*** and *(Let's Go) Where There Are Horses*, both of which appeared as B-side tracks to the first single from the enterprise, ***Somewhere over the Rainbow/What a Wonderful World***. The latter of the two songs was another Tarney and Black composition.
As with the other material from the project, the song is heavily laden with programmed percussion and keyboards but it is the lush instrumentation and the backing vocals that are the high points of the song. It is a shame that the song wasn't given wider distribution because of its inherent whimsical beauty.

Track Specification
Composed by Alan Tarney and Don Black

Musicians

John Brant	additional programming
Anthony Clark	backing vocals
Cliff Richard	vocals, backing vocals
Alan Tarney	arranger, backing vocals, keyboards, programming

Recording Details

Producer	Alan Tarney
Engineered by	John Brant and Gerry Kitchingham
Recording location	Wilmer Studios, London
Recording date	January-April 2001

♫ Where You Are

B-side of **Saviour's Day** *(twelve-inch and CD singles) and from the album* **Songs of Life: Music from Mission '89** *(Various)*

Written and recorded specifically for the charity album *Songs of Life: Music from Mission '89* by Cliff Richard and Dave Cooke, *Where You Are* – sometimes mistyped as *Where Are You?* – was re-recorded a month later. When ***Saviour's Day*** was released, there was still a lot of hype over the Wembley Stadium concerts from 1989 and so the principal B-side track was the ***Oh Boy! Medley*** that opened ***The Event*** and the subsequent album. For the twelve-inch and CD versions of the singles, an additional track was chosen to complete the package and that was the new recording of *Where You Are*. In 1995, it was added as a track to ***The Winner*** compilation album and has appeared on a few others since then, including ***My Songs***.
Littered with synthesisers and electric piano, the melody is simple, while the backing vocals, created from a choir of Cliff's own voice creates beautiful harmonies. There is a gentle saxophone on the track, the player of which is unknown.

Track Specification
Composed by Dave Cooke and Cliff Richard

1. Songs of Life: Music from Mission '89

Musicians	
Dave Cooke	piano
Cliff Richard	vocals

Recording Details	
Producer	Dave Cooke
Engineered by	Wally Duguid and David Hofer
Recording location	J. F. M. Studios, Twickenham, London
Recording date	26th June 1989

2. B-side (Saviour's Day)

Musicians	
Cliff Richard	vocals, backing vocals
Unknown	synthesiser
Unknown	bass
Unknown	drums, percussion
Unknown	saxophone

Recording Details	
Producer	Dave Cooke
Engineered by	Unknown
Recording location	J. F. M. Studios, Twickenham, London
Recording date	September 1989

♫ While Shepherds Watched

From the EP **Carol Singers**

Although the words to *While Shepherds Watched Their Flocks* are sometimes attributed to an Irish hymnist by the name of Nahum Tate, the uncertainty of its pedigree exists, although it appeared in a collection of hymns in 1700 compiled by Tate and Nicholas Brady. The tune most commonly associated with it carol services the world over is the one called *Cranbrook* written in 1805 by Thomas Clark, a cobbler from Canterbury. However, originally, it was more often performed to the tune of *On Ilkla Moor Baht'at*, a version that is gaining popular ground in contemporary services. In addition to choirs and choral societies, the carol has been recorded by Burl Ives, George Guest and Maddy Prior among a few others.
Cliff Richard's version of *While Shepherds Watched Their Flocks*, with its foreshortened title, was arranged by a music teacher acquaintance of Cliff's, Geoffrey Keating, who, with other Christian teachers, formed the Mastersingers and accompanied Cliff *a capella*. Recorded at a dual session on the same day, the final edit was spliced from multiple takes and issued in mono format only on the ***Carol Singers*** EP. The stereo version was released in 1988 on the ***Carols*** LP album.
As with all of the songs recorded for the EP, whether released or not, the *a capella* arrangement and the beauty of the blending voices makes the rendition very special. Cliff, singing the lead melody, performs with love and reverence and with a restraint not heard on other recordings at the time.

Track Specification
Composed by Traditional, arranged by Geoffrey Keating

Musicians	
Mastersingers:	backing vocals
John Horrex	
Geoffrey Keating	
George Pratt	
Michael Warrington	
Cliff Richard	vocals

Recording Details	
Producer	Norrie Paramor
Engineered by	Peter Vince and John Barrett
Recording location	Abbey Road Studio 2, St. John's Wood, London
Recording date	10th September 1967

♫ While She's Young

From the album **Green Light**

As with ***Devil Woman***, which he wrote with the story's provider Christine Holmes, Terry Britten wrote *While She's Young* with Margaret Christie, who again provided the detail of the lyrics. Recorded at one of the main sessions for the ***Green Light*** album sessions in January 1978, it was ostensibly completed in three takes with just a few overdubs added at a session two months later.
The song is reasonably fast-paced ballad that talks of problems in love being surmountable when a girl is young in this highly observational and lyrical song. The guitar solo in the middle eight is typical of the period and the occasional backing vocals of the type that Cliff fans had become familiar with, which included Cliff supplying his own in certain points of the song.

Track Specification
Composed by Terry Britten and Margaret Christie

Musicians	
Brian Bennett	drums, percussion
Terry Britten	guitar
Stuart Calver	backing vocals
Alan Jones	bass
Duncan MacKay	keyboards
Alan Parker	guitar
John Perry	backing vocals
Tim Renwick	guitar
Cliff Richard	vocals
Tony Rivers	backing vocals
Trevor Spencer	drums, percussion
Alan Tarney	backing vocals, guitar, bass, keyboards
Graham Todd	keyboards

Recording Details	
Producer	Bruce Welch
Engineered by	Tony Clark and Haydn Bendall
Recording location	Abbey Road Studio 3, St. John's Wood, London
Recording date	13th January 1978 and 15th March 1978

♬ White Christmas

From the album **Together with Cliff Richard**

White Christmas was a *tour de force* by Irving Berlin and Bing Crosby's famous version of it has become the world's biggest selling single of all time. Originally part of the soundtrack to the 1942 hit film, *Holiday Inn*, the power of the song ensured that a 1954 remake was centred on it and, indeed, took its name. Both films starred Crosby and both won the Academy Award (or Oscar) for the Best Original Song: *White Christmas* for *Holiday Inn* and *Count Your Blessings Instead of Sheep* for the *White Christmas* film. One of the most familiar contemporary Christmas songs, it has been covered by several artists including the Moody Blues, the Calico Consort, Frankie Avalon, the Bachelors and the Beach Boys among others.
The extraordinary affection in which people hold the Crosby version of *White Christmas* makes it almost impossible to do a cover that won't garner unwanted negative criticism or to do it almost verbatim and thereby making it a shadow of the original. Cliff successfully carries off the arrangement, which is performed slowly and with chiming synthesisers. The second repetition of the song title, too, features a full-blown close harmony vocal group led by Cliff and this adds something that was missing from Crosby's version: the blended vocals with the harmonies crying out to be exploited.

Track Specification
Composed by Irving Berlin

Musicians	
Mick Clarke	backing vocals
Dave Cunliffe	violin
Andrew Greasley	violin
Peter Howarth	backing vocals
Mae McKenna	backing vocals
Paul Moessl	keyboards
Sonia Morgan	backing vocals
Mick Mullins	backing vocals
Keith Murrell	backing vocals
Tessa Niles	backing vocals
Cliff Richard	arranger, vocals, backing vocals
Miriam Stockley	backing vocals
Steve Stroud	bass
Anthony Thompson	backing vocals

Recording Details	
Producer	Cliff Richard and Paul Moessl
Engineered by	Gerry Kitchingham, Andrew Greasley and Ben Robbins
Recording location	R. G. Jones Studios, Wimbledon, London
Recording date	24th June 1991 to July 1991

♬ Who Are We to Say?

From the album **32 Minutes and 17 Seconds with Cliff Richard**

One of four songs recorded and of three completed, *Who Are We to Say?* was the last to be recorded in the session that provided an A-side (***I'm Looking out the Window***) and a track for the ***Love Songs*** EP (***Love Letters***). The sixth and final take and edit were used for the mono and stereo recordings issued on the ***32 Minutes and 17 Seconds with Cliff Richard*** album, albeit with differing mixes for the audio channels. The penultimate track on the second side of the album, it also featured on the track listing of the ***Cliff Sings Don't Talk to Him*** EP.
The dramatic string introduction belies the tempo of the performance that follows it. Cliff Richard had proven himself capable of singing songs that had syrupy strings and twinkling percussion and this is no different. There are female backing vocals, provided by the Mike Sammes Singers, which are not mentioned on either session notes or track listings.

Track Specification
Composed by Ira Kosloff and Tom Pray

Musicians	
Mike Sammes Singers	backing vocals
Norrie Paramor Orchestra	orchestra
Norrie Paramor	arranger, conductor
Cliff Richard	vocals

Recording Details	
Producer	Norrie Paramor
Engineered by	Malcolm Addey
Recording location	Abbey Road Studio 2, St. John's Wood, London
Recording date	11th December 1961

♫ Whole Lotta Shakin' Goin' On

Unreleased live track and from the albums **The Rock 'n' Roll Years 1958-1963**, **Cliff**, **From a Distance ***** The Event** *(two versions) and* **World Tour Live**

The first hit for Jerry Lee Lewis, *Whole Lotta Shakin' Goin' On* set him on the stratospheric rise to rock and roll superstardom. Its thrilling, driving melody and the emulation of the naughty boys of the genre appealed to the wakening teenage audience of America, made all the more delicious given his Deep South religious upbringing. In the UK, the song reached number eight in the singles charts but it fared even better back home in the US.

The origins of the song have been long disputed. On the first recording of it in 1954 by James Faye Hall, there was only the one credit on the listing and that was David Williams. It is since revealed that Hall has had his name added along with a Native American by the name of Crow.

Lewis's version of the song was recorded at his second session for Sun Records in Memphis and has since been covered by a veritable star-studded list of entertainers, including Elvis Presley, Bill Haley and his Comets, Rick Nelson, Gerry and the Pacemakers, Wanda Jackson and Chubby Checker to name but a few.

It was on the repertoire for Cliff Richard and the Drifters' short residency at the Clacton-on-Sea Butlin's Holiday Camp in August 1958, since Lewis was a major star in the UK and the US, thereby guaranteeing the popularity of the performance. Stan Edwards recorded one of their performances on a two-track tape machine. Some of these songs were included on the rarities retrospective, ***The Rock 'n' Roll Years 1958-1963***, while others were in too poor a condition to be considered for commercial release: fortunately *Whole Lotta Shakin' Goin' On* was rescued and included on the track listing.

The next version that Cliff and the Drifters recorded was in the so-called 'live' set that was performed over two nights at the Abbey Road Studio complex in front of an audience made up from the invited fans of the band and Cliff. It is altogether far more competent than the earlier version, with Cliff talking in the middle eight, in a similar style to Elvis Presley, where he intersperses his words with mumbled lines from the song before resuming from where they were.

In 1981, Cliff was the subject of a four-part BBC documentary and a number of songs were recorded live at the Hammersmith Odeon and the Manchester Apollo. Of the dozen or so songs, only about half of them have been licensed for release; this version of *Whole Lotta Shakin' Goin' On* is not one of them and, to date, it remains unissued. Eight years later, it also appeared in the opening set at ***The Event***, the thirtieth anniversary celebratory performance at Wembley Stadium, as part of the ***Oh Boy! Medley***, where it was reprised at the end with a slightly different line-up performing the song. Started off with a rocking piano behind the Vernons Girls, followed by the voices of the Dallas Boys and the Kalin Twins, Cliff joins in during the chorus and this is repeated in the reprise at the end of the medley.

A favourite in his shows when performing rock and roll nostalgia, Cliff picked *Whole Lotta Shakin' Goin' On* for inclusion on his 2003 world tour set list, which was filmed for DVD release at the New Zealand show. The accompanying CD album, also titled *World Tour Live*, released in 2004 featured a small subset of the songs filmed and the track listing included this performance. Joined once again on the stage by the dancers, Cliff takes the heavy-guitar-led production at a slightly slower pace than usual but once again, it is an exciting performance.

Track Specification

Composed by Crow, James Hall and David Williams

1. The Rock 'n' Roll Years 1958-1963

Musicians

Cliff Richard	vocals, guitar
Ian Samwell	guitar
Terry Smart	drums, percussion

Recording Details

Producer	Unknown
Engineered by	Stan Edwards
Recording location	Rock 'n' Roll Ballroom, Butlin's Holiday Camp, Clacton-on-Sea, Essex
Recording date	August 1958

2. Cliff

Musicians

Jet Harris	bass
Hank Marvin	guitar
Tony Meehan	drums, percussion
Cliff Richard	vocals
Bruce Welch	rhythm guitar

Recording Details

Producer	Norrie Paramor
Engineered by	Peter Bown and Stuart Eltham
Recording location	Abbey Road Studio 2, St. John's Wood, London
Recording date	10th February 1959

3. Unissued track (BBC Documentary)

Musicians

Stuart Calver	backing vocals
Howie Casey	saxophone, trumpet, trombone
John Clark	guitar
Mark Griffiths	bass
Graham Jarvis	drums, percussion
Martin Jenner	guitar
Alan Park	keyboards
John Perry	backing vocals
Cliff Richard	vocals
Tony Rivers	backing vocals
Graham Todd	keyboards

Recording Details

Producer	Cliff Richard
Engineered by	Unknown
Recording location	Hammersmith Odeon, London
Recording date	1st May 1981

4. *From a Distance *** The Event (first version)***

Musicians		*Recording Details*	
Dallas Boys:		Producer	Cliff Richard
Nicky Clarke	backing vocals	Engineered by	Keith Bessey and Mick McKenna
Leon Fisk	backing vocals	Recording location	Rolling Stones Mobile Studio, Wembley Stadium, Wembley, North-west London
Stan Jones	backing vocals	Recording date	16th-17th June 1989
Joe Smith	backing vocals		
Bob Wragg	backing vocals		
Kalin Twins:			
Harold Kalin	backing vocals		
Herbie Kalin	backing vocals		
Oh Boy! Band	rock 'n' roll band		
Cliff Richard	vocals		
Vernons Girls:			
Lyn Cornell	backing vocals		
Maureen Kennedy	backing vocals		
Frances Lee	backing vocals		
Jean Owen	backing vocals		

5. *From a Distance *** The Event (second version)***

Musicians		*Recording Details*	
Dallas Boys:		Producer	Cliff Richard
Nicky Clarke	backing vocals	Engineered by	Keith Bessey and Mick McKenna
Leon Fisk	backing vocals	Recording location	Rolling Stones Mobile Studio, Wembley Stadium, Wembley, North-west London
Stan Jones	backing vocals	Recording date	16th-17th June 1989
Joe Smith	backing vocals		
Bob Wragg	backing vocals		
Kalin Twins:			
Harold Kalin	backing vocals		
Herbie Kalin	backing vocals		
Oh Boy! Band	rock 'n' roll band		
Cliff Richard	vocals		
Vernons Girls:			
Lyn Cornell	backing vocals		
Maureen Kennedy	backing vocals		
Frances Lee	backing vocals		
Jean Owen	backing vocals		

6. *World Tour Live*

Musicians		*Recording Details*	
Anthony Clark	backing vocals, guitar	Producer	Keith Bessey
John Clark	guitar	Engineered by	Keith Bessey
Dave Cooke	keyboards	Recording location	The Mission Winery, Napier, New Zealand
Mike Haughton	saxophone	Recording date	22nd February 2003
Peter Howarth	backing vocals		
Pete May	drums, percussion		
Mick Mullins	backing vocals		
Keith Murrell	backing vocals		
Alan Park	keyboards		
Cliff Richard	vocals		
Steve Stroud	bass		

♫ Who's Gonna Take You Home?

From the album **The Rock 'n' Roll Years 1958-1963**

According to *The Complete Chronicle* (written by Mike Read, Peter Lewry and Nigel Goodall and published in 1995), an acetate surfaced on the market that had two tracks: *Who's Gonna Take You Home?* and ***Let's Stick Together***. However, the authors also go on to say that the sessions for recording the songs are untraceable since no paper records exist, although it is believed that they were recorded at some point in 1959.

Like *Let's Stick Together*, *Who's Gonna Take You Home?* also struggles with information on its provenance. The lyrics and music appear to be original rather than a cover although records of the composer and the performers (other than Cliff Richard, of course) are also unavailable. To this end, the entry for this song simply catalogues this information as unknown until further research unearths more details. The track and its acetate stablemate was eventually released as one of the tracks on the collation of early rock and roll songs and rarities ***The Rock 'n' Roll Years 1958-1963***, which was released in 1997.

Cliff performs the song in simple style accompanied only by one guitar (which may or may not be himself or it could conceivably be Hank Marvin). *Who's Gonna Take You Home?* also shows Cliff's burgeoning vocal capabilities with arpeggiated runs long chords and occasional falsetto interludes (a device he used to great critical acclaim in the seventies). The song is gentle and quite beautiful and, given that this appears to be a rehearsal run of the song, it would be interesting to hear how it might have possibly been built up into a single or album track.

Track Specification
Composed by Unknown
Musicians

Cliff Richard	vocals
Unknown	guitar

Recording Details

Producer	Unknown
Engineered by	Unknown
Recording location	Unknown
Recording date	1959

♬ Who's in Love?
From the album **Stronger**

The second track on the ***Stronger*** album, *Who's in Love?* was recorded using the same techniques developed during the ***Always Guaranteed*** album with Alan Tarney creating a musical idea, building on it and getting a basic track down in the studio before getting Cliff Richard to overdub his vocals and then tidying it up.
A straightforward piece of synthesiser pop, Cliff sings his vocal line with meaning in this song questioning love and the emotions and feelings that are associated with it. There is a generous echo added to each of the words at the end of the second and fourth lines of the verses. In the choruses, Cliff and Tarney supply the backing vocals but it is kept simple.

Track Specification
Composed by Alan Tarney
Musicians

Cliff Richard	vocals, backing vocals
Alan Tarney	arranger, backing vocals, synthesisers, drum and percussion sequencers

Recording Details

Producer	Alan Tarney
Engineered by	Gerry Kitchingham and Ben Robbins
Recording location	R. G. Jones Studios, Wimbledon, London
Mixed by	John Hudson and Noel Rafferty
Mixing location	Mayfair Studios, London
Recording date	27th February 1989, 9th March 1989, 13th-17th March 1989 and 22nd-23rd March 1989

♬ Why?
From the film soundtrack album of **Take Me High**

For some uncatalogued reason, *Why?* appears out of sequence on the ***Take Me High*** film soundtrack: it should appear after ***The Anti-Brotherhood of Man*** and before ***Life*** but instead is placed as the third song instead of the fifth. In the film, Tim Matthews (played by Cliff) and his banking rival Hugo Flaxman (Anthony Andrews) have been playing off each other in order to win a lucrative account from Sir Harry Cunningham (Hugh Griffith); Cunningham finds Flaxman's suggestion too lacklustre while Tim's suggestion is too inflammatory since it involves working with the unions. Having been chased off by Cunningham firing guns at them and throwing grenades from his seat on the bonnet of the Land Rover, Flaxman and Tim run away and abscond in their car. The song is played out as they drive along country lanes, with each thought sung separately or in unison and this is reflected in the camerawork focusing on the face of the person singing. Anthony Andrews is clearly not a singer, but his portrayal of the vastly egotistical Flaxman is extended to the song and, while Tim is trying to understand why getting the account is so important and what he is doing with his life, Flaxman is thinking about how to capitalize on the failure and not believing in his own inadequacies, and the matching of his almost spoken pompous vocals to Cliff's clarity of the notes actually works exceedingly well.
The song was recorded at a final sessions at the beginning of September 1973, with *Why?* completed first. There is some suggestion in Peter Lewry's and Nigel Goodall's book *The Complete Recording Sessions 1958-1990* that several of the songs had the backing track recorded in May with the vocals overdubbed in September. While *Why?* is annotated as being recorded wholly in September, should further information be revealed, this will be updated in future editions.
With a simple guitar accompaniment, joined by tom-toms then a brilliantly evocative bass line, the song is highly effective in displaying the introspection at this stage of the film's narrative. Cliff provides his own backing vocals in the chorus, while the middle eight features a slide guitar solo before the main melody is picked up by the lead guitar and finishing with a slide guitar chord.

Track Specification
Composed by Tony Cole
Musicians

Anthony Andrews	vocals
David MacKay Orchestra	orchestra
David MacKay	arranger, conductor
Cliff Richard	vocals, backing vocals

Recording Details

Producer	David MacKay
Engineered by	Tony Clark and Mike Jarrett
Recording location	Abbey Road Studio 3, St. John's Wood, London
Recording date	3rd September 1973

♬ Why Don't They Understand?
From the EP **Why Don't They Understand?**

Also recorded by Dave Berry, Petula Clarke, Lem Winchester and Patty Duke, it was George Hamilton IV who had the most successful hit with it, taking it into the UK singles charts in early 1958 when it reached number twenty-two as his first single (of two) before taking up acting as his dominant career.

Cliff Richard's version, destined for the EP of the same name, was recorded at the final session before he travelled to Nashville and New York in the summer of 1964 for a series of recording sessions planned there. One of five tracks to be completed at the session, the final (unknown) take and edit were used for the mono and stereo recordings but with different mixes for the separate audio channels. The parent EP was only released in mono but was not a commercial success in EP chart terms and the title track was a collector's item until a stereo version of the song was included almost forty-five years later on the celebratory compilation ***...And They Said It Wouldn't Last! (My 50 Years in Music)*** in 2008.
With a guitar and bass combination from the Norrie Paramor orchestra rather than the Shadows, there is a harmonica that makes the occasional appearance throughout. The simple melody, harmonies and foot-tapping beat makes it unclear why the track was never given broader release. Cliff falls into a natural groove with his vocal performance on this track.

Track Specification
Composed by Joe Henderson and Jack Fishman

Musicians		*Recording Details*	
Mike Sammes Singers	backing vocals	Producer	Norrie Paramor
Norrie Paramor Orchestra	orchestra	Engineered by	Malcolm Addey
Norrie Paramor	arranger, conductor	Recording location	Abbey Road Studio 2, St. John's Wood, London
Cliff Richard	vocals	Recording date	24th July 1964

♬ Why Me?
Unissued track and from the album **Small Corners**

With the most familiar versions being recorded by actor and singer Kris Kristofferson and Elvis Presley, *Why Me?* has also been covered by Johnny Cash, Kelly Hogan, the Gaither Vocal Band, Loretta Lynn, Shawn Camp, the Oak Ridge Boys, Roy Clark, Jack Greene, Shirley Caesar, the Emeralds, Daniel O'Donnell, Hank Snow, Carroll Baker, Presley's backing group the Jordanaires, Conway Twitty and Steve Warner among several others. The song is often entitled *Why Me Lord?* but both of Cliff Richard's recorded versions drop the last word (although it is given the full title in Peter Lewry's and Nigel Goodall's book *The Complete Recording Sessions 1958-1990*).
As a committed Christian, Cliff regularly performed at close-knit gospel sessions or fronted large rallies such as the Way of Life, which took place at the Empire Pool (now the Arena) at Wembley. In April, 1975, he performed three songs: ***Love Never Gives Up***, *Why Me?* and ***Didn't He?*** In addition, he spoke of his conversion to Christianity and what his faith meant to him. All three songs were recorded but only the first was issued when it appeared on the album *10th Way of Life Rally* later in 1975 to raise funds for charity. The album is a major rarity and many of the details regarding the recording are unknown or unavailable.
Almost two years after the Way of Life rally, Cliff recorded *Why Me?* again at the second session for the ***Small Corners*** album, and was the first song completed as the first song in three takes. Further overdubs were added nine days later.
The gentleness of the song belies an undercurrent of passion and joy that comes out of the lyrics, and, as the song is built up into the chorus that features Cliff's vibrato matched with the close harmony of the backing vocals, the posture becomes evangelical while still being suitably reverential.

Track Specification
Composed by Kris Kristofferson

1. Unissued track (Way of Life Rally)

Musicians		*Recording Details*	
Cliff Richard	vocals	Producer	Unknown
Unknown	other instrumentation	Engineered by	Unknown
		Recording location	Empire Pool, Wembley, Middlesex
		Recording date	19th April 1975

2. Small Corners

Musicians		*Recording Details*	
Brian Bennett	drums, percussion	Producer	Cliff Richard
Terry Britten	guitar	Engineered by	Tony Clark, Haydn Bendall and Alan Rouse
Stuart Calver	backing vocals	Recording location	Abbey Road Studio 3, St. John's Wood, London
Bryn Haworth	guitar	Recording date	18th and 27th January 1977
John Perry	backing vocals		
Cliff Richard	vocals, backing vocals		
Tony Rivers	backing vocals		
Alan Tarney	bass		
Graham Todd	piano		

♬ Why Should the Devil Have All the Good Music?
From the albums **Small Corners** *and* **Thank You Very Much**

Written and recorded by Larry Norman in 1977, *Why Should the Devil Have All the Good Music?* was also covered by Geoff Moore and the Distance. It was then picked up and arranged by Cliff Richard for his next spiritual and religious album ***Small Corners*** later that year.

Recorded as the last song in the first very long session for the album, it was completed in three takes with additional overdubs recorded later in the month. In addition to its inclusion on the track listing of the album, *Why Should the Devil Have All the Good Music?* was also released as a single, but in France only. Backed with **Hey Whatcha' Say**, also taken rom the *Small Corners* album, the song was issued on the EMI Pathé Marconi label (catalogue number 2C008-06623) in early 1978 but didn't register in the French charts. Because of the message in the song, the non-rhetorical question in the title and the power behind the track, Cliff regularly performed the song during his later concerts and it remains one of his favourites from the album.

The track begins with a small group of children struggling, as they do so sweetly, with the first verse of *Jesus Bids Us Shine*, before the rock beat of a drum, guitar and bass are faded up initiating the perfect antidote to all those people who think religious songs should all be of a particular genre. The children are uncredited and there is no information available as to where they were recorded or the studio personnel involved. *Why Should the Devil Have All the Good Music?* is a foot-tapping rock and roll song featuring Cliff giving a creditable lead vocal performance that is given a bit of reverb. The rocking instrumentation, particularly the Jerry Lee Lewis style of piano and the accompanying guitar solo, brilliantly portray the intent of the song's lyrics, effectively answering the question in one fell swoop, while the close harmony vocals add another dimension to the song.

The penultimate song from the ***Thank You Very Much*** album recorded live at the London Palladium saw the song being slowly built up from the drums with a lengthy introduction, joined by oohing vocals and chugging guitars. Once again, it is the rocking piano that takes the credit for the proof to the song's question.

Track Specification
Composed by Larry Norman

1. Small Corners

Musicians

Brian Bennett	drums, percussion
Terry Britten	guitar
Stuart Calver	backing vocals
Bryn Haworth	guitar
John Perry	backing vocals
Cliff Richard	vocals
Tony Rivers	backing vocals
Alan Tarney	bass
Graham Todd	piano
Unknown	children's chorus

Recording Details

Producer	Cliff Richard
Engineered by	Tony Clark and Haydn Bendall
Recording location	Abbey Road Studio 3, St. John's Wood, London
Recording date	17th January 1977 (backing track and vocals), 31st January 1977 (overdubs) and Unknown (children's chorus)

2. Thank You Very Much

Musicians

Terry Britten	guitar
Stuart Calver	backing vocals
Clem Cattini	drums, percussion
Dave Christopher	guitar
Mo Foster	bass
Graham Jarvis	drums, percussion
Graham Murray	guitar
John Perry	backing vocals
Cliff Richard	vocals
Tony Rivers	backing vocals
Graham Todd	keyboards

Recording Details

Producer	Bruce Welch
Engineered by	Tony Clark, remixed by Peter Vince
Recording location	London Palladium, London
Remix location	Abbey Road Studios, St. John's Wood, London
Recording date	4th March 1978

♬ Why Wasn't I Born Rich?

Unissued track and from the pantomime cast recording album of **Cinderella**

After the incredible success of Cliff Richard's first foray into pantomime in 1965 with ***Aladdin and His Wonderful Lamp***, accompanied by the Shadows, who were also responsible for the story and the musical compositions, it was no surprise that they would return to the London Palladium the following year with another show: this time with the timeless story of the rags to riches fairytale adventure of ***Cinderella***. Written in its entirety once again by the highly prolific collaboration of all of the Shadows, the first song to feature them was *Why Wasn't I Born Rich?*, thereby setting the scene for the rags part of the story.

Two attempts were made at recording the song: the first was at the mid-October session that resulted in the completion of only one soundtrack song, ***Come Sunday***, while after the sixth take of *Why Wasn't I Born Rich?*, the recording was abandoned; the second attempt saw it completed over a month later, where it was the only song to be finished at that session. The final (unknown) take and edit was used for both the mono and stereo recordings but with different mixes for the split audio channel requirements. After the pantomime season was complete, the song was also chosen as the B-side of the non-show tune ***It's All Over*** but in mono format only.

The second song in the soundtrack but the first to feature Cliff, it tells the story of the poverty he finds himself in the pantomime story. The backing vocals are somewhat subdued, while the rhythm drives the song relentlessly onwards.

Track Specification
Composed by Hank Marvin, Bruce Welch, Brian Bennett and John Rostill

1. Unissued track (Cinderella)

Musicians	
Brian Bennett	drums, percussion
Hank Marvin	backing vocals, guitar
Norrie Paramor Orchestra	orchestra
Norrie Paramor	arranger, conductor
Cliff Richard	vocals
John Rostill	backing vocals, bass
Bruce Welch	backing vocals, rhythm guitar

Recording Details	
Producer	Norrie Paramor
Engineered by	Peter Vince and Richard Lush
Recording location	Abbey Road Studio 2, St. John's Wood, London
Recording date	14th October 1966

2. Cinderella

Musicians	
Brian Bennett	drums, percussion
Hank Marvin	backing vocals, guitar
Norrie Paramor Orchestra	orchestra
Norrie Paramor	arranger, conductor
Cliff Richard	vocals
John Rostill	backing vocals, bass
Bruce Welch	backing vocals, rhythm guitar

Recording Details	
Producer	Norrie Paramor
Engineered by	Peter Vince and Richard Lush
Recording location	Abbey Road Studio 2, St. John's Wood, London
Recording date	19th November 1966

♬ Wide Open Space

B-side of **Just Don't Have the Heart**

Cliff Richard recorded *Wide Open Space* during the ***Stronger*** sessions, although it wasn't included on the album's track listing. However, it was chosen as the B-side for the second single release from the project, ***Just Don't Have the Heart***, and it appeared on all the single's variants of format. A rarity outside of this release, *Wide Open Space* was added as a bonus track on the remaster of *Stronger* in 2004.

As expected from the much of the material recorded at the time, Cliff performs the song against the accompaniment of a synthesiser track. Cliff sings the song with assuredness along with of a choir engendered from his own backing vocals, which, as always with his harmonies, lifts the song in the tuneful chorus. With a contemporary feel, there is a throwback acknowledgment towards his early roots with a healthy guitar solo. While the song is good enough and pleasant to listen to, *Wide Open Space* isn't particularly memorable enough to have increased exposure and, as it didn't make it into anything other than a B-side, this was the right commercial choice for it.

Track Specification
Composed by Judith Walmsley and Martin Abbot

Musicians	
Keith Bessey	drum and percussion programming
Dave Bishop	saxophone
John Clark	guitar
Paul Moessl	arranger
Mick Mullins	backing vocals
Keith Murrell	backing vocals
Cliff Richard	vocals, backing vocals

Recording Details	
Producer	Cliff Richard
Engineered by	Gerry Kitchingham and Ben Robbins
Recording location	R. G. Jones Studios, Wimbledon, London
Recording date	27th February 1989, 9th March 1989, 13th-17th March 1989 and 22nd-23rd March 1989

♬ Wild Geese

B-side of **Two Hearts** *(twelve-inch and CD single only)*

The writing team that had given Cliff Richard a minor hit with ***Ocean Deep*** a few years earlier returned with *Wild Geese*. The song was recorded in the early spring of 1987 and was amalgamated with the ***Always Guaranteed*** album project. When the fourth and final single, ***Two Hearts***, was released, the principal B-side across all formats was ***Yesterday, Today, Forever***, while the twelve-inch and CD single versions added *Wild Geese* as a B-side bonus track. The song was subsequently included on the 1995 compilation album *The Winner* and again as one of the eight bonus tracks on the 2004 remaster of *Always Guaranteed*.

The thudding bass and percussion follow a glissando on the guitar into Cliff's vocal line with a quacking synthesiser to represent the honk of the geese in the song's title. Cliff supplies his own backing vocals that are arranged in close harmony behind the lead vocal.

Track Specification
Composed by Rod Trott and Jon Sweet

Musicians	
John Clark	guitar, bass
Alan Park	keyboards, drum and percussion programming
Cliff Richard	vocals, backing vocals

Recording Details	
Producer	Cliff Richard, Keith Bessey and Alan Park
Engineered by	Keith Bessey
Recording location	C. R. O. Studios, Esher, Surrey
Recording date	April 1987

♫ Willie and the Hand Jive

B-side of **Fall in Love with You** *and from the albums* **Rock on with Cliff Richard**, **40th Anniversary Complete**, **Thank You Very Much**, **The Rock Connection** *and* **Reunited** *and unissued live track*

Using a style of hambone rhythm (so created from a dance that required the dancer to beat out a rhythm by slapping parts of his body), Johnny Otis managed to incorporate the more constrained hand-jive dance (fists bumping on top of one another, fingers touching the elbows and so on in time to the music) into the song that would appear as the B-side of Cliff Richard and the Shadows eighth single. Otis himself had a hit with it in his native America and, while it was immensely popular as an uplifting song that has been covered by George Thorogood and the Destroyers, Eric Clapton, Taj Mahal and Kim Carnes amongst others, it has not been a hit in the singles charts in the UK.

When Cliff Richard's ***Fall in Love with You*** was released as the A-side, the belief among the band and the studio executives was that Ian Samwell's song was the better one and more likely to be a commercial success. However, the fans wanted to hear *Willie and the Hand Jive* almost as much as the A-side; despite this clamour for its recognition, though, the song was never elevated to the status of being a double A-side but is now a regular favourite in the concerts.

A prior attempt to record *Willie and the Hand Jive* had been made on 6th November 1959 but abandoned after twelve takes, before deciding to use the tenth take at the 18th November sessions. In addition, two other studio versions have been released: one the undubbed stereo version (the eighth take), which was the same as the mono but recorded on a different machine and mixed differently for the stereo channel without the overdubbed backing vocals; and a take, possibly from the same session but not confirmed, that appeared on an Australian album called *40th Anniversary Complete*.

The performance of the song has an increasing energy throughout as it tells the tale of the eponymous Willie who starts the hand-jive craze in his home town until his new-born son is witnessed doing it on television. The song gives Cliff and the Shadows an excellent opportunity to show off their close harmony vocals and, in concert, Hank Marvin and Bruce Welch would usually stand either side of Cliff and perform the staccato harmonies into the same microphone. Hank's lead guitar is slightly distorted while Jet Harris's bass line sounds as if is performed either on a double bass or the strings on his guitar are muted. A staple of many concerts, it is always received well by the audience.

The reunion concert in 1978 at the London Palladium showed how special the joint vocals of Bruce, Hank and Cliff are and how perfectly blended they are. The magic of Hank's guitar also comes to the fore in the performance.

A new arrangement was created for Cliff's 1984 album, ***The Rock Connection***, imbuing the result with a contemporary feel while still maintaining a nod towards the song's fifties roots. Indeed, as was the vogue at the time, there is a strong use of the synthesiser as an instrument, although the rhythm guitar is more in evidence than on many tracks. Cliff's lead vocal is far more subdued than is usual and he eschews the natural urge to the call and respond feature of this style of music. Cliff provides his own backing vocals and, overall, it is a gentler trawl through the song.

In spite of the restoration of all other previously unreleased tracks to the 2005 remaster of ***From a Distance ***** The Event***, *Willie and the Hand Jive* was one of six Cliff and the Shadows performances to remain unissued (with no information given as to why the decision was taken).

More successful for release was a new recording of *Willie and the Hand-Jive* by Cliff and the Shadows for their ***Reunited*** album in 2009, which was released to celebrate fifty years in the music business the previous year and was then promoted on tour around the world. A jazz-like introduction leads into the hambone approach to the song, which features the fantastic blend of Cliff's, Bruce's and Hank's vocals.

Track Specification
Composed by Johnny Otis

1. Unissued track

Musicians		*Recording Details*	
Jet Harris	backing vocals, bass	Producer	Norrie Paramor
Hank Marvin	backing vocals, guitar	Engineered by	Malcolm Addey and Alan Kane (mono) and Stuart Eltham and Peter Bown (stereo)
Tony Meehan	drums, percussion		
Cliff Richard	vocals	Recording location	Abbey Road Studio 2, St. John's Wood, London
Bruce Welch	backing vocals, rhythm guitar	Recording date	6th November 1959

2. B-side (Fall in Love with You)

Musicians		*Recording Details*	
Jet Harris	backing vocals, bass	Producer	Norrie Paramor
Hank Marvin	backing vocals, guitar	Engineered by	Malcolm Addey and Alan Kane (mono) and Stuart Eltham and Peter Bown (stereo)
Tony Meehan	drums, percussion		
Cliff Richard	vocals	Recording location	Abbey Road Studio 2, St. John's Wood, London
Bruce Welch	backing vocals, rhythm guitar	Recording date	19th November 1959

3. Rock on with Cliff Richard

Musicians		*Recording Details*	
Jet Harris	bass	Producer	Norrie Paramor
Hank Marvin	guitar	Engineered by	Malcolm Addey and Alan Kane (mono) and Stuart Eltham and Peter Bown (stereo)
Tony Meehan	drums, percussion		
Cliff Richard	vocals	Recording location	Abbey Road Studio 2, St. John's Wood, London
Bruce Welch	rhythm guitar	Recording date	19th November 1959

4. 40th Anniversary Complete (Australia only)

Musicians		*Recording Details*	
Jet Harris	backing vocals, bass	Producer	Norrie Paramor
Hank Marvin	backing vocals, guitar	Engineered by	Malcolm Addey and Alan Kane (mono) and Stuart Eltham and Peter Bown (stereo)
Tony Meehan	drums, percussion	Recording location	Abbey Road Studio 2, St. John's Wood, London
Cliff Richard	vocals	Recording date	Unknown but likely to be November 1959
Bruce Welch	backing vocals, rhythm guitar		

5. Thank You Very Much

Musicians		*Recording Details*	
Brian Bennett	drums, percussion	Producer	Bruce Welch
Alan Jones	bass	Engineered by	Tony Clark, remixed by Peter Vince
Cliff Hall	keyboards	Recording location	London Palladium, London
Hank Marvin	backing vocals, guitar	Remix location	Abbey Road Studios, St. John's Wood, London
Cliff Richard	vocals	Recording date	4th March 1978
Bruce Welch	backing vocals, rhythm guitar		

6. The Rock Connection

Musicians		*Recording Details*	
John Clark	guitar	Producer	Cliff Richard and Keith Bessey
Dave Cooke	keyboards	Engineered by	Keith Bessey
Mark Griffiths	bass	Recording location	Strawberry Studios South, Surrey
Alan Park	keyboards	Recording date	30th July 1984-3rd August 1984
Cliff Richard	vocals, backing vocals		
Stuart Tosh	drums, percussion		

7. Unissued track (From a Distance *** The Event)**

Musicians		*Recording Details*	
Ray Beavis	saxophone	Producer	Cliff Richard
Brian Bennett	drums, percussion	Engineered by	Keith Bessey and Mick McKenna
Mark Griffiths	bass	Recording location	Rolling Stones Mobile Studio, Wembley Stadium, Wembley, North-west London
Cliff Hall	keyboards	Recording date	16th-17th June 1989
Hank Marvin	backing vocals, guitar		
Cliff Richard	vocals		
Bruce Welch	backing vocals, rhythm guitar		

8. Reunited

Musicians		*Recording Details*	
Brian Bennett	drums, percussion	Producer	Warren Bennett (co-ordination)
Warren Bennett	piano	Engineered by	James Collins (Honeyhill Studios), Ethan Carlson (Middle Ear Studios), Les Williams (Nivram Studios) and Keith Bessey (mixing and mastering)
Mark Griffiths	bass	Recording location	Middle Ear Studios, Miami, Florida, USA (Cliff's vocals), Nivram Studios, Perth, Western Australia (Hank's guitars and vocals) and Honeyhill Studios, Hertfordshire, England (all other vocals and instruments)
Hank Marvin	backing vocals, guitar	Recording date	Early 2009
Cliff Richard	vocals, backing vocals		
Bruce Welch	backing vocals, rhythm guitar		

♫ Will You Love Me Tomorrow?

From the album **Sincerely Cliff Richard**

Recorded by Cliff Richard at the first October session in 1968, *Will You Love Me Tomorrow?* was held back for over a year before being included on the track listing of the 1969 album ***Sincerely Cliff Richard***. Originally a hit for the Shirelles, it is notable for being the first single to reach the US number one spot by an all-girl act. In the UK, it reached number four in February 1961, before being covered by Melanie in 1974 (reaching number thirty-seven) and Bryan Ferry who had a number twenty-three hit with it in June 1993. Other artists to have covered it include Cher, Mike Berry, Carole King (on her *Tapestry* album), Linda Ronstadt, the Four Seasons, Roberta Flack, Elton John, Laura Brannigan, Dionne Warwick and Amy Winehouse among several others.

Arranged by Shadows drummer Brian Bennett, *Will You Love Me Tomorrow?* was recorded at a Cliff Richard session that resulted in another album track (***Bang Bang (My Baby Shot Me Down)***) and a B-side (***Leave My Woman Alone***). With a jauntier beat than the original and an accompaniment that evokes a sound of Tijuana brass style trumpets, the song matches the purity of Cliff's vocal line perfectly.

Track Specification

Composed by Carole King and Gerry Goffin

Musicians		*Recording Details*	
Brian Bennett	arranger	Producer	Norrie Paramor
Norrie Paramor Orchestra	orchestra	Engineered by	Peter Vince
Norrie Paramor	conductor	Recording location	Abbey Road Studio 2, St. John's Wood, London
Cliff Richard	vocals	Recording date	10th October 1968

♫ Wind Me Up (Let Me Go)

*32nd **UK single** and unissued live track*

Recorded first by Johnny Tillotson for one of his albums in the sixties, *Wind Me Up (Let Me Go)* became a favourite at his concerts. For this reason, it was on the list of songs for Cliff Richard to record during his August 1964 sojourn at the Nashville and New York Columbia studios. The final (unknown) take and edit were used for the mono and stereo takes but with different mixes for the separate audio channels.

Originally only released in mono, both as a single and on the later ***Wind Me Up*** EP, it was backed with ***In the Night*** from a London session and issued on the Columbia label (catalogue number DB 7745) on 29th October 1965 reaching the number two spot in the UK singles charts, held off the top spot by the Beatles' double A-side of *Day Tripper* and *We Can Work It Out*. The stereo recording of the song was not issued until its inclusion on ***The Best of Cliff*** in 1969.

The arpeggio in the woodwind along with the military snare drum evokes the image of soldiers marching, which matches the image in the lyrics of a spurned soldier transposed into being a toy. The backing vocals are gentle and at one or two points, a very deep voice can be heard, which is quite possibly Scotty Moore of the Jordanaires.

In October 1965, Cliff entered the studio to record a German version of the song (***Nur Bei Dir Bin Ich zu Haus***), with his new vocals overdubbed on the original backing track. It was released in November 1965 and reached number twenty-one in the German chart. The song was included on the 1974 Japanese tour but this was left off the resultant album probably for reasons of space both in the vinyl and CD editions.

Track Specification

Composed by John Talley and Bob Montgomery

1. Single

Musicians

Jordanaires	backing vocals
Cliff Richard	vocals
Unknown	female backing vocals
Unknown	guitar
Unknown	bass
Unknown	orchestra
Unknown	drums, percussion

Recording Details

Producer	Bob Morgan and Billy Sherrill
Engineered by	Mort Thomason
Recording location	Columbia Studios, Nashville
Recording date	24th August 1964

2. Unissued track (Japan Tour '74)

Musicians

Barrie Guard	arranger, conductor
Cliff Hall	piano
Brian Lewis	backing vocals, guitar
Kevin Peak	acoustic guitar
Cliff Richard	vocals
Shambles Symphonet	orchestra
Trevor Spencer	drums, percussion
Alan Tarney	backing vocals, bass
Bruce Welch	backing vocals, rhythm guitar

Recording Details

Producer	Toshiba EMI (no individual detailed)
Engineered by	Toshiba EMI (no individual detailed)
Recording location	Shinjuku Koseinenkin, Tokyo, Japan
Recording date	7th-8th October 1974

♫ Winner, The

B-side of **Silhouettes**

Written by Cliff Richard and Dave Cooke, *The Winner* was recorded late in 1989 and chosen as the principal B-side of the first single to be released from the ***From a Distance ***** The Event*** album, ***Silhouettes***. *The Winner* gave its name to a CD compilation in 1995 and subsequently appeared on the compilation album ***My Songs***, which featured a selection of songs to which Cliff had contributed an element of composition.

Very much of its time with a wall of sophisticated synthesiser performances, *The Winner* is a song that takes a number of listens before its intrinsic beauty becomes apparent. The elements are there: an interesting melody line, the thudding bass line, the strong percussion and the backing vocals created by Cliff himself.

Track Specification

Composed by Cliff Richard and Dave Cooke

Musicians

Cliff Richard	vocals, backing vocals
Unknown	synthesisers
Unknown	bass
Unknown	drums, percussion

Recording Details

Producer	Dave Cooke
Engineered by	Unknown
Recording location	J. F. M. Studios, Twickenham, London
Recording date	December 1989

♫ Winning

From the film soundtrack album of **Take Me High** *and from the album* **Japan Tour '74**

Incongruously and perhaps due to the space considerations on the vinyl album for ***Take Me High***, the songs are presented in a different sequence from that in the film's narrative. One of the most obvious is *Winning*, which is the tenth song placed after ***The Anti-Brotherhood of Man*** and before ***Join the Band*** on the soundtrack, while the film has it as the third

song placed after ***Midnight Blue*** and before *The Anti-Brotherhood of Man*. But none of this detracts from the listening pleasure since, although the songs are all written to support the storyline, they all stand up pretty much on their own and the narrative therefore is inconsequential for the album.
In the film, merchant banker Tim Matthews (played by Cliff Richard) has been thwarted in his expectations of being transferred to America. Instead, he has to move to Birmingham and go up against his rival Hugo Flaxman (Anthony Andrews). He needs to find a place to live and he is seen walking through concrete structures, edifices and tower blocks before despondently giving up, just as he reaches a canal and spies a longboat that is ripe for conversion.
Winning was recorded in just one take at a suite of sessions to finalize the soundtrack recording. There is a suggestion that some (and possibly all) of the songs were basically recorded at the May sessions with vocal overdubs applied during the September sessions. However, this is unlikely for this song and, therefore, the recording details reflect that, although will be updated should further research dictate the necessity.
A guitar-driven song, Cliff enjoys singing a song such as this and it suits his voice well. The message in the song, to keep on trying against adversity, picks up its pace in the joyous chorus before returning to the next verse. The first song in the Japanese tour set list of 1974 also features some feedback from the microphone on top of the fuzzed heavy rocking guitar.

Track Specification
Composed by Tony Cole

1. Take Me High

Musicians		*Recording Details*	
David MacKay Orchestra	orchestra	Producer	David MacKay
David MacKay	arranger, conductor	Engineered by	Tony Clark and Mike Jarrett
Cliff Richard	vocals	Recording location	Abbey Road Studio 3, St. John's Wood, London
Unknown	backing vocals	Recording date	26th May 1973

2. Japan Tour '74

Musicians		*Recording Details*	
Cliff Hall	piano	Producer	Toshiba EMI (no individual detailed)
Brian Lewis	backing vocals, guitar	Engineered by	Toshiba EMI (no individual detailed)
Kevin Peak	acoustic guitar	Recording location	Shinjuku Koseinenkin, Tokyo, Japan
Cliff Richard	vocals	Recording date	7th-8th October 1974
Trevor Spencer	drums, percussion		
Alan Tarney	backing vocals, bass		
Bruce Welch	backing vocals, rhythm guitar		

♫ Winter Wonderland

From the album **Cliff at Christmas**

A Christmas standard, *Winter Wonderland* was written in 1934 and was inspired by lyricist Richard Smith's childhood growing up in Pennsylvania. The first recording was by Richard Himber and His Hotel Carleton Orchestra in the same year as its composition. By far the most familiar reasonably contemporary version is by Johnny Mathis, who reached number seventeen in 1958, while the Cocteau Twins attained a number fifty-eight in 1993. It has been covered by a variety of artists including the Calico Consort, Goldfrapp, Chet Atkins, Dean Martin, Mantovani, Anne Murray, Connie Francis, Engelbert Humperdinck, Perry Como, Dave Brubeck, Frank Sinatra, Elvis Presley, Annie Lennox, Eurhythmics, Andy Williams and the Three Tenors among hundreds of others.
Cliff Richard picked the song for the final new song to be included on the track listing of his new Christmas album, ***Cliff at Christmas***. It was recorded at the same session that produced ***Santa's List*** and ***Come to Us*** for the same album.
The crooner's favourite, the jazzy piano and percussion leads into Cliff's particular arrangement that is familiar while successfully being a contemporary version.

Track Specification
Composed by Richard B. Smith and Felix Bernard

Musicians		*Recording Details*	
Chris Cameron	conductor	Producer	Chris Porter
Peter Gordeno	keyboards	Engineered by	Chris Porter
Rick Mitra	drums, percussion	Recording location	Sony Studios, London (orchestra) and Porterhouse Studios, London (other instruments and vocals)
Phil Palmer	guitar		
Cliff Richard	vocals		
Unknown	orchestra	Recording date	2003
Gavin Wright	violin, leader		

♫ Wired for Sound

81st UK single *and from the album* **From a Distance ***** The Event** *and unissued live track*

Alan Tarney, once again in the driving seat for producing Cliff Richard's next album, ***Wired for Sound*** in 1981, wrote around half of the songs that can be found on the album's track listing. The album's eponymous track was the first to be recorded and started life as an instrumental. B. A Robertson, who had had a short-lived solo career at the time and who had worked with Terry Britten to provide the lyrics on several of the ***Rock 'n' Roll Juvenile*** album's tracks, was contacted by Tarney with a suggestion that he might like to write the words to the tune he had already composed. Robertson tells the story that he was scheduled to be at a meal with Mickey Dolenz, and left after the starters to drive to the studio where Tarney was working pick up the cassette and return home for dessert. The next day, listening to the song, Robertson immediately came up with the title (and thence giving the album its title in the process) and the rest of the lyrics flowed easily after that. Although there was much criticism from some quarters about the love for tall speakers and small speakers, it is nevertheless a considerably contemporary song that continued Cliff's rehabilitation in the charts started by Bruce Welch in the mid-seventies.

Backed with a non-album track, ***Hold On***, which had been recorded during the ***I'm No Hero*** sessions, *Wired for Sound* was released as a single on the EMI label (catalogue number EMI 5221) on 17th August 1981 and reached number four in the charts, continuing his regular top ten entries of recent times. With a resurgence of success in the US, the single was also released there but only reached number seventy-seven in the Billboard charts. As was more common in the late seventies and onwards, the single was also incorporated on the album rather than being separate. The associated promotional video was filmed in Milton Keynes on 23rd July 1981 and it features everything that was quintessentially eighties fashion: the bomber jacket, the large teardrop glasses, roller disco and, of course, the now omnipresent personal stereo devices (or Sony Walkman as was the most popular brand at the time). Cliff is clearly a talented roller-skater and, although the video looks quite dated today, it was considered very fresh and innovative at the time.

The shuffling syncopation of the drum introduction and the synthesiser line firmly indicated to listeners that Cliff had changed his musical outlook to match the time. As with *I'm No Hero*, Alan Tarney and Cliff sang all the backing vocals, but it is Cliff's voice that can be heard principally on the accompaniment.

Although it was performed and recorded at the *Live & Guaranteed 1988!* concert in Denmark, the track wasn't issued on the eventual CD. In addition, the following year, starting off *Cliff's Set* during his two-day Wembley Stadium concerts in June 1989, *Wired for Sound* was originally not released on the ***From a Distance ***** The Event*** track listing. Instead, it was included on the twelve-inch and CD single release of ***From a Distance***, before being restored to its rightful place in the two-CD remaster of the live album in 2005. This version has a slow introduction based around guitars rather than synthesisers but then the keyboards take over for the chorus. The performance is a little subdued but is still a great opener to the second event of the day.

Track Specification
Composed by B. A. Robertson and Alan Tarney

1. Single

Musicians		*Recording Details*	
Graham Jarvis	drums, percussion	Producer	Alan Tarney
Cliff Richard	vocals, backing vocals	Engineered by	Michael Boddicker and Ian Little
Alan Tarney	arranger, backing vocals, guitar, bass, keyboards	Recording location	Gallery Studios, Chertsey, Surrey
		Recording date	27th May-9th July 1981

2. Unissued track (Live & Guaranteed 1988!)

Musicians		*Recording Details*	
John Clark	guitar	Producer	Unknown
Rosemarie Ford	backing vocals	Engineered by	Unknown
Mark Griffiths	bass	Recording location	Fyens Forum, Odense, Denmark
Peter Howarth	backing vocals	Recording date	22nd May 1988
Steve Lauri	guitar		
Paul Moessl	keyboards		
Mick Mullins	backing vocals		
Alan Park	keyboards		
Cliff Richard	vocals		
Henry Spinetti	drums, percussion		

3. From a Distance ** The Event***

Musicians		*Recording Details*	
John Clark	guitar	Producer	Cliff Richard
Sonia Jones-Morgan	backing vocals	Engineered by	Keith Bessey and Mick McKenna
Steve Lauri	guitar	Recording location	Rolling Stones Mobile Studio, Wembley Stadium, Wembley, North-west London
Peter May	drums, percussion		
Paul Moessl	keyboards	Recording date	16th-17th June 1989
Tessa Niles	backing vocals		
Alan Park	keyboards		
Provox:			
Peter Howarth	backing vocals		
Mick Mullins	backing vocals		
Keith Murrell	backing vocals		
Cliff Richard	vocals		
Steve Stroud	bass		

♫ With a Hmm-Hmm on My Knee

From the Shadows' album **Jigsaw** *(The Shadows)*

One of the last albums to be recorded before the Shadows disbanded the first time was 1967's *Jigsaw*, which featured the track *With a Hmm-Hmm on My Knee*. This was written by Cliff Richard for the Shadows and, with the plucked banjo, it is reminiscent of the red-necked bluegrass sound from mid-America and the title is a tongue-in-cheek play on the cowboy song *With a Banjo on My Knee* but with a nod towards the *Carry On* style of double entendre with audiences left to guess what the 'hmm-hmm' refers to. It fits with the Shadows' sense of humour very well with the variety of amusing titles that they provided to their own compositions. Cliff doesn't appear on the recording but, on the sleeve of the album, above the composition credits against the song, are written the words 'also a singer!'

Track Specification
Composed by Cliff Richard

Musicians		*Recording Details*	
Brian Bennett	drums, percussion	Producer	Norrie Paramor
Hank Marvin	guitar, banjo	Engineered by	Peter Vince
John Rostill	bass	Recording location	Abbey Road Studio 2, St. John's Wood, London
Bruce Welch	rhythm guitar	Recording date	March 1967

♫ Without You

From the album **21 Today**

The second of three home-grown songs on the ***21 Today*** album featured co-composition credits for Cliff Richard alongside Hank Marvin and Bruce Welch (the third chronological song that featured Cliff on the copyright). *Without You* was the first of three songs to be recorded in the session, with four takes attempted. The final take was used for the mono and stereo edits but with different mixes for the respective audio channels.

With a rhythm reminiscent of a steam train on a railroad track, this steady piece of rock and roll keeps the pace up with another exemplary set of vocal harmonies between the Shadows and Cliff. The inevitable guitar solo in the middle eight bridge is mixed quite low down and is difficult to hear with everything else that is going on (although that might be the effect of the mixes for the audio channels).

Track Specification
Composed by Cliff Richard, Hank Marvin and Bruce Welch

Musicians		*Recording Details*	
Jet Harris	backing vocals, bass	Producer	Norrie Paramor
Hank Marvin	backing vocals, guitar	Engineered by	Malcolm Addey
Tony Meehan	drums, percussion	Recording location	Abbey Road Studio 2, St. John's Wood, London
Cliff Richard	vocals	Recording date	11th July 1961
Bruce Welch	backing vocals, rhythm guitar		

♫ With the Eyes of a Child

48th UK single

Recorded at the same session as the B-side of ***Throw Down a Line***, ***Reflections***, the song *With the Eyes of a Child* is a tender ballad that saw Cliff Richard performing darker material that included what can be construed as either religious or protest songs. Written by Guy Fletcher and Doug Flett, who had given a number of tracks to Cliff to record, *With the Eyes of a Child* sees the world through a child's eyes and makes a commentary of it. Backed with ***So Long***, which was recorded three months before, *With the Eyes of a Child* was issued as a single on the Columbia label (catalogue number DB 8641) on 16th November 1969 but only reached number twenty in the UK singles charts, allowing his critics to suggest that the previous two top ten singles were just a blip on the inevitable downward trend. This is unfair because the music world was changing rapidly and the messages in the songs of this period are heartfelt and the performance and beauty under-rated. Originally released in mono format only, the stereo version was eventually added to the second hit compilation album ***The Best of Cliff Vol. 2***. Strangely, for such a strong song, it rarely appears on other compilations.

Strummed guitars and an organ backing suggest something a little more spiritual than the standard pop song. The song slowly builds up by adding further instruments, with the same sort of rhythm as the opening bars. Cliff sings the lyrics with meaning and emotion, as he refers to how a child sees the world and how adults turn the world into a bad place, and employs a beautiful vibrato that add to the expression he is invoking. The final verse and chorus is a full-blown orchestral and vocal piece, which then slows down and ends quietly with Cliff hitting a high note in his vocal range. Critics might have hated the song but this is one of the best singles that Cliff released during what was his musically fallow period.

Track Specification
Composed by Guy Fletcher and Doug Flett

Musicians		*Recording Details*	
Mike Vickers Orchestra	orchestra	Producer	Norrie Paramor
Cliff Richard	vocals	Engineered by	Peter Vince
Unknown	backing vocals	Recording location	Abbey Road Studio 2, St. John's Wood, London
Mike Vickers	arranger, conductor	Recording date	29th May 1969

♫ Woman and a Man

From the album **Real as I Wanna Be**

The track listing to Cliff Richard's ***Real as I Wanna Be*** album suggests that Green is credited as a co-writer of *Woman and a Man*, while the lyric entry gives it solely to the three mentioned here in the track specification; no other reputable sources can confirm if this a typographical or not. As such, the credits are given to the three stated people.

Using a variety of percussive instruments and the insistent bass, *Woman and a Man* is probably the most curious of the tracks on the album, since it is unlike anything else Cliff has performed. Reliant on the staccato rhythm section, the track is driven insistently. In spite of its construction, the song is memorable and worth more than one listen for its nuances.

Track Specification

Composed by Noel McCoy, Shelly Peiken and Michelle Wolf

Musicians

Vinnie Colaiuta	drums, percussion
Cliff Richard	vocals, backing vocals
Jeff Richman	guitar
Michelle Wolf	backing vocals
Peter Wolf	arranger, bass, keyboards, synclavier, drums, percussion

Recording Details

Producer	Peter Wolf
Engineered by	Christian Leitgeb, Chris Heil, Paul Erickson and/or Keith Bessey
Recording location	Little America Recording Studios, Weiler, Austria, Ocean Recording Studios, Burbank, California, USA, Arco Recording Studios, Munich, Germany, R. G. Jones Recording Studios, Wimbledon, London, England and/or The Pierce Room, London, England
Recording date	March-April 1996 and November 1997

♫ Wonderful Life

From the film soundtrack album of **Wonderful Life** *and from the album* **Cliff Richard at the Movies 1959-1974**

The film ***Wonderful Life*** was the first outing in celluloid for new Shadows bassist John Rostill but the title track featured his predecessor, Brian Locking. The song is performed only the once in the film and that over the opening titles, after the introductory premise of the film's plot is initiated. Johnny Craig (played by Cliff Richard), Jerry (Cliff film stalwart Melvyn Hayes) and Edward (Richard O'Sullivan) are stewards on a cruise liner, with their friends the Shadows (Hank Marvin, Bruce Welch, Brian Bennett and John Rostill) playing onboard musicians (including miming the cello, violin, harp and flute). Desperate to get the tedious problem of their job out of the way, they try tricks to persuade the last diner to go to his berth by swaying gently in front of him. Then the group of seven friends get back to their shared accommodation to play music, with Edward blowing the ships fuses as he plugs the amplifiers in, causing everything to short out, resulting in the ship running aground. The angry captain turfs them off the ship in a dinghy. As they row across a placid sea towards a distant shore, the *Wonderful Life* theme tune is performed with the running title captions.

One of two tracks recorded in the session (the other being the only single from the project, ***On the Beach***), the final (unknown) take and edit was used for the mono and stereo recordings but with different mixes for the requirements of the audio channels. The song also appeared on the first EP to be released from the film, ***Wonderful Life No. 1***. The film version is similar to the soundtrack version, although the orchestral accompaniment is different, and was probably recorded some time in the first three months of 1964. To date, the film version of the song has not been released in any aural format.

On the album ***Cliff Richard at the Movies 1959-1974***, a different take was issued. The difference is in the guitar work and, unlike the prior version, had no backing vocals. The version is described as take number eighteen, which, according to *The Complete Recording Sessions 1958-1990*, this was the final take, although it was the last take that was actually released, giving rise to some inaccuracy of information availability.

The orchestral introduction cleverly evokes life on the high seas and the exuberance of the song matches the title. There are uncredited backing vocals, likely to be the Mike Sammes Singers, who were on other soundtrack songs. Sources suggest that the Shadows appeared but this is unlikely, since the approach to recording the song is entirely orchestral.

Track Specification

Composed by Bruce Welch and Brian Bennett

1. Wonderful Life

Musicians

Associated British Studio Orchestra	orchestra
Stanley Back	arranger, conductor
Cliff Richard	vocals
Unknown	backing vocals

Recording Details

Producer	Norrie Paramor
Engineered by	Malcolm Addey
Recording location	Abbey Road Studio 3, St. John's Wood, London
Recording date	5th November 1963

2. Cliff Richard at the Movies 1959-1974

Musicians

Associated British Studio Orchestra	orchestra
Stanley Back	arranger, conductor
Cliff Richard	vocals
Unknown	backing vocals

Recording Details

Producer	Norrie Paramor
Engineered by	Malcolm Addey
Recording location	Abbey Road Studio 3, St. John's Wood, London
Recording date	5th November 1963

♫ Wonderful Summer

Single by **Richard Loring**

Little-known in the UK, Richard Loring was born in the British Channel Islands and, after working as an executive for the Ford Motor Company, he decided to change his career to be a singer and actor. To assist with the direction he wanted to take, he also moved to South Africa and, in 1966, his first single was released on the EMI international label. Most popular in South Africa with a huge number one, his career with EMI lasted for fifteen years. In 1977, Cliff Richard became involved in producing a number of tracks, including a single that was only released in Loring's adoptive South Africa, *Wonderful Summer*, which had also been recorded by Robin Ward in 1963. Backed with ***Are You Sincere?***, the single was released on the EMI label (catalogue number EMIJ 11129) in 1978.

Track Specification

Composed by Garfield and P. L. Botkin, Jr.

Musicians

Richard Loring	vocals
Unknown	other instrumentation

Recording Details

Producer	Cliff Richard
Engineered by	Unknown
Recording location	Abbey Road Studios, St. John's Wood, London
Recording date	August 1977

♫ Wonderful to Be Young

Unissued track and American single and from the **A Forever Kind of Love** *EP and from the albums* **Cliff Richard at the Movies 1959-1974** *and* **The Young Ones – The Remaster**

When Cliff Richard's film ***The Young Ones***, featuring him in his first headlining role, was released in the US, the distributors (Paramount Pictures) requested a title change to *Wonderful to Be Young*, although the purpose behind the request is largely lost to history. Since there was therefore no title song, Burt Bacharach was commissioned to write one with long-term compositional partner Hal David. It should be noted that *Wonderful to Be Young* was recorded after the release of the film and, for this reason, may be instructive as to why it didn't chart in the US. The first attempt at recording the song was made on 20th July (along with another unissued track ***Sweet Dreams***), where fourteen takes were recorded. Three weeks later with an overnight session running until quarter to five in the morning, a further twenty-eight takes were recorded with the same final take used for mono and stereo but with a different edit and mix for the audio channel: the stereo version has a slightly longer fade-out. For the ***A Forever Kind of Love*** EP, the previous version was remixed with louder orchestral string parts (possibly new overdubs) and the fade out starts much later. A further version was released on the anthology ***Cliff Richard at the Movies 1959-1974***, which is the original undubbed version without the orchestra. Finally, on the reissued album ***The Young Ones – The Remaster***, a different take (the fourteenth) was included on the track listing; this one has no backing vocals.

Often retitled incorrectly to *(It's) Wonderful to Be Young* on some track listings, the song was issued as a single in the US, backed with ***Got a Funny Feeling***, on the Dot label (catalogue number Dot 16399) in September 1962. Each version includes a female backing group, which is uncredited but could possibly be representation from the Mike Sammes Singers who had been involved in the original film soundtrack.

With a vibe similar to the beginning of ***Spanish Harlem***, the song doesn't quite have the same impact as Tepper and Bennett's original film title track. The principal instrumentation is focused on Bruce Welch's rhythm guitar with an occasion interpolation from Hank Marvin's lead. Cliff's vocals are as strong as ever, although, more than many other tracks, he tends to over-emphasize the American burrs in his accent.

Track Specification

Composed by Burt Bacharach and Hal David

1. Unissued track

Musicians

Brian Bennett	drums, percussion
Max Harris	piano
Brian 'Licorice' Locking	bass
Hank Marvin	guitar
Cliff Richard	vocals
Unknown	female backing vocals
Bruce Welch	rhythm guitar

Recording Details

Producer	Norrie Paramor
Engineered by	Malcolm Addey and Peter Vince
Recording location	Abbey Road Studio 2, St. John's Wood, London
Recording date	20th July 1962

2. American single

Musicians

Brian Bennett	drums, percussion
Max Harris	piano
Brian 'Licorice' Locking	bass
Hank Marvin	guitar
Cliff Richard	vocals
Unknown	female backing vocals
Bruce Welch	rhythm guitar

Recording Details

Producer	Norrie Paramor
Engineered by	Malcolm Addey
Recording location	Abbey Road Studio 1, St. John's Wood, London
Recording date	11th August 1962

3. *A Forever Kind of Love* EP

Musicians

Brian Bennett	drums, percussion
Max Harris	piano
Brian 'Licorice' Locking	bass
Hank Marvin	guitar
Cliff Richard	vocals
Unknown	female backing vocals
Bruce Welch	rhythm guitar

Recording Details

Producer	Norrie Paramor
Engineered by	Malcolm Addey
Recording location	Abbey Road Studio 1, St. John's Wood, London
Recording date	11th August 1962

4. *Cliff Richard at the Movies 1959-1974*

Musicians

Brian Bennett	drums, percussion
Max Harris	piano
Brian 'Licorice' Locking	bass
Hank Marvin	guitar
Cliff Richard	vocals
Unknown	female backing vocals
Bruce Welch	rhythm guitar

Recording Details

Producer	Norrie Paramor
Engineered by	Malcolm Addey
Recording location	Abbey Road Studio 1, St. John's Wood, London
Recording date	11th August 1962

5. *The Young Ones – The Remaster*

Musicians

Brian Bennett	drums, percussion
Max Harris	piano
Brian 'Licorice' Locking	bass
Hank Marvin	guitar
Cliff Richard	vocals
Bruce Welch	rhythm guitar

Recording Details

Producer	Norrie Paramor
Engineered by	Malcolm Addey
Recording location	Abbey Road Studio 1, St. John's Wood, London
Recording date	11th August 1962

♫ Wonderful World

From the EP **Congratulations** *and B-side of* **Zärtliche Sekunden**

Coming third in a national mail poll from the candidates that Cliff Richard sang each week on *The Cilla Black Show* for the UK's entry into 1968's Eurovision Song Contest, *Wonderful World* was written by the partnership of Guy Fletcher and Doug Flett, who would go on to write some of Cliff's later hits including the winner of the candidacy for the 1973 Contest. In a challenge against ***Congratulations***, which polled 69% of the vote, it is hardly surprising that the other five songs would receive such a relatively small portion; *Wonderful World* polled 8% coming behind ***High 'n' Dry*** which received just 12.4%. *Wonderful World* has only been released in mono format (primarily the ***Congratulations*** EP) with the exception of its inclusion on the 1968 German compilation *Congratulations und 13 Weitere Hits*. The mono version was made more widely available with its inclusion as a bonus track on the 2007 remaster of ***Live at the Talk of the Town***.

A more traditional arrangement than the other candidate songs with sweeping strings, a plodding bass and a tinkling glockenspiel, *Wonderful World* is an upbeat love song that tells of the happiness and joy he feels by falling in love with a girl. Cliff sings it with a spirited enthusiasm but it really was not the best song of the bunch.

Maintaining its English title for the German language album *Hier Ist Cliff* sessions, *Wonderful World* was the first track to be recorded in a set of four sessions designated for the album. The song was chosen to be the B-side of the only single, ***Zärtliche Sekunden*** (the German version of ***Don't Forget to Catch Me***), and was originally only released in mono but, having been a major rarity for almost thirty years, it was added to the track listing of ***On the Continent*** appearing there in stereo for the first time. The arrangement is in the same style as the Eurovision original and sounds very similar as a result. The backing vocals are uncredited but are likely to be the Breakaways with whom Cliff regularly worked at the time; certainly, their sound is purer than the shrill vocals created in the original by the Mike Sammes Singers.

Track Specification

1. *Congratulations EP*

Composed by Guy Fletcher and Doug Flett

Musicians

Bernard Ebbinghouse Orchestra	orchestra
Bernard Ebbinghouse	conductor
John Paul Jones	bass
Mike Sammes Singers	backing vocals
Norrie Paramor	arranger
Cliff Richard	vocals

Recording Details

Producer	Norrie Paramor
Engineered by	Peter Vince
Recording location	Abbey Road Studio 2, St. John's Wood, London
Recording date	2nd February 1968

2. *B-side (Zärtliche Sekunden)*

Composed by Guy Fletcher and Doug Flett; German lyrics by Loose

Musicians

Norrie Paramor Orchestra	orchestra
Norrie Paramor	arranger, director
Cliff Richard	vocals

Recording Details

Producer	Norrie Paramor
Engineered by	Peter Vince
Recording location	Abbey Road Studio 2, St. John's Wood, London
Recording date	31st October 1968

♫ Word Is Love, The

From the film soundtrack album of **Take Me High**

With the opening night publicity completed for their Brumburger joint, Tim Matthews (Cliff Richard) and Sarah (Debbie Watling) are in the restaurant, she preparing some of the food and he walking through the tables watching her as she works. As he walks, he sings this song that explores his feelings for her, confirming that the word he is looking for is love and he enters the central cooking kiosk and the camera blurs as they bend into each other for a kiss.

Recorded in five takes at one the many sessions in May for the soundtrack, *The Word Is Love*, as suggested in Peter Lewry's and Nigel Goodall's *The Complete Recording Sessions 1958-1990*, is one of the selection of songs that were basically recorded in May and then had vocal overdubs applied in September 1973, although other sources suggest otherwise. Until other information is found, this entry will use the earlier recording without overdubs but this will be updated if appropriate.

A beautiful love song, Cliff sings such ballads well and it requires him to sing notes at the top of his register, which he peforms with an easy confidence.

Track Specification

Composed by Tony Cole

Musicians		*Recording Details*	
David MacKay Orchestra	orchestra	Producer	David MacKay
David MacKay	arranger, conductor	Engineered by	Tony Clark and Mike Jarrett
Cliff Richard	vocals	Recording location	Abbey Road Studio 3, St. John's Wood, London
		Recording date	28th May 1973

♫ Words

From the album **...And They Said It Wouldn't Last! (My 50 Years in Music)**

Recorded at the last of the half-dozen or so sessions for Cliff Richard's religious album ***Good News***, *Words* is not really in keeping with the religious tenor of the other songs. It remained unissued for over forty years, when it was released on the collection ***...And They Said It Wouldn't Last! (My 50 Years in Music)***. The liner notes of the album suggests that there is no information regarding the track or its writer. However, looking back to the session on 25th April 1967, which saw the German language recordings of ***Ein Girl Wie Du*** and ***Bilder von Dir***, it is clear that *Ein Girl Wie Du* (translated as *A Girl Like You* but not to be confused with Cliff's hit of the same name) is the same song as *Words* with German lyrics – the information on the writer and recording details are found on ***On the Continent***. What is not clear is whether the same backing track was used for the German and English versions, although it is likely that both were recorded from scratch.

Given a similar arrangement and treatment to the German equivalent, this lilting ballad is kept moving by the andante bass line and exquisite string accompaniment. Given the strength and quality of the melody, it is extraordinary that EMI decided not to release it until forty years after it was recorded. Simply a list of words that he used to say replaced by sad words since his lover has gone, the song is a perfect love song that would have had considerable appeal were it given broader release (other than Germany) at the time.

Track Specification

Composed by Peter Poll

Musicians		*Recording Details*	
Norrie Paramor Orchestra	orchestra	Producer	Norrie Paramor
Mike Leander	arranger, conductor	Engineered by	Peter Vince and Mike Stone
Cliff Richard	vocals	Recording location	Abbey Road Studio 2, St. John's Wood, London
		Recording date	13th May 1967

♫ Working after School

From the album **Me and My Shadows**

For the final song on the album, two different takes from the same session (the ninth and eleventh) were spliced together to form the completed track. The mono and stereo versions of *Working after School* took this splice and edit and mixed it according to the needs of their aural medium. As the final album track, it was the only song not to be issued on any of the three associated EPs (***Me and My Shadows No. 1***, ***No. 2*** and ***No. 3***, which each had five tracks on their listings).

Staccato guitar chords introduce this upbeat song that is a different view of a love song where the singer depicts the reason for not getting together with his girl after school is that he is working to get money to buy her a ring and their future. It is a straightforward progression through a traditional rock and roll style of song, where Hank Marvin's guitar is prominent in the mix, ending on staccato chords just as it had begun.

Track Specification

Composed by Vic Abrams and P. Medley

Musicians		*Recording Details*	
Jet Harris	bass	Producer	Norrie Paramor and John Schroeder
Hank Marvin	guitar	Engineered by	Malcolm Addey and Norman Smith (mono) and Peter Bown and Alan Kane (stereo)
Tony Meehan	drums, percussion		
Cliff Richard	vocals	Recording location	Abbey Road Studio 2, St. John's Wood, London
Bruce Welch	rhythm guitar	Recording date	1st April 1960

♬ World of Difference

From the album **Did He Jump... Or Was He Pushed?** *(Garth Hewitt)*

World of Difference was one of the ten songs written by the protagonist of ***Did He Jump... Or Was He Pushed?***, Garth Hewitt, and it features the backing vocals and production talents of Cliff Richard. The song was subsequently released on CD for the first time on the Hewitt collection *30 Songs Spanning 30 Years 1973-2003*.

Beginning with backing vocals supported by a guitar and the string synthesiser, the track leads into a quite beautiful song that looks forward to a time when people will realize they should help each other and that they have the power to heal and live in peace. The brilliance of the vocal line stands out above he instrumentation, which consists of the strings and the arpeggiated plucked acoustic guitar, played by Kevin Peek.

Track Specification

Composed by Garth Hewitt

Musicians

Garth Hewitt	vocals
Dave Lawson	string synthesiser
Kevin Peek	acoustic guitar
Cliff Richard	backing vocals

Recording Details

Producer	Cliff Richard
Engineered by	Tony Clark and Haydn Bendall
Recording location	Odyssey Studios, London
Recording date	1979

♬ Wouldn't You Know It (Got Myself a Girl)?

B-side of **(There's a) Honky Tonk Woman**

Written by Alan Tarney and Trevor Spencer, who were now firmly ensconced in Cliff Richard's backing band on tour and in the studio, *Wouldn't You Know It (Got Myself a Girl)?* was a highly unfortunate casualty of circumstances for the composers' royalties. Chosen as the B-side of ***(There's a) Honky Tonk Angel,*** the single sold no more than a thousand copies because of the furore about Cliff, a committed Christian, singing a song that was ostensibly about prostitution. The naïvety of the singer was brought out when he denied knowledge of honky tonks nor that the term 'honky tonk angel' was used to describe a prostitute trawling the bars for custom. Cliff promptly pulled the single and guaranteed its hasty demise and has since refused to perform the song again. Both A-side and B-side became an instant rarity, with the price bumped up by its notoriety, and it would seem that *Wouldn't You Know It (Got Myself a Girl)?* had unfortunately missed its moment in the limelight until both single sides were remastered and reissued on the 2001 release of ***I'm Nearly Famous*** as bonus tracks.

The extraordinary ebullience of the song's performance is made even more quirky by the use of falsetto backing vocal echoes of Cliff's lead and the finger-pop of the mouth as part of the indiosyncratic percussion. The ensemble piece would have made a suitable A-side for Cliff and, for this reason more than any, it is unfortunate that it was not made more widely available until the remastering programme was underway.

Track Specification

Composed by Alan Tarney and Trevor Spencer

Musicians

Terry Britten	guitar
Clem Cattini	drums, percussion
Tony Harding	backing vocals
John Perry	backing vocals
Cliff Richard	vocals, backing vocals
Tony Rivers	backing vocals
Alan Tarney	bass
Graham Todd	electric piano
Unknown	saxophones

Recording Details

Producer	Hank Marvin, Bruce Welch and John Farrar
Engineered by	Tony Clark
Recording location	Abbey Road Studio 2, St. John's Wood, London
Recording date	29th May 1975

X - X - X - X - X - X - X - X - X - X - X - X - X - X - X - X - X - X

No entries available.

Y - Y - Y - Y - Y - Y - Y - Y - Y - Y - Y - Y - Y - Y - Y - Y - Y - Y

♫ Y'Arriva

From the album **21 Today**

Y'Arriva, translated approximately as *I'm Here* from the Spanish, is one of three home-grown compositions by Bruce Welch and Hank Marvin, opens the second side of the album ***21 Today***. The second of three songs attempted at the session, there were eighteen takes attempted of this song, of which the final was chosen for the stereo and mono edits with different mixes for the audio channels. The song also appears on the track listing of the ***Cliff Richard No. 2*** EP.
A Spanish style introduction on the guitar heads into rolling guitars and ticking percussion supported ably by a swift lick on the bass guitar. The wit that was the Shadows trademark can be heard on this track, with Hank Marvin doing a stereotypical version of a Mexican shouting 'Andalay' at the top of his voice. A very catchy song, it cannot fail to raise a smile as the vocal harmonies gel together.

Track Specification
Composed by Bruce Welch and Hank Marvin

Musicians

Jet Harris	backing vocals, bass
Hank Marvin	vocals, backing vocals, guitar
Tony Meehan	drums, percussion
Cliff Richard	vocals
Bruce Welch	backing vocals, rhythm guitar

Recording Details

Producer	Norrie Paramor
Engineered by	Malcolm Addey
Recording location	Abbey Road Studio 2, St. John's Wood, London
Recording date	11th July 1961

♫ Yes He Lives

71st UK single *and from the albums* **Thank You Very Much Remaster**, **Greenbelt Live!** *(Various) and* **Drifting** *(Sheila Walsh)*

Written by long-time guitarist with Cliff Richard's band, Terry Britten, *Yes He Lives* was recorded at the second of three main sessions for the ***Small Corners*** album. It was completed in just one take, although overdubs were recorded nine days later. *Yes He Lives* was issued as a single, backed with ***Good on the Sally Army***, on the EMI label (catalogue number EMI 2730) on 27th January 1978, a couple of weeks before the parent album. Although the album charted, the single appeared nowhere, making it Cliff's fourth flop in as many years.
Featuring uncredited strings, the song has a guitar line redolent of ***Devil Woman*** in its strength and understated power. The backing vocals provide another point of interest as they help to usher in a dramatic key change to the middle eight.
The song was included on the set list of the twentieth anniversary concert but was unreleased until it was included on the remastered ***Thank You Very Much*** in 2004. The track appears out of sequence on the album, since the recording is in mono having been generated from the concert video of the song. Because of the quality between the pre-existing stereo tracks and those in mono, it was decided to add them as bonus tracks to avoid a potential dip in listening pleasure.
It was resurrected in 1979 for the Greenbelt concert and featured Snowy White, Mike Moran and others in the band. The song is a major rarity, after appearing on the *Greenbelt Live!* album, and has never been issued in any other format.
Subsequently, it was chosen as the closing track to the first side of Sheila Walsh's first album, ***Drifting***. Featuring Cliff on backing vocals, he is joined by mother and daughter session singers, Vicki and Sammy Brown. The electronic introduction is very different to the original and the jerky rhythm and careful vocal create a wary atmosphere until the chorus, which has extra beauty in Cliff's subdued multi-layered harmonies.

Track Specification
Composed by Terry Britten

1. Single

Musicians

Brian Bennett	drums, percussion
Terry Britten	guitar
Stuart Calver	backing vocals
Bryn Haworth	guitar
John Perry	backing vocals
Cliff Richard	vocals
Tony Rivers	backing vocals
Alan Tarney	bass
Graham Todd	keyboards
Unknown	orchestra
Unknown	conductor

Recording Details

Producer	Cliff Richard
Engineered by	Tony Clark, Haydn Bendall and Alan Rouse
Recording location	Abbey Road Studio 3, St. John's Wood, London
Recording date	18th January 1977 (backing track and vocals) and 27th January 1977 (overdubs)

2. Thank You Very Much Remaster

Musicians

Terry Britten	guitar
Stuart Calver	backing vocals
Clem Cattini	drums, percussion
Dave Christopher	guitar
Mo Foster	bass
Graham Jarvis	drums, percussion
Graham Murray	guitar
John Perry	backing vocals
Cliff Richard	vocals
Tony Rivers	backing vocals
Graham Todd	keyboards

Recording Details

Producer	Bruce Welch
Engineered by	Tony Clark
Recording location	London Palladium, London
Recording date	4th March 1978

3. Greenbelt Live!

Musicians

Derek Beauchemin	keyboards
Stuart Calver	backing vocals
George Ford	bass
Graham Jarvis	drums, percussion
Mart Jenner	guitar
Mike Moran	keyboards
John Perry	backing vocals
Cliff Richard	vocals
Tony Rivers	backing vocals
Snowy White	guitar

Recording Details

Producer	Doug Hopkins and Tony Tew
Engineered by	Tim Summerhayes
Recording location	Odell, Bedfordshire, England
Recording date	26th August 1979

4. Drifting

Musicians

Sammy Brown	backing vocals
Vicki Brown	backing vocals
John Clark	electric guitar
Craig Pruess	arranger, synthesiser, percussion
Cliff Richard	backing vocals
Sheila Walsh	vocals

Recording Details

Producer	Cliff Richard and Craig Pruess
Engineered by	Keith Bessey
Recording location	Riverside Studios, London, Strawberry Studios, London, Ramp Studios, London and/or Sonoptics Studios, London
Recording date	September 1982-January 1983

♫ Yesterday Once More

137th UK single (download only)

Written for the Carpenters' 1973 album *Now & Then*, it was then released as a single, reaching number two in the Billboard Hot 100 chart. It was their best-selling UK single and, with *Please Mr. Postman*, their highest-placed single reaching number two. It has been covered by Moe Bandy, Ray Coniff, Richard Clayderman and Sanchez among a few others.

Cliff Richard was working on his duets album, ***Two's Company***, in 2005 and 2006 and leaked to the press that he had recorded *Yesterday Once More* with Daniel O'Donnell. The song was released as a download single on the same day as the album (6th November 2006) but didn't make an impression on the singles charts.

A complex vocal arrangement introduces the track, with Cliff singing the lead first before handing over to O'Donnell. The pair's voices blend together well, with Cliff taking the upper harmonies while O'Donnell sings the principal melody, but it is the vocal arrangement that makes this song special and, while a tribute to the original, is not a straight copy.

Track Specification

Composed by Richard Carpenter and John Bettis

Musicians

Richard Cardwell	keyboards
Mickey Féat	bass
Gavin Harrison	drums, percussion
Jakko M. Jakszyk	backing vocals
Daniel O'Donnell	vocals
Phil Palmer	guitar
Cliff Richard	vocals, backing vocals

Recording Details

Producer	Chris Porter
Engineered by	Chris Porter
Recording location	Metropolis Studios, London and Stanley House Studio, west London
Recording date	2006

♫ Yesterday's Memories

B-side of **Healing Love**

Cliff Richard's joint composition with old friend Dave Cooke has no information on the musicians and technical staff involved, nor on the location or date. What is known is that Cooke and Cliff produced it and it was released as the principal B-side of ***Healing Love*** in 1993, appearing on the seven-inch vinyl and CD boxed set issues of the single.

The synthesiser is the primary instrument on the recording, while the bass and percussion keeps the song moving. Cliff supplies his own backing harmony vocals but these are used sparingly. The song is sung in slightly breathless anticipation and the bridge features a short saxophone solo before the final verse and chorus return. The song finishes in an incomplete way with the saxophone and Cliff singing snatches of the lyrics but never resolves to the expected dominant or tonic key.

Track Specification
Composed by Cliff Richard and Dave Cooke

Musicians		*Recording Details*	
Cliff Richard	vocals, backing vocals	Producer	Cliff Richard and Dave Cooke
Unknown	guitar	Engineered by	Unknown
Unknown	bass	Recording location	Unknown
Unknown	synthesisers	Recording date	Unknown
Unknown	drums, percussion		
Unknown	saxophone		

♫ Yesterday, Today, Forever

From the album **Help It Along** *and B-side of* **Two Hearts**

Written by Cliff Richard to express some of his feelings about his Christian religion, *Yesterday, Today, Forever* was one of seventeen songs recorded at the studio-based concert sessions in front of a small audience and one of the thirteen eventually released with *Yesterday, Today, Forever* appearing on the charity album ***Help It Along*** in aid of the Tear Fund.

Gently guitar-led from the beginning, there is a complex accompaniment to Cliff's lead vocals that slowly builds up but is always there to underpin the meaning of the lyrics. The melody is surprisingly intricate with its diminished intervals and Cliff employs his increasing use of vibrato to great effect on the sustained notes.

In the spring of 1987, Cliff revisited the song for his own purposes, choosing *Yesterday, Today, Forever* as one of eight songs that were amalgamated with the ***Always Guaranteed*** album project. It became the principal B-side of ***Two Hearts*** – the final and fourth single to be released from the album – in all its formats and was first released on ***The Winner*** in CD album form in 1995, before giving its name to a compilation album in 1998. *Yesterday, Today, Forever* was one of eight bonus tracks to be added to the 2004 remaster of *Always Guaranteed.*

This second version is more upbeat and, because of the times, synthesiser-led, while still providing elements of the original with a guitar solo by John Clark. This time there are backing vocals, which Cliff also sings.

Track Specification
Composed by Cliff Richard

1. Help It Along

Musicians		*Recording Details*	
Terry Britten	guitar	Producer	David MacKay
Barrie Guard	arranger, conductor, percussion	Engineered by	Roger Quested
Cliff Hall	keyboards	Recording location	Morgan Studios, London
Kevin Peek	guitar	Recording date	24th, 25th and 26th September 1973
Cliff Richard	vocals		
Unknown	orchestra		

2. B-side (Two Hearts)

Musicians		*Recording Details*	
John Clark	guitar, bass	Producer	Cliff Richard, Keith Bessey and Alan Park
Alan Park	keyboards, drum and percussion programming	Engineered by	Keith Bessey
		Recording location	C. R. O. Studios, Esher, Surrey
Cliff Richard	vocals, backing vocals	Recording date	April 1987

♫ You

Unissued track

During the February 1974 sessions for the album ***The 31st of February Street***, there were three songs that were recorded that have never been released. One of these was *You*, which was abandoned after three takes, and about which there is scant information. Until further information is unearthed, the known musicians at the sessions (from the other released tracks completed) are highlighted against the track specification.

Track Specification
Composed by Unknown

Musicians		*Recording Details*	
Terry Britten	backing vocals, guitar	Producer	David MacKay
Barrie Guard	arranger, conductor, percussion	Engineered by	Tony Clark and Mike Jarrett
Cliff Hall	keyboards	Recording location	Abbey Road Studio 2, St. John's Wood, London
Jean Hawker	backing vocals	Recording date	12th February 1974
Gordon Huntley	steel guitar		
David MacKay	backing vocals		
Dave MacRae	keyboards		
Anna Peacock	backing vocals		
Kevin Peek	acoustic guitar		
Cliff Richard	vocals		
Trevor Spencer	drums, percussion		
Alan Tarney	backing vocals, bass		
Unknown	orchestra		

♫ You and I

From the album **Me and My Shadows**

The second track on the ***Me and My Shadows*** album is another in-house creation, composed as it was by guitarists Hank Marvin and Bruce Welch. For the final release of the album, the seventh take was used and, since the album was issued in both mono and stereo, these versions were the same take but with different mixes for the stereo channels. There was also further work carried out on the stereo version, although the detail of the work, dates and studio personnel is unknown.
With the now familiar guitar introduction played by Hank Marvin, it ushers in an archetypal Cliff Richard and the Shadows song with echoes of the earlier single release ***Fall in Love with You***. An assessing love song that looks at the state of a relationship, this is Cliff very much in his vocal comfort zone.

Track Specification
Composed by Bruce Welch and Hank Marvin

Musicians

Jet Harris	bass
Hank Marvin	guitar
Tony Meehan	drums, percussion
Cliff Richard	vocals
Bruce Welch	rhythm guitar

Recording Details

Producer	Norrie Paramor and John Schroeder
Engineered by	Malcolm Addey and Norman Smith (mono) and Peter Bown and Alan Kane (stereo)
Recording location	Abbey Road Studio 2, St. John's Wood, London
Recording date	1st April 1960 (backing track and vocals) and Unknown (stereo mixing)

♫ You and Me

Unissued track

During the February 1974 sessions for the album ***The 31st of February Street***, there were three songs that were recorded that have never been released. One of these was *You and Me*, which was abandoned after two takes, about which there is scant information. Until further information is unearthed, the known musicians at the sessions (from the other released tracks completed) are highlighted against the track specification.

Track Specification
Composed by Unknown

Musicians

Terry Britten	backing vocals, guitar
Barrie Guard	arranger, conductor, percussion
Cliff Hall	keyboards
Jean Hawker	backing vocals
Gordon Huntley	steel guitar
David MacKay	backing vocals
Dave MacRae	keyboards
Anna Peacock	backing vocals
Kevin Peek	acoustic guitar
Cliff Richard	vocals
Trevor Spencer	drums, percussion
Alan Tarney	backing vocals, bass
Unknown	orchestra

Recording Details

Producer	David MacKay
Engineered by	Tony Clark and Mike Jarrett
Recording location	Abbey Road Studio 3, St. John's Wood, London
Recording date	11th February 1974

♫ You Belong to My Heart

From the album **Cliff Richard**

Literally translated from the original Spanish as *Only Once*, ***Solamente Una Vez*** was published in 1944, with the English subtitle *You Belong to My Heart*. With new English lyrics added by Ray Gilbert and taking the subtitle as the recording title, it was covered most by non-Latin musicians, which included Gene Autrey, Little Joe, Engelbert Humperdinck, Roy Hamilton, Lord Tanamo, Gracie Fields, Marty Robbins, the Flamingoes, Elvis Presley and Pérez Prado. A further set of lyrics were added by Janis and Rick Carnes in 1998, this time taking the closer translation of *Only Once in My Life*.
Cliff Richard recorded the English version for his ***Cliff Richard*** album, but first it was recorded as one of the Spanish lyric songs that he recorded over four days at the EMI Studios based in Barcelona. It was a sequence of sessions that first laid down the backing track in Barcelona, followed by Norrie Paramor's orchestral strings and the backing vocals by Cliff and Bruce Welch; a further session ensued in early 1965 to overdub a number of English lyric vocals on the foreign language songs already recorded of which *You Belong to My Heart* was one. The combined final take and edit was used for the mono and stereo recordings but with different mixes for the needs of the audio channels. The stereo version was narrowed for the CD reissue of the parent album in 1992. It should be noted that, at the time of recording the new lead vocal, John Rostill was the permanent bassist with the Shadows but that Brian Locking appeared on this track since the instrumentation was originally recorded almost two years prior to this session.
There is little to distinguish the two versions other than the language but, of course, Cliff's lead vocals carry the song particularly well, perfectly accompanied by the muted guitars of the Shadows and the piano played by Norrie Paramor. The mix for the stereo is, however, an improvement on the Spanish version since the apportionment of the instrumentation is better laid out across the two channels.

Track Specification
Composed by Augustín Lara; English lyrics by Raymond Gilbert

Musicians

Brian Bennett	drums, percussion
Brian 'Licorice' Locking	bass
Hank Marvin	guitar
Norrie Paramor Strings	orchestra
Norrie Paramor	arranger, conductor, piano
Cliff Richard	vocals, backing vocals
Bruce Welch	backing vocals, rhythm guitar

Recording Details

Producer	Norrie Paramor
Engineered by	Malcolm Addey
Recording location	EMI Studios, Barcelona (backing track) and Abbey Road Studio 2, St. John's Wood, London (vocals, backing vocals and strings)
Recording date	29th April 1963 (backing track), 14th May 1963 (strings), 28th May 1963 (backing vocals) and 31st January 1965 (vocals)

♫ You Can't Get to Heaven...

Unissued track

A song much beloved of Scout and Guide jamborees and camps, usually with additional lyrics (some unprintable), Cliff Richard attempted to record *You Can't Get to Heaven...* during the three main sessions for the ***Small Corners*** album. At the second session, it was the penultimate song to be tried but was, although six takes were completed and further overdub work was done, the song has ever been released.

Track Specification
Composed by Gary S. Paxton

Musicians

Brian Bennett	drums, percussion
Terry Britten	guitar
Stuart Calver	backing vocals
Bryn Haworth	guitar
John Perry	backing vocals
Cliff Richard	vocals
Tony Rivers	backing vocals
Alan Tarney	bass
Graham Todd	keyboards

Recording Details

Producer	Cliff Richard
Engineered by	Tony Clark, Haydn Bendall and Alan Rouse
Recording location	Abbey Road Studio 3, St. John's Wood, London
Recording date	18th and 31st January 1977

♫ You Don't Know

From the album **32 Minutes and 17 Seconds with Cliff Richard**

The first song to be completed (in just seven takes) in the session that resulted in two songs for the track listing of the ***32 Minutes and 17 Seconds with Cliff Richard*** album, the mono and stereo *You Don't Know* recordings used the final take and edit but employed different mixes for the needs of the audio channels. The song was also included on the track listing of the ***Time for Cliff and the Shadows*** EP.
With a vibe that is very similar to *Fever* (made popular by Peggy Lee and Elvis Presley), the Shadows accompaniment is edited quite far back in the mix with echo applied. The lazy, plodding rhythm is perfectly adapted to Cliff's lead vocal.

Track Specification
Composed by Walter Spriggs

Musicians

Jet Harris	bass
Hank Marvin	guitar
Tony Meehan	drums, percussion
Cliff Richard	vocals
Bruce Welch	rhythm guitar

Recording Details

Producer	Norrie Paramor
Engineered by	Malcolm Addey
Recording location	Abbey Road Studio 2, St. John's Wood, London
Recording date	11th December 1961

♫ You Got Me Wondering

From the albums **Every Face Tells a Story** *and* **My Kinda Life**

Recorded in the ***Every Face Tells a Story*** sessions during September 1976, *You Got Me Wondering* was completed in three takes with additional vocal overdubs recorded three days later – something that Bruce Welch as producer preferred as a mode of working. On some releases of the song, it is referred to as *You've Got Me Wondering* although the album issues have referred to it as the original *You Got Me Wondering*. The song was included as the joint B-side with ***Spider Man*** for the promotional record for the album with the title track on the A-side.
With a guitar introduction that comes straight out of the mid-West of America, the song builds up into the chorus with a rattling drum and percussion rhythm that settles back down for the next verse. An understated song that stands out from the other brilliant album tracks, the middle eight features a near *a capella* performance between the vocalists.
The song was revisited when compiling the track listing for ***My Kinda Life*** in 1992. For this album, the original recordings were taken and either remixed or had additional instrumentation or vocals overdubbed. In the case of *You Got Me Wondering*, there are some additional keyboards and percussion by Paul Moessl and the vocals have been remixed slightly in places, as well as fading out earlier than the original track. This updated version of *You Got Me Wondering* was added as a track on the CD single release of ***Never Let Go*** in September 1993.

Track Specification
Composed by Terry Britten

1. Every Face Tells a Story

Musicians		*Recording Details*	
Brian Bennett	drums, percussion	Producer	Bruce Welch
Terry Britten	guitar	Engineered by	Tony Clark and Alan Rouse
John Perry	backing vocals	Recording location	Abbey Road Studio 2, St. John's Wood, London
Cliff Richard	vocals, backing vocals	Recording date	10th and 13th September 1976
Frank Ricotti	percussion		
Tony Rivers	backing vocals		
Alan Tarney	bass		
Graham Todd	keyboards		

2. My Kinda Life

Musicians		*Recording Details*	
Brian Bennett	drums, percussion	Producer	Bruce Welch (original track) and Cliff Richard and Paul Moessl (new instrumentation)
Terry Britten	guitar		
Paul Moessl	drum sequencing, synthesisers	Engineered by	Tony Clark and Alan Rouse (original track) and Gerry Kitchingham and Ben Robbins (new instrumentation)
John Perry	backing vocals		
Cliff Richard	vocals		
Frank Ricotti	percussion	Recording location	Abbey Road Studio 2, St. John's Wood, London (original track) and R. G. Jones Studios, Wimbledon, London (new instrumentation)
Tony Rivers	backing vocals		
Alan Tarney	bass		
Graham Todd	keyboards	Recording date	10th and 13th September 1976 (original track) and 20th-23rd April 1992 (new instrumentation)

♬ You Gotta Tell Me

From the album **Don't Stop Me Now!**

The penultimate track on the first vinyl side of Cliff Richard's ***Don't Stop Me Now!*** album was recorded at a dual session on 11th October 1966. The final (unknown) take and edit were used for the mono and stereo recordings.
Although the accompaniment is orchestral with an uncredited piano, the ensemble is a classic Cliff Richard period track, purely by dint of the inclusion of Bruce Welch and Hank Marvin singing close harmonies.

Track Specification
Composed by Roy Williams

Musicians		*Recording Details*	
Bernard Ebbinghouse Orchestra	orchestra	Producer	Norrie Paramor
Bernard Ebbinghouse	arranger, conductor	Engineered by	Peter Vincent and Richard Lush
Hank Marvin	backing vocals	Recording location	Abbey Road Studio 2, St. John's Wood, London
Cliff Richard	vocals	Recording date	11th October 1966
Unknown	piano		
Bruce Welch	backing vocals		

♬ You Held My Hand

Unissued track

In early 1969, Tyne Tees Television commissioned six playlets called *Life with Johnny*, featuring Cliff Richard in the title role as each episode updated a Biblical parable. Records are unclear on most episodes although *Johnny Come Home* and *Johnny Faces Facts* are complete, *Johnny and the Good Samaritan* is partially available, while the remainder are unavailable.
The songs had some relevance to the parable and, in all, there were about five songs per episode. *You Held My Hand* appeared in one of *Johnny on the Rocks, Johnny and the Blind Rage* or *Johnny in Love*. The end credits of the episode stated that all songs were original and written in collaboration between Cliff, the Settlers and the programme's writer David Winter. The instrumentation and performance details are unknown.

Track Specification
Composed by Cliff Richard, David Winter, Cindy Kent, Mike Jones, John Fyffe and Geoffrey Srodzinski

Musicians		*Recording Details*	
John Fyffe	backing vocals, guitar	Producer	Norrie Paramor
Cindy Kent	backing vocals	Engineered by	Peter Vince
Mike Jones	backing vocals, guitar	Recording location	Abbey Road Studio 3, St. John's Wood, London
Cliff Richard	vocals	Recording date	8th January 1969
Geoffrey Srodzinski	backing vocals, bass		

♬ You Know That I Love You

From the album **Rock 'n' Roll Juvenile**

The fourth of ten songs provided by co-producer Terry Britten for Cliff Richard's ***Rock 'n' Roll Juvenile*** album, *You Know That I Love You* was recorded in two parts with the backing track completed in the Parisian EMI studios followed by a vocal overdub session eight months later.

The funky beat created in the bass by in-demand session musician Herbie Flowers is joined by the slinking synthesiser, while Cliff keeps up the evocatively lazy atmosphere with a laidback vocal performance, accompanied by his own backing vocals.

Track Specification
Composed by Terry Britten

Musicians		*Recording Details*	
Terry Britten	guitar, percussion	Producer	Cliff Richard and Terry Britten
Herbie Flowers	bass	Engineered by	Tony Clark and Haydn Bendall
Graham Jarvis	drums, percussion	Recording location	Pathé Marconi, Paris, France (backing track) and Abbey Road Studio, St. John's Wood, London (vocals)
Cliff Richard	vocals, backing vocals	Recording date	18th-20th July 1978 (backing track) and 17th March 1979 (vocals)
Graham Todd	keyboards		

♫ You'll Never Be the Same

From the album **Don't Hide Your Heart** *(Sheila Walsh)*

Another Chris Eaton song from Sheila Walsh's third album, ***Don't Hide Your Heart***, *You'll Never Be the Same* featured Cliff Richard on backing vocals recorded at some of the very few sessions he carried out in 1985. Cliff had produced her first album but relinquished that control to collaborator Craig Pruess and limited himself to providing backing vocals only.
The gentle beat is ushered in by a syncopated percussion and synthesiser motif. Walsh's voice is almost tremulous as she sings the main melody and this is lifted with greater energy by the multi-layered harmonizing vocals by Cliff.

Track Specification
Composed by Chris Eaton

Musicians		*Recording Details*	
Rick Fenn	guitar	Producer	Craig Pruess and Keith Bessey
Graham Jarvis	drums, percussion	Engineered by	Keith Bessey
Craig Pruess	keyboards, electronics	Recording location	Gallery Studios, Chertsey, Surrey
Cliff Richard	backing vocals	Recording date	November 1984-February 1985
Sheila Walsh	vocals		

♫ You'll Want Me

From the album **Sincerely Cliff Richard**

Roger Cook and Roger Greenaway had become regular suppliers of recording material for Cliff Richard and, at the session that resulted in the completion of *You'll Want Me*, the single ***Good Times (Better Times)***, which was also written by them with Jerry Lordan, was also recorded with *You'll Want Me* the first song to be completed at the evening session.
Introducing the song with a close harmony *a capella* arrangement that sounds like a hymn in the way it is performed, the song moves on to a straightforward and gentle orchestral accompaniment. The vocalists in the backing group are not credited but they are reminiscent of the Mastersingers who performed with Cliff on his ***Carol Singers*** EP.

Track Specification
Composed by Roger Cook and Roger Greenaway

Musicians		*Recording Details*	
Mike Vickers Orchestra	orchestra	Producer	Norrie Paramor
Cliff Richard	vocals	Engineered by	Peter Vince
Mike Vickers	arranger, conductor	Recording location	IBC Studios, London
Unknown	backing vocals	Recording date	31st January 1969

♫ You, Me and Jesus

B-side of **Little Town** *and from the album* **Dressed for the Occasion Remaster**

You, Me and Jesus, a Cliff Richard composition, was recorded during the sessions for the ***Now You See Me... Now You Don't*** album, but it wasn't issued on the track listing. Instead, it was released as one of the two songs forming the B-side of the third single release, ***Little Town***. ***Love and a Helping Hand***, which was recorded later on and also written by Cliff, was the other track. Both tracks were also included on the 1985 LP and CD collation of Cliff's faith and inspiration recordings, ***Walking in the Light***, as well as forming bonus tracks on the 2002 remaster of *No You See Me... Now You Don't*.
Cliff asserts regularly, and most recently in his ***My Songs*** album, that he isn't a songwriter and that he doesn't rate what he produces: this is unfortunate because much of what he writes has a simplistic beauty about it and *You, Me and Jesus* exemplifies the point perfectly. With acoustic guitars accompanying him throughout, the song is carried forward on the simple melody and the arpeggiated guitar chords.
Since the timing of the single's release matched the date of the concert at the Royal Albert Hall, *Little Town* and *You, Me and Jesus* were incorporated on the set list. Although both were recorded and prepared for release, neither made it on to the track listing of ***Dressed for the Occasion***. However, when the album was remastered in 2004, all five missing tracks, left off due to time and space considerations, were replaced as bonus items. The song is accompanied by a simple guitar even though the overall performance on the night was accompanied by the London Philharmonic Orchestra.

Track Specification
Composed by Cliff Richard

1. B-side (Little Town)

Musicians		*Recording Details*	
John Clark	acoustic guitar	Producer	Cliff Richard and Craig Pruess
Cliff Richard	vocals, guitar	Engineered by	John Walker and Steve Cook
		Recording location	Strawberry Studios South, Surrey
		Recording date	4th-15th January 1982

2. Dressed for the Occasion

Musicians		*Recording Details*	
Cliff Richard	vocals, guitar	Producer	Cliff Richard and Richard Hewson
		Engineered by	John Kurlander
		Mixed by	Keith Bessey
		Recording location	Royal Albert Hall, London
		Mixed at	Strawberry Studios South, Surrey
		Recording date	23rd November 1982

♬ You Move Heaven
From the album **Cliff Richard - The Album**

You Move Heaven was the first track on the second side of the original vinyl release of Cliff Richard's ***Cliff Richard - The Album*** and was one of the first to be completed for the track listing.
As would be expected of Paul Moessl, there is a predominance of synthesized accompaniment with a number of key changes adding interest to a pretty main melody and backing harmonies. The middle eight features a lengthy guitar solo that has reverberations from an earlier decade but manages to fit perfectly with the ensemble piece.

Track Specification
Composed by Paul Moessl and Glen

Musicians		*Recording Details*	
John Clark	guitar	Producer	Paul Moessl and Cliff Richard
Peter Howarth	backing vocals	Engineered by	Gerry Kitchingham and Ben Robbins
Peter May	drums, percussion	Recording location	R. G. Jones Studios, Wimbledon, London
Paul Moessl	arranger, drum programming, keyboards	Recording date	25th-31st May 1992, 8th June 1992 (backing track) and 10th June 1992 (vocals)
Keith Murrell	backing vocals		
Tessa Niles	backing vocals		
Cliff Richard	vocals, backing vocals		
Steve Stroud	bass		
Judith Walmsley	backing vocals		

♬ You Never Can Tell
B-side of **Goodbye Sam, Hello Samantha**

Written by Hank Marvin for Cliff Richard to record, he would later pick it up and record it himself with John Farrar on the *Marvin & Farrar* album which was released in 1973. Cliff's original was recorded some nineteen months before it was released and at the session that saw three songs recorded, only *You Never Can Tell* was initially released with ***If I Do*** and ***Note in a Bottle*** waiting until 2008. The song will have had a mono edit created but by the time of release as the B-side of Cliff's fiftieth UK single, ***Goodbye Sam, Hello Samantha,*** Columbia had altered its policy and now only issued singles in stereo only. One other point of note was that the song was recorded in the largest studio in the Abbey Road complex rather than the more familiar Studio 2. Although Cliff is perfectly suited to sing this song, the arrangement by Norrie Paramor doesn't quite do justice to the observational world-weariness of Hank's later version. Given what is going on in the lyrics, with people failing and usually dying, it is all expressed in too much of an upbeat way. However, that denigrates Cliff's vocal performance, which, as ever, is very strong right through to the final lengthy sustained note.

Track Specification
Composed by Hank Marvin

Musicians		*Recording Details*	
Norrie Paramor Orchestra	orchestra	Producer	Norrie Paramor
Norrie Paramor	conductor	Engineered by	Peter Vince
Cliff Richard	vocals	Recording location	Abbey Road Studio 1, St. John's Wood, London
Unknown	female backing vocals	Recording date	24th October 1968

♬ Young Love
From the album **Wired for Sound**

Another Alan Tarney song recorded for the ***Wired for Sound*** album by Cliff Richard, *Young Love* is almost a Tarney track with guest vocals by Cliff, given that he arranged, produced and played almost every instrument on the album, although engineer Michael Boddicker performs the piano in addition to his old friend and collaborator Trevor Spencer on drums.

After the gentle expression of ***Summer Rain*** that precedes it on the album, the upbeat rhythm and major key of *Young Love* surges with energy. The backing vocals by Cliff and Tarney match Cliff's lead vocal and add an extra dimension to the straightforward pleasance of the track.

Track Specification
Composed by Alan Tarney

Musicians		*Recording Details*	
Michael Boddicker	piano	Producer	Alan Tarney
Cliff Richard	vocals, backing vocals	Engineered by	Michael Boddicker and Ian Little
Trevor Spencer	rums, percussion	Recording location	Gallery Studios, Chertsey, Surrey
Alan Tarney	arranger, backing vocals, guitar, bass, keyboards	Recording date	27th May-9th July 1981

♫ Young Ones, The

16th ***UK single*** *and from the film soundtrack album of* **The Young Ones** *(early versions) and from the albums* **Live at the ABC Kingston 1962, Cliff in Japan, Cliff Live in Korea, Cliff "Live" in Japan '72, Thank You Very Much, Live & Guaranteed 1988!, From a Distance ***** The Event** *and* **Reunited** *and unissued live tracks and B-side of* **Be with Me Always**

Contracted to compose three songs for ***The Young Ones***, Sid Tepper and Roy Bennett delivered ***When the Girl in our Arms Is the Girl in Your Heart***, *The Young Ones* and ***Outsider***. The latter wasn't used in the film but was recorded for release on the album ***21 Today***. The song is incorporated into the film twice: once when Nicky Black (Cliff Richard's character) is singing to Toni Crowthier (played by Carole Gray) and finally over the end credits of the film.
In addition to Cliff Richard's song, it has been recorded by several acts such as the Angelic Upstarts, Menace, Foster and Allen, The Resistors, Hank Marvin himself and, of course, The Young Ones. Famously, the latter comedy troupe made two series of anarchic situation comedy that ran from 1982 to 1984 on the BBC and featured the comedic talents of Rik Mayall (whose character Rick was always embarrassed to admit his fondness for Cliff Richard and his music – hence the title of the series), Ade Edmondson, Nigel Planer and Christopher Ryan. These four tunelessly bellowed a version of *The Young Ones* for the title sequence and, in truth, it was intended to be a swipe at the establishment (of which Cliff was firmly a part) but, because of the good nature that Cliff took this ribbing accolade, either the comedians were viewed as having sold out to the mainstream or Cliff was seen as cool. Their collaboration continued on stage for charity, Cliff's face was seen on a giant billboard in the last episode before a big red bus crashed through it and over a cliff (visual puns and cultural references galore) and it culminated in Cliff and Hank Marvin recording the 1986 Comic Relief record with the four comedians on a new version of ***Living Doll***. Meanwhile, in Spain, Los Mustang, which were very similar in style to Cliff and the Shadows, recorded a cover of the song with Spanish lyrics and retitled to ***Los Jovenes***.
In the film, after despondency at news that the Youth Club is soon scheduled for closure after its purchase by property magnate Hamilton Black (Robert Morley), Nicky Black (Cliff Richard) takes his girlfriend, Toni Crowthier (Carole Gray), for a drive to a local park and lido, where he reveals he is Black's son and she suggests that it would be unwise to tell the rest of their friends. Trying to find a reason for Black Senior's actions, Nicky begins to sing this song as they walk through the crowds on the small beach. As he sings the verse ending with the suggestion of looking after their own kids, they are surrounded by strangely attentive children. Nicky and Toni move in for a kiss and the kids mob them shouting and screaming (possibly to avoid censorship, probably to hype up the comedy quotient). The song plays as the end credits roll.
There have been several versions recorded for the film as well as commercial release. The first was the single, which took thirty-six takes to perfect. The mono and stereo edits used the same take but with different mixes for the audio channels. Backed with ***We Say Yeah***, also from the film, it was issued on the Columbia label (catalogue number 45-DB 4761) on 11th January 1962 and it went straight into the number one spot in the UK charts entirely due to presales orders of one million units and stayed there for six weeks (before being displaced by Elvis Presley's *Rock-a-Hula Baby*). For the domestic market – and most international markets, too – the undubbed single version that was essentially the single but without the swooping strings appeared on the film soundtrack album and the associated ***Hits from the Young Ones*** EP; however, later album releases incorporated the single version. The mono track has not been released is now a major rarity.
Often the versions of the songs recorded for the film were not formally released in record or tape form. However, the 1996 compilation ***Cliff Richard at the Movies 1959-1974*** included the film version rather than the familiar single version. There are different vocal inflections, some changed lyrics and the mix is quite different with a focus on the orchestra. Finally there is the end title version (two verses and a chorus with the heavier orchestral brass), which has not been released.
The introductory two-chord thump on guitar, bass and drums are so indelibly linked to Cliff Richard and the Shadows, as is the step forward, over and back routine (although not in the film), that it can be instantly recognized before the melody comes in, which is played on Hank's lead guitar. In addition, the string accompaniment and the beautiful instrumental harmonies and intervals help make this song a classic. The rhythm section (Tony Meehan having a ball on the drums and Bruce Welch working hard on the chord sequences) drives the song ever onwards to the middle eight with Hank's guitar interlude accompanied by the swooping orchestral strings. As with the introduction, the rallentando in the lead guitar at the end of the song is a hallmark that makes this song instantly recognizable.
In subsequent concerts to support and promote the film, Cliff and the Shadows built a selection of songs into a medley, one of which was *The Young Ones*. For the ABC Kingston concert, this was recorded but remained unreleased until the 2002 album ***Live at the ABC Kingston 1962***, which was released in stereo only.

On Cliff's other tours in the sixties, he created other medleys of songs not performed elsewhere in the show. For the Far East tour at the end of 1967, which resulted in the ***Cliff in Japan*** album, *The Young Ones* was the second of five songs taken from the era of that film and ***Summer Holiday***: ***Let's Make a Memory***, *The Young Ones*, ***Lucky Lips***, ***Summer Holiday*** and ***We Say Yeah***, all accompanied by orchestral instruments only. This was followed the next year with a medley at the Talk of the Town shows in May 1968 that included *The Young Ones*, *Lucky Lips*, ***Living Doll*** and ***In the Country***. Although this performance was released as another live album, the medley remains unissued. For the mono-only, ultra-rare album *Cliff Live in Korea*, this time the song formed part of the ***Shadows Medley***: *The Young Ones*, *Living Doll* and *In the Country*, while the ***Cliff "Live" in Japan '72*** album features a version that moves straight to the vocal rather than building up from the extended guitar introduction, which sounds as if it had gone wrong – if it had, it was successfully covered up.
The reunion concert in 1978 is quite a tame rendition that takes a bit of time to pick up, which really gets going once the singers get together providing their unique close harmonies. The strings are replicated by the latest synthesiser technology, which sounds very modern in the original setting of the London Palladium.
Extraordinarily, given the Shadows' impact on Cliff's career, the celebratory ***Event*** at Wembley Stadium in 1989 only featured eight songs with the Shadows and, more curiously, only two of them have been released (even on the remastered 2005 album which restored all of the other unissued tracks on to two CDs). Hank's harmonious guitar shines out in the performance, while the strings are replicated on the synthesiser. In the middle eight, the blended harmonies of the three singers' vocals work well together and it is a faithful rendition against the original.
The original track was released alongside the 1968 recording of *Congratulations* and the revisited version of ***You Got Me Wondering*** as B-side elements to the CD single release of ***Never Let Go*** in 1993.
The early summer of 1996 was particularly disastrous for the annual Wimbledon tennis tournament and Cliff was handed a microphone to entertain the crowds with an impromptu concert. A number of songs were performed but four were released as B-sides, included *The Young Ones* which appeared on the B-side of ***Be with Me Always***.
Returning to the original recording and its cover by Los Mustang, in 1999, Cliff was invited by the group to record a new version of their cover *Los Jovenes* in Spanish. Santi Carulla Hernandez and Cliff shared the lead vocals while Cliff also supplied the backing vocals on a version that was again very close to the original in its spirited rendition.
Always a welcome addition to any tour set list to get the fans shouting for more, Cliff added *The Young Ones* to his 2003 world tour, the New Zealand show of which was filmed for DVD release later that year. While the DVD included all of the songs performed, the complementary CD album, *World Tour Live*, only had a selection of songs and *The Young Ones* didn't make it to the track listing.
In early 2009 in preparation for going out on the road as a reunited team, Cliff reformed with the Shadows once again and recording a number of their most famous tracks from the first ten years of working together, including *The Young Ones*, which was issued on the track listing of the ***Reunited*** album. As would be expected after performing it so many times, this new version is close to the original, with supporting strings and familiar rock instrumentation.

Track Specification
Composed by Sid Tepper and Roy C. Bennett

1. Single

Musicians		*Recording Details*	
Jet Harris	bass	Producer	John Schroeder and Norrie Paramor
Hank Marvin	guitar	Engineered by	Malcolm Addey and David Lloyd (main session) and Malcolm Addey (orchestra session)
Tony Meehan	drums, percussion		
Norrie Paramor Orchestra	orchestra	Recording location	Abbey Road Studio 2, St. John's Wood, London
Norrie Paramor	conductor	Recording date	11th August 1961 (main session) and 5th December 1961 (orchestra)
Cliff Richard	vocals		
Bruce Welch	rhythm guitar		

2. The Young Ones (early versions)

Musicians		*Recording Details*	
Jet Harris	bass	Producer	John Schroeder and Norrie Paramor
Hank Marvin	guitar	Engineered by	Malcolm Addey and David Lloyd
Tony Meehan	drums, percussion	Recording location	Abbey Road Studio 2, St. John's Wood, London
Norrie Paramor	conductor	Recording date	11th August 1961
Cliff Richard	vocals		
Unknown	orchestra		
Bruce Welch	rhythm guitar		

3. Cliff Richard at the Movies 1959-1974

Musicians		*Recording Details*	
Jet Harris	bass	Producer	John Schroeder and Norrie Paramor
Hank Marvin	guitar	Engineered by	Malcolm Addey and Norman Smith
Tony Meehan	drums, percussion	Recording location	Abbey Road Studio 2, St. John's Wood, London and possibly Elstree Sound Stage
Norrie Paramor Orchestra	orchestra		
Norrie Paramor	conductor	Recording date	23rd May 1961 with possible overdubs later in the year
Cliff Richard	vocals		
Bruce Welch	rhythm guitar		

4. Live at the ABC Kingston 1962

Musicians	
Brian Bennett	drums, percussion
Jet Harris	bass
Hank Marvin	guitar
Cliff Richard	vocals
Bruce Welch	rhythm guitar

Recording Details	
Producer	Norrie Paramor
Engineered by	Malcolm Addey and Ken Townsend
Recording location	ABC Theatre, Kingston, Surrey
Recording date	7th March 1962

5. Cliff in Japan

Musicians	
Norrie Paramor Orchestra	orchestra
Norrie Paramor	arranger, conductor
Cliff Richard	vocals

Recording Details	
Producer	Norrie Paramor
Engineered by	Unknown
Recording location	Shibuya Public Hall, Tokyo, Japan
Recording date	18th October 1967

6.Unissued track (Live at the Talk of the Town)

Musicians	
Breakaways:	backing vocals
Vicki Hasemen	
Margo Quantrell	
Jean Ryder	
Norrie Paramor	arranger, conductor
Cliff Richard	vocals
Talk of the Town Orchestra	orchestra

Recording Details	
Producer	Norrie Paramor
Engineered by	Peter Vince
Recording location	Talk of the Town Theatre, London
Recording date	30th May 1968

7. Cliff Live in Korea

Musicians	
Brian Bennett	drums, percussion
Alan Hawkshaw	keyboards
Hank Marvin	guitar
Cliff Richard	vocals
John Rostill	bass
Bruce Welch	rhythm guitar

Recording Details	
Producer	Unknown
Engineered by	Unknown
Recording location	Citizen Hall, Seoul, South Korea
Recording date	16th October 1969

8. Cliff "Live" in Japan '72

Musicians	
Brian Bennett	drums, percussion
Pat Carroll	backing vocals
John Farrar	bass
Alan Hawkshaw	piano
Hank Marvin	guitar
Olivia Newton-John	backing vocals
Cliff Richard	vocals
Bruce Welch	rhythm guitar

Recording Details	
Producer	Norrie Paramor
Engineered by	Unknown
Recording location	Kosei Nenkin Hall, Tokyo, Japan
Recording date	22nd-23rd September 1972

9. Thank You Very Much

Musicians	
Brian Bennett	drums, percussion
Alan Jones	bass
Cliff Hall	keyboards
Hank Marvin	backing vocals, guitar
Cliff Richard	vocals
Bruce Welch	backing vocals, rhythm guitar

Recording Details	
Producer	Bruce Welch
Engineered by	Tony Clark, remixed by Peter Vince
Recording location	London Palladium, London
Remix location	Abbey Road Studios, St. John's Wood, London
Recording date	4th March 1978

10. Live & Guaranteed 1988!

Musicians	
John Clark	guitar
Rosemarie Ford	backing vocals
Mark Griffiths	bass
Peter Howarth	backing vocals
Steve Lauri	guitar
Paul Moessl	keyboards
Mick Mullins	backing vocals
Alan Park	keyboards
Cliff Richard	vocals
Henry Spinetti	drums, percussion

Recording Details	
Producer	Unknown
Engineered by	Unknown
Recording location	Fyens Forum, Odense, Denmark
Recording date	22nd May 1988

*11. From a Distance ***** The Event*

Musicians	
Brian Bennett	drums, percussion
Mark Griffiths	bass
Cliff Hall	synthesiser
Hank Marvin	backing vocals, guitar
Cliff Richard	vocals
Bruce Welch	backing vocals, rhythm guitar

Recording Details	
Producer	Cliff Richard
Engineered by	Keith Bessey and Mick McKenna
Recording location	Rolling Stones Mobile Studio, Wembley Stadium, Wembley, North-west London
Recording date	16th-17th June 1989

12. *Unissued (Knebworth - The Album)*

Musicians

Ray Beavis	saxophone
Brian Bennett	drums, percussion
John Earle	saxophone
Chris Gower	trombone
Mark Griffiths	bass
Cliff Hall	keyboards
Dick Hanson	trumpet
Peter Howarth	backing vocals
Hank Marvin	backing vocals, guitar
Paul Moessl	keyboards
Mick Mullins	backing vocals
Keith Murrell	backing vocals
Cliff Richard	vocals
Bruce Welch	backing vocals, guitar

Recording Details

Producer	Chris Kimsey and Steve Smith
Engineered by	Unknown
Recording location	Knebworth House, Hertfordshire, England
Recording date	30th June 1990

13. *B-side (Be with Me Alwas)*

Musicians

Cliff Richard	vocals

Recording Details

Producer	Unknown
Engineered by	Unknown
Recording location	Wimbledon Lawn Tennis Association
Recording date	3rd July 1996

14. *Unissued track (World Tour Live)*

Musicians

Rachel Allen	violin
Elena Bulgakova	violin
Jenni Champion	violin
Anthony Clark	backing vocals, guitar
John Clark	guitar
Dave Cooke	keyboards
Cornelia Didenco	violin
Gina Ferguson	violin
Peter Howarth	backing vocals
Cathy Irons	violin
Pete May	drums, percussion
Mick Mullins	backing vocals
Keith Murrell	backing vocals
Alan Park	keyboards
Hee-Jung Park	violin
Cliff Richard	vocals
Eva Schwanen-Lilley	violin
Steve Stroud	bass

Recording Details

Producer	Keith Bessey
Engineered by	Keith Bessey
Recording location	The Mission Winery, Napier, New Zealand
Recording date	22nd February 2003

15. *Reunited*

Musicians

Brian Bennett	arranger (strings), drums, percussion
Warren Bennett	arranger (strings)
Mark Berrow	violin
Mark Griffiths	bass
Bogustan Kostecki	violin
Martin Loveday	cello
Hank Marvin	backing vocals, guitar
Perry Montague-Mason	violin
Cliff Richard	vocals, backing vocals
Emlyn Singleton	violin
Chris Tombling	violin
Kevin Townsend	arranger (strings), conductor
Bruce Welch	backing vocals, rhythm guitar
Warren Zeilinski	violin

Recording Details

Producer	Warren Bennett (co-ordination)
Engineered by	James Collins (Honeyhill Studios), Ethan Carlson (Middle Ear Studios), Les Williams (Nivram Studios) and Keith Bessey (mixing and mastering)
Recording location	Middle Ear Studios, Miami, Florida, USA (Cliff's vocals), Nivram Studios, Perth, Western Australia (Hank's guitars and vocals) and Honeyhill Studios, Hertfordshire, England (all other vocals and instruments)
Recording date	Early 2009

♫ Young Ones Medley, The

From the album **Live at the ABC Kingston 1962**

After the successful release of the third Cliff Richard film, ***The Young Ones***, Cliff and the Shadows regularly performed a medley of the best songs from the album. This featured:

a) ***Lessons in Love***
b) ***Got a Funny Feeling***
c) ***The Young Ones***

The live version that appears on ***Live at the ABC Kingston 1962*** was released finally in 2003 but only in stereo, after the recordings languished in the EMI vaults since the March 1962 concert.

♫ You're Just the One to Do It

From the album **Me and My Shadows**

You're Just the One to Do It is the penultimate track on the first side of the original vinyl release of ***Me and My Shadows*** and also features on the ***Me and My Shadows No. 2*** EP. Recorded in both stereo and mono, the same session take was used (the fifteenth) but the editing and mixing process is subtly different to allow for the dual channels of stereo.
With a clucking guitar and tambourine as principal percussion, these usher in this love song that is driven along by Bruce Welch's rhythm guitar and the strong tambourine beat. The song comes to a halt to express a sudden thought of the singer, before the instrumentation resumes as before. While slow-paced, the song has a surprising effervescent energy.

Track Specification
Composed by Otis Blackwell

Musicians

Jet Harris	bass
Hank Marvin	guitar
Tony Meehan	drums, percussion, tambourine
Cliff Richard	vocals
Bruce Welch	rhythm guitar

Recording Details

Producer	Norrie Paramor
Engineered by	Malcolm Addey and Norman Smith (mono) and Peter Bown and Alan Kane (stereo)
Recording location	Abbey Road Studio 2, St. John's Wood, London
Recording date	16th March 1960

♫ You're Only Lonely

Single by **Marietta**

Written and recorded by J. D. Souther for the *Coast to Coast* film soundtrack released in 1977, *You're Only Lonely* has been covered by relatively unknown acts such as Schuyler Fisk, Raul Malo and Feels Like Home and it was chosen as Marietta's first single release. Marietta Parfitt was the wife, at the time of recording, of Status Quo guitarist and singer Rick, who also co-produced the track. At the time, Rick was helping Marietta to forge a music career and invited Cliff Richard to provide backing vocals. Backed with *Making Up My Mind*, which didn't involve Cliff, *You're Only Lonely* was issued on the Polydor label (catalogue number POSP 305) in January 1982 and, although there was radio interest, the song didn't chart.
Marietta's vocal line is a little nasal in a song that sounds like a mixture of nostalgic rock and roll ballad and slow Status Quo. However, the song is pleasant enough and is lifted by the support of the backing vocals and instrumentation arranged by her husband. Cliff sings multi-layered harmonies and these are obvious throughout the track.

Track Specification
Composed by J. D. Souther

Musicians

Andy Bown	bass, keyboards
Marietta Parfitt	vocals
Rick Parfitt	guitar
Cliff Richard	backing vocals
Unknown	keyboards
Unknown	drums, percussion

Recording Details

Producer	John Eden and Rick Parfitt
Engineered by	Unknown
Recording location	Unknown
Recording date	1981

♫ You're the One

B-side of **It's Only Me You've Left Behind**

Alan Tarney and Trevor Spencer had, by the time *You're the One* was recorded, become regular members of Cliff Richard's backing band, and they had written a number of fine tunes together for Cliff to record. *You're the One* was recorded at a session on its own two days after its eventual A-side, ***It's Only Me You've Left Behind***. With the force of Shadows friends and occasional guests on his television programme, Hank Marvin, Bruce Welch and John Farrar, at the production desk, both songs were worth a lot more than the commercial results dictated, which saw the single sink without getting into the charts. As a result of the poor sales, both songs were collector's items until they were dusted off and remastered for inclusion as bonus tracks for the reissue of the ***I'm Nearly Famous*** album in 2001.
There is a pseudo-steel guitar in the mix as well as the gentle backing vocals that Bruce Welch brought to Cliff's recordings during this period. The percussion in the middle eight is evocative of the Caribbean before the song returns to a typical rock treatment. Although ostensibly a love song, it has the dual advantage for Cliff of being a veiled religious track.

Track Specification
Composed by Alan Tarney and Trevor Spencer

Musicians

Terry Britten	guitar
Clem Cattini	drums, percussion
Tony Harding	backing vocals
Richard Hewson	arranger, conductor
John Perry	backing vocals
Cliff Richard	vocals
Tony Rivers	backing vocals
Alan Tarney	bass
Graham Todd	keyboards
Unknown	orchestra

Recording Details

Producer	Hank Marvin, Bruce Welch and John Farrar
Engineered by	Unknown
Recording location	Abbey Road Studio 2 and 3, St. John's Wood, London
Recording date	29th January 1975

♬ Your Eyes Tell on You

B-side of **It's All in the Game**

The only song to be recorded at its session, which was only the second of 1963, there were ten takes tried, the final one and its edit used for the mono and stereo recordings of *Your Eyes Tell on You*. Written by Shadows guitarist Hank Marvin, it was chosen as the B-side of Cliff Richard's twenty-second single, the cover of Tommy Edwards's ***It's All in the Game***, and was also on the track listing of the ***Cliff's Lucky Lips*** EP. Until the 2000 French release *Do You Want to Dance with Cliff Richard* and then the 2008 anthology ***...And They Said It Wouldn't Last! (My 50 Years in Music)***, the track was a scarce rarity much sought after by fans and musicologists alike.
The song is a typical Shadows-based song with a strong rhythm section that appears in the right channel, while the backing vocals appear in the left and Cliff's lead in the centre. The song is a tale of betrayal by a lover, which is at odds with the upbeat and thrumming foot-tapper of a song that results. The instrumental bridge features Hank providing a complex melody on the guitar. Towards the end, the vocal harmonies are spread across both channels.

Track Specification
Composed by Hank Marvin

Musicians		*Recording Details*	
Brian Bennett	drums, percussion	Producer	Norrie Paramor
Brian 'Licorice' Locking	bass	Engineered by	Malcolm Addey
Hank Marvin	backing vocals, guitar	Recording location	Abbey Road Studio 2, St. John's Wood, London
Cliff Richard	vocals	Recording date	10th April 1963
Bruce Welch	backing vocals, rhythm guitar		

♬ Your Heart's Not in Your Love

From the album **Tracks 'n' Grooves**

Cliff recorded the Neil Sedaka and Carole Bayer song at a dual session in September 1969, which also successfully completed two other tracks destined for the ***Tracks 'n' Grooves*** album, released the following year. The second of three songs to be completed at the first session, the song appeared on the second side of the original vinyl release. The omnipresent uncredited backing vocals tend to overtake the lyrical quality of Nick Ingman's arrangement but the ensemble piece is rescued by Cliff's able vocal line.

Track Specification
Composed by Neil Sedaka and Carole Bayer

Musicians		*Recording Details*	
Nick Ingman	arranger, conductor	Producer	Norrie Paramor
Nick Ingman Orchestra	orchestra	Engineered by	Peter Vince
Cliff Richard	vocals	Recording location	Abbey Road Studio 2, St. John's Wood, London
Unknown	backing vocals	Recording date	22nd September 1969

♬ Youth and Experience

From the film soundtrack album of **Wonderful Life**

The final song from the film ***Wonderful Life*** is sung as a duet between the principal film director (Walter Slezak) and Johnny (Cliff Richard). Johnny has been making a musical version of the director's film, with recordings of the action sequences filmed at the same time, while the songs were filmed separately and spliced in. As the group of friends watch their musical version, they are embarrassed, but at least he has proven his love for Jenny (Susan Hampshire) who is revealed as the director's daughter (thereby making him a future father-in-law). The older and younger men agree that their film is terrible although it had good parts: the director's film in the action sequences, while Johnny's had the songs as the best elements. They agree to combine the two films and shoot anther ending. As the film finishes (with Hank Marvin dabbing away another tear in the stalls), the director stands up to take the applause and invites Johnny to join him, entering into the song that expresses the success being down to youth and experience. There is audience participation with Chelsea pensioners and scouts and guides to ram home the generation divide. Towards the end, there is a brief reprise of ***All Kinds of People***, before the credits roll very quickly over the dying moments of the song and the applause.
The song was recorded in two sections, with the orchestra recorded first (divided into two parts with the second and fourth takes and edits used respectively) and then, six days later, the vocals and backing vocals, where the fifth and final take and edit was used. The eventual combination was used for both mono and stereo recordings but with different mixes for the separate audio channels. The film version, probably recorded in the first three months of 1964 although no information on musicians (other than Cliff and Walter Slezak), studio personnel or recording location is available. The film arrangement is slightly faster than the album version, and it's unclear who is taking the lead in the duet on the soundtrack other than an uncredited member of the Mike Sammes Singers. The film version has not been released in any other commercial format to date.
There are, it has to be said, far better songs in the soundtrack, and it is a shame that this particular track was chosen to close the show. The stand-out tracks are those composed by or involving the Shadows in some way and given that the film ends suddenly during this performance, it is somewhat lacking. There is a starring role for one of the session singers singing in duet with Cliff, who performs adroitly and adeptly, and rescues another humdrum song on the soundtrack.

Track Specification
Composed by Peter Myers and Ronald Cass

Musicians

Associated British Studio Orchestra	orchestra
Stanley Black	conductor
Mike Sammes Singers	vocals, backing vocals
Cliff Richard	vocals

Recording Details

Producer	Bob Barratt (orchestra) and Norrie Paramor (vocals)
Engineered by	Malcolm Addey and Alan Kane (orchestra) and Malcolm Addey and Richard Langham (vocals)
Recording location	Abbey Road Studio 2, St. John's Wood, London (orchestra and vocals)
Recording date	20th May 1964 (orchestra) and 26th May 1964 (vocals)

♫ You've Got a Friend

From the album **Wanted**

Written in 1971 by Carole King for her *Tapestry* album, it was made famous by James Taylor in the August, reaching number four in the UK charts and number one in the US Billboard Hot 100. As a result of this exposure, it won a Grammy for Song of the Year and another for Taylor as Best Pop Vocal Performance, Male. The Brand New Heavies recorded a version, featuring one-time Cliff Richard backing vocalist Siedah Garrett, in 1997 which reached number nine. VH1, the music video channel brought together a number of 'divas' to record the song: Céline Dion, Shania Twain, Gloria Estefan and Carole King performed the song for the *VH1 Divas Live* album and this was released as a single in Belgium, reaching number seventy-four. McFly then took their version to number one in 2005 and, naturally, it has become a popular song to cover as well as being successfully used in the television advertisements for the AA in 2006. Some of the artists to record a version include *EastEnders* actors Barbara Windsor and Steve McFadden, Johnny Mathis, Michael Jackson, Alanis Morrisette, Jimmy Cliff, Acker Bilk, Tom Jones, Aled Jones, Barry Manilow and the Housemartins among several others.
Cliff chose the song to feature on his first album since leaving EMI, ***Wanted***, which incorporated principally covers of well-known songs. From the start, Cliff supplies his own backing vocals and is then joined by the other vocalists before taking his lead vocal to perform the verse. The original is lugubrious and quite dark, while Cliff's cover is much more upbeat and optimistic. The best part of the performance remains the lush backing vocal arrangement in the choruses.

Track Specification
Composed by Carole King

Musicians

John Brant	additional programming
Anthony Clark	backing vocals
Cliff Richard	vocals, backing vocals
Alan Tarney	arranger, backing vocals, keyboards, programming

Recording Details

Producer	Alan Tarney
Engineered by	John Brant and Gerry Kitchingham
Recording location	Wilmer Studios, London
Recording date	January-April 2001

♫ You've Got Me Wondering

Misnomer for **You Got Me Wondering**

Some releases of the song ***You Got Me Wondering***, which appears on the ***Every Face Tells a Story*** album, incorrectly refer to it as *You've Got Me Wondering* although the album refers to it as the original *You Got Me Wondering*.

♫ You've Got to Give Me All Your Lovin'

From the album **I'm Nearly Famous**

Recorded and completed in one take only at the first session for the ***I'm Nearly Famous*** album, there was a follow-up session ten days later for a set of vocal overdubs to finalize *You've Got to Give Me All Your Lovin'*.
The foot-tapping nature of *You've Got to Give Me All Your Lovin'* is juxtaposed against the spiritual strength gleaned from the predecessor track, ***Such Is the Mystery***, but this serves to show the maturity of the material Cliff was now singing and therefore instrumental in his seventies renaissance. As with much on the album, the focus is firmly on the backing vocals with the instrumentation coming a close second, and this is proven in the middle eight where the vocalists are almost *a capella* save the percussion tapping away in syncopated form.

Track Specification
Composed by Ken Gold and Michael Denne

Musicians

Terry Britten	guitar
Clem Cattini	drums, percussion
Tony Harding	backing vocals
John Perry	backing vocals
Cliff Richard	vocals
Tony Rivers	backing vocals
Alan Tarney	bass
Graham Todd	keyboards

Recording Details

Producer	Bruce Welch
Engineered by	Tony Clark and John Barrett
Recording location	Abbey Road Studio 3, St. John's Wood, London
Recording date	1st and 11th December 1975

♫ You've Lost That Lovin' Feelin'

From the album **Japan Tour '74**

Credited to Barry Mann and Cynthia Weil on the ***Japan Tour '74*** sleeve, it is often co-credited to Phil Spector (correctly so as confirmed by Weil) as he was the producer of the most famous version of the song recorded by the Righteous Brothers (which also features Cher on backing vocals). In the UK, it was Cilla Black who had a hit with it at exactly the same time as the Righteous Brothers, although she hit number two while theirs reached number one. After the unlikely success of *If*, by *Kojak* actor Telly Savalas, he went on to talk his way through his unlikely version of *You've Lost That Lovin' Feelin'*, but it only reached number forty-seven in June 1975, while Daryl Hall and John Oates fared even worse when their version only reached number fifty-five in 1980. It has also been covered by a wide variety of artists, including Roberta Flack and Donny Hathaway, Long John Baldry, Elvis Presley, Sugar Minott, Pat Boone and Fontella Bass among many others.

Cliff Richard regularly performed songs in concert that were popular or resonated in some other was but that he had never (and would never) record in the studio. For the 1974 tour of Japan, this included *You've Lost That Lovin' Feelin'*. The CD reissue of the album saw a slightly edited version of the song - presumably due to space limitations on the disc - with part of the introductory guitar cut out.

Accompanied by syrupy strings and the backing rock band, Cliff carries off the vocals with assuredness and feeling, and it is only marred slightly by the over-emphasis on the guitar. Alan Tarney's bass line is interesting to listen too because of its complexity while Cliff Hall's piano is beautifully understated but adds perfectly to the mix.

Track Specification

Composed by Phil Spector, Barry Mann and Cynthia Weil

Musicians

Barrie Guard	arranger, conductor
Cliff Hall	piano
Brian Lewis	backing vocals, guitar
Kevin Peak	acoustic guitar
Cliff Richard	vocals
Shambles Symphonet	orchestra
Trevor Spencer	drums, percussion
Alan Tarney	backing vocals, bass
Bruce Welch	backing vocals, rhythm guitar

Recording Details

Producer	Toshiba EMI (no individual detailed)
Engineered by	Toshiba EMI (no individual detailed)
Recording location	Shinjuku Koseinenkin, Tokyo, Japan
Recording date	7th-8th October 1974

♫ You Will Never Know

From the album **The 31st of February Street**

Cliff Richard recorded *You Will Never Know* at one of the intense recording sessions for ***The 31st of February Street*** that took place in the middle of February 1974. The song was completed in eight takes.

A string quartet sound introduces the song which then becomes a staccato rhythmic piece that owes much to the Eurovision Song Contest approach to song accompaniment but it settles down in the chorus and then returns to the original pace set. A saxophone and over-exuberant backing choir kicks in the middle eight but then it settles back into its subdued pace.

Track Specification

Composed by Richard Kerr and George Osborne

Musicians

Bob Bertles	saxophone
Terry Britten	backing vocals, guitar
Barrie Guard	arranger, conductor
Cliff Hall	keyboards
Jean Hawker	backing vocals
David MacKay	backing vocals
Dave MacRae	keyboards
Anna Peacock	backing vocals
Kevin Peek	acoustic guitar
Cliff Richard	vocals
Trevor Spencer	drums, percussion
Alan Tarney	backing vocals, bass
Unknown	orchestra

Recording Details

Producer	David MacKay
Engineered by	Tony Clark and Mike Jarrett
Recording location	Abbey Road Studio 2, St. John's Wood, London
Recording date	12th and 14th February 1974

♫ Zärtliche Sekunden
German single

The German translation of Cliff Richard's forty-fourth UK single, ***Don't Forget to Catch Me***, was chosen for his first fully German album and as a single, backed with ***Wonderful World*** (the German version of the 1968 Eurovision Song Contest contender for the UK but maintaining the English title), on the Columbia label (catalogue number 1C 006-28032) in March 1969 but failed to chart in Germany. It was included two months later on *Hier Ist Cliff* and remained a rarity until it was included on the foreign language collation set ***On the Continent*** in 1997.
Cliff's recording of *Zärtliche Sekunden* (literally *Tender Seconds*, which is obviously a different meaning from the English version of the song) was original rather than opting for performing the vocals and overdubbing them on the English backing track – instead of the Shadows, *Zärtliche Sekunden* is an orchestral setting. The single was released, as was still the policy for singles by Columbia, in mono only but the subsequent release on the albums were in stereo.
As with the English version, Cliff sings the song gently, while orchestra plods along underneath him, including a thumping bass drum that threatens to overwhelm the recording. In addition there is a backing group that sings softly alongside him but there is no information regarding who they are.

Track Specification
Composed by Hank Marvin, Bruce Welch and Brian Bennett; German lyrics by Kurt Hertha

Musicians		*Recording Details*	
Norrie Paramor Orchestra	orchestra	Producer	Norrie Paramor
Norrie Paramor	arranger, director	Engineered by	Peter Vince
Cliff Richard	vocals	Recording location	Abbey Road Studio 2, St. John's Wood, London
Unknown	backing vocals	Recording date	28th November 1968

♫ Zip-A-Dee-Doo-Dah
From the album **...And They Said It Wouldn't Last! (My 50 Years in Music)**

One of the long-term favourites for many years from the Disney studios was the film *Song of the South*, which was a blend of cartoon and live action, much like *Mary Poppins*, and based on the Joel Chandler Harris's Uncle Remus stories. Originally released in 1946, the film was last shown in 1986 and now remains hidden from public view because studio executives fear a backlash against the racially insensitive stereotypes portrayed within the film. Regardless of the changes in points of view over the years and the rights and wrongs of its content, the film did produce a number of memorable tunes, one of which, ***Zip-a-Dee-Doo-Dah***, won an Academy Award for Best Song. Also used as the theme tune to the long-running television series *The Wonderful World of Disney*, it is sung by James Baskett at Uncle Remus as he is walking along the path talking to the birds that alight on him and it is an upbeat song of hope and optimism based on the simple premise that it is a wonderful day. It has also been covered by Bing Crosby, Miley Cyrus, Doris Day, Freddie and the Dreamers, Frank Sinatra, Louis Armstrong, the Hollies, Connie Francis, the Jackson 5, Bob B. Soxx and the Blue Jeans (who had their only UK chart hit when they reached number forty-five in February 1963) and Dionne Warwick.
At the last recording session of 1965 for Cliff Richard, he recorded four tracks taken from Disney films (two from *Song of the South* and two from *Mary Poppins*), of which *Zip-a-Dee-Doo-Dah* was one. Although they were successfully recorded, they were not immediately released – indeed, it is unclear what the original intention was for the songs, although there is strong evidence that it might have been an abandoned Disney-related EP project – until they were included over forty years later on the rarity collation of the celebratory ***...And They Said It Wouldn't Last! (My 50 Years in Music)***. The fourth and final take and edit were used for both mono and stereo recordings, although it has only been released in stereo.
Disney songs tend towards the saccharine and twee; however, *Zip-a-Dee-Doo-Dah* is a different case and, besides, Cliff's version is given the full swing arrangement treatment and Cliff is obviously enjoying the experience (as he commented at the time to press) and with the exuberance of his performance, it is perplexing as to why EMI didn't see fit to release the song earlier.

Track Specification
Composed by Allie Wrubel and Ray Gilbert

Musicians		*Recording Details*	
Cliff Richard	vocals	Producer	Norrie Paramor
Unknown	backing vocals	Engineered by	Malcolm Addey
Unknown	orchestra	Recording location	Abbey Road Studio 2, St. John's Wood, London
Unknown	arranger, conductor	Recording date	18th November 1965

♫ Zum Heiraten Bin Ich Kein Typ

From the album **Ich Träume Deine Träume**

Originally recorded in English for his ***Sincerely Cliff Richard*** album as the prophetic *I'm Not Getting Married*, the German translated version, *Zum Heiraten Bin Ich Kein Typ* was recorded by Cliff Richard for his second German language album, *Ich Träume Deine Träume*, which was released in 1971. *Zum Heiraten Bin Ich Kein Typ* – translated as *I'm Not the Type to Get Married* – was recorded in the last of a marathon four sessions over two days in November 1970, which was made easier by having the orchestral backing tracks recorded prior to the event. The song was eventually remastered and reissued on the anthology of Cliff's foreign language recordings, ***On the Continent***, in 1997.
The foot-tapping song is curiously upbeat for the meaning of the song, but it is one of the best tracks on the album. There is some spirited whistling that may be provided by the uncredited backing vocalists, while Cliff appears to be enjoying the performance in a non-native tongue.

Track Specification

Composed by Albert Hammond and Mike Hazelwood; German lyrics by Hans Bradtke

Musicians		*Recording Details*	
Norrie Paramor Orchestra	orchestra	Producer	Norrie Paramor (backing track and vocals)
Norrie Paramor	arranger, conductor	Engineered by	Phil McDonald (backing track and vocals)
Cliff Richard	vocals	Recording location	Cologne, Germany (backing track) and Abbey Road Studio 2, St. John's Wood, London (vocals)
Unknown	backing vocals		
Unknown	whistling	Recording date	November 1970 (backing track) and 25th November 1970 (vocals)

♫ Zuviel Allein

German single

Using the instrumental track that was recorded for the English version (***I'm the Lonely One***), *Zuviel Allein* had two more overdubs: first, Cliff Richard's lead vocals with the German lyrics and then, next, a further overdub with the backing vocals in Germany with the Botho Lucas Quartet. *Zuviel Allein* (literally translated to *Too Much Alone*, and keeping the same tenor of the original title and lyrics) was released as single, backed with ***Sag 'No' zu Ihm*** (itself a translation of ***Don't Talk to Him***), on the Columbia label (catalogue number C-22707) in April 1964, but it made no impression on the German singles charts. The various takes and edits of the original track and later overdubs used the combined edit for the mono and stereo recordings but with different mixes for the audio channels, although it was originally released in mono only. The single was a considerable rarity for many years until the stereo version was incorporated in on the 1997 CD compilation album ***On the Continent***, which featured all of Cliff's foreign language recordings.
In many respects, other than the German lyrics, *Zuviel Allein* is a reproduction of the English original – this is hardly surprising given is provenance. What doesn't work that well is the German backing vocals, which are too musical theatre and it misses the close harmonisation that Cliff and the Shadows provide on their recordings.

Track Specification

Composed by Gordon Mills; German lyrics by Kurt Hertha

Musicians		*Recording Details*	
Brian Bennett	drums, percussion	Producer	Norrie Paramor
Botho Lucas Quartet	backing vocals	Engineered by	Malcolm Addey
Hank Marvin	guitar	Recording location	Abbey Road Studio 2, St. John's Wood, London (Shadows track and lead vocals) and Germany (backing vocals)
Cliff Richard	vocals		
John Rostill	bass		
Unknown	piano	Recording date	23rd November 1963 (Shadows track), 20th March 1964 (lead vocals) and March 1964 (backing vocals)
Bruce Welch	rhythm guitar		

THE

CLIFF RICHARD

RECORDING CATALOGUE

1958-2010

—

Appendices

THE CLIFF RICHARD RECORDING CATALOGUE

Appendix A: The Stage Shows

♬ Aladdin and His Wonderful Lamp

1st UK stage show

The story of *Aladdin* is one of the most familiar from *The Arabian Nights*, alongside *Ali Baba and the Forty Thieves*, although it is not an integral part of that story. However, the story of the boy Aladdin, who lives in the mountains of China with his widowed mother, and who is requested by an evil sorcerer to locate an oil lamp in a cave brimming full of treasures, is one that endures particularly with children, thereby making it a hugely suitable subject for a pantomime, which is primarily targeted at youngsters as an audience. Of course, the lamp holds a genie who can grant wishes for freeing him when the lamp is rubbed and this action results in Aladdin's fortunes changing where he becomes rich and he s finally able to marry a beautiful Arabian princess.

The Shadows wrote the music for the 1964-1965 London Palladium performance of the pantomime, for which a cast album was recorded (the cover of which was one of only three in Cliff Richard's career not to bear some kind of likeness of him) with Cliff in the title role of Aladdin.

♬ Cinderella

2nd UK stage show

After the success of ***Aladdin and His Wonderful Lamp*** at the London Palladium, Cliff Richard and the Shadows repeated the success in the 1965-1966 winter season with *Cinderella*. Like its predecessor, it is another highly enduring story originally written by Charles Perrault (as *Cendrillon, ou la Petite Pantoufle de Vair*) updated from the traditional fairy story. It tells of a beautiful girl, Cinderella, who is banished to the scullery and kitchen to slave away for her stepmother and stepsisters, while they swan around with the cream of society attempting to ingratiate themselves in the process. The Prince decides to throw a ball and invites all the eligible ladies in the kingdom but this seems to exclude Cinderella as she has no finery with which to dress up. Then, after an appearance by her fairy godmother, her rags are turned into a beautiful ball-gown, mice into footmen, pumpkin into a stagecoach and so on but she is given strict instructions to return by midnight when everything will return to its original state. She dances with the Prince who is enchanted with her but she runs off as the clock starts striking midnight, leaving a glass slipper behind. The Prince then embarks on a journey throughout the kingdom to find the foot of the girl that can fit into the slipper. Eventually arriving at the stepmother's house, Cinderella's stepsisters try to force the slipper on but fail and then gasp in surprise when the Prince notices Cinderella and that the shoe fits. They marry and live happily ever after.

This plot is wrong since the slipper would have reverted to its original state; however, ignoring that, there is a failure of translation too. Originally thought to be a 'glass slipper' (pantoufle de verre), it is in fact a slipper made from squirrel fir (pantoufle de vair).

The Shadows wrote all of the songs for the show, as they had with *Aladdin*, and Cliff played the role of Buttons. One single was released from the cast soundtrack album, ***In the Country***.

♬ Heathcliff

4th UK stage show

Ever since he read the book of *Wuthering Heights* by Emily Brontë at school, Cliff Richard was keen to see a stage version of the story covering the character of Heathcliff from his point of view. While the book focuses on the central character of Cathy, Cliff wanted to explore what made Heathcliff the man he was.

Taken in by the Earnshaws as a ragamuffin living on the streets of north-west England, Cathy and Heathcliff would become firm friends and stroll on their beloved moors. However, as they enter adulthood, Cathy is swayed by the society in which the Lintons move and becomes betrothed to Edgar. Heathcliff, riven with jealousy goes off on his travels determined to become as rich and show her what she is missing. In so doing, he also creates a sham marriage to Cathy's sister-in-law Isabella, treating her cruelly and beating her. Later, he finds Cathy on the moors, dying in childbirth.

With lyrics written by Sir Tim Rice and music by John Farrar, the songs were trialled in late December 1995. At Earl's Court in London, there were two public previews before the premiere at the National Indoor Arena in Birmingham on 16th October 1996. Although critics were largely unkind about the show, Cliff managed to get into the record books after the fastest sales of tickets in history at the time. A studio album of ten songs was produced, featuring the vocal talents of Olivia Newton-John, while Helen Hobson took the role for a live album of the complete song list and the associated video and DVD.

♫ Time – The Musical

3rd UK stage show

In the sixties, Dave Clark was one of the most successful artists in popular music, with songs such as *Glad All Over* and *Bits and Pieces*, drumming with his band the Dave Clark Five. In the early eighties, he took the seventies musical, *The Time Lord* (presumably based at least a little on the story of *Doctor Who*), which had been written by Jeff Daniels and David Soames and updated it into *Time – The Musical*.

Starting with a rock musician, Chris Wilder, performing with his backing singers in concert, he is transported to the Andromeda Galaxy to the High Court of the Universe to represent Earth. Essentially, because of the strides in man's space exploration, the High Court wants to assess the suitability of humankind to spread the word of peace on their eventual interstellar travels. This means Wilder and his band members must defend the Earth and what atrocities humans have perpetrated. In many ways, it can also be seen as an allegory for Judgment Day in the Christian religion.

Performed at the Dominion Theatre for two years from 1986, the special effects and set design called for the theatre to be gutted so that the steel frame could be installed. There was also a large suspended head (wrongly called a hologram) of Laurence Olivier in his role of Akash the narrator. Directed by Larry Fuller, the premiere was on 9th April 1986 with Cliff Richard in the role of Wilder and, later on in the run, Cliff was replaced by David Cassidy. An album was released alongside the musical, although technically it wasn't a cast recording since it also included the likes of Freddie Mercury, Julian Lennon and Dusty Springfield. Cliff released three singles from the project: ***Born to Rock 'n' Roll, It's in Every One of Us*** and ***She's So Beautiful***, the latter being a collaboration with Stevie Wonder.

THE CLIFF RICHARD RECORDING CATALOGUE

Appendix B: The Films

♫ Expresso Bongo

2nd film appearance

After the success of Cliff Richard's almost cameo appearance in ***Serious Charge***, a lighter topic (in some respects) was chosen for a starring vehicle featuring Cliff in joint top billing with Laurence Harvey. Based on a musical play of the same name that was performed in 1958 with a cast recording album issued later that year, *Expresso Bongo* starred Paul Scofield and contained original songs by Monty Norman, David Heneker and Julian More. In the play, Scofield played a music promoter, Johnny, who cannily observes the teenage frenzy whipped up by the performances on the bongo drums played by the young Herbert Rudge. He is renamed Bongo Herbert for obvious reasons and a new contract gives the promoter fifty percent of whatever he makes. Getting the stardom he desires, Herbert attracts the sleazy types of the music industry who want to exploit his unlikely popularity. Johnny finds himself out of his depth and this is not helped by the Herbert's manipulation of the situation.

Only one of the play's songs made it into the film version the following year, ***The Shrine on the Second Floor***, which was intended to be a cynical attempt at producing a sickeningly sentimental song about Herbert's mother and fleecing the easily foold audience. The other songs added to the film were ***A Voice in the Wilderness*** and ***Love***, which were written specifically for the updated screenplay, while the Shadows were represented also by the instrumental *Bongo Blues*. Following a similar line to the theatrical plot, Johnny Jackson (Harvey) is a hustler looking to exploit new entertainment talent and he discovers Bert Rudge (Cliff) in a coffee shop and organizes his rise to stardom. The name change to Bongo Herbert remains and he manages to secure a record deal. The only difference is that the lack of talent expressed by Herbert in the play has been upgraded to having a great talent because there were fears that this might impact Cliff's fan base if he were to play someone who is supposed to be an untalented musician.

A Voice in the Wilderness was released as a single as a project, while the public demand for the undeniably cynical but pretty *The Shrine on the Second Floor* pushed the associated EP from the project into the singles charts - remaining the only one of Cliff's EPs to have that notoriety. Released in black and white only, *Expresso Bongo* was written by Wolf Mankowitz with a credit to the playwright Julian More and directed by Val Guest. Distributed by British Lion Films, it was released in 1959 in the UK to a limited number of cinemas. The incidental music score was by Robert Farnon, while the new songs were written by Norrie Paramor, Bunny Lewis and Lionel Bart, in addition to the credts for the original writers of *The Shrine on the Second Floor*. All three songs plus the Shadows instrumental appeared on the associated EP, while the film has since been released on video and subsequently on DVD.

♫ Finders Keepers

6th film appearance

Cliff Richard's sixth film was a radical change from its immediate predecessors. After the success of the first two of a triumvirate of films, ***The Young Ones*** and ***Summer Holiday***, the third, ***Wonderful Life*** - all three written by Peter Myers and Ronald Cass - was somewhat of a disappointment. It was short for a feature film and felt disconnected and a rehash of *The Young Ones* plot. For *Finders Keepers*, screenwriter Michael Pertwee was brought in while the Shadows wrote all of the tunes. In addition, the Shadows had central roles, which was something that had only just started to be realized in *Wonderful Life*. Finally, all of the musicians were playing themselves.

Essentially, the plot is this: Cliff and the Shadows are booked to appear in concert in a pokey Spanish town but arrive to find it empty (prompting the glorious ***Time Drags By*** in the hotel foyer). They find that the villagers have all left because a bomb has been inadvertently dropped in the area by the local military and they are afraid it will go off. The story then follows Cliff and the Shadows as they endeavour to find it and restore peace to the area and therefore allow them to carry out their booking.

Only *Time Drags By* was issued as a UK single from the film - there were no instrumentals issued separately by the Shadows, although the quality of the music is a significant improvement on the unfortunately tired format by Myers and Cass in the previous films. The soundtrack album was short, however, on material, so three additional tracks were released on it from Cliff's earlier sessions. In the mean time, and unusually, there were no EPs released to accompany the film. Directed by Sidney Hayers, the plot and action are tightly and effectively controlled throughout and *Finders Keepers* was released nationally on 8th December 1966 and the following year in the US. But, in spite of its many qualities, this style of musical was falling out of favour with the cinema-going public and it would take another seven years before Cliff would try something similar in ***Take Me High***. The film has been issued on VHS only but it is now a collector's item; even though the *Daily Mail* ran an offer for 'all' of Cliff's films on DVD, *Finders Keepers* was not included in that list.

♫ His Land

9th film appearance

Cliff Richard's penultimate film was another departure after the gritty drama of ***Two a Penny***. Although it was billed as 'a musical journey into the soul of a nation', the film was much less a film as was generally expected from Cliff with a dramatic message, than more a documentary about the state of Israel, its history, how it was coping on the international stage contemporaneously and what it could look forward to in the future. Featuring American Cliff Barrows, the pair walks through the Holy Lands discussing tracts from the Bible, some of which appears very heavily scripted, interspersed with Cliff singing a number of very good songs, sometimes with Barrows, often on his own – the title track is a surprising gem that is much forgotten from Cliff's oeuvre. Released in 1970, the film was only shown in limited outlets and was issued on both VHS video and DVD formats in 2004.

♫ Serious Charge

1st film appearance

The first film to feature Cliff Richard, *Serious Charge* is a very dark film. Cliff plays Curley Thompson, whose brother (played by Andrew Ray) has been sleeping with a girl, who is now pregnant – in those days such a problem would have made the girl and her family social pariahs and so would have been seen as a profound predicament – and who refuses to have anything to do with it. In the ensuing chase, the girl runs in front of a vehicle and is killed. The new vicar, the Reverend Howard Phillips (Anthony Quayle), hears of the accident and blames the would-be father in part for the death. As revenge, the youth accuses the vicar of molesting him, which is given credence by the malice of a local woman whose advances were spurned. The story then becomes one of this serious but refuted charge levelled at the vicar.
Cliff appears in a part that has little in the way of speaking, and performs thee songs in the coffee bar, where the teenagers are all hanging out: an upbeat version of ***Living Doll*** (as opposed to the countrified and more recognizable version that was released as the single from the project), ***No Turning Back*** and ***Mad About You***. Backed by Hank Marvin, Bruce Welch and the others, they were still working under the name of the Drifters (they would change it later in 1959 to avoid confusion with the American vocal group, once *Living Doll* became Cliff's first big hit in the US) and they also performed an instrumental, *Chinchilla*. All four tracks appeared on the associated EP, with the now familiar arrangement of *Living Doll* developed by Bruce Welch. At the time, Norrie Paramor, Cliff, music director and producer, fought back against the film's producers by releasing ***Livin' Lovin' Doll*** in an attempt to confuse things, although he irony was that *Living Doll* shot to the top of the charts making it Cliff's first number one.
The film was based on a stage play that had been written by Philip King, with the screenplay written by Mickey Delamar and Guy Elmes. Directed by Terence Young (who would go on to significant success with the early films in the Bond series), the film was given parochial release in the UK in black and white only in the middle of 1959, distributed by Eros Films Limited. The music score was written by Leighton Lewis, while the featured songs (which were only played in small excerpts) were written by Lionel Bart. The film has been released on video as well as subsequently being remastered for DVD release.

♫ Summer Holiday

4th film appearance

Along with ***The Young Ones***, *Summer Holiday* is probably the best-known of Cliff Richard's films, helped by the ubiquitous powerhouse performance by the London Transport AEC Regent RT bus. The plot is simple: a group of London Transport bus mechanics, led by Don (Cliff), spend time converting a London bus into a kind of caravan with sleeping, showering and living quarters spread out on the two decks. The idea is to take the bus to Athens and back again. On the way, they pick up an American stowaway, Barbara (played by Laurie Peters initially dressed as a boy), and a girl trio who are driven off the road in France by the bus. The plot twists on the girl's mother wanting to get Barbara's inheritance and with her friend and agent, they eventually get Don and his friends arrested for kidnap, after Barbara reveals her love for Don and that, of course, she is a girl. Don states that he loves her at the end of the film and the mother instantly warms to him once it is also announced that London Transport are interested in investing in a company to take converted London Buses on continental holidays.
What makes the film stand out, too, is the exotic (for the times) locations and the spirited performances from the cast, which included Melvyn Hayes (who also appeared in *The Young Ones*) and Una Stubbs, a firm fixture from that point on in many of Cliff's film and television projects. Once again, most of the songs were provided by Peter Myers and Ron Cass, who were also responsible for the screenplay. Other songs were composed by the Shadows, including the title song and the instrumentals *Les Girls, Round and Round* and *Foot Tapper*. Cliff himself co-wrote ***Bachelor Boy*** and ***Big News***, both of which were last minute additions, with the latter being written in the last days of filming and the former being an afterthought once it was realized that the film was a song or two short. Cliff and Bruce Welch wrote the song and the available actors made their way to Elstree Studios to film the segment that, in retrospect, is clearly a studio-based piece of action immersed into the film. The soundtrack was issued alongside the release of the film, while *Foot Tapper, Summer Holiday, Bachelor Boy,* ***Dancing Shoes*** and ***The Next Time*** were all released as singles. In addition, two EPs were issued: ***Hits from Summer Holiday*** and ***More Hits from Summer Holiday***. In the mid-nineties, Darren Day took a touring show on

the road featuring several songs from Cliff's back catalogue weaved into the narrative, and Cliff contributed to the associated album by supplying backing vocals.
Distributed by Associated British Studios, *Summer Holiday* was directed by Peter Yates in his début and filmed on location in Europe and at the Elstree Studios based in Hertfordshire (where he BBC's *EastEnders* continuing serial is now filmed). Additional incidental music was composed and conducted by Stanley Black (who also conducted the orchestra on a number of the soundtrack songs). *Summer Holiday* was premiered at the Warner Theatre in London's Leicester Square on 11th January 1963 and given a full national release on 18th February 1963. The film has since been released on video and subsequently DVD, where it has also been issued in a boxed set collection along with *The Young Ones* and ***Wonderful Life***.

♫ Take Me High

***10th** film appearance*

When Cliff Richard filmed *Take Me High*, it wasn't known at the time that it was going to be his last. During the early seventies, Cliff was heavily involved in his television programmes for the BBC, which also included short story films such as *The Case*. Once he had finished this, the pop star film vehicle had pretty much petered out as a genre and Cliff would go back to the theatre instead.
The story, written by Christopher Penfold, follows Tim Matthews (Cliff) as a merchant banker looking to head up an office in New York for the company, beating off competition from Hugo Flaxman (Anthony Andrews). However, instead he is despatched to Birmingham and there meets up with Sarah (Deborah Watling) after he buys a longboat as a home from her parents. She has already met both Matthews and Flaxman after she has tried to extend the loan for her overly smart French restaurant. On a trip on the boat, Matthews and Sarah stop for a burger but after one bite, they throw it in the canal because it was disgusting and this gives them the idea to create a restaurant in the centre of Birmingham dishing out good fast food. Some of the action is preposterous but it is good to see Cliff back on form as the slightly bewildered leading man trying to do right for the girl and creating the business that makes him feel better about himself than the banking sector ever did and also answers the quandary regarding what he is doing wth his life.
The songs are all written by Tony Cole and it is the first film that does not feature Norrie Paramor as the nominal producer, since he had retired the year before. Instead, that fell to David Mackay. Only one single was released from the project and that was the title track, which reached number twenty-seven in the British charts. The performances are strong and the soundtrack memorable of the film directed by David Askley and released in 1973. *Take Me High* was issued on VHS video in 1988 but, to date, has never found a commercial release on DVD, although it was issued as part of a *Daily Mail* promotional offer running from 18th September 2010 for a week, where all the films except *Finders Keepers* and *His Land* were released on a selection of DVD discs.

♫ Thunderbirds Are Go!

***7th** film appearance*

For *Thunderbirds Are Go!*, Cliff Richard and the Shadows appeared as puppets, performing one song (written by the Shadows), ***Shooting Star***. The year is 2065, and the Zero-X spacecraft is scheduled for take -off for the first manned mission to Mars. The Hood, who is the resident criminal and nemesis throughout the television series, has designs on the ship and, after a spot of industrial espionage, he causes a power shortage after tripping on cables and the craft crashes into the sea. International Rescue and the Tracy family are called in to help and this creates the need to factor in their English agent, Lady Penelope. Alan Tracy, the pilot of Thunderbird 3, feels unappreciated after his brothers Scott and Virgil accompany Penelope to the Swinging Star night club and he has a dream where he is escorting her to a club in the stars where Cliff Richard Jr. (although the timeline on this doesn't really work given the relative ages) and the Shadows perform for them on a makeshift moon and huge guitar.
Written by the originators of the franchise, Gerry and Sylvia Anderson, the film was directed by David Lane and was an extraordinary feat to complete a feature length film using puppets as the principal characters. Made by Anderson's Century 21 Cinema and distributed by United Artists and the Rank Organisation, it premiered on 12th December 1966 (the same week as ***Finders Keepers***). Popular with fans, a soundtrack album was released with incidental music by Barry Gray and others, while Cliff and the Shadows released the last EP connected to a film at the same time as the premiere (although it failed to chart). The track listing incorporated *Shooting Star* as well as three instrumentals played by the Shadows: *Lady Penelope*, the *Thunderbirds Theme* and the *Zero X Theme*. Released on video in the eighties, the film has yet to be issued on DVD. The *Daily Mail* ran a promotional offer in September 2010 but *Thunderbirds Are Go!* was not included.

♫ Two a Penny

8th film appearance

After the frivolous nature of the films, ***The Young Ones***, ***Summer Holiday***, ***Wonderful Life*** and ***Finders Keepers***, Cliff Richard's next film was a complete surprise in the direction that it took. First of all, it was not a comedy; second, it wasn't a romance; and, third and most surprising, it wasn't a musical. Although Cliff played Jamie Hopkins who was an artist and a frustrated pop star, the focus of the film's narrative was on the gritty drama. He lives with his mother (played by Dora Bryan), of whom he takes regular advantage. She has a job as a receptionist with a doctor who is experimenting with psychedelic drugs. Needing money quickly to prove his London gangster credentials, Hopkins plots a raid on the doctor's drugs and framing the man to whom he owes money (played by Geoffrey Bayldon). Meanwhile, his girlfriend (Ann Holloway) is converted to Christianity and attends one of the London Crusades held by Billy Graham at Earl's Court in London. She tries to teach her boyfriend that what he is doing is wrong but he refuses to listen. He is caught stealing the drugs and slowly comes to terms with his girlfriend's epiphany. Although he inveigles himself on to the stage at the Crusade, Hopkins is questioning what God and faith is all about but never quite converts, ending the film singing the song ***Questions***. It's a clever technique because the viewer is left to think about the message themselves.

Cliff's performance is very strong in this film even though he looks too clean-cut and his sober public persona is at odds with what is on the screen but, nevertheless, he carries the film well and even writes three of the four songs featured in the film.

It was written by Stella Linden and directed by James F. Collier while being financed in part by the Billy Graham Organisation. Distributed by World Wide Pictures, the film was released in the autumn of 1967, although it didn't have the wide appeal of the previous films. *Two a Penny* was issued on VHS video and DVD for the first time in 2002.

♫ Wonderful to Be Young

American film title

In 1961, Cliff's first colour film and the first to be publicized across the Atlantic, ***The Young Ones***, was retitled to *Wonderful to Be Young* at the insistence of the American distributors. As a result, a new title song had to be written and recorded and Burt Bacharach and Hal David were given the commission. This song appeared on the ***A Forever Kind of Love*** EP in September 1964, but was issued as a single in the American territory only.

♫ Wonderful Life

5th film appearance

Filmed in the Canaries as the primary location, *Wonderful Life* is another feel-good film that follows on from ***The Young Ones*** and ***Summer Holiday*** in its style. However, it is not as successful, because of two reasons: the script is largely a rehash of *The Young Ones* albeit set on a film set rather than in a theatre and Susan Hampshire doesn't evoke the chemistry that was prevalent in the earlier films between Cliff Richard and his leading ladies, despite his best efforts. The film feels rushed and, while there are some good sections, they don't seem to fit together well as a whole. Cliff plays Johnny, a steward on a cruise ship, and, with his friends (including Richard O'Sullivan and Melvyn Hayes again as well as the Shadows pretending to play orchestral instruments throughout the film while dressed in morning dress), enjoy listening to the latest music. However the Heath Robinson construction of plugs and sockets forces a power failure and the ship has a small accident, forcing the captain to set them all adrift in a dinghy. They cast up on the Canaries and soon Johnny is trying to save a girl in a yashmack (Hampshire) on a runaway camel before realizing it is part of the action in a film. As a result, and given the group has no money, Johnny is offered the job of stuntman on the film by the director (Walter Slezak). The director is giving the girl a very hard time by wanting her to wear the yashmack and so on and Johnny and his friends come up with an idea to help her self-esteem: to make another film with her in the starring role. Johnny starts falling in love with her and, of course, once it is revealed that he has been clandestine about the project, she becomes angry and vouches never to see him again. Meanwhile, it is also revealed that she is the director's daughter. The dénouement comes when the competing films are shown together and neither is particularly good. After burying the hatchet, Johnny and the director decide to splice the best bits together creating a film that is a critical triumph.

Written once again by Peter Myers and Ronald Cass, who also composed a lot of the songs, the film was directed by Sidney J. Furie, who had also directed *The Young Ones*. This time the Shadows wrote more of the tunes including the title track, the instrumentals *Walkin'* and *Theme for Young Lovers*, ***A Matter of Moments*** (released as a single in some countries) and ***On the Beach***, which was the only UK single by Cliff to be issued from the project (the Shadows had a hit with *Theme for Young Lovers*, too). The soundtrack album was pretty much released in its entirety on three EPs: ***Wonderful Life No. 1***, ***Wonderful Life No. 2*** and ***Hits from Wonderful Life***. The film was distributed by the Associated British Studios in 1964 but was not popular with cinema-goers in comparison with the two earlier films. It has subsequently been released on both video and DVD, with a boxed set DVD version being released with the other two films. The next film, ***Finders Keepers***, was a considerable improvement but fared even less well at the cinema.

♫ Young Ones, The

3rd film appearance

In the first colour release and the film that set the tone for the next three Cliff Richard films, *The Young Ones* is firmly a starring vehicle for Cliff. The premise of the film is simple, Nicky Black (Cliff) and his friends are frequenters of a youth club in London, which is coming up for a lease renewal, although the benefactor who provided the premises wants to sell it. Hamilton Black (Robert Morley) is a property magnate who uses all his wiles to try to purchase the prime piece of land in order to build major complexes including a skyscraper. What isn't known to Nicky's friends is that Black is his father. The group decides to put on a show in a run-down theatre to garner funds, while Black Senior attempts to scupper them by buying the theatre from them. In the end, the rougher element of the youth club kidnaps Hamilton Black and threatens him, at which point Nicky reveals who he is and goes to his aid. The result is that his father relents and the show goes on. Much of the action is about outwitting the architect and preparing for the show in the dusty London theatre.

With two songs from Hank Marvin and Bruce Welch, ***We Say Yeah*** and ***Got a Funny Feeling***, as well as an instrumental by Norrie Paramor for the Shadows to perform, *Peace Pipe*, the music was predominantly provided by the partnership of Peter Myers and Ronald Cass, who also wrote the screenplay. The title song was written by Sid Tepper and Roy C. Bennett, who would go on to write a number of other songs for Cliff, including the pivotal single from the soundtrack, ***When the Girl in Your Arms (Is the Girl in Your Heart)***. However, when the film was released in the US, it was retitled ***Wonderful to Be Young*** with a commissioned title song by Burt Bacharach and Hal David, which Cliff recorded and released as a single in the US only. As well as the soundtrack album, Cliff also issued the ***Hits from The Young Ones*** EP.

Originally, the Shadows were supposed to play a more significant set of roles in the film, with a bespectacled solicitor's clerk set for Hank Marvin but taken by Richard O'Sullivan and a blond-haired youth club member (designated for Jet Harris but taken by Melvyn Hayes, who had to bleach his hair for the role); instead they played the incidental musicians who appear throughout and finally backing Cliff at the show that the youngsters put on.

Distributed by the Associated British Studios, *The Young Ones* as directed by Sidney J. Furie with incidental music by Stanley Black (who also conducted the orchestra for the soundtrack) and was released on 19th December 1961. Perhaps Cliff's most famous film other than ***Summer Holiday***, *The Young Ones* was the biggest grossing British film of the year and Cliff topped polls of favourite actors as a consequence. The film has since been issued on both video and DVD, with a collection of *The Young Ones*, *Summer Holiday* and ***The Young Ones*** being collated and issued in a DVD boxed set collection.

The film also gave its title to an anarchic situation comedy (of sorts) that ran on the BBC from 1982, based on one of the main characters, played by Rik Mayall, professing a love for Cliff and his music (intended to be horrendously uncool but paradoxically making it cool in the process). The final scene of the programme sees the comic group driving a London Transport bus into a large poster billboard of Cliff and disappearing over a cliff (an homage to the following film, *Summer Holiday*). The group later reunited to join Cliff on the Comic Relief single version of ***Living Doll***.

Appendix C: The Extended Players (EPs)

♫ The EP – A Brief History

Although extended play (or EP) releases had been in circulation since the 1920s, it was in the fifties and sixties that they came into their own with the huge surge in the purchase of popular music formats. Like singles, they were played at 45 revolutions per minute and, by lowering the cutting levels and in certain instances the sound quality, it was possible to fit seven and a half minutes of music on each side, thereby allowing at least four songs of standard length to become an EP.

In part, the move was designed to be competition for the long-player but also made commercial sense since, while many teenagers with the purchasing power to buy the records owned record-players, usually they were only capable of playing seven-inch discs (such as the ubiquitous Dansette machine). Therefore, to issue albums of material on three or four EPs made the exercise commercially viable since these same teenagers would buy the segmented versions of the albums. Later in the sixties, the cost and size of record players capable of playing the twelve-inch records as well as the singles in addition to the reduction in the cost of production of albums had made both highly affordable to a group of people who had more disposable income than their forebears.

As a consequence, EPs and the associated chart died out, although occasionally new collections of material are referred to as EPs, although the space capacity and length of musical performance afforded by the CD format makes the definition almost meaningless. The Official Chart Company defined an EP for vinyl as being twenty-five minutes of musical material or four tracks of different songs (including different versions), while the CD definition has been extended to thirty-six minutes (coincidentally, roughly around the target for most album lengths in the sixties).

Cliff Richard was at the forefront of EP generation and the number of his EPs far outweighs that of many of his contemporaries. This section is intended to give an insight into the activity of the medium and how Cliff affected the charts as a consequence.

♫ 40 Golden Greats

Promotional EP

Issued on the EMI label in October 1977 as a double EP (catalogue numbers PSR 414 and PSR 415), the two promotional discs featured small excerpts from the songs from the track listing of the double LP ***40 Golden Greats*** spread across the four sides of the EP to mirror the LP release.

Track Listing

Move It
Living Doll
Travellin' Light
Fall in Love with You
Please Don't Tease
Nine Times out of Ten
Theme for a Dream
Gee Whiz It's You
When the Girl in Your Arms (Is the Girl in Your Heart)
A Girl Like You
The Young Ones
Do You Wanna Dance?
I'm Looking out the Window
It'll Be Me
Bachelor Boy
The Next Tim
Summer Holiday
Lucky Lips
It's All in the Game
Don't Talk to Him
Constantly
On the Beach
I Could Easily Fall (in Love with You)
The Minute You're Gone
Wind Me Up (Let Me Go)
Visions
Blue Turn to Grey
In the Country
The Day I Met Marie
All My Love
Congratulation
Throw Down a Line
Goodbye Sam, Hello Samantha
Sing a Song of Freedom
Power to All Our Friends
(You Keep Me) Hangin' On
Miss You Nights
Devil Woman
I Can't Ask for Anything More Than You
My Kinda Life

♫ Angel

37th UK EP

Angel took its title from the first track on the EP, which was also the first song on the ***Cliff Richard*** album released a few months earlier. The *Angel* EP featured two singles from the Nashville sessions, ***On My Word*** and ***The Minute You're Gone***, as well as the first two tracks from the album, making it a strange mix of songs for the title's concept, although it was most likely exploiting that song's popularity. The title song, ***Angel***, had been released overseas and had success over there, while it had generated demand in the domestic market too. Issued on the Columbia label, the EP was released in mono format only (catalogue number SEG 8444) in September 1965, but itself failed to chart.

Track Listing

Angel
I Only Came to Say Goodbye
On My Word
The Minute You're Gone

♫ Carol Singers

45th UK EP

Cliff Richard's penultimate vinyl EP was an oddity in a number of respects. First it was performed entirely without instruments; second, it was the first time he had recorded and issued Christmas music; and, third, the *a capella* group performing with him were music teachers from a Christian group calling themselves the Mastersingers rather than being professional performers. Nevertheless, the content of the EP is mesmerically beautiful in its arrangement, managed by one of the group's members, Geoffrey Keating. In spite of the rarity of the material that made up the five tracks that were released on the EP of the eight that had been recorded, the EP was not a commercial success and failed to chart, confirming that the format was a dying breed. Issued on the Columbia label, *Carol Singers* was released in mono only (catalogue number SEG 8533) in November 1967. The tracks have ubsequently been reissued on the ***Carols*** LP in 1988 and on the celebratory ***...And They Said It Wouldn't Last! (My 50 Years in Music)***.

Track Listing

God Rest Ye Merry Gentlemen
In the Bleak Midwinter
Unto Us a Boy Is Born
While Shepherds Watched
O Little Town of Bethlehem

♫ Cinderella

44th UK EP

The second of Cliff's two pantomimes at the London Palladium was the familiar rags-to-riches fairytale story of ***Cinderella***. The tie-in EP to the cast soundtrack album was the simply titled *Cinderella* EP, which incorporated four tracks randomly chosen from the track listing. By far the best of the four is ***Hey Doctor Man*** but, in spite of this, the EP format was dying and it failed to chart. *Cinderella* was issued on the Columbia label (catalogue number SEG 8527) in May 1967 and in mono only.

Track Listing

Come Sunday
Peace and Quiet
She Needs Him More Than Me
Hey Doctor Man

♫ Cliff No. 1

2nd UK EP

Cliff Richard's second EP was the first to be associated with an album release, which was simply entitled ***Cliff*** in spite of the fact that the Drifters (still four or five months off changing their name to the Shadows) contributed three tracks of their own. The album was a 'live' recording performed at Abbey Road in front of an invited audience of unfortunately screaming fans, who threaten to overwhelm the primitive technology and recording levels. There were two EPs released as part of the project, imaginatively entitled *Cliff No. 1* and ***Cliff No. 2***, which featured several of the tracks from the album, with the first being the initial six tracks with the last two being rearranged in order so that the Drifters' *Jet Black* appeared at the end of the second side. *Cliff No. 1* was released on the Columbia label in both mono (catalogue number SEG 7903) and stereo (ESG 7754) in June 1959, although neither of the EPs made any impression on the British UK EP charts. The second EP in the collection was released a month later.

Track Listing

Apron Strings
My Babe
Down the Line
I Gotta Feeling
Baby I Don't Care
Jet Black

♫ Cliff No. 2

3rd UK EP

The second and final EP associated with Cliff Richard's first album, which had been simply entitled ***Cliff***, was his third to be released. While the first EP from the parent album, imaginatively called ***Cliff No. 1***, took the first six tracks from the album and included a Drifters' vocal-cum-instrumental track, *Jet Black*, the second EP, ***Cliff No. 2*** missed out ***Baby I Don't Care*** and then took only the next five tracks, this time all featuring Cliff on lead vocals backed by the Drifters. The album was recorded at Abbey Road 'live' in front of a small invited audience of female fans whose incessant screaming adds nothing to the listening experience and often threatens to overwhelm the recording machines on occasion, although it does instil some atmosphere to what is supposed to be a live performance. The EP was issued on the Columbia label in both mono (catalogue number SEG 7910) and stereo (ESG 7769) in July 1959 but, like its predecessor failed to make any impression on the UK EP charts.

Track Listing

Donna
Move It
Ready Teddy
Too Much
Don't Bug Me Baby

♫ Cliff Richard No. 1

17th UK EP

Cliff Richard turned twenty-one in October 1961 and Columbia released an album to celebrate the fact. They had pared back their policy of issuing a suite of EPs that had all of the album's tracks on by the time ***21 Today*** was issued and, renaming two EPs simply *Cliff Richard*, each had a selection of songs taken from its track listing. The first EP, *Cliff Richard No. 1*, included the second to the fifth tracks (the first was studio banter overlaid on an instrumental version of ***Happy Birthday***) from the A-side and was issued in mono only (catalogue number SEG 8151) on the Columbia label in April 1962. The EP followed its predecessor, ***Cliff's Hit Parade***, by reaching number four in the British EP charts.

Track Listing

Forty Days
Catch Me
How Wonderful to Know
Tough Enough

♫ Cliff Richard No. 2

19th UK EP

The second of two EPs to include material originally released on Cliff Richard's celebratory ***21 Today*** album continued where the first left off with the provision of the tracks from the second half of the album's A-side. Earlier, Columbia had adopted a policy of depositing the album's tracks on a suite of EPs but, since ***Listen to Cliff!***, had stopped at the first side of the album instead. Released on the Columbia label, *Cliff Richard No. 2* (as the EP had been retitled rather than inheriting the name of the parent album) was issued in mono format only (catalogue number SEG 8168) in June 1962 and reached number nineteen in the British EP charts.

Track Listing

Fifty Tears for Every Kiss
The Night Is So Lonely
Poor Boy
Y'Arriva

♫ Cliff's Hit Parade

16th UK EP

Cliff Richard had had unprecedented success in the singles charts throughout the end of the fifties and early sixties and Columbia decided to capitalize on the success by issuing an EP that collated the best from 1961 (excluding the unofficially released ***Gee Whiz It's You***). All of the songs had managed a top three position in the singles charts and the EP almost achieved the same success. The first EP for a while to only be released in mono (catalogue number SEG 8133), *Cliff's Hit Parade* was issued on the Columbia label in February 1962. It reached number four in the British EP charts, just missing out on the accolade achieved by the singles.

Track Listing

I Love You
Theme for a Dream
A Girl Like You
When the Girl in Your Arms (Is the Girl in Your Heart)

♫ Cliff's Hits

20th UK EP

Cliff Richard's third EP anthology of hits is a bit of a misnomer. In fact it is the double A-side of ***I'm Looking out the Window*** and ***Do You Wanna Dance?*** alongside the single ***It'll Be Me*** and it's B-side ***Since I Lost You***. In essence, it is two single releases in their entirety placed on one disc. *Cliff's Hits* was issued on the Columbia label in mono format only (catalogue number SEG 8203) in November 1962.

Track Listing

It'll Be Me
Since I Lost You
Do You Wanna Dance?
I'm Looking out the Window

♫ Cliff's Hits from *Aladdin and His Wonderful Lamp*

35th UK EP

Cliff Richard started his two-year annual run of pantomimes at the London Palladium in the winter of 1964 with ***Aladdin and His Wonderful Lamp***. The inevitable EP gleaned from the cast soundtrack of the show is not quite as stated, since there is only the one single hit: ***I Could Easily Fall (in Love with You)***. Written by the Shadows, the rest of the material features songs where Cliff takes the lead (note that the Shadows also released their own EP of material associated with the show). Issued on the Columbia label, the EP was only released in mono format (catalogue number SEG 8395) in March 1965 and scraped into number twenty in the British EP charts.

Track Listing

Havin' Fun
Evening Comes
Friends
I Could Easily (Fall in Love with You)

♫ Cliff Sings *Don't Talk to Him*

28th UK EP

Cliff Sings Don't Talk to Him is a bit of a curio in that it features the number two single ***Don't Talk to Him*** and its B-side but the reverse side of the EP features apparently random choices from the B-side of his earlier album ***32 Minutes and 17 Seconds with Cliff Richard***. It therefore appears to be little more than a cynical cash-in on the success of his single. Released on the Columbia label, it was issued in mono only (catalogue number SEG 8299) in March 1964 and reached number fifteen in the British EP charts.

Track Listing

Don't Talk to Him
Say You're Mine
Spanish Harlem
Who Are We to Say?
Falling in Love with Love

♫ Cliff Sings No. 1

5th UK EP

For Cliff Richard's second album, ***Cliff Sings***, each side was split into two groups of four songs with the first of each being rock and roll songs accompanied by the Shadows, while the second group of four was Cliff singing standards accompanied by Norrie Paramor and his orchestra. The entire album was transposed on to a set of four EPs, with the first two being the rock and roll selection and the last two being the standards. *Cliff Sings No. 1* was a rearrangement of the track listing of the first four songs on side one of the album. *Cliff Sings No. 1* was issued on the Columbia label in both mono (catalogue number SEG 7979) and stereo (ESG 7788) formats in February 1960 and reached number four in British EP charts.

Track Listing

Here Comes Summer
I Gotta Know
Blue Suede Shoes
The Snake and the Bookworm

♫ Cliff Sings No. 2

6th UK EP

The four EPs associated with Cliff Richard's second album, ***Cliff Sings***, were split across the rock and roll songs, featuring the Shadows, and the standards, accompanied by Norrie Paramor and his orchestra. The second of these EPs was the second set of four rock and roll songs, which initiated the second side of the album, and is presented in the sequence found on *Cliff Sings*. Issued on the Columbia label in mono (catalogue number SEG 7987) and stereo ESG 7794) formats in March 1960, *Cliff Sings No. 2* reached number three in the British EP charts.

Track Listing

Twenty Flight Rock
Pointed Toe Shoes
Mean Woman Blues
I'm Walkin'

♫ Cliff Sings No. 3

7th UK EP

Cliff Richard's second album, ***Cliff Sings***, was divided into two sections on each side with the first four songs of each being accompanied by the Shadows and the second four by Norrie Paramor's orchestra. The entire album was transposed on to EP format with four discs being issued: the first two covered the rock and roll tracks while the second looked after the orchestral standards. *Cliff Sings No. 3* was the first of the two standards EPs and was issued on the Columbia label in both mono (catalogue number SEG 8005) and stereo (ESG 7808) in June 1960 and reached number two in the British EP charts, doing better than both of the rock and roll songs EPs in the set.

Track Listing

I'll String Along with You
Embraceable You
As Time Goes By
The Touch of Your Lips

♫ Cliff Sings No. 4

8th UK EP

The final EP connected to Cliff Richard's second album, ***Cliff Sings***, completed the full transposition of the album on to the EP format. The EPs reflected the division of songs on both sides of the album, which had the first four songs supported by the Shadows and the second by Norrie Paramor's orchestra: the first two EPs were the rock and roll songs and the second two, the standards. Issued on the Columbia label in both mono (catalogue number SEG 8021) and stereo (ESG 7816) formats in September 1960, *Cliff Sings No. 4* was the only one of the set that failed to get into the British EP charts.

Track Listing

I Don't Know Why (I Just Do)
Little Things Mean a Lot
Somewhere Along the Way
That's My Desire

♫ Cliff's Lucky Lips

25th UK EP

As with the ***Cliff's Hits*** EP, *Cliff's Lucky Lips* is the A- and B-sides of two singles, ***Lucky Lips*** (of course) and ***It's All in the Game***, essentially bringing two complete single packages into one. The EP was issued on the Columbia label in mono only (catalogue number SEG 8269) on 18th October 1963 and only reached number seventeen in the British EP charts.

Track Listing

It's All in the Game
Your Eyes Tell on You
Lucky Lips
I Wonder

♫ Cliff's Silver Discs

9th UK EP

Cliff Richard experienced almost unchallenged dominance of the charts at the end of the fifties and into the sixties. A number of his singles had reached the top three in the UK charts and Columbia released an anthology of four best hits in recent years, two of which had reached number one, one a number two and the final song a number three. The concept of the EP was the receipt of a silver disc for single sales and issued as Cliff's ninth EP to capitalize on these single's success. Only issued in mono format on the Columbia label (catalogue number SEG 8050) on 1st December 1960, it whipped up sufficient interest to reach number one in the British EP charts; his second to achieve that position in as many years.

Track Listing

Please Don't Tease
Fall in Love with You
Nine Times out of Ten
Travellin' Light

♫ Cliff's Palladium Success

29th UK EP

Cliff Richard's success as a live performer was well-known and he enjoyed performing at the London Palladium, often returning there for reunion concerts with the Shadows and for his pantomimes in the mid-sixties. However, it does appear odd that his twenty-ninth EP should be titled *Cliff's Palladium Success* since it contains the single ***I'm the Lonely One*** and its B-side and two tracks that had not been placed on the track listing of an album. Released on the Columbia label in mono format only (catalogue number SEG 8320) in May 1964, the EP failed to get anywhere in the British EP charts.

Track Listing

I'm the Lonely One
Watch What You Do with My Baby
Perhaps Perhaps Perhaps
Frenesi

♫ Congratulations

46th UK EP

In 1968, Cliff Richard was chosen to represent the UK at the annual Eurovision Song Contest and it was hoped that he would follow the success of Sandie Shaw's *Puppet on a Strong* the year before. The six contending songs were performed on Cilla Black's show in the first few weeks of 1968 and opened up to a public vote. As is well known, ***Congratulations*** was the winner by a stupendous margin, while ***High 'n' Dry*** came in second. These are the tracks that open either side of the associated *Congratulations* EP, which included all six songs. The EP was the last ever vinyl EP to be released under Cliff's name and, in spite of the attendant publicity, Cliff's second position in the contest and the rarity of the material, the EP was not a hit and marked the final demise of the medium for future releases. Issued on the Columbia label, *Congratulations* was released in mono format only (catalogue number SEG 8540) in April 1968.

Track Listing

Congratulations
Wonderful World
Do You Remember?
High 'n' Dry
The Sound of the Candyman's Trumpet
Little Rag Doll

♫ Dream

14th UK EP

Apart from the early film-related EPs, *Dream* was Cliff Richard's first to include material not available either in single or album form and it was his first to be themed. In this case, with its obvious title, it comprised a set of songs that had the word 'dream' somewhere in the title. *Dream* was issued on the Columbia label in both mono (catalogue number SEG 819) and stereo (ESG 7867) formats in November 1961 and reached number three in the British singles charts, its popularity possibly boosted by the rarity of the material in other forms.

Track Listing

Dream
All I Do Is Dream of You
I'll See You in My Dreams
When I Grow Too Old to Dream

♫ Expresso Bongo
4th UK EP

Expresso Bongo was Cliff Richard's second film and the first with him publicized as the headline star. Playing an obnoxious and manipulative character who, along with his obsequious manager, attempts to pull the wool over the public's and the record company's eyes and goes for saccharine schmaltz in his performances of songs such as ***The Shrine on the Second Floor***, which is the only original song to survive the transition from play to film. The associated EP includes all the songs from the film and also featured the associated single release, ***A Voice in the Wilderness***, to propel it into the charts, as well as the Shadows instrumental *Bongo Blues*.

However, in spite of the premise of the film and the purpose of the song to the narrative, fans fell for *The Shrine on the Second Floor*, citing it as a beautiful song with perfect lyrics often calling on a bewildered Cliff to prform it in concert after the film's release. As a result, and unusually, *Expresso Bongo* became the first EP to cross over and get a position in the British singles charts, when it reached number fourteen. Released on the Columbia label, *Expresso Bongo* was issued in mono (catalogue number SEG 7971) and stereo (ESG 7783) formats in January 1960 and was the first in a long run of Cliff's EPs to chart, when it reached number one in the British EP charts.

Track Listing

Love	The Shrine on the Second Floor
A Voice in the Wilderness	Bongo Blues

♫ Forever Kind of Love, A
31st UK EP

Featuring a song recorded two years earlier from which the *A Forever Kind of Love* EP took its title, Cliff Richard's then recent number four single, ***Constantly***, and its B-side, ***True True Lovin'***, also feature (taking up the flip-side of the EP) while a relatively rare track in the UK was also issued on the EP's A-side. When the film ***The Young Ones*** was looking for distribution in America, the film company insisted on retitling it ***Wonderful to Be Young*** and commissioned Burt Bacharach and Hal David to write a new title song, which Cliff recorded and released as an unsuccessful single in the US. This song was given its first British release on the *A Forever Kind of Love* EP, although there is an erroneous 'It's' prefixed to the song's title. The EP was issued on the Columbia label in mono format only (catalogue number SEG 8347) in September 1964 but, in spite of the rarity of the two tracks that appear on its A-side, it failed to make any headway in the British EP charts.

Track Listing

A Forever Kind of Love	Constantly
It's Wonderful to Be Young	True True Lovin'

♫ Hits from *Summer Holiday*
23rd UK EP

As with ***The Young Ones***, when ***Summer Holiday*** was released, the inevitable EP collation of songs was issued from the film. But, whereas *The Young Ones* was predominantly B-sides and other tracks loosely associated to hits, the *Summer Holiday* version was different. This time it was all the singles released from the project. Issued on the Columbia label in both mono (catalogue number SEG 8250) and stereo (ESG 7896) formats in June 1963 and reached number four in the British EP charts. The associated ***More Hits from Summer Holiday*** was a different affair, however, since it was four other tracks from the film not otherwise associated with hits or singles. Once again, the term 'more hits' means more accurately 'favourite' or 'other'.

Track Listing

Summer Holiday	Dancing Shoes
The Next Time	Bachelor Boy

♫ Hits from *The Young Ones*
18th UK EP

The breakthrough film for Cliff Richard was ***The Young Ones*** in 1961 and was the first truly musical film with the emphasis on music as much as it was on piecing the details of the plot around those songs. The only EP to be released from the project was issued five months after the soundtrack album, and it featured four tracks from the album under the rather misnamed title of *Hits from The Young Ones*, although the term 'hits' could simply be replaced by 'favourites'. The disc was issued on the Columbia in mono only (catalogue number SEG 8159) in May 1962 and reached number eleven in the specialist British EP charts.

Track Listing

The Young Ones	Lessons in Love
Got a Funny Feeling	We Say Yeah

♬ Hits from *When in Rome*
40th UK EP

Calling the EP *Hits from When in Rome* is a little disingenuous to the rest of Cliff Richard's material since none of the tracks was issued as a single nor had they charted anywhere else in their own right. Taken from the track listing of, as the title suggests, his then new album ***When in Rome*** from August 1965, all of the tracks are familiar tunes made popular by other artists in recent years, thereby giving credence to the title, but sung in Italian. *Hits from When in Rome* was issued on the Columbia label and released in mono format only (catalogue number SEG 8478) in April 1966 but was the second of a run of seven not to chart.

Track Listing

Come Prima (For the First Time)
Nel Blu di Pinto di Blu (Volare)
Dicitencello Vuie (Just Say I Love Her)
Arrivederci Roma

♬ Hits from *Wonderful Life*
33rd UK EP

Following the process initiated by previous films, the third EP from Cliff Richard's ***Wonderful Life*** film was entitled *Hits from Wonderful Life*, although, once again, this is a misnomer, since there is only one track, ***On the Beach***, that was a hit. Indeed, the remaining tracks are slim pickings since there had already been two other EPs released from the film's soundtrack. Released on the Columbia label, it was issued in mono (catalogue number SEG 8376) and stereo (ESG 7906) formats only in December 1964 but failed to make an impression on the British EP charts.

Track Listing

On the Beach
We Love a Movie
Home
All Kinds of People

♬ Holiday Carnival
22nd UK EP

Other than EPs associated with film projects, *Holiday Carnival* was the second of Cliff Richard's EPs after ***Dream*** to be based around a concept or word: in this case, it was the spirit of being away from home in some exotic place and enjoying the ability to relax and exploiting the parties and it was also matched with the timing of the release of the ***Summer Holiday*** film. Featuring songs not issued elsewhere, *Holiday Carnival* was released on the Columbia label in both mono (catalogue number SEG 8246) and stereo (ESG 7892) formats in May 1963 and reached number one in the British EP charts.

Track Listing

Carnival
Moonlight Bay
Some of These Days
For You For Me

♬ La La La La La
43rd UK EP

Cliff Richard regularly released new material in EP form that was unavailable elsewhere and this was the case with the curiously titled *La La La La La* EP, which took its name from the first track. As well as two other vocal tracks by Cliff, there is also an unusual vocal contribution from Hank Marvin and Bruce Welch in *Solitary Man*. Issued on the Columbia label, it was only released in mono format (catalogue number SEG 8517) in December 1966 (roughly the same time as the ***Thunderbirds Are Go!*** EP) but failed to chart.

Track Listing

La La La La La
Solitary Man
Things We Said Today
Never Knew What Love Could Do

♬ Listen to Cliff!
13th UK EP

Although the practice had been to deploy an album's material on to a suite of EPs, Cliff Richard's fourth album only saw its first side transferred to two EPs. ***Listen to Cliff!*** was organized like the earlier ***Cliff Sings*** album with half the tracks on each side being rock and roll-based songs while the remainder were standards accompanied by an orchestra. The first EP to be released covered the tracks performed with the Shadows and reorganised into a different order from the album. The EP was issued on the Columbia label in both mono (catalogue number SEG 8105) and stereo (ESG 7858) formats in October 1961 and only reached number seventeen in the British EP charts.

Track Listing

What'd I Say
True Love Will Come to You
Blue Moon
Lover

♫ Listen to Cliff! No. 2

15th UK EP

In between the only two EPs to be released for the ***Listen to Cliff!*** album project was released the ***Dream*** EP comprising all original non-album material. The usual process of transposing entire albums on to a suite of EPs was largely stopped with this album, possibly because of poorer sales than anticipated on the two that were released. Comprising the second half of the tracks from the album's A-side and the first from the B-side in a slightly different order, this selection was those standards accompanied by Norrie Paramor's orchestra. Issued on the Columbia label in both mono (catalogue number SEG 8105) and stereo (ESG 7870) in December 1960, the EP was the last for a while to be issued in stereo. It was also a commercial failure in that it didn't manage to get into the British EP charts.

Track Listing

Unchained Melody
First Lesson in Love
Idle Gossip
Almost Like Being in Love
Beat Out Dat Rhythm on a Drum

♫ Look in My Eyes Maria

36th UK EP

Another of Cliff Richard's loosely conceptual EPs, *Look in My Eyes Maria* focused on two songs with Maria in the title and they are all love songs of the sort that have conditions or confrontation within them. As with the other EPs, the material on the track listing had not, at the time, been released in any other format. Issued on the Columbia label in mono format label only (catalogue number SEG 8405) in May 1965 and reached number fifteen in the British EP charts.

Track Listing

Look in My Eyes Maria
Where Is Your Heart?
Maria
If I Give My Heart to You

♫ Love Is Forever

41st UK EP

A tie-in EP release to Cliff Richard's November 1965 album of the same name, *Love Is Forever* featured a selection from the album's track listing. Issued on the Columbia label in mono format only (catalogue number SEG 8488) in April 1966, it was the third in a run of seven that failed to chart and was perhaps an indication of the demise of the medium that would take another two years to be stopped in Cliff's case.

Track Listing

My Colouring Book
Fly Me to the Moon
Someday (You'll Want Me to Want You)
Everyone Needs Someone to Love

♫ Love Songs

26th UK EP

Another of Cliff Richard's concept EPs, *Love Songs* is simply a collection of songs that centre on unconditional love. All of the songs are covers of songs made famous by other people but, for Cliff, they had never appeared on any associated album at the time. Released on the Columbia label, *Love Songs* was issued in both mono (catalogue number SEG 8272) and stereo (ESG 7900) in November 1963 and fared better than its two predecessors by reaching number four in the British EP charts.

Track Listing

I'm in the Mood for Love
Secret Love
Love Letters
I Only Have Eyes for You

♫ Me and My Shadows No. 1

10th UK EP

As detailed in the introduction, the EP was a cost-effective way for record companies to release their albums piecemeal to the record-buying public who might not have had the funds afford the more expensive album or the equipment to play it on. *Me and My Shadows No. 1* was the first of three EPs to be released connected to the ***Me and My Shadows*** album project and its track listing was simply the first five tracks that appeared on the album's A-side. Issued on the Columbia label in both mono (catalogue number SEG 8065) and stereo (ESG 7837) formats in February 1961 and reached number five on the British EP charts.

Track Listing

I'm Gonna Get You
You and I
I Cannot Find a True Love
Evergreen Tree
She's Gone

♫ Me and My Shadows No. 2

11th UK EP

The second EP from the ***Me and My Shadows*** project featured the final three tracks from the album's A-side and the first two from the B-side. Released on the Columbia label in both mono (catalogue number SEG 8071) and stereo (ESG 7481) formats in March 1961, the *Me and My Shadows No. 2* EP reached number eight in the British EP charts, the worst performance of the three issued from the project.

Track Listing

Let Out Again
You're Just the One to Do It
Lamp of Love
Choppin' and Changin'
We Have It Made

♫ Me and My Shadows No. 3

12th UK EP

In late 1960, Cliff Richard's third album, ***Me and My Shadows***, was released. At the time, it was Columbia's policy to transfer the albums on to a sequence of EPs in order to make sure the entire available market had access to the products. For this album, three EPs were released, each with five tracks on them, over a period of three months in 1961. The third in the sequence was comprised the third to the penultimate track on the second album side. Since there were sixteen tracks on the album, it meant that, in this case, ***Working after School*** was not released in this format. Issued on the Columbia label in mono (catalogue number SEG 8078) and stereo (ESG 7843) in April 1961 and reached number six in the British EP charts. The popularity of this EP was boosted slightly by the inclusion of the unofficial single release ***Gee Whiz It's You***.

Track Listing

Tell Me
Gee Whiz It's You
I'm Willing to Learn
I Love You So
I Don't Know

♫ More Hits from *Summer Holiday*

24th UK EP

The first EP from Cliff Richard's most famous film ***Summer Holiday*** was truly a collection of his hits that he had garnered from the project. The follow-up EP, *More Hits from Summer Holiday*, is a misnomer since it is only a collection of other tracks featuring him from the soundtrack. However, the success of the film and the material released from it made its release inevitable. It was issued on the Columbia label in both mono (catalogue number SEG 8263) and stereo (ESG 7898) formats in September 1963 and but failed to reach anywhere in the specialized chart of British EPs.

Track Listing

Seven Days to a Holiday
Stranger in Town
Really Waltzing
All at Once

♫ Serious Charge

1st UK EP

The first EP to be released by Cliff Richard, rather than being associated with his first studio single recordings and B-sides or his then recently released first album, ***Cliff***, the month before, was actually connected to his first screen role in the film ***Serious Charge***. Not a musical but with music in it performed by Cliff and the Drifters, this helped publicity for the black and white British film that was quite gritty in its premise of a callow youth accusing a well-meaning priest of paedophilia. The *Serious Charge* EP featured all three Cliff songs that were featured in the film, as well as a Drifters instrumental *Chinchilla*, but not necessarily the versions that appeared in it: for example, ***Living Doll*** is the countrified and less rocky version that was released as a single and applied to this EP to propagate the success of Cliff's first number on single into the EP. Released in mono format only, *Serious Charge* was issued on the Columbia label (catalogue number SEG 7895) in May 1959 but, in spite of the attendant publicity, failed to get anywhere in the UK EP charts.

Track Listing

Living Doll
No Turning Back
Mad About You
Chinchilla

♫ Take Four

38th UK EP

With less predictable success in the EP market than in the singles market, Cliff Richard nevertheless exploited the medium as much as possible and released a number of tracks not issued in any other format. This was the case with the *Take Four* EP, which was simply four tracks not found elsewhere with no concet, two of which were recorded in 1964 and two in 1965. Issued on the Columbia label in mono only (catalogue number SEG 8450) in October 1965, *Take Four* reached number four in the British EP charts, making it his best-placed EP since ***Wonderful Life No. 1*** and the last of Cliff's EPs to chart.

Track Listing

Boom Boom (That's How My Heart Beats)
My Heart Is an Open Book
Lies and Kisses
Sweet and Gentle

♫ Thunderbirds Are Go!

42nd UK EP

In 1966, Cliff Richard and the Shadows were immortalized in puppet form as they lent their voices and performance to the film ***Thunderbirds Are Go!*** For the film, Cliff only sang the one song, ***Shooting Star***, during a dream sequence with Alan Tracy dating Lady Penelope, while the Shadows provided three instrumentals including a thundering version of the television show's theme. The associated EP tie-in was issued on the Columbia label in mono format only (catalogue number SEG 8510) in December 1966 but was the latest in a sequence of seven not to chart, marking the precipitation of the medium's demise.

Track Listing

Shooting Star
Lady Penelope
Thunderbirds Theme
Zero X Theme

♫ Time for Cliff and the Shadows

21st UK EP

Time for Cliff Richard and the Shadows eschews the former policy of issuing more than one EP per Cliff Richard album and instead gives the listener five tracks from the album ***32 Minutes and 17 Seconds with Cliff Richard*** picked from both sides of the album. The EP was issued on the Columbia label in both mono (catalogue number SEG 8228) and stereo (ESG 7887) formats in March 1963 but didn't get anywhere in the British EP charts.

Track Listing

So I've Been Told
I'm Walkin' the Blues
When My Dreamboat Comes Home
Blueberry Hill
You Don't Know

♫ When in France

27th UK EP

Cliff Richard had had an amount of success on the continent with foreign language versions of songs he had recorded in English, or, on occasions, songs that he had not recorded even in English. In late 1963, he released an album of Spanish songs, ***When in Spain***, and followed this up with an EP of French songs, *When in France*. These were not released on any album until all the songs were featured on the 1976 album, *When in France... Chante en Français*, and then later on the compendium, ***On the Continent***. The EP was issued on the Columbia label for domestic issue in mono format only (catalogue number SEG 8290) in February 1964 but wasn't placed in the British EP charts.

Track Listing

La Mer
Boum
J'Attendrai
C'est Si Bon

♫ Why Don't They Understand?

34th UK EP

Featuring Cliff Richard's twenty-seventh single, ***The Twelfth of Never*** and its B-side on the EP's flip-side, *Why Don't They Understand?* also featured two tracks not available in any other format at the time: the title track and ***Where the Four Winds Blow***. Issued on the Columbia label, *Why Don't They Understand?* was released in mono format only (catalogue number SEG 8384) in February 1965 but, in spite of the strength of the material, it didn't chart.

Track Listing

Why Don't They Understand?
Where the Four Winds Blow
The Twelfth of Never
I'm Afraid to Go Home

♫ Wind Me Up

39th UK EP

Cliff Richard's EPs were a mixture when taken as a collection: some had new material on them, others were tie-ins with film or stage projects, while others were simply re-releases of singles with their B-sides pressed on to the EP format. *Wind Me Up* is a case in point, which features ***Wind Me Up (Let Me Go)*** and ***The Time in Between*** and their respective B-sides. Released on the Columbia label, it was issued in mono format only (catalogue number SEG 8474) in February 1966 but was the first of a run seven EPs until the final vinyl EP ***Congratulations*** not to chart

Track Listing

Wind Me Up
The Night
The Time in Between
Look Before You Love

♬ Wonderful Life No. 1

30th UK EP

The first of three EPs to be released from Cliff Richard's film ***Wonderful Life***, the simply titled *Wonderful Life No. 1* was a selection of tracks from the soundtrack album, which also featured the Shadows instrumental *Walkin'*. Issued on the Columbia label in both mono (catalogue number SEG 8338) and stereo (ESG 7902) in August 1964, *Wonderful Life No. 1* reached number three in the British EP charts.

Track Listing

Wonderful Life
Do You Remember?
What've I Gotta Do?
Walkin'

♬ Wonderful Life No. 2

32nd UK EP

The second of three EPs to be issued from the ***Wonderful Life*** film project, *Wonderful Life No. 2* was another selection of tracks from the soundtrack that featured Cliff Richard. While ***A Matter of Moments*** and ***A Little Imagination*** are reasonably strong songs the other two are rather mediocre in comparison. Perhaps for this reason, the EP failed to chart in the British EP charts. *Wonderful Life No. 2* was issued on the Columbia label in both mono (catalogue number SEG 8354) and stereo (ESG 7903) formats in October 1964.

Track Listing

A Matter of Moments
Girl in Every Port
A Little Imagination
In the Stars

THE CLIFF RICHARD RECORDING CATALOGUE

Appendix D: The Long Players (LPs)

♫ 21 Today
5th studio album

Released on his twenty-first birthday (14th October 1961), Cliff Richard's fifth album was called appropriately ***21 Today***. Featuring another mixture of original material (including compositions by Hank Marvin and Bruce Welch), there was also a song written by Cliff himself, ***Without You***, and a number of covers of older songs. Issued on the Columbia label in mono (catalogue number 33SX 1368) and stereo (SCX 3409) formats, the album became Cliff's first number one in Britain, although it only stayed on the listings for sixteen weeks, less than half of the time appreciated by any of its four predecessors. No singles or EPs were included in the project, although two were released the following year simply called ***Cliff Richard No. 1*** and ***Cliff Richard No. 2***. The album was reissued on CD for the first time as part of the Cliff Richard CD Collection programme alongside ***Listen to Cliff!*** in stereo only on the EMI label (catalogue number 0777 7 80420 2 0) on 5th October 1992. The mono version of the album was issued on CD (7243 4 95442 2 2) on 5th June 1998.

Track Listing

Happy Birthday to You
Forty Days
Catch Me
How Wonderful to Know
Tough Enough
Fifty Tears for Every Kiss
The Night Is So Lonely
Poor Boy
Y'Arriva
Outsider
Tea for Two
To Prove My Love for You
Without You
A Mighty Lonely Man
My Blue Heaven
Shame on You

♫ 31st of February Street, The
28th studio album

The 31st of February Street was Cliff Richard's only real attempt at a sort of concept album - about leaving home and returning and the mix of emotions associated with it. With mostly new material, including a number of songs written by Cliff himself, there was also a re-recording of his 1959 number one single ***Travellin' Light***. No singles were released from the album as EMI were still generally operating a policy of keeping singles and albums distinct and it was the last album to be produced by David Mackay before Bruce Welch took control of the renaissance of Cliff's career. *The 31st of February Street* was issued on the EMI label (catalogue number EMC 3048) in November 1974 but it didn't sell well enough to bother the album charts. The album was first reissued on CD format combined with ***I'm Nearly Famous*** (catalogue number 0777 7 80491 2 8) on 4th October 1993, later being digitally remastered and reissued on its own (7243 4 73358 2 2) on 26th July 2004 with four bonus tracks.

Track Listing

31st of February Street (Opening)
Give Me Back That Old Familiar Feeling
The Leaving
Travellin' Light
There You Go Again
Nothing to Remind Me
Our Love Could Be So Real
No Matter What
Fireside Song
Going Away
Log Long Time
You Will Never Know
The Singer
31st of February Street (Closing)

Bonus tracks (2004 CD)
Celestial Houses
Days of Love
Ashes to Ashes
Love Is Here

♫ 32 Minutes and 17 Seconds with Cliff Richard
7th studio album

Cliff Richard's seventh album in less than four years featured a single in the first track, ***It'll Be Me***. A collection of tracks that had the Shadows accompanying him on some, an orchestra on the others led by producer Norrie Paramor, the songs were covers of contemporary and older hits as well as some new material supplied by Bruce Welch and a number by the writing team of Tepper and Bennett, who had given Cliff a number one hit with ***The Young Ones***. One EP was issued from the album in mono and stereo formats, called ***Time for Cliff and the Shadows***. The album was issued in on the Columbia label in mono (catalogue number 33SX 1431) and stereo (SCX 3436) in October 1962 and it reached number three in Britain staying the charts for twenty-one weeks. When EMI remastered and reissued Cliff's earlier albums under the CD Collection programme the stereo version was issued alongside ***When in Spain*** (catalogue number 0777 7 80423 2 7) on the 5th October 1992. The mono format was finally issued on CD (7243 4 95443 2 1) on 5th June 1998 for completists.

Track Listing

It'll Be Me
So I've Been Told
How Long Is Forever?
I'm Walkin' the Blues
Tun Around
Blueberry Hill
Let's Make a Memory
When My Dreamboat Comes Home
I'm on My Way
Spanish Harlem
You Don't Know
Falling in Love with Love
Who Are We to Say?
I Wake Up Cryin'

♫ 40 Golden Greats

Compilation album

Capitalizing on Cliff Richard's musical renaissance and getting in just before the twentieth anniversary celebrations would start, EMI released a double LP collection of forty of Cliff's singles to date (of the seventy that had been officially released in the UK up to that point). Whereas previous collections had pretty much faithfully collated all the singles of the period it was covering, the focus here was on the chronology and the most successful of the singles. Most of them are at least top ten, while the last few were a deliberate ploy to assist the recent studio album sales. A separate sampler EP (on four discs, one per side of the double LP) was released with snippets of all he tracks on the compilation. *40 Golden Greats* was issued on the EMI label (catalogue number EMTVS 6) in October 1977 and became Cliff's fourth number one album (and the first since ***Summer Holiday*** in 1963), staying in the charts for nineteen weeks. The album was subsequently issued on a double CD (catalogue number CDS 7924252) in July 1989.

♫ 50th Anniversary Album

Compilation album

Inevitably, to celebrate Cliff Richard's extraordinary fifty years in the music business, EMI wanted to capitalize on it by issuing another compilation of his best work. Featuring a broad spread across his career from the first, ***Move It***, to what was then his last, ***Thank You for a Lifetime***, the album justly provides a glimpse at what Cliff had achieved over those fifty years. The two-disc album was issued on the EMI label (catalogue number 50999 2 42389 2 2) on 3rd November 2008.

♫ About That Man

23rd studio album

Cliff Richard had had reasonable success with his first religious album, ***Good News***, in late 1967 and, for his twenty-third studio album, he decided to delve deeper into the story of Christ. Reading passages from the Gospels according to Matthew, Mark, Luke and John, Cliff also recorded four new songs, one of which had been recorded earlier with the Settlers but remains unreleased (***Where Is That Man?***). The album was issued on the Columbia label and was the first studio album by Cliff to be issued in stereo format only (catalogue number SCX 6408) in October 1970. Perhaps unsurprisingly, given the nature of the album, and the lack of songs within the listing, the album was of limited appeal and therefore failed to make an impression on the charts. Combined with ***His Land***, the album was subsequently issued on CD by EMI (catalogue number 0777 780482 2 0) on 2nd November 1992. The album is unusual in that it has no depiction of Cliff on the cover as all bar three albums did; instead there is a painting of Christ on the cross which is more apposite to the material on the record.

Track Listing

The Birth of John the Baptist
Sweet Little Jesus Boy *(song)*
The Visit of the Wise Men and the Escape to Egypt
John the Baptist Points out Jesus
Jesus Recruits His Helpers and Heals the Sick
Where Is That Man? *(song)*
Jesus Addresses the Crowd on the Hillside
Can It Be True? *(song)*
Jesus Is Betrayed and Arrested
The Trial of Jesus
His Execution and Death
The Fist Easter – The Empty Tomb
Reflections *(song)*

♫ Aladdin and His Wonderful Lamp

11th studio album

Written in its entirety by the Shadows, ***Aladdin and His Wonderful Lamp*** was their and Cliff Richard's first pantomime, which took place over the winter of 1964 at the London Palladium. Cliff had a number six single with ***I Could Easily Fall (in Love with You)***, while the Shadows released the tongue-in-cheek *Genie with the Light Brown Lamp* as an instrumental. One EP was issued from the project, ***Cliff's Hits from Aladdin and His Wonderful Lamp***, while the album was released on the Columbia label in mono (catalogue number 33SX 1676) and stereo (SCX 3522) formats in December 1964 and reached number thirteen in the charts, the first time one of Cliff's albums had not got into the top ten, staying there for only five weeks. The album was reissued on CD in stereo format only alongside ***Wonderful Life*** on the EMI label (catalogue number 0777 7 80426 2 4) on 5th October 1992. The album has the almost unique distinction in that the album cover has no depiction of Cliff anywhere (the others are its pantomime counterpart *Cinderella* and ***About That Man***).

Track Listing

Emperor Theme
Chinese Street Scene
Me Oh My
I Could Easily Fall (in Love with You)
Little Princess
This Was My Special Day
I'm in Love with You
There's Gotta Be a Way
Ballet: Rubies, Emeralds, Sapphires, Diamonds
Dance of the Warriors
Friends
Dragon Dance
Genie with the Light Brown Lamp
Make Ev'ry Day a Carnival Day
Widow Twankey's Song
I'm Feeling Oh So Lonely
I've Said Too Many Things
Evening Comes
Havin' Fun

♫ Album, The

42nd studio album

Over the years of his recording career, Cliff Richard has been able to change with the times and the musical genres and produce music that is of its time, and in so doing managing to sound fresh and challenging to younger acts within the charts. And so it was with his *The Album* in the early nineties. This studio album moved away from the electronic instrumentation, keyboards and sequencers of his eighties recordings and worked on a jazzier, saxophone-based sound for the songs making up *The Album*. The album saw five tracks being released from its listing: ***I Still Believe in You, Peace in Our Time, Human Work of Art, Never Let Go*** and ***Healing Love***, all of which successfully charted. The album was released on the EMI label (catalogue numbers EMD 1043 and CDEMD 1043 for the LP and CD, respectively) on 19th April 1993 and became his first studio album to reach number one since ***Summer Holiday*** in 1963, and it stayed in the charts for fifteen weeks.

Track Listing

Peace in Our Time
Love Is the Strongest Emotion
I Still Believe in You
Love's Salvation
Only Angel
Handle My Heart with Love
Little Mistreater
You Move Heaven
I Need Love
Hold Us Together
Human Work of Art
Never Let Go
Healing Love
Brother to Brother

♫ Always Guaranteed

39th studio album

For his first album in almost three years, Cliff returned to Alan Tarney for help on the production and generation of the songs and they used a very different technique for making the recordings. Completely written by Tarney, the songs were generated in the studio on the instruments that Tarney had to hand and built up in preparation for Cliff's visit to the studio. His time was at a premium because of the evening job he had performing on stage in ***Time – The Musical*** in London, making the process work very well for all concerned. The album relinquished four singles: ***Some People, Two Hearts, My Pretty One*** and ***Remember Me***. The vinyl album was issued alongside a boxed set version that included some pictures and a seven-inch one-sided vinyl disc with ***Another Christmas Day***. The album was issued on the EMI label (catalogue numbers EMD 1004 (LP), TCEMD 1004 (CD) and EMDB 1004 (boxed set), respectively) on 14th September 1987, with the boxed set appearing on 9th November 1987. The album reached number five in the UK album charts, staying in the listings for twenty-five weeks and became Cliff's most successful album to date in terms of sales. The album was digitally remastered and reissued (catalogue number 7243 5 83393 2 1) on 19th January 2004, with a number of bonus tracks, culled from the B-sides of the singles.

Track Listing

One Night
Once upon a Time
Some People
Forever
Two Hearts
Under Your Spell
This Time Now
My Pretty One
Remember Me
Always Guaranteed

Bonus tracks (2004 CD)

Under the Gun
Brave New World
Wild Geese
Love Ya
One Time Lover Man
Another Christmas Day
Yesterday, Today, Forever
Reunion of the Heart

♫ ...And They Said It Wouldn't Last! (My 50 Years in Music)

Compilation album

The extraordinary longevity of Cliff Richard in the music business meant that, over his fifty-year career, he had recorded hundreds of songs either in the studio or live. To celebrate the milestone anniversary, EMI released a boxed set of eight discs, which featured a number of tracks that had never been released or alternative takes to the known record as well as a live performance and compilations of favourite tunes from his oeuvre. These were divided across these titles:

1. Early years
2. Rare B-sides
3. Rare EP tracks: 1961-1991
4. Film and theatre
5. Best-sellers
6. Faith and inspirational songs
7. Live in Japan '72
8. Lost & Found (unreleased tracks)

The ***Early Years, Rare B-sides, Lost & Found, Rare EP Tracks*** and ***Live in Japan '72*** have all been released as separate albums in their own right. The main boxed set album is an extraordinary historical document of Cliff's career and it was released on the EMI label (catalogue number 5099921659225) on 15th September 2008.

Track Listing

Move It
Schoolboy Crush
High Class Baby
My Feet Hit the Ground
Apron Strings (B-side)
Livin' Lovin' Doll
Never Mind
Mean Woman Blues
Don't Bug Me Baby
Blue Suede Shoes
Dynamite
Mean Streak
She's Gone
I Cannot Find a True Love
Willie and the Hand-Jive
'D' in Love
Nine Times out of Ten
Choppin' n' Changin'
Mumblin' Mosie
Tough Enough
Gee Whiz It's You
Now's the Time to Fall in Love
Nine Times out of Ten (Alternative take)
A Girl Like You (Alternative take)
Fall in Love with You (Alternative take)
Never Mind (Alternative take)
I Love You (Undubbed version)
Dynamite Alternative take)
Michelle
Poor Boy (Alternative take)

Say You're Mine
True, True Lovin'
Just another Guy
Just a Little Too Late
Somebody Loses
I Get the Feelin'
Our Story Book
Sweet Little Jesus Boy
Occasional Rain
She's Leaving You
So Long
Monday Comes Too Soon
I Was Only Fooling Myself
Time Flies
Annabella Umbrella
Pigeon
A Thousand Conversations
Mr. Cloud
Empty Chairs
The Old Accordion
Come Back, Billie Jo
I Only Know I Love You
Back in Vaudeville
Stronger than That (Extended mix)
Just Don't Have the Heart (X Mix)

Dream
I'll See You in My Dreams
Carnival
Some of These Days
For You, For Me
Your Eyes Tell on You
I Wonder
I'm in the Mood for Love
Watch What You Do with My Baby
Perhaps, Perhaps, Perhaps (English version)
Frenesi (English version)
Why Don't They Understand?
I'm Afraid to Go Home
Where Is Your Heart?
Lies and Kisses
Me Lo Dijo Adela
The Night
Look Before You Love
La La La La La
Never Knew What Love Could Do
The Twelve Days of Christmas
The Holly and the Ivy
Wonderful to Be Young (Alternative take)
It Came upon a Midnight Clear
Sooner or Later
A Spoonful of Sugar
Zip-a-Dee-Doo-Dah
Chim-Chim-Cheree

Mad About You
Love
Lessons in Love
Dancing Shoes
On the Beach
This Was My Special Day
I Could Easily Fall (in Love with You)
Time Drags By
Shooting Star
Why Wasn't I Born Rich?
In the Country
Two a Penny
His Land
Take Me High
Midnight Blue
Born to Rock 'n' Roll
She's So Beautiful
It's in Every One of Us
A Misunderstood Man
Be with Me Always (Live)
Had to Be (Live)

Living Doll
Travellin' Light
Please Don't Tease
I Love You
Them for a Dream
When the Girl in Your Arms (Is the Girl in Your Heart)
The Young Ones
It'll Be Me
The Next Time
Bachelor Boy
Summer Holiday
Lucky Lips
It's All in the Game
Constantly
The Minute You're Gone
Congratulations
Power to All Our Friends
Devil Woman
We Don't Talk Anymore
Living Doll
Mistletoe and Wine
Saviour's Day
The Millennium Prayer

Help It Along
Higher Ground
Such Is the Mystery
I Wish We'd All Been Ready
Up in Canada
Why Should the Devil Have All the Good Music?
Yes He Lives
When I Survey the Wondrous Cross
Walking in the Light
Better than I Know Myself
Discovering
Be in My Heart
Little Town
Love and a Helping Hand
Yesterday Today Forever
Where You Are
There's No Power in Pity
Free (Live)
Faithful One

Backscratcher *(instrumental)*
Can't Let You Go
Have a Little Talk with Myself
Sunny Honey Girl
The Minute You're Gone
Flying Machine
The Day I Met Marie
Silvery Rain
My Way
Move It
Living in Harmony
Walk on By/The Look of Love
Early in the Morning
Goodbye Sam, Hello Samantha
Living Doll Bachelor Boy
The Young Ones
Congratulations
Rock 'n' Roll Medley: The Girl Can't Help It; Great Balls of Fire; Lucille; Jailhouse Rock; Good Old Rock 'n' Roll; Do You Wanna Dance?
Sing a Song of Freedom

Deep Purple
I Love You the Way You Are
Words
The Letter
If I Do
Note in a Bottle
All My Love (Solo Tu) (Alternative take)
The Day I Met Marie (Alternative take)
No Name No Fame
Love Is Like a Crescendo
Postmark Heaven
When You Are There
A Sad Song with a Happy Soul
'Cause I Believe in Loving
I (Who Have Nothing)
Run for Shelter
Sweet Lovin' Ways
Love of My Life
(There's a) Honky Tonk Angel (Alternative take)
Song of Yesterday
Mobile Alabama School-Leaving Hullabaloo

♫ Best of Cliff, The

Compilation album

The previous compilation of hits, ***More Hits by Cliff***, had taken the singles up to ***I Could Easily Fall (in Love with You)***. *The Best of Cliff* picked up where that left off with ***The Minute You're Gone*** and took the sequence of singles up to ***Congratulations***. Curiously, the next single, ***I'll Love You Forever Today***, was not included but instead, the compilers added its B-side, ***Girl, You'll Be a Woman Soon***. The album was issued on the Columbia label in mono (catalogue number SX 6343) and stereo (SCX 6343) in June 1969, and reached number five – the best showing since the ***Finders Keepers*** soundtrack three years earlier – and stayed in the charts for seventeen weeks. The album was released on CD combined with ***Established 1958*** (catalogue number 0777 7 80450 2 1) on 2nd November 1992.

♫ Best of Cliff Volume 2, The

Compilation album

The fourth hit compilation of Cliff Richard singles was the last of his albums to be issued on the Columbia label and was also the last of his albums to feature the full work of Norrie Paramor as producer (tracks produced by Paramor would of course appear on other compilations later in Cliff's career but these were combined with other producers' work). What differs slightly on this album is that the tracks are not presented in chronological sequence. It picks up after ***The Best of Cliff***, which had finished on ***Congratulations***, with ***I'll Love You Forever Today*** and continues through to ***Jesus***; however, it also misses out ***Don't Forget to Catch Me*** and ***I Ain't Got Time Any More***. Issued on the Columbia label (catalogue number SCX 6519) in November 1972, it was only a minor hit reaching number forty-nine and only staying in the charts for two weeks, possibly due to the lack of popularity of the assigned singles in general. The album was combined with ***Tracks 'n' Grooves*** and issued on the EMI label (catalogue number 0777 7 80485 2 7) on 4th October 1993.

♫ Carols

Compilation album

Cliff Richard had had phenomenal success with ***Mistletoe and Wine*** at the Christmas of 1988 and, alongside it, a compilation album was produced that brought together several Christmas themed tracks from his repertoire, including a number of the carols recorded *a capella* with the Mastersingers for the ***Carol Singers*** EP in 1967. The album was issued on the Word label (catalogue number WRD 3034) in October 1988 but didn't get anywhere in the album charts.

Track Listing

Little Town
In the Bleak Midwinter
Sweet Little Jesus Boy
While Shepherds Watched
Mary, What Ya Gonna Name That Pretty Little Baby?
Joseph
God Rest Ye Merry Gentlemen
Unto Us a Child is Born
Can It Be True?
Little Town of Bethlehem

♫ Christmas Story, The

Christmas album by the **Exeter Cathedral Choristers**

The Christmas story is a familiar one, particularly to those of the Christian faith or those living in the northern hemiphere of countries, in particular. Premier Christian Radio asked Cliff Richard to assist in creating an album to tell the story. This he did by reading excerpts from the Gospel according to St. Matthew and two psalms. These readings were interspersed with performances of carols by the choristers of Exeter Cathedral to underline what Cliff had read out. Recorded at the cathedral, the album was released on the RTD/Universal label (catalogue number PREMSIG2) on 19th November 2007 but, although receiving a number of plaudits, didn't sell enough to get into the album charts.

Track Listing

Psalm 150 *(Cliff)*
O Come All Ye Faithful
Deck the Halls
Extract from St. Matthew's Gospel Ch. 2 *(Cliff)*
We Three Kings
Extract from St. Matthew's Gospel Ch. 2 *(Cliff)*
O Little Town of Bethlehem
Once in Royal David's City
Extract from St. Matthew's Gospel Ch. 2 *(Cliff)*
Rocking Carol
Away in a Manger
Extract from St. Matthew's Gospel Ch. 2 *(Cliff)*
In Dulci Jubilo
Extract from St. Matthew's Gospel Ch. 2 *(Cliff)*
Silent Night
Extract from St. Matthew's Gospel Ch. 2 *(Cliff)*
Ding Dong Merrily on High
Psalm 106 Extract *(Cliff)*
Further Extract Psalm 106 *(Cliff)*
Reprise (last verse) O Come All Ye Faithful

♫ Cinderella

17th studio album

After ***Aladdin and His Wonderful Lamp*** in December 1965, the Shadows followed it up with ***Cinderella*** the following year. The cast recording featured one single, ***In the Country***, while four other tracks were released on an associated EP. The album was issued on the Columbia label in mono (catalogue number SX 6103) and stereo (SCX 6103) in January 1967 but only reached number thirty, staying in the charts for six weeks. The album was subsequently released alongside ***Finders Keepers*** on the CD Collection programme by EMI (catalogue number 0777 7 80435 2 2) on 2nd November 1992. The album is almost unique (the others are its pantomime counterpart *Aladdin and His Wonderful Lamp* and ***About That Man***) in that the album cover has no depiction of Cliff anywhere.

Track Listing

Welcome to Stoneybroke
Why Wasn't I Born Rich?
Peace and Quiet
The Flyder and the Spy *(The Shadows)*
Poverty
The Hunt
In the Country
Come Sunday
Dare I Love Him Like I Do?
If Our Dreams Come True
Autumn
The King's Place
Peace and Quiet (Reprise)
She Needs Him More Than Me
Hey Doctor Man

♫ Cliff

1st studio album

For Cliff Richard's first album outing, it was decided to invite a small selection of fans into the Abbey Road Studios to watch the performance being recorded. In some ways, this was a novel approach to recording and in others, it was a failure, largely because the screams of the presumably pubescent audience of girls threaten to overwhelm the music and the recording levels. However, the album also sounds very fresh because of the live element. Released on the Columbia label in mono only (catalogue number 33SX 1147) on 1st April 1959, the album reached number four in the middle of the month and stayed on the charts for thirty-one weeks. Stereo versions of the songs were recorded and mixed but were only released on the two EPs issued from the project, ***Cliff No. 1*** and ***Cliff No. 2***, with the remaining tracks added to the1997 release ***The Rock 'n' Roll Years 1958-1963***. Three tracks from the two sessions were left off any release and remain unissued. Although titled *Cliff*, the album is in fact the first album released by Cliff and the Drifters – it would be another seven months before they changed it to the more familiar Shadows – and they provide three of the tracks on the album. The album was finally released in CD format on the EMI label (catalogue number CDP 7 48277 2) in 1987 in mono format and was eventually issued in stereo (catalogue number 7243 4 95438 2 9) in May 1998.

Track Listing

Apron Strings
My Babe
Down the Line
I Got a Feeling
Jet Black *(The Drifters)*
Baby I Don't Care
Donna
Move It
Ready Teddy
Too Much
Don't Bug Me Baby
Driftin' *(The Drifters)*
That'll Be the Day
Be Bop a Lula *(The Drifters)*
Danny
Whole Lotta Shakin' Goin' On

♫ Cliff at Christmas

46th studio album

Cliff Richard had been dropped by EMI at the beginning of the millennium but he fought back with the excellent ***Wanted***, which was released on the Papillon label. EMI recognized that Cliff's popularity was still strong among his legion of fans and persuaded him to come back to record some new songs for some albums that followed a theme. The first was *Cliff at Christmas*, which took the track listing of ***Together with Cliff Richard*** and added a number of new Christmas-based recordings, to capitalize on the release and success of ***Santa's List***. The album was released on the EMI label (catalogue number 7243 5 93498 2 4) on 17th November 2003 and reached number nine, staying in the charts for eight weeks.

Track Listing

Have Yourself a Merry Little Christmas
Mistletoe and Wine
Walking in the Air
Little Town
Mary's Boy Child
Christmas Is Quit
Let It Snow
Saviour's Day
White Christmas
Silent Night
Santa's List
When a Child Is Born
Come to s
The Christmas Song
We Should Be Together
Winter Wonderland
The Millennium Prayer

♫ Cliff in Japan

Live album

Although Cliff Richard had performed on many international tours in the first ten years of his singing career and even though other performances (such as that at the ABC in Kingston in 1962) had been recorded, it was his performance on 18th October 1967 in Tokyo that was issued as his first live album. Featuring a number of tracks from his then recently released album, ***Don't Stop Me Now!***, it surprisingly also included relatively unknown tracks such as ***La La La La La***, previously only available on a EP. In addition, of course, there were the familiar hits selected from the previous few years. The album was first issued in the Japanese market on the Odeon label (catalogue number OP 9701) in stereo only and then internationally on the Columbia label in both mono (SX 6244) and stereo (SCX 6244) formats in May 1968. Reaching number twenty-nine, it stayed in the British charts for two weeks. It was issued on CD for the first time in stereo only by EMI as part of its programme to reissue Cliff's back catalogue of albums (catalogue number 0777 7 80441 2 3) combined with ***Two a Penny***. The album was remastered and reissued (catalogue number 0946 3 81962 2 8) on 12th March 2007 and featured a couple of bonus tracks, which were songs recorded at the time but left off the track listing of the international release, although they were on the Japanese album. These have been restored to their correct running position and are highlighted in bold in the track listing below.

Track Listing

Shout
I'll Come Running
The Minute You're Gone
Bachelor Boy
On the Beach
Hang on to a Dream
Spanish Harlem
Finders Keepers
Visions
Move It
Living Doll
It's All in the Game
La La La La La
Twist and Shout
Evergreen Tree
What'd I Say
Dynamite
Medley: Let's Make a Memory; The Young Ones; Lucky Lips; Summer Holiday; We Say Yeah

♫ Cliff Richard

12th studio album

Cliff Richard, the self-titled album, was not a planned album release but rather a collection of songs that Cliff had recorded over the previous two or so years but hadn't found a mechanism to release them previously. These included tracks from his sojourn in the summer 1964 to Nashville and New York as well as the English originals of songs overdubbed with Spanish lyrics for ***When in Spain***. There was one EP issued from the project, entitled ***Angel***, while that EP's title track and the first of the album enjoyed life as a single in the Far Eastern territories. The album was issued on the Columbia label in mono (catalogue number 33SX 1709) and stereo (SCX 3456) formats on 15th April 1965 and reached number nine, staying in the charts for just five weeks. The stereo version of the album only was issued on CD on the EMI label, alongside ***When in Rome***, (catalogue number 0777 7 80429 2 1) on 5th October 1992.

Track Listing

Angel
Sway
I Only Came to Say Goodbye
Take Special Care
Magic Is the Moonlight
House without Windows
Razzle Dazzle
I Don't Wanna Love You
It's Not for Me to Say
You Belong to My Heart
Again
Perfidia
Kiss
Reelin' and Rockin'

♫ Cliff Richard at the Movies 1959-1974

Compilation album

Cliff's extraordinary career in music has been marked by a number of different facets to his skills, including several films and stints in the theatre in both serious musical roles and pantomime. In particular, the golden age for his movies came in the sixties, when he was regularly voted Britain's best actor. In 1996, EMI compiled a collection of songs that best represented his performances on celluloid and included a number of different takes, film versions (that is, those not appearing on the associated soundtrack albums, singles or EPs but hard in the films) and a song never before released in the UK, the eponymous song to the retitled American version of ***The Young Ones***, ***Wonderful to Be Young***. The album was released on the EMI label (catalogue number 7423 8 52790 2 7) on 29th July 1996 and reached number seventeen in the UK album charts. The films represented on the album are:

1. ***Serious Charge***
2. ***Expresso Bongo***
3. ***The Young Ones***
4. ***Summer Holiday***
5. ***Wonderful Life***
6. ***Thunderbirds Are Go!***
7. ***Finders Keepers***
8. ***Two a Penny***
9. ***Take Me High***

What is missing is anything from the documentary film ***His Land*** and the charity documentary ***It's a Small World***.

Track Listing

No Turning Back
Living Doll
Mad About You
Love
A Voice in the Wilderness
The Shrine on the Second Floor
Friday Night
Got a Funny Feeling
Nothing Is Impossible
The Young Ones
Lessons in Love
When the Girl in Your Arms (Is the Girl in Your Heart)
We Say Yeah
Wonderful to Be Young
Outsider
Seven Days to a Holiday
Summer Holiday
Let Us Take You for a Ride
A Stranger in Town
Bachelor Boy
A Swingin' Affair
Dancing Shoes
The Next Time
Big News
Wonderful Life
A Girl in Every Port
A Little Imagination
On the Beach
Do You Remember?
Look Don't Touch
In the Stars
What've I Gotta Do?
A Matter of Moments
Shooting Star
Finders Keepers
Time Drags By
Washerwoman
La La La Song
Oh Señorita
This Day
Paella
Two a Penny
Twist and Shout
I'll Love You Forever Today
Questions
It's only Money
Midnight Blue
Game
Brumburger Duet
Take Me High
The Anti-Brotherhood of Man
Winning

♫ Cliff's Hit Album

Compilation album

Cliff Richard had had extraordinary success both on his own but also backed by the Shadows since starting out in 1958. It took almost five years for Columbia to pull together the first collection of hits and covered the period from his first hit ***Move It*** through to the ***I'm Looking out the Window*** and ***Do You Wanna Dance?*** double A-side single from May 1962. Featuring fourteen songs out of the twenty that had been hits for him, the six that were missing from the listing were ***High Class Baby, Livin' Lovin' Doll, Mean Streak, Never Mind, Dynamite*** and ***Gee Whiz It's You,*** the latter possibly not being chosen since it wasn't an official British release and had only charted after demanding fans bught the imported release. Issued on the Columbia label in mono (catalogue number 33SX 1512) and stereo (SCX 1512) in July 1963, *Cliff's Hit Album* reached number two in the charts and remained on the British album charts for nineteen weeks.

♫ Cliff Sings

2nd studio album

Cliff Sings was the first album to be released that was credited to Cliff Richard and the Shadows – who had changed their name from the Drifters after the success of ***Living Doll*** in the US to avoid confusion with the singing group of the same name, although they had recorded all the tracks under their original name – and it was also the last album to be issued in mono format only. The album was divided into rock and roll (the first half of each side) and orchestral-backed ballads (the second half) and was released in both mono and stereo format on four EPs, ***Cliff Sings No. 1, Cliff Sings No. 2, Cliff Sings No. 3*** and ***Cliff Sings No. 4***. None of the tracks was original material and the album was released on the Columbia label (catalogue number 33SX 1192) on 6th November 1959 and reached number two in the UK album charts, staying five weeks longer than its predecessor, ***Cliff,*** when it remained in the chart for thirty-six weeks. The album was eventually released on CD format as part of the dual CD programme on the EMI label (catalogue number 0777 7 80417 2 6) on 5th October 1992 alongside ***Me and My Shadows***. The stereo version of the album (essentially the tracks released on the stereo EPs) was issued in May 1998 (catalogue number 7243 4 95439 2 8).

Track Listing

Blue Suede Shoes
The Snake and the Bookworm
I Gotta Know
Here Comes Summer
I'll String Along with You
Embraceable You
As Time Goes By
The Touch of Your Lips
Twenty Flight Rock
Pointed Toe Shoes
Mean Woman Blues
I'm Walking
I Don't Know Why (I Just Do)
Little Things Mean a Lot
Somewhere Along the Way
That's My Desire

♫ Did He Jump... Or Was He Pushed?

Album by **Garth Hewitt**

A regular collaborator with Garth Hewitt in the following few years, Cliff Richard produced his debut album *Did He Jump... Or Was He Pushed?*, following on from a project that he did with Dave Pope called ***Sail Away***. The album has heavily rock-orientated songs and the quality of the material deserved greater success than it did. The album was issued on the Patch Records label, a subsidiary of EMI (catalogue number WOOF 1001) in 1979 but didn't make it into the charts.

Track Listing

Not Afraid to Rock 'n' Roll
On and On
Always on the Run
Physical Pain
Let's Go Out
Big Black Mamba
Did He Jump?
He's the One
World of Difference
We Sure Do
Roll On

♫ Don't Stop Me Now!

18th studio album

Taking a different musical turn with orchestral arrangements of songs that are now quintessential examples of Cliff Richard from this period, *Don't Stop Me Now!* was Cliff's eighteenth studio album in nine years and is a selection of covers of contemporary titles as well as a revisited version of ***Good Golly Miss Molly, Dizzy Miss Lizzy*** and his first single hit ***Move It***. There were no singles or EPs released from the album project, in part because the latter genre was on the verge of being abandoned by Columbia. The album was issued on the Columbia label in both mono (catalogue number SX 6133) and stereo (SCX 6133) on 8th April 1967 and reached number twenty-three and stayed in the British album charts for nine weeks. It was reissued on CD format for the first time in stereo only as part of EMI's programme to convert Cliff's back catalogue of albums (catalogue number 0777 7 80438 2 9) on 2nd November 1992) coupled with ***Good News***.

Track Listing

Shout
One Fine Day
I'll Be Back
Heartbeat
I Saw Her Standing There
Hang on to a Dream
You Gotta Tell Me
Homeward Bound
Good Golly Miss Molly
Don't Make Promises
Move It
Don't
Dizzy Miss Lizzy
Baby It's You
My Babe
Save the Last Dance for Me

♫ Dressed for the Occasion

Live album

In 1983, Cliff was celebrating his twenty-fifth anniversary in the music business and, to mark the occasion, he released a double album of material and also recorded a live show from the Royal Albert Hall in London with the London Philharmonic Orchestra. The set of songs chosen were a selection of his hits as well as a lot of new material such as a cover of the Marvin & Farrar song ***Galadriel (Sprit of Starlight)***. The original album was cut down to twelve titles but all of the missing songs were restored on the CD remaster into their running position – for ease, these have been added to the track listing in bold below. The album was released on the EMI label (catalogue number EMC 3432) on 9th May 1983 and reached number seven, spending seventeen weeks in the charts. It was first released on CD on the EMI label (catalogue number CDP 792420) in July 1989, with the same track listing as the original album but was digitally remastered and reissued (7243 5 83389 2 8) with the full set list on 19th January 2004.

Track Listing

Green Light
We Don't Talk Anymore
True Love Ways
Softly as I Leave You
Carrie
The Treasure of Love
The Golden Days Are Over
Galadriel (Spirit of Starlight)
You, Me and Jesus
Maybe Someday
Miss You Nights
Thief in the Night
Up in the World
Discovering
Devil Woman
Daddy's Home
Little Town

♫ Drifting

Album by **Sheila Walsh**

Aspiring Christian singer Sheila Walsh was assisted by Cliff Richard on her first album, *Drifting*, with Cliff taking the production duties as well as helping out on backing vocals on several of the tracks. In addition, the title song, ***Drifting***, was released as a duet between the pair, although it charted lowly in the UK. The album was originally released in the US under the title *War of Love*, before being picked up by the DJM Records label (catalogue number DJF 20581) and being released in June 1983. In spite of the pedigree, the album didn't chart.

Track Listing

Turn! Turn! Turn!
Mystery
Sunset Skies
Private Life
Yes He Lives
Drifting
Fooled by a Feeling
Sleepwalking
It's Lonely When the Lights Go On
Fighter

♫ Early Years, The

Compilation album

Cliff Richard's fiftieth anniversary in the music business was marked by an eight-disc boxed set of material, much of it rare out-takes, alternative versions and previously unreleased material. The first of those albums was *The Early Years*, which was subsequently issued on a CD in its own right. Issued on the EMI label (catalogue number 5099921659324), *The Early Years* was released on 12th April 2010.

♫ EP Collection, The: Ballads and Love Songs

Compilation album

Colin Miles was one of the first music entrepreneurs to see the value in pulling together archive material from vinyl and transferring them to CD once the boom in that format took off in the middle of the eighties. As well as producing three albums worth of rare Shadows EP tracks, amongst other artists, he also oversaw the collation of the ballads and love songs from Cliff Richard's multitude of EPs. On the listing were songs from ***Look in My Eyes, Maria, Love Songs, Dream, Take Four, Holiday Carnival, A Forever Kind of Love, When in France, Expresso Bongo, Why Don't They Understand?, La La La La La*** and ***Congratulations***. *The EP Collection: Ballads and Love Songs* was issued on the See For Miles label (catalogue numbers SEE 280 and SEE CD 280 for the LP and CD respectively) on 29th September 1989 but didn't make any impression on the album charts. Out of print, the album in any format has become a collector's item.

Track Listing

Look in My Eyes, Maria
If I Give My Heart to You
Maria
Secret Love
Love Letters
I Only Have Eyes for You
All I Do Is Dream of You
When I Grow Too Old to Dream
My Heart Is an Open Book
Boom Boom (That's How My Heart Beats)
Moonlight Bay
A Forever Kind of Love
La Mer
J'Attendrai
The Shrine on the Second Floor
Where the Four Winds Blow
Solitary Man
Things We Said Today
Carnival
Little Rag Doll

♫ Established 1958

21st studio album

August 1968 saw the tenth year of the partnership between Cliff Richard and the Shadows and the phenomenal success they had had and were continuing to have. Although the cracks were showing and the Shadows were on the verge of breaking up, the celebratory tenth anniversary album, suitably titled *Established 1958*, had a selection of songs, none of which was released as a single even though the material was strong enough, with the track listing adopting a sequence of a Cliff song followed by a Shadows tune. One of the tracks features Cliff backed only by an orchestra, while two of the tracks feature the Shadows exercising their vocal capabilities. The album was issued on the Columbia label in mono (catalogue number SX 6282) and stereo (SCX 6282) in September 1968 and, despite the pedigree, only reached number thirty, staying in the charts for just four weeks. The stereo version of the album was issued on CD for the first time alongside ***The Best of Cliff*** on the EMI label (catalogue number 0777 7 80450 2 1) on 2nd November 1992 and was remastered and reissued again (0946 3 81968 2 2) on 12th March 2007 but with four bonus tracks originally released on vinyl around this period.

Track Listing

Don't Forget to Catch Me
Voyage to the Bottom of the Bath *(The Shadows)*
Not the Way It Should Be
Poem *(The Shadows)*
The Dreams I Dream
The Average Life of a Daily Man *(The Shadows)*
Somewhere By the Sea
Banana Man *(The Shadows)*
Girl on the Bus
The Magical Mrs. Clamps *(The Shadows)*
Ooh La La
Here I Go Again Loving You *(The Shadows)*
What's Behind the Eyes of Mary?
Maggie's Samba *(The Shadows)*

Bonus tracks (2007 CD)
High 'n' Dry
Girl, You'll Be a Woman Soon
Mr. Nice
What's More I Don't Need Her

♫ Every Face Tells a Story

30th studio album

After the phenomenal commercial and critical success of ***I'm Nearly Famous***, Cliff Richard repeated the formula with Bruce Welch on production duties for the follow-up album, *Every Face Tells a Story*. Featuring all new material, the album ceded three singles, ***My Kinda Life, When Two Worlds Drift Apart*** and ***Hey Mr. Dream Maker*** with another, ***Don't Turn the Light Out***, being released in the US, which helped cement the critics' view that Cliff was now a renewed force in music. The album was issued on the EMI label (catalogue number EMC 3172) in March 1977 and peaked at number eight, staying in the UK album charts for ten weeks. It was first issued on CD as part of the EMI programme to reissue Cliff's albums (catalogue number 0777 7 80494 2 5) on 4th October 1993 when it was combined with ***Small Corners***. On 2nd July 2002, the album was digitally remastered and released in its own right (catalogue number 7243 5 38370 2 0) with three bonus tracks that had been the B-sides of the three main singles.

Track Listing

My Kinda Life
Must Be Love
When Two Worlds Drift Apart
You Got Me Wondering
Every Face Tells a Story (It Never Tells a Lie)
Try a Smile
Hey Mr. Dream Maker
Give Me Love Your Way
Up in the World
Don't Turn the Light Out
It'll Be Me Babe
Spider Man

Bonus tracks (2002 CD)
No-One Waits
Nothing Left for Me to Say
That's Why I Love You

♫ Finders Keepers

16th studio album

Although ***Wonderful Life*** was a reasonable success, it was by no means anywhere near as popular as ***Summer Holiday*** or ***The Young Ones***. Dropping Peter Myers and Ronald Cass as screenwriters and composers, the entire musical was composed by the Shadows. The resultant album also featured three additional songs not in the film to pad the album out because it was short: ***Run to the Door, Where Did the Summer Go?*** and ***Into Each Life Some Rain Must Fall***. There were no EPs released associated with the project, while only ***Time Drags By*** was released as a single. The album was issued on the Columbia label in mono (catalogue number SX 6079) and stereo (SCX 6079) in December 1966 and reached number six in the charts, remaining for eighteen weeks. The album was reissued in stereo only alongside ***Cinderella*** on the EMI label (catalogue number 0777 7 80435 2 2) on 2nd November 1992. It was remastered and reissued on its own (7243 4 77716 2 0) on 22nd August 2005 and incorporated a number of bonus tracks.

Track Listing

Finders Keepers
Time Drags By
Washerwoman
La La La Song
My Way
Oh Señorita
Spanish Music/Fiesta
This Day
Paella
Finders Keepers/My Way/Paella/Fiesta *(The Shadows)*
Run to the Door
Where Did the Summer Go?
Into Each Life Some Rain Must Fall

Bonus tracks (2005 CD)
Oh Señorita (Extended version)
Visions
What Would I Do (for the Love of a Girl)
In the Country

♫ For Life

Reissue of **Something's Goin' On**

Cliff Richard bounced back with a very fresh sounding album in ***Something's Goin' On*** in late 2004 with three singles issued from the project. Although the album reached number seven, Cliff was generally reported as being unhappy with its reception because the tracks are some of the best he has ever produced. The album was reorganized and had four extra tracks (previously B-sides and a download track) added to the listing and was reissued in Europe as *For Life* (after one of Cliff's favourite tracks on the album) on the Edel label (catalogue number 163652ERE) on 17th June 2005.

Track Listing

She's All Mine
Somethin' Is Goin' On
How Many Sleeps?
Sometimes Love
I Cannot Give You My Love
The Day that I Stop Loving You
Simplicity
What Car?
How Did She Get Here?
Field of Love
Faithful One
Slow Down
I Will Not Be a Mistake
I Don't Wanna Lose You
Diamonds on a Chain
For Life
Thousand Miles to Go

♫ From a Distance ***** The Event

Live album

Cliff Richard reached his thirtieth anniversary in the music business in 1988 in spectacular style with a commercially successful album in ***Always Guaranteed*** and still getting top ten singles. To celebrate, he booked Wembley Stadium for two days on 16th and 17th June 1989 to celebrate and thank those with whom he had worked and also his fans. The first set was called the *Oh Boy! Set* and featured the Dallas Boys, the Oh Boy! Band, the Vernons Girls, the Kalin Twins and the Shadows. The second set was called *Cliff's Set* and brought everything up to date with much of the material coming from ***Stronger*** and *Always Guaranteed*. This set featured Jet Harris, Tony Meehan, Stock, Aitken and Waterman and Aswad. The original album was quite short on a lot of the material and, indeed, it included three tracks that were studio recordings (represented in italics in the track listing). The remastered CD included everything from the set, removing the studio tracks, reordering some items (these are highlighted in bold in the track listing), but missed six tracks featuring the Shadows, which is unfortunate given their influence on Cliff's career. The programme was issued in album and boxed set form on the EMI label (catalogue numbers CRTV 31 (LP), CDCRTV 31 (CD), CRTVB 31 (LP boxed set) and CDCRTVB 31 (CD boxed set)) on 5th November 1990 (albums) and 3rd December 1990 (boxed sets). It reached number three in the charts and stayed in the listings for fifteen weeks. The remastered album was extended to two discs (7243 5 63730 2 0) and reissued on 21st March 2005 alongside the DVD version of the previously released VHS video of the event.

Track Listing

Oh Boy! Medley: Oh Boy!; Whole Lotta Shakin' Goin' On; Bird Dog; Let's Have a Party; It's My Party; C'mon Everybody; Whole Lotta Shakin' Goin' On
Zing Went the Strings of My Heart *(The Dallas Boys)*
Always
When *(The Kalin Twins)*
The Glory of Love
Wired for Sound
Dreamin'
Daddy's Home
I Could Easily Fall (in Love with You)
Some People
We Don't Talk Anymore
Two Hearts

Hoots Mon *(The Oh Boy! Band)*
Don't Look Now *(The Vernons Girls)*
The Girl Can't Help It
Sea Cruise
Medley: Book of Love; Blue Moon; Do You Wanna Dance?; Chantilly Lace; At the Hop; Rock 'n' Roll Is Here to Stay
The Young Ones
In the Country
Move It
Shake, Rattle and Roll
Joanna
Remember Me
Stronger than That
Silhouettes
Good Golly Miss Molly
Miss You Nights
Summer Holiday
Just Don't Have the Heart
Fighter/Thief in the Night
The Best of Me
From a Distance
Share a Dream
All the Time You Need
Saviour's Day

♫ Good News

19th studio album

Norrie Paramor was the one to suggest to Cliff Richard that he ought to consider creating an album of religious material, perhaps arranged in such away to help broaden its appeal. At the time, Cliff was spending a lot of his time on Christian rallies, particularly with the American evangelist Billy Graham, and this came as a highly opportune suggestion and was pretty much completed in a set of sessions planned over a week in April and May of 1967. The album was issued on the Columbia label in mono (catalogue number SX 6167) and stereo (SCX 6167) on 21st October 1967 and, in spite of the narrow appeal of the album's contents, it still reached number thirty-seven for a week. The album was subsequently paired with ***Don't Stop Me Now!*** and issued on CD for the first time on the EMI label (catalogue number 0777 7 80438 2 9) on 2nd November 1992.

Track Listing
Good News
It Is No Secret
We Shall Be Changed
The 23rd Psalm (Crimond)
Go Where I Send Thee
What a Friend We Have in Jesus
All Glory Laud and Honour
Just a Closer Walk with Thee
The King of Love My Shepherd Is
Mary, What You Gonna Name That Pretty Little Baby?
When I Survey the Wondrous Cross
Take My Hand, Precious Lord
Get on Board, Little Children
May the Good Lord Bless and Keep You

♫ Green Light

32nd studio album

After Cliff Richard self-produced his religious album, ***Small Corners***, Bruce Welch returned to carry out the production on his next album, *Green Light*. There were high hopes for the album and, while it was critically well-received, it fared less well than ***I'm Nearly Famous*** and ***Every Face Tells a Story***. The album produced three singles: the title track, ***Can't Take the Hurt Any More*** and ***Please Remember Me***, none of which set the singles charts alight. The album was issued on the EMI label (catalogue number EMC 3231) on 29th September 1979 and reached number twenty-five, staying in the charts for only three weeks. It was combined with ***Thank You Very Much*** as part of the EMI programme to release Cliff's first two-and-a-half decades of albums on CD (catalogue number 0777 7 80496 2 3) on 4th October 1993 before being digitally remastered and reissued (7243 5 38369 2 4) on 2nd July 2002 , this time with three bonus tracks culled from the B-sides.

Track Listing
Green Light
Under Lock and Key
She's a Gypsy
Count Me Out
Please Remember Me
Never Even Thought
Free My Soul
Start All Over Again
While She's Young
Can't Take the Hurt Anymore
Ease Along

Bonus tracks (2002 CD)
Please Don't Tease
Needing a Friend
Imagine Love

♫ Heathcliff Live

Live album

After producing a studio version of ten of the songs to be included in the eventual stage show, Cliff Richard decided to release an album of a live show. Spread across two discs, the album includes a number of new songs not previously available, including ***The Gambling Song*** and ***The Nightmare***. Featuring Helen Hobson as Cathy, Daryl Knock as Edgar Linton and Sara Haggerty as Isabella Linton, the atmosphere from the audience adds more excitement to the performance. Released in a boxed set with a luxury pamphlet describing the history of the show, how it was created and the lyrics to the songs, it was issued on the EMI label (catalogue number 7243 8 54768 2 2) on 2nd December 1996 but he release didn't generate enough interest for it to chart.

Track Listing

Overture *(instrumental)*
A Misunderstood Man
Funeral Cortege *(instrumental)*
The Sleep of the Good
Gypsy Bundle
The Grange Waltz *(instrumental)*
Each to His Own
Had to Be
Mrs. Edgar Linton *(Helen Hobson)*
The Journey: Africa/India/China *(instrumental)*
When You Thought of Me
Overture (Reprise) Entr'Acte Music *(instrumental)*
When You Thought of Me (Reprise)
Dream Tomorrow
I Do Not Love You Isabella (Bridge) *(Sara Haggerty)*
The Gambling Song
I Do Not Love You Isabella
Isabella (Reprise)
Choosing When It's Too Late
The Madness of Cathy *(Helen Hobson)*
Marked with Death
Be with Me Always
The Nightmare
Be with Me Always (Reprise) *(Helen Hobson)*
Overture (Reprise) *(instrumental)*
A Misunderstood Man (Reprise)
Music for Curtain Calls *(instrumental)*

♫ Help It Along

27th studio album

Cliff Richard's fourth album was devoted to the more religiously inspirational side of the material that he recorded and took its name from one of the songs that were entered as candidates for the UK's song for the 1973 Eurovision Song Contest. Like his first album, *Help It Along* was recorded in front of a quietly reverential group of invited fans and featured all new recordings of some familiar songs from Cliff's repertoire as well as some new titles. There was also a handful of songs recorded but not issued (even on the remastered CD in the new millennium). The album was issued on the EMI label (catalogue number EMA 768) in June 1974 but didn't find a placing in the album charts. Combined with the soundtrack to Cliff's last film, ***Take Me High***, EMI released the album on CD for the first time (catalogue number 0777 7 80488 2 4) on 4th October 1993, before remastering it and reissuing it again (0946 3 81970 2 7) on 12th March 2007, with the four lowest placed candidates for the Eurovision Song Contest, which had made it into the singles charts as a maxi-single.

Track Listing

Day By Day
Celestial Houses
Jesus
Silvery Rain
Jesus Loves You
Fire and Rain
Yesterday Today Forever
Mr. Businessman
Help It Along
Amazing Grace
Higher Ground
Sing a Song of Freedom

Bonus tracks (2007 CD)
Help It Along
Tomorrow Rising
The Days of Love
Ashes to Ashes

♫ His Land

24th studio album

A month after releasing a truly religious album full of scripture readings and telling the story of Christ, ***About That Man***, Cliff Richard issued another religious album, this time with more songs. Touted as a soundtrack to a new film, this is only partly true, since it was more of a Christian documentary. *His Land* tells the story of Israel, its history and how it was succeeding contemporaneously in the modern day. Alongside American Cliff Barrows, Cliff discusses tracts of the Bible as they walk around the holy lands and he sings a number of songs along the way. The album was released on the Columbia label (catalogue number SCX 6443) on 27th November 1970 but, like its predecessor, it made no impression on the charts (although this was not entirely the point of the project). The album was paired with *About That Man* and released on CD by EMI (catalogue number 0777 780482 2 0) on 2nd November 1992.

Track Listing

Ezekiel's Vision
Dry Bones
His Land *(Cliff)*
Jerusalem Jerusalem *(Cliff)*
The New 23rd *(Cliff)*
His Land *(Cliff)*
Hava Nagila
Over in Bethlehem *(Cliff)*
Keep Me Where Love Is *(Cliff)*
He's Everything to Me *(Cliff)*
Narration and Hallelujah Chorus

♫ Hit List, The

Compilation album

In 1993, Cliff had successfully completed thirty-five years at the top of the music business. Coincidentally (and perhaps spookily) he had also achieved thirty-five top five UK hits. The subsequent tour worked on that premise with a random trawl through this list and the associated album, with its two discs, selected many of those songs adding ***Green Light*** and ***Miss You Nights*** because they were Cliff's favourites. The album was issued on the EMI label on CD only (catalogue number CDEMTV 84) on 3rd October 1994 (in time, of course, for Christmas) and reached number three, staying in the charts for twenty-one weeks.

♫ I'm Nearly Famous
29th studio album

Cliff Richard's twenty-ninth studio album marked a significant milestone in his musical career. Having been somewhat in the doldrums from a chart perspective and from a critical point of view for a few years, this was turned around once former Shadows band-mate Bruce Welch came on board as producer, furnishing Cliff with stronger material and amore defined musical direction. Many see this album as the turning point in Cliff's career and the start of the renaissance that would continue until the early nineties. It spawned three very successful singles in ***I Can't Ask for Anything More than You***, ***Miss You Nights*** and ***Devil Woman***, with the last two songs being cited as Cliff's eternal favourites. The album was issued on the EMI label (catalogue number EMC 3122) in May 1976 and Cliff was rewarded with his first top ten studio album – it peaked at number five, staying in the charts for twenty-one weeks – since the ***Finders Keepers*** soundtrack album in December 1966. The album was combined with ***The 31st of February Street*** and issued on CD for the first time (catalogue number 0777 7 80491 2 8) on 4th October 1993, and it was digitally remastered and reissued (7243 5 33114 2 1) on 9th July 2009 with a number of bonus tracks not previously available on CD, including the controversial single ***(There's a) Honky Tonk Angel***.

Track Listing

I Can't Ask for Any More than You
It's No Use Pretending
I'm Nearly Famous
Lovers
Junior Cowboy
Miss You Nights
I Wish You'd Change Your Mind
Devil Woman
Such Is the Mystery
You've Got to Give Me All Your Lovin'
If You Walked Away
Alright, It's Alright

Bonus tracks (2001 CD)
Love Enough
Love On (Shine On)
(There's a) Honky Tonk Angel
Wouldn't You Know It?
It's Only Me You've Left Behind
You're the One

♫ I'm No Hero
34th studio album

Cliff Richard turned away from Bruce Welch as producer and, having co-produced his previous album, ***Rock 'n' Roll Juvenile***, he now turned to Alan Tarney to take up the duties for *I'm No Hero*, which also featured a large number of songs that had also been written by Tarney and this would seed the point of his continued dominance in the studio with Cliff for most of the eighties. The album was issued on the EMI label (catalogue number EMA 796) in August 1980 and reached number four, staying in the album charts for twelve weeks. It was first released on CD in its own right on the Fame label (catalogue number CD-FA 3148) in 1988, before being digitally remastered and reissued on the EMI label (7243 5 33113 2 2) on 9th July 2001, with two B-sides as bonus tracks.

Track Listing

Take Another Look
Anything I Can Do
A Little in Love
Here (So Doggone Blue)
Give a Little Bit More
In the Night
I'm No Hero
Dreamin'
A Heart Will Break
Everyman

Bonus tracks (2001 CD)
Dynamite
Keep on Looking

♫ It's a Small World
Compilation album

Cliff Richard had had a long association with the Tear Fund charity and in the early eighties made a film documentary called *It's a Small World*. Featured on that short film were three songs written by Cliff and released on the album: ***Tiny Planet***, which was completely new, ***Small World***, originally released as a B-side of ***Shooting from the Heart*** and ***La Gonave***, originally found on the track listing of ***The Rock Connection***. The other songs were a selection of inspirational songs from his albums. The album was issued on the Myrrh label (catalogue numbers MYRR 1209 and MYRCD 1209 for the LP and CD, respectively) in May 1985. The album was subsequently reissued on the Alliance label (ALD 023) in CD format only in 1994.

Track Listing

Tiny Planet
Small World
Devil Woman
Moving In
It Has to Be You, It Has to Be Me
La Gonave
I Will Follow You
The Only Way Out
Rock 'n' Roll Juvenile
Where Do We Go from Here?

♫ Japan Tour '74
Live album

For some reason, Cliff Richard's tours to Japan were regularly recorded and released as albums. One such was the concert performed at the Shinjuku Koseinenkin Hall in Tokyo on the 7th and 8th October 1974. Originally only released in Japan on the EMI label (catalogue number EMS-67037 38) on 5th July 1975 as a two-record album, it was subsequently dusted off and transferred to CD (5099926843728) on 6th April 2009.

Track Listing

Winning
Do You Wanna Dance?
(You Keep Me) Hangin' On
Make It Easy on Yourself/ The Sun Ain't Gonna Shine Any More
Get Back
Fireside Song
Travellin' Light
Give Me Back That Old Familiar Feeling
Early in the Morning
Take Me High
Hit Medley: Congratulations; In the Country; Dancing Shoes; The Day I Met Marie; On the Beach; Sing a Song of Freedom
Constantly
You've Lost That Lovin' Feeling
Gospel Medley: Jesus; Amazing Grace; Jesus Is My Kind of People
Don't Talk to Him
Bachelor Boy
Rock Medley: His Latest Flame; Chantilly Lace; Bony Maronie; Do You Wanna Dance?; Crocodile Rock
Higher Ground
Sing a Song of Freedom
Visions
Power to All Our Friends

♫ Kinda Latin

15th studio album

Keeping firmly in the same mould as his previous album, ***Love Is Forever,*** Cliff Richard followed that album up six months later with *Kinda Latin,* again featuring a number of Latin-rhythm-inspired songs sung in English. Although no singles or EPs were issued against the project, the album was released on the Columbia label in mono (catalogue number SX 6039) and stereo (SCX 6039) formats – the first time Cliff's Columbia mono and stereo album catalogue numbers had been synchronized – in May 1966, reaching number nine and staying n the charts for twelve weeks, which proved to be Cliff's best showing in the album charts for over a year. The album was combined with *Love Is Forever* and released as part of the EMI Cliff Richard CD Collection programme (catalogue number 0777 7 80432 2 5) on 5th October 1992 and was issued in stereo only.

Track Listing

Blame It on the Bossa Nova
Blowing in the Wind
Quiet Nights of Quiet Stars
Eso Beso
The Girl from Ipanema
One Note Samba
Fly Me to the Moon
Our Day Will Come
Quando, Quando, Quando
Come Closer to Me
Meditation
Concrete and Clay

♫ Listen to Cliff!

4th studio album

Cliff Richard's fourth album, like its predecessor ***Me and My Shadows,*** featured a mixture of original and cover material as well as accompaniment by the Shadows or an orchestra. Two EPs were eventually issued from the project, ***Listen to Cliff!*** and ***Listen to Cliff! No. 2,*** while there was still no single to appear on its track listing, as was the policy of Columbia to keep LPs and singles quite separate. Issued on the Columbia label in mono (catalogue number 33SX 1320) and stereo (SCX 3375) formats on 14th April 1961, the album reached the highest point of number two and stayed in the UK album charts for twenty-eight weeks. Regularly reissued in different packages on vinyl, *Listen to Cliff!* was first issued in stereo format on CD as part of the Cliff Richard CD Collection programme and was combined with ***21 Today*** on the EMI label (catalogue number 0777 7 80420 2 0) on 5th October 1992. The mono version was also given a CD release (catalogue number 7243 4 95441 2 3) on 5th June 1998.

Track Listing

What'd I Say
Blue Moon
True Love Will Come to You
Lover
Unchained Melody
Idle Gossip
First Lesson in Love
Almost Like Being in Love
Beat Out Dat Rhythm on a Drum
Memories Linger On
Temptation
I Live for You
Sentimental Journey
I Want You to Know
We Kiss in a Shadow
It's You

♫ Live at the ABC Kingston 1962

Live album

Although Cliff Richard's first live album released was ***Cliff in Japan,*** it was actually the concert performed with the Shadows at the ABC theatre in Kingston, London that was recorded first. For an unknown reason, it was left in the EMI vaults before being unearthed and released during Cliff's fiftieth anniversary celebrations. Featuring a number of familiar tracks from that period, it also had a number of songs, such as ***Save My Soul, Dim, Dim the Lights*** and ***Rovin' Gambler,*** which Cliff never recorded in the studio. The album was issued on the EMI label in two formats: the first as a straight CD album (catalogue number 7243 537342 2 0) and the second as a boxed set that include a seven inch presentation single (7243 537931 2 8) both released on 4th March 2002.

Track Listing

Tony Marsh Intro *(Tony Marsh)*
Apache/Shazam *(The Shadows)*
Shadoogie *(The Shadows)*
Wonderful Land *(The Shadows)*
All My Sorrows *(The Shadows)*
Quarter to Three *(The Shadows)*
Nivram *(The Shadows)*
Little B *(The Shadows)*
FBI *(The Shadows)*
Tony Marsh Intro *(Tony Marsh)*
Do You Wanna Dance?
Dim, Dim the Lights
My Blue Heaven
Razzle Dazzle
Rovin' Gambler
Save My Soul
When the Girl in Your Arms (Is the Girl in Your Heart)
I Got a Woman
The Young Ones Medley: Lessons in Love; Got a Funny Feeling; The Young Ones
We Say Yeah

♫ Live at the Talk of the Town

2nd live album

Following the moderate success of the live album, ***Cliff in Japan***, a performance by Cliff Richard backed with an orchestra from the Talk of the Town theatre in London recorded on 30th May 1968 was released in the middle of 1970. The set list, unsurprisingly, is very similar to that of the earlier live album, largely because they were performed in roughly the same period. But there are some differences: Cliff performs a guitar solo version of ***A Taste of Honey*** and also performs a number of tracks that he hasn't recorded in the studio or released in any other capacity since, such as ***The Lady Came from Baltimore*** and ***Something Good***. The album was released in stereo only on the Regal Starline (rather than the more familiar Columbia) label (catalogue number SRS 5031) in July 1970 but failed to make any impression on the charts. Paired with ***Sincerely Cliff Richard***, it was issued on CD for the first time on the EMI label as part of an ongoing programme to reissue Cliff's earlier albums (catalogue number 0777 7 80444 2 0) on 2nd November 1992 and then again on 12th March 2007 (0946 3 8969 2 1) with a number of bonus tracks, which were four of the candidates for the 1968 Eurovision Song Contest for the UK, previously only available on a French CD compilation and the ***Congratulations*** EP.

Track Listing

Introduction
Congratulations
Shout
All My Love
Ain't Nothing But a House Party
Something Good
If Ever I Should Leave You
Girl, You'll Be a Woman Soon
Hank's Medley: London's Not Too Far; The Dreams I Dream; The Day I Met Marie
La La La La La
A Taste of Honey
The Lady Came from Baltimore
When I'm 64
What's More I Don't Need Her
Bows and Fanfare
Congratulations
Visions
Finale: Congratulations

Bonus tracks (2007 CD)
Wonderful World
Do You Remember?
The Sound of the Candyman's Trumpet
Little Rag Doll

♫ "Live" in Japan '72

Live album

Cliff Richard's 1972 Japanese concert in the Kosei Nenkin Hall in Tokyo on 22nd and 3rd September 1972 featured Olivia Newton-John, Hank Marvin and Brian Bennett and was recorded. However, it was not released until it formed one of the eight discs in the ***...And They Said It Wouldn't Last! (My 50 Years in Music)*** retrospective of favourite tracks and rare material. The album was subsequently given its own release on the EMI label (catalogue number 5099921659928) on 12th April 2010.

♫ Lost & Found (from the Archives)

Compilation album

...And They Said It Wouldn't Last! (My 50 Years in Music) was the celebratory eight-disc album release featuring a collection of favourite tunes as well as a wealth of material never released before, including alternative versions, songs not released on CD and material recorded but never released. The latter was given its own album release on the EMI label (catalogue number 50999 2 16600 2 3) on 6th April 2009.

♫ Love Is Forever

14th studio album

As with the self-titled ***Cliff Richard***, *Love Is Forever* is a collection of songs that Cliff recorded over a number of months. One EP was issued against the project, taking the same title, while the album was released on the Columbia label in mono (catalogue number 33SX 1769) and stereo (SCX 3569) in November 1965 and reached number nineteen, staying in the charts for just one week. The CD version was released as part of EMI's Cliff Richard CD Collection (catalogue number 0777 7 80432 2 5) in stereo only, alongside ***Kinda Latin*** on 5th October 1992.

Track Listing

Everyone Needs Someone to Love
Long Ago (and Far Away)
(All of a Sudden) My Heart Sings
Have I Told You Lately That I Love You?
Fly Me to the Moon
Theme from *A Summer Place*
I Found a Rose
My Foolish Heart
Through the Eye of a Needle
My Colouring Book
I'll Walk Alone
Someday (You'll Want Me to Love You)
Paradise Lost
Look Homeward Angel

♫ Love Songs

Compilation album

A reasonably unique idea was tried with the collection of Cliff Richard's songs to date by corralling the greatest hit ballads and love songs on to one album. The coverage is extensive with ***A Voice in the Wilderness*** being the earliest and ***A Little in Love*** being the latest, with the remainder being a spread in between (although largely missing the late sixties and early seventies period). The album was released on the EMI label (catalogue number EMTV 27) in July 1981 and became Cliff's fifth number one album, staying in the charts for an amazing forty-three weeks - his best ever tenure on the album charts since he started recording. It was subsequently released as a CD (CDP 7 48049 2) on 28th March 1987.

Love... The Album

49th studio album

When EMI dropped Cliff Richard from their roster of talent at the beginning of the millennium after an association lasting more than forty years, Cliff fought back with ***Wanted*** and proved his worth. EMI, for their part, recognized that he was an integral part of their history and convinced him to record new material for what were otherwise essentially three compilation albums. The third was *Love... The Album*, which featured a selection of his ballads over the years with new material recorded, including a cover of Leo Sayers' ***When I Need You***, which was subsequently released as a single from the project. The album was released on the EMI label (catalogue number 50999 509370 2 8) on 12th November 2007.

Track Listing

Waiting for a Girl Like You
It's Al in the Game
Miss You Nights
If You're Not the One
Constantly
The Best of Me
When I Need You
True Love Ways
The Twelfth of Never
When You Say Nothing at All
Ocean Deep
For Life
All out of Love
I Still Believe in You
Some People

♫ Me and My Shadows

3rd studio album

The first album with Cliff Richard and the Shadows on every track was also the first to be released in mono and stereo simultaneously. In addition, there were some original compositions amongst the covers and it saw the emerging writing talents of Hank Marvin and Bruce Welch. Issued on the Columbia label in mono (catalogue number 33SX 1261) and stereo (SCX 3330) on 7th October 1960, the album reached number two and remained in the album charts for thirty-three weeks. Three EPs were issued from the project, ***Me and My Shadows No. 1***, ***Me and My Shadows No. 2*** and ***Me and My Shadows No. 3***, while ***Gee Whiz It's You*** became an unofficial single hit in the UK after it was released in foreign territories and precipitated unprecedented demand back home. The album was first released in stereo on the dual CD reissue of Cliff's albums alongside the mono version of ***Cliff Sings*** on the EMI label (catalogue number 0777 7 80417 2 6) on 5th October 1992, with the mono release following (catalogue number 7243 4 95440 2 4) on 5th June 1998.

Track Listing

I'm Gonna Get You
You and I
I Cannot Find a True Love
Evergreen Tree
She's Gone
Left Out Again
You're Just the One to Do It
Lamp of Love
Choppin' and Changin'
We Have It Made
Tell Me
Gee Whiz It's You
I Love You So
I'm Willing to Learn
I Don't Know
Working After School

♫ More Hits by Cliff

Compilation album

The second compilation of Cliff Richard's hits followed directly on from ***Cliff's Hit Album*** from July 1963 with ***It'll Be Me*** and took the chronology through to ***I Could Easily Fall (in Love with You)***. This time, none of the hits from this period is left off the track listing, although two non-single tracks were added to the collection: ***Dancing Shoes*** (from ***Summer***

Holiday and B-side of the title single) and ***A Matter of Moments*** (from ***Wonderful Life*** and a single in some territories). The album was issued on the Columbia label in mono (catalogue number 33SX 1737) and stereo (SCX 3555) in July 1965. Perhaps because of the popularity of the singles and the likely ownership of those discs, the album only reached number twenty, staying in the British charts for only one week, which was the worst showing for any type of Cliff album to date.

♫ My Kinda Life

French album

Cliff Richard was riding high on his success and popularity at the beginning of the nineties and he spent some time reworking a number of tracks mainly from albums and recordings made during the first half of the eighties. Taking the original track, new vocals, or guitars or other instrumentation would be added to give the chosen songs a fresher feel. This was released on CD only on the EMI label (catalogue number 7994322) on 18th May 1992 but only in France. However, a number of imports were sold in the UK but insufficient to make its presence felt in the album charts.

Track Listing

Born to Rock 'n' Roll
Hot Shot
Devil Woman
Remember
Carrie
Lean n You
We Don't Talk Anymore
Monday Thru' Friday
Lucille
You've Got Me Wondering
Never Even Thought
Two Hearts
Language of Love
My Kinda Life

♫ My Life, My Way

Audio-book

Cliff Richard has written a number of versions of his autobiography over the years but it was in 2008 that he published *My Life, My Way* to mark the fiftieth anniversary of his time at the top of the music business. The text of the book was subsequently abridged by Yvonne Antrobus and read by Cliff for a two CD set released on the Hachette Digital label (catalogue number 978 1 4055 0537 6) on 9th July 2009.

♫ My Songs

Compilation album

Cliff Richard has regularly asserted that he is not a songwriter, so it came as a surprise when he realized the number of them that he had actually written. The album *My Songs* was created to provide acknowledgment of this facet of his talents and features some familiar tracks as well as some not so well-known. In addition there are some tracks, such as the superlative ***Bulange Downpour*** that appear on the album for the first time. The album was issued on the EMI label (catalogue number 7243 5 90965 2 0) on 18th August 2003.

Track Listing

Without You
Bachelor Boy
Don't Talk to Him
On the Beach
I'll Love You Forever Today
31st of February Street (Opening)
Nothing to Remind Me
Fireside Song
Love On (Shine On)
Nothing Left for Me to Say
Rock 'n' Roll Juvenile
La Gonave
Over You
Love Ya
Lindsay Jane
The Winner
Where You Are
Bulange Downpour
Hold Us Together

♫ Now You See Me... Now You Don't

36th studio album

Cliff Richard's star was back on the ascendency from the end of the seventies and throughout the eighties and he had a run of successful top ten albums, including his latest, quasi-religious album, *Now You See Me... Now You Don't*. Featuring two singles, the opening track ***The Only Way Out*** and ***Little Town***, the album was released on 23rd August 1982 on the EMI label (catalogue number EMC 3415) and reached the number four spot, staying in the chart for fourteen weeks. It was first released on CD on the EMI label (catalogue number CDP 7 48276 2) in August 1987 and then digitally remastered and reissued (7243 5 38371 2 9) on 2nd July 2002 with three bonus tracks that formed the B-sides of the two singles.

Track Listing

The Only Way Out
First Date
Thief in the Night
Where Do We Go from Here
Son of Thunder
Little Town
It Has to Be You, It Has to Be Me
The Water Is Wide
Now You See Me, Now You Don't
Be in My Heart
Discovering

Bonus tracks (2002 CD)

Under the Influence
Love and a Helping Hand
You, Me and Jesus

♫ On the Continent

Compilation album

Cliff Richard regularly recorded songs in foreign languages and most prominent was his predilection for aiming songs at the German market, for which he recorded two albums: *Hier Ist Cliff* and *Ich Träume Deine Träume*. For the French fans, he released *When in France... Chante en Français*, while Spain and Italy already had ***When in Spain*** and ***When in Rome*** respectively. Other recordings included several singles and B-sides as well as the different language versions of his two Eurovision songs. These were collated together, remastered and issued on the Bear Family Records label (catalogue number BCD 15 903 EI) on 24th November 1997 in Germany and in stereo. Coming in a box with four CDs, there was also a reproduction of a German fan magazine and hardback booklet crammed with pictures from the period covered by the songs. Purporting to be all his continental songs, this is not quite true since it doesn't include ***Remember***, the French version of ***When Two Worlds Drift Apart***, recorded for the French ***My Kinda Life*** album.

Track Listing

Bin Verliebt
Die Stimme der Liebe
Schön Wie ein Traum
Vreneli
Rote Lippen Soll Man Küssen
Zuviel Allein
Sag 'No' zu Ihm
Das Ist die Frage Aller Fragen
Nur mit Dir
Es War Keine so Wunderbar Wie Du
Es Könnte Schon Morgen Sein
Glaub' Nur Mir
Nur Bei Dir Bin Ich zu Haus
Du Bis Mein Erster Gedanke
Was Ist Dabei?
Das Glück Ist Rosarot
Was Kann Ich Tun?
Ein Girl Wie Du
Bilder von Dir
Ein Sonntag mit Marie
Es Ist Nict Gut Allein zu Sein
Mrs. Emily Jones
Ch Kann Treu Sein
Sternengold
London Ist Nicht Weit
Man Gratuliert Mir
Wonderful World
Marianne
Geh Deinen Weg Nicht So Allein
Twist im Blut
Mr. Niemand
Die Liebe Ist Immer Nur Heute
Fragen
Stell Mich Deinen Eltern Vor
Deine Augen Träumen Mary
Ooh La La (Sagte Cäsar zu Cleopatra)
Zärtliche Sekunden
Shoom Llama Boom Boom
Story Ohne Happy End
Kein Zug nach Gretna Green
Du, Du Gefällst Mir So
Lieben Kann Man Einmal Nur
Goodbye Sam, Das Ist die Liebe
Umbarella
Laß Uns Schnell Vegessen
Das Girl von Nebenan
Du Fragst Mich Immer Wieder
Wenn Du Lachst, Lacht das Glück
Ein Spiel ohne Grenzen
Concerto
Neben Dir Wird's Keine Geben
Zum Heiraten Bin Ich Kein Typ
Der Mann Neben Dir
Ich Träume Deine Träume
Kleine Taube
Gut Daß Es Freunde Gibt
Es Gehören Zwei zum Glücklichsein
Liebesleid
O Mio Signore
Come Prima
Concerto d'Autumno
Arrividerci Roma
Legata ad un Granello di Sabbia
Per un Bacio Mia Amore
Che Cosa Farai di Questo Mia Amore
Carina
Nel Blu Dipinto di Blu (Volare)
Dicitencello Vuie
Casa Senze Finestre
Maria Ninguem
Non l'Ascoltare
Imagina un Giorno
Oh, No, No
Il Mondo et Tondo
Chi Lo Sa
Non Dimenticare Chi Ti Arma
Chi Lo Sa (Original version)
Boum
La Mer
J'Attendrai
C'Est Si Bon
A Quelle Histoire
Relève Mon Défi
Je Suis Formidale
La Ballade de Baltimore
L'Amandier Sauvage
Il Faut Chanter la Vie
Je T'Aime pour Toujours Ce Jour
Perfidia
Frenesi
Tus Besos
Amor, Amor, Amor
Solamente una Vez
Quizas, Quizas, Quizas
Cancia de Orfeo
Quien Sera
Te Quiero Dijeste
Vaya con Dios
Me Lo Diz Adela
Maria No Mas
Que Buena Suerte (Felicidades)
Todo el Pder a los Amigos

♫ Private Collection

Compilation album

Chosen by Cliff Richard as his favourite songs from the end of the seventies through to 1988, the album featured a number of his most successful single releases. The CD issue had fewer tracks than the cassette and vinyl releases, mainly from the later selection of singles. The album was released on the EMI label (catalogue numbers CRTV 30 (LP) and CDCRTV 30 (CD)) on 7th November 1988 and became Cliff's sixth number one and stayed in the charts for twenty-six weeks.

♫ Rare B-Sides: 1963-1989

Compilation album

EMI released ***...And They Said It Wouldn't Last! (My 50 Years in Music)*** as an eight-disc boxed set to celebrate Cliff Richard's fiftieth anniversary in the music business. The collection had several favourites and was a major document of his career, while the rare B-sides section had tracks not previously released on CD and it was one of the first to be released as a disc in its own right. It was issued on the EMI label (catalogue number 5099921659423) on 6th April 2009.

♫ Rare EP Tracks: 1961-1991

Compilation album

To mark Cliff Richard's fiftieth anniversary in the music business, EMI issued an eight-disc collation of rare and previously unreleased material alongside favourite tracks called ***...And They Said It Wouldn't Last! (My 50 Years in Music)***. One of these discs collated together EP tracks not previously seen on CD before, which was subsequently given its own album released. It was issued on the EMI label (catalogue number 50999 2 16595 2 2) on 12th April 2010.

♫ Real as I Wanna Be

44th studio album

At the start of the nineties, Cliff Richard's star was in the ascendency and at the height of his renewed popularity. But, almost a decade later, something had changed: the old guard of DJs at Radio 1 had been turfed out and boy bands and rap music were the in-thing; no longer did labels want to nurture talent or invest in existing stars, rather they only wanted to make money. This meant that stars like Cliff suffered at the hands of the cynical music machine. By the time *Real as I Wanna Be* was released, no-one wanted to play Cliff songs because it was deemed to be uncool. Cleverly, Cliff released the album's first single ***Can't Keep This Feeling In*** under the name of Blacknight and it received a lot of airplay. When it was revealed that it was Cliff, the airtime vanished, this proving the point. One other single was released from the project, ***The Miracle***, and the album was issued on the EMI label (catalogue number 7243 4 97406 2 4) on 19th October 1998. A version with a digipak cover was released simultaneously (7243 4 97951 2 9) and the album reached number ten, staying in the charts for nine weeks. It was to be his last full studio album for EMI after they dropped him – until 2009's ***Reunited*** album with the Shadows, although he did record new material for three EMI compilation albums in that period.

Track Listing

Real as I Wanna Be
Even If It Breaks My Heart
Can't Keep This Feeling In
Climbing Up Mount Everest
United for Evermore
She Makes Me Feel Like a Man
Butterfly Kisses
Snowfall on the Sahara
Woman and a Man
Till I'm Home Again
Come Back to Me
The Miracle
Vita Mia

♫ Reunited

50th studio album

Fittingly, to celebrate Cliff Richard's and the Shadows' fiftieth year in the music business, they released the fiftieth studio album. This was a collection of the band's back catalogue re-arranged and recorded with up-to-date techniques – essential since Hank Marvin lives in Australia. Most tracks have the same feel as the originals but there is enough difference and freshness to ensure it isn't a compilation album. In addition, they recorded a three covers, one of which, ***Singing the Blues***, was issued as a single. EMI had abandoned Cliff earlier in the decade but this saw them signing Cliff and the Shadows again. Issued on the EMI label (catalogue number 50999 687883 2 2), it was also released in a special edition box with an extra disc containing three extra tracks and a jigsaw of the front cover (50999 687875 2 3) both on 21st September 2009.

Track Listing

I Could Easily Fall (in Love with You)
The Young Ones
Move It
Living Doll
Bachelor Boy
Nine Times out of Ten
C'mon Everybody
Travellin' Light
It'll Be Me
In the Country
On the Beach
The Next Time
Please Don't Tease
Sea Cruise
Willie and the Hand-Jive
Summer Holiday
Do You Wanna Dance?
Don't Talk to Him
Time Drags By
Gee Whiz It's You
Lucky Lips
Singing the Blues

♫ Rock Connection, The

38th studio album

Having recorded a number of albums in quick succession, Cliff Richard's *The Rock Connection* was to be the last studio album for almost three years, while he concentrated on his performance in the stage musical ***Time – The Musical*** in London. The album featured a number of new arrangements of familiar songs from the rock and roll era, some padded out from the track listing of ***Rock 'n' Roll Silver***. The album was released on the EMI label (catalogue number EJ 26 03091) on 19th November 1984 but only reached number forty-five, staying in the charts for just five weeks. It was combined with ***Silver***/*Rock 'n' Roll Silver* and issued on CD (0777 7 80499 2 0) on 4th October 1993 with the track listings from the albums moved around and songs missing altogether. These were restored on the remastered version (7243 5 83402 2 8) on 19th January 2004, incorporating much of the track listing from *Rock 'n' Roll Silver*, which had not had the same remastering treatment, as well as a duet with Phil Everly previously only released on Everly's solo album.

Track Listing

Heart User
Willie and the Hand-Jive
Lovers and Friends
There'll Never Be Anyone Else But You
La Gonave
Over You
Shooting from the Heart
Learning How to Rock 'n' Roll
Lucille
Be Bop-a-Lula
Donna
Dynamite
She Means Nothing to Me
Makin' History

Bonus tracks (2004 Rock Connection *CD)*
Move It
Teddy Bear
It'll Be Me
Little Bitty Pretty One
Tutti Frutti
I'll Mend Your Broken Heart

♫ Rock 'n' Roll Juvenile

33rd studio album

Self-producing with the help of one of his chief songwriters, Terry Britten, Cliff Richard's thirty-third studio album was an insular affair with much of the material written or co-written by Britten as well as the title track by Cliff. There were three singles from the project: ***Carrie, Hot Shot*** and ***We Don't Talk Anymore***. Technically, though, this latter song was never intended for release on the album but, with its phenomenal success in the singles charts, EMI forced Cliff's hand against his better judgment, to tack it on to the end of the track listing to assist in the album's sales. A neat commercial trick, it was for sure, but Cliff's general misgivings were correct because it didn't fit well with the rest of the album. Released on the EMI label (catalogue number EMC 3307) on 7th September 1979, *Rock 'n' Roll Juvenile* reached number three and stayed in the charts for twenty-two weeks (the longest tenure since ***Wonderful Life*** back in 1964). It was issued as a CD in its own right (the first of Cliff's albums to be treated in this way, possibly because of the proximity of the original release) on the EMI label (catalogue number CDP 792422 2) in 1989, and was digitally remastered and reissued (7243 5 33115 2 0) on 9th July 2001 with two bonus tracks, which were B-sides not previously available on CD.

Track Listing

Monday Thru' Friday
Doing Fine
Cities May Fall
You Know That I Love You
My Luck Won't Change
Rock 'n' Roll Juvenile
Sci-Fi
Fallin' in Luv
Carrie
Hot Shot
Language of Love
We Don't Talk Anymore

Bonus tracks (2001 CD)
Walking in the Light
Moving In

♫ Rock 'n' Roll Silver

37th studio album (joint)

For Cliff Richard's twenty-fifth anniversary in the music business, he recorded an album of new material called ***Silver***. The boxed version of the released included another disc, called *Rock 'n' Roll Silver*, which had a number of covers and updated arrangements of rock and roll classic songs. Released on the EMI label (the *Silver* boxed set had the catalogue number EMCS 1077873, while the *Rock 'n' Roll Silver* disc was given EMC 1077881) on 3rd October 1983, it helped the parent album reach the seven position in the charts with its sales. The album was released on CD under the *Silver* title in 1983 (catalogue number CDP 7 46008 2) but it was the reissued alongside ***The Rock Connection*** under *Rock 'n' Roll Silver*, although several of the tracks were missing, on the EMI label (0777 7 80499 2 0) on 4th October 1993, while the missing tracks were added as bonuses to the eventual reissue of *The Rock Connection* in 2004.

Track Listing

Makin' History
Move It
Donna
Teddy Bear
It'll Be Me
Lucille
Little Bitty Pretty One
There'll Never Be Anyone Else But You
Be Bop-a-Lula
Tutti Frutti

♫ Rock 'n' Roll Years 1958-1963, The

Compilation album

In 1997, a year before Cliff Richard enjoyed his fortieth anniversary in the music business, EMI compiled a four-disc set of Cliff's material from the start of his career to the end of 1963 (with the release of ***Summer Holiday***). Although there are some familiar tracks on the album, much of it is made up from hugely rare out-takes and early recordings, including performances at Butlin's before his career took off and the first known recording that he made at HMV in London in July 1958. The track listing is an enormously interesting trawl through rehearsal takes, alternative takes, live recordings and excerpts from his Radio Luxembourg show, *Me and My Shadows*, and is an important historical document of the genesis of one of the most enduring performers the country has ever produced. The album was issued on the EMI label (catalogue number CDEMD 1109) on 9th June 1997 and reached number thirty-two in the charts, with some buyers perhaps being put off by its price, and stayed for three weeks.

Track Listing

Schoolboy Crush
High Class Baby
My Feet Hit the Ground
Don't Bug Me Baby
King Creole
TV Hop
Rockin' Robin
I'll Try
High School Confidential
Early in the Morning
Somebody Touched Me
Livin' Lovin' Doll
Mean Woman Blues
Pointed Toe Shoes
I'm Walkin'
Don't Be Mad at Me
Willie and the Hand-Jive
Nine Times out of Ten
Thinking of Our Love
Evergreen Tree
She's Gone
Tell Me
Where s My Heart?
Lamp of Love
Tough Enough
Mumblin' Mosie
Fifty Tears for Every Kiss
Unchained Melody
What'd I Say?
Forty Days
Without You
Shame on You
Spanish Harlem
Do You Remember?
I'm Looking out the Window
You Don't Know
Lawdy Miss Clawdy (Private recording)
Breathless (Private recording)
Twenty Flight Rock (Live)
Jailhouse Rock (Live)
Money Honey (Live)
Heartbreak Hotel (Live)
Turn Me Loose (Live)
Who's Gonna Take You Home? (Acetate)
Let's Stick Together (Acetate)
What'd I Say? (Alternative South

Mean Streak
Never Mind
Steady with You
My Babe (Live)
Move It (Live)
That'll Be the Day (Live)
Danny (Live)
Whole Lotta Shakin' Goin' On (Live)
One Night (Live)
Apron Strings (B-side)
Dynamite (B-side)
I Gotta Know
The Snake and the Bookworm
Here Comes Summer
Twenty Flight Rock
Blue Suede Shoes
I'm Gonna Get You
I Cannot Find a True Love
Working After School
You and I
I'm Willing to Learn
We Have It Made
Choppin' 'n' Changin'
It's You
I Love You
'D' in Love
Catch Me
Now's the Time to Fall in Love
True Love Will Come to You
First Lesson in Love
I Want You to Know
Blue Moon
Take Special Care
Do You Wanna Dance? (Rehearsal take)
Do You Wanna Dance? (Alternative take)
Do You Wanna Dance? (Undubbed master)
Do You Wanna Dance? (Remaster)
Since I Lost You
Dim, Dim the Lights (Live)
Save My Soul (Live)
I'm Walkin' the Blues
Summer Holiday (Undubbed original)
The Next Time (Undubbed version)
Blueberry Hill
A Forever Kind of Love
Razzle Dazzle
Reelin' and Rockin'
It's All in the Game (Alternative take)
African version)
Forty Days (Radio Luxembourg)
Got a Funny Feeling (Radio Luxembourg)
Rosalie (Come Back to Me) (Radio Luxembourg)
Me and My Shadows (Radio Luxembourg)
Lessons in Love (Solo version)
We Say Yeah (Undubbed version)
Hang up Your Rock and Roll Shoes (Radio broadcast)
Dancing Shoes (Radio broadcast)
It'll Be Me (Radio broadcast)
Summer Holiday Advertising EP
Cliff's Personal Message to You

♫ Sail Away

Album by **Dave Pope**

The first album to be produced for someone else by Cliff Richard was *Sail Away* by Dave Pope. A fellow Christian, Pope recorded ten songs for the album and featured Cliff on backing vocals. It was issued on the Myrrh label (catalogue number MYR 1068) in 1978 but didn't sell sufficiently to make any impression on the charts.

Track Listing

It Only Goes to Show
Love Song
Once Again
Lord, I Love You
Sail Away
Couldn't Care Less
Dying Embers
Lord, I Miss the Rain
It's You
We're All One

♫ Silver

37th studio album (joint)

To celebrate Cliff Richard's achievement of twenty-five years in the music business and his continuing success, he recorded a double album of new material and covers of rock 'n' roll standards. The first disc was simply called *Silver*, while the second was entitled ***Rock 'n' Roll Silver***, incorporated into the boxed set release of the album. The album was released as a double LP and a boxed set on the EMI label (catalogue numbers EMC 1077871 and EMCS 1077873 respectively) on 3rd October 1983 and reached number seven, staying in the UK album charts for twenty-four weeks. It was one of the first albums to be released on CD (catalogue number CDP 7 46008 2) in 1983 but packaged up with ***The Rock Connection*** for a reissue (0777 7 80499 2 0) on 4th October 1993, although not all of the original tracks were carried forward on to the track listing, with some being transposed to *The Rock Connection*. It was subsequently reissued on CD in digitally remastered form (7243 5 38372 2 8) on 2nd July 2002 with two bonus B-side tracks from the singles ***Please Don't Fall in Love*** and ***Never Say Die (Give a Little Bit More)***.

Track Listing

Silver's Home Tonight
Hold On
Never Say Die (Give a Little Bit More)
Front Page
Ocean Deep
Locked Inside Your Prison
Please Don't Fall in Love
Baby You're Dynamite
The Golden Days Are Over
Love Stealer

Bonus tracks (2002 CD)

Too Close to Heaven
Lucille

♫ Sincerely Cliff Richard

22nd studio album

Another collection of covers of contemporary material, *Sincerely Cliff Richard* continues to show the musical direction that Cliff was taking at the time, particularly with the quintessentially sixties arrangement of the tracks. The album was issued on the Columbia label and was the last of Cliff's albums to be released in both mono (catalogue number SX 6357) and stereo (SCX 6357) formats in October 1969 but it only reached number twenty-four and stayed in the British charts no longer than three weeks. The album was subsequently issued on CD in stereo only for the first time by EMI coupled with ***Live at the Talk of the Town*** (catalogue number 0777 7 80444 2 0) on 2nd November 1992, while it was remastered and released separately on 26th July 2004 (catalogue number 7243 4 73392 2 6) but with a number of bonus tracks, which were singles and a B-side released from the period.

Track Listing

In the Past
Always
Will You Love Me Tomorrow
You'll Want Me
I'm Not Getting Married
Time
For Emily Wherever I May Find Her
Baby I Could Be So Good at Loving You
Sam
London's Not Too Far
Take Action
Take Good Care of Her
When I Find You
Punch and Judy

Bonus tracks (2004 CD)
The Joy of Living
Throw Down a Line
Reflections

♫ Small Corners

31st studio album

Small Corners was Cliff Richard's fifth album of religious-orientated songs and featured a number of new tracks, as well as one that had been previously produced by Bruce Welch (***Joseph***). Bruce is reported to have said that he wasn't interested in recording an album of Christian music and therefore Cliff stepped in to self-produce the remaining tracks for the first time in that role. The album was issued on the EMI label (catalogue number EMC 3219) on 10th February 1978 and succeeded in reaching number thirty-three, staying in the UK charts for five weeks. It was first released on CD (and LP simultaneously) on the Word label (catalogue number WRDD 3036) in 1987, before being combined with ***Every Face Tells a Story*** and reissued on the EMI label (0777 7 80494 2 5) on 4th October 1993. It was digitally remastered and again reissued (0946 3 81971 2 6) on 12th March 2007 with three bonus tracks: Cliff's single theme tune to *Trainer* and two B-sides from the nineties.

Track Listing

Why Should the Devil Have All the Good Music?
I Love
Why Me, Lord?
I've Got News for You
Hey Watcha Say
I Wish We'd All Been Ready
Joseph
Good on the Sally Army
Goin' Home
Up in Canada
Yes He Lives
When I Survey the Wondrous Cross

Bonus tracks (2007 CD)
More to Life
There's No Power in Pity
Peace in Our Time (Gospel Mix)

♫ Something's Goin' On

47th studio album

Cliff Richard powered back on the music scene in 2004 with his next studio album, *Something's Goin' On*. Commissioning groups of writers to come up with fresh material, he transplanted himself to American studios, including working with Barry Gibb in Miami, to work on a selection of songs that sounded very contemporary but also had strong echoes of his rock 'n' roll roots. Three songs were issued as singles: ***Somethin' Is Goin' On***, ***What Car?*** and ***I Cannot Give You My Love***. The album was issued on the Decca label (catalogue number 475 6408) on 25th October 2004 and reached number seven in the charts, although it only stayed in the listings for four weeks. The album was subsequently revisited and reissued as ***For Life*** but with additional tracks that had previously only been available as B-sides or in download format.

Track Listing

Thousand Miles to Go
Somethin' Is Goin' On
I Will Not e a Mistake
Simplicity
Sometimes Love
I Cannot Give You My Love
The Day That I Stop Loving You
What Car?
How Did She Get Here?
Field of Love
For Life
I Don't Wanna Lose You
Faithful One

♫ Songs from Heathcliff

42nd studio album

Cliff Richard had long nurtured the idea of creating a musical based on the character of Heathcliff from *Wuthering Heights* by Emily Brontë, ever since he read the book at school. This came to fruition in the middle of the nineties when the story was completed and Sir Tim Rice and John Farrar had composed a selection of ten songs. These were recorded in the studio with the help of Olivia Newton-John and released as an album before the remaining songs were completed. The *Songs from Heathcliff* album was released – the first of Cliff's albums to be released in CD format only – on the EMI label (catalogue number CDEMD 1091) on 30th October 1995 and only reached number fifteen in the UK charts – Cliff's first non-top ten album since ***The Rock Connection*** eleven years before – and stayed in the charts for nine weeks.

Track Listing

A Misunderstood Man
Sleep of the Good
Gypsy Bundle
Had to Be
When You Thought of Me
Dream Tomorrow
I Do Not Love You Isabella (Heathcliff's Wedding Song)
Choosing When It's Too Late
Marked with Death
Be with Me Always

♫ Stronger

40th studio album

Following on from the success of ***Always Guaranteed,*** Cliff Richard and Alan Tarney followed the process in creating most of the songs, with Tarney generating the song in the studio for Cliff to apply his vocals later. In addition, there were collaborations with Aswad and Stock, Aitken and Waterman, while the album garnered some publicity because it was to feature the one hundredth single ***The Best of Me*** (although this was not truly the case). The other songs to be released from the album were ***Stronger than That, Just Don't Have the Heart*** and ***Lean on You***. The album was issued on the EMI label (catalogue numbers EMD 1012 and CDEMD 1012 for the vinyl and CD releases respectively) on 30th October 1989 and reached number seven, staying in the charts for twenty-one weeks. The album was digitally remastered and reissued (catalogue number 7243 5 83392 2 2) on 19th January 2004, with five bonus tracks gleaned from the B-sides of the singles.

Track Listing

Stronger than That
Who's in Love?
The Best of Me
Clear Blue Skies
Keep Me Warm
Lean on You
Just Don't Have the Heart
Joanna
Everybody Knows
Share a Dream
Better Day
Forever You Will Be Mine

Bonus tracks (2004 CD)

Wide Open Space
Just Don't Have the Heart (remix)
Hey Mister
Lindsay Jane
Marmaduke

♫ Summer Holiday

8th studio album

After the huge success of ***The Young Ones,*** it was inevitable that Cliff Richard would follow it up with another film. ***Summer Holiday*** was it and its premise and the songs ensured that it was even more popular. A double A-side, ***The Next Time*** and ***Bachelor Boy,*** plus the film's title song were released as singles and both were number ones. In addition, two EPs were also released: ***Hits from Summer Holiday*** and ***More Hits from Summer Holiday***. The Shadows also had their share of success releasing *Foot Tapper* as a single. The album was issued on the Columbia label in mono (catalogue number 33SX 1472) and stereo (SCX 3462) on 18th January 1963, a week after the film's premiere, and reached number one. The third of Cliff's albums to do so, it remained in the album charts for thirty-six weeks. Like *The Young Ones,* the album has only ever been issued in stereo in CD format, when it was released on the Music for Pleasure label (catalogue number MFP 6021) in 1988. Reissued again on 15th September 2003, the package included reproductions of the original cinema poster and lobby cards, a souvenir booklet called *Inside Summer Holiday* and a number of previously unreleased tracks.

Track Listing

Seven Days to a Holiday
Summer Holiday
Let Us Take You for a Ride
Les Girls *(The Shadows)*
Round and Round *(The Shadows)*
Foot Tapper ***(The Shadows)***
Stranger in Town
Orlando's Mime
Bachelor Boy
A Swingin' Affair
Really Waltzing
All at Once
Dancing Shoes
Yugoslav Wedding
The Next Time
Big News

Bonus tracks (2003 CD)

Summer Holiday Advertising EP
The Next Time
Bachelor Boy
Les Girls
Summer Holiday Advertising EP
Brass Band Opening/Summer Holiday
Bachelor Boy
The Next Time
Big News
Summer Holiday

♫ Take Me High

26th studio album

Cliff Richard released his final feature-length film, ***Take Me High,*** in 1973 to mixed reviews, in spite of the quality and contemporary nature of the story and the songs. The soundtrack album was issued over three years after ***Tracks 'n' Grooves,*** but it marked a new era in Cliff's career. It was the first album to be issued on the EMI label and the first studio album not to be produced by Norrie Paramor, who had since retired. The track listing itself is presented out of sequence with the film's narrative, although the listening pleasure is not denigrated by that. There was one single released from the enterprise – the title song – and the album was released on the EMI label (catalogue number EMC 3016) in December 1973, when it reached number forty-one, staying in the charts for four weeks. The album was issued on CD for the first time, paired with Help ***It Along*** (catalogue number 0777 7 80488 2 4) on 4th October 1993. Remastered and reissued on 22nd August 2005 (7243 4 77731 2 9), bonus tracks including the songs from the ***Two a Penny*** film were added to the disc.

Track Listing

It's Only Money
Midnight Blue
Hover *(instrumental)*
Why?
Life
Driving *(instrumental)*
The Game
Brumburger Duet
Take Me High
The Anti-Brotherhood of Man
Winning
Driving
Join the Band
The Word Is Love
Brumburger (Finale)

Bonus tracks (2005 CD)

Two a Penny
I'll Love You Forever Today
Questions
Twist and Shout
Fragen
Celestial Houses

♫ Thank You Very Much

Live album

Cliff Richard and the Shadows had been successful in showbusiness for twenty years in 1978. Although the Shadows had split up at the end of the sixties, they had continued to work together on various projects such as the Marvin, Welch & Farrar albums and solo material. They reformed fully in 1975 to represent the UK at the Eurovision Song Contest with *Let Me Be the One* two years after Cliff's second appearance at the Contest. As a result, it seemed apposite to come together again to celebrate this enduring anniversary with a set of concerts at the London Palladium, entitled *Thank You Very Much,* in deference to their legion of fans. Split between Cliff supported by the Shadows and with his main band and the Shadows on their own, a number of tracks were missed of the original album release, although these were later restored from the video at a later date (out of sequence because of the relative quality of the sound recording). The album was released on the EMI label (catalogue number EMTV 15) alongside a video of the event, which was broadcast on television. It reached number five, starting a long run of top ten albums for Cliff, and stayed in the charts for twelve weeks. Matched with ***Green Light,*** the album was first released on CD on the EMI label (catalogue number 0777 7 80496 2 3) on 4th October 1993 and then digitally remastered and reissued (7243 4 73356 2 4) in its own right on 26th July 2004 with three tracks drawn from the video recording.

Track Listing

The Young Ones
Do You Wanna Dance?
The Day I Met Marie
Shadoogie *(The Shadows)*
Atlantis *(The Shadows)*
Nivram *(The Shadows)*
Apache *(The Shadows)*
Please Don't Tease
Miss You Nights
Move It
Willie and the Hand-Jive
All Shook Up
Devil Woman
Why Should the Devil Have All the Good Music?
The End of the Show

Bonus tracks (2004 CD)
Up in Canada
Yes He Lives
Let Me Be the One *(The Shadows)*

♫ Together with Cliff Richard

41st studio album

Because of the success that Cliff Richard had had with ***Mistletoe and Wine*** in 1988 and ***Saviour's Day*** in 1990, he was beginning to be associated with the tag of churning out nothing but Christmas records. But, to capitalize on this, Cliff recorded an album of Christmas songs, which musically showed a different direction again. Although Alan Tarney had created a number of songs with electronic instrumentation on albums throughout the eighties, *Together with Cliff Richard* took their use to another level. The choice of songs include his three Christmas hits (with ***Little Town*** making up the third) as well as a select collection of familiar Christmas popular songs such as ***Christmas Alphabet*** and ***Have Yourself a Merry Little Christmas*** and revisited Christmas carols such as ***Venite*** and ***Silent Night*** and some original songs. Two singles were released from the project: ***We Should Be Together*** and ***This New Year,*** while ***Scarlet Ribbons*** was also released in some territories. Issued on the EMI label (catalogue numbers EMD 1028 and CDEMD 1028 for the LP and CD respectively) on 18th November 1991, *Together with Cliff Richard* reached number ten and stayed in the charts for seven weeks (dropping out at the end of January 1992).

Track Listing

Have Yourself a Merry Little Christmas
Venite (O Come All Ye Faithful)
We Should Be Together
Mistletoe and Wine
Christmas Never Comes
Christmas Alphabet
Saviour's Day
The Christmas Song (Merry Christmas to You)
Little Town
Scarlet Ribbons
Silent Night
White Christmas
This New Year

♫ Tracks 'n' Grooves

25th studio album

Tracks 'n' Grooves marks a turning point in Cliff Richard's career: it was the last studio album to be produced by his mentor Norrie Paramor, who retired in 1972, it was the last studio album to be released on the Columbia label before he signed on to EMI and it was to be his last album for over three years after twelve prolific years releasing a huge volume of material in that time. The songs were a collection of covers and other material that Cliff had recorded over the previous year or two, with one single lifted, ***Early in the Morning,*** for the Far Eastern market, while a mooted British single release of the track ***Love, Truth and Emily Stone*** never materialized. The album was issued on the Columbia label (catalogue number SCX 6435) in November 1970 reaching number thirty-seven and staying in the charts for two weeks, thus helping to cement the critics' viewpoint that Cliff was no longer a major musical force. The album was paired with the compilation ***The Best of Cliff Vol. II*** and issued on CD for the first time on the EMI label (catalogue number 0777 7 0485 2 7) on 4th October 1993. It was remastered and reissued on its own on 26th July 2004 (7243 4 73364 2 3) with a number of bonus tracks which had formed B-sides from singles of the immediate period.

Track Listing

Early in the Morning
As I Walk into the Morning of Your Life
Love, Truth and Emily Stone
My Head Goes Around
Put My Mind at Ease
Abraham, Martin and John
The Girl Can't Help It
Bang Bang (My Baby Shot Me Down)
I'll Make It All up to You
I'd Just Be Fool Enough
Don't Let Tonight Ever End
What a Silly Thing to Do
Your Heart's Not in Your Love
Don't Ask Me to Be Friends
Are You Only Fooling Me?

Bonus tracks (2004 CD)
Don't Move Away
Leave My Woman Alone
You Never Can Tell

♫ Two a Penny

20th studio album

Moving completely away from the slapstick style that had been the signature of the four major sixties films starring Cliff Richard, ***Two a Penny*** was a far more thoughtful affair with a moralistic, indeed religious, message. As such, the drama was the focus of the film while the music was secondary. Although there is incidental music in the film (as represented here by three instrumental tunes on the track listing), the four Cliff performances from the film are all represented with the first three tracks on side one plus ***Twist and Shout***, while the remainder of the album is padded out with songs recorded at various times but not previously released. In some ways, it's a misnomer to describe it as a soundtrack album, but the film tracks are great examples of the direction Cliff was taking musically (and in his life). ***I'll Love You Forever Today*** was the only track to be released as a single, while Columbia had dispensed with EPs earlier in the year. The album was issued on the Columbia label in mono (catalogue number SX 6262) and stereo (SCX 6262) in August 1968 but became the second of Cliff's albums not to make any impression on the charts. The album was issued only once on CD as part of the EMI programme to reissue Cliff's earlier albums, coupled with ***Cliff in Japan*** (catalogue number 0777 7 80441 2 3) on 2nd November 1992. The four songs from the film were later added as bonus tacks to the reissue of ***Take Me High*** in August 2005.

Track Listing

Two a Penny
I'll Love You Forever Today
Questions
Long Is the Night *(instrumental)*
Lonely Girl
And Me (I'm on the Outside Now)
Daybreak *(instrumental)*
Twist and Shout
Celeste *(instrumental)*
Wake Up, Wake Up
Cloudy
Red Rubber Ball
Close to Cathy
Rattler

♫ Two's Company

48th studio album

At the beginning of the new millennium, EMI took the extraordinary decision to drop Cliff Richard after an association lasting more than forty years. Cliff fought back and proved his worth with two fine studio albums, ***Wanted*** and ***Something's Goin' On***. EMI recognized that they had not made the right decision and asked Cliff to provide new recorded material for three albums throughout the decade to capitalize on his back catalogue and continued success. The second was *Two's Company*, which was an album of duets, some of which were new – Barry Gibb, Tammy Wynette, Anne Murray and others including a new version of ***Move It*** – while the others were from his back catalogue – Elton John, Olivia Newton-John, G4, Phil Everly and others. The album was released on the EMI label (catalogue number 0094637707227) on 6th November 2006.

Track Listing

Move It
Anyone Who Had a Heart
Miss You Nights
Yesterday Once More
She Means Nothing to Me
All I Ask of You
Let There Be Love
Throw Down a Line
Fields of Gold
Up Where We Belong
Slow Rivers
Suddenly
Danny Boy
Reunited

♫ Wanted

45th studio album

Having been unceremoniously dumped by EMI after a collaboration lasting over forty years (encompassing the earlier Columbia recordings), Cliff Richard was determined to prove the company wrong in its decision to focus on making money quickly on the swift turnover of newer performers fed on a diet of the *X Factor* generation. *Wanted* was the result and featured a few new songs as well as a number of brilliant arrangements of more familiar songs, not the least being the melding of ***Somewhere over the Rainbow*** with ***What a Wonderful World***. That combination was released as the first single and followed up by ***Let Me Be the One***. The album was released on the Papillon label (catalogue number WANTED1) on 6th November 2001 and reached number eleven, staying in the charts for eight weeks (by that time a very strong showing).

Track Listing

Somewhere over the Rainbow/What a Wonderful World
Right Here Waiting
What's Love Got to Do with It?
Let Me Be the One
And I Love Her
All Shook Up
Love Me Tender
Do You Wonder?
You've Got a Friend
Moon River
This Love You Will Never Forget
Like Strangers
When You Walk in the Room

♫ When in Rome

13th studio album

Following the comparatively reasonable success of Cliff Richard's first non-English language album, ***When in Spain***, two years earlier, the formula was repeated with Italian tracks on *When in Rome*. Featuring some new recordings and a few songs that were vocal overdubs on the original backing track, while there were no singles released from the project, there was an EP issued, which was curiously entitled ***Hits from When in Rome***. *When in Rome* has only ever been issued in mono format and was first released on the Columbia label (catalogue number 33SX 1762) in August 1965 and the album had the dubious distinction of being the first album bearing Cliff's name not to chart. It has been issued on CD as part of the EMI Cliff Richard CD Collection programme (catalogue number 0777 7 80429 2 1) alongside ***Cliff Richard*** on 5th October 1992 and was released in its entirety n the boxed set ***On the Continent*** featuring all of Cliff's foreign language recordings.

Track Listing

Come Prima
Nel Blu Dipinto di Blu (Volare)
Concerto d'Autumno
O Mio Signore
Maria Ninguem
Non L'Acoltare
Dicitencello Vuie
Arrivederci Roma
Carina
Legata ad un Granello di Sabbia
Casa Senza Finestre
Che Cosa del Farai Mia Amore
Per un Bacio d'Amor

♫ When in Spain

9th studio album

Showing just how broad his capabilities as a performer and singer were, Cliff Richard's next studio album was a selection of covers of songs sung in the Spanish language, brought together under the title *When in Spain*, a choice of title predating the more familiar saying ***When in Rome*** by almost two years. Featuring the Shadows on all of the tracks, but additionally with Norrie Paramor's orchestra on four of the songs, the opening track, ***Perfidia***, has been covered by the Shadows as an instrumental and several of the tracks have been previously recorded in English, with Cliff providing new vocals on the original backing tracks. No singles or EPs were issued from the project, while the album was released on the Columbia label in mono (catalogue number 33SX 1541) and stereo (SCX 3488) in September 1963, reaching number eight but only staying in the British charts or ten weeks, perhaps underlining the overall lack of appeal of the songs sung in a language other than English. The stereo version of the album was issued on CD alongside ***32 Minutes and 17 Seconds with Cliff Richard*** on the EMI label (catalogue number 0777 7 80423 2 7) on 5th October 1992, and was later included on the foreign language compilation of Cliff's songs on the ***On the Continent*** boxed set. The mono version of the album was later released on CD alongside ***Kinda Latin*** on the EMI label (catalogue number 7243 541086 2 4) on 2nd September 2002.

Track Listing

Perfidia
Amor, Amor, Amor
Frenesi
Solamente una Vez
Vaya con Dios
Me Lo Dijo Adela
Maria No Mas
Tus Besos
Quizas, Quizas, Quizas
Te Quiero Dijiste
Cançion de Orfeo
Quien Sera

♫ Wired for Sound

35th studio album

Irrepressibly continuing his musical rehabilitation since the mid-seventies in the eyes of the critics, Cliff Richard turned to Alan Tarney once more to produce his next studio album. Once again featuring most songs written by Tarney himself with him providing most of the instrumentation too, *Wired for Sound* was another commercial success. It resulted in two singles: the title track and ***Daddy's Home***, which was, in fact, taken from a live a performance and added to the track listing. The album was issued on the EMI label (catalogue number EMC 3377) in November 1981 and reached number four in the charts, staying for twenty-five weeks. The CD version was issued seven years later on the Fame label (catalogue number CD-FA 3159) before being digitally remastered and reissued on the EMI label (7243 5 33112 2 3) on 9th July 2001, incorporating the two B-sides from the singles as bonus tracks.

Track Listing
Wired for Sound
Once in a While
Better Than I Know Myself
Oh No, Don't Let Go
'Cos I Love That Rock 'n' Roll
Broken Doll
Lost in a Lonely World
Summer Rain
Young Love
Say You Don't Mind
Daddy's Home

Bonus tracks (2001 CD)
Shakin' All Over
Hold On

♫ Wonderful Life
10th studio album

After the enormous success of ***The Young Ones*** and ***Summer Holiday***, it looked like Cliff Richard's film career was on a roll. But with the third film, ***Wonderful Life***, something faltered with the presentation. Well-acted and performed with gusto, it didn't seem to have quite the same magic as the other films. By now, too, the Ronald Cass and Peter Myers contributions to the songs were sounding somewhat tired and arcane, so it was left to the members of the Shadows to help add the spice which they successfully did. Only one single was released, ***On the Beach***, while Columbia pushed hard with releasing three EPs, ***Wonderful Life No. 1***, ***Wonderful Life No. 2*** and ***Hits from Wonderful Life***, the latter being somewhat of a misnomer. In addition, the Shadows had some success with the instrumental *Theme for Young Lovers* as a single. The album was issued on the Columbia label in mono (catalogue number 33SX 1628) and stereo (SCX 3515) formats in July 1964 and managed to reach number two staying in the album charts for twenty-three weeks. Only the stereo version of the album was issued on CD, when EMI ran a programme of remastering Cliff's back catalogue of albums (catalogue number 0777 7 80426 2 4) on 5th October 1992 alongside ***Aladdin and His Wonderful Lamp***. A remastered version was issued on 22nd August 2005, also on EMI (catalogue number 7243 4 77718 2 8), and featured a number of bonus tracks not previously available.

Track Listing
Wonderful Life
A Girl in Every Port
Walkin' *(The Shadows)*
A Little Imagination
Home
On the Beach
In the Stars
We Love a Movie
Do You Remember?
What've I Gotta Do?
Theme for Young Lovers *(The Shadows)*
All Kinds of People
A Matter of Moments
Youth and Experience

Bonus tracks (2005 CD)
Look Don't Touch
Do You Remember? (Alternative version)
Wonderful Life (Alternative version)
Angel (Non-album Import A-side)

♫ Young Ones, The
6th studio album

Cliff Richard's first major film musical, *The Young Ones*, was hugely popular, spurred on as it was a brilliant theme song and ***When the Girl in Your Arms Is the Girl in Your Heart*** released as highly successful singles plus two instrumentals issued by the Shadows, which also reached the charts (*Peace Pipe* and *The Savage*). Only one EP was released from the project, ***Hits from The Young Ones***, and only in mono format. The sound track album also featured a solo by Grazina Frame, who was doubling the vocals of the lead actress Carole Gray – *No-one for Me but Nicky*. The album was issued on the Columbia label in mono (catalogue number 33SX 1384) and stereo (SCX 3397) formats on 15th December 1961 four days before the film's release date and reached number one – the second in succession for Cliff – remaining in the British album charts for forty-two weeks. The mono version of the album has never been released in CD format, while the stereo version was one of the first to be released on CD on the Music for Pleasure label (catalogue number MFP 5823) on 5th April 1988. On 22nd August 2005, a remastered version was issued on the EMI label (catalogue number 743 4 77723 2 0) which incorporated three bonus tracks including a different version of the title song of the US film release, ***Wonderful to Be Young***.

Track Listing
Friday Night
Got a Funny Feeling
Peace Pipe *(The Shadows)*
Nothing's Impossible
The Young Ones
All for One
Lessons in Love
No One for Me But Nicky *(Grazina Frame)*
What D'You Know, We've Got a Show – Vaudeville Routine
When the Girl in Your Arms (Is the Girl in Your Heart)
Just Dance
Mood Mambo *(The Shadows)*
The Savage *(The Shadows)*
We Say Yeah

Bonus tracks (2005 CD)
(It's) Wonderful to Be Young (Alternative version)
The Young Ones (Undubbed version)
Got a Funny Feeling (Alternative version)

THE CLIFF RICHARD RECORDING CATALOGUE

Appendix E: A Foretaste of *Bold as Brass*

♬ Introduction

In this section, there is a brief introduction to the history of the tracks intended for the release of Cliff Richard's 2010 album, *Bold as Brass*, to be released at the time of his seventieth birthday in October 2010. The special edition includes a bonus CD with two extra tracks and, like ***Reunited***, has a jigsaw included. The tracks are:

a) Love Me or Leave Me
b) Lazy River
c) I've Got You Under My Skin
d) I Just Want to Make Love to You
e) They Can't Take That Away from Me
f) Let's Fall in Love
g) I Didn't Know What Time It Was
h) Accentuate the Positive
i) Teach Me Tonight
j) Don't Get Around Much Any More
k) Night and Day
l) Bewitched, Bothered and Bewildered
m) When I Take My Sugar to Tea (special edition release only)
n) Every Time We Say Goodbye (special edition release only)

These are presented in alphabetical order below.

♬ Accentuate the Positive

Published in 1944, *Accentuate the Positive* was written by Harold Arlen and Johnny Mercer, often with the phonetic title of *Ac-Cent-Tchu-Ate the Positive*. Inspired by a religious sermon and hence its usual performance in an ecclesiastical style, the first recording appeared in that year by the writer Mercer, assisted by the Pied Pipers and Paul Weston's Orchestra ad this was swiftly followed by covers from Bing Crosby and the Andrews Sisters, Kay Kyser and Artie Shaw. In the UK, it was Johnny Green who produced the first single there on Decca, although was not a commercial hit. A number of other artists have recorded the song, including Ella Fitzgerald, Aretha Franklin, Perry Como and even a punk version from The Vindictives. However, culturally speaking, it is more familiar as a song interpolated into the score of many a popular film television, including *Bugsy*, *The Singing Detective*, *Quantum Leap* and *Blast from the Past* among several other worthy projects.

♬ Bewitched, Bothered and Bewildered

Bewitched, Bothered and Bewildered was written by Richard Rodgers and Lorenz Hart for their 1940 Broadway musical *Pal Joey*. Originally, the lyrics were viewed by some as a little too hot for some audiences, with its overt references to female sexuality and women's desires, and has often been covered in a toned down version. The song has been recorded by, amongst others, Helen Forrest with the Benny Goodman Orchestra in 1941, followed by Doris Day (who had a Billboard number nine with the song), Mel Tormé, Oscar Peterson, Frank Sinatra (from the film version of *Pal Joey*, which was released in 1957), Ella Fitzgerald, Barbra Streisand, Linda Ronstadt, Rufus Wainwright and a duet by Rod Stewart and Cher, while Frederica von Stade resurrected the original lyrics in 1990.

♬ Don't Get Around Much Any More

Originally written by Duke Ellington as an instrumental dance tune with a big band sound, it was also recorded by him under the title *Never No Lament* in 1940. It was Bob Russell who, a couple of years later added lyrics and thereby changing the title to *Don't Get Around Much Any More*. This evolution of the song was by far the most popular and it has since become a jazz standard performed by a number of artists across the years. For recordings, it has been covered by several artists, including The Ink Spots the year after it was written (and achieving a number two in the American charts with the result), Harry Connick, Jr., Paul McCartney (known for his love of the music from this period and earlier), Rod Stewart, Chicago, B. B. King and Willie Nelson.

♫ Every Time We Say Goodbye

More familiarly titled *Ev'ry Time We Say Goodbye*, with the second syllable of the first word removed, Cole Porter's 1944 song from the musical revue *Seven Lively Arts*, the song is most popularly associated with what some consider to be the definitive version by Ella Fitzgerald in 1956. Porter was known for his clever use of imagery and wordplay and many commentators point to *Every Time We Say Goodbye* as an exemplar of his work in this area. In addition, the clever and often unexpected key changes (particularly between the major and minor keys reflecting the lyrics) prove Porter's credentials as superlative composer. Long since a jazz standard, it has been covered by Simply Red (who reached number eleven in the UK charts in May 1987), Robbie Williams, Ray Charles, Diana Krall, Dinah Washington, Nina Simone, Annie Lennox, Natalie Cole and Jack Jones.

♫ I Didn't Know What Time It Was

Another Richard Rodgers and Lorenz Hart composition, *I Didn't Know What Time It Was* was written for the 1939 musical *Too Many Girls.* First recorded by Artie Shaw and Bennie Goodman, who both had hits with it, in the film version of the play, it was sung by Trudy Erwin, who was providing the singing vocals for Lucille Ball, the star of the film, and then it was inculcated into the *Pal Joey* score for Frank Sinatra to sing in that film. In addition to these artists, the song has also been covered by Ray Charles (who also had a chart hit with it in America), Nat King Cole, Bobby Darrin, Doris Day, Jack Teagarden, Oscar Peterson, Charlie Parker, Ted Heath and Julie London among many others.

♫ I Just Want to Make Love to You

The most popular and generally familiar version of *I Just Want to Make Love to You* in the UK was recorded by Etta James in 1961 but only became a number five hit in 1996 when it was used in a television advertising campaign for Diet Coke. For those interesting in blues music, the Willie Dixon song was made popular in 1954 by Muddy Waters when his single entered the US Billboard Charts that same year. Since then, it has been covered numerous times with versions by the Rolling Stones, Tom Petty and the Heartbreakers, Chuck Berry, the Grateful Dead, the Kinks, Van Morrison, the Animals, Bo Diddley, the Righteous Brothers and Lou Rawls.

♫ I've Got You Under My Skin

One of two or three signature songs for Frank Sinatra when he recorded it in 1966, *I've Got You Under My Skin* was written by Cole Porter in 1936 for inclusion in the musical film *Born to Dance*. The lead actress Virginia Bruce was the first to perform it and the song was nominated for that year's Academy Award for best song. In the UK, it was first a hit for the Four Seasons when it reached number twelve in the same year as Sinatra released his version, with Neneh Cherry reaching number twenty-five almost twenty-four years later. Before Cliff Richard tried a duet with Matt Monro using the original recording of ***Let There Be Love***, Bono had already succeeded in obtaining agreement from the Sinatra estate to record his vocals over the top of Sinatra's 1966 recording and the pairing reached number four in the UK charts in December 1993. In addition, several artists have recorded covers and a selection of them includes Al Bowlly, Ella Fitzgerald, Dinah Washington, Peggy Lee, Ella Fitzgerald, Michael Bolton and Can Calloway.

♫ Lazy River

More correctly titled *(Up a) Lazy River* with the initial parenthesised phrase, this Hoagy Carmichael and Sidney Arodin composition was a hit for Carmichael in 1930, the year that it was published. In the UK, it was in March 1961 that Bobby Darin had a number two hit with his cover, while several acts have covered the song since it was written: Acker Bilk, Bing Crosby, Kenny Ball, Kay Starr, Sammy Davis, Jr., Pat Boone, Paul Whiteman and His Orchestra, the Ink Spots, Glenn Miller and His Orchestra, Brenda Lee, Louis Armstrong, Rosemary Clooney and Tennessee Ernie Ford among several others.

♫ Let's Fall in Love

Without access to the track listing of the album, it is assumed that this track is not the Cole Porter track, which is more correctly titled *Let's Do It, Let's Fall in Love*, since this doesn't seem to easily fit in with the remainder of the chosen tracks for ***Bold as Brass***.

Rather, *Let's Fall in Love* is likely to be the 1933 hit for Eddy Duchin, written by Harold Arlen and Ted Koehler and is usually played, as a jazz standard, with an upbeat swing feel. In addition to Duchin, *Let's Fall in Love* has been covered by Ella Fitzgerald, who recorded two versions of it (one in 1959 and the following cover in 1961), Peaches and Herb, Carl Risely, Diana Krall and Shirley Bassey.

However, this dictation of the song by the author that is used on the album may be possibly an error of assumption and the author will be happy to rectify any possible errors in this respect once the album has been released and, should it be necessary, will add the information to the next edition of the *Recording Catalogue*.

♫ Love Me or Leave Me

Written by the famous pairing of early twentieth century composers Walter Donaldson and Gus Kahn, the song first came to prominence in *Whoopee!*, a Broadway play that opened in late 1928. Just over a year later, the popularity of the song from that show meant that it was also included in *Simple Simon*, another Broadway play that opened in early 1930.The first artist to record it was Ruth Etting, who also performed it in both of the Broadway plays, in December 1928 and it went on to become the biggest selling version. In September 1955, two versions entered the UK charts simultaneously: while the song is contemporaneously most associated with Doris Day, who only reached number twenty with her single, it was actually Sammy Davis, Jr. who had the bigger hit when his only British top ten single hit number eight. Other than these, *Love Me or Leave Me* has been covered by a number of artists including Bing Crosby, Perry Como, Elkie Brooks, Benny Goodman, Sarah Vaughan, Miles Davis and Olivia Newton-John among several others.

♫ Night and Day

Written for the 1932 stage musical *Gay Divorce* by the prolific Cole Porter, *Night and Day* was first performed by Fred Astaire and, when he recorded it, he reached number one in the US charts. Astaire resurrected his role once again in the film version of the play in 1934, which had by now been retitled *The Gay Divorcee*, and went on to become his signature song. Several artists have recorded covers of the song, including Peter Skellern (as part of his tribute album *Astaire* and also featuring a brass band as Cliff Richard's new version does), Frank Sinatra, Shirley Bassey, Ringo Starr, Nelson Riddle, Everything But The Girl, U2, while Allan Sherman parodied the song by inserting spoken punctuation marks for comedic effect.

♫ Teach Me Tonight

Published in 1953 and written by Gene de Paul and Sammy Cahn, a new verse was written for Frank Sinatra to record on his 1984 album, *L.A. Is My Lady*, with reference to Sinatra's oft-reported dalliances with a number of women. A Cuban female vocal group, the De Castro Sisters, had the only UK hit with *Teach Me Tonight* with their only charting single release, reaching number twenty in February 1955. Other artists to cover the song over the years have included Natalie Cole, Chaka Khan, Oscar Peterson, Errol Garner, Barry Manilow, Neil Diamond, Marvin Gaye, Ella Fitzgerald and Paul Anka.

♫ They Can't Take That Away from Me

Composed by brothers George and Ira Gershwin for the 1937 film *Shall We Dance*, it was performed by George Gershwin towards Ginger Rogers and became one of his signature songs. The song was nominated for the Academy Award for Best Original Song, posthumously in George Gershwin's case, since he died a couple of months prior to the release of the film. Other artists to cover the song include Peter Skellern (on his tribute album *Astaire*, which, like Cliff Richard's version, is accompanied by a brass band), Frank Sinatra, Robbie Williams and actor Rupert Everett in duet, Ella Fitzgerald, Rod Stewart, Brian Wilson, Jamie Cullum, Tony Bennett and Diana Krall.

♫ When I Take My Sugar to Tea

Written by Pierre Connor, Sammy Fain and Irving Kahal, the song is most associated with the Rat Pack and with Sammy Davis, Jr. and Frank Sinatra specifically. A big hit, too, for the Boswell Sisters, *When I Take My Sugar to Tea* has also been covered by Nat King Cole, Bing Crosby, the Dorsey Brothers, Cleo Laine, King Oliver, Jack Hylton and Billy May.

THE CLIFF RICHARD RECORDING CATALOGUE

Appendix F: The Lists

♬ Introduction

In this section, I have tried to create a number of reference lists about Cliff's music and his recordings that might be of interest and to help the direct the reader on particular journeys in the book.
Specifically, the following lists are available:

1. The chronology of singles and their UK chart peaks
2. The alphabet of songs written by Cliff
3. The top 50 of different versions (live and studio) of songs
4. The short inventory of Cliff's duets
5. The long catalogue of all of Cliff's foreign language recordings
6. The facts and figures around the alphabetical sequence of songs

♬ Cliff Richard's UK Singles List

This section features al of Cliff's singles released in the UK, their chart status and other relevant information. The single release title is highlighted in bold. Top ten chart positions are highlighted in italics, while the top position is also highlighted in bold.

Title	Backed with	Label	Catalogue number	Chart position
Move It	Schoolboy Crush	Columbia	DB 4178	2
High Class Baby	My Feet Hit the Ground	Columbia	DB 4203	*7*
Livin' Lovin' Doll	Steady with You	Columbia	DB 4249	20
Mean Streak	Never Mind	Columbia	DB 4290 (A)	*10*
Never Mind	Mean Streak	Columbia	DB 4290 (B)	21
Living Doll	Apron Strings	Columbia	DB 4306	***1***
Travellin' Light	Dynamite	Columbia	DB 4351 (A)	***1***
Dynamite	Travellin' Light	Columbia	DB 4351 (B)	16
A Voice in the Wilderness	Don't Be Mad at Me	Columbia	DB 4398	2
Fall in Love with You	Willie and the Hand-Jive	Columbia	DB 4431	2
Please Don't Tease	Where Is My Heart?	Columbia	DB 4479	***1***
Nine Times out of Ten	Thinking of Our Love	Columbia	DB 4506	*3*
I Love You	'D' in Love	Columbia	DB 4547	***1***
Theme for a Dream	Mumblin' Mosie	Columbia	DB 4593	*3*
Gee Whiz It's You	I Cannot Find a True Love	Columbia	DC 756	*4*
A Girl Like You	Now's the Time to Fall in Love	Columbia	DB 4667	*3*
When the Girl in Your Arms Is the Girl in Your Heart	Got a Funny Feeling	Columbia	DB 4716	*3*
The Young Ones	We Say Yeah	Columbia	DB 4761	***1***
I'm Looking out the Window	**Do You Wanna Dance?**	Columbia	DB 4828	2
It'll Be Me	Since I Lost You	Columbia	DB 4886	2
The Next Time	**Bachelor Boy**	Columbia	DB 4950	***1***
Summer Holiday	Dancing Shoes	Columbia	DB 4977	***1***
Lucky Lips	I Wonder	Columbia	DB 7034	*4*
It's All in the Game	Your Eyes Tell on You	Columbia	DB 7089	2
Don't Talk to Him	Say You're Mine	Columbia	DB 7150	2
I'm the Lonely One	Watch What You Do with My Baby	Columbia	DB 7203	*8*
Constantly	True, True Lovin'	Columbia	DB 7272	*4*
On the Beach	A Matter of Moments	Columbia	DB 7305	*7*
The Twelfth of Never	I'm Afraid to Go Home	Columbia	DB 7372	*8*
I Could Easily Fall (in Love with You)	I'm in Love with You	Columbia	DB 7420	*6*
The Minute You're Gone	Just another Guy	Columbia	DB 7496	***1***
On My Word	Just a Little Bit Too Late	Columbia	DB 7596	12
The Time in Between	Look Before You Love	Columbia	DB 7660	22
Wind Me Up (Let Me Go)	The Night	Columbia	DB 7745	2
Blue Turns to Grey	Somebody Loses	Columbia	DB 7866	15

Title	Backed with	Label	Catalogue number	Chart position
Visions	What Would I Do (for the Love of a Girl)?	Columbia	DB 7968	7
Time Drags By	The La La Song	Columbia	DB 8017	10
In the Country	Finders Keepers	Columbia	DB 8094	6
It's All Over	Why Wasn't I Born Rich?	Columbia	DB 8150	9
I'll Come Running	I Get the Feeling	Columbia	DB 8210	26
The Day I Met Marie	Our Story Book	Columbia	DB 8245	10
All My Love	Sweet Little Jesus Boy	Columbia	DB 8293	6
Congratulations	High 'n' Dry	Columbia	DB 8376	1
I'll Love You Forever Today	Girl, You'll Be a Woman Soon	Columbia	DB 8437	27
Marianne	Mr. Nice	Columbia	DB 8476	22
Don't Forget to Catch Me	What's More, I Don't Need Her	Columbia	DB 8503	21
Good Times (Better Times)	Occasional Rain	Columbia	DB 8548	12
Big Ship	She's Leaving You	Columbia	DB 8581	8
Throw Down a Line	Reflections	Columbia	DB 8615	7
With the Eyes of a Child	So Long	Columbia	DB 8641	20
The Joy of Living	Leave My Woman Alone	Columbia	DB 8657	25
	Boogitoo			
Goodbye Sam, Hello Samantha	You Never Can Tell	Columbia	DB 8685	6
I Ain't Got Time Anymore	Monday Comes Too Soon	Columbia	DB 8708	21
Sunny Honey Girl	Don't Move Away	Columbia	DB 8747	19
	I Was Only Foolin'			
Silvery Rain	Annabella Umbrella	Columbia	DB 8774	27
	Time Flies			
Flying Machine	Pigeon	Columbia	DB 8797	37
Sing a Song of Freedom	A Thousand Conversations	Columbia	DB 8836	13
Jesus	Mr. Cloud	Columbia	DB 8864	35
Living in Harmony	Empty Chairs	Columbia	DB 8917	12
A Brand New Song	The Old Accordion	Columbia	DB 8957	-
Power to All Our Friends	Come Back Billy Jo	EMI	EMI 2012	4
Help It Along/Tomorrow Rising	The Days of Love	EMI	EMI 2022	29
	Ashes to Ashes			
Take Me High	Celestial Houses	EMI	EMI 2088	27
(You Keep Me) Hangin' On	Love Is Here	EMI	EMI 2150	13
It's Only Me You've Left Behind	You're the One	EMI	EMI 2279	-
(There's a) Honky Tonk Angel	Wouldn't You Know It (Got Myself a Girl)?	EMI	EMI 2344	-
Miss You Nights	Love Enough	EMI	EMI 2376	15
Devil Woman	Love On, Shine On	EMI	EMI 2458	9
I Can't Ask for Anything More Than You	Junior Cowboy	EMI	EMI 2499	17
Hey Mr. Dream Maker	No-One Waits	EMI	EMI 2559	31
My Kinda Life	Nothing Left for Me to Say	EMI	EMI 2584	15
When Two Worlds Drift Apart	That's Why I Love You	EMI	EMI 2633	46
Yes He Lives	Good on the Sally Army	EMI	EMI 2730	-
Please Remember Me	Please Don't Tease	EMI	EMI 2832	-
Can't Take the Hurt Anymore	Needing a Friend	EMI	EMI 2885	-
Green Light	Imagine Love	EMI	EMI 2920	57
We Don't Talk Anymore	Count Me Out	EMI	EMI 2975	1
Hot Shot	Walking in the Light	EMI	EMI 5003	46
Carrie	Movin' In	EMI	EMI 5006	4
Dreamin'	Dynamite	EMI	EMI 5095	8
Suddenly	*You Made Me Love You*	Jet	Jet 7002	15
A Little in Love	Keep on Lookin'	EMI	EMI 5123	15
Wired for Sound	Hold On	EMI	EMI 5221	4
Daddy's Home	Shakin' All Over	EMI	EMI 5251	2
The Only Way Out	Under the Influence	EMI	EMI 5318	10
Where Do We Go from Here?	Discovering	EMI	EMI 5341	60
Little Town	Love and a Helping Hand	EMI	EMI 5348	11
	You, Me and Jesus			
She Means Nothing to Me	*A Man and a Woman*	Capitol	CL 276	9
True Love Ways	Galadriel (Spirit of Starlight)	EMI	EMI 5385	8
Drifting	It's Lonely When the Lights Go On	DJM	SHEIL 1	64
Never Say Die (Give a Little Bit More)	Lucille	EMI	EMI 5415	15
Please Don't Fall in Love	Too Close to Heaven	EMI	EMI 5437	7
Baby You're Dynamite	**Ocean Deep**	EMI	EMI 5457	27
Two to the Power of Love	*Don't Mess up a Good Thing*	A&M	AM210	-
Shooting from the Heart	Small World	EMI	RICH 1	51
Heart User	I Will Follow You	EMI	RICH 2	46

Title	Backed with	Label	Catalogue number	Chart position
She's So Beautiful	She's So Beautiful	EMI	EMI 5531	17
It's in Every One of Us	Alone	EMI	EMI 5537	45
Living Doll	*(All the Little Flowers Are) Happy*	WEA	YZ 65	*1*
Born to Rock 'n' Roll	*The Law of the Universe*	EMI		-
All I Ask of You	*Phantom of the Opera Act II Overture*	Polydor	POSP 802	*3*
	Only You			
Slow Rivers	*Billy and the Kids*	Rocket	EJS 13	44
My Pretty One	Love Ya	EMI	EM 4	*6*
	Under the Gun			
Some People	One Time Lover Man	EMI	EM 18	*3*
	Reunion of the Heart			
Remember Me	Another Christmas Day	EMI	EM 31	35
	Brave New World			
Two Hearts	Yesterday, Today, Forever	EMI	EM 42	34
	Wild Geese			
Mistletoe and Wine	Marmaduke	EMI	EM 78	*1*
	Little Town			
	La Gonave			
The Best of Me	Move It	EMI	EM 92	*2*
	Lindsay Jane			
	High Class Baby			
Just Don't Have the Heart	Wide Open Space	EMI	EM 101	*3*
Lean on You	Hey Mister	EMI	EM 105	17
Whenever God Shines His Light	*I'd Love to Write another Song*	Polydor	VANS 2	20
Stronger than That	Joanna	EMI	EM 129	14
	Stronger than That (extended)			
Silhouettes	The Winner	EMI	EM 152	*10*
	All the Time You Need			
From a Distance	Lindsay Jane II	EMI	EM 155	11
	Wired for Sound			
Saviour's Day	Oh Boy! Medley	EMI	XMAS 90	*1*
	Where Are You?			
More to Life	*More to Life (instrumental)*	EMI	EM 205	23
We Should Be Together	Miss You Nights	EMI	XMAS 91	*10*
	Mistletoe and Wine			
This New Year	Scarlet Ribbons	EMI	EMS 218	30
	We Don't Talk Anymore			
I Still Believe in You	Bulange Downpour	EMI	EM 255	*7*
	There's No Power in Pity			
	Remember			
	Ocean Deep			
Peace in Our Time	Somebody Loves You	EMI	CDEM 265	*8*
	Living Doll			
	That's Alright Mama			
Human Work of Art	Ragged	EMI	CDEM 267	24
	Move It			
	Never Even Thought			
	Free			
	Devil Woman			
Never Let Go	Congratulations	EMI	CDEM 281	32
	The Young Ones			
	You Got Me Wondering			
Healing Love	Yesterday's Memories	EMI	CDEM 294	19
	Carrie			
	Daddy's Home			
	Some People			
All I Have to Do Is Dream/Miss You Nights	When Will I Be Loved	EMI	CDEM 359	14
	Tribute to the Legends			
	True Love Ways			
	Party Megamix			
A Misunderstood Man	*A Misunderstood Man (instrumental)*	EMI	CDEM 394	19
Had to Be	Had to Be	EMI	CDEM 410	22
	Don't Move Away			
The Wedding	The Sleep of the Good	EMI	CDEM 422	40
	I Do Not Love You Isabella			

Title	Backed with	Label	Catalogue number	Chart position
Be with Me Always	Summer Holiday The Young Ones Bachelor Boy	EMI	CDEM 453	52
Can't Keep This Feeling In	Larger Design Can't Keep This Feeling In (Little America mix) Can't Keep This Feeling In (Step Child mix) Can't Keep This Feeling In (Phil Chills mix) After This Love	EMI	CDEM 526	*10*
The Miracle	Don't Say Goodbye Move It Hope, Faith and You The Twelfth of Never	EMI/Blacknight	CDEM 546	23
The Millennium Prayer	Two Worlds	Papillon	PROMISECD 01	*1*
Somewhere over the Rainbow/What a Wonderful World	The Millennium Prayer (*a capella*) Lay All Your Love on Me Let's Go Where There Are Horses	Papillon	CLIFF CD1	11
Let Me Be the One	I Gotta Woman This Can't Be Love My Funny Valentine	Papillon	CLIFF CD2	29
Santa's List	Mistletoe and Wine Mary's Boy Child	EMI	SANTA 1	*5*
Somethin' Is Goin' On	How Many Sleeps? Slow Down	Decca/UCJ	4756419	*9*
I Cannot Give You My Love	She's All Mine	Decca/UCJ	4756611	13
What Car?	Slow Down Sentimental Journey Diamonds on a Chain	Decca/UCJ	756943	12
Yesterday Once More	***download only***	-	-	-
21st Century Christmas	**Move It**	EMI	946 3799312	*2*
When I Need You	Never Let Go My Pretty One	EMI	50999 511452	38
Thank You for a Lifetime	Mobile Alabama School Leaving Hullabaloo	EMI	50999 236462	*3*
Singing the Blues	Dancing Shoes A Voice in the Wilderness We Say Yeah	EMI	50999 687887	40

♫ Cliff Richard's Compositions

This section features all of the songs for which Cliff has a writing credit, whether he recording them or not. The information is presented so that co-writers are identified, as well as giving pertinent chart information where relevant.

Title	Co-writers	Source	Chart position
31st of February Street (Closing)	-	The 31st of February Street	-
31st of February Street (Opening)	-	The 31st of February Street	-
And Me (I'm on the Outside Now)	Mike Leander	Two a Penny	-
Another Christmas Day	-	B-side (Remember Me)	-
Bachelor Boy	Bruce Welch	Single	1
Big News	Mike Condon, Ronald Cass	Summer Holiday	-
Bulange Downpour	-	B-side (I Still Believe in You)	-
Can It Be True?	David Winter, Cindy Kent, Mike Jones, John Fyffe, Geoffrey Srodzinski	Unissued track	-
The Carnival's Just for Me	David Winter, Cindy Kent, Mike Jones, John Fyffe, Geoffrey Srodzinski	Unissued track	-
Celebrate	David Winter, Cindy Kent, Mike Jones, John Fyffe, Geoffrey Srodzinski	Unissued track	-
Chi Lo Sà	Hank Marvin, Bruce Welch, Cino Tortorella	When in Rome	-
Compassion Road	David Winter, Cindy Kent, Mike Jones, John Fyffe, Geoffrey Srodzinski	Unissued track	-
Count Us Out	David Winter, Cindy Kent, Mike Jones, John Fyffe, Geoffrey Srodzinski	Unissued track	-
Don't Blame Me	David Winter, Cindy Kent, Mike Jones, John Fyffe, Geoffrey Srodzinski	Unissued track	-
Don't Listen to Him	David Winter, Cindy Kent, Mike Jones, John Fyffe, Geoffrey Srodzinski	Unissued track	-
Don't Talk to Him	Bruce Welch	Single	
The Fellow Next to Me	David Winter, Cindy Kent, Mike Jones, John Fyffe, Geoffrey Srodzinski	Unissued track	-
Fireside Song	-	The 31st of February Street	-
Forgive Me	David Winter, Cindy Kent, Mike Jones, John Fyffe, Geoffrey Srodzinski	Unissued track	-
For You, For Me	Bruce Welch	Holiday Carnival EP	-
Fragen	Jim Collier, Carl Ulrich Blecher	German track	-
La Conave	-	The Rock Connection	-
Happy Like a Bell (Ding Dong)	-	Cherry Wainer single	-
Happy World	David Winter, Cindy Kent, Mike Jones, John Fyffe, Geoffrey Srodzinski	Unissued track	-
Hold Us Together	Paul Moessl	The Album	-
I'll Love You Forever Today	Jim Collier	Single	
I Love You, I Need You	-	Patti Brook single	-
I Love You So	Ian Samwell, Jet Harris	Me and My Shadows	-
Is There an Answer?	David Winter, Cindy Kent, Mike Jones, John Fyffe, Geoffrey Srodzinski	Unissued track	-
It Just Happened That Way	Ian Samwell, Jet Harris	Brian James single	-
I Will Arise and Go	David Winter, Cindy Kent, Mike Jones, John Fyffe, Geoffrey Srodzinski	Unissued track	-
I Will Follow You	-	B-side (Heart User)	-
I Wonder	Hank Marvin	B-side (Lucky Lips)	-
Je Suis Formidable	Unknown	French track	-
Jesus Loves You	-	Help It Along	-
Je T'Aime Pour Toujours Ce Jour	Jim Collier, Unknown	French track	-
Johnny	David Winter, Cindy Kent, Mike Jones, John Fyffe, Geoffrey Srodzinski	Unissued track	-
Johnny Wake Up to Reality	David Winter, Cindy Kent, Mike Jones, John Fyffe, Geoffrey Srodzinski	Unissued track	-
Die Liebe Ist Immer Nur Heute	Jim Collier, Joachim Relin	German track	-
Lindsay Jane	-	B-side (The Best of Me)	-
Lindsay Jane II	-	B-side (From a Distance)	-
Lonely Girl	Mike Leander	Two a Penny	-
Lord, I Love You	-	Sail Away (Dave Pope)	-
Love and a Helping Hand	-	B-side (Little Town)	-

Title	Co-writers	Source	Chart position
Love Is More Than Words	David Winter, Cindy Kent, Mike Jones, John Fyffe, Geoffrey Srodzinski	Unissued track	-
Love Never Gives Up	-	10th Way of Life Rally	-
Love On (Shine On)	-	B-side (Devil Woman)	-
Love's Salvation	Paul Moessl	The Album	-
Love Ya	-	B-side (My Pretty One)	-
Moving In	-	B-side (Carrie)	-
Mr. Niemand	Unknown	German track	-
Needing a Friend	Gary Isherwood	B-side (Can't Take the Hurt Anymore)	-
The Night	Hank Marvin	B-side (Wind Me U (Let Me Go))	-
Non l'Ascoltare	Bruce Welch, Cassia	Italian track	-
No-One Seems to Care	David Winter, Cindy Kent, Mike Jones, John Fyffe, Geoffrey Srodzinski	Unissued track	-
No-One Waits	Gary Isherwood	B-side (Hey Mr. Dream Maker)	-
Nothing Left for Me to Say	-	B-side (My Kinda Life)	-
Nothing to Remind Me	-	The 31st of February Street	-
Now I've Done It	David Winter, Cindy Kent, Mike Jones, John Fyffe, Geoffrey Srodzinski	Unissued track	-
Nur Mit Dir	Hank Marvin, Bruce Welch, Hans Bradtke	German track	-
One Time Lover Man	-	B-side (Some People)	-
On the Beach	Hank Marvin, Bruce Welch	Single	7
Our Love Could Be So Real	-	The 31st of February Street	-
Over You	Dave Cooke	The Rock Connection	-
Questions	Jim Collier	Two a Penny	-
Reflections	Keith Craddock	B-side (Throw Down a Line)	-
Relève Mon Défi	Jim Collier, Unknown	French track	-
Rock 'n' Roll Juvenile	-	Rock 'n' Roll Juvenile	-
Sag 'No' zu Ihm	Bruce Welch, Carl Ulrich Blecher	German track	-
Seeing Is Believing	David Winter, Cindy Kent, Mike Jones, John Fyffe, Geoffrey Srodzinski	Unissued track	-
She Makes Me Feel Like a Man	Peter Wolf, Michelle Wolf	Real as I Wanna Be	-
Silent Night	Joseph Mohr, Franz Gruber, John Freeman Young, Paul Moessl	Together with Cliff Richard	-
Small World	-	It's a Small World	-
Some Are Lonely	-	Out of the Shadows	-
That's My Kind of Life	David Winter, Cindy Kent, Mike Jones, John Fyffe, Geoffrey Srodzinski	Unissued track	-
That's What Love Is	David Winter, Cindy Kent, Mike Jones, John Fyffe, Geoffrey Srodzinski	Unissued track	-
There's No Power in Pity	-	B-side (I Still Believe in You)	-
There You Go Again	-	The 31st February Street	-
Till Winter Follows Spring	David Winter, Cindy Kent, Mike Jones, John Fyffe, Geoffrey Srodzinski	Unissued track	-
Tiny Planet	-	It's a Small World	-
Turn It into Cash	David Winter, Cindy Kent, Mike Jones, John Fyffe, Geoffrey Srodzinski	Unissued track	-
Two a Penny	-	Two a Penny	-
The Water Is Wide	Traditional, Craig Pruess	Now You See Me, Now You Don't	-
Where Is That Man?	David Winter, Cindy Kent, Mike Jones, John Fyffe, Geoffrey Srodzinski	About That Man	-
Where You Are	Dave Cooke	B-side (Saviour's Day)	-
The Winner	Dave Cooke	B-side (Silhouettes)	-
With a Hmm-Hmm on My Knee	-	Jigsaw	-
Without You	Hank Marvin, Bruce Welch	21 Today	-
Yesterday's Memories	Dave Cooke	B-side (Healing Love)	-
Yesterday, Today, Forever	-	Help It Along	-
You Held My Hand	David Winter, Cindy Kent, Mike Jones, John Fyffe, Geoffrey Srodzinski	Unissued track	-
You, Me and Jesus	-	B-side (Little Town)	-

♫ Cliff Richard's Top 100 Most Frequently Recorded Songs

This section features all of the songs that Cliff has recorded (live or in the studio), including unissued tracks, presented in the order of the most to the fewest – all the songs have at least three unique versions. Other information provided includes highest chart position, where appropriate.

	Song title	Number of recordings	Number unissued	Number released	Highest chart position
1	Move It	20	2	18	2
2	Living Doll	17	4	13	1
3	Do You Wanna Dance?	15	0	15	10
	The Young Ones	15	3	12	1
5	Bachelor Boy	13	2	11	1
6	In the Country	12	6	6	6
7	Miss You Nights	10	0	10	14
8	Summer Holiday	9	2	7	1
9	The Day I Met Marie	8	1	7	10
	Willie and the Hand-Jive	8	2	6	-
11	I Could Easily Fall (in Love with You)	7	2	5	6
	The Next Time	7	2	5	1
	On the Beach	7	0	7	7
	We Don't Talk Anymore	7	1	6	1
15	Born to Rock 'n' Roll	6	1	5	-
	Congratulations	6	0	6	1
	Devil Woman	6	0	6	9
	Dynamite	6	1	5	16
	It'll Be Me	6	2	4	2
	Visions	6	1	5	7
	Whole Lotta Shakin' Goin' On	6	2	4	-
22	Got a Funny Feeling	5	0	5	-
	I Love You	5	0	5	1
	Just Don't Have the Heart	5	0	5	3
	La La La La La	5	1	4	-
	Lucky Lips	5	2	3	4
	The Millennium Prayer	5	0	5	1
	Peace in Our Time	5	0	5	8
	Please Don't Tease	5	1	4	1
	She's So Beautiful	5	0	5	17
	Some People	5	0	5	3
	Stronger than That	5	0	5	14
	What'd I Say?	5	2	3	-
	Wonderful to Be Young	5	1	4	-
35	Can't Keep This Feeling In	4	0	4	10
	Carrie	4	0	4	4
	Daddy's Home	4	1	3	2
	Dancing Shoes	4	0	4	-
	Early in the Morning	4	0	4	-
	Gee Whiz It's You	4	1	3	4
	Good on the Sally Army	4	2	2	-
	It's All in the Game	4	0	4	2
	It's in Every One of Us	4	0	4	45
	Lessons in Love	4	0	4	-
	Little Town	4	1	3	11
	Lucille	4	0	4	-
	The Minute You're Gone	4	0	4	1
	Nine Times out of Ten	4	0	4	3
	Remember Me	4	0	4	35
	Share a Dream	4	1	3	-
	Shout	4	0	4	-
	Sing a Song of Freedom	4	0	4	13
	Thief in the Night	4	1	3	-
	Travellin' Light	4	0	4	1
	Two Hearts	4	0	4	34
	A Voice in the Wilderness	4	0	4	2
	We Have It Made	4	2	2	-
	We Say Yeah	4	0	4	-
	Yes He Lives	4	0	4	-

	Song title	Number of recordings	Number unissued	Number released	Highest chart position
60	All My Love	3	0	3	6
	All Shook Up	3	0	3	-
	Angel	3	2	1	-
	Baby You're Dynamite	3	0	3	27
	C'mon Everybody	3	0	3	-
	Don't Forget to Catch Me	3	2	1	21
	Don't Talk to Him	3	0	3	2
	Dreamin'	3	0	3	8
	Every Face Tells a Story (It Never Tells a Lie)	3	2	1	-
	Fall in Love with You	3	1	2	2
	Fighter	3	0	3	-
	The Girl Can't Help It	3	0	3	-
	A Girl Like You	3	0	3	3
	Girl, You'll Be a Woman Soon	3	0	3	-
	Great Balls of Fire	3	0	3	-
	Had to Be	3	0	3	22
	Healing Love	3	0	3	19
	I Cannot Give You My Love	3	0	3	13
	If Ever I Would Leave You	3	0	3	-
	I'll Come Running	3	0	3	26
	It's All Over	3	1	2	9
	It's No Use Pretending	3	2	1	-
	Jesus	3	0	3	35
	Living in Harmony	3	1	2	12
	A Misunderstood Man	3	0	3	19
	My Pretty One	3	1	2	6
	Now's the Time to Fall in Love	3	0	3	-
	One Fine Day	3	2	1	-
	Rattler	3	0	3	-
	Rock 'n' Roll Juvenile	3	2	1	-
	Saviour's Day	3	1	2	1
	Silvery Rain	3	0	3	27
	The Sleep of the Good	3	0	3	-
	Spanish Harlem	3	1	2	-
	Under the Gun	3	1	2	-
	Up in the World	3	0	3	-
	What's Behind the Eyes of Mary?	3	2	1	-
	When I Survey the Wondrous Cross	3	0	3	-
	Wired for Sound	3	1	2	4

♫ Cliff Richard's Duets and Collaborations

Although Cliff Richard is most associated with his huge volume of songs that he has recorded solo, there are also several tracks, in a surprisingly long list, of songs that he has performed while sharing the lead vocal honours. Several songs come from his musicals in the theatre and on film but many others are specific recordings with other people. This list addresses those songs with information on who he partnered on the recording and whether it charted:

	Song title	Singing partner(s)	Highest chart position
1	All I Ask of You	Sarah Brightman	3
2	All I Have to Do Is Dream	Phil Everly	14
3	Anyone Who Had a Heart	Dionne Warwick	-
4	Brumburger Duet	Debbie Watling	-
5	Choosing When It's Too Late (1)	Olivia Newton-John	-
6	Choosing When It's Too Late (2)	Sara Haggerty, Helen Hobson, Darryl Knock	-
7	Danny Boy	Helmut Lotti	-
8	Devoted to You	Denise Black	-
9	Different Is Beautiful	Vincenzo La Scola	-
10	Don't Move Away	Olivia Newton-John	-
11	Dream Tomorrow (1)	Olivia Newton-John	-
12	Dream Tomorrow (2)	Helen Hobson	-
13	Drifting	Sheila Walsh	64
14	Each to His Own	Helen Hobson	-
15	The Escapade	Art Garfunkel, Julian Lennon, Deniece Williams	-
16	Fields of Gold	Barry Gibb	-
17	Find a Little Faith	Olivia Newton-John	-
18	The Gambling Song	Jimmy Johnston	-
19	Had to Be (1)	Olivia Newton-John	22
20	Had to Be (2)	Helen Hobson, Darryl Knock	-
21	He's Everything to Me	Cliff Barrows	-
22	I Could Be Persuaded	The Bellamy Brothers	-
23	I Do Not Love You Isabella (1)	Olivia Newton-John, Kristina Nichols	-
24	I Do Not Love You Isabella (2)	Sara Haggerty, Helen Hobson, Darryl Knock	-
25	If Ever I Would Leave You	Helen Hobson	-
26	If It Were Up to Me	Vincenzo La Scola	-
27	If Our Dreams Came True	Jackie Lee	-
28	I'll Mend Your Broken Heart	Phil Everly	-
29	Imagine	Cilla Black	-
30	Isabella (Reprise)	Sara Haggerty	-
31	Jesus, Call Your Lambs	Sheila Walsh	-
32	Los Jovenes	Los Mustang	-
33	The Joy of Living	Hank Marvin	25
34	Let It Be Me (1)	Elaine Paige	-
35	Let It Be Me (2)	Olivia Newton-John	-
36	Let There Be Love	Matt Monro	-
37	Living Doll	The Young Ones featuring Hank Marvin	1
38	Look Up, Look Down	The Olsen Brothers	-
39	Love Is More Than Words	Cindy Kent	-
40	Love Is the Strongest Emotion	Judith Walmsley	-
41	Love That Knows No End	Aleksander Mežek	-
42	Marked with Death (1)	Olivia Newton-John	-
43	Marked with Death (2)	Helen Hobson	-
44	Mary's Boy Child	Helmut Lotti	-
45	Miss You Nights (1)	Elaine Paige	-
46	Miss You Nights (2)	G4	-
47	A Misunderstood Man (Reprise)	Sara Haggerty, Helen Hobson, Jimmy Johnston, Darryl Knock	-
48	Move It	Brian May, Brian Bennett	2
49	My Love	Vincenzo La Scola	-
50	The Nightmare	Sara Haggerty, Helen Hobson, Jimmy Johnston, Darryl Knock	-
51	Nothing's Impossible	Grazina Frame	-
52	Oh, Señorita	Ronnie Brodie, Unknown others	-
53	Only You	Sarah Brightman	-
54	Over in Bethlehem	Cliff Barrows	-
55	Paella	Unknown, possibly Vivianne Ventura	-
56	Prijatelju	Aleksander Mežek	-
57	Reunited	Lulu	-
58	The Rock That Doesn't Roll	Larry Norman	-

	Song title	Singing partner(s)	Highest chart position
59	Saviour's Day	Claudia Jung	-
60	She Means Nothing to Me	Phil Everly	9
61	Slow Rivers	Elton John	44
62	Suddenly	Olivia Newton-John	15
63	A Swingin' Affair	Grazina Frame	-
64	That's What Friends Are For	Cilla Black	-
65	This Love	Tammy Wynette	-
66	This Was My Special Day	Audrey Bayley, Faye Fisher, Joan Palethorpe	-
67	Throw Down a Line	Hank Marvin	8
68	To a Friend	Aleksander Mežek	-
69	Tribute to the Legends Medley	Phil Everly	-
70	The Twelfth of Never	Michelle Wolf	-
71	Two to the Power of Love	Janet Jackson	-
72	Up Where We Belong	Anne Murray	-
73	Vita Mia	Vincenzo La Scola	-
74	Vodna Pot	Aleksander Mežek	-
75	We Being Many	Helen Shapiro	-
76	The Wedding	Helen Hobson	40
77	Weihnachtszeit – Mistletoe and Wine	Claudia Jung	-
78	Whenever God Shines His Light	Van Morrison	20
79	When Will I Be Loved?	Phil Everly	-
80	Where Is That Man?	Cindy Kent	-
81	Why?	Anthony Andrews	-
82	Yesterday Once More	Daniel O'Donnell	-

♫ Cliff Richard's Foreign Language Recordings

Cliff Richard has a long and successful history of recording songs in foreign languages, principally the popular European tongues, although he has also tried his hand at Slovenian with Aleksander Mežek. Most of the continental songs have been collated and issued on the anthology boxed set ***On the Continent***, but this list is the definitive set of **107** foreign songs involving Cliff:

	Song title	Translated title	Cliff's English language version
1	Ah! Quelle Histoire	Ah! What a Story	Congratulations
2	L'Amandier Sauvage	The Wild Almond	-
3	Amor, Amor Amor	Love, Love, Love	*Amor, Amor, Amor* (possible)
4	Arrivederci Roma	Goodbye Rome	-
5	La Ballade de Baltimore	The Baltimore Ballad	The Lady Came from Baltimore (live)
6	Bilder von Dir	Pictures of You	Visions
7	Bin Verliebt	Am Loved	Fall in Love with You
8	Boum	Boom	-
9	Canción de Orfeo	Orfeo's Song	Carnival
10	Carina	Carina (or Cute)	-
11	Casa sense Finestre	House without Windows	House without Windows
12	C'est Si Bon	It's So Good	-
13	Che Chosa del Farai Mia Amore?	What Are You Doing About It, My Love?	-
14	Chi Lo Sà	Search Me	On the Beach
15	Come Prima	Like the First Time	-
16	Concerto d'Autumno	Autumn Concerto	-
17	Das Ist die Frage Aller Fragen	That Is the Question of All Questions	Spanish Harlem
18	Deine Augen Träumen Mary	Your Eyes Dream of Mary	What's Behind the Eyes of Mary?
19	Dicitencello Vuie	Say to You	-
20	Du Bist Mein Erster Gedanke	You Are My First Thought	-
21	Du, Du Gefällst Mir So	You, You Give Me So Much Pleasure	-
22	Du Fragst Mich Immer Wieder	You Ask Me Time and Time Again	-
23	Es Gehören Zwei zum Glücklichsein	Happiness Takes Two	(You Keep Me) Hangin' On
24	Es Ist Nicht Gut, Allein zu Sein	It's Not Good to Be Alone	-
25	Es Könnte Schön Morgen Sein	It Could Already Be Morning	The Minute You're Gone
26	Es War Keine So Wunderbar Wie Du	It Wasn't So Wonderful as You	I Could Easily Fall (in Love with You)
27	Fragen	Questions	Questions
28	Frenesi	Frenzy	-
29	Geh' Deinen Weg Nicht So Allein	Don't Go Your Own Way So Alone	The Dreams I Dream
30	Das Girl von Nebenan	The Girl Next Door	-
31	Ein Girl Wie Du	A Girl Like You	Words
32	Glaub' Nur Mir	Believe only Me	Wind Me Up (Let Me Go)
33	Das Glück Ist Rosarot	Luck Is Rose-Red	-
34	Goodbye Sam, Das Ist die Liebe	Goodbye Sam, That's Love	Goodbye Sam, Hello Samantha
35	Gut, Daß Es Freunde Gibt	It's Good That It Gives You Friends	Power to All Our Friends
36	Ich Kann Treu Sein	I Can Be Faithful	I'll Come Running
37	Ich Träume Deine Träume	I Dream Your Dreams	-
38	Il Faut Chanter la Vie	It's Necessary to Sing about Life	Power to All Our Friends
39	Imagina un Giorno	Imagine a Day	The Day I Met Marie
40	J'Attendrai	I Will Wait	-
41	Je Suis Formidable	I Am Strong	Two a Penny
42	Je T'Aime pour Toujours Ce Jour	I Love You Forever This Day	I'll Love You Forever Today
43	Los Jovenes	The Young Ones	The Young Ones
44	Kein Zug Nach Gretna Green	No Train to Gretna Green	-
45	Kleine Taube	Little Pigeon	Pigeon
46	Laß Uns Schnell Vergessen	Let's Forget Quickly	-
47	Legata ad un Granelo di Sabbia	Tied to a Little Grain of Sand	-
48	Die Liebe Ist Immer Nur Heute	Love Is Only for Today	I'll Love You Forever Today
49	Lieben Kann Man Einmal Nur	Can You Only Love Once	-
50	Liebeslied	Love Song	Love Is Here
51	London Ist Nicht Weit	London Is Not Far	London's Not Too Far
52	Man Gratuliert Mir	One Congratulates Me	Congratulations
53	Der Mann Neben Dir	The Man Next to You	-
54	Maria Ninguém	Maria Nobody	-
55	Maria No Mas	Maria No More	-
56	Me Lo Dijo Adela	Say It to Me Sweetly	Sweet and Gentle
57	La Mer	The Sea	-
58	Il Mondo et Tondo	The World Is Round	Congratulations
59	Mrs. Emily Jones	Mrs. Emily Jones	-
60	Mr. Niemand	Mr. Nobody	Two a Penny

	Song title	Translated title	Cliff's English language version
61	'Na Voce, 'Na Chitarra, e'o Poco 'e Luna	A Voice, a Guitar and a Little Moonlight	I Only Know I Love You
62	Neben Dir Wird's Keine Geben	No-One Compares with You	Early in the Morning
63	Nel Blu Dipinto di Blu	In the Blue Painted Blue	-
64	Non Dimenticare Chi Ti Ama	Don't Forget Who Loves You	Don't Forget to Catch Me
65	Non l'Ascoltare	Don't Listen to Him	Don't Talk to Him
66	Nur Bei Dir Bin Ich zu Haus	Only with You Am I at Home	Wind Me Up (Let Me Go)
67	Nur Mit Dir	Only with You	On the Beach
68	O Mio Signore	Oh My Lord	-
69	Ooh La La (Sagte Cäsar zu Cleopatra)	Ooh La La (as Ceasar Said to Cleopatra)	Ooh La La
70	Perfidia	Treachery	Perfidia
71	Per un Bacio d'Amor	For a Kiss of Love	-
72	Prijatelju	Friend	To a Friend
73	Quando, Quando, Quando	When, When, When?	-
74	¡Qué Buena Suerte!	How Lucky!	Congratulations
75	¿Quién Serà?	Whoever It Will Be	-
76	Quizás, Quizás, Quizás	Perhaps, Perhaps, Perhaps	Perhaps, Perhaps, Perhaps
77	Relève Mon Défi	Take Up My Challenge	Questions
78	Remember	Remember	When Two Worlds Drift Apart
79	Rote Lippen Soll Man Küssen	Red Lips Can One Kiss	Lucky Lips
80	Sag'No' zu Ihm	Say No to Him	Don't Talk to Him
81	Schön Wie ein Traum	As Beautiful as a Dream	Theme for a Dream
82	Shoom Llamma Boom Boom	Shoom Llamma Boom Boom	*Shoom Llamma Boom Boom* (possible)
83	Solamente una Vez	Only Once	You Belong to My Heart
84	Ein Sonntag mit Marie	A Sunday with Marie	The Day I Met Marie
85	Ein Spiel ohne Grenzen	A Game without Boundaries	-
86	Stell' Mich Deinen Eltern Vor	Introduce Me to Your Parents	Not the Way That It Should Be
87	Sternengold	Gold Star	All My Love
88	Die Stimme der Liebe	The Voice of Love	A Voice in the Wilderness
89	Story ohne Happy-End	Story without a Happy End	Girl on the Bus
90	Te Quiero Dijiste	I Want You to Say	Magic Is the Moonlight
91	Todo el Poder a los Amigos	All the Power to the Friends	Power to All Our Friends
92	Tus Besos	Your Kisses	Kiss
93	Tu, Tu, Mi Piaci	You, You, My Pleasure	True, True Lovin'
94	Twist im Blut	Twist in the Blood	Twist and Shout
95	Umbarella	Umbrella	Annabella Umbrella
96	Vaya con Dios	Go with God	May God Be with You
97	Vita Mia	My Life	-
98	Vodna Pot	Waterway	Strong Is the Current
99	Vreneli	Vreneli	-
100	Was Ist Dabei?	What Is with Her?	The Time in Between
101	Was Kann Ich Tun?	What Can I Do?	What Would I Do (for the Love of a Girl)?
102	Weihnachtszeit – Mistletoe and Wine	Christmas Time – Mistletoe and Wine	Mistletoe and Wine
103	Wenn Du Lachst, Lacht das Glück	When You Laugh, Laugh with Happiness	-
104	Wonderful World	Wonderful World	Wonderful World
105	Zärtliche Sekunden	Tender Seconds	Don't Forget to Catch Me
106	Zum Heiraten Bin Ich Kein Typ	I'm Not the Type to Get Married	-
107	Zuviel Allein	Too Much Alone	I'm the Lonely One

♬ Some Facts and Figures About Cliff Richard Songs

Prior to the recording of his latest album, *Bold as Brass*, Cliff Richard had recorded **1191** unique song titles (notwithstanding the multiple versions of those songs listed earlier). Breaking the songs down into their initial alphabetic and following the rules stated in the How to... section of this book, there are some interesting facts that begin to surface:

1. If Cliff records a song, there is a one in ten chance that it will start with an I or an S, slightly less to begin with W
2. There is a one in twenty chance that any new song will begin with a C, D, H and slightly more that it will begin with an L or a T
3. Although it would be skewed by the time of year that the songs are recorded, every twenty-second son is likely to be connected to Christmas
4. More obviously, every tenth song will have the word 'love' somewhere in the title

Taking this data and extrapolating the information, including the two bonus tracks on the special edition of *Bold as Brass*, there are fourteen tracks in total, which means that:

a) There will be at least one song beginning with I, S and W
b) There will likely be a song that starts with C, D, H, L or T
c) Give the release date, there is a better chance that one song might have a reference to Christmas
d) At least one but nearer two songs will have 'love' somewhere in the title

In reality, the run-down looks like this:

- There are three songs beginning with I, one with S and none with W
- There are also three beginning with L, two with T and one with D
- The others are one each for A, N, B and E, which are also statistically significant
- None of the tracks, however, mention Christmas, while there are three songs that talk of love

However, any statistician will suggest that fourteen tracks is insufficient for any pattern to adequately establish itself; but, this analysis shows that the choice of songs does lean significantly towards the initial statements of expectation in the opening paragraph. What would be interesting is to apply the statistical analysis over the choice of songs performed in concert, although this would be skewed by the proximity of any new studio material released.

Also, there is a strong statistical correlation to suggest that at least two of the songs would be performed in another language; but, again, since the early seventies, Cliff has only rarely recorded in anything other than English, thereby forcing the statistical nuances down to near to nothing.

Finally, should any of the songs be released from the album as a single, there is a strong probability that it will be placed in the top twenty in the British singles charts: time will tell!

These are the hard facts about Cliff's recording career (excluding the new album):

- **1191** unique songs recorded in the studio or as part of a live album at a rate of **23** new songs a year
- **50** studio albums released
- **92** songs composed at least in part by Cliff, making his composition rate almost **2** a year
- The **most prolific writers** of Cliff's songs are **the Shadows**, although the accolade for an individual falls to **Alan Tarney**, followed by Terry Britten, Bruce Welch, Hank Marvin and Chris Eaton
- For the singles charts, Cliff holds the record for the **most number of weeks on the singles charts** as well as being the only artist to have a **number one in five consecutive decades**, and the only artist to achieve **top five singles in six consecutive decades**, while the individual statistics are:
    - **139 singles** released in the UK (including the import ***Gee Whiz It's You***)
    - **14 number one** singles
    - **11 number two** singles
    - **8 number three** singles
    - **6 number four** singles
    - **1 number five** single
    - **40 top five** singles
    - **68 top ten** singles
    - **96 top twenty** singles
    - **114 top thirty** singles

And still Sir Cliff keeps going. Keep the faith!